XINHUA DICTIONARY

新华字典

汉英双语版

Chinese-English

商務印書館
The Commercial Press

商务印书馆有限公司，2020
《新华字典》（第 11 版）汉英双语版由商务印书馆有限公司授权出版发行。

新华字典（汉英双语版）

Xinhua Dictionary (Chinese-English)

出　　版　商务印书馆（马来西亚）有限公司
马来西亚吉隆坡苏丹街 63C 号
Publisher　K.L. Commercial Book Co. (M) SDN. BHD.
No. 63C, Jalan Sultan, Kuala Lumpur 50000, W.P. Kuala Lumpur, Malaysia
Email: editorial@commercialpress.com.hk
发　　行　香港联合书刊物流有限公司
香港新界荃湾德士古道 220-248 号荃湾工业中心 16 楼
Distributor　SUP Publishing Logistics (HK) Limited
16/F, Tsuen Wan Industrial Centre, 220-248 Texaco Road, Tsuen Wan, N.T., Hong Kong
印　　刷　南京爱德印刷有限公司
Printer　Nanjing Amity Printing Co., Ltd.
NO.99, Mozhou Zhonglu, Dong Shan Qiao, Jiangning, Nanjing, China
版　　次　2023 年 6 月第 1 版第 1 次印刷
Printing　First edition, First printing, June 2023

ISBN　978 629 98 2560 9

汉英双语版翻译、审订及编辑人员名单

Translation, Review and Editorial Team

of the Chinese-English Edition

审订 Reviewers:

〔英〕Elisabeth Hallett

〔英〕Alastair E. MacDonald

〔英〕Michael G. Murray

翻译 Translators:

曹　飞　胡龙彪　黄克群　陶志健

赵根宗　郑定欧　周殊平

责任编辑 Executive Editor: 马浩岚

封面设计 Cover Designer: 涂　慧

编辑 Editors:

杜茂莉　李昆之　刘　彤

郄一帆　吴　冰　赵宇琪

校對 Proofreaders:

商务印书馆出版中心

排版 Typesetting:

商务印书馆全媒体制作中心

目　　录

Contents

出版说明

《新华字典》是新中国最有影响的、权威的现代汉语字典，1953 年首版后历经数次修订，一直畅销不衰，至今累计发行 6 亿余册，是中国小学生入学后人手一册的汉语学习必备工具书。

随着中国经济、社会的发展，汉语在世界范围内的影响力日益增强，国外读者了解、学习汉语的需求也不断增加，《新华字典》这本权威规范的汉语字典就成为汉语与国际上众多语种的沟通基础。也正因此，《新华字典》的汉英双语版得以面世。

这次出版的《新华字典》(汉英双语版)是在《新华字典》(第 11 版)的基础上进行翻译编纂的。商务印书馆经过征询英美等国出版社、词典专家、国外读者的意见建议后，组建了十余人的翻译团队和外籍审订专家团队，在保留《新华字典》汉语原文的同时，提供英文对译，在准确传达汉语词典原文的释义、例证含义的基础上，尽量以汉英双语间时态、语态、词性的对应表达来协助读者理解和使用汉语，尽可能以便于国外读者理解的英语体现《新华字典》原文中的中国历史、社会、文化背景知识。这本汉英双语版的字典，主要服务于需要学习汉语和了解中国语言文化的非汉语母语读者，同时也可作为我国读者学习英文和从事汉英翻译的参考工具书。

在词典出版之际，我们谨向《新华字典》(第 11 版)的修订作者中国社会科学院语言研究所，以及本双语版的翻译、审订、编辑团队表示敬意。翻译编纂如此博大精深的权威汉语工具书是一项极具挑战性的工作，纰漏之处在所难免，欢迎各界读者提出改进意见、建议。

商务印书馆编辑部

2019 年 6 月

Foreword

The *Xinhua Dictionary* has been the most influential and authoritative modern Chinese language dictionary in China since its first publication in 1953. With many revisions, it has been a best seller with a total print run of over 600 million copies as well as a must for every primary student in China.

Stimulated by the growing influence of the Chinese language in the new era, a larger group of readers worldwide is interested in knowing and learning Chinese. As an authoritative Chinese dictionary, the *Xinhua Dictionary* is the best choice to serve as a communication bridge connecting the Chinese with other languages in the world. Hence, its Chinese-English Edition comes into being.

The *Xinhua Dictionary* (*Chinese-English Edition*) is translated and compiled on the basis of the eleventh edition of the *Xinhua Dictionary*.

After adopting comments and suggestions from publishers, lexicographers and readers in UK, USA and some other countries, the Commercial Press organized an expert team of over ten translators and native English reviewers, who have provided and reviewed the English translation of the full text of the original dictionary. In addition to accurately translating the Chinese text, we have paid special attention to preserving its tense, voice and part of speech so as to help learners understand and use Chinese. Accurate and direct English is also provided to explain the Chinese history, society and culture embodied in the Chinese dictionary. This bilingual dictionary is a rich resource that aims at facilitating the non-Chinese speaking readers in learning the Chinese language and its culture. It may also serve the Chinese readers who need to learn English or engage in Chinese-English translation.

At the publication of this dictionary, we would like to extend our sincere gratitude to the Language Research Institute of the Chinese Academy of Social Sciences, the reviser of the *Xinhua Dictionary (11th edition)*, and the translators, reviewers and editors of the Chinese-English Edition. It is no easy task to translate such an authoritative dictionary as the *Xinhua Dictionary*. We would greatly appreciate the readers' comments and suggestions for this Chinese-English edition.

The Editorial Department
The Commercial Press
June 2019

第 11 版修订说明

《新华字典》是新中国第一部现代汉语字典，首次出版于 1953 年，原由新华辞书社编写，著名语言文字学家魏建功先生主持编写工作。1956 年，新华辞书社并入当时的中国科学院语言研究所（1977 年改属中国社会科学院）词典编辑室。《新华字典》历经多次修订出版，深受广大读者欢迎。在第 11 版出版之际，谨向为《新华字典》的编写、修订工作做出重要贡献的前辈学者们致以崇高的敬意。

本次修订在保持《新华字典》原有特色的基础上，以贯彻执行国家语言文字规范为重点，同时根据时代发展变化和读者的需求，对全书进行了谨慎而系统的修订，主要修订内容有：

一、新增正体字 800 多个，以姓氏、人名、地名用字和科技术语用字为主；根据专家学者和广大读者的意见，对某些繁体字、异体字做了相应处理，增收繁体字 1 500 多个，异体字 500 多个。

二、对个别体例做了改动。

三、酌情删去了个别过于陈旧的异读音；有选择地增收了某些字的读音。

四、对个别释义进行修改，简化或更新了某些词语的释义；适当增补了一些新的义项。对复音词进行了适量的增补和删减。

五、对部分例证进行修改，删改了一些难懂或过时、过长的例证；根据中小学教学的需求，适当增加了一些例证。

本次修订听取了部分所内外专家、中小学教师以及广大读者的意见，商务印书馆的领导和有关编辑对修订工作大力支持，提出不少中肯的修改意见，在此一并表示衷心的感谢。限于水平，本次修订或有不当和错误之处，诚恳欢迎广大读者批评指正。

中国社会科学院语言研究所

2010 年 11 月

About the 11th Revised Edition

The *Xinhua Dictionary*, first published in 1953, is the first modern Chinese Dictionary of the People's Republic of China. This dictionary was originally compiled by *Xinhua Dictionary* Editorial Department with the well-known linguist Wei Jiangong as the chief editor. In 1956, it was annexed into the Dictionary Editing Department of the Language Research Institute, which was affiliated to the Chinese Academy of Science then and to the Chinese Academy of Social Sciences in 1977. The *Xinhua Dictionary* has been revised for many editions and well received by the reading public. At the publication of the 11th edition of the *Xinhua Dictionary*, we sincerely express our respect to the scholars and forerunners who have made such significant efforts during the process of editing the dictionary.

While preserving the original features of the dictionary, we give priority to implementing the national standards for the Chinese language and characters and satisfying readers' changing needs as time develops in the process of revision. The revision is done in a fastidious and systematic way. Main revisions are as follows.

1. Over 800 standard characters are added, mostly related to family names, given names, place names, scientific and technological terms. Some adjustments are made to the traditional characters and variant forms of characters by taking suggestions of experts, scholars and readers: over 1 500 traditional characters and over 500 variants are added respectively.

2. Some formats are adjusted.

3. Some out-of-date variant pronunciations are deleted and some pronunciations are added.

4. Some definitions are adjusted, simplified or updated; new definitions of some characters are added; some multi-syllabic words are added and some deleted.

5. Some difficult, old-fashioned or unnecessarily long examples are deleted and some new ones

added to satisfy the learning and teaching needs of primary and secondary schools.

We would like to extend our thanks to the experts, primary and secondary school teachers and readers for their suggestions and to the Commercial Press for their assistance and support during our revision process. Some revisions may not be proper or correct due to the limitation of our capacity. We sincerely hope that the readers will continue to offer comments and suggestions to the dictionary.

Language Research Institute
Chinese Academy of Social Sciences
November 2010

第 10 版修订说明

《新华字典》1953 年首次出版，此后经多次修订再版，深受广大读者欢迎。为了使《新华字典》在新世纪更好地服务于社会，我们在第 9 版的基础上，对字典进行了修订。

修订中我们认真研究了 1953 年原版的风格特点，对比参考了历次修订版本，在加强规范性和科学性的同时，特别注重保持原书的简明性和实用性。

本次修订的主要方面有：根据中华人民共和国教育部、国家语言文字工作委员会发布的《第一批异形词整理表》对本字典中所涉及的异形词作了相应处理；增补了部分新词、新义、新例和少量字头，删除了部分陈旧的词条和例证；订正了一些过时的内容和个别的错误以及表述不够准确的地方；统查整理了部分体例；调整了个别字头和部分复音词的顺序；增补了几幅插图和一个附录《地质年代简表》；按照国家有关规定重新编制了《部首检字表》。

本次修订吸收了一些读者意见，得到了有关专家和商务印书馆的热情帮助和支持，在此谨表谢意。欢迎广大读者继续提出宝贵意见。

中国社会科学院语言研究所

2003 年 10 月

About the 10th Revised Edition

The *Xinhua Dictionary*, first published in 1953 and revised for many editions, has been well received by the reading public. The present revision is done on the basis of the 9th edition in order to better serve the society in the new century.

In doing the revision, we have made a serious study of styles and features of the 1953 edition and made comparisons and references to all the other successive editions. Special attention has been paid to preserving the conciseness and practicality of the original edition, in addition to its further conformity to the criteria and the scientific spirit.

In the present revision, the variant forms of the same word in the dictionary are adjusted according to the First Batch of Standardized Forms of Chinese Words with Non-Standardized Variant Forms issued by the Ministry of Education and the State Language Working Committee of the

PRC. Some new words, new meanings, new examples, and a few headwords are added, while some obsolete entries and examples are deleted. Some out-of-date material, errors and inaccuracies are corrected. Some format guidelines are checked and rearranged throughout the dictionary. The order of some headwords and multi-syllabic words are adjusted. Some illustrations and an appendix the Table of Geological Time Scale are added. The Radical Index is re-compiled according to the relevant national stipulations.

We would like to extend our thanks to the readers for their suggestions, and to the experts and The Commercial Press for their assistance and support during our revision process. We sincerely hope that the readers will continue to offer their comments and suggestions to the dictionary.

Language Research Institute
Chinese Academy of Social Sciences
October 2003

凡　例

一、本字典的字头用大字排印。繁体字、异体字附在字头后面，外加圆括号。不带 * 号的为繁体字，带一个 * 号的为《第一批异体字整理表》中的异体字，带两个 * 号的是《第一批异体字整理表》以外的异体字。有些繁体字、异体字的左上方附有义项序号，表示只适用于某义项；有些繁体字、异体字的左上方带△号，表示另外也做字头。

二、一个字头有几个音的，就列为几个字头，各在注解之末附列其余的音及其所见页码，按音序连排。

三、字头下所收的带注解的复音词或词组，外加［　］号，按音序排列。意义上有联系的，分别放在重点字的相关义项之下；意义上联系不明确的，放在本字注解最后，并另起行。对于《第一批异形词整理表》中的非推荐词形，在左上角加 * 号，外加圆括号，附列于推荐词形之后。

四、本字典的字音依据普通话语音系统，用汉语拼音字母及注音字母标音。

五、有些字头连注两个音，第二个音后面附注“（又）”，表示“又音”。有时某义项内注“also pronounced 某音”，表示“又音”用于某义。

六、有些字头注有“（formerly pronounced）”，表示旧时的不同读法。有时某义项内注“（formerly pronounced）”，表示某义旧时的不同读法。

七、对行文中一些生僻字、多音字或复音词中读轻声的字加注读音。

八、字头的意义不止一项的，分条注解，用❶❷❸等表示义项。一个义项下如果再分条以及前面有总括性文字说明的，用①、②、③等表示。［ ］中的复音词或词组，如果分条注解，用1、2、3等表示。

九、注解中㊀、㊁、㊂的用法如下：

“㊀”表示由原义引申出来的意义。如287页“急 jí”字条❶义下，“㊀气恼，发怒”是由“焦躁”引申出来的。

“㊁”表示由比喻形成的意义（包括独立使用的比喻义和在复音词或词组中用于比喻而产生的意义）。如328页“晶 jīng”字条［结晶］下注“㊁成果”；180页“蜂 fēng”字条下注“㊁成群地：～起｜～拥”。

“㊂”表示由风俗、故事、成语等转化而成的意义，或由没有直接的理据而产生的意义。如14页“白 bái”字条❶义下注“㊂①有关丧事的……②反动的”；665页“推 tuī”字条❶义下［推敲］条注“㊂斟酌文章字句”。

十、注解中的（-子）、（-儿）、（-头）表示本字可以加上这类词尾，构成大致同义的词，不另加注解。

十一、注解中的“㊃”表示本字可以重叠。放在注解前的表示必须叠用，如315页“喈”字；放在注解后的表示可以叠用也可以不叠用，如407页“凛”字❷。

十二、注解中的“㊄”表示本字可以跟一个意义相同或相近的字并列起来构成大致同义的词，不另加注解。

十三、注解中的“〈方 dialect〉”表示本字是方言地区用的字或者本义项所注的是方言地区的用法。“〈古 ancient〉”表示本字是古代用的字或者本义项所注的是古代的用法。

十四、从兄弟民族语言中来的词，加注民族简称。如237页“哈 hǎ”字条［哈达］是从藏语来的，注“（藏 *Tibetan*）”。

十五、有些词的后面注“（外 *loanword*）”，表示是近代的外来语。历史上相沿已久的外来语，一般不注来源。

十六、在注解后举例中，用“～”号代替所释的字或复音词。一个“～”号代替一个字或一个复音词。不止一个例子的，中间用“|”号隔开。

十七、“－”和“-”（短横）的用法如下：

1. 在“－子、－儿、－头”中，在“㊦”字后，“－”代替所释字。

2. 在拼音字母标音中，“－”代替省略的音节，“-”（短横）表示连接转行的音节。

十八、“·”（圆点）用于注音字母的标音时，表示后面的音节读轻声。

Guide to the Text

1. The headwords in the dictionary are printed in the larger type. The Chinese characters of the original complex forms or variant forms are placed in brackets following the headwords. If a bracketed character is without an asterisk (*) following it, it is of the complex form; if it has an asterisk (*) following it, it is of the variant form collected in the First Batch of Standardized Forms of Chinese Characters with Non-standardized Variant Forms (FBSFCCNVF); if it has two asterisks, it is of the variant form not collected in FBSFCCNVF. The small number to the upper left of some complex-formed or variant-formed characters indicates that these characters are applicable only in certain senses while a small triangle (△) to the upper left of some complex-formed or variant-formed characters indicates that these characters are also used as headwords.

2. A headword with more than one pronunciation is treated as separate entries. At the end of its definition, the other pronunciations and their page numbers therein are listed in phonetic order for cross references.

3. The multi-syllabic words or phrases with definitions under a headword are placed in square brackets [ ] in the order of their phonetic sequences. The words semantically related to the headword are placed under their relevant senses and those not closely related semantically are placed at the end of the definitions in a separate line. The forms of the characters not recommended in the First Batch of Standardized Forms of Chinese Words with Non-standardized Variant Forms are placed after the recommended ones in brackets with an asterisk (*) to its upper left.

4. The pronunciation system adopted in this dictionary is that of mandarin Chinese (*putonghua*) and every entry is noted with the Chinese phonetic transcription (*hanyupinyin*) and the Phonetic Symbols of the Chinese Language (*hanyuzhuyin*).

5. Some headwords have two phonetic transcriptions and the second one is noted with (又), which means "also pronounced". Sometimes in certain senses there is a note"also pronounced+pinyin", which indicates that the pronunciation is only applicable to this sense of the character.

6. Some headwords are noted with " (formerly pronounced) ", which indicates that there was a different pronunciation in the former times. When this label appears in a certain sense of a character, it indicates that the former pronunciation is only applicable to this sense of the character.

7. Rarely used characters, polysyllabic characters or multi-syllabic words with a neutral-tone character are specially noted in the pronunciation.

8. When there are more than one sense in the definition of the headword, these senses are respectively marked with ❶, ❷, ❸, etc. If there are sub-senses under a sense or there are senses under a general definition, they are marked with ①, ②, ③, etc. If polysyllabic characters or multi-syllabic words in the square brackets [ ] need to be noted with different sense items, they are marked with 1, 2, 3, etc.

9. The use of labels, "㉛, ㊡, ㊕", is as follows:

The label "㉛" indicates that the meaning of the character here is extended from its original meaning. For instance,"㉛气恼，发怒 be angry" under the definition ❶ of entry "急 jí" on page 278 is extended from "焦躁 worried".

The label "㊡" indicates that the meaning of the character here is used figuratively (when the character is used alone or in multi-syllabic words or phrases). For instance, [结晶] under the entry of "晶 jīng" on page 328 is defined as "㊡成

果 achievement"; the entry " 蜂 fēng"on page 180 is defined as " ㊗成群地 in swarms".

The label " ㊟ " indicates that the meaning of the character here is transferred from a custom, a story, or a proverb, etc., or transferred from certain indirect understanding. For instance, definition ❶ of the entry " 白 bái"on page 14 is noted with " ㊟ ①有关丧事的 funerary...... ②反动的 reactionary" and the definition of ［推敲］ under the entry of " 推 tuī" on page 665 is noted with "㊟斟酌文章字句 to deliberate".

10. Such Chinese suffixes as (一子), (一儿), and (一头) in the definition mean that they can be added to the headword to form its synonymous word without a further definition.

11. The label " ㊣ " in the definition means that the character can be reduplicated. When it is placed before the definition, it indicates that the character must be reduplicated in use, such as in the case of " 喈 " on page 315. When it is placed after the definition, it indicates that the character can be either reduplicated or used singly such as in the case of " 凛 " on page 407.

12. The label "㊤" in the definition indicates that the character can be used together with a synonymous or near synonymous character to form a near-synonymous expression without a further definition.

13. The label "〈方 dialect〉" in the definition indicates that the character is used in dialect areas or this sense defines its use in a dialect area. The label "〈古 ancient〉" means that the character is an archaic one, or this sense defines its use in the ancient times.

14. If a character is borrowed from the language of an ethnic group of China, it is marked with the shortened form of its ethnic group. For instance, the word [哈达] under the entry of "哈 hǎ" on page 237 marked with （藏 *Tibetan*） indicates that it is borrowed from Tibetan.

15. Some characters followed by （外 *loanword*） means that they are modern loanwords. Loanwords that have become common through long usage are not given their origins.

16. In the illustration examples after a definition, the sign "～" replaces the illustrated character or multi-syllabic word. One "～" replaces only one character or multi-syllabic word. More than one examples after a definition are separated with the sign "|".

17. The use of "—" and "-" is as follows:

1）When used in "—子, —儿, and —头" or after the label "㊁", the sign "—" replaces the headword.

2）The sign "—" in the phonetic transcriptions replaces the omitted syllable and the hyphen "-" is used to connect the syllable which is moved to the next line.

18. The dot " · " used in the phonetic symbols of the Chinese characters shows that the following symbol is in the neutral tone.

汉语拼音音节索引

Index of Syllables of Hanyupinyin

1. 每一音节后举一字做例，可按例字读音去查同音的字。
   There's an example character after each syllable. Characters with the same pronunciation shall be consulted in accordance with the pronunciation of this example character.
2. 数字指本字典正文页码。
   The numerals indicate the page numbers of the text in this dictionary.

新旧字形对照表

Old and New Forms of Characters

（字形后圆圈内的数字表示字形的笔画数）

(Number in circle indicating number of strokes)

旧字形 Old form	新字形 New form	新字举例 Example	旧字形 Old form	新字形 New form	新字举例 Example
⺾④	艹③	花草	直⑧	直⑧	值植
⻍④	辶③	连速	黽⑧	黾⑧	绳鼋
幵⑥	开④	型形	咼⑨	呙⑧	過蝸
丰④	丰④	艳沣	垂⑨	垂⑧	睡郵
巨⑤	巨④	苣渠	飠⑨	飠⑧	飲飽
屯④	屯④	纯顿	郎⑨	郎⑧	廊螂
瓦⑤	瓦④	瓶瓷	彔⑧	录⑧	渌箓
反④	反④	板饭	昷⑩	昷⑨	温瘟
丑④	丑④	纽杻	骨⑩	骨⑨	滑骼
犮⑤	犮⑤	拔茇	鬼⑩	鬼⑨	槐嵬
印⑥	印⑤	茚	俞⑨	俞⑨	偷渝
耒⑥	耒⑥	耕耘	既⑪	既⑨	溉厩
呂⑦	吕⑥	侣营	蚤⑩	蚤⑨	搔骚
攸⑦	攸⑥	修倏	敖⑪	敖⑩	傲遨
爭⑧	争⑥	净静	莽⑫	莽⑩	漭蟒
产⑥	产⑥	彦産	眞⑩	真⑩	慎填
𦍌⑦	𦍌⑥	差养	䍃⑩	䍃⑩	摇遥
幷⑧	并⑥	屏拼	殺⑪	殺⑩	摋鎩
吳⑦	吴⑦	蜈虞	黃⑫	黄⑪	廣横
角⑦	角⑦	解确	虛⑫	虚⑪	墟歔
奐⑨	奂⑦	换痪	異⑫	異⑪	冀戴
㡀⑧	㡀⑦	敝弊	象⑫	象⑪	像橡
耳⑧	耳⑦	敢嚴	奧⑬	奥⑫	澳襖
者⑨	者⑧	都著	普⑬	普⑫	谱氆

部首检字表
Radical Index

〔说明〕

1. 本表采用的部首依据《汉字部首表》，共 201 部；归部依据《GB13000.1 字符集汉字部首归部规范》；编排次序依据《GB13000.1 字符集汉字笔顺规范》和《GB13000.1 字符集汉字字序（笔画序）规范》，按笔画数由少到多顺序排列，同画数的，按起笔笔形横（一）、竖（丨）、撇（丿）、点（丶）、折（乛）顺序排列，第一笔相同的，按第二笔，依次类推。

2. 在《部首目录》中，主部首的左边标有部首序号；附形部首大多加圆括号单立，其左边的部首序号加有方括号。

3. 在《检字表》中，繁体字和异体字加有圆括号；同部首的字按除去部首笔画以外的画数排列。

4. 查字时，需先在《部首目录》里查出待查字所属部首的页码，然后再查《检字表》。

5. 为方便读者查检，《检字表》中有些字仍采取"多开门"的方式，分别收在所属规定部首和传统习用部首之下，收在后者的字右上角加有"◦"的标志。如"思"字在"田"部和"心"部都能查到，在"心"部的"思"右上角带"◦"。

6.《检字表》后面另有《难检字笔画索引》备查。

[Directions]

1. The radicals in this Radical Index are adopted from *The Chinese Character Radical Index*, which totals 201 volumes; the indexing method is based on *The Criterion on Radical Indexing of the Chinese Character in GB13000.1 Character Set*. The layout sequence is based on *The Criterion on Stroke Orders of the Chinese Character in GB13000.1 Character Set* and *The Criterion on Character Orders (Stroke Orders) of the*

Chinese Character in GB13000.1 Character Set, and arranged in accordance with the stroke numbers increasingly. As to characters with the same stroke number, the layout sequence is arranged in accordance with the starting stroke of horizontal(一), vertical(丨), left-falling stroke(丿), dot (丶)and the turning stroke(→). If the first starting stroke is still the same, the second will in turn function.

2. In *List of Radicals*, the sequence number of the radicals is marked on the left of the major radical; the form-attached radicals are mostly listed solely with parenthesis, and the radical numbers to the left are marked with square brackets.

3. In *Character Index*, the original complex form of a simplified Chinese character and the variant form of a Chinese character are both marked with parenthesis; characters of the same radical shall be arranged in accordance with the stroke numbers except the stroke number of the radical.

4. When looking up a character, one shall get to know the page number of the radical of the character in *List of Radicals*, then check it out in *Character Index*.

5. For readers' convenience, some characters are listed under different radicals, the radical defined in The Criterion and the radical in traditional understanding with a "◦" sign on the right top of the character under the latter radical. For example, 思 is listed under both radicals 田 and 心 while the 思 under radical 心 is marked with a "◦" on its right top.

6. Following *Character Index*, *Stroke Index for Difficult Characters* is provided.

(一) 部首目录

List of Radicals

(部首左边的号码是部首序号;右边的号码指《检字表》的页码。)

(The number to the left of the radicals is the sequence number of the radical and the number to the right is the page number of the *Index*.)

（二）检字表

Character Index

（字右边的号码指正文的页码；带圆括号的字是繁体字或异体字；字右上角带“◦”的是非规定的归部。）

(The number to the right of each character indicates the page number in the dictionary. Characters in parentheses are the original complex forms or variant forms. Characters with a “◦” on the right top are not listed in the Criterion but adopted as in traditional understanding.)

2
丨部

3
丿部

4 丶部

5 乛(𠃍乁乚乙)部

6 十部

[12] 入部

13 勹部

14 儿部

15 匕部

16 几部

[16] ⺇部

17 亠部

1—4 画

15 画以上

[29] 士部

30 艹部

1—3 画

4 画

5 画

6 画

42 彡部

43 夕部

44 夂部

45 丬部

[45] 爿部

46 广部

49 辶部

55 屮部

[55] 屮部

56 女部

(獵) 405
(獺) 632
獾 265
(獼) 448
(玁) 709
(玀) 428
玃 345

67 歹部

歹 111
2—4 画
列 404
死 618
夙° 623
歼 300
(殀) 759
殁 461
5—6 画
残 57
殂 101
殃 756
殇 580
殄 650
殆 112
殊 607
殉 744
毙° 34
7 画以上
殒 813
殓 398
殍 505
殖 604
853
(殘) 57
殚 114
殛 287
殢 648
殨 276
(飱) 628
(殞) 813
殡 44
殣 326
(殢) 648
(殤) 580
殪 778
(殨) 276
(殫) 114
(殭) 307
(殮) 398
(斃)° 34
(殯) 44
(殲) 300

[67] 步部

粲° 58
餐° 57

68 车(车)部

车 72
335
1—4 画
轧 193
747
826
轨 232
军° 345
轩 737
轪 111
𫐄 810
轫 559
轰 253
转 872
872
轭 158
斩 830
轮 426
轼 518
软 565
5 画
轱 217
轲 354
轳 422
轴 864
865
轵 854
轶 775
轷 218
轸 257
轸 844
轹 395
轺 760
轻 540
6 画
载 816
817
轼 601
轾 856
轿 229
辀 313
辁 863
辁 550
辂 421
较 313
晕° 811
814
7—8 画
辄 839
辅 187
辆 401
辇 477
辊 234
辋 676
辊 475
辌 399
辍 96
辎 881
辈° 27
辉° 272
9—10 画
毂° 221
辏 100
辐 186
辑 288
辒 685
输 608
辐 793
辑 563
辔° 496
辕 807
辖 703
辗 831
舆° 799
11 画以上
辘 421
辙 840
辚 407
辚 627
镮 267
268

[68] 車部

(車) 72
335
1—7 画
(軋) 193
747
826
(軌) 232
(軒) 737
(軑) 111
(軏) 810
(軔) 559
(軔) 559
(軛) 158
(斬) 830
(軝) 518
(軟) 565
(軲) 217
(軻) 354
(軸) 864
865
(軹) 854
(軼) 775
(軱) 218
(軤) 257
(軫) 844
(軺) 760
(載) 816
817
(軾) 601
(輊) 856
(輈) 229
(輈) 863
(輇) 550
(輅) 421
(較) 313
(暈)° 811
814
(輒) 839
(輔) 187
(輕) 540
(輓) 674
8 画以上
(輦) 477
(輒) 839
(輛) 401
(輥) 234
(輞) 676
(輗) 475
(輪) 426
(輬) 399
(輟) 96
(輜) 881
(輩)° 27
(輝)° 272
(輳) 100
(輻) 186
(輭) 565
(輯) 288
(轀) 685
(輸) 608
(輶) 793
(輮) 563
(轅) 807
(轄) 703
(輾) 831
(輿)° 799
(轉) 872
872
(槧)° 818
(轆) 421
(轎) 313
(轍) 840
(轔) 407
(轙) 627
(轘) 267
268

75 日(曰)部

[75] 冃部

[88] ⺝部

89 氏部

90 欠部

2—7 画

8 画以上

91 风部

[91] 風部

92 殳部

93 文部

94 方部

95 火部

[98] 忄部

[98]
⺌部

99
毋部

[99]
母部

100
示部

[100]
礻部

1—4 画

5 画

6 画以上

101
甘部

102
石部

2—4 画

5 画

6—7 画

8 画

103 龙部

[103] 龍部

104 业部

105 目部

[130] 虎部

131 虫部

132 肉部

133 缶部

134 舌部

135 竹(⺮)部

[148] 糸部

150 走部

151 赤部

152 豆部

153 酉部

154 辰部

155 豕部

156 卤部

［156］鹵部

157 里部

158 足部

[158] ⻊部

159 邑部

[159] 阝右部

175 阜部

[175] 阝左部

2—4 画

5 画

6—8 画

9 画

10 画以上

176 金部

1—2 画

3 画

4 画

5 画

6 画

[176] 钅部

[177] 魚部

178 隶部

179 革部

5—6 画

7—9 画

10 画以上

186 音部

187 首部

188 髟部

189 鬲部

190 鬥部

191 高部

192 黄部

193 麻部

194 鹿部

195 鼎部

（三）难检字笔画索引

Stroke Index for Difficult Characters

（字右边的号码指正文的页码；带圆括号的字是繁体字或异体字。）

(The number to the right of each character indicates the page number in the dictionary. Characters in parentheses are the original complex forms or variant forms.)

A ㄚ

A ㄚ

吖 ā ㄚ ［吖嗪］（－qín）有机化合物的一类，呈环状结构，含有一个或几个氮原子，如吡啶、嘧啶等 azine

阿 ā ㄚ 〈方 dialect〉词头 prefix ①加在排行、小名或姓的前面 prefix of seniority among family members, or used before a childhood name or surname：～大 *the eldest*｜～根 *A Gen*｜～王 *A Wang* ②加在某些亲属称谓的前面 prefix used before forms of address related to some relatives：～妹 *younger sister*｜～公 *grandpa* ［阿姨］1 称跟母亲年纪差不多的、没有亲属关系的女性 form of address for a woman of one's mother's generation and not related to one's family 2 对保育员或保姆等的称呼 form of address for a female childcare worker or housekeeper 3〈方 dialect〉姨母 aunt

［阿昌族］我国少数民族，参看附录四 the Achang people (one of the ethnic groups in China. See Appendix Ⅳ.)

⇨ see also ē on p.157

呵 ā ㄚ same as "啊 (ā)"

⇨ see also á on p.1,ǎ on p.1, à on p.2, a on p.2, hē on p.246

啊 ā ㄚ 叹词，表示赞叹或惊异 (exclamation) used to express admiration or surprise：～，这花多好哇！ *Ah, what a beautiful flower!*｜～，下雪了！ *Ah, it's snowing!*

⇨ see also á on p.1, ǎ on p.1, à on p.2, a on p.2

锕(錒) ā ㄚ 放射性金属元素，符号 Ac。actinium (Ac)

腌 ā ㄚ ［腌臜］（－za）〈方 dialect〉不干净 dirty

⇨ see also yān on p.750

呵 á ㄚˊ same as "啊 (á)"

⇨ see also ā on p.1,ǎ on p.1, à on p.2, a on p.2, hē on p.246

啊 á ㄚˊ 叹词，表示追问 (exclamation) used to make further inquiry：～，你说什么？ *Eh, what did you say?*｜～，你再说！ *Excuse me, say it again!*

⇨ see also ā on p.1, ǎ on p.1, à on p.2, a on p.2

嗄 á ㄚˊ same as "啊 (á)"

⇨ see also shà on p.575

呵 ǎ ㄚˇ same as "啊 (ǎ)"

⇨ see also ā on p.1,á on p.1, à on p.2, a on p.2, hē on p.246

啊 ǎ ㄚˇ 叹词，表示疑惑 (exclamation) used to express doubt：～，这是怎么回事？ *Well, what's the matter?*

⇨ see also ā on p.1, á on p.1, à on p.2, a on p.2

A

呵 à ㄚˋ same as "啊 (à)"
⇨ see also ā on p.1, á on p.1, ǎ on p.1, ɑ on p.2, hē on p.246

啊 à ㄚˋ 叹词 exclamation ① 表示应诺或醒悟（音较短） used to express agreement or sudden realization (pronounced with a shorter sound)：～，好吧！ *Eh, OK!* | ～，原来是你呀！ *Ah, so it's you!* ②表示惊异或赞叹（音较长） used to express surprise or admiration (pronounced with a longer sound)：～，伟大的祖国！ *Ah, our great homeland!*
⇨ see also ā on p.1, á on p.1, ǎ on p.1, ɑ on p.2

呵 ɑ ·ㄚ same as "啊 (ɑ)"
⇨ see also ā on p.1, á on p.1, ǎ on p.1, à on p.2, hē on p.246

啊 ɑ ·ㄚ 助词 auxiliary word ①用在句末，表示赞叹、催促、嘱咐等语气（常因前面字音不同而发生变音，可用不同的字来表示） used at the end of a sentence to express praise, urging or exhortation, often with sound or form variations depending on its context：快些来～（呀）！ *Come here quickly!* | 您好～(哇)! *How are you doing?* | 同志们加油干～（哪）！ *Step up efforts, comrades!* ②用在列举的事项之后 used when enumerating items：纸～、笔～，摆满了一桌子。 *The desk is covered with things like sheets of paper, pens and what not.*
⇨ see also ā on p.1, á on p.1, ǎ on p.1, à on p.2

AI ㄞ

哎 āi ㄞ 叹词，表示不满或提醒 (exclamation) used to express dissatisfaction or call for attention：～，你怎么能这么说呢！ *Hey, how can you say that?* | ～，你们看，谁来了！ *Well, look who's coming!* ［哎呀］叹词，表示惊讶 (exclamation) used to express surprise ［哎哟］（－yō）叹词，表示惊讶、痛苦 (exclamation) used to express surprise or pain

哀 āi ㄞ ❶悲痛（㊟悲－） grief：喜怒～乐 *delight, anger, grief and joy* ❷悼念 to mourn：默～ *pay silent tribute* ❸怜悯，同情 to show compassion; to sympathize：～怜 *show compassion* | ～其不幸 *show compassion for sb's misfortune*

锿(鎄) āi ㄞ 人造的放射性金属元素，符号Es。einsteinium (Es)

埃 āi ㄞ 灰尘（㊟尘－） dust

挨 āi ㄞ ❶靠近 to be close to：居民区～着一条河。 *The residential area is close to a river.* ❷顺着（一定次序） in the order of：～家查问 *question from door to door* | ～着号叫 *call (a group of people) sequentially*
⇨ see also ái on p.3

唉 āi ㄞ 叹词 exclamation ①表示答应 used to express acknowledgment：～，听见了。 *Yes, I hear you.* ②表示叹息 used to express disappointment：～，一天的工夫

又白费了！ *Oh no! Another day's work came to nothing!* ③表示招呼 used to express a call：～，你来一下。*Hey you, come here.*

⇨ see also ài on p.4

嗳(噯) āi ㄞ same as "哎"

⇨ see also ǎi on p.3, ài on p.4

挨(捱)** ái ㄞ ❶遭受，亲身受到 to suffer：～饿 *suffer from hunger*｜～打 *suffer a beating*｜～骂 *be given a scolding* ❷困难地度过（岁月） to pull through (bad times)：～日子 *drag out a miserable existence day after day* ❸拖延 to delay：他～到晚饭后才开始写作业。*He delayed doing his homework until after dinner.*

⇨ see also āi on p.2

骇(騃) ái ㄞ 傻 silly; foolish：痴～ *foolish; stupid*

皑(皚) ái ㄞ 白 ㊂ snow white：～～白雪 *pure white snow*

癌 ái ㄞ (formerly pronounced yán) 生物体细胞变成恶性增生细胞所形成的肿瘤 cancer：胃～ *stomach cancer*｜肝～ *liver cancer*｜肺～ *lung cancer*｜乳腺～ *breast cancer*

毐 ǎi ㄞ 用于人名，嫪毐（lào－），战国时秦国人 used in given names, e.g. Lao Ai from State Qin, the era of the Warring States

欸 ǎi ㄞ ［欸乃］形容摇橹声 creak (when rowing)：～一声山水绿。*With the sound of rowing, the green landscape turns up.*

⇨ see also ē on p.160, é on p.160, ě on p.160, è on p.160

嗳(噯) ǎi ㄞ 叹词，表示否定或不同意 (exclamation) used to express negation or disagreement：～，别那么说。*No, don't say that.*｜～，不是这样放。*No, don't place it like that.*

⇨ see also āi on p.3, ài on p.4

矮 ǎi ㄞ 身材短 (of stature) short：他比他哥哥～。*He's shorter than his elder brother.* ㊀ ①高度小的 short; low (in height)：几棵小～树 *some low trees* ②等级、地位低 low (in rank or status)：我比他～一级。*I am his junior by one grade.*

蔼(藹) ǎi ㄞ 和气，和善 amiable; friendly：和～ *amiable; affable*｜～然可亲 *amiable and accessible*

霭(靄) ǎi ㄞ 云气 mist：云～ *haze*｜暮～ *evening mist*

艾 ài ㄞ ❶草本植物，又叫艾蒿，叶有香味，可制成艾绒，供灸病用 Chinese mugwort (also called 艾蒿) ❷止，绝 to cease; to stop：方兴未～ *be just unfolding and far from ending; be in the ascendant* ❸漂亮，美 beautiful; handsome：少～（年轻漂亮的人） *a young and handsome person* ❹姓 (surname) Ai

⇨ see also yì on p.773

砹 ài ㄞ 放射性非金属元素，符号 At。astatine (At)

A

唉 ài ㄞ 叹词，表示伤感或惋惜 (exclamation) used to express sadness or sympathy：～，病了两个月，把工作都耽搁了。*Oh dear, I've been ill for two months, which has delayed my work.*

⇨ see also āi on p.2

爱(愛) ài ㄞ ❶喜爱，对人或事物有深挚的感情 to love：拥军～民 *support the army and love the people* | ～祖国 *love one's homeland* | ～人民 *love the people* | 友～ *friendly and affectionate* ❷喜好 to like：～游泳 *enjoy swimming* | ～干净 *enjoy cleanliness* | ～劳动 *like physical labour* ❸爱惜，爱护 to cherish; to take good care of：～集体荣誉 *cherish the collective honour* ❹容易（出现某种变化），常常（发生某种行为）to be apt to; to tend to：铁～生锈。*Iron tends to get rusty.* | 小王～迟到。*Xiao Wang is often late for work.*

嗳(噯) ài ㄞ 叹词，表示懊恼、悔恨 (exclamation) used to express annoyance or remorse：～，早知道是这样，我就不来了。*If I had known this earlier, I wouldn't have come.*

⇨ see also āi on p.3, ǎi on p.3

嫒(嬡) ài ㄞ ［令嫒］［令爱］对对方女儿的敬称 (polite speech) your daughter

瑷(璦) ài ㄞ ［瑷珲］（— huī）地名，在黑龙江省，今作“爱辉” Aihui (a place in Heilongjiang Province, now written as 爱辉)

叆(靉) ài ㄞ ［叆叇］（— dài）云彩很厚的样子 (of clouds) dense：乌云～ *dark and cloudy*

暧(曖) ài ㄞ 日光昏暗㊀(of daylight) dim ［暧昧］1 态度不明朗 ambiguous 2 行为不光明 dubious

餲(餲) ài ㄞ 食物经久而变味 (of food) to spoil

⇨ see also hé on p.248

隘 ài ㄞ ❶险要的地方 place strategically located and difficult to approach：要～ *narrow pass of strategic importance* ❷狭窄，狭小（㊀狭一）narrow; cramped：路～林深 *narrow path in dense forest*

嗌 ài ㄞ 噎，食物塞住嗓子 to choke (on food)

⇨ see also yì on p.777

碍(礙) ài ㄞ 妨害，阻挡 to hinder; to obstruct：～口（不便说）*be too awkward to mention* | ～事不～事？ *Does it matter or not?* | ～手～脚 *be a hindrance*

AN ㄢ

厂 ān ㄢ 同“庵”，多用于人名 same as 庵 (often used in given names)

⇨ see also chǎng on p.70

广 ān ㄢ 同“庵”，多用于人名 same as 庵 (often used in given names)

⇨ see also guǎng on p.229

安 ān ㄢ ❶平静，稳定 calm; stable：～定 *quiet and stable*｜～心（心情安定）*(of mind) at ease; at peace*｜～居乐业 *live and work in peace and contentment* ❷使平静，使安定（多指心情）(often of mood) to ease; to calm down：～神 *calm the nerves*｜～民告示 *notice to reassure the public* ❸安全，平安，跟"危"相对 safe; secure (opposite of 危)：～康 *safe and well*｜治～ *public order*｜转危为～ *to turn the corner* ❹安置，装设（㊀－装）to set; to install：～排 *to arrange*｜～营扎寨 *set up (temporary) camp*｜～电灯 *install electric lights* ❺存着，怀着（多指不好的念头）to harbour (often ill intentions)：你～的什么心？ *What are you up to?* ❻代词，哪里 (pronoun) where; what; how：而今～在？ *Where is it now?*｜～能如此？ *How can it be like this?* ❼电流强度单位名安培的简称，符号 A。ampere (A)

垵 ān ㄢ 用于地名 used in place names：曾厝～（在福建省厦门）*Zengcuo'an (in Xiamen, Fujian Province)*

⇨ see also ǎn on p.5

桉 ān ㄢ 桉树，常绿乔木，又叫有加利树，树干高而直，木质坚韧，供建筑用，树皮和叶可入药，叶可提制桉油 eucalyptus (also called 有加利树)

氨 ān ㄢ 无机化合物，气体，无色而有恶臭，可用来制硝酸、肥料和炸药 ammonia

鮟（鮟） ān ㄢ［鮟鱇］(－kāng) 鱼名，俗称老头儿鱼，身体前半部平扁，圆盘形，尾部细小，全身无鳞，能发出像老人咳嗽的声音，生活在深海 anglerfish (informal 老头儿鱼)

鞍（△*鞌） ān ㄢ（－子）放在骡马等背上承载重物或供人骑坐的器具 saddle (on a horse, etc.)

鞌 ān ㄢ ❶ see 鞍 on page 5 ❷用于古地名 used in ancient place names：～之战 *the Battle of An*

庵（*菴） ān ㄢ ❶圆形草屋 round thatched hut：结草为～ *thatch a cottage* ❷小庙（多指尼姑居住的）small temple (often nunnery)：～堂 *nunnery*

鹌（鵪） ān ㄢ［鹌鹑］(－chun) 鸟名，头小尾短，羽毛赤褐色，杂有暗黄色条纹，雄的好斗 common quail

谙（諳） ān ㄢ 熟悉 to know well：不～水性 *not know how to swim*［谙练］熟习，有经验 well versed in; experienced

盦 ān ㄢ ❶古代一种器皿 (ancient) a kind of container (for food) ❷同"庵"，多用于人名 same as 庵 (often used in given names)

玵 án ㄢˊ 美玉 fine jade

垵 ǎn ㄢˇ same as "埯"

⇨ see also ān on p.5

铵（銨） ǎn ㄢˇ 铵根，从氨衍生所得的带正电荷的根，在化合物中的地位相当于金

A

属离子 ammonium

俺 ǎn ㄢˇ 〈方 dialect〉代词，我，我们 (pronoun) I / me / my; we / us / our：～村 *my village* | ～们 *we* | ～那里出棉花。*We produce cotton at our place.*

埯 ǎn ㄢˇ ❶点播种子挖的小坑 small hole for planting seeds ❷挖小坑点种 to dibble in seeds：～瓜 *sow melon* | ～豆 *sow beans* ❸（-儿）量词，用于点种的植物 (measure word) cluster of plants to be sowed：一～儿花生 *a cluster of peanut seedlings*

唵 ǎn ㄢˇ ❶把食物放在手里吞食 to eat food from one's hand：～了几口炒米 *eat a few mouthfuls of fried rice from one's hand* ❷佛教咒语的发声词 word of sound of Buddhist incantation

揞 ǎn ㄢˇ 用手指把药粉等按在伤口上 to apply medicinal powder to the wound with one's fingers

犴 àn ㄢˋ see 狴犴 (bì-) at 狴 on page 35

⇨ see also hān on p.239

岸（*屽） àn ㄢˋ ❶江、河、湖、海等水边的陆地 shore; bank：河～ *river bank* | 船靠～了。*The ship pulled in to shore.* ❷高大 tall and big：伟～ *tall and sturdy*

按 àn ㄢˋ ❶用手压或摁（èn）to push down; to press：～脉 *take the pulse (of a patient)* | ～电铃 *ring an electric bell* | ～摩 *to massage* ❷止住，压住 to cease; to suppress：～兵不动 *stand by; take no action* | ～下此事先不表 *leave this aside for the moment* ❸介词，依照 (preposition) according to：～理说你应该去。*Normally you should go.* | ～人数算 *calculate according to the number of people* | ～部就班（依照程序办事）*proceed in the prescribed order* | ～图索骥（喻办事拘泥，也指根据线索去寻求）*search for a fine horse according to its picture; (figuratively) do sth mechanically, or try to locate sth by following clues* ❹经过考核研究后下论断 to arrive at a conclusion (after careful examination)：～语 *note (by an author or editor)* | 编者～ *editor's note*

胺 àn ㄢˋ 有机化合物，是氨的氢原子被烃（tīng）基取代而成的 amine

案 àn ㄢˋ ❶长形的桌子 a long table/desk ❷机关或团体中记事的案卷 official file：备～ *put on file* | 有～可查 *can be checked against a file* ❸提出计划、办法等的文件 document containing plans; proposal：提～ *motion* | 议～ *proposal* ❹事件 incident：五卅惨～ *the May 30th Massacre* 特指涉及法律问题的事件 (specifically) law case：～情 *details of a case* | 犯～ *be caught for committing a crime* | 破～ *crack a criminal case* ❺古时候端饭用的木盘 (ancient) wooden tray (for serving food)：举～齐眉（形容夫妇互相敬重）*treat one's spouse with respect (literally means 'to hold the tray level with* *one's eyebrows')* ❻ same as "按❹"

暗(❶❸* 闇) àn ㄢˋ ❶不亮，没有光，跟"明"相对 dark (opposite of 明)：～中摸索 *grope in the dark*| 这间屋子太～。*This room is too dark.* [暗淡] 昏暗，不光明 dim; dull; gloomy：颜色～ *have a dull colour* | 前途～ *have a bleak future* ❷不公开的，隐藏不露的，跟"明"相对 hidden (opposite of 明)：～号 *secret signal* | ～杀 *assassinate* | 心中～喜 *rejoice inwardly* ❸愚昧，糊涂 ignorant; muddled：明于知彼，～于知己 *understand others but not oneself*

黯 àn ㄢˋ 昏黑 dusky [黯然] 昏暗的样子 gloomy ㊖心神沮丧 depressed：～泪下 *shed tears in depression*

ANG ㄤ

肮(骯) āng ㄤ [肮脏](－zāng) 不干净 dirty

卬 áng ㄤˊ ❶人称代词，我 (personal pronoun) I; me ❷ same as "昂" ❸姓 (surname) Ang

⇨ see also yǎng on p.758

昂 áng ㄤˊ ❶仰，高抬 to raise：～首挺胸 *with one's chin up and chest out* ❷高，贵 expensive; costly：～贵 *expensive*| 价～ *at a high price* ❸情绪高 ㊂ spirited：～扬 *high-spirited* | 激～ *roused; excited* | 气～～ *in high spirits*

盎 àng ㄤˋ ❶古代的一种盆，腹大口小 (ancient) a kind of vessel, with a large belly and a small mouth ❷盛 (shèng) abundant：春意～然。*Spring is in the air.* | 兴味～然 *be greatly interested*

AO ㄠ

凹 āo ㄠ 洼下，跟"凸"相对 concave (opposite of 凸)：～透镜 *concave lens* | ～凸不平 *uneven*

熬 āo ㄠ 煮 to stew：～菜 *stewed vegetables*

⇨ see also áo on p.8

爊(** 爊) āo ㄠ ❶放在微火上煨熟 to simmer ❷ same as "熬(āo)"

敖 áo ㄠˊ ❶ same as "遨" ❷姓 (surname) Ao

嶅 áo ㄠˊ 嶅山，山名，一在山东省新泰，一在广东省东北部 Aoshan Mountain (one in Xintai, Shandong Province, one in the northeast of Guangdong Province) [嶅阴] 地名，在山东省新泰 Aoyin (a place in Xintai, Shandong Province)

遨 áo ㄠˊ 遨游，游逛 to tour; to travel; to roam

嗷 áo ㄠˊ 嘈杂声，喊叫声 ㊂ ouch; the sound of howling：～～待哺 *howling for food*

廒(** 厫) áo ㄠˊ 收藏粮食的仓房 granary：仓～ *granary*

璈 áo ㄠˊ 古代的一种乐器 (ancient) musical instrument

獒 áo ㄠˊ 一种狗，身体大，凶猛善斗，能帮助人打猎 mastiff

A

熬 áo ㄠˊ ❶久煮 to cook for a long time on a low fire：～粥 *make congee* | ～药 *decoct medicinal herbs* ❷忍受，耐苦支撑 to endure (distress, hard times, etc.)：～夜 *stay up late or all night* | ～红了眼睛 *have bloodshot eyes from lack of sleep*

⇨ see also āo on p.7

聱 áo ㄠˊ 话不顺耳 (of words) unpleasant to the ear［聱牙］文句念着不顺口 (of sentences) awkward to read：诘屈～ *(of texts) awkward to read*

螯 áo ㄠˊ 螃蟹等甲壳动物变形的第一对脚，形状像钳子，能开合，用来取食、自卫(of crustaceans) chela; pincer

謷 áo ㄠˊ 诋毁 to slander：訾(zǐ)～ *to defame*［謷謷］1 不考虑别人的话 to ignore other people's view 2 悲叹声 sigh of sorrow

鳌（鼇、*鰲） áo ㄠˊ 传说中海里的大鳖 (in Chinese legend) a huge softshell turtle in the sea

翱（*翶） áo ㄠˊ ［翱翔］(-xiáng) 展开翅膀回旋地飞 to hover; to soar：雄鹰在天空～。*Eagles hovered in the sky.*

鏖 áo ㄠˊ 激烈地战斗 to fight hard：～战 *engage in fierce battle* | 赤壁～兵 *the Battle of Chibi*

拗（*抝） ǎo ㄠˇ 〈方 dialect〉弯曲使断，折 to bend and break：竹竿～断了。*The bamboo was bent and broken.*

⇨ see also ào on p.8, niù on p.482

袄（襖） ǎo ㄠˇ 有衬里的上衣 lined jacket：夹～ *lined jacket* | 棉～ *quilted jacket* | 皮～ *fur-lined jacket*

媪 ǎo ㄠˇ 年老的妇人 old woman

岙（**嶴） ào ㄠˋ 浙江、福建等沿海一带把山间平地叫"岙" level ground in a mountain (used in coastal regions like Zhejiang and Fujian provinces)

垇 ào ㄠˋ 同"坳"。多用于地名 same as 坳 (often used in place names)：黄～（在江西省井冈山市）*Huang'ao (a place in Jinggangshan municipality, Jiangxi Province)*

坳（*坳） ào ㄠˋ 山间平地 level ground between mountains：山～ *level ground between mountains*

拗（*抝） ào ㄠˋ 不顺，不顺从 to defy; to disobey：～口 *difficult to pronounce* | 违～ *to disobey*

⇨ see also ǎo on p.8, niù on p.482

奡 ào ㄠˋ ❶ same as "傲" ❷矫健 vigorous：排～（文章有力）*(of writing) vigorous and forceful*

傲 ào ㄠˋ ❶自高自大（㊥骄－）conceited：～慢 *arrogant* | 高～ *haughty* ❷藐视，不屈 to look down on; to despise：红梅～霜雪。*In defiance of snow and frost, the red plum tree blossomed.*

骜（驁） ào ㄠˋ ❶快马 fine horse ❷马不驯良 (of

horses) intractable ⑩傲慢，不驯顺 arrogant; intractable：桀～不驯 *wild and intractable*

鏊 ào ㄠ 一种铁制的烙饼的炊具，平面圆形，中间稍凸 griddle

奥 ào ㄠ 含义深，不容易懂 profound and difficult to understand：深～ *recondite* | ～妙 *profound and subtle*

薁 ào ㄠ 有机化合物，是萘(nài)的同分异构体，青蓝色，有特殊气味，用作药物 azulene

⇨ see also yù on p.805

澳 ào ㄠ ❶海边弯曲可以停船的地方 inlet ❷指澳门 Macao：港～（香港和澳门）同胞 *Hong Kong and Macao compatriots* ❸指澳洲（现称大洋洲），世界七大洲之一 Oceania (now called 大洋洲) ❹指澳大利亚 Australia

懊 ào ㄠ 烦恼，悔恨 restless; regret：～悔 *to regret* [懊丧]（－sàng）因失意而郁闷不乐 depressed (from frustration)

B

B ㄅ

BA ㄅㄚ

八 bā ㄅㄚ 数目字 eight

扒 bā ㄅㄚ ❶抓住，把着 to hold on to; to cling to：～着栏杆 *hold on to the railing* | ～着树枝 *clutch the branch of a tree* ❷刨开，挖 to dig: 城墙～了个豁口。*A breach was made in the city wall.* [扒拉]（–la）拨动 to prod; to pluck：～算盘 *flick abacus beads* | ～开众人 *push one's way through a crowd* ❸剥，脱 to strip off; to take off：～皮 *to skin; (figuratively) exploit harshly* | ～下衣裳 *strip off one's clothes*

⇨ see also pá on p.488

叭 bā ㄅㄚ 形容物体的断裂声、枪声等 crack; bang：～的一声，弦断了。*The string broke with a snap.* | ～，～，两声枪响。*Bang! Bang! Two shots rang out.*

朳 bā ㄅㄚ 无齿的耙子 toothless rake

巴 bā ㄅㄚ ❶黏结着的东西 crust：锅～ *rice crust* ❷〈方 dialect〉粘住，依附在别的东西上 to stick to ; to cling to：饭～锅了。*The rice has stuck to the pot.* | 爬山虎～在墙上。*The Boston ivy clings to the wall.* ❸〈方 dialect〉贴近 to be close to; to be next to：前不～村，后不～店 *with neither village ahead nor inn behind; be stranded in a desolate place* [巴结]（–jie）奉承，谄媚 to flatter; to fawn on ❹巴望，盼，期望 to hope; to look forward to：～不得马上到家 *cannot wait to get home* ❺古代国名，在今重庆市一带 Ba (an ancient state, near today's Chongqing Municipality) ❻（ba）词尾 used as a suffix ①在名词后 used as a nominal suffix：尾～ *tail* ②在动词后 used as a verbal suffix：眨～眼 *to blink* | 试～试～ *have a try* ③在形容词后 used as an adjectival suffix：干～ *dried up; shrivelled* | 皱～ *crumpled; wrinkled* ❼压强的非法定计量单位，符号 bar，1 巴合 10^5 帕 bar (unofficial unit of pressure, equal to 10^5 pascal)

芭 bā ㄅㄚ [芭蕉]（–jiāo）草本植物，叶宽大。果实也叫芭蕉，跟香蕉相似，可以吃 Japanese banana

吧 bā ㄅㄚ ❶ same as "叭" [吧嗒]（–dā）形容物体轻微撞击声、液体滴落声等 (of sound) to click; (of water) to patter [吧唧]（–jī）形容嘴唇开合声、脚踩泥水声等 to smack (one's lips); to squelch ❷（外 *loanword*）具备特定功能或设施的休闲场所 bar：酒～ *bar* | 网～ *Internet café* |

氧～ *oxygen bar* | ～台 *bar counter*

⇨ see also bɑ on p.13

岜 bā ㄅㄚ （壮 zhuang）石山 rocky mountain ［岜关岭］地名，在广西壮族自治区扶绥 Baguanling (a place in Fusui, Guangxi Zhuang Autonomous Region)

疤 bā ㄅㄚ ❶疤瘌（lɑ），伤口或疮平复以后留下的痕迹 scar：疮～ *scar* | 伤～ *scar* | 伤口结～了。*A scar has formed over the wound.* ❷器物上像疤的痕迹 mark (on a vessel)

蚆 bā ㄅㄚ 蚆蛸（shāo）岛，岛名，在辽宁省长海县 Bashaodao Island (in Changhai County, Liaoning Province)

笆 bā ㄅㄚ 用竹子、柳条等编成的片状物 flat object woven from bamboo or wicker：竹篾～ *fence woven from bamboo* | ～篓 *basket (carried on the back) made from bamboo or wicker* | 荆～ *chaste-tree basketry* | 篱～ *fence*

羓 bā ㄅㄚ ❶干肉。泛指干制食品 dried meat; (generally) dried food ❷一种品种好的羊 a high-quality breed of sheep

粑 bā ㄅㄚ 〈方 dialect〉饼类食物 叠 cake：玉米～～ *corn cake*

鲃（鲃） bā ㄅㄚ 鱼名，身体侧扁或略呈圆筒形，生活在淡水中 common barbel

捌 bā ㄅㄚ “八”字的大写 elaborate form of 八, used in commercial or financial context

拔 bá ㄅㄚˊ ❶抽，拉出，连根拽（zhuài）出 to pull out; to root up：～草 *pull up weeds* | ～牙 *extract a tooth* | 一毛不～（形容吝啬）*miserly (literally means 'unwilling to give up even a hair')* | 不能自～ *unable to extricate oneself* 引夺取军事上的据点 to capture a military stronghold：连～数城 *capture several cities in succession* | ～去敌人的据点 *seize an enemy stronghold* ❷吸出 to suck out; to draw out：～毒 *draw out poison* | ～火罐 *fire cupping; short detachable stove chimney (used to help draw fire)* ❸挑选，提升 to select; to promote：选～ *select (talents)* ［提拔］挑选人员使担任更高的职务 to promote sb ❹超出 to surpass; to stand out：出类～萃（人才出众）*stand out from one's peers* ［海拔］地面超出海平面的高度 altitude; height above sea level

茇 bá ㄅㄚˊ 草根 grass roots

妭 bá ㄅㄚˊ 美妇 beautiful woman

胈 bá ㄅㄚˊ 大腿上的毛 hairs on the thigh

菝 bá ㄅㄚˊ ［菝葜］（－qiā）藤本植物，叶卵圆形，茎有刺，花黄绿色，浆果红色。根状茎可入药 China root

跋 bá ㄅㄚˊ ❶翻过山岭 to cross mountains：～山涉水 *cross mountains and ford rivers* ［跋涉］爬山蹚水，形容行路辛苦 make an arduous journey：长途～ *trudge over a long distance* ❷写在文章、书籍等后面的短文，多是评介内

容的 postscript; epilogue：～文 *postscript*

［跋扈］（－hù）骄傲而专横 bossy; domineering

B

魃 bá ㄅㄚˊ 传说中造成旱灾的鬼怪 (in Chinese legend) demon of drought：旱～ *demon of drought*

鼥 bá ㄅㄚˊ see 鮀鼥 (tuó－) at 鮀 on page 668

把 bǎ ㄅㄚˇ ❶拿，抓住 to hold; to grasp：～盏 *raise a wine cup* | 两手～住门 *hold the door with both hands* ❷控制，掌握 to control：～舵 *hold the rudder; to steer* | ～犁 *handle a plough* ［把持］专权，一手独揽，不让他人参与 to dominate; to monopolize：～财权 *monopolize financial power* ［把握］1 掌握，控制，有效地处理 to grasp; to seize：～时机 *seize an opportunity* 2 事情成功的可靠性 assurance; certainty：这次试验，他很有～。*He is quite sure of this experiment.* ❸把守，看守 to guard; to watch：～门 *guard a gate* | ～风（守候，防有人来）*keep watch* ❹手推车、自行车等的柄 handlebar：车～ *handlebar* ❺（－儿）可以用手拿的小捆 bundle：草～儿 *bundle of straw* ❻介词，表示后边的名词是处置的对象 preposition, indicating that the noun that follows is the object of disposal：～一生献给党 *devote one's whole life to the Party* | ～衣服洗干净了。*The clothes were washed clean.* ❼量词 measure word ①用于有柄的 used for things with a handle：一～刀 *a knife* | 一～扇子 *a fan* ②用于可以一手抓的 a handful of：一～粮食一～汗。*A drop of sweat brings a handful of grain.* ③用于某些抽象的事物 used for sth abstract：一～年纪 *old age* | 努～力 *make an effort* ❽放在量词或"百、千、万"等数词的后面，表示约略估计 used after certain measure words, or numerals such as hundred, thousand, ten thousand, to express approximation：丈～高的树 *a tree about ten feet high* | 个～月以前 *about a month ago* | 有百～人 *there are about a hundred people* ❾指拜把子（结为异姓兄弟）的关系 sworn brotherhood：～兄 *sworn older brother*

［把势］［把式］（－shi）1 武术 martial arts：练～ *practise martial arts* 2 专精一种技术的人 skilled person：车～（赶车的）*cart-driver*

［把戏］魔术、杂耍一类的技艺 acrobatics; jugglery ⑩手段，诡计 trick：你又想玩什么～？*What tricks are you up to now?*

⇨ see also bà on p.13

钯（鈀） bǎ ㄅㄚˇ 金属元素，符号 Pd，银白色，能吸收多量的氢，可用来制催化剂。它的合金可制电器、仪表等 palladium (Pd)

⇨ see also pá on p.488

靶 bǎ ㄅㄚˇ （－子）练习射击用的目标 target (to shoot at)：打～ *practise target-shooting* | ～心 *bullseye*

坝(❸垻、壩) bà ㄅㄚˋ ❶截住河流的建筑物 dam：拦河～ *barrage (across a river)* ❷河工险要处巩固堤防的建筑物 dyke ❸（一子）〈方 dialect〉平地。常用于西南各省地名 flat land (often used in place names in provinces of southwest China)

把(** 欛) bà ㄅㄚˋ （一儿）物体上便于手拿的部分，柄 handle; grip：刀～儿 *handle of a knife* | 茶壶～儿 *handle of a teapot* [话把儿] 被人作为谈笑资料的言论或行为 subject of ridicule

➪ see also bǎ on p.12

爸 bà ㄅㄚˋ 称呼父亲 ㊀ Dad

耙 bà ㄅㄚˋ ❶用来把土块弄碎、弄平的农具 harrow：钉齿～ *spike-tooth harrow* | 圆盘～ *disc harrow* ❷用耙弄碎土块 to harrow：地已经～过了。*The field has been harrowed.*

➪ see also pá on p.488

䶕(齙) bà ㄅㄚˋ 〈方 dialect〉牙齿外露 (of front teeth) projecting：～牙 *bucktooth*

罢(罷) bà ㄅㄚˋ ❶停，歇（㊥一休）to stop; to cease：～工 *go on strike* | ～手 *give up* | 欲～不能 *be unable to stop in spite of oneself* ❷免去（官职）（㊥一免）to dismiss (from office)：～官 *dismiss from office* | ～职 *remove from position* ❸完了，毕 to finish：吃～饭 *after a meal*

〈古 ancient〉also same as 疲 (pí)

➪ see also ba on p.14

䎬(羅) bà ㄅㄚˋ same as "耙 (bà)"

鲅(鮁) bà ㄅㄚˋ 鱼名，即马鲛，身体侧扁而长，性凶猛，生活在海洋里 Japanese seerfish (also 马鲛)

鲌(鮊) bà ㄅㄚˋ same as "鲅"

➪ see also bó on p.49

霸(* 覇) bà ㄅㄚˋ ❶依靠权势横行无忌，迫害人民的人 tyrant; bully：他过去是码头上的一～。*He used to be a bully at the wharf.* ㊁以武力或经济力量侵略、压迫别国，扩大自己势力的国家 hegemonic power; hegemony [霸道] 1 蛮横 overbearing：横行～ *tyrannize over* 2（-dao）猛烈的，厉害的 strong; potent：这药够～的。*This medicine is really strong.* ❷强占 to seize; to occupy by force：～占 *take by force* | ～住不让 *occupy by force and refuse to give up* ❸古代诸侯联盟的首领 (ancient) leader of an alliance of princedoms：春秋五～ *the Five Overlords in the Spring and Autumn Period (770–476BC)*

灞 bà ㄅㄚˋ 灞河，水名，在陕西省西安 Bahe River (in Xi'an, Shaanxi Province)

吧 ba · ㄅㄚ 助词，用在句末或句中。也作"罢" (auxiliary word) used at the end or in the middle of a sentence (also written as 罢) ①表示可以，允许 expressing consent or approval：好～，就这么办～。*All right, let's*

B

do it this way. ②表示推测，估量 expressing supposition：今天不会下雨～？ *Looks as if it won't rain today, doesn't it?* ③表示命令，请求 expressing a command or request：快出去～！*Quickly, get out!* | 还是你去～！*It would be better for you to go.* ④用于停顿处 used to mark a pause：说～，不好意思；不说～，问题又不能解决。*It is embarrassing to talk about it, but the issue will remain unsolved if not.*

⇨ see also bā on p.10

罢(罷) ba・ㄅㄚ same as "吧(ba)"

⇨ see also bà on p.13

BAI ㄅㄞ

刏 bāi ㄅㄞ [刏划](-huai)〈方 dialect〉1 处置，安排 to deal with; to arrange：这件事让他～吧。*Let him deal with it.* 2 修理，整治 to repair; to fix：这孩子把闹钟～坏了。*The child damaged the alarm clock by trying to fix it.*

掰 bāi ㄅㄞ 用手把东西分开或折断 to break off; to snap off：～月饼 *break a moon cake into pieces* | ～老玉米 *break off corn cobs* | 把这个蛤蜊～开。*Split the clam open.*

擘 bāi ㄅㄞ same as "掰"

⇨ see also bò on p.51

白 bái ㄅㄞˊ ❶像雪或乳汁的颜色，跟"黑"相对 white (opposite of 黑)：～面 *wheat flour* | 他头发～了。*His hair has turned white.* ㊕①有关丧事的 funerary：办～事 *manage funeral affairs* ②反动的 reactionary：～军 *the White Army* | ～匪 *White bandits* [白领] 一般指从事脑力劳动的管理人员、技术人员、政府公务人员等 white-collar worker ❷清楚(㊈明-) clear：真相大～。*The truth has come out.* | 蒙受不～之冤 *suffer from an unredressed injustice* ❸亮 bright：东方发～。*Day breaks.* ❹空空的，没有加上其他东西的 blank; plain：～卷(juàn) *unanswered exam paper* | ～水 *plain water* | ～地(没有庄稼的地) *unplanted land* ㊁副词 adverb ①没有效果地 in vain：这话算～说。*The words have fallen on deaf ears.* | 烈士们的鲜血没有～流。*The martyrs did not shed their blood in vain.* ②不付代价地 free of charge：～给 *give away for free* | ～饶 *give as an extra* | ～吃 *eat for free* ❺陈述，说明 to state; to explain：自～ *vindicate oneself* | 表～ *explain oneself* | 道～(戏曲中不用唱的语句) *spoken parts (in Chinese opera)* [白话] 1 口头说的话 spoken words (seen as unrealizable / unfounded) 2 在口语基础上形成的汉语书面语，跟"文言"相对 vernacular language (opposite of 文言) ❻指字形或字音有错 (of Chinese characters) wrongly written or pronounced：写～了 *(it's) incorrectly written* | 念～了 *(it's) mispronounced* [白字] 别字 wrongly written or pronounced character

［白族］我国少数民族，参看附录四 the Bai people (one of the ethnic groups in China. See Appendix Ⅳ.)

拜 bái ㄅㄞˊ ［拜拜］(外 loan-word) 再见 bye-bye ㊀结束某种关系 to break off a relationship

⇨ see also bài on p.16

百 bǎi ㄅㄞˇ ❶数目，十个十 hundred ㊀表示众多或所有的 numerous; all kinds of: ～花齐放，～家争鸣。*Let a hundred flowers blossom and a hundred schools of thought contend.* | ～战～胜 *be ever-victorious* ［百姓］人民 common people ❷法定计量单位中十进倍数单位词头之一，表示 10^2，符号 h。(decimal unit prefix) hecto- (h)

佰 bǎi ㄅㄞˇ "百"字的大写 elaborate form of 百, used in commercial or financial context

伯 bǎi ㄅㄞˇ ［大伯子］(—— zi) 丈夫的哥哥 brother-in-law (elder brother of one's husband)

⇨ see also bó on p.48

柏(*栢) bǎi ㄅㄞˇ ❶常绿乔木，有侧柏、圆柏、罗汉柏等多种。木质坚硬，纹理致密，可供建筑或制器物用 Chinese weeping cypress ❷姓 (surname) Bai

⇨ see also bó on p.48, bò on p.51

捭 bǎi ㄅㄞˇ 分开 to divide; to separate: ～阖(hé)(开合) *to divide or unite*

摆(擺、❺襬) bǎi ㄅㄞˇ ❶陈列，安放 to put; to arrange: 把东西～整齐。*Put things in order.* ㊀故意显示 to show off: ～阔 *parade one's wealth* | ～架子 *put on airs* ［摆布］任意支配 to order about; to manipulate: 受人～ *to be at sb's beck and call* ❷陈述，列举 to state; to spell out: ～事实，讲道理 *to present the facts and reason things out* ❸来回地摇动 to sway; to wave: ～手 *wave one's hand* | 摇头～尾 *assume an air of complacency or levity (literally means 'shake the head and wag the tail')* | 大摇大～ *to swagger* ［摆渡］1 用船运载过河 to ferry 2 过河用的船 ferry boat ［摆脱］挣脱，甩开 to shake off; to break away from: ～贫困 *shake off poverty* ❹钟表等用于控制摆动频率的装置 pendulum: 钟～ *pendulum* ❺衣裙的下边 lower hem: 下～ *lower hem of a garment* (see picture of 上衣 on page 767)

呗(唄) bài ㄅㄞˋ ［梵呗］(fàn—) 佛教徒念经的声音 Buddhist chanting of prayers

⇨ see also bei on p.28

败(敗) bài ㄅㄞˋ ❶输，失利，跟"胜"相对 to lose; to be defeated (opposite of 胜): 一～涂地 *suffer a crushing defeat* | 敌军～了。*The enemy troops have been defeated.* ❷打败，使失败 to defeat; to beat: 人民军队大～侵略军。*The people's army inflicted a crushing defeat on the invading army.* ❸做事没有达

B

到目的，不成功，跟"成"相对 to fail (opposite of 成)：功～垂成 *fail on the verge of success* ❹败坏，毁坏 to spoil; to ruin：～血症 *septicemia* | 身～名裂 *lose all standing and reputation* ❺解除，消散 to relieve; to counteract：～火 *relieve internal heat* | ～毒 *counteract a toxin* ❻衰落，使衰落 to wither; to weaken：花开～了。*The flowers faded.* | ～兴（xìng）（情绪低落）*be disappointed; low-spirited* | ～家子儿 *spendthrift*

拜 bài ㄅㄞ ❶过去表示敬意的礼节 to respect：对～ *salute each other* | 叩～ *to kowtow* | 跪～ *to show respect by kneeling down* ㊀恭敬地 courteously：～托 *to entrust* | ～访 *pay a visit* | ～望 *call on sb* | ～请 *cordially invite* [礼拜] 宗教徒对神敬礼或祷告 attend a religious service ㊕周、星期的别称 week ❷行礼祝贺 to send greetings; to extend congratulations：～年 *pay a New Year call* | ～寿 *present birthday greetings* ❸用一定的礼节授予某种名义或结成某种关系 to confer a title or establish a relationship with ceremony：～将（jiàng）*confer the title of general* | ～师 *formally acknowledge sb as tutor/teacher*

⇨ see also bái on p.15

稗 bài ㄅㄞ （-子）草本植物，长在稻田里或低湿的地方，叶像稻叶，是稻田的害草 common barnyard grass ㊗微小的，琐碎的 insignificant; unofficial：～史（记载逸闻琐事的书）*book of historical anecdotes*

韛（鞴） bài ㄅㄞ 〈方 dialect〉风箱 bellows：风～ *bellows* | ～拐子（风箱的拉手）*bellows handle*

呗 bai · ㄅㄞ 助词，用法相当于"呗"（bei）auxiliary word, with the same function as 呗

BAN ㄅㄢ

扳 bān ㄅㄢ ❶把一端固定的东西往下或往里拉，使改变方向 to pull; to turn：～枪栓 *unlock a rifle bolt* | ～着指头算 *count on one's fingers* ❷把输了的赢回来 to win back：～回一局 *win back a game*

攽 bān ㄅㄢ 分给，发给 to distribute; to issue

颁（頒） bān ㄅㄢ 发下（㊐一发）to issue：～布 *to promulgate* | ～证 *issue certificate to sb* | ～奖 *give out an award*

班 bān ㄅㄢ ❶工作或学习的组织 class; group：学习～ *study class* | 机修～ *maintenance team* ❷工作按时间分成的段落，也指工作或学习的场所 shift; work or study place：排～ *arrange shifts (of work)* | 上～ *go to work* | 下～ *come off work* | 值～ *be on duty* ❸定时开行的 regular; scheduled：～车 *regular bus; shuttle bus* | ～机 *scheduled flight* ❹军队编制中的基层单位，在排以下 squad (in the army) ❺量词 measure word ①用于人群 used for groups of people：这～年轻人真有力气。

These young people are really strong. ②用于定时开行的交通运输工具 used for scheduled transport services: 我搭下一～飞机走。*I'll leave on the next flight.* ❻调回或调动（军队）to withdraw or redeploy (troops): ～师 *withdraw troops* | ～兵 *redeploy troops*

斑 bān ㄅㄢ 一种颜色中夹杂的别种颜色的点子或条纹（㊀一驳）spot; stripe: ～马 *zebra* | ～竹 *giant timber bamboo* | ～白（花白）*grizzled; greying* | 雀～ *freckles* [斑斓]（—lán）灿烂多彩 multicoloured: 色彩～ *in bright colours*

瘢 bān ㄅㄢ 皮肤上生斑点的病 macula

般 bān ㄅㄢ ❶样，种类 type: 如此这～ *in this way; thus and thus* | 百～照顾 *show every possible consideration* | 兄弟～的友谊 *fraternal friendship* [一般] 1 同样 same as; as...as: 我们两个人～高。*The two of us are the same height.* 2 普通，普遍 ordinary; common: ～的读物 *general reading materials* | ～人的意见 *general opinion* ❷ (ancient) same as "搬"

搬 bān ㄅㄢ 移动，迁移 to move; to relocate; to remove: 把这块石头～开。*Move the rock away.* | ～家 *move house*

瘢 bān ㄅㄢ 疤，伤口或疮平复以后留下的痕迹 scar: ～痕 *scar*

斒 bān ㄅㄢ 文武全才 a master of both the pen and the sword

阪 bǎn ㄅㄢˇ ❶ (old) same as "坂" ❷用于地名 used in place names: 大～（在日本）*Osaka* (in Japan)

坂（*岅）bǎn ㄅㄢˇ 山坡，斜坡 hillside; slope: ～上走丸（形容迅速）*as fast as a ball rolling down a slope*

板（❺闆）bǎn ㄅㄢˇ ❶（—子、—儿）成片的较硬的物体 board; plank: ～材 *planking* | 铁～ *iron plate* | 玻璃～ *glass plate* | 黑～ *blackboard* ❷演奏民族音乐或戏曲时打节拍的乐器 clappers (used in traditional music or operas): 檀～ *hardwood clappers* ㊁歌唱的节奏 rhythm (in singing): 一～三眼 *one accented beat followed by three unaccented ones* | 离腔走～ *off the beat* [板眼] 民族音乐或戏曲中的节拍 metre (in traditional music or opera)㊉做事的条理 orderliness in doing things ❸不灵活，少变化 stiff; inflexible: 表情太～ *look too stiff* ❹露出严肃或不高兴的表情 rigid; stern: ～起面孔 *put on a stern expression* ❺[老板] 1 私营工商业的业主 proprietor; boss 2 过去对著名戏曲演员的尊称 a respectful form of address for well-known opera actors in former times

昄 bǎn ㄅㄢˇ 用于地名 used in place names: ～大（在江西省德兴）*Banda (in Dexing, Jiangxi Province)*

版 bǎn ㄅㄢˇ ❶用木板或金属等制成供印刷用的东西，上

B

面有文字或图形 printing plate; block：木～书 *block-printed book*| 活字～ *movable-type plate* ㉤底版，相片的底片 negative; photographic plate：修～ *retouching* ❷印刷物排印的次数 edition：第一～ *first edition* | 再～ *second edition* [出版] 书籍报刊等编印发行 to publish; to come out ❸报纸的一面叫一版 (of a newspaper) page：头～头条新闻 *front page headline* ❹打土墙用的夹板 clamping board (for making an earthen wall)：～筑 *build a wall with clamping boards* ❺户籍 household register [版图] 户籍和地图 household registers and maps ㉕国家的疆域 domain; territory

钣(鈑) bǎn ㄅㄢˇ 金属板材 metal plate：铅～ *lead plate* | 钢～ *steel plate*

舨 bǎn ㄅㄢˇ see 舢板 (shān—) at 舢 on page 576

办(辦) bàn ㄅㄢˋ ❶处理 to handle；to deal with：～公 *handle official business* | ～事 *handle affairs* | 好，就这么～。*OK, let's do it this way.* ㉤处分，惩治 to punish：重（zhòng）～ *punish severely* | 首恶者必～。*The principal culprits must be punished severely.* ❷创设 to set up; to establish：～工厂 *set up a factory* ❸置备 to prepare：～货 *buy goods* | ～酒席 *prepare a feast*

半 bàn ㄅㄢˋ ❶二分之一 half：十个的一～是五个。*Half of ten is five.* | ～米布 *half a metre of cloth* | 一吨～ *one and a half tons*| 分给他一～。*Give him half.* ❷在中间 in the middle：～夜 *midnight* | ～途而废 *give up halfway* ❸不完全的 semi-; partly：～透明 *semi-transparent* | ～脱产 *partly released from one's regular work*

伴 bàn ㄅㄢˋ ❶（一儿）同在一起生活或活动的人（㉠一侣）companion; partner：同～ *companion* | 老～儿 *(of an old married couple) husband; wife* | 找个～儿学习 *find a companion to study with* ❷陪着，伴随 to accompany：～游 *accompany sb on a journey; travelling companion* | ～奏 *to accompany (on a musical instrument)*

拌 bàn ㄅㄢˋ 搅和 to mix：搅～ *stir and mix* | ～种子 *dress seeds* | ～草喂牛 *prepare cattle fodder (by mixing hay with bran, etc.)*

绊(絆) bàn ㄅㄢˋ 行走时被别的东西挡住或缠住 to stumble; to trip：～马索 *rope for tripping a horse; heel rope* | 一不留神被石头～倒了 *trip over a stone by accident* [羁绊]（jī—）束缚 trammels; fetters：挣脱封建礼教的～ *cast off the fetters of feudal ethics*

柈 bàn ㄅㄢˋ （一子）大块的木柴 large piece of firewood

靽 bàn ㄅㄢˋ 驾车时套在牲口后部的皮带 breeching; croup strap

扮 bàn ㄅㄢˋ 化装成（某种人物）（㉠装一）to dress up as; to play the part of：～老头儿 *dress up as an old man* | ～演（化装成某种人物出场表演）*act the role of* [打扮] 1 化装，装饰 to dress up; to make up: ～得很漂亮 *be beautifully dressed* 2 衣着穿戴 the way one is dressed

湴 bàn ㄅㄢˋ 〈方 dialect〉烂泥 mire

瓣 bàn ㄅㄢˋ ❶（一儿）花瓣，组成花冠的各片 petal: 梅花五～。*A plum blossom has five petals.* ❷（一儿）植物的种子、果实或球茎可以分开的片状物 segment/section (of fruits, seeds, etc.): 豆～儿 *bean segment* | 蒜～儿 *clove of garlic* | 橘子～儿 *tangerine wedge* ❸（一儿）量词，用于自然分开或破碎后分成的部分等 measure word for fragment of an object: 一～蒜 *a clove of garlic* | 杯子摔成了好几～儿。*The cup was broken into several pieces.*

BANG ㄅㄤ

邦(**邦) bāng ㄅㄤ 国 country: 友～ *friendly country* | 盟～ *allied country* [邦交] 国与国之间的正式外交关系 diplomatic relations: 建立～ *establish diplomatic relations*

帮(幫、*幇、*幚) bāng ㄅㄤ ❶辅助（㊣一助）to help; to assist: ～忙 *give sb a hand; do sb a favour* | ～手 *assistant* | ～凶 *serve as an accomplice; accomplice* | 我～你做。*I'll help you do it.* ❷集团，帮会 clique; gang: 匪～ *bandit gang* | 青红～ *the Green Gang and the Red Gang* ❸（一子、一儿）旁边的部分 outer part of sth: 船～ *side of a boat; gunwale* | 鞋～儿 *the upper of a shoe* | 白菜～子 *outer leaves of Chinese cabbage* ❹量词，群，伙 (measure word) group; gang; band: 大～人马 *a large group of people*

哪 bāng ㄅㄤ 形容敲打木头等的声音 bang: ～～的敲门声 *noise of banging on the door*

梆 bāng ㄅㄤ ❶梆子，打更用的响器，用竹或木制成。又指戏曲里打拍子用的两根短小的木棍，是梆子腔的主要乐器 watchman's clapper; clappers used in Chinese operas [梆子腔] 戏曲的一种，敲梆子加强节奏。简称"梆子"。有陕西梆子、河南梆子、河北梆子等 (short form 梆子) a type of traditional opera using clappers to stress the rhythm ❷ bang (same as 哪)

浜 bāng ㄅㄤ 〈方 dialect〉小河沟 creek; brook

绑(綁) bǎng ㄅㄤˇ 捆，缚（㊣捆一）to bind; to tie up: 把两根棍子～在一起 *tie two sticks together*

榜(*牓) bǎng ㄅㄤˇ 张贴出来的文告或名单 placard; public notice: 张～招贤 *put up a notice to solicit the service of capable people* | 光荣～ *a roster of honour* [榜样] 样子，行动的模范 model; example: 雷锋是我们学习的～。*Lei Feng is a fine example for us to follow.*

膀 bǎng ㄅㄤˇ ❶（一子）胳膊上部靠肩的部分 upper arm:

他的两 ～真有劲。*He has strong arms.* ❷（～儿）鸟类等的翅膀 wing

⇨ see also pāng on p.492, páng on p.493

玤 bàng ㄅㄤˋ ❶质量次于玉的美石 gemstone inferior to jade ❷古地名，春秋时虢地，在今河南省渑池 an ancient place name (in State Guo in Spring-Autumn Period,in today's Mianchi, Henan Province)

蚌（**蜯）bàng ㄅㄤˋ 软体动物，贝壳长圆形，黑褐色，生活在淡水里，壳内有珍珠层，有的可以产出珍珠 mussel

⇨ see also bèng on p.30

棒 bàng ㄅㄤˋ ❶棍子 stick：棍～ *cudgel*［棒子］（-zi）1 棍子 stick 2〈方 dialect〉玉米 corn：～面 *corn flour* ❷指在某方面优秀，如体力强、能力高、成绩好等 strong; outstanding; excellent：这小伙子真～。*This young fellow is terrific.* | 画得～。*The painting is excellently done.*

傍 bàng ㄅㄤˋ ❶靠 to be close to; to approach：依山～水 *be near the mountains and rivers* ❷临近（多指时间）close to (usually refers to time)：～亮 *at dawn* | ～晚 *at dusk*

谤（**謗**）bàng ㄅㄤˋ ❶恶意攻击（㊀诽－、毁－）to slander; to defame ❷公开指责 to denounce publicly：妄～前辈 *make irresponsible comments about one's seniors*

塝 bàng ㄅㄤˋ〈方 dialect〉田边土坡，沟渠或土埂的边，多用于地名 slope (beside a field); edge of a ditch (often used in place names)：张～（在湖北省蕲春）*Zhangbang (in Qichun, Hubei Province)*

搒 bàng ㄅㄤˋ 摇橹使船前进，划船 to row a boat with sculls

⇨ see also péng on p.498

蒡 bàng ㄅㄤˋ［牛蒡］草本植物，叶心脏形，很大，花紫红色。果实、根、叶可入药 edible burdock

磅 bàng ㄅㄤˋ（外 *loanword*）❶英美制重量单位，1 磅合 453.6 克 pound (unit of weight) ❷磅秤 platform scale：过～ *to weigh (on a scale)*

⇨ see also páng on p.493

镑（**鎊**）bàng ㄅㄤˋ（外 *loanword*）英国、埃及等国的货币单位 pound (unit of currency)

BAO ㄅㄠ

包 bāo ㄅㄠ ❶用纸、布等把东西裹起来 to wrap; to envelop：把书～起来 *wrap up a book* ❷（～儿）包好了的东西 parcel; package; packet：邮～ *postal parcel* | 行李～ *luggage pack*［包裹］1 缠裹 to wrap up; to bind up：把伤口～起来 *bandage a wound* 2 指邮寄的包 postal parcel ❸装东西的袋 bag; sack：书～ *school bag* | 皮～ *leather bag* ❹量词，用于成包的东西 (measure word) pack;

package：一～花生米 *a packet of peanuts* ❺（一子、一儿）一种带馅儿的、蒸熟的食物 steamed bun with filling：糖～儿 *steamed bun with sugar filling* | 肉～子 *steamed bun with meat filling* ❻肿起的疙瘩 swelling; lump：腿上起个大～ *have a bump on one's leg* ❼容纳在内，总括在一起（㊀一含、一括）to include; to contain：无所不～ *all-inclusive* [包涵]（一han）客套话，请人宽容或原谅 (a polite form of address) to excuse ❽总揽，负全责 exclusive; fully responsible：～销 *have exclusive selling rights; assume the responsibility of selling sth* | ～换 *guarantee replacement of goods* [包办] 总负全责办理 to take full responsibility; to take sole charge of㊁专断独行，不让别人参与 to monopolize; to arrange arbitrarily：～婚姻 *arranged marriage* ❾保证 to guarantee：～你喜欢。*I bet you'll like it.* | ～你玩得痛快。*I'm sure you'll have a good time.* ❿约定专用 to charter：～饭 *to board* | ～场 *book all the (cinema, etc.) tickets* | ～了一辆车 *hired a car*

苞 bāo ㄅㄠ ❶花苞，苞片，花或花序下面像叶的小片 (of a flower) bud：含～未放 *in bud; budding* ❷茂盛 profuse; luxuriant：竹～松茂 *bamboos and pines growing in profusion*

孢 bāo ㄅㄠ 孢子，某些低等生物在无性繁殖或有性生殖中所产生的生殖细胞 spore

枹 bāo ㄅㄠ 枹树，落叶乔木，叶子互生，略呈倒卵形，边缘锯齿形。种子可用来提取淀粉，树皮可以制栲胶 *Quercus serrata* (a deciduous tree whose seed can be used to extract starch and bark can be made into rubber)

⇨ see also fú on p.186

胞 bāo ㄅㄠ ❶胞衣，包裹胎儿的膜和胎盘 afterbirth ❷同一父母所生的 born of the same parents：～兄 *elder brother* | ～叔（父亲的同父母的弟弟）*paternal uncle* [同胞] 1 同父母的兄弟姊妹 siblings 2 称同祖国、同民族的人 compatriot

炮 bāo ㄅㄠ ❶把物品放在器物上烘烤或焙 to dry with heat：把湿衣服搁在热炕上～干 *spread damp clothes on the heated brick bed for drying* ❷烹饪方法，在旺火上急炒 to quick-fry：～羊肉 *sauté mutton*

⇨ see also páo on p.494, pào on p.495

龅(齙) bāo ㄅㄠ [龅牙] 突出唇外的牙齿 bucktooth

剥 bāo ㄅㄠ 去掉外面的皮、壳或其他东西（常用于口语）(usually in spoken Chinese) to shell; to peel; to skin：～花生 *shell peanuts* | ～皮 *peel the skin off*

⇨ see also bō on p.48

煲 bāo ㄅㄠ 〈方 dialect〉❶壁较陡直的锅 deep cooking pot：沙～ *casserole* | 瓦～ *earthen pot* | 电饭～ *electric rice cooker* ❷用

B

煲煮或熬 to cook in a deep cooking pot：～粥 *cook congee* | ～汤 *make soup*

褒(*襃) bāo ㄅㄠ 赞扬，夸奖，跟"贬"相对（㊀一奖）to praise; to commend (opposite of 贬)：～扬 *to praise* | ～义词 *complimentary word*

雹 báo ㄅㄠˊ （一子）冰雹，空中水蒸气遇冷结成的冰粒或冰块，常在夏季随暴雨降下 hail

薄 báo ㄅㄠˊ ❶扁平物体上下两个面之间的距离较小的，跟"厚"相对 thin (opposite of 厚)：～片 *thin slice* | ～饼 *pancake* | ～纸 *thin sheet of paper* | 这块布太～。*This piece of cloth is too thin.* ❷（感情）冷淡，（情义）不深 (to treat sb) with disrespect; with indifference：待我不～。*(He/She) is rather nice to me.* ❸（味道）淡 (of taste) bland：酒味很～。*The wine tastes light.* ❹不肥沃 infertile：土地～。*The land is infertile.*

⇨ see also bó on p.50, bò on p.51

饱(飽) bǎo ㄅㄠˇ ❶吃足了，跟"饿"相对 full (opposite of 饿) ㊁足，充分 to the full：～学 *erudite* | ～经风霜 *have had one's fill of hardships* [饱和] 在一定的温度和压力下，溶液内所含被溶解物质的量已达到最大限度，不能再溶解 to saturate ㊁ 事物发展到最高限度 to reach the ultimate limit [饱满] 充实，充足 plump：谷粒长得很～。*The grains are plump.* | 精神～ *full of vigour and vitality* ❷满足 to feel satisfied：大～眼福 *feast one's eyes*

宝(寶、*寳) bǎo ㄅㄠˇ ❶珍贵的 precious：～刀 *precious sword* | ～石 *gemstone* | ～物 *treasure* 敬辞，称与对方有关的人或事物，如家眷、店铺等 (polite speech) used to refer to the other party's family, property, etc.：～眷 *your respected family* | ～号 *your company; your name* ❷珍贵的东西 treasure：珠～ *jewellry* | 国～ *national treasure* | 粮食是～中之～。*Grain is the treasure of all treasures.* [宝贝] 1 珍贵的东西 treasure 2（一儿）对小孩儿亲昵的称呼 (endearment for child) darling

保 bǎo ㄅㄠˇ ❶看守住，护着不让受损害或丧失（㊀一卫、一护）to protect：～家卫国 *to protect one's homes and defend one's country* | ～健 *maintain health* | ～育 *to rear* [保持] 维持，使持久 to maintain：～艰苦奋斗的作风 *maintain a style of plain living and hard struggle* [保守] 1 保住，使不失去 to keep：～机密 *keep secret* 2 守旧，不改进 conservative：这个想法太～了。*The idea is too conservative.* [保障] 1 维护 to safeguard：～群众的合法权益 *safeguard the legal rights of the people* 2 作为卫护的力量 guarantee：人民解放军是祖国安全的～。*The PLA is the guarantee of the safety of our motherland.* ❷

负责，担保 to guarantee：～证 *to pledge; to ensure; guarantee* | ～荐 *recommend and guarantee* | 我敢～他一定做得好。*I can assure you that he'll do it well.* [保险] 1 因自然灾害或意外事故等造成损失而给付保险金的一种经济补偿制度。参与保险的个人或企业按期向保险公司交保险费，发生灾害或遭受损失时，由保险公司按预定保险数额赔偿 insurance 2 靠得住 to be sure：这样做～不会错。*It's sure not to be wrong doing it this way.* ❸旧时户口的一种编制，若干户为一甲，若干甲为一保 (old) an administrative system organized on the basis of households, each 保 being made up of several 甲 and each 甲 of several households

[保安族] 我国少数民族，参看附录四 the Bonan people (one of the ethnic groups in China. See Appendix Ⅳ.)

葆 bǎo ㄅㄠˇ ❶草木繁盛 (of plants) luxuriant ❷保持 to preserve：永～青春 *stay young forever*

堡 bǎo ㄅㄠˇ ❶堡垒 fortress：碉～ *pillbox* | 桥头～ *bridgehead* [堡垒] 军事上防守用的建筑物 stronghold：攻下敌人最坚固的～ *capture the enemy's strongest fortress* ⓦ难于攻破的事物 barrier：攻克科学～ *overcome the challenges of science* ❷小城 small town

⇨ see also bǔ on p.52, pù on p.514

褓(*緥) bǎo ㄅㄠˇ see 襁褓 (qiǎng —) at 襁 on page 532

鸨(鴇) bǎo ㄅㄠˇ ❶大鸨，鸟名，比雁略大，背上有黄褐色和黑色斑纹，不善飞而善走 great bustard ❷指鸨母（开设妓院的女人）brothel keeper; madam：老～ *procuress*

报(報) bào ㄅㄠˋ ❶传达，告知 to report; to announce：～喜 *announce good news* | ～信 *to inform* [报告] 向上级或群众陈述，也指向上级或群众所做的陈述 to report; report：～大家一个好消息。*I have some good news for you all.* | 起草～ *draft a report* ❷传达消息和言论的文件或信号 documents or signals that transmit news or messages：电～ *telegram* | 情～ *intelligence* | 警～ *alarm* ❸报纸，也指某些刊物 newspapers; periodical：日～ *daily paper* | 晚～ *evening paper* | 画～ *pictorial* | 黑板～ *blackboard bulletin* ❹回答，回应 to reply; to respond：～恩 *pay a debt of gratitude* | ～仇 *revenge oneself* [报酬] 由于使用别人的劳动或物件而付给的钱或实物 remuneration [报复] 用敌对的行动回击对方 to retaliate

刨(*鉋、*鑤) bào ㄅㄠˋ ❶（～子）推刮木料等使平滑的工具 plane (a tool) ❷用刨子或刨床推刮 to plane：～得不光 *not well planed* | ～平 *plane sth smooth*

⇨ see also páo on p.493

B

B

抱(❸**菢) bào ㄅㄠˋ ❶用手臂围住(㊟拥—) to hold in the arms: ～着孩子 *holding a child in one's arms*|～头鼠窜 *flee helter-skelter* ㊥ 围绕 to surround: 山环水～ *surrounded by mountains and rivers* [合抱] 两臂围拢(多指树木、柱子等的粗细)(of a tree, pillar, etc.) circumference big enough to wrap one's arms around [抱负] 愿望，志向 aspiration; ambition: 做有志气有～的青年 *become an ambitious young man* ❷心里存着 to harbour: ～不平 *be outraged by an injustice*|～歉 *be sorry*|～着必胜的决心 *having the determination to win* ❸孵(fū) to hatch: ～窝 *sit on eggs*|～小鸡 *hatch out chicks* ❹量词，表示两臂合围的量 (measure word) (of a person's arms) span; armful: 树干有两～粗。*The trunk of the tree is two spans in circumference.*

鲍(鮑) bào ㄅㄠˋ ❶软体动物，俗叫鲍鱼，古称鳆(fù)，肉味鲜美 abalone (informal 鲍鱼, called 鳆 in ancient times) ❷鲍鱼，盐腌的干鱼 salted fish

趵 bào ㄅㄠˋ 跳 to bounce: ～突泉(在山东省济南) *Baotuquan Spring (in Jinan, Shandong Province)*

豹 bào ㄅㄠˋ 兽名，像虎而小，毛黄褐或赤褐色，多有黑色斑点。性凶猛，善跳跃，能上树 leopard

暴 bào ㄅㄠˋ ❶强大而突然来的，又猛又急的 sudden and violent: ～风雨 *tempest*|～病 *sudden illness* [暴力] 武力，强制性的力量 violence: 滥施～ *use physical violence abusively*|家庭～ *domestic violence* ❷过分急躁的，容易冲动的 quick-tempered: 这人脾气真～。*This guy is really quick-tempered.* ❸凶恶残酷的(㊟—虐、残—、凶—) fierce; cruel: ～行(xíng) *act of brutality*|～徒 *thug* ❹糟蹋，损害 to spoil; to ruin: 自～自弃 *give oneself up as hopeless* ❺露出来 to expose: ～露 *to expose*|自～家丑 *reveal a scandal in one's own family* ❻姓 (surname) Bao

⇨ see also pù on p.514

瀑 bào ㄅㄠˋ ❶暴雨 downpour ❷瀑河，水名，一在河北省东北部，一在河北省中部 Baohe River (two rivers, both located in Hebei Province, one in the northeast and the other in the centre)

⇨ see also pù on p.514

曝 bào ㄅㄠˋ [曝光] 使感光纸或摄影胶片感光 to expose (in photography) ㊐隐蔽的事情暴露出来，被众人知道 to lay bare: 事情～后，他压力很大。*After the matter came out, he was under great pressure.*

⇨ see also pù on p.514

爆 bào ㄅㄠˋ ❶猛然破裂(㊟—炸) to burst: 豆荚熟得都～了。*The pods were so ripe that they burst open.* [爆竹] 用纸卷火药，点燃引线爆裂发声的东西。又叫爆仗、炮仗 firecracker (also called 爆仗、炮仗) ❷突然发

生 to happen unexpectedly：～发 *break out* | ～冷门 *turn out an unexpected result* ❸烹饪方法，用滚水稍微一煮或用滚油稍微一炸 to quick-cook：～肚（dǔ）儿 *quick-boiled tripe* | ～炒 *quick stir-fry*

BEI ㄅㄟ

陂 bēi ㄅㄟ ❶池塘 pond：～塘 *pond* | ～池 *pond* ❷池塘的岸 (of a pond) edge ❸山坡 slope

⇨ see also pí on p.500，pō on p.509

杯（*盃） bēi ㄅㄟ （一子）盛酒、水、茶等的器皿 cup; glass：酒～ *wine glass* | 玻璃～ *glass* | ～水车薪（用一杯水救一车着火的柴，喻无济于事）*utterly inadequate measures (literally means 'to use a cup of water to put out a cartload of burning wood')*

卑 bēi ㄅㄟ 低下 low：地势～湿 *low and damp terrain* | 自～ *have an inferiority complex* ㊀低劣（㊖一鄙）inferior：～劣 *despicable*

椑 bēi ㄅㄟ ［椑柿］柿子的一种，果实小，青黑色，可用来制柿漆 *Diospyros oleifera Cheng* (a deciduous tree with dark yellow fruits that can be used for making paint)

碑 bēi ㄅㄟ 刻上文字纪念事业、功勋或作为标记的石头 stele：人民英雄纪念～ *Monument to the People's Heroes* | 里程～ *milestone* | 有口皆～（喻人人都说好）*win universal praise*

鹎（鵯） bēi ㄅㄟ 鸟名，羽毛大部分为黑褐色，腿短而细。种类很多 bulbul

背（*揹） bēi ㄅㄟ 人用背（bèi）驮（tuó）东西to carry on one's back：把小孩儿～起来 *carry the child on one's back* | ～包袱 *have a burden on one's mind; bear the financial burden* | ～枪 *shoulder a gun*

⇨ see also bèi on p.26

悲 bēi ㄅㄟ ❶伤心，哀痛（㊖一哀、一伤、一痛）sad; sorrowful：～喜交集 *mixed feelings of grief and joy* ❷怜悯（㊖一悯）have compassion for：慈～ *merciful*

北 běi ㄅㄟˇ ❶方向，早晨面对太阳左手的一边，跟"南"相对 north (opposite of 南)：～门 *north gate* | 由南往～ *from south to north* ❷败北，打了败仗往回跑 to suffer a defeat; to be defeated：三战三～ *lose three battles in succession* | 追奔逐～（追击败逃的敌人）*pursue an enemy in full retreat*

贝（貝） bèi ㄅㄟˋ ❶有壳的软体动物的统称，如蛤蜊、蚌、鲍、田螺等 shellfish ❷古代用贝壳做的货币 cowrie

狈（狽） bèi ㄅㄟˋ 传说中的一种兽 (in Chinese legend) a kind of animal (hunting with wolves)：狼～为奸 *act in collusion with each other*

浿（浿） bèi ㄅㄟˋ 用于地名 used in place names：

B

B

虎～（在福建省宁德）*Hubei (in Ningde, Fujian Province)*

钡(鋇) bèi ㄅㄟˋ 金属元素，符号Ba，银白色，燃烧时发黄绿色火焰 barium (Ba)

孛 bèi ㄅㄟˋ 古书上指彗星 (in ancient Chinese texts) comet

悖(*誖) bèi ㄅㄟˋ 混乱，违反 to be confused; to go against：并行不～ *not to be mutually exclusive* | 有～常理 *go against common sense*

邶 bèi ㄅㄟˋ 周代诸侯国名，在今河南省汤阴东南 Bei (a state in the Zhou Dynasty, in the southeast of today's Tangyin, Henan Province)

背 bèi ㄅㄟˋ ❶躯干后部自肩至后腰的部分 back (see picture of 人体 on page 647) [背地] 不当人面 behind sb's back：不要当面不说，～乱说。*When you won't say it to one's face, don't gossip behind one's back.* [背景] 1 舞台上的布景 backdrop 2 图画上或摄影时衬托主体事物的景物 background ㊋对人物、事件起作用的环境或关系 background：政治～ *political background* | 历史～ *historical background* [背心] 没有袖子和领子的短上衣 vest ❷物体的反面或后面 back：～面 *reverse side* | 手～ *back of a hand* | 刀～ *back of a knife* ❸用背部对着，跟"向"相对 with one's back towards (opposite of 向)：～水作战 *fight a last-ditch battle* | ～光 *with one's back to the light; backlit* | ～灯 *backlight* ㊀①向相反的方向 in the opposite direction：～道而驰 *run in the opposite direction* | ～地性（植物向上生长的性质）*apogeotropism* ② 避 behind sb's back：～着他说话 *talk behind one's back* ③离开 to leave：离乡～井 *be far away from one's hometown (especially against one's will)* ❹凭记忆读出 to recite from memory：～诵 *to recite* | ～书 *recite a text from memory* ❺违背，违反 to break; to violate：～约 *break a contract* | ～信弃义 *break faith with sb* [背叛] 投向敌对方面，反对原来所在的方面 to betray ❻不顺 unfortunate：～时 *ill-timed; unlucky* ❼偏僻，冷淡 remote; (of business) slack：这条胡同太～。*The alley is out-of-the-way.* | ～月（生意清淡的季节）*slack season* ❽听觉不灵 hard of hearing：耳朵有点ㄦ～ *be a little hard of hearing*

⇨ see also bēi on p.25

褙 bèi ㄅㄟˋ 把布或纸一层一层地粘在一起 to glue layers of cloth or paper together：裱～ *to mount (a picture, painting, etc.)*

备(備、*俻) bèi ㄅㄟˋ ❶具备，完备 to have; to possess：德才兼～ *have both integrity and ability* | 求全责～ *be too demanding* ㊀完全，全 all; completely：艰苦～尝 *have experienced all hardships* | 爱护～至 *take utmost care of* ❷预备，防备 to prepare; to take precautions against：～耕 *make preparations for ploughing and planting* | ～荒

be prepared for famine | ～课 *(of a teacher) prepare lessons* | 准～ *get ready* | 有～无患。*Where there is precaution, there is no peril.* [备案] 向主管机关做书面报告，以备查考 to put on record [备份] 备用的重（chóng）份文件、数据或资料等 backup copy ❸设备 equipment：装～ *to equip; equipment* | 军～ *military establishment and equipment*

惫(憊) bèi ㄅㄟˋ 极度疲乏 exhausted：疲～ *tired out*

糒 bèi ㄅㄟˋ 干饭 solid food

鞴 bèi ㄅㄟˋ 把鞍辔（pèi）等套在马身上 to saddle：～马 *saddle a horse*

倍 bèi ㄅㄟˋ ❶跟原数相同的数，某数的几倍就是用几乘某数 times：二的五～是十。*Five times two is ten.* | 精神百～（精神旺盛）*full of vigour* ❷加倍 to double; to redouble：事半功～ *half the work, double the outcome* | 勇气～增 *with redoubled courage* | ～加努力 *redouble one's effort*

棓 bèi ㄅㄟˋ [五棓子] 盐肤木的叶子受五棓子蚜虫刺激后形成的虫瘿，可入药。也作"五倍子" Chinese gall (also written as 五倍子)

焙 bèi ㄅㄟˋ 把东西放在器皿里，用微火在下面烘烤 to bake over a slow fire：把花椒～干研成细末 *bake the seeds of Chinese prickly ash over a slow fire and grind them into a fine powder*

蓓 bèi ㄅㄟˋ [蓓蕾]（－lěi）花骨朵儿，还没开的花 (of flower) bud

碚 bèi ㄅㄟˋ [北碚] 地名，在重庆市 Beibei (a place in Chongqing Municipality)

被 bèi ㄅㄟˋ ❶（－子）睡觉时覆盖身体的东西 quilt：棉～ *cotton-padded quilt* | 夹～ *double layered quilt* ❷盖，遮盖 to cover：～覆 *to cover* ❸介词，引进主动的人物并使动词含有受动的意义 (preposition) used in the passive voice to introduce an active agent：他～父亲骂了一顿。*He was scolded by his father.* | ～大家评选为生产能手。*(He) was elected a model worker by all.* ❹放在动词前，表示受动 used before the verb to express the passive voice：～压迫 *be oppressed* | ～批评 *be criticized*

〈古 ancient〉also same as 披(pī)

鞁 bèi ㄅㄟˋ ❶古时套车用的器具 (old) saddlery ❷ same as "鞴"

琲 bèi ㄅㄟˋ 珠子串儿 string of beads

辈(輩) bèi ㄅㄟˋ ❶代，辈分 generation; seniority (among relatives)：长～ *member of elder generation* | 晚～ *member of younger generation* | 革命前～ *revolutionary predecessors* [辈子]（－zi）人活着的时间 lifetime：一～ *a lifetime* | 半～ *half of one's lifetime* ❷等，类（指人）people of a certain kind：彼～ *they* | 我～ *we* | 无能之～ *the incompetent*

B

鐾 bèi ㄅㄟˋ 把刀在布、皮、石头等物上反复摩擦几下，使锋利 to sharpen a knife on a strop：～刀 *sharpen a knife* | ～刀布 *canvas strop*

呗(唄) bei·ㄅㄟ 助词 auxiliary word ① 表示"罢了""不过如此"的意思 to show that sth is self-evident：这就行了～。*Well, that's it.* ②表示勉强同意的语气，跟"吧"相近 to show concession (similar to 吧)：你愿意去就去～。*Well, go if you want to.*

⇨ see also bài on p.15

臂 bei·ㄅㄟ see 胳臂 (gē－) at 胳 on page 204

⇨ see also bì on p.36

BEN ㄅㄣ

奔(❶△*犇) bēn ㄅㄣ ❶急走，跑(㊀－跑) to move quickly; to run：狂～ *to dash* | ～驰 *to speed* | 东～西跑 *run around* [奔波] 劳苦奔走 bustle around ❷姓 (surname) Ben

⇨ see also bèn on p.29

锛(錛) bēn ㄅㄣ ❶(－子) 削平木料的一种工具，用时向下向内用力 adze ❷用锛子一类东西削、砍 to cut with an adze or sth similar：～木头 *cut wood with an adze* | 用镐～地 *dig with a pickaxe*

贲(賁) bēn ㄅㄣ ❶奔走，快跑 to move quickly [虎贲] 古时指勇士 (ancient) warrior ❷姓 (surname) Ben [贲门] 胃与食管相连的部分 cardia

⇨ see also bì on p.35

栟 bēn ㄅㄣ [栟茶] 地名，在江苏省如东 Bencha (a place in Rudong, Jiangsu Province)

⇨ see also bīng on p.45

犇 bēn ㄅㄣ ❶ see 奔 on page 28 ❷用于人名 used in given names ❸姓 (surname) Ben

本 běn ㄅㄣˇ ❶草木的根，跟"末"相对 root (opposite of 末)：无～之木 *tree without roots* | 木～水源 *the origin of sth (literally means 'root of tree and source of river')* ㊂事物的根源 origin：翻身不忘～ *not to forget one's past after emancipation* [本末] 头尾，始终，事情整个的过程 course of events from beginning to end：～倒置 *put the cart before the horse* | 纪事～(史书的一种体裁) *a genre of historical writing in which every chapter is devoted to the recording of a particular event of significance* [根本] 1 事物的根源或主要的部分 foundation ㊂彻底 radically：～解决 *solve (problems) once and for all* 2 本质上 in essence：～不同 *completely different* [基本] 1 主要的部分 base; foundation：～建设 *capital construction* 2 大体上 on the whole：大坝已经～建成。*The dam has been mostly completed.* ❷草的茎或树的干 (of grass) stem; (of tree) trunk：草～植物 *herb plant* | 木～植物 *woody plant* ❸

中心的，主要的 central; principal：校～部 *main campus* ❹本来，原来 original：～意 *original intention* | 我～想去游泳，结果没去成。*Originally I planned to go swimming, but failed.* ❺自己这方面的 one's own：～国 *our country* | ～厂 *this factory* [本位] 1 自己的责任范围 within the call of duty：做好～工作 *get one's own job done* 2 计算货币用作标准的单位 standard unit：～货币 *standard coin* ❻现今的 current：～年 *this year* | ～月 *this month* ❼（一儿）本钱，用来做生意、生利息的资财 capital：小～儿生意 *business with little capital* | 老～儿 *capital; one's assets so far* | 够～儿 *gain enough to cover the cost* ❽根据 base on：有所～ *be well based on* | ～着负责的态度去做 *do sth conscientiously* ❾（一子、一儿）册子 book：日记～ *diary* | 笔记～ *notebook* ❿（一儿）版本或底本 edition; script：刻～ *wood-block edition* | 稿～ *manuscript* | 剧～儿 *script* ⓫量词，用于书籍等 (measure word for book) copy：一～书 *a book* | 两～账 *two account books*

苯 běn ㄅㄣˇ 有机化合物，无色液体，有特殊气味，可用来制染料，是化学工业的原料和溶剂 benzene

畚 běn ㄅㄣˇ 簸箕，用竹、木、铁片等做的撮土器具 dustpan

夯 bèn ㄅㄣˋ 同"笨"（多见于明清白话小说）same as 笨 (often in the vernacular fictions during Ming-Qing period)

⇨ see also hāng on p.242

坌 bèn ㄅㄣˋ ❶灰尘 dust：尘～满室。*The room was covered all over with dust.* ❷聚集 to gather：响应者～集。*The supporters gathered together.*

奔（*逩） bèn ㄅㄣˋ ❶直往，投向 to head for：投～ *go to a place/sb for shelter* | 直～工厂 *go straight to the factory* | ～向祖国最需要的地方 *run to a place where you are most needed by the motherland* ㊉接近（某年龄段）to be getting on (in years)：他是～七十的人了。*He is almost seventy.* ❷为某种目的而尽力去做 to be after：～材料 *be busy procuring materials* | ～来两张球票 *manage to get two game tickets*

⇨ see also bēn on p.28

倴 bèn ㄅㄣˋ ［倴城］地名，在河北省滦南 Bencheng (a place in Luannan, Hebei Province)

笨 bèn ㄅㄣˋ ❶不聪明(㊥愚一) stupid ❷不灵巧 clumsy：嘴～ *inarticulate* | ～手～脚 *be clumsy* ❸粗重，费力气的 cumbersome：箱子太～。*The crate is too cumbersome.* | ～活 *heavy manual labour*

BENG ㄅㄥ

伻 bēng ㄅㄥ 〈古 ancient〉使，使者 envoy

祊（鬃）** bēng ㄅㄥ ❶古代宗庙门内的祭祀，也指门内祭祀之处 sacrifice

(site) inside the gate of ancestral shrine in ancient times ❷ 祊河，水名，在山东省中部偏南，沂（yí）河支流 Benghe River (a tributary of Yihe River, in the central by south of Shandong Province)

崩 bēng ㄅㄥ ❶倒塌 to collapse：山～地裂 *cataclysm; deafening noise (literally means 'mountains collapse and the earth cracks')*［崩溃］垮台，彻底失败 to collapse; to crumble：敌军～了。*The enemy collapsed.* ❷破裂 to burst：把气球吹～了 *blow the balloon up so hard that it bursts* | 俩人谈～了。*The two of them failed to make an agreement through talk.* ❸爆裂或弹（tán）射出来的东西击中 to get hurt by sth bursting：放爆竹～了手。*The firecracker hurt (his) hand when it went off.* ❹崩症，又叫血崩，一种妇女病 metrorrhagia (also called 血崩) ❺封建时代称帝王死 (of an emperor) to die

嘣 bēng ㄅㄥ 形容东西跳动或爆裂的声音 bang：气球～的一声破了。*The balloon burst with a bang.*

绷（繃、*綳） bēng ㄅㄥ ❶张紧，拉紧 to stretch; to strain：衣服紧～在身上。*The clothes fit too tightly around the body.* | ～紧绳子 *tighten the rope*［绷带］包扎伤口的纱布条 bandage［绷子］（—zi）刺绣用的架子，把绸布等材料张紧在上面，免得皱缩 embroidery frame ❷粗粗地缝上或用针别上 to baste; to pin：～被头 *baste the upper part of the quilt*

⇨ see also běng on p.30

甭 béng ㄅㄥˊ〈方 dialect〉副词，不用 (adverb) needn't：你～说了。*You save the breath.* | ～惦记他。*Don't worry about him.*

绷（繃、*綳） běng ㄅㄥˇ ❶板着 to pull (a long face)：～着个脸 *pull a long face* ❷强忍住 to restrain oneself：他～不住笑了。*He couldn't restrain himself from laughing.*

⇨ see also bēng on p.30

琫 běng ㄅㄥˇ 古代刀鞘近口处的装饰 (ancient) ornaments on the rim of a knife sheath

泵 bèng ㄅㄥˋ（外 loanword）把液体或气体抽出或压入用的机械装置 pump：气～ *air pump* | 油～ *oil pump*

迸 bèng ㄅㄥˋ 爆开，溅射 to burst：～裂 *to burst (open)* | ～溅 *to splatter* | 火星儿乱～。*Sparks flew about.*

蚌 bèng ㄅㄥˋ［蚌埠］（—bù）地名，在安徽省 Bengbu (a place in Anhui Province)

⇨ see also bàng on p.20

甏 bèng ㄅㄥˋ〈方 dialect〉瓮、坛子一类的器皿 earthen jar/vat

镚（鏰） bèng ㄅㄥˋ（—子、—儿）原指清末发行的无孔的小铜币，今泛指小的硬币 small coin：金～子 *gold coin* | 钢～儿 *coin*

蹦 bèng ㄅㄥˋ 两脚并着跳，也泛指跳 to jump：欢～乱

跳 *dancing and jumping with joy; exuberant* | ～了半米高 *jump as high as half a metre* [蹦跶]（－dɑ）蹦跳 jump about ⑩挣扎 to struggle：秋后的蚂蚱～不了几天了。*One is nearing its end. (literally mean 'Late autumn grasshoppers have but a few days left to struggle'.)*

BI ㄅㄧ

屄（**屄）bī ㄅㄧ 女子阴道口的俗称 vaginal orifice, cunt

逼（*偪）bī ㄅㄧ ❶强迫，威胁（㊣－迫）to force; to compel：～债 *press for debt repayment* | ～上梁山 *be driven to revolt* | 寒气～人。*There is a nip in the air.* ❷切近，接近 to approach：～近 *to approach* | ～真 *lifelike; clear* ❸狭窄 narrow：～仄 *cramped*

鲾（鰏）bī ㄅㄧ 鱼名，身体小而侧扁，青褐色，鳞细，口小，生活在近海。种类很多 ponyfish

荸 bí ㄅㄧˊ [荸荠]（－qi）草本植物，生长在池沼或栽培在水田里。地下茎也叫荸荠，球状，皮赤褐色，肉白色，可以吃 water chestnut

鼻 bí ㄅㄧˊ ❶（－子）嗅觉器官，也是呼吸器官之一 nose (see picture of 头 on page 660) ❷（－儿）器物上面突出带孔的部分或带孔的零件 object or part of a machine with a hole in it：门～儿 *bolt staple (of a door)* | 针～儿 *eye of a needle* | 扣～儿 *buttonhole*

[鼻祖] 始祖，创始人 originator; founder

匕 bǐ ㄅㄧˇ 古代一种类似汤勺的餐具 (ancient) ladle [匕首] 短剑 dagger

比 bǐ ㄅㄧˇ ❶比较，较量 to compare; to compete：～干劲 *compete with each other in drive* | ～大小 *compare in size* | ～优劣 *compare in terms of quality* [比赛] 用一定的方式比较谁胜谁负 to compete ❷表示比赛双方得分的对比 refers to a comparison of scores on both sides of the competition：三～二 *3 to 2* ❸两个数相比较，前项和后项的关系是被除数和除数的关系，如 3:5，3 是前项，5 是后项，比值是 3/5。ratio [比例] 1 表示两个比相等的式子，如 6:3=10:5。ratio 2 数量之间的倍数关系 proportion：～合适 *suitable proportion* | 不成～ *disproportional* [比重] 1 一定体积的物体的重量跟在 4℃时同体积的纯水重量的比值，现常改用相对密度表示 specific gravity 2 某一事物在整体中所占的分量 proportion：硕士、博士在科研队伍中的～迅速上升。*The proportion of master's and doctor's degree holders in scientific research personnel increases rapidly.* | 我国工业在整个国民经济中的～逐年增长。*The proportion of industry within our country's national economy as a whole is growing year by year.* ❹比方，模拟，做譬喻（㊣－

B

喻）to make an analogy：把儿童～作祖国的花朵 *compare children to the flowers of our country* | 用手～了一个圆形 *made a circle with one's hand* [比画]（-hua）用手做样子 to gesticulate：他一边说一边～。*He gesticulated while talking.* [比照] 大致依照 in line with; in the light of：你～着这个做一个。*Make one after this model.* ❺介词，用来比较程度或性状的差别 (preposition) used to show comparison (in degree,quality, shape, etc.)：他～我强。*He's better than me.* | 今天的雨～昨天还大。*It's raining even harder today than yesterday.* ❻（formerly pronounced bì）靠近，挨着 close to; next to：～邻 *neighbour; be in the neighbourhood of* | ～肩 *shoulder to shoulder; be as good as* [比比] 一个挨一个 one by one：～皆是 *can be seen everywhere* [比及] 等到 by the time that：～敌人发觉，我们已经冲过火线了。*We had already passed the front line before the enemy realized what had happened.* [朋比] 互相依附，互相勾结 to gang up：～为奸 *gang up to do evil*

芘 bǐ ㄅㄧˇ 有机化合物，棱形晶体，浅黄色，不溶于水。可用来制合成树脂和染料等 pyrene

⇨ see also pí on p.501

吡 bǐ ㄅㄧˇ [吡啶]（-dìng）有机化合物，无色液体，有臭味。可用作溶剂、化学试剂 pyridine

沘 bǐ ㄅㄧˇ 沘江，水名，在云南省西北部，澜沧江支流 Bijiang River (a tributary of Lancangjiang River, in the northwest of Yunnan Province)

妣 bǐ ㄅㄧˇ 原指母亲，后称已经死去的母亲 one's late mother：先～ *my late mother* | 如丧考～（像死了父母一样）*be sorrowful (as if one had lost their parents)*

秕（*粃）bǐ ㄅㄧˇ 籽实不饱满 (of grain) not fully developed [秕子]（-zi）不饱满的籽实 immature grain

舭 bǐ ㄅㄧˇ 船底与船侧之间的弯曲部分 bilge

彼 bǐ ㄅㄧˇ 代词 pronoun ①那，那个，跟"此"相对 that, the other (opposite of 此)：～岸 *(of a river, sea, etc.) the other side* | ～处 *that place* | 顾此失～ *attend to one thing while losing sight of another* ②他，对方 the other (party)：知己知～ *know both the other party and oneself* [彼此] 那个和这个。特指对方和自己两方面 this and that; each other：～有深切的了解 *know each other well* | ～互助 *help each other*

笔（筆）bǐ ㄅㄧˇ ❶写字、画图的工具 pen：毛～ *Chinese writing brush* | 画～ *painting brush* | 钢～ *fountain pen* | ～直（像笔杆一样直）*straight (as a pen)* ❷笔画，组成汉字的横竖撇点折，一画就是一笔。character stroke ❸写 to write：亲～ *write in one's own hand* | 代～ *write on behalf of sb* | ～之于

书 *set sth down in writing* [笔名] 著作人发表作品时用的别名 pen name ❹（写字、绘画、作文的）笔法 technique (in drawing or writing)：败～ *flaw (in drawing or writing)*｜伏～*foreshadowing*｜工～画 *meticulous brushwork* ❺量词 measure word ①用于款项等 for money：收到一～捐款 *receive a donation* ②用于字的笔画 for stroke (of character)："人"字有两～。*The character* 人 *has two strokes.* ③用于书画艺术 for technique (in drawing or writing)：写一～好字 *write in a neat hand*

俾 bǐ ㄅㄧˇ 使 to cause：～便考查 *facilitate the checking process*

鄙 bǐ ㄅㄧˇ ❶粗俗，低下 vulgar; low：～陋 *coarse and shallow* 谦辞 used as a humble speech：～人 *your humble servant; I*｜～意 *my humble opinion*｜～见 *my humble view* ❷低劣 of poor quality：卑～ *mean; despicable* ❸轻蔑 to disdain：可～ *contemptible*｜～视 *look down upon*｜～薄 *to disdain*｜～夷 *to scorn* ❹边远的地方 outlying area：边～ *remote area*

币（幣） bì ㄅㄧˋ 钱币，交换各种商品的媒介 currency; money：银～ *silver coin*｜纸～ *bank note*｜硬～ *coin*｜人民～ *Renminbi; RMB*

必 bì ㄅㄧˋ 副词 adverb ①必定，一定 surely; definitely：～能成功 *will surely succeed*｜骄兵～败。*An arrogant army is bound to be defeated.* [必然] 必定如此 inevitably：种族歧视制度～要灭亡。*A racial discrimination system will inevitably perish.* [必需] 一定要有，不可少 to be essential; to be indispensable：～品 *necessities* ②必须，一定要 must; ought to：事～躬亲 *make sure to see to everything in person*｜不～着急 *need not worry* [必须] 副词，一定要 (adverb) necessarily：个人利益～服从整体利益。*Personal interests must be subordinated to the overall interests.*

佖 bì ㄅㄧˋ 相挨排列，布满 abreast of; be everywhere

邲 bì ㄅㄧˋ 古地名，在今河南省荥（xíng）阳东北 Bi (a place name in ancient times, in the northeast of today's Xingyang, Henan Province)

苾 bì ㄅㄧˋ 芳香 fragrant

咇 bì ㄅㄧˋ 用于地名 used in place names：哈～嘎（在河北省康保）*Habiga (in Kangbao, Hebei Province)*

閟（閟） bì ㄅㄧˋ ❶闭门，关闭 to close (door) ❷谨慎 prudent

泌 bì ㄅㄧˋ [泌阳] 地名，在河南省 Biyang (a place in Henan Province)

⇨ see also mì on p.449

珌（琿）** bì ㄅㄧˋ 刀鞘下端的饰物 ornament at the lower end of a sheath

毖 bì ㄅㄧˋ 谨慎 cautious：惩前～后 *learn from past mistakes to avoid future ones*

铋(鉍) bì ㄅㄧˋ 金属元素，符号 Bi，银白色或粉红色。合金熔点很低，可用来做保险丝和汽锅上的安全塞等 bismuth (Bi)

秘(△*祕) bì ㄅㄧˋ 姓 (surname) Bi

[秘鲁] 国名，在南美洲 Peru

⇨ see also mì on p.449

⇨ see 祕 at mì on p.449

馝 bì ㄅㄧˋ [馝馞] (-bó) 形容香气很浓 very fragrant

毕(畢) bì ㄅㄧˋ ❶完，完结 to finish; to terminate: ～业 *to graduate* | 话犹未～ *not to have finished speaking* [毕竟] 副词，究竟，到底 (adverb) after all; all in all: 他虽态度生硬，但说的话～不错。*Although his attitude is harsh, after all he hasn't said anything wrong.* ❷全，完全 fully, completely: ～生 *all one's life* | 真相～露 *show one's true colours* ❸星宿名，二十八宿之一 *bi* (one of the twenty-eight constellations in ancient Chinese astronomy)

荜(蓽) bì ㄅㄧˋ ❶ [荜拨] (-bō) 藤本植物，叶卵状心形，浆果卵形。果穗可入药 long pepper ❷ same as "筚"

哔(嗶) bì ㄅㄧˋ [哔叽] (-jī) (外 *loanword*) 一种斜纹的纺织品 serge

筚(篳) bì ㄅㄧˋ 用荆条、竹子等编成的篱笆或其他遮拦物 bamboo or wicker fence: 蓬门～户 (指穷苦人家) *a house with a wicker fence; a humble abode*

跸(蹕) bì ㄅㄧˋ ❶帝王出行时清道，禁止行人来往 to clear the way to let the emperor through: 警～ *stop all traffic for the imperial carriage* ❷帝王出行的车驾 emperor's carriage on tour: 驻～ (帝王出行时沿途停留暂住) *(of an emperor on tour) stop over*

闭(閉) bì ㄅㄧˋ ❶关，合 to shut; to close: ～上嘴 *close one's mouth* | ～门造车 (喻脱离实际) *work blindly, out of touch with reality (literally means 'shut the door and make a cart')* ㊞结束，停止 to terminate; to end: ～会 *close a meeting* ❷塞，不通 to obstruct; to block up: ～气 *hold one's breath* [闭塞] (-sè) 堵住不通 to obstruct ㊞交通不便，消息不灵通 inaccessible; ill-informed: 这个地方很～。*The place is very inaccessible and backward.*

毖 bì ㄅㄧˋ ❶毗邻，相连 contiguous; adjacent to ❷用于地名 used in place names: 六～ (在浙江省慈溪) *Liubi (in Cixi, Zhejiang Province)*

庇 bì ㄅㄧˋ 遮蔽，掩护 (㊟-护) to shelter; to shield: 包～ *to harbour* | ～佑 *to bless*

陛 bì ㄅㄧˋ 宫殿的台阶 flight of steps leading to a palace hall [陛下] 对国王或皇帝的敬称 Your Majesty

毙(斃、*獘) bì ㄅㄧˋ ❶死 to die: ～命 *get killed* | 击～ *shoot dead* ❷用

枪打死 to shoot dead：～了一个凶犯 *shot a criminal dead*

狴 bì ㄅㄧˋ ［狴犴］（－àn）传说中的一种走兽。古代牢狱门上常画着它的形状，因此又用为牢狱的代称 prison (literally the name of a legendary beast painted on a prison door in ancient times)

梐 bì ㄅㄧˋ ［梐枑］（－hù）古代官署前拦住行人的东西，用木条交叉制成。又叫行马 a barrier to prevent entry placed in front of a government office in ancient times (also called 行马)

诐（詖） bì ㄅㄧˋ 偏颇，邪僻（㊥－邪）bias; wickedness：以德正天下之～ *overcome all kinds of wickedness in the world by the force of virtue*

畀 bì ㄅㄧˋ 给予 to give

痹（*痺） bì ㄅㄧˋ 痹症，中医指由风、寒、湿等引起的肢体疼痛或麻木的病 numbness; paralysis

箅 bì ㄅㄧˋ （－子）有空隙而能起间隔作用的片状器物，如竹箅子、铁箅子、纱箅子、炉箅子 grid; grating

贲（賁） bì ㄅㄧˋ 装饰得很好 well adorned：～临（客人盛装光临）*honour my place with your presence*

⇨ see also bēn on p.28

萆 bì ㄅㄧˋ ❶［萆薢］（－xiè）藤本植物，叶略呈心脏形，根状茎横生，圆柱形，表面黄褐色，可入药 *Dioscorea septemloba Thunb* ❷(old) same as "蓖"

庳 bì ㄅㄧˋ ❶低下 low-lying：堕高堙～（削平高丘，填塞洼地）*flatten hills and fill out low-lying terrain* ❷矮 short; low

婢 bì ㄅㄧˋ 旧时被有钱人家役使的女孩子 servant girl：～女 *servant girl* | 奴～ *(male or female) servant*

睥 bì ㄅㄧˋ（又） see pì on page 502

裨 bì ㄅㄧˋ 补益，益处 benefit; advantage：无～于事 *be of no help* | 对工作大有～益 *be of great benefit to one's work*

⇨ see also pí on p.501

髀 bì ㄅㄧˋ 大腿，也指大腿骨 thigh; thighbone

敝 bì ㄅㄧˋ 破旧 worn-out; shabby：～衣 *shabby clothes* 谦辞，称跟自己相关的事物 (humble speech, prefix) my; our：～姓 *my surname* | ～处 *my place* | ～公司 *our firm*

蔽 bì ㄅㄧˋ ❶遮，挡（㊥遮－、掩－）to hide; to cover：旌旗～日 *a huge army (literally means 'banners and flags are hiding the sun')* ❷概括 to sum up：一言以～之 *in a word*

弊（*獘） bì ㄅㄧˋ ❶欺蒙人的行为 fraud：作～ *commit fraud* | 营私舞～ *practice graft* ❷弊病，害处，跟"利"相对 disadvantage; harm (opposite of 利)：兴利除～ *promote what is beneficial and abolish what is harmful* | 流～ *corrupt practices*

B

皕 bì ㄅㄧˋ 二百 two hundred

弼 bì ㄅㄧˋ 辅助 to assist

赑(贔) bì ㄅㄧˋ [赑屃](—xì) 1 用力的样子 straining hard 2 传说中的一种动物，像龟。旧时大石碑的石座多雕刻成赑屃形状 a legendary tortoise-shaped creature, providing support for a stele

愎 bì ㄅㄧˋ 乖戾，固执 wilful; stubborn：刚～自用（固执己见）*self-willed*

蓖 bì ㄅㄧˋ [蓖麻](—má) 草本植物，叶子大。种子可榨油，医药上用作轻泻剂，工业上用作润滑油等 castor-oil plant

篦 bì ㄅㄧˋ ❶(—子) 齿很密的梳头用具 a fine-toothed comb ❷用篦子梳 to comb with such a tool：～头 *do one's hair with a fine-toothed comb*

滗(潷) bì ㄅㄧˋ 挡住渣滓或泡着的东西，把液体倒出 to drain; to strain; to decant：壶里的茶～干了。*The tea in the teapot has been drained.* | 把汤～出去 *strain soup*

辟 bì ㄅㄧˋ ❶君主 monarch [复辟] 失位的君主恢复君位 to restore a dethroned monarch ㊀被打垮的统治者恢复原有的统治地位或被推翻的制度复活 to restore (a king to the throne); to revive (a toppled system) ❷旧指君主召见并授予官职 (of a sovereign) to summon sb and confer on him an official post in ancient times ❸ (ancient) same as "避"

⇨ see also pì on p.502

薜 bì ㄅㄧˋ [薜荔](—lì) 常绿灌木，爬蔓，叶卵形。果实球形，可做凉粉。茎、叶可入药 climbing fig

壁 bì ㄅㄧˋ ❶墙(㊥墙—) wall：四～ *four walls (of a room)* | ～报 *wall newspaper* | 铜墙铁～ *impregnable fortress (literally means 'walls of bronze and iron')* ❷陡峭的山石 cliff：绝～ *precipice* | 峭～ *precipice* ❸壁垒，军营的围墙 rampart：坚～清野 *strengthen defences and clear fields* | 作～上观（坐观双方胜败，不帮助任何一方）*sit by and watch; be an onlooker* ❹星宿名，二十八宿之一 *bi* (one of the twenty-eight constellations in ancient Chinese astronomy)

避 bì ㄅㄧˋ ❶躲，设法躲开(㊥躲—) to avoid：～暑 *avoid the summer heat; prevent sunstroke* | ～雨 *seek shelter from the rain* | 不～艰险 *brave hardships and perils* ❷防止 to prevent：～孕 *avoid pregnancy* | ～雷针 *lightning conductor*

嬖 bì ㄅㄧˋ ❶宠幸 to show favour toward：～爱 *to favour* ❷被宠幸 to enjoy favour：～臣 *favoured minister* | ～人 *favoured one*

臂 bì ㄅㄧˋ 胳膊 arm：振～高呼 *raise one's arm(s) and shout (slogans, etc.)*

⇨ see also bei on p.28

璧 bì ㄅㄧˋ 古代玉器，平圆形，中间有孔 a round flat piece of jade with a hole in its centre ［璧还］（-huán）㊕敬辞，用于归还原物或辞谢赠品 (polite speech) to return a borrowed object or decline a gift：谨将原物～。*I'd like to return what I borrowed from you.*

襞 bì ㄅㄧˋ 古代指给衣裙打褶（zhě）子，也指衣裙上的褶子 (ancient) to make pleats/folds; to pleat; folds; pleats

躄（**躃） bì ㄅㄧˋ ❶腿瘸（qué），不能行走 to limp ❷仆倒 to fall down

碧 bì ㄅㄧˋ ❶青绿色的玉石 jade ❷青绿色 bluish-green：～草 *green grass*｜～波 *blue waves*｜金～辉煌 *(of a palace, etc.) resplendent and magnificent*

觱（**篳） bì ㄅㄧˋ ［觱篥］（-lì）古代的一种管乐器 a wind instrument in ancient times

滭 bì ㄅㄧˋ ［漾滭］（yàng-）地名，在云南省 Yangbi (a place in Yunnan Province)

BIAN ㄅㄧㄢ

边（邊） biān ㄅㄧㄢ ❶（-儿）物体周围的部分 edge：纸～儿 *paper edge*｜桌子～儿 *edge of a table* ㊀旁边，近旁，侧面 side：身～ *by one's side*｜马路～ *by the roadside* ❷国家或地区之间的交界处 frontier; border：～防 *frontier defence*｜～境 *border*｜～疆 *frontier* ❸几何学上指夹成角的射线或围成多边形的线段 side (of a geometrical figure) ❹方面 side：双～会谈 *bilateral talks*｜两～都说定了。*Both sides have reached an agreement.* ❺（一）边……（一）边……，用在动词前，表示动作同时进行 used before verbs to express simultaneity of two actions：～干～学 *learn on the job*｜～走～说 *talk while walking* ❻（bian）表示位置、方向，用在"上""下""前""后""左""右"等字后 used after 上，下，前，后，左，右，etc., to indicate location or direction：东～ *east*｜外～ *outside*｜左～ *left*

笾（籩） biān ㄅㄧㄢ 古代祭祀或宴会时盛果品等的竹器 bamboo fruit container (used at banquets or sacrifices in ancient times)

砭 biān ㄅㄧㄢ 古代用石针扎皮肉治病 (ancient treatment of illnesses) to perform acupuncture with stone needles ［针砭］㊥指出过错，劝人改正 to admonish; to criticize：～时政 *criticize the current politics*

萹 biān ㄅㄧㄢ ［萹蓄］（-xù）草本植物，又叫萹竹，叶狭长，略像竹叶，花小。全草可入药 common knotgrass (also called 萹竹)

编（編） biān ㄅㄧㄢ ❶用细条或带子形的东西交叉组织起来 to weave：～草帽 *weave a straw hat*｜～筐子 *weave*

B

a basket ❷按一定的次序或条理来组织或排列 to organize; to arrange：～号 *to number* | ～队 *organize into teams* | ～组 *organize into groups* [编辑] 把资料或现成的作品加以适当的整理、加工做成书报等，也指从事这一工作的人 to edit; to compile; editor; compiler [编制] 军队或机关中按照工作需要规定的人员或职务的配置 authorized personnel (in army, government, etc.) ❸成本的书，书里因内容不同自成起讫的各部分 part of a book; volume：正～ *main part* | 下～ *second part* | 简～ *concise edition* ❹创作 to write; to compose：～歌 *compose a song* | ～剧本 *write a play* ❺捏造，把没有的事情说成有 to fabricate：～了一套瞎话 *fabricated a story*

煸 biān ㄅㄧㄢ 把蔬菜、肉等放在热油里炒 to sauté：干(gān)～ *to stir-fry (without adding any water)* | ～炒 *to sauté*

蝙 biān ㄅㄧㄢ [蝙蝠]（－fú）哺乳动物，头和身体像老鼠，前后肢都有薄膜和身体连着，夜间在空中飞，捕食蚊、蛾等 bat (an animal)

鳊(鯿) biān ㄅㄧㄢ 鱼名，身体侧扁，头尖，尾巴小，鳞细，生活在淡水中 white Amur bream

鞭 biān ㄅㄧㄢ ❶（－子）驱使牲畜的用具 whip ❷用鞭子抽打 to whip：～尸 *whip the body of a dead person* [鞭策] ㊗督促前进 to spur on ❸一种旧式武器，用铁做成，没有锋刃，有节 (old) an iron nodular staff used as a weapon ❹编连成串的爆竹 a string of firecrackers：～炮 *firecrackers*

贬(貶) biǎn ㄅㄧㄢˇ ❶给予不好的评价，跟"褒"相对 to disparage (opposite of 褒)：一字之～ *criticize with a single word* | ～义词 *derogatory word* [褒贬] 1 评论好坏 to assess 2（－bian）指出缺点 to point out the shortcomings ❷减低，降低 to reduce; to devalue：～价 *reduce a price* | ～值 *to devalue; (of a currency) to depreciate* | ～职 *to demote*

窆 biǎn ㄅㄧㄢˇ 埋葬 to bury

扁 biǎn ㄅㄧㄢˇ 物体平而薄 flat and thin：～豆 *hyacinth bean* | ～担 *shoulder pole* | 鸭子嘴～。*A duck has a flat beak.*

⇨ see also piān on p.503

匾 biǎn ㄅㄧㄢˇ 匾额，题字的横牌，挂在门、墙的上部 horizontal inscribed board (hung above the door or on the upper part of a wall)：金字红～ *red board with characters inscribed in gold* | 光荣～ *board of honour*

碥 biǎn ㄅㄧㄢˇ 在水旁斜着伸出来的山石 rock hanging obliquely over water

褊 biǎn ㄅㄧㄢˇ 狭小，狭隘(ài)(㊀－狭、－窄) narrow; cramped

藊 biǎn ㄅㄧㄢˇ [藊豆] 草本植物，爬蔓，开白色或紫色的花，种子和嫩荚可以吃。现作"扁

豆”hyacinth bean (now written as 扁豆)

卞 biàn ㄅㄧㄢˋ 急躁(㊀—急) impatient; irritable

抃 biàn ㄅㄧㄢˋ 鼓掌 to clap (one's hands); to applaud：～掌 *clap one's hands*

苄 biàn ㄅㄧㄢˋ [苄基]一种有机化合物的基，又叫苯甲基 benzyl (also called 苯甲基)

汴 biàn ㄅㄧㄢˋ 河南省开封的别称 another name for Kaifeng, Henan Province

忭 biàn ㄅㄧㄢˋ 高兴，喜欢(㊀—欣) happy; glad：欢呼～舞 *dance happily amidst cheers*

弁 biàn ㄅㄧㄢˋ ❶古代男子戴的一种帽子 (ancient) man's cap [弁言]书籍或长篇文章的序文，引言 foreword; preface ❷旧时称低级武官 (old) junior military officer：马～ *officer's bodyguard*

邴 biàn ㄅㄧㄢˋ 姓 (surname) Bian

昪 biàn ㄅㄧㄢˋ ❶日光明亮 (of sunlight) bright ❷欢乐 joyful

变(變) biàn ㄅㄧㄢˋ 性质、状态或情形和以前不同，更改(㊀—更、—化) to change：沙漠～良田。*Deserts have been turned into cultivated land.* | 天气～了。*The weather has changed.* | 思想～了。*Ideas have changed.* ㊁事变，突然发生的非常事件 incident; unexpected turn of events：政～ *coup d'état* [变通]改动原定的办法，以适应新情况的需要 accommodate to new conditions

便 biàn ㄅㄧㄢˋ ❶方便或使方便，顺利，没有困难或阻碍(㊀—利) convenient; smooth; easy：行人称～。*All passers-by appreciate the convenience.* | ～于携带 *easy to carry* | ～民 *convenient for the public* ❷简单的，非正式的 simple; informal：家常～饭 *simple home-style cooking* | ～衣 *plain/civilian clothes; plainclothesman* | ～条 *note* [便宜]根据实际需要而灵活、适当地 convenient and appropriate：～行事 *act as one sees fit* (also pronounced piányi, see 便 pián) [随便]不勉强，不拘束 ready and willing ❸便利的时候 at one's convenience：～中请来信。*Please write to me at your convenience.* | 得～就送去 *send it at a convenient time* ❹屎尿或排泄屎尿 excreta; to excrete：粪～ *excrement and urine* | 小～ *to urinate; urine* ❺就 in that case：没有一个人民的军队，～没有人民的一切。*Without an army of the people, no one would have anything.*

⇨ see also pián on p.503

遍(*徧) biàn ㄅㄧㄢˋ ❶普遍，全面 be everywhere：我们的朋友～天下。*We have friends all over the world.* | ～布 *spread all over; be found everywhere* | 满山～野 *all over the mountains and plains* ❷量词，次，回 (measure word) time：念一～ *read once* | 问了两～ *asked twice*

辨 biàn ㄅㄧㄢˋ 分别，分析(㊀—别、分—) to discriminate; to differentiate：明～是非 *tell right*

from wrong | 不～真伪 *can't tell true from false* | ～认 *to identify*

辩（辯） biàn ㄅㄧㄢˋ 说明是非或真假，争论（㊀－论）to argue; to debate：～驳 *to refute* | ～护 *to defend* | 争～ *to argue*

辫（辮） biàn ㄅㄧㄢˋ ❶（－子）把头发分股编成的带状物 plait; braid：梳小～儿 *to plait* ❷（－子、－儿）像辫子的东西 braid-like object：草帽～儿 *plaited straw (for making hats)* | 蒜～子 *a braid of garlic*

BIAO ㄅㄧㄠ

杓 biāo ㄅㄧㄠ 勺子等物的柄，特指北斗柄部的三颗星 scoop; the three stars forming the handle of the Big Dipper

⇨ see also sháo on p.584

标（標） biāo ㄅㄧㄠ ❶树木的末梢 tip of a tree ㊁事物的表面，非根本的部分 surface; outward appearance：治～不如治本。*Radical treatment is better than symptomatic relief.* ❷记号，标志 mark; sign：浮～（浮在水上的行船航线标志）*buoy* | 商～ *trademark* | ～点符号 *punctuation* [标榜] 吹捧，夸耀 to flaunt; to parade：互相～ *flatter each other* | ～民主 *flaunt democracy* [标语] 用文字写出的有鼓动宣传作用的口号 slogan [标准] 衡量事物的准则 standard; criterion：实践是检验真理的唯一～。*Practice is the sole criterion of truth.* [指标] 计划中规定达到的目标 target：数量～ *quota* | 质量～ *quality index* ❸用文字或其他事物表明 to express：～题 *title* | ～价 *mark a price; marked price* | ～新立异 *start sth new in order to be different* [标本] 保持原样供学习研究参考的动物、植物、矿物 sample; specimen ❹发承包工程或买卖大宗货物时公布的标准和条件 bid; tender：投～ *to bid* | 招～ *invite tenders* | 竞～ *compete for a bid*

[标致]（－zhi）容貌美丽，多用于女子 (usually of women) pretty

飑（飑） biāo ㄅㄧㄠ 气象学上指风向突然改变，风速急剧增大且常伴有阵雨的天气现象 squall

骉（驫） biāo ㄅㄧㄠ 许多马奔跑的样子 galloping horses

彪 biāo ㄅㄧㄠ 小虎 young tiger：～形大汉（形容身材魁梧的男子）*big, strong man*

幖 biāo ㄅㄧㄠ 用作标志的旗帜或其他物品 flag or other item used as a symbol

骠（驃） biāo ㄅㄧㄠ [黄骠马] 一种黄毛夹杂着白点子的马 horse with a yellow coat and white spots

⇨ see also piào on p.506

膘（*臕） biāo ㄅㄧㄠ 肥肉（多指牲畜）(usually of livestock) fat meat：～满肉肥 *(of a domestic animal) plump* | 上～（长肉）*put on weight*

熛 biāo ㄅㄧㄠ 火星迸飞，也指迸飞的火星或火焰 to blaze; to spark; blaze; spark

镖（鏢） biāo ㄅㄧㄠ 旧时以投掷方式杀伤敌人的武器，形状像长矛的头 (old) dart-like weapon

瘭 biāo ㄅㄧㄠ ［瘭疽］（—jū）手指头肚儿或脚趾头肚儿发炎化脓的病，症状是局部红肿，剧烈疼痛，发热 inflammation of the pad of a finger or toe

飙（飆、飇、**飈）** biāo ㄅㄧㄠ 暴风 violent wind：狂～ *hurricane*

儦 biāo ㄅㄧㄠ ［儦儦］1 行走的样子 milling around 2 众多 numerous

藨 biāo ㄅㄧㄠ 藨草，草本植物，茎三棱形，可用来织席、编草鞋，也是造纸原料 bulrush

瀌 biāo ㄅㄧㄠ ［瀌瀌］形容雨雪大 (of rain, snow, etc.) heavy

镳（鑣） biāo ㄅㄧㄠ ❶马嚼子两头露在嘴外的部分 two ends of a bit (for a horse)：分道扬～（喻趋向不同）*part company; separate and go different ways* ❷ same as “镖”

表（❺錶） biǎo ㄅㄧㄠˇ ❶外部，跟“里”相对 surface (opposite of 里) ①在外的 exterior：～面 *surface*｜～皮 *epidermis* ②外面，外貌 exterior; appearance：外～ *outward appearance*｜～里如一 *consistent in thought and action*｜虚有其～ *be more apparent than real* ❷表示，显示 to show; to demonstrate：略～心意 *only serve as a token of one's regard*［表白］对人解释说明自己的意思 to clarify; to explain［表决］会议上用举手、投票等方式取得多数意见而做出决定 to vote：这个议案已经～通过了。*The motion has been voted through.*［表现］1 显露 to display; to manifest：医疗队的行动充分～了救死扶伤的人道主义精神。*The medical team's actions fully displayed the humanitarian spirit of rescuing the dying and healing the wounded.* 2 所显露出来的行为，作风 behaviour; performance：他在工作中的～还不错。*He is doing quite well in his job.*［表扬］对集体或个人，用语言、文字公开表示赞美、夸奖 to praise：～好人好事 *praise good people and good deeds* ❸中医指用药物把感受的风寒发散出来 (of traditional Chinese medicine) to administer medicine to dispel cold ❹分类分项记录事物的东西 table; form：历史年～ *chronological table of history*｜时间～ *timetable*｜统计～ *table of statistics* ❺计时间的器具，通常比钟小，可以带在身边 watch; clock：手～ *wrist watch*｜怀～ *pocket watch* ❻计量某种量的器具 gauge：温度～ *thermometer*｜电～ *electric meter*｜水～ *water meter* ❼树立的标志 sign post［表率］（—shuài）榜样 model：干部要做群众的～。*Cadres should*

B

be models for the masses. [华表] 古代宫殿、陵墓等大建筑物前面做装饰用的巨大石柱，柱身多雕刻龙凤等图案，顶端有云板和蹲兽 ornamental column (erected in front of a palace, tomb, etc.) ❽称呼父亲或祖父的姊妹、母亲或祖母的兄弟姊妹生的子女，用来表示亲属关系 prefix indicating relationship between the children or grandchildren of a brother and a sister, or of sisters：～兄弟 *male cousins* | ～叔 *uncle (son of paternal grandfather's sister, or son of paternal grandmother's sister or brother)*| ～姑 *aunt (daughter of paternal grandfather's sister, or daughter of paternal grandmother's sister or brother)* ❾封建时代称臣子给君主的奏章 memorial (submitted by feudal officials to the emperor)

婊 biǎo ㄅㄧㄠˇ [婊子] (—zi) 对妓女的称呼。多用作骂人的话 whore

脿 biǎo ㄅㄧㄠˇ 用于地名 used in place names：法～(在云南省双柏) *Fabiao (in Shuangbai, Yunnan Province)*

裱 biǎo ㄅㄧㄠˇ 用纸、布或丝织物把书、画等衬托装饰起来 to mount (calligraphy or painting)：双～纸 *double mount paper*| 揭～字画 *remove (calligraphy or painting) from an old mount and put on a new one* [裱糊] 用纸或其他材料糊屋子的墙壁或顶棚 to paper (wall or ceiling)：把这间屋子～一下。*Please paper this room.*

俵 biào ㄅㄧㄠˋ 〈方 dialect〉俵分，把东西分给人 to distribute

摽 biào ㄅㄧㄠˋ ❶紧紧地捆在器物上 to fasten：把口袋～在车架子上 *fasten a sack to the bicycle rack* ❷用手、胳膊钩住 to hook one's hand or arm around sth：他俩～着膀子走。*The two of them are walking arm in arm.* ❸由于利害相关而互相亲近、依附或纠结 to cling together for mutual support：这伙人老～在一块儿。*The gang always sticks together.*

鳔(鰾) biào ㄅㄧㄠˋ ❶鱼体内可以胀缩的气囊，膨胀时鱼上浮，收缩时鱼下沉 swim bladder ❷鳔胶，用鳔或猪皮等熬成的胶，很黏 fish glue; isinglass ❸用鳔胶粘上 to stick with fish glue：把桌子腿儿～一～ *to stick the table leg on with isinglass*

BIE ㄅㄧㄝ

瘪(癟、*癟) biē ㄅㄧㄝ [瘪三] 〈方 dialect〉旧时上海人对城市中无正当职业而以乞讨或偷窃为生的游民的称呼 (old, a term used by Shanghai people) vagrant who lived by begging or stealing

⇨ see also biě on p.43

憋 biē ㄅㄧㄝ ❶气不通 be airless：门窗全关着，真～气。*It is stifling in the room with all the doors and windows closed.* [憋闷]

(一men) 心里不痛快 to be depressed: 这事真叫人～。*This is really depressing.* ❷勉强忍住 to try hard to hold back: 把嘴一闭，～足了气 *hold one's breath with one's mouth shut* | 心里～了许多话要说。*With so much bottled up, (he) wanted to speak out.*

鳖(鱉、*鼈) biē ㄅㄧㄝ 爬行动物，又叫甲鱼、团鱼，俗叫王八，像龟，背甲无纹，边缘柔软，生活在水里 soft-shelled turtle (also called 甲鱼 or 团鱼, informal 王八)

癿 bié ㄅㄧㄝˊ 用于地名 used in place names: ～藏(在甘肃省积石山县) *Biezang (in Jishishan County, Gansu Province)*

别 bié ㄅㄧㄝˊ ❶分离(㊀分一、离一) to part: 告～ *say goodbye to* | 临～赠言 *parting advice* ❷分辨，区分(㊀辨一) to distinguish; to differentiate: 分门～类 *to classify* | 分～清楚 *make a clear distinction* ㊂差别，差异 difference; distinction: 天渊之～ *a world of difference* [区别] 1 划分 to distinguish: 正确～和处理不同性质的矛盾 *correctly differentiate and deal with different kinds of contradictions* 2 差异 difference: ～不大。*There is little difference.* ❸类别，分类 classification; category: 性～ *gender* | 职～ *occupation* ❹另外，另外的 other; another: ～人 *somebody else* | ～名 *alias* | ～开生面 *break fresh ground* [别致] 跟寻常不同，新奇 unconventional; original: 式样～ *be unique in style* [别字] 写错了的或念错了的字。又叫白字 wrongly written or mispronounced character (also called 白字) ❺副词，不要(表示禁止或劝阻) (adverb of negation) don't: ～动手！*Stop that!* | ～开玩笑！*Don't joke!* ❻绷住或卡(qiǎ)住 to fasten; to get stuck: ～针 *pin* | 用大头针把两张表格～在一起 *pin the two forms together* | 腰里～着一支手枪 *with a gun stuck in one's belt* ❼姓 (surname) Bie

⇨ see also biè on p.43

蹩 bié ㄅㄧㄝˊ 〈方 dialect〉扭了脚腕子或手腕子 to sprain (one's ankle or wrist) [蹩脚] 〈方 dialect〉质量不好，本领不强 of poor quality; poorly skilled: ～货 *shoddy goods*

瘪(癟、*癟) biě ㄅㄧㄝˇ 不饱满，凹下 shrivelled; deflated: ～花生 *blighted peanuts* | 干(gān)～ *shrunken* | 车带～了 *have a flat tyre*

⇨ see also biē on p.42

别(彆) biè ㄅㄧㄝˋ [别扭] (一niu) 1 不顺心，不相投 awkward; at odds: 心里～ *feel awkward and uncomfortable* | 闹～ *be at odds with sb* 2 不顺从，难对付 hard to get along with; difficult to deal with: 这人脾气很～。*This person is really difficult to get along with.* 3 (话语、文章)不顺畅、有毛病 (of speech or writing) unnatural; awkward: 他的英语听起来有点儿～。*His English sounds* *a little strange.*

⇨ see also bié on p.43

BIN ㄅㄧㄣ

B

邠 bīn ㄅㄧㄣ 邠县，在陕西省。今作"彬县" Binxian (in Shaanxi Province; now written as 彬县)

玢 bīn ㄅㄧㄣ 玉名 a kind of jade

⇨ see also fēn on p.176

宾(賓) bīn ㄅㄧㄣ 客人，跟"主"相对（㊣－客）guest (opposite of 主)：来～ *guest* | 外～ *foreign guest* | ～馆 *guesthouse* | 喧～夺主（喻次要事物侵占主要事物的地位）*the secondary supercedes the primary (literally means 'a guest speaks louder than the host')*

傧(儐) bīn ㄅㄧㄣ 引导 to usher; to lead：～者 *usher* [傧相]（－xiàng）旧指为主人接引宾客的人，今指婚礼时陪伴新郎新娘的人 (old) receptionist; (present-day) best man or bridesmaid：女～ *bridesmaid* | 男～ *best man*

滨(濱) bīn ㄅㄧㄣ ❶水边 water's edge; shore; bank：湖～ *lakeside* | 海～ *seaside* ❷靠近 to be close to：～海 *coastal*

缤(繽) bīn ㄅㄧㄣ [缤纷]（－fēn）繁盛而交杂的样子 flourishing; abundant：五彩～ *multicoloured*

槟(檳、梹)** bīn ㄅㄧㄣ 槟子，苹果树的一种，果实也叫槟子，比苹果小，熟后紫红色，味酸甜 applecrab

⇨ see also bīng on p.45

镔(鑌) bīn ㄅㄧㄣ [镔铁] 精炼的铁 refined iron

彬 bīn ㄅㄧㄣ [彬彬] 形容文雅 elegant; refined：文质～ *be cultured and refined*

斌 bīn ㄅㄧㄣ [斌斌] same as "彬彬"

濒(瀕) bīn ㄅㄧㄣ ❶紧靠（水边）to be close to (water)：～海 *border the sea* ❷接近，将，临 to be on the verge of：～危 *be in imminent danger* | ～死 *be on the verge of death*

豳 bīn ㄅㄧㄣ 古地名，在今陕西省旬邑一带 Bin (a place name in ancient times, located in the area of present-day Xunyi, Shaanxi Province)

摈(擯) bìn ㄅㄧㄣˋ 排除，遗弃（㊣－弃）to exclude; to discard：～斥异己 *dismiss people who hold dissenting opinions*

殡(殯) bìn ㄅㄧㄣˋ 停放灵柩或把灵柩送到墓地去 to lay a coffin in a memorial hall or to carry it to the grave：出～ *hold a funeral procession* | ～仪馆（代人办理丧事的场所）*funeral parlour*

膑(臏) bìn ㄅㄧㄣˋ same as "髌"

髌(髕) bìn ㄅㄧㄣˋ ❶髌骨，膝盖骨 patella; kneecap (see picture of 人体骨骼 on page 220) ❷古代剔除髌骨的酷刑 patella removing (a cruel torture in ancient times)

鬓(鬢) bìn ㄅㄧㄣˋ 脸旁边靠近耳朵的头发 hair on the temples：两～斑白 *grey at the temples* | ～角 *sideburns*

BING ㄅㄧㄥ

冰(*氷) bīng ㄅㄧㄥ ❶水因冷凝结成的固体 ice ❷使人感到寒冷 chilly：河里的水有点儿～手。*The water of the river is a bit cold.* ❸用冰贴近东西使变凉 to ice; to make sth cold：把汽水～上 *chill soda water*

并 bīng ㄅㄧㄥ 并州，山西省太原的别称 Bingzhou (another name for Taiyuan, Shanxi Province)

⇨ see also bìng on p.46

栟 bīng ㄅㄧㄥ ［栟榈］(－lǘ) 古书上指棕榈 palm (in ancient Chinese texts)

⇨ see also bēn on p.28

兵 bīng ㄅㄧㄥ ❶武器 arms; weapons：～器 *weapons* | 短～相接 *fight fiercely at close quarters (literally means 'to fight face to face with short weapons')* ❷战士，军队 soldier; army：官～一致 *unity between officers and men* | 步～ *infantry* ❸指军事或战争 of war or military affairs：～法 *art of war* | 纸上谈～ *be an armchair strategist*

槟(檳、梹)** bīng ㄅㄧㄥ ［槟榔］(－lang) 常绿乔木，羽状复叶，生长在热带、亚热带。果实也叫槟榔，可以吃，也可入药 betel palm

⇨ see also bīn on p.44

丙 bǐng ㄅㄧㄥˇ ❶天干的第三位，用作顺序的第三 *bing* (the third of the ten Heavenly Stems, a system used in the Chinese calendar); third：～等 *grade C* ❷指火 fire：付～(烧掉) *burn sth*

邴 bǐng ㄅㄧㄥˇ 姓 (surname) Bing

柄 bǐng ㄅㄧㄥˇ ❶器物的把(bà)儿 handle：刀～ *handle of a knife* ［把柄］㊗可被人用来要挟或攻击的事情 information that can be used against someone ［笑柄］被人当作取笑的资料 butt of a joke：一时传为～ *become the subject of ridicule for some time* ❷植物的花、叶或果实跟枝或茎连着的部分 stem：花～ *stem of a flower* | 叶～ *leafstalk* | 果～ *stem of a fruit* ❸执掌 to wield (power)：～国 *rule a country* | ～政 *be in power* ❹权 power：国～ *state power*

昺(昞)** bǐng ㄅㄧㄥˇ 明亮，光明 bright

炳 bǐng ㄅㄧㄥˇ 光明，显著 bright; distinctive：～如观火(形容看得清楚) *see clearly (literally means 'as clear as looking at fire')*

蛃 bǐng ㄅㄧㄥˇ ［石蛃］昆虫，身体长，棕褐色，体表有鳞片，触角丝状细长，生活在阴湿处。种类很多 campodeoid

B

秉 bǐng ㄅㄧㄥˇ ❶拿着，持 to hold; to grasp：～烛 *hold a candle* | ～笔 *hold a pen* ㊀掌握，主持 to preside over：～公处理 *act with impartiality* ❷古代容量单位，一秉为十六斛（hú）an ancient Chinese unit of capacity, equal to 16 斛

饼(餅) bǐng ㄅㄧㄥˇ ❶扁圆形的面制食品 round flat cake, made from flour：肉～ *meat pie* | 大～ *large pancake* ❷像饼的东西 sth shaped like a cake：铁～ *discus* | 豆～ *soya-bean cake*

屏 bǐng ㄅㄧㄥˇ ❶除去，排除（㊀一除）to remove; to eliminate：～弃不用 *to reject* | ～退左右 *order one's attendants to withdraw* ❷抑止（呼吸）to hold one's breath：～气 *hold one's breath* | ～息 *hold one's breath*

⇨ see also píng on p.509

禀(*稟) bǐng ㄅㄧㄥˇ ❶承受，生成的（㊀一受）to receive; to be endowed with：～性 *disposition* ❷下对上报告（㊀一报、一告）to report (sth to people in authority)：～明一切 *report everything in detail (to one's superior)*

鞞 bǐng ㄅㄧㄥˇ 刀鞘 sheath; scabbard

并(❶*併、❷-❹*並、❷-❹*竝) bìng ㄅㄧㄥˋ ❶合在一起（㊀合一）to combine：归～ *to merge* | ～案办理 *combine related cases and handle them together* ❷一齐，平排着 together; alongside：～驾齐驱 *keep pace with sb* | ～肩作战 *fight side by side* | ～排坐着 *sit side by side* ❸连词，并且 (conjunction) and (also)：讨论～通过了这项议案 *discussed and passed this resolution* [并且] 连词，表示进一层，有时跟"不但"相应 (conjunction) but (also)：他不但赞成，～愿意帮忙。*He not only agreed but also offered to help.* ❹副词 adverb ①放在否定词前面，加强否定语气，表示不像预料的那样 used before a negation marker for emphasis, indicating unexpectedness：～不太冷 *not as cold as expected* | ～非不知道 *not really unaware of it* ②同时，一起，同样 at the same time：两说～存 *two theories coexist* | 相提～论 *discuss very different things indiscriminately; place on a par* | 二者～重 *lay equal stress on both of them*

⇨ see also bīng on p.45

摒 bìng ㄅㄧㄥˋ 排除（㊀一除）to get rid of

病 bìng ㄅㄧㄥˋ ❶生物体发生的不健康的现象（㊀疾一）illness：害了一场～ *suffered from an illness* ❷患病 to have an illness：他～了。*He was ill.* [毛病]（-bing）1 疾病 disease 2 缺点 shortcoming 3 指器物损坏或发生故障的情况 defect：勤检修，机器就少出～。*With regular maintenance, the machine will have few problems.* ❸弊端，错误 fault;

error：语～ *grammatical error* | 通～ *common failing*

BO ㄅㄛ

拨(撥) bō ㄅㄛ ❶用手指或棍棒等推动或挑动 to move (with a finger, a stick, etc.)：把钟～一下。*Set the clock, please.* [拨冗]（-rǒng）推开杂事，抽出时间 to find time to do sth in the midst of pressing affairs：务希～出席。*Your presence is cordially requested.* ❷分给 to allocate：～款 *allocate funds* | ～点儿粮食 *allocate some grain* ❸（-儿）量词，用于成批的、分组的人或事物 (measure word) batch; group：一～儿人 *a group of people* | 分～儿进入会场 *enter the conference hall in groups*

波 bō ㄅㄛ ❶江、河、湖、海等因振荡而一起一伏的水面（㊀-浪、-涛、-澜）wave [波动] ㊃事物起变化，不稳定 to fluctuate [波及] ㊃牵涉到，影响到 to involve; to affect ❷物理学上指振动在物质中的传播，是能量传递的一种形式 (in physics) wave：光～ *light wave* | 声～ *sound wave* | 电～ *electric wave* | 微～ *microwave*

玻 bō ㄅㄛ [玻璃]（-li）1 一种质地硬而脆的透明物体，是用石英砂、石灰石、纯碱等混合起来，加高热熔解，冷却后制成的 glass 2 透明、像玻璃的质料 transparent and glass-like material：有机～ *PMMA; acrylic glass* | ～纸 *cellophane*

菠 bō ㄅㄛ [菠菜] 草本植物，叶略呈三角形，根带红色。可用作蔬菜 spinach

铍(鈹) bō ㄅㄛ 人造的放射性金属元素，符号 Bh。bohrium (Bh)

砵 bō ㄅㄛ 用于地名 used in place names：东～（在广东省阳江市）*Dongbo (in Yangjiang, Guangdong Province)*

钵(鉢、*缽、*盋) bō ㄅㄛ ❶盛饭、菜、茶水等的陶制器具 earthen bowl for food, drinks, etc.：饭～ *earthen bowl for cooked rice* [乳钵] 研药使成细末的器具 mortar ❷梵语音译"钵多罗"的省称，和尚用的饭碗 (short for 钵多罗, from Sanskrit) alms bowl (of a Buddhist monk)：～盂 *alms bowl (of a Buddhist monk)* [衣钵] 原指佛教中师父传授给徒弟的袈裟和钵盂，后泛指传下来的思想、学术、技能等 originally referring to a Buddhist monk's mantle and alms bowl, handed down to his disciple; (generally) teaching, skill, etc. handed down from a master to his pupil：继承～ *inherit the mantle of sb*

哱 bō ㄅㄛ [哱罗] 1 古代军中的一种号角 horn (used in armies in ancient times) 2 用于地名 used in place names：～寨（在山东省宁津）*Boluozhai (in Ningjin, Shandong Province)*

饽(餑) bō ㄅㄛ [饽饽]（-bo）〈方 dialect〉1 馒

B

头或其他块状的面食 steamed bun, pastry 2 甜食，点心 sweet food; snack

B

剥 bō ㄅㄛ 义同“剥”（bāo），用于复合词 (in compound) same as 剥 (bāo) in meaning [剥夺] 1 用强制的方法夺去 to deprive; to expropriate 2 依照法律取消 to deprive by law：～政治权利 *deprive of political rights* [剥削]（-xuē）凭借生产资料的私人所有权、政治上的特权无偿地占有别人的劳动或产品 to exploit

⇨ see also bāo on p.21

播 bō ㄅㄛ ❶ 撒种 to sow (seeds)：条～ *to drill (seeds)* | 点～ *to dibble (seeds)* ❷传扬，传布 to spread：～音 *to broadcast* [广播] 利用电波播送新闻、文章、文艺节目等 to broadcast

蕃 bō ㄅㄛ [吐蕃]（tǔ-）我国古代民族，在今青藏高原。唐时曾建立政权 an ancient ethnic group in China, on the present-day Qinghai-Tibet Plateau, who established a regime during the Tang Dynasty

⇨ see also fān on p.165, fán on p.166

嶓 bō ㄅㄛ [嶓冢]（-zhǒng）古山名，在今甘肃省成县东北 Bozhong, ancient name of a mountain, in the northeast of present-day Chengxian, Gansu Province

伯 bó ㄅㄛˊ ❶兄弟排行（háng）常用“伯”“仲”“叔”“季”做次序，伯是老大 the eldest in the order of seniority among brothers [伯仲] 比喻不相上下的人或事物 about the same：二者在～之间。*Both are on a par with each other.* | 两人难分～。*It is hard to tell who is better between the two.* ❷伯父，父亲的哥哥，大爷（ye）。又对年龄大、辈分高的人的尊称 uncle; elder brother of one's father; respectful form of address for a man of one's father's generation：老～ *uncle* ❸古代五等爵位（公、侯、伯、子、男）的第三等 count (the third of the five ranks of nobility in ancient China) ❹姓 (surname) Bo

⇨ see also bǎi on p.15

帛 bó ㄅㄛˊ 丝织品的总称 silk fabric [玉帛] 古代往来赠送的两种礼物，表示友好交往 jade objects and silk fabrics, presented as state gifts in ancient times as a sign of friendship：化干戈为～ *turn hostility into friendship*

泊 bó ㄅㄛˊ ❶停船靠岸（㊥停-）to berth; to anchor; to moor：～船 *to berth* [泊车] 把汽车停放在某处 to park ❷恬静 tranquil; peaceful [淡泊]（*澹泊）不贪图功名利禄 to seek no fame nor wealth

⇨ see also pō on p.510

柏 bó ㄅㄛˊ [柏林] 德国的首都 Berlin

⇨ see also bǎi on p.15, bò on p.51

铂(鉑) bó ㄅㄛˊ 金属元素，符号 Pt，银白色，熔点高。可用来制坩埚、蒸发皿，也用作催化剂 platinum (Pt)

舶 bó ㄅㄛˊ 大船 big ship：船～ *boats and ships* | 巨～ *huge ship* | ～来品（外国输入的货物）*imported goods*

鲌（鮊） bó ㄅㄛˊ 鱼名，身体侧扁，嘴向上翘，生活在淡水中 topmouth culter

⇨ see also bà on p.13

箔 bó ㄅㄛˊ ❶用苇子、秫秸等做成的帘子 curtain (made of reeds, sorghum stalks, etc.) ❷ 蚕箔，又叫蚕帘，养蚕的器具，多用竹篾制成，像筛子或席子 bamboo tray for breeding silkworms (also called 蚕帘) ❸金属薄片 thin metal sheet：金～ *gold leaf* | 铜～ *copper foil* ❹敷上金属薄片或粉末的纸 foil (paper covered in thin metal sheets or metal powder)：锡～ *tinfoil*

驳（駁、❶❸*駮） bó ㄅㄛˊ ❶说出自己的理由来，否定别人的意见 to refute：真理是～不倒的。*Truth can't be refuted.* | 反～ *to refute* | 批～ *criticize and refute* ❷大批货物用船分载转运 to transport by barge or lighter：起～ *start shipment by lighter* | 把大船上的米～卸到货栈里 *unload the rice from the ship by lighter and transfer it to the warehouse* [驳船] 转运用的小船。又叫拨船 barge; lighter (also called 拨船) ❸马的毛色不纯。泛指颜色不纯，夹杂着别的颜色（㊃斑一、一杂）mottled; variegated

勃 bó ㄅㄛˊ 旺盛 ㊂ vigorous：～起 *have an erection; erection* | 蓬～ *flourishing* | 生气～～ *full of vitality* | 英姿～～ *dashing and vigorous* [勃然] 1 兴起或旺盛的样子 vigorously：～而兴 *thrive with fresh vigour* 2 变脸色的样子 (to change countenance) abruptly：～大怒 *fly into a rage*

浡 bó ㄅㄛˊ 〈古 ancient〉兴起，涌出 to thrive; to spring up：～然而兴 *develop vigorously*

脖（*頖） bó ㄅㄛˊ ❶（一子）颈，头和躯干相连的部分 neck ❷像脖子的部分 neck-shaped part：脚～子 *ankle*

鹁（鵓） bó ㄅㄛˊ [鹁鸪]（一gū）鸟名，又叫水鸪鸪，羽毛黑褐色。天要下雨或天刚晴的时候，常在树上咕咕地叫 common wood pigeon (also called 水鸪鸪)

渤 bó ㄅㄛˊ 渤海，在辽东半岛和山东半岛之间 Bohai Sea (between the Liaodong Peninsula and the Shandong Peninsula)

馞 bó ㄅㄛˊ see 馝馞 (bì一) at 馝 on page 34

钹（鈸） bó ㄅㄛˊ 打击乐器，铜质，圆片形，中心鼓起，两片相击作声 cymbals

亳 bó ㄅㄛˊ [亳州] 地名，在安徽省 Bozhou (a place in Anhui Province)

袯（襏） bó ㄅㄛˊ [袯襫]（一shì）1 古蓑衣 straw or palm-bark rain cape in ancient China 2 粗糙结实的衣服 coarse and durable clothes

艴 bó ㄅㄛˊ fú ㄈㄨˊ（又）艴然，生气的样子 to look angry

B

博(❶❷*愽) bó ㄅㄛˊ ❶多，广(㊀广一) abundant; vast：地大物～ *vast in territory and rich in resources* | ～学 *erudite* | ～览 *read extensively* [博士] 1 学位名，在硕士之上 doctor (degree) 2 古代掌管学术的官名 official rank in ancient times, in charge of academic affairs [博物] 动物、植物、矿物、生理等学科的总称 natural science ❷知道得多 well-informed：～古通今 *be acquainted with things both ancient and modern* ❸用自己的行动换取 to win; to gain：～得同情 *win sympathy* ❹古代的一种棋戏，后泛指赌博 chess game in ancient times; gambling

搏 bó ㄅㄛˊ ❶对打 to exchange blows：～斗 *fight fiercely against* | ～击 *fight with* | 肉～(徒手或用短兵器搏斗) *fight hand to hand* ❷跳动 to pulsate：脉～ *pulse*

馎(餺) bó ㄅㄛˊ [馎饦](－tuō)一种面食 a kind of wheaten food

膊 bó ㄅㄛˊ 胳膊(bo)，肩膀以下手腕以上的部分 arm [赤膊] 光膀子，赤裸上身 be stripped to the waist：～上阵(喻不讲策略或不加掩饰地做某事) *do sth without disguise or tactics (literally means 'go into battle bare-chested')*

镈(鎛) bó ㄅㄛˊ ❶大钟，古代的一种乐器 large bell (a kind of musical instrument in ancient times) ❷古代一种锄类农具 a kind of hoe in ancient times

薄 bó ㄅㄛˊ ❶义同"薄"(báo)。用于合成词或成语，如厚薄、单薄、淡薄、浅薄、薄田、薄弱、尖嘴薄舌、厚古薄今等 same as 薄 (thin) in meaning, used in compound words or idioms ❷轻微，少 slight; meagre：～技 *inadequate skill* | ～酬 *meagre reward* ❸不庄重 frivolous：轻～*flirtatious* ❹看不起，轻视，慢待 to despise：鄙～ *to despise* | 厚此～彼 *discriminate against one and favour the other* | 妄自菲～ *belittle oneself* ❺迫近 to approach：～暮(天快黑) *dusk* | 日～西山 *be near one's end (literally means 'the sun is setting beyond the western hills')* ❻姓 (surname) Bo

⇨ see also báo on p.22, bò on p.51

欂 bó ㄅㄛˊ [欂栌]古代指斗拱 (ancient) same as 斗拱

礴 bó ㄅㄛˊ see 磅礴 (páng－) at 磅 on page 493

僰 bó ㄅㄛˊ 我国古代西南地区的少数民族 Bo (an ancient ethnic group in southwest China)

踣 bó ㄅㄛˊ 跌倒 to fall down：屡～屡起 *persist in doing sth (literally means 'fall down and set up repeatedly')*

跛 bǒ ㄅㄛˇ 瘸(qué)，腿或脚有毛病，走路身体不平衡 to limp：一颠一～ *walk with a limp* | ～脚 *lameness*

簸 bǒ ㄅㄛˇ ❶用簸(bò)箕颠动米粮，扬去糠秕和灰尘

to winnow ❷上下颠动，摇晃 to toss：～荡 *pitch and roll* | 船在海浪中颠～起伏。*The ship tosses in the waves.*

⇨ see also bò on p.51

柏 bò ㄅㄛˋ ［黄柏］即黄檗 same as 黄檗

⇨ see also bǎi on p.15, bó on p.48

薄 bò ㄅㄛˋ ［薄荷］（—he）草本植物，茎四棱形。叶和茎有清凉香味，可入药 mint

⇨ see also báo on p.22, bó on p.50

檗 bò ㄅㄛˋ 黄檗（也作“黄柏”），落叶乔木，羽状复叶，花黄绿色。木质坚硬，茎可制黄色染料，树皮可入药 Amur cork tree (also written as 黄柏)

擘 bò ㄅㄛˋ 大拇指 thumb ［巨擘］㊞杰出的人物 top authority

⇨ see also bāi on p.14

簸 bò ㄅㄛˋ ［簸箕］（—ji）扬糠除秽的用具 winnowing pan; dustpan

⇨ see also bǒ on p.50

卜（蔔） bo · ㄅㄛ see 萝卜 at 萝 on page 427

⇨ see also bǔ on p.51

啵 bo · ㄅㄛ 助词，相当于“吧” (auxiliary word) equivalent to 吧

BU ㄅㄨ

逋 bū ㄅㄨ ❶逃亡（㊀一逃）to flee ❷拖欠 to be in arrears：～租 *be behind in paying one's rent*

晡 bū ㄅㄨ 〈古 ancient〉申时，指下午三点到五点 the period from 3 p.m. to 5 p.m.

醭 bú ㄅㄨˊ （formerly pronounced pú）（—ㄦ）醋、酱油等表面上长（zhǎng）的白色的霉 white mould (on the surface of vinegar or soya sauce, etc.)

卜 bǔ ㄅㄨˇ ❶占卜，古时用龟甲、兽骨等预测吉凶的一种活动。后泛指用其他方法预测吉凶 to practise divination; to predict ㊀料定，先知道 to foretell; to predict：预～ *to foretell* | 吉凶未～。*No one knows how it will turn out.* ［卜辞］商代刻在龟甲、兽骨上记录占卜事情的文字 oracle inscriptions of the Shang Dynasty on tortoise shells or animal bones ❷姓 (surname) Bu

⇨ see also bo on p.51

吓 bǔ ㄅㄨˇ ［吓吩］有机化合物，是叶绿素、血红蛋白等的重要组成部分 porphin

补（補） bǔ ㄅㄨˇ ❶把残破的东西加上材料修理完整 to mend; to repair：～衣服 *patch clothes* | ～锅 *repair a pan* ❷把缺少的充实起来或添上（㊀—充、贴—）to supplement：～空（kòng）子 *fill a vacancy* | ～习 *attend make-up lessons* | 候～委员 *alternate member* | 滋～ *nourish* ［补白］报刊上填补空白的短文 filler in a newspaper or magazine ❸益处 benefit：不无小～ *not be without some benefit*

捕 bǔ ㄅㄨˇ 捉，逮 to seize; to arrest：～获 *to capture* | ～风

捉影（喻言行没有事实根据）*speak or act on hearsay (literally means 'chase the wind and clutch at shadows')*

哺 bǔ ㄅㄨˇ ❶喂不会取食的幼儿 to feed (a baby)：～养 *raise (a baby)* | ～育 *feed and take care of* | ～乳 *to breast-feed* ❷嘴里嚼着的食物 food in one's mouth：一饭三吐（tǔ）～ *stop three times in the middle of a meal to welcome talented people*

鵏（鵏） bǔ ㄅㄨˇ ［地鵏］鸟名，又叫大鸨，雄鸟体长约1米，背部有黄褐色和黑色斑纹，腹部灰白色，不善飞而善走，吃谷类和昆虫 great bustard (also called 大鸨)

堡 bǔ ㄅㄨˇ 堡子，有围墙的村镇。又多用于地名 walled village or town; also often used in place names：吴～（在陕西省）*Wubu (in Shaanxi Province)*

⇨ see also bǎo on p.23, pù on p.514

不 bù ㄅㄨˋ 副词 adverb ①表示否定的意义 no; not：他～来。*He's not coming.* | ～好 *no good* | ～错 *not bad* | ～简单 *not simple* ②表示否定对方的话 (used as a negative reply) no：他刚来农村吧？——～，他到农村很久了。*He has just arrived in the countryside, hasn't he? — No, he has been here for a long time.* ③表示不可能达到某种结果，用法上跟"得"相反 used to express inability to achieve sth (opposite of 得)：拿～动 *too heavy to carry* | 说～明白 *fail to make oneself understood* | 跑～很远 *be unable to run very far* ④跟"就"搭用，表示选择 used with 就 to express 'either...or'：他一有空儿，～是看书，就是看报。*He'll read a book or a newspaper when he's free.* ⑤〈方 dialect〉用在句末，表示疑问 used as an ending to form a question：他来～？ *Is he coming or not?* | 你知道～？ *Do you know it?* ［不过］1 副词，仅仅，不超过 (adverb) only, not more than：一共～五六个人。*There are only about five or six people altogether.* 2 连词，但是，可是 (conjunction) but, however：时间虽然很紧，～我们会按时完成的。*Time presses, but we can manage to get the job done on time.*

吥 bù ㄅㄨˋ see 唝吥 (gòng—) at 唝 on page 214

钚（鈈） bù ㄅㄨˋ 放射性金属元素，符号 Pu，化学性质跟铀相似。可作为核燃料用于核工业中 plutonium (Pu)

布（❷–❹*佈） bù ㄅㄨˋ ❶用棉纱、麻纱等织成的、可以做衣服或其他物件的材料 cloth; fabric ［布匹］布的总称 cloth ❷宣布，宣告，对众陈述 to declare; to proclaim; to announce：发～ *to issue* | 开诚～公 *in all sincerity and frankness* ［布告］张贴出来通知群众的文件 notice; bulletin ❸散布，分布 to spread; to disseminate：阴云密～ *be overcast* | 星罗棋～ *be scat-*

tered all over like stars in the sky or pieces on a chessboard ❹布置，安排 to dispose; to arrange: ～防 *deploy troops for defence* | ～局 *make overall arrangement* | ～下天罗地网 *spread an unescapable net (of law, etc.)* ❺古代的一种钱币 a kind of coin in ancient times

[布朗族][布依族]都是我国少数民族，参看附录四 the Blang people; the Bouyei people (Both are ethnic groups in China. See Appendix Ⅳ.)

埗 bù ㄅㄨˋ [茶埗]地名，在福建省建阳 Chabu (a place in Jianyang, Fujian Province)

怖 bù ㄅㄨˋ 惧怕(㊊恐一) to fear: 情景可～。*The scene is horrific.* [白色恐怖]反动统治者迫害人民所造成的令人恐惧的情势 White Terror

步 bù ㄅㄨˋ ❶脚步，行走时两脚之间的距离 step; pace: 一～跟不上，～～跟不上。*Miss one step and you'll never catch up with others.* | 稳～前进 *to move forward steadily* [步伐]队伍行进时的脚步 pace; step: ～整齐 *march in step* ❷阶段 stage: 初～ *initial* [步骤]事情进行的程序 step (in a process) ❸行，走 to go; to walk: ～其后尘(追随在人家后面) *follow sb's footsteps* ❹用脚步量地面 pace off (distance): ～一～看这块地有多长。*Try to pace off this piece of land to see how long it is.* ❺旧制长度单位，一步为五尺 a former unit of length, 1 步 equal to 5 尺 ❻地步，境地，表示程度 (of extent) situation, plight: 没想到他竟会落到这一～。*I never expected he would be in such a plight.* ❼ (ancient) same as "埠"

埗 bù ㄅㄨˋ 同"埠"。多用于地名 (often in place names) same as 埠: 深水～(在香港) *Shenshuibu (in Hong Kong)*

埔 bù ㄅㄨˋ [大埔]地名，在广东省 Dabu (a place in Guangdong Province)

⇨ see also pǔ on p.513

部 bù ㄅㄨˋ ❶部分，全体中的一份 part: 内～ *interior* | 南～ *southern part* | 局～ *part* [部位]位置 position ❷机关企业按业务范围分设的单位 ministry; department: 农业～ *Ministry of Agriculture* | 编辑～ *editorial department* | 门市～ *retail department* [部队]军队 army [部首]按汉字形体偏旁所分的门类，如"山"部、"火"部等 radical (of Chinese characters) ❸统属 to have as one's subordinate; to be subordinate to: ～领 *to command* | 所～三十人 *have 30 people under one's control* [部署]布置安排 to make arrangements for ❹量词 measure word ①用于书籍、影片等 used for books, films, etc.: 一～小说 *a novel* | 两～电影 *two films* ②用于车辆或机器 for car or machine: 一～收割机 *a reaper* | 三～汽车 *three cars*

瓿 bù ㄅㄨˋ 小瓮 small jar

B

蔀 bù ㄅㄨˋ ❶遮蔽 to shelter; to cover ❷古代历法称七十六年为一蔀 in ancient Chinese calendar system, one 蔀 equals 76 years ❸用于地名 used in place names: 蓁（zhēn）～（在浙江省龙泉市）*Zhenbu (in Longquan, Zhejiang Province)*

埠 bù ㄅㄨˋ 埠头，停船的码头。多指有码头的城镇 pier; wharf; often refers to a town or city with a port: 本～ *this town* | 外～ *other towns* [商埠] 1 旧时与外国通商的城镇 (old) trading city 2 指商业发达的城市 commercially developed town or city

簿 bù ㄅㄨˋ （一子）本子 notebook: 账～ *account book* | 发文～ *register of outgoing documents, letters, etc.*

C ㄘ

CA ㄘㄚ

擦 cā ㄘㄚ ❶抹(mā), 揩(kāi) 拭 to wipe: ～桌子 *wipe the table* | ～脸 *wipe one's face* ❷摩, 搓 to rub: 摩拳～掌 *be itching for action* ❸贴近 next to, close to: ～黑儿(傍晚) *at nightfall* | ～着屋檐飞过 *skim over the eaves and fly away*

嚓 cā ㄘㄚ 形容物体摩擦声 used to describe scraping sounds: 摩托车～的一声停住了。*The motorcycle screeched to a stop.*

⇨ see also chā on p.62

礤 cā ㄘㄚ see 礓礤儿(jiāngcār) at 礓 on page 307

礤 cǎ ㄘㄚˇ 粗石 rough stone [礤床儿] 把瓜、萝卜等擦成丝的器具 grater

CAI ㄘㄞ

偲 cāi ㄘㄞ 有才能 talented

⇨ see also sī on p.617

猜 cāi ㄘㄞ ❶推测, 推想 to guess: ～谜 *guess a riddle* | 你～他来不来? *Do you think he will come?* ❷疑心(连一疑) to suspect: ～忌 *be suspicious and hostile* | ～嫌 *be suspicious of*

才(❸纔) cái ㄘㄞˊ ❶能力(连一能) ability; talent: 口～ *eloquence* | ～干 *ability* ❷从才能方面指称某类人 person of certain ability: 干(gàn)～ *able person* | 奇～ *genius* | 庸～ *mediocre person* ❸副词 adverb ①表示事情发生在前不久或结束得晚, 刚刚(连刚一、方一) just (now); not until (used to indicate that sth happened a very short time ago or finished later than expected): 昨天～来 *arrived only yesterday* | 现在～懂得这个道理。*The truth didn't dawn on me until now.* ②仅仅 only: ～用了两元 *cost only two yuan* | 来了～十天 *have been here for just ten days*

材 cái ㄘㄞˊ ❶木料 timber; lumber: 美木良～ *premium timber* 引材料, 原料或资料 material: 器～ *equipment* | 教～ *teaching material* ❷资质, 能力 ability; competence: 因～施教 *teach according to student's ability* ❸棺木 coffin: 一口～ *a coffin*

财(財) cái ㄘㄞˊ 金钱或物资(连一产、资一、钱一) wealth: 理～ *manage one's money* | ～务 *financial affairs* [财富] 具有价值的东西 wealth: 物质～ *material wealth* | 精神～ *spiritual wealth* [财政] 国家的收支及其他有关经济的事务 (public) finance

C

裁 cái ㄘㄞˊ ❶用剪子剪布或用刀子割纸 to cut (cloth or paper)：～衣服 *cut out a garment* | 对～（把整张纸平均裁为两张）*cut (a sheet of paper) in half* [裁缝]（-feng）以做衣服为职业的人 tailor ❷削减，去掉一部分 to cut down：～军 *reduce armaments* | ～员 *lay off employees* ❸决定，判断 to judge; to adjudicate：～夺 *deliberate and decide* | ～判 *give judgment or verdict; to referee; referee* ❹安排取舍 to select and plan：独出心～ *adopt an original approach* |《唐诗别～》*An Anthology of Tang Poems*

采（❶-❸*採）cǎi ㄘㄞˇ ❶摘取 to pick：～莲 *pick lotus flowers* | ～茶 *pick tea* ❷开采 to mine：～煤 *mine coal* | ～矿 *to mine* ❸选取，取 to select：～购 *to purchase for an institution, etc.* | ～取 *to adopt* [采访] 搜集寻访，多指记者为搜集材料进行调查访问 (often of journalists) to interview [采纳] 接受（意见）to adopt (an opinion)：～群众的意见 *adopt suggestions from the public* ❹神采，神色，精神 facial expression; countenance：兴高～烈 *elated* ❺ same as "彩"

⇨ see also cài on p.56

彩（❷*綵）cǎi ㄘㄞˇ ❶各种颜色 colour：～色 *colour* | ～虹 *rainbow* | ～排（化装排演）*have a dress rehearsal* [挂彩] 指在战斗中受伤 to be wounded in action ❷彩色的绸子 coloured silk：剪～ *cut a ribbon (during a ceremony)* | 悬灯结～ *be decked out in lanterns and coloured silk streamers* ❸指赌博或某种竞赛中赢得的东西 (in a game or competition) winnings; prize：得～ *win at gambling* | ～金 *winnings; lottery prize* ❹称赞、夸奖的欢呼声 applause：喝（hè）～ *to applaud*

睬（*倸）cǎi ㄘㄞˇ 理会，答理（㊀理－）to pay attention to：对群众的意见不理不～ *turn a deaf ear to public opinion* | 叫他，他～也不～。*He took absolutely no notice when someone called out to him.*

踩（*跴）cǎi ㄘㄞˇ 用脚蹬在上面，踏 to step on; to trample：～了一脚泥 *got one's feet covered in mud*

采（*寀、**埰）cài ㄘㄞˋ 采地，采邑，古代卿大夫的封地 fief

⇨ see also cǎi on p.56

菜 cài ㄘㄞˋ ❶蔬菜，供作副食品的植物 vegetable ❷主食以外的食品，如经过烹调的鱼、肉、蛋等 dish：做了几个～ *cooked a few dishes*

蔡 cài ㄘㄞˋ ❶周代诸侯国名，在今河南省上蔡、新蔡一带 Cai (a state in the Zhou Dynasty, in Shangcai and Xincai in today's Henan Province) ❷〈古 ancient〉大龟 large turtle：蓍（shī）～（占卜用的东西）*yarrow stalks and turtle shells (used in divination)*

CAN ㄘㄢ

参(參、*桼) cān ㄘㄢ ❶参加，加入 to join; to participate in: ～军 *join the army* | ～战 *enter a war* [参半] 占半数 account for half of the total: 疑信～ *half believing, half doubting* [参观] 实地观察（事业、设施、名胜等）to visit (a business, facility, place of interest, etc.) [参考] 用有关的材料帮助了解、研究某事物 to consult (reference material) [参天] 高入云霄 to soar; to tower: 古木～。*The ancient trees tower into the sky.* ❷进见 to call to pay one's respect: ～谒 *pay a formal visit to (a respected or old person)* | ～拜 *pay homage to* ❸探究并领会 to ponder; to meditate on: ～不透这句话的意思 *can't work out what the sentence means* ❹封建时代指弹劾（tánhé）to impeach (an official in imperial China): ～他一本 *impeach him in a memorial to the emperor*

⇨ see also cēn on p.61, shēn on p.588

骖(驂) cān ㄘㄢ 古代驾在车前两侧的马 outer pair of carriage horses in ancient times

餐(飡、**湌)** cān ㄘㄢ ❶吃 to eat: 饱～一顿 *eat one's fill* | 聚～ *have a dinner party* ❷饭食 meal: 一日三～ *three meals a day* | 午～ *lunch* | 西～ *Western food*

残(殘) cán ㄘㄢˊ ❶毁坏，毁害（㊟－害）to damage: 摧～ *to wreck* | 自～ *harm oneself* ❷凶恶（㊟－暴、－忍）ferocious ❸不完全的，有毛病的（㊟－缺）incomplete; defective: ～疾 *physical disability* | ～品 *defective product* | ～破不全 *fragmentary* ㊪余下的（㊟－余）remaining: ～局 *endgame* | ～茶剩饭 *leftovers*

蚕(蠶) cán ㄘㄢˊ 家蚕，昆虫，又叫桑蚕，吃桑叶长大，蜕（tuì）皮时不食不动，俗叫眠。蚕经过四眠就吐丝做茧，蚕在茧里变成蛹，蛹变成蚕蛾。家蚕的丝可织绸缎。另有柞（zuò）蚕，又叫野蚕，吃柞树的叶子。柞蚕的丝可织茧绸 silkworm (also called 桑蚕); tussah silkworm (also called 柞蚕，野蚕)

惭(慚、*慙) cán ㄘㄢˊ 羞愧（㊟－愧）to feel ashamed: 自～ *feel ashamed of oneself* | 大言不～ *brag unashamedly*

惨(慘) cǎn ㄘㄢˇ ❶凶恶，狠毒 cruel: ～无人道 *cruel and inhuman* ❷使人悲伤难受（㊟凄－、悲－）miserable; wretched: 她的遭遇太～了。*She's been through hell.* [惨淡] 1 暗淡无色 pale; gloomy: 病容～ *look pallid and sick* 2 凄凉，萧条 desolate: ～的人生 *wretched life* | 生意～。*Business is poor.* 3 指辛苦 laborious: ～经营 *keep (sth) going through painstaking*

C

effort ❸程度严重 seriously; terribly：敌人～败。*The enemy was crushed.* | 可累～了 *be completely exhausted*

穇（穇） cǎn ㄘㄢˇ 穇子，草本植物，茎粗，穗在顶端，像鸡爪。籽实可以吃，也可用作饲料 finger millet

篸（篸） cǎn ㄘㄢˇ 〈方 dialect〉一种簸箕 winnowing tray; dustpan

黪（黲） cǎn ㄘㄢˇ ❶浅青黑色 bluish-black：～发 *dark hair* ❷昏暗 dim

灿（燦） càn ㄘㄢˋ 光彩耀眼 glorious; resplendent：～若云霞 *radiant as rosy clouds* [灿烂] 鲜明，耀眼 brilliant; resplendent：阳光～。*The sun is shining brilliantly.* | 光辉～ *dazzling*

孱 càn ㄘㄢˋ same as 孱 (chán), only used in 孱头 [孱头] (－tou) 〈方 dialect〉软弱无能的人 weakling

➪ see also chán on p.66

粲 càn ㄘㄢˋ 鲜明的样子 brilliant [粲然] 笑的样子 (of a smile) radiant：～一笑 *give a radiant smile*

璨 càn ㄘㄢˋ ❶美玉 fine jade ❷ same as "粲"

CANG ㄘㄤ

仓（倉） cāng ㄘㄤ 收藏谷物的建筑物 granary; barn：米～ *rice barn* | 谷～ *granary* [仓库] 储藏东西的房子 warehouse [仓促] [仓猝] (－cù) 匆忙 in haste

伧（傖） cāng ㄘㄤ 古代讥人粗俗，鄙贱 (ancient) vulgar, crude：～俗 *coarse and vulgar*

➪ see also chen on p.75

苍（蒼） cāng ㄘㄤ ❶青色 blue：～天 *blue sky; Heaven* ❷草色，深绿色 dark green：～松 *green pine* ❸灰白色 grey; ashen：～白 *pale* | 两鬓～～ *be greying at the temples* [苍老] 1 容貌、声音老 (of appearance, voice) aged 2 书画笔力雄健 (of calligraphy or painting) firm and vigorous：字迹～。*The handwriting is firm and vigorous.*

沧（滄） cāng ㄘㄤ 暗绿色（指水）(of water) dark blue：～海 *the sea* [沧海桑田] 大海变成农田，农田变成大海，形容世事变化很大。Time wreaks drastic changes in the world (literally means 'seas change into mulberry fields; the fields change into seas').

鸧（鶬） cāng ㄘㄤ [鸧鹒] (－gēng) 黄鹂。也作"仓庚" oriole (same as 黄鹂, also written as 仓庚)

舱（艙） cāng ㄘㄤ 船或飞机内用于载人或物的部分 cabin; hold (in a ship or plane)：货～ *hold* | 客～ *cabin* | 底～ *bottom tank*

藏 cáng ㄘㄤˊ ❶隐避（㊀隐－）to hide：埋～ *to bury and hide* | 他～在树后头。*He was*

hidden behind the tree. ❷收存（㊵收一）to collect; to store：～书 *collect books* | 储～ *to store*

⇨ see also zàng on p.820

CAO ㄘㄠ

操 cāo ㄘㄠ ❶拿，抓在手里 to grasp：～刀 *hold a knife* | ～戈 *take up arms* ㊀掌握，控制 to control; to operate (machinery, etc.)：～舟 *take the helm* | ～必胜之券(quàn) *be sure of success*［操纵］随着自己的意向来把持支配 to manipulate：～股市 *manipulate the stock market* | ～民意 *manipulate public opinion* ❷拿出力量来做 to do with effort：～劳 *work hard* | ～持 *to handle; to plan*［操作］按照一定的程序和技术要求进行活动，也泛指劳动 to operate; (generally) to work：田间～ *field operation* ❸从事，做某种工作 to take (a job)：重～旧业 *return to one's old trade* ❹用某种语言或方言说话 to speak (a language or dialect)：～俄语 *speak Russian* | ～闽语 *speak the Min dialect* ❺操练 (of soldiers or athletes) to drill：出～ *have drill* | ～演 *to drill* | 下～ *finish drilling* ❻由一套动作编排成的体育或军事活动 (set-up) exercises：体～ *gymnastics* | 徒手～ *free-standing exercises* | 做了几节～ *did a few rounds of exercise* ❼行为，品行 behaviour; conduct：节～ *moral integrity* | ～行 *conduct*

糙 cāo ㄘㄠ ❶糙米，脱壳未去皮的米 brown rice ❷不细致，粗（㊵粗一）coarse：这活儿做得太～。*This work is very shoddy.*

曹 cáo ㄘㄠ ❶等，辈 people of the same kind：尔～ *you people* | 吾～ *the lot of us* ❷古代分科办事的官署 (ancient) division of a governmental department：部～ *head of division (under the central government)* | 功～ *regional merit officer*

嘈 cáo ㄘㄠ 杂乱（多指声音）(often of sounds) chaotic; riotous：人声～杂 *hubbub of voices*

漕 cáo ㄘㄠ 利用水道转运食粮 to transport grain by water：～运 *transport grain by water* | ～河（运粮的河道）*waterway for transporting grain*

槽 cáo ㄘㄠ ❶一种长方形或正方形的较大的容器 trough (container in general)：石～ *stone trough* | 水～ *water trough* ❷特指喂牲畜食料的器具 (specifically) trough (for animal feed)：猪食～ *pig trough* | 马～ *horse manger* ❸（一儿）东西上凹下像槽的部分 groove：挖个～儿 *carve a groove* | 河～ *river bed*

碽 cáo ㄘㄠ 用于地名 used in place names：斫（zhuó）～（在湖南省邵东）*Zhuocao (in Shaodong, Hunan Province)*

螬 cáo ㄘㄠ see 蛴螬 (qí —) at 蛴 on page 517

艚 cáo ㄘㄠ （一子）载货的木船 wooden cargo boat

C

草(*艸、❺**騲) cǎo ㄘㄠˇ ❶高等植物中栽培植物以外的草本植物的统称 grass：野～ *weed* | 青～ *green grass* [草本植物] 茎干通常比较柔软的植物，如小麦、豌豆等 herb ❷马虎，不细致 ㊄ careless; sloppy：潦～ *(of handwriting) sloppy; (of work) careless* | ～～了(liǎo)事 *do sth carelessly* | ～率 *careless* [草书] 汉字形体的一种，笔画牵连曲折，写起来快 Chinese cursive script ❸草稿，文稿 draft：起～ *to draft* ㊀还没有确定的(文件等) (of documents, etc.) draft：～约 *draft agreement* | ～案 *(of law) draft* | ～图 *sketch* ❹打稿 to draft：～拟 *to draft* | ～檄 *draft a call for war; prepare an official document* [草创] 开始创办或创立 to start (an enterprise) ❺雌性的(指某些家禽、家畜) female (domestic fowls or animals)：～鸡 *hen* | ～驴 *jenny*

CE ㄘㄜ

册(*冊) cè ㄘㄜˋ ❶古时称编串好的许多竹简，现在指装订好的纸本子 binded paper; (ancient) stringed bamboo slips：第三～ *volume three* | 纪念～ *commemorative album* ❷量词，用于书籍 (measure word for books) copy; volume：一～书 *a book*

厕(厠、*廁) cè ㄘㄜˋ ❶厕所，大小便的地方 toilet; lavatory：公～ *public toilet* ❷参与(yù)，混杂在里面 to be involved in; to participate in：～身其间 *occupy a place among them*

侧(側) cè ㄘㄜˋ ❶旁 side：楼～ *the side of a building* | ～面 *side* ❷斜着 to incline; lean to one side：～耳细听 *be all ears* | ～身而入 *enter sideways* [侧目] 斜着眼睛看，表示畏惧而又愤恨 to glance sidelong (in fear and indignation)：世人为之～。*People raised their eyebrows.* [侧重] (-zhòng) 偏重 to lay special emphasis on

⇨ see also zè on p.824, zhāi on p.828

测(測) cè ㄘㄜˋ ❶测量，利用仪器来度量 to measure：～角器 *goniometer* | ～绘 *to survey and map* | ～一下高度 *measure the height* [测验] 用一定的标准检定 to test ❷推测，料想 to surmise; to speculate：预～ *to predict* | 变幻莫～ *change unpredictably*

恻(惻) cè ㄘㄜˋ 悲痛 sorrowful; sad [恻隐] 对遭难(nàn)的人表示同情 compassionate; full of pity：动了～之心 *feel compassion*

策(*筞、*筴) cè ㄘㄜˋ ❶计谋，主意(㊄计一) plan; idea：决～ *make a decision; decision-making* | 献～ *offer suggestions* | 下～ *unwise idea* | 对～ *countermeasure* | 束手无～

be rendered utterly helpless [策略] 根据形势发展而制定的行动方针和方法 strategy ❷谋划 to plan: ～反 *incite a rebellion/defection* | ～应 *support by coordinated action* [策动] 设法鼓动或促成 to instigate ❸古代的一种马鞭子，头上有尖刺 (ancient) pointed riding crop ❹鞭打 to whip: ～马 *whip a horse on* | 鞭～ *spur on* ❺古代称编连好的竹简 (ancient) stringed bamboo slips for writing on: 简～ *stringed bamboo slips; historical works; official documents* ❻古代考试的一种文体 (ancient) style of writing used in examinations: ～论 *political treatise*

CEN ㄘㄣ

参(**參**、*****叅**) cēn ㄘㄣ [参差] (－cī) 长短、大小、高低等不齐 not uniform: ～不齐 *uneven*

⇨ see also cān on p.57, shēn on p.588

岑 cén ㄘㄣˊ 小而高的山 high hill

涔 cén ㄘㄣˊ 连续下雨，积水成涝 waterlogged [涔涔] 1 雨多的样子 rainy 2 流泪的样子 streaming (with tears)

CENG ㄘㄥ

噌 cēng ㄘㄥ 形容短促摩擦或快速行动的声音 used to describe the sound of friction or quick action: ～的一声，火柴划着了。*The match sparked to life with a single strike.* | ～地站了起来 *sprang to one's feet*

层(**層**) céng ㄘㄥˊ ❶重复，重叠 to layer: ～出不穷 *emerge in an endless stream* | ～峦叠翠 *chain after chain of verdant mountains* ❷重叠的事物或其中的一部分 layer: 云～ *clouds* | 大气～ *atmosphere* | 基～ *basic level* ❸量词，重 (chóng) (measure word) storey, tier: 二～楼 *a two-storey building* | 三～院子 *triple-conjoined courtyards* | 絮两～棉花 *pad with two layers of cotton* | 还有一～意思 *have another shade of meaning*

曾 céng ㄘㄥˊ 副词，曾经，表示从前经历过 (adverb) once; previously: 未～ *not...before* | 何～ *ever* | 他～去北京两次。*He's been to Beijing twice.* | ～几何时 (表示时间过去没多久) *not long ago*

⇨ see also zēng on p.824

嶒 céng ㄘㄥˊ see 崚嶒 (léng －) at 崚 on page 386

蹭 cèng ㄘㄥˋ 摩擦 to rub: ～了一身泥 *got oneself covered in mud* | ～破了皮 *scraped one's skin* ㊀ ①就着某种机会占便宜，揩油 to scrounge: ～吃 *scrounge meals* | ～车 *cadge a lift* ②拖延 to dawdle: 快点儿，别～了。*Hurry up. Stop dawdling.* | 磨～ (ceng) *to dawdle*

[蹭蹬] (－dèng) 遭遇挫折 to suffer a setback

CHA ㄔㄚ

叉 chā ㄔㄚ ❶（一子）一头有两个以上长齿便于扎取东西的器具 fork：鱼～ *fishing spear* | 三齿～ *three-pronged fork* | 粪～子 *manure pitchfork* ❷用叉子扎取 to fork; to spear：～鱼 *spear fish* ❸ 交错 crossed：～着手站着 *standing with folded hands* ❹形状为"×"的符号，表示错误或不同意等 cross (×, a mark used to indicate a mistake, disagreement, etc.)：反对的打～。*Put a cross if you object.*

⇨ see also chá on p.62, chǎ on p.63, chà on p.63

扠 chā ㄔㄚ same as "叉❷"

杈 chā ㄔㄚ 一种用来挑（tiǎo）柴草等的农具 pitchfork

⇨ see also chà on p.64

臿 chā ㄔㄚ ❶〈古 ancient〉same as "锸" ❷〈方 dialect〉舂 to pound (rice, etc.)

插（*揷） chā ㄔㄚ 扎进去，把细长或薄的东西扎进、放入 to insert：～秧 *transplant rice seedlings* | ～门卡 *insert a room card* | 把花～在瓶子里 *put the flowers in a vase* 引 加入，参与 to join (in the middle of sth)：～班 *join a class mid-semester* | ～嘴 *cut in*

锸（鍤） chā ㄔㄚ 铁锹（qiāo），掘土的工具 spade

差 chā ㄔㄚ ❶不同，不同之点（连 -别、-异、偏-）different; difference ❷大致还可以 partly; slightly：～强人意（大体上还能使人满意）*tolerable* ❸错误 mistake; error：～错 *error* | 阴错阳～ *(by) a twist of fate; accidental error* ❹差数，减法运算的得数 (mathematical) difference：五减二的～是三。*Five minus two is three.*

⇨ see also chà on p.64, chāi on p.64, cī on p.96

喳 chā ㄔㄚ ［喳喳］1（-chā）形容小声说话的声音 sound of low voices：喊喊～ *whispering* 2（-cha）小声说话 to speak in a low voice：打～ *whisper*

⇨ see also zhā on p.826

馇（餷） chā ㄔㄚ ❶拌煮猪、狗的食料 to cook and stir (feed for pigs and dogs)：～猪食 *cook feed for pigs* ❷〈方 dialect〉熬（粥）to make (porridge)：～锅豆粥 *cook a pot of bean porridge*

嚓 chā ㄔㄚ see 咔嚓 (kā-) at 咔 on page 347

⇨ see also cā on p.55

叉 chá ㄔㄚˊ 挡住，堵塞住，互相卡住 to jam; to block：车把路口～住了。*The cars blocked the crossroads.*

⇨ see also chā on p.62, chǎ on p.63, chà on p.63

垞 chá ㄔㄚˊ 小土山。多用于地名 earthen mound (often used in place names)

茬 chá ㄔㄚˊ ❶（-儿）庄稼收割后余留在地上的短根和茎 stubble：麦～儿 *wheat stubble* | 豆～儿 *bean stubble* ❷（-儿）在同一块土地上庄稼种植或收割

的次数 a crop：换～ *change of crops* | 头～ *first crop* | 二～ *second crop* ❸短而硬的头发、胡子 (of hair or beard) stubble

茶 chá ㄔㄚˊ ❶茶树，常绿灌木，叶长椭圆形，花白色。嫩叶采下经过加工，就是茶叶 tea (plant) ❷用茶叶沏成的饮料 tea (drink) ㊀某些饮料的名称 drink：果～ *fruit drink* | 杏仁～ *almond drink*

搽 chá ㄔㄚˊ 涂抹 to apply：～药 *apply medication* | ～粉 *powder (one's face, etc.)*

查（*查）chá ㄔㄚˊ ❶检查 to check：～账 *audit an account* ❷翻检着看 to look up：～地图 *look at a map* | ～字典 *consult a dictionary* ❸调查 to investigate：把案子～清楚 *get to the bottom of the case*

➩ see also zhā on p.826

嵖 chá ㄔㄚˊ ［嵖岈］（－yá）山名，在河南省遂平 Chaya (a mountain in Suiping, Henan Province)

猹 chá ㄔㄚˊ 〈方 dialect〉鲁迅小说《故乡》提到的一种像獾的野兽，喜欢吃瓜 badger-like animal (mentioned in Lu Xun's story *Hometown*)

楂 chá ㄔㄚˊ same as "茬"

➩ see also zhā on p.826

碴（*鑑）chá ㄔㄚˊ ❶（－儿）小碎块 shard; fragment：冰～儿 *ice shard* | 玻璃～儿 *fragment of glass* ❷（－儿）器物上的破口 chip：碗上有个破～儿。*The bowl is chipped.* ㊃争执的事由 cause of dispute：找～儿打架 *pick a fight* ❸〈方 dialect〉皮肉被碎片碰破 to cut (one's flesh)：手让碎玻璃～破了 *cut one's hand on broken glass*

糌 chá ㄔㄚˊ （－子）〈方 dialect〉玉米等磨成的碎粒儿 coarsely ground grain (such as maize)

槎 chá ㄔㄚˊ ❶木筏 raft：乘～ *ride a raft* | 浮～ *legendary raft travelling between the sea and the Milky Way; wooden boat* ❷ same as "茬"

察（*詧）chá ㄔㄚˊ 仔细看，调查研究 to examine：考～ *to research* | 视～ *to inspect*

檫 chá ㄔㄚˊ 檫木，落叶乔木，树干高大，木质坚韧，可供建筑、造船等用 sassafras

叉 chǎ ㄔㄚˇ 分开，张开 to splay：～腿 *splay out one's legs*

➩ see also chā on p.62, chá on p.62, chà on p.63

衩 chǎ ㄔㄚˇ ［裤衩］短裤 briefs; knickers; underpants：三角～ *Y-front briefs*

➩ see also chà on p.64

蹅 chǎ ㄔㄚˇ 踩，在泥水里走 to tread (through mud or water)：～雨 *tread through rainwater* | 鞋都～湿了。*The shoes have got wet from the walk.*

镲（鑔）chǎ ㄔㄚˇ 钹（bó），一种打击乐器 small cymbal

叉 chà ㄔㄚˋ ［劈叉］两腿分开成一字形，臀部着地。是

体操或武术动作 to do the splits

⇨ see also chā on p.62, chá on p.62, chǎ on p.63

汊 chà ㄔㄚˋ 河流的分支 branch of a river

杈 chà ㄔㄚˋ （～子、～儿）植物的分枝 (of a plant) offshoot：树～儿 *tree branch* | 打棉花～ *prune the side shoots of a cotton plant*

⇨ see also chā on p.62

衩 chà ㄔㄚˋ 衣服旁边开口的地方 slit (in a garment)

⇨ see also chǎ on p.63

岔 chà ㄔㄚˋ ❶分歧的，由主干分出的 divergent; branch：～道 *side road* | 三～路 *three-forked road* ❷转移主题 to change the topic：拿话～开 *change the topic of the conversation* | 打～ *to interrupt* ❸互相让开（多指时间）to stagger (events,etc.)：把这两个会的时间～开 *stagger the two meetings* ❹（～子、～儿）乱子，事故 accident：仔细点儿，别出～子。*Be careful. Don't mess up.*

侘 chà ㄔㄚˋ [侘傺]（-chì）形容失意 frustrated

诧(詫) chà ㄔㄚˋ 惊讶，觉着奇怪 surprised：～异 *astounded* | 惊～ *astonished*

姹 chà ㄔㄚˋ 美丽 beautiful：～紫嫣红（形容百花艳丽）*(of flowers) in a riot of colour*

刹 chà ㄔㄚˋ 梵语音译"刹多罗"的省称，原义是土或田，转指佛寺 Buddhist temple (short for 刹多罗 , from Sanskrit, originally referring to earth or field)：宝～ *Buddhist pagoda; your (honourable) temple* | 古～ *ancient Buddhist temple*

[刹那] 梵语音译，指极短的时间 (from Sanskrit) instant

⇨ see also shā on p.574

差 chà ㄔㄚˋ ❶错误 wrong：说～了 *said it wrong* ❷不相当，不相合 unequal; different：～得远 *radically different* | ～不多 *about the same* ❸缺，欠 short of; wanting：～一道手续 *have one more procedure to go through* | 还～一个人 *be one person short* ❹不好，不够标准 inferior：成绩～ *have poor grades*

⇨ see also chā on p.62, chāi on p.64, cī on p.96

CHAI ㄔㄞ

拆 chāi ㄔㄞ 把合在一起的弄开，卸下来（㊟-卸）to take apart; to dismantle：～信 *open a letter* | ～房子 *demolish a house*

钗(釵) chāi ㄔㄞ 妇女发髻上的一种首饰 hairpin：金～ *gold hairpin* | 荆～布裙（旧形容妇女装束朴素）*(old, of a woman) plainly dressed*

差 chāi ㄔㄞ ❶派遣去做事（㊟-遣）to dispatch ❷旧时称被派遣的人，差役 (old) errand-boy (in local authorities) ❸差事，被派遣去做的事 errand; assignment：兼～ *take on more than one job; part-time job* | 出～ *go on business*

⇨ see also chā on p.62, chà on p.64, cī on p.96

侪(儕) chái ㄔㄞˊ 同辈，同类的人们 peers：吾～（我们）*we; us*

柴 chái ㄔㄞˊ 烧火用的草木 firewood：打～ *gather firewood* | 砍～ *chop firewood*[火柴] 用细小的木条蘸上磷、硫等制成的能摩擦生火的东西 match (for lighting fire)

豺 chái ㄔㄞˊ 兽名，像狼而嘴较短，性凶猛，常成群侵袭家畜 dhole [豺狼] ㊗贪心残忍的恶人 greedy villain

茝 chǎi ㄔㄞˇ 古书上说的一种香草，即白芷（zhǐ）a kind of fragrant grass in ancient Chinese texts (same as 白芷, Chinese Angelica)

䶪 chǎi ㄔㄞˇ （一儿）碾碎了的豆子、玉米等 ground beans (or maize, etc.)：豆～儿 *ground beans*

虿(蠆) chài ㄔㄞˋ 古书上说的蝎子一类的毒虫 poisonous insects like scorpion in ancient Chinese texts

瘥 chài ㄔㄞˋ 病愈 to recuperate：久病初～ *have just recovered from a lingering illness*

⇨ see also cuó on p.105

CHAN ㄔㄢ

辿(**䟞) chān ㄔㄢ 用于地名 used in place names：龙王～（在山西省吉县）*Longwangchan (in Jixian, Shanxi Province)* | 黄草～（在山西省黎城）*Huangcaochan (in Licheng, Shanxi Province)*

觇(覘) chān ㄔㄢ 看，窥视 to observe; to spy on [觇标] 一种测量标志，标架用木料或金属制成，高几米到几十米，架在被观测点上作为观测目标，也可在此处观测其他地点 surveyor's beacon

梴 chān ㄔㄢ 形容树长得高 (of a tree) lofty

掺(摻) chān ㄔㄢ 混合（㊟一杂、一和）to mix：在粥里～点儿水 *add some water to the porridge* | 不要～假。*Do not adulterate.*

搀(攙) chān ㄔㄢ ❶用手轻轻架住对方的手或胳膊（㊟一扶）to support (sb) by the hand or arm：～着老人过马路 *help the elderly across the street* ❷ same as "掺"

襜 chān ㄔㄢ ❶古代系在身前的围裙 (ancient) apron ❷[襜褕]（一yú）古代一种长的单衣 (ancient) long casual jacket

单(單) chán ㄔㄢˊ [单于]（一yú）古代匈奴的君主 Chanyu, (ancient) king of the Xiongnu

⇨ see also dān on p.114, shàn on p.578

婵(嬋) chán ㄔㄢˊ [婵娟]（一juān）1（姿态）美好 graceful 2 旧时指美人 (old) beauty; belle 3 古诗文中指明月 (in classical Chinese literature) moon：千里共～ *share the beauty of the full moon though a thousand miles apart*

禅(禪) chán ㄔㄢˊ ❶梵语音译"禅那"的省称，佛教指静思 Zen (short for 禅那, from Sanskrit), meditation in Buddhism：坐～ *sit in meditation (in Zen)* ❷关于佛教的 Buddhist：～杖 *Buddhist monk's staff* | ～师 *Zen master*

⇨ see also shàn on p.578

蝉(蟬) chán ㄔㄢˊ 昆虫，又叫知了，雄的腹面有发声器，叫的声音很大。种类很多 cicada (also called 知了)

[蝉联] 连续（多指连任某职或继续保持某称号）to retain (one's post or title)：～冠军 *retain the championship*

铤(鋋) chán ㄔㄢˊ 古代一种铁把（bà）儿的短矛 (ancient) short spear with an iron handle

谗(讒) chán ㄔㄢˊ 在别人面前说陷害某人的坏话 to slander：～言 *slander*

馋(饞) chán ㄔㄢˊ ❶贪吃，专爱吃好的 greedy (for food)：嘴～ *be greedy for food* | ～涎欲滴 *drool with longing* ❷贪，羡慕 to hunger for：眼～ *to covet*

儳 chán ㄔㄢˊ 〈古 ancient〉杂乱不齐 disorderly

巉 chán ㄔㄢˊ 山势险峻 (of mountains) precipitous：～岩 *sheer precipice*

镵(鑱) chán ㄔㄢˊ ❶古代一种铁制的刨土工具 (ancient) iron shovel ❷刺 to stab：以刃～腹 *stab sb in the abdomen with a knife*

孱 chán ㄔㄢˊ 懦弱，弱小（连 一弱）cowardly; weak

⇨ see also càn on p.58

潺 chán ㄔㄢˊ [潺潺] 形容溪水、泉水等流动的声音 (of flowing water) to burble：～流水 *burbling water* [潺湲]（一yuán）水慢慢流动的样子 flowing slowly：溪水～。*The stream is flowing gently.*

缠(纏) chán ㄔㄢˊ ❶绕，围绕（连 一绕）to wind; to wrap：头上～着一块布。*One's head was wrapped with a piece of cloth.* [缠绵] 纠缠住不能解脱（多指感情或疾病）(often of illness or feelings) lingering ❷搅扰 to pester：胡搅蛮～ *harass sb with unreasonable demands*

廛 chán ㄔㄢˊ 古代指一户人家拥有的土地和房子，特指房屋，也泛指城邑民居 (ancient) family-owned estate; commoner's house [市廛] 店铺集中的地方 market; high street

瀍 chán ㄔㄢˊ 瀍河，水名，在河南省洛阳 Chanhe River (in Luoyang, Henan Province)

躔 chán ㄔㄢˊ ❶兽的足迹 animal track ❷日月星辰的运行 (of a celestial body) to orbit

澶 chán ㄔㄢˊ [澶渊] 古地名，在今河南省濮阳西南 Chanyuan (an ancient place name, in the south-west of present day Puyang, Henan Province)

镡(鐔) chán ㄔㄢˊ 姓 (surname) Chan

➪ see also tán on p.637, xín on p.725

蟾 chán ㄔㄢˊ 蟾蜍，两栖动物，俗叫癞蛤蟆、疥蛤蟆，皮上有许多疙瘩，内有毒腺。吃昆虫等，对农业有益 toad (informal 癞蛤蟆 or 疥蛤蟆)：～宫（指月亮）*the moon*

产（產） chǎn ㄔㄢˇ ❶人或动物生子 to give birth to：～子 *give birth to a son*｜～卵 *lay eggs*｜～科 *obstetrics department* ［产生］生，出现 to produce; to bring out：～好的效果 *produce positive results* ㊀由团体中推出 to choose (from a group of people)：每个小组～一个代表 *choose a representative from each group* ❷制造、种植或自然生长 to manufacture; to yield：沿海盛～鱼虾。*The coastal areas teem with fish and shrimps.*｜我国～稻、麦的地方很多。*Many regions in our country grow rice and wheat.*｜增～ *increase production* ❸制造、种植或自然生长的东西 product; produce：土特～ *local speciality*｜水～ *aquatic product* ❹财产 property：房～ *house property*｜地～ *real estate*｜遗～ *legacy* ［产业］1 家产 family property 2 构成国民经济的行业和部门，也特指工业生产 industry：信息～ *information industry*｜文化～ *cultural industry*｜～工人 *industrial worker*

浐（滻） chǎn ㄔㄢˇ 浐河，水名，在陕西省西安 Chanhe River (in Xi'an, Shaanxi Province)

铲（鏟、*剷） chǎn ㄔㄢˇ ❶（～子、～儿）削平东西或把东西取出来的器具 shovel：铁～ *iron shovel*｜饭～儿 *rice scoop* ❷用锹（qiāo）或铲子削平或取出来 to shovel：把地～平 *level the ground with a shovel or spade*｜～土 *shovel earth*｜～菜 *lift vegetables with a shovel or spade* ［铲除］去掉 to eradicate：～恶习 *get rid of bad habits*

刬（剗） chǎn ㄔㄢˇ (old) same as "铲❷"

➪ see also chàn on p.68

冁 chǎn ㄔㄢˇ ❶日光照耀 (of the sun) to shine ❷冁山，山名，又地名，都在安徽省泾县 Mount Chanshan, Chanshan Village (both in Jingxian, Anhui Province)

谄（諂） chǎn ㄔㄢˇ 巴结，奉承 to fawn on; to flatter：～媚 *to flatter*｜不骄不～ *neither proud nor ingratiating*

啴（嘽） chǎn ㄔㄢˇ 宽舒，和缓 relaxed; mellow：～缓 *slow and relaxed*

➪ see also tān on p.635

阐（闡） chǎn ㄔㄢˇ 说明，表明 to explain：～述 *to expound*｜～明 *to elucidate* ［阐发］深入说明事理 to explicate

焊（燀） chǎn ㄔㄢˇ ❶烧火做饭 to start a fire to cook ❷炽热 red-hot; scorching ❸中药炮制方法，将桃仁、杏仁等放在沸水内浸泡，以便去皮 to scald (some ingredients of traditional Chinese medicine to remove

C

their skin)

辴(囅) chǎn 彳ㄢ 笑的样子 used to describe the way someone laughs：～然而笑 *laugh heartily*

蒇(蕆) chǎn 彳ㄢ 完成，解决 to complete：～事（把事情办完）*complete a job*

骣(驏) chǎn 彳ㄢ 骑马不加鞍辔 to ride (a horse) without a saddle：～骑 *ride (a horse) bareback*

忏(懺) chàn 彳ㄢ 梵语音译“忏摩”的省称。佛教指请人宽恕。又指佛教、道教讽诵的一种经文(short for 忏摩, from Sanskrit) to repent; a type of chanted scripture in Buddhism and Taoism［忏悔］悔过 to repent

刬(剗) chàn 彳ㄢ ［一刬］〈方 dialect〉全部，一律 without exception：～新 *brand new*｜～都是平川。*All around was open country.*

⇨ see also chǎn on p.67

颤(顫) chàn 彳ㄢ 物体振动 to tremble; to vibrate：这条扁担（dan）担上五六十斤就～了。*This carrying pole starts to sway under a weight of fifty or sixty jin.*｜～动 *to quiver*

⇨ see also zhàn on p.832

羼 chàn 彳ㄢ 掺杂 to mix; to mingle：～入 *mix in*

韂 chàn 彳ㄢ 垫在马鞍下的东西，垂于马背两侧，用来遮挡泥土 saddle pad：鞍～ *saddle and pad*

CHANG 彳尢

伥(倀) chāng 彳尢 古代传说中被老虎咬死的人变成的鬼，它常助虎伤人 (in ancient Chinese legend) the ghost of someone killed by a tiger, who helps it to entice other people for food：为（wèi）虎作～（喻帮恶人作恶）*help an evil person to do evil*

昌 chāng 彳尢 兴盛 prosperous; thriving：～盛 *thriving and prosperous*｜科学～明。*Science is thriving.*

菖 chāng 彳尢 ［菖蒲］草本植物，生长在水边，花穗像棍棒。根状茎可做香料，也可入药 sweet flag

猖 chāng 彳尢 凶猛，狂妄 rampant［猖狂］狂妄而放肆 arrogant and unbridled：打退了敌人的～进攻 *repulsed the enemy's savage attack*［猖獗］（–jué）放肆地横行，闹得很凶 rampant：～一时 *run rampant for a time*

阊(閶) chāng 彳尢 ［阊阖］（–hé）1 传说中的天门 (in Chinese legend) gate of Heaven 2 宫门 gate of a palace［阊门］苏州城门名 Changmen (city gate of Suzhou)

娼 chāng 彳尢 妓女（㊥–妓）prostitute

鲳(鯧) chāng 彳尢 鱼名，又叫平鱼，身体短而扁，没有腹鳍，鳞小，生活在海洋里 butterfish (also called 平鱼)

长(長) cháng ㄔㄤˊ ❶两端的距离大，跟“短”相对 long (opposite of 短) ①指空间 (of space)：这条路很～。*This road is very long.* | ～篇大论 *long-winded discourse* ②指时间 (of time)：天～夜短 *days are long while nights are short* | ～远利益 *long-term interests* [长短] 1 长度 length 2 意外的变故（多指生命的危险）accident (often life-threatening)：万一有什么～可怎么办？*What if an accident occurs?* ❷长度 length：波～ *wavelength* | 那张桌子～1米，宽70厘米。*The desk is 1 metre long and 70 centimetres wide.* ❸长处，专精的技能，优点 forte; strength：专～ *speciality* | 特～ *forte* | 一技之～ *a professional skill* ❹对某事做得特别好 to be good at：他～于写作。*He's good at writing.*

⇨ see also zhǎng on p.833

苌(萇) cháng ㄔㄤˊ 姓 (surname) Chang

场(場、*塲) cháng ㄔㄤˊ ❶平坦的空地，多半用来脱粒、晒粮食 level open space (usually used as a threshing or sunning ground)：打～ *to thresh* | ～院 *threshing ground* ❷量词，多用于一件事情的经过 (measure word) often used to describe the course of an event：经历了一～激烈的搏斗 *had a fierce fight* | 下了一～大雨 *rained heavily* | 害了一～病 *had an illness*

⇨ see also chǎng on p.70

肠(腸、*膓) cháng ㄔㄤˊ ❶（－子）人和高等动物的消化器官之一，长管形，分大肠、小肠两部分。intestine (see picture of 人体内脏 on page 819) [断肠] 形容非常悲痛 be heartbroken [牵肠挂肚] 形容挂念 be deeply concerned ❷借指心思，情怀 feelings：愁～ *pent-up feelings of sadness* | 衷～ *heart-felt words* ❸在肠衣（脱去脂肪晾干的羊或猪的肠子）里塞进肉、淀粉等制成的食物 sausage：香～ *sausage* | 腊～ *Chinese sausage* | 火腿～ *ham sausage*

尝(嘗、❶*嚐、❶*甞) cháng ㄔㄤˊ ❶辨别滋味 to taste：～～咸淡 *taste food for saltiness* ㊗ 经历，体验 to experience：备～艰苦 *suffer all manner of hardships* [尝试] 试 to try：～一下 *give it a go* ❷曾经 ever：未～ *not ever*

偿(償) cháng ㄔㄤˊ ❶归还，补还（㊎赔－）to repay：～还 *pay back* | 补～ *compensate for* | 得不～失。*The gain does not make up for the loss.* ❷满足 to fulfil; to satisfy：如愿以～。*One's dream has come true.*

鲿(鱨) cháng ㄔㄤˊ 毛鲿鱼，鱼名，身体侧扁，体长1米多，头较大，眼小，生活在海里 Megalonibea fusca (a saltwater fish)

倘 cháng ㄔㄤˊ [倘佯]（－yáng）(old) same as “徜徉”

⇨ see also tǎng on p.640

C

徜 cháng 彳九 [徜徉](– yáng) 安闲自在地来回走 to stroll: ～湖畔 *stroll along the lake*

常 cháng 彳九 ❶长久 constant; long-lasting: ～绿树 *evergreen tree* | 冬夏～青 *remain green throughout the year* ❷副词，经常，时时 ㊀ (adverb) frequently; often: ～～见面 *meet regularly* | ～和工人一起劳动 *often work with the workers* ❸平常，普通的，一般的 ordinary; common: ～识 *common sense* | ～态 *normality* | ～事 *common occurrence* | 反～ *unusual* | 习以为～ *be used to*

嫦 cháng 彳九 [嫦娥] 神话中月宫里的仙女 Chang'e (moon goddess in Chinese mythology)

裳 cháng 彳九 遮蔽下体的衣裙 skirt-like lower garment (for both men and women in ancient China)

⇨ see also shang on p.583

厂(廠、厰)** chǎng 彳九 ❶工厂 factory: 机械～ *machinery works* | 造纸～ *paper mill* | 纱～ *cotton mill* ❷有空地可以存货或进行加工的场所 yard (for storage or processing): 木材～ *timber yard* | 煤～ *coal yard* ❸跟棚子类似的房屋 shed

⇨ see also ān on p.4

场(場、*塲) chǎng 彳九 ❶(－子、－儿) 处所，能适应某种需要的较大地方 venue: 会～ *meeting venue* | 市～ *market* | 广～ *(open) square* | 飞机～ *airport* ㊁特定的地点或范围 site: 当～ *on the spot* | 现～ *site* | 情～ *arena of love* | 生意～ *business field* | ～合 *occasion* ❷戏剧的一节 (of play or opera) scene: 三幕五～ *three acts, five scenes* ❸量词，用于文体活动 (measure word) used for sports and recreation: 一～电影 *a film* | 一～球赛 *a ball game* ❹物质相互作用的范围 field: 电～ *electric field* | 磁～ *magnetic field* | 引力～ *gravitational field*

⇨ see also cháng on p.69

钅长(鋹) chǎng 彳九 锐利 (of knife, etc.) sharp

昶 chǎng 彳九 ❶白天时间长 (of day) long ❷舒畅，畅通 unimpeded

惝 chǎng 彳九 tǎng 去九(又) 失意 disheartened

敞 chǎng 彳九 ❶没有遮蔽，宽绰(chuo) spacious: ～亮 *bright and spacious* | 宽～ *spacious* ❷打开 to open: ～开大门 *open the door wide*

氅 chǎng 彳九 大氅，大衣 cloak; overcoat

怅(悵) chàng 彳九 失意，不痛快 ㊀ dejected: ～～离去 *leave in dejection* | ～然 *dejected*

韔(韔) chàng 彳九 古代盛(chéng) 弓的袋子 (ancient) bow case

畅(暢) chàng 彳九 ❶没有阻碍 smooth; unimpeded: ～达 *smooth; free-flowing* | ～行 *move freely* | ～销 *sell well* ❷痛快，尽情地 uninhibited: ～谈 *talk freely* | ～饮 *drink one's fill*

倡 chàng ㄔㄤˋ 发动，首先提出 to initiate: ～议 *to propose* | ～导 *to advocate*

唱 chàng ㄔㄤˋ ❶歌唱，依照音律发声 to sing: ～歌 *to sing* | ～戏 *sing in an opera* | ～曲 *sing a tune* ㊂ 高呼 to call out: ～名 *call the roll* | ～票 *call out the votes* ❷（～儿）歌曲 song: 小～儿 *folk song* | 唱个～儿 *sing a song*

鬯 chàng ㄔㄤˋ 古代祭祀用的一种香酒 fragrant sacrificial wine in ancient times

CHAO ㄔㄠ

抄 chāo ㄔㄠ ❶誊写，照原文写 to transcribe; to copy: ～文件 *transcribe documents* | ～书 *copy out a book* ❷把别人的文章或作品照着写下来当自己的 to plagiarize: ～袭 *to plagiarize* ❸搜查并没（mò）收 to search and confiscate: ～家 *search sb's house and confiscate his/her property* ❹走近便的路 to take (a shortcut): ～小道走 *take a shortcut* ❺same as "绰 (chāo)❷": ～起镰刀就去割麦子 *seize a sickle to harvest wheat*

吵 chāo ㄔㄠ [吵吵]（-chao）吵嚷 to be noisy

⇨ see also chǎo on p.72

钞（鈔） chāo ㄔㄠ ❶same as "抄❶" ❷钞票，纸币 banknote: 外～ *foreign currency*

怊 chāo ㄔㄠ 悲伤，失意 sad and disappointed

弨 chāo ㄔㄠ ❶弓弦松弛的状态 (of a bow) loose ❷弓 bow

超 chāo ㄔㄠ ❶越过，高出 to exceed: ～龄 *be overage* | ～额 *exceed a quota* | ～声波 *ultrasonic wave; supersonic wave* ❷在某种范围以外，不受限制 to transcend: ～现实 *surrealist* | ～自然 *supernatural*

绰（綽） chāo ㄔㄠ ❶same as "焯 (chāo)" ❷匆忙地抓起 to seize: ～起一根棍子 *snatch up a stick*

⇨ see also chuò on p.96

焯 chāo ㄔㄠ 把蔬菜放在开水里略微一煮就拿出来 to scald (vegetables): ～菠菜 *scald spinach*

⇨ see also zhuō on p.877

剿（*勦、*剿） chāo ㄔㄠ 因袭套用别人的语言文句作为自己的 to plagiarize: ～说 *to plagiarize*

⇨ see also jiǎo on p.313

晁（鼂）** cháo ㄔㄠˊ 姓 (surname) Chao

巢 cháo ㄔㄠˊ 鸟搭的窝，也指蜂、蚁等的窝 nest: 鸟～ *bird's nest* | 蜂～ *beehive; wasp's nest*

朝 cháo ㄔㄠˊ ❶面对 to face: 坐北～南 *face south* | 窗户～着大街。*The window faces the street.* ㊂介词，向着，对着 (preposition) towards: ～前看 *look ahead* | ～着目标前进 *march towards one's destination* ❷封建时代臣见君 to have an audience with (the emperor in imperial China) ㊂宗教徒参拜 to go on a pilgrim-

C

age：～圣 *make a pilgrimage* ❸朝廷，皇帝接见官吏、发号施令的地方，跟“野”相对 imperial court (opposite of 野) [在朝] ㉄当政 to be in power ❹朝代，建立国号的帝王世代连续统治的时期 dynasty：唐～ *the Tang Dynasty* | 改～换代 *change the dynasty* ❺姓 (surname) Chao

[朝鲜族] (–xiǎn–) 1 我国少数民族，参看附录四 the Korean people (one of the ethnic groups in China. See Appendix Ⅳ.) 2 朝鲜和韩国的主要民族 the Korean people (the biggest ethnic group in North and South Korea)

⇨ see also zhāo on p.836

嘲(** 謿) cháo ㄔㄠˊ (formerly pronounced zhāo) 讥笑，取笑(㊟–笑、–讽) to laugh at; to jeer：冷～热讽 *biting sarcasm (literally means 'freezing irony and burning satire')*

⇨ see also zhāo on p.836

潮 cháo ㄔㄠˊ ❶海水因为受日、月的引力而定时涨落的现象 tide：～水 *tidal wave* | ～汐 *tide* ❷像潮水那样汹涌起伏的事物 tide; trend：思～ *ideological trend* | 风～ *craze* | 革命高～ *climax of the revolution* ❸湿（程度比较浅）damp; moist：～气 *dampness* | 受～了 *be dampened* | 阴天返～ *become damp on a cloudy day* ❹成色差，技术低 inferior：～金 *impure gold* | 手艺～ *have poor craftsmanship*

吵 chǎo ㄔㄠˇ ❶声音杂乱搅扰人 noisy：～得慌 *very noisy* | 把他～醒了。*The noise woke him up.* ❷打嘴仗，口角 to quarrel：～架 *have an argument* | 争～ *to quarrel* | 他俩～起来了。*The two of them started arguing.*

⇨ see also chāo on p.71

炒 chǎo ㄔㄠˇ 把东西放在锅里加热，翻动着弄熟 to stir-fry：～鸡蛋 *scrambled egg* | ～菜 *stir-fried dishes* | 糖～栗子 *sugar roasted chestnuts*

耖 chào ㄔㄠˋ ❶耙(bà)地后用来把土块弄得更碎的农具 a harrow-like implement for pulverizing soil ❷用耖整地，使地平整 to level land with the implement

CHE ㄔㄜ

车(車) chē ㄔㄜ ❶陆地上有轮子的交通工具 vehicle：火～ *train* | 汽～ *car* | 马～ *horse-drawn carriage* | 轿～ *curtained carriage; saloon car* | 跑～ *sports car* | 自行～ *bicycle* ❷用轮轴来转动的器具 wheeled instrument：纺～ *spinning wheel* | 水～ *waterwheel* | 滑～ *pulley* ㉃指机器 machinery：开～ *start a machine* | 试～ *make a test run* ❸用旋(xuàn)床旋东西 to lathe：～圆 *make sth round with a lathe* | ～光 *polish on a lathe* | ～一个零件 *lathe a machine part* ❹用水车打水 to raise (water) with a waterwheel：～水 *raise water with a waterwheel* ❺姓 (surname) Che

⇨ see also jū on p.335

砗(硨) chē ㄔㄜ ［砗磲］(— qú) 软体动物，比蛤蜊大，壳略呈三角形，很厚，生活在热带海里 giant clam

尺 chě ㄔㄜˇ see 工尺 at 工 on page 210

⇨ see also chǐ on p.81

扯(*撦) chě ㄔㄜˇ ❶拉 to pull; to yank: ～住他不放 *grab him and not let go* ❷不拘形式、不拘内容地谈 to chat: 闲～ *to chitchat* | 不要把问题～远了。*Don't stray too far from the issue.* ❸撕，撕破 to tear; to rip: ～几尺布 *buy a few chi of cloth* | 他把信～了。*He ripped up the letter.*

彻(徹) chè ㄔㄜˋ 通，透 thorough; penetrating: 冷风～骨。*The wind was chilling to the bone.* | ～头～尾(自始至终，完完全全) *out-and-out* | ～夜(通宵) *all night long* ［彻底］一直到底，深入透彻 thorough; complete: ～解决问题 *solve the problem once and for all*

坼 chè ㄔㄜˋ 裂开 to crack: 天寒地～。*The earth cracks in the extreme cold.*

掣 chè ㄔㄜˋ ❶拽(zhuài)，拉 to pull: ～后腿 *hold sb back* | 风驰电～(形容迅速) *with lightning speed* ［掣肘］拉住别人的胳膊 to hold sb back by the elbow ㊗阻碍别人做事，牵制 to prevent sb from doing sth: 被杂事～ *be bogged down in trivialities* ❷抽 to draw: ～签 *draw lots*

撤 chè ㄔㄜˋ ❶除去，免除 to dismiss; to remove: ～职 *dismiss from post* | ～销 *to revoke* ❷向后转移，收回 to withdraw: ～兵 *withdraw troops* | ～资 *withdraw investment* | ～回 *to withdraw*

澈 chè ㄔㄜˋ ❶水清 (of water) clear: 清～ *clear* ❷ same as "彻"

瞮 chè ㄔㄜˋ 明亮，明晰 bright; clear

CHEN ㄔㄣ

抻 chēn ㄔㄣ 扯，拉 to stretch: ～面(抻面条或抻的面条) *pull noodles by hand; hand-pulled noodles* | 把衣服～～ *stretch the clothes* | 把袖子～出来 *pull out the sleeve*

郴 chēn ㄔㄣ 郴州，地名，在湖南省 Chenzhou (a place in Hunan Province)

綝(綝) chēn ㄔㄣ ❶止 to cease ❷善 good

⇨ see also lín on p.406

棽 chēn ㄔㄣ(又) see shēn on page 589

捵 chēn ㄔㄣ same as "抻"

⇨ see also tiǎn on p.650

琛 chēn ㄔㄣ 珍宝 treasure

嗔 chēn ㄔㄣ 生气(㊀—怒) to get angry: ～怪 *to reproach* | ～责 *to rebuke* | 转～为喜 *turn from anger to happiness* ［嗔着］(— zhe) 对人不满，嫌 to reproach; to be displeased: ～他多事 *reproach him for being meddlesome*

C

C

瞋 chēn ㄔㄣ 睁大眼睛瞪人 to glare at：～目而视 *to glower*

臣 chén ㄔㄣˊ ❶奴隶社会的奴隶 slave ❷帮助皇帝进行统治的官僚 official (in imperial China) ❸封建时代官吏对君主的自称 your servant (used by an official to refer to himself before the emperor in imperial China)

尘(塵) chén ㄔㄣˊ ❶尘土，飞扬的灰土 dust ❷尘世（佛家道家指人间，和他们所幻想的理想世界相对）this world：～俗 *worldliness* | 红～（指人世）*this mortal life*

辰 chén ㄔㄣˊ ❶地支的第五位 *chen* (the fifth of the twelve Earthly Branches, a system used in the Chinese calendar) ❷辰时，指上午七点到九点 *chen* (the period from 7 a.m. to 9 a.m.) ❸指时日 day; time：生～ *birthday* | 诞～ *birthday* ❹日、月、星的统称 celestial body

宸 chén ㄔㄣˊ ❶屋宇，深邃（suì）的房屋 mansion ❷旧指帝王住的地方 (old) imperial palace ⓘ称王位、帝王 emperor; king

晨 chén ㄔㄣˊ 清早，太阳出来的时候 morning：清～ *early morning* | ～昏（早晚）*dawn and dusk* | ～练（早晨锻炼身体）*to exercise in the morning*

沈 chén ㄔㄣˊ same as "沉"
⇨ see also shěn on p.590

忱 chén ㄔㄣˊ 真实的心情 true sentiment：热～ *enthusiasm* | 谢～ *gratitude*

沉 chén ㄔㄣˊ ❶没(mò)入水中，跟"浮"相对 to sink (opposite of 浮)：船～了。*The ship sank.* ⓘ落下，陷入 to subside：地基下～。*The foundations subside.* ❷重，分量大 heavy：～重 *heavy* | 铁比木头～。*Iron is heavier than wood.* [沉着]（-zhuó）镇静，不慌张 calm; composed：～应(yìng)战 *rise to a challenge with composure* ❸深入，程度深 deep; intensive：～思 *to contemplate* | ～醉 *be intoxicated* | 天阴得很～。*The sky was overcast and sullen.*

陈(陳) chén ㄔㄣˊ ❶排列，摆设（㊥-列、-设）to lay out：～放 *to display* ❷述说（㊥-述）to state; to explain：详～ *to elaborate* ❸旧的，时间久的（㊥-旧）old：～腐 *hackneyed* | ～酒 *mellow wine* | 新～代谢 *metabolism* ❹周代诸侯国名，在今河南省淮阳一带 Chen (a state in the Zhou Dynasty, in present-day Huaiyang, Henan Province) ❺ 朝代名，南朝之一，陈霸先所建立（公元557－589年）Chen Dynasty (557－589, one of the Southern Dynasties, founded by Chen Baxian)

〈古 ancient〉 also same as 阵(zhèn)

梣 chén ㄔㄣˊ qín ㄑㄧㄣˊ（又）落叶乔木，通称白蜡树，羽状复叶，木质坚韧，树皮可入药，叫秦皮 Chinese ash (usually known as 白蜡树, whose bark can be used in traditional Chinese medicine, called 秦皮)

谌(諶) chén ㄔㄣˊ ❶相信 to believe ❷的确，诚然 indeed ❸（也有读 shèn 的）姓 (surname) Chen (also pronounced shèn)

煁 chén ㄔㄣˊ 古代一种可移动的火炉 (ancient) movable stove

碜(磣、**碜) chěn ㄔㄣˇ ❶东西里夹杂着沙子 gritty［牙碜］（－chen）食物中夹杂着沙子，嚼起来牙不舒服 (of food) gritty：米饭有些～。*The rice is a bit gritty.* ❷丑，难看 ugly［寒碜］（*寒伧）（－chen）1 丑，难看 ugly：长得～ *be ugly* 2 使人没面子 to embarrass：说起来怪～人的。*It's rather embarrassing to mention it.*

衬(襯) chèn ㄔㄣˋ ❶在里面再托上一层 to line：～绒 *line with fleece*｜～上一张纸 *line with a sheet of paper* ❷搭配上别的东西 to set off; to contrast with：红花～着绿叶。*The red flowers contrast with the green leaves.*

疢 chèn ㄔㄣˋ 热病，也泛指病 febrile disease; (generally) disease：～毒 *heat-toxicity*｜～疾 *heat disease*

龀(齔) chèn ㄔㄣˋ 小孩儿换牙（乳牙脱落长出恒牙）(of a child) to grow permanent teeth

称(稱) chèn ㄔㄣˋ 适合 to suit; to match：～心 *gratifying*｜～职 *fully qualified*｜相～ *matching*［对称］两边相等或相当 symmetrical

⇨ see also chēng on p.75, chèng on p.79

趁(*趂) chèn ㄔㄣˋ ❶利用机会 to take advantage of：～热打铁 *strike while the iron is hot*｜～着晴天晒麦子。*Dry the wheat while it is sunny.* ❷〈方 dialect〉富有 well off：～钱 *be wealthy*

榇(櫬) chèn ㄔㄣˋ 棺材（㊧棺－）coffin

谶(讖) chèn ㄔㄣˋ 迷信的人指将来要应验的预言、预兆 portent; prophecy

伧(傖) chen·ㄔㄣ［寒伧］(old) same as 寒碜, see 碜 (chěn) on page 75 for reference

⇨ see also cāng on p.58

CHENG ㄔㄥ

柽(檉) chēng ㄔㄥ 柽柳，落叶小乔木，又叫三春柳、红柳，老枝红色，叶像鳞片，花淡红色，性耐碱抗旱，适于盐碱地区造林防沙 five-stamen tamarisk (also called 三春柳, 红柳)

蛏(蟶) chēng ㄔㄥ （－子）软体动物，贝壳长方形，淡褐色，生活在沿海泥中 razor clam

琤 chēng ㄔㄥ 形容玉石碰击声、琴声或水流声 ㊟(of jade or stone) clink; twang; gurgle：泉水～～ *tinkling spring*

称(稱) chēng ㄔㄥ ❶量轻重 to weigh：把这包米～一～ *weigh this bag of rice* ❷

叫，叫作 to call; to be called：自～ *call oneself; to claim* | ～得起英雄 *worthy of being called a hero* ❸名称 name：简～ *abbreviation* | 别～ *another name* ❹说 to say：～病（以生病为借口）*plead illness* | 连声～好 *keep praising* | 拍手～快 *clap and cheer* ❺赞扬 to praise：～许 *to commend* | ～道 *speak approvingly of* ❻举事 stage an uprisiging：～兵 *wage war*

⇨ see also chèn on p.75, chèng on p.79

铛(鐺) chēng ㄔㄥ 烙饼或做菜用的平底浅锅 frying pan; griddle：饼～ *griddle*

⇨ see also dāng on p.118

偁 chēng ㄔㄥ ❶用于人名。王禹偁，宋代人 used in given names, e.g. Wang Yucheng in Song Dynasty ❷姓 (surname) Cheng

赪(赬) chēng ㄔㄥ 红色 red

撑(*撐) chēng ㄔㄥ ❶抵住，支撑 to prop up; to support：～竿跳高 *the pole vault* | ～腰 *back up* | ～门面 *keep up appearances* ❷用篙使船前进 to pole (a boat)：～船 *pole a boat* ❸充满到容不下的程度 to fill to bursting：少吃些，别～着。*Don't eat too much. You'll burst.* | 麻袋装得太满，都～圆了。*The sacks are bulging to the point of bursting.* ❹使张开 to open：～伞 *put up an umbrella* | 把口袋～开 *hold open a sack*

樘 chēng ㄔㄥ 用于人名。朱祐樘，明代孝宗 used in given names, e.g. Zhu Youcheng, Emperor Xiao of the Ming Dynasty

⇨ see also táng on p.640

瞠 chēng ㄔㄥ 直看，瞪着眼 to stare：～目结舌（形容受窘或惊呆的样子）*be dumbfounded; to gape* | ～乎其后（指赶不上）*be left far behind and unable to catch up*

成 chéng ㄔㄥˊ ❶做好了，办好了，跟"败"相对（㊥完一）to accomplish (opposite of 败)：～事 *succeed in doing sth* | 事情已～。*Mission accomplished.* ❷事物生长发展到一定的形态或状况 to mature：～虫 *adult (insect)* | ～人 *adult* | ～熟 *to mature; mature* ❸成为，变为 to become：他～了专家。*He became an expert.* | 雪化～水 *snow melting into water* ❹成果，成绩 achievement：坐享其～ *sit idle and enjoy the fruits of someone else's work* | 一事无～ *(of a person) be a complete failure* ❺可以，能行 to be fine：这么办可不～。*This won't do.* | ～，就那么办吧。*All right, let's go with it.* ❻称赞人能力强 capable：你真～，又考了个第一。*Well done. You finished top in the exam again.* ❼够，达到一定的数量 to amount to：～千上万 *thousands of thousands* | ～车的慰问品 *truckloads of relief supplies* [成年累月]（——lěi—）形容经历的时间长 year in, year out ❽已定的，定形的 established：～规 *established convention* | ～见 *stereotype* ❾（—儿）十分之一 ten per cent：八～ *eighty per cent*

诚(誠) chéng ㄔㄥˊ ❶真心(㊀—实) sincere: ～心～意 *whole-heartedly* | ～恳 *sincere* ❷实在，的确 indeed: ～然 *admittedly* | ～有此事。*That is indeed the case.*

城 chéng ㄔㄥˊ ❶城墙 city wall: 万里长～ *the Great Wall* ❷城市，都市 city: ～乡互助 *urban-rural mutual support* 也指城区 (also) part of a city: 东～ *eastern part of the city*

宬 chéng ㄔㄥˊ 姓 (surname) Cheng

宬 chéng ㄔㄥˊ 古代的藏书室 (ancient) library: 皇史～(明清两代保藏皇室史料的处所，在北京) *Archive of the Imperial Family (in Ming and Qing dynasties)*

珹 chéng ㄔㄥˊ 一种玉 a type of jade

盛 chéng ㄔㄥˊ ❶把东西放进去 to put sth in a container: ～饭 *fill a bowl with rice* ❷容纳 to hold; to have the room/capacity for: 这座大剧院能～几千人。*The theatre can seat thousands of people.*

⇨ see also shèng on p.594

铖(鋮) chéng ㄔㄥˊ 用于人名 used in given names

丞 chéng ㄔㄥˊ ❶帮助，辅佐 to assist: ～辅 *to assist* [丞相](—xiàng)古代帮助皇帝处理政务的最高一级官吏 (ancient) prime minister ❷古代起辅佐作用的官吏，副职 (ancient) assistant official, deputy: 县～ *assistant county magistrate* | 府～ *deputy prefectural magistrate*

呈 chéng ㄔㄥˊ ❶显出，露出 to appear: 皮肤～红色。*The skin looks red.* | ～现 *to appear* ❷恭敬地送上去 to present respectfully: 送～ *to submit* | 谨～ *submit respectfully* ❸呈文，下级报告上级的书面文字 official document submitted to a higher authority: 辞～ *letter of resignation*

埕 chéng ㄔㄥˊ ❶蛏埕，福建、广东沿海一带饲养蛏类的田 razor clam farm ❷〈方 dialect〉酒瓮 wine jar

珵 chéng ㄔㄥˊ 一种玉 a type of jade

程 chéng ㄔㄥˊ ❶里程，道路的段落(㊀路—) journey; leg of a journey: 起～ *start a journey* | 登～ *set off on a journey* | 送他一～ *accompany him part of the way* [过程]事物变化、发展的经过 process ❷进度，限度 progress; limit: 日～ *schedule* | ～序 *procedure* ❸法式(㊀—式) rule: 操作规～ *operating rule* ❹计量，计算 to measure; to assess: 计日～功 *have the completion of a project well in sight*

裎 chéng ㄔㄥˊ 脱衣露体 to be naked

酲 chéng ㄔㄥˊ 喝醉了神志不清 be intoxicated; drunkenness: 忧心如～ *be deeply perturbed*

枨(棖) chéng ㄔㄥˊ ❶古时门两边竖的木柱，泛指支柱 (ancient) gate jamb; (generally) pillar ❷触动 to touch：～触 *to touch*

承 chéng ㄔㄥˊ ❶在下面接受，托着 to support (from below)：～尘（天花板）*ceiling* ❷承担，担当 to undertake：～应（yìng）*agree to undertake* | ～包 *to contract* | ～当 *to bear (responsibility)* ㊀蒙，受到，接受（别人的好意）to be indebted to：～情 *owe sb a debt of gratitude* | ～教（jiào）*stand instructed* | ～大家热心招待。*(I'm) grateful to you all for your kind hospitality.* [承认] 表示肯定，同意，认可 to admit：～错误 *admit one's mistake* | 他～有这么回事。*He admitted it was indeed the case.* ❸继续，接连 to continue：～上启下 *be a connecting link between the preceding and the following* | 继～ *to inherit* | ～接 *to continue*

乘（*乗、*椉）chéng ㄔㄥˊ ❶骑，坐 to ride; to travel by：～马 *ride a horse* | ～车 *take a bus/car* | ～飞机 *by air* ❷趁，就着 taking advantage of：～便 *at one's convenience* | ～机 *seizing the opportunity* | ～势 *avail oneself of an opportune moment* | ～兴（xìng）*when in high spirits* ❸进行乘法运算，一个数使另一个数变成它自身的若干倍 to multiply：五～二等于十。*Five times two is ten.*

⇨ see also shèng on p.594

惩（懲）chéng ㄔㄥˊ 处罚，警戒 to punish：严～ *punish severely* | ～前毖（bì）后 *learn from the past to avoid future mistakes*

塍（*堘）chéng ㄔㄥˊ 田间的土埂子 ridge between fields：田～ *ridge between fields*

澂 chéng ㄔㄥˊ ❶ see 澄 on page 78 ❷用于人名。吴大澂，清代文字学家 used in given names, e.g. Wu Dacheng, a philologist in the Qing Dynasty

澄（△*澂）chéng ㄔㄥˊ 水清 (of water) limpid [澄清] 1 清澈，清亮 clear：溪水～。*The stream is crystal clear.* 2 搞清楚，搞明白 to clarify：把问题～一下 *clarify the problem*

⇨ see also dèng on p.126

憕 chéng ㄔㄥˊ 平，平均 level; equal

橙 chéng ㄔㄥˊ ❶常绿乔木，果实叫橙子，圆球形，黄绿色，味酸甜，种类很多 orange (tree) ❷红和黄合成的颜色 orange (colour)

逞 chěng ㄔㄥˇ ❶炫耀，卖弄 to show off：～能 *show off one's skill* | ～强 *show off one's prowess* ❷施展，实现 to succeed (in doing sth bad)：敌人的阴谋没能得～。*The enemy's plot was foiled.*

骋（騁）chěng ㄔㄥˇ 骑马奔驰，奔跑（㊇驰—）。to gallop ㊀放任，尽量展开 to give free rein to：～目 *look far into the distance* | ～望 *look as far as the eye can see*

庱 chěng ㄔㄥˇ ❶古地名，在今江苏省丹阳东 Cheng (an

ancient place name, in the east of today's Danyang, Jiangsu Province) ❷姓 (surname) Cheng

秤 chèng ㄔㄥˋ 衡量轻重的器具 scales

称(稱) chèng ㄔㄥˋ same as "秤"

⇨ see also chèn on p.75, chēng on p.75

牚 chèng ㄔㄥˋ ❶斜柱 slanted pillar ❷（一儿）桌椅等腿中间的横木 rung (between the legs of a table, chair, etc.)

CHI ㄔ

吃(*喫) chī ㄔ ❶咀嚼（jǔjué）食物后咽下（包括喝、吸）to take (food, drink, etc.); to eat (including 喝 and 吸): ～饭 *have a meal* | ～奶 *suck milk* | ～药 *take medicine* ⓐ消灭（多用于军事、棋戏）(in war) to destroy (enemy forces); (in chess games) to capture (a piece): ～掉敌人一个团 *wipe out an enemy regiment* | 黑方的炮被～了。*The black side's cannon was taken.* ❷靠某种事物生活 to live off: ～老本 *rest on one's laurels; live off one's skills without improving oneself* | 靠山～山，靠水～水 *make use of what is readily available* ❸吸（液体）to absorb (liquid): ～墨纸 *blotting paper* ⓒ耗费 to exhaust: ～力 *arduous* | ～劲 *bear weight; strenuous* ❹挨，遭受 to suffer: ～惊 *be surprised* | ～官司 *be taken to court* | ～亏 *suffer losses* ⓒ被（宋元小说、戏曲里常用）used to form the passive voice in stories or operas in Song and Yuan dynasties: ～那厮骗了 *was taken in by the bastard* ❺承受 to endure: 这个任务很～重。*This is an arduous task.* | ～不住太大的分量 *not able to bear much weight*

[口吃] (吃 formerly pronounced jī) 结巴 to stammer

哧 chī ㄔ 形容笑声或布、纸等的撕裂声 used to describe the sound of laughing or tearing cloth or paper, etc.: ～～地笑 *to giggle* | ～地撕下一块布 *rip off a piece of cloth*

蚩 chī ㄔ 无知，痴愚 idiotic

嗤 chī ㄔ 讥笑 to jeer: ～之以鼻 *snort in contempt*

媸 chī ㄔ 面貌丑 ugly: 妍（yán）～（美丑）*beautiful and ugly*

鸱(鴟) chī ㄔ 鹞（yào）鹰 harrier [鸱鸮]（-xiāo）[鸱鸺]（-xiū）猫头鹰一类的鸟 eagle owl

绨(絺) chī ㄔ 细葛布 fine kudzu cloth

瓻 chī ㄔ 古代的一种酒器 (ancient) a type of wine container

眵 chī ㄔ 眼眵，又叫眵目糊、眼屎，眼睛分泌出来的淡黄色黏稠液体 eye discharge (also called 眵目糊，眼屎）

笞 chī ㄔ 用鞭、杖或竹板打 to whip; to cane; to flog: ～杖 *cane* | 鞭～ *to flog*

C

摛 chī ㄔ 舒展，散布 to spread out：～藻（铺张辞藻）*write in an ornate style*

螭 chī ㄔ 古代传说中一种没有角的龙，古代建筑或工艺品上常用它的形状做装饰 (in ancient Chinese legend) hornless dragon (often used as a decorative motif)

魑 chī ㄔ ［魑魅］（－mèi）传说中山林里能害人的怪物 (in Chinese legend) mountain-or forest-dwelling monster

痴（*癡） chī ㄔ 傻 stupid：～呆 *idiotic*｜～人说梦（喻完全胡说）*talk absolute nonsense*

池 chí ㄔ ❶（－子）水塘，多指人工挖的（㊀－沼）(artificial) pond; pool：游泳～ *swimming pool*｜养鱼～ *fish pond* ❷像水池的东西 enclosed space that resembles a pond：便～ *urinal*｜花～ *enclosed flower bed* ❸护城河 moat：城～ *city*｜金城汤～（形容城池极为坚固，不易攻破）*impregnable fortress*

弛 chí ㄔ (formerly pronounced shǐ) 放松，松懈，解除 to relax; to slacken：一张一～ *alternate between tension and relaxation*｜废～ *(of decree, discipline, etc.) become lax*｜～禁 *lift a ban*

驰（馳） chí ㄔ ❶快跑（多指车马）（㊀－骋）to gallop：背道而～ *run counter to*｜飞～ *to race*｜奔～ *run fast* ㊁向往 to yearn：神～ *one's thoughts fly to sth*｜情～ *be lost in one's yearning* ❷传播 to spread：～名 *be famous*

迟（遲） chí ㄔ ❶慢，缓 slow：说时～，那时快 *in the blink of an eye*｜～缓 *tardy*｜～～不去 *drag one's feet in going* ㊁不灵敏 slow (in response)：心～眼钝 *be dull; be slow-witted*［迟疑］犹豫不决 hesitant ❷晚 late：～到 *arrive late*｜睡得太～ *go to bed too late*

坻 chí ㄔ 水中的小块高地 islet
⇨ see also dǐ on p.128

茌 chí ㄔ ［茌平］地名，在山东省 Chiping (a place in Shandong Province)

持 chí ㄔ ❶拿着，握住 to hold：～笔 *hold a pen*｜～枪 *carry a gun* ❷遵守不变 to maintain：坚～ *stick to*｜～久 *lasting*［持续］延续不间断 to continue：～发展 *sustained development*［相持］各不相让 to be locked in stalemate and refuse to back down：～不下 *be locked in a stalemate* ❸料理，主管 to manage：勤俭～家 *run a household with industry and economy*｜主～ *preside over; campaign for (justice, etc.); organizer*

匙 chí ㄔ 舀（yǎo）汤用的小勺子，又叫调羹（tiáogēng）soup spoon (also called 调羹)
⇨ see also shi on p.604

漦 chí ㄔ（又）see sī on page 618

墀 chí ㄔ 台阶上面的空地，又指台阶 landing at the top of a flight of steps; step

踟 chí ㄔ ［踟蹰］（－chú）心里犹豫，要走不走的样子

hesitant to move：～不前 *hesitant to move forward*

篪（**篪、**箎）chí 彳 古代的一种竹管乐器，像笛子 (ancient) a flute-like musical instrument made of bamboo

尺 chǐ 彳 ❶市制长度单位，10 寸是 1 尺，10 尺是 1 丈，1 尺约合 33.3 厘米 *chi* (a traditional Chinese unit for measuring length, equal to 33.3 cm. There are 10 寸 in 1 尺 and 10 尺 in 1 丈.)[尺寸]（-cun）衣物的大小长短 (of clothes, etc.) size：照着～做 *make to measure* | ～要量准确。*Make sure the measurements are accurate.* [尺牍] 书信（因古代的书简长约 1 尺）letter (The bamboo strips on which a letter was written in ancient times were about 1 尺 in length.) ❷尺子，一种量长短的器具 ruler ❸画图的器具 instrument for drawing graphs：放大～ *pantograph* ❹像尺的东西 sth like a ruler：计算～ *slide rule*

⇨ see also chě on p.73

呎 chǐ 彳 又读 yīngchǐ，现写作"英尺"，英美制长度单位，1 呎是 12 吋，合 0.304 8 米 (also pronounced yīngchǐ，now written as 英尺) foot (equal to 12 inches or 0.304 8 metre)

齿（齒）chǐ 彳 ❶牙齿，人和动物嘴里咀嚼食物的器官 tooth [挂齿] 谈到，提到（只用在否定的句子里）mention (only in negation)：不足～ *not worth mentioning* | 何足～ *not worth mentioning* ❷（-儿）牙齿状的或像牙齿状的东西 tooth-like part of sth：～轮 *gear* | 锯～ *saw tooth* | 梳子～儿 *tooth of a comb* ❸年龄 age：马～徒增（自谦年长无能）*(humble speech) older but not wiser*

[不齿] ㊕不认为是同类的人，表示鄙弃 to despise

侈 chǐ 彳 ❶浪费，用财物过度(㊀奢一) wasteful：～靡(mí) *extravagant* ❷夸大 to exaggerate：～谈 *be an armchair theorist; high-sounding words*

胣 chǐ 彳 剖开腹部掏出肠子 to disbowel

耻（*恥）chǐ 彳 羞愧，耻辱（㊀羞一）shame：雪～ *avenge an insult* | 可～ *shameful* | 无～ *shameless*

豉 chǐ 彳 豆豉，一种用豆子制成的食品 fermented soya beans

褫 chǐ 彳 剥夺 to divest：～职 *relieve sb of their post* | ～夺 *to deprive*

彳 chì 彳 [彳亍]（-chù）小步慢走或走走停停的样子 to walk slowly

叱 chì 彳 呼呵（hē），大声斥骂 to rebuke loudly [叱咤]（-zhà）发怒吆喝 to roar：～风云 *be all-powerful*

斥 chì 彳 ❶责备（㊀一责）to scold; to denounce：痛～谬论 *denounce a falsehood* ❷使退去，使离开 to repel：排～ *to repel* | ～退 *to dismiss* ❸多，广 extensive [充斥] 多得到处都是（含贬义）(derogatory) to be full

C

of：满纸～着谎言。*The whole paper is full of lies.*
［斥资］支付费用，出资 to fund：～百万建造福利院 *provide one million yuan in funding to build welfare institutions*

赤 chì ㄔ ❶比朱红稍浅的颜色，泛指红色 a shade of red slightly lighter than vermilion; (generally) red：～小豆 *red bean*｜～铜矿 *cuprite*［赤子］初生婴儿 newborn baby［赤字］财政上亏空的数字 deficit ❷忠诚 loyal：～诚 *most sincere*｜～心 *total sincerity*｜～胆忠心 *utter devotion* ❸空无所有 empty：～手空拳 *bare-handed; unarmed*｜～贫 *destitute* ❹裸露 to be naked：～脚 *be barefoot*｜～背（bèi）*be bare-backed*

饬（飭） chì ㄔ ❶整顿，使整齐（㊟整－）to put in order ❷旧时指上级命令下级 (old) to order：～知 *notify by an edict*｜～令 *to order*

炽（熾） chì ㄔ 旺盛 vigorous：～热 *white-hot; blazing*｜～烈 *fervent*

翅（*翄） chì ㄔ ❶翅膀，鸟和昆虫等用来飞行的器官 wing ❷鱼翅，指用鲨鱼的鳍制成的食物 shark's fin (as food) ❸ (ancient) same as "啻"

敕（*勅、*勑） chì ㄔ 帝王的诏书、命令 royal edict：～文 *imperial decree*｜～令 *issue an imperial edict; imperial edict*｜～旨 *royal edict*

鶒（鶒） chì ㄔ see 鸂鶒 (xī－) at 鸂 on page 698

瘛 chì ㄔ 中医指筋脉痉挛、强直的病症 (in traditional Chinese medicine) spasm of the sinews and muscles

啻 chì ㄔ 但，只 merely［不啻］1 不只，不止 to be more than：～如此 *be more than this* 2 不异于，如同 to be like：～兄弟 *be as close as brothers*

傺 chì ㄔ see 侘傺 (chà－) at 侘 on page 64

瘈 chì ㄔ same as "瘛"
⇨ see also zhì on p.860

瘛 chì ㄔ ［瘛疭］（－zòng）中医指手脚痉挛、口眼㖞斜的症状，抽风 (in traditional Chinese medicine) to convulse

CHONG ㄔㄨㄥ

冲（❷－❹衝、❶❺沖）** chōng ㄔㄨㄥ ❶用开水等浇，水流撞击 to pour (boiling water, etc.) on; (of water) to flush：～茶 *make tea*｜用水～服 *take (medicine) after dissolving it in water*｜这道堤不怕水～。*The levee is water resistant.* ㊕〈方 dialect〉山区的平地 flatland in a mountainous area：韶山～（地名，在湖南省韶山市）*Shaoshanchong (a place in Shaoshan City, Hunan Province)*［冲淡］加多液体，降低浓度 to dilute ㊑使某种效果、气氛等减弱 to weaken (an effect, atmosphere, etc.) ❷向上钻 to shoot up：～入云霄 *soar into the clouds* ❸通行的大道 thoroughfare：要～ *strategic pass*｜

这是～要地方。*This is a place of strategic importance.* ❹ 快速向前闯 to dash: ～锋 *charge (at the enemy)* | ～入敌阵 *charge into the enemy line* | 横～直撞 *barge about; dash around* [冲动] 1 神经兴奋而突然产生的情绪或行动 impulse; urge 2 感情强烈，不能自制 impulsive [冲突] 1 互相撞击或争斗 to collide; to clash 2 意见不同，互相抵触 to conflict ❺ 互相抵消 to cancel out: ～账 *(of accounts) to balance; to offset*

⇨ see also chòng on p.84

忡(**㤝) chōng ㄔㄨㄥ 忧虑不安 ㊂ anxious; disturbed: 忧心～～ *be deeply disturbed and worried*

翀 chōng ㄔㄨㄥ 鸟向上直飞 (of a bird) to soar

充 chōng ㄔㄨㄥ ❶满，足（㊀－足）full: ～其量 *at most* | ～分 *full; sufficient; as far as possible* | ～实 *rich; substantial; to enrich; to substantiate* ❷ 填满，装满 to fill: ～电 *to charge (a battery, etc.)* | ～耳不闻 *turn a deaf ear to* | ～满 *be full of* ❸ 当，担任 to act as: ～当 *serve as* | ～任 *take up the post of* ❹ 假装 to pose as: ～行家 *pose as an expert* | ～能干 *pretend to be capable*

茺 chōng ㄔㄨㄥ [茺蔚]（－wèi）草本植物，即益母草，茎四棱形，叶掌状分裂，花红色或白色。茎、叶、籽实都可入药 Chinese motherwort (same as 益母草)

浺 chōng ㄔㄨㄥ ❶ 山泉流下 (of a spring) to flow down ❷ 形容水流声 (used to describe the sound of flowing water) gushing

珫 chōng ㄔㄨㄥ [珫耳] 古代冠冕上垂在耳朵两旁的玉饰，可用来塞耳避听 (ancient) jade ear plug

涌 chōng ㄔㄨㄥ 〈方 dialect〉河汊，多用于地名 (often used in place names) river branch: 霞～（在广东省惠阳）*Xiachong (in Huiyang, Guangdong Province)* | 鲗鱼～（在香港）*Quarry Bay (in Hong Kong)*

⇨ see also yǒng on p.789

舂 chōng ㄔㄨㄥ 捣去皮壳或捣碎 to pound in a mortar: ～米 *husk rice in a mortar* | ～药 *pound medicinal herbs in a mortar*

摏 chōng ㄔㄨㄥ 撞击 to pound

憧 chōng ㄔㄨㄥ 心意不定 hesitant; uneasy [憧憧] 往来不定，摇曳不定 to flicker: 人影～ *shadows of people flickering* [憧憬]（－jǐng）向往 long for: ～未来 *cherish hopes for the future*

艟 chōng ㄔㄨㄥ see 艨艟 (méng －) at 艨 on page 446

虫(蟲) chóng ㄔㄨㄥˊ ❶ 虫子，昆虫 worm; insect ❷ 称呼某类人（多含轻蔑或诙谐意）used to refer to a person, often contemptuously or humorously: 可怜～ *miserable wretch* | 懒～ *idler* | 书～ *bookworm*

种 chóng ㄔㄨㄥˊ 姓 (surname) Chong

⇨ see also zhǒng on p.861, zhòng on p.862

C

重 chóng ㄔㄨㄥˊ ❶重复，再 to repeat; again：书买～了。*This book was a duplicate purchase.* | 旧地～游 *revisit a place* | ～整旗鼓 *rally after a setback* | ～来一次 *have another go* [重阳] [重九] 农历九月九日，我国传统节日，有登高的习俗 Double Ninth Festival (a traditional Chinese festival, on the ninth of the ninth lunar month) ❷层 layer; tier：双～领导 *dual leadership* | ～～围住 *encircle ring upon ring*

⇨ see also zhòng on p.862

崇 chóng ㄔㄨㄥˊ ❶高 lofty：～山峻岭 *soaring mountains* | ～高 *lofty; noble* ❷尊重 to esteem：推～ *hold in high esteem* | ～拜 *to worship* | 尊～ *to venerate*

漴 chóng ㄔㄨㄥˊ ❶形容水声 ㊂ (used to describe the sound of flowing water) gushing ❷漴河，水名，在安徽省五河县 Chonghe River (in Wuhe County, Anhui Province)

⇨ see also shuāng on p.613

宠(寵) chǒng ㄔㄨㄥˇ ❶偏爱，过分地爱 to spoil; to dote on：不能老～着孩子。*Don't always indulge your children.* ❷光耀，荣耀 honour：～辱不惊 *maintain one's equanimity whether in glory or in disgrace*

冲(衝) chòng ㄔㄨㄥˋ ❶对着，向 to face; towards：～南的大门 *south-facing gate* | 别～着我说。*Don't speak to me.* ❷猛烈 strong; vigorously：水流得真～。*The water is gushing.* | 大蒜气味～。*Garlic has a pungent smell.* [冲劲儿] 1 敢做、敢向前冲（chōng）的劲头儿 gusto; vigour 2 强烈的刺激性 pungency：这酒有股～。*The wine has quite a kick.* ❸介词，凭，根据 (preposition) because of; considering：～他这股子钻劲儿，一定能攻克这道难关。*With his drive, there is no doubt he will overcome this difficulty.*

⇨ see also chōng on p.82

铳(銃) chòng ㄔㄨㄥˋ ❶旧时指枪一类的火器 (old) blunderbuss ❷（-子）用金属做成的一种打眼器具 pin punch ❸用铳子打眼或除去 to punch or remove (with a pin punch)

CHOU ㄔㄡ

抽 chōu ㄔㄡ ❶从事物中提出一部分 to draw (sth from sth else)：～签 *draw lots* | ～调干部 *to transfer officials* | ～空（kòng）儿 *manage to find time* [抽象] 1 从事物中抽取本质并形成概念的思维活动 to abstract 2 笼统，不具体 abstract：别讲得太～，最好举一个实例。*Don't be too abstract. It would be helpful to give a specific example.* [抽绎]（-yì）引出头绪 to sort out one's thoughts ❷长出 to put forth：～芽 *to bud* | ～穗 *to head; to ear* ❸吸 to draw：～水 *pump water* | ～气机 *air pump* | ～烟 *to smoke* ❹减缩，收缩 to shrink; to contract：这布一洗～了一厘米。*The cloth shrank by a centimetre* *after the wash.* ❺用细长的、软的东西打 to lash; to whip: 用鞭子～牲口 *whip a draught animal*

䌷(紬) chōu ㄔㄡ 引出，缀辑 to draw/sort out [䌷绎] (－yì) same as "抽绎"

⇨ see also chóu on p.85

瘳 chōu ㄔㄡ ❶疾病减轻，病愈 to recover from illness: 病体已～ *have recovered from illness* ❷减损，消除 to reduce; to dispel

犨 chōu ㄔㄡ ❶牛喘息声 wheeze of an ox ❷突出 to protrude

仇(*讐、△*讎) chóu ㄔㄡˊ 很深的怨恨 animosity; grudge: ～人 *enemy* | 报～ *to revenge* | 恩将～报 *bite the hand that feeds you* | ～视 *be hostile to*

⇨ see also qiú on p.544

⇨ 讎 see also 雠 on p.86

䌷(紬) chóu ㄔㄡˊ (old) same as "绸"

⇨ see also chōu on p.85

俦(儔) chóu ㄔㄡˊ 同伴，伴侣 companion; partner

帱(幬) chóu ㄔㄡˊ ❶帐子 bed curtain ❷车帷 carriage curtain

⇨ see also dào on p.122

畴(疇) chóu ㄔㄡˊ ❶田地 field: 田～ *farmland* ❷类，同类 kind: 范～ *category* [畴昔] 过去，以前 yesteryear

筹(籌) chóu ㄔㄡˊ ❶计数的用具，多用竹子制成 chip; counter (usually made of bamboo): ～码 *(bargaining) chip/counter; one's stock holding* ❷谋划 to plan: ～款 *raise funds* | ～备 *to prepare* | 统～ *to make overall plans* | 一～莫展 *be at one's wits' end*

踌(躊) chóu ㄔㄡˊ [踌躇] (－chú) 1 犹豫，拿不定主意 hesitant: 他～了半天才答应了。*He agreed only after much hesitation.* 2 自得的样子 smug: ～满志 *feel smug with oneself*

惆 chóu ㄔㄡˊ [惆怅] (－chàng) 失意，伤感 melancholy; despondent

绸(綢) chóu ㄔㄡˊ (－子) 一种薄而软的丝织品 silk

椆 chóu ㄔㄡˊ 用于地名 used in place names: ～树塘 (在湖南省武冈) *Choushutang (in Wugang, Hunan Province)*

稠 chóu ㄔㄡˊ ❶多而密 (㊟－密) dense: 棉花棵很～。*The cotton plants are very dense.* ❷浓，跟"稀"相对 thick (opposite of 稀): 这粥太～了。*The porridge is too thick.*

酬(*酧、*醻、❷-❹*詶) chóu ㄔㄡˊ ❶向客人敬酒 to toast; to propose a toast [酬酢] (－zuò) 主客互相敬酒 to exchange toasts ❷交际往来 to socialise: ～答 *repay (with money or gifts, etc.)* [应酬] (yìngchou) 1 交际往来 to socialise: 不善～ *be socially inept* 2 表面应付 to deal with courtesy: 心里不愿意，不得不～一下 *be forced to make*

some polite exchanges 3 指私人间的聚会等 private gathering：明晚还有个～。*I still have a dinner party tomorrow evening.* ❸ 用财物报答 to repay (sb with money, gifts, etc.)：～劳 *to remunerate; remuneration* ❹ 报酬 pay：同工同～ *equal pay for equal work*

C

愁 chóu ㄔㄡˊ 忧虑（㊟忧－）to worry：发～ *be worried* | 不～吃，不～穿 *not to have to worry about food and clothing* | ～死人了 *be worried to death*

雠（讎、*讐） chóu ㄔㄡˊ 校（jiào）对文字（㊟校－）to proofread

⇨ 讎 see also 仇 on p.85

丑（❹❺醜） chǒu ㄔㄡˇ ❶地支的第二位 *chou* (the second of the twelve Earthly Branches, a system used in the Chinese calendar) ❷丑时，指夜里一点到三点 *chou* (the period from one am to three am) ❸（－儿）戏剧里的滑稽角色 clown (in traditional Chinese opera) ❹相貌难看 ugly：长得～ *be ugly* ❺可厌恶的，可耻的，不光彩的 despicable：～态 *despicable demeanour* | ～名 *infamy* ㊀ 不好的、不光彩的事情 scandal：出～ *make a fool of oneself* | 家～ *skeleton in the cupboard*

杻 chǒu ㄔㄡˇ 古代刑具，手铐之类 (ancient) manacle

⇨ see also niǔ on p.482

俞 chǒu ㄔㄡˇ 姓 (surname) Chou

瞅（*瞧、*田） chǒu ㄔㄡˇ 〈方 dialect〉看 to look：我没～见他。*I didn't see him.* | 让我～～。*Let me have a look.*

臭 chòu ㄔㄡˋ ❶气味难闻，跟"香"相对 smelly (opposite of 香)：～气 *bad smell* | ～味 *foul smell* ㊀ ①惹人厌恶的 disgusting：遗～万年 *be condemned to eternal infamy* | 放下～架子。*Stop putting on airs and graces.* ② 低劣 poor：～棋 *bad move in chess* | 这球踢得真～！ *What a lousy kick!* ❷ 狠狠地 severely：～骂 *scold angrily*

⇨ see also xiù on p.732

CHU ㄔㄨ

出（❿齣） chū ㄔㄨ ❶ 跟"入""进"相对 to go out (opposite of 入 or 进) ① 从里面到外面 to come out：～门 *go out* | 从屋里～来 *come out of the room* | ～汗 *to sweat* ②支付，往外拿 to give out：～一把力 *lend a hand* | ～主意 *make a suggestion* | 量入为～ *live within one's means* ❷来到 to arrive：～席 *be present* | ～勤 *turn up at work* ❸ 离开 to depart from：～格 *exceed what is proper* | ～轨 *to derail; go beyond the limits of convention* ❹ 出产，产生 to produce：～品 *to produce; product* | 这里～稻米。*This is a rice-growing region.* | 这个县～过好几个状元。*This county has produced quite a few people* *who came first in the national imperial examinations.* ❺ 发生 to happen：～事 *have an accident*｜～问题了。*Something has gone wrong.* ❻ 显得量多 to produce in volume：这米很～饭。*The rice rises well when cooked.* ❼ 显露 to emerge：～名 *famous*｜～头 *jut out; take the lead* ❽ 超过 to exceed：～众 *outstanding*｜～人头地 *rise above others* [出色]（-sè）特别好，超出一般的 outstanding：～地完成了任务 *did an excellent job* ❾ 放在动词后，表示趋向或效果 used after a verb to indicate direction or effect：提～问题 *raise a question*｜做～贡献 *make a contribution* ❿ 量词，传（chuán）奇中的一回，戏曲的一个独立剧目 (measure word) chapter (in a romance); or used for a play：第二～ *chapter two*｜一～戏 *a play*

岀 chū ㄔㄨ 用于地名 used in place names：～江镇（在四川省大邑）*Chujiang Town (in Dayi, Sichuan Province)*

初 chū ㄔㄨ 开始，表示时间、等级、次序等都在最前的 first; initial：～一 *the first day of a lunar calendar month*｜～伏 *the first of the three hottest ten-day periods in summer*｜～稿 *first draft*｜～学 *be a beginner*｜～等教育 *primary education*｜红日～升 *rising sun* ㊀ ①开始的一段时间 beginning：年～ *beginning of the year*｜开学～ *beginning of a semester* ②原来的，原来的情况 original：～衷 *original intention*｜和好如～ *be reconciled*

貙（貙） chū ㄔㄨ 古代指一种虎属猛兽，又名貙虎 a tiger-like animal in ancient times (also 貙虎)

摴 chū ㄔㄨ [摴蒱]（-pú）same as "樗蒲"

樗 chū ㄔㄨ ❶樗树，即臭椿树 tree of heaven; *Ailanthus* (same as 臭椿树) ❷[樗蒲]古代博戏，像后代的掷色子(shǎizi)，也作"摴蒱" ancient game similar to dice-throwing (also written as 摴蒱)

刍（芻） chú ㄔㄨˊ ❶喂牲畜的草 hay ❷割草 to cut (grass)

鸲（鶵） chú ㄔㄨˊ ❶ same as "雏" ❷ see 鹓鸲 (yuān-) at 鹓 on page 805

雏（雛） chú ㄔㄨˊ 幼小的鸟，生下不久的 nestling; fledging：～鸡 *chick*｜～莺乳燕 *young orioles and swallows* [雏形] ㊁ 事物初具的规模 embryonic form：略具～ *begin to take shape*

除 chú ㄔㄨˊ ❶去掉 to get rid of：～害 *get rid of a scourge*｜斩草～根 *stamp out the source of trouble* ❷不计算在内 besides; apart from; except for：～此以外 *apart from this*｜～了这个人，我都认识。*I know everybody but this one.* [除非] 1 连词，表示唯一的条件，只有 (conjunction) only if：若要人不知，～己莫为。*The only way to keep a guilty secret is to have none.* 2 介词，表示不计

算在内，除了 (preposition) except：这类怪字，～王老师没人认识。*No one but Mr Wang knows these arcane characters.* ❸ 进行除法运算，用一个数去平分另一个数 to divide：用二～四得二。*Four divided by two equals two.* ❹ 台阶 step：庭～ *courtyard*

滁 chú ㄔㄨˊ 滁州，地名，在安徽省 Chuzhou (a place in Anhui Province)

蜍 chú ㄔㄨˊ ［蟾蜍］see 蟾 (chán) on page 67

篨 chú ㄔㄨˊ see 籧篨 (qú—) at 籧 on page 548

厨(*廚、*厨) chú ㄔㄨˊ 厨房，做饭做菜的地方 kitchen：下～ *do some cooking*

橱(*櫥) chú ㄔㄨˊ （一子、一儿）一种放置东西的家具，前面有门 cabinet：衣～ *wardrobe* | 碗～儿 *cupboard (for crockery, etc.)* | ～柜 *cupboard*

蹰(*躕) chú ㄔㄨˊ see 踟蹰 (chí—) at 踟 on page 80

锄(鋤、*鉏、*耡) chú ㄔㄨˊ ❶用来弄松土地和除草的农具 hoe：大～ *big hoe* | 三齿耘～ *three-tine hoe* ❷用锄弄松土地，除草 to hoe：～田 *hoe a field* | ～草 *hoe weeds* ❸ 铲除 to eliminate：～奸 *eliminate a traitor*

躇 chú ㄔㄨˊ see 踌躇 (chóu—) at 踌 on page 85

处(處、**處、**処) chǔ ㄔㄨˇ ❶居住 to dwell; to reside：穴居野～ *dwell in caves and in the wild* ［处女］1 没有发生过性行为的女子 virgin 2 指第一次的 first：～作 *first effort* | ～航 *maiden voyage* ［处女地］未开垦的土地 virgin land ❷存在，置身 to be situated：设身～地 *put oneself in sb's shoes* | ～在有利位置 *be in a favourable position* ❸跟别人一起生活，交往 to get along with：相～ *get along with each other* | 容易～ *easy to get on with* | ～得来 *get along well with* ❹办理，决定 to handle：～理 *deal with* 引 处罚 to punish：惩～ *to punish* | ～以徒刑 *give a prison sentence*

⇨ see also chù on p.89

杵 chǔ ㄔㄨˇ ❶舂米或捶衣的木棒 pestle; washing bat (for beating clothes) ❷用长形的东西戳或捅 to poke (with sth long)：用手指头～他一下 *jab at him with a finger*

础(礎) chǔ ㄔㄨˇ 础石，垫在房屋柱子底下的石头 plinth：基～ *foundation*

楮 chǔ ㄔㄨˇ same as 构树，see 构❹ on page 215 转 纸 paper

储(儲) chǔ ㄔㄨˇ (formerly pronounced chú) ❶储蓄，积蓄 to store：～存 *to store* | ～藏 *to store* | ～备 *to stockpile* ❷已经确定为继承皇位等最高统治权的人 heir (to the throne)：立～ *appoint sb crown prince* | 王～ *crown prince*

褚 chǔ ㄔㄨˇ 姓 (surname) Chu
⇨ see also zhǔ on p.868

C

楚 chǔ ㄔㄨˇ ❶古书上指牡荆（一种落叶灌木）(in ancient Chinese texts) five-leaved chaste tree; *Vitex negundo* ❷周代诸侯国名，疆域在今湖北省和湖南省北部，后来扩展到河南省南部及江西、安徽、江苏、浙江等省 Chu (a state in the Zhou Dynasty, in today's Hubei and other neighbouring provinces) ❸痛苦（㊀苦－、凄－）painful

[楚楚] 1 鲜明，整洁 neat：衣冠～ *smartly dressed* 2 娇柔，秀美 dainty：～动人 *delicate and graceful*

滍 chǔ ㄔㄨˇ 古水名，济水支流，在今山东省定陶一带 Chuhe River (a tributary of the ancient Jishui River, in today's Dingtao, Shandong Province)

齼（齼）chǔ ㄔㄨˇ 吃酸味食物而牙齿发酸，不舒服 (of teeth) sensitive (caused by acidic food)

亍 chù ㄔㄨˋ see 彳亍 (chì－) at 彳 on page 81

处（處、**䖏、**処）chù ㄔㄨˋ ❶地方 place：住～ *dwelling* | 各～ *everywhere* ㊁部分，点 part; point：长～ *strength* | 好～ *benefit* | 益～ *benefit* ❷机关，或机关、团体里的部门 (of an organization) division：办事～ *office* | 总务～ *general affairs department*

⇨ see also chǔ on p.88

怵 chù ㄔㄨˋ 恐惧，害怕 to fear：～惕（恐惧警惕）*be fearful and wary* | 发～ *be afraid*

绌（絀）chù ㄔㄨˋ 不足，不够 insufficient：经费支～ *be underfunded* | 相形见～ *be dwarfed in comparison*

黜 chù ㄔㄨˋ 降职或罢免（㊀罢－）to demote; to dismiss：～退 *relieve sb of their post* | ～职 *dismiss sb from their post*

柷 chù ㄔㄨˋ 用于人名。李柷，唐代哀帝 used in given names, e.g. Li Chu, Emperor Ai of the Tang Dynasty

⇨ see also zhù on p.870

俶 chù ㄔㄨˋ 〈古 ancient〉开始 to commence

[俶尔] 忽然 suddenly：～远逝 *suddenly dart off into the distance*

⇨ see also tì on p.648

琡 chù ㄔㄨˋ 一种玉器，即八寸的璋 a type of jade ware

畜 chù ㄔㄨˋ 禽兽，有时专指家养的兽类 beast; (sometimes) domestic animal：牲～ *livestock* | ～力 *animal power*

⇨ see also xù on p.736

搐 chù ㄔㄨˋ 牵动 to twitch [抽搐] 肌肉不自主地收缩 to have a tic

滀 chù ㄔㄨˋ 水聚积 (of water) to collect

⇨ see also xù on p.736

触（觸）chù ㄔㄨˋ ❶抵，顶 to touch; to butt：羝（dī）羊～藩 *in a dilemma (literally means 'A ram butts up against a fence and gets its horns entangled.')* ❷碰，遇着 to encounter; to touch：～礁 *strike a reef/rock* | ～电 *have an electric shock; act in a film/TV series (usually for the first time)*| ～景生情。*The sight strikes an emotional chord.*|一～即发 *(of a situation) erupt at the slightest trigger* [触觉]（-jué）皮肤、毛发等与物体接触时所产生的感觉 sense of touch

斶 chù ㄔㄨˋ 用于人名。颜斶，战国时齐国人 used in given names, e.g. Yan Chu, a person of the State of Qi in the Warring States Period

憷 chù ㄔㄨˋ 害怕，畏缩 to fear; to flinch：发～ *be afraid*|任何难事，他都不～。*He doesn't shy away from any difficulty.*

矗 chù ㄔㄨˋ 直立，高耸 to stand tall and upright; to tower：～立 *to stand tall and upright*|高～ *stand tall and erect*

CHUA ㄔㄨㄚ

欻 chuā ㄔㄨㄚ 形容短促迅速的声音 used to describe a short and quick sound：～地一下拉开了窗帘 *jerked back the curtains*

⇨ see also xū on p.734

CHUAI ㄔㄨㄞ

揣 chuāi ㄔㄨㄞ 藏在衣服里 to hide in one's clothes：～手 *tuck each hand into the opposite sleeve*|～在怀里 *tuck into one's bosom*

⇨ see also chuǎi on p.90, chuài on p.90

搋 chuāi ㄔㄨㄞ 用拳头揉，使掺入的东西和（huó）匀 to knead well：～面 *knead dough*

膗 chuái ㄔㄨㄞˊ 〈方 dialect〉肥胖而肌肉松 flabby：看他那～样。*Look how flabby he is.*

揣 chuǎi ㄔㄨㄞˇ 估量，忖度 to surmise; to conjecture; to guess：～测 *to surmise*|不～浅陋（谦辞，指不顾自己的浅陋）*(polite) may I venture in my humble opinion*[揣摩] 1 研究，仔细琢磨 to try to work out：～写作的方法 *study writing techniques carefully* 2 估量，推测 to reckon：我～你也能做。*I guess you can do it, too.*

⇨ see also chuāi on p.90, chuài on p.90

阐（闡） chuài ㄔㄨㄞˋ see 阐阐 (zhèng—) at 阐 on page 849

啜 chuài ㄔㄨㄞˋ 姓 (surname) Chuai

⇨ see also chuò on p.95

揣 chuài ㄔㄨㄞˋ [挣揣](zhèng—) 挣扎 to struggle

⇨ see also chuāi on p.90, chuǎi on p.90

踹 chuài ㄔㄨㄞˋ 践踏，用脚底蹬踏 to trample; to kick：一脚把门～开 *kick the door open*

嘬 chuài ㄔㄨㄞˋ 咬，吃 to bite; to eat

⇨ see also zuō on p.891

膪 chuài ㄔㄨㄞˋ [囊膪]（nāng—）猪的胸腹部肥而松软的肉 fat and soft pork belly meat

CHUAN ㄔㄨㄢ

川 chuān ㄔㄨㄢ ❶河流 river：高山大～ *towering mountains and broad rivers* | ～流不息 *flow in an endless stream* ❷平地，平原 plain：平～ *level plain* | 米粮～ *land of rice and grain* ❸指四川 Sichuan Province：～马 *Sichuan pony* | ～贝 *Sichuan fritillary bulb*
[川资]旅费 travel expenses

氚 chuān ㄔㄨㄢ 氢的同位素之一，符号 T，质量数 3，有放射性，用于热核反应 tritium (T)

穿 chuān ㄔㄨㄢ ❶破，使通透 to pierce：屋漏瓦～ *leaking roof and cracked tiles* | 用锥子～一个洞 *pierce a hole with an awl* ❷放在动词后，表示通透或揭开 used after a verb to indicate penetration or exposure：说～ *lay bare* | 看～ *see through* ❸通过孔洞 to go through (a hole)：～针 *thread a needle* | 把这些珠子～成一串 *string these beads* ㊀通过 to pass：从小胡同～过去 *go through the narrow alley* | 横～马路 *walk across the street* ❹把衣服鞋袜等套在身上 to put on (clothes, shoes, socks, etc.)：～衣服 *dress oneself*

传(傳) chuán ㄔㄨㄢˊ ❶递，转授(㊀一递) to pass：～球 *pass a ball* | ～令 *dispatch an order* | 言～身教(jiào) *teach by example as well as verbal instruction* [传统]世代相传，具有特点的风俗道德、思想作风等 tradition：发扬艰苦奋斗的优良～ *carry forward the great tradition of arduous hard work* ❷推广，散布 to spread：～单 *leaflet* | 宣～ *to publicize* | 消息～遍全国。*The news has been spread throughout the country.* [传媒]传播的媒介，多指报纸、广播、电视等 media [传染]因接触或由其他媒介而感染疾病 to be infected ❸叫来 to summon：～人 *summon sb* | ～呼 *page (sb about a phone call)* ❹传导 to transmit：～电 *conduct electricity* | ～热 *conduct heat* ❺表达 to convey：～神 *lifelike* | 眉目～情 *dart amorous glances*

⇨ see also zhuàn on p.872

舡 chuán ㄔㄨㄢˊ ❶〈古 ancient〉same as "船" ❷姓 (surname) Chuan

船(*舩) chuán ㄔㄨㄢˊ 水上的主要交通工具，种类很多 boat; ship：帆～ *sailing boat* | 轮～ *ship*

遄 chuán ㄔㄨㄢˊ 快，迅速 swiftly：～往 *go promptly*

篅 chuán ㄔㄨㄢˊ 一种盛粮食等的器物，类似囤(dùn) a type of grain bin

椽 chuán ㄔㄨㄢˊ (一子)放在檩上架着屋顶的木条 rafter (see picture of 房屋的构造 on page 170)

舛 chuǎn ㄔㄨㄢˇ ❶错误，错乱(㊀一错) erroneous ❷违背 to run counter to

喘 chuǎn ㄔㄨㄢˇ ❶急促地呼吸 to pant：～息 *to pant* | 累得直～ *pant with exhaustion* | 苟延

残～ *drag out a feeble existence*［喘气］呼吸 to breathe ❷气喘的简称 to gasp：爷爷一到冬天就～。*Grandpa always starts to wheeze when winter comes.*

踳 chuǎn ㄔㄨㄢˇ same as "舛"［踳驳］错谬杂乱 erroneous and confused

串 chuàn ㄔㄨㄢˋ ❶许多个连贯成一行（háng）to string together：把羊肉块儿用竹签子～起来 *skewer the mutton with bamboo skewers*｜～联 *link up with*｜～讲 *explain (a text) word by word; give a summing-up of a text after going over it paragraph by paragraph* ㊂（一儿）连贯起来的东西 string：珠子～儿 *bead string*｜羊肉～儿 *skewered mutton cubes; shashlik* ❷（一儿）量词，用于成串儿的东西 (measure word) string：一～儿项链 *a necklace*｜两～钥匙 *two bunches of keys*｜一～铃声 *a peal of bells* ❸互相勾结、勾通 to collude：～通 *to collude*｜～骗 *collude in fraud*［串供］（-gòng）互相串通，捏造口供 to collude (in confession) ❹由这里到那里走动 to move around：～亲戚 *visit relatives*｜～门儿 *drop in (for a chat)* ❺指演戏剧、杂耍等，现多用于扮演非本行当的戏曲等角色 to act (usually an unaccustomed role)：客～ *be a guest performer*｜反～ *play a role other than one's customary role*

钏（釧） chuàn ㄔㄨㄢˋ （一子）用珠子或玉石等穿起来做成的镯子 bracelet

CHUANG ㄔㄨㄤ

创（創） chuāng ㄔㄨㄤ 伤（㊀一伤）wound：刀～ *knife wound*｜重（zhòng）～ *inflict serious damage on*

⇨ see also chuàng on p.93

疮（瘡） chuāng ㄔㄨㄤ 皮肤或黏膜上肿烂溃疡的病 sore; skin ulcer：褥～ *bedsore*｜口～ *mouth ulcer*｜背上长～ *have a sore on the back*

窗（*窓、*窻、*窸、*牕、*牎） chuāng ㄔㄨㄤ（一子、一儿）窗户，房屋通气透光的装置 window：～明几（jī）净 *(of a room) bright and clean* (see picture of 房屋的构造 on page 170)

床（*牀） chuáng ㄔㄨㄤˊ ❶床铺 bed ❷像床的东西 sth like a bed：车～ *lathe*｜河～（河身）*river bed*｜琴～ *guqin table* ❸量词，用于被褥等 (measure word for duvet, etc.) set：一～被褥 *a set of bedding*

噇 chuáng ㄔㄨㄤˊ 〈方 dialect〉大吃大喝 to pig out (on)

幢 chuáng ㄔㄨㄤˊ ❶古代指旗子一类的东西 (ancient) streamer ❷佛教的经幢。在绸伞上写经的叫经幢，在石柱上刻经的叫石幢 silk umbrella, stone pillar (on which Buddhist scriptures are written)

⇨ see also zhuàng on p.874

闯（闖） chuǎng ㄔㄨㄤˇ ❶猛冲 to charge：往里

～ *burst in* | 刀山火海也敢～ *be ready to go through hell* ❷历练，经历 to temper oneself：～练 *temper oneself* ❸为一定的目的奔走活动 to venture (for some purpose)：～关东 *(of poor people) leave one's hometown to eke out a living in north-east China* | ～江湖 *make a living as an itinerant* | ～荡 *to venture out into the world* ❹惹起 to cause (trouble, etc.)：～祸 *get into trouble*

创(創、*剏、*刱) chuàng ㄔㄨㄤˋ 开始，开始做 to start (doing sth); to create：～办 *set up* | ～造 *to create* | 首～ *to originate* [创举] 从未有过的举动或事业 pioneering undertaking [创刊号] 报刊开始刊行的一期 first issue [创意] 独创、新颖的构思 original idea：颇具～ *very original*

⇨ see also chuāng on p.92

怆(愴) chuàng ㄔㄨㄤˋ 悲伤 sorrowful：凄～ *sorrowful* | ～然泪下 *shed sad tears*

CHUI ㄔㄨㄟ

吹 chuī ㄔㄨㄟ ❶合拢嘴唇用力出气 (of a person) to blow：～灯 *blow out a lamp* | ～笛 *play the flute* ❷夸口 to boast：瞎～ *to brag* [吹牛] 说大话，自夸 to talk big [吹嘘] 自夸或替人夸张 to boast ❸奉承 to praise excessively：～捧 *to flatter* ❹类似吹的动作 action similar to blowing:～风机 *hairdryer* | 风～日晒 *be exposed to the elements* ❺(事情)失败，(感情)破裂 to fail; to break up：事情～了。*It fell through.* | 他们俩～了。*They have broken up.*

炊 chuī ㄔㄨㄟ 烧火做饭 to cook：～烟 *cooking smoke* | ～事员 *cook; kitchen staff* | ～帚（zhou）（刷洗锅碗等的用具）*kitchen scrubing brush*

垂 chuí ㄔㄨㄟˊ ❶东西一头挂下来 to hang down：～直 *be perpendicular* | ～杨柳 *weeping willow* | ～钓 *angle (for fish)* | ～涎（形容羡慕）*to covet* 敬辞，多用于长辈或上级对自己的行为 (polite speech, of a senior person) to condescend：～询 *condescend to enquire* | ～念 *show kind concern for* ❷传下去，传留后世 to bequeath to posterity：永～不朽 *live forever* | 名～千古 *go down in history* ❸接近，快要 to approach：～危 *be critically ill* | 功败～成（快要成功的时候遭到失败）*fall at the last hurdle*

倕 chuí ㄔㄨㄟˊ 古代传说中的巧匠名 Chui (name of a famous craftsman in ancient Chinese legend)

陲 chuí ㄔㄨㄟˊ 边疆，国境，靠边界的地方 borderland：边～ *frontier*

捶(*搥) chuí ㄔㄨㄟˊ 敲打 to thump; to beat (with a stick)：～衣裳 *pound clothes (with a washing bat)* | ～腿 *beat one's leg with one's fist (as in massage)*

C

棰(❸❹*箠) chuí ㄔㄨㄟˊ ❶短棍子 cudgel ❷用棍子打 to cudgel ❸鞭子 whip ❹鞭打 to whip

锤(錘、*鎚) chuí ㄔㄨㄟˊ ❶秤锤，配合秤杆称分（fèn）量的金属块 (metal) weight (used on a steelyard) ❷（一子、一儿）敲打东西的器具 hammer：铁～ *iron hammer* | 木～ *mallet* ❸用锤敲打 to hammer：千～百炼 *(to be) tempered and steeled*

椎 chuí ㄔㄨㄟˊ ❶敲打东西的器具 hammer：木～ *mallet* ❷敲打 to pound; to beat：～鼓 *beat a drum*

⇨ see also zhuī on p.875

陲 chuí ㄔㄨㄟˊ 陲山，山名，在江苏省镇江 Chuishan Mountain (in Zhenjiang, Jiangsu Province)

槌 chuí ㄔㄨㄟˊ （一子、一儿）敲打用具 a tool used for beating or breaking：棒～（chui）*washing bat* | 鼓～儿 *drum stick*

CHUN ㄔㄨㄣ

春(*旾) chūn ㄔㄨㄣ ❶春季，四季中的第一季 spring ㊜生气，生机 vitality：大地回～。*Spring has returned.* | 妙手回～ *(of a doctor) effect a miraculous cure* [春秋] 1 春季和秋季，泛指岁月 spring and autumn; year：不知过了多少～。*Untold years have rolled by.* 2 年龄，年岁 age：～已高 *well advanced in years* 3 我国古代最早的一部编年体史书 *Spring and Autumn Annals* (the earliest chronicle of ancient China) 4 泛指历史 history：甘洒热血写～ *be willing to sacrifice one's life to earn a place in history* 5 我国历史上的一个时代（公元前 770—公元前 476 年），因鲁国编年体史书《春秋》而得名 Spring and Autumn Period (770BC—476 BC) [青春] 青年时代 youth ❷指男女情欲 sexual desire：～情 *amorous feelings* | ～心 *sexual stirrings*

堾 chūn ㄔㄨㄣ ❶〈方 dialect〉地边上用石块垒起来的挡土的墙 stone wall (at the edge of a field serving as an embankment) ❷用于地名 used in place names：～坪（在山西省五台）*Chunping (in Wutai, Shanxi Province)*

瑃 chūn ㄔㄨㄣ 一种玉 a type of jade

椿 chūn ㄔㄨㄣ ❶植物名 plant names ①香椿，落叶乔木，叶初生时有香味，可以做菜吃，木质坚实细致 mahogany; Chinese toon ②臭椿，落叶乔木，又叫樗（chū），花白色，叶有臭味，木质不坚固 tree of heaven; ailanthus (also called 樗 chū) ❷椿庭，代指父亲 father：～萱（父母）*parents*

蝽 chūn ㄔㄨㄣ 昆虫，即椿象，身体圆形或椭圆形，头部有单眼，种类很多，有的能放出恶臭，多数是害虫 stink bug (same as 椿象)

鰆(鰆) chūn ㄔㄨㄣ 鱼名，即马鲛，身体侧扁而长，性凶猛，生活在海洋里 mackerel (same as 马鲛)

纯(純) chún ㄔㄨㄣˊ ❶专一不杂(㊣ー粹) pure：水质不～。*The water contains some impurities.* | ～洁 *pure* | ～钢 *clean steel* | ～蓝 *true blue* ㊀ 完全 absolutely：～系捏造 *sheer fabrication* | ～属谎言 *downright lie* ❷熟练 skillful; versed：～熟(shú) *skillful* | 功夫不～。*Skills are unpolished.*

莼(蒓、*蓴) chún ㄔㄨㄣˊ 莼菜，水草，叶椭圆形，浮生在水面，花暗红色，茎和叶表面都有黏液，可以做汤吃 water shield

唇(*脣) chún ㄔㄨㄣˊ 嘴唇，嘴边缘的肌肉组织 lip [唇齿]㊥关系密切的两个方面 mutual dependency (like that between lips and teeth)：～相依 *be mutually dependent*

淳 chún ㄔㄨㄣˊ 朴实，厚道 pure; simple; honest：～朴 *pure and simple* | ～厚 *pure and honest*

錞(錞) chún ㄔㄨㄣˊ [錞于]古代一种铜制乐器 (ancient) bronze musical instrument

⇨ see also duì on p.152

鹑(鶉) chún ㄔㄨㄣˊ 即鹌(ān)鹑 quail (same as 鹌鹑) [鹑衣]㊥破烂的旧衣服 tattered clothes

醇(*醕) chún ㄔㄨㄣˊ ❶酒味浓厚，纯 (of alcohol) pure; mellow：～酒 *full-bodied wine* | 大～小疵(优点多，缺点少) *great despite minor blemishes* ❷ same as "淳" ❸有机化合物的一大类，酒精(乙醇)就属醇类 alcohol

蠢(❶*惷) chǔn ㄔㄨㄣˇ ❶愚笨，笨拙(㊣愚ー) stupid：～才 *idiot* ❷虫子爬动 (of worms) to wriggle [蠢动]㊥坏人进行活动 scheme to stir up trouble

CHUO ㄔㄨㄛ

逴 chuō ㄔㄨㄛ 远 far

踔 chuō ㄔㄨㄛ ❶跳 to leap：～腾 *to jump* ❷超越 to go beyond; to surpass

戳 chuō ㄔㄨㄛ ❶用尖端触击 to jab; to poke：用手指头～他的额头 *poke him in the forehead with a finger* ❷因猛触硬物而受伤 to get injured (by pushing into sth hard with a sudden strong movement)：打球～伤了手 *sprain one's hand while playing a ball game* ❸竖立 to stand sth on end; to erect：把秫秸～起来 *stand the sorghum stalks up* ❹(一子、一儿)图章 seal; stamp：邮～ *postmark* | 盖～子 *apply a seal*

娖 chuò ㄔㄨㄛˋ 谨慎㊍ cautious; prudent

齪(齪) chuò ㄔㄨㄛˋ see 龌龊 (wò—) at 龌 on page 689

啜 chuò ㄔㄨㄛˋ ❶饮，吃 to sip; to eat：～茗(喝茶) *sip tea* | ～粥

have some porridge ❷哭泣的时候抽噎的样子 to sob：～泣 *to sob*

⇨ see also chuài on p.90

惙 chuò ㄔㄨㄛˋ ❶忧愁 ⓐ worried ❷疲乏 fatigued

辍(輟) chuò ㄔㄨㄛˋ 中止，停止 to stop halfway：～学 *drop out of school* | 中～ *stop halfway* | 日夜不～ *non-stop day and night*

歠 chuò ㄔㄨㄛˋ ❶吸，喝 to sip; to drink ❷指可以喝的汤、粥等 liquid food (such as soup, porridge, etc.)

绰(綽) chuò ㄔㄨㄛˋ 宽裕 ample; spacious：～～有余 *more than enough* | 宽～(chuo) *spacious*

[绰号] 外号 nickname

⇨ see also chāo on p.71

CI ㄘ

刺 cī ㄘ 形容撕裂声、摩擦声等 sound of ripping or scratching, etc.：～～地冒火星儿 *hiss with flying sparks* [刺棱] (-lēng) 形容动作迅速的声音 sound of a swift movement [刺溜] (-liū) 形容脚底下滑动的声音，东西迅速滑过的声音 sound of slipping or sliding

⇨ see also cì on p.98

呲 cī ㄘ (一儿) 斥责，责骂 to scold：挨～儿 *get told off* | ～儿了他一顿 *told him off*

⇨ see also zī on p.879

玼 cī ㄘ 玉上的斑点 blemish in a piece of jade

⇨ see also cǐ on p.97

疵 cī ㄘ 毛病 flaw; fault：吹毛求～(指故意挑剔) *nitpick*

跐 cī ㄘ 脚下滑动 to slip：蹬～了(脚没有踏稳) *lose one's footing*

⇨ see also cǐ on p.97

差 cī ㄘ see 参差 (cēn-) at 参 on page 61

⇨ see also chā on p.62, chà on p.64, chāi on p.64

词(詞、*䛐) cí ㄘˊ ❶在句子里能自由运用的最小的语言单位，如"人""跑""甜""他""而且"等 word [词组] 两个或两个以上的词的组合，又叫短语 phrase (also called 短语) ❷语言，特指有组织的语言、文字 wording：歌～ *lyrics* | 演讲～ *speech* | 义正～严 *speak sternly out of a sense of justice* ❸一种长短句押韵的文体 *ci* (a poetic form in rhymes consisting of variable line lengths)：宋～ *ci of the Song Dynasty* | 填～ *compose ci*

祠 cí ㄘˊ 供奉祖宗、鬼神或有功德的人的庙宇或房屋 shrine：～堂 *ancestral hall/temple* | 先贤～ *worthies and sages shrine*

茈 cí ㄘˊ [凫茈] (fú-) 古书上指荸荠 water chestnut (in ancient Chinese texts)

⇨ see also zǐ on p.882

雌 cí ㄘˊ (formerly pronounced cī) 母的，阴性的，跟"雄"相对 female (opposite of 雄)：～花 *female flower* | ～鸡 *hen* | ～蕊

pistil [雌黄] 矿物名，橙黄色，可用作颜料，古时用来涂改文字 orpiment (used in ancient times for correcting writing)：妄下～（乱改文字，乱下议论）*make careless alterations (in a text); make irresponsible comments* | 信口～（随意讥评）*make irresponsible criticism* [雌雄] 指胜负，强弱 victory or defeat：一决～ *battle it out*

茨 cí ㄘ ❶用茅或苇盖房子 to thatch ❷蒺藜 puncture vine

瓷（** 甆）cí ㄘ 用高岭土（江西省景德镇高岭产的黏土，泛指做瓷器的土）烧成的一种质料，所做器物比陶器细致而坚硬 porcelain; china

兹（** 茲）cí ㄘ see 龟兹 (qiū —) at 龟 on page 543

⇨ see also zī on p.880

慈 cí ㄘ ❶慈爱，和善 loving; kind; benign：敬老～幼 *respect the old and care for the young* | 心～面善 *have a kind face and a heart of gold* ❷指母亲 mother：家～ *my mother*

磁 cí ㄘ ❶磁性，物质能吸引铁、镍等的性质 magnetism：～石 *magnet* | ～卡 *magnetic card* | ～盘 *(magnetic) disc* ❷ same as "瓷"

鹚（鶿、* 鷀）cí ㄘ see 鸬鹚 (lú —) at 鸬 on page 419

糍（* 餈）cí ㄘ 一种用江米（糯米）做成的食品 food made of glutinous rice：～粑（bā）*glutinous rice cake* | ～团 *glutinous rice balls*

辞（辭、* 辤）cí ㄘ ❶告别 to bid farewell：～行 *take leave (of sb)* ❷不接受，请求离去 to resign：～职 *to resign* ⓘ躲避，推托 to shy away from; to shrink from：虽死不～ *not to shirk from sth even at the risk of one's life* | 不～辛苦 *not shrink from any hardship* ❸解雇 to sack; to dismiss; to fire：他被老板～了。*He was sacked by his boss.* ❹ same as "词❷"：～藻 *ornate language; retoric* ❺古典文学的一种体裁 a form of classical Chinese poetry：～赋 *a form of classical Chinese poetry*

此 cǐ ㄘ 代词 pronoun ①这，这个，跟"彼"相对 this (opposite of 彼)：彼～ *each other* | ～人 *this person* | ～时 *this moment* | 特～布告。*It is hereby announced that...* ②这儿，这里 here：由～往西 *go west from here* | 到～为止 *stop here*

泚 cǐ ㄘ ❶清，鲜明 (of water) clear; limpid ❷用笔蘸墨 to dip (a brush in ink)：～笔作书 *dip the brush into ink and start writing*

玼 cǐ ㄘ 玉色明亮 (of jade) bright

⇨ see also cī on p.96

跐 cǐ ㄘ 踩，踏 to step on：～着门槛 *stand on the threshold* | 脚～两只船 *have a foot in both camps*

⇨ see also cī on p.96

鲨（鮆）cǐ ㄘ 鱼名，身体侧扁，上颌骨向后延

长，有的可达臀鳍，生活在海里 anchovy

次 cì ㄘˋ ❶第二 second：～日 *next day* | ～子 *second son* ❷质量或品质较差 inferior; shoddy：～货 *inferior goods* | ～品 *defective product* | 这人太～。*That person is really horrible.* ❸等第，顺序（㊥—序）order; sequence：名～ *ranking* | 车～ *train number* | 依～前进 *march in file* ❹量词，回 (measure word) time：第一～来北京 *come to Beijing for the first time* ❺临时驻扎，也指途中停留的处所 to stop over; stopover：舟～ *quay* | 旅～ *lodging (during a trip)*

佽 cì ㄘˋ 帮助 to help：～助 *to help*

伺 cì ㄘˋ same as 伺 (sì), used in 伺候［伺候］（-hou）1 旧指侍奉或受役使 (old) to serve：～主子 *wait on one's master* 2 照料 to look after：～病人 *look after the patient*

⇨ see also sì on p.619

刺 cì ㄘˋ ❶用有尖的东西穿进或杀伤 to pierce; to prick; to stab：～绣 *to embroider; embroidery* | ～杀 *to assassinate* ㊂感觉器官受刺激而感到不舒服 to irritate (one's senses)：～耳 *jarring on the ears* | ～鼻 *pungent* | ～眼 *dazzling; harsh on the eye*［刺激］1 光、声、热等引起生物体活动或变化 (of light, sound, heat, etc.) to stimulate ㊂一切使事物起变化的作用 stimulation 2 推动事物，使起积极的变化 to stimulate (sth to make it more active)：～经济发展 *stimulate economic growth* 3 使人精神上受到挫折、打击 to upset：考试不及格对他～很大。*Failing the exam was a heavy blow to him.* ❷暗杀 to assassinate：～客 *assassin* | 被～ *be assassinated* ❸打听，侦探 to pry：～探 *make secret enquiries* ❹用尖刻的话指摘、嘲笑 to scoff：讽～ *to mock* ❺尖锐像针的东西 thorn：鱼～ *fish bone* | ～猬 *hedgehog* | ～槐 *black locust* ❻名片 visiting card：名～ *calling card*

⇨ see also cī on p.96

莿 cì ㄘˋ 用于地名 used in place names：～桐乡（在台湾省）*Citongxiang (in Taiwan Province)*

赐（賜）cì ㄘˋ ❶给，指上级给下级或长辈给晚辈（㊥赏—）(of a senior person) to bestow：恩～ *to bestow* ❷敬辞，用于他人对自己或自己一方的指示、答复等 (polite speech) your instruction, reply, etc.：～教（jiào）*grant instructions* | 希～回音。*I'm looking forward to your reply.* ❸赏给的东西，给予的好处 favours; gift：皆受其～ *have all received favours from him* | 受～良多 *receive many favours and gifts*

CONG ㄘㄨㄥ

匆（*怱、*悤）cōng ㄘㄨㄥ 急促㊣ hasty; hurried：～忙 *in haste* | 来去～～ *come and go in a hurry*

葱（*蔥）cōng ㄘㄨㄥ ❶草本植物，叶圆筒状，中空，花白色，茎叶有辣味，可

用作蔬菜，又可供调味用 spring/green onion ❷青色 green：～翠 *lush green* | 郁郁～～ *luxuriantly green*

苁(蓯) cōng ㄘㄨㄥ [苁蓉] (-róng) 植物名 general name of several plants with 苁蓉 in their names 1 草苁蓉，草本植物，寄生，茎和叶黄褐色，花淡紫色 northern groundcone 2 肉苁蓉，草本植物，寄生，茎和叶黄褐色，花紫褐色，茎可入药 saline cistanche

瑽(瑽) cōng ㄘㄨㄥ [瑽瑢] (-róng) 形容佩玉相碰的声音 (used to describe jade pieces striking each other) to tinkle

枞(樅) cōng ㄘㄨㄥ 常绿乔木，又叫冷杉，树干高大，耐寒，木材供建筑或做器具用 fir (also called 冷杉)

⇨ see also zōng on p.884

囱 cōng ㄘㄨㄥ 烟囱，炉灶、锅炉出烟的通路 chimney

骢(驄) cōng ㄘㄨㄥ 青白色的马 piebald horse

璁 cōng ㄘㄨㄥ 像玉的石头 jade-like stone

熜 cōng ㄘㄨㄥ ❶微火 low fire ❷热气 heat

聪(聰) cōng ㄘㄨㄥ ❶听觉 hearing：失～ *become deaf* ❷听觉灵敏 sharp-eared：耳～目明 *have sharp eyes and ears* ❸聪明，智力强 clever：～颖 *bright* | ～慧 *intelligent*

从(從) cóng ㄘㄨㄥˊ (❻❼❽ formerly pronounced zòng) ❶跟随 to follow：愿～其后 *wish to follow in sb's footsteps* ❷依顺 to obey：服～ *to obey* | 胁～ *be an accomplice under duress* | 言听计～ *accept advice without questioning* ❸参与 to participate in：～政 *enter politics* | ～军 *join the army* ❹介词，表示起点或经由 (preposition) from：～南到北 *from the south to the north* | ～古到今 *from ancient times till now* | ～小路走 *take the shortcut* [从而]连词，由此 (conjunction) thus：坚持改革开放，～改变了贫穷和落后的面貌。*(We) adhered to reform and opening up and thus relieved poverty and backwardness.* [从来]副词，向来，一向 (adverb) always：他～不说假话。*He never lies.* ❺采取某种态度或方式 to adopt (a certain attitude or method)：～速解决 *resolve (a problem) as soon as possible* | 一切～简 *do away with all unnecessary formalities* | ～宽处理 *treat leniently* ❻跟随的人 follower; attendant：仆～ *servant* | 随～ *entourage* ❼指同宗而非嫡亲的(亲属) one's first cousin or cousin once removed on the paternal side who bears the same family name：～兄弟 *paternal male cousins* | ～伯叔 *father's male cousins once removed ascending* ❽次要的 secondary：主～ *principal and subordinate* | 分别首～ *distinguish between the principal and an accessory*

[从容] 不慌不忙 composed; calm：举止～ *carry oneself with ease* | ～不迫 *calm and steady* ㊀充裕 ample：手头～ *have ample funds* | 时间～ *have ample time*

〈古 ancient〉also same as 纵 in 纵横

从(叢、**菆) cóng ㄘㄨㄥˊ ❶聚集，许多事物凑在一起 to cluster; to grow together：草木～生 *overgrown with grass and trees* | 百事～集。*A whole heap of issues have piled up.* ❷聚在一起的人或物 crowd; cluster：人～ *crowds of people* | 草～ *clumps of grass*

淙 cóng ㄘㄨㄥˊ 形容水流声 ㊂ (used to describe the sound of flowing water) to gurgle

悰 cóng ㄘㄨㄥˊ ❶快乐 joy ❷心情 mood

琮 cóng ㄘㄨㄥˊ 古时的一种玉器，筒状，外边八角，中间圆形 a type of jade piece in ancient times

賨(賨) cóng ㄘㄨㄥˊ 秦汉时期今湖南、重庆、四川一带少数民族所缴的一种赋税，后也指这部分少数民族 tax paid by people in the Qin and Han dynasties in present-day Hunan, Chongqing and Sichuan; (later) the people there

COU ㄘㄡ

凑(*湊) còu ㄘㄡˋ ❶聚合 to gather：～在一起 *come together* | ～钱 *pool money* [凑合]（—he）1 same as "凑" ❶ 2 将就 to make do：～着用吧 *make do with it* ❷接近 to approach：～上去 *move closer* | 往前～ *move forward* [凑巧] 碰巧 by chance; as chance would have it

辏(輳) còu ㄘㄡˋ 车轮的辐聚集到中心 (of spokes) to converge：辐～ *to converge (like spokes)*

腠 còu ㄘㄡˋ 肌肤上的纹理 skin texture; interstices of the skin and muscles

CU ㄘㄨ

粗(*粡、*麤、**麁) cū ㄘㄨ ❶跟"细"相对 opposite of 细 ①颗粒大的 coarse：～沙子 *coarse sand* | ～面 *coarse flour* ②长条形东西直径大的 thick：～线 *thick thread* | 这棵树长(zhǎng)得很～。*The tree trunk is very thick.* | ～枝大叶（形容不细致）*rough and careless* ③声音低而大 (of voice) gravelly and loud：嗓音很～ *speak in a rough voice* ④毛糙，不精致的 crude：工艺很～ *of shoddy workmanship* | ～瓷 *crude porcelain* | ～布 *coarse cloth* | 去～取精 *discard the dross and retain the fine essence* ⑤疏忽，不周密 careless：～心 *careless* | ～～一想 *have a quick think* ❷鲁莽，粗俗（㊀—鲁）rude：～暴 *(of attitude) harsh; rough* | ～人 *uncouth person* | 这话太～。*It is very rude to speak like that.*

徂 cú ㄘㄨˊ ❶往 to go to ❷过去 to elapse ❸开始 to commence ❹ same as “殂”

殂 cú ㄘㄨˊ 死亡 to die: 崩～ *(of an emperor or king) to die*

卒 cù ㄘㄨˋ same as “猝”
⇨ see also zú on p.887

猝 cù ㄘㄨˋ 忽然 abruptly: ～生变化。*There is a sudden turn of events.* | ～不及防 *be taken by total surprise*

促 cù ㄘㄨˋ ❶靠近 to be close to: ～膝谈心 *have a heart-to-heart talk* ❷时间极短，急迫 rushed; hurried: 急～ *hurried* | 短～ *brief* ❸催，推动 to urge; to promote: 督～ *supervise and urge* | ～进 *to promote* | ～销 *promote sales*

酢 cù ㄘㄨˋ same as “醋”
⇨ see also zuò on p.892

醋 cù ㄘㄨˋ 一种调味用的液体，味酸，用酒或酒糟发酵制成，也可用米、麦、高粱等直接酿制 vinegar

蔟 cù ㄘㄨˋ 蚕蔟，用麦秆等做成，蚕在上面做茧 bundle of straw for silkworms to spin a cocoon on

簇 cù ㄘㄨˋ ❶丛聚，聚成一团 to cluster: ～拥 *crowd around* | 花团锦～ *colourful and splendid* ❷量词，用于聚成团的东西 (measure word) cluster: 一～鲜花 *a bunch of flowers*

踧 cù ㄘㄨˋ ❶[踧踖] (－jí) 恭敬而不安的样子 awed and uneasy ❷ same as “蹙”

蹙 cù ㄘㄨˋ ❶急促 pressed: 气～ *be short of breath* ❷困窘 in a tight corner; in straitened circumstances: 穷～ *be in dire straits* ❸缩小，收敛 to contract: ～眉 *knit one's brows* | 颦～（皱眉头） *furrow one's brows*

蹴(*蹵) cù ㄘㄨˋ ❶踢 to kick: ～鞠(jū)(踢球) *kick a ball* ❷踏 to stamp on: 一～而就（一下子就成功） *succeed at the first attempt*

CUAN ㄘㄨㄢ

汆 cuān ㄘㄨㄢ ❶把食物放到开水里稍微一煮 to quick-boil: ～汤 *quick-boil some soup* | ～丸子 *quick-boiled meatballs in soup* ❷(－子、－儿) 烧水用的薄铁筒，能很快地把水煮开 slender cylindrical metal pot used for boiling water quickly ❸用汆子把水烧开 to boil (water) in a slender cylindrical metal pot: ～了一汆子水 *boiled a pot of water*

撺(攛) cuān ㄘㄨㄢ 〈方 dialect〉 ❶抛掷 to throw ❷匆忙地做，乱抓 to do sth in a hurry: 事先没准备，临时现～ *rush to do sth without due preparation* ❸(－儿) 发怒，发脾气 to fly into a rage: 他一听就～儿了。*He flared up the instant he heard about it.*

[撺掇] (－duo) 怂恿，劝诱别人做某种事情 to egg sb on: 我再三～，他也不去。*I kept urging him to go but he wouldn't.*

镩(鑹) cuān ㄘㄨㄢ ❶冰镩，一种金属凿冰器具，头部尖，有倒钩 ice pick ❷

C

用冰镩凿（冰）to chip (ice) with an ice pick

蹿（躥） cuān ㄘㄨㄢ 向上或向前跳 to leap：猫～到房上去了。*The cat leapt onto the roof.*

酇（酇） cuán ㄘㄨㄢˊ（又）see cuó on page 105

攒（攢、欑）** cuán ㄘㄨㄢˊ 聚，凑集，拼凑 to gather; to put together：～凑 *put together* | ～钱 *collect money* | ～电视机 *assemble a TV set*

⇨ see also zǎn on p.818

窜（竄） cuàn ㄘㄨㄢˋ ❶逃走，乱跑 to flee：东跑西～ *flee in all directions* | ～逃 *flee in disorder* | 抱头鼠～ *flee like a frightened rat* ❷放逐，驱逐 to exile; to expel ❸修改文字 to alter (words)：～改 *alter (words)* | 点～ *alter the wording*

篡（*簒） cuàn ㄘㄨㄢˋ ❶封建时代指臣子夺取君位 to usurp (the throne) ❷用阴谋手段夺取地位或权力 to seize (a position or power)

爨 cuàn ㄘㄨㄢˋ ❶烧火做饭 to cook：分～（旧时指分家）*(old) divide up family property and start a new household* | 同居各～ *live under the same roof but have separate kitchens* ❷灶 cooking stove

CUI ㄘㄨㄟ

衰 cuī ㄘㄨㄟ 〈古 ancient〉❶等差，等次，等级 hierarchy：等～（等次）*rank* ❷same as "缞"

⇨ see also shuāi on p.612

缞（縗） cuī ㄘㄨㄟ 古时用粗麻布制成的丧服，也作"衰" (in old times) funeral clothing made of coarse linen (also written as 衰)

榱 cuī ㄘㄨㄟ 古代指椽子 (ancient) rafter

崔 cuī ㄘㄨㄟ 姓 (surname) Cui

［崔嵬］（—wéi）山高大不平 (of a mountain) lofty and craggy

催 cuī ㄘㄨㄟ ❶催促，使赶快行动 to urge：～办 *urge (sb) to do sth* | ～他早点儿动身 *press him to set out earlier* ❷使事物的产生、发展变化加快 to speed up; to expedite：～生 *induce labour* | ～化剂 *catalyst*

摧 cuī ㄘㄨㄟ 破坏，折断 to break; to snap：～毁 *to destroy* | ～残 *to wreck* | 无坚不～ *be all-conquering* | ～枯拉朽（形容腐朽势力很容易打垮）*easily destroy (a weakened power)*

漼 cuǐ ㄘㄨㄟˇ ❶水深的样子 (of water) deep ❷眼泪流下的样子 (of tears) coursing down

璀 cuǐ ㄘㄨㄟˇ ［璀璨］（—càn）形容玉石的光泽鲜明夺目 (of jade) brilliant：～的明珠 *dazzling pearl* | 星光～ *luminous star*

脆（*脃） cuì ㄘㄨㄟˋ ❶容易折断，容易碎，跟"韧"相对 (of things) brittle (opposite of 韧)：～枣 *fresh ju-*

jube | 这纸太～。*The paper is too fragile.* [脆弱] 懦弱，不坚强 (of a person) weak ❷声音响亮、清爽 (of voice or sound) crisp：嗓音挺～ *have a crisp voice* ❸〈方 dialect〉干脆，说话做事爽利痛快 straightforward and decisive：办事很～ *be straightforward and decisive*

萃 cuì ㄘㄨㄟˋ 草丛生 (of grass) to grow in a clump ⑪聚在一起的人或物 assemblage：出类拔～（超出同类）*outstanding; out of the ordinary run*

啐 cuì ㄘㄨㄟˋ 用力从嘴里吐出来 to spit：～一口痰 *spit phlegm*

淬 (** 焠) cuì ㄘㄨㄟˋ 淬火，通称蘸火，把合金制品或玻璃加热到一定温度，随即在水、油或空气中急速冷却，以提高合金或玻璃的硬度和强度 to quench (usually known as 蘸火) [淬砺] ⑩刻苦锻炼，努力提高 temper (oneself)

悴 (* 顇) cuì ㄘㄨㄟˋ see 憔悴 (qiáo—) at 憔 on page 534

瘁 cuì ㄘㄨㄟˋ 过度劳累 overworked：鞠躬尽～ *give every ounce of energy* | 心力交～ *be physically and mentally drained*

粹 cuì ㄘㄨㄟˋ ❶不杂 pure：纯～ *pure* ❷精华 (㊀精一) essence：国～（指我国传统文化的精华，如中医、国画、京剧等）*essence of Chinese culture (such as traditional Chinese medicine, painting and Peking Opera, etc.)*

翠 cuì ㄘㄨㄟˋ ❶翠鸟，鸟名，又叫鱼狗，羽毛青绿色，尾短，捕食小鱼 kingfisher (also called 鱼狗) ❷绿色的玉，翡翠 jadeite; emerald：珠～ *pearls and jade* ❸绿色 green：～绿 *emerald green* | ～竹 *green bamboo*

膵 (** 脺) cuì ㄘㄨㄟˋ 膵脏 (zàng)，胰腺的旧称 (old) pancreas

毳 cuì ㄘㄨㄟˋ 鸟兽的细毛 (of birds or animals) down [毳毛] 即寒毛，人体表面生的细毛 (same as 寒毛) vellus hair

CUN ㄘㄨㄣ

邨 cūn ㄘㄨㄣ ❶ see 村 on page 103 ❷用于人名 (used in given names) Cun

村 (❶△* 邨) cūn ㄘㄨㄣ ❶ (一子、一儿) 乡村，村庄 village ❷粗俗 vulgar; rustic：～话 *vulgar language*

皴 cūn ㄘㄨㄣ ❶皮肤因受冻或受风吹而干裂 (of skin) to be chapped：手都～了。*Hands are chapped.* ❷皮肤上积存的泥垢和脱落的表皮 grime：一脖子～。*The neck is covered with grime.* ❸中国画的一种画法，涂出山石的纹理和阴阳向背 *cun* (a type of stroke in traditional Chinese painting to show the shade and texture of rocks and mountains)

存 cún ㄘㄨㄣˊ ❶在，活着 to exist; to live：～在 *to exist* | ～亡 *survive or perish* ❷保留，留下 to retain; to keep：～留 *to pre-*

serve | 去伪~真 *discard the false and retain the true* [存心] 1 居心，怀着某种想法 to harbour：~不良 *harbour evil intentions* 2 故意 intentionally：~捣乱 *deliberately cause trouble* ❸ 储蓄 to deposit (money)：~款 *savings* | 整~整取 *lump-sum saving and withdrawal* ❹寄放 leave (sth for safe-keeping); to check (one's belongings in an official place)：~车 *park (one's car or bicycle)* ❺ 停聚 to retain：小孩儿~食了。*The baby has indigestion.* | 雨后，街上~了一些水。*There were puddles on the street after the rain.* ❻ 慰问 to extend one's regards to：~问 *extend one's regards to* | ~慰 *express sympathy and solicitude* | ~恤 *express sympathy and provide relief*

蹲 cún ㄘㄨㄣˊ 〈方 dialect〉脚、腿猛然着地，使腿或脚受伤 to sustain an impact injury (to the feet or legs through a heavy landing)：他跳下来~了腿了。*He landed hard from his jump and injured his legs.*

⇨ see also dūn on p.153

忖 cǔn ㄘㄨㄣˇ 揣度(chuǎiduó)，思量 to ponder; to turn over in one's mind：~度(duó) *to speculate* | 自~ *think to oneself*

寸 cùn ㄘㄨㄣˋ 市制长度单位，1尺的十分之一，约合3.33厘米 *cun* (a traditional Chinese unit for measuring length, equal to 3.33 centimetres. There are 10 寸 in 1 尺) ㊥短小 short：~阴 *a very short time* | ~步 *a very short distance* | 手无~铁 *be completely unarmed* | 鼠目~光 *be very short-sighted*

吋 cùn ㄘㄨㄣˋ 又读yīngcùn，现写作"英寸"，英美制长度单位，1呎的十二分之一，1吋合2.54厘米 inch (also pronounced yīngcùn, now written as 英寸)

CUO ㄘㄨㄛ

搓 cuō ㄘㄨㄛ 两个手掌相对或把手掌放在别的东西上反复揉擦 to rub one's hands together; to rub with one's hands：~手 *rub one's hands together* | ~绳子 *make cords by twisting hemp fibres between the palms*

瑳 cuō ㄘㄨㄛ 玉色明亮洁白，也泛指颜色洁白 (of jade) white and bright; white

磋 cuō ㄘㄨㄛ 把骨、角磨制成器物 to grind and polish (bones or horns) [磋商] 商量 to negotiate; to consult

蹉 cuō ㄘㄨㄛ ❶跌，倒(㊥一跌) to fall; to slip ❷失误，差错(㊥一失) to err; to slip up

[蹉跎] (-tuó) 把时光白耽误过去 to idle away one's time：岁月~ *time pass by without any achievement*

撮 cuō ㄘㄨㄛ ❶聚起，现多指把聚拢的东西用簸箕等物铲起 to scoop up：~成一堆 *gather into a pile* | 把土~起来 *scoop up the dirt* [撮合] 给双方拉关系 to act as a go-between ❷取，摘取 to extract, to summarize (main ideas)：～要（摘取要点）*summarize the main points* ❸〈方 dialect〉吃 to eat：请你～一顿 *invite you to dinner* ❹市制容量单位，1 升的千分之一 *cuo* (a traditional unit for measuring capacity, equal to one thousandth of 1 升) ❺（一儿）量词 measure word ①用于手所撮取的东西 pinch：一～米 *a pinch of rice* | 一～儿土 *a pinch of earth* ②用于极少的坏人 handful (of bad people)：一小～坏人 *a handful of bad people*

⇨ see also zuǒ on p.891

嵯 cuó ㄘㄨㄛˊ ［嵯峨］（—é）山势高峻 (of mountains) precipitous

瘥 cuó ㄘㄨㄛˊ 病 disease

⇨ see also chài on p.65

鹾（鹺） cuó ㄘㄨㄛˊ ❶盐 salt ❷咸 salty：～鱼 *salted fish*

矬 cuó ㄘㄨㄛˊ 〈方 dialect〉矮 (of a person) short：他长得太～。*He's a little too midget.*

痤 cuó ㄘㄨㄛˊ 痤疮，俗称粉刺，一种皮肤病，多生在青年人的面部，通常是有黑头的小红疙瘩 acne (informal 粉刺)

酂（酇） cuó ㄘㄨㄛˊ cuán ㄘㄨㄢˊ（又）［酂阳］［酂城］地名，都在河南省永城 Cuoyang, Cuocheng (places in Yongcheng, Henan Province)

⇨ see also zàn on p.818

脞 cuǒ ㄘㄨㄛˇ 小而繁 trivial and tortuous［丛脞］细碎，烦琐 loaded down with trivial details

挫 cuò ㄘㄨㄛˋ ❶挫折，事情进行不顺利，失败 setback：屡次受～ *suffer a series of setbacks* | 事遭～阻。*There has been a setback.* ❷压下，使音调降低 to subdue：～了坏人的威风 *cut the evil-doers down to size* | 语音抑扬顿～ *speak in a cadence*

莝 cuò ㄘㄨㄛˋ 莝草，铡碎的草 chopped hay/grass

锉（銼、*剉） cuò ㄘㄨㄛˋ ❶条形多刃工具，多用钢制成，用来磨铜、铁、竹、木等 file (a tool) ❷用锉磨东西 to file：把锯～一～ *file the saw*

厝 cuò ㄘㄨㄛˋ ❶放置 to place：～火积薪（把火放在柴堆下，喻隐藏祸患）*hidden danger (literally means 'put fire under faggots')* ❷停柩（jiù），把棺材停放待葬，或浅埋以待改葬 to place a coffin in a temporary place before permanent burial

措 cuò ㄘㄨㄛˋ ❶安放，安排 to place; to arrange：～辞 *to word* | ～手不及（来不及应付）*be caught off guard* ❷筹划办理 to plan and handle sth：～借 *to borrow* | 筹～ *to raise (money, grain, etc.)* | ～施（对事情采取的办法）*measure*

楷 cuò ㄘㄨㄛˋ 用于地名 used in place names：～树园（在湖南省湘潭）*Cuoshuyuan (in Xiangtan, Hunan Province)*

错（錯） cuò ㄘㄨㄛˋ ❶不正确，不对，与实际不符（㊣一误）wrong：你弄～了。

You got it wrong. | 没～儿。*That's right.* [错觉]（-jué）跟事实不符的知觉，视、听、触各种感觉都有错觉 misconception ❷差，坏（用于否定式）bad (in negation)：他的成绩～不了。*His marks are unlikely to be bad.* | 你的身体真不～。*You are really in good shape.* ❸交叉着 to be interlaced：～杂 *mixed* | ～落 *be scattered randomly* | ～综复杂 *complicated* | 犬牙交～ *jagged and interlocked* ❹岔开 to stagger sth：～车 *(of vehicles) give way* | ～过机会 *miss an opportunity* ❺磨玉的石 grindstone (for polishing jade)：他山之石，可以为～。*One can always learn from others to improve oneself. (literally means 'Stones from other mountains can be used to polish jade.')* ❻(ancient) same as "措"

C

D ㄉ

DA ㄉㄚ

哒 dā ㄉㄚ （发音短促）吆喝牲口前进的声音 gee up (short sound made to drive animals forward)

耷 dā ㄉㄚ 大耳朵 big ear [耷拉]（－la）向下垂 hang down：狗～着尾巴跑了。*The dog ran off with its tail hanging between its legs.* | 饱满的谷穗～着头。*The plump ears of millet hang down.*

哒（噠） dā ㄉㄚ same as "嗒 (dā)"

搭 dā ㄉㄚ ❶支起，架起 to put up; to construct：～棚子 *build a shed* | ～架子 *put up a shelf* | ～桥 *build a bridge* [搭救] 帮助人脱离危险或灾难 go to the rescue of sb ❷共同抬 to lift sth together：把桌子～起来。*Let's lift up the table together.* ❸相交接 to join up ①连接，接触 to connect：两根电线～上了。*The two wires are connected.* ②凑在一起 to join together：～伙 *join for the group meal; form a partnership* ③搭配，配合 to combine：粗粮细粮～着吃 *eat a mixture of coarse and refined grains* ④放在支撑物上 to hang over：把衣服～在竹竿上。*Hang the clothes on a bamboo pole.* | 身上～着一条毛毯 *cover the body with a blanket* ❹乘坐车船、飞机等 to take (bus, plane, etc.)：～载（zài）*to transport; to carry* | ～车 *to hitchhike* | ～船 *take a boat* | ～班机 *take a flight*

嗒 dā ㄉㄚ 形容马蹄声、机关枪声等 ㊀ repetitive sound made by galloping horses, machine guns, etc.

⇨ see also tà on p.632

铬（鎝） dā ㄉㄚ 铁铬，翻土的农具 iron rake

褡 dā ㄉㄚ [褡裢]（－lian）一种口袋，中间开口，两头装东西 a long, rectangular bag that opens in the middle with both ends for storage

答（荅）** dā ㄉㄚ 同"答"（dá），用于口语"答应""答理"等词 (spoken; used in 答应, 答理, etc.) same as 答 (dá) [答理]（－li）打招呼，理睬 to greet; to acknowledge [答应]（－ying）1 应声回答 to respond 2 允许 to allow：父母不～我转学。*My parents do not allow me to change schools.*

⇨ see also dá on p.108

打 dá ㄉㄚˊ （外 loanword）量词，12个为1打 (measure word) dozen

⇨ see also dǎ on p.109

达（達） dá ㄉㄚˊ ❶通，到达 to reach：抵～ *to*

D

reach | 四通八～ *(of transport) accessible from all directions* | 火车从北京直～上海。*The train goes straight to Shanghai from Beijing.* ❷通达，对事理认识得透彻 to know sth inside out：知书～理 *well-read and refined* | 通权～变（不拘常规，采取变通办法）*adaptable to circumstances* | ～观（对不如意的事情看得开）*philosophical (about disappointing things)* ❸达到，实现 to reach; to realize：目的已～。*The goal is reached.* | ～成协议 *reach an agreement* ❹告知，表达 to inform; to express：转～ *pass on message, information, etc.* | 传～ *to convey; to receive and register caller (at government office, school, factory, etc.)* | 词不～意。*Words fail to express the meaning.* ❺指官位高，有权势（㊦显－）of high official rank and powerful：～官 *high official*

［达斡尔族］（－wò－－）我国少数民族，参看附录四 the Daur people (one of the ethnic groups in China. See Appendix Ⅳ.)

荙（薘） dá ㄉㄚˊ see 莙荙菜 (jūn－－) at 莙 on page 345

跶（躂） dá ㄉㄚˊ ❶〈方 dialect〉卵石 smooth pebble：～石（地名，在广东省云浮）*Dashi (a place in Yunfu, Guangdong Province)* ❷古代用石头修筑的水利设施 (ancient) irrigation works constructed from rocks

⇨ see also tǎ on p.632

钛（鐽） dá ㄉㄚˊ 人造的放射性金属元素，符号 Ds。darmstadtium (Ds)

鞑（韃） dá ㄉㄚˊ ［鞑靼］（－dá）1 我国古代对北方少数民族的统称 Tartar (collective name used in ancient times for ethnic groups north of China) 2 俄罗斯联邦的一个民族 Tartar people in Russia

沓 dá ㄉㄚˊ （－子、－儿）量词，用于重叠起来的纸张或其他薄的东西 (measure word for paper and other thin items) pile：一～子信纸 *a stack of letter paper*

⇨ see also tà on p.632

怛 dá ㄉㄚˊ 忧伤，悲苦 sad; sorrowful

妲 dá ㄉㄚˊ 用于人名，妲己，商纣王的妃子 used in given names, e.g. Daji, concubine of King Zhou of the Shang Dynasty

炟 dá ㄉㄚˊ 用于人名，刘炟，东汉章帝 used in given names, e.g. Liu Da, Emperor Zhang of the Eastern Han Dynasty

笪 dá ㄉㄚˊ ❶用粗竹篾编的像席的东西，用来晾晒粮食等 woven bamboo mat (for drying food) ❷拉船的竹索 bamboo rope (for pulling boats) ❸姓 (surname) Da

靼 dá ㄉㄚˊ see 鞑靼 (dá－) at 鞑 on page 108

答（荅）** dá ㄉㄚˊ ❶回答，回复（㊦－复）to answer; to respond：问～ *to question and answer* | ～话 *to answer* ❷还报（㊦报－）to repay：

～谢 *to thank (for sb's hospitality, kindness, etc.)* | ～礼 *return a salute;give a present in return*

⇨ see also dā on p.107

瘩(*瘩) dá ㄉㄚˊ [瘩背] 中医指生在背部的痈 (in traditional Chinese medicine) carbuncle on the back

⇨ see also da on p.110

打 dǎ ㄉㄚˇ ❶击 to hit: ～击 *to strike; a blow (of mind)* | ～铁 *forge iron* | ～门 *knock on a door* | ～鼓 *strike a drum; feel nervous* | ～靶 *shoot at a target* | ～垮 *to smash; to destroy* ㉛放射 to shoot: ～枪 *fire a shot* | ～闪 *(of lightning) flash* ❷表示各种动作，代替许多有具体意义的动词 used to replace specific verbs to indicate various actions ①除去 to remove: ～虫 *remove parasites from the body* | ～枝杈 *remove branches and twigs* | ～食（服药帮助消化）*to relieve indigestion (by taking medicine)* ②毁坏，损伤，破碎 to damage; to harm; to break: 衣服被虫～了。*The clothes are damaged by insects.* | 碗～了。*The bowl is broken.* ③取，收，捕捉 to obtain; to collect; to catch: ～鱼 *catch fish* | ～粮食 *harvest grain* | ～柴 *collect firewood* | ～水 *fetch water* ④购买 to buy: ～车票 *buy bus/train tickets* | ～酒 *buy liquor* ⑤举 to raise: ～伞 *hold an umbrella* | ～灯笼 *carry a lantern* | ～旗子 *hoist a flag* ⑥揭开，破开 to open; to break: ～帐子 *open a bed curtain* | ～鸡蛋 *break an egg* ⑦建造，修筑 to build: ～井 *dig a well* | ～墙 *build a wall* ⑧制作，编织 to make; to weave: ～镰刀 *make a sickle* | ～桌椅 *make tables and chairs* | ～毛衣 *knit a sweater* ⑨捆扎 to bind; to tie up: ～行李 *pack one's luggage* | ～裹腿 *wrap puttees* ⑩涂抹 to apply (sth to sth else); to paint: ～蜡 *polish with wax* | ～桐油 *coat with tung oil* ⑪玩耍，做某种文体活动 to play; to take part in (cultural or sporting activities): ～秋千 *play on a swing* | ～球 *play (a ball game)* ⑫通，发 (of communication) to connect; to send: ～电话 *make a telephone call* | ～电报 *send a telegram* ⑬计算 to calculate: 精～细算 *meticulously calculate* | 设备费～十万元。*The estimation of total equipment cost is 100 000 yuan.* ⑭立，定 to set; to establish: ～下基础 *lay a foundation* | ～主意 *come up with an idea* | ～草稿 *write a draft* ⑮从事或担任某些工作 to do (a certain kind of work): ～杂儿 *do odd jobs* | ～前站 *do the work of an advance party* ⑯表示身体上的某些动作 used to indicate certain physical actions: ～手势 *make a hand gesture* | ～冷战 *to shiver* | ～哈欠 *to yawn* | ～前失（马前腿跌倒）*(of horse, etc.) to stumble* | ～滚儿 *to roll; (figurative) to live under certain difficult circumstances for a long time* ❸与某些动词结合为一个动词 used to combine with certain verbs to form another verb: ～扮 *dress up* | ～扫

D

clean up | ～搅 *to disturb; (polite expression) to trouble* | ～扰 *to disturb; (polite expression) to bother* ❹ 介词，从，自 (preposition) from; since：～去年起 *since last year* | ～哪里来？ *Where are (you) from?*

⇨ see also dá on p.107

大 dà ㄉㄚˋ ❶跟"小"相对 big (opposite of 小) ①占的空间较多，面积较广，容量较多 (of space or volume) big; large：～山 *big mountain* | ～树 *big tree* | 这间房比那间～。*This room is bigger than that one.* ②数量较多 (of quantity) big; large：～众 *the public* | ～量 *a large quantity of* ③程度深，范围广 (adverb) very：～冷天 *a very cold day* | ～干一场 *go all out to do sth* | ～快人心 *to the general satisfaction (when a villain is punished or frustrated)* ④声音响 loud：雷声～ *loud thunder* | ～嗓门儿 *loud voice* ⑤年长，排行第一 the oldest; highest in rank：～哥 *oldest brother; (honorific speech) brother* | 老～ *the oldest; the most senior* ⑥敬辞，称跟对方有关的事物 (polite speech) used to refer to things associated with the person addressed：～作 *your wonderful work* | 尊姓～名 *your name* [大夫] 古代官职名称 *dafu* (an official post in ancient times)(also dàifu, see 大 dài) [大王] 1 古代尊称国王 (ancient) honorific form of address for a king 2 指最擅长某种事情的人 expert; master：爆破～ *a master of explosives* 3 指垄断某种行业的人 tycoon; mogul (in a certain trade)：钢铁～ *a steel mogul* (also dàiwang, see 大 dài) ❷时间更远 (of time) further：～前年 *three years ago* | ～后天 *three days from now* ❸不很详细，不很准确 not very detailed/accurate：～略 *basic facts; roughly* | ～概 *basic facts; approximate, rough; perhaps* | ～约 *approximate; perhaps* ❹〈方 dialect〉称父亲或伯父 used to refer to one's father, father's older brother or a senior man in father's generation

〈古 ancient〉 also same as 太，泰 (tài), e.g. 大子，大山，etc.

⇨ see also dài on p.111

垯(墶) da ·ㄉㄚ see 圪垯 (gē—) at 圪 on page 203

纮(縫) da ·ㄉㄚ see 纥纮 (gē—) at 纥 on page 203

跶(躂) da ·ㄉㄚ see 蹦跶 (bèng—) at 蹦 on page 30

瘩(*瘩) da ·ㄉㄚ see 疙瘩 (gē—) at 疙 on page 203

⇨ see also dá on p.109

DAI ㄉㄞ

呆(❶❷*獃) dāi ㄉㄞ ❶傻，愚蠢 stupid; foolish ❷死板，发愣 rigid; in a daze：两眼发～ *stare blankly* | 他～～地站在那里。*He stood there in a daze.* | ～板 *inflexible; rigid* ❸ same as "待 (dāi)"

呔 dāi ㄉㄞ 叹词，突然大喝一声，使人注意 (exclamation) hey

待 dāi ㄉㄞ 停留，逗留，迟延，也作“呆”to stay; to delay (also written as 呆)：你～一会儿再走。*Stay a while before you go.*

⇨ see also dài on p.113

歹 dǎi ㄉㄞˇ 坏，恶 bad; evil：～人 *bad person* | ～意 *ill will* | 为非作～ *do all kinds of bad things* [好歹] 1 好和坏 good and bad：不知～ *can not tell right from wrong; be ungrateful* 2 危险（多指生命危险）(mortal) danger：他要有个～，就惨了。*It would be terrible if something bad were to happen to him.* 3 无论如何 no matter what：～你得(děi)去一趟。*You have to go no matter what.*

逮 dǎi ㄉㄞˇ 捉，捕，用于口语 (spoken) to catch：～老鼠 *catch rats* | ～蝗虫 *catch locusts*

⇨ see also dài on p.113

傣 dǎi ㄉㄞˇ [傣族] 我国少数民族，参看附录四 the Dai people (one of the ethnic groups in China. See Appendix Ⅳ.)

大 dài ㄉㄞ˙ [大夫]（—fu）医生 doctor (also dàfū, see 大 dà) [大王]（—wang）旧戏曲、小说中对国王、山寨头领或大帮强盗首领的称呼 form of address for a king or leader of bandits in old drama and novels (also dàwáng, see 大 dà)

⇨ see also dà on p.110

轪(軑) dài ㄉㄞ˙ 包在车毂(gǔ)端的铜皮、铁皮，也指车轮 hubcap; (also) wheel of a vehicle

代 dài ㄉㄞ˙ ❶替(㊀—替、替—) to replace; to substitute：～理 *act on behalf of sb in a responsible position; serve as an agent* | ～办 *do sth for sb; (in diplomacy) chargé d'affaires* | ～耕 *farm the land for sb* [代表] 1 受委托或被选举出来替别人或大家办事 to represent：我～他去。*I will go and represent him.* 2 被选派的人 a representative：工会～ *union representative* | 全权～ *plenipotentiary* [代词] 代替名词、动词、形容词、数量词的词，如“我、你、他、谁、什么、这样、那么些”等 pronoun [代价] 获得某种东西所付出的价钱 price (to buy sth) ㊂为达到某种目的所花费的物质和精力 price (to achieve sth) ❷历史上划分的时期，世，朝代(㊀世—、时—) historical period; era; dynasty：古～ *ancient times; (specifically) slave society* | 近～ *modern times; the capitalist era* | 现～ *contemporary age* | 清～ *Qing Dynasty* [年代] 1 泛指时间 (generally) time：～久远 *a long time ago* 2 十年的时期（前面须有确定的世纪）a decade：20世纪50～（1950—1959年）*the 1950s* ❸世系的辈分 generation：第二～ *second generation* | 下一～ *next generation* [代沟] 指两代人之间在思想观念、心理状态、生活方式等方面的巨大差异 generation gap ❹地质年代分期的第二级，在“宙”之下、“纪”之上

D

(geology) era：古生～ *Paleozoic Era* | 中生～ *Mesozoic Era* | 新生～ *Cenozoic Era*

垈 dài ㄉㄞˋ 用于地名 used in place names：封家～ *Fengjiadai* | 夏家～（都在江苏省泰兴）*Xiajiadai (both in Taixing, Jiangsu Province)*

岱 dài ㄉㄞˋ 五岳中东岳泰山的别称，又叫岱宗、岱岳，在山东省 (another name for Taishan Mountain in Shandong Province) Dai (also called 岱宗，岱岳)

玳(*瑇) dài ㄉㄞˋ ［玳瑁］（－mào）爬行动物，像龟，甲壳黄褐色，有黑斑，很光滑，生活在海里 (formerly pronounced －mèi) hawksbill (turtle)

贷(貸) dài ㄉㄞˋ ❶借贷，借入或借出（会计工作上专指借出）to borrow; to lend (especially in accounting)：从银行～到 50 万元 *borrow 500 000 yuan from the bank* ❷ 贷款 to loan; loan：农～ *agricultural loan* | 信～ *credit* ❸推卸给别人 to shirk：责无旁～ *be duty bound* ❹ 宽恕，饶恕 to forgive：严惩不～ *punish mercilessly*

袋 dài ㄉㄞˋ （－子、－儿）衣兜或用布、皮等做成的盛东西的器物 pocket; bag：布～ *cloth bag* | 衣～ *pocket* | 面口～ *flour sack*

黛 dài ㄉㄞˋ 青黑色的颜料，古代女子用来画眉 greenish black pigment used by women in ancient times to draw their eyebrows：～眉 *a woman's drawn eyebrows* | 粉～（借指妇女）*cosmetics (also refers to women)*

甙 dài ㄉㄞˋ former name for 苷 (gān)

迨 dài ㄉㄞˋ ❶等到，达到 to wait until; to reach ❷ 趁 to take the opportunity

骀(駘) dài ㄉㄞˋ ［骀荡］1 使人舒畅 comfortable：春风～ *the pleasant springtime breeze* 2 放荡 debauched; dissolute

⇨ see also tái on p.634

绐(紿) dài ㄉㄞˋ 欺哄 to deceive

殆 dài ㄉㄞˋ ❶几乎，差不多 almost; approximately：财产损失～尽。*The loss of property is almost total.* ❷危险 dangerous：危～ *dangerous* | 知彼知己，百战不～。*Win all battles by knowing both yourself and your enemy.*

怠 dài ㄉㄞˋ 懒惰，松懈（㊣－惰、懒－、懈－）lazy; lax ［怠慢］冷淡 (of attitude) cold：态度～ *cold attitude* 谦辞，表示招待不周 (humble speech) used to express insufficient hospitality shown to guests：对不起，～各位了。*Apologies, everyone. I've been a bad host.*

带(帶) dài ㄉㄞˋ ❶（－子、－儿）用皮、布或纱线等物做成的长条 belt; ribbon：皮～ *leather belt* | 腰～ *belt* | 鞋～儿 *shoelace* ㊀轮胎 tyre：外～ *tyre* | 里～ *inner tube* ❷ 地带，区域 area; region：温～ *temperate zone* | 寒～ *cold zone* | 沿海一～ *coastal zone* ❸携带 to carry：腰里～着盒子枪 *carrying a Mauser pistol on one's belt* | ～着行李 *carrying luggage* ❹捎，顺便做，连着一起做 to do sth incidentally; to do sth without extra trouble：你给他～个口信去。*Pass this message to him.* | 把门～上。*Close the door behind you.* | 连寄信～买菜 *go to the market on the way to post a letter* ❺显出，有 to display;to have：面～笑容 *have a smile on one's face* | ～花纹的玻璃 *patterned glass* ❻领，率领（㊄—领）to lead：～路 *lead the way* | ～兵 *lead the troops* | ～头 *take the lead* ❼白带，女子阴道分泌的白色黏液 leucorrhoea

待 dài ㄉㄞˋ ❶等，等候（㊄等—）to wait：～业 *be a job seeker* | ～机出击 *wait for an opportunity to launch an attack* | 尚～研究 *await research* ❷对待，招待 to treat; to host：～人接物 *the way one gets along with people* | 大家～我太好了。*All of you treat me so well.* | ～客 *entertain guests* [待遇] 在社会上享有的权利、地位等 treatment (according to status)：政治～ *political treatment* | 物质～ *material reward* 特指工资、食宿等 (specifically) remuneration：调整～ *adjust remuneration* ❸需要 to need：自不～言 *it goes without saying* ❹将，要（古典戏曲小说和现代某些方言的用法）about to (used in ancient dramas and novels, and some contemporary dialects)：正～出门，有人来了。*I was just about to go out when someone came.*

⇨ see also dāi on p.111

埭 dài ㄉㄞˋ 土坝 earthen dam

逮 dài ㄉㄞˋ ❶到，及 to reach：力有未～ *beyond one's ability* | ～乎清季（到了清代末年）*by the late Qing Dynasty* ❷逮捕，捉拿 to arrest; to capture

⇨ see also dǎi on p.111

叇（靆） dài ㄉㄞˋ see 叆叇 (ài—) at 叆 on page 4

戴 dài ㄉㄞˋ ❶加在头、面、颈、手等处 to wear; to put on：～帽子 *wear a hat* | ～眼镜 *wear glasses* | ～红领巾 *wear a red scarf* ❷尊奉，推崇 to respect; to honour：推～ *support sb as leader* | 拥～ *to support (sb as a leader)* | 爱～ *to love and support*

襶 dài ㄉㄞˋ see 褦襶 (nài—) at 褦 on page 469

DAN ㄉㄢ

丹 dān ㄉㄢ ❶红色 red：～心 *sincerity* | ～砂（朱砂）*cinnabar* ❷依成方配制成的中药，通常是颗粒状或粉末状的 traditional Chinese medicine in pill or powdered form：丸散（sǎn）膏～ *different forms of traditional Chinese medicine (literally means 'pill, powder, ointment and pellet')* | 灵～妙药 *panacea*

担（擔） dān ㄉㄢ ❶用肩膀挑 to carry on the shoulder; to shoulder：～水 *carry water (on shoulder pole)* | ～着两筐

D

青菜 *carrying two baskets of vegetables on one's shoulder* [担心] 忧虑，顾虑 to worry; to be anxious：我～他身体受不了。*I worry that his body cannot take it.* ❷ 担负，承当 to bear; to take：～风险 *take risk* | ～责任 *bear responsibility*

⇨ see also dàn on p.116

单(單) dān ㄉㄢ ❶ 种类少，不复杂 simple：简～ *simple; (of experience, ability, etc.) ordinary; cursory* | ～纯 *innocent; merely* ㉷ 副词，只，仅 (adverb) only：做事～靠热情不够。*Passion alone is not enough to achieve something.* | 不提别的，～说这件事。*Let us speak only of this matter and nothing else.* [单位] 1 计算物体轻重、长短及数量的标准 unit (of measure) 2 指机关、团体或属于一个机关、团体的各个部门 organization; group; (subordinate) department：事业～ *public sector organization* | 直属～ *unit under the direct jurisdiction of a higher authority* ❷ 独，一 single：～身 *(of relationship status) single* | ～打一 *have a one-track mind; concentrate on one thing or one aspect only* | ～枪匹马 *single-handedly* | ～数（跟"复数"相对）*singular (opposite of* 复数*)* ❸ 奇（jī）数的 (of numbers) odd：～日 *odd-number days* | ～号 *odd numbers* | ～数（一、三、五、七等，跟"双数"相对）*odd number (opposite of* 双数*)* [单薄]（－bó）1 薄，少 thin; few：穿得很～ *wearing very little* 2 弱 weak：他身子骨儿太～。*His constitution is too weak.* | 人力～ *insufficient manpower* ❹（－子、－儿）记载事物用的纸片 paper for written records：～据 *receipt* | 传～ *flyer* | 账～儿 *bill* | 清～ *inventory* | 药～ *prescription* ❺ 衣服被褥等只有一层的 (of clothing, blankets, etc.) single-layered：～衣 *unlined shirt* | ～裤 *unlined trousers* ❻（－子、－儿）覆盖用的布 cloth cover：被～ *blanket cover* | 床～ *bed sheet* | 褥～儿 *(bed) sheet*

⇨ see also chán on p.65, shàn on p.578

郸(鄲) dān ㄉㄢ [郸城] 地名，在河南省 Dancheng (a place in Henan Province)

殚(殫) dān ㄉㄢ 尽，竭尽 to use up; to exhaust：～力 *do one's best* | ～心 *with all one's heart* | ～思极虑 *rack one's brains*

瘅(癉) dān ㄉㄢ [瘅疟]（－nüè）中医指疟疾的一种 (in traditional Chinese medicine) a strain of malaria

⇨ see also dàn on p.116

箪(簞) dān ㄉㄢ 古代盛饭的圆竹器 (ancient) round bamboo receptacle for cooked rice：～食壶浆（百姓用箪盛饭、用壶盛汤来慰劳所爱戴的军队）*(of civilians) welcome troops with food and drink*

眈 dān ㄉㄢ [眈眈] 注视的样子 gazing：虎视～（凶狠

贪婪地看着）*gaze greedily*

耽(❶* 躭) dān ㄉㄢ ❶迟延 to delay [耽搁]（-ge）迟延，停止没进行 to delay：这件事～了很久。*This matter has been delayed for a long time.* [耽误]（-wu）因耽搁或错过时机而误事 hold up; to delay：不能～生产。*Production cannot be held up.* ❷沉溺，入迷 addicted：～乐（lè）*be addicted to pleasure* | ～色（沉迷女色）*be addicted to sex* | ～于幻想 *abandon oneself in fantasy*

酖 dān ㄉㄢ same as "耽❷"

⇨ see also zhèn 鸩 on p.845

聃(** 耼) dān ㄉㄢ 古代哲学家老子的名字 name of the ancient philosopher Laozi

儋 dān ㄉㄢ 儋州，地名，在海南省 Danzhou (a place in Hainan Province)

纨(紞) dǎn ㄉㄢˇ 古代冠冕两旁用来悬挂塞耳玉坠的带子 (ancient) ribbons on a crown for hanging ear ornaments

胆(膽) dǎn ㄉㄢˇ ❶胆囊，体内储存胆汁的袋状器官，胆汁黄绿色，味苦，有帮助消化、杀菌、防腐等作用 gall bladder (see picture of 人体内脏 on page 819) ❷（-子、-儿）胆量 courage：～怯 *timid; cowardly* | ～子小 *timid* | ～大心细 *bold but cautious* ❸某些器物的内层 (of some objects) inner layer：球～ *bladder of a ball* | 暖瓶～ *inner container of a vacuum flask*

疸 dǎn ㄉㄢˇ 黄疸，人的皮肤、黏膜和眼球巩膜等发黄的症状，由血液中胆红素大量增加引起 jaundice

掸(撣、** 撢) dǎn ㄉㄢˇ 拂，打去尘土 to brush; to dust：～桌子 *dust a table* | ～衣服 *dust down one's clothes*

⇨ see also shàn on p.578

赕(賧) dǎn ㄉㄢˇ（傣 *Dai*）奉献 to make an offering：～佛 *make an offering to the Buddha*

亶 dǎn ㄉㄢˇ 实在，诚然 really; truly

石 dàn ㄉㄢˋ 市制容量单位，1石是10斗，合100升（此义在古书中读shí，如"二千石"）(pronounced shí in ancient Chinese texts) *dan* (a traditional Chinese unit for measuring volume. There are 10 斗 or 100 升 in 1石.)

⇨ see also shí on p.596

旦 dàn ㄉㄢˋ ❶早晨 morning：～暮 *morning and evening; a whole day; within a short time* | 枕戈待～ *maintain combat readiness (literally means 'sleep on the dagger-axe and wait for the dawn')* ㊀天，日 day：元～ *New Year's Day* [一旦] 1 一天之间（形容时间短）in a day (used to describe a short time)：毁于～ *destroyed in a moment* 2 副词，表示不确定的一天（既可用于已然，也可用于未然）(adverb) one day：同学三

年，～分别，大家都依依不舍。*When it came to leave, none of us could bear to say goodbye after three years of being in the same class.* | ～发现问题，立刻想法解决。*When you discover a problem, think of a solution at once.* [旦夕] 1 早晨和晚上 morning and night 2 在很短的时间内 within a very short time：危在～ *imminent danger* ❷传统戏曲里扮演妇女的角色 *dan* (female role in traditional dramas)：～角（jué）*female role* | 花～ *vivacious young female role*

但 dàn ㄉㄢˋ ❶只，仅 only：～愿能成功。*I only hope that it will succeed.* [不但] 连词，不只，不仅 (conjunction) not only：我们～要按时完成任务，还要保证质量。*Not only do we have to complete the task on time, but we also have to ensure its quality.* [但凡] 只要 as long as：～有工夫，我就去看他。*As long as I have time, I will visit him.* ❷连词，但是，不过 (conjunction) but：我们热爱和平，～也不怕战争。*We love peace, but we are not afraid of war.*

担(擔) dàn ㄉㄢˋ ❶扁担，挑东西的用具，多用竹、木做成 carrying pole (usually made of bamboo or wood) ❷（一子）一挑ㄦ东西 (of objects) load：货郎～ *pedlar's load* ⓨ 担负的责任 responsibility：重～ *heavy responsibility* ❸市制重量单位，1 担是 100 斤，合 50 千克 *dan* (a traditional Chinese unit of weight, equal to 50 kilograms. There are 100 斤 in 1 担.) ❹量词，用于成担的东西 (measure word) load：一～水 *a load of water (carried on a shoulder pole)*

⇨ see also dān on p.113

疍 dàn ㄉㄢˋ [疍民]过去广东、广西、福建内河和沿海一带的水上居民，多以船为家，从事渔业、运输业 The Tanka people (boat-dwellers who used to live on the rivers and along the coasts of Guangdong, Guangxi and Fujian provinces)

诞(誕) dàn ㄉㄢˋ ❶诞生，人出生 to be born：～辰（生日）*birthday* ❷生日 birthday：华～（敬称他人的生日）*(polite speech) sb's birthday* ❸荒唐的，不合情理的 absurd; unreasonable：荒～不经 *absurd* | 怪～ *weird; strange*

僤(僤) dàn ㄉㄢˋ 大，盛 big; great

惮(憚) dàn ㄉㄢˋ 怕，畏惧 afraid; fearful：不～烦 *not afraid of trouble* | 肆无忌～ *without scruple*

弹(彈) dàn ㄉㄢˋ ❶可以用弹（tán）力发射出去的小丸 pellet (used as fired projectile)：～丸 *pellet;bullet* ❷装有爆炸物可以击毁人、物的东西 bomb：炮～ *artillery shell* | 炸～ *bomb* | 手榴～ *hand grenade*

⇨ see also tán on p.636

瘅(癉) dàn ㄉㄢˋ ❶因劳累造成的病 illness (caused by overwork) ❷憎恨 to hate：彰善～恶 *extol good and* *abhor evil*

⇨ see also dān on p.114

萏 dàn ㄉㄢˋ see 菡萏 (hàn—) at 菡 on page 242

啖(*啗、*噉) dàn ㄉㄢˋ ❶吃或给人吃 to eat; to give sb sth to eat ❷拿利益引诱人 entice: ～以私利 *to entice sb with personal gain*

淡 dàn ㄉㄢˋ ❶含的盐分少，跟"咸"相对 not salty; bland (opposite of 咸): 菜太～。*The food is too bland.* | ～水湖 *freshwater lake* ❷含某种成分少，稀薄，跟"浓"相对 diluted; light (opposite of 浓): ～绿 *light green* | ～酒 *mild liquor* | 云～风轻 *light clouds and mild wind; fine weather* ❸不热心 indifferent; unpassionate: 冷～ *(of attitude) cold* | 他～～地应了一声。*He gave an unpassionate response.* ❹营业不旺盛 (of business) slack: ～月 *slack month* | ～季 *off-peak season*

氮 dàn ㄉㄢˋ 气体元素，符号 N，无色、无臭、无味，化学性质不活泼，可制氮肥 nitrogen (N)

蛋 dàn ㄉㄢˋ ❶鸟、龟、蛇等生的带有外壳的卵，受过精的可以孵出小动物 egg: 鸡～ *egg* | 鸭～ *duck egg* | 蛇～ *snake egg* ❷(－子、－儿) 形状像蛋的东西 egg-like object: 山药～ *Chinese yam tuber* | 驴粪～儿 *donkey faeces*

澹 dàn ㄉㄢˋ ❶ ㊀水波起伏的样子 undulating; rippling ❷安静 quiet: 恬～ *indifferent to fame or wealth*

⇨ see also tán on p.637

憺 dàn ㄉㄢˋ ❶安定 peaceful ❷忧愁 sorrowful

DANG ㄉㄤ

当(當、❼噹) dāng ㄉㄤ ❶充当，担任 to serve as; to hold the post of: 开会～主席 *chair a meeting* | 人民～了主人。*The people have become the masters.* ㊀承担 to bear (responsibility): 好汉做事好汉～。*A real man takes responsibility for what he does.* [当选] 选举时被选上 to be elected: 他～为人民代表。*He was elected as the people's representative.* ❷掌管，主持 to be in charge of: ～家 *manage the household* | ～权 *be in power* | ～局 *the authorities* ❸介词，正在那时候或那地方 (preposition) when, where: ～他工作的时候，不要打搅他。*Do not disturb him when he is working.* | ～胸就是一拳 *punch sb right on the chest* [当面] 副词，在面前，面对面 (adverb) face-to-face: ～说清 *clarify in person* [当初] 指从前的时候 in the past; originally [当即] 立刻 immediately: ～散会。*The meeting was immediately dismissed.* [当年] [当日] 从前 at that time (also dàng—, see 当 dàng): 想～我离家的时候，这里还没有火车。*There were no trains here when I left home.* [当前] 目前，眼下，现阶段 the present; the current time: ～任务 *the task at hand* [当下] 马上，立刻 im-

D

mediately：～就去 *go immediately* ❹相当，相称（chèn），相配 to match; to correspond to：旗鼓相～ *be well-matched in strength* | 门～户对 *be well-matched socially and economically (for marriage)* ❺应当，应该 should：～办就办。*Do what should be done.* | 不～问的不问。*Do not ask what should not be asked.* ❻顶端，头 top; head：瓜～（瓜蒂）*stalk of a gourd* | 瓦～（屋檐顶端的盖瓦头，俗叫猫头）*eaves tile (informal* 猫头*)* ❼形容撞击金属器物的声音 clanging (sound of a metal object being struck)：小锣敲得～～响 *the incessant clanging of a small gong* [当啷]（-lāng）形容摇铃或其他金属器物撞击的声音 ring (sound of bell ringing or other metal objects being struck)：～～，上课铃响了。*Ring, the bell for class has sounded.*

[当心]留心，小心 to be careful：～受骗。*Be careful not to get cheated.*

⇨ see also dàng on p.119

珰(璫) dāng ㄉㄤ ❶妇女戴在耳垂上的装饰品 ear ornaments worn by women ❷汉代武职宦官帽子上的装饰品，后来借指宦官 ornaments on the hats of military eunuchs in the Han Dynasty; (metonymy) eunuch

铛(鐺) dāng ㄉㄤ same as “当(dāng)❼”

⇨ see also chēng on p.76

裆(襠) dāng ㄉㄤ 裤裆，两裤腿相连的地方 (of trousers) crotch：横～ *(of trousers) upper part* | 直～ *(of trousers) front or back rise* | 开～裤 *open-crotch trousers* (see picture of 裤子 on page 767) ㊂两腿相连的地方 (of human body) crotch：从～下钻过去 *crawl between sb's legs*

筜(簹) dāng ㄉㄤ see 筼筜(yún-) at 筼 on page 813

挡(擋、*攩) dǎng ㄉㄤˇ ❶阻拦，遮蔽(㊀阻-、拦-) to block; to obstruct：水来土～ *build an earthen dam when the water comes; (figurative) deal with a problem when it arises* | 把风～住 *block the wind* | 拿扇子～着太阳 *use a fan to block the sunlight* ❷(-子、-儿)用来遮蔽的东西 protective cover：炉～ *stove cover* | 窗户～儿 *shutters*

⇨ see also dàng on p.119

党(黨) dǎng ㄉㄤˇ ❶政党，在我国特指中国共产党 political party; (in China specifically) the Communist Party of China ❷由私人利害关系结成的集团 clique; gang：死～ *very close friend; sworn follower* | 结～营私 *form a clique for selfish interests* [党羽]附从的人(指帮同作恶的) follower (of doer of bad deeds) ❸偏袒 to show favouritism：不偏不～ *without bias or favour* | ～同伐异 *to unite within one's faction and attack outsiders* ❹旧时指亲族 (old) relatives：父～ *paternal relatives* | 母～ *maternal relatives* | 妻～ *wife's relatives*

谠(讜) dǎng ㄉㄤˇ 正直的(言论)(of speech and ideas) upright: ～言 *upright speech* | ～论 *unbiased comments*

棁(欓) dǎng ㄉㄤˇ 落叶乔木，即食茱萸，又叫棁子，枝上有刺，果实红色，可入药 ailanthus prickly ash; *Zanthoxylum ailanthoides* (also called 棁子)

凼 dǎng ㄉㄤˇ 用于地名 used in place names: ～村(在广西壮族自治区灵川) *Dangcun (in Lingchuan, Guangxi Zhuang Autonomous Region)*

⇨ see also hán on p.240

氹 dàng ㄉㄤˋ same as "凼"

凼 dàng ㄉㄤˋ 〈方 dialect〉塘，水坑 pond: 水～ *pond* | ～肥 *compost*

当(當) dàng ㄉㄤˋ ❶恰当，合宜 suitable; proper: 得～ *apt* | 用词不～ *inappropriate wording* | 妥～ *(of actions or arrangements) appropriate* | 适～ *suitable* ❷抵得上，等于 worth; equal to: 一个人～俩人用。*The work of one person is worth that of two.* ❸当作，作为 to regard as: 安步～车 *walk leisurely as if riding in a carriage* | 不要把他～外人。*Do not treat him as an outsider.* ㊀认为 to think; to believe: 你～我不知道吗? *Do you think I don't know?* ❹表示在同一时间 in the same time period [当年] 本年，在同一年 the same year (also dāng—, see 当 dāng): ～种，～收 *plant and harvest in the same year* | ～受益 *benefit within the same year* [当天][当日] 本日，在同一天 the same/very day (also dāng—, see 当 dāng): ～的火车票 *train tickets for the very day* ❺用实物做抵押向当铺借钱 to pawn: 这块表～了200块钱。*This watch was pawned for 200 yuan.* ❻押在当铺里的实物 (in a pawnshop) pledge; sth pawned: 赎～ *redeem a pawned item*

[上当] 吃亏，受骗 be cheated

⇨ see also dāng on p.117

垱(壋) dàng ㄉㄤˋ 〈方 dialect〉为便于灌溉而筑的小土堤 earthen embankment built for irrigation

挡(擋) dàng ㄉㄤˋ [摒挡](bìng—) 收拾，料理 to put in order; to arrange: ～行装 *pack the necessities for a journey*

⇨ see also dǎng on p.118

档(檔) dàng ㄉㄤˋ ❶存放案卷用的带格子的橱架 filing cabinet: 归～ *to file* ❷档案，分类保存的文件、材料等 archive; file: 查～ *check a file* ❸等级 grade: ～次 *grade* | 高～ *of superior quality* ❹(—子、—儿) 量词，件，桩 (measure word) used of an event, issue, etc.: 一～子事 *a matter*

砀(碭) dàng ㄉㄤˋ [砀山] 地名，在安徽省 Dangshan (a place in Anhui Province)

D

荡(蕩、❶-❸* 盪) dàng ㄉㄤˋ ❶清除，弄光 to remove; to empty out: 扫～ *to raid* | 倾家～产 *go bankrupt* ❷洗 涤 to wash: 涤～ *clean up* ❸摇动(㊀摇－) to shake; to sway: ～舟 *row a boat* | ～秋千 *play on a swing* [荡漾](－yàng)水波一起一伏地动 (of water) rippling ❹不受约束或行为不检点(㊀浪－、放－) unconstrained; dissipated ❺浅水湖 shallow lake: 芦花～ *reed marshes*

瑬(璗) dàng ㄉㄤˋ tāng ㄊㄤ(又) ❶黄金 gold ❷一种玉 a type of jade

宕 dàng ㄉㄤˋ ❶延迟，拖延 to delay: 延～ *to delay* ❷不受拘束 to be unrestrained: 豪～ *bold and uninhibited*

菪 dàng ㄉㄤˋ see 莨菪(làng－) at 莨 on page 380

DAO ㄉㄠ

刀 dāo ㄉㄠ ❶(－子、－儿)用来切、割、斩、削、刺的工具 knife; any kind of cutting tool: 镰～ *sickle* | 菜～ *kitchen knife* | 刺～ *bayonet* | 旋～ *rotary knife* | 铅笔～儿 *pencil sharpener* ❷量词，纸张单位，通常为100张 measure word for paper, usually 100 sheets ❸古代的一种钱币 (a kind of knife-shaped coins in ancient time): ～币 dao *coins*

叨 dāo ㄉㄠ [叨叨](－dao)[叨唠](－lao)翻来覆去地说 to say sth repeatedly

⇨ see also tāo on p.641

氻 dāo ㄉㄠ [氻氻]灵活，流动 agile; flowing

忉 dāo ㄉㄠ [忉忉]忧愁，焦虑 sad; anxious

舠 dāo ㄉㄠ 古书上说的一种小船 small boat (in ancient Chinese texts)

鱽(魛) dāo ㄉㄠ 鱽鱼，现多写作"刀鱼"，鱼名，身体很长，像刀 (now often written as 刀鱼) fish shaped like a knife/sword ①我国北方指带鱼 (in northern China) cutlassfish ②鲚(jì)鱼的一种，即刀鲚 grenadier anchovy (same as 刀鲚)

氘 dāo ㄉㄠ 氢的同位素之一，符号D，质量数2，用于热核反应 deuterium (D)

捯 dáo ㄉㄠˊ 两手不住倒换着拉回线、绳子等 to pull (string, rope, etc) hand over hand; to reel in (string, rope, etc.) with both hands: 把风筝～下来。*Reel in the kite.* ㊀追溯，追究原因 to trace (the reason of sth): 这件事到今天还没～出头儿来呢。*We have yet to trace the reason for this matter.*

[捯饬](－chi)〈方 dialect〉打扮，修饰 to dress up; to decorate

导(導) dǎo ㄉㄠˇ ❶指引，带领 to guide; to lead: 领～ *to lead; leader* | ～游 *tour guide* | ～航 *to navigate* ㊀指教，教诲 to instruct; to teach: 开～ *to enlighten* | 教～ *to teach* | 劝～ *to persuade* ❷疏导 to dredge; to redirect：～管 *dredge pipe* | ～尿 *urethral catheterization* | ～淮入海 *channelling the Huai River into the sea* ❸传导 to conduct：～热 *conduct heat* | ～电 *conduct electricity* | ～体 *conductor*

岛(島、*嶋) dǎo ㄉㄠˇ 海洋或河流、湖泊里四面被水围着的陆地叫岛，突入海洋或湖泊里，三面被水围着的陆地叫半岛 island (半岛 peninsula)

捣(擣、*擣、*擣) dǎo ㄉㄠˇ ❶砸，舂，捶打 to pound; to hammer：～蒜 *pound garlic* | ～米 *pound rice* | ～衣 *pound on clothing when doing laundry by hand* ㊀冲，攻打 to charge; to attack：～毁 *to destroy* | 直～敌巢 *storm the enemy's base* ❷搅扰 to disturb：～乱 *create trouble* | ～鬼 *do mischief*

倒 dǎo ㄉㄠˇ ❶竖立的东西躺下来 to fall：墙～了。*The wall has collapsed.* | 摔～ *trip and fall* ㊀失败，垮台 to fail; to collapse：～台 *fall from power* | ～闭 *go bankrupt* 也指使垮台 (also) to cause ... to fall from power：～阁 *topple a cabinet (of a government)* [倒霉]（*倒楣）事情不顺利，受挫折 to have bad luck ❷转移，更换 to transfer; to change：～手 *change hands* | ～车 *change buses/trains* | ～换 *to exchange* ❸倒买倒卖，进行投机活动 to buy and sell speculatively：～汇 *speculate in foreign currency* | ～邮票 *trade in postage stamps* ❹指食欲变得不好 to dampen the appetite：老吃白菜，真～胃口。*I am so sick of eating cabbages all the time.*

⇨ see also dào on p.122

祷(禱) dǎo ㄉㄠˇ ❶教徒或迷信的人向天、神求助 to pray：祈～ *to pray* ❷敬辞（书信用语）polite speech used in letters：为～。*Looking forward to hearing from you and regards.* | 盼～。*Looking forward to hearing from you and regards.*

蹈 dǎo ㄉㄠˇ ❶踩，践踏 to step on：～白刃而不顾（形容不顾危险）*ignore danger (literally means 'fearless despite stepping on blades')* | 赴汤～火 *ready to risk one's life (literally means 'leap into boiling water and tread on fire')* ㊀实行，遵循 to carry out; to abide by：循规～矩 *follow the rules* ❷跳动 to jump about：手舞足～ *gesticulate in happiness with hands and feet*

到 dào ㄉㄠˋ ❶到达，达到 to reach; to arrive (at / in)：～北京 *arrive in Beijing* | ～十二点 *until 12 o'clock* | 不～两万人 *fewer than 20 000 people* | 坚持～最后 *persist until the end* [到处] 处处，不论哪里 everywhere ❷往 to go to：～祖国最需要的地方去 *go to where our country needs it most* ❸周到，全顾得着 considerate; satisfactory：有不～的地方请原谅。*Please accept our apologies if you are not satisfied in any way.* ❹表示动作有效果 used to indicate that an action is effective：办得～ *can* be done | 做不～ *cannot be done* | 达～ *reach*

倒 dào ㄉㄠˋ ❶上下或前后颠倒 upside down; reversed: 这面镜子挂～了。*This mirror has been hung upside down.* | 把那几本书～过来。*Turn those few books right-side up.* | ～数第一 *first from the bottom* ❷把容器反转或倾斜使里面的东西出来 to pour (out): ～茶 *pour tea* | ～水 *pour water* ❸向后，往回退 to reverse; to move backwards: ～退 *go backwards* | ～车（车向后退）*(of vehicles) to reverse* ❹副词，反而，却，相反 (adverb) but, yet: 跑了一天，～不觉得累。*I was busy the whole day, but I am not tired.*

⇨ see also dǎo on p.121

帱（幬） dào ㄉㄠˋ 覆盖 to cover

⇨ see also chóu on p.85

焘（燾） dào ㄉㄠˋ tāo ㄊㄠ （又） 覆盖 to cover

盗 dào ㄉㄠˋ ❶偷（㊣—窃）to steal: ～卖 *steal sth and offer it for sale* | ～取 *steal* | 掩耳～铃 *deceive oneself (literally means 'covering one's ears while stealing a bell')* ㊀用不正当的方法谋得 to obtain sth by dishonest means: 欺世～名 *obtain fame by deceiving the public* [盗版] 未经版权所有者同意，大量偷录或偷印，非法牟利 to pirate (a copy) ❷偷窃或抢劫财物的人（㊣—贼）thief; robber: 强～ *robber* | 海～ *pirate*

悼 dào ㄉㄠˋ 悲伤，哀念（㊣哀—）to mourn: 追～（追念死者）*mourn one's death*

道 dào ㄉㄠˋ ❶（—儿）路（㊣—路）road: 火车～ *railway track* | 水～ *waterway* | 街～ *street* ❷方向，途径 direction; way: 志同～合 *have a common goal* ❸道理，正当的事理 principle; reason: 无～ *unprincipled; without morals* | 得～多助。*A just cause enjoys much support.* [道具] 佛家修道用的物品 religious paraphernalia (for Buddhists) ㊁演剧等用的设备和用具 (in theatre) prop ❹（—儿）方法，办法，技术 means; technique: 门～ *way of doing sth* | 医～ *(esp. of traditional Chinese medicine) medical skill* | 照他的～儿办。*Do it according to his way.* ❺道家，我国古代的一个思想流派，以老聃和庄周为代表 Taoist school ❻道教，我国主要宗教之一，创立于东汉 Taoism: ～观（guàn）（道教的庙）*Taoist temple* ❼指某些迷信组织 superstitious sect: 一贯～ *Yiguandao (literally means 'Consistent Way', a secret society)* | 会～门 *cults and secret societies* ❽说 to say: 说长～短 *gossip about sb* | 一语～破 *lay bare the truth with a single utterance* | 常言～ *as the saying goes* ㊀用话表示情意 to express emotions with spoken words: ～贺 *to congratulate* | ～谢 *to thank* | ～歉 *to apologise* | ～喜 *to congratulate* ❾历史上的行政区域 administrative division in Chinese history ①唐太宗时分全国为十道 *dao* (one of the ten administrative divisions of China in the reign of Emperor Taizong of the Tang Dynasty) ②清代和民国初年每省分成几个道 *dao* (an administrative division under a province during the Qing Dynasty and the early Republican Period) ❿（一子、一儿）线条 line：红～儿 *red line*｜铅笔～儿 *line drawn with a pencil* ⓫量词 measure word ①用于长条状的东西 used for long objects：一～河 *a river*｜画一～红线 *draw a red line* ②用于路上的关口，出入口 used for road passes, entrances and exits：两～门 *two doors*｜过一～关 *go through a pass* ③则，条 (used for questions, orders, etc.)：三～题 *three questions (on a test or examination paper)*｜一～命令 *an order* ④次 used for number of times：洗了三～ *washed three times*

稻 dào ㄉㄠˋ （一子）谷类作物，叶狭长，有水稻、旱稻之分，通常指水稻，籽实椭圆形，有硬壳，去壳后就是大米，供食用 rice

纛 dào ㄉㄠˋ 古代军队里的大旗 (ancient) military flag

DE ㄉㄜ

嘚 dē ㄉㄜ 形容马蹄踏地声 clip-clop; clatter of a horse's hoofs［嘚啵］（一bo）〈方 dialect〉唠叨 chat garrulously：别瞎～了，赶紧干活儿吧。*Stop chatting and get back to work.*

得 dé ㄉㄜˊ ❶得到（㊀获一）to obtain; to get：大～人心 *win popular support*｜～奖 *win a prize*｜～胜 *win a victory* ㊁遇到 to get by chance：～空（kòng）*have spare time*｜～便 *when it is convenient* ❷适合 suitable：～当（dàng）*appropriate*｜～法 *in the proper manner*｜～手（顺利）*run smoothly; bring sth off*｜～劲 *easy to use; feeling comfortable* ❸得意，满意 to be proud or satisfied with oneself：扬扬自～ *complacent* ❹完成 to complete：衣服做～了。*The clothes are finished.*｜饭～了。*Dinner is ready.* ❺用于某种语气 used in certain tones of voice ①表示禁止 used to express prohibition：～了，别说了。*Stop it. Don't say anymore.* ②表示同意 used to express agreement：～，就这么办。*Great, let's do it this way.* ③表示无可奈何 used to express helplessness：～，今天又迟到了。*Oh no, I'm late again today.* ❻可以，许可 can; to be permitted：不～随地吐痰。*No spitting.*｜正式代表均～参加表决。*All official representatives can vote.*

⇨ see also de on p.124, děi on p.124

锝（鍀） dé ㄉㄜˊ 人造的放射性金属元素，符号 Tc，是第一种人工合成的元素 technetium (Tc)

德（*悳） dé ㄉㄜˊ ❶好的品行 virtue：～才兼备 *have both integrity and ability* ❷道德，人们共同生活及其行为的准则、规范 morals：公～ *social ethics*｜缺～ *unscrupulous*｜～行

morality and conduct ❸ 信念 belief; conviction：同心同～ *share a common belief* ❹ 恩惠 favour; grace：感恩戴～ *be deeply grateful*

［德昂族］原名崩龙族，我国少数民族，参看附录四 the De'ang people (originally called 崩龙族，one of the ethnic groups in China. See Appendix Ⅳ.)

地 de ·ㄉㄜ 助词，用在状语后，状语与后面的动词、形容词是修饰关系 auxiliary word placed after an adverbial to modify verb or adjective that follows：胜利～完成任务 *complete the task successfully* | 天色渐渐～黑了。*The sky was gradually turning dark.*

⇨ see also dì on p.129

的 de ·ㄉㄜ 助词 auxiliary word ①用在定语后 placed after an attribute1 定语与后边的名词是修饰关系 placed after an attribute to modify noun that follows：美丽～风光 *beautiful scenery* | 宏伟～建筑 *magnificent building* 2 定语与后边的名词是所属关系，旧时也写作"底" placed after an attribute to indicate possession of noun that follows (formerly also written as 底)：我～书 *my book* | 社会～性质 *the nature of society* ②用在词或词组后，组成"的"字结构，表示人或事物 placed after a word/phrase to indicate sb or sth：吃～*food* | 穿～*clothing* | 红～*red* | 卖菜～*greengrocer* ③用在句末，表示肯定的语气，常跟"是"相应 placed at the end of a sentence to express affirmation, often corresponds with 是：他是刚从北京来～。*He has just come from Beijing.*

⇨ see also dī on p.127, dí on p.127, dì on p.130

底 de ·ㄉㄜ (auxiliary word) same as "的 (de) ① 2"

⇨ see also dǐ on p.129

得 de ·ㄉㄜ 助词 auxiliary word ①在动词后表可能或许可 placed after a verb to indicate possibility or permission 1 再接别的词 followed by another word/phrase：冲～出去 *can rush out* | 拿～起来 *can be lifted* 2 不再接别的词 not followed by another word/phrase：要～*good* | 要不～*bad* | 说不～*unspeakable* ②用在动词或形容词后，连接表结果或程度的补语 placed after a verb or an adjective to connect complement that indicates result/degree：跑～快 *run quickly* | 急～满脸通红 *so anxious that one's face turned red* | 香～很 *very fragrant*

⇨ see also dé on p.123, děi on p.124

脦 de ·ㄉㄜ te ·ㄊㄜ(又) see 肋脦 (lē—) at 肋 on page 383

DEI ㄉㄟ

得 děi ㄉㄟˇ ❶必须，需要 must; have to; need to：你～用功。*You must work hard.* | 这活儿～三个人才能完成。*This work requires three people to complete.* ❷

会，估计必然如此 would：时间不早了，要不快走，就～迟到。*It's late. If we don't leave, we would be late.* ❸〈方 dialect〉满意，高兴，舒适 contented; comfortable：躺着听音乐挺～。*It's rather comfortable to listen to music lying down.*

⇨ see also dé on p.123, de on p.124

DEN ㄉㄣ

扽（**揼）dèn ㄉㄣˋ〈方 dialect〉用力拉 to pull hard：把绳子～一～。*Tug on the rope.*｜～线 *pull a string*

DENG ㄉㄥ

灯（燈）dēng ㄉㄥ 照明或利用光线达到某种目的的器具 lamp; light：电～ *electric light*｜路～ *street light*｜探照～ *searchlight*｜一盏～ *a lamp*

登 dēng ㄉㄥ ❶上，升 to go up; to ascend：～山 *climb a mountain*｜～高 *ascend a height*｜～峰造极（喻达到顶点）*reach the pinnacle of sth* ❷ same as "蹬" ❸刊载，记载 to publish; to record：～报 *publish in a newspaper*｜把这几项～在簿子上。*Write these few items down in a notebook.* [登记] 为了特定的目的，向主管机关或部门按表填写事项 to register：～结婚 *register to marry*｜参观前请～。*Please register before you visit.* ❹（谷物）成熟 (of crops) to ripen：五谷丰～ *bountiful harvest*

[登时] 即时，立刻 immediately

噔 dēng ㄉㄥ 形容重东西落地或撞击物体的响声 thump; thud

璒 dēng ㄉㄥ 一种像玉的石头 a kind of jade-like stone

簦 dēng ㄉㄥ 古代有柄的笠，类似现在的雨伞 a bamboo device with a top and a central rod, used as protection against rain in ancient times, similar to present-day umbrella

蹬 dēng ㄉㄥ 踩，践踏 to step on：～在凳子上 *step on a bench* 🄘 脚向下用力 to step on with force：～三轮车 *pedal a trishaw*｜～水车 *pedal a water wheel*

⇨ see also dèng on p.126

等 děng ㄉㄥˇ ❶数量一般大，地位或程度一般高 equal：～同 *equivalent*｜相～ *equal*｜平～ *equality*｜一加二～于三。*One plus two equals three.* [等闲] 平常 ordinary 🄘 轻易地，不在乎地 easily; nonchalantly：莫作～看！*You mustn't see it as ordinary!* ❷级位，程度的分别（㊈一级）grade：一～功 *first class merit*｜特～英雄 *special class hero*｜何～快乐！*Such immense joy!* ❸类，群 category; group ①表示多数 indicating plurality：我～ *we*｜你～ *you (plural)*｜彼～ *they* ②列举后煞尾 placed at the end of a list of examples：北京、天津、上海、重庆～四个直辖市 *the four municipalities of Beijing, Tianjin,*

D

Shanghai and Chongqing ③ 表示列举未完 ㊂et cetera; and so on: 派老张、老王～五人去。*Send five people there—Zhang, Wang, and so on.* | 这里煤、铁～～蕴藏都很丰富。*This area has large deposits of coal, iron, etc.* ❹ 待，候（㊈一待、一候）to wait: ～一下再说。*Let's wait a while first.* | ～～我。*Wait for me.* | ～不得 *cannot wait* ❺ same as "戥"

戥 děng ㄉㄥˇ ❶（一子）一种小型的秤，用来称金、银、药品等分量小的东西 a small steelyard for weighing gold, silver, medicine, etc. ❷用戥子称 to weigh with a small steelyard: 把这包药～一～。*Weigh this bag of medicine.*

邓(鄧) dèng ㄉㄥˋ 邓州，地名，在河南省 Dengzhou (a place in Henan Province)

僜 dèng ㄉㄥˋ 僜人，生活在西藏自治区察隅一带 the Deng people (who live in the Chayu area of the Tibet Autonomous Region)

凳(*櫈) dèng ㄉㄥˋ （一子、一儿）有腿没有靠背的坐具 stool: 板～ *wooden stool* | 小～儿 *small stool*

嶝 dèng ㄉㄥˋ 山上可攀登的小路 mountain path

澄 dèng ㄉㄥˋ 让液体里的杂质沉下去 (of liquid) to become clear: 水～清了再喝。*Allow the water to clear before drinking it.*

⇨ see also chéng on p.78

磴 dèng ㄉㄥˋ ❶石头台阶 stone steps: ～道 *path with stone steps* ❷量词，用于台阶或楼梯的层级 measure word for the number of steps/stairs

瞪 dèng ㄉㄥˋ 睁大眼睛 to open (one's eyes) wide; to stare: 把眼一～ *give sb a stare* | 你～着我做什么？*Why are you staring at me?* | ～眼 *glare at sb/sth*

镫(鐙) dèng ㄉㄥˋ 挂在马鞍子两旁的东西，是为骑马的人蹬踩用的 stirrup

〈古 ancient〉also same as 灯 (dēng)

蹬 dèng ㄉㄥˋ see 蹭蹬 (cèng—) at 蹭 on page 61

⇨ see also dēng on p.125

DI ㄉㄧ

氐 dī ㄉㄧ ❶我国古代西部的少数民族名 Di (an ethnic group in western China in ancient times) ❷星宿名，二十八宿之一 *di* (one of the twenty-eight constellations in ancient Chinese astronomy)

⇨ see also dǐ on p.128

低 dī ㄉㄧ ❶跟"高"相对 low (opposite of 高) ①由下到上距离近的 (vertically) short: 这房子太～。*This flat is too low.* | 弟弟比哥哥～一头。*The younger brother is one head shorter than his older brother.* ②等级在下的 (of grade) low: ～年级 *junior grade* ③在一般标准或平均程度之下 lower than average: ～能 *incompetent* | 眼高手～ *have great ambition but little ability* | 政治水

平～ *low political awareness* ④声音细小 (of voice) low：～声讲话 *speak softly* ❷俯，头向下垂 (of head) to lower：～头 *bow one's head; (figurative) submit*

羝 dī ㄉㄧ 公羊 ram (male sheep)

的 dī ㄉㄧ （外 loanword）"的士"（出租车）的省称 taxi (short for 的士)：打～ *take a taxi* | ～哥（称男性出租车司机）*male taxi driver*

⇨ see also de on p.124, dí on p.127, dì on p.130

堤（*隄） dī ㄉㄧ 用土、石等材料修筑的挡水的高岸 embankment：河～ *river dyke* | 修～ *repair an embankment* | ～防 *embankment*

提 dī ㄉㄧ ［提防］（－fɑng）小心防备 to take precautions ［提溜］（－liu）手提（tí）to carry by hand

⇨ see also tí on p.646

鞮 dī ㄉㄧ ❶古代的一种皮鞋 (ancient) a kind of leather footwear ❷姓 (surname) Di

磾（磾） dī ㄉㄧ 用于人名，金日（mì）磾，汉代人 used in given names, e.g. Jin Midi, a person in the Han Dynasty

滴 dī ㄉㄧ ❶一点一点地落下的少量液体 (of liquid) a drop：汗～ *drop of sweat* | 水～ *drop of water* ［点滴］1 形容零星，少，也指零星的事物 a bit; droplet 2 通称静脉滴注为打点滴 to be on an intravenous drip (usually known as 打点滴) ❷液体一点一点地落下，使液体一点一点地落下 to drip：汗水直往下～。*Sweat is falling in drops.* | ～眼药 *drip eye drops* ［滴沥］（－lì）形容雨水下滴的声音 used to describe the sound of falling rain ❸量词，用于一点一点下滴的液体 (measure word for liquid) drop：一～血 *a drop of blood* | 一～汗 *a drop of sweat*

［滴溜］（－liū）1 滚圆的样子 like a sphere：～圆 *round like a sphere* 2 形容很快地旋转 used to describe sth spinning quickly：～转 *spin rapidly*

镝（鏑） dī ㄉㄧ 金属元素，符号 Dy，银白色，用于核工业等 dysprosium (Dy)

⇨ see also dí on p.128

狄 dí ㄉㄧˊ 我国古代称北方的民族 Di (a name used in ancient times for ethnic groups in northern China)

荻 dí ㄉㄧˊ 草本植物，生长在水边，叶像苇叶，秋天开紫色花 Amur silver-grass

迪 dí ㄉㄧˊ 开导（㊟启－）to guide; to enlighten

頔（頔） dí ㄉㄧˊ 美好 fine

笛 dí ㄉㄧˊ （－子、－儿）管乐器，通常是竹制的，有八孔，横着吹 flute (Chinese flutes are usually made of bamboo) ㊀响声尖锐的发音器 sth that makes a sharp noise：汽～ *whistle* | 警～ *police siren*

的 dí ㄉㄧˊ 真实，实在 real：～当（dàng）*proper* | ～确 *really*

⇨ see also de on p.124, dī on p.127, dì on p.130

籴(糴) dí ㄉㄧˊ 买粮食，跟"粜"相对 to buy grain (opposite of 粜)：～米 *buy rice*

敌(敵) dí ㄉㄧˊ ❶敌人 enemy：分清～我 *draw a clear line between our side and the enemy* ❷ 相当 equivalent：势均力～ *evenly matched* ❸ 抵挡 to withstand：军民团结如一人，试看天下谁能～。*Nothing in the world can withstand the united front of the army and the people.*

涤(滌) dí ㄉㄧˊ 洗(㊀洗一) to wash：～除 *wash away* | ～荡 *clean up; to eradicate*

觌(覿) dí ㄉㄧˊ 相见 to meet (sb)：～面 *meet sb*

髢 dí ㄉㄧˊ (formerly pronounced dì) 假头发 ㊃ wig

嘀(啾)** dí ㄉㄧˊ ［嘀咕］(一gu) 1 小声说私话 to wisper in private：他们俩～什么呢？*What are those two whispering about?* 2 心中不安，犹疑不定 to feel unsettled; to hesitate：拿定主意，别犯～。*Be decisive and don't hesistate.*

嫡 dí ㄉㄧˊ ❶封建宗法制度中称正妻 (in feudal times) principal wife (as distinguished from a concubine) ㊀正妻所生的 principal wife's offspring：～子 *son of a principal wife* | ～嗣 *descendant of a principal wife* ❷ 亲的，血统最近的 closely related by blood：～亲哥哥 *older brother (by the same mother)* | ～堂兄弟 *first cousins (sons of father's brothers)* ㊀系统最近的 of closest bloodline/system：～系 *direct line of descent; one's own clique*

镝(鏑) dí ㄉㄧˊ 箭头 arrowhead：锋～ *weapons; war (literally means 'blades and arrows')* | 鸣～（响箭）*whistling arrow*

⇨ see also dī on p.127

蹢 dí ㄉㄧˊ 〈古 ancient〉蹄子 hoof

⇨ see also zhí on p.853

翟 dí ㄉㄧˊ ❶长尾野鸡 long-tailed pheasant ❷古代哲学家墨子名翟 Di (given name of ancient Chinese philosopher 墨子)

⇨ see also zhái on p.829

氐 dǐ ㄉㄧˇ 根本 root; basis

⇨ see also dī on p.126

邸 dǐ ㄉㄧˇ 高级官员的住所 residence (of a high-ranking official)：官～ *official residence*

诋(詆) dǐ ㄉㄧˇ 毁谤(㊀一毁) to slander：丑～（辱骂）*abuse verbally*

坻 dǐ ㄉㄧˇ 山坡 mountain slope

［宝坻］地名，在天津市 Baodi (a place in Tianjin Municipality)

⇨ see also chí on p.80

抵(❷*牴、❷*觝) dǐ ㄉㄧˇ ❶挡，拒，用力支撑着(㊀一挡、一拒) to hold; to resist：～住门，别让风刮开。*Hold the door shut against the wind.* ［抵制］抵抗，阻止，不让侵入或发生作用 to resist; to reject ❷牛、羊等有角的兽用角顶、触 (of an animal) to butt (with its horns) [抵触] 发生冲突 to conflict with：他的话前后～。*What he says now contradicts what he said before.* ❸ 顶，相当 to be equal to：～债 *pay a debt in kind* | ～押 *to mortgage* | 一个～俩。*One is equal to two.* [抵偿] 用价值相等的事物作为赔偿或补偿 to compensate in kind ❹ 到达 to arrive; to reach：～京 *arrive in Beijing* ❺ 抵消 to offset：收支相～ *income and expenditure offset each other*

[大抵] 大略，大概 approximately：～是这样，详细情况我说不清。*I don't have the specific details but this is roughly what happened.*

茋 dǐ ㄉㄧˇ 有机化合物，无色晶体，可用来制染料等 stilbene

⇨ see also zhǐ on p.855

底 dǐ ㄉㄧˇ ❶（一子、一儿）最下面的部分 bottom：锅～ *bottom of a pot* | 鞋～儿 *sole of a shoe* | 海～ *sea bottom* ㊀ 末了 end：月～ *end of the month* | 年～ *end of the year* ❷（一子、一儿）根基，基础，留作根据的 foundation; kept as a record：～稿 *manuscript* | ～账 *(in finance) original account* | 刨（páo）根问～ *inquire into the root of the matter* | 那文件要留个～儿。*A copy of that document must be kept.* [底细] 内情，详情，事件的根底 detail; (of a matter) root ❸（一儿）图案的底子 (of a design) ground; background：白～儿红花碗 *bowl with red flowers on a white ground* ❹ 〈古 ancient〉达到 to reach：终～于成 *succeed in the end* ❺ 何，什么 what：～事？*What is the matter?* | ～处？*Where is the place?*

⇨ see also de on p.124

柢 dǐ ㄉㄧˇ 树木的根(㊥根－) (of a tree) root：根深～固 *deep-rooted*

砥 dǐ ㄉㄧˇ (formerly also pronounced zhǐ) 细的磨刀石 fine grindstone [砥砺] 1 磨炼 to temper; to toughen：～意志 *strengthen one's resolve* 2 勉励 to encourage：相互～ *encourage one another*

骶 dǐ ㄉㄧˇ 腰部下面尾骨上面的部分 sacrum (see picture of 人体骨骼 on page 220)

地 dì ㄉㄧˋ ❶地球，太阳系八大行星之一，人类居住的星球 the Earth：天～ *Heaven and Earth; field of activity* | ～心 *the Earth's core* | ～层 *stratum* ㊀ ①指土地、地面 land; ground：～大物博 *(of a country) large in area and abundant in resources* | 草～ *lawn; grassland* | 两亩～ *two* mu *of land* ②指某一地区，地点 area; place; spot：此～ *this place* | 华东各～ *regions in eastern China* | 目的～ *destination* ③指路程，用在里数或站数后 (used after unit of distance or number of stops) distance：三十里～ *distance of thirty* li | 两站～ *distance of two stops* [地道] 1 地下挖成的隧道 underground tunnel：～战 *tunnel warfare* 2（一dao）真正原产地出产的，也说“道地” authentic

D

(also 道地)：～药材 *authentic medicinal herbs* ⓘ 真正的，纯粹 genuine; pure：一口～北京话 *a pure Beijing dialect* [地方] 1 中央下属的省、市、县等各级行政区划的统称 (of government) local：～各级人民政府 *all levels of local People's Governments* | ～服从中央。*Local governments obey the central government.* 2 军队指军队以外的部门 civilian：从军队转业到了～ *be transferred from the military to civilian work* 3（—fang）区域 region：飞机在什么～飞？*Where is the plane flying over?* | 那～出高粱。*That region produces sorghum.* 4（—fang）点，部分 point; part：他这话有的～很对。*He made some good points in his speech.* [地位] 人在社会关系中所处的位置 social status [地下] 1 地面下，土里 underground：～铁道 *underground railway* ⓘ 秘密的，不公开的 secret; concealed：～工作 *underground work* 2（—xia）地面上 on the ground：掉在～了 *fell on the ground* ❷表示思想活动的领域 mind; thinking：见～ *insight* | 心～ *character; mood* ❸底子（ⓘ质—）base; background：蓝～白花布 *fabric with a pattern of white flowers on a blue background*

⇨ see also de on p.124

玓 dì ㄉㄧˋ [玓珠]（—lì）形容珠光闪耀 (of jewellery) brilliant

的 dì ㄉㄧˋ 箭靶的中心 bullseye：中（zhòng）～ *hit the bullseye* | 有～放矢 *have a definite objective* [目的] 要达到的目标、境地 aim; objective：～明确 *clear objective*

⇨ see also de on p.124, dī on p.127, dí on p.127

菂 dì ㄉㄧˋ〈古 ancient〉莲子 lotus seed

杕 dì ㄉㄧˋ 形容树木孤立 (of a tree) lone

⇨ see also duò on p.156

弟 dì ㄉㄧˋ ❶同父母或亲属中同辈而年龄比自己小的男子 ⓘ younger brother; younger male relative of the same generation [弟兄]（—xiong）1 包括所有的兄和弟（口语里跟"兄弟（di）"有分别，"兄弟（di）"专指弟弟）brothers (when spoken, 兄弟 (di) specifically refers to younger brother)：我们～三个 *we three brothers* 2 同辈共事的朋友间亲热的称呼 brother (friendly reference to a peer whom one works with) ❷称呼年龄比自己小的男性 younger brother (reference to a male person who is younger than one)：小～ *little brother* | 师～ *junior (male student who enrolled in a course of study later than oneself)* [弟子] 学生对老师自称或别人指称 (self-designation) your humble student; disciple ❸ (ancient) same as "第❶❷❹"

〈古 ancient〉also same as 悌 (tì)

递（遞） dì ㄉㄧˋ ❶传送，传达（ⓘ传—）to deliver; to convey：投～ *to deliver* | 请把书～给我。*Please* *pass the book to me.* | ～话 *pass a message* | ～眼色（以目示意）*signal with one's eyes* ❷顺着次序 successively：～补 *fill vacancies in the proper order* | ～加 *increase successively* | ～进 *go forward in order of sequence*

娣 dì ㄉㄧˋ ❶古代称丈夫的弟妇 (ancient) wife of husband's younger brother: ～姒(sì)(妯娌) *wives of brothers* ❷古时姐姐称妹妹为娣 (ancient) younger sister (used by an elder sister)

睇 dì ㄉㄧˋ 斜着眼看 to cast a sidelong glance at：～视 *cast a sidelong glance at*

第 dì ㄉㄧˋ ❶次序（㊥等一、次一）sequence; order ㊀科举时代考中（zhòng）叫及第，没考中叫落第 in feudal times, passing the imperial examination was referred to as 及第; failing it 落第 ❷表次序的词头 placed in front of a word/phrase to indicate sequence：～一 *first* | ～二 *second* ❸封建社会官僚贵族的大宅子（㊥宅一、一宅）(in feudal times) large residences of officials and nobles：府～ *mansion* ❹〈古 ancient〉仅，只 only：此物世上多有，～人不识耳。*There are many of these in the world, but only humans do not know it.*

帝 dì ㄉㄧˋ ❶古代指天神 (ancient) deity：上～ *Supreme Deity; God* ❷君主，皇帝 monarch; emperor：称～ *declare oneself emperor* | 三皇五～ *(in Chinese mythology) the Three Sovereigns and Five Emperors*

谛（諦） dì ㄉㄧˋ ❶仔细 careful：～听 *listen carefully* | ～视 *look carefully* ❷意义，道理（原为佛教用语）(originally Buddhist term) meaning; doctrine：妙～ *exquisite truth* | 真～ *true meaning*

蒂（*蔕） dì ㄉㄧˋ 花或瓜果跟枝茎相连的部分 (of flowers and fruits) stalk; receptacle：并～莲 *two lotus flowers on one stalk; (figurative) a devoted married couple* | 瓜熟～落。*A gourd falls when it is ripe; (figurative) Things will fall into place when conditions are ripe.*

媂 dì ㄉㄧˋ 古书上指主管茅厕的女神 Di (goddess of toilets in ancient Chinese texts)

缔（締） dì ㄉㄧˋ 结合（㊥一结）to join：～交 *make friends; establish diplomatic relations* | ～约 *sign a treaty*

[缔造] 创立，建立 to found; to establish：中国共产党～了新中国。*The Communist Party of China founded the New China.*

碲 dì ㄉㄧˋ [玛碲脂]即沥青胶，用沥青加填充料制成的黏合材料，膏状，可用于黏结油毡等 bitumen mastic (same as 沥青胶)

禘 dì ㄉㄧˋ 古代一种祭祀 (ancient) a kind of religious offering ceremony

碲 dì ㄉㄧˋ 非金属元素，符号 Te，银白色晶体或灰色粉末，是半导体材料，也用于钢铁工业等 tellurium (Te)

棣 dì ㄉㄧˋ ❶植物名 plant name ①棠棣（也作“唐棣”），古书上说的一种植物 *cerasus japonica* (also written as 唐棣, a plant mentioned in ancient texts) ②棣棠，落叶灌木，叶近卵形，花黄色，花和枝叶可入药 kerria ❷同“弟”，旧多用于书信 (often used in letters in old times) same as 弟：贤～ *my worthy younger brother*

螮（蝃） dì ㄉㄧˋ ［螮蝀］（—dōng）古书上指虹 (in ancient Chinese texts) rainbow

踶 dì ㄉㄧˋ 踢，踏 to kick; to step on

DIA ㄉㄧㄚ

嗲 diǎ ㄉㄧㄚˇ 〈方 dialect〉形容撒娇的声音或姿态 (of voice and manner) coquettish：～声～气 *in a coquettish manner* | ～得很 *very coquettish*

DIAN ㄉㄧㄢ

战 diān ㄉㄧㄢ ［战敠］（—duo）same as “掂掇”

掂 diān ㄉㄧㄢ 用手托着东西估量轻重 to estimate the weight of sth (with one's hand)：～一～ *estimate the weight (of sth)* | ～着不轻。*It feels heavy in my hand.*［掂掇］（—duo）1 斟酌 to consider; to deliberate 2 估量 to assess

滇 diān ㄉㄧㄢ ❶滇池，湖名，在云南省昆明，又叫昆明湖 Dianchi Lake (in Kunming, Yunnan Province; also called 昆明湖) ❷云南省的别称 (another name for Yunnan Province) Dian

颠（顛） diān ㄉㄧㄢ ❶头顶 (of head) top; crown：华～（头顶上黑发白发相杂）*greyish hair* ㊀最高最上的部分 the peak; the summit：山～ *mountain peak* | 塔～ *top of a tower* ❷始 beginning：～末 *beginning and end* ❸倒，跌（㊁—覆）to fall; to trip：～扑不破（指理论正确不能推翻）*irrefutable; indisputable*［颠倒］（—dǎo）1 上下或前后的次序倒置 to invert; to overturn：书放～了。*The book is placed upside down.* ㊀使颠倒 to reverse：～是非 *turn right into wrong; distort facts* 2 错乱 to be confused：神魂～ *be intoxicated; be in a confused state of mind* ❹颠簸，上下震动 to jolt：山路不平，车～得厉害。*The mountain road is uneven so the vehicle jolted a lot.* ❺same as “癫”

攧（攧） diān ㄉㄧㄢ 跌 to fall; to trip

巅（巔） diān ㄉㄧㄢ 山顶，也作“颠” the peak; the summit (also written as 颠)

癫（癲） diān ㄉㄧㄢ 精神错乱、失常（㊁—狂、疯—）insane

典 diǎn ㄉㄧㄢˇ ❶可以作为标准、典范的书籍 (of book) classics：～籍 *ancient books and records* | 词～ *dictionary* | 字～ *dictionary of (Chinese) characters* | 引经据～ *quote authoritative works* ㊀标准，法则 standard; regulation：～范 *model* | ～章 *decrees and regulations* | 据为～要 *cite as the standard* [典礼] 郑重举行的仪式 ceremony：开学～ *opening ceremony (of the school year)* | 开幕～ *(of performances or events) opening ceremony* [典型] 1 有概括性或代表性的人或事物 archetype 2 具有代表性的 typical：这个案例很～。*This is a very typical case.* 3 文艺作品中，用典型化的方法创造出来的能够反映一定社会本质而又具有鲜明个性的艺术形象 (in the arts) typical character ❷ 典礼 ceremony：盛～ *grand ceremony* | 大～ *formal ceremony* ❸典故，诗文里引用的古书中的故事或词句 literary quotation; allusion：用～ *cite from classical allusion* ❹ 旧指主持，主管 (old) to supervise; to preside over：～试 *supervise an examination* | ～狱 *be in charge of a prison* ❺活买活卖，到期可以赎 to pawn; to mortgage: ～当(dàng) *to pawn* | ～押 *to mortgage*

碘 diǎn ㄉㄧㄢˇ 非金属元素，符号I，黑紫色晶体，有金属光泽。可用来制药、染料等。人体中缺少碘能引起甲状腺肿大 iodine (I)

点(點) diǎn ㄉㄧㄢˇ ❶（-子、-儿）小的痕迹或水滴 small spot; drop：墨～儿 *ink spot* | 雨～儿 *rain drop* | 斑～ *spots* ㊀少量 a small quantity of：一～小事儿 *a small matter* | 吃～儿东西 *eat something* ❷几何学上指只有位置，没有长、宽、厚的图形 (in geometry) point ❸一定的处所或限度 location; limit; threshold：起～ *starting point* | 终～ *finishing point* | 据～ *stronghold; (disapproving) base* | 焦～ *focus; focal point* | 沸～ *boiling point* ❹ 项，部分 item; part：优～ *advantage; strong point* | 重～ *emphasis; stress* | 要～ *essential point; important stronghold* | 补充三～ *make three additional points* ❺（-儿）汉字的一种笔形（丶）(in a Chinese character) dot：三～水 *(in Chinese characters) the three drops of water radical* ❻加上点子 to dot：～句 *(in writing) to punctuate* | 评～ *to annotate and highlight (with circles); to comment* | 画龙～睛 *add the finishing touches (to a work of art); add a word to clinch a point* [点缀]（-zhuì）在事物上略加装饰 to adorn; to embellish：～风景 *embellish the scenery* ❼一落一起地动作 to nod：～头 *nod one's head* | 蜻蜓～水 *a dragonfly darts about on the water; (figurative) to be superficial* ❽ 使一点一滴地落下 to drop：～眼药 *apply eye drops* | ～播种子 *dibble seeds* ❾引火，燃火 to set alight ; to light：～灯 *light a lamp* | ～火 *set fire; stir up trouble* ❿ 查数（shǔ） to check and count：～收 *check and accept* | ～数（shù） *to count; check an amount* | ～验 *check item by item* ⓫指示，指定（㊀指-） to instruct; to specify：～破 *bring sth into the open* | ～菜 *order food* | ～歌 *choose a song* ⓬时间单位，

D

即小时，一昼夜的二十四分之一 hour ⓭钟点，规定的时间 the time; time table：误～ *(of transport) be delayed*｜准～ *(of transport) be on time*｜到～了，该下班了。*It is time to get off work.* ⓮点心 snack：糕～ *cake; dessert*｜早～ *morning snack; breakfast*

踮(跕)** diǎn ㄉㄧㄢˇ ❶跛足人走路用脚尖点地 to limp：～脚 *limp on one's feet*（也作"点" also written as 点）❷提起脚跟，用脚尖着地 to stand on tiptoe：～着脚才够到书架上的书。*(I) have to stand on my toes to reach the book on the bookshelf.*（也作"点"also written as 点）

电(電) diàn ㄉㄧㄢˋ ❶物质中存在的一种能，可利用它来使电灯发光、机械转动等 electricity［电脑］指电子计算机 computer［电子］构成原子的一种带负电的粒子 electron ❷闪电，阴雨天气空中云层放电的现象 lightning：雷～交加 *thunder and lightning* ❸电流打击，触电 electric shock：电门有毛病，～了我一下。*The switch was faulty so I got an electric shock.* ❹指电报 telegram; telegraph：急～ *urgent telegram*｜通～ *(send) a public telegram (for political reasons)* ❺打电报 to send a telegram：～汇 *telegraphic transfer (of money)*｜～告 *inform by telegraph*

佃 diàn ㄉㄧㄢˋ 一般指旧社会无地或少地的农民，被迫向地主、富农租地耕种 to be a tenant farmer：～户 *tenant farming household*｜～农 *tenant farmer*

⇨ see also tián on p.649

甸 diàn ㄉㄧㄢˋ ❶古时称郊外的地方 (ancient) countryside ❷〈方 dialect〉甸子，放牧的草地，多用于地名 (often used in place names) grazing field

钿(鈿) diàn ㄉㄧㄢˋ ❶把金属、宝石等镶嵌（qiàn）在器物上做装饰 to inlay (metals, gemstones, etc.)：宝～ *ornament inlayed with precious stones*｜螺～（一种手工艺，把贝壳镶嵌在器物上）*ornament inlayed with sea shell and conch* ❷古代一种嵌金花的首饰 (ancient) a kind of jewellery with inlayed golden flowers

⇨ see also tián on p.649

阽 diàn ㄉㄧㄢˋ yán ㄧㄢˊ（又）临近（危险）to be near (danger)：～于死亡 *near death*

坫 diàn ㄉㄧㄢˋ ❶古时室内放东西的土台子 (ancient) earthern platform in a room for food, drinkware, etc. ❷屏障 screen (furniture)

玷 diàn ㄉㄧㄢˋ 白玉上面的污点 blemish on white jade［玷污］使有污点 to sully; to tarnish

扂 diàn ㄉㄧㄢˋ〈古 ancient〉门闩 door bolt

店 diàn ㄉㄧㄢˋ ❶商店，铺子 shop：书～ *book shop*｜零售～ *retail store*｜～员 *shop assistant*［饭店］1 较大的卖饭食的铺子 restaurant 2 都市中的大旅馆 hotel ❷旧式的旅馆 old-style inn：住～ *put up at an inn*｜大车～ *inn for carters*

惦 diàn ㄉㄧㄢˋ 惦记，记挂，不放心 to miss; to worry about: ～念 *worry about* | 心里老～着工作 *bear work in mind*

垫(墊) diàn ㄉㄧㄢˋ ❶衬托，放在底下或铺在上面 to cushion; to support; to lay sth below or above: ～桌子 *put sth under the legs of a table to make it stable or higher* | ～上个褥子 *lay a mattress* | 路面～上点儿土 *fill the surface of the road with a bit of earth* ❷(－子、－儿) 衬托的东西 lining; filling: 草～子 *straw pallet* | 鞋～儿 *insole* | 椅～子 *chair cushion* ❸替人暂付款项 to temporarily pay on sb's behalf: ～款 *pay for sb in the first instance* | ～钱 *pay for sb in the first instance*

淀(❷澱) diàn ㄉㄧㄢˋ ❶浅的湖泊 shallow lake: 白洋～(在河北省) *Baiyangdian Lake (in Hebei Province)* ❷渣滓，液体里沉下的东西 sediment [淀粉]有机化合物，白色，不溶于水，米、麦、甘薯、马铃薯中含量很多。工业上应用很广 starch

琔 diàn ㄉㄧㄢˋ 玉色 colour of jade

靛 diàn ㄉㄧㄢˋ ❶靛青，蓝靛，用蓼蓝叶泡水调和石灰沉淀所得的蓝色染料 indigo (dye) ❷蓝和紫合成的颜色 indigo

奠 diàn ㄉㄧㄢˋ ❶陈设祭品向死者致敬(㊀祭－) to hold a memorial service with offerings: ～酒 *pour wine onto the ground as offering for the dead* | ～仪 *condolence money/gift* ❷奠定，稳稳地安置 to lay; to put sth firmly in place: ～基 *lay foundation* | ～都(dū) *establish as a capital*

殿 diàn ㄉㄧㄢˋ ❶高大的房屋，特指封建帝王受朝听政的地方，或供奉神佛的地方 hall; imperial court; temple: 宫～ *palace* | 佛～ *Buddhist temple* ❷在最后 last place: ～后 *bring up the rear* [殿军] 1 行军时走在最后的部队 rearguard 2 体育、游艺竞赛中的最末一名，也指入选的最末一名 (in competitions) last; last among the winners

癜 diàn ㄉㄧㄢˋ 皮肤病名，常见的是白癜，俗称白癜风，皮肤生斑点后变白色 vitiligo (informal 白癜风)

簟 diàn ㄉㄧㄢˋ 竹席 bamboo mat: ～席 *bamboo mat* | 竹～ *bamboo mat*

DIAO ㄉㄧㄠ

刁 diāo ㄉㄧㄠ ❶狡猾，无赖 cunning; roguish: ～棍(恶人) *rascal; rogue* | 这个人真～。*This person is such a rogue.* ❷挑剔，难应付 picky; difficult: 嘴～ *picky about food* | 眼～ *overly discerning* [刁难] (－nàn) 故意难为人 to make things difficult for sb

叼 diāo ㄉㄧㄠ 用嘴衔住 to carry sth in one's mouth: 猫～着老鼠。*The cat is carrying the mouse in its jaws.* | 嘴里～着烟斗 *have a pipe in one's mouth*

汈 diāo ㄉㄧㄠ [汈汊]湖名，在湖北省汉川 Diaocha Lake

(in Hanchuan, Hubei Province)

凋 diāo ㄉㄧㄠ 草木零落，衰落（㊣－谢、－零）(of plants) to wilt; to wither：松柏后～。*Honest and virtue will last. (literally means 'Pine and cypress will be the last to wither.')* | ～敝 *destitute; (in) poor condition*

碉 diāo ㄉㄧㄠ 碉堡，防守用的建筑物 (military) pillbox; blockhouse

D

雕（❶*鵰、❷–❹*彫、❷❸*琱）diāo ㄉㄧㄠ ❶鸟名，即老雕，羽毛褐色，上嘴钩曲，性凶猛，捕食野兔、鼠类等 eagle ❷刻竹、木、玉、石、金属等 to carve; to engrave：木～泥塑 *carved wood and molded clay; (figurative) perfectly still or rigid (person)* | 浮～ *relief sculpture* | ～版 *printing block* ❸用彩画装饰 to decorate with coloured patterns：～弓 *bow carved with patterns* | ～墙 *wall decorated with relief sculpture* ❹ same as "凋"

鲷（鯛）diāo ㄉㄧㄠ 鱼名，身体侧扁，头大，口小，生活在海洋里，种类很多，如真鲷、黄鲷、黑鲷等 sea bream

貂 diāo ㄉㄧㄠ 哺乳动物，嘴尖，尾巴长，毛皮黄黑色或带紫色，很珍贵 marten; sable; mink

屌 diǎo ㄉㄧㄠˇ 男子阴茎的俗称 (informal) dick (penis)

吊（*弔）diào ㄉㄧㄠˋ ❶祭奠死者或对遭到丧事的人家、团体给予慰问 to pay respects to the dead; to offer one's condolences：～丧（sāng）*pay a condolence call* | ～唁 *offer one's condolences* ❷悬挂 to hang：房梁上～着四盏大红灯。*Four big red lanterns are hanging from the beam.* ❸把毛皮缀在衣面上 to stitch fur on clothing：～皮袄 *line a coat with fur* ❹提取，收回 to extract; to take back：～卷 *ask to see the files* | ～销 *to revoke; to withdraw* ❺旧时货币单位，一般是一千个制钱叫一吊 *diao* (a traditional Chinese currency unit; usually 1 000 copper coins equals 1 吊)

铞（銱）diào ㄉㄧㄠˋ see 钌铞儿 (liàodiàor) at 钌 on page 403

钓（釣）diào ㄉㄧㄠˋ 用饵诱鱼上钩 to fish (with hook and bait)：～鱼 *to fish* ㊧施用手段取得 to acquire through underhand means：沽名～誉 *seek fame through underhand means*

莜（蓧）diào ㄉㄧㄠˋ 古代一种除草的农具 (ancient) a farming tool to remove weeds

窎（窵）diào ㄉㄧㄠˋ 深远（㊣－远）remote; distant

调（調）diào ㄉㄧㄠˋ ❶调动，安排 to transfer; to arrange：～职 *be transferred to another job* | ～兵遣将 *move troops; (figurative) deploy manpower* ❷（－子）曲调，音乐上高、低、长、短配合和谐的一组音（㊣腔－）melody; tune：民间小～儿 *folk melody* | 这个～子很好听。

This melody is nice. ❸多指调式类别和调式主音高度 tonality：C大～ *C major* ❹语言中字音的声调 (in language) word tone：～号 *diacritical mark* | ～类 *tone category* [声调] 1 字音的高低升降。古汉语的声调是平、上、去、入四声。普通话的声调是阴平、阳平、上声、去声 (in language) tone 2 读书、说话、朗诵的腔调 intonation; accent

⇨ see also tiáo on p.652

掉 diào ㄉㄧㄠ ❶落 to fall：～眼泪 *shed tears* | ～在水里 *fall into the water* ❷落在后面 to fall behind：～队 *lag behind* ❸〈方 dialect〉遗漏，遗失 to lose/miss sth; to be missing：文章～了几个字。*The essay has a few words missing.* | 钱包～了。*The wallet has been lost.* ❹减损，消失 to diminish; to lose：～膘ル *(of livestock) lose weight* | ～色 *lose colour* ❺回转 to turn back：～头 *turn around* | ～过来 *turn round* ❻摇摆 to wag：尾大不～（喻指挥不灵或难以驾驭）*a tail that is too heavy to wag; (figurative) (of an organization) too cumbersome to manage* ❼对换 to exchange：～一个个ル *exchange the position with one another* ❽在动词后表示动作的完成 used after a verb to indicate completion of action：丢～ *throw away* | 卖～ *sell off* | 改～ *to change*

铫(銚) diào ㄉㄧㄠ （～子、～ル）煮开水熬东西用的器具 vessel for boiling and simmering：药～ル *medicine pot* | 沙～ *clay pot*

⇨ see also yáo on p.761

DIE ㄉㄧㄝ

爹 diē ㄉㄧㄝ ❶父亲 ㊀ father ❷对老人或长（zhǎng）者的尊称 honorific speech for elderly person：老～ *Dear Sir*

跌 diē ㄉㄧㄝ 摔倒 to fall：～了一跤 *trip and fall* | ～倒 *to fall* ㊁下降，低落 to drop; to lower：～价 *go down in price* [跌足] 顿足，跺脚 stamp one's foot

迭 dié ㄉㄧㄝ ❶交换，轮流 to alternate; to take turns：更～ *to alternate* | ～为宾主 *take turns to host* ❷屡，连着 repeatedly：～次会商 *negotiate repeatedly* | 近年来，地下文物～有发现。*There has been a succession of archaeological discoveries in recent years.* ❸及，赶上 to catch up ; to be in time for：忙不～ *in a hurry*

昳 dié ㄉㄧㄝ 〈古 ancient〉日过午偏西 (of the sun) to move towards the west

⇨ see also yì on p.775

瓞 dié ㄉㄧㄝ 小瓜 small gourd

垤 dié ㄉㄧㄝ 小土堆（㊄丘～）small earthen mound：蚁～ *anthill*

咥 dié ㄉㄧㄝ 咬 to bite

⇨ see also xì on p.702

绖(絰) dié ㄉㄧㄝ 古代丧服用的麻带ル(ancient) linen ribbon on mourning clothes：首～ *head band worn by*

D

mourners | 腰～ *belt worn by mourners*

耋 dié ㄉㄧㄝˊ 年老，七八十岁的年纪 old age (in one's seventies or eighties)：耄（mào）～ *advanced/old age* | ～老 *old age; elderly person*

谍（諜） dié ㄉㄧㄝˊ 秘密探察军事、政治及经济等方面的消息 espionage：～报 *intelligence report*［间谍］（jiàn－）潜入敌方或外国，刺探军事情报、国家机密或进行颠覆活动的人 spy

堞 dié ㄉㄧㄝˊ 城墙上呈⊓⊓形的矮墙 battlements; crenellated wall

喋 dié ㄉㄧㄝˊ ［喋喋］形容说话烦琐 used to describe annoying, trivial speech：～不休 *talk non-stop*［喋血］血流满地 shed much blood

⇨ see also zhá on p.827

楪 dié ㄉㄧㄝˊ 用于地名 used in place names：～村（在广东省新兴）*Diecun (in Xinxing, Guangdong Province)*

牒 dié ㄉㄧㄝˊ 文书，证件 official document：～文 *government document* | 通～（两国交换意见用的文书）*diplomatic note*

碟 dié ㄉㄧㄝˊ （－子、－儿）盛食物等的器具，扁而浅，比盘子小 (tableware) saucer

蝶（*蜨） dié ㄉㄧㄝˊ 蝴蝶，昆虫名。静止时四翅竖立在背部，喜在花间、草地飞行，吸食花蜜。幼虫多对作物有害。有粉蝶、蛱（jiá）蝶、凤蝶等多种 butterfly

蹀 dié ㄉㄧㄝˊ 蹈，顿足 to stamp one's foot［蹀躞］（－xiè）迈着小步走路的样子 to walk with small steps

鲽（鰈） dié ㄉㄧㄝˊ 鱼名，身体侧扁，两眼都在身体的一侧，有眼的一侧褐色，无眼的一侧大都为白色。种类很多，如星鲽、高眼鲽等 flatfish

嵽（嵽） dié ㄉㄧㄝˊ ［嵽嵲］（－niè）形容山高 (of mountains) high

叠（*疊、*疉、*曡） dié ㄉㄧㄝˊ ❶重复地堆，累积（㊀重－）to stack; to accumulate：～床架屋（形容重复累赘）*needless repetition* | ～假山 *create artificial mountain (for a garden)* | ～罗汉 *form a human pyramid* ❷重复 to repeat：层见～出 *appear repeatedly* ❸折叠 to fold：～衣服 *fold clothes* | 铺床～被 *make a bed*

DING ㄉㄧㄥ

丁 dīng ㄉㄧㄥ ❶天干的第四位，用作顺序的第四 *ding* (the fourth of the ten Heavenly Stems, a system used in the Chinese calendar); fourth ❷成年男子 adult male：壮～ *able-bodied man* ㊀①指人口 (of humans) population：人～ *the number of people (in a family)* | ～口 *population* ②指从事某种劳动的人 person working in a certain trade：园～ *gardener* ❸当，遭逢 when; to encounter：～兹盛

世 *live in prosperous times* | ～忧(旧指遭父母丧) *(old) be afflicted with death of one's parent* ❹(～儿) 小方块 small cube: 肉～儿 *meat cubes* | 咸菜～儿 *cubes of pickled vegetable* [丁点儿] 表示极少或极小 a tiny amount: 一～毛病都没有。*There is not even the tiniest bit of problem.* ❺姓 (surname) Ding

[丁当] (－dāng) same as "叮当"

⇨ see also zhēng on p.846

仃 dīng ㄉㄧㄥ see 伶仃 (líng－) at 伶 on page 408

叮 dīng ㄉㄧㄥ ❶再三嘱咐 to exhort repeatedly: ～嘱 *urge repeatedly* ❷蚊子等用针形口器吸食 (of insects) to sting; to bite: 被蚊子～了一口 *be bitten by a mosquito* ❸追问 to question closely: ～问 *inquire closely*

[叮当] 形容金属等撞击的声音 (of the sound of metal) ding dong, tinkle; jingle

[叮咛] (*丁宁) 反复地嘱咐 to exhort repeatedly: ～再三 *urge repeatedly*

玎 dīng ㄉㄧㄥ [玎玲] (－líng) 形容玉石等撞击的声音 (of the sound of jade pieces) jingle; tinkle

盯 dīng ㄉㄧㄥ 注视，集中视力看 to stare at: 眼睛一直～着他 *eyes kept staring at him*

町 dīng ㄉㄧㄥ see 畹町 (wǎn－) at 畹 on page 674

⇨ see also tǐng on p.655

钉(釘) dīng ㄉㄧㄥ ❶(－子、－儿) 竹、木、金属制成的可以打入他物的细条形的东西 nail; spike: 螺丝～儿 *screw* | 碰～子 (喻受打击或被拒绝) *receive a blow; be rejected* ❷紧跟着不放松 to follow closely: ～住对方的前锋。*Mark the opponent's forward closely.* ❸督促，催问 to supervise and urge: 这事得～着他点儿。*You must watch and guide him on this matter.*

⇨ see also dìng on p.140

疔 dīng ㄉㄧㄥ 疔疮，一种毒疮，硬而根深，形状像钉 hard furuncle

耵 dīng ㄉㄧㄥ [耵聍] (－níng) 耳垢，耳屎 cerumen; earwax

酊 dīng ㄉㄧㄥ (外 loanword) 医药上用酒精和药配合成的液剂 tincture: 碘～ *iodine tincture*

⇨ see also dǐng on p.140

顶(頂) dǐng ㄉㄧㄥˇ ❶(－儿) 人体或物体的最高最上的部分 top: 头～ *crown (of one's head)* | 山～ *mountain peak* | 房～ *roof* ❷用头支承 to support using one's head: 用头～东西 *support sth on one's head* | ～天立地 (形容英雄气概) *heroic; indomitable* 引 ①用东西支撑 to prop up with sth: 用门杠把门～上。*Prop up the door with a pole.* ②冒 to brave sth: ～着雨走了。*Braving the rain, (he) left.* ③担当，担得起 to bear responsibility: 出了事我来～。*I will take the responsibility if anything happens.* | 他一个人去不～事。*He cannot handle it by going alone.* ❸

用头或角撞击 to butt (with head or horns)：～球 *(in sports) head a ball*｜公牛～人。*The bull gores people.* ❹自下而上用力拱起 to raise with great strength：用千斤顶把汽车～起来。*Raise the car with a jack.*｜麦芽～出土来了。*The wheat seedlings have broken through the soil.* ❺相逆，对面迎着 in opposition to：～风 *go against the wind; head wind; go against a law/rule/policy* ❻顶撞（多指下对上）(often by junior to senior persons) to contradict; to talk back：他气冲冲地～了班长两句。*He gave a couple of angry retorts to the class monitor.* ❼代替（㊎一替）to take the place of：～名 *assume sb's name*｜冒名～替 *be an imposter* ❽相当，等于 to be equal to：一个人～两个人工作。*One person is doing the job of two persons.* ❾〈方 dialect〉直到 until：昨天～十二点才到家。*It wasn't until twelve o'clock that (I) reached home yesterday.* ❿副词，最，极 (adverb) most：～好 *best*｜～多 *at most*｜～会想办法 *be best at coming up with solutions* ⓫量词 measure word for hats, sedan chairs, etc.：两～帽子 *two hats*

酊 dǐng ㄉㄧㄥˇ see 酩酊 (mǐng—) at 酩 on page 457

⇨ see also dīng on p.139

鼎 dǐng ㄉㄧㄥˇ ❶古代烹煮用的器物，一般是三足两耳 (ancient) cooking vessel (usually with two handles and three legs)［鼎立］三方并立 (of three forces) confront each other on an equal footing：三国～ *confrontation of three kingdoms* ❷大 ㊢ big;great：～力 *great effort*｜～～大名 *great fame* ❸〈方 dialect〉锅 cooking pot：～间(厨房) *kitchen* ❹正当，正在 at this time; while：～盛 *at the height of power or prosperity*

订(訂) dìng ㄉㄧㄥˋ ❶改正，修改 to revise; to correct：～正 *make corrections*｜考～ *do textual research (into historical texts)*｜校（jiào）～ *check against an authoritative text* ❷立（契约），约定 to enter into (an agreement)：～报 *subscribe to a newspaper*｜～货 *order goods*｜～婚 *be engaged (to be married)*｜～合同 *lay down a contract* ❸用线、铁丝等把书页等连在一起 (for pages of books, etc.) to bind (with thread, wires, etc.)：装～ *bind (books, etc.)*｜～一个笔记本ル *bind the pages into a notebook*

饤(飣) dìng ㄉㄧㄥˋ see 饾饤 (dòu—) at 饾 on page 145

钉(釘) dìng ㄉㄧㄥˋ ❶把钉子或楔（xiē）子打入他物 to nail：拿个钉子～一～。*Fasten it with a nail.*｜墙上～着木橛。*A wooden peg is nailed into the wall.* ❷连接在一起 to join：～扣子 *sew a button*

⇨ see also dīng on p.139

定 dìng ㄉㄧㄥˋ ❶不可变更的，规定的，不动的 unchangeable; stipulated; fixed：～理 *theorem*｜～论 *final conclusion*｜～量

fixed quantity | ～期 *fixed period of time; regular* 引 副词，必然地 (adverb) certainly：～能成功。*It will definitely succeed.* ❷确定，使不移动 to fix; to secure：～编 *fix the number of staff* | ～岗 *define job responsibility* | ～案 *reach a final conclusion (on a case, proposal, etc.)* | ～胜负 *determine success or failure* | 否～ *negate; refute* | 决～ *decide* | ～章程 *lay down the constitution/charter* 引固定，使固定 to be fixed; to fix：表针～住不走了。*The hand of the watch has stopped and does not move.* | ～影 *(in photography) fix* ❸安定，平定（多指局势）(often of situations) stabilized; pacified：大局已～。*The outcome is a foregone conclusion.* ❹镇静，安稳（多指情绪）(often of emotions) calm; stable：心神不～ *anxious and distracted* | ～～神再说。*Calm down before saying anything.* ❺预先约妥 to agree in advance：～金 *deposit money* | ～票 *book a ticket* | ～酒席 *book a banquet*

� dìng ㄉㄧㄥˋ 用于地名 used in place names：茄（jiā）～乡（在台湾省）*Jiadingxiang (in Taiwan Province)*

啶 dìng ㄉㄧㄥˋ see 吡啶 (bǐ—) at 吡 on page 32, and 嘧啶 (mì—) at 嘧 on page 450

腚 dìng ㄉㄧㄥˋ 〈方 dialect〉屁股 buttocks：光～ *bare-bottomed*

碇（*椗、*矴） dìng ㄉㄧㄥˋ 系船的石礅 stone piling (for tying up a boat)：下～（停船）*drop anchor (to stop a boat)* | 起～（开船）*weigh anchor (to start a boat)*

锭（錠） dìng ㄉㄧㄥˋ ❶（—子）纺车或纺纱机上绕纱的机件 spindle：纱～ *silk spindle* ❷（—子、—儿）金属或药物等制成的块状物 ingot; tablet：钢～ *steel ingot* | 金～儿 *gold ingot* | 紫金～ *a kind of traditional Chinese medicinal tablet*

DIU ㄉㄧㄡ

丢 diū ㄉㄧㄡ ❶失去，遗落 to lose; to be missing：钱包～了。*The wallet is missing.* | ～脸（失面子）*lose face* | ～三落（là）四 *scatterbrained* ❷放下，抛开 to set aside：这件事可以～开不管。*This matter can be ignored.*

铥（銩） diū ㄉㄧㄡ 金属元素，符号 Tm，银白色，质软。可用来制 X 射线源等 thulium (Tm)

DONG ㄉㄨㄥ

东（東） dōng ㄉㄨㄥ ❶方向，太阳出来的那一边，跟“西”相对 east：～方红，太阳升。*The east is turning red; the sun is rising.* | 面朝～ *facing east* | 黄河以～ *east of the Yellow River* | 华～ *eastern China* [东西]（—xi）物件，有时也指人或动物 thing; (sometimes) a person or an animal ❷主人 owner：房～ *landlord/landlady* ❸东道（请

人吃饭出钱的人，也简称“东”）host (also shortened as 东)：做～ *be the host*

[东乡族] 我国少数民族，参看附录四 the Dongxiang people (one of the ethnic groups in China. See Appendix Ⅳ.)

岽(崬) dōng ㄉㄨㄥ [岽罗] 地名，在广西壮族自治区扶绥，今作“东罗”(now written as 东罗) Dongluo (a place in Fusui, Guangxi Zhuang Autonomous Region)

鸫(鶇) dōng ㄉㄨㄥ 鸟名，羽毛多淡褐色或黑色，叫得很好听。吃昆虫，是益鸟。种类很多 (bird) thrush

蝀(蝀) dōng ㄉㄨㄥ see 蝃蝀 (dì—) at 蝃 on page 132

冬(❷鼕) dōng ㄉㄨㄥ ❶四季中的第四季，气候最冷 winter：过～ *pass the winter* | 隆～ *midwinter* ❷ same as “咚”

咚 dōng ㄉㄨㄥ 形容敲鼓、敲门等的声音 ㊀(the sound of drumbeats, knocking on doors, etc.) rat-a-tat-tat

氡 dōng ㄉㄨㄥ 放射性气体元素，符号 Rn，无色、无臭，不易跟其他元素化合，在真空玻璃管中能发荧光 radon (Rn)

董 dǒng ㄉㄨㄥˇ 监督管理 to supervise [董事] 某些企业、学校等推举出来代表自己监督和主持业务的人 (in companies, schools, etc.) director; trustee：～会 *board of directors* 也省称“董”(also shortened as 董)：校～ *school board trustee* | 刘～ *Director Liu*

懂 dǒng ㄉㄨㄥˇ 了解，明白 to understand; to know about：一看就～ *to understand sth at the first sight* | ～点儿中医 *know a little about traditional Chinese medicine*

动(動) dòng ㄉㄨㄥˋ ❶改变原来的位置或脱离静止状态，跟“静”相对 to move (opposite of 静)：站住别～！*Stand still and don't move!* | 风吹草～ *the slightest sign of movement* | ～弹 (tan) *to move* ㊀①能动的 able to move：～物 *animal* ②可以变动的 movable：～产 *movables* ❷行动，动作，行为 action; behaviour：一举一～ *every single action* [动词] 表示动作、行为、变化的词，如“走、来、去、打、吃、爱、拥护、变化”等 verb [动静] (—jing) 动作或情况 activity or movement：没有～ *no activity* | 侦察敌人的～ *reconnoitre the enemy's activities* ❸使动，使有动作 to move; to make sth move：～手 *get to work; to touch; strike sb* | ～脑筋 *use one's brains* | ～员 *mobilize* ❹感动，情感起反应 (of emotions) to move; to react emotionally：～心 *be attracted/lured* | ～人 *moving* ❺开始做 to begin：～工 *start work* | ～身 (起行) *set off (on a journey)* ❻往往 often：观众～以万计。*The size of the audience is often in the tens of thousands.* [动不动] 表示很容易发生，常跟“就”连用 (often used with 就) easily：～就引古

书 *quote from ancient books at the drop of a hat* | ～就争吵 *quarrel at the slightest provocation* ❼ 放在动词后，表示有效果 used after a verb to indicate effectiveness：拿得～ *can be lifted* | 搬不～ *cannot be moved*

冻(凍) dòng ㄉㄨㄥˋ ❶液体或含水分的东西遇冷凝结 to freeze：河里～冰了。*The river is frozen.* | 天寒地～ *extremely cold weather (literally means 'The weather is cold and the ground is frozen.')* ❷（～儿）凝结了的汤汁 gelatinised soup/gravy：肉～儿 *meat jelly* | 鱼～儿 *fish in aspic* | 果子～儿 *fruit jelly* ❸感到寒冷或受到寒冷 to be cold：外面很冷，真～得慌。*It's cold outside and I'm freezing.* | 小心别～着。*Be careful not to catch a chill.*

栋(棟) dòng ㄉㄨㄥˋ ❶古代指房屋的脊檩 (ancient) roof ridge［栋梁］㊉担负国家重任的人 pillar of a state ❷量词，用于房屋 measure word for houses：一～房子 *a house*

胨(腖) dòng ㄉㄨㄥˋ 蛋白胨，有机化合物，医学上用作细菌的培养基 peptone

侗 dòng ㄉㄨㄥˋ［侗族］我国少数民族，参看附录四 the Dong people ; the Kam people (one of the ethnic groups in China. See Appendix Ⅳ.)

⇨ see also tóng on p.657, tǒng on p.658

垌 dòng ㄉㄨㄥˋ ❶田地 farmland：田～ *field; paddy field* ❷用于地名 used in place names：麻～（在广西壮族自治区桂平）*Madong (in Guiping, Guangxi Zhuang Autonomous Region)*

⇨ see also tóng on p.657

峒(*峝) dòng ㄉㄨㄥˋ 山洞，石洞 cave

⇨ see also tóng on p.657

洞 dòng ㄉㄨㄥˋ ❶洞穴，窟窿 hole：山～ *cave* | 老鼠～ *mouse hole* | 衣服破了一个～。*There's a hole in these clothes.* ❷透彻，清楚 penetrating：～察 *have an insight into* | ～若观火 *see very clearly* ❸在某些场合说数字时用来代替0。zero (used as a code word for 0 on certain occasions)

注：山西省洪洞县的"洞"习惯上读 tóng。Note: the 洞 in 洪洞县 (a county in Shanxi Province) is pronounced tóng.

恫 dòng ㄉㄨㄥˋ 恐惧，恐吓 to scare; to intimidate［恫吓］（－hè）吓（xià）唬 to scare sb

⇨ see also tōng on p.656

胴 dòng ㄉㄨㄥˋ ❶躯干，整个身体除去头部、四肢和内脏余下的部分 eviscerated torso; body：～体 *body* ❷大肠 large intestine

硐 dòng ㄉㄨㄥˋ 山洞、窑洞或矿坑 cave; mine pit：～产（矿产）*mined product*

DOU ㄉㄡ

都 dōu ㄉㄡ 副词 adverb ①表示总括，全，完全 all; both：事情不论大小，～要做好。

You must do everything properly, no matter how big or small it is. ② 表示语气的加重 used to show intensified tone：～十二点了还不睡。*It's already 12 o'clock and you're still not in bed!* | 连小孩子～搬得动。*Even a child can move it.*

⇨ see also dū on p.146

哣 dōu ㄉㄡ 斥责声，多见于旧小说或戏曲中 sound of rebuke often used in old novels or traditional dramas

兜(*兠) dōu ㄉㄡ ❶（一子、一儿）作用和口袋相同的东西 pocket：裤～ *trouser pocket* | ～儿布 *cloth used to make inner pockets* ❷做成兜形把东西拢住 to hold sth (in a pocket-like container)：用手巾～着鸡蛋 *carry eggs in a handkerchief* | 船帆～风 *wind fills the sails* ㊀ 兜揽，招揽 to solicit; to tout：～售 *to sell; to peddle* ❸承担 to bear：没关系，有问题我～着。*It's all right. If anything goes wrong, I'll handle it.* ❹环绕，围绕 to encircle; to surround：～抄 *to envelop (an enemy, etc.)* | ～圈子 *go round in circles*

蔸 dōu ㄉㄡ 〈方 dialect〉❶指某些植物的根和靠近根的茎 (of certain plants) roots and stems near the roots：禾～ *roots of rice* | 树～脑（树墩儿）*tree stump* ❷量词，相当于“丛”或“棵” (measure word) equivalent to 丛 or 棵：一～草 *a patch of grass* | 两～白菜 *two heads of Chinese cabbage*

篼 dōu ㄉㄡ ❶（一子）走山路坐的竹轿 bamboo sedan chair (usually used in hilly terrains) ❷竹、藤、柳条等做成的盛东西的器物 container made of bamboo, rattan, wicker, etc.

斗 dǒu ㄉㄡˇ ❶市制容量单位，1 斗是 10 升 *dou* (a traditional Chinese unit for measuring volume. There are 10 升 in 1 斗.) ❷量（liáng）粮食的器具，容量是 1 斗，多为方形 *dou* (often square-shaped measuring tool for grain with a capacity of 1 斗) ㊓ ①形容小东西的大 used to describe the largeness of sth small：～胆 *(often used as humble speech) boldly* ②形容大东西的小 used to describe the smallness of sth large：～室 *tiny room* | ～城 *small city* ❸像斗的东西 sth that resembles a *dou*：漏～ *funnel* | 熨～ *iron (for clothes)* [斗拱]（一gǒng）拱是建筑上的弧形承重结构，斗是垫拱的方木块，合称斗拱 bucket arch (a system of interlocking wood brackets in traditional Chinese architecture) ❹呈圆形的指纹 (of fingerprints) whorl ❺星宿名，二十八宿之一 *dou* (one of the twenty-eight constellations in ancient Chinese astronomy)

⇨ see also dòu on p.145

阧 dǒu ㄉㄡˇ 〈古 ancient〉 same as “陡”

抖 dǒu ㄉㄡˇ ❶使振动 to shake：～床单 *flick open bed sheets* | ～空竹 *play with a diabolo* | ～～身上的雪 *shake the snow off*

one's body [抖搂] (—lou) 1 same as "抖❶": ～衣服上的土 *shake the dirt off one's clothes* 2 任意挥霍 to squander: 别把钱～光了。*Don't waste all your money.* 3 揭露 to reveal: ～老底儿 *reveal sb's unsavoury past* ❷哆嗦，战栗 to shiver; to tremble: 冷得发～ *shiver from the cold* ❸讽刺人突然得势或生活水平突然提高 to put on airs (because one has suddenly come up in the world): 他最近～起来了。*He has recently started to put on airs.*

钭(鈄) dǒu ㄉㄡˇ (又) see tǒu on page 661

蚪 dǒu ㄉㄡˇ see 蝌蚪 (kē—) at 蝌 on page 354

陡 dǒu ㄉㄡˇ ❶斜度很大，近于垂直 steep: 悬崖～壁 *sheer cliffs and steep crags* | ～峭 *precipitous* | 这个山坡太～。*This mountain slope is too steep.* ❷突然 suddenly: 气候～变。*The weather changed suddenly.* | ～起歹心。*(He) suddenly had an evil thought.*

斗(鬥、*鬭、*鬦、*鬪) dòu ㄉㄡˋ ❶对打 (㊀战—) to fight: 搏～ *to fight* | ～殴 *to fight with fists* [斗争] 1 矛盾的双方互相冲突，一方力求战胜另一方 to struggle: 思想～ *mental struggle* 2 用说理、揭露、控诉等方式打击 to accuse and denounce: ～汉奸 *accuse and denounce sb as a traitor of the Chinese people* | 开～会 *convene a denunciation meeting* 3 奋斗 to strive; to fight for sth: 为真理而～ *strive for the truth* [奋斗] 为了达到一定的目的而努力干 to work hard towards a goal ❷比赛胜负 to contest: ～智 *engage in a battle of wits* | ～力 *battle with strength* ❸〈方 dialect〉拼合，凑近 to join; to put together: 那条桌子腿还没有～榫 (sǔn)。*The leg of the table has not been dovetailed.* | 用碎布～成一个口袋。*Make a pocket by sewing oddments of cloth together.*

⇨ see also dǒu on p.144

豆(❶*荳) dòu ㄉㄡˋ ❶豆类植物，有大豆、豌豆、蚕豆等，又指这些植物的种子 bean ❷(—儿) 形状像豆粒的东西 bean-like object: 山药～儿 *Chinese yam bulbil* | 花生～儿 *peanut* ❸古代盛肉或其他食品的器皿，形状像高脚盘 tall-stemmed dish for meat and other foods in ancient times

逗 dòu ㄉㄡˋ ❶停留 (㊀—留) to stay ❷引，惹弄 to tease; to provoke: ～笑 *make sb laugh* | ～趣 *try to induce laughter by making jokes* | 把弟弟～哭了。*(He) made his younger brother cry.* 特指引人发笑 (specifically) to induce laughter: 爱说爱～ *be chatty and jovial* ❸有趣 amusing: 他说话真～。*He is such a funny talker.* ❹ same as "读 (dòu)"

饾(餖) dòu ㄉㄡˋ [饾饤] (—dìng) 供陈设的食品 food for display ㊗ 文辞堆砌 verbose writing

D

脰 dòu ㄉㄡˋ 脖子，颈 neck

痘 dòu ㄉㄡˋ ❶水痘，一种传染病，小儿容易感染 chickenpox ❷痘疮，即天花，一种急性传染病，病原体是病毒 smallpox

读(讀) dòu ㄉㄡˋ 指文章里一句话中间念起来要稍稍停顿的地方 slight pause in a sentence：句～ *full stops and commas*

⇨ see also dú on p.147

窦(竇) dòu ㄉㄡˋ 孔，洞 hole：鼻～ *nasal sinus* | 狗～ *dog hole* [疑窦] 可疑的地方 point of suspicion：顿生～ *immediately feel suspicious*

D

DU ㄉㄨ

厾(**㞘) dū ㄉㄨ 用指头、棍棒等轻击轻点 to tap lightly with finger, stick, etc.：～一个点儿 *make a small dot* [点厾] 画家随意点染 (of an artist) to make random dots and splashes

都 dū ㄉㄨ ❶首都，全国最高领导机关所在的地方 capital：建～ *establish a capital* ❷大城市（㊀一市）big city：通～大邑 *metropolis* ❸姓 (surname) Du

⇨ see also dōu on p.143

阇(闍) dū ㄉㄨ 城门上的台 terrace above a city gate

⇨ see also shé on p.585

嘟 dū ㄉㄨ 形容喇叭等的声音 toot (the sound of a trumpet, etc.)：喇叭～～响。*Trumpets are tooting.* [嘟囔]（—nang）小声、连续地自言自语，常带有抱怨的意思 (often grumbling) to mutter to oneself：别瞎～啦！ *Stop this muttering!* [嘟噜]（—lu）1 向下垂着 hang downwards：～着脸，显得很不高兴 *pull a long face to show displeasure* 2 量词，用于连成一簇的东西 (measure word) bunch：一～钥匙 *a bunch of keys* | 一～葡萄 *a bunch of grapes* 3（—儿）舌或小舌连续颤动发出的声音 trill：打～儿 *to trill*

督 dū ㄉㄨ 监督，监管，察看 to monitor; to oversee：～战 *supervise military operations* | ～促 *supervise and urge* | ～着他干。*Supervise him in his work.*

毒 dú ㄉㄨˊ ❶对生物体有危害的性质，或有这种性质的东西 poison：～气 *poisonous gas* | 中（zhòng）～ *be poisoned* | 消～ *disinfect; sterilise* | 砒霜有～。*Arsenic is poisonous.* ㊂对思想品质有害的事物 poison (to the mind and morality)：肃清流～ *eliminate pernicious influence* ❷毒品 drugs; narcotics：吸～ *take drugs* | 贩～ *traffic drugs* | 禁～ *ban narcotics* ❸用有毒的东西使人或物受到伤害 to poison (sb/sth)：用药～老鼠。*Poison mice.* | ～杀害虫。*Kill insect pests with poison.* ❹毒辣，凶狠，厉害 cruel; fierce：心～ *vicious-hearted* | ～计 *diabolical plot* | 下～手 *use vicious means to harm or kill sb* | 太阳真～。*The sun is scorchingly hot.*

独(獨) dú ㄉㄨˊ ❶单一(㊀单一) single; only: ～唱 *sing solo* | ～幕剧 *one-act play* | ～生子女 *only child* | 无～有偶。*It is not unique but has its counterpart.* ❷没有依靠或帮助(㊀孤一) alone and helpless [独立]自立自主，不受人支配 independent ❸没有子孙的老人 childless elderly person: 鳏寡孤～ *widowers, widows, orphans and the childless* ❹只，唯有 only: 大家都到了，～有他没来。*Everyone is here except him.*

[独龙族]我国少数民族，参看附录 四 the Derung people (one of the ethnic groups in China. See Appendix Ⅳ.)

顿(頓) dú ㄉㄨˊ see 冒顿(mò —) at 冒 on page 461

⇨ see also dùn on p.154

读(讀) dú ㄉㄨˊ 依照文字念 to read sth out: 宣～ *proclaim* | 朗～ *read aloud* | ～报 *read a newspaper* ㊁①阅读，看书，阅览 to read: ～书 *read a book* | ～者 *reader* ②求学 to study at school: ～大学 *study at university*

⇨ see also dòu on p.146

渎(瀆、❷凟)** dú ㄉㄨˊ ❶水沟，小渠(㊀沟一) gutter; drain ❷亵渎，轻慢，对人不恭敬 to show disrespect or contempt [渎职]不尽职，在执行任务时犯错误 neglect one'e duty

椟(櫝) dú ㄉㄨˊ ❶柜子 cabinet ❷匣子 small box; casket

犊(犢) dú ㄉㄨˊ (一子、一儿)牛犊，小牛 calf: 初生之～不怕虎。*A young calf does not fear the tiger.*

牍(牘) dú ㄉㄨˊ 古代在上面写字的木简 (ancient) strip of wood with writing ㊁①文牍，公文 official document: 案～ *official document* ②尺牍，书信 correspondence

讟(讟) dú ㄉㄨˊ 诽谤，怨言 to slander; to grumble

黩(黷) dú ㄉㄨˊ ❶污辱 to insult; to humiliate ❷随随便便，不郑重 to act flippantly [黩武]滥用武力 indiscriminate use of military power: 穷兵～ *be militaristic and aggressive*

髑 dú ㄉㄨˊ [髑髅](—lóu)死人头骨 skull of a dead person

肚 dǔ ㄉㄨˇ (一子、一儿)动物的胃用作食品时叫肚 tripe: 猪～子 *pig tripe* | 羊～儿 *sheep tripe*

⇨ see also dù on p.148

笃(篤) dǔ ㄉㄨˇ ❶忠实，全心全意 earnest; sincere: ～学 *be devoted to study* | ～信 *sincerely believe in* ❷病沉重 be seriously ill: 病～ *be critically ill*

堵 dǔ ㄉㄨˇ ❶阻塞(sè)，挡 to obstruct; to block: 水沟～住了。*The ditch is blocked.* | ～老鼠洞 *block a mouse hole* | 别～着门站着! *Don't stand there and block the doorway!* ㊂心中不畅快 unhappy; oppressed: 心里～得慌 *feel oppressed* ❷墙 wall: 观者如～ *a wall of spectators* [安堵]

安定地生活，不受骚扰 to live an untroubled life ❸量词，用于墙 measure word for walls：一～高墙 *a high wall*

赌（賭） dǔ ㄉㄨˇ 赌博，用财物作注争输赢 to gamble：～钱 *gamble with money* | 聚～ *get together to gamble* ㉑争输赢 to wager; to bet：打～ *to bet*

［赌气］因不服气而任性做事 to act wilfully because one feels wronged or discontented：他～走了。*He left in a fit of pique.*

睹（*覩） dǔ ㄉㄨˇ 看见 to see：耳闻目～ *to see and hear* | 熟视无～ *pay no attention to sth familiar* | ～物思人 *be reminded of sb by the sight of sth related*

芏 dù ㄉㄨˋ see 茳芏 (jiāng—) at 茳 on page 306

杜（❷Ⓐ 敥）** dù ㄉㄨˋ ❶杜梨树，落叶乔木，果实圆而小，味涩，可以吃。是嫁接梨的主要砧木 birch-leaf pear ❷阻塞（sè），堵塞（sè）to obstruct; to block：以～流弊 *stop corrupt or harmful practices*

［杜绝］堵死，彻底防止 to block/prevent completely：～漏洞 *close loopholes* | ～事故发生 *prevent any accident from happening*

［杜鹃］（—juān）1 鸟名，又叫布谷、杜宇或子规，身体黑灰色，胸腹常有横斑点，吃害虫，是益鸟 cuckoo (also called 布谷，杜宇 or 子规) 2 常绿或落叶灌木，又叫映山红，春天开花，多为红色，供观赏 Indian azalea (also called 映山红)

［杜撰］（—zhuàn）凭自己的意思捏造 to make sth up; to fabricate

肚 dù ㄉㄨˋ ❶（—子）腹部，胸下腿上的部分 abdomen; belly; stomach ㉑（—儿）器物中空的部分 the empty part of a vessel：大～儿坛子 *full-bodied jar* ❷（—子、—儿）物体上圆而凸起像肚子的部分 abdomen-like mound protruding from sth：腿～子 *calf of the leg* | 手指头～儿 *pad of a finger*

⇨ see also dǔ on p.147

钍（釷） dù ㄉㄨˋ 人造的放射性金属元素，符号 Db。dubnium (Db)

妒（*妬） dù ㄉㄨˋ 因为别人好而忌恨（㊀嫉—）to be jealous; to envy：嫉贤～能 *resent the good and the able*

度 dù ㄉㄨˋ ❶计算长短的器具或单位 ruler or unit for measuring length：～量（liàng）衡 *weights and measures* ❷依照计算的标准划分的单位 standard unit of measure：温～ *temperature* | 湿～ *humidity* | 经～ *longitude* | 用了 20 ～电。*Twenty units of electricity were used.* ❸事物所达到的程度 extent; level attained by sth：知名～ *level of fame* | 高～的爱国热情 *strong sense of patriotism* ❹法则，应遵行的标准（㊀制—、法—）rule; standard ❺度量，能容纳承受的量 capacity：气～ *one's bearing and magnanimity* | 适～ *moderate* | 过～ *excessive* ❻过，由此到彼 to pass from one point to another：～日 *pass one's days* ❼所打算或考虑的 calculation;

consideration：置之～外 *give no thought to* ❽ 量词，次 (measure word) number of times：一～ *once* | 再～ *again* | 前～ *former*

⇨ see also duó on p.155

渡 dù ㄉㄨˋ ❶ 横过水面 to cross (a body of water)：～河 *cross a river* | ～江 *cross a river* ㊀ 过，由此到彼 to cross from one point to another：～过难关 *overcome a crisis* | 过～时期 *transitional period* ❷渡口，渡头，过河的地方 ferry; crossing：荒村野～ *remote countryside with an abandoned crossing*

镀（鍍）dù ㄉㄨˋ 用物理或化学方法使一种物质附着在别的物体的表面 to plate：～金 *gilding* | 电～ *electroplating*

蠹（**蝩、**螙）dù ㄉㄨˋ ❶蛀蚀器物的虫子 insect that infests things：木～ *woodworm* | 书～ *bookworm* | ～鱼 *silverfish* ❷ 蛀蚀，侵害 to worm into; to encroach on：流水不腐，户枢不～ *activity keeps one healthy (literally means 'Flowing water does not stagnate; a door hinger never gets worm-eaten.')*

DUAN ㄉㄨㄢ

耑 duān ㄉㄨㄢ ❶ ancient written form of 端 ❷姓 (surname) Duan

⇨ see also zhuān 专 on p.871

端 duān ㄉㄨㄢ ❶端正，不歪斜 regular; upright：五官～正 *regular facial features* | ～坐 *sit upright* ㊀ 正派 decent; upright：品行不～ *indecent behaviour* ❷ 东西的一头 tip; end：两～ *both ends* | 末～ *terminal end* | 笔～ *tip of a pen or writing brush* ㊀ ① 事情的开头 beginning (of sth)：开～ *beginning* ② 起因 cause：无～ *with no cause* ③ 项目，方面 aspect; point：不只一～ *more than one aspect* | 举其大～ *point out the main features* [端午] [端阳] 农历五月初五日。民间在这一天包粽子、赛龙舟，纪念两千多年前的楚国诗人屈原（相传屈原在这一天投江自尽）Duanwu Festival; Duanyang Festival; Dragon Boat Festival (the 5th day of the 5th month in Chinese lunar calendar) [端详] 1 从头到尾的详细情形 details：听～ *hear the details of sth* | 说～ *tell the details of sth* 2 仔细地看 to scrutinise：她久久地～着孩子的相片。*She scrutinised the child's photograph for a long time.* ❸用手很平正地拿着 hold sth level in one's hands：～碗 *hold the bowl* | ～茶 *hold up a cup of tea; serve tea*

短 duǎn ㄉㄨㄢˇ ❶长度小，跟"长"相对 short (opposite of 长) ① 指空间 (of space) short：～距离 *short distance* | ～裤 *short trousers* | ～视（目光短浅）*short-sighted* ② 指时间 (of time) short; brief：～期 *short-term* | 天长夜～。*The days are long and the nights short.* | ～工（指短期雇用的工人、农民等）*seasonal worker* ❷ 缺少，欠（㊀—少）to be

D

short of：别人都来了，就～他一个人了。*Everyone is here except him.* ❸短处，缺点 shortcoming; weakness：护～ *shield a fault* | 取长补～ *take the strengths to offset the weaknesses*

段 duàn ㄉㄨㄢˋ ❶量词，用于事物、时间的一节，截 measure word for sections of objects or time：一～话 *a section of a speech*| 一～时间 *a period of time* | 一～木头 *a section of wood*［段落］文章、事情等根据内容划分成的部分 paragraph; section：工作告一～ *the end of a phase of work*| 这篇文章可以分两个～。*This essay can be divided into two paragraphs.* ❷工矿企业中的行政单位 administrative unit in industrial and mining enterprises：工～ *work section*| 机务～ *maintenance department*

塅 duàn ㄉㄨㄢˋ 〈方 dialect〉指面积较大的平坦地形，多用于地名 (often used in place names) large flat terrain：李家～（在湖南省汨罗）*Lijiaduan (in Miluo, Hunan Province)*

缎(緞) duàn ㄉㄨㄢˋ （一子）质地厚密，一面光滑的丝织品，是我国的特产之一 satin

瑖 duàn ㄉㄨㄢˋ 一种像玉的石头 jade-like stone

椴 duàn ㄉㄨㄢˋ 椴树，落叶乔木，像白杨，木质细致，可用来制器具等 Tuan linden

煅 duàn ㄉㄨㄢˋ ❶ same as "锻" ❷放在火里烧，减少药石的烈性（中药的一种制法）(in traditional Chinese medicine) to calcine (to reduce the strength of medicines)：～石膏 *calcined plaster (used in traditional Chinese medicine)*

锻(鍛) duàn ㄉㄨㄢˋ 把金属加热，然后锤打 to forge (metal)：～件 *forged product* | ～工 *(person) blacksmith; (process) forging* | ～造 *forge*［锻炼］1 通过体育活动，增强体质 to train physically：～身体 *exercise and strengthen the body* 2 通过生产劳动、社会斗争和工作实践，使思想觉悟、工作能力提高 to temper：在工作中～成长 *grow through work*

断(斷) duàn ㄉㄨㄢˋ ❶长形的东西截成两段或几段 (of a long object) to break：棍子～了。*The stick broke.* | 风筝线～了。*The string of the kite has snapped.* | 把绳子剪～了。*The rope is cut.* ❷隔绝，不继续 to cut off; to stop：～奶 *wean*| ～了关系 *cut off ties* ㊀戒除 to give up; to abstain from：～酒 *give up drinking*| ～烟 *quit smoking*［断送］丧失、毁弃、败坏原来所有而无可挽回 to wreck; to ruin：～前程 *ruin one's future* ❸判断，决定，判定 to make a judgement; to decide：诊～ *to diagnose* | ～案 *settle a lawsuit* | 当机立～ *decide promptly*| 下～语 *make a judgement* ❹一定，绝对 definitely：～无此理 *definitely impossible*［断然］1 坚决，果断 resolutely：～拒绝 *re-*

ject resolutely 2 绝对 absolutely: ～不可妄动 *must absolutely not act rashly*

簖(籪) duàn ㄉㄨㄢˋ 插在水里捕鱼、蟹用的竹栅栏 bamboo trap for catching fish and crabs

DUI ㄉㄨㄟ

堆 duī ㄉㄨㄟ ❶(一子、一儿) 累积在一起的东西 pile: 土～ *mound of earth* | 草～ *hay stack* | 柴火～ *pile of firewood* ❷累积，聚集在一块(㊥一积) to pile up: ～肥 *compost* | 粮食～满仓。*Grain fills the warehouse.* [堆砌]㊐写文章用大量华丽而无用的词语 to fill one's writing with verbose language ❸量词，用于成堆的事物 (measure word) pile: 两～土 *two piles of earth* | 一～事 *a pile of work* | 一～人 *a group of people*

队(隊) duì ㄉㄨㄟˋ ❶有组织的集体或排成的行(háng)列 team: 乐～ *musical band* | 工程～ *construction team* | 排～ *stand in line* [队伍](一wu) 1 军队 military unit; army 2 有组织的群众行列或群体 organised group of people: 游行～过来了。*The marchers are coming.* | 干部～ *team of cadres* ❷在我国特指中国少年先锋队 (specifically in China) Young Pioneers of China: 入～ *join the Young Pioneers of China* ❸量词，用于排成队列的人或物 (measure word) procession; team: 一～人马 *a troop of soldiers*

对(對) duì ㄉㄨㄟˋ ❶答话，回答 to answer; to reply: 无词可～ *be unable to reply* | ～答如流 *answer fluently without hesitation* ❷向着 to face: 面～大海 *face the sea* [对象] 1 思考或行动时作为目标的事物或人 target; object 2 特指恋爱的对方 boyfriend; girlfriend ❸对面的 opposite: ～门 *two houses facing each other; the building or room opposite* | ～岸 *opposite bank* ❹互相 mutually: ～调 *exchange* | ～流 *convection* | ～比 *contrast; antithesis* | ～照 *contrast* ❺介词。对于，引进对象或事物的关系者 (preposition) to; about: ～他说明白。*Explain it clearly to him.* | ～人很和气 *friendly towards people* | 我～这件事情还有意见。*I still have my own opinions about this matter.* | 他～历史很有研究。*He is very knowledgeable about history.* ❻对待，看待，对付 to treat; to deal with: ～事不～人。*It is business and nothing personal.* | 刀～刀，枪～枪 *fight (literally means 'sword against sword and spear against spear')* ❼照着样检查 to check sth against sth else: ～笔迹 *compare handwriting* | 校(jiào)～ *proofread; proofreader* ❽相合，适合 to match; to agree with: ～劲 *compatible; right* | ～症下药 *prescribe the right medicine for an illness; (figurative) prescribe the right remedy for a problem* ❾正

确 correct; right：这话很～。*What is said is absolutely right.* ⓨ用作答语，表示同意 to express agreement：～，你说得不错！*Yes, what you say is right!* ❿双，成双的 pair：～联 *couplet* | 配～ *to pair* ⓨ ①（一子、一儿）联语 couplet：喜～ *congratulatory couplet* ②平分，一半 to halve：～开 *divide into halves* | ～半 *fifty-fifty* ⓫掺和（多指液体）to mix (often liquid)：～水 *add water* ⓬（一儿）量词，双 (measure word) pair; couple：一～鸳鸯 *a pair of mandarin ducks* | 两～夫妻 *two married couples*

怼（懟） duì ㄉㄨㄟˋ 怨恨 resentment

兑 duì ㄉㄨㄟˋ ❶交换（㊀一换）to exchange：～款 *redeem sth for money* | 汇～ *remittance* | ～现 *to cash (a cheque)* ❷掺和，混合 to mix：勾～ *mix* ❸八卦之一，符号是☱，代表沼泽 *dui* (one of the Eight Trigrams used in ancient divination, symbol ☱, representing swamps)

祋 duì ㄉㄨㄟˋ ❶古代的一种兵器 a type of weapon in ancient times ❷姓 (surname) Dui

敦 duì ㄉㄨㄟˋ 古时盛黍稷的器具 container for millet in ancient times

⇨ see also dūn on p.152

镦（鐓） duì ㄉㄨㄟˋ 矛戟柄末端的金属套 metal cap covering the ends of the shafts of spears and halberds

⇨ see also chún on p.95

憝 duì ㄉㄨㄟˋ ❶怨恨 resentment ❷坏，恶 bad; evil：元凶大～ *the arch-criminal*

镦（鐓） duì ㄉㄨㄟˋ same as "镦 (duì)"

⇨ see also dūn on p.153

碓 duì ㄉㄨㄟˋ 捣米的器具，用木、石制成 wood or stone pestle for pounding rice

DUN ㄉㄨㄣ

吨（噸） dūn ㄉㄨㄣ（外 *loan-word*）❶质量单位，法定计量单位中1吨等于1 000千克。英制1吨（长吨）等于2 240磅，合1 016.05千克，美制1吨（短吨）等于2 000磅，合907.18千克 ton ❷指登记吨，计算船只容积的单位，1吨相当于100立方英尺，合2.83立方米 register ton (unit of a ship's internal volume)

惇（*憞） dūn ㄉㄨㄣ 敦厚 honest and sincere

敦（❶❷*敦） dūn ㄉㄨㄣ ❶敦厚，厚道 honest and sincere; kind：～睦邦交 *promote good relations between states* ❷诚心诚意 in all honesty and sincerity：～聘 *earnestly invite (sb to serve in a position)* | ～请 *cordially invite* ❸姓 (surname) Dun

⇨ see also duì on p.152

墩（*墪） dūn ㄉㄨㄣ ❶土堆 mound of earth ❷（一子、一儿）厚而粗的木头、石头等，座儿 a thick block of wood, stone, etc.: 门～ₗ *door buttress* | 桥～ *bridge pier* ❸ 量词，用于丛生的或几棵合在一起的植物 (measure word for plants grouped together) clump: 栽稻秧两万～ *plant 20 000 bundles of rice seedlings* | 每～五株 *bundles of five tree trunks each*

撴 dūn ㄉㄨㄣ 〈方 dialect〉揪住 to grasp

礅 dūn ㄉㄨㄣ 厚而粗的石头 stone block: 石～ *stone block*

镦(鐓) dūn ㄉㄨㄣ 用锤击、加压的方法使坯料变短、变粗。在常温下加工叫冷镦，加热后再加工叫热镦 (in metallurgy) to upset; to stamp

⇨ see also duì on p.152

蹾(撉)** dūn ㄉㄨㄣ 猛地往下放，着(zháo)地很重 to put sth down with force: 篓子里是鸡蛋，别～。*There are eggs in the basket; don't put it down heavily.*

蹲 dūn ㄉㄨㄣ 两腿尽量弯曲，像坐的样子，但臀部不着地 to squat: ～在地上 *squat on the ground* 㐅 闲居 to stay at home idly: 不能再～在家里了。*(I) can't idle at home anymore.* [蹲班] 留级 repeat a year at school: ～生 *(in school) sb who repeats a year* [蹲点] 深入到基层单位，参加实际工作，进行调查研究等 to work/research at grassroots level

⇨ see also cún on p.104

盹 dǔn ㄉㄨㄣˇ (～ₗ) 很短时间的睡眠 nap: 打～ₗ (打瞌睡) *take a nap*

趸(躉) dǔn ㄉㄨㄣˇ ❶整，整数 whole; wholesale: ～批 *wholesale* | ～卖 *sell wholesale* ❷整批地买进 to buy in bulk: ～货 *buy in bulk* | ～菜 *buy vegetables in bulk* | 现～现卖 *teach sb what one has just learnt (literally means 'sell right after buying')*

囤 dùn ㄉㄨㄣˋ 用竹篾、荆条等编成的或用席箔等围成的盛粮食等的器物 grain bin (made of bamboo strips, twigs of chaste tree, or reed): 大～满，小～流。*All bins, big or small, are bursting with grain (from a bumper harvest).*

⇨ see also tún on p.666

沌 dùn ㄉㄨㄣˋ see 混沌 (hùn－) at 混 on page 278

⇨ see also zhuàn on p.872

炖(燉)** dùn ㄉㄨㄣˋ ❶煨煮食物使熟烂 to stew; to simmer: 清～鸡 *stewed chicken in light broth* | ～肉 *stewed meat* ❷〈方 dialect〉把汤药、酒等盛在碗里，再把碗放在水里加热 to heat herb soup, wine, etc. in a bain-marie

砘 dùn ㄉㄨㄣˋ ❶(－子) 耩(jiǎng)完地之后用来轧(yà)地的石磙子 (in agriculture) stone roller for compressing the ground after planting ❷用砘子轧地 to compress the ground using a stone roller

钝(鈍) dùn ㄉㄨㄣˋ ❶不锋利，不快，跟"锐""利""快"相对 blunt (opposite of 锐，利，快): 这把刀真～。*This knife is so blunt.* | 镰

刀～了，磨一磨吧。*The sickle is blunt; please sharpen it.* ❷笨，不灵活 stupid; dull-witted：迟～ *obtuse* | 拙嘴～舌 *inarticulate*

顿(頓) dùn ㄉㄨㄣˋ ❶很短时间的停止（㊀停一）pause：抑扬～挫 *cadence* | 念到这个地方应该～一下。*When you read to this point you should pause.* ❷忽然，立刻，一下子 suddenly; at once：～悟 *be enlightened suddenly* | ～时 *at once* ❸叩，碰 to knock：～首 *kowtow* ㊁ 跺 to stamp one's foot：～足 *stamp one's foot* ❹处理，放置 to handle; to place：整～ *to rectify* | 安～ *to help settle down* ❺书法上指运笔用力向下而暂不移动 (in Chinese calligraphy) a pause in a brushstroke ❻疲乏 tired; fatigued：劳～ *exhausted* | 困～ *exhausted; impoverished* ❼量词，次 measure word for number of times：一天三～饭 *three meals a day* | 说了一～ *gave sb a talking-to* | 打了他一～。*(Sb) gave him a beating.* ❽姓 (surname) Dun

⇨ see also dú on p.147

盾 dùn ㄉㄨㄣˋ ❶古代打仗时防护身体，挡住敌人刀、箭等的牌 (ancient) shield［后盾］指后方护卫、支援的力量 backing; support ❷盾形的东西 shield-shaped object：金～ *gold shield-shaped coin* | 银～ *silver shield-shaped coin* ❸越南等国的货币单位 the currency of Vietnam (Dong), Indonesia (Rupiah), etc.

遁(*遯) dùn ㄉㄨㄣˋ 逃走，逃避（㊀逃一）to escape; to evade：～去 *to escape* | 夜～ *take flight by night*［遁词］［遁辞］理屈词穷时所说的应付话 evasive word

楯 dùn ㄉㄨㄣˋ same as "盾"

⇨ see also shǔn on p.615

DUO ㄉㄨㄛ

多 duō ㄉㄨㄛ ❶跟"少"相对 many; a lot of (opposite of 少) ①数量大的 a large number of：人很～。*There are many people.* | ～打粮食 *harvest more grain* ②有余，比一定的数目大（㊀一余）more; in excess of：十～个 *over ten* | 一年～ *over a year* | 只预备五份，没有～的。*(I) prepared only five; there is no extra.*［多少］1 未定的数量 undetermined quantity: 你要～拿～。*Take as much as you want.* 2 问不知道的数量 how much; how many：这本书～钱？*How much does this book cost?* | 这班有～学生？ *How many students are there in this class?* 3 许多 many; much：没有～ *not many/much* 4 或多或少 more or less：～有些困难。*There will be some difficulties to a certain extent.* ❷过分，不必要的 excessive; unnecessary：～嘴 *have a big mouth* | ～心 *overly sensitive/suspicious* ❸表示相差的程度大 much (used to show a big difference in comparison)：好得～ *much better* | 厚～了 *much* *thicker* ❹副词 adverb ①多么，表示惊异、赞叹 how (used to show surprise, admiration)：～好！*How splendid!*｜～大！ *How big it is!*｜～香！ *How fragrant it is!* ②表疑问 how (used in questions)：有～大？ *How big is it?* [多会儿]（－huir）[多咱]（－zan）什么时候，几时 when; what time

哆 duō ㄉㄨㄛ [哆嗦]（－suo）发抖，战栗 to shiver; to tremble：冷得打～ *shiver with cold*｜吓得浑身～ *tremble all over with fear*

咄 duō ㄉㄨㄛ 呵斥或表示惊异 to berate; to show surprise [咄咄] 表示惊怪 to show amazement：～怪事 *extremely absurd thing* [咄嗟]（－jiē）吆喝 to cry out：～立办（马上就办到）*carry out (an order) immediately*

剟 duō ㄉㄨㄛ ❶刺，击 to stab; to hit ❷削，删除 to cut; to delete

埩 duō ㄉㄨㄛ 用于地名 used in place names：埩～（在广东省吴川）*Tangduo (in Wuchuan, Guangdong Province)*

掇 duō ㄉㄨㄛ ❶拾取（㊇－拾）to pick up ❷〈方 dialect〉用双手拿（椅子、凳子等），用手端 to carry (chairs, benches, etc.) with both hands; to hold

敠 duō ㄉㄨㄛ see 战敠 (diān-duo) at 战 on page 132

裰 duō ㄉㄨㄛ ❶缝补破衣 to patch clothing：补～ *to patch* ❷直裰，古代士子、官绅穿的长袍便服，也指僧道穿的袍子 (ancient) casual long robe (worn by literati and officials); robe worn by Buddhist and Taoist clergy

夺（奪）duó ㄉㄨㄛˊ ❶抢，强取（㊇抢－）to take by force; to wrest：把敌人的枪～过来 *take the enemy's gun by force* [夺目] 耀眼 dazzling：光彩～ *dazzlingly brilliant* ❷争取得到 to strive for：～丰收 *reap a bumper harvest*｜～冠 *win the championship* ❸冲出 to rush out：泪水～眶而出 *tears gush from the eyes*｜～门而出 *dash out through the door* ❹做决定 to decide：定～ *make a final decision*｜裁～ *judge and decide* ❺漏掉（文字）(of written words) to be missing：讹～ *error or omission* ❻失去，使失去 to lose sth; to cause sth to be lost：勿～农时 *do not miss the farming season*｜剥～ *take away*

度 duó ㄉㄨㄛˊ 忖度，揣度，计算，推测 to appraise; to estimate：～德量力 *appraise one's morality and ability*

⇨ see also dù on p.148

踱 duó ㄉㄨㄛˊ 慢慢地走 to walk slowly：～来～去 *pace to and fro*

铎（鐸）duó ㄉㄨㄛˊ 大铃，古代宣布政教法令时或有战事时用 (ancient) large bell used for announcing policies and laws, or in military campaigns

朵（*朶）duǒ ㄉㄨㄛˇ ❶花朵，植物的花或苞 flower; blossom; bud ❷量词，用于花或成团的东西 measure word for flowers,clouds, flower-shaped things, etc.: 三～花 *three flowers*｜一～蘑菇 *one mushroom*｜两～云彩 *two clouds*

垛(*垜) duǒ ㄉㄨㄛˇ (－子) 用泥土、砖石等筑成的掩蔽物 battlements; bulwark: 箭～子 *battlements target for arrows*｜门～子 *door jamb*｜城墙～口 *crenel*

⇨ see also duò on p.156

哚(**哚) duǒ ㄉㄨㄛˇ see 吲哚 (yǐn－) at 吲 on page 782

躲(**躱) duǒ ㄉㄨㄛˇ 隐藏，避开 (㊀－藏、－避) to hide; to avoid: ～雨 *take shelter from the rain*｜他～在哪里? *Where is he hiding?*｜明枪易～，暗箭难防。*An open attack is easy to deal with, but an underhanded assault is not.*

埵 duǒ ㄉㄨㄛˇ 坚硬的土 hard soil

亸(軃、**嚲) duǒ ㄉㄨㄛˇ 下垂 to hang down; to droop

驮(馱) duò ㄉㄨㄛˋ (－子) 骡马等负载的成捆的货物 pack (carried on horseback, etc.): 把～子卸下来，让牲口歇会儿。*Take the pack down and let the animals rest a while.*

⇨ see also tuó on p.668

杕 duò ㄉㄨㄛˋ same as "舵"

⇨ see also dì on p.130

剁(**刴) duò ㄉㄨㄛˋ 用刀向下砍 to chop: ～碎 *chop into small pieces*｜～饺子馅儿 *make the* jiaozi *filling by mincing*

垛(*垜、**稑) duò ㄉㄨㄛˋ ❶整齐地堆成的堆 a neat pile: 麦～ *wheat stack*｜砖～ *brick pile* ❷整齐地堆积 to stack neatly: 柴火～得比房还高。*The firewood is stacked higher than the house.* ❸量词，用于成垛的东西 (measure word) pile: 一～砖 *a pile of bricks*｜两～柴火 *two piles of firewood*

⇨ see also duǒ on p.156

跺(*跥) duò ㄉㄨㄛˋ 顿足，提起脚来用力踏 to stamp: ～脚 *stamp one's foot*

饳(飿) duò ㄉㄨㄛˋ see 馉饳 (gǔ－) at 馉 on page 220

柮 duò ㄉㄨㄛˋ see 榾柮 (gǔ－) at 榾 on page 220

柁 duò ㄉㄨㄛˋ same as "舵"

⇨ see also tuó on p.668

舵 duò ㄉㄨㄛˋ 控制行船方向的设备，多装在船尾 rudder; helm: 掌～ *steer a boat; helmsman*｜～手 *helmsman* 泛指飞机、汽车等控制方向的装置 steering equipment in planes, cars, etc.: ～轮 *steering wheel*｜～盘 *steering wheel*

堕(墮) duò ㄉㄨㄛˋ 掉下来，坠落 to fall: ～地 *fall on the ground* [堕落] ㊋思想行为向坏的方向变化 to degenerate: ～分子 *degenerate person*｜腐化～ *corrupt and degenerate*

惰 duò ㄉㄨㄛˋ 懒，懈怠，跟"勤"相对 (㊀懒－、怠－) lazy (opposite of 勤)

E ㄜ

E ㄜ

阿 ē ㄜ ❶迎合，偏袒 to play up to：～附 *toady to* | ～其所好 *pander to sb's whims* | ～谀逢迎 *butter up* ❷凹曲处 winding area：山～ *mountain bend*

[阿胶] 中药名，用驴皮加水熬成的胶，有滋补养血的作用，原产山东省东阿 E-gelatin (a traditional Chinese tonic made by stewing donkey hide in water)

⇨ see also ā on p.1

屙 ē ㄜ 〈方 dialect〉排泄大小便 to discharge (excrement or urine)：～屎 *to shit* | ～尿 *to piss*

婀 ē ㄜ [婀娜] (-nuó) 姿态柔美的样子 lithe and graceful

讹(訛、❶*譌) é ㄜˊ ❶错误(㊣-误) wrong; erroneous：以～传～ *believe in a wrong message and spread it as such* ❷敲诈，假借某种理由向人强行索取财物或其他权利 to blackmail; to extort：～人 *blackmail sb* | ～诈 *to blackmail*

囮 é ㄜˊ (-子) 捕鸟时用来引诱同类鸟的鸟，又叫圝(yóu)子 decoy bird (also called 圝子)

俄 é ㄜˊ 短时间 shortly; presently [俄而] [俄顷] 一会儿，不久 before long; presently

[俄罗斯族] 1 我国少数民族，参看附录四 the Russian people (one of the ethnic groups in China. See Appendix Ⅳ.) 2 俄罗斯联邦的主要民族 the Russians (the majority people in the Russian Federation)

莪 é ㄜˊ 莪蒿，草本植物，叶像针，生长在水边 sagebrush

[莪术] (-zhú) 草本植物，叶长椭圆形，根状茎可入药 zedoary (*Curcuma zedoaria*) (a plant whose root-stock can be used as Chinese medicine)

哦 é ㄜˊ 吟哦，低声地唱 to chant softly

⇨ see also ó on p.486, ò on p.486

峨(*峩) é ㄜˊ 高 high：巍～ *(of mountains, buildings) lofty* | ～冠 *high hat*

[峨眉] [峨嵋] 山名，在四川省 Emei Mountain (in Sichuan Province)

涐 é ㄜˊ 古水名，即今大渡河 E River (an ancient river name, now called 大渡河)

娥 é ㄜˊ ❶美好(指女性姿态) (of a woman's posture) charming ❷指美女 beauty：宫～ *palace maid* [娥眉] 指美女细长、弯曲的眉毛，也指美女，也作“蛾眉” delicate eyebrows; beauty

E

(also written as 蛾眉)

锇(鋨) é ㄜˊ 金属元素，符号Os，银白色，质硬而脆。可用来制催化剂。它的合金可制耐腐蚀、耐磨部件 osmium (Os)

鹅(鵝、*鵞、*䳘) é ㄜˊ 家禽，身体比鸭子大，颈长，头部有黄色或黑褐色的肉质突起，雄的突起较大，脚有蹼，能游泳 goose

蛾 é ㄜˊ （一子、一儿）昆虫，略像蝴蝶，静止时，翅左右平放 moth：灯～ *moth* | 蚕～ *silk moth* | 飞～投火 *bring destruction upon oneself (literally means 'like a moth darting into flame')*

〈古 ancient〉also same as 蚁 (yǐ)

额(額、*頟) é ㄜˊ ❶额头，俗叫脑门儿，眉毛以上头发以下的部分 (informal 脑门儿) forehead (see picture of 头 on page 660) ❷规定的数量 quota：定～ *set a quota; quota* | 名～ *quota of people* | 超～ *exceed the quota* | ～外 *additional* ❸牌匾 horizontal inscribed board：横～ *horizontal inscribed board* | 匾～ *horizontal inscribed board*

恶(惡、△噁) ě ㄜˇ ［恶心］（—xin）要呕吐 sick; nauseous ⑭厌恶（wù）to detest; to loathe

⇨ see also è on p.158, wū on p.690, wù on p.693

⇨ see also 噁 at è 噁 on p.158

厄(❸*阨、*戹) è ㄜˋ ❶困苦，灾难 adversity; disaster：～运 *misfortune* ❷阻塞，受困 to be stranded：～于海上 *be stranded at sea* ❸险要的地方 strategic point：险～ *place difficult of access*

扼(*搤) è ㄜˋ 用力掐着，抓住 to grip：力能～虎 *strong enough to subdue a tiger* ［扼守］把守要地，防止敌人侵入 to guard (a strategic point) ［扼要］抓住要点 to the point：文章简明～。*The article is brief and to the point.*

苊 è ㄜˋ 有机化合物，无色针状晶体，有致癌作用，可用作媒染剂 acenaphthene

呃 è ㄜˋ 呃逆，因膈痉挛引起的打嗝儿 to hiccup

轭(軛) è ㄜˋ 驾车时搁在牛颈上的曲木 yoke

垩(堊) è ㄜˋ ❶粉刷墙壁用的白土 chalk ❷用白土涂饰 to whitewash

恶(惡) è ㄜˋ ❶恶劣，不好 bad; evil：～感 *ill feeling* | ～习 *bad habit* ❷凶狠（㊀凶一）vicious; ferocious：～狗 *ferocious dog* | ～战 *fierce fighting* | ～霸 *local tyrant* ❸犯罪的事，极坏的行为，跟"善"相对 evil (opposite of 善)：罪～ *crime* | 无～不作 *one's evil doings know no bounds*

⇨ see also ě on p.158, wū on p.690, wù on p.693

噁(噁) è ㄜˋ ［二噁英］一类有毒的含氯有机化合物，有强烈的致畸或致癌作用，进入人体的主要途径是饮食

dioxin

⇨ see also 噁 at ě 恶 on p.158

姶 è ㄜ see 媢 (zhōu) on page 863

饿（餓） è ㄜ 肚子空，想吃东西，跟"饱"相对 hungry (opposite of 饱)：肚子～了 *be hungry*

鄂 è ㄜ 湖北省的别称 another name for Hubei Province [鄂伦春族][鄂温克族] 都是我国少数民族，参看附录四 the Oroqen people; the Ewenki people (Both are ethnic groups in China. See Appendix Ⅳ.)

谔（諤） è ㄜ 言语正直 (of speech) honest and righteous [谔谔] 直言争辩的样子 outspoken

萼（*蕚） è ㄜ 花萼，在花瓣下部的一圈绿色小片 calyx

崿 è ㄜ 山崖 cliff：危岩峭～ *dangerous crags and sheer cliffs*

愕 è ㄜ 惊讶（㊟惊－）astonished：～然 *astounded*

腭（*齶） è ㄜ 口腔的上壁，分为前后两部，前部叫硬腭，后部叫软腭 palate

碍 è ㄜ 用于地名 used in place names：～嘉（在云南省双柏）*Ejia (in Shuangbai, Yunnan Province)*

鹗（鶚） è ㄜ 鸟名，即鱼鹰，背暗褐色，腹白色，常在水面上飞翔，性凶猛，捕食鱼类 (same as 鱼鹰) osprey; fish hawk

锷（鍔） è ㄜ 刀剑的刃 blade (of a sword); edge (of a knife)

颚（顎） è ㄜ ❶某些节肢动物摄取食物的器官 mandible (of some arthropod) ❷ same as "腭"

鳄（鰐、*鱷） è ㄜ 爬行动物，俗叫鳄鱼，皮和鳞很坚硬，性凶恶，生活在热带、亚热带的沿海和河流、池沼中，主要捕食小动物 (informal 鳄鱼) crocodile

堨 è ㄜ 〈方 dialect〉堤坝，多用于地名 dam (often used in place names)：富～（在安徽省歙县）*Fu'e (a place in Shexian, Anhui Province)* | ～头（在浙江省建德）*Etou (a place in Jiande, Zhejiang Province)*

遏 è ㄜ 阻止（㊟－止、阻－）to stop; to hold back：怒不可～ *be beside oneself with anger* [遏制] 制止，控制 to contain：～敌人的进攻 *contain the attack from the enemy* | ～不住满腔的激情 *cannot contain one's passion*

频（頞） è ㄜ 鼻梁 bridge (of the nose)

噩 è ㄜ 可怕而惊人的 shocking：～梦 *nightmare* | ～耗（指亲近或敬爱的人死亡的消息）*sad news (as of the death of a beloved)*

Ê ㄝ

诶（誒） ē ㄝ ēi ㄟ（又）same as "欸 (ē)"

⇨ see also é on p.160, ě on p.160,

ề on p.160

欸 ê̄ ㄝ ēi ㄟ(又) 叹词，表示招呼 (exclamation) used to call attention：～，你快来！*Hey, come over here!*

⇨ see also ǎi on p.3, ế on p.160, ễ on p.160, ề on p.160

诶（誒） ế ㄝ éi ㄟ(又) same as "欸(ế)"

⇨ see also ê̄ on p.159, ễ on p.160, ề on p.160

欸 ế ㄝ éi ㄟ(又) 叹词，表示诧异 (exclamation) used to express surprise：～，怎么回事！*Hey, what's the matter!*

⇨ see also ǎi on p.3, ê̄ on p.160, ễ on p.160, ề on p.160

诶（誒） ễ ㄝ ěi ㄟ(又) same as "欸(ễ)"

⇨ see also ê̄ on p.159, ế on p.160, ề on p.160

欸 ễ ㄝ ěi ㄟ(又) 叹词，表示不以为然 (exclamation) used to express disagreement：～，你这话可不对呀！*Now, you shouldn't say that.*

⇨ see also ǎi on p.3, ê̄ on p.160, ế on p.160, ề on p.160

诶（誒） ề ㄝ èi ㄟ(又) same as "欸(ề)"

⇨ see also ê̄ on p.159, ế on p.160, ễ on p.160

欸 ề ㄝ èi ㄟ(又) 叹词，表示应声或同意 (exclamation) used to express an answer or consent：～，我这就来！*All right, I'm coming.* | ～，就这么办！*Yes, let's do it this way.*

⇨ see also ǎi on p.3, ê̄ on p.160, ế on p.160, ễ on p.160

EI ㄟ

唉 éi ㄟ 叹词，表示诧异或忽然想起 (exclamation) used to express surprise or a sudden idea：～，他怎么病了！*Why, how come he's got ill!* | ～，我三点钟还有一场电影呢！*Oh, I've got a film at 3 o'clock.*

EN ㄣ

恩（*恖） ēn ㄣ 好处，深厚的情谊（㊟－惠、－德）favour; kindness：～情 *loving kindness* | 感～ *feel grateful* [恩爱]（夫妻）亲爱 (of a couple) affectionate to each other

蒽 ēn ㄣ 有机化合物，无色晶体，有紫色荧光，是制染料的原料 anthracene

摁 èn ㄣ 用手按压 to press (with hand)：～电铃 *ring an electric bell* | ～钉儿 *drawing pin* | ～扣儿 *press stud*

ENG ㄥ

鞥 ēng ㄥ 马缰绳 reins (for a horse)

ER 儿

儿（兒） ér 儿 ❶小孩子（㊟－童）child：婴～ *baby* | 幼～ *infant* | ～科 *paediatrics* | ～戏 *trifling matter (lit-*

erally means 'child's play') ❷年轻的人（多指青年男子）youngster (often referring to man)：健～ *strong and energetic youngster* ❸儿子，男孩子 son; boy：他有一～一女。*He has a son and a daughter.* ㊂雄性的 male：～马 *stallion* ❹父母对儿女的统称，儿女对父母的自称 a general term to address one's children; a term used to refer to oneself when addressing one's parents ❺词尾，同前一字连成一个卷舌音 used as a suffix to form a retroflexion with the character before it ①加在名词后，表示小 added to a noun to indicate smallness：小孩～ *kid*｜乒乓球～ *table tennis ball*｜小狗～ *puppy* ②使动词、形容词等名词化 added to a verb or an adjective to turn it into a noun：没救～ *beyond cure*｜拐弯～ *make a turn*｜挡着亮～ *block the light*｜叫好～ *applaud* ③表示具体事物抽象化 used to turn a concrete noun into an abstract one：门～ *way (to do sth)*｜根～ *root cause*

而 ér ㄦˊ 连词 conjunction ①连接同类的词或句子 used to join words or sentences of the same kind 1 顺接 and：聪明～勇敢 *clever and brave*｜通过实践～发现真理，又通过实践～证实真理和发展真理。*Truth is discovered through practice and in turn truth is proved and developed through practice.* 2 转接 but：有其名～无其实 *in name but not in fact*［而且］连词 conjunction 1 表示平列 (used to indicate coordination) and：这篇文章写得长～空。*The article is lengthy and empty.* 2 表示进一层，常跟"不但"相应 often used with 不但 to indicate progression：鲁迅不但是伟大的文学家，～是伟大的思想家和革命家。*Lu Xun is not only a great writer, but also a great thinker and revolutionary.*［而已］助词，罢了 (auxiliary word) only; just：不过如此～ *just so-so* ②把表时间、原因或情状的词连接到动词上 used to connect an adverbial phrase of time, cause or manner with a verb：匆匆～来 *come in a hurry*｜因公～死 *die in the line of duty*｜侃侃～谈 *talk with ease and fluency*｜挺身～出 *step forward bravely* ③（从）……到…… (from)...to...：自上～下 *from top to bottom*｜由小～大 *from small to large*

陑 ér ㄦˊ 古山名，在今山西省永济南 Er Mountain (ancient name for a mountain in the south of today's Yongji, Shanxi Province)

耏 ér ㄦˊ ❶面颊上的胡须 whiskers ❷姓 (surname) Er

⇨ see also nài on p.469

洏 ér ㄦˊ see 涟洏 (lián－) at 涟 on page 396

鸸（鴯） ér ㄦˊ ［鸸鹋］（－miáo）鸟名，外形像鸵鸟，嘴短而扁，脚有三个趾。善走，不能飞，产于澳大利亚的草原和开阔的森林中 emu

鲕（鮞） ér ㄦˊ 鱼苗 (of fish) fry

尔(爾、*尒) ěr ㄦˇ ❶代词 pronoun ①你，你的 you; your：～辈 *you people* | ～父 *your father* | 出～反～（指反复无常）*go back on one's word* [尔汝] 你我相称，关系亲密 intimate：相为～ *be very intimate* | ～交 *be on very intimate terms* ②如此 ㊀so：果～ *if so* | 偶～ *occasionally* | 不过～～ *just so-so* ③那，其（指时间）(of time) that：～时 *at that time* | ～日 *that day* | ～后 *thereafter* ❷ same as "耳❸" ❸词尾，相当于"然" suffix, equivalent to 然：卓～ *outstanding* | 率～（轻率）*rashly*

迩(邇) ěr ㄦˇ 近 close：遐(xiá)～闻名(遐：远) *be well-known far and near* | ～来（近来）*(in) recent days*

耳 ěr ㄦˇ ❶耳朵，人和动物的听觉器官 ear：～聋 *deaf* | ～熟（听着熟悉）*familiar to the ear* | ～生（听着生疏）*unfamiliar to the ear* | ～语（嘴贴近别人耳朵小声说话）*whisper in sb's ear* ❷像耳朵的 ear-like ①指形状 (of shape)：木～ *edible tree fungus* | 银～ *tremella* ②指位置在两旁的 on either side：～房 *side room* | ～门 *side door* ❸文言助词，表示罢了，而已 (auxiliary word in classical Chinese) only; just：前言戏之～。*What I just said was only a joke.* | 此无他，唯手熟～。*It is just that I am an old hand at it.*

饵(餌) ěr ㄦˇ ❶糕饼 cakes：香～ *nice cakes* | 果～ *sweets and snacks* ❷钓鱼用的鱼食 bait：鱼～ *bait* ❸引诱 to entice：以此～敌 *entice the enemy with this*

洱 ěr ㄦˇ 洱海，湖名，在云南省大理 Erhai Lake (in Dali, Yunnan Province)

駬(駬) ěr ㄦˇ see 騄駬 (lù–) at 騄 on page 420

珥 ěr ㄦˇ 用珠子或玉石做的耳环 jade or pearl earrings

铒(鉺) ěr ㄦˇ 金属元素，符号 Er，银灰色，质软，可用来制特种合金、激光器等 erbium (Er)

二 èr ㄦˋ ❶数目字 two：十～个 *twelve* | 两元～角 *two yuan and two* jiao (see the note for 两 on page 399 for the differences between 二 and 两) ❷第二，次的 second; secondary：～等货 *second-class goods* | ～把刀（指技术不高）*incompetent* [二手] 1 旧的，用过的 second-hand; used：～车 *second-hand car* | ～货 *second-hand goods* 2 间接的 second-hand; indirect：～资料 *second-hand materials* ❸两样 different：心无～用。*One should concentrate on one thing at a time.*

弍 èr ㄦˋ same as "二"

贰(貳) èr ㄦˋ "二"字的大写 elaborate form of 二

佴 èr ㄦˋ 置，停留 to stay
⇨ see also nài on p.469

咡 èr ㄦˋ ❶口旁；两颊 cheek ❷用于地名 used in place names：咪～（在云南省彝良）*Mi'er (in Yiliang, Yunnan Province)*

F ㄈ

FA ㄈㄚ

发(發) fā ㄈㄚ ❶交付，送出，跟“收”相对 to give out; to send out (opposite of 收)：分～ *hand out* | ～选民证 *hand out elector's certificate* | ～货 *dispatch goods* | 信已经～了。*The letter has been sent out.* [发落] 处理，处分 to deal with：从轻～ *deal with sb leniently* [打发] (—fa) 1 派遣 to dispatch sb on an errand：～专人去办 *send sb to do it* 2 使离去 to dismiss; to send away：好不容易才把他～走了。*It took much effort to send him away.* 3 消磨(时日) to kill (time)：～时光 *kill time* ❷表达，说出 to express：～言 *make a speech* | ～问 *ask a question* | ～誓 *take an oath* | ～表 *to issue; to publish* ❸放射 to launch; to fire：～炮 *fire a cannon* | ～光 *give off light* ㊀ 量词，用于枪弹、炮弹 measure word for bullets and shells：五十～子弹 *fifty bullets* ❹散开，分散 to disperse; to spread out：～汗 *induce perspiration* | 挥～ *volatilize* | 蒸～ *evaporate* [发挥] 把意思尽量地说出，把能力尽量地表现出 to elaborate; to bring into play：借题～ *seize upon a pretext and make a fuss* | ～群众的智慧和力量 *give play to the wisdom and strength of the masses* ❺开展，扩大，膨胀 to expand; to develop：～扬 *carry forward* | ～展 *to develop* | ～海带 *soak dried kelp* | 面～了。*The dough has risen.* [发育] 生物逐渐成长壮大 to grow：身体～正常。*The physical development is normal.* ❻因得到大量资财而兴旺 to become rich：～家 *build up a family fortune* | 暴～户 *upstart* | 这几年他做买卖～了。*He has made a fortune in business these years.* ❼打开，揭露 to open up; to expose：～掘潜力 *tap potential* | 揭～ *expose* [发明] 创造出以前没有的事物 to invent：印刷术是我国首先～的。*Printing was first invented in China.* [发现] 1 找出原先存在而大家不知道的事物或道理 to discover：～新油田 *discover a new oil-field* 2 发觉 to notice：～问题就及时解决。*Deal with a problem as soon as it is detected.* ❽显现，散发 to appear; to become：脸上～黄。*The face appears sallow.* | ～潮 *become damp* | ～臭 *smell bad* | ～酸 *turn sour* ❾产生，发生 to produce：～芽 *to sprout* | ～病 *fall ill* ㊀ 流露 to show：～怒 *get angry* | ～笑 *burst out laughing* ❿感到(多用于令人不快的情况) to feel (usually sth unpleasant)：～麻 *feel numb* | ～烧

have a fever ⓫开始动作，起程 to start; to set out：～端 *make a start* | 朝～夕至 *set off in the morning and arrive in the evening* | ～动 *to start; call into action* | 出～ *set out*

⇨ see also fà on p.164

乏 fá ㄈㄚˊ ❶缺少（㊀缺－）to lack：～味 *tasteless; dull* | 不～其人。*There is no lack of such people.* ❷疲倦（㊀疲－）tired：人困马～ *be completely worn out* | 跑了一天，身上有点儿～。*(I've) been busy all day, so feel a little tired.*

伐 fá ㄈㄚˊ ❶砍 to fell; to cut down：～树 *fell trees* | 采～ *to fell* ❷征讨，攻打（㊀讨－）to attack：北～ *northward expedition* | 口诛笔～ *condemn both in speech and in writing*

垡 fá ㄈㄚˊ ❶〈方 dialect〉耕地，把土翻起来 to turn up soil：秋～地（秋耕）*autumn ploughing* 也指翻起来的土块 upturned soil：晒～ *aerate the soil* ❷用于地名 used in place names：榆～（在北京市大兴）*Yufa (in Daxing, Beijing)*

阀（閥） fá ㄈㄚˊ ❶封建时代指有权势的家庭、家族 powerful family (in feudal times)：门～ *family of power and influence* | ～阅之家 *distinguished family* ❷凭借权势造成特殊地位的个人或集团 powerful person/group：军～ *warlord* | 财～ *tycoon* ❸（外 loanword）阀门，管道、唧筒或机器中调节控制流体的流量、压力和流动方向的装置 valve：水～ *water valve* | 气～ *air valve* | 油～ *oil valve*

筏（*栰） fá ㄈㄚˊ （－子）用竹、木平摆着编扎成的水上交通工具，也有用牛羊皮或橡胶制成的 raft

罚（罸、*罰） fá ㄈㄚˊ 处分犯错误和犯罪的人（㊀惩－、责－）to punish：他因违纪而受～了。*He was punished for breaking the rules.*

法（❶–❺*灋、❶–❺*㳒） fǎ ㄈㄚˇ ❶法律、法令、条例等的总称 law：婚姻～ *marriage law* | 犯～ *break the law* | 合～ *legitimate* | 依～治国 *rule the state by law* ❷（－子、－儿）方法，处理事物的手段 method：写～ *way of writing* | 办～ *method* | 用～ *usage* | 没～儿办 *be impossible to do* ❸仿效 to follow：效～ *follow the example of* | 师～ *model oneself after (a great master)* ❹标准，模范，可仿效的 standard; model：～书 *model calligraphy* | ～绘 *model painting* | ～帖 *model calligraphy* ❺佛教徒称他们的教义，民间传说的所谓"超人力"的本领 dharma; magic：佛～ *Buddhist doctrine; power of Buddha* | ～术 *magic arts* ❻电容单位名法拉的简称，符号 F。farad (F)

砝 fǎ ㄈㄚˇ ［砝码］（－mǎ）天平上用作重量标准的东西，用金属制成 (on a balance) weight

发（髮） fà ㄈㄚˋ 头发 hair：理～ *have a haircut* | 脱～ *lose one's hair* | 令人～指

（形容使人非常气愤）*make one feel extremely angry*

⇨ see also fā on p.163

珐（*琺） fà ㄈㄚˋ ［珐琅］（—láng）用石英、长石、硼砂、纯碱等烧制成的像釉子的物质。涂在铜质或银质器物的表面作为装饰，又可防锈。用来制景泰蓝、证章、纪念章等。也指珐琅制品 enamel; enamelware

FAN ㄈㄢ

帆（*帆、*颿） fān ㄈㄢ 利用风力使船前进的布篷 sail：白～ *white sail* | ～船 *sailing boat* | 一～风顺 *plain sailing*

番 fān ㄈㄢ ❶称外国的或外族的 foreign：～茄 *tomato* | ～薯 *sweet potato* | ～椒 *chilli; pepper* ❷量词 measure word ①遍，次 times：三～五次 *time and again* | 费了一～心思 *take some thinking* | 解说一～ *give an explanation* | 产量翻了一～。*The output doubled.* ②种，样 kind：别有一～滋味 *have an altogether different flavour; (figurative) have a different and special feeling*

⇨ see also pān on p.490

蕃 fān ㄈㄢ same as “番（fān）❶”

⇨ see also bō on p.48, fán on p.166

幡（**旛） fān ㄈㄢ 用竹竿等挑起来直着挂的长条形旗子 streamer

藩 fān ㄈㄢ 藩篱，篱笆 fence ⑩用作保卫的屏障，封建时代用来称属国、属地 screen; vassal; feudatory：～国 *vassal state* | ～属 *vassal state*

翻（*飜） fān ㄈㄢ ❶歪倒（dǎo），或上下、内外移位 to turn over / upside down / inside out：～身 *turn over; (figurative) free oneself* | 车～了。*The car turned over.* | ～修 *to renovate* | 别把书～乱了。*Don't mess up the books.* ❷改变 to change; to overturn：～改 *to make over (clothes)* | ～案 *overturn a verdict* ❸数量成倍增加 to multiply; to double：产量～一番。*The output doubled.* ❹翻译，把一种语文译成另一种语文 to translate; to interpret：把外国名著～成中文。*Translate foreign masterpieces into Chinese.* ❺（—儿）翻脸 to fall out; to turn hostile：闹～了 *fell out (with sb)*

凡（*凢） fán ㄈㄢˊ ❶平常，普通 commonplace; ordinary：～人 *ordinary people* | 平～ *ordinary* ❷宗教、神话或迷信的人称人世间 this mortal world：神仙下～。*Immortals descend to the earth.* ❸凡是，所有的 all：～事要跟群众商量。*Whatever (we) do, (we) must consult with the masses.* ❹概要，要略 gist; outline; summary：发～起例 *introduce (a book) and give a guide (to its use)* ［凡例］书前面说明内容和体例的文字 editorial guide ❺总共 altogether：全书～十卷。*The book has altogether 10 volumes.*

F

矾(礬) fán ㄈㄢˊ 某些金属硫酸盐的含水结晶。如明矾（硫酸钾铝，又叫白矾）、胆矾（硫酸铜）、绿矾（硫酸亚铁） vitriol

钒(釩) fán ㄈㄢˊ 金属元素，符号V，银白色，质硬。可用来制合金钢等 vanadium (V)

氾 fán ㄈㄢˊ 姓 (surname) Fan
⇨ see also fàn 泛 on p.168

烦(煩) fán ㄈㄢˊ ❶苦闷，急躁 restless; vexed: ～恼 *worried* | 心～意乱 *perturbed* | 心里有点儿～ *feel a little upset* ❷厌烦，使厌烦 fed up; tired; annoying: 不耐～ *impatient* | 这些话都听～了。*(I) am tired of listening to all this.* | ～人 *annoying* ❸又多又乱 superfluous and confusing: 要言不～ *succinct* | 絮～ *fed up (with monotonous repetition)* [烦琐] 繁杂琐碎 complicated and overloaded ❹敬辞，表示请托 (polite speech) to trouble: ～你做点儿事。*Would you please do me a favour?*

墦 fán ㄈㄢˊ 坟墓 tomb

蕃 fán ㄈㄢˊ 草木茂盛 (of vegetation) luxuriant: ～盛 *luxuriant* ㊟繁多 various: ～衍（逐渐增多或增广，现作“繁衍”）*to multiply; increase gradually (now written as* 繁衍*)*
⇨ see also bō on p.48, fān on p.165

璠 fán ㄈㄢˊ 美玉 jade

膰 fán ㄈㄢˊ 古代祭祀时用的熟肉 sacrificial meat in ancient times

燔 fán ㄈㄢˊ ❶焚烧 to burn ❷烤 to toast

镭(鐇) fán ㄈㄢˊ 古代的一种铲子 an ancient shovel

鷭(鷭) fán ㄈㄢˊ 鸟名，即骨顶鸡，头颈黑色，额部有角质骨顶，生活在河流、沼泽地带，善游泳 coot (same as 骨顶鸡)

蹯 fán ㄈㄢˊ 兽足 paw: 熊～（熊掌）*bear's paw*

樊 fán ㄈㄢˊ 篱笆 fence [樊篱] 篱笆 fence ㊟限制人或事物的制度、习俗等 barrier

繁(*緐) fán ㄈㄢˊ ❶复杂，跟“简”相对（㊧—杂）complicated (opposite of 简): 删～就简 *simplify sth by cutting out the superfluous* ❷滋生 to multiply: ～衍 *to multiply* | ～殖 *to breed; to reproduce* ❸许多，不少 numerous: ～多 *various* | ～密 *dense* | ～星 *constellations* | 实～有徒（这种人实在很多）。*Such people are to be found everywhere.* [繁华] 市面热闹，工商业兴盛 thriving; flourishing [繁荣] 兴旺发展或使兴旺发展 prosperous; to prosper: 市场～ *flourishing market* | ～经济 *boost the economy*
⇨ see also pó on p.510

蘩 fán ㄈㄢˊ 草本植物，即白蒿，可入药 wormwood (same as 白蒿)

反 fǎn ㄈㄢˇ ❶翻转，颠倒 to turn over: ～败为胜 *convert*

defeat into victory | ～守为攻 *turn defence into offence* | 易如～掌 *as easy as turning one's palm over* ⓨ 翻转的，颠倒的，跟"正"相对 reverse (opposite of 正)：～面 *reverse side* | ～穿皮袄 *wear one's fur coat inside out* | 放～了 *put sth the opposite way around* | 图章上刻的字是～的。*Characters inscribed on a stamp are reversed.* [反复] 1 翻来覆去 to chop and change：～无常 *changeable* 2 重复 repeatedly; again and again：～练习 *practise repeatedly* ❷表示和原来的或预想的不同 on the contrary; instead：～常 *abnormal*| 画虎不成～类犬 *set out to draw a tiger and end up with the likeness of a dog; (figurative) aim high but achieve little; (figurative) make a poor imitation* [反而] [反倒] (－dào) 副词，表示跟上文意思正相反或出乎预期和常情 (adverb) conversely; on the contrary：希望他走，他～坐下了。*It was hoped he would leave, but instead he sat down.* ❸反对，反抗 to oppose：～浪费 *combat waste* | ～腐败 *combat corruption* | ～封建 *oppose feudalism* | ～法西斯 *fight against fascism* ❹类推 to analogise：举一～三 *make inferences by analogy* ❺回，还 to return; to counter：～攻 *to counter-attack* | ～求诸己 *seek the cause in oneself; impose a demand on oneself* [反省] (－xǐng) 对自己的思想行为加以检查 to introspect ❻ (ancient) same as "返"

返 fǎn ㄈㄢˇ 回，归 to return：往～ *travel to and fro* | 一去不复～ *once gone will not return* [返工] 工作没有做好再重做 redo sth poorly done

犯 fàn ㄈㄢˋ ❶抵触，违反 to violate：～法 *break the law* | ～规 *to foul* ❷犯罪的人 criminal：战～ *war criminal* | 要～ *principal criminal* | 贪污～ *embezzler* ❸侵犯，进攻 to attack：人不～我，我不～人；人若～我，我必～人。*We will not attack unless we are attacked; if we are attacked, we will certainly counterattack.* ❹发作，发生 to suffer; to recur; to commit：～病 *suffer recurrence of an illness* | ～脾气 *flare up* | ～错误 *make a mistake* [犯不着] (－－zháo) [犯不上] 不值得 not worthwhile：你～和他生气。*It is not worth your while to get angry at him.*

范 (❶–❹範) fàn ㄈㄢˋ ❶模(mú)子 mould：钱～ *coin mould* ❷范围，一定的界限 boundary：就～ (喻听从支配和控制) *to submit; give up* [范畴] 1 概括性最高的基本概念，如化合、分解是化学的范畴；矛盾、质和量等是哲学的范畴 category 2 类型，范围 scope ❸模范，榜样 example; model：示～ *to demonstrate; to show how* | 师～ *teacher-training school; model* | ～例 *example* ❹限制 restriction：防～ *be on guard* ❺姓 (surname) Fan

饭 (飯) fàn ㄈㄢˋ ❶煮熟的谷类食品，特指大米

F

饭 cooked cereals; (specifically) cooked rice ❷每日定时吃的食物 meal：午～ *lunch* | 开～ *serve a meal; (of a canteen) to open*

贩（販）fàn ㄈㄢˋ ❶为获利而买货出卖 to buy to resell for profit：～货 *buy goods for resale* | ～了一群羊来 *bought a flock of sheep for resale* ❷（－子）买货出卖的人 trader：菜～子 *greengrocer* | 摊～ *street pedlar*

畈 fàn ㄈㄢˋ 〈方 dialect〉田地，多用于村镇名 (often used in names of villages and towns) land

泛（*汎、❸❹△*氾）fàn ㄈㄢˋ ❶漂浮 to float：～舟 *go boating* ㊀浮现，透出 to emerge; to penetrate through sth：脸上～红。*The cheeks were suffused with blushes.* ❷浮浅，不深入 ㊂superficial：～～之交（友谊不深）*nodding acquaintance* | 浮～之论 *superficial argument* ❸广泛，一般地 general：～览 *to read extensively* | ～问 *aimless question* | ～论 *general discussion; make casual comments* | ～称 *general term* ❹水向四处漫流 to overflow：～滥 *to flood; (figurative) spread unchecked*

⇨ 氾 see also fán on p.166

梵 fàn ㄈㄢˋ 梵语音译"梵摩"的省称，意思是清静，常指关于古印度或佛教的 short for 梵摩, from Sanskrit, meaning peaceful and quiet, usually of ancient India or Buddhism：～文 *Sanskrit* | ～宫 *Buddhist temple* | ～刹 *Buddhist temple* [梵语] 印度古代的一种语言 Sanskrit

FANG ㄈㄤ

方 fāng ㄈㄤ ❶四个角全是直角的四边形或六个面全是方形的六面体 square; cuboid：正～ *square* | 长～ *rectangle* | 见～（长宽或长宽高相等）*square* | 平～米 *square metre* | 立～米 *cubic metre* ㊀乘方，一个数自乘若干次的积数 (in mathematics) power：平～（自乘两次）*to square* | 立～（自乘三次）*to cube* [方寸] 指内心 state of mind：～已乱 *greatly agitated* [方圆] 周围 circumference：这个城～有四五十里。*The town is about forty to fifty* li *in circumference.* ❷正直 upright; virtuous：品行～正 *be honest and fair* ❸方向，方面 direction; side：前～ *ahead; the front* | 四～ *four directions* | 双～ *both sides* | 对～ *the other/opposite side* | 四面八～ *all directions* ㊀一个区域的，一个地带的 regional; local：～言 *dialect* | ～志 *local records* [方向] 1 东、西、南、北的区分 direction：航行的～ *navigation direction* 2 目标 orientation：做事情要认清～。*When doing sth go in the right direction.* ❹方法，法子 way; method：教导有～ *good at teaching and providing guidance* | 千～百计 *by every conceivable means* ㊀（－子、－儿）药方，配药的单子 prescription：偏～ *folk*

F

prescription | 秘～ *secret prescription* | 开～子 *write a prescription* [方式] 说话、做事所采取的方法和形式 way; approach ❺副词，才 (adverb) just; only：书到用时～恨少。*You will only realize your knowledge is not enough when you need it.* ❻副词，正，正当 (adverb) just when：来日～长。*There will be plenty of time.* ❼量词 measure word ①指平方米（用于墙、地板等）或立方米（用于土、沙、石、木材等）square metre; cubic metre ②用于方形的东西 of square things：一～图章 *a seal* | 三～砚台 *three ink-stones*

邡 fāng ㄈㄤ [什邡] 地名，在四川省 Shifang (a place in Sichuan Province)

坊 fāng ㄈㄤ ❶里巷，多用于街巷的名称 (often used in names of streets or lanes) lane ㊥ 街市，市中店铺 street stall：～间 *in the market; (especially) book store* ❷牌坊，旧时为旌表功德、宣扬封建礼教而建造的建筑物 (old) memorial arch：贞节～ *chastity arch*

⇨ see also fáng on p.169

芳 fāng ㄈㄤ 芳香，花草的香味 fragrance ㊥ 美好的德行或声名 virtue; good reputation：流～百世 *leave a lasting reputation*

枋 fāng ㄈㄤ 方柱形木材 squared timber

牥 fāng ㄈㄤ 古代传说中的一种牛，能在沙漠中行走 a legendary ox that can walk in the desert

钫（鈁） fāng ㄈㄤ ❶放射性金属元素，符号 Fr。francium (Fr) ❷古代一种酒壶，方口大腹 a kind of square-mouthed and big-bellied wine vessel in ancient times

蚄 fāng ㄈㄤ see 虸蚄（zǐ－）at 虸 on page 882

防 fáng ㄈㄤˊ ❶防备，戒备 to prevent; to guard against：～御 *guard against* | ～守 *to defend* | 预～ *to prevent* | 军民联～ *army-civilian joint defence* | 冷不～ *suddenly* | 谨～假冒。*Beware of imitation.* [国防] 为了保卫国家的领土、主权而部署的一切防务 national defence：～军 *national defence forces* | ～要地 *strategic national defence point* ❷堤，挡水的建筑物 dyke

坊 fáng ㄈㄤˊ 作（zuō）坊，某些小手工业的工作场所 workshop：染～ *dyeworks* | 油～ *oil mill* | 粉～ *starch-noodle mill* | 磨～ *mill*

⇨ see also fāng on p.169

妨 fáng ㄈㄤˊ 妨害，阻碍（㊥－碍）to hinder; to hamper; to obsruct：无～ *do no harm* [不妨] 没有什么不可以 might as well：～试试。*You might as well give it a try.* [何妨] 用反问语气表示"不妨" used in rhetorical question to mean 不妨：你～去看看。*Why don't you go and have a look?*

肪 fáng ㄈㄤˊ see 脂肪 at 脂 on page 852

房 fáng ㄈㄤˊ ❶（－子）住人或放东西用的建筑物（㊥

一屋）house：楼～ *multi-storey building* | 瓦～（见下图）*tile-roofed house (see picture below)* | 库～ *storehouse* ❷形状、作用像房子的 house-like structure：蜂～ *beehive* | 莲～ *lotus pod* | 心～ *atrium (of the heart); heart* ❸称家族的一支 branch of an extended family：大～ *eldest branch* | 长（zhǎng）～ *eldest branch* ❹星宿名，二十八宿之一 *fang* (one of the twenty-eight constellations in ancient Chinese astronomy)

鲂（魴） fáng ㄈㄤˊ 鱼名，像鳊（biān）鱼，银灰色，背部隆起，生活在淡水中 triangular bream

仿（❶-❸*倣、❹*髣） fǎng ㄈㄤˇ ❶效法，照样做（㊎一效）to imitate：～造 *model on/after* | ～制 *copy (in making sth)* ❷依照范本写的字 characters written after a calligraphy model：写

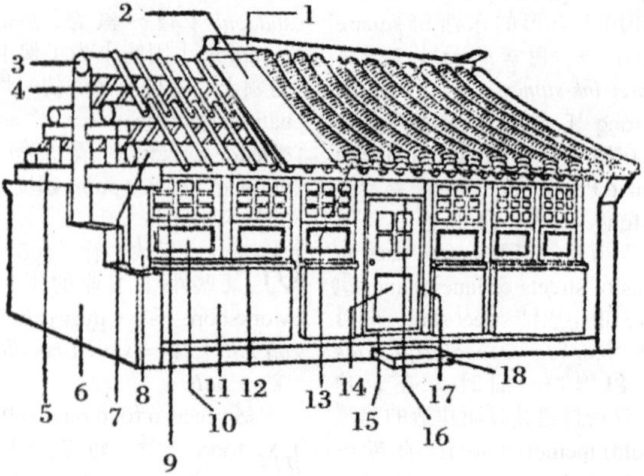

房屋的构造 structure of a house

1 屋脊 *roof ridge*
2 苫背 *thatch with straw mat, tarpaulin, etc.*
3 脊檩 *ridgepole*
4 椽子 *rafter*
5 梁 *roof beam*
6 山墙 *gable*
7 檩 *purlin*
8 柱子 *pillar*
9 窗格子 *window lattice*
10 窗户 *window*
11 墙 *wall*
12 窗台 *windowsill*
13 檐 *eaves*
14 门 *door*
15 门槛 *threshold*
16 门楣 *lintel*
17 门框 *doorframe*
18 台阶 *steps*

了一张～ *have written a page of Chinese characters after a calligraphy model* ❸类似 to resemble：二人年纪相～。*The two are about the same age.* ❹［仿佛］（*彷佛、*髣髴）（—fú）1 好像 seemingly：这个人我～在哪里见过。*I seem to have met this person somewhere.* 2 像，类似 to be similar：弟兄俩长得相～。*The two brothers look very much alike.*

访（訪） fǎng ㄈㄤˇ ❶向人询问调查 to inquire：～查 *to investigate* | ～贫问苦 *visit the impoverished and the wretched* | 采～ *(of journalist) to interview* ❷探问，看望 to visit：～友 *call on a friend* | ～古（古迹）*search for ancient relics* ［访问］有目的地看望，探问 to visit：～劳动模范 *call on model workers* | 出国～ *visit a foreign country*

彷 fǎng ㄈㄤˇ ［彷佛］(ancient) same as "仿佛" (see 仿❹ on page 170 for reference)

⇨ see also páng on p.492

纺（紡） fǎng ㄈㄤˇ ❶把丝、棉、麻、毛或人造纤维等做成纱 to spin：～纱 *spin yarn* | ～棉花 *spin cotton* ❷纺绸，一种绸子 thin silk cloth：杭（杭州）～ *Hangzhou silk* | 富春～ *Fuchun silk*

昉 fǎng ㄈㄤˇ ❶明亮 bright ❷起始 to begin

舫 fǎng ㄈㄤˇ 船 boat：画～（装饰华美专供游览用的船）*gaily-painted pleasure boat* | 游～ *pleasure boat*

放 fàng ㄈㄤˋ ❶解除约束，得到自由 to let go; to set free：～行 *allow to pass* | 释～ *to release* | 把笼子里的鸟～了。*Let the birds out of the cage.* ㊀ ①赶牲畜、家禽到野外去觅食 to put out to feed：～牛 *graze cattle* | ～羊 *graze sheep* | ～鸭子 *tend ducks* ②散（sàn）to dismiss; to let out：～工 *(of workers) knock off* | ～学 *dismiss class; have school holidays* ［放晴］阴雨后转晴 (of weather) to clear up ❷任意，随便 to act with abandon; to give way to：～任 *give free reign to* | ～纵 *to indulge; self-indulgent* | ～肆 *wanton* ❸发出 to give off：～枪 *fire a gun* | ～光 *emit light* | ～电 *discharge electricity* ❹发物给人 to distribute; to hand out：～粮 *distribute relief grain* | ～赈 *provide disaster relief* ㊀ 借钱给人，收取利息 to loan：～款 *grant a loan* ❺点燃 to light：～火 *set on fire* | ～鞭炮 *let off firecrackers* ❻扩展 to expand：～大 *to enlarge* | ～宽 *to relax (requirements); to lift (restriction)* | 把领子～出半寸。*Let out the collar by half a* cun. ㊀ 花开 to bloom：芦花～，稻谷香。*The reeds are flowering and the paddy fields are fragrant.* | 心花怒～ *be elated* ❼搁，置 to put：存～ *to store* | ～在箱子里 *put in the box* ［放心］安心，解除忧虑和牵挂 to rest assured：～吧，一切都准备好了！ *Rest assured! Everything is ready.* ❽流放，旧时把人驱逐到边远的地方去 to exile：～逐 *to*

F

exile

FEI ㄈㄟ

飞(飛) fēi ㄈㄟ ❶鸟类或虫类等用翅膀在空中往来活动 to fly：～行 *to fly* | ～鸟 *flying bird* | ～虫 *winged insect* ㉠物体在空中飘荡或行动 to float; to fly：～沙走石 *sand flying and pebbles rolling* | 飞机向东～。*The plane flies eastwards.* ❷快，像飞似的 rapidly：～奔 *to dash* | ～跑 *run very fast* ❸指无根据的，无缘无故的 groundless：流言～语 *unfounded rumours* | ～灾 *unexpected disaster* ❹（外 loanword）法定计量单位中十进分数单位词头之一，表示 10^{-15}，符号 f。(one of the prefixes of legal units of measurement in decimal fractions for 10^{-15}) femto (f)

妃 fēi ㄈㄟ ❶古代皇帝的妾，地位次于皇后 imperial concubine ❷太子、王、侯的妻 wife of a prince, etc.：王～ *princess consort; consort of a prince*

非 fēi ㄈㄟ ❶不，不是 no; not: 莫～ *can it be that* | 答～所问 *give an irrelevant answer* [非常] 1 异乎寻常的 extraordinary：～时期 *time of emergency* 2 副词，十分，极 (adverb) very; extremely：～光荣 *very honourable* | ～高兴 *very happy* ❷错误，跟"是"相对 wrong (opposite of 是)：明辨是～ *make a clear distinction between right and wrong* | 为～作歹 *do evils* | 痛改前～ *make a clean break with one's past errors* ❸名词词头，表示不属于某个范围 (noun prefix) non-：～卖品 *article not for sale* | ～金属 *nonmetal* | ～对抗性矛盾 *non-antagonistic contradiction* ❹不合于 to run counter to：～法 *illegal* | ～礼 *impolite; harass sexually* ❺副词，跟"不"搭用，表示必须，一定（有时后面没有"不"字）(adverb, used in combination with 不, but sometimes without 不) must：他～去不可。*He's got to go.* | 不让他去，他～去。*(We) didn't want him to go, but he insisted.* ❻以为不对，不以为然 to blame; to find fault with：～笑（讥笑）*to ridicule* | ～议 *to reproach* [非难]（－nàn）责备 to reproach ❼指非洲，世界七大洲之一 Africa

菲 fēi ㄈㄟ 花草茂盛 (of flowers and grass) luxuriant：芳～ *(of flowers and grass) fragrant and gorgeous; flowers and grass*

⇨ see also fěi on p.174

啡 fēi ㄈㄟ see 吗啡 (mǎ－) at 吗 on page 432, and 咖啡 (kā－) at 咖 on page 347

騑(騑) fēi ㄈㄟ 古时一车驾四马，中间两马叫服马，两旁的马叫騑马，又叫骖马 (of horse-drawn carriage) side horses (near the shaft)(also called 骖马)

绯(緋) fēi ㄈㄟ 红色 red：两颊～红 *bright red cheeks* | ～闻（跟不正当的男女关系有关的消息）*sex scandal*

扉 fēi ㄈㄟ 门扇 door leaf：柴～ *wicker gate* [扉页] 书

刊封面之内印着书名、著者等项的一页 title page［扉画］书籍正文前的插图 illustration before the text of a book

蜚 fēi ㄈㄟ (ancient) same as "飞"

➪ see also fěi on p.174

霏 fēi ㄈㄟ ❶（雨、雪、云气等）很盛的样子 ㊜ (of rain and snow) thick and fast; (of clouds and fog) heavy: 雨雪～～。*It is snowing thick and fast.* ❷ 云气 thin, floating cloud: 日出而林～开。*The sun rises and the thin clouds in the forest disperse.* ❸ 飘扬 drift in the air: 烟～云敛。*The smoke diffuses while the clouds disperse.*

鲱（鯡） fēi ㄈㄟ 鱼名，身体侧扁而长，生活在海洋里。种类很多，是世界上重要的经济鱼类 Pacific herring

肥 féi ㄈㄟˊ ❶含脂肪多，跟"瘦"相对 fat (opposite of 瘦): ～猪 *fat pig* | ～肉 *fat meat* | 牛～马壮 *fat cattle and strong horses* ❷好处多 lucrative: ～活儿 *lucrative work* | ～差（chāi）*lucrative job* ❸肥沃，土质含养分多的 (of land or soil) fertile: 地很～。*The land is fertile.* ❹ 肥料，能增加田地养分的东西 fertilizer: 施～ *apply fertilizer* | 追～ *apply top-dressing; top-dressing* | 氮～ *nitrogenous fertilizer* | 化～ *chemical fertilizer* ❺使田地增加养分 to fertilize: 用草灰～田 *fertilize the soil with plant ash* ❻衣服鞋袜等宽大，跟"瘦"相对 (of clothes, shoes, socks, etc.) loose; large (opposite of 瘦): 袖子太～了。*The sleeves are too wide.*

淝 féi ㄈㄟˊ 水名，南淝河、北淝河、东淝河、西淝河等，都在安徽省。东淝河古称淝水 Feihe River. There are South/North/East/West Feihe rivers, which are all in Anhui Province. East Feihe River was called Feishui River in ancient China: ～水之战 *Battle of the Feishui River*

蜰 féi ㄈㄟˊ 臭虫 bedbug

腓 féi ㄈㄟˊ 腓肠肌，俗称腿肚子，胫骨和腓骨后的肌肉 (informal 腿肚子) calf (of the leg) ［腓骨］小腿外侧的骨头，比胫骨细小 fibula（see picture of 人体骨骼 on page 220）

朏 fěi ㄈㄟˇ ❶新月开始发光 (of the crescent moon) to begin to shine: 月～星堕。*The moon begins to shine as the stars fade.* ❷ 用于地名 used in place names: ～头（在福建省福州）*Feitou (in Fuzhou, Fujian Province)*

匪 fěi ㄈㄟˇ ❶强盗，抢劫财物的坏人 bandit: 惯～ *professional bandit* | 土～ *bandit* ❷ 不，不是 not; no: 获益～浅 *reap substantial benefits* | ～夷所思（不是常人所能想到的）*incredible; unimaginable*

诽（誹） fěi ㄈㄟˇ 说别人的坏话（㊥ —谤）to slander: 腹～心谤 *vent one's grievances secretly*

F

菲 fěi ㄈㄟˇ ❶微，薄（㊀ —薄）humble：～礼 *my humble gift* | ～ 材 *my humble talent* ❷古书上说的一种像蔓菁的菜 a kind of vegetable like turnip in ancient Chinese texts

⇨ see also fēi on p.172

悱 fěi ㄈㄟˇ 想说可是不能够恰当地说出来 speechless

棐 fěi ㄈㄟˇ ❶辅助 to assist ❷(ancient) same as "榧" or "篚"

斐 fěi ㄈㄟˇ 有文采 rich in literary grace［斐然］1 有文采的样子 of striking literary talent：～成章 *show striking literary talent* 2 显著 brilliant; outstanding：成绩～ *splendid results*

榧 fěi ㄈㄟˇ 常绿乔木，木质坚硬，可供建筑用。种子叫榧子，种仁可以吃，也可榨油，又可入药 Chinese torreya

蜚 fěi ㄈㄟˇ ［蜚蠊］（—lián）蟑螂 cockroach

⇨ see also fēi on p.173

翡 fěi ㄈㄟˇ ［翡翠］（—cuì）1 鸟名，嘴长而直，有蓝色和绿色的羽毛，捕食鱼和昆虫 halcyon (a kind of kingfisher) 2 一种半透明、有光泽的玉，多为绿色、蓝绿色，也有红色、紫色或无色的，很珍贵 jadeite

篚 fěi ㄈㄟˇ 古代盛东西的竹器 (ancient) round bamboo basket

芾 fèi ㄈㄟˋ ［蔽芾］形容树干及树叶小 (of tree trunk or leaves) small

⇨ see also fú on p.184

肺 fèi ㄈㄟˋ 肺脏，人和高等动物体内的呼吸器官之一 lung (see picture of 人体内脏 on page 819)［肺腑］借指内心 the bottom of one's heart：～之言 *words from the bottom of one's heart*

吠 fèi ㄈㄟˋ 狗叫 to bark：狂～ *bark furiously* | 蜀犬～日（喻少见多怪）*make a fuss about common things (literally means 'Sichuan dogs bark at the sun because it is a rare sight in that misty region')*

狒 fèi ㄈㄟˋ ［狒狒］哺乳动物，头部像狗，面部肉色，光滑无毛，体毛褐色，吃果实和鸟卵等。多产于非洲 baboon

沸 fèi ㄈㄟˋ 开，滚，液体受热到一定温度时急剧转化为气体，产生大量气泡 to boil：～点 *boiling point* | ～腾 *to boil; (figurative) boil over with excitement* | 人声鼎～ *a hubbub of voices*

费（費） fèi ㄈㄟˋ ❶花费，消耗得多，跟"省"相对 to spend; to consume (opposite of 省)：～力 *exert great effort* | ～心 *take much trouble* | ～神 *exert great mental effort* | ～事 *involve a lot of trouble* | ～工夫 *be time-consuming* | 浪～ *to waste* | 这孩子穿鞋太～。*The child wears out shoes too quickly.* ❷费用，为某种需要用的款项 fee; expenditure：学～ *tuition (fees)* | 办公～ *administrative expenses*

镄（鐨） fèi ㄈㄟˋ 人造的放射性金属元素，符号 Fm。fermium (Fm)

废（廢、❸*癈） fèi ㄈㄟˋ ❶停止，放弃 to abandon; to give up：半

途而～ *give up halfway* | ～寝忘食 *forget to eat and sleep; (figurative) be absorbed / occupied* | ～除 *to abolish*㊀失去效用的，没有用的 useless：～纸 *waste paper* | ～物 *waste materials* | 修旧利～ *repair and utilize old or discarded things* ❷荒芜，衰败 deserted：～园 *deserted garden* | ～墟 *ruins* ❸残疾 disabled：～疾 *disability*

剕 fèi ㄈㄟˋ 古代把脚砍掉的酷刑 amputation of the feet (a cruel punishment in ancient times)

痱（*疿）fèi ㄈㄟˋ 痱子，皮肤病，暑天皮肤上生出来的红色或白色小疹，很刺痒 prickly heat

FEN ㄈㄣ

分 fēn ㄈㄣ ❶分开，区划开，跟"合"相对 to separate; to divide (opposite of 合)：～离 *to separate* | ～类 *to classify* | ～工 *divide up the work* | ～散 *to divert; to distribute; scattered* | ～解 *to break into parts or pieces; to resolve; to decompose; to explain* ㊀①由整体中取一部分 to take one's share of sth：他～到了五千元。*He was allotted five thousand yuan.* ②由机构分出的，分设的 (of an organization) branch：～会 *(of an association or society) branch* | ～队 *contingent; detachment* | ～局 *branch (office); sub-bureau* | ～社 *(of an agency, etc.) branch*［分化］由一种事物演变成几种不同的事物 to split up：两极～ *to polarize* | "他"字～成"他""她""它"。*The character* 他 *has evolved into* 他, 她 *and* 它.［分析］把事物、现象、概念等划分成简单的部分，找出它的本质、属性或相互联系 to analyse：～问题 *analyse problems* | 化学～ *chemical analysis* ❷分配 to distribute：～红 *distribute dividends* | ～工 *divide up the work* ❸辨别（㊄一辨）to distinguish：不～青红皂白 *make no distinction between right and wrong* | ～清是非 *distinguish right from wrong* ❹表示分数 used to express fraction：二～之一 *a half* | 百～之八 *eight per cent*［分数］数学中表示除法的式子，画一道横线，叫分数线，被除数写在线上面，叫分子，除数写在线下面，叫分母 fraction［分子］1 物体分成的最细小而不失原物性质的颗粒 molecule：水的一个～，含有两个氢原子和一个氧原子。*A molecule of water consists of two hydrogen atoms and one oxygen atom.* 2 see 分数 at this entry (see also fènzǐ at 分 fèn) ❺法定计量单位中十进分数单位词头之一，表示 10^{-1}，符号 d。one of the prefixes of the legal units of measurement in decimal fractions for 10^{-1}(d) ❻计量单位名 unit of measurement ①市制长度，10 分是 1 寸，1 分约合 3.33 毫米 a traditional Chinese unit for measuring length, roughly equal to 3.33 millimetre. There are 10 分 in 1 寸. ②市制地积，10 分是 1 亩，1 分约合 66.67 平方米 a traditional Chinese unit for measuring area, roughly equal to 66.67 square metres. There are 10 分 in 1 亩 . ③市制重量，10 分是 1 钱，1 分合 0.5 克 a traditional Chinese unit for measuring weight, equal to 0.5 gram. There are 10 分 in 1 钱 . ④币制，10 分是 1 角 a Chinese unit of money. 10 分 is equal to 1 角 . ⑤时间，60 秒是 1 分，60 分是 1 小时 (of time) minute ⑥圆周或角，60秒是1分，60分是1度 (of angles) minute ⑦（－儿）表示成绩 point：赛篮球赢了三～。*(We) won the basketball match by three points.* | 考试得了一百～。*(I) got 100 marks in the exam.* ⑧利率，月利一分按百分之一计算，年利一分按十分之一计算 (of interest rate) 1 per cent (on a monthly basis); 10 per cent (on an annual basis) [分寸]（－cun）指说话或办事的适当标准或限度 sense of propriety：说话要有～。*One should have a sense of propriety when speaking.*

⇨ see also fèn on p.177

芬 fēn ㄈㄣ 芬芳，花草的香气 fragrance

吩 fēn ㄈㄣ [吩咐]（*分付）（－fu）口头指派或命令 to tell; to order：母亲～他早去早回。*His mother told him to go early and come back early.*

纷(紛) fēn ㄈㄣ 众多，杂乱（㊧－乱、－杂）㊂numerous; disorderly：众说～纭 *opinions vary* | 大雪～飞 *snow falling thick and fast* | 议论～～ *be widely discussed*

玢 fēn ㄈㄣ [赛璐玢]（外 *loanword*）玻璃纸的旧称，可染成各种颜色，多用于包装 (old) Cellophane™

⇨ see also bīn on p.44

氛(△*雰) fēn ㄈㄣ 云气 thin clouds ㊖气象，情势 atmosphere：战～ *war atmosphere* | ～围 *atmosphere* | 气～ *atmosphere*

翂 fēn ㄈㄣ [翂翂] 形容鸟飞的样子 (of birds) flying

棻 fēn ㄈㄣ 有香味的木头 fragrant wood

酚 fēn ㄈㄣ 有机化合物的一类，由羟基与芳香环连接而成，苯酚是最简单的酚 phenol

雰 fēn ㄈㄣ 雾气 mist [雰雰] 形容霜雪很盛的样子 (of snow or frost) heavy

坟(墳) fén ㄈㄣˊ 埋葬死人之后筑起的土堆（㊧－墓）tomb

汾 fén ㄈㄣˊ 汾河，水名，在山西省 Fenhe River (in Shanxi Province)

蚡 fén ㄈㄣˊ ❶〈古 ancient〉same as “鼢” ❷姓 (surname) Fen

棼 fén ㄈㄣˊ 纷乱 confused：治丝益～（整理丝不找头绪，越理越乱。喻做事没有条理，越搞越乱）*make a confused situation only worse*

鼢 fén ㄈㄣˊ 鼢鼠，哺乳动物，尾短，眼小，身体灰色。在地下打洞，损害农作物和树木的根，甚至危害河堤 zokor

焚 fén ㄈㄣˊ 烧 to burn：～香 *burn incense* | ～毁 *destroy by fire* | 忧心如～ *be burning with anxiety* | 玩火自～。*One who plays with fire will get burnt.*

濆（濆） fén ㄈㄣˊ 水边 waterside

豮（豶） fén ㄈㄣˊ 〈方 dialect〉雄性的牲畜 male domestic animal：～猪 *boar*

粉 fěn ㄈㄣˇ ❶细末儿 powder：药～ *medicinal powder* | 藕～ *lotus root starch* | 漂白～ *bleaching powder* 特指化妆用的粉末 face powder：香～ *cosmetic powder* | 涂脂抹～ *apply powder and paint; (figurative) prettify* ❷粉刷，用涂料抹刷墙壁 to whitewash：这墙是才～的。*The wall has just been whitewashed.*［粉饰］装饰表面 to whitewash ㊖ 掩盖污点或缺点 to gloss over：门面～一新。*The shop front was given a facelift.* | ～太平 *present a false picture of peace and prosperity* ❸使破碎，成为粉末 to pulverise：～碎 *shatter (into pieces)* | ～身碎骨 *have one's body ground to powder* ❹浅红色 pink：这朵花是～的。*The flower is pink.* ❺白色的或带粉末的 white; powdered：～蝶 *white butterfly* | ～墙 *plaster wall* ❻用淀粉做成的食品 food made from starch：～条 *starch noodles* | 凉～ *bean-starch noodles* | 米～ *rice noodles*

分 fèn ㄈㄣˋ ❶名位、职责、权利的限度 extent of one's duty or rights：～所当然 *just doing one's duty; be duty-bound* | 本～ *one's duty* | 非～ *overstepping one's bounds; not belonging to oneself* | 过～ *excessive* ❷成分 content; ingredient：水～ *moisture content* | 糖～ *sugar content* | 养～ *nutrient* ❸same as "份"［分子］(－zǐ) 属于一定阶级、阶层、集团或具有某种特征的人 element (in a group or society)：积极～ *activist* | 知识～ *intellectual* (see also fēnzǐ at 分 fēn)

⇨ see also fēn on p.175

份 fèn ㄈㄣˋ ❶整体分成几部分，每一部分叫一份 part：分成三～ *divide into three parts* | 每人一～ *one share for each person* | ～子 *share of expenses for buying a gift; cash gift* | 股～ *(in business) share* ❷（－儿）量词，多用于成组的东西或报刊文件 measure word for newspapers or sets of things：一～儿工作 *a job* | 一～儿礼 *a present* | 一～报 *a copy of newspaper* ❸用在"省、县、年、月"后面，表示划分的单位 used after 省，县，年 or 月 to indicate a unit of division：省～ *province* | 年～ *a particular year*

〈古 ancient〉also same as 彬 (bīn)

坋 fèn ㄈㄣˋ 用于地名 used in place names：长～（在福建省屏南）*Changfen (in Pingnan, Fujian Province)*

忿 fèn ㄈㄣˋ 生气，恨（㊃ －怒、－恨）㊂ angry; indignant：～～不平 *be indignant* 现多作"愤"now often written as 愤［不忿］不服气，不平 resentful; be indignant［气不忿儿］看到不平

的事，心中不服气 feel resentful about injustice

奋(奮) fèn ㄈㄣˋ 振作，鼓劲 to exert oneself: ～翅 *spread and flutter the wings* | ～斗 *to struggle* | 兴～ *be excited* | ～不顾身 *dash ahead regardless of one's safety* | ～发图强 *go all out to achieve success*

偾(僨) fèn ㄈㄣˋ 败坏，破坏 to spoil; to destroy: ～事 *spoil an affair* | ～军之将 *a general that ruins the army*

愤(憤) fèn ㄈㄣˋ 因为不满意而感情激动，发怒 ㊀ to be angry: 气～ *be furious* | ～～不平 *be indignant* [发愤] 自己感觉不满足，努力地做 to resolve: ～图强 *make determined efforts to better oneself*

鲼(鱝) fèn ㄈㄣˋ 鱼名，身体扁平，呈菱形，尾部像鞭子，生活在热带和亚热带海洋里 eagle ray

粪(糞) fèn ㄈㄣˋ ❶屎，粪便，可用作肥料 excrement ❷施肥，往田地里加肥料 to manure: ～地 *manure the fields*| ～田 *manure the fields* ❸扫除（㊄－除）to clear away

瀵 fèn ㄈㄣˋ 水从地面下喷出漫溢 (of underground water) to gush out and overflow: ～涌 *gush out and overflow*

FENG ㄈㄥ

丰(❷❸豐) fēng ㄈㄥ ❶容貌、姿态美好 good-looking [丰采] [丰姿] see 风采，风姿 at 风 on page 178 ❷盛，多（㊄－盛）rich; plentiful: ～年 *bumper year* | ～衣足食 *be well fed and well clad* ❸大 great: ～碑 *monument* | ～功伟绩 *tremendous achievements*

沣(灃) fēng ㄈㄥ 沣河，水名，在陕西省西安 Fenghe River (in Xi'an, Shaanxi Province)

风(風) fēng ㄈㄥ ❶跟地面大致平行的流动着的空气 wind: 北～ *north/northerly wind* | 旋（xuàn）～ *whirlwind* | 刮一阵～。*The wind blew for a while.* | ～行（像风那样快地流行）*be in fashion ; be popular* [风化] 1 风俗教化 decency; morals and manners: 有伤～ *corrupt public morals* 2 岩石在地表因长期受风雨等侵蚀而受到破坏或分解 to weather 3 化学上称结晶体在空气中因失去结晶水而分解 to effloresce [风头]（－tou）1 指形势的发展方向或有关个人利害的情势 trend of events: 不要看～办事。*Don't just act according to circumstances.* 2 出头露面，显示自己的表现（含贬义）(disapproving) publicity; limelight: 出～ *seek the limelight* ❷消息 news: 闻～而至 *arrive without delay on getting wind of sth* ❸没有确实根据的 rumoured: ～传 *(of news or rumours) get about; to rumour* | ～闻 *get wind of* ❹表现在外的景象或态度 scene; bearing: ～景 *scenery* | ～光 *scenery;*

honourable | 作～*style* | ～度 *demeanour; bearing* [风采] 风度神采。也作"丰采" graceful demeanour (also written as 丰采) [风姿] 风度姿态。也作"丰姿" graceful carriage/being (also written as 丰姿) ❺风气，习俗 custom; convention: 世～*social customs* | 勤俭成～。*Diligence and frugality have become the order of the day.* | 移～易俗 *change the prevailing habits and customs* | ～土人情 *local customs and practices* ❻病名 used in some disease names: 抽～*convulsion* | 羊痫(xián)～*epilepsy* ❼古代称民歌 (ancient) ballad: 国～*Folksongs of the States (from* The Book of Songs《诗经》*)* | 采～*collect folk songs*

〈古 ancient〉 also same as 讽 (fěng)

沨(渢) fēng ㄈㄥ 形容水声 (of water) gurgle

枫(楓) fēng ㄈㄥ 落叶乔木，又叫枫香，叶掌状三裂，秋季变红色 maple (also called 枫香)

砜(碸) fēng ㄈㄥ 有机化合物，是硫酰(xiān)基与烃(tīng)基或芳香基结合而成的，如二甲砜、二苯砜 sulfone

疯(瘋) fēng ㄈㄥ 精神错乱、失常(㊀—癫、—狂) mad; crazy ㊁ ①指农作物生长旺盛，不结果实 (of crops) overgrown: 长～杈 *(of a plant) to grow a spindling stem* | 棉花长～了。*The cotton plants have bolted.* ②言行狂妄 unbridled: ～言～语 *nonsense*

封 fēng ㄈㄥ ❶严密堵住或关住，使不能随便打开或通行 to close; to seal: ～存 *seal up for safekeeping* | ～门 *seal up a door* | ～禁 *close down; to ban* | ～瓶口 *seal a bottle* | ～河(河面冻住) *(of a river) be frozen over* [封锁] 采取军事、政治、经济等措施使跟外界断绝联系 to block off: ～港口 *seal a port* | ～消息 *block the news* | 军事～线 *military blockade* ❷(－儿)封起来的或用来封东西的纸袋、纸包 enveloped object; envelope: 信～*envelope* | 赏～*enveloped gratuity* ❸量词，用于封起来的东西 measure word for sth enveloped: 一～信 *a letter* | 一～厚礼 *an enveloped generous gift* ❹古代帝王把土地或爵位给予亲属、臣属 confer (a title, territory, etc.) upon: ～侯 *make sb a marquis* ❺指疆界，范围 boundary: ～疆 *boundary*

葑 fēng ㄈㄥ same as "芜菁", also 蔓(mán)菁

⇨ see also fèng on p.181

崶 fēng ㄈㄥ 用于地名 used in place names: ～源庄(在河北省涿州) *Fengyuanzhuang (in Zhuozhou, Hebei Province)*

峰(*峯) fēng ㄈㄥ 高而尖的山头 peak: 山～*mountain peak* | 顶～*peak* | ～峦 *ridges and peaks* ㊂形状像峰的事物 peak-like thing: 洪～*flood peak* | 波～*(wave) crest* | 驼～

camel hump

烽 fēng ㄈㄥ 烽火，古时边防报警点的烟火，敌人来侵犯时，守卫的人就点火报警 beacon fire

锋(鋒) fēng ㄈㄥ 刃，刀剑等器械的锐利或尖端部分（㊟－刃）cutting edge：交～（双方作战或比赛）*cross swords* | 刀～ *blade* ㉄①器物的尖锐部分 sharp point of sth：笔～ *tip of a writing brush* ②在前面带头的人 vanguard：先～ *pioneer* | 前～ *vanguard*

蜂(*蠭、*逢) fēng ㄈㄥ 昆虫，会飞，多有毒刺，能蜇（zhē）人。多成群住在一起。有蜜蜂、熊蜂、胡蜂、细腰蜂等多种。特指蜜蜂 bee; (specifically) honey bee：～糖 *honey* | ～蜡 *beeswax* | ～蜜 *honey* ㉅成群地 in swarms：～起 *rise in swarms* | ～拥 *to swarm*

酆 fēng ㄈㄥ ［酆都］地名，在重庆市。今作"丰都"(now written as 丰都) Fengdu (a place in Chongqing Municipality)

冯(馮) féng ㄈㄥˊ 姓 (surname) Feng
〈古 ancient〉also same as 凭 (píng)

逢 féng ㄈㄥˊ ❶遇到 to meet：～人便说 *tell whoever happens to come across* | 每～星期三开会。*A meeting is arranged every Wednesday.* ❷迎合 to curry favour with［逢迎］迎合别人的意图，巴结人 curry favour with

浲 féng ㄈㄥˊ 用于地名 used in place names：杨家～（在湖北省京山县）*Yangjiafeng (in Jingshan County, Hubei Province)*

缝(縫) féng ㄈㄥˊ 用针线连缀 to sew：把衣服的破口～上。*Sew up the hole in the clothes.*［缝纫］裁制服装 to tailor (clothes)：学习～ *learn tailoring*

⇨ see also fèng on p.181

讽(諷) fěng ㄈㄥˇ (formerly pronounced fèng) ❶不看着书本念，背书（㊟－诵）to recite ❷用含蓄的话劝告或讥刺（㊟讥－）to mock; to imply：～刺 *to satirize* | 冷嘲热～ *taunt and jeer*

唪 fěng ㄈㄥˇ 唪经，佛教徒、道教徒高声念经 (of Buddhist or Taoist) to recite scriptures loudly

凤(鳳) fèng ㄈㄥˋ 凤凰（huáng），传说中的鸟王。又说雄的叫"凤"，雌的叫"凰"（古作"皇"），通常单称作"凤" phoenix：～毛麟角（喻罕见而珍贵的东西）*as rare as phoenix feathers and unicorn horns*

奉 fèng ㄈㄥˋ ❶恭敬地用手捧着 to carry respectfully with both hands ㉄尊重，遵守 to revere; to abide by：～行 *abide by* | ～公守法 *act for public interests and follow the law* 敬辞 polite speech：～陪 *keep sb company* | ～劝 *may I suggest* | ～送 *offer as a gift* | ～还 *gratefully return*［奉承］恭维，谄媚 to flatter ❷献给（多指对上级或长辈）to submit respectfully (often to superiors or elders)：双

F

手～上 *offer with both hands* ❸接受（多指上级或长辈的）to receive (often from superiors or elders)：～命 *follow orders* | 昨～手书。*I received your letter yesterday.* ❹信奉，信仰 to believe in：素～佛教 *have always believed in Buddhism* ❺供养，伺候（㊟一养、供一、侍一）to serve; to wait on

俸 fèng ㄈㄥˋ 旧时称官员等所得的薪金 (old) (of an official) salary：～禄 *government salary* | 薪～ *salary*

葑 fèng ㄈㄥˋ 古书上指菰的根 (in ancient Chinese texts) root of Manchurian wild rice

⇨ see also fēng on p.179

赗（賵） fèng ㄈㄥˋ 古时指用财物帮助人办丧事 (ancient) to help sb hold a funeral with money or gifts：赙（fù）～ *present a gift to a bereaved family*

缝（縫） fèng ㄈㄥˋ ❶（一子、一儿）缝隙，裂开或自然露出的窄长口子 crack; slot：裂～ *to crack; crack* | 墙～ *wall crack* ❷（一儿）物体接合的地方 seam：这道～儿不直。*The seam is not straight.*

⇨ see also féng on p.180

FO ㄈㄛ

佛 fó ㄈㄛˊ 梵语音译"佛陀"的省称，是佛教徒对修行圆满的人的称呼。特指佛教的创始人释迦牟尼 (short for 佛陀, from Sanskrit) Buddha; (specifically) Sakyamuni Buddha [佛教] 宗教名。相传公元前6世纪—公元前5世纪释迦牟尼所创 Buddhism

⇨ see also fú on p.183

FOU ㄈㄡ

缶 fǒu ㄈㄡˇ ❶瓦器，大肚子小口 an earthen pot with a large belly and a narrow mouth ❷古代一种瓦质的打击乐器 an ancient clay percussion instrument

否 fǒu ㄈㄡˇ ❶不 no ①用在表示疑问的词句里 (used to indicate a question) or not：是～？ *Whether...or not?* | 可～？ *Is it possible...?* | 能～？ *Is it possible...?* ②用在答话里，表示不同意对方的意思 (used in a reply to express disagreement) no：～，此非吾意。*No, that is not what I mean.* [否定] 1 不同意的，反面的 negative 2 不承认，做出相反的判断 to negate [否决] 对问题做不承认、不同意的决定 to veto [否认] 不承认 to deny ❷不如此，不然 not such; not in this way [否则] 连词，如果不这样 (conjunction) otherwise：必须确定计划，～无法施工。*The plan must be determined, otherwise construction is impossible.*

⇨ see also pǐ on p.502

FU ㄈㄨ

夫 fū ㄈㄨ ❶成年男子的通称 man：农～ *farmer* | 渔～ *fisherman* ㊁旧时称服劳役的人（㊟一役）(old) conscripted la-

F

bourer ❷丈夫(fu)，跟"妻""妇"相对 husband (opposite of 妻 or 妇)：～妻 *husband and wife* | ～妇 *husband and wife* | 姐～ *brother-in-law (elder sister's husband)* | 妹～ *brother-in-law (younger sister's husband)*

[夫人] 对别人妻子的敬称 (polite speech) Mrs.

[夫子] 1 旧时尊称老师或学者 (old, honorific speech) teacher, scholar 2 旧时妻称丈夫 (old) my husband

⇨ see also fú on p.182

呋 fū ㄈㄨ [呋喃] (—nán) 有机化合物，无色液体。可用来制药品，也是重要的化工原料 furan

玞 fū ㄈㄨ see 珷玞 (wǔ—) at 珷 on page 692

肤(膚) fū ㄈㄨ 皮肤，人体表面的皮 skin：～色 *skin colour* | 肌～ *muscle and skin* | 切～之痛 *acute pain* ⓔ 表面的，浅薄的 superficial; shallow：～浅 *superficial*

砆 fū ㄈㄨ 用于地名 used in place names：～石村(在湖南省浏阳) *Fushicun (in Liuyang, Hunan Province)*

鈇(鈇) fū ㄈㄨ 铡刀 fodder chopper

麸(麩、*粰、*稃) fū ㄈㄨ (—子)麸皮，小麦磨面过罗后剩下的皮儿和碎屑 bran

趺 fū ㄈㄨ ❶ same as "跗" ❷ 碑下的石座 pedestal of a stone tablet：龟～ *tortoise-shaped base of a stone tablet*

跗 fū ㄈㄨ 脚背 tarsus：～骨 *tarsus bone* | ～面 *instep* 也作"趺" also written as 趺 (see picture of 人体骨骼 on page 220)

稃 fū ㄈㄨ 小麦等植物的花外面包着的硬壳 husk：内～ *palea* | 外～ *lemma*

孵 fū ㄈㄨ 鸟类伏在卵上，使卵内的胚胎发育成雏鸟，也指用人工的方法使卵孵化 to hatch; to incubate

鄜 fū ㄈㄨ 鄜县，地名，在陕西省。今作"富县" (now written as 富县) Fuxian (a place in Shaanxi Province)

敷 fū ㄈㄨ ❶涂上，搽上 to apply：～粉 *apply powder* | 外～药 *medicine for external application* ❷布置，铺开 to lay out：～设路轨 *lay a railway track* ❸ 足够 to suffice：～用 *to suffice* | 入不～出 *live beyond one's means*

[敷衍] (—yǎn) 做事不认真或待人不真诚，只是表面应酬 go through the motions：～了(liǎo)事 *muddle through one's work* | 这人不诚恳，对人总是～。*This man is insincere and always takes a perfunctory attitude to others.*

夫 fú ㄈㄨˊ ❶文言发语词 used at the beginning of a sentence to introduce a subject in classical Chinese：～战，勇气也。*When it comes to fighting, courage is vital.* ❷文言助词 auxiliary word in classical Chinese：逝者如斯～。*Thus do things flow away.*

⇨ see also fū on p.181

F

扶 fú ㄈㄨˊ ❶搀，用手支持人或物使不倒 to support (with hands)：～老携幼 *help the aged and lead the young* | ～犁 *hold the plough* ❷支撑在别的物体上，使自己不倒或立起 to hold onto sth for support; to support oneself against：～杖而行 *walk with the support of a stick* | ～墙 *support oneself against a wall* | ～栏杆 *hold onto a rail* [扶手] 手扶着可以当倚靠的东西，如楼梯旁的栏杆等 handrail; armrest ❸用手帮助躺或倒的人坐或立；用手使倒下的东西竖直 to help sb/sth up：把病人～起来。*Help the patient up.* | ～苗 *straighten up the seedlings* ❹帮助，援助 to help：～贫 *aid the poor* | 救死～伤 *heal the wounded and rescue the dying* | ～危济困 *help those in danger and relieve those in need*

芙 fú ㄈㄨˊ [芙蓉] (－róng) 1 落叶灌木，又叫木芙蓉，花有红、白等颜色 cotton rose mallow (also called 木芙蓉) 2 荷花的别名 another name for 荷花

蚨 fú ㄈㄨˊ 青蚨，古代用作铜钱的别名 (ancient) copper coin

弗 fú ㄈㄨˊ 文言副词，不 (adverb in classical Chinese) not：～去 *not go* | ～许 *not allow*

佛 (*彿、*髴) fú ㄈㄨˊ see 仿佛 (fǎng－) at 仿 on page 170

⇨ see also fó on p.181

拂 fú ㄈㄨˊ ❶掸 (dǎn) 去，轻轻擦过 to flick; to whisk; to touch lightly：～尘 *horsetail whisk* | 春风～面。*A spring breeze caresses the cheeks.* [拂晓] 天将明的时候 dawn ❷甩动 to fling [拂袖] 甩袖子，表示生气 shake out one's sleeves in anger ❸违背，不顺 to go against：～意 (不如意) *go against sb's wishes*

〈古 ancient〉also same as 弼 (bì)

茀 fú ㄈㄨˊ 道路上草太多，不便通行 overgrown with grass

怫 fú ㄈㄨˊ 忧郁或愤怒的样子 gloomy; angry：～郁 *gloomy and indignant* | ～然作色 *take on an angry expression*

绋 (紼) fú ㄈㄨˊ 大绳，特指出殡时拉棺材用的大绳 thick rope; (specifically) tow rope for a coffin：执～ (指送殡) *serve as a pall-bearer*

氟 fú ㄈㄨˊ 气体元素，符号 F，淡黄色，味臭，有毒。液态氟可用作火箭燃料的氧化剂，含氟塑料和含氟橡胶有特别优良的性能 fluorine (F)

艴 fú ㄈㄨˊ (又) see bó on page 49

伏 fú ㄈㄨˊ ❶趴，脸向下，体前屈 to lie prostrate：～在地上 *lie prostrate on the ground* | ～案读书 *bend over one's desk to read* ❷低下去 to go down：此起彼～ *rise one after another* | 时起时～ *now rise, now fall* ❸隐藏 to hide：～兵 *troops in ambush* | ～击 *to ambush* | 潜～ *to hide* ❹屈服，承认错误或受到惩罚 to yield; to give in：～辜 (承认自己的罪过)

admit one's guilt | ～法（被执行死刑）*be put to death* ❺伏日，夏至后第三个庚日叫初伏，第四个庚日叫中伏，立秋后第一个庚日叫末伏，统称三伏。从初伏到末伏一般是一年中天气最热的时期 dog days; hot summer days ❻ 电压单位名伏特的简称，符号 V。(short for 伏特) volt (V)

茯 fú ㄈㄨˊ ［茯苓］（－líng）寄生在松树根上的一种真菌，球状，皮黑色，有皱纹，内部白色或粉红色。可入药 Indian bread

洑 fú ㄈㄨˊ ❶ 旋涡 vortex; whirlpool ❷水在地下潜流 (of water) to flow underground

⇨ see also fù on p.191

栿 fú ㄈㄨˊ 古书上指房梁 (in ancient Chinese texts) beam (of the roof)

袱 fú ㄈㄨˊ 包裹、覆盖用的布单 cloth covering; cloth wrapper［包袱］（－fu）1 包裹衣物的布单 cloth wrapper 2 用布单包成的包裹 cloth-wrapped bundle：胳膊上挎着白布～ *carry a bundle wrapped in white cloth in one's arm* ㊞ 思想上的负担或使行动受到牵制的障碍 burden：放下～，轻装前进 *lay down one's burdens and move forward* 3 指相声、快书等曲艺中的笑料 joke or laughing-stock in Chinese comic dialogue：抖～ *crack a joke*

凫（鳧）fú ㄈㄨˊ ❶鸟名，即野鸭，雄的头部绿色，背部黑褐色，雌的黑褐色，能飞，常群游在水中 wild duck (same as 野鸭）❷在水里游 to swim：～水 *to swim*

芾 fú ㄈㄨˊ ❶草木茂盛 (of trees and plants) luxuriant ❷同"黻"。宋代书画家米芾，也作米黻 same as 黻, e.g. 米芾 (Mi Fu, a painter and calligrapher in Song Dynasty, also written as 米黻）

⇨ see also fèi on p.174

苯 fú ㄈㄨˊ ［苯苢］（－yǐ）古书上指车前，草本植物，花淡绿色，叶和种子可入药 (in ancient Chinese texts) Chinese plantain

罘 fú ㄈㄨˊ ［罘罳］［罦罳］（－sī）1 一种屋檐下防鸟雀的网 net under eaves to ward off birds 2 古代一种屏风 (ancient) screen

［芝罘］山名，靠黄海，在山东省烟台 Zhifu Mountain (in Yantai, Shandong Province)

孚 fú ㄈㄨˊ ❶信用 credibility ❷使人信服 inspire confidence in：深～众望 *have great credibility with the public*

俘 fú ㄈㄨˊ ❶打仗时捉住的敌人（㊀－虏）prisoner of war; captive：战～ *prisoner of war* | 遣～ *repatriate prisoners of war* ❷打仗时捉住敌人（㊀－虏）(in a war) to capture：被～ *be taken prisoner* | ～获 *to capture*

郛 fú ㄈㄨˊ 古代城圈外围的大城 (ancient) outer city

垺 fú ㄈㄨˊ 用于地名 used in place names：南仁～（在天津市宝坻）*Nanrenfu (in Baodi,*

Tianjin Municipality)

莩 fú ㄈㄨˊ 芦苇秆子里面的薄膜 (of reed stalk) membrane

⇨ see also piǎo on p.505

浮 fú ㄈㄨˊ ❶漂，跟"沉"相对(㊥漂－) to float (opposite of 沉): ～萍 *duckweed* | ～桥 *pontoon bridge* | ～在水面上 *float on water* ❷表面的 superficial; on the surface: ～面 *surface* | ～皮 *(of organisms) outer skin; surface* | ～土 *surface soil; surface dust* [浮雕] 雕塑的一种，在平面上雕出凸起的形象 (of decoration) relief ❸暂时的 temporary: ～记 *keep a temporary account* | ～支 *provisional accounts of expenditure* ❹不沉静，不沉着(zhuó) frivolous: 心粗气～ *be hot-headed* | 心～气躁 *flighty and impetuous* ❺空虚，不切实 hollow; empty: ～名 *hollow reputation* | ～华 *showy* | ～泛 *superficial* ❻超过，多余 to exceed: 人～于事 *be over-staffed* | ～额 *surplus number*

[浮屠][浮图] 1 佛教徒称释迦牟尼 (a term used by Buddhists to refer to Sakyamuni) Buddha 2 古时称和尚 (ancient) monk 3 塔 pagoda: 七级～ *seven-storeyed pagoda*

琈 fú ㄈㄨˊ 玉的色彩 colour of jade

桴 fú ㄈㄨˊ ❶小筏子 small raft: 乘～渡河 *cross a river by raft* ❷鼓槌 drumstick: ～鼓相应 *work in perfect coordination (literally means 'the drum responds to the drumstick')*

罦 fú ㄈㄨˊ 古书上指捕鸟的网 (in ancient Chinese texts) bird net [罦罳](－sī) same as "罘罳" (see 罘 fú on page 184 for reference)

蜉 fú ㄈㄨˊ [蜉蝣](－yóu) 昆虫，幼虫生在水中，成虫有两对翅，在水面飞行。成虫生存期极短，交尾产卵后即死。种类很多 mayfly

苻 fú ㄈㄨˊ ❶ same as "莩(fú)" ❷姓 (surname) Fu

符 fú ㄈㄨˊ ❶朝廷传达命令或征调(diào)兵将用的凭证，用金、玉、铜、竹、木制成，刻上文字，分成两半，一半存朝廷，一半给外任官员或出征将帅 tally (issued by a government): 兵～ *commander's tally* | 虎～ *tiger-shaped tally* ❷代表事物的标记，记号 symbol: 音～ *musical note* | 星～ *prophetic sign (of being a future king)* | ～号 *symbol* ❸相合(㊥－合) to tally with; be in line with: 言行相～ *one's deeds match one's words* | 与事实不～ *not correspond to facts* ❹道士、巫婆等画的驱使鬼神的东西(迷信) charm (special drawing to expel the evils): 护身～ *amulet*

服 fú ㄈㄨˊ ❶衣服，衣裳(㊥－装) clothes: 制～ *uniform* | 便～ *casual wear* 旧时特指丧服 (old, specifically) mourning dress ❷穿(衣裳) to wear (clothes): ～布袍 *wear a cloth robe* ❸承当，担任 to serve: ～刑 *serve a prison term* | ～兵役 *serve in the army* ❹

F

信服，顺从（㊀－从）to obey; to be convinced：说～ *to persuade* | 心悦诚～ *obey willingly; to have a heartfelt admiration* | 心里不～ *not genuinely convinced* | ～软（认输，认错）*admit defeat; acknowledge one's mistake* 也指使信服 to convince：～众 *to convince the public* | 以理～人 *convince people by reasoning* ❺习惯，适应 to be accustomed to：水土不～ *not be acclimatized* ❻吃（药）to take (medicine)：～药 *take medicine*

⇨ see also fù on p.190

菔 fú ㄈㄨˊ ［莱菔］（lái－）萝卜 radish

箙 fú ㄈㄨˊ 古代盛箭的器具 (ancient) quiver (for carrying arrows)

绂（紱）fú ㄈㄨˊ 古代系（jì）印章或佩玉用的丝带 silk ribbon used to tie a seal or jade in ancient times

韨（韍）fú ㄈㄨˊ ❶古代朝见或祭祀时遮在衣前的一种服饰，用熟皮制成 a kind of adornment on ceremonial gowns in ancient times ❷ same as "绂"

祓 fú ㄈㄨˊ 古代一种习俗，用斋戒沐浴等方法除灾求福 exorcistic ceremony in ancient times㊁清除 to get rid of

黻 fú ㄈㄨˊ ❶古代礼服上绣的半青半黑的花纹 half-blue, half-black pattern embroidered on a ceremonial gown in ancient times ❷ same as "韨" ❸ same as "绂"

枹 fú ㄈㄨˊ ❶用于地名 used in place names：～罕（在甘肃省临夏）*Fuhan (in Linxia, Gansu Province)* ❷ (old) same as "桴❷"

⇨ see also bāo on p.21

匐 fú ㄈㄨˊ see 匍匐 (pú－) at 匍 on page 512

幅 fú ㄈㄨˊ ❶布匹、呢绒等的宽度 (of cloth) width：～面 *(of textile and wool fabric) width* | 这种料子是双～的。*This kind of cloth is of double width.* ❷物体振动或摇摆所展开的宽度 (of vibration or swing) amplitude; breadth：～度 *extent; range* | 振～ *amplitude* ㊃事物变动的大小 extent of change：产品质量大～提高。*The quality of the product has been greatly improved.* ［幅员］宽窄叫幅，周围叫员 size (of a country)㊁疆域 territory：我国～广大。*Our country is vast in territory.* ❸量词，用于布帛、书画等 measure word for cloth, painting, etc.：一～字画 *a work of calligraphy and painting* | 两～锦缎 *two lengths of brocade*

辐（輻）fú ㄈㄨˊ 连接车辋和车毂的直条 spoke：～条 *spoke*（see picture of 旧式车轮 on page 426）［辐辏］［辐凑］（－còu）车辐聚于车毂 (of spokes) to converge to the wheel hub㊃人、物聚集 (of people, things) to gather ［辐射］光、热、粒子等向四周放射的现象 to radiate; radiation

福 fú ㄈㄨˊ 幸福，跟"祸"相对 good fortune; happiness (opposite of 祸)：为人类造～ *work for the well-being of human beings* |

～利 *well-being; bring benefits to* | ～如东海 *boundless happiness* [福祉]（－zhǐ）幸福 well-being: 为人民谋～ *work for the well-being of the people*

蝠 fú ㄈㄨˊ see 蝙蝠 (biān－) at 蝙 on page 38

涪 fú ㄈㄨˊ 涪江，发源于四川省，入嘉陵江 Fujiang River (originating in Sichuan Province and flowing into Jialingjiang River)

榑 fú ㄈㄨˊ [榑桑] 传说中的神树，太阳升起的地方。今作"扶桑" sacred tree in Chinese legend where the sun rises (now written as 扶桑)

幞 fú ㄈㄨˊ same as "袱" [幞头] 古代男子用的一种头巾 (ancient) headdress for a man

襆 fú ㄈㄨˊ 〈古 ancient〉❶布单、巾帕等 sheet; handkerchief ❷包裹 to bundle: ～被（用包袱包裹衣被等，即准备行装）*pack up one's clothes and quilts* ❸ same as "袱"

父 fǔ ㄈㄨˇ ❶老年人 old man: 田～ *old farmer* | 渔～ *old fisherman* ❷ same as "甫❶"

⇨ see also fù on p.189

㕮 fǔ ㄈㄨˇ 㕮咀 to chew [㕮咀] 中医指把药物切成片或弄碎，以便煎服 (in traditional Chinese medicine) shred herbal medicine for decoction

斧 fǔ ㄈㄨˇ ❶（－子、－头）砍东西用的工具，头呈楔形，装有木柄 axe ❷一种旧式武器 battleaxe

釜 fǔ ㄈㄨˇ ❶古代的一种锅 (ancient) a kind of cauldron: ～底抽薪（喻从根本上解决）*strike at the root (literally means 'take away firewood from under the cauldron')* | 破～沉舟（喻下决心去干，不留后路）*burn one's boats/bridges (literally means 'break the cauldrons and sink the boats')* ❷古代量器名 (ancient) a measuring tool

滏 fǔ ㄈㄨˇ 滏阳河，水名，在河北省西南部 Fuyanghe River (in the south-west of Hebei Province)

抚(撫) fǔ ㄈㄨˇ ❶慰问 to console: ～恤 (xù) *console and compensate* | ～慰 *to comfort* ❷扶持，保护 to nurture: ～养 *bring (sb) up* | ～育 *to nurture (children); to tend (forest)* ❸轻轻地按着 to stroke: ～摩 *to stroke* ❹ same as "拊"

甫 fǔ ㄈㄨˇ ❶古代在男子名字下加的美称。也作"父" (ancient) male courtesy name (also written as 父) [台甫] 旧时询问别人名号的用语 (old, used to ask another's name) your name ❷刚，才 just: ～入门 *have just entered the house* | 年～十岁 *be just ten years old*

辅(輔) fǔ ㄈㄨˇ ❶帮助，佐助（㊣－助）to assist: ～导 *to tutor* | 相～而行 *complement each other* [辅音] 发音的时候，从肺里出来的气经过口腔或鼻腔受到障碍所成的音。汉语拼音字母 b、d、g 等都是辅音 consonant ❷人的颊骨

cheekbone：～车相依（车：牙床。喻二者关系密切，互相依存）*be cheek by jowl with (sb/sth) (literally means 'be close like cheek and gum')*

脯 fǔ ㄈㄨˇ ❶肉干 dried meat：鹿～ *dried venison* ❷蜜饯果干 preserved fruit：果～ *preserved fruit* | 桃～ *preserved peach* | 杏～ *preserved apricot*

⇨ see also pú on p.513

䩉 fǔ ㄈㄨˇ ❶〈古 ancient〉same as "釜" ❷姓 (surname) Fu

簠 fǔ ㄈㄨˇ 古代祭祀时盛稻、粱的器具。长方形，有盖和耳 (ancient) utensil for grain used in sacrifice

黼 fǔ ㄈㄨˇ 古代礼服上绣的半黑半白的花纹 (ancient) black and white pattern embroidered on official robes

拊 fǔ ㄈㄨˇ 拍 to clap：～掌大笑 *clap one's hands and laugh heartily* 也作"抚" (also written as 抚)

府 fǔ ㄈㄨˇ ❶储藏文书或财物的地方（㊜-库）repository (for books or other property)：天～（喻物产富饶的地方）*land of abundance* ❷贵族或高级官员办公或居住的地方 official residence：王～ *residence for the nobility* | 总统～ *presidential residence* | 相（xiàng）～ *(old) prime minister's residence* 泛指政权机关 (generally) organs of state power：官～ *local authorities* | 政～ *government* [府上] 对对方的籍贯、家庭或住宅的敬称 (honorific speech) your home; your hometown ❸旧时行政区域名，等级在县和省之间 (old) prefecture (an administrative division that ranks between a county and a province)

俯（△*頫、*俛）fǔ ㄈㄨˇ 脸向下，低头，跟"仰"相对 to bow (one's head)(opposite of 仰)：～视 *to overlook* | ～仰之间（很短的时间）*in the twinkling of an eye*

⇨ 頫 see also 頫 on p.188

腑 fǔ ㄈㄨˇ 中医把胃、胆、大肠、小肠、三焦、膀胱叫六腑 fu (the stomach, gallbladder, large intestine, small intestine, *sanjiao* and bladder are referred to as *liufu* in traditional Chinese medicine)

腐 fǔ ㄈㄨˇ 烂，变质（㊜-败、-烂、-朽）to go bad; to rot：流水不～。*Running water is never stale.* | 鱼～肉败 *rotten food* ㊀思想陈旧或行为堕落 (of ideas or behaviour) old-fashioned; corrupt：陈～ *hackneyed* | ～化 *become corrupt* [腐蚀] 通过化学作用使物体逐渐消损或毁坏 to corrode：～剂 *corrosive agent* ㊒使人腐化堕落 to corrupt (sb)[豆腐]（-fu）用豆子制成的一种食品 tofu; bean curd：～皮 *dried skin of soy bean milk* | ～乳 *fermented bean curd*

頫（頫）fǔ ㄈㄨˇ 用于人名。赵孟頫，元代书画家 used in given names, e.g. Zhao Mengfu, calligrapher and painter of the Yuan Dynasty

F

⇨ 頫 see also 俯 on p.188

父 fù ㄈㄨˋ ❶父亲，爸爸 father ❷对男性长辈的称呼 a term to refer to one's male relative of a senior generation：叔～ *uncle* | 姨～ *uncle (husband of mother's sister)* | 师～ *master* | ～老 *elders (of a country or district)*

⇨ see also fǔ on p.187

洑 fù ㄈㄨˋ 用于地名 used in place names：湖～（在江苏省宜兴）*Hufu (in Yixing, Jiangsu Province)*

讣(訃) fù ㄈㄨˋ 报丧，也指报丧的通知 to notify of sb's death; obituary：～闻 *obituary* | ～告 *notify of sb's death; obituary*

赴 fù ㄈㄨˋ 往，去 to go to：～北京 *go to Beijing* | ～宴 *attend a banquet* | ～汤蹈火（喻不避艰险）*go through fire and water*

付 fù ㄈㄨˋ ❶交，给 to hand over; to give; to pay：～款 *to make payment* | ～印 *send to the press; turn over to printing house* | ～表决 *put to a vote* | ～诸实施 *put into practice* | ～出 *to pay* ❷量词 (measure word) ① same as "副❹"：一～手套 *a pair of gloves* | 一～笑脸 *a smiling face* ② same as "服 (fù)"

附(*坿) fù ㄈㄨˋ ❶另外加上，随带着 to attach：～录 *appendix* | ～设 *have as an attached institution* | ～注 *annotation* | 信里面～着一张相片。*A photograph is enclosed in the letter.* ❷依附，依从 to rely on; to comply with：～和（hè）*to echo (view or behaviour of another person)* | ～议 *second a motion* | ～庸 *dependency; appendage* | 魂不～体 *feel as if the soul had left the body* ❸靠近 to get close：～近 *nearby (regions)* | ～耳交谈 *talk in whispers*

咐 fù ㄈㄨˋ see 吩咐 (fēnfu) at 吩 on page 176

驸(駙) fù ㄈㄨˋ 几匹马共同拉一辆车，在旁边的马叫"驸" horse hitched up by the side of the shaft horse [驸马] 驸马都尉，汉代官名。后来皇帝的女婿常做这个官，因此驸马专指公主的丈夫 official in charge of the horses of an imperial escort; (specifically) emperor's son-in-law

鲋(鮒) fù ㄈㄨˋ 古书上指鲫鱼 (in ancient Chinese texts) crucian carp：涸（hé）辙之～（喻处在困难中急待援助的人）*person in a desperate situation*

负(負) fù ㄈㄨˋ ❶背 to carry on one's back：～重 *carry a heavy load; shoulder a heavy burden* | ～荆请罪 *offer a humble and sincere apology* ⓘ 担任 to shoulder：～责 *be responsible for* [负担] 1 担当，承担 to bear：邀请方～往返旅费。*The inviter shall bear the round-trip travel expenses.* 2 责任，所担当的事务 burden (duty or responsibility)：减轻～ *ease the burden* ⓨ感到痛苦的不容易解决的思想问题 burden (worry) ❷仗恃，倚靠 to rely on：～险固守 *take advantage of a*

F

natural barrier to put up a strong defence｜～隅（yú）顽抗 *put up a desperate resistance by taking advantage of a natural barrier*［负气］赌气 to do sth in a fit of anger［自负］自以为了不起 self-important ❸遭受 to suffer：～伤 *sustain an injury*｜～屈 *suffer wrongful treatment* ❹具有 to enjoy; to have：～有名望 *enjoy a prestige*｜素～盛名 *have always enjoyed a good reputation* ❺欠（钱）to owe：～债 *be in debt; debt* ❻违背，背弃 to betray：～盟 *break one's promise*｜忘恩～义 *forget sb's kindness and turn one's back on him/her in return*｜不～人民的希望 *live up to the expectations of the people* ❼败，跟"胜"相对 to lose (opposite of 胜)：～于对方 *lose to an opponent* ❽小于零的，跟"正"相对 minus (opposite of 正)：～数 *negative number* ❾指相对的两方面中反的一面，跟"正"相对 negative (opposite of 正)：～极 *negative electrode*｜～电 *negative electricity*｜～面 *negative*

妇(**婦**、* **媍**) fù ㄈㄨˋ ❶已经结婚的女子 married woman㊀女性的通称 woman：～科 *gynaecology*｜～女 *woman* ❷妻，跟"夫"相对 wife (opposite of 夫)：夫～ *husband and wife* ❸儿媳 daughter-in-law：长～ *eldest daughter-in-law*｜媳～ *daughter-in-law*

阜 fù ㄈㄨˋ ❶土山 mound ❷盛，多 abundant：物～民丰。*Goods are abundant and the people live in plenty.*

服 fù ㄈㄨˋ 量词，用于中药 (measure word for traditional Chinese medicine) dose：吃～药就好了。*Take a dose of medicine and (you) will be well.*（也作"付" also written as 付）

⇨ see also fú on p.185

复(❶-❹**復**、❺❻**複**) fù ㄈㄨˋ ❶回去，返 to turn back; to return：反～ *repeatedly; go back on one's word; (of illness, etc.) to recur; seeback*｜循环往～ *move in cycles* ❷回答，回报 to reply; to pay back：～仇 *to avenge*｜～命 *report upon completion of a task*｜函～ *reply by letter* ❸还原，使如旧 to recover：光～ *recover (lost territory)*｜～原 *recover from an illness; restore to former condition*｜～员 *return to peacetime conditions; be demobilized* ❹副词，又，再 (adverb) again：死灰～燃 *revival of sth assumed dead (literally means 'dying embers flaring up again')*｜一去不～返 *gone for ever* ❺重复，重叠 to repeat：～习 *to revise*｜～印 *to photo copy*｜山重水～ *(of a place) surrounded by mountain ranges and girdled by winding rivers* ❻不是单一的，许多的 compound：～杂 *complex*｜～分数 *mixed fraction*｜～音词 *disyllabic and polysyllabic word*

腹 fù ㄈㄨˋ 肚子，在胸部的下面 belly：～部 *abdomen*｜～背（前后）受敌 *be exposed to attacks* *from the front and the rear* [腹地] 内地，中部地区 hinterland

蝮 fù ㄈㄨˋ 蝮蛇，一种毒蛇，身体灰褐色，头部略呈三角形，生活在山野和岛上 Pallas' pit viper

鳆(鰒) fù ㄈㄨˋ 鳆鱼，鲍(bào)的古称 (ancient name for 鲍) abalone (see 鲍❶ on page 24 for reference)

覆 fù ㄈㄨˋ ❶遮盖，蒙(㊌-盖) to cover: 天～地载 *infinite bounties bestowed by the emperor; all under heaven and upon earth* ❷翻，倒(dào)过来 to overturn: ～舟 *capsized boat; (figurative) collapse* | 天翻地～ *(of changes) earth-shaking turbulent* [覆没](-mò)船翻沉 (of boat) capsize and sink㊎军队被消灭 (of an army) be annihilated [覆辙]路上留下的翻过车的车辙 track of an overturned cart㊎失败的道路、方法 unsuccessful way [颠覆]车翻倒 (of vehicles) to overturn㊎用阴谋推翻合法政权，也指政权垮台 to subvert; (of regime) to collapse ❸ same as "复❶❷"

馥 fù ㄈㄨˋ 香气 fragrance [馥郁]香气浓厚 strongly fragrant

洑 fù ㄈㄨˋ 在水里游 to swim: ～水 *to swim*

⇨ see also fú on p.184

副 fù ㄈㄨˋ ❶居第二位的，辅助的(区别于"正"或"主") (contrast to 正 or 主) assistant; vice: ～主席 *vice chairman* | ～排长 *auxiliary platoon leader* ❷附带的或次要的 auxiliary; subsidiary: ～食 *non-staple food* | ～业 *side occupation* | ～作用 *side effect* | ～产品 *by-product* [副本] 1 书籍原稿以外的誊录本 transcript; copy 2 文件正式、标准的一份文本以外的若干份 duplicate [副词]修饰动词或形容词的词，如"都、也、很、太、再三"等 adverb ❸相称(chèn)，符合 to correspond to: 名不～实 *be unworthy of the name* | 名实相～ *the name matches the reality* ❹量词 measure word ①用于成组成套的东西 used for a pair or set of things: 一～对联 *a pair of couplets* | 一～担架 *a stretcher* | 全～武装 *be armed to the teeth* ②用于面部表情、态度等 used for facial expressions: 一～笑容 *a smiling face* | 一～和蔼的面孔 *an amiable face*

富 fù ㄈㄨˋ ❶富有，跟"贫""穷"相对 rich (opposite of 贫 or 穷): ～人 *the rich* | ～豪 *rich and powerful person* | ～强 *prosperous and powerful* [富丽]华丽 beautiful and magnificent: 宫殿～堂皇。*The palace is magnificent.* ❷资源、财产 resource: ～源 *natural resources* | 财～ *wealth* ❸充裕，多，足(㊌-裕、-足、-饶、丰-) abundant: ～于创造精神 *highly creative*

赋(賦) fù ㄈㄨˋ ❶旧指田地税 (old) land tax: 田～ *land tax (in feudal times)* [赋税]旧时田赋和各种捐税的总

F

称 tax ❷我国古典文学中的一种文体，盛行于汉魏六朝 prose poem ❸念诗或作诗 to read/compose a poem：～诗 *compose a poem* ❹交给，给予 to bestow：～予重任 *assign an important task (to sb)*

傅 fù ㄈㄨˋ ❶辅助，教导 to instruct ❷师傅，教导人的人 instructor ❸附着，使附着 to adhere：～粉 *to powder*

缚(縛) fù ㄈㄨˋ 捆绑 to tie up; to bind：束～ *to bind* | 手无～鸡之力 *be weak physically (literally means 'have no strength to truss a chicken')*

赙(賻) fù ㄈㄨˋ 拿钱财帮人办理丧事 to give money to help with a funeral：～金 *money presented to a bereaved family* | ～仪 *gift presented to a bereaved family*

F

G ㄍ

GA ㄍㄚ

夹(夾) gā ㄍㄚ [夹肢窝](－zhiwō)腋窝 armpit

⇨ see also jiā on p.295, jiá on p.296

旮 gā ㄍㄚ [旮旯](－lá)(－子、－儿)角落 nook; corner: 墙～ *corner of a wall* | 门～ *door nook* ㊗偏僻的地方 remote, out-of-the-way location: 山～ *mountain recess*

伽 gā ㄍㄚ [伽马射线]通常写作"γ 射线"，又叫丙种射线。波长极短，一些放射性元素的原子能放出这种射线，在工业和医学上用途很广 gamma ray (usually written as γ 射线, also called 丙种射线)

⇨ see also jiā on p.295, qié on p.535

咖 gā ㄍㄚ [咖喱](－lí)(外 *loanword*)用胡椒、姜黄等做的调味品 curry

⇨ see also kā on p.347

戛 gā ㄍㄚ [戛纳]法国地名 Cannes (French city)

⇨ see also jiá on p.297

嘎(*嘠) gā ㄍㄚ 拟声词 onomatopoeia [嘎吧][嘎叭](－bā)形容树枝等折断的声音 crack (as in a tree branch breaking); snap [嘎吱](－zhī)形容物体受压发出的声音 creak; squeak

[嘎巴](－ba)1 黏东西凝结在器物上 to form into crust 2(－儿)凝结在器物上的东西 crust (formed on things): 衣服上有好多～。*There is a lot of dried gunge on the clothes.*

[嘎渣](－zha)1 疮口或伤口结的痂 scab (over a wound) 2(－儿)食物烤黄的焦皮 (of bread, cake, etc.) burnt crust: 饭～ *rice crusts* | 饼子～儿 *crust of pan-baked bread*

⇨ see also gá on p.194, gǎ on p.194

轧(軋) gá ㄍㄚˊ 〈方 dialect〉❶挤，拥挤 to push; to squeeze ❷结交(朋友) to associate with ❸查对(账目) to check (financial accounts)

⇨ see also yà on p.747, zhá on p.826

钆(釓) gá ㄍㄚˊ 金属元素，符号 Gd，银白色，磁性强，用于微波技术、核工业等 gadolinium (Gd)

尜 gá ㄍㄚˊ [尜尜](－ga) 1 一种儿童玩具，两头尖中间大，又叫尜儿 *gaga* (olive /spindle-shaped toy, also called 尜儿) 2 像尜尜的 spindle-shaped: ～枣 *spindle-shaped dates* | ～汤(用玉米面等做的食品) gaga *soup (soup with spindle-shaped corn flour pieces)*

嘎(*嘎) gá ㄍㄚˊ [嘎嘎](— gɑ) same as "尜尜"

⇨ see also gā on p.193, gǎ on p.194

噶 gá ㄍㄚˊ 译音用字 used in phonetic translation

生 gǎ ㄍㄚˇ same as "嘎(gǎ)"

尕 gǎ ㄍㄚˇ 〈方 dialect〉小 small; little: ～娃 *little child* | ～李 *Young Li (used before a younger person's surname as a form of endearment)*

嘎(*嘎) gǎ ㄍㄚˇ 〈方 dialect〉❶ 乖僻 odd; eccentric ❷ 调皮 naughty; mischievous: ～小子 *naughty boy*

⇨ see also gā on p.193, gá on p.194

尬 gà ㄍㄚˋ see 尴尬(gān—) at 尴 on page 197

GAI ㄍㄞ

该(該) gāi ㄍㄞ ❶应当，理应如此(㊀应—) should; to deserve: ～做的一定要做。*What should be done must be done.* ❷表示根据情理或经验推测必然的或可能的结果 (to express an inference) will: 不学习，就～跟不上时代了。*We won't keep up with the times if we don't keep learning.* ❸代词，指前面说过的人或事物，多用于公文 (pronoun) above-mentioned (often in official documents): ～地 *this place* | ～员 *the said person* | ～书 *the afore-mentioned book* ❹ 欠，欠账 to owe (money, etc.): ～他几块钱 *owe him a few yuan* ❺ same as "赅"

陔 gāi ㄍㄞ ❶近台阶的地方 place near steps ❷级，层，台阶 step; storey; stair ❸ 田埂 ridge in a field

垓 gāi ㄍㄞ ❶垓下，古地名，在今安徽省灵璧东南，是汉刘邦围困项羽的地方 Gaixia (an ancient place where a famous battle was fought, in the south-east of the present day Lingbi, Anhui Province) ❷古代数目名，是京的十倍，指一万万 (ancient Chinese number word) one hundred million (ten times as 京)

荄 gāi ㄍㄞ 草根 grass roots

晐 gāi ㄍㄞ 兼备，完备 complete; inclusive

赅(賅) gāi ㄍㄞ ❶完备 complete; comprehensive: 言简意～ *(of words, speech, etc.) concise but complete* ❷包括 to include: 举一～百 *give one example and account for all cases*

改 gǎi ㄍㄞˇ ❶变更，更换(㊀—革、—变、更—) to change; to replace: 住址～了。*The address is changed.* | ～天再谈 *continue the discussion another day* ❷修改 to revise; to modify: ～文章 *revise/edit an article* | ～衣服 *make alterations to clothing* ❸改正 to rectify: 知过必～ *always correct a mistake when one becomes aware of it*

丐(△*匄、*匃) gài ㄍㄞˋ ❶乞求 to

beg ❷乞丐，讨饭的人 beggar ❸给予 to give; to bestow

钙（鈣） gài ㄍㄞˋ 金属元素，符号 Ca，银白色，是生物体的重要组成元素。它的化合物在工业和医药上用途很广 calcium (Ca)

丐 gài ㄍㄞˋ ❶ see 丐 on page 194 ❷用于人名。姬丐，东周敬王 used in given names, e.g. Ji Gai, King Jing of Eastern Zhou Dynasty

芥 gài ㄍㄞˋ 芥菜（也作“盖菜”），是芥（jiè）菜的变种，叶大，表面多皱纹，可用作蔬菜 leaf mustard (also written as 盖菜, a variant of 芥 jiè 菜)

⇨ see also jiè on p.319

隑（隑） gài ㄍㄞˋ 〈方 dialect〉 ❶斜靠 to lean against ❷依仗 to rely on ❸站立 to stand

盖（蓋） gài ㄍㄞˋ ❶（一子、一儿）器物上部有遮蔽作用的东西 lid; cover：锅～ *lid of pot* | 瓶～ *bottle top* ❷伞 umbrella：华～（古代车上像伞的篷子）*canopy (awning on a cart in ancient times)* ❸由上向下遮、蒙（㊀覆一）to cover：～上锅 *cover a pot* | ～被 *cover with a quilt* ㊁ ①压倒 to surpass; to excel; to outclass：～世无双 *unequalled on earth* ②用印打上 to impress (seal); to stamp：～章 *to stamp* | ～印 *impress a seal on* ③掩饰（㊀掩一）to cover up; to conceal：问题～是～不住的。*Problems will not be covered up.* ❹建造 to build; to construct：～楼 *construct a building* | ～房子 *build a house* ❺动物的甲壳 (of animals) top shell：螃蟹～ *crab shell* ❻文言虚词 function word in classical Chinese writing ①发语词 function word used to begin a phrase：长安一别，～有年矣。*It's been years since we parted in Chang'an.* ②表不能确信，大概如此 approximately; about：观者如云，～近千人也。*There were about a thousand onlookers.* ③连词，表原因 (conjunction) used to indicate a cause：有所不知，～未学也。*If there are things (we) do not know, it is because (we) have not learnt them.* ❼姓 (surname) Gai

〈古 ancient〉 also same as 盍 (hé)

⇨ see also gě on p.206

溉 gài ㄍㄞˋ 浇灌（㊀灌一）to irrigate; to water

概（*槩） gài ㄍㄞˋ ❶大略，总括 general：～论 *general introduction* | 大～ *general idea; approximate (ly); likely* | ～况 *general overview* ❷一概，一律 without exception; categorically：未预约者～不接待。*Those without appointments absolutely will not be seen.* [概念] 人们在反复的实践和认识过程中，将事物共同的本质特点抽出来，加以概括，从感性认识飞跃到理性认识，就成为概念 concept; notion; idea ❸情况，景象 circumstance; scene：胜～ *beautiful scenery* ❹气度 manner; deportment：气～ *lofty spirit* ❺刮平斗、斛用的小木板 wooden scraper (used for levelling the content of a measuring bucket)

G

戤 gài ㄍㄞ 〈方 dialect〉冒牌图利 to counterfeit

GAN ㄍㄢ

干(❼—⓭△乾、❼—⓭*乹、❼—⓭*乾) gān ㄍㄢ ❶关联，涉及 to relate to; to have to do with：相～ *be related* | 这事与你何～？ *What has this to do with you?* ❷冒犯，触犯 to offend; to violate：～犯 *to offend* | 有～禁例 *go against the prohibitions* [干涉]过问或制止，常指不应管硬管 to interfere：互不～内政 *not interfere in each other's internal affairs* ❸追求，旧指追求职位俸禄 (formerly) to pursue (an official position or salary)：～禄 *seek an official position* ❹盾 shield：动～戈（指发动战争）*resort to arms* ❺天干，历法中用的"甲、乙、丙、丁、戊、己、庚、辛、壬、癸"十个字，也用来编排次序 Heavenly Stems (a system used in the Chinese calendar or to arrange things into a sequence) [干支]天干和地支，历法上把这两组字结合起来，共配成六十组，表示日子或年份，周而复始，循环使用 the Heavenly Stems and Earthly Branches (a system used in the Chinese calendar) ❻水边 waterside：江～ *riverbank* | 河～ *riverside* ❼没有水分或水分少，跟"湿"相对（㊀—燥）dry (opposite of 湿)：～柴 *fire wood* | ～粮 *solid food (for a journey); field ration* [干脆]㊉爽快，简捷 clear-cut; straightforward：说话～，做事也～ *crisp in talking, and brisk in doing* ❽(—儿)干的食品或其他东西 dried food or other things：饼～ *biscuits* | 豆腐～儿 *dried bean curd* ❾枯竭，净尽，空虚 dried up; empty：大河没水小河～。*When a river has no water, streams run dry.* | ～杯 *drink a toast; 'cheers!'(when proposing a toast)* | 外强中～ *outwardly strong but inwardly weak* ❿副词，空，徒然 (adverb) in vain; to no avail：～着急 *fret in vain* | ～等 *wait to no avail* | ～看着 *look on helplessly* ⓫拜认的（亲属）关系 nominal kinship：～娘 *nominally adoptive mother* ⓬当面说怨恨、气愤的话使对方难堪 to discomfit; to put ill at ease with words：今天，我又～了他一顿。*I made him ill at ease again today.* ⓭〈方 dialect〉慢待，不理睬 to cold shoulder (sb)：把来人～在一旁 *leave guests in the cold* ⓮量词，伙 (measure word) group：一～人 *a group of people* ⓯姓 (surname) Gan

[干将]（—jiāng）古宝剑名 Ganjiang (name of an ancient sword)

⇨ see also gàn on p.199

⇨ 乾 see also qián on p.527

玕 gān ㄍㄢ [琅玕]（láng—）像珠子的美石 pearl-like stone

杆 gān ㄍㄢ （—子、—儿）较长的木棍或类似的东西 pole; staff：旗～ *flagstaff* | 电线～子 *utility pole* | 栏～儿 *railing*

G

⇨ see also gǎn on p.197

肝 gān ㄍㄢ 肝脏，人和高等动物的消化器官之一，功能是分泌胆汁，储藏糖原，进行蛋白质、脂肪和碳水化合物的代谢及解毒等 liver (see picture of 人体内脏 on page 819) [肝胆] ㊕ 1 诚心，诚意 sincerity: ～相照（喻真诚相见）*be true to each other (literally means 'as close as liver and gall bladder')* | 2 勇气，血性 heroic spirit; courage

矸 gān ㄍㄢ 矸子，夹杂在煤里的石块 gangue: 煤～石 *coal gangue*

虷 gān ㄍㄢ 〈古 ancient〉干犯 to offend

⇨ see also hán on p.240

竿 gān ㄍㄢ （－子、－儿）竹竿，竹子的主干，竹棍 bamboo pole

酐 gān ㄍㄢ 酸酐，是含氧的无机或有机酸缩水而成的氧化物，如二氧化硫、醋酸酐 anhydride

甘 gān ㄍㄢ ❶甜，味道好，跟"苦"相对 sweet (opposite of 苦): ～苦 *sweetness and bitterness; weal and woe* | ～泉 *sweet spring* | 苦尽～来。*When bitterness ends, sweetness begins.* ㊗ 美好 pleasant: ～雨 *timely rainfall* ❷甘心，自愿，乐意 to be willing to; to be contented with: 心～情愿 *of one's free will* | 不～失败 *not take a defeat lying down*

坩 gān ㄍㄢ 盛东西的陶器 earthen pot/jar [坩埚]（－guō）用来熔化金属或其他物质的器皿，多用瓷土、石墨或铂制成，能耐高热 crucible

苷 gān ㄍㄢ 有机化合物的一类，即糖苷，旧叫甙（dài），由糖类和其他有机化合物失水缩合而成 glycoside (same as 糖苷, formerly called 甙 dài)

泔 gān ㄍㄢ 泔水，洗过米的水 rice water (leftover after washing rice) ㊊ 洗碗洗菜用过的脏水 slops; swill

柑 gān ㄍㄢ 常绿灌木或小乔木，花白色，果实圆形，比橘子大，红黄色，味甜，种类很多 mandarin orange

疳 gān ㄍㄢ 疳积，中医指小儿面黄肌瘦、腹部膨大的病 infantile malnutrition (in traditional Chinese medicine)

尴（尷、尲）** gān ㄍㄢ [尴尬]（－gà）1 处境窘困，不易处理 awkward 2 神态不自然 embarrassed

杆（*桿） gǎn ㄍㄢˇ ❶（－子、－儿）较小的圆木条或像木条的东西（指作为器物的把儿的）shaft; rod; stem: 笔～儿 *barrel of a pen; shaft of a writing brush* | 枪～儿 *barrel of a gun* | 烟袋～儿 *stem of a pipe* ❷量词，用于有杆的器物 measure word for objects with a shaft: 一～枪 *a rifle* | 一～笔 *a pen; a writing brush*

⇨ see also gān on p.196

秆（*稈） gǎn ㄍㄢˇ （－子、－儿）稻麦等植物的茎 stalk; stem: 高粱～儿 *sorghum*

G

stalk | 高～作物 *long-stalked crops*

赶(趕) gǎn ㄍㄢˇ ❶追，尽早或及时到达 to catch up with; to get to in time：再不走就～不上他了。*(We) won't catch up with him if (we) don't start now.* | ～集 *go to a fair/market* | ～火车 *catch a train* | 学先进，～先进 *learn from and catch up with progressive people* ㊕从速，快做 to hurry through：～写文章 *dash off an article* | ～任务 *hurry through a task* | ～活 *work against the clock* ❷驱使，驱逐 to drive; to expel：～羊 *herd sheep* | ～马车 *drive a cart* | 把侵略者～出国门 *chase the aggressors out of the land* ❸介词，等到（某个时候）(preposition) till：～明儿再说 *put it off till one of these days* | ～年下再回家 *not go home until Spring Festival* ❹遇到（某种情形）to happen to; to run into：我去时，正～上他没在家。*He happened not to be home when I went.*

擀 gǎn ㄍㄢˇ 用棍棒碾轧(yà) to roll (pastry etc.)：～面条 *make noodles* | ～毡（制毡）*make felt*

敢 gǎn ㄍㄢˇ ❶有勇气，有胆量 to dare：～于斗争 *dare to struggle* | ～负责任 *dare to take the responsibility* ❷谦辞 (humble speech) May I...?：～问尊姓大名？*May I know your name?* | ～请光临。*May I ask for your presence?* ❸莫非 maybe; perhaps：～是哥哥回来了？*Could it be (our) elder brother back home?*

澉 gǎn ㄍㄢˇ ［澉浦］地名，在浙江省海盐 Ganpu (a place in Haiyan, Zhejiang Province)

橄 gǎn ㄍㄢˇ ［橄榄］(－lǎn) 1 橄榄树，常绿乔木，花白色。果实也叫橄榄，又叫青果，绿色，长圆形，可以吃，种子可用来榨油 olive tree; Chinese olive (its fruit also called 青果) 2 油橄榄，常绿小乔木，又叫齐墩果，花白色，果实黑色。欧美用它的枝叶作为和平的象征 olive; Olea europaea (also called 齐墩果)

感 gǎn ㄍㄢˇ ❶感觉，觉到 to feel; to sense：～想 *thoughts* | ～到很温暖 *feel warm feelings* ［感觉］1 客观事物的个别性质作用于人的感官（眼、耳、鼻、舌、皮肤）所引起的直接反应 perception; sensation; feeling 2 觉得 to feel：我～事情还顺手。*I feel that things are handled smoothly.* ［感性］指感觉和印象，是认识的初级阶段 perception：～认识 *perceptual knowledge* ❷使在意识、情绪上起反应 (in feelings) to move; to touch：～动 *to move; be moved* | ～人 *touching; moving* | ～化 *educate an erring person by persuasion, example, etc.* ❸情感，感情，因受刺激而引起的心理上的变化 feeling; sense; reaction：读后～ *reflections (after reading sth)* | 百～交集 *a myriad of feelings surge up* | 自豪～ *sense of pride* ❹感谢，对人家的好意表示谢意 to be grateful：～恩 *feel thankful* | 深～厚谊 *much appreciate the friend-*

G

ship | 请寄来为～。*I should be much obliged if you could mail it to me.*

鳡(鱤) gǎn ㄍㄢˇ 鱼名，又叫黄钻（zuàn），身体长，青黄色，嘴尖。性凶猛，捕食其他鱼类，生活在淡水中 yellowcheek carp (also 黄钻, an aggressive freshwater fish)

干(幹、❶*榦) gàn ㄍㄢˋ ❶事物的主体，重要的部分 trunk; main body：树～ *tree trunk* | 躯～ *torso* | ～线 *main line; trunk road* [干部] 1 指机关团体的领导或管理人员 cadre (people at the leadership or management level) 2 指一般公职人员 public official ❷做，搞 to do; to work：～工作 *perform a job* | 你在～什么？*What are you doing?* ㊕有才能的，善于办事的 able; capable：～才 *ability; capable person* | ～员 *competent official* [干练] 办事能力强，很有经验 capable and experienced [干事]（-shi）负责某些事务的人 clerk：宣传～ *publicity officer* ❸〈方 dialect〉坏，糟 to mess up：不好，事情要～。*Oh dear, things don't look good.* | ～了，要迟到了。*Oh no, we'll be late.*

⇨ see also gān on p.196

旰 gàn ㄍㄢˋ 晚上 evening：～食 *eat late*

骭 gàn ㄍㄢˋ ❶小腿骨 shank ❷肋骨 rib

绀(紺) gàn ㄍㄢˋ 微带红的黑色 reddish black or deep purple

淦 gàn ㄍㄢˋ 用于地名 used in place names：～井沟（在重庆市忠县）*Ganjinggou (a place in Zhongxian, Chongqing Municipality)*

淦 gàn ㄍㄢˋ 淦水，水名，在江西省 Ganshui River (in Jiangxi Province)

赣(贑、*赣、*灨) gàn ㄍㄢˋ ❶赣江，水名，在江西省 Ganjiang River (in Jiangxi Province) ❷江西省的别称 Gan (another name for Jiangxi Province)

GANG ㄍㄤ

冈(岡) gāng ㄍㄤ 山脊 (of a hill) ridge：山～ *low hill* | 景阳～ *Jingyang Ridge* | 井～山 *Jinggang Mountain*

刚(剛) gāng ㄍㄤ ❶坚强，跟"柔"相对(㊟-强) hard; unyielding (opposite of 柔)：～正 *principled* ❷副词，正好，恰巧㊫(adverb) just; just about：～～合适 *just right* | ～好一杯 *exactly a cupful* ❸副词，才，刚才 (adverb) just; just now：～来就走 *barely arrive before leaving* | 她～走，还追得上。*She just left, and (you) can still catch up with her.*

㧏(㨣) gāng ㄍㄤ same as "扛 (gāng)"

岗(崗) gāng ㄍㄤ same as "冈"

⇨ see also gǎng on p.200

纲(綱) gāng ㄍㄤ ❶提网的总绳 headrope of a fishing net ㊐事物的关键部分

G

key link; guiding principle：大～ *outline* | ～目 *detailed outline* | ～领 *programme; guiding principle* ❷ 从唐朝起，转运大量货物时，把货物分批运行，每批的车辆、船只计数编号，叫作一纲 (in ancient China from Tang Dynasty) convoy; goods transported under convoy: 盐～ *salt convoy* | 茶～ *tea convoy* | 花石～ *convoy of precious stones and plants* ❸生物的分类单位之一，在“门”之下、“目”之上 class (a category in taxonomic classification)：鸟～ *Aves* | 单子叶植物～ *Monocotyledoneae*

棡(㭎) gāng ㄍㄤ 青㭎，落叶乔木，叶椭圆形，木质坚实，可供建筑用 glaucous-leaf oak

钢(鋼) gāng ㄍㄤ 含碳量低于2%的铁碳合金，并含有少量锰、硅、硫、磷等，比熟铁硬度高，比生铁韧性好，是重要的工业原料 steel [钢铁] 钢和铁的合称，也专指钢 iron and steel; steel ㊖坚强，坚定不移 firm; unbreakable：～的意志 *iron will*

⇨ see also gàng on p.201

江 gāng ㄍㄤ 姓 (surname) Gang

扛 gāng ㄍㄤ ❶两手举东西 to lift / raise with both hands：～鼎 *lift a tripod (big vessel); (figurative) shoulder big responsibilities* ❷〈方 dialect〉抬东西 (of two or more persons) to carry together

⇨ see also káng on p.351

肛 gāng ㄍㄤ 肛门，直肠末端的出口 anus

矼 gāng ㄍㄤ ❶石桥 stone bridge ❷用于地名 used in place names：大～（在浙江省永嘉）*Dagang (in Yongjia, Zhejiang Province)*

缸(甌)** gāng ㄍㄤ 盛东西的陶器，圆筒状，底小口大 earthen vat

罡 gāng ㄍㄤ [天罡星] 即北斗星 the Plough; the Big Dipper

堽 gāng ㄍㄤ 用于地名 used in place names：～城屯（在山东省宁阳）*Gangchengtun (in Ningyang, Shandong Province)*

岗(崗) gǎng ㄍㄤˇ ❶（一子、一儿）高起的土坡 mound; hillock：黄土～儿 *loess hill* ❷（一子、一儿）平面上凸起的一长道 ridge; welt：肉～子 *muscle ridge* ❸守卫的位置 post; sentry：站～ *keep guard; stand sentry* | 门～ *gate sentry* | 布～ *post a sentry* [岗位] 守卫、值勤的地方，也指职位 post; station; position：工作～ *post of duty*

⇨ see also gāng on p.199

港 gǎng ㄍㄤˇ ❶江河的支流 tributary ❷可以停泊大船的江海口岸 port; harbour：军～ *military harbour* | 商～ *commercial port* | 不冻～ *non-freezing port* ❸指香港 (short for) Hong Kong：～人治～。*Hong Kong people administer Hong Kong.*

杠(*槓) gàng ㄍㄤˋ ❶（一子）较粗的棍子 thick pole/stick：铁～ *metal bar* | 木～ *wooden pole* | 双～（一种运

动器具）*parallel bars*［杠杆］（－gǎn）简单机械，剪刀、辘轳、秤等就是利用杠杆的原理制作的 lever (simple machine) ❷（用笔等画的）粗的直线 thick line (as a mark)：在书中重要的地方画上了红～。*Red lines are drawn in the book to highlight key points.*

埄 gàng ㄍㄤˋ 〈方 dialect〉山冈，多用于地名 low hill (often used in place names)：浮亭～（在浙江省景宁）*Futinggang (a place in Jingning, Zhejiang Province)*

钢（鋼） gàng ㄍㄤˋ 把刀在布、皮、石或缸沿等上用力摩擦几下，使锋利 to sharpen：这把刀钝了，要～一～。*This blunt knife needs sharpening.*

⇨ see also gāng on p.200

筻 gàng ㄍㄤˋ ［筻口］地名，在湖南省岳阳 Gangkou (a place in Yueyang, Hunan Province)

戇（戇） gàng ㄍㄤˋ 〈方 dialect〉鲁莽 crude; reckless：～头～脑 *be slow-witted*

⇨ see also zhuàng on p.874

GAO ㄍㄠ

皋（*臯、*皐） gāo ㄍㄠ 水边的高地 waterside highland：江～ *river bank*

槔（橰）** gāo ㄍㄠ see 桔槔 (jié－) at 桔 on page 317

高 gāo ㄍㄠ ❶跟"低"相对 high; tall (opposite of 低) ①由下到上距离远的 tall; high：～山 *high mountain*｜～楼大厦 *high-rise buildings* ②等级在上的 above; higher：～年级 *higher (senior) grade*｜～等学校 *institution of higher learning* ③在一般标准或平均程度之上 (of standard or level) high：质量～ *of high quality*｜～速度 *high speed*｜～价 *high price* ④声音响亮 loud：～歌 *sing aloud*｜～声 *loudly*［高低］1 高低的程度 height 2 优劣 relative superiority 3 深浅轻重（指说话或做事）sense of propriety：不知～ *have no sense of propriety* 4 〈方 dialect〉到底，终究 at long last; after all：这事儿～让他办成了。*He did it after all.* 5 无论如何 anyway; on any account：再三请求，他～不答应。*He simply would not give his consent despite repeated requests.* ❷高度 height：身～ *body height*｜书桌～80厘米。*The desk is 80cm high.* ❸敬辞 (polite speech) your：～见（高明的见解）*your opinion*｜～寿（问老人的年纪）*your age (in asking the age of an elderly person)*

［高山族］我国少数民族，参看附录四 the Gaoshan people (one of the ethnic groups in China. See Appendix Ⅳ.)

膏 gāo ㄍㄠ ❶肥或肥肉 fat; fatty meat：～粱（肥肉和细粮）*rich food (fatty meat and fine grain)*［膏腴］（－yú）土地肥沃 fertile ❷脂，油 cream; grease; oil ❸很稠的、糊状的东西 paste; ointment：梨～ *pear syrup (cough* *medicine in China)* | 牙～ *tooth paste* | ～药 *(medicated) plaster; patch*

⇨ see also gào on p.203

篙 gāo ㄍㄠ 用竹竿或杉木等做成的撑船的器具 punt-pole

羔 gāo ㄍㄠ （一子、一儿）羊羔，小羊 lamb：～儿皮 *lamb skin* 泛指幼小的动物 (generally) young animal：狼～ *wolf pup*

糕(*餻) gāo ㄍㄠ 用米粉或面粉等掺和其他材料做成的食品 cake; pastry：鸡蛋～ *(sponge) cake* | 年～ *New Year cake (made of glutinous rice flour)*

睾 gāo ㄍㄠ 睾丸，又叫精巢、外肾，男子和雄性哺乳动物生殖器官的一部分，在体腔或阴囊内，能产生精子 testicle; testis (also called 精巢，外肾)

杲 gǎo ㄍㄠˇ 明亮 ㊣ bright; brilliant：～～出日。*The sun rises bright.*

搞 gǎo ㄍㄠˇ 做，弄，干，办 to do：～工作 *engage in work* | ～通思想 *straighten out one's thinking* | ～清问题 *get to the bottom of an issue*

缟(縞) gǎo ㄍㄠˇ 一种白色的丝织品 a kind of thin white silk：～衣 *white silk clothing* [缟素] 白衣服，指丧服 white mourning garment

槁(*槀) gǎo ㄍㄠˇ 枯干（㊀枯一）parched; withered：～木 *withered tree*

镐(鎬) gǎo ㄍㄠˇ 刨土的工具 pickaxe

⇨ see also hào on p.246

稿(*稾) gǎo ㄍㄠˇ ❶谷类植物的茎秆 straw; stalk of crops：～荐（稻草编的垫子）*straw mattress* ❷（一子、一儿）文字、图画的草底 draft; sketch：文～儿 *manuscript* | 打～儿 *make a draft* ㊙ 事先考虑的计划 plan：做事没准～子可不成。*It won't do to not have a good plan.*

藁 gǎo ㄍㄠˇ 藁城，地名，在河北省 Gaocheng (a place in Hebei Province)

告 gào ㄍㄠˋ ❶把事情说给别人，通知（㊀一诉）to tell; to inform：报～ *to report* | 奔走相～ *run around telling people* [告白] 对公众的通告 public notice [忠告] 规劝，也指规劝的话 to advise; advice ❷提起诉讼（㊀控一）to accuse; to sue：～发 *report on; inform against* | 原～ *plaintiff; complainant* | 被～ *defendant; accused* ❸请求 to ask for; to plead：～假（jià）*ask for leave* | ～饶 *beg for mercy* ❹表明 to express; to make known：～辞 *say goodbye* | 自～奋勇 *volunteer for a task* ❺宣布或表示某种情况的出现 to announce：大功～成 *mission accomplished* | ～急 *report an emergency*

郜 gào ㄍㄠˋ 姓 (surname) Gao

诰(誥) gào ㄍㄠˋ 古代帝王对臣子的命令 imperial mandate：～命 *imperial mandate; titled lady* | ～封 *confer an honorary title by imperial mandate*

G

锆(鋯) gào ㄍㄠˋ 金属元素，符号Zr，银灰色，质硬，耐腐蚀。用于核工业等 zirconium (Zr)

筶 gào ㄍㄠˋ 东筶杯岛、西筶杯岛，岛名，都在福建省莆田 East Gaobei Island and West Gaobei Island (both in Putian, Fujian Province)

膏 gào ㄍㄠˋ ❶把油加在车轴或机械上 to lubricate; to grease: ～油 *to oil* | ～车 *lubricate a vehicle* ❷把毛笔蘸上墨汁在砚台边上掭 to dip in ink and smooth (a writing brush) on an ink stone: ～笔 *dip a writing brush in ink and smooth it* | ～墨 *dip in ink and smooth a brush*

➪ see also gāo on p.201

GE ㄍㄜ

戈 gē ㄍㄜ 古代的一种兵器，横刃长柄 dagger-axe (a weapon in ancient times)

[戈壁]（蒙 *Mongolian*）沙漠地区 Gobi Desert

仡 gē ㄍㄜ [仡佬族]（一lǎo一）我国少数民族，参看附录四 the Gelao people (one of the ethnic groups in China. See Appendix Ⅳ.)

➪ see also yì on p.774

圪 gē ㄍㄜ [圪垯]（一da）1 同"疙瘩2"。多用于土块等 same as 疙瘩 2 (often of clay etc.): 土～ *clay lump* | 冰～ *ice chunk* 2 小土丘，多用于地名 mound; knoll (often in place names) [圪塄]（一láo）〈方 dialect〉角落，也用于地名 corner (also used in place names): 炕～ *corner of a* kang | 周家～（在陕西省子洲县）*Zhoujiagelao (a place in Zizhou, Shaanxi Province)*

纥(紇) gē ㄍㄜ [纥繨]（一da）同"疙瘩2"。多用于纱线、织物等 same as 疙瘩 2 (often of yarn, fabric, etc.): 线～ *thread knot* | 解开头巾上的～ *untie the knot of a scarf*

➪ see also hé on p.247

疙 gē ㄍㄜ [疙瘩]（一da）1 皮肤上突起或肌肉上结成的病块 pimple;(of skin) lump: 头上起了个～ *have a bump on the head* 2 小球形或块状的东西 lump; knot: 面～ *dough pieces* | 芥菜～ *swede* 3 比喻不易解决的问题 thorny issue; knotty problem: 思想～ *hang-up* | 这件事有点ル～。*There's something knotty about the matter.* 4 比喻不通畅、不爽利的话 (figurative) uneven sentence: 文字上有些～。*There's something uneven about the writing.* 5〈方 dialect〉量词，用于球形或块状的东西 measure word for lump-shaped objects: 一～石头 *a (lump of) rock* | 一～糕 *a piece of cake*

咯 gē ㄍㄜ [咯噔]（一dēng）形容皮鞋踏地或物体撞击等声音 click: ～～的皮鞋声 *the click of leather shoes* [咯咯]形容笑声或咬牙声等 chuckle; giggle: 传来一阵～的笑声。*There came a burst of giggling.* | 牙齿咬得～响 *grit one's teeth* [咯吱]

G

（－zhī）形容竹、木等器物受挤压发出的声音 creak：把地板踩得～～直响。*There are creaks of the floor when walked on.*

⇨ see also kǎ on p.347, lo on p.414

胳（*肐）gē ㄍㄜ ［胳膊（－bo）］［胳臂］（－bei）上肢，肩膀以下手腕以上的部分 (human) arm

袼 gē ㄍㄜ ［袼褙］（－bei）用纸或布裱糊成的厚片，多用来做纸盒、布鞋等 scrap pieces of cloth, rags or paper pasted together in layers for making boxes or cloth shoes

搁（擱）gē ㄍㄜ 放，置 to put; to place：把书～下 *put down a book*｜在汤里～点儿味精 *add some MSG to the soup*㊂耽搁，放在那里不做 to lay aside; to shelve：这事～了一个月。*It has been on the shelf for a month.*［搁浅］船停滞在浅处，不能进退 (of a boat or ship) to run aground; to be grounded ㊔事情停顿 to reach a deadlock; to be shelved

⇨ see also gé on p.205

哥 gē ㄍㄜ ❶兄，同父母（或只同父、只同母）或亲属中同辈而年龄比自己大的男子㊋ elder brother：大～ *eldest brother*｜表～ *elder male cousin* ❷称呼年龄跟自己差不多的男子 (used to address a male person of older or similar age) brother：张大～ *Brother Zhang*

歌（*謌）gē ㄍㄜ ❶（－儿）能唱的文辞 song：山～ *folk song*｜唱～ *sing a song* ❷唱（㊄－唱、－咏）to sing：高～一曲 *sing a song loudly*［歌颂］颂扬 to extol; to eulogize：～祖国 *sing praise of one's motherland*

鿔（鎶）gē ㄍㄜ 人造的放射性金属元素，符号Cn。copernicium (Cn)

鸽（鴿）gē ㄍㄜ （－子）鸟名，有家鸽、野鸽等多种，常成群飞翔。有的家鸽能够传递书信。常用作和平的象征 pigeon; dove

割 gē ㄍㄜ 切断，截下 to cut; to mow：～麦 *cut/reap wheat*｜～草 *cut grass*｜～阑尾 *surgically remove the appendix*㊂舍去 to give up; to part with：～舍 *give up*｜～爱 *part with sth dear*［割据］一国之内拥有武力的人占据部分地区，形成分裂对抗的局面 divide up a country by force［交割］一方交付，一方接收，双方结清手续 to complete a business transaction［收割］把成熟的庄稼割下收起 to harvest

革 gé ㄍㄜˊ ❶去了毛，经过加工的兽皮（㊄皮－）leather; hide：制～ *to process hide; to tan* ❷改变（㊄改－、变－）to change; to reform：～新 *to reform; to innovate*｜洗心～面 *reform oneself thoroughly*㊂革除，撤销（职务）to expel; to dismiss：～职 *remove from office*［革命］1 被压迫阶级用暴力夺取政权，摧毁旧的腐朽的社会制度，建立新的进步的社会制度 start a revolution 2 事物的根本变革 revolution; radical change：思想～ *ideological rev-*

olution | 技术 ～ *technical revolution*

⇨ see also jí on p.287

阁(閤) gé ㄍㄜˊ 小门，旁门 small door; side door

⇨ 閤 see also 阁 on p.205, hé 合 on p.247

蛤 gé ㄍㄜˊ 蛤蜊(li)，软体动物，介壳颜色美丽，生活在近海泥沙中 clam

[蛤蚧](-jiè)爬行动物，像壁虎而大，头大，尾部灰色，有红色斑点，可入药 Gekko gecko

⇨ see also há on p.237

颌(頜) gé ㄍㄜˊ 口 mouth

⇨ see also hé on p.247

阁(閣、△*閤) gé ㄍㄜˊ ❶类似楼房的建筑物 pavilion：亭台楼～ *pavilions, terraces and towers*[阁下]对人的敬称，今多用于外交场合 (polite speech, now often in diplomatic settings) Your/His/Her Excellency/Honour [阁子]小木头房子 cabin [内阁]明清两代的中央政务机构，民国初年的国务院和现在某些国家的最高行政机关也叫内阁，省称"阁"(government) cabinet (shortened as 阁)：组～ *form a cabinet* | 入～ *become cabinet member* ❷闺房 boudoir：出～(指女子出嫁) *(of a woman) get married*

⇨ 閤 see also 阁 on p.205, hé 合 on p.247

格 gé ㄍㄜˊ ❶(-子、-儿)划分成的空栏和框子 square (formed by crossed lines); grid：方～儿布 *chequered cloth* | ～子纸 *squared paper* | 打～子 *draw a grid (on paper, etc.)* | 架子上有四个～。*The frame/case has four shelves.* ❷规格，标准 standard; pattern：～言 *maxim; motto* | 合～ *qualified* ⓨ人的品质(ⓛ品－)(of a person) character：人～ *personality* [格外]副词，特别地 (adverb) especially：～小心 *be especially careful* | ～帮忙 *be of great help* ❸阻碍，隔阂 ⓓ hindrance：～～不入 *be incompatible (with)* ❹击，打 to hit：～斗(dòu) *to grapple;to wrestle* | ～杀 *fight to kill* ❺推究 to study carefully：～物致知(推究事物的道理取得知识) *study the nature of things and obtain knowledge*

搁(擱) gé ㄍㄜˊ 禁(jīn)受，承受 to endure; to bear：～不住这么沉 *cannot stand the weight* | 骂得他有些～不住。*The rebuke was almost too much for him to take.*

⇨ see also gē on p.204

骼 gé ㄍㄜˊ 骨头 bone：骨～ *skeleton*

鬲 gé ㄍㄜˊ 鬲津河，古水名，旧称四女寺减河，即今漳卫新河，是河北、山东两省的界河 Gejin River (ancient name for former Sinüsijian River, and now called Zhangweixin River, boundary river between Hebei and Shandong Provinces)

⇨ see also lì on p.395

隔 gé ㄍㄜˊ ❶遮断，阻隔 to separate; to partition：分～ *to divide* | ～离 *to isolate; to quaran-*

tine | ～着一条河 *separated by a river* | ～靴搔痒（喻不中肯，没抓住关键）*fail to get to the point (literally means 'scratch an itch from outside a boot')* [隔阂]（— hé）same in meaning as 隔膜 1 [隔离] 使互相不能接触，断绝来往 to isolate; to quarantine [隔膜] 1 情意不相通，彼此有意见 rift; estrangement 2 不通晓，外行 unfamiliar：我对于这种技术实在～。*I am unfamiliar with this technology.* ❷间（jiàn）隔，距离 (in space or time) separation; interval：～一周再去 *go again in a week's time* | 相～很远 *far apart*

塥 gé ㄍㄜˊ 〈方 dialect〉水边的沙地，多用于地名 sandy ground by the water (often used in place names)：青草～（在安徽省桐城）*Qingcaoge (in Tongcheng, Anhui Province)*

嗝 gé ㄍㄜˊ （—儿）胃里的气体从嘴里出来而发出的声音，或因膈痉挛，气体冲过关闭的声带而发出的声音 burp; hiccup：打～ *to belch; to hiccup*

滆 gé ㄍㄜˊ 滆湖，湖名，在江苏省南部 Gehu Lake (in the south of Jiangsu Province)

膈 gé ㄍㄜˊ 旧叫膈膜或横膈膜，人或哺乳动物胸腔和腹腔之间的膜状肌肉 diaphragm (formerly called 膈膜 or 横膈膜)

镉（鎘） gé ㄍㄜˊ 金属元素，符号 Cd，银白色，质软，可用来制合金、颜料等，也用于核工业 cadmium (Cd)

葛 gé ㄍㄜˊ 藤本植物，花紫红色。茎皮纤维可织葛布。根肥大，叫葛根，可提制淀粉，也可入药 kudzu

⇨ see also gě on p.206

个（個） gě ㄍㄜˇ [自个儿] 自己 oneself

⇨ see also gè on p.206

合 gě ㄍㄜˇ ❶市制容量单位，1 升的十分之一 a traditional Chinese unit for capacity, equal to one tenth of a 升 ❷旧时量粮食的器具 (old) implement for measuring grain

⇨ see also hé on p.247

各 gě ㄍㄜˇ 〈方 dialect〉特别，与众不同 unusual; odd：那人挺～。*That guy is a real oddity.*

⇨ see also gè on p.207

哿 gě ㄍㄜˇ 赞许，可，嘉 to praise; to commend

舸 gě ㄍㄜˇ 大船 barge; ship

盖（蓋） gě ㄍㄜˇ 姓 (surname) Ge

⇨ see also gài on p.195

葛 gě ㄍㄜˇ 姓 (surname) Ge

⇨ see also gé on p.206

个（個、*箇） gè ㄍㄜˋ ❶量词 measure word：洗～澡 *take a bath* | 一～人 *one person* | 离开学还有～七八天。*There's some seven or eight days to go before school starts.* | 一～不留神摔倒了 *fell down out of some carelessness* | 打他～落花流水 *beat him/her all to pieces* ❷单独的 single; individual：～人 *individual; I (used to call oneself*

on formal occasions) | ～体 *individual (person or organism)* ❸（一子、一儿）身材或物体的大小 height; size：高～子 *tall person* | 小～儿 *short person* | 馒头～儿不小。*These steamed buns are rather big.*

⇨ see also gě on p.206

各 gè ㄍㄜˋ ❶代词，指每个，彼此不同的人或事物 (pronoun) every; each：～种 *all kinds; various* | ～处 *everywhere* | ～人 *each one; every one* | ～不相同 *each different from another* ❷ 副词，表示分别做或分别具有 (adverb) each individually：～尽所能 *let each person do his/her best* | ～有利弊。*Each has its pros and cons.*

⇨ see also gě on p.206

硌 gè ㄍㄜˋ 凸起的硬东西跟身体接触使身体感到难受或受到损伤 (of sth hard or bulging) to press/rub against：～脚 *stick into one's foot* | ～牙 *hurt one's tooth*

⇨ see also luò on p.429

铬(鉻) gè ㄍㄜˋ 金属元素，符号 Cr，银灰色，质硬，耐腐蚀，可用来制不锈钢等，也用于电镀 chromium (Cr)

虼 gè ㄍㄜˋ ［虼蚤］（一zao） see 蚤 (zǎo) on page 821

GEI ㄍㄟ

给(給) gěi ㄍㄟˇ ❶交付，送与 to give; to hand over：～他一本书 *give him a book* | 是谁～你的？*Who gave it to you?* ㊀把动作或态度加到对方 to inflict sth on sb：～他一顿批评 *make a criticism of him* ❷介词 preposition ①替，为 for; to：医生～他看病。*The doctor treats him.* | ～大家帮忙 *lend a hand to everybody* ②被，表示遭受 (in passive voice) by：房子～火烧掉了。*The house was burnt down by fire.* | 他～拉走了。*He was dragged away.* ③向，对 to; toward：快～大伙儿说说。*Come on, tell everybody about it.* | ～人家赔不是 *say sorry to him/her* ❸助词，跟前面"让""叫""把"相应，可有可无 auxiliary word used after 让，叫，把 (not indispensable)：窗户叫风(～)吹开了。*The window was blown open by wind.* | 羊让狼（～）吃了。*The sheep was taken by a wolf.* | 狼把小羊（～）叼走了。*A wolf took the lamb in its mouth.*

⇨ see also jǐ on p.290

GEN ㄍㄣ

根 gēn ㄍㄣ ❶植物茎干下部长在土里的部分。能从土壤里吸收水分和溶解水中的无机盐，还能把植物固定在地上，有的还有储藏养料的作用（㊣一柢）(of a plant) root：树～ *tree root* | 草～ *grass root* | 直～（如向日葵、甜菜的根）*(of sunflower, beet etc.) taproot* | 须～（如小麦、稻的根）*(of wheat, rice etc.) fibrous root* | 块～（如甘薯等可以吃的部分）*(of sweet potato, etc.) tuberous root* ㊀

(－儿)①比喻后辈儿孙(figurative) descendant; offspring：他是刘家一条～。*He is the Liu family's only offspring.* ②物体的基部和其他东西连着的部分(㊀一基) base; bottom：耳～ *basal part of ear* | 舌～ *root of the tongue* | 墙～儿 *foot of a wall* ③事物的本源 root; origin：祸～ *root of trouble* | 斩断穷～ *chop off the root of poverty* ④彻底 completely; thoroughly：～绝 *to eradicate* | ～治 *cure completely* [根据]凭依，依据 basis; grounds; on the basis of; according to：～什么？*On what grounds?* | 有什么～？*Is there anything to back it up?* ❷量词，用于长条的东西 measure word for long and thin objects：一～木料 *a piece of timber* | 两～麻绳 *two flax ropes* ❸代数方程式中未知数的值 (in algebra equation) solution ❹化学上指带电的原子团 (in chemistry) radical：氢～ *hydrogen radical* | 硫酸～ *sulphate radical*

跟 gēn ㄍㄣ ❶(－儿)脚的后部 (of foot) heel：脚后～ *heel* ㊀鞋袜的后部 (of a shoe or sock) heel：袜后～儿 *sock heal* ❷随在后面，紧接着 to follow; to go/come after：一个～一个别掉队。*Follow one another closely and don't fall behind.* | 开完会～着就参观。*There will be a visit right after the meeting.* ㊀赶，追赶 to catch up：后续部队也～上来了。*The follow-up troops have also caught up.* ❸介词，对，向 (preposition) to; with：已经～他说过了。*He has been informed (of it).* ❹连词，和，同 (conjunction) and：我～他都是山东人。*He and I are both from Shandong.*

[跟头](－tou) 1 身体摔倒的动作 fall; tumble：摔～ *have a fall* | 栽 ～ *fall headfirst; (figurative) suffer a setback* 2 身体向下翻转的动作 somersault：翻～ *turn a somersault*

哏 gén ㄍㄣˊ 〈方 dialect〉❶滑稽，可笑，有趣 funny：这话真～。*That's so funny.* ❷滑稽的话或表情 clownish speech or behaviour：捧～ *(to perform) a supporting role in a cross-talk* | 逗～ *(to perform) a leading role in a cross-talk*

艮 gěn ㄍㄣˇ 〈方 dialect〉食物韧而不脆 (of food) tough; leathery：～萝卜不好吃。*Leathery turnips don't taste good.*

⇨ see also gèn on p.208

亘(*亙) gèn ㄍㄣˋ 空间或时间上延续不断 (of space or time) to extend; to stretch：绵～数十里 *extend for scores of* li | ～古及今 *from time immemorial down to the present day*

艮 gèn ㄍㄣˋ 八卦之一，符号是☶，代表山 *gen* (one of the Eight Trigrams used in ancient divination, symbol ☶, representing mountain)

⇨ see also gěn on p.208

茛 gèn ㄍㄣˋ [毛茛]草本植物，喜生在水边湿地，花黄色，果实集合成球状。全草有毒，可用作外用药 buttercup

GENG ㄍㄥ

更 gēng ㄍㄥ ❶改变，改换（㊊－改、－换、变－）to change; to replace：～动 *to change* | 万象～新。*Everything takes on a new look.* | ～番（轮流调换）*alternately* | ～正 *to correct; make corrections* ❷经历 to experience：少（shào）不～事 *young and inexperienced* ❸旧时一夜分五更 watch (one of the five periods into which the night was formerly divided)：三～半夜 *in the dead of night* | 打～（打梆敲锣报时巡夜）*sound the night watches*

⇨ see also gèng on p.210

浭 gēng ㄍㄥ 浭水，古水名，即今还乡河，河北省与天津市交界处蓟运河的上游 Gengshui River (ancient name of the present Huanxiang River, in the upper reaches of Ji Canal River which flows between Hebei Province and Tianjin Municipality)

庚 gēng ㄍㄥ ❶天干的第七位，用作顺序的第七 *geng* (the seventh of the ten Heavenly Stems, a system used in the Chinese calendar); seventh ❷年龄 age：同～ *of the same age*

赓（賡） gēng ㄍㄥ 继续（㊊－续）to continue

鹒（鶊） gēng ㄍㄥ see 鸧鹒（cāng－）at 鸧 on page 58

耕（*畊） gēng ㄍㄥ ❶用犁把土翻松 to plough：～耘（yún）*to plough and weed; to farm* | 深～细作 *deep ploughing and intensive farming* ❷比喻从事某种劳动 (figurative) to work on：笔～ *engage in writing (as a profession)* | 舌～ *make a living by teaching*

羹 gēng ㄍㄥ 煮或蒸成的汁状、糊状、冻状的食品 liquid：鸡蛋～ *steamed egg custard* | 肉～ *meat soup* | 豆腐～ *thick tofu soup* [调羹]（tiáo－）喝汤用的小勺子，又叫羹匙（chí）soup spoon (also called 羹匙)

埂 gěng ㄍㄥˇ ❶（－子、－儿）田间稍稍高起的小路 foot path between fields：田～儿 *field ridge* | 地～子 *ridge between fields* ❷地势高起的地方 long narrow mound

哽 gěng ㄍㄥˇ 声气阻塞 to choke：～咽（yè）*choke with sobs*

绠（綆） gěng ㄍㄥˇ 汲水用的绳子 well rope：～短汲深（喻才力不能胜任）*ability inadequate for the task (literally means 'a short rope for a deep well')*

梗 gěng ㄍㄥˇ ❶（－子、－儿）植物的枝或茎 stem; stalk：花～ *flower stem* | 荷～ *lotus stalk* [梗概] 大略的情节 synopsis ❷直，挺立 to straighten up：～着脖子 *stiffen one's neck* ❸阻塞，妨碍（㊊－塞）to obstruct; to hinder：从中作～ *put obstacles in sb's way*

鲠（鯁、*骾） gěng ㄍㄥˇ ❶鱼骨 fishbone ❷骨头卡在嗓子里 to have (a

fishbone, etc.) stuck in the throat [骨鲠] 正直 upright; righteous

耿 gěng ㄍㄥˇ ❶光明 bright ❷正直 upright; honest: ～介 *upright in character* [耿直] (*梗直、*鲠直) 直爽，正直 upright and straightforward

[耿耿] 1 形容忠诚 devoted; loyal: 忠心～ *loyal and faithful* 2 心里老想着，不能忘怀 take sth to heart; have sth in mind: ～于怀 *take sth to heart; hold a grudge*

颈(頸) gěng ㄍㄥˇ same in meaning as 颈 (jǐng), used in 脖颈子

⇨ see also jǐng on p.329

硁 gěng ㄍㄥˇ 用于地名 used in place names: 石～(在广东省佛山市) *Shigeng (in Foshan, Guangdong Province)*

更 gèng ㄍㄥˋ 副词 adverb ①再，又 more; further: ～上一层楼 *go up one more storey; to the next level* ②越发，愈加 still more: ～好 *better* | ～明显了 *even more obvious*

⇨ see also gēng on p.209

晅 gèng ㄍㄥˋ 晒。多用于人名 (often used in given names) to bask

GONG ㄍㄨㄥ

工 gōng ㄍㄨㄥ ❶工人 worker; labourer: 矿～ *miner* | 技～ *skilled worker* | 农民～ *migrant worker (from a rural area)* | ～农联盟 *worker-peasant alliance* ❷工业 industry: 化～ *chemical industry* | ～商界 *industrial and commercial circles* ❸工作，工程 work; project: 做～ *do manual work* | ～具 *tools* | 手～ *handwork; work cost* | 动～ *begin construction; start a project* [工程] 关于制造、建筑、开矿等，有一定计划进行的工作 industrial project; engineering: 土木～ *civil engineering* | 水利～ *water conservancy project; irrigation works* | 文化～ *cultural project* ❹一个工人或农民一个劳动日的工作 person-day: 这件工程需要二十个～才能完成。*This project will take twenty person-days to complete.* ❺技术，本领 skill; craftsmanship: 唱～ *singing skills* | 做～精细 *be of excellent workmanship* ❻精细 fine; delicate: ～笔画 *traditional Chinese realistic painting style characterized by fine brushwork and attention to detail* ❼善于，长于 to be good at; to be versed in: ～书善画 *be versed in calligraphy and painting* ❽旧时乐谱的记音符号 a note in traditional Chinese musical scale [工尺] (-chě) 我国旧有的音乐记谱符号，计有合、四、一、上、尺(chě)、工、凡、六、五、乙，分别相当于简谱的 5̣、6̣、7̣、1、2、3、4、5、6、7。"工尺"是这些符号的总称 *gongche (traditional Chinese musical scale)*

[工夫][功夫](-fu) 1 时间(多用"工夫") time (often as 工夫): 有～来一趟。*Come round when (you) have time.* 2 长期努力实践的成果，本领(多用"功夫") (often as 功夫) practised skill or ability: ～深 *having well versed skills*

功 gōng ㄍㄨㄥ ❶功劳，贡献较大的成绩 meritorious service; exploit: 记大～一次 *award sb a citation for a major achievement* | 立～ *render meritorious service* | ～臣 *person who has rendered outstanding service hero* ❷功夫 practised skill or ability: 用～ *diligent; work hard* | 下苦～ *make painstaking effort* ❸成就，成效 success; result: 成～ *success; to succeed* | 徒劳无～ *futile efforts* ❹物理学上指在外力作用下，物体顺力的方向移动，这个力就对物体做了功 (in physics) work

红(紅) gōng ㄍㄨㄥ [女红] 旧指女子所做的缝纫、刺绣等工作。也作"女工"(old, also written as 女工) needlework done by women

⇨ see also hóng on p.253

攻 gōng ㄍㄨㄥ ❶攻击，打击，进击，跟"守"相对 to attack; to take the offensive (opposite of 守): ～守同盟 *offensive and defensive alliance; (of accomplices) shield each other* | ～势 *offensive* | ～城 *attack a city* ㉇ 指摘别人的错误 to accuse; to charge: ～人之短 *attack sb where he/she is weak* ❷致力学习、研究 to study; specialize in: ～读 *assiduously study* | 专～化学 *specialize in chemistry*

弓 gōng ㄍㄨㄥ ❶射箭或发弹（dàn）丸的器具 bow; catapult: 弹～ *catapult* | ～箭 *bow and arrow* ❷（一子）像弓的用具 anything bow-shaped: 胡琴～子 *bow of a fiddle* ❸旧时丈量地亩的器具，也是计量单位，1弓为5市尺，240平方弓为1亩 (old) a tool, as well a unit, for measuring the field (equal to 5 尺) ❹弯曲 to bend: ～腰 *bend down (from the waist)*

躬(*躳) gōng ㄍㄨㄥ ❶身体 body ㉇ 自身，亲自 in person: ～行 *practice personally* | ～耕 *do farm work in person* | 事必～亲 *personally attend to all matters* ❷弯曲（身体）to bend forward; to bow: ～身 *bend forward; to bow*

公 gōng ㄍㄨㄥ ❶属于国家或集体的，跟"私"相对 public (opposite of 私): ～物 *public property* | ～务 *public affairs; official business* | ～文 *official document* | 因～出差 *go on a business trip* | 大～无私 *unselfish; perfectly impartial* ❷公平，公道 fair and just; equitable: ～允 *fair and just* | ～正 *impartial; righteous* | 秉～办事 *act impartially* ❸让大家知道 to make public: ～开 *make public* | ～告 *issue a public notice; public announcement* | ～布 *to announce* | ～示 *make known to the public* ❹共同的，大家承认的，大多数适用的 common: ～海 *international waters* | ～约 *convention; treaty* | ～理 *self-evident truth; axiom* [公司] 合股（或单股）经营的一种工商业组织，经营产品的生产、商品的流转或某些建设事业 company; corporation: 百货～ *department*

G

store | 运输～ *transport company* | 煤气～ *gas company* ❺公制的 metric：～里 *kilometre* | ～尺 *metre* | ～斤 *kilogramme* ❻雄性的 (of an animal) male：～鸡 *cock* | ～羊 *ram* ❼对祖辈和老年男子的称呼㊀term of address for a man of one's grandfather's generation, or an elderly man：外～ *grandfather on the mother's side* | 老～～ *venerable elder man* ❽丈夫的父亲㊀one's husband's father：～婆 *one's husband's parents* ❾古代五等爵位（公、侯、伯、子、男）的第一等 duke (the first of the five ranks of nobility in ancient China) ❿对年长男子的尊称 polite address for an older man：诸～ *dear sirs* | 丁～ *Mr. Ding*

蚣 gōng ㄍㄨㄥ see 蜈蚣 (wúgong) at 蜈 on page 691

郱 gōng ㄍㄨㄥ 姓 (surname) Gong

供 gōng ㄍㄨㄥ 供给（jǐ），准备着钱物等给需要的人使用 to supply; to furnish：～养 *provide for (parents or elders)* | 提～ *to supply* | ～销 *supply and marketing* | ～求相应 *balance between supply and demand* | ～参考 *for reference* [供给制] 对工作人员不给工资，只供给生活必需品的一种分配制度 supply system for payment in kind

⇨ see also gòng on p.213

龚（龔） gōng ㄍㄨㄥ 姓 (surname) Gong

肱 gōng ㄍㄨㄥ 胳膊由肘到肩的部分，泛指胳膊 (upper) arm：曲～ *bend the arm* [股肱] 大腿和胳膊，比喻得力的助手 legs and arms; (figurative) right-hand man

宫 gōng ㄍㄨㄥ ❶房屋，封建时代专指帝王、太子等的住所 palace：～殿 *palace* | 故～ *the Imperial Palace* | 东～ *Eastern Palace; crown prince* ❷神话中神仙居住的房屋或庙宇的名称 (in Chinese mythology) palace：天～ *heavenly palace* ❸一些文化娱乐场所的名称 palace (building for cultural and recreational activities)：少年～ *children's palace* | 文化～ *cultural palace* ❹宫刑，古代阉割生殖器的酷刑 castration (a punishment in ancient times) ❺古代五音"宫、商、角（jué）、徵（zhǐ）、羽"之一 one of the five notes in the ancient Chinese pentatonic scale

恭 gōng ㄍㄨㄥ 肃敬，谦逊有礼貌（㊀一敬）respectful; courteous：～贺 *to congratulate* [出恭] 排泄大小便 to go to the toilet

塨 gōng ㄍㄨㄥ 用于人名。李塨，清代人 used in given names, e.g. Li Gong of Qing Dynasty

觥 gōng ㄍㄨㄥ 古代用兽角做的一种饮酒器皿 a wine vessel made of horn in ancient times

巩（鞏） gǒng ㄍㄨㄥˇ [巩固] 坚固，结实，使牢固 consolidated; to consolidate：基础～ *solid foundation* | ～学习成果 *consolidate what is learnt* | ～政

权 *consolidate political power*

汞 gǒng ㄍㄨㄥˇ 金属元素，通称水银，符号 Hg，银白色液体，有毒，能溶解金、银、锡、钾、钠等。可用来制温度表、气压计、水银灯等 mercury (Hg)

拱 gǒng ㄍㄨㄥˇ ❶拱手，两手向上相合表示敬意 to cup one hand in the other before the chest (a salute) ❷两手合围 to encircle/surround with both arms：～抱 *to embrace (with arms)* | ～木 *a thick tree* ⓘ 环绕 to encircle：～卫 *surround and protect* ❸肩膀向上耸 to hunch one's shoulders：～肩膀 *shrug one's shoulders* ❹建筑物上呈弧形的结构，大多中间高两侧低 arch：～门 *archway* | ～桥 *arch bridge* | 连～坝 *multiple-arch dam* ❺顶动，向上或向前推 to squeeze upward or forward：～芽 *to sprout* | 虫子～土。*Worms wriggle through the earth.* | 猪用嘴～地。*Pigs dig earth with the snout.*

珙 gǒng ㄍㄨㄥˇ ❶大璧 a precious stone ❷珙县，地名，在四川省 Gongxian (a place in Sichuan Province)

硔 gǒng ㄍㄨㄥˇ 用于地名 used in place names：～池（在山西省陵川）*Gongchi (in Lingchuan, Shanxi Province)*

共 gòng ㄍㄨㄥˋ ❶相同的，都具有的 common; general：～识 *consensus* | ～性 *common nature* ❷在一起，一齐（㊣一同）together：和平～处 *peaceful coexistence* | 同甘～苦 *share weal and woe* | ～鸣 *resonance* | ～事 *be colleagues* ❸副词，总，合计（㊣总－）(adverb) altogether; in all：～二十人 *twenty people in all* | ～计 *amount to* ❹共产党的简称 short for the Communist Party：中～ *the Communist Party of China*

〈古 ancient〉 also same as 恭 (gōng)

〈古 ancient〉 also same as 供 (gōng)

供 gòng ㄍㄨㄥˋ ❶向神佛或死者奉献祭品 to make an offering (at a shrine or tomb)：～佛 *make offerings to Buddha* ❷指奉献的祭品 offerings：上～ *make offerings* ❸被审者述说案情 to confess; to own up：～出同谋 *give the name of an accomplice* | ～状 *written confession* | ～认 *to confess* ⓘ口供，供词 oral confession：录～ *take down a confession* | 问出～来 *obtain a confession by questioning*

⇨ see also gōng on p.212

贡(貢) gòng ㄍㄨㄥˋ ❶古代指属国或臣民向君主献东西 (ancient) to pay tribute [贡献] 1 拿出力量或财物来给国家和人民 to contribute：为祖国～出自己的一切 *contribute all one has for the motherland* 2 对人民、人类社会所做的有益的事 contribution：革命导师创立的学说，是对人类的伟大～。*The theories established by the revolutionary mentors are a great contribution to humanity.* ❷贡品 (an article of) tribute：进～ *pay tribute* ❸封建时代指选拔人才，推荐给朝廷

G

to recommend talent (to imperial court): ～举 *to recommend* | ～生 *tribute student/scholar (selected/recommended to study in the capital)*

唝(嗊) gòng ㄍㄨㄥˋ ［唝吥］（-bù）柬埔寨地名，今作"贡布" Kampot (a place in Cambodia, now written as 贡布)

GOU ㄍㄡ

勾 gōu ㄍㄡ ❶用笔画出符号，表示删除或截取 to cross out; to strike out: ～了这笔账 *cancel the debt* | 一笔～销 *write off at one stroke; cancel once and for all* | 把精彩的文句～出来 *mark out exceptionally good texts* ❷描画，用线条画出形象的边缘 to sketch; to draw: ～图样 *draw a sketch* ㊀用灰涂抹建筑物上砖、瓦或石块之间的缝 to point (a brick wall, tiles, etc.): ～墙缝 *point the wall* | 用灰～抹房顶 *point the roof* ❸招引，引（㊀-引）to evoke; to entice: ～魂 *to bewitch* | 这一问～起他的话来了。*The question induced him to talk.* ❹结合 to collude; to gang up: ～结 *collude with* | ～通 *collude/collaborate with* ❺我国古代称不等腰直角三角形中构成直角的较短的边 (in ancient Chinese geometry) the shorter leg of a right triangle

［勾留］停留 to stop over; to stay: 在那里～几天 *stop over there for a few days*

⇨ see also gòu on p.215

沟(溝) gōu ㄍㄡ ❶流水道 ditch; drain; sewer: 阴～ *covered drain* | 阳～ *open drain; ditch* ［沟通］使两方通达 to link up; to connect: ～文化 *link up cultures* ❷像沟的东西 groove; furrow: 车道～ *ruts on road*

钩(鈎、*鉤) gōu ㄍㄡ ❶（-子、-儿）悬挂或探取东西用的器具，形状弯曲，头端尖锐 hook: 秤～儿 *steelyard hook* | 钓鱼～儿 *fishhook; angle* | 挂～儿 *coat hanger* | 火～子 *poker; fire iron* ❷（-子、-儿）形状像钩子的 hook-like thing: 鹰～鼻 *aquiline nose* | 蝎子的～子 *sting of a scorpion* ❸（-儿）汉字的一种笔形（㇀ ㇂ ㇄等）hook stroke in Chinese characters ❹（-儿）形状为"√"的符号，表示正确或同意 check mark; tick (to indicate correct or agreed): 打～ *to tick* ❺用钩状物探取 to hook out: 把小洞里的东西～出来 *pull the thing out of a small hole* ㊀研究，探寻 to explore: ～深致远 *probe deep into a subject* ❻ same as "勾❷" ❼用带钩的针编织，或用针缝合衣边 to crochet; to sew with large stitches: ～毛衣 *crochet a sweater* | ～贴边 *sew on an edging* ❽在某些场合说数字时用来代替 9 used to replace the number 9 on certain occasions

句 gōu ㄍㄡ (ancient) same as "勾" ［高句丽］［高句骊］（--lí）古族名，古国名 Gaogouli (ancient nation and ethnic group)

G

[句践]春秋时越王名 Goujian (King of the state of Yue in the Spring and Autumn Period)

⇨ see also jù on p.339

佝 gōu ㄍㄡ [佝偻]（—lóu）病名，俗叫小儿软骨病，因身体缺钙、磷和维生素 D 而引起，症状是方头、鸡胸、驼背、两腿弯曲等 rickets

枸 gōu ㄍㄡ [枸橘]（—jú）same as "枳 (zhǐ)" (see 枳 on page 854 for reference)

⇨ see also gǒu on p.215, jǔ on p.338

缑(緱) gōu ㄍㄡ 刀剑等柄上所缠的绳 cord binding on the hilt of a sword, knife, etc.

篝 gōu ㄍㄡ 熏笼 bamboo or wire frame over a brazier for drying things [篝火] 原指用笼子罩着的火，现指在野外或空旷的地方燃烧的火堆 bonfire; campfire

鞲 gōu ㄍㄡ [鞲鞴]（—bèi）活塞的旧称 (former name for 活塞) piston

苟 gǒu ㄍㄡˇ 姓 (surname) Gou

苟 gǒu ㄍㄡˇ ❶姑且，暂且 barely; temporarily：～安 *go with momentary ease* | ～延残喘 *subsist in a worsening condition (literally means 'linger on with one's last breath of life')* ❷马虎，随便 careless; casual：一丝不～ *meticulously attentive* ❸文言连词，假如 (conjunction in classical Chinese) if; provided：～可以利民，不循其礼。*If it benefits the people, there is no need to observe the rituals.* ❹姓 (surname) Gou

岣 gǒu ㄍㄡˇ [岣嵝]（—lǒu）山峰名，衡山的主峰，也指衡山，在湖南省中南部 Goulou Mountain (the main peak of Hengshan Mountain, also the name of the mountain itself, in the mid-south of Hunan Province)

狗 gǒu ㄍㄡˇ 家畜，听觉、嗅觉都很灵敏，种类很多，有的能帮人打猎、牧羊、看守门户等 dog [狗腿子] 指走狗，为有权势的人奔走做坏事的人 lackey; henchman

耇(耈)** gǒu ㄍㄡˇ 年老，长寿 old; aged; long-lived

枸 gǒu ㄍㄡˇ [枸杞]（—qǐ）落叶灌木，花淡紫色。果实红色，叫枸杞子，可入药 goji berry

⇨ see also gōu on p.215, jǔ on p.338

笱 gǒu ㄍㄡˇ 竹制的捕鱼器具 bamboo basket fishing trap

勾 gòu ㄍㄡˋ ❶[勾当]（—dang）事情（多指坏事）(often derogatory) business; deal：见不得人的～ *shameful deed* ❷ same as "够" ❸姓 (surname) Gou

⇨ see also gōu on p.214

构(構、❶-❸*搆) gòu ㄍㄡˋ ❶构造，组合 to construct; to form; to compose：～屋 *build a house* | ～图 *compose a picture* | ～

G

词 *form a word*［构造］各组成部分及其相互关系 structure; construction; formation：人体～ *anatomy of the human body*｜飞机的～ *structure of an aeroplane*｜句子的～ *sentence structure* ❷结成（用于抽象事物）to fabricate; to make up; to cause：～怨 *form resentment*｜虚～ *fabricate*［构思］做文章或进行艺术创作时运用心思 to plot (a literary composition); to conceive ❸作品 a literary composition：佳～ *a good piece of writing*｜杰～ *masterpiece* ❹构树，落叶乔木，又叫榖（gǔ）或楮（chǔ），叶卵形，花淡绿色。树皮纤维可用来造纸 paper mulberry (also called 榖，楮)

购（購） gòu ㄍㄡˋ 买（㊀—买）to buy; to purchase：～物 *do/go shopping*｜～置 *to purchase (durable goods)*｜采～ *to purchase*

诟（詬） gòu ㄍㄡˋ ❶耻辱 shame; humiliation; disgrace：含～忍辱 *silently endure humiliation and insult* ❷辱骂 to rebuke; to revile：～病 *to denounce*｜～骂 *to revile*

垢 gòu ㄍㄡˋ ❶污秽，脏东西 dirt; filth：油～ *oil stain*｜牙～ *tartar*｜藏污纳～ *shelter evil people and uphold evil practices (literally means 'store dirt and conceal filth')* ❷耻辱。也作"诟" shame; humiliation; disgrace (also written as 诟)

姤 gòu ㄍㄡˋ ❶same as "遘(gòu)" ❷善，美好 good; kind

够（*夠） gòu ㄍㄡˋ ❶足，满足一定的限度 to suffice; to be enough：～数 *be sufficient*｜～用 *be enough*｜钱不～了。*There is not enough money left.* ㊀用在动词后，多含不耐烦义 (used after verbs) to be fed up：受～了 *have had enough*｜这个话我真听～了。*I have had enough of these remarks.* ❷达到，及 to reach：～得着 *be able to reach*｜～格 *be qualified* ❸副词，表示程度高 (adverb) quite; really：东西～贵的。*Things are quite expensive.*｜天气真～冷的。*It's rather cold.*

雊 gòu ㄍㄡˋ 野鸡叫 (of a pheasant) to crow

遘 gòu ㄍㄡˋ 相遇 to meet; to encounter

媾 gòu ㄍㄡˋ ❶结合，交合 to wed; to copulate：婚～（两家结亲）*(of two families) to become related by marriage*｜交～（性交，交配）*to copulate* ❷交好 to be on friendly terms：～和（讲和）*make peace*

觏（覯） gòu ㄍㄡˋ 遇见 to meet; to encounter：罕～（很少见）*rarely seen*

彀 gòu ㄍㄡˋ ❶same as "够" ❷使劲张弓 to draw a bow with one's full force［彀中］（—zhōng）箭能射及的范围 shooting range of an arrow ㊁牢笼，圈套 trap：入我～ *fall into my trap*［入彀］㊁进牢笼，入圈套 to fall into the trap：诱敌～ *lure the enemy into a trap*

G

GU ㄍㄨ

估 gū ㄍㄨ 揣测，大致地推算 to estimate; to assess：～计 *to estimate* | ～量 *to estimate* | 不要低～了群众的力量。*Do not underestimate the power of the masses.* | ～一～价钱 *estimate the price*

⇨ see also gù on p.221

咕 gū ㄍㄨ 形容母鸡、某些鸟叫的声音 cluck; coo：布谷鸟～～地叫。*The cuckoos were cooing.* [咕咚]（－dōng）形容重东西落下的声音 thud; plump; plop [咕嘟] 1（－dū）形容液体沸腾、水流涌出或大口喝水的声音 bubble; gurgle 2（－du）煮，用火长时间煮 to boil for a long time：再～几分钟，粥就好了。*The porridge should be done after bubbling for a few more minutes.* 3（－du）（嘴）鼓起 to purse/pout (one's lips)：他气得把嘴～起来。*He pursed his lips in annoyance.* [咕唧] [咕叽]（－ji）小声交谈或自言自语 to whisper/murmur (to oneself) [咕噜]（－lū）形容水流动或东西滚动的声音 the sound of rumbling or rolling [咕哝]（－nong）小声说话（多指自言自语，并带不满情绪）to mutter/grumble (often to oneself in a bad-tempered way)

沽 gū ㄍㄨ ❶买 to buy; to purchase：～酒 *buy wine* | ～名钓誉（有意做使人赞扬的事，捞取个人声誉）*fish for fame and compliments* ❷卖 to sell：待价而～（喻等到有了较高的待遇才肯答应替人做事）*wait to sell for the right price; (figurative) wait for the right terms before accepting an employment*

姑 gū ㄍㄨ ❶父亲的姊妹 ㊂ father's sister ❷丈夫的姊妹 husband's sister：～嫂 *sisters-in-law* | 大～子 *husband's older sister* ❸妻称夫的母亲 husband's mother：翁～（公婆）*husband's parents* ❹姑且，暂且 for the time being：～妄言之 *say sth for what it's worth* | ～置勿论 *leave the subject aside for now* [姑息] 暂求苟安 to seek temporary peace ㊀ 无原则地宽容 to appease; to indulge：对错误的行为绝不～。*We should never indulge erroneous behaviour.*

轱（軲） gū ㄍㄨ [轱辘]（－lu）1 车轮 wheel 2 滚动，转（zhuàn）to roll：球～到沟里了。*The ball rolled into the ditch.*

鸪（鴣） gū ㄍㄨ see 鹧鸪 (zhè－) at 鹧 on page 841, and 鹁鸪 (bó－) at 鹁 on page 49

菇 gū ㄍㄨ 蕈（xùn），蘑菇 mushroom：香～ *shiitake* | 金针～ *enokitake*

蛄 gū ㄍㄨ see 蝼蛄 (lóu－) at 蝼 on page 417, and 蟪蛄 (huì－) at 蟪 on page 276

辜 gū ㄍㄨ ❶罪 guilt：无～ *innocent* | 死有余～ *even death would be too good for sb* ❷亏负，违背 to let down; to disappoint：～负 *fail to live up to*

酤 gū ㄍㄨ ❶买酒 to buy wine ❷卖酒 to sell wine

苽 gū ㄍㄨ 〈古 ancient〉same as "菰❶"

呱 gū ㄍㄨ [呱呱] 古书上指小儿哭声 (in ancient Chinese literature) baby's cry: ~坠地(指婴儿出生) *be born with a cry*

⇨ see also guā on p.223, guǎ on p.223

孤 gū ㄍㄨ ❶幼年丧父或父母双亡 fatherless (since childhood); orphan: ~儿 *orphan* ❷单独(㊃-独) solitary; lonely; alone: ~雁 *a solitary goose* | ~掌难鸣(喻力量单薄,难以有所作为) *alone and helpless (literally means 'it is impossible to clap with only one hand')* | ~立 *be isolated* ❸古代君主的自称 used by ancient monarchs to refer to themselves: ~家 *my humble self* | ~王 *my humble self, the King* ❹ same as "辜❷": ~恩负义 *be devoid of all gratitude*

轱(軲) gū ㄍㄨ 大骨 big bone

菰 gū ㄍㄨ ❶草本植物,生长在浅水里,花紫红色。嫩茎经黑粉病菌寄生后膨大,叫茭白,果实叫菰米,都可以吃 Manchurian wild rice ❷ same as "菇"

觚 gū ㄍㄨ ❶古代一种盛酒的器具 a wine vessel in ancient times ❷古代写字用的木板 wooden writing tablet in ancient times: 操~(执笔写作) *engage in writing* ❸棱角 edge and corner

骨 gū ㄍㄨ [骨朵儿] (-duor) 没有开放的花朵 flower bud [骨碌] (-lu) 滚动 to roll

⇨ see also gǔ on p.219

蓇 gū ㄍㄨ [蓇葖] (-tū) 1 果实的一种,成熟时在一面开裂,如芍药、八角的果实 follicle (a kind of fruit) 2 骨朵儿 flower bud

箍 gū ㄍㄨ ❶用竹篾或金属条束紧器物 to bind fast; to hoop (with a bamboo or metal strip): ~木盆 *hoop a wooden basin* ❷(-儿) 紧束器物的圈 hoop; band: 铁~ *iron hoop*

古 gǔ ㄍㄨˇ ❶时代久远的,过去的,跟"今"相对(㊃-老) ancient; age-old (opposite of 今): ~书 *ancient book* | ~迹 *ancient relic* | ~为今用 *make past serve the present* [古板] 守旧固执,呆板 old-fashioned and rigid [古怪] 奇怪,罕见,不合常情 eccentric; odd ❷古体诗 a form of pre-Tang poetry: 五~ *a form of pre-Tang poetry with five characters to a line* | 七~ *a form of pre-Tang poetry with seven characters to a line*

[古董] (*骨董) 古代留传下来的器物 antique ㊕ 顽固守旧的人或过时的东西 old fogey

诂(詁) gǔ ㄍㄨˇ 用通行的话解释古代语言文字或方言字义 to interpret archaic or dialectal words in current language: 训~ *interpretation of ancient texts* | 解~ *interpret archaic or dialectal words in current lan-*

guage | 字～ *dictionary on archaic Chinese*

牯 gǔ ㄍㄨˇ 牯牛，指公牛 bull：黄～ *brown bull* | 黑～ *black bull*

脵 gǔ ㄍㄨˇ 用于地名 used in place names：宋～（在山西省介休）*Songgu (in Jiexiu, Shanxi Province)*

罟 gǔ ㄍㄨˇ 〈古 ancient〉捕鱼的网 fishing net

钴（鈷） gǔ ㄍㄨˇ 金属元素，符号 Co，银白色。可用来制合金等，医学上用放射性钴（钴-60）治疗恶性肿瘤 cobalt (Co)

嘏 gǔ ㄍㄨˇ jiǎ ㄐㄧㄚˇ（又）福 felicity; good fortune

鹽 gǔ ㄍㄨˇ （一子）烹饪用具，周围陡直的深锅 deep pot: 瓷～子 *porcelain pot* | 沙～子 *earthen pot*

谷（❷–❹穀） gǔ ㄍㄨˇ ❶山谷，两山中间狭长的水道。又指两山之间 valley; gorge：万丈深～ *very deep ravine* ❷庄稼和粮食的总称 cereal; grain：五～ *the five cereals;(generally) food crops* ❸（一子）谷类作物，籽实碾去皮以后就成小米，供食用，茎可喂牲口 millet ❹〈方 dialect〉稻，也指稻的籽实 unhusked rice：糯～ *glutinous rice* | 粳（jīng）～ *non-glutinous rice* | 轧（yà）～机 *threshing machine* ❺姓 (surname) Gu

⇨ see also yù on p.802

汩 gǔ ㄍㄨˇ 水流的声音或样子 叠 (of water) gurgling

股 gǔ ㄍㄨˇ ❶大腿 thigh (see picture of 人体 on page 647) ❷事物的一部分 a section or part ①股份，指集合资金的一份 share; stock：～东 *shareholder* | ～票 *share* | ～市 *stock market* ②机关团体中的一个部门 section (of an organization)：总务～ *general affairs section* | 卫生～ *health section* ③合成绳线等的部分 strand; ply：合～线 *plied thread* | 三～绳 *three-ply rope* ❸我国古代称不等腰直角三角形中构成直角的较长的边 (in ancient Chinese geometry) the longer leg of a right-angled triangle ❹量词 measure word ①用于成条的东西 for long and narrow things：一～道（路）*a road* | 一～线 *a skein of thread* | 一～泉水 *a stream of spring water* ②用于气味、力气 for smell or strength：一～香味 *a whiff of fragrance* | 一～劲 *a burst of energy* ③用于成批的人（多含贬义）for group of people (often disapproving)：一～残匪 *a pack of remaining bandits* | 一～势力 *a force of influence*

骨 gǔ ㄍㄨˇ ❶骨头，人和脊椎动物支持身体的坚硬组织 bone：颅～ *skull* | 肋～ *rib* [骨骼] 全身骨头的总称 skeleton [骨干]（一gàn）能起中坚作用的人或事物 backbone; mainstay：～分子 *core member* | ～作用 *main role* [骨肉] 喻最亲近的有血统关系的人，指父母、子女、兄弟、姊妹 your (own) flesh and blood; kindred ❷像骨的东西 framework;

G

skeleton：钢～水泥 *reinforced concrete* ❸品格，气概 character; mettle; spirit：～气 *moral integrity* | 媚～ *obsequiousness*

⇨ see also gū on p.218

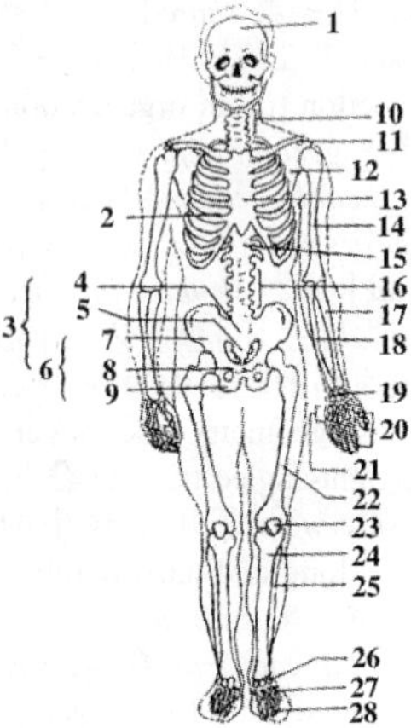

人体骨骼 Human Bone Structure

1 颅 *cranium*
2 肋骨 *ribs*
3 骨盆 *pelvis*
4 骶骨 *sacrum*
5 尾椎 *coccyx*
6 髋骨 *hip bone*
7 髂骨 *ilium*
8 耻骨 *pubis*
9 坐骨 *ischium*
10 颈椎 *vertebrae*
11 锁骨 *clavicle*
12 肩胛骨 *scapula*
13 胸骨 *sternum*
14 肱骨 *humerus*
15 胸椎 *thoracic vertebra*
16 腰椎 *lumbar vertebra*
17 桡骨 *radius*
18 尺骨 *ulna*
19 腕骨 *carpus*
20 指骨 *phalanx*
21 掌骨 *metacarpus*
22 股骨 *femur*
23 髌骨 *patella*
24 胫骨 *tibia*
25 腓骨 *fibula*
26 跗骨 *tarsus*
27 跖骨 *metatarsus*
28 趾骨 *phalanx*

馉(餶) gǔ ㄍㄨˇ ［馉饳］（－duò）一种面制食品 a wheaten food with a filling

榾 gǔ ㄍㄨˇ ［榾柮］（－duò）截成一段一段的短木头 wood block

鹘(鶻) gǔ ㄍㄨˇ ［鹘鸼］（－zhōu）古书上说的一种鸟，羽毛青黑色，尾巴短 a short-tailed black bird in ancient Chinese texts

⇨ see also hú on p.259

贾(賈) gǔ ㄍㄨˇ ❶商人（⊜商－）。古时特指坐商 merchant (especially shopkeeper in ancient times) ❷卖 to sell：余勇可～（还有多余的力量可以使出）*still having plenty of fight left*

⇨ see also jiǎ on p.298

羖(羖)** gǔ ㄍㄨˇ 公羊 ram

蛊(蠱) gǔ ㄍㄨˇ 古代传说把许多毒虫放在器皿里，使互相吞食，最后剩下不死的毒虫叫蛊，可用来毒害人 in ancient legend, someone had put many venomous insects in a utensil so that they ate each other, and the one survived was called 蛊 which could be used to poison people [蛊惑] 迷惑，毒害 to poison and bewitch：～人心 *to rabble-rouse*

鹄(鵠) gǔ ㄍㄨˇ 射箭的靶子 (in archery) target [鹄的]（－dì）箭靶子的中心，练习射击的目标 bullseye; target

⇨ see also hú on p.259

鼓(*皷) gǔ ㄍㄨˇ ❶打击乐器。多为圆柱形，中空，一面或两面蒙皮，有军鼓、腰鼓等多种 drum ❷敲鼓 to beat a drum：一～作气 *in one vigorous effort* ㊀①击，拍，弹（tán）to beat; to strike; to play (an instrument)：～掌 *to applaud* | ～琴 *play the* qin ②发动，使振作起来 to arouse; to inspire：～足干劲 *gather up all one's vigour* | ～励 *to encourage* | ～动 *to incite* | ～舞 *to inspire* [鼓吹] 1 打击乐和管乐合奏 to play in a percussion and wind ensemble 2 传播，宣扬（现多用于贬义）to propagandize; to advocate; to preach (now often disapproving) ❸凸出，使凸出 to bulge; to swell：～起个包 *get a bump* | ～起两颊 *blow out one's cheeks* ❹饱满 ㊂ full; bulging：口袋装得～～的。*The pocket is filled to the full.*

臌 gǔ ㄍㄨˇ 膨胀，中医指肚子胀起的病，通常有水臌、气臌两种。也作"鼓" distension of abdomen (also written as 鼓)

瞽 gǔ ㄍㄨˇ 瞎 blind：～者 *blind person*

毂(轂) gǔ ㄍㄨˇ 车轮的中心部分，有圆孔，可以插轴 hub (of a wheel)(see picture of 旧式车轮 on page 426)

榖 gǔ ㄍㄨˇ same as "构树" (see 构 ❹ on page 215 for reference)

瀔 gǔ ㄍㄨˇ 瀔水，地名，在湖南省湘乡。又水名，在河南省。今均作"谷水" Gushui (a place in Xiangxiang, Hunan Province; also a river in Henan Province. Both now written as 谷水.)

估 gù ㄍㄨˋ [估衣]（－yi）旧指贩卖的旧衣服。贩卖旧衣的行业叫估衣业 (old) second hand clothes for sale (business dealing in such is called 估衣业)

⇨ see also gū on p.217

故 gù ㄍㄨˋ ❶意外的事情 accident; unexpected event：变～ *unforeseen event* | 事～ *accident* | ～障 *break down* ❷缘故，原因 cause; reason：不知何～ *not knowing why* | 无缘无～ *for no reason at all* ❸故意，存心 intentionally; on purpose：明知～犯 *knowingly violate* | ～弄玄虚 *deliberately make things look mysterious* ❹老，旧，过去的 old; past; former：～书 *old book* | ～人（老朋友）*old friend* | ～宫 *palace of a former dynasty; the Imperial Palace* ❺本来的，原来的 original：～土 *native land* | ～乡（老家）

hometown ❻死（用于人）(of a person) to die：～去 *pass away*｜病～ *die of illness*［物故］指人死 (of a person) to pass away ❼连词，所以 (conjunction) so; therefore：他有坚强的意志，～能克服困难。*He has strong willpower so he can overcome the difficulties.*

固 gù ㄍㄨˋ ❶结实，牢靠（㊟坚－）firm; solid：稳～ *firm*｜牢～ *well-fixed* ㊀使坚固、牢固 to solidify; to strengthen;to consolidate：～本 *consolidate the basis*｜～防 *beef up defence* ❷坚定，不变动 steadfast：～请 *insistently request*｜～守阵地 *tenaciously defend one's position* ❸本，原来 innate; inborn：～有 *inherent*［固然］连词，表示先承认原来的意思，后面还要否定那个意思或者转到另一方面去 (conjunction) admittedly; no doubt: 这项工作～有困难，但是一定能完成。*This is admittedly a difficult job, but it will be done.* ❹坚硬 hard; solid：～体 *solid*

堌 gù ㄍㄨˋ 堤。多用于地名 dyke (often used in place names)：牛王～（在河南省夏邑）*Niuwanggu (a place in Xiayi, Henan Province)*

崮 gù ㄍㄨˋ 四周陡峭而顶部较平的山。多用于地名 mesa (often used in place names)：孟良～（在山东省临沂）*Mengliänggu (a place in Linyi, Shandong Province)*

锢（錮） gù ㄍㄨˋ ❶把金属熔化开来，堵塞金属器物的空隙 to plug with melted metal ❷禁锢，禁闭起来不许跟人接触 to confine; to hold in custody

痼 gù ㄍㄨˋ 痼疾，积久不易治的病 chronic illness ㊀长期养成不易克服的 deep-rooted：～习 *deep-rooted habit*｜～癖 *addiction*

鲴（鯝） gù ㄍㄨˋ 鱼名，又叫黄鲴，身体侧扁，口小无须，生活在江河湖泊中 silver xenocypris (also 黄鲴)

顾（顧） gù ㄍㄨˋ ❶回头看，泛指看 to look back; to look at：回～ *to review*｜环～ *look around*｜～视左右 *look back round* ❷拜访 to visit; to call on：三～茅庐 *repeatedly invite sb to take up a post* ❸照管，注意 to take care of; to heed：～面子 *heed one's image*｜～全大局 *consider the big picture*｜奋不～身 *dash ahead heedless of personal safety* ㊀商店称来买货物 (used in a shop) to patronize：惠～ *to patronize*｜～客 *customer*｜主～ *customer*［照顾］1 照管，特别关心 to care for; to look after：～群众的生活 *take care of the general public's livelihood* 2 旧时商店称顾客来买货 (old term used in a shop) to patronize ❹文言连词，但，但是 (conjunction in classical Chinese) but

梏 gù ㄍㄨˋ 古代束缚罪人两手的木制刑具 wooden handcuffs in ancient times

牿 gù ㄍㄨˋ ❶绑在牛角上使牛不得顶人的横木 length of wood tied to an ox horns to prevent them from injuring people ❷ 养牛马的圈（juàn）stable; cattleshed

雇(*僱) gù ㄍㄨˋ ❶出钱让人给自己做事 to employ：～工 *hire labour; hired labourer* | ～保姆 *hire a nanny* ❷租赁交通运输工具 to hire：～车 *hire a taxi* | ～牲口 *rent a draught animal*

GUA ㄍㄨㄚ

瓜 guā ㄍㄨㄚ 蔓生植物，叶掌状，花多为黄色，果实可吃。种类很多，有西瓜、南瓜、冬瓜、黄瓜等 any kind of melon or gourd [瓜分] 像切瓜一样地分割 to divide up; to carve up [瓜葛]（－gé）㊙亲友关系或相牵连的关系 connection; association

呱 guā ㄍㄨㄚ [呱嗒]（－dā）形容短而脆的撞击声 clack; clip-clop [呱嗒板儿] 1 唱莲花落（lào）等打拍子的器具 bamboo clappers 2 木拖鞋 wooden sandals [呱呱] 形容鸭子、青蛙等的响亮叫声 (of a duck) quack; (of a frog) croak ㊕形容好 tiptop; top-notch：～叫 *superb* | 顶～ *first-rate*

⇨ see also gū on p.218, guǎ on p.223

胍 guā ㄍㄨㄚ 有机化合物，无色晶体，易潮解。可用来制药 guanidine

刮(❷颳) guā ㄍㄨㄚ ❶用刀子去掉物体表面的东西 to scrape; to shave：～脸 *to shave (the face)* | ～冬瓜皮 *peel a white gourd* ㊙搜刮民财 to extort; to plunder：贪官污吏只会～地皮。*Corrupt officials just thrive on extortion.* ❷(风)吹动 (of wind) to blow：～风 *wind blows* | ～倒了一棵树。*The wind blew a tree down.*

括 guā ㄍㄨㄚ [挺括]〈方 dialect〉（衣服、纸张等）较硬而平整 (of clothing, paper, etc.) stiff and neat

⇨ see also kuò on p.372

栝 guā ㄍㄨㄚ 古书上指桧（guì）树 juniper (in ancient Chinese texts)

[栝楼]（－lóu）草本植物，爬蔓（wàn），花白色，果实卵圆形。块根和果实都可入药 Chinese snake gourd

鸹(鴰) guā ㄍㄨㄚ [老鸹]〈方 dialect〉乌鸦 crow

騧(騧) guā ㄍㄨㄚ 黑嘴的黄马 yellow horse with a black mouth

G

蜗(緺) guā ㄍㄨㄚ ❶古代青紫色的绶带 (in ancient times) purple and blue ribbon ❷量词，用于妇女盘结的发髻 (measure word) lock (of a woman's bun)

呱 guǎ ㄍㄨㄚˇ [拉呱儿]（lāguǎr）〈方 dialect〉聊天 to chat

⇨ see also gū on p.218, guā on p.223

剐(剮) guǎ ㄍㄨㄚˇ ❶被尖锐的东西划破 to cut; to slit：把手～破了 *cut one's hand* | 裤子上～了个口子 *get a cut on the trousers* ❷古代把人的身体割成许多块的酷刑 to cut off flesh from the bones (an ancient form of punishment)：千刀万～ *hack to pieces*

寡 guǎ ㄍㄨㄚˇ ❶少，缺少 few; lacking：～言 *taciturn* | 优柔～断 *weak and irresolute* | 多～不等 *vary in quantity or amount* ❷古代君主的自称 used by ancient monarchs to refer to themselves：称孤道～ *address oneself as king* ❸妇女死了丈夫 widowed：～妇 *widow*

卦 guà ㄍㄨㄚˋ 八卦，我国古代用来占卜的象征各种自然或人事现象的八种符号，相传是伏羲氏所创 the Eight Trigrams (symbols used in ancient Chinese divination) [变卦] ㊈已定的事情忽然改变（含贬义）(disapproving) to go back on one's word; to break an agreement

诖(註) guà ㄍㄨㄚˋ 失误 to err [诖误] 1 被牵连而受谴责或处分 to be implicated in some trouble：为人～ *be implicated* 2 旧时也指撤职、失官 (old) to be removed from office

挂(*掛、❷*罣) guà ㄍㄨㄚˋ ❶悬（㊀悬一）to hang (up); to suspend：红灯高～ *red lantern hanging high* | ～图 *wallchart* ❷惦记（㊀牵一）to be concerned about：～念 *miss and worry about sb absent* | ～虑 *be anxious about* | 记～ *be concerned about* ❸登记 to register：～号 *to register (at a hospital etc.)* | ～失 *report a loss* ❹量词，多用于成串的东西 (measure word) often for things in a string：一～鞭 *a string of firecrackers* | 一～珠子 *a string of beads*

褂 guà ㄍㄨㄚˋ （一子、一儿）上身的衣服 Chinese-style unlined garment：大～子（长衫）*long gown* | 小～儿 *(Chinese-style) shirt*

GUAI ㄍㄨㄞ

乖 guāi ㄍㄨㄞ ❶不顺，不和谐（㊀一僻）perverse; contrary to reason ❷指小孩听话，懂事 well-behaved; obedient：宝宝很～，大人省事多了。*The baby is so well-behaved it saves a lot of work for the parents.* ❸机灵，伶俐（㊀一巧）smart; quick-witted：这孩子嘴～。*The child has a quick tongue.*

掴(摑) guāi ㄍㄨㄞ guó ㄍㄨㄛˊ(又) 打耳光 to slap; to smack：被～了一记耳光 *be given a slap on the face*

拐(❹*柺) guǎi ㄍㄨㄞˇ ❶转折 to turn：～过去就是大街。*The street is just round the corner.* | ～弯抹角 *zigzag along;(figurative) beat about the bush* | ～角 *corner* | ～点（转折点）*turning point* ❷骗走人或财物 to abduct; to swindle：～骗 *to swindle* | ～卖 *abduct and traffic* | 钱被人～走了。*(He was) swindled out of money.* ❸腿脚有毛病，失去平衡，走路不稳 to limp：走道一瘸（qué）一～ *limp along;*

walk with a limp ❹走路时帮助支持身体的棍子 walking stick; crutch：～杖 *crutch* | ～棍 *walking stick* | 架～ *use a crutch* ❺在某些场合说数字时用来代替7。used to represent the number 7 on some specific occasions

夬 guài ㄍㄨㄞˋ 坚决，果断 resolute

怪(*恠) guài ㄍㄨㄞˋ ❶奇异，不平常(㊥奇一、一异) strange; odd; unusual：～事 *oddity* | ～模～样 *odd-looking* ㊀惊奇 to find sth strange：少见多～ *find things unusual out of ignorance* | 大惊小～ *be alarmed at sth normal* ❷怪物，神话传说中的妖魔之类(㊥妖一) monster; fiend; evil spirit ㊤ 性情乖僻的人或形状异样的东西 eccentric; freak; oddity ❸副词，很，非常 (adverb) rather; quite：～好的天气 *a rather nice day* | 这孩子～讨人喜欢的。*The child is quite cute.* ❹怨，责备 to blame; to rebuke：责～ *to blame* | ～罪 *to blame* | 这事儿不能～他。*This is not his fault.*

GUAN ㄍㄨㄢ

关(關、**関) guān ㄍㄨㄢ ❶闭，合拢(㊥一闭) to close; to shut：～门 *close the door* | ～上箱子 *shut the chest* ㊀拘禁 to lock up; to confine：～监狱 *put behind bars* ❷古代在险要地方或国界设立的守卫处所 guarded pass; (mountain) pass：～口 *strategic pass* | 山海～ *Shanhaiguan Pass* ㊀征收出口、入口货税的机构 customs; customhouse：海～ *customs* | ～税 *tariff* ❸重要的转折点，不易度过的一段时间 turning point; barrier：难～ *barrier* | 紧要～头 *critical moment* ❹起转折关联作用的部分 hinge; crux：～节 (两骨连接的地方) *joint (of bones)* | ～键 *key point* ❺牵连，连属 connection; relation：相～ *be related* | 无～紧要 *inconsequential* [关系] 1 事物之间的关涉牵连 relation; connection: 这个电门和那盏灯没有～。*This switch has nothing to do with that lamp.* 2 人事的联系 relationship：同志～ *comrade relationship* | 亲戚～ *related of kinship* 3 影响 bearing; impact: 这件事～太大。*It matters a lot.* [关于] 介词，引进某种行为或事物的关系者 (preposition) about; on; concerning：～促进就业的措施 *measures to promote employment* | ～社会学方面的书 *a book on sociology* ❻旧指发给或支领(薪饷) (old) to pay or receive (salary)：～饷 *pay salary*

观(觀) guān ㄍㄨㄢ ❶看(㊥一看) to look; to watch; to observe：坐井～天 *have a narrow view of things (literally means 'look at the sky from the bottom of a well')* | ～摩 *to view and emulate* | 走马～花 *get a superficial view of things (literally means 'view flowers riding on horseback')* | ～察 *to observe* | ～光 *go sightseeing* ❷看到的景象

G

（㊇景一、一瞻）view; sight：奇～ *wonder* | 壮～ *magnificent (sight)* | 洋洋大～ *spectacular sight* ❸对事物的认识，看法 outlook; concept; conception：乐～ *optimistic* | 人生～ *view of life* | 宇宙～ *world outlook*［观点］从某一角度或立场出发形成的对事物的看法 point of view［观念］1 思想，理性认识 idea; concept 2 客观事物在意识中构成的形象 sense; perception

⇨ see also guàn on p.228

纶（綸） guān ㄍㄨㄢ 青丝带 black silk ribbon［纶巾］古代配有青丝带的头巾。传说三国时诸葛亮平常戴这种头巾 black silk ribbon scarf (an ancient headdress, said to have been worn often by Zhuge Liang)

⇨ see also lún on p.426

官 guān ㄍㄨㄢ ❶政府机关或军队中经过任命的、一定级别以上的公职人员 government official; officer：～吏 *government official* | ～员 *official* | 当～ *hold a public office* ❷旧时称属于国家的 (old) government-owned; of the state：～办 *state-run* | ～款 *public money*［官话］1 旧时指通行于广大区域的北方话，特指北京话 (old) Mandarin (Chinese, specially Beijing dialect) 2 官腔 official jargon; bureaucratic tone ❸器官，生物体上有特定机能的部分 organ：五～ *the five sense organs* | 感～ *sensory organ*

倌 guān ㄍㄨㄢ ❶农村中专管饲养某些家畜的人 herdsman; livestock keeper：牛～儿 *cowherd* | 羊～儿 *shepherd* ❷旧时称服杂役的人 (old) hired hand：堂～儿（茶、酒、饭馆的服务人员）*waiter*

棺 guān ㄍㄨㄢ 棺材，装殓死人的器物 coffin：～木 *coffin* | 入～ *lay a corpse in a coffin*

冠 guān ㄍㄨㄢ ❶帽子 hat：～冕堂皇 *high-sounding* | 衣～楚楚 *immaculately dressed* ❷（一子）鸟类头上的肉瘤或高出的羽毛 (of bird) crest; comb; crown：鸡～子 *cockscomb*

⇨ see also guàn on p.228

蒄 guān ㄍㄨㄢ 有机化合物，针状晶体，淡黄色，可看作是六个苯环组成的环烃 coronene

矜 guān ㄍㄨㄢ 〈古 ancient〉 ❶ same as “鳏” ❷ same as “瘝”

⇨ see also jīn on p.321, qín on p.538

瘝 guān ㄍㄨㄢ 病，痛苦 illness; pain

鳏（鰥） guān ㄍㄨㄢ 无妻或丧妻的男人 bachelor; widower：～夫 *bachelor; widower* | ～寡孤独 *widowers, widows, orphans and the childless (those who are on their own and unable to support themselves)*

莞 guǎn ㄍㄨㄢˇ ［东莞］地名，在广东省 Dongguan (a place in Guangdong Province)

⇨ see also wǎn on p.674

筦 guǎn ㄍㄨㄢˇ ❶ see 管 on page 227 ❷姓 (surname) Guan

馆（館、*舘） guǎn ㄍㄨㄢˇ ❶招待宾客

或旅客食宿的房舍 accommodation; guesthouse; hotel: 宾～ *hotel*| 旅～ *hotel* ❷一个国家在另一个国家办理外交的人员常驻的处所 embassy; legation; consulate: 大使～ *embassy* ❸（一子、一儿）某些服务性商店的名称 a service establishment; shop: 照相～ *photo studio* | 理发～ *barber's* | 饭～儿 *restaurant* ❹开展文化等活动的场所 place for cultural activities, etc.: 体育～ *gymnasium* | 图书～ *library* | 博物～ *museum* ❺旧时指教学的地方 (old) school: 家～ *family school* | 蒙～ *primary school*

琯 guǎn ㄍㄨㄢˇ 玉管，古代的一种管乐器 an ancient jade flute

管（△*筦）guǎn ㄍㄨㄢˇ ❶吹奏的乐器 wind instrument: 丝竹～弦 *wind and strings; music* | ～乐器 *wind instrument* ❷（一子、一儿）圆筒形的东西 tube; pipe: ～道 *pipeline* | 竹～儿 *bamboo pipe* | 无缝钢～ *seamless steel pipe* | ～见（指浅陋的见识）*(my) humble opinion* ㊀ 量词，用于细长圆筒形的东西 (measure word) for tube-shaped objects: 一～毛笔 *a writing brush* ❸负责，管理 to manage; to be responsible; to run: ～家 *butler* | ～账 *keep account* | ～伙食 *be in charge of catering* ㊀干预，过问 to interfere; to be concerned with: ～闲事 *poke one's nose into other people's business* | 这事我们不能不～。*We can't leave this matter unattended.* ❹管教，约束 to keep under control; to discipline; to restrain: ～孩子 *keep one's child(ren) under control*| ～住自己的嘴，不说粗话 *keep one's language in check* [管制] 1 监督，管理 to control: ～灯火 *enforce a blackout* 2 刑事处分的一种，对某些有罪行的人，由政府和群众监督教育，使能改过自新 to put under surveillance [不管] 连词，跟"无论"义相近 (conjunction, similar to 无论) no matter (what, how, etc.); regardless of: ～有多大困难，我们都能克服。*We can overcome any difficulties, no matter what.* ❺负责供给 to supply: ～吃～住 *provide food and accommodation* | 生活用品都～。*All daily necessities are supplied.* ㊀保证 to assure: ～用 *effective* | 不好～换 *replacement of defective goods assured* | ～保 *to guarantee* ❻介词，把（与动词"叫"连用）(preposition) used with the verb 叫 to introduce the object: 有的地区～玉米叫苞谷。*In some areas* 玉米 *is called* 苞谷.

鳤（鰥）guǎn ㄍㄨㄢˇ 鱼名，身体长筒形，银白色，鳞小，生活在淡水中 *Ochetobius elongatus* (a fish found in eastern Asia)

毌 guàn ㄍㄨㄢˋ ❶ancient form of 贯 ❷姓 (surname) Guan

贯（貫）guàn ㄍㄨㄢˋ ❶连贯，穿通（㊥一穿）to connect; to link up; to pass through: 学～中西 *well versed in* *both Chinese and Western learning*| 一直～串下去 *run all the way through* | 融会～通 *master sth through thorough study* [贯彻] 使全部实现 to carry out; to implement: ～执行 *carry out* | ～党的政策 *implement the Party's policies* [一贯] 向来如此，始终一致 all along; consistent: 艰苦朴素是他的～作风。*Hardworking and plain-living has been his style all along.* ❷旧时把方孔钱穿在绳子上，每一千个叫一贯 (old) *guan* (string of 1 000 coins) ❸原籍，出生地 place of one's birth or origin; native place: 籍～ *native place* ❹姓 (surname) Guan

掼(摜) guàn ㄍㄨㄢˋ 〈方 dialect〉❶掷，扔 to hurl; to throw; to fling: 往地下一～ *throw to the ground* ❷跌；使跌 to fall; to tumble: ～了一跤。*(He) fell down.* | 把他～倒在地 *throw him to the ground*

惯(慣) guàn ㄍㄨㄢˋ ❶习以为常的，积久成性的 habitual; customary: ～技 *old trick* | ～例 *convention* | 穿～了休闲装 *be used to wearing casual clothing* [惯性] 物体没有受外力作用时保持原有的运动状态或静止状态，这种性质叫惯性 inertia ❷纵容，放任 to spoil; to indulge: ～坏了孩子 *have spoiled the child* | 娇生～养 *spoiled and pampered*

观(觀) guàn ㄍㄨㄢˋ 道教的庙宇 Taoist temple: 道～ *Taoist temple*

⇨ see also guān on p.225

冠 guàn ㄍㄨㄢˋ ❶把帽子戴在头上 to put on a hat ❷居第一位 to be in first place;be the best: 勇～三军 *be peerless in battle* [冠军] ㊕ 比赛的第一名 champion ❸在前面加上某种名号 to crown sb/sth with: ～名权 *naming right* | ～以诗人的桂冠 (guān) *be crowned poet*

⇨ see also guān on p.226

涫 guàn ㄍㄨㄢˋ 沸 to boil: ～汤 *boiling soup*

祼 guàn ㄍㄨㄢˋ 古代祭祀时把酒浇在地上的礼节 wine spilling (an ancient sacrificial rite)

盥 guàn ㄍㄨㄢˋ 洗（手、脸）to wash (face or hands): ～洗室 *washroom*

灌 guàn ㄍㄨㄢˋ ❶浇，灌溉 to irrigate: 引水～田 *irrigate fields with channelled water* ❷倒进去或装进去（液体、气体、颗粒状物体）to fill; to pour in: 风雪往门里～。*Wind and snow sweep in through the door.* | ～一瓶水 *fill up a bottle with water* [灌木] 主茎不发达，丛生而矮小的树木，如茶树、酸枣树等 bush; shrub

瓘 guàn ㄍㄨㄢˋ 古玉器名 (ancient) a jade ware

爟 guàn ㄍㄨㄢˋ ❶古代祭祀用的火炬 a torch used in sacrifices in ancient times ❷报警的烽火 beacon-fire

鹳(鸛) guàn ㄍㄨㄢˋ 鸟名，像鹤，羽毛灰色、白色或黑色，生活在水边，捕食鱼

虾等，种类很多 stork

罐(*鑵、**鏆) guàn ㄍㄨㄢˋ (一子、一儿) 盛东西或汲水用的瓦器，泛指各种圆筒形的盛物器 jar; pot; tin：铁～儿 *iron jar* | 易拉～儿 *ring-pull can* | 煤气～儿 *gas tank*

GUANG ㄍㄨㄤ

光 guāng ㄍㄨㄤ ❶光线，照射在物体上能使视觉感知物体的那种物质 light; ray：一束～ *a beam of light* | 灯～ *lamplight* | 阳～ *sunlight* | 激～ *laser* | ～盘 *compact disc* [光明] 亮 bright 喻襟怀坦白，没有私心 openhearted; guileless：心地～ *openhearted* [光盘] 用激光束记录和读取信息的圆盘形存储载体，可分为只读光盘和可刻录光盘 compact disc [激光] 一种由激光器产生的颜色很纯、能量高度集中并朝单一方向发射的光。广泛应用在工业、军事、医学、通信、探测等方面 laser ❷光彩，荣誉 honour; glory：为国增～ *win honour for one's country* | ～荣 *glory* ❸敬辞 polite speech：～临 *be present* | ～顾 *to patronize* ❹景物 scenery; sight：春～ *spring scene* | 风～ *scenery* | 观～ *go sightseeing* [光景] 1 same as "光❹" 2 生活的情况 circumstances of life：～一年好似一年。*Life is getting better each year.* ❺光滑，平滑 smooth; glossy：磨～ *to polish* | ～溜 (liu) *smooth* ❻完了，一点儿不剩 used up; finished：把敌人消灭～ *wipe out the enemy* ❼露着 to be bare/naked：～头 *go bareheaded; baldhead; shaven head* | ～膀子 *naked to the waist* ❽副词，单，只 (adverb) only; alone：大家都走了，～剩下他一个人了。*Everybody is gone, leaving only him.*

垙 guāng ㄍㄨㄤ ❶田间小路 footpath through a field ❷用于地名 used in place names：上～（在北京市延庆）*Shangguang (in Yanqing, Beijing)*

咣 guāng ㄍㄨㄤ 形容撞击或振动的声音 bang; gong：～的一声，门被关上了。*The door was shut with a bang.*

洸 guāng ㄍㄨㄤ see 浛洸 (hán—) at 浛 on page 240

珖 guāng ㄍㄨㄤ 一种玉 a kind of jade

桄 guāng ㄍㄨㄤ [桄榔] (—láng) 常绿乔木，大型羽状叶，生于茎顶。花序的汁可制糖，茎髓可制淀粉 gomuti sugar palm

⇨ see also guàng on p.230

轱(軲) guāng ㄍㄨㄤ 古代指车厢底部的横木 (ancient) wooden cross beam on the bottom of a cart

胱 guāng ㄍㄨㄤ see 膀胱 (páng—) at 膀 on page 493

广(廣) guǎng ㄍㄨㄤˇ ❶宽，大 broad; wide; vast：～场 *square* | 我国地～人多。*Our country has a vast territory and a large population.* [广泛] 范围大，普遍 extensive; widespread：～宣传 *give wide publicity* | 意义～ *have*

G

extensive significance ❷ 宽度 width：长五十米，～三十米 *50 metres in length, and 30 metres in width* [广袤]（-mào）东西的长度叫广，南北的长度叫袤，指土地的面积。也形容辽阔 the length and breath (of a land); vast：～的大地 *vast earth* ❸多 many; numerous：大庭～众 *in public* ❹扩大，扩充 to broaden; to spread：～播 *to broadcast; broadcast* | 推～ *to promote* ❺姓 (surname) Guang

⇨ see also ān on p.4

犷（獷） guǎng ㄍㄨㄤˇ 粗野 tough; uncouth：粗～ *rough and unsophisticated* | ～悍 *uncouth and valiant*

桄 guàng ㄍㄨㄤˋ ❶绕线的器具 reel ❷量词，用于线 (measure word) reel：一～线 *a reel of thread*

⇨ see also guāng on p.229

逛 guàng ㄍㄨㄤˋ 闲游，游览（㊀游-）to stroll; to roam; to wander about：～大街 *stroll through streets* | ～公园 *stroll about the park*

GUI ㄍㄨㄟ

归（歸） guī ㄍㄨㄟ ❶返回，回到本处（㊀回-）to return; go back to：～家 *return home* | ～国 *return to one's country* ㊁还给 to return sth to; give sth back to：物～原主 *return sth to its owner* | ～本还原 *return to original state* ❷趋向 to converge：殊途同～。*Different roads lead to the same end.* | 众望所～ *command public confidence and support* ❸归并，合并 to merge; to come together：把书～在一起 *pile the books together* | 这两个机构～成一个。*These two institutions will merger into one.* | ～里包堆（总共）*in all* [归纳] 由许多的事例概括出一般的原理 to induce ❹由，属于 to belong to; to be in sb's charge：这事～我办。*I am in charge of this.* ❺珠算中指一位数的除法 (on the abacus) division with a one-digit divisor：九～ *rules for doing division with a one-digit divisor*

圭 guī ㄍㄨㄟ ❶古代帝王、诸侯在举行典礼时拿的一种玉器，上尖下方 jade tablet with a tip held by ancient rulers in ceremonies ❷古代测日影的器具 ancient Chinese sundial [圭臬]（-niè）标准，法度 standard; criterion：奉为～ *hold as standard* ❸古代容量单位名，一升的十万分之一 an ancient Chinese unit for capacity, equal to one hundred thousandth of 升）❹姓 (surname) Gui

邽 guī ㄍㄨㄟ [下邽] 地名，在陕西省渭南 Xiagui (a place in Weinan, Shaanxi Province)

闺（閨） guī ㄍㄨㄟ ❶上圆下方的小门 small arched door ❷旧时指女子居住的内室 (in old times) boudoir：深～ *lady's inner chamber* [闺女] 1 未出嫁的女子 girl; maiden 2 女儿 daughter

珪 guī ㄍㄨㄟ ❶ same as "圭❶" ❷姓 (surname) Gui

硅 guī ㄍㄨㄟ 非金属元素，旧叫矽（xī），符号 Si，褐色粉末或灰色晶体，是重要的半导体材料。硅酸盐在玻璃、水泥工业中很重要 silicon (Si) (formerly called 矽)

鲑(鮭) guī ㄍㄨㄟ 鱼名，身体大，略呈纺锤形，鳞细而圆。种类很多 trout

龟(龜) guī ㄍㄨㄟ 爬行动物，腹背都有硬甲，头尾和脚能缩入甲中，寿命长。种类很多。龟甲可入药，古人用龟甲占卜 tortoise; turtle: ～卜 *divination using tortoiseshell*

⇨ see also jūn on p.345, qiū on p.543

妫(嬀、媯)** guī ㄍㄨㄟ 妫河，水名，在北京市延庆 Guihe River (in Yanqing, Beijing)

规(規、*槼) guī ㄍㄨㄟ ❶圆规，画圆形的仪器 compasses: 两脚～ *a pair of dividers* ❷法则，章程(㊂一则、一章) regulation; rule: 成～ *set rule* | 常～ *convention* [规格] 产品质量的标准，如大小、轻重、精密度、性能等 specifications; norms; standards: 合～ *comply with specifications* [规矩](-ju) 1 标准，法则 rule; established practice: 守～ *go by the rules* | 老～ *old practice* 2 合标准，守法则 well-behaved; well-disciplined: 做事～老实 *honest and law-abiding in behaviour* [规模] 1 格局(多指计划、设备) (often of plans, equipments) scale: 略具～ *having achieved a certain scale* | 这座工厂～宏大。*This is a large-scale factory.* 2 范围 scope: 大～的经济建设 *economic construction on a large scale* ❸相劝 to admonish; to advise: ～劝 *to admonish* | ～勉 *admonish and encourage* ❹谋划 to plan; to map out: ～划 *to plan* | ～定 *to stipulate* | ～避(设法避开) *to evade*

鬶(鬹) guī ㄍㄨㄟ 古代炊具(多为陶制)，嘴像鸟喙，有把柄和三个空心的短足 a pottery cooking vessel with three short hollow feet and a beak-shaped lip, used in ancient China

皈 guī ㄍㄨㄟ [皈依] 原指佛教的入教仪式，后泛指信仰佛教或参加其他宗教组织。也作"归依" to be converted to (originally referring to Buddhist initiation ceremony, also written as 归依)

傀 guī ㄍㄨㄟ 古山名，在今河南省洛阳西 ancient name of a mountain, in the west of the present-day Luoyang, Henan Province

⇨ see also wěi on p.681

瑰(*瓌) guī ㄍㄨㄟ ❶一种像玉的石头 a jade-like stone ❷奇特，珍奇 rare; precious: ～丽 *magnificent* | ～异 *extraordinary* | ～宝 *rarity*

氿 guǐ ㄍㄨㄟˇ 氿泉，从侧面喷出的泉 spring that spurts side ways

G

⇨ see also jiǔ on p.333

宄 guǐ ㄍㄨㄟˇ 坏人 treacherous person; evil-doer: 奸～ *evil-doer*

轨（軌） guǐ ㄍㄨㄟˇ ❶车辙 track ❷轨道，一定的路线，特指铺设轨道的钢条 rail; track: 钢～ *steel rail* | 铁～ *railway rail* | 铺～ *lay a railway track* ㊗应遵循的规则 regulation; rule: 越～ *violate a rule* | 步入正～ *get onto the right course*

匦（匭） guǐ ㄍㄨㄟˇ 箱子，匣子 box; basket: 票～ *ballot box*

庋 guǐ ㄍㄨㄟˇ ❶放东西的架子 shelf ❷搁置 to lay aside; to keep: ～藏 *store up*

诡（詭） guǐ ㄍㄨㄟˇ ❶欺诈，奸滑 sly; deceitful; treacherous: ～辩（无理强辩）*use sophistry* | ～计多端 *full of craft and tricks* ❷怪异，出乎寻常（㊟一异）weird; uncanny: ～秘 *secretive*

姽 guǐ ㄍㄨㄟˇ［姽婳］（— huà）形容女子娴静美好 (of women) quiet and graceful

鬼 guǐ ㄍㄨㄟˇ ❶迷信的人以为人死之后有灵魂，叫鬼 ghost; spirit: 妖魔～怪 *devils and spirits* | 这话～才相信（指无人信）。*Nobody but a ghost would believe such nonsense.* | ～话（虚妄不实的话）*lie* | ～胎（喻不可告人之事）*ulterior motive* ❷躲躲闪闪，不光明正大 deceitful; evasive: ～～祟祟 *sneaky* | ～头～脑 *secretive* ❸指阴谋，不可告人的打算 sinister plot: 心里有～ *have a guilty conscience* | 捣～ *play dirty tricks* ❹机灵（多指小孩子）(often of a child) clever: 这孩子真～。*That child is so clever.* ❺对人的蔑称或憎称 a derogatory term for sb: 酒～ *drunkard* | 吸血～ *vampire* ❻糟糕的，恶劣的 terrible; bad: ～主意 *wicked idea* | ～天气 *terrible weather* ❼星宿名，二十八宿之一 *gui* (one of the twenty-eight constellations in ancient Chinese astronomy)

癸 guǐ ㄍㄨㄟˇ 天干的第十位，用作顺序的第十 *gui* (the tenth of the ten Heavenly Stems, a system used in the Chinese calendar); tenth

晷 guǐ ㄍㄨㄟˇ 日影 shadow cast by the sun ㊕时间 time: 日无暇～ *having no time to spare* ［日晷］古代按照日影测定时刻的仪器。又叫日规 sundial (also called 日规)

簋 guǐ ㄍㄨㄟˇ 古代盛食物的器具，多为圆形，两耳 a food container in ancient China,often round-shaped with two handles

柜（櫃） guì ㄍㄨㄟˋ （—子）一种收藏东西用的器具，通常作长方形，有盖或有门 cabinet; chest; cupboard: 衣～ *wardrobe* | 保险～ *safe*

⇨ see also jǔ on p.337

炅 guì ㄍㄨㄟˋ 姓 (surname) Gui

⇨ see also jiǒng on p.332

刿（劌） guì ㄍㄨㄟˋ 刺伤 to stab and wound

G

刽(劊) guì ㄍㄨㄟˋ 砍断 to cut/chop off [刽子手] 旧指执行斩刑的人 (old) executioner ㊀ 杀害人民的人 slaughterer

桧(檜) guì ㄍㄨㄟˋ 常绿乔木，即圆柏，幼树的叶子针状，大树的叶子鳞片状，果实球形。木材桃红色，有香味，可供建筑等用 Chinese juniper

⇨ see also huì on p.275

贵(貴) guì ㄍㄨㄟˋ ❶价钱高，跟"贱"相对 expensive; costly (opposite of 贱): 这本书不～。*This book is not expensive.* | 金比银～。*Gold costs more than silver.* ❷指地位高，跟"贱"相对 of high rank; noble (opposite of 贱): ～族 *nobility* | 达官～人 *dignitaries* 敬辞，称与对方有关的事物 (polite speech) your: ～姓 *your family name* | ～处 *your place* | ～校 *your school/university* | ～宾 *distinguished guest* ❸值得珍视或重视（㊥宝一、一重）highly valued; valuable: 可～ *commendable* | 珍～ *precious* ❹以某种情况为可贵 to value; to cherish: ～精不～多 *quality over quantity* | ～在坚持 *perseverance is most valuable* | 人～有自知之明。*Self-knowledge is valuable.*

桂 guì ㄍㄨㄟˋ ❶植物名 name for several kinds of plants with 桂 in their names ①肉桂，常绿乔木，花白色。树皮有香味，可入药，又可做香料 Chinese cinnamon; cassia ②月桂树，常绿乔木，叶长椭圆形，花黄色，叶可做香料 laurel; bay tree ③桂花，常绿小乔木或灌木，又叫木樨，花白色或黄色，有特殊香味，可做香料 osmanthus (also called 木樨) ❷广西壮族自治区的别称 Gui (another name for Guangxi Zhuang Autonomous Region)

筀 guì ㄍㄨㄟˋ [筀竹] 古书上说的一种竹子 a kind of bamboo in ancient Chinese texts

跪 guì ㄍㄨㄟˋ 屈膝，使膝盖着地 to kneel; go down on one's knees: 下～ *kneel down* | ～姿射击 *shoot from a kneeling position*

鳜(鱖) guì ㄍㄨㄟˋ 鱼名，身体侧扁，青黄色，有黑色斑点，口大鳞细，尾鳍呈扇形，生活在淡水中。是我国的特产 mandarin fish

GUN ㄍㄨㄣ

衮 gǔn ㄍㄨㄣˇ 古代君王的礼服 ceremonial robe worn by rulers in ancient China: ～服 *ceremonial robe of rulers in ancient China*

滚 gǔn ㄍㄨㄣˇ ❶水流翻腾 ㊂ (of water) to churn: 白浪翻～ *white waves churning* | 大江～～东去。*The river flows to the east.* ㊀ 水煮开 to boil: 水～了。*The water is boiling.* ❷旋转着移动 to roll: 小球～来～去。*The little ball rolls about.* | ～铁环 *roll a hoop* | 打～ *roll about* ❸走，离开（含斥责意）go/get away (imperative, rebuking): ～出去！ *Get out of here!* ❹极，特 extremely;

very：～烫 *boiling hot* | ～圆 *round as a ball*

磙 gǔn ㄍㄨㄣˇ （一子）用石头做的圆柱形的压、轧用的器具 stone roller

绲(緄) gǔn ㄍㄨㄣˇ ❶织成的带子 braided band; tape ❷绳 string; cord ❸沿衣服等的边缘缝上布条、带子等 to bind; to trim (a piece of clothing with bands or cords)：～边ㄦ *embroidered border*

辊(輥) gǔn ㄍㄨㄣˇ 机器上能滚动的圆柱形机件 roller：皮～花 *(of textiles) roller waste* | ～轴 *roll shaft*

鲧(鯀、鮌)** gǔn ㄍㄨㄣˇ ❶古书上说的一种大鱼 a huge fish in ancient Chinese texts ❷古人名，传说是夏禹的父亲 Gun (father of Yu the legendary ruler of the Xia Dynasty)

棍 gùn ㄍㄨㄣˋ ❶（一子、一ㄦ）棒 stick; rod ❷称坏人 rascal; scoundrel：赌～ *gambler* | 恶～ *ruffian*

GUO ㄍㄨㄛ

过(過) guō ㄍㄨㄛ 姓 (surname) Guo

⇨ see also guò on p.236

彍(彉) guō ㄍㄨㄛ 拉满弩弓 to draw a bow to the full

呙(咼) guō ㄍㄨㄛ 姓 (surname) Guo

埚(堝) guō ㄍㄨㄛ see 坩埚 (gān—) at 坩 on page 197

涡(渦) guō ㄍㄨㄛ 涡河，水名，发源于河南省，流至安徽省注入淮河 Guohe River (originating from Henan Province, and reaching Huaihe River in Anhui Province)

⇨ see also wō on p.687

锅(鍋) guō ㄍㄨㄛ ❶烹煮食物的器具 pot; pan; wok [锅炉] 1 一种烧开水的设备 boiler (an apparatus for heating water) 2 使水变成蒸汽以供应工业或取暖需要的设备。又叫汽锅 steam boiler ; boiler (an equipment to produce steam, also called 汽锅) ❷（一ㄦ）器物上像锅的部分 pot-shaped part (of an utensil)：烟袋～ *bowl of a pipe*

郭 guō ㄍㄨㄛ 城外围着城的墙（㊐城一）outer city wall

崞 guō ㄍㄨㄛ 崞县，旧地名，在山西省。现叫原平县 Guo County (old name of present-day Yuanping County, Shanxi Province)

啯(嘓) guō ㄍㄨㄛ 形容蛙鸣声 ㊂ croak (of frogs)：蛙鸣～～ *frogs croaking*

蝈(蟈) guō ㄍㄨㄛ [蝈蝈ㄦ]（—guor）昆虫，身体绿色或褐色，翅短，腹大，雄的前翅根部有发声器，能振翅发声。对植物有害 bush cricket; katydid

聒 guō ㄍㄨㄛ 声音嘈杂，使人厌烦 noisy：～耳 *grating on one's ears* | ～噪 *noisy*

国(國、囯)** guó ㄍㄨㄛˊ ❶国家

country; nation; state：保家卫～ *protect our home and defend our country* | ～内 *domestic* | ～际 *international* | 外～ *foreign country* | 祖～ *homeland* [国家] 1 阶级统治和管理的工具，是统治阶级对被统治阶级实行专政的暴力组织，主要由军队、警察、法庭、监狱等组成。国家是阶级矛盾不可调和的产物和表现，它随着阶级的产生而产生，也将随着阶级的消灭而自行消亡 state 2 一个独立的国家政权所领有的区域 country ❷代表国家的，属于本国的 national：～旗 *national flag* | ～徽 *national emblem* | ～歌 *national anthem* | ～产 *domestically produced* | ～画 *traditional Chinese painting* | ～货 *domestic goods*

掴(摑) guó ㄍㄨㄛˊ(又) see guāi on page 224

帼(幗) guó ㄍㄨㄛˊ 古代妇女包头的巾、帕 women's headdress in ancient times：巾～英雄（女英雄）*woman hero*

涠(漍) guó ㄍㄨㄛˊ [北涠] 地名，在江苏省江阴 Beiguo (a place in Jiangyin, Jiangsu Province)

腘(膕) guó ㄍㄨㄛˊ 膝部的后面 knee pit：～窝（腿弯曲时腘部形成的窝）*popliteal fossa*

虢 guó ㄍㄨㄛˊ 周代诸侯国名。在今陕西、河南一带 a state in the Zhou Dynasty (around present-day Shaanxi and Henan Provinces)

馘(** 聝) guó ㄍㄨㄛˊ 古代战争中割取敌人的左耳以计数献功。也指割下的左耳 (in ancient wars) to cut off the left ears of enemies as a measure of a soldier's merit; left ears cut off in this way

果(❶* 菓) guǒ ㄍㄨㄛˇ ❶（一子）果实，某些植物花落后含有种子的部分 fruit：水～ *fruit* | 干～（如花生、栗子等）*nuts (peanut, chestnut, etc.)* ❷结果，事情的结局或成效 result; consequence：成～ *achievement* | 恶～ *disastrous result* | 前因后～ *cause and effect* ❸果断，坚决（㊀一决）resolute; decisive：～敢 *resolute and courageous* | 言必信，行必～ *truthful in speech and firm in action* ❹果然，确实，真的 as expected; sure enough：～不出所料。*It happened just as expected.* | ～真 *really*

馃(餜) guǒ ㄍㄨㄛˇ （一子）一种油炸的面食 deep-fried dough stick

蜾 guǒ ㄍㄨㄛˇ [蜾蠃]（-luǒ）一种蜂，常捕捉螟蛉等小虫存在窝里，留作将来幼虫的食物。旧时误认蜾蠃养螟蛉为己子，所以有把抱养的孩子称为“螟蛉子”的说法 thread-waisted wasp (a wasp that catches corn earworms 螟蛉, which the ancients mistook to be its adopted offspring, hence the term 螟蛉子, meaning adopted children)

G

裹 guǒ ㄍㄨㄛˇ 包，缠 to bind; to wrap：～伤口 *dress a wound* | 用纸～上 *wrap sth up in paper* | ～足不前（停止不进行，多指有所顾虑）*hesitate to move forward* ⑩ 把东西卷在里头 to wrap in：洪水～着泥沙 *flood thick with silt*

粿 guǒ ㄍㄨㄛˇ 用米粉等制成的食品 foodstuff made with rice flour

椁（*槨） guǒ ㄍㄨㄛˇ 棺材外面套的大棺材 outer coffin

过（過） guò ㄍㄨㄛˋ ❶ 从这儿到那儿，从甲方到乙方 to cross; to pass; to transfer：～江 *cross a river* | 没有～不去的河。*There is no river so wide that one cannot cross.* | ～户 *transfer ownership* | ～账 *transfer items (as from a daybook to a ledger)* ㊀ ①传 to transmit; to pass：～电 *get an electric shock* | 别把病～给孩子。*Don't pass the disease to the child.* ②交往 to interact (with people)：～从 *to associate*［过去］1（－qù）已经经历了的时间 the past 2（－qu）从这儿到那儿去 to pass; to cross ❷ 经过，度过 to spend (time)：～冬 *pass the winter* | ～节 *celebrate a festival* | 日子越～越好。*Life is getting better each day.* ㊀使经过某种处理 to undergo (a process); to go through：～秤 *to weigh* | ～目 *read over (to check or approve)* | ～一～数 *to count* | 把菜～一～油 *pass the ingredients of a dish through hot oil* ❸ 数量或程度等超出 to exceed in quantity or extent：～半数 *more than half* | ～了一百 *over a hundred* | ～分（fèn）*excessive* | ～火 *to overdone* | 这样说，未免太～。*These remarks went too far.* ❹（－儿）量词，次，回，遍 (measure word) time：衣服洗了好几～儿。*The clothes have been washed several times.* ❺错误（㊥－错）error; mistake：改～自新 *turn over a new leaf* | 知～必改。*Always correct a mistake once it is found.* ❻（guo）放在动词后 used after a verb ① 助词，表示曾经或已经 (auxiliary word) to indicate a past or finished action：看～ *have seen* | 听～ *have heard* | 用～了 *have used* | 你见～他吗？*Have you met him before?* ② 跟"来""去"连用，表示趋向 (used with 来 or 去) toward; to：拿～来 *take (sth) over here* | 转～去 *turn away/around* ❼放在单音节形容词后，表示超过 used behind a monosyllabic adjective, to express a higher level：弟弟高～哥哥。*The younger brother is taller than his older brother.* | 今年好～去年。*This year is better than last year.*

⇨ see also guō on p.234

G

H 厂

HA 厂Y

哈(❸** 蝦) hā 厂Y ❶张口呼气 exhale with mouth wide open：～一口气 *to exhale* [哈哈]笑声 ha-ha ❷叹词，表示得意或惊喜 ㊟(exclamation) expressing complacency or joyful excitation：～，我赢啦！*Ha! I won!* ❸哈腰，稍微弯腰，表示礼貌 to bow

[哈喇](—lɑ) 1 含油的食物日子久了起了变化的味道 rancid 2 杀死（元曲多用）to kill (mainly used in *Yuanqu*, a type of verse popular in the Yuan Dynasty)

[哈尼族]我国少数民族，参看附录四 the Hani people (one of the ethnic groups in China. See Appendix Ⅳ.)

[哈萨克族] 1 我国少数民族，参看附录四 the Kazak people (one of the ethnic groups in China. See Appendix Ⅳ.) 2 哈萨克斯坦的主要民族 Kazakhs; Qazaks (the main ethnic group of Kazakhstan)

⇨ see also hǎ on p.237, hà on p.237

铪(鉿) hā 厂Y 金属元素，符号 Hf，银白色，熔点高，可用来制耐高温合金，也用于核工业等 hafnium (Hf)

虾(蝦) há 厂Ý [虾蟆](—mɑ)(old) same as "蛤蟆"

⇨ see also xiā on p.702

蛤 há 厂Ý [蛤蟆](—mɑ)青蛙和癞蛤蟆的统称 general term for frog and toad

⇨ see also gé on p.205

哈 hǎ 厂Y̌ 姓 (surname) Ha [哈达](藏 *Tibetan*)一种长条形薄绢，藏族和部分蒙古族人用以表示敬意或祝贺 khata; khatag (a ceremonial strip of silk used by Tibetans and some Mongolians)

[哈巴狗](—bɑ—)一种狗，又叫狮子狗、巴儿狗，个儿小腿短，常用来比喻驯顺的奴才 Pekinese dog; (figurative) obedient minion

⇨ see also hā on p.237, hà on p.237

哈 hà 厂Y̌ [哈什蚂](—shimǎ)一种蛙，又叫哈士蟆，身体灰褐色，生活在阴湿的地方。雌的腹内有脂肪状物质，叫哈什蚂油，可入药。主要产于我国东北各省 Chinese forest frog (also called 哈士蟆)

⇨ see also hā on p.237, hǎ on p.237

HAI 厂历

咍 hāi 厂历 ❶讥笑 to ridicule：为众人所～ *be laughed at by others* ❷欢笑，喜悦 happy; delightful：欢～ *joyful* ❸ same as "咳 (hāi) ❷"

咳 hāi ㄏㄞ ❶叹息 to sigh: ～声叹气 *moan and groan* ❷叹词 exclamation ①表示惋惜或后悔 Oh (expressing sorrow or regret): ～，我为什么这么糊涂! *Oh, how could I be so foolish!* ②招呼人，提醒人注意 hey: ～，到这儿来。*Hey, come here!*

⇨ see also ké on p.355

嗨 hāi ㄏㄞ (exclamation) same as "咳 (hāi) ❷"

⇨ see also hēi on p.250

还(還) hái ㄏㄞˊ 副词 adverb ①仍旧，依然 still: 你～是那样。*You are still like that.* | 这件事～没有做完。*It has still not been finished.* ② 更 even more: 今天比昨天～热。*It is even hotter today than yesterday.* ③再，又 once again: 另外～有一件事要做。*There is one more thing to do.* | 提高产量，～要保证质量。*We have to ensure quality as well as increase production.* ④尚，勉强过得去 fairly: 身体～好 *in pretty good health* | 工作进展得～不算慢。*The work is progressing not too slowly.* ⑤尚且 even, still: 他那么大年纪～这么干，咱们更应该加油干了。*He works so hard even at his advanced age, so we should work even harder.* [还是] (－shi) 1 副词，表示这么办比较好 (adverb) indicating a better way to do something: 咱们～出去吧。*It is better that we go out.* 2 连词，用在问句里表示选择 (conjunction) used in the second part of a question to indicate choice: 是你去呢，～他来? *Will you go or he come?* ⑥表示没想到如此，而居然如此（多含赞叹语气）used to show surprise (mostly in admiration): 他～真有办法。*He is really resourceful.*

⇨ see also huán on p.265

孩 hái ㄏㄞˊ （－子、－儿）幼童 child: ～童 *child* | 小～儿 *child* ㉄子女 one's son or daughter [孩提] 指幼儿时期 childhood

骸 hái ㄏㄞˊ ❶骨头（㊥－骨）bones: 尸～ *corpse* ❷指身体 body: 病～ *ailing body* [残骸] 人或动物的尸体，借指残破的建筑物、机械、交通工具等 corpse; remains; wreckage

胲 hǎi ㄏㄞˇ 有机化合物的一类，是 NH_2OH 的烃基衍生物 hydroxylamine

海 hǎi ㄏㄞˇ ❶靠近大陆比洋小的水域 sea: 黄～ *the Yellow Sea* | 渤～ *the Bohai Sea* | ～岸 *seashore* ❷用于湖泊名称 used in the name of some lakes: 青～ *Qinghai Lake* | 洱～ *Erhai Lake* ❸容量大的器皿 big container: 墨～ *ink slab* ❹比喻数量多的人或事物 (figurative) a great number of people or things: 人～ *a sea of people* | 文山会～ *mountains of paperwork and seas of meetings* ❺巨大的 huge: ～碗 *big bowl* | ～量 *a great amount* | 夸下～口 *to boast*
[海报] 文艺、体育演出或比赛等活动的招贴 poster; playbill

醢 hǎi ㄏㄞˇ ❶古代用肉、鱼等制成的酱 sauce made of

minced meat or fish ❷古代把人杀死后剁成肉酱的酷刑 a form of torture by killing people and mincing the flesh

亥 hài ㄏㄞˋ ❶地支的第十二位 *hai* (the twelfth of the twelve Earthly Branches) ❷亥时，指晚上九点到十一点 *hai* (the period from 9 p.m.to 11 p.m.)

骇(駭) hài ㄏㄞˋ 惊惧 alarmed and frightened: 惊涛～浪（可怕的大浪）*terrifying waves*|～人听闻 *appalling; shocking*

氦 hài ㄏㄞˋ 气体元素，符号 He，无色、无臭，很轻，不易跟其他元素化合，可用来充入气球或电灯泡等 helium (He)

害 hài ㄏㄞˋ ❶有损的 harmful: ～虫 *(of insect) pest*|～鸟 *(of bird) pest* ❷祸害，坏处，跟“利”相对 damage; harm (opposite of 利): 为民除～ *rid the people of the scourge*|喝酒过多对身体有～。*Drinking too much alcohol is harmful to your health.* ❸灾害，灾患 disaster; calamity: 虫～ *insect pestilence* ❹使受损伤 to cause injury: ～人不浅 *inflict great harm on people*|伤天～理 *do evil against Heaven and reason*|危～ *to harm; to injure* ❺发生疾病 to suffer from (an illness): ～病 *to fall ill*|～眼 *to have eye disease* ❻心理上发生不安的情绪 to feel (ashamed, afraid, etc.): ～羞 *shy; bashful*|～臊 *shy; ashamed*|～怕 *to fear*

〈古 ancient〉also same as 曷 (hé)

嗐 hài ㄏㄞˋ 叹词，表示伤感、惋惜、悔恨等 exclamation, expressing sadness, regret, remorse, etc.: ～！想不到他病得这样重。*Oh no! I didn't realize he was so seriously ill.*

HAN ㄏㄢ

犴 hān ㄏㄢ 哺乳动物，即驼鹿，又叫堪达罕 elk (same as 驼鹿，also called 堪达罕)

⇨ see also àn on p.6

顸(頇) hān ㄏㄢ 粗，圆柱形的东西直径大的 (of cylinder-shaped object) thick: 这线太～。*The thread is too thick.*|拿根～杠子来抬。*Bring a thick stick here to lift it.*

鼾 hān ㄏㄢ 熟睡时的鼻息声 snore: 打～ *to snore*|～声如雷 *snore thunderously*

蚶 hān ㄏㄢ （-子）软体动物，俗叫瓦垄子，贝壳厚，有突起像瓦垄的纵线，种类多，生活在浅海泥沙中 blood clam (informal 瓦垄子)

酣 hān ㄏㄢ 酒喝得很畅快 (to drink) to one's heart's content: ～饮 *drink to one's heart's content*|酒～耳热 *be mellow with drink* ㊀尽兴，痛快 heartily; to one's heart's content: ～睡 *sleep soundly*|～战（长时间紧张地战斗）*fight a fierce battle*

憨 hān ㄏㄢ ❶傻，痴呆 foolish; dull-witted: ～笑 *smile guilelessly* ❷朴实，天真 simple; honest; naive: ～直 *straightforward; ingenuous*|～态 *naive but charming appearance* [憨厚] 朴实，厚

H

道 simple and honest

邗 hán ㄏㄢˊ ［邗江］地名，在江苏省扬州 Hanjiang (a place in Yangzhou, Jiangsu Province)

汗 hán ㄏㄢˊ 指可汗 Khan (see 可 kè on page 356 for reference)

⇨ see also hàn on p.241

虷 hán ㄏㄢˊ 〈古 ancient〉孑孓，蚊子的幼虫 mosquito larva; wriggler

⇨ see also gān on p.197

邯 hán ㄏㄢˊ ［邯郸］（－dān）地名，在河北省 Handan (a place in Hebei Province)

含 hán ㄏㄢˊ ❶嘴里放着东西，不吐出来也不吞下去 to hold sth in the mouth：嘴里～着块糖 *have a sweet in one's mouth* ❷里面存在着 to contain：眼里～着泪 *have tears in one's eyes* | ～水分 *contain water* | ～养分 *contain nutritious substances* ［含糊］（*含胡）（－hu）1 不明确，不清晰 unclear; ambiguous 2 不认真，马虎 not serious; careless：这事可不能～。*We must not deal with the matter carelessly.* 3 怯懦，畏缩（多用于否定）timid; cowardly (often in negative)：上场比赛，绝不～。*In contests, we should never show any cowardice.* ❸带有某种意思、感情等，不完全表露出来 to harbour (a certain idea or feeling)：～怒 *harbour resentment* | ～羞 *look shy* | ～笑 *wear a smile*

浛 hán ㄏㄢˊ ［浛洸］（－guāng）地名，在广东省英德 Hanguang (a place in Yingde, Guangdong Province)

琀 hán ㄏㄢˊ 死者口中所含的珠玉 a pearl or jade in the mouth of a dead person

晗 hán ㄏㄢˊ 天将明 dawn

焓 hán ㄏㄢˊ 单位质量的物质所含的全部热能 enthalpy

函（*圅） hán ㄏㄢˊ ❶匣，套子 case; envelope：石～ *stone casket* | 镜～ *case for a mirror* | 全书共四～。*The book comprises four volumes.* ㊟信件（古代寄信用木函）letter; correspondence (in ancient times, wooden cases were used to mail letters)：～件 *letter* | 来～ *incoming letter* | 公～ *official letter* | ～授 *teaching by correspondence* ❷包容，包含 to contain; to include

崡 hán ㄏㄢˊ 古地名，即函谷，在今河南省灵宝北 the ancient name of 函谷 (a place in the north of today's Lingbao, Henan Province)

涵 hán ㄏㄢˊ 包容，包含（㊟包－）contain; include：海～ *be generous enough to forgive or tolerate* | 内～ *connotation; content* | ～养 *self-restraint*

韩（韓） hán ㄏㄢˊ 战国国名，在今河南省中部、山西省东南一带 a state in the Warring States period (in the middle part of today's Henan Province and the south-east part of Shanxi Province)

嵅 hán ㄏㄢˊ 岚嵅，山名 Lanhan (name of a mountain)

⇨ see also dǎng on p.119

H

寒 hán ㄏㄢˊ ❶冷（㊥—冷）cold：御～ *keep out the cold*｜天～。*It's cold.*［寒噤］因受冷或受惊而发抖的动作 shiver：打～ *shiver with cold*［寒心］灰心，痛心失望 bitterly disappointed［胆寒］害怕 terrified ❷穷困 poverty stricken：贫～ *impoverished* ❸谦辞 (humble speech) my：～门 *my humble abode*｜～舍 *my humble abode*

罕 hǎn ㄏㄢˇ 稀少（㊥稀—）rare; scarce：～见 *seldom seen*｜～闻 *rarely heard of*｜～物 *rare thing*

喊 hǎn ㄏㄢˇ 大声叫，呼（㊥呼—、叫—）to cry out; to shout：～口号 *shout slogans*｜～他一声 *give him a shout*

蔊 hǎn ㄏㄢˇ（又）see hàn on page 242

阚（闞） hǎn ㄏㄢˇ 虎叫声 (of a tiger) roar

⇨ see also kàn on p.351

㘚（㘚） hǎn ㄏㄢˇ 同"阚"(hǎn)（柳宗元文《黔之驴》用此字）same as 阚 (hǎn) (used in Liu Zongyuan's essay *The Donkey of Guizhou*)

汉（漢） hàn ㄏㄢˋ ❶汉江，又叫汉水，发源于陕西省南部，在湖北省武汉入长江 Hanjiang River (also called 汉水) ❷朝代名 name of dynasties ①汉高祖刘邦所建立（公元前206—公元220年）Han Dynasty (206 B.C.—220 A.D., founded by Liu Bang, Emperor Gaozu) ② 五代之一，刘知远所建立（公元947—950年），史称后汉 Later Han Dynasty (947—950, one of the Five Dynasties, founded by Liu Zhiyuan) ❸（—子）男人，男子 man：老～ *old man*｜好～ *true man*｜英雄～ *hero* ❹汉族，我国人数最多的民族 Han ethnic group (the largest ethnic group in China)［汉奸］出卖我们国家民族利益的败类 traitor (to China)

扞 hàn ㄏㄢˋ ❶触犯 to offend; to violate［扞格］互相抵触 to contradict each other：～不入 *incompatible with* ❷ see 捍 on page 241

闬（閈） hàn ㄏㄢˋ〈古 ancient〉❶里巷门 gate to a lane/an alley ❷墙 wall

汗 hàn ㄏㄢˋ 人和高等动物由身体的毛孔里排泄出来的液体 sweat

⇨ see also hán on p.240

旱 hàn ㄏㄢˋ ❶长时间不下雨，缺雨，跟"涝"相对 drought (opposite of 涝)：防～ *prevent drought*｜天～ *dry weather* ❷陆地，没有水的 land; dryland：～路 *overland route*｜～田 *dry farmland*｜～稻 *upland rice*

垾 hàn ㄏㄢˋ 小堤，多用于地名 small dyke (often used in place names)：中～（在安徽省巢湖市）*Zhonghan (a place in Chaohu City, Anhui Province)*

捍（△*扞） hàn ㄏㄢˋ 保卫，抵御（㊥—卫）to defend; to safeguard：～海堰（挡海潮的堤）*sea wall*

悍（*猂） hàn ㄏㄢˋ ❶勇敢 valiant; brave：强～

H

strong and intrepid | 短小精～ *(of person) small in stature but capable and agile; (of articles, etc.) pithy* ❷凶暴（㊥凶一）fierce：～然不顾 *in flagrant defiance of*

焊（*釬、*銲）hàn ㄏㄢˋ 用熔化的金属或某些非金属把工件连接起来，或用熔化的金属修补金属器物 to weld; to solder：电～ *electric welding* | 铜～ *copper brazing* | ～接 *weld*

蔊 hàn ㄏㄢˋ hǎn ㄏㄢˇ（又）［蔊菜］草本植物，茎部叶长椭圆形，花小，黄色，嫩茎叶可以吃，全草入药 variable-leaf yellowcress

菡 hàn ㄏㄢˋ ［菡萏］（—dàn）荷花的别称 another name for 荷花 (lotus)

颔（頷）hàn ㄏㄢˋ ❶下巴颏儿 chin ❷点头 to nod：～首 *to nod* | ～之而已 *just give a nod*

撖 hàn ㄏㄢˋ 姓 (surname) Han

暵 hàn ㄏㄢˋ ❶曝晒 to expose to the sun ❷使干枯 to dry

撼 hàn ㄏㄢˋ 摇动 to shake：震～ *to shake; to shock* | 蚂蚁～大树，可笑不自量。*It is ridiculous to overrate one's own strength, just like an ant shaking a big tree.*

憾 hàn ㄏㄢˋ 悔恨，心中感到有所缺欠 to regret：～事 *matter for regret* | 遗～ *regret*

翰 hàn ㄏㄢˋ 长而坚硬的羽毛，古代用来写字 quill (used for writing in ancient times)㊕①毛笔 writing brush：～墨 *pen and ink; stationery* | 染～ *dip a writing brush into ink* ②诗文，书信 poetry; prose; letter：文～ *prose; official correspondence* | 华～ *(polite speech) your letter* | 书～ *letter*

瀚 hàn ㄏㄢˋ 大 vast：浩～（广大，众多）*vast; numerous*

HANG ㄏㄤ

夯（**硌）hāng ㄏㄤ ❶砸地基的工具 rammer：打～ *ram; pound* ❷用夯砸 to ram; to pound：～地 *ram the ground* | ～实 *to ram; to tamp*

⇨ see also bèn on p.29

行 háng ㄏㄤˊ ❶行列，排 line; row：单～ *single line/row; odd number of lines/rows* | 双～ *double lines/rows; even number of lines/rows* | 雁飞成～。*Wild geese fly in line.* ❷行业 profession; industry：同～ *people engaged in the same occupation* | 外～ *layperson; layman*［行家］精通某种事务的人 professional; expert ❸某些营业性机构 business organization：银～ *bank* | 车～ *motor shop; car store* | 电料～ *shop selling electrical materials*［行市］（—shi）市场上商品的一般价格 current market price ❹兄弟、姊妹长幼的次第 order of birth among siblings：排～ *rank in order of seniority* | 您～几？我～三。*Where do you come among your brothers and sisters? I am the third.* ❺量词，

用于成行的东西 measure word for things in line：几～字 *a few lines of words/characters* | 两～树 *two rows of trees*

⇨ see also xíng on p.727

绗（絎） háng ㄏㄤˊ 做棉衣、棉被、棉褥等，粗粗缝，使布和棉花连在一起 to sew with long stitches：～被褥 *sew long stitches on a quilt*

吭 háng ㄏㄤˊ 喉咙，嗓子 throat：引～（拉长了嗓音）高歌 *sing lustily at the top of one's voice*

⇨ see also kēng on p.359

迒 háng ㄏㄤˊ ❶野兽、车辆经过的痕迹 track; trail ❷道路 road; way

杭 háng ㄏㄤˊ 杭州，地名，在浙江省 Hangzhou (a city in Zhejiang Province)

航 háng ㄏㄤˊ 行船 to sail a boat/ship; to navigate：～海 *navigation* ㊋飞机等在空中飞行 (of planes, etc.) flight：～空 *aviation* | ～天 *space flight* | 宇～（宇宙航行）*space flight*

颃（頏） háng ㄏㄤˊ see 颉颃 (xié－) at 颉 on page 721

沆 hàng ㄏㄤˋ 大水 vast stretch of water［沆瀣］（－xiè）夜间的水汽 evening mist［沆瀣一气］㊖气味相投的人勾结在一起 act in collusion

巷 hàng ㄏㄤˋ ［巷道］采矿或探矿时挖的坑道 roadway; tunnel; drift (in a mine)

⇨ see also xiàng on p.714

HAO ㄏㄠ

蒿 hāo ㄏㄠ 青蒿、茵陈蒿、艾蒿一类植物，用手揉时常有香味，有的可入药 sweet wormwood; artemisia

嚆 hāo ㄏㄠ 呼叫 to yell; to cry［嚆矢］带响声的箭 whistling arrow ㊖发生在先的事物，事物的开端 precursor; beginning

薅 hāo ㄏㄠ 拔，除去 to pull out; to get rid of：～草 *pull up weeds*

号（號） háo ㄏㄠˊ ❶大声呼喊（㊀呼－）to howl：～叫 *to howl* ❷大声哭 to wail; to cry：悲～ *cry mournfully* | 干～（哭声大而无泪）*cry loudly without tears*［号啕］［号咷］（－táo）大声哭喊 wail at the top of one's voice

⇨ see also hào on p.245

蚝（*蠔） háo ㄏㄠˊ 牡蛎 oyster：～油（用牡蛎肉制成的浓汁，供调味用）*oyster sauce*

毫 háo ㄏㄠˊ ❶长而尖细的毛 long, fine hair：狼～笔 *weasel-hair writing brush* ❷秤或戥（děng）子上的提绳 loop handle of a steelyard：头～ *first loop handle of a steelyard* | 二～ *second loop handle of a steelyard* ❸法定计量单位中十进分数单位词头之一，表示 10^{-3}，符号 m。milli- (m) ❹计量单位名，10 丝是 1 毫，10 毫是 1 厘 unit of measurement that equals 10 丝 or 1/10 厘 ❺〈方 dialect〉货币单位，角，毛 same

H

as 角 or 毛, a unit of money in China ❻用在否定词前，加强否定语气，表示一点儿也没有或一点儿也不 not at all (used before a negative word to reinforce the negative tone)：～无诚意 *no sincerity at all* | ～不费力 *with little effort*

嗥(*嘷) háo ㄏㄠˊ 野兽吼（hǒu）叫 to howl; to growl：虎啸熊～。*A tiger roars and a bear growls.*

貉 háo ㄏㄠˊ same as 貉 (hé), used in 貉子 and 貉绒

⇨ see also hé on p.249

豪 háo ㄏㄠˊ ❶具有杰出才能的人（㊟-杰）person of extraordinary power or ability：文～ *literary giant; great writer* | 英～ *hero; outstanding figures* [自豪] 自己感到骄傲 to be proud of oneself：我们为祖国而～。*We are proud of our motherland.* ❷气魄大，直爽痛快，没有拘束的 bold; straightforward; unrestrained：～放 *bold and unconstrained* | ～爽 *generous and forthright* | ～迈 *courageous; heroic* ❸强横的，有特殊势力的 despotic; tyrannical：～门 *wealthy and powerful family or clan* | 土～劣绅 *local tyrants and evil gentry* | 巧取～夺 *to take away other's belongings by trickery or force*

壕 háo ㄏㄠˊ 沟 trench; ditch：战～ *trench (used during a battle)*

嚎 háo ㄏㄠˊ 大声叫或哭喊 to cry; to yell; to howl [嚎啕] [嚎咷] same as "号啕"

濠 háo ㄏㄠˊ ❶护城河 moat ❷濠水，水名，在安徽省 Haoshui (a river in Anhui Province)

好 hǎo ㄏㄠˇ ❶优点多的或使人满意的，跟"坏"相对 good; nice (opposite of 坏)：～人 *nice person* | ～汉 *true man* | ～马 *good horse* | ～东西 *good things* | ～事 *good thing; good deed* ㊀指生活幸福、身体健康或疾病消失 happy; healthy; well：您～哇！*Hello,how are you?* | 他的病完全～了。*He has fully recovered.* [好手] 擅长某种技艺的人，能力强的人 good hand; capable person ❷友爱，和睦 friendly; harmonious：相～ *be on intimate terms* | 我跟他～。*I get along very well with him.* | 友～ *friendly* ❸易于，便于 easy; convenient：这件事情～办。*It is easy to do.* | 请你闪开点，我～过去。*Please move out of the way so that I can pass.* ❹完，完成 done (indicating completion of an action or readiness)：计划已经订～了。*The plan has already been made.* | 我穿～衣服就去。*I'll go once I've dressed.* | 预备～了没有？*Are you ready?* ❺副词，很，甚 (adverb) very：～冷 *very cold* | ～快 *very fast* | ～大的风 *very strong winds* [好不] 副词，很 (adverb) very：～高兴 *very happy* ❻表示赞许、应允或结束等口气的词 all right; OK：～，你真不愧是专家！*All right, it is no wonder that you are an expert.* | ～，就照你的意

H

见做吧！ *OK, let's do as you suggest.* | ～，会就开到这里。*Right, that's the end of the meeting.*

⇨ see also hào on p.245

郝 hǎo ㄏㄠˇ 姓 (surname) Hao

号(號) hào ㄏㄠˋ ❶名称 name：国～ *name of a country* | 别～ *another name; alias* | 牌～ *name/sign/mark of a shop; trademark; name of a product* ㊕ 商店 shop; store：本～ *this shop; our shop* | 分～ *(of a shop) branch* ❷记号，标志 mark; sign：暗～ *cipher; secret sign* | 信～ *signal* ❸表示次第或等级 numbering; sequence：挂～ *register (in a hospital, etc.)* | 第一～ *No. 1* | 大～ *large size* | 中～ *medium size* | ～码 *number* [号外] 报社报道重要消息临时印发的报纸 extra (edition of a newspaper) ❹指某种人 certain groups of people：病～ *the patient* | 伤～ *the wounded* ❺量词，用于人数 measure word for number of people：全队有几十～人。*The whole team comprises dozens of people.* ❻标上记号 to mark a sign：把这件东西～上。*Mark a sign on this item.* ❼号令，命令 order; command：发～施令 *issue orders* [号召] (—zhào) 召唤(群众共同去做某一件事) call (other people jointly to do sth)：响应～ *to respond to a call* [口号] 号召群众或表示纪念等的语句 slogan ❽军队或乐队里所用的西式喇叭 brass wind instrument：吹～ *blow a bugle; sound a trumpet* | ～兵 *bugler* ❾用号吹出的表示一定意义的声音 bugle call：熄灯～ *lights-out; taps* | 冲锋～ *bugle call to charge*

⇨ see also háo on p.243

好 hào ㄏㄠˋ 爱，喜欢(㊣爱—、喜—) to love; to be apt to：～学 *enjoy learning* | ～劳动 *to enjoy doing labour* | 这孩子不～哭。*The baby seldom cries.*

⇨ see also hǎo on p.244

昊 hào ㄏㄠˋ 广大的天 vast sky

淏 hào ㄏㄠˋ 水清 (of water) clear

耗 hào ㄏㄠˋ ❶减损，消费(㊣—费、消—) to cost; to consume：～神 *consume one's energy* | ～电 *to consume electricity* ❷拖延 to delay; to dawdle：～时间 *waste time* | 别～着了，快去吧！*Don't dawdle, go right now!* ❸音信，消息 message; news：噩(è)～(指亲近或敬爱的人死亡的消息) *sad news (as of the death of sb)*

浩 hào ㄏㄠˋ ❶盛大，广大 ㊂(㊣—大) great; vast：～茫 *far and wide* | ～～荡荡 *boundless and mighty* ❷众多 a great many：～如烟海 *a great number of; as vast as the open sea*

皓(*皜、*暠) hào ㄏㄠˋ 洁白，明亮 white; bright：～齿 *white teeth* | ～首(白发，指老人) *white hair; old people* | ～月当空 *the bright moon high in the sky*

鄗 hào ㄏㄠˋ 古县名，在今河北省柏乡 Hao (an ancient

H

county in today's Baixiang, Hebei Province)

滈 hào ㄏㄠˋ 滈河，水名，在陕西省西安 Haohe (a river in Xi'an, Shaanxi Province)

镐(鎬) hào ㄏㄠˋ 西周的国都，在今陕西省长安西北 Hao (the capital of the Western Zhou Dynasty, to the north-west of today's Chang'an in Shaanxi Province)

⇨ see also gǎo on p.202

皞 hào ㄏㄠˋ 明亮 bright; luminous

颢(顥) hào ㄏㄠˋ 白的样子 white

灏(灝) hào ㄏㄠˋ 水势大 vast water

HE ㄏㄜ

诃(訶) hē ㄏㄜ same as "呵(hē)❶"

[诃子]（-zǐ）常绿乔木，果实像橄榄，叶子、幼果（藏青果）、果实（诃子）、果核均可入药 myrobalan

呵 hē ㄏㄜ ❶怒责（㊄-斥、-责）to scold：～禁 *angrily warn sb not to do sth* ❷呼气 to breathe out; to exhale：～冻 *defrost (ink, etc.) with breath*｜～气 *exhale with the mouth open* [呵呵] 笑声 sound of laughter：笑～ *smile cheerfully* [呵护] 爱护，保护 take good care of; protect ❸ same as "嗬"

⇨ see also ā on p.1, á on p.1, ǎ on p.1, à on p.2, a on p.2

喝(欱)** hē ㄏㄜ 吸食液体饮料或流质食物，饮 to drink：～水 *drink water*｜～酒 *drink alcohol*｜～粥 *eat porridge*

⇨ see also hè on p.250

嗬 hē ㄏㄜ 叹词，表示惊讶 (exclamation) wow：～，真不得了！*Wow, that's great!*

禾 hé ㄏㄜˊ ❶谷类植物的统称 grain crop ❷古代特指粟（谷子）(in ancient times) millet

和(❶❷△*龢、❶❷*咊)

hé ㄏㄜˊ ❶相安，谐调 peaceful; harmonious：～睦 *harmonious* ㊀平静，不猛烈 quiet; gentle：～气（qi）*kind; amiable*｜温～ *mild; gentle*｜心平气～ *even-tempered and good-humoured*｜风～日暖 *gentle breeze and warm sunshine* [和平] 1 没有战争的状态 peace：～环境 *peaceful environment* 2 温和，不猛烈 gentle; mild：药性～ *mild medicine* [和谐] 配合得适当 harmonious：乐调～ *harmonious tunes*｜色彩～ *harmonious colours* ㊁融洽，友好 harmonious; friendly：气氛～ *harmonious atmosphere*｜～社会 *harmonious society* ❷平息争端 to settle conflicts：讲～ *negotiate a peace*｜～解 *become reconciled* ❸和数，加法运算的得数 sum：二加三的～是五。*The sum of two and three is five.* ❹连带 with; together with：～盘托出（完全说出来）*bring all out; to speak all in one's mind*｜～衣而卧 *lie down with one's clothes* on ❺ 连词，跟，同，与 (conjunction) and: 我～他都不同意。*Both he and I disagree.* ❻介词，对，向 (preposition) toward; to: 你～孩子讲话要讲得通俗些。*When you speak to children, try to use simple words.* ❼ 姓 (surname) He

[和尚] 佛教男性僧侣的通称 monk

⇨ see also hè on p.249, hú on p.258, huó on p.279, huò on p.280

盉 hé ㄏㄜˊ 古代盛酒和水的器皿，形状像壶，三足或四足 vessel for liquids in ancient times

龢 hé ㄏㄜˊ ❶ see 和 on page 246 ❷用于人名。翁同龢，清代人 used in given names, e.g. Weng Tonghe, a person of the Qing Dynasty

合(❸△閤) hé ㄏㄜˊ ❶闭，对拢 to close: ～眼 *close one's eyes* | ～抱 *get one's arms around sth* | ～围（四面包围）*to surround* [合龙] 修筑堤坝或桥梁时从两端施工，最后在中间接合 (of construction of dams or bridges) join up/close two sections ❷聚，集，共同，跟“分”相对 to assemble; to join (opposite of 分): ～力 *join forces; resultant force* | ～办 *work collaboratively* | ～唱 *sing in chorus* [合同]（-tong）两方或多方为经营事业或在特定的工作中规定彼此权利和义务所订的共同遵守的条文 contract: 产销～ *production and selling contract* [合作] 同心协力做某事 to cooperate ❸总共，全 in total; altogether: ～计 *add up to* | ～家 *the whole family* ❹相合，符合 to conform to; to suit: ～格 *qualified* | ～法 *lawful* | ～理 *reasonable* ㊂应该 should; ought to: 理～如此。*It should be like this.* ❺计，折算 to amount to; to be equal to; to convert: 这件衣服做成了～多少钱? *How much will this garment cost after it is finished?* | 一米～多少市尺? *How many* chi *are equal to 1 metre?* ❻ 姓 (surname) He

⇨ see also gě on p.206

⇨ 閤 see also gé 阁 on p.205, gé 阁 on p.205

郃 hé ㄏㄜˊ [郃阳] 地名，在陕西省，今作“合阳” Heyang (a place in Shaanxi Province, now written as 合阳)

饸(餄) hé ㄏㄜˊ [饸饹](-le) 一种条状食品，多用荞麦面轧（yà）成，有的地区叫“河漏” buckwheat noodle (also called 河漏 in some places)

䶎 hé ㄏㄜˊ 牙齿咬合 (of teeth) occlusion

盒 hé ㄏㄜˊ （-子、-儿）底盖相合的盛东西的器物 box; case: 饭～儿 *lunch box* | 墨～儿 *ink cartridge*

颌(頜) hé ㄏㄜˊ 构成口腔上部和下部的骨头和肌肉组织叫作颌，上部的叫上颌，下部的叫下颌 jaw

⇨ see also gé on p.205

纥(紇) hé ㄏㄜˊ see 回纥 at 回 on page 273

⇨ see also gē on p.203

龁(齕) hé ㄏㄜˊ 咬 to bite; to gnaw

何 hé ㄏㄜˊ 代词，表示疑问 pronoun, indicating query ① 什么 what; who; whom; which: ～人？*who?*｜～事？*What?*｜为～？*Why?*｜有～困难？*What's the difficulty?* ②为什么 why: ～不尝试一下？*Why not have a try?*｜～必如此。*Why do (you) have to do it this way?* ③ 怎样 how: ～如？*How about this?*｜如～？*How do you think of it?* ④ 怎么 how; why: 他学习了好久，～至于一点进步也没有？*He's been studying for so long, so how come he's made no progress at all?* ⑤哪里 where: 欲～往？*Where will you go?*

〈古 ancient〉 also same as 荷 (hè)

河 hé ㄏㄜˊ ❶水道的通称 river; waterway: 运～ *canal*｜淮～ *the Huaihe River* [河汉] 银河，又叫天河，天空密布如带的星群 the Milky Way (also called 天河) ❷专指黄河，我国的第二大河，发源于青海省，流入渤海 the Yellow River: ～西 *west of the Yellow River*｜～套 *Hetao, the Great Bend of the Yellow River*｜江淮～汉 *the Yangtze River, the Huaihe River, the Yellow River and the Hanjiang River*

荷 hé ㄏㄜˊ 即莲 lotus (same as 莲)

⇨ see also hè on p.249

菏 hé ㄏㄜˊ [菏泽] 地名，在山东省 Heze (a place in Shandong Province)

劾 hé ㄏㄜˊ 揭发罪状(㊎弹－) to impeach (a public official)

阂(閡) hé ㄏㄜˊ 阻隔不通 blocked; hindered: 隔～ *alienation; estrangement*

核(❹*覈) hé ㄏㄜˊ ❶果实中坚硬并包含果仁的部分 kernel; stone (of fruit) ❷像核的东西 nucleus: 菌～ *sclerotium*｜细胞～ *cell nucleus* [核心] 中心，主要部分 core; centre: 领导～ *core of the leadership*｜～作用 *key role* ❸指原子核、核能、核武器等 atomic nucleus; nuclear: ～潜艇 *nuclear submarine*｜～试验 *nuclear test*｜～战争 *nuclear war* ❹仔细地对照、考察(㊎－对、－查) to check; to examine: ～算 *check accounts*｜～实 *to verify*｜考～ *to evaluate; to assess*｜复～ *to recheck*

⇨ see also hú on p.259

曷 hé ㄏㄜˊ 文言代词，表示疑问 pronoun in classical Chinese, indicating query ①怎么 how ② 何时 when

饸(餄) hé ㄏㄜˊ 一种油炸的面食 a kind of deep-fried cake

⇨ see also ài on p.4

鹖(鶡) hé ㄏㄜˊ 古书上说的一种善斗的鸟 a kind of fighting bird in classical Chinese literature

鞨 hé ㄏㄜˊ see 靺鞨 (mò－) at 靺 on page 460

盍(*盇) hé ㄏㄜˊ 何不 why not: ～往观之？

Why not go and see it?

阖(闔) hé ㄏㄜˊ ❶全，总共 whole; entire: ～家 *the whole family* | ～城 *the whole town* ❷关闭 to close; to shut down: ～户 *close the door*

涸 hé ㄏㄜˊ 水干（㊀干一）to dry up: 枯～ *dry* | ～辙（水干了的车辙）*dry rut*

貉 hé ㄏㄜˊ 哺乳动物，耳小，嘴尖，毛棕灰色，昼伏夜出，捕食虫类。毛皮珍贵 raccoon dog [一丘之貉] 比喻彼此相似，没什么差别的坏人 raccoon dogs from the same mound; (figurative) people of similar evil character

〈古 ancient〉also same as 貊 (mò)

➪ see also háo on p.244

翮 hé ㄏㄜˊ ❶鸟翎的茎，翎管 quill; shaft of a feather ❷翅膀 wing: 奋～高飞 *strive to fly high*

吓(嚇) hè ㄏㄜˋ ❶恫(dòng)吓，恐吓 to intimidate ❷叹词，表示不满 (exclamation) indicating dissatisfaction; humph: ～，怎么能这样呢! *Humph!How could it be like this?*

➪ see also xià on p.705

和 hè ㄏㄜˋ 声音相应 to join in singing: 一人唱，众人～。*When one person sings, others join in.* 特指依照别人所做诗词的题材和体裁而写作 (specifically) compose a poem (following the theme, style and rhyme of another): ～诗 *write a poem echoing the theme and the rhyme of another* | 唱～ *sing along with others; compose a poem in response to the theme and rhyme sequence of another*

➪ see also hé on p.246, hú on p.258, huó on p.279, huò on p.280

垎 hè ㄏㄜˋ ❶土干燥坚硬 (of soil/clay/earth) dry and hard ❷用于地名 used in place names: ～塔埠（在山东省枣庄）*Hetabu (in Zaozhuang, Shandong Province)*

贺(賀) hè ㄏㄜˋ 庆祝，祝颂（㊀庆一、祝一）to celebrate; to congratulate: ～年 *extend New Year's greetings* | ～喜 *congratulate sb on a happy event* | ～功 *congratulate sb on his/her achievements* | ～电 *congratulatory telegram*

荷 hè ㄏㄜˋ ❶担，扛 to shoulder: ～锄 *carry a hoe on one's shoulder* | ～枪 *carry a gun/rifle* [电荷] 构成物质的许多基本粒子所带的电。有的带正电（如质子），有的带负电（如电子），习惯上也把物体所带的电叫电荷 electric charge: 正～ *positive charge* | 负～ *negative charge* ❷承受恩惠（常用在书信里表示客气）be grateful (often used in letters to show politeness): 感～ *be grateful (for)* | 请予批准为～。*I would be grateful for your approval.*

➪ see also hé on p.248

隺 hè ㄏㄜˋ 〈古 ancient〉❶鸟往高处飞 bird flying high ❷same as "鹤"

鹤(鶴) hè ㄏㄜˋ 鸟名，颈、腿细长，翼大善飞，叫的声音很高、很清脆。种类很

H

多，如丹顶鹤、白鹤、灰鹤、黑颈鹤等 crane (a kind of bird)

喝 hè ㄏㄜˋ 大声喊叫 to shout：～令 *shout out an order* | 呼～ *bawl to pedestrians to make way for government officials in ancient times; to reproach* | 大～一声 *shout loudly* [喝彩] 大声叫好 cheer loudly

⇨ see also hē on p.246

褐 hè ㄏㄜˋ ❶粗布或粗布衣服 coarse cloth or clothing ❷ 黑黄色 brown

赫 hè ㄏㄜˋ ❶显明，盛大 ㊟ grand; imposing：显～ *significant; eminent* | 声势～～ *have a great reputation and influence* ❷ 频率单位名赫兹的简称，符号 Hz。hertz (Hz)

[赫哲族] 我国少数民族，参看附录 四 the Hezhen people (one of the ethnic groups in China. See Appendix Ⅳ.)

熇 hè ㄏㄜˋ [熇熇] 烈火燃烧的样子 blazing

翯 hè ㄏㄜˋ [翯翯] 羽毛洁白润泽的样子 (of feather) white and smooth

壑 hè ㄏㄜˋ 山沟或大水坑 gully：沟～ *gully; ravine* | 以邻为～（喻把灾祸推给别人）*use one's neighbour's field as a drain; (figurative) shift one's troubles onto others*

HEI ㄏㄟ

黑 hēi ㄏㄟ ❶像煤或墨的颜色，跟"白"相对 black (opposite of 白)：～布 *black cloth* | ～头发 *black hair* ❷暗，光线不充足 dark：天～了。*It is getting dark.* | 那间屋子太～。*The room is too dark.* ❸秘密的，隐蔽的，非法的 secret; covert; illegal：～话 *(of underworld gangs, bandits, etc.) argot* | ～市 *black market* | ～社会 *underworld* ❹ 恶毒 evil; vicious：～心 *evil mind; evil-minded*

[黑客]（外 *loanword*）1 精通电子计算机技术，善于发现网络系统缺陷的人 white-hat hacker 2 通过互联网非法侵入他人电子计算机系统进行破坏活动的人 hacker

嘿 hēi ㄏㄟ 叹词 exclamation ①表示惊异或赞叹 hey (expressing surprise or admiration)：～，你倒有理啦！*Hey! You think you are right!* | ～，这个真好！*Wow!How nice it is!* ②表示招呼或提醒注意 hey (to greet or warn)：～，老张，快走吧！*Hey! Old Zhang, hurry up!* | ～，小心点儿，别滑倒！*Hey!Be careful, don't slip and fall.*

[嘿嘿] 形容冷笑声 ha-ha (sound of sneer)

⇨ see also mò on p.462

𫟼(鐽) hēi ㄏㄟ 人造的放射性金属元素，符号 Hs。hassium (Hs)

嗨 hēi ㄏㄟ same as "嘿 (hēi)"

⇨ see also hāi on p.238

HEN ㄏㄣ

痕 hén ㄏㄣˊ 痕迹，事物留下的印迹 trace; mark：水～ *water*

trace; water stain | 泪～ *tear stain* | 伤～ *scar* | 裂～ *crack*

垠(詪) hěn ㄏㄣˇ 乖戾，不顺从 grumpy; disobedient

很 hěn ㄏㄣˇ 副词，非常，表示程度高 (adverb) very; quite: ～好 *very good* | 好得～ *very good; excellent*

狠 hěn ㄏㄣˇ ❶凶恶，残忍（㊟凶一）cruel; ruthless: 心～ *merciless; malicious* | ～毒 *malevolent* ㊀不顾一切，下定决心 harden one's heart: ～着心送走了孩子 *steel oneself and send the child away* ❷严厉地 ㊟ sternly; rigorously: ～～地打击敌人 *fight enemies fiercely* ❸全力 with all one's forces: ～抓科学研究 *devote every effort to scientific research* [狠命] 拼命，用尽全力 desperately: ～地跑 *run with all one's might* ❹ same as "很"

恨 hèn ㄏㄣˋ ❶怨，仇视（㊟怨一、仇一）to resent; to hate: ～入骨髓 *hate to the marrow of one's bones* ❷懊悔，令人懊悔或怨恨的事 to regret; something to regret: 悔～ *to regret* | 遗～ *eternal regret*

HENG ㄏㄥ

亨 hēng ㄏㄥ ❶通达，顺利（㊟一通）smooth; successful [大亨] 称某地或某一行业有势力的人 tycoon; magnate: 房地产～ *real estate tycoon* ❷（外 *loanword*）电感单位名亨利的简称，符号 H。henry (H)

〈古 ancient〉 also same as 烹 (pēng)

哼 hēng ㄏㄥ ❶鼻子发出痛苦的声音 to groan; to snort: 他病很重，却从不～一声。*He is seriously ill, but has never given out a groan.* ❷轻声随口地唱 to hum; to croon: 他一面走一面～着歌。*He was crooning a song while walking.*

⇨ see also hng on p.252

脝 hēng ㄏㄥ see 膨脝 (péng 一) at 膨 on page 498

啈 hēng ㄏㄥ 叹词，表示禁止 humph (exclamation, indicating prohibition)

恒(*恆) héng ㄏㄥˊ ❶持久（㊟一久）lasting; permanent: ～心 *perseverance* | 永～ *eternal* ❷经常的，普通的 often; common; usual: ～言 *common saying*

姮 héng ㄏㄥˊ [姮娥] 嫦娥 Heng'e (also Chang'e, legendary goddess of the moon)

珩 héng ㄏㄥˊ 古代一组成套佩饰上面的横玉 top jade laid horizontally in a set of ornamental accessories in ancient times

桁 héng ㄏㄥˊ 檩 purlin

鸻(鴴) héng ㄏㄥˊ 鸟名，身体小，嘴短而直，只有前趾，没有后趾，多生活在水边，种类很多 plover

衡 héng ㄏㄥˊ ❶称东西轻重的器具 weighing apparatus ❷称量（㊟一量）to weigh; to measure：～其轻重 *judge/estimate the significance/value of something* ❸平，不倾斜 level; balanced：平～ *balanced; to balance* | 均～ *balanced* ❹ (ancient) same as "横"

蘅 héng ㄏㄥˊ ［杜蘅］草本植物，花暗紫色，全草可入药，今作"杜衡" *Asarumforbesii* (herbaceous plant, can be used for medicine, now written as 杜衡)

横 héng ㄏㄥˊ ❶跟地面平行的，跟"竖""直"相对 horizontal; transverse (opposite of 竖 or 直)：～额 *horizontal inscription of a couplet; banner* | ～梁 *crossbeam; cross girder* ❷地理上指东西向的，跟"纵"相对 across; crosswise (opposite of 纵)：～渡太平洋 *cross the Pacific Ocean* ❸从左到右或从右到左的，跟"竖""直""纵"相对 horizontal; transverse (opposite of 竖, 直 or 纵)：～写 *write words horizontally* | ～队 *rank; row* ❹跟物体的长的一边垂直的 horizontal; transverse：～剖面 *transverse section* | 人行～道 *cross walk* ❺使物体成横向 put sth horizontally/crosswise：把扁担～过来。*Put the shoulder pole crosswise.* ❻纵横杂乱 unrestrained; random：蔓草～生。*Creepers grow wild.* ❼蛮横，不合情理的 rude; unreasonable：～加阻拦 *impede violently* | ～行霸道 *abuse one's power and commit all kinds of outrages* ❽汉字平着由左向右写的一种笔形（一）horizontal stroke："王"字是三～一竖。王 *is composed of three horizontal strokes and one vertical stroke.* ［横竖］副词，反正，表示肯定 (adverb, indicating affirmation) whatever; no matter how：不管怎么着，～我要去。*Anyway, I'm going.*

⇨ see also hèng on p.252

堼 hèng ㄏㄥˋ 用于地名 used in place names：大～上（在天津市蓟州区）*Dahengshang (in Jizhou District, Tianjin Municipality)*

横 hèng ㄏㄥˋ ❶凶暴，不讲理（㊀蛮一）fierce; brutal：这个人说话很～。*This person speaks very rudely.* ❷意外的 unexpected：～财 *ill-gotten wealth* | ～事 *sudden misfortune* | ～死 *violent and sudden death*

⇨ see also héng on p.252

HM ㄏㄇ

噷 hm ㄏㄇ 〔h 跟单纯的双唇鼻音拼合的音〕叹词，表示申斥或禁止 ugh (exclamation, indicating reprimand or prohibition)：～，你还闹哇！*Darn it, you are still making trouble!* | ～，你还想骗我！*Ugh, you still want to cheat me!*

HNG ㄏㄫ

哼 hng ㄏㄫ 〔h 跟单纯的舌根鼻音拼合的音〕叹词，表示不满意或不信任 humph (exclamation, indicating dissatisfaction or distrust)：～，走着瞧吧！*Hum! Let's wait and see!* | ～，你信他的！

Humph! How can you believe him!

⇨ see also hēng on p.251

HONG ㄏㄨㄥ

吽 hōng ㄏㄨㄥ 佛教咒语用字 a word used in Buddhist incantation

轰(轟、❸揈)** hōng ㄏㄨㄥ ❶形容雷鸣、炮击等发出的巨大声音 boom; bang [轰动] 同时引起许多人的注意 cause a stir; create a sensation: ～全国 *create a sensation around the country* [轰轰烈烈] 形容气魄雄伟，声势浩大 with vigour and vitality: ～的群众运动 *a vigorous mass movement* ❷用大炮或炸弹破坏(连一击) to bombard: ～炸 *to bombard* | 炮～ *to bombard; to shell* ❸驱逐，赶走 to shoo; to drive: 把猫～出去 *shoo the cat out* | 把侵略者～出国门 *drive the invaders out of the country*

哄 hōng ㄏㄨㄥ 好多人同时发声 a chorus of roars/clamours: ～传 (chuán) *(of rumours) spread widely* | ～堂大笑。*Everyone in the hall roared with laughter.*

⇨ see also hǒng on p.254, hòng on p.255

烘 hōng ㄏㄨㄥ 用火或蒸汽等使身体暖和或使东西变热、变熟、变干燥 to dry or warm (using fire or steam): 衣裳湿了，～一～。*The clothes are wet. Please dry them.* | ～干机 *dryer* | ～箱 *drying oven* [烘托] 用某种颜色衬托另外的颜色，或用某种事物衬托另外的事物，使在对比下表现得更明显 set off by contrast

訇 hōng ㄏㄨㄥ 形容声响很大 loud sound/noise: ～然 *with a loud sound* | ～的一声 *with a resounding crash*

[阿訇] 我国伊斯兰教称主持教仪、讲授经典的人 imam

薨 hōng ㄏㄨㄥ 古代称诸侯或有爵位的大官的死 (ancient) death of feudal lords or high officials

弘 hóng ㄏㄨㄥˊ ❶大 great; vast: ～愿 (现写作"宏愿") *great ambition (now written as 宏愿)* | ～图 (现写作"宏图") *great plan/prospect (now written as 宏图)* ❷扩充，光大 to enlarge; to glorify: ～扬 *to promote; carry forward* | 恢～ *splendid; bring into full play*

泓 hóng ㄏㄨㄥˊ 水深而广 (of water) wide and deep

红(紅) hóng ㄏㄨㄥˊ ❶像鲜血的颜色 red ㊕①喜庆 happy; joyful: 办～事 *hold a wedding* ②象征革命或觉悟高 red; revolutionary: ～军 *Red Army* | ～色政权 *red regime* | 又～又专 *be both red and expert* ③象征顺利、成功或受欢迎、重视 successful; popular: 唱～了 *win fame by singing* | 走～ *be in favour; be in vogue* | 开门～ *a successful opening/beginning* ❷指人受宠信 favoured: ～人 *favourite; fair-haired boy* ❸红利 bonus; dividend: 分～ *distribute or draw*

H

dividends ❹ 姓 (surname) Hong

⇨ see also gōng on p.211

荭(葒) hóng ㄏㄨㄥˊ 荭草，草本植物，叶卵形，花粉红或白色。全草可入药 Princess feather

玒 hóng ㄏㄨㄥˊ 一种玉 a kind of jade

虹 hóng ㄏㄨㄥˊ 雨后天空中出现的彩色圆弧，有红、橙、黄、绿、蓝、靛、紫七种颜色。是空中的小水珠经日光照射发生折射和反射作用而形成的。这种圆弧常出现两个，红色在外，紫色在内，颜色鲜艳的叫虹，又叫正虹；红色在内，紫色在外，颜色较淡的叫霓，又叫副虹 rainbow

⇨ see also jiàng on p.308

鸿(鴻) hóng ㄏㄨㄥˊ ❶鸿雁，鸟名，即大雁 swan goose (same as 大雁)［鸿毛］比喻轻微的东西 (figurative) something very light or insignificant: 轻于～ *lighter than a goose feather* ❷大 great: ～儒 *great scholar* ［鸿沟］楚汉（项羽和刘邦）分界的一条水，比喻明显的界限 an ancient canal used as the dividing line of the Chu army commanded by Xiang Yu and Han army commanded by Liu Bang; (figurative) a distinctive boundary

闳(閎) hóng ㄏㄨㄥˊ ❶里巷门 gate of a lane ❷宏大 grand; huge

宏 hóng ㄏㄨㄥˊ 广大 grand; magnificent: ～伟 *magnificent; majestic* | 宽～大量 *generous and lenient* | 规模～大 *grand in size; immense*

纮(紘) hóng ㄏㄨㄥˊ 古代帽子（冠冕）上的系带 lace on an ancient hat or crown

竑 hóng ㄏㄨㄥˊ 广大 vast; immense

翃(** 翝) hóng ㄏㄨㄥˊ 飞 to fly

铉(鋐) hóng ㄏㄨㄥˊ 宏大 grand; vast

洪 hóng ㄏㄨㄥˊ ❶大 huge; immense: ～水 *flood* ❷大水 flood: 山～ *flash flood* | ～峰 *flood peak* | 溢～道 *spillway*

铁(鉷) hóng ㄏㄨㄥˊ 弩弓上射箭的装置 device on a crossbow used for shooting arrows

谼 hóng ㄏㄨㄥˊ ❶大的山谷，深沟 vast valley; ravine ❷鲁谼山，山名，又地名，都在安徽省桐城 Luhongshan (name of a mountain as well as a place in Tongcheng, Anhui Province)

蕻 hóng ㄏㄨㄥˊ ［雪里蕻］草本植物，芥（jiè）菜的变种，茎、叶可用作蔬菜，也作"雪里红" snow mustard (also written as 雪里红)

⇨ see also hòng on p.255

黉(黌) hóng ㄏㄨㄥˊ 古代称学校 (ancient) school

哄 hǒng ㄏㄨㄥˇ ❶说假话骗人（㊣一骗）to cheat; to fool: 你不要～我。*Don't kid me.* ❷用语言或行动使人欢喜 to coax; to keep in good humour: 他很会～小孩儿。*He is very good at handling children.*

⇨ see also hōng on p.253, hòng on p.255

讧(訌) hòng ㄏㄨㄥˋ 乱，溃败 disorder; defeat: 内～ *engage in internal conflict or strife*

澒(澒) hòng ㄏㄨㄥˋ [澒洞] 弥漫无际 all-pervasive

哄(*鬨) hòng ㄏㄨㄥˋ 吵闹，搅扰 to clamour: 一～而散 *disperse in an uproar*| 起～(故意吵闹扰乱) *stir up disturbances in a crowd*

⇨ see also hōng on p.253, hǒng on p.254

蕻 hòng ㄏㄨㄥˋ ❶茂盛 flourishing; luxuriant ❷〈方 dialect〉某些蔬菜的长茎 stem (of certain vegetables): 菜～ *stem of a vegetable*

⇨ see also hóng on p.254

HOU ㄏㄡ

齁 hōu ㄏㄡ ❶鼻息声 snore; snort ❷很，非常(多表示不满意) very; awfully (often indicating dissatisfaction): ～咸 *very salty* | ～冷 *very cold* | ～麻烦的 *very troublesome* ❸太甜或太咸的食物使喉咙不舒服 to cause throat discomfort by consuming food that is too sweet or salty: 糖吃多了～人。*Eating too much sugar affects one's throat.*

侯 hóu ㄏㄡˊ ❶古代五等爵位(公、侯、伯、子、男)的第二等 marquis (the second of the five ranks of nobility in ancient China): 封～ *confer the rank of marquis upon sb* ❷泛指达官贵人 a high official or nobleman: ～门 *home/family of a high official or nobleman* ❸姓 (surname) Hou

⇨ see also hòu on p.256

喉 hóu ㄏㄡˊ 介于咽和气管之间的部分，喉内有声带，又是发音器官 larynx

猴 hóu ㄏㄡˊ (～子、～儿) 哺乳动物，略像人，毛灰色或褐色，颜面和耳朵无毛，有尾巴，两颊有储存食物的颊囊，种类很多 monkey

锻(鍭) hóu ㄏㄡˊ 古代指一种箭 (ancient) a kind of arrow

瘊 hóu ㄏㄡˊ (～子) 疣的俗称 wart (informal name for 疣)

篌 hóu ㄏㄡˊ see 箜篌 (kōng－) at 箜 on page 359

糇(*餱) hóu ㄏㄡˊ 〈古 ancient〉干粮 dry cooked food: ～粮 *food*

骺 hóu ㄏㄡˊ 骨骺，长形骨两端的膨大部分 epiphysis

吼 hǒu ㄏㄡˇ 兽大声叫 to roar; to bellow: 牛～。*A cow moos.*| 狮子～。*The lion roars.* 也指人因愤怒而呼喊 to shout; to yell: 怒～ *yell in rage*

后(❸❹後) hòu ㄏㄡˋ ❶上古称君王 (in remote ancient times) king; emperor: 商之先～(先王) *former sovereigns of the Shang Dynasty* ❷皇后，帝王的妻子 queen; empress ❸跟"前"相对 rear; back; behind (opposite of 前) ①指空间，在背面的，在反面的 (of space)

H

behind; back: ～门 *rear door* | 村～ *at the back of the village* ②指时间，较晚的，未到的 (of time) later; after; afterwards: 日～ *in days to come* | 先来～到 *in order of arrival* ③指次序靠末尾的 (of order) rear; back; behind: ～排 *back row*| ～十名 *the last 10 (persons)* [后备] 准备以后使用的 reserve: ～军 *the reserves* ❹后代，子孙 offspring: ～嗣 *descendant; offspring* | 无～ *without heir*

郈 hòu ㄏㄡˋ 姓 (surname) Hou

茩 hòu ㄏㄡˋ see 薢茩 (xiè—) at 薢 on page 722

垕 hòu ㄏㄡˋ ❶用于地名 used in place names: 神～(在河南省禹州) *Shenhou (in Yuzhou, Henan Province)* ❷用于人名 used in given names

逅 hòu ㄏㄡˋ see 邂逅 (xiè—) at 邂 on page 723

鲘(鮜) hòu ㄏㄡˋ 用于地名 used in place names: ～门(在广东省海丰) *Houmen (in Haifeng, Guangdong Province)*

厚 hòu ㄏㄡˋ ❶扁平物体上下两个面的距离较大的，跟"薄"相对 thick (opposite of 薄): ～纸 *thick paper* | ～棉袄 *thick cotton-padded jacket* ❷厚度 thickness; depth: 长宽～ *length, width and thickness* | 木板～五厘米。*The plank is 5cm thick.* ❸深，重，浓，大 deep; great: ～望 *great expectation* | ～礼 *generous gift* | ～情 *profound feelings* | ～味 *strong taste* | 深～的友谊 *profound friendship* ❹不刻薄 (bó)，待人好 kind; generous: ～道 *honest and kind* | 忠～ *loyal and honest* ❺重视，注重 to lay emphasis on; to stress: ～今薄古 *(in academic research) stress the present and disdain the past* | ～此薄彼 *favour this more than the other*

侯 hòu ㄏㄡˋ [闽侯] 地名，在福建省 Minhou (a place in Fujian Province)

⇨ see also hóu on p.255

候 hòu ㄏㄡˋ ❶等待 (㊀等—) to wait: ～车室 *waiting room*| 你先在这儿～一～，他就来。*Please wait here for a while, he will come soon.* ❷问候，问好 send one's regards/greetings to: 致～ *send one's greetings/regards to* ❸时节 time; season: 时～ *time*| 气～ *climate* | 季～ *season* [候鸟] 随气候变化而迁移的鸟，如大雁、家燕 migratory bird ❹事物在变化中间的情状 condition; state: 症～ *symptom* | 火～ *(of heating, cooking, etc.) degree and duration* ❺古代称五天为一候，现在气象学上仍沿用。In ancient times every five days was called one 候 . This term is still used in meteorology.

堠 hòu ㄏㄡˋ 古代瞭望敌情的土堡 (ancient) earthen watch-tower

鲎(鱟) hòu ㄏㄡˋ ❶节肢动物，俗叫鲎鱼，身体黄褐色，尾剑状，生活在浅海里 horseshoe crab (informal 鲎鱼) ❷〈方 dialect〉虹 rainbow

HU ㄏㄨ

乎 hū ㄏㄨ ❶文言助词，表示疑问、感叹等语气 auxiliary word in classical Chinese, indicating query, exclamation, etc. ①同白话的"吗" same as 吗：天雨～？ *Is it raining?* ②同白话的"呢"，用于选择问句 same as 呢，used in choice-type questions：然～？否～？ *Yes?Or no?* ③同白话的"吧"，表推测和疑问 same as 吧，indicating speculation and suspicion：日食饮得无衰～？ *I don't think you have reduced your daily diet, have you?* ④同白话的"啊" same as 啊：天～！ *Good Heavens!* ❷词尾，相当于"于"（放在动词或形容词后）suffix, equivalent to 于 (put after a verb or adjective)：异～寻常 *uncommon; unusual* | 合～情理 *reasonable* | 不在～好看，在～实用。 *We don't mind how good it looks as much as how useful it is.*

呼（*嘑） hū ㄏㄨ ❶喊（㊥－喊）to shout：高～万岁 *cheer loudly to show respect to sb; to hurrah* | 欢～ *to cheer* ❷唤，叫（㊥－唤、－叫）to call：～之即来 *respond instantly to a call* | ～应（yìng）（彼此声气相通，互相照应）*respond to each other's call* [呼声] 群众的希望和要求 people's voice [呼吁]（－yù）向个人或社会公众提出要求 appeal to ❸把体内的气体排出体外，跟"吸"相对 breathe out; to exhale (opposite of 吸)：～吸 *to breathe* | ～出一口气 *exhale a breath* ❹形容风声等 ㊥ howl; whistle：风～～地吹。 *The wind is whistling.*

轷（軤） hū ㄏㄨ 姓 (surname) Hu

烀 hū ㄏㄨ 半蒸半煮，把食物弄熟 stew in shallow water：～白薯 *stew sweet potato*

滹 hū ㄏㄨ [滹沱河] 水名，从山西省流入河北省 Hutuohe River (a river that flows from Shanxi Province to Hebei Province)

戏（戲、*戲） hū ㄏㄨ see 於戏 (wū－) at 於 on page 689

⇨ see also xì on p.701

昒 hū ㄏㄨ 天将亮未亮之时 dawn; daybreak：～昕 *dawn; before sunrise* | ～爽 *dawn; daybreak*

曶 hū ㄏㄨ ❶疾速，转眼之间 swiftly; in a trice ❷古人名 Hu (name in ancient times)：～鼎（西周中期青铜器，作者名曶）*bronzeware made by Hu (a person), in the middle period of the Western Zhou Dynasty*

忽 hū ㄏㄨ ❶粗心，不注意 careless; negligent：～略 *to overlook; to neglect* | ～视 *to ignore; to overlook* | 疏～ *to overlook; to neglect* ❷副词，忽然，忽而 (adverb) suddenly; unexpectedly：～见一人闯来 *suddenly saw a person rushing in* | 情绪～高～低 *spirits suddenly high, suddenly low* ❸计量单位名，10忽是1丝 centimillimetre (unit of measurement.

H

There are 10 忽 in a 丝.)

唿 hū ㄏㄨ [唿哨]同"呼哨", 把手指放在嘴里吹出的高尖音 to whistle (same as 呼哨): 打～ *to whistle*

滹 hū ㄏㄨ 水流出的声音，用于地名 (used in place names) sound of flowing water: ～～水村（在河北省平山县）*Huhushui Village (in Pingshan County, Hebei Province)*

[滹浴]〈方 dialect〉洗澡 have a bath

惚 hū ㄏㄨ see 恍惚 (huǎng—) at 恍 on page 270

糊 hū ㄏㄨ 涂抹或黏合使封闭起来 to plaster; to paste: 用泥把墙缝～上 *plaster mud over the cracks on the wall*

⇨ see also hú on p.259, hù on p.261

囫 hú ㄏㄨˊ [囫囵]（—lún）整个的，完整 whole; entire: ～吞枣（喻不加分析地笼统接受）*swallow a date in one gulp; (figurative) learn sth without careful thinking*

和 hú ㄏㄨˊ 打麻将或斗纸牌用语，表示获胜 to win (in mahjong or cards)

⇨ see also hé on p.246, hè on p.249, huó on p.279, huò on p.280

狐 hú ㄏㄨˊ 狐狸，兽名，略像狼而小，耳朵三角形，性狡猾多疑 fox [狐媚] 曲意逢迎，投人所好 flirtatiously bewitching [狐疑] 多疑 suspicious; oversensitive

弧 hú ㄏㄨˊ ❶木弓 wooden bow ❷圆周的一段 arc: ～形 *arc* | ～线 *arc*

胡（❹鬍、❻*衚）hú ㄏㄨˊ ❶我国古代泛称北方和西方的民族 general name of non-Han nationalities in the north and west of ancient China: ～人 *people of non-Han nationalities in the north and west of ancient China* | ～服 *Hu clothing* 引古称来自北方和西方民族的（东西），也泛指来自国外的（东西）(in ancient China) things coming from either northern or western nationalities, or from abroad: ～琴 *a general term for musical instruments comprising two strings and a bow* | ～萝卜 *carrot* | ～椒 *pepper* ❷乱，无道理 disorderly; unreasonable: ～来 *fool with sth* | ～闹 *be mischievous* | ～说 *speak unreasonably; talk nonsense* | 说～话 *to drivel* ❸文言代词，表示疑问，为什么 why (pronoun in classical Chinese, indicating query): ～不归？ *Why haven't you come back?* ❹（—子）胡须 beard; moustache; whiskers ❺古指兽类颔间下垂的肉 (in ancient times) jowls of a beast ❻[胡同]（—tòng）巷 lane; alleyway

葫 hú ㄏㄨˊ [葫芦]（—lu）草本植物，爬蔓，花白色，果实中间细，像大小两个球连在一起，可以做器皿或供观赏。还有一种瓢葫芦，又叫匏（páo），果实梨形，对半剖开，可做舀水的瓢 bottle gourd

猢 hú ㄏㄨˊ [猢狲]（—sūn）猴的俗称，特指猕猴 monkey

(informal name for 猴); (specifically) macaque

湖 hú ㄏㄨˊ 陆地上围着的大片水域 lake: 洞庭～ *Dongtinghu Lake* | 太～ *Taihu Lake*

[湖色] 淡绿色 light green

瑚 hú ㄏㄨˊ see 珊瑚 (shān—) at 珊 on page 577

煳 hú ㄏㄨˊ 烧得焦黑 (of food) burnt: 馒头烤～了。*The bun is burnt.*

鹕(鶘) hú ㄏㄨˊ see 鹈鹕 (tí—) at 鹈 on page 646

蝴 hú ㄏㄨˊ [蝴蝶] see 蝶 (dié) on page 138

糊(❷* 餬) hú ㄏㄨˊ ❶ 黏合，粘贴 to glue; to paste: 拿纸～窗户 *paste a sheet of paper over a window* | 裱(biǎo)～ *glue paper on ceiling, walls, etc.* [糊涂] (—tu) 不清楚，不明事理 muddled; confused ❷粥类 porridge; conjee: 玉米面～～ *corn porridge* [糊口] 指勉强维持生活 eke out a living; keep body and soul together ❸ same as "煳"

⇨ see also hū on p.258, hù on p.261

醐 hú ㄏㄨˊ see 醍醐 (tí—) at 醍 on page 646

壶(壺) hú ㄏㄨˊ 一种有把儿有嘴的容器，通常用来盛茶、酒等液体 pot; kettle: 酒～ *flagon; wine jar* | 茶～ *teapot*

核 hú ㄏㄨˊ (—儿) 义同"核(hé)❶❷"，用于某些口语词，如杏核儿、煤核儿等 same in meaning as 核 (hé) ❶❷, used in some colloquial terms, e.g. 杏核儿 and 煤核儿

⇨ see also hé on p.248

斛 hú ㄏㄨˊ 量器名，方形，口小底大。古时以十斗为一斛，后又以五斗为一斛 a measuring vessel, square shaped with a small mouth and a large base

槲 hú ㄏㄨˊ 落叶乔木或灌木，花黄褐色，果实球形。叶子可喂柞蚕，树皮可做染料，果壳可入药，木质坚实，可供建筑或制器具用 daimyo oak

鹄(鵠) hú ㄏㄨˊ 鸟名，即天鹅，像鹅而大，羽毛白色，飞得高而快，生活在水边 Whooper Swan: ～立 (直立) *stand straight*

⇨ see also gǔ on p.221

鹘(鶻) hú ㄏㄨˊ 隼 (sǔn) falcon

⇨ see also gǔ on p.220

縠 hú ㄏㄨˊ 有皱纹的纱 crepe

觳 hú ㄏㄨˊ [觳觫] (—sù) 恐惧得发抖 shiver from fear

虎 hǔ ㄏㄨˇ 老虎，兽名，毛黄褐色，有条纹，性凶猛 tiger ㊉威武，勇猛 bold; valiant: 一员～将 *a brave general* [虎口] 1㊉危险境地 tiger's mouth; (figurative) dangerous situation: ～余生 *survive from the jaws of a tiger; (figurative) escape narrowly from a dangerous situation* 2 手上拇指和食指相交的地方 first web space of hand (part of the hand between the thumb and the index finger)

唬 hǔ ㄏㄨˇ 威吓 (hè) 或蒙混 to bluff; to deceive: 你别～人

H

了。*Stop bluffing.*

⇨ see also xià on p.705

琥 hǔ ㄏㄨˇ ［琥珀］（—pò）古代松柏树脂的化石，黄褐色透明体，可做装饰品，也可入药 amber

浒（滸） hǔ ㄏㄨˇ 水边 waterside

⇨ see also xǔ on p.735

互 hù ㄏㄨˋ 互相，彼此 mutually: ～助 *help each other* | ～动 *to interact* | ～致问候 *exchange greetings* | ～为因果 *interact as both cause and effect; reciprocal causation* ［互联网］由若干个计算机网络相互连接而成的网络 internet

冱（沍）** hù ㄏㄨˋ 水因寒冷冻结、凝固 (of water) freeze solid

桓 hù ㄏㄨˋ see 梐桓 (bì—) at 梐 on page 35

户 hù ㄏㄨˋ ❶一扇门 a door ㉑门 door：夜不闭～ *keep the door unlocked at night* ❷人家 household; family：农～ *peasant household* | 千家万～ *thousands of families; numerous households* ［户口］住户和人口 households and population：报～ *apply for a residence permit; register for residence* | ～簿 *household register* ❸量词，用于家庭 (measure word for household) household; family：村里有五十～人家。*The village comprises 50 households.* ❹门第 (of family) social status and educational background：门当～对 *well-matched in social status and financial situation* ❺户头 (bank) account：开～ *open a bank account* | 账～ *account*

护（護） hù ㄏㄨˋ 保卫（㊀保—、—卫）to protect; to guard：爱～ *to cherish; care for* | ～路 *maintain a road/railway; patrol/guard a road/railway* ㉑袒护，包庇 to shield：～短 *cover up one's mistakes* | 不要一味地～着他。*Don't always shield his faults.* ［护士］医院里担任护理工作的人员 nurse

沪（滬） hù ㄏㄨˋ ❶沪渎，吴淞江下游的古称，在今上海 Hudu (ancient name for the area in the lower reaches of the Wusong jiang River, in today's Shanghai) ❷上海的别称 another name for Shanghai：～剧 *Shanghai opera* | ～杭铁路 *the Shanghai-Hangzhou Railway*

昈 hù ㄏㄨˋ ❶文采斑斓 rich and bright colours ❷分明，清楚 clear; distinct

戽 hù ㄏㄨˋ ❶戽斗，汲水灌田用的旧式农具 bailing bucket (for irrigation) ❷用戽斗汲水 draw water with a bailing bucket

扈 hù ㄏㄨˋ 随从（㊀—从、随—）retinue; attendant

岵 hù ㄏㄨˋ 多草木的山 hill covered with grass and trees

怙 hù ㄏㄨˋ 依靠，仗恃 rely on：～恶不悛（quān）（坚持作恶，不肯悔改）*stick to one's evil doings and refuse to repent*

祜 hù ㄏㄨˋ 福 happiness

糊 hù ㄏㄨˋ 像粥一样的食物 paste：辣椒～ *chilli paste* [糊弄]（—nong）1 敷衍，不认真做 do sth in a perfunctory manner：做事不应该～。*(We) should not work in such a perfunctory way.* 2 蒙混，欺骗 to fool; to deceive：你不要～人。*Don't cheat people.*

⇨ see also hū on p.258, hú on p.259

笏 hù ㄏㄨˋ 古代大臣上朝拿着的手板 (ancient) tablet held by officials when received by the emperor

瓠 hù ㄏㄨˋ [瓠瓜] 草本植物，俗叫瓠子，爬蔓，花白色，果实长圆形，嫩时可用作蔬菜 white-flowered gourd (informal 瓠子)

鄠 hù ㄏㄨˋ 鄠县，地名，在陕西省，今作"户县" Huxian (in Shaanxi Province, now written as 户县)

嫮 hù ㄏㄨˋ ❶美好 beautiful ❷美女 beauty; beautiful woman

鹱(鸌) hù ㄏㄨˋ 鸟名，身体大，嘴的尖端略呈钩状，趾间有蹼，会游泳和潜水，生活在海边，吃鱼类和软体动物等 shearwater

鳠(鱯) hù ㄏㄨˋ 鱼名，身体细长，灰褐色，有黑色斑点，无鳞，口部有四对须，生活在淡水中 spotted long-barbel catfish

HUA ㄏㄨㄚ

化 huā ㄏㄨㄚ same as "花❻"

⇨ see also huà on p.263

华(華) huā ㄏㄨㄚ 〈古 ancient〉 same as "花❶"

⇨ see also huá on p.262, huà on p.264

哗(嘩) huā ㄏㄨㄚ 形容撞击、水流等的声音 sound of crashing or flowing water：水～～地流。*The water is gurgling.* | 老师走进教室，学生们～的一声站了起来。*When the teacher entered the classroom, the students stood up with one accord.*

⇨ see also huá on p.263

花(❶–❺*苍、❶–❺*蘤) huā ㄏㄨㄚ ❶（—儿）种子植物的有性生殖器官，有各种的形状和颜色，一般花谢后结成果实 flower; blossom ㉠ 供观赏的植物 flower ❷（—儿）样子或形状像花的东西 anything resembling a flower：雪～儿 *snow flake* | 浪～ *spindrift* | 火～儿 *spark; sparkle* | 葱～儿 *chopped green onion* | 印～ *stamp; revenue stamp* | 礼～ *fireworks* | 棉～ *cotton* ㉡年轻漂亮的女子 beautiful girl：校～ *school beauty; campus belle* | 交际～ *social butterfly* [挂花] 指在战斗中受伤流血 wounded in action ❸颜色或式样错杂的 colourful; variegated：～布 *patterned cloth* | 头发～白 *grizzled; grey-haired* | ～边 *decorative border; lace* | 那只猫是～的。*That cat is multi-coloured.* [花哨]（—shao）颜色鲜艳，花样多，变化多 multicoloured; variegated：这块布真～。*The cloth is really*

H

colourful. [花搭] 错综搭配 diversified; mixed: 粗粮细粮～着吃 *diversify one's diet with fine and coarse grains* [花甲] 天干地支配合用来纪年，从甲子起，六十年成一周，因称六十岁为花甲 sixty years of age (according to Chinese chronology, each of the ten Heavenly Stems is matched with each of the twelve Earthly Branches; sixty years compose a cycle beginning with 甲子; thus the sixtieth year of age is called 花甲) ❹虚伪的、用来迷惑人的 hypocritical; delusive: ～招 *trick* | ～言巧语 *plausible words spoken to cheat sb* ❺模糊不清 blurred; dim: ～眼 *presbyopia* | 眼～了 *suffer from presbyopia* ❻用掉 to use up: ～钱 *spend money* | ～一年工夫 *spend a year* [花销] (－xiao) 费用，也作"花消" expense; cost (also witten as 花消)

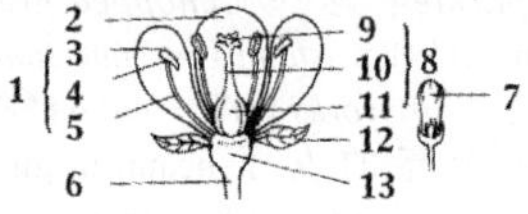

花 flower

1 雄蕊 *stamen* 7 花蕾 *bud*
2 花瓣 *petal* 8 雌蕊 *pistil*
3 花粉 *pollen* 9 柱头 *stigma*
4 花药 *anther* 10 花柱 *style*
5 花丝 *filament* 11 子房 *ovary*
6 花梗 *pedicel* 12 萼片 *sepal*
13 花托 *receptacle*

砉 huā ㄏㄨㄚ 形容迅速动作的声音 swish (sound): 乌鸦～的一声飞了。*The crow flew away with a swish.*

➪ see also xū on p.733

划(❶劃) huá ㄏㄨㄚˊ ❶用刀或其他东西把别的东西分开或从上面擦过 to scratch; to cut: 用刀把瓜～开 *cut the melon with a knife* | ～了一道口子 *scratched a cut* | ～火柴 *strike a match* ❷用桨拨水使船行动 to row; to paddle: ～船 *row a boat* [划子] (－zi) 用桨拨水行驶的小船 small rowing boat ❸合算，按利益情况计较相宜不相宜 to be profitable: ～算 *cost-efficient* | ～得来 *worthwhile; profitable* | ～不来 *not worthwhile; unprofitable*

➪ see also huà on p.264, huai on p.265

华(華) huá ㄏㄨㄚˊ ❶美丽有光彩的（㊣－丽）gorgeous; splendid: ～灯 *resplendently decorated lantern* | 光～ *brilliance; honour* 敬辞，用于跟对方有关的事物 polite term used to refer to another person: ～诞（生日）*your / his / her birthday* | ～翰（书信）*your letter* ❷繁荣昌盛 flourish; boom: 繁～ *flourishing and bustling* ❸事物最好的部分 best part; essence: 精～ *essence; cream* | 英～ *outstanding person; extraordinary thing* ❹指时光，岁月 time: 韶～ *prime years of youth* | 年～ *time; year* ❺（头发）花白 (of hair) grizzled; grey: ～发（fà）*grey hair* ❻指中华民族或中国 Chinese people; China: ～夏 *Huaxia (an ancient name for*

China) | ～侨 *overseas Chinese* | ～北 *north China*

⇨ see also huā on p.261, huà on p.264

哗(嘩、*譁) huá ㄏㄨㄚˊ 人多声杂，乱吵（㊀喧一）noisy; clamorous：全体大～。*The crowd began to clamour.* | ～众取宠（在别人面前夸耀自己，以博取别人称赞）*try to please the crowd with claptrap*

⇨ see also huā on p.261

骅(驊) huá ㄏㄨㄚˊ ［骅骝］（一liú）古代称赤色的骏马 (ancient) red fine steed

铧(鏵) huá ㄏㄨㄚˊ 犁铧，安装在犁的下端用来破土的厚铁片 ploughshare

猾 huá ㄏㄨㄚˊ 狡猾，奸诈 cunning; duplicitous

滑 huá ㄏㄨㄚˊ ❶滑溜，光溜 slippery; smooth：下雪以后地很～。*The ground is slippery after the snowfall.* | 桌面光～。*The table top is smooth.* ❷在光溜的物体表面上溜动 to slip; to slide：～了一跤 *slip* | ～雪 *ski* | ～冰 *skate* ［滑翔］航空上指借着大气浮力飘行 to glide (in the air)：～机 *glider* ❸狡诈，不诚实 cunning; dishonest：～头 *sly fellow* | 耍～ *play tricks; do sth dishonestly* | 这人很～。*This person is very sly.*

［滑稽］（一ji）诙谐，使人发笑 humorous; funny：他说话很～。*He speaks very comically.*

搳 huá ㄏㄨㄚˊ ［搳拳］饮酒时两人同时伸出手指并各说一个数，谁说的数目跟双方所伸手指的总数相符，谁就算赢，输的人喝酒。现作“划拳”a finger-guessing game often played while enjoying alcoholic drinks (now written as 划拳)

化 huà ㄏㄨㄚˋ ❶性质或形态改变，使改变 to change; to transform：变～ *to change* | 熔～ *fuse; melt* | 消～ *digest* | ～石 *fossil* | 冰都～了。*The ice has melted.* | ～整为零 *break the whole into pieces/parts* | ～压力为动力 *convert pressure into power* ❷使思想、行为等有所转变 to transform; to convert：感～ *cause sb to reform their errant ways by words or deeds* | 教～ *enlighten sb through education* | 潜移默～ *subtly influence sb's thinking, character, etc.* ❸指化学 chemistry：～工 *chemical industry* | ～肥 *chemical fertilizer* ❹佛教徒、道教徒募集财物 (of Buddhist monks or Taoist priests) to beg for alms：～缘 *(of Buddhist monks or Taoist priests) beg for alms* | ～斋（乞食）*(of Buddhist monks or Taoist priests) beg for vegetarian meals* ❺词尾，放在名词或形容词后，表示转变成某种性质或状态 suffix (used to indicate a change of state)：革命～ *revolutionize* | 机械～ *mechanize; mechanization* | 现代～ *modernize; modernization* | 绿～ *greening; afforestation*

⇨ see also huā on p.261

华(華) huà ㄏㄨㄚˋ ❶华山，五岳中的西岳，在陕西省华阴 Huashan Mountain (the west mountain of the Five Sacred Mountains, in Huayin, Shaanxi Province) ❷姓 (surname) Hua

⇨ see also huā on p.261, huá on p.262

桦(樺) huà ㄏㄨㄚˋ 白桦树，落叶乔木，树皮白色，容易剥离，木质致密，可用来制器具 birch

划(劃) huà ㄏㄨㄚˋ ❶分开 to divide; to partition: ～拨 *to appropriate* | ～分 *to divide* | ～清界限 *demarcate; make a clean break with* [划时代] 由于出现了具有伟大意义的新事物，在历史上开辟一个新的时代 epoch making ❷设计（㊀计－、筹－）to plan; to design: 策～ *to plan; to plot* [划一] 一致，使一致 to make uniform: 整齐～ *unified; uniform* | ～制度 *standardization of systems* ❸ same as "画❸❹"

⇨ see also huá on p.262, huai on p.265

画(畫) huà ㄏㄨㄚˋ ❶用笔等做出图形 to paint; to draw: ～画儿 *paint a picture* | ～人像 *paint a portrait* ❷（－儿）画成的作品（㊀图－）picture; painting: 一张～儿 *a picture; a painting* | 年～儿 *New Year picture* | 油～ *oil painting* ❸用笔或手等做出线或作为标记的文字 to draw; to mark: ～个圈 *draw a circle* | ～十字 *(of Christians) cross oneself; make the sign of the cross* | ～押 *(old) sign with a mark (on a document)* ❹汉字的一笔叫一画 stroke (of a Chinese character): "人"字是两～。*The character* 人 *comprises two strokes.* | "天"字是四～。*The character* 天 *comprises four strokes.* ❺〈古 ancient〉same as "划 (huà)"

婳(嫿) huà ㄏㄨㄚˋ see 姽婳 (guǐ－) at 姽 on page 232

话(話、*語) huà ㄏㄨㄚˋ ❶语言 language; words: 说～ *speak; say; talk* | 谈了几句～ *say a few words; speak/talk for a while* [话剧] 用平常口语和动作表演的戏剧 modern drama ❷说，谈 to say; to talk; to speak: ～别 *say goodbye; bid farewell* | 茶～ *tea party* | ～旧 *talk over old times*

觟 huà ㄏㄨㄚˋ ❶有角的母羊 ewe with horns ❷姓 (surname) Hua

HUAI ㄏㄨㄞ

怀(懷) huái ㄏㄨㄞˊ ❶思念（㊀－念）to miss; to cherish the memory of: ～友 *miss a friend* | ～旧 *feel nostalgic for the past/old friends* ❷包藏，心里存有 to carry in one's body; to conceive; to have/keep in mind: ～胎 *conceive (a child); be pregnant* | ～疑 *suspect; doubt* | ～恨 *harbour hatred* | 胸～壮志 *cherish lofty aspirations* ❸胸前 bosom: 把小孩抱在～里 *carry the baby in one's* *arms* ❹心意 mind; intention; feeling：无介于～ *do not mind* | 正中(zhòng)下～ *exactly fit one's expectations*

徊 huái ㄏㄨㄞˊ see 徘徊 (pái－) at 徘 on page 489

淮 huái ㄏㄨㄞˊ 淮河，源出河南省，流经安徽省，至江苏省注入洪泽湖 the Huaihe River (originating in Henan Province, flowing through Anhui Province, and joining Hongze Lake in Jiangsu Province)

槐 huái ㄏㄨㄞˊ 槐树，落叶乔木，花黄白色，果实长荚形。木材可供建筑和制家具用，花蕾可做黄色染料 Chinese scholar tree; *Sophora japonica*

踝 huái ㄏㄨㄞˊ 脚腕两旁凸起的部分 ankle：内～ *medialis malleolus; inner ankle* | 外～ *lateral malleolus; outer ankle* (see picture of 人体 on page 647)

耲 huái ㄏㄨㄞˊ 用耲耙翻土 to harrow [耲耙] (－bà) 用来翻土并播种的农具 a harrow

坏(壞) huài ㄏㄨㄞˋ ❶缺点多的或使人不满意的，跟"好"相对 bad (opposite of 好)：向～人～事做斗争 *fight against evildoers and bad deeds* ❷东西受了损伤，被毁(㊀破－) to damage; to destroy：手机～了。*The mobile phone is broken.* ❸坏主意 evil ideas; dirty tricks：使～ *play a dirty trick; be up to mischief* ❹放在动词或形容词后，表示程度深 very; terribly：忙～了 *be terribly busy* | 气～了 *be terribly angry* | 高兴～了 *be extremely happy*

划(劃) huai ·ㄏㄨㄞ see 刉划 (bāi－) at 刉 on page 14

⇨ see also huá on p.262, huà on p.264

HUAN ㄏㄨㄢ

欢(歡、*懽、*讙、*驩) huān ㄏㄨㄢ ❶快乐，高兴(㊀－喜、－乐) happy; merry; joyful：～庆 *celebrate joyfully* | ～迎 *welcome* | ～声雷动 *thunderous sound of cheering* | ～天喜地 *very happy; extremely elated* ❷活跃，起劲 vigorously; in full swing：孩子们真～。*The children are having a lot of fun.* | 机器转得很～。*The machine is running at full strength.* ㊀旺，盛 flourishing; booming：雨下得正～。*It is raining hard.* | 炉子里的火很～。*The fire in the stove is burning vigorously.* ❸喜爱，也指所喜爱的人 to love; lover：～心 *love; favour* | 喜～ *love; like* | 新～(新的相好) *new lover; new sweetheart*

獾(*貛、*獾) huān ㄏㄨㄢ 哺乳动物，毛灰色，有的头部有三条白色纵纹。脂肪炼油可入药 badger

还(還) huán ㄏㄨㄢˊ ❶回，归(㊀回－) to go back; to return：～家 *go back home* | ～原(恢复原状) *restore; resume* ❷

H

回报 give sth in return：～礼 *give a gift in return; return a salute* | ～手 *hit back* | 以眼～眼，以牙～牙 *an eye for an eye and a tooth for a tooth* ❸归还（㊀偿－）to return; to give back; to repay：～钱 *pay back the money* ❹ 姓 (surname) Huan

〈古 ancient〉also same as 旋 (xuán)

⇨ see also hái on p.238

环（環） huán ㄏㄨㄢˊ ❶（－儿）圈形的东西 ring; loop：连～ *chain of rings* | 铁～ *iron hoop* ❷围绕（㊀－绕）to surround; to encircle：～城马路 *ring road; round-the-city road* | ～视 *look around* [环境] 周围的一切事物 environment; surroundings：～优美 *beautiful environment* | 保护～ *protect the environment* ❸指射击、射箭比赛中射中环靶的环数 (of shooting and archery) number of rings

郇 huán ㄏㄨㄢˊ 姓 (surname) Huan

⇨ see also xún on p.742

萱 huán ㄏㄨㄢˊ 草本植物，根状茎粗壮，叶心脏形，花白色带紫色条纹，果实椭圆形。全草入药 *viola moupinesis*

峘 huán ㄏㄨㄢˊ ❶与大山相连时显得较高的小山 hill higher than the mountain connected with it ❷姓 (surname) Huan

洹 huán ㄏㄨㄢˊ 洹河，水名，又叫安阳河。在河南省安阳 Huanhe River (also called Anyanghe River, in Anyang, Henan Province)

桓 huán ㄏㄨㄢˊ 古代立在驿站、官署等建筑物旁作为标志的木柱，后称华表 wooden column erected beside a public building in ancient times, later called 华表

貆 huán ㄏㄨㄢˊ ❶幼小的貉 young raccoon dog ❷豪猪 porcupine

綄（綄） huán ㄏㄨㄢˊ 古代测风的一种装置 a device used to measure wind in ancient times

萑 huán ㄏㄨㄢˊ 古书上指芦苇一类的植物 a reed-like plant in ancient Chinese texts

锾（鍰） huán ㄏㄨㄢˊ 古代重量单位，约合旧制六两 an ancient Chinese unit for measuring weight, about equal to six 两 of the old unit for measuring weight

圜 huán ㄏㄨㄢˊ 围绕 to surround

⇨ see also yuán on p.808

阛（闤） huán ㄏㄨㄢˊ [阛阓]（－huì）街市 street market

澴 huán ㄏㄨㄢˊ 澴水，水名，在湖北省东北部 Huanshui River (in the northeast part of Hubei Province)

寰 huán ㄏㄨㄢˊ 广大的地域 vast area; extensive territory [寰球] [寰宇] 全世界。也分别作“环球”“环宇” the whole world; the earth (also written as 环球 and 环宇 respectively)

嬛 huán ㄏㄨㄢˊ see 嫏嬛 (láng－) at 嫏 on page 379

H

缳(繯) huán ㄏㄨㄢˊ ❶绳套 loop：投～（自缢）*hang oneself* ❷绞杀 to strangle to death：～首 *hang (sb)*

轘(轘) huán ㄏㄨㄢˊ [轘辕]（-yuán）古关名，在河南省偃师东南 (ancient) Huanyuan Pass (in southeast Yanshi, Henan Province)

⇨ see also huàn on p.268

鹮(䴉) huán ㄏㄨㄢˊ 鸟名，嘴细长而向下弯曲，腿长，生活在水边。种类较多，如朱鹮、白鹮、彩鹮等 ibis

镮(鐶) huán ㄏㄨㄢˊ 圆形有孔可贯穿的东西 ring; a round item with a hole to go through

鬟 huán ㄏㄨㄢˊ 古代妇女梳的环形的发结（fàjié）(ancient) ring-shaped hairstyle [丫鬟]（yāhuan）[小鬟] 旧称年轻的女仆 (old) servant girl

瓛(瓛) huán ㄏㄨㄢˊ 古代的一种玉圭 jade tablet used in ancient times

缓(緩) huǎn ㄏㄨㄢˇ ❶慢，跟"急"相对(㊟-慢) slow; unhurriedly (opposite of 急)：轻重～急 *degree of importance or urgency; the order of priority* | ～步而行 *walk slowly* | ～不济急。*A slow action cannot help in an urgent situation.* ❷延迟 to delay; to put off; to postpone：～兵之计 *(of an army) stalling tactics* | ～刑 *probation; temporarily suspend the execution of a sentence* | ～两天再办 *put off for a couple of days* ❸平和，不紧张 relaxed; at ease ㊞ 使不紧张 to ease up; to relax：和～ *mild; gentle* | ～和 *to relax; to moderate* [缓冲] 使紧张的局势缓和 to buffer; to mitigate：～地带 *buffer zone* | ～作用 *buffering* [缓和] 使紧张的情势转向平和 to calm down; to ease off ❹恢复正常的生理状态 to recover; to resume a normal physical condition：病人昏过去又～了过来。*The patient lost consciousness, then came to.* | 下过雨，花都～过来了。*After the rain, the flowers revived.* | ～～气再往前走。*Walk forward after refreshing ourselves.*

鲩 huǎn ㄏㄨㄢˇ 姓 (surname) Huan

幻 huàn ㄏㄨㄢˋ ❶空虚的，不真实的 imaginary; unreal：梦～ *dream; illusion* | ～境 *dreamland; phantasmagoria* | ～想 *imagination; fantasy* [幻灭] 幻想或不真实的事受到现实的打击而消灭 to vanish into thin air ❷奇异地变化（㊟变-）to change magically：～术（魔术）*magic*

奂 huàn ㄏㄨㄢˋ ❶盛，多 plenty; abundant ❷文采鲜明 (of writing) bright; splendid

换 huàn ㄏㄨㄢˋ ❶给人东西同时从他那里取得别的东西 to exchange; to trade：互～ *exchange; interchange* | 交～ *exchange* ❷变换，更改 to change：～衣服 *change one's clothes* | ～汤不～药 *change the form but not the content; (literally means 'change the liquid rather than the herbs in de-*

coction') ❸兑换（用证券换取现金或用一种货币换另一种货币）to cash; to exchange

唤 huàn ㄏㄨㄢˋ 呼叫，喊（连呼一）to call out; to shout：～鸡 *call the chickens* | ～醒 *wake up; awaken*

涣 huàn ㄏㄨㄢˋ 散（sàn）开 to scatter; to disperse：～散 *be lax; be slacken* | ～然冰释 *melt away; vanish* [涣涣] 水势盛大 (of water) overflowing

焕 huàn ㄏㄨㄢˋ 光明 bright; shining：～然一新 *take on a completely new look* [焕发] 1 光彩外现的样子 to shine; to glow：容光～ *look very healthy; have a glowing complexion* 2 振作 keep up one's spirits：～斗志 *boost one's fighting will*

痪 huàn ㄏㄨㄢˋ [瘫痪] see 瘫 on page 636

宦 huàn ㄏㄨㄢˋ 官（连官一、仕一）official [宦官] 封建时代经过阉割在皇宫里伺候皇帝及其家族的男人。又叫太监 eunuch (also called 太监)

浣（*澣） huàn ㄏㄨㄢˋ ❶洗 to wash：～衣 *wash clothes* | ～纱 *rinse yarn; wash clothes* ❷旧称每月的上、中、下旬为上、中、下浣 (old) each of the three 10-day divisions of a month

皖 huàn ㄏㄨㄢˋ ❶明亮 bright; luminous ❷美好 wonderful; beautiful

鲩（鯇） huàn ㄏㄨㄢˋ 鱼名，即草鱼，身体微绿色，鳍微黑色，生活在淡水中。是我国的特产 grass carp (same as 草鱼)

患 huàn ㄏㄨㄢˋ ❶灾祸（连一难、灾一、祸一）disaster; calamity：有备无～。*Effective preparations can prevent disasters.* | 防～未然 *be prepared against future misfortune* | 水～ *flood* ❷忧虑（连忧一）to worry：～得～失 *anxious about one's gains and losses* ❸害病 suffer from an illness; contract an illness：～病 *fall ill* | ～脚气 *suffer from athlete's foot*

漶 huàn ㄏㄨㄢˋ [漫漶] 文字图像等磨灭、模糊 (of words, pictures, etc.) illegible

逭 huàn ㄏㄨㄢˋ 逃，避 to escape; to evade; to get away from

豢 huàn ㄏㄨㄢˋ 喂养牲畜（连一养）to feed/raise animals; to breed livestock

擐 huàn ㄏㄨㄢˋ 穿 to put on; to wear：～甲执兵 *clad in one's armour and take up arms*

轘（轘） huàn ㄏㄨㄢˋ 古代用车分裂人体的酷刑 (ancient) a kind of cruel torture that tears up a human body using wheeled vehicles

⇨ see also huán on p.267

HUANG ㄏㄨㄤ

肓 huāng ㄏㄨㄤ [膏肓] 心脏和膈膜之间。我国古代医学把心尖脂肪叫膏，膈膜叫肓，认为膏肓之间是药力达不到的地方 the section between heart and diaphragm (According to ancient Chinese medicine, this part was beyond the reach of any medicine.): 病入～（指病重到无法医治的地步）*be beyond cure (literally means 'the disease has attacked the vitals')*

荒 huāng ㄏㄨㄤ ❶庄稼没有收成或严重歉收 crop failure; grain shortage: 饥～ *famine* | ～年 *year of famine; lean year* | 备～ *be prepared against famine* ㊀ 严重缺乏 severe shortage; scarcity: 煤～ *coal shortage* | 房～ *shortage of houses* ❷长满野草或无人耕种（㊀－芜）deserted; waste: ～地 *wasteland; deserted land* | 垦～ *reclaim virgin land* | 开～ *reclaim a deserted land* ㊀ ①废弃 to discard: ～废 *neglect; leave uncultivated* ②荒凉，偏僻 desolated; remote: ～村 *desolated village* | ～郊 *wild suburbs* [荒疏] 久未练习而生疏 become rusty; become out of practice: 学业～ *haven't done enough school work* ❸不合情理，不正确 unreasonable; incorrect: ～谬 *absurd* | ～诞 *preposterous; absurd* [荒唐] 1 浮夸不实 excessively exaggerated; absurd: 这话真～。*What was said is absurd.* 2 行为放荡 dissipated act

塃 huāng ㄏㄨㄤ 〈方 dialect〉开采出来的矿石 mineral; ore

慌 huāng ㄏㄨㄤ ❶慌张，急忙，忙乱（㊀－忙）flustered; hurried: 他做事太～。*He does things too hastily.* | ～里～张 *in a confused rush* ❷恐惧，不安（㊀恐－）panicky; disturbed: 心里发～ *be panic stricken* | 惊～ *scared; panicked* ❸用作补语，表示难忍受 very; awfully; unbearably: 累得～ *completely exhausted* | 闷（mèn）得～ *awfully bored*

皇 huáng ㄏㄨㄤ ❶君主（㊀－帝）emperor ❷大 ㊂ magnificent; grand: ～～巨著 *a great work/book* ❸ (ancient) same as "遑" and "惶"

凰 huáng ㄏㄨㄤ see 凤凰 at 凤 on page 180

隍 huáng ㄏㄨㄤ 没有水的城壕 dry moat along a city wall

喤 huáng ㄏㄨㄤ ㊂形容钟鼓声、小儿啼哭声 sound of bells and drums; sound of a baby wailing

遑 huáng ㄏㄨㄤ ❶闲暇 leisure; free time: 不～（没有工夫）*have no spare time* ❷匆忙 ㊂ in a hurry

徨 huáng ㄏㄨㄤ see 彷徨 (páng－) at 彷 on page 492

湟 huáng ㄏㄨㄤ 湟水，水名，在青海省 Huangshui River (in Qinghai Province)

惶 huáng ㄏㄨㄤ 恐惧(㊀－恐) scared; terrified: 惊～ *shocked and scared* | 人心～～。*Everyone is terrified and anxious.*

媓 huáng ㄏㄨㄤ ❶〈古 ancient〉母亲 mother ❷传说中舜的妻子的名字 Huang (name of Emperor Shun's wife in Chinese legend)

瑝 huáng ㄏㄨㄤ 形容玉碰撞发出的声音 sound of jade pieces knocking against each other

H

煌 huáng ㄏㄨㄤˊ 明亮 ⓐbright: 星火~~ *sparkling; twinkling* | 灯火辉~ *ablaze with lights*

锽(鍠) huáng ㄏㄨㄤˊ ❶古代的一种兵器 ancient weapon ❷形容钟鼓声 ⓐsound of bells and drums

蝗 huáng ㄏㄨㄤˊ 蝗虫，昆虫，又叫蚂蚱（màzha），后肢发达，常成群飞翔，吃庄稼 locust (also called 蚂蚱 màzha)

篁 huáng ㄏㄨㄤˊ 竹林，泛指竹子 bamboo grove; (generally) bamboo

艎 huáng ㄏㄨㄤˊ see 艅艎 (yú—) at 艅 on page 798

鳇(鰉) huáng ㄏㄨㄤˊ 鱼名，像鲟鱼，有五行硬鳞。嘴突出，半月形，两旁有扁平的须 *Huso dauricus*

黄 huáng ㄏㄨㄤˊ ❶像金子或向日葵花的颜色 yellow［黄色］1 黄的颜色 yellow 2 指腐朽堕落，与色情有关的 obscene; pornographic: ~小说 *pornographic novel* ❷指黄河 the Yellow River: 引~工程 *the Yellow River Diversion Project* ❸事情失败或计划不能实现 to fail; to be unsuccessful: 这件事~不了。*This affair cannot fail.* ❹指黄帝，传说中的我国上古帝王 (in Chinese legend) the Yellow Emperor (a ruler of China in ancient times): 炎~子孙 *descendants of the Yan and Yellow Emperors; the Han Chinese people; Chinese Nation*

潢 huáng ㄏㄨㄤˊ ❶积水池 pool; pond ❷染纸 to dye paper［装潢］裱褙字画 to mount a picture/painting ⓨ装饰货物的包装 package

璜 huáng ㄏㄨㄤˊ 半璧形的玉 semi-annular jade pendant

磺 huáng ㄏㄨㄤˊ 硫黄旧作“硫磺” sulphur (formerly written as 硫磺)

锁(鐄) huáng ㄏㄨㄤˊ ❶大钟 big bell ❷钟声 sound of bells ❸same as “簧”

癀 huáng ㄏㄨㄤˊ 癀病，牛马猪羊等家畜的炭疽（jū）病 anthrax

蟥 huáng ㄏㄨㄤˊ see 蚂蟥 (mǎ—) at 蚂 on page 432

簧 huáng ㄏㄨㄤˊ ❶乐器里用铜等制成的发声薄片 reed in musical instrument: 笙~ *the reed in a* sheng | ~乐器 *reed musical instrument* ❷器物里有弹力的机件 spring (in devices): 锁~ *locking spring* | 弹~ *spring (in devices)*

恍(*怳) huǎng ㄏㄨㄤˇ ❶忽地，忽然 suddenly; all of a sudden: ~然大悟 *become suddenly enlightened; suddenly understand sth* ❷仿佛 seem; as if: ~若置身其境 *as if be in the place or situation in person*［恍惚］（—hū）1 神志不清，精神不集中 dazed; in a trance; absent-minded: 精神~。*One's mind is wandering/in a trance.* 2（看得、听得、记得）不真切，不清楚 blurred; faint: 我~看见他了。*I saw him faintly.*

晃 huǎng ㄏㄨㄤˇ ❶明亮 bright; shining: 明~~的刺刀 *a*

shining bayonet ❷光芒闪耀 dazzling：～眼（光线刺眼）*dazzling* ❸很快地闪过 to flash：窗户外有个人影，一～就不见了。*A figure flashed by the window.*

➪ see also huàng on p.271

幌 huǎng ㄏㄨㄤˇ 帐幔，帘帷 heavy curtain [幌子]（—zi）商店、饭店等门外的标志物 shop sign; signboard ⑳为了进行某种活动所假借的名义 (figurative) pretence; cover; shield：打着募捐的～骗钱 *cheat sb out of money under the pretence of making a donation*

谎(謊) huǎng ㄏㄨㄤˇ ❶谎话，不真实的话 lie; untruth：撒～ *lie; tell a lie*｜说～ *lie; tell a lie* ㊀商贩要的虚价 false price：要～ *ask a false price* ❷说谎话 tell a lie：～称 *claim falsely*

晃(*搖) huàng ㄏㄨㄤˋ 摇动，摆动（㊖摇—）to shake; to sway：树枝来回～。*The branches are swaying gently in the wind.*｜～动 *shake; rock; quake*｜～悠（you）*sway; wobble*

➪ see also huǎng on p.270

滉 huàng ㄏㄨㄤˋ [滉瀁]（—yǎng）形容水广大无边 (of water) vast; extensive

皝 huàng ㄏㄨㄤˋ 因气血虚少而面部发白的病色 pale

䀮 huàng ㄏㄨㄤˋ 用于人名。慕容皝，东晋初年鲜卑族的首领 Huang (used in given names, e.g. Murong Huang, a leader of the Xianbei people in the early years of the Eastern Jin Dynasty)

HUI ㄏㄨㄟ

灰 huī ㄏㄨㄟ ❶物体燃烧后剩下的粉末状的东西 ash：炉～ *coal ash from a stove*｜烟～ *soot; cigarette ash*｜～肥 *ash fertilizer* [石灰]一种建筑上常用的材料，俗叫白灰，又叫生石灰，是用石灰石烧成的，化学成分是氧化钙。生石灰遇水变成氢氧化钙，叫熟石灰 lime (informal 白灰, also called 生石灰) ❷灰尘 dust：桌上一层～。*The table is covered with dust.* ❸灰色，介于黑和白之间的颜色 grey ❹消沉，失望 depressed; disappointed：心～意懒 *downhearted; dispirited*｜～心丧气 *disheartened; discouraged*

诙(詼) huī ㄏㄨㄟ 诙谐，说话有趣 humorous; jocular

咴 huī ㄏㄨㄟ [咴ㄦ咴ㄦ]形容马叫声 neigh

恢 huī ㄏㄨㄟ 大，宽广㊇（㊖—弘）grand; extensive: ～～有余 *very spacious; extensive*｜天网～～。*Justice has long arms. (literally means 'The net of the Heaven is extensive.')*

[恢复] 1 回到原来的状态 to resume; to return to：～健康 *recover one's health* 2 使回到原来的状态，把失去的收回来 to return; to restore：～旧貌 *restore the old appearance*｜～失地 *restore lost territory*

㧑(撝) huī ㄏㄨㄟ ❶指挥 to conduct; to command ❷谦逊 modest: ～谦 *modest; humble*

挥(揮) huī ㄏㄨㄟ ❶舞动，摇摆 to wave; to wield: ～刀 *wield a sword* | ～手 *wave one's hand* | 大笔一～ *wield one's writing brush forcefully* [指挥] 1 指导，调度 to direct; to dispatch 2 指导、调度的人 director; conductor: 工程总～ *general director of a project* | 乐队～ *conductor in an orchestra* ❷散（sàn）出，甩出 to scatter; to disperse: ～金如土 *squander one's money lavishly as if it were dirt* | ～汗如雨。*Sweat falls like rain.* | ～发 *to volatilize* [挥霍]（－huò）用钱浪费，随便花钱 to squander; spend money extravagantly

珲(琿) huī ㄏㄨㄟ see 瑷珲 (ài－) at 瑷 on page 4

⇨ see also hún on p.277

晖(暉) huī ㄏㄨㄟ ❶阳光 sunshine; sunlight: 春～ *sunlight in spring* | 朝～ *sunshine in the morning* | 余～ *after glow of sunset* ❷same as "辉"

辉(輝、*煇) huī ㄏㄨㄟ 闪射的光彩（㊥光－）brilliance; lustre: 夕阳的余～ *last rays of sunset* [辉煌] 光彩耀眼 dazzling; resplendent: 金碧～ *brilliantly decorated with gold and jade; splendid and magnificent* ㊞极其优良，出色 excellent; outstanding: ～的成绩 *brilliant achievements* [辉映] 光彩照耀 to shine; to reflect: 烟花～着夜空。*The fireworks were flashing in the night sky.* ㊋事物互相对照 to reflect: 交相～ *reflect each other* | 前后～。*The front part and the back part reflect each other.*

翚(翬) huī ㄏㄨㄟ ❶飞 flight ❷古书上指具有五彩羽毛的雉 (in ancient Chinese texts) pheasant with colourful feathers

虺 huī ㄏㄨㄟ [虺隤]（－tuí）疲劳生病（多用于马）。也作"虺隤" (often of horses) to fall ill with fatigue (also written as 虺隤)

⇨ see also huǐ on p.273

豗 huī ㄏㄨㄟ 撞击 to hit against; to dash [喧豗] 形容轰响声 loud noise like thunder

袆(褘) huī ㄏㄨㄟ 古代王后穿的祭服 (in ancient times) ceremonial robe worn by an empress

麾 huī ㄏㄨㄟ 古代指挥用的旗子 (in ancient times) standard used by a commander ㊋指挥 to command; to conduct: ～军 *command an army*

徽(❶❷*微) huī ㄏㄨㄟ ❶标志 badge; emblem: 国～ *national emblem* | 校～ *school badge* ❷美好的 wonderful, glorious: ～号 *title of honour* ❸指安徽省徽州 Huizhou (a place in Anhui Province): ～墨 *Huizhou inkstick (inkstick produced in Huizhou of Anhui Province)*

隳 huī ㄏㄨㄟ 毁坏 to damage; to destroy

回(❸迴、❸*廻、**囬) huí ㄏㄨㄟˊ ❶还(huán), 走向原来的地方 to return to: ～家 *go back home* | ～国 *return to one's country* | ～到原单位工作 *return to work at one's former workplace* ❷掉转 to turn over: ～过身来 *turn around* [回头] 1 把头转向后方 turn one's head: ～观望 *turn around and look* 2 回归, 返回 to come back; to return: 一去不～ *go away and never return* 3 等一会儿 wait a while: ～再说吧。*We will talk it over later.* 4 改邪归正 renounce one's evil doings and turn over a new leaf: 现在～还不晚。*It is never too late to turn from one's evil ways.* ❸曲折, 环绕, 旋转 to encircle; to wind: ～形针 *paper clip* | 巡～ *go the rounds; make a circuit tour* [回避] 避免, 躲开 to avoid; to evade ❹答复, 报答 to reply; to pay back: ～信 *write in reply* | ～话 *to reply; to answer* | ～敬 *to return a compliment/gift; to retaliate* ❺量词, 指事件的次数 (measure word) time: 两～ *twice* | 他来过一～。*He has been here once.* ㊕我国长篇小说分的章节 chapter: 《红楼梦》一共一百二十～。A Dream of Red Mansions *comprises 120 chapters.*

[回纥] (—hé) 唐代西北的民族。又叫回鹘(hú) Huihe (an ethnic group in the north-west of the Tang Dynasty, also called 回鹘 hú)

[回族] 我国少数民族, 参看附录四 the Hui people (one of the ethnic groups in China. See Appendix Ⅳ.)

茴 huí ㄏㄨㄟˊ [茴香] 1 小茴香, 草本植物, 叶分裂像毛, 花黄色, 茎叶嫩时可用作蔬菜。籽实大如麦粒, 可做香料, 又可入药 fennel 2 大茴香, 常绿小乔木, 叶长椭圆形, 花红色, 果实呈八角形, 也叫八角茴香或大料, 可做调料或入药 anise (also called 八角茴香, 大料)

洄 huí ㄏㄨㄟˊ 水流回旋 (of water) to whirl

蛔(*蚘、*蛕、*痐、*蜖) huí ㄏㄨㄟˊ 蛔虫, 像蚯蚓, 白色, 寄生在人或其他动物的肠子里。能损害人畜的健康 roundworm

烠 huí ㄏㄨㄟˊ 古书上指光或光的颜色 (in ancient Chinese texts) light; colour of light

虺 huǐ ㄏㄨㄟˇ 古书上说的一种毒蛇 (in ancient Chinese texts) poisonous snake

[虺虺] 〈古 ancient〉形容打雷的声音 sound of thundering

⇨ see also huī on p.272

悔 huǐ ㄏㄨㄟˇ 后悔, 懊恼 to regret; to repent: 懊～ *to regret; to repent* | ～过 *repent one's mistakes* | ～之已晚。*It is now too late to regret.*

毁(❷*燬、❹*譭) huǐ ㄏㄨㄟˇ ❶破坏, 损害 to damage; to destroy: ～坏 *to destroy; to ruin* | 这把椅子是谁～的? *Who destroyed this chair?* | 别～了个人前途。*Do not damage your own prospects.*

［毁灭］彻底地消灭 to exterminate; to wipe out：给敌人以～性的打击 *give the enemy a crushing attack* ❷烧掉 to burn down; to destroy by fire：烧～ *burn down* | 焚～ *destroy by fire* ㊀使不存在 to exterminate; to destroy completely：拆～ *to demolish; to dismantle* | 炸～ *bomb down; blow up* | 摧～ *to destroy; to impair* | 销～ *destroy by burning or melting* | 捣～ *to demolish; to devastate* | 撕～ *tear up* ❸〈方 dialect〉把成件的旧东西改造成别的东西 to refashion; to make over：这两个小凳是一张旧桌子～的。*The two small stools were made from an old table.* ❹诽谤，说别人的坏话（㊉诋－、－谤）to slander; to malign

卉 huì ㄏㄨㄟˋ 草的总称 grass：花～ *flowers and grasses*

汇（**匯**、❷❸**彙**、*** 滙**）huì ㄏㄨㄟˋ ❶河流会合在一起 (of rivers) to converge：～成巨流 *converge into a mighty current* ❷会聚在一起的东西 assemblage; collection：总～ *flow together; confluence* | 词～ *vocabulary* ❸聚合（㊉－聚、－集）to converge; to aggregate：～报 *to report* | ～印成书 *compile a book* ❹由甲地把款项寄到乙地 make a remittance; remit money：～款 *remit money* | ～兑 *to exchange (one currency for another)* ❺指外汇 foreign exchange：出口创～ *earn foreign exchange through export* | ～市 *foreign currency market*

会（**會**）huì ㄏㄨㄟˋ ❶聚合，合在一起（㊉－合）to get together; to assemble：就在这里～齐吧。*Let us assemble here.* | ～审 *hold a joint trial; make a joint check-up* | ～师 *join forces* | ～话（对面说话）*have a conversation (face to face)* ❷众人的集合 gathering; meeting ①有一定目的的集会 conference; meeting：纪念～ *commemorative meeting* | 群众大～ *mass meeting* | 开个～ *have a meeting* ②指某些团体 organization; union：工～ *trade union* | 学生～ *student union* ❸城市（通常指行政中心）city; metropolis：都（dū）～ *city; metropolis* | 省～ *provincial capital* ❹彼此见面 to meet; to see each other：～客 *receive a guest* | ～一～面 *see each other* | 你～过他没有？*Have you ever seen him?* ❺付钱 to pay the money：～账 *pay a bill* | 饭钱我～过了。*I have paid for the meal.* ❻理解，领悟，懂 to understand; to comprehend：误～ *to misunderstand; misunderstanding* | ～意 *to understand* | 领～ *to understand; to comprehend* ❼能 can ①表示懂得怎样做或有能力做 to be able to：他～游泳。*He can swim.* ②可能 to be likely to：我想他不～不懂。*I think he could not have not understood.* ③能够 can：我们的理想一定～实现。*Our ideal will surely come true.* ④善于 to be good at：能说～道 *good at talking; eloquent* ❽机会，时机，事情变化的一个时

H

间 opportunity; occasion：适逢其～ *happen to be present at the right moment* ❾一定，应当（㊜一当）be sure; should：长风破浪～有时。*I am sure some day I can ride the wind and cleave the waves.* ❿恰好，正好 to happen to; as it happens：～天大雨，道不通。*It happened to rain and the road was obstructed.* ⓫（一儿）一小段时间 a short period of time：一～儿 *a moment* | 这～儿 *at this moment* | 那～儿 *at that moment* | 多～儿 *when* | 用不了多大～儿。*It will not take much time.*

⇨ see also kuài on p.364

荟（薈）huì ㄏㄨㄟˋ 草木繁多 (of plants) luxuriant［荟萃］（一cuì）聚集 to get together; to assemble：人才～。*Many talents gather together.*

浍（澮）huì ㄏㄨㄟˋ ❶浍河，水名，发源于河南，流入安徽 Huihe River (originating in Henan Province and flowing into Anhui Province) ❷浍河，水名，汾河的支流，在山西 Huihe River (a tributary of Fenhe River in Shanxi Province)

⇨ see also kuài on p.364

绘（繪）huì ㄏㄨㄟˋ 画，描画 to paint; to draw：～图 *paint/draw a picture* | ～形～声 *vivid; true to life*

桧（檜）huì ㄏㄨㄟˋ 用于人名。秦桧，南宋奸臣 Hui (used in given names, e.g. Qin Hui, a treacherous official of the South Song Dynasty)

⇨ see also guì on p.233

烩（燴）huì ㄏㄨㄟˋ 加浓汁或多种食物混在一起烹煮 to braise：～豆腐 *braise bean curd* | ～饭 *braised food* | 杂～ *mixed stew; hotchpotch*

讳（諱）huì ㄏㄨㄟˋ ❶避忌，有顾忌不敢说或不愿说（㊜忌一）to avoid as taboo：～疾忌医 *conceal one's illness and refuse the doctor's treatment; (figurative) conceal one's faults for fear of criticism* | 直言不～ *speak straight without any concealment* ❷封建时代称死去的皇帝或尊长的名字 name of deceased emperor or head of a family in the feudal age

诲（誨）huì ㄏㄨㄟˋ 教导，劝说（㊜教一）to teach; to instruct：～人不倦 *be tireless in teaching*

晦 huì ㄏㄨㄟˋ ❶昏暗不明（㊜一暗）gloomy; obscure［晦气］1 不顺利，倒霉 unlucky; unfortunate 2 指人不顺利或生病时难看的气色 pale and gloomy appearance：一脸～ *gloomy look* ❷夜晚 night：风雨如～ *wind and rain making the sky dark as night; (figurative) a turbulent and grim society* ❸农历每月的末一天 the last day of a lunar month

恚 huì ㄏㄨㄟˋ 恨，怒 hatred; resentment

贿（賄）huì ㄏㄨㄟˋ ❶财物 wealth ❷贿赂，用财物买通别人，也指用来买通别人的财物 to bribe; bribe：行～ *to*

H

bribe | 受～ *accept bribes*

彗（**篲）huì ㄏㄨㄟˋ (formerly pronounced suì) 扫帚（sàozhou）broom［彗星］拖有长光像扫帚的星体，俗叫扫帚星 comet (informal 扫帚星)

蔧 huì ㄏㄨㄟˋ (formerly pronounced suì) 王蔧，草本植物，即地肤，俗叫扫帚菜，分枝多，叶狭长。嫩苗可以吃，老株可以做扫帚 summer cypress (same as 地肤，informal 扫帚菜)

慧 huì ㄏㄨㄟˋ 聪明，有才智（㊥智一、聪一）clever; intelligent：～眼 *discerning eyes* | 明～ *wise; intelligent* | 秀外～中 *have an elegant appearance and a wise mind; beautiful and intelligent*

槥 huì ㄏㄨㄟˋ 〈古 ancient〉一种小棺材 a kind of small coffin

鏏（鏏）huì ㄏㄨㄟˋ（又）see wèi on page 684

硊 huì ㄏㄨㄟˋ ［石硊］地名，在安徽省芜湖市 Shihui (a place in Wuhu City, Anhui Province)

秽（穢）huì ㄏㄨㄟˋ 肮脏 dirty：～土（垃圾）*rubbish; dirt* ㊞丑恶 ugly：～行 *immoral behaviour; vile conduct* | 自惭形～ *feel inferior and ashamed of oneself*

翙（翽）huì ㄏㄨㄟˋ ［翙翙］形容鸟飞的声音 sound of a bird in flight

惠 huì ㄏㄨㄟˋ 好处 benefit; favour：恩～ *kindness; favour* | 实～ *tangible benefit; substantial benefit* | 加～于人 *do sb a favour; give sb benefits* ㊂给人好处 to give benefits to sb：互～ *reciprocal; mutually beneficial* | ～及全体人民 *give benefits to all people* 敬辞，用于对方对自己有益的行动 (polite speech) kind; generous：～赠 *your kind presentation of the gift* | ～临 *your honorable presence/visit*

谌（譓）huì ㄏㄨㄟˋ ❶辨察 to distinguish and inspect ❷顺服 obedient; compliant

蕙 huì ㄏㄨㄟˋ 蕙兰，兰花的一种，花淡黄绿色，气味香 faber cymbidium (a species of orchid)

橞 huì ㄏㄨㄟˋ 古书上说的一种树 a kind of tree in ancient Chinese texts

蟪 huì ㄏㄨㄟˋ ［蟪蛄］（一gū）一种蝉，又叫伏天儿，身体小，青紫色，有黑纹 *Platypleura kaempferi* (also called 伏天儿), a kind of cicada

喙 huì ㄏㄨㄟˋ 嘴，特指鸟兽的嘴 (specifically) beak; snout：毋庸置～（不要插嘴）。*Don't butt in.*

阓（闠）huì ㄏㄨㄟˋ see 阛阓 (huán一) at 阛 on page 266

溃（潰）huì ㄏㄨㄟˋ 疮溃（kuì）烂 to fester：～脓 *suppuration*

⇨ see also kuì on p.370

殨（殨）huì ㄏㄨㄟˋ same as "溃 (huì)"

HUN ㄏㄨㄣ

昏（*昬）hūn ㄏㄨㄣ ❶黄昏，天将黑的时

候 dusk：晨～（早晚）*dawn and dusk* ❷黑暗（㊎－暗、－黑）dark; dim：天～地暗 *dark all round* ❸神志不清楚，认识糊涂 confused; muddled: 发～ *muddled; confused* | ～～沉沉 *in a daze; befuddled* ㊎失去知觉 lose consciousness：～迷 *be in a coma* | 他～过去了。*He lost consciousness.* ❹ (ancient) same as "婚"

阍（閽） hūn ㄏㄨㄣ ❶宫门 palace gate ❷看（kān）门 guard a gate

惛 hūn ㄏㄨㄣ 糊涂 muddle-headed; confused

婚 hūn ㄏㄨㄣ 结婚，男女结为夫妇 to get married：已～ *married* | 未～ *unmarried* | ～配 *to marry* [婚姻] 嫁娶、结婚的事 matrimony; marriage：～自主 *freedom of marriage*

䃅 hūn ㄏㄨㄣ 〈方 dialect〉一种类似涵洞而较小的地下排水建筑，多用于地名 (often used in place names) a culvert-like underground drainage：赵家～（在湖南省常德）*Zhaojiahun (a place in Changde, Hunan Province)*

荤（葷） hūn ㄏㄨㄣ ❶鸡鸭鱼肉等食物，跟"素"相对 meat or fish dishes (opposite of 素)：～素 *meat and vegetables* | ～菜 *dish with meat or fish* | 不吃～ *vegetarian; not eat meat or fish* ❷葱蒜等有特殊气味的菜 dishes with special tastes like onion or garlic：五～ *five pungent vegetables* ❸粗俗的，下流的 vulgar; obscene：～话 *obscene words*

浑（渾） hún ㄏㄨㄣˊ ❶水不清，污浊 (of water) muddy; turbid：～水坑 *muddy puddle* ❷糊涂，不明事理 stupid; unreasonable：～人 *unreasonable person; a person lacking in common sense* | ～话 *unreasonable words* | 这人太～了。*The person is too stupid.* ❸全，满 all over; whole：～身是汗。*The body is covered in sweat.* ❹天然的 natural：～朴 *simple and honest* | ～厚 *(of a person) simple and honest; (of art styles) simple and vigorous; (of a voice) sonorous*

珲（琿） hún ㄏㄨㄣˊ [珲春] 地名，在吉林省 Hunchun (a place in Jilin Province)

⇨ see also huī on p.272

馄（餛） hún ㄏㄨㄣˊ [馄饨]（－tun）一种煮熟连汤吃的食品，用薄面片包上馅做成 wonton

混 hún ㄏㄨㄣˊ same as "浑❶❷"

⇨ see also hùn on p.278

魂（*䰟） hún ㄏㄨㄣˊ ❶迷信的人指能离开肉体而存在的精神（㊎－魄）soul：～不附体 *as if the soul has left the body; (figurative) to be scared out of one's wits* ❷泛指精神或情绪 (generally) spirit; mood：神～颠倒。*One's mind is in a confused state.* 特指崇高的精神 (specifically) lofty spirit: 民族～ *national spirit* | 国～ *national spirit* [灵魂] ㊍1 指人的精神、思想 spirit; thought：教师是人类～的工程师。*Teachers are the engineers of* *the human spirit.* 2 事物的最精粹、最主要的部分 gist; essence：这一句是全诗的～。*This sentence is the gist of the whole poem.*

诨(諢) hùn ㄏㄨㄣˋ 开玩笑的话 joke; jest：打～ *crack a joke* | ～名（外号）*nickname*

圂 hùn ㄏㄨㄣˋ ❶猪圈 pigsty ❷厕所 toilet; lavatory

溷 hùn ㄏㄨㄣˋ ❶肮脏(㊥—浊) dirty; filthy ❷厕所 toilet; lavatory ❸猪圈 pigsty

混 hùn ㄏㄨㄣˋ ❶掺杂在一起 to mix; to mingle：～合 *to mix; to blend* | ～杂 *mix up; to blend* | ～入 *sneak into* | ～充 *pretend to be sb else; palm sth off as* | ～为一谈 *lump different items together; confuse different topics* ❷苟且度过 to muddle along：～日子 *muddle along* | 鬼～ *fool around; live aimlessly* ❸蒙混 to cheat/mislead people：～过去了 *muddled through; bluffed it out* | 鱼目～珠 *deceive people with fish eyes for pearls; (figurative) pass off sham as being genuine* ❹胡乱 at random; irresponsibly：～乱 *chaotic; disorderly* | ～出主意 *randomly put forward an idea*

[混沌]（—dùn）1 传说中指世界开辟前的状态 chaos 2 糊涂，不清楚 muddled; unclear

⇨ see also hún on p.277

HUO ㄏㄨㄛ

耠 huō ㄏㄨㄛ ❶（—子）用来翻松土壤的农具，比犁轻便 hoe ❷用耠子翻土，代替耕、锄或耩的工作 to hoe (the earth)：～地 *to hoe* | ～个八九厘米深就够了。*It is enough to hoe eight or nine centimeters deep.*

䂄(騞、剨)** huō ㄏㄨㄛ 形容用刀解剖东西的声音 sound of a knife dissecting sth

锪(鍃) huō ㄏㄨㄛ 一种金属加工方法，用专门的刀具对金属工件已有的孔进行加工，刮平端面或切出锥形、圆柱形凹坑 to ream

劐 huō ㄏㄨㄛ ❶用刀、剪的尖ㄦ插入物体后顺势划开 to slit; to cut：用剪刀～开 *slit with a pair of scissors* ❷ same as "耠❷"

嚄 huō ㄏㄨㄛ 叹词，表示惊讶 (exclamation, expressing surprise) wow：～，好大的水库！*Wow! What a big reservoir it is!*

⇨ see also ǒ on p.486

豁 huō ㄏㄨㄛ ❶残缺，裂开 crack; slit：～口 *breach; opening* | ～了一个口子 *cracked an opening* | ～唇 *harelip* [豁子]（—zi）残缺的口子 breach; chip：碗上有个～。*There is a chip on the edge of the bowl.* | 城墙拆了一个～。*A breach was made in the city wall.* ❷舍弃，狠心付出高代价 to give up; to make up one's mind to pay a high price：～出性命 *give up one's life* | ～出几天时间 *make up one's mind to spend a few days doing sth*

⇨ see also huò on p.281

H

攉 huō ㄏㄨㄛ 把堆在一起的东西铲起倒（dǎo）到另一处去 to shovel：～土 *shovel the soil* | ～煤机 *coal shovel*

和 huó ㄏㄨㄛˊ 在粉状物中加水搅拌或揉弄使粘在一起 to mix with water：～面 *mix flour with water; to knead dough* | ～泥 *mix earth with water*

⇨ see also hé on p.246, hè on p.249, hú on p.258, huò on p.280

佸 huó ㄏㄨㄛˊ 相会，聚会 to meet; to gather

活 huó ㄏㄨㄛˊ ❶生存，能生长，跟"死"相对 to live; to be alive (opposite of 死)：鱼在水里才能～。*Fish can only live in water.* | 新栽的树～了。*The newly planted tree is alive.* ㊀使生存 to keep alive; to save (the life of sb)：～命之恩 *indebted to sb for saving one's life* | 养家～口 *support a family* ❷不固定，可移动的 movable; mobile：～期存款 *current deposit* | ～页本 *loose-leaf notebook* | ～塞 *piston* | ～扣 *slipknot* [活泼] 活跃自然，不呆板 lively; vivacious：孩子们很～。*The children are very lively.* ❸真正，简直 exactly; simply：～像一只老虎 *look exactly like a tiger* | 神气～现 *high and mighty; excessively proud* ❹（－儿）工作或产品 work; product：做～ *to work* | 这～儿做得真好。*The work is well done.*

[活该] 表示就应该这样，一点儿也不委屈 serve sb right：～如此。*It serves sb right.*

火 huǒ ㄏㄨㄛˇ ❶东西燃烧时所发的光和焰 fire：着（zháo）～ *to catch fire; to be on fire* | 大～ *big fire* | ～苗 *flame* ㊉紧急 urgent; pressing：～速 *at top speed; post-haste* | ～急 *extremely urgent* ❷指枪炮弹药 firearms; ammunition：军～ *arms and ammunition; munitions* | ～器 *firearms* | 开～ *open fire; to fire* [火药] 炸药的一类，主要用作引燃药或发射药。是我国古代四大发明之一 gunpowder [火线] 1 两军交战枪炮子弹交接的地带 line of battle：轻伤不下～。*Those who were slightly wounded would not leave the line of battle.* 2 从电源输送电的导线 power line; live wire ❸红色的 red：～狐 *red fox* | ～鸡 *turkey* ❹古代军队的组织，十个人为一火 army unit in ancient China, one 火 consisting of ten persons ❺中医指引起发炎、红肿、烦躁等症状的病因 (in traditional Chinese medicine) internal heat：上～ *suffer from excessive internal heat* | 败～ *relieve internal heat* ❻（－儿）怒气 anger; rage：好大的～儿！*What a hot temper!* ❼（－儿）发怒 to get angry; to fly into a rage：他～儿了。*He got angry.* ❽兴隆，旺盛 flourishing; thriving：生意很～。*The business is going very well.*

伙（❶–❺△夥） huǒ ㄏㄨㄛˇ ❶（－儿）伙计，同伴，一同做事的人（㊥－伴）partner; peer; colleague：同～儿 *people working in partnership;*

people colluding with each other in doing sth ❷旧指店员 (old) salesperson：店～ *shop assistant* ❸合伙，结伴，联合起来 to form a partnership; to join up：～办 *do sth jointly* | ～同 *cooperate with* ❹由同伴组成的集体 group; partnership：合～ *join into a partnership* | 入～ *join a group/gang/company* ❺量词，用于人群 (measure word for people) group; crowd：一～歹徒 *a band of ruffians* | 十人一～ *ten people in each group* ❻伙食 meal; diet：～补 *food allowance* | 起～ *cook meals*

钬(鈥) huǒ ㄏㄨㄛˇ 金属元素，符号 Ho，银白色，质软，可用来制磁性材料 holmium (Ho)

漷 huǒ ㄏㄨㄛˇ ［漷县］地名，在北京市通州 Huoxian (a place in Tongzhou, Beijing)

夥 huǒ ㄏㄨㄛˇ ❶多 plenty; abundant：获益甚～ *achieve a great many benefits* ❷ see 伙 on page 279

或 huò ㄏㄨㄛˋ ❶连词，表示选择 (conjunction, indicating choice) or：同意～反对 *for or against* ❷副词，也许 (adverb) perhaps; probably: 明晨～可抵达。*We may arrive tomorrow morning.* ❸文言代词，某人，有人 (pronoun in classical Chinese) somebody; some people：～谓之曰："何不为学？" *Somebody asked: "Why not start to learn?"*

惑 huò ㄏㄨㄛˋ ❶疑惑，不明白对与不对 to doubt; to be confused：困～ *puzzled; perplexed* | 大～不解 *deeply puzzled* | 智者不～。*A wise person is not confused.* ❷使迷乱（㊀迷～）to bewilder; to confuse：～乱人心 *confuse people's minds* | 谣言～众 *delude people with rumour*

和 huò ㄏㄨㄛˋ ❶粉状或粒状物掺和在一起，或加水搅拌 to mix; to blend：～药 *mix medicine* ❷量词 measure word ①洗衣物换水的次数 number of times of changing water when washing：衣裳已经洗了两～。*The clothes have been washed twice.* ②煎药加水的次数 number of times of adding water when boiling medicinal herbs：头～药 *the first decoction of herbal medicines* | 二～药 *the second decoction of herbal medicines*

⇨ see also hé on p.246, hè on p.249, hú on p.258, huó on p.279

货(貨) huò ㄏㄨㄛˋ ❶货物，商品 goods; commodity：进～ *to stock; replenish one's stock* | 订～ *order goods* | 水～ *smuggled goods* | 山～ *mountain products* ［货郎］卖零星商品的流动小贩 itinerant vendor/pedlar ❷钱币 money; currency：通～ *currency; current money* | ～币 *money; currency* ❸卖 to sell：～卖（出售）*to sell* ❹骂人时指人 used to denote a person when cursing：他不是个好～。*He is not a good man.* | 笨～ *idiot* | 蠢～ *blockhead*

获(❶獲、❷穫) huò ㄏㄨㄛˋ ❶得到，

H

取得（㊀一得）to get; to gain：俘～ *to capture* | 不～全胜，决不收兵。*Without a complete victory, we would not withdraw.* ㊀ 能得到机会或空闲 to obtain an opportunity; to have leisure time：不～面辞 *have no opportunity to say goodbye to sb* ❷收割庄稼 to reap; to harvest [收获] 割取成熟的农作物 to harvest; to reap ㊀所得到的成果 gains; results：这次学习有很大的～。*We have gained a great deal from the study.*

祸（禍、*旤）huò ㄏㄨㄛˋ ❶灾殃，苦难（nàn），跟"福"相对（㊀灾一）disaster; misfortune (opposite of 福)：大～临头 *imminent catastrophe* | 闯～ *cause trouble; bring disaster upon* ❷损害，使受灾殃 to harm; to wreck：～国殃民 *cause great calamity to the country and bring misfortune to the people*

謋（謋）huò ㄏㄨㄛˋ 形容迅速分裂的声音 sound of fast splitting：动刀甚微，～然已解。*Only a slight movement of the knife was enough to cause immediate separation of flesh and bones.*

霍 huò ㄏㄨㄛˋ 迅速，快 quick; speedy; fast：～然病愈。*(The patient) has made a fast recovery.*

[霍霍] 形容磨刀声 sound of sharpening a knife; scrape：磨刀～ *sharpen a knife with a loud scraping noise*

藿 huò ㄏㄨㄛˋ 藿香，草本植物，茎四棱形，叶对生，茎叶香味浓，可入药 wrinkled giant hyssop

嚯 huò ㄏㄨㄛˋ ❶叹词，表示惊讶或赞叹 (exclamation, indicating surprise or praise) oh; wow：～，几年不见，孩子长这么高了！ *Wow! I have not seen her/him for several years, and the child has grown so tall!* ❷形容笑声 (sound of laughing) ho ho：～～一笑 *laugh*

㸌 huò ㄏㄨㄛˋ 形容光亮闪烁 (of light) flickering; twinkling

濩 huò ㄏㄨㄛˋ ❶雨水从屋檐向下流的样子 (of rain) to drip from eaves ❷ 姓 (surname) Huo

镬（鑊）huò ㄏㄨㄛˋ ❶〈方 dialect〉（一子）锅 pot; wok：～盖 *pot cover* ❷古代的大锅 (ancient) cauldron：鼎～（常用为残酷的刑具）*a kind of cauldron usually used as an instrument of torture*

蠖 huò ㄏㄨㄛˋ 尺蠖，尺蠖蛾的幼虫，生活在树上，身体一屈一伸地前进，是害虫 looper; inchworm

豁 huò ㄏㄨㄛˋ ❶开通，敞亮 clear; spacious and light：～达 *open-minded; generous* | ～然开朗 *become suddenly enlightened/clear-minded* ❷免除（㊀一免）to remit; to exempt

⇨ see also huō on p.278

J ㄐ

JI ㄐㄧ

几(❷❸幾) jī ㄐㄧ ❶(一儿)小或矮的桌子 small table：茶～儿 *tea table*｜条～ *long narrow table* ❷差一点儿，近乎 nearly; almost：～乎 *nearly*｜～为所害 *narrowly avoided being hurt/murdered*｜迄今～四十年 *nearly forty years by now* ❸苗头 (of things to come) early sign：知～其神乎 *see the earliest sign of things to come borders on the prescience of a god*

⇨ see also jǐ on p.289

讥(譏) jī ㄐㄧ 讽刺，挖苦(㊥一讽、一刺) to take a swipe at：冷～热嘲 *make sarcastic comments*｜～笑 *to mock*

叽(嘰) jī ㄐㄧ 形容小鸟、小鸡等的叫声 ㊢(of birds) to chirp：小鸟～～地叫。*The birds are twittering.*［叽咕］(一gu) 小声说话 to mutter

饥(❶飢、❷饑) jī ㄐㄧ ❶饿(㊥一饿) hungry：～不择食。*Beggars can't be choosers.*｜～寒交迫 *suffer from cold and hunger* ❷庄稼收成不好或没有收成 famine：～馑 *famine*

玑(璣) jī ㄐㄧ ❶不圆的珍珠 baroque pearl：珠～ *bead; (figurative) beautiful articles or lines* ❷古代测天文的仪器 (ancient) astronomical instrument：璇～ *armillary sphere*

机(機) jī ㄐㄧ ❶事物发生、变化的枢纽 turning point：生～ *chance for survival*｜危～ *crisis*｜转～ *turn for the better* ㊀ ①对事情成败有重要关系的中心环节，有保密性质的事件 crucial point; confidential matter：军～ *military plan; military secret*｜～密 *(a) secret*｜～要 *confidential* ②机会，合宜的时候 opportunity：～不可失。*The opportunity cannot be missed.*｜随～应变 *play it by ear*｜勿失良～。*Don't let the opportunity slip.*｜时～ *opportunity* ❷指生命 life：～能 *function*｜～体 *organism* ❸心思，念头 idea：动～ *motive*｜心～ *calculation*｜暗藏杀～ *conceal a death trap* ❹灵巧，能迅速适应事物的变化的 agile：～巧 *adroit*｜～智 *sharp-witted*｜～警 *alert*［机动］1 依照客观情况随时灵活行动 flexible：～处理 *deal with flexibility*｜～作战 *manoeuvre warfare* 2 利用机器开动的 motorized：～车 *motorized vehicle*［机灵］聪明，头脑灵活 clever ❺机器，由许多零件组成可以做功或有特殊作用的装置或设备 machine：织布～ *loom*｜发电～ *generator*｜收音

～ *radio* | 拖拉 ～ *tractor* | 计算 ～ *computer* | 手 ～ *mobile phone* [机械] 1 利用力学原理组成的各种装置，各种机器、杠杆、滑轮以及枪炮等都是机械 machinery：～化 *to mechanize* | ～工业 *machinery industry* 2 方式死板，不灵活 mechanical：～地工作 *work mechanically* | ～唯物论 *mechanical materialism* | 你的办法太～了。*Your approach is too inflexible.* ❻指飞机 plane：～场 *airport* | 客 ～ *passenger airplane*

肌 jī ㄐㄧ 肌肉，人和动物体的组织之一，由许多肌纤维组成，具有收缩特性 muscle：心 ～ *cardiac muscle* | 平滑 ～ *smooth muscle* | 骨骼 ～ *skeletal muscle*

矶(磯) jī ㄐㄧ 水边突出的岩石。多用于地名 rocky headland (often used in place names)：采石～（在安徽省马鞍山市）*Caishiji (in Ma'anshan City, Anhui Province)* | 燕子～（在江苏省南京）*Yanziji (in Nanjing, Jiangsu Province)*

击(擊) jī ㄐㄧ ❶打，敲打 to strike; to hit：～鼓 *beat a drum* | ～柝（tuò）（敲梆子）*(of a night watchman) strike a clapper* ❷攻打 to attack：袭～ *make a surprise attack* | 游 ～ *fight guerrilla warfare* | 痛 ～ *to thrash* ❸碰 to bump into：冲 ～ *to lash; to charge; have an impact on* | 撞～ *slam into* | 肩摩毂（gǔ）～（形容来往人多，拥挤）*crowded* ㊀接触 to come into contact：目～（亲眼看见）*to witness*

圾 jī ㄐㄧ see 垃圾 (lā－) at 垃 on page 373

芨 jī ㄐㄧ [白芨] 草本植物，叶长形，块茎白色，可入药 Chinese ground orchid

乩 jī ㄐㄧ [扶乩] 迷信的人占卜问疑 practise planchette writing (for the purpose of divination)

鸡(鷄、*雞) jī ㄐㄧ 家禽，公鸡能报晓，母鸡能生蛋 chicken

枅 jī ㄐㄧ 古代指柱子或门上所垫的方木 (ancient) bracket

笄 jī ㄐㄧ 古代盘头发用的簪子 (ancient) hairpin

奇 jī ㄐㄧ ❶数目不成双的，跟"偶"相对 odd (opposite of 偶)：一、三、五、七、九是～数。*One, three, five, seven and nine are odd numbers.* ❷零数，余数 remainder：长八分有 ～ *eight* fen *odd in length*

⇨ see also qí on p.519

剞 jī ㄐㄧ [剞劂]（－jué）1 雕刻用的弯刀 curved blade (used in carving) 2 雕版，刻书 to engrave; to carve a woodblock

犄 jī ㄐㄧ [犄角] 1（－儿）物体的两个边沿相接处，棱角 corner (formed by two adjacent sides)：桌子 ～儿 *corner of a table* 2（－儿）角落 corner：墙 ～儿 *corner of a wall* 3（－jiɑo）兽角 horn：牛 ～ *ox horn*

畸 jī ㄐㄧ ❶不规则的，不正常的 irregular; deformed：～形 *malformed* ❷数的零头 part of a number discarded when rounding

J

down：～零（零数）*part of a number discarded when rounding down* ❸偏 unbalanced：～轻～重 *swing between too little and too much*

畸 jī ㄐㄧ 同"奇❶"，单数 same as 奇❶, odd (number)

隮(隮) jī ㄐㄧ ❶登，上升 to ascend ❷ 虹 rainbow

跻(躋) jī ㄐㄧ 登，上升 to ascend [跻身] 上升到某位置，跨入某行列 join the ranks of：～前三名 *rank among the top three* | ～文坛 *break into the literary world*

唧 jī ㄐㄧ ❶用水射击 to squirt：～筒 *pump* | ～他一身水。*The water squirted all over him.* ❷形容虫叫声 ㊥(of an insect) to chirp [唧咕]（-gu）same as "叽咕"

积(積) jī ㄐㄧ ❶聚集 to accumulate：～少成多 *build up bit by bit* | ～年累月 *year in, year out* | ～习 *(often disapproving) ingrained habit* | ～劳 *be constantly overworked* [积淀] 1 积累沉淀 to accumulate 2 积累沉淀下来的事物（多指文化、知识、经验等）accumulation (usually of culture, knowledge and experience, etc.) [积极] 向上的，进取的，跟"消极"相对 active (opposite of 消极)：工作～ *be hard-working* | ～分子 *active member* ❷乘积，乘法运算的得数 product (in maths)：二乘四的～是八。*Two times four is eight.*

屐 jī ㄐㄧ 木头鞋 clog：木～ *clog* 泛指鞋 (generally) shoes

姬 jī ㄐㄧ ❶古代对妇女的美称 (ancient) complimentary term of address for women ❷旧时称妾 (old) concubine ❸旧时称以歌舞为业的女子 (old) professional female singer or dancer：歌～ *professional female singer*

基 jī ㄐㄧ ❶建筑物的根脚 foundation：地～ *foundation* | 墙～ *foundation for a wall* ㊞最下面的，根本的 basic：～数 *cardinal number* | ～层 *grass roots* [基础] 建筑物的根脚和柱石 foundation ㊞事物的根基 basis：钢铁是工业的～。*Industry is built on steel.* [基金] 1 国民经济中有特定用途的资金 fund：消费～ *consumption fund* | 生产～ *production fund* 2 为兴办或发展某一事业而集聚、储备的资金或专门的拨款 funding：教育～ *funding for education* | 福利～ *welfare fund* ❷化学上指不带电的原子团 (in chemistry) group：烃（tīng）～ *hydrocarbyl group* | 氨～ *amino* ❸根据 on the basis of：～于上述理由 *for the above reasons*

[基督]（外 *loanword*）基督教徒称耶稣，意为"救世主" Christ

[基督教] 宗教名。公元1世纪犹太人耶稣所创。11世纪分为罗马教会（天主教）和希腊教会（东正教）两派；16世纪罗马教会又分为新教和旧教。现在一般称新教为基督教 Christianity; (now usually referring to) Protestantism

[基诺族] 我国少数民族，参看附

录 四 the Jino people (one of the ethnic groups in China. See Appendix Ⅳ.)

期(*朞) jī ㄐㄧ 〈古ancient〉一周年，一整月 one whole year; one whole month: ～年 *one whole year* | ～月 *one whole month*

⇨ see also qī on p.515

錤(錤) jī ㄐㄧ see 镃錤 (zī —) at 镃 on page 880

箕 jī ㄐㄧ ❶簸箕（bòji），用竹篾、柳条或铁皮等制成的扬去糠麸或清除垃圾的器具 dustpan ❷不成圆形的指纹 loop (in fingerprints) ❸星宿名，二十八宿之一 *ji* (one of the twenty-eight constellations in ancient Chinese astronomy)

鿓(鈓) jī ㄐㄧ 古书上说的金圭 a pointed tablet made of gold and jade (in ancient Chinese texts)

赍(賫、*齎、*賷) jī ㄐㄧ ❶怀抱着，带着 to cherish: ～志而殁（mò）（志未遂而死去）*die with unfulfilled ambitions* | ～恨 *harbour hatred* ❷把东西送给别人 to give

嵇 jī ㄐㄧ 姓 (surname) Ji

稽 jī ㄐㄧ ❶停留（㊥—留）to tarry: ～迟 *to delay* | ～延 *to procrastinate* ❷考核（㊥—核）to examine: ～查 *investigate; investigator* | 无～之谈 *unfounded story* ❸计较，争论 to dispute: 反唇相～（反过来责问对方）*to retort* ❹姓 (surname) Ji

⇨ see also qǐ on p.522

缉(緝) jī ㄐㄧ 搜捕，捉拿 to arrest: ～私 *clamp down on smuggling* | 通～ *order the arrest of*

⇨ see also qī on p.516

襀(襀) jī ㄐㄧ 衣服的褶儿 pleat

齑(齏) jī ㄐㄧ ❶捣碎的姜、蒜、韭菜等 crushed ginger, garlic, or Chinese chives, etc. ❷细，碎 powdered: 化为～粉 *to pulverize*

畿 jī ㄐㄧ 古代称靠近国都的地方 (ancient) environs (of a capital city): 京～ *capital city and its environs*

墼 jī ㄐㄧ 土坯 adobe [炭墼] 用炭末做成的块状物 charcoal briquette [土墼] 未烧的砖坯 unfired clay brick

激 jī ㄐㄧ ❶水冲击或急速浇淋 (of water) to surge, to cascade: ～起浪花 *churn up waves* | 他被雨～病了。*He was caught in the rain and fell ill.* ㊞使发作，使人的感情冲动 to rouse: 刺～ *to provoke* | 用话～他 *say sth provocative to him* [激昂]（情绪、语调等）激动昂扬 impassioned: 慷慨～ *passionate* ❷急剧的，强烈的（㊥—烈）drastic: ～变 *have a drastic change* | ～战 *fight a fierce battle*

羁(羈、*覊) jī ㄐㄧ ❶马笼头 bridle ❷束缚 to restrain: ～绊 *to fetter* | ～押 *to detain* ❸停留 to stay: ～留 *to stay (in a strange place)* [羁旅] 寄居作客 live in an alien land for a long time

及 jí ㄐㄧˊ ❶到 to reach; to arrive ①从后头跟上 catch up with: 来得～ *be in time* | 赶不～ *not have enough time* ㊀比得上 to match: 我不～他。*I can't compare with him.* ②达到 to reach: 由表～里 *from the surface to the core* | 将～十载 *be approaching ten years* | ～格 *to pass (an exam)* ㊀牵涉到，推广到 extend to: 言不～义 *talk only about trivialities* | 不～其余 *fail to see the whole picture* ❷趁着，乘 taking advantage of: ～时 *timely* | ～早 *as soon as possible* ❸连词，和，跟（通常主要成分在"及"字前）(conjunction) and (usually used after the most important information): 给老人买了烟、酒～其他一些东西 *bought cigarettes, alcohol and some other items for the old person/people* [以及] 连词，连接并列的词、词组，意义和"及❸"相同 (conjunction) and (same in meaning as 及❸): 花园里种着状元红、矢车菊、夹竹桃～其他各色花木。*In the garden, there are Kaempfer's glorybower, cornflowers, oleander and various other trees and flowers.*

伋 jí ㄐㄧˊ 用于人名。孔伋，字子思，孔子的孙子 Ji (used in given names, e.g. Kong Ji, grandson of Confucius)

岌 jí ㄐㄧˊ ❶山高 (of a mountain) precipitous ❷危险 dangerous [岌岌] 1 形容山高 (of a mountain) precipitous 2 形容危险 dangerous: ～可危 *in imminent danger*

汲 jí ㄐㄧˊ ❶从井里打水 to draw (water from a well): ～水 *draw water* [汲引] 旧时喻提拔人才 (old) to promote (talented people) ❷ ㊂急切的样子 craving: 不可～～于名利。*Do not crave fame and fortune.*

级(級) jí ㄐㄧˊ ❶层，层次 level: 那台阶有十多～。*That flight of stairs has over ten steps.* | 七～浮屠（七层的塔）*seven-storey pagoda* ❷等次 grade: 高～ *advanced; high-grade* | 低～ *low-level; vulgar* | 初～ *primary* | 上～ *senior* | 下～ *junior* ❸年级，学校编制的名称，学年的分段 school year; grade: 同～不同班 *in the same year group but different classes* | 三年～ *Year Three; Grade Three* | 高年～ *upper years*

极(極) jí ㄐㄧˊ ❶顶端，最高点，尽头处 peak; extreme: 登峰造～ *reach the pinnacle* ❷指地球的南北两端，磁体的两端或电路的正负两端 (of the earth, or of a magnet or circuit) pole: 南～ *South Pole* | 北～ *North Pole* | 阳～ *anode* | 阴～ *cathode* [南极洲] 世界七大洲之一 Antarctica ❸副词，最，表示达到顶点 (adverb) extremely: 大～了 *extremely big* | ～好 *extremely good* | 穷凶～恶 *thoroughly vicious and evil* ❹竭尽 to exhaust: ～力 *to the utmost* | ～目远眺（tiào）*look*

J

as far as the eye can see

笈 jí ㄐㄧˊ ❶书箱 book trunk ❷书籍，典籍 book; ancient book and record

吉 jí ㄐㄧˊ ❶幸运的，吉利的，跟"凶"相对(㊥—祥、—庆) auspicious (opposite of 凶)：～日 *auspicious day* | ～期 *happy day; wedding day* ❷(外 loanword) 法定计量单位中十进倍数单位词头之一，表示 10^9，符号 G。giga (G)

佶 jí ㄐㄧˊ 健壮 robust [佶屈][诘屈] 曲折 convoluted: ～聱(áo)牙(文句拗口) *(of writing) twisted and convoluted*

诘(詰) jí ㄐㄧˊ [诘屈] same as "佶屈" (see 佶 jí on page 287 for reference)

➪ see also jié on p.316

姞 jí ㄐㄧˊ 姓 (surname) Ji

即 jí ㄐㄧˊ ❶就是 namely：番茄～西红柿。番茄 *and* 西红柿 *both mean "tomato".* ❷当时或当地 as of; at the very place：～日 *this very day; recently* | ～刻 *immediately* | ～席 *(do sth) over a banquet; be seated* | ～景生情 *be moved by the scenery* ❸副词，便，就 (adverb) immediately：胜利～在眼前。*Victory is well in sight.* | 用毕～行奉还。*It will be returned immediately when it is finished with.* [即使] 连词，常和"也"字连用表示假设性让步 (conjunction, often used with 也 to indicate hypothetical concession) even though：～我们的工作取得了很大的成绩，也不能骄傲自满。*Even if we achieve great success in our work, we shouldn't feel arrogant.* ❹靠近 to approach：不～不离 *keep a discreet distance* [即位] 指封建统治者登上帝王的位子，做君主或诸侯 ascend the throne

垐 jí ㄐㄧˊ 〈古 ancient〉 ❶烧土为砖 make and fire bricks ❷烛灰 candle ash

亟 jí ㄐㄧˊ 文言副词，急切地 (adverb in classical Chinese) urgently：～待解决 *demand an immediate solution* | 缺点～应纠正。*The shortcomings must be rectified without delay.*

➪ see also qì on p.523

殛 jí ㄐㄧˊ 杀死 to kill：雷～ *be killed by a thunderbolt*

革 jí ㄐㄧˊ 〈古 ancient〉(病)危急 (of illness) critical

➪ see also gé on p.204

急 jí ㄐㄧˊ ❶焦躁(㊥焦—) worried：真～死人了。*I'm worried sick.* | 着～ *worried* ㊀气恼，发怒 be angry：他一听就～了。*He flared up the moment he heard about it.* ❷匆促 in a hurry：～～忙忙 *hastily* | ～就 *complete in haste* | ～于完成任务 *eager to get the job done* ㊀迅速，又快又猛 rapid：水流得～。*The water is flowing rapidly.* | ～病 *sudden illness* ❸迫切，要紧 urgent：～事 *urgent matter* | 不～之务 *non-urgent matter* | ～件 *urgent item for delivery* ㊀严重 serious：情况紧～。*The situation is urgent.* | 告～ *ask for help in an emergency* | 病～乱投

J

医（喻临事慌乱）。*A drowning man will clutch at a straw.* ❹对大家的事或别人的困难赶快帮助 be eager to help：～公好义 *be public-spirited* | ～难（nàn）*be eager to help with an emergency*

湒 jí ㄐㄧˊ 用于地名 used in place names：～滩（在河南省邓州）*Jitan (in Dengzhou, Henan Province)*

疾 jí ㄐㄧˊ ❶病，身体不舒适（㊀-病）illness：目～*eye disease* | 积劳成～*fall ill due to burnout* ㊁痛苦 suffering：～苦 *hardship* ❷恨 to hate：～恶如仇 *hate evil with a passion* ❸快，迅速，猛烈 swift; fierce：～走 *walk swiftly* | ～风知劲草。*Adversity is the touchstone of character.* | ～言厉色（形容发怒的样子）*look stern and speak harshly* ❹疼痛 ache：痛心～首 *hold the utmost hatred*

蒺 jí ㄐㄧˊ ［蒺藜］（-li）1 草本植物，茎横生在地面上，花黄色。果实也叫蒺藜，有刺，可入药 puncture vine (its fruit is also called 蒺藜 and has medicinal uses) 2 像蒺藜的东西 refers to objects resembling the puncture vine：铁～ *caltrop (weapon)*

嫉 jí ㄐㄧˊ ❶因别人比自己好而怨恨（㊀-妒、妒-）envious：～才 *be envious of a talented person* | ～贤妒能 *envy the talented and the capable* ❷憎恨 to hate：～恶如仇 *hate evil with a passion*

棘 jí ㄐㄧˊ ❶酸枣树，落叶灌木，茎上多刺，花黄绿色，果实小，味酸 sour jujube ❷针形的刺 thorn：～皮动物 *echinoderm* ［棘手］刺手，扎手 thorny ㊂事情难办 thorny; tricky ❸指有刺的草木 bramble：披荆斩～ *plough through obstacles*

集 jí ㄐㄧˊ ❶聚，会合，总合（㊀聚-）to gather; to assemble：～思广益 *pool ideas* | ～会 *gather for meeting; assembly* | ～中 *to gather; to concentrate* ［集体］许多人合起来的有组织的总体 collective：～利益 *collective interests* | ～所有制 *collective ownership* ❷会合许多单篇或单张作品编成的书 (of book) collection：诗～ *anthology of poems* | 文～ *collected writings* | 选～ *selected anthology* ❸某些篇幅较长的著作或作品中相对独立的部分 (of a literary or artistic work) part：影片分上下～。*The film is in two parts.* | 十～电视纪录片 *ten-part documentary series* ❹定期交易的市场 market; fair：～市 *market* | 赶～ *go to a fair* ❺完成 to accomplish：大业未～。*One's enterprise has not been accomplished.*

楫（*檝） jí ㄐㄧˊ 划船用的桨 oar

辑（輯） jí ㄐㄧˊ ❶聚集。特指聚集材料编书 to gather; (specifically) to compile：～录 *to compile* | 纂～ *collect and edit* ❷整套书籍、资料等按内容或发表次序分成的各个部分 (of a series of books, etc.) volume：专～ *album* | 丛书第一～ *first volume in a series* ❸和睦 harmonious：～睦 *harmonious*

戢 jí ㄐㄧˊ 收敛，收藏 store up：载～干戈（把兵器收藏起来）*put away arms* ㉖止，停止 to cease：～怒 *stop being angry*

蕺 jí ㄐㄧˊ 蕺菜，草本植物，又叫鱼腥草，茎上有节，花小而密。茎和叶有腥味。根可用作蔬菜，全草可入药 heart-leaved houttuynia (also called 鱼腥草)

嵴 jí ㄐㄧˊ 山脊 ridge (of a mountain)

瘠 jí ㄐㄧˊ ❶瘦弱 emaciated ❷土地不肥沃（㉘贫一）(of land) barren：～土 *barren land*｜～田 *infertile field*

鹡（鶺）jí ㄐㄧˊ ［鹡鸰］（—líng）鸟名，种类较多，常见的头黑额白，背部黑色，腹部白色，尾巴较长，生活在水边 wagtail

蹐 jí ㄐㄧˊ 小步行走 walk in short steps

耤 jí ㄐㄧˊ 耤河，水名，在甘肃省东南部，渭河支流 Jihe River (in the south-east of Gansu Province; branch of Weihe River)

踖 jí ㄐㄧˊ see 蹴踖 (cù—) at 蹴 on page 101

藉 jí ㄐㄧˊ ❶践踏，凌辱 to trample［狼藉］（*狼籍）乱七八糟 clutter：杯盘～ *used cups and dishes in a clutter*｜声名～ *be infamous* ❷姓 (surname) Ji

⇨ see also jiè on p.320, jiè 借 on p.320

籍 jí ㄐㄧˊ ❶书，书册（㉘书一）book; volume：六～（六经）*six canons*｜古～ *ancient books* ❷登记隶属关系的簿册，隶属关系 register (indicating membership or belonging)：户～ *household register*｜国～ *nationality*｜党～ *party membership*｜学～ *student status*［籍贯］自身出生或祖居的地方 native place

几（幾）jǐ ㄐㄧˇ ❶询问数量多少 how many：～个人？ *How many people?*｜来～天了？ *How many days have (you) been here?*［几何］1 多少 how much：人生～？ *Life is short!* 2 几何学，研究点、线、面、体的性质、关系和计算方法的学科 geometry ❷表示不定的数目 several：他才十～岁。*He is only a teenager.*｜所剩无～ *have very little left*

⇨ see also jī on p.282

虮（蟣）jǐ ㄐㄧˇ （—子）虱子的卵 nit

麂 jǐ ㄐㄧˇ （—子）哺乳动物，像鹿而小，毛黄黑色，雄的有很短的角 muntjac

己 jǐ ㄐㄧˇ ❶代词，自己，对人称本身 (pronoun) self：舍～为人 *sacrifice oneself for others*｜身不由～ *in spite of oneself* ❷天干的第六位，用作顺序的第六 *ji* (the sixth of the ten Heavenly Stems, a system used in the Chinese calendar)；sixth

纪（紀）jǐ ㄐㄧˇ 姓 (surname) Ji

⇨ see also jì on p.291

鱾（紀）jǐ ㄐㄧˇ 鱼名，身体侧扁，略呈椭圆形，头小，口小，生活在海底岩石间 girella

J

挤(擠) jǐ ㄐㄧˇ ❶许多人、物很紧地挨着，不容易动转 to crowd：一间屋子住十来个人，太～了。*It's too cramped for a dozen people to live in one room.* ❷在拥挤的环境中推、拥 to jostle：人多～不过去。*It's impossible to squeeze through so many people.* | ～进会场 *squeeze into the meeting room* ㊄ 排斥（㊥排－）crowd out：甲队被～出前三名。*Team A was edged out of the top three.* ❸用压力使排出 squeeze out：～牛奶 *milk a cow* | ～牙膏 *squeeze toothpaste*

济(濟) jǐ ㄐㄧˇ 济水，古水名，发源于今河南省，流经山东省入渤海 Jishui River (an ancient river that originated in Henan Province) [济南] [济宁] 地名，都在山东省 Jinan, Jining, place names, both in Shandong Province

[济济] 众多 (of people) numerous：人才～ *have a wealth of talented people*

⇨ see also jì on p.292

给(給) jǐ ㄐㄧˇ ❶供应 to supply：自～自足 *be self-sufficient* | 补～ *to supply (ammunition, army provision, etc.)* | ～养（军队中主副食、燃料，以及牲畜饲料等物资供应的统称）*(military) supplies* ❷富裕，充足 ample：家～人足。*Every family is well provided for.*

⇨ see also gěi on p.207

脊 jǐ ㄐㄧˇ ❶人和动物背中间的骨头 spine：～椎 *spine* | ～髓 *spinal cord* | ～梁 *back* | ～柱 *vertebral column* ❷物体中间高起、形状像脊柱的部分 ridge：屋～ *ridge of a roof* | 山～ *ridge of a mountain*

掎 jǐ ㄐㄧˇ 拖住，牵制 pull from behind; hold back

戟 jǐ ㄐㄧˇ 古代的一种兵器，由矛和戈组合而成 halberd

计(計) jì ㄐㄧˋ ❶算（㊥－算）to calculate：不～其数 *innumerable* ❷测量或计算度数、时间等的仪器 gauge：时～ *chronometer* | 体温～ *thermometer* ❸主意，策略（㊥－策）idea; plan：妙～ *ingenious idea* | 百年大～ *project of lasting impact* ❹计划，打算 to plan：为工作方便～ *in order to make one's work easier* [计较]（－jiào）1 打算，商量 to think over：此事日后再做～。*We'll think about it later.* 2 争论，较量 to argue：是他不对，但大家都没有跟他～。*He was the one in the wrong, but no one argued with him.*

痣(痣) jì ㄐㄧˋ 皮肤上生来就有的深色斑，现多写作“记” birthmark (now often written as 记)

记(記) jì ㄐㄧˋ ❶记忆，把印象保持在脑子里 to remember：～住这件事 *keep this in mind* | ～性 *memory* ❷把事物写下来 write down：～录 *(to) record* | ～账 *keep the books* | 把这些事情都～在笔记本上 *write all these things in a notebook* [记者] 报刊、电台、电视台、通讯

社里做采访报道工作的人员 journalist ❸记载事物的书册或文字 chronicle; note：游～*travelogue*｜日～*diary*｜大事～*chronicle of events* ❹记号，标志 mark：以红色为～*marked in red*｜戳～*seal* ❺ same as "疳" ❻量词，用于某些动作的次数 measure word, used to indicate how many times sth happens：一～耳光 *a slap in the face*｜一～劲射 *a powerful shot*

纪(紀) jì ㄐㄧˋ ❶记载 to record：～事 *keep a record of events; (often in book titles) account* [纪念] 用事物或行动对人或事表示怀念 to commemorate [纪元] 纪年的开始，如公历以传说的耶稣出生那一年为元年 beginning of an era ❷古时把十二年算作一纪 (ancient) twelve years [世纪] 一百年叫一世纪 century ❸制度，法度 discipline：军～*military discipline*｜违法乱～*break the law and violate discipline*｜～律 *discipline* ❹地质年代分期的第三级，在"代"之下 period (the subdivision of era in geological time scale)：第四～*Quaternary Period*｜侏罗～*Jurassic Period*

⇨ see also jǐ on p.289

忌 jì ㄐㄧˋ ❶嫉妒，憎恨 be jealous and resentful：猜～*be suspicious and resentful*｜～才 *be jealous of talented people* ❷怕，畏惧 to fear：顾～*have scruples*｜肆无～惮 *unscrupulous* ❸禁戒 abstain from：～酒 *stop drinking*｜～口 *avoid certain food*｜～食生冷 *avoid cold or uncooked food*｜～讳 *treat as a taboo; to avoid; taboo*

跽 jì ㄐㄧˋ 长跪，挺直上身两膝着地 to kneel with one's upper body erect

伎 jì ㄐㄧˋ ❶技巧，才能 skill [伎俩]（-liǎng）手段，花招 ploy ❷古代称以歌舞为业的女子 (ancient) professional female singer or dancer：歌舞～*professional female singer or dancer*

技 jì ㄐㄧˋ 才能，手艺（㊥-艺、-能）skill：～巧 *skill*｜口～*vocal mimicry*｜～师 *technician*｜一～之长 *professional skill* [技术] 1 进行物质资料生产所凭借的方法、能力或设备等 technology：～革新 *technical innovation* 2 专门的技能 expertise：他打球的～很高明。*He is an excellent ball game player.*

芰 jì ㄐㄧˋ 古书上指菱 water caltrop (in ancient Chinese texts)

妓 jì ㄐㄧˋ 妓女，以卖淫为生的女人 prostitute

系(繫) jì ㄐㄧˋ 打结，扣 to tie：把鞋带～上 *tie shoelaces*

⇨ see also xì on p.701

际(際) jì ㄐㄧˋ ❶交界或靠边的地方 border：林～*edge of the forest*｜水～*waterside*｜天～*horizon*｜春夏之～*in late spring and early summer* ❷彼此之间 between：国～*international*｜厂～竞赛 *competition between factories* ❸时候 moment：目前正是用人之～。*Talent is in short supply at the moment.* ❹

当，适逢其时 on the occasion of：～此盛会 *on this grand occasion*

季 jì ㄐㄧˋ ❶兄弟排行，有时用伯、仲、叔、季做次序，季是最小的 youngest among brothers (伯，仲，叔 and 季 are often used to indicate birth order)：～弟 *little brother* | ～父（小叔叔）*youngest paternal uncle* ⓘ末了 last period：～世 *end period* | ～春（春季末一月）*last month of spring (i.e. the third month in lunar calender)* ❷三个月为一季 season：一年分春、夏、秋、冬四～。*There are four seasons in a year: spring, summer, autumn and winter.* | ～度 *quarter* ⓘ（一儿）一段时间 period of time：瓜～儿 *melon season* | 淡～ *off-season* | 雨～ *rainy season*

悸 jì ㄐㄧˋ 因害怕而心跳 to palpitate：～栗（心惊肉跳）*palpitate with terror* | 惊～ *to palpitate* | 心有余～ *one's heart is still pounding (at the memory of a terrifying experience)*

剂（劑） jì ㄐㄧˋ ❶配合而成的药 medical preparation：药～ *pharmaceutical preparation* | 清凉～ *freshener* [调剂]（tiáo－）1 配制药物 make up a prescription 2 适当调整 to adjust ❷量词，用于水煎服的中药 (measure word for concoctions of herbal medicine) dose：一～药 *a dose of medicine*

荠（薺） jì ㄐㄧˋ 荠菜，草本植物，叶羽状分裂，花白色。茎、叶嫩时可用作蔬菜，全草可入药 shepherd's purse

⇨ see also qí on p.517

济（濟） jì ㄐㄧˋ ❶对困苦的人加以帮助 to provide relief for：救～ *provide relief for* | ～困扶危 *come to the rescue of those in need and peril* ❷补益 to benefit：无～于事 *to be of no avail* ❸渡，过河 to cross (a river)：同舟共～ *be in the same boat*

⇨ see also jǐ on p.290

霁（霽） jì ㄐㄧˋ ❶雨、雪停止，天放晴 (of rain or snow) clear up：雪初～。*The sky has cleared after the snow.* ❷怒气消除 (of anger) to subside：色～ *calm down*

鲚（鱭） jì ㄐㄧˋ 鱼名，身体侧扁，头小而尖，尾尖而细。生活在海洋里。有刀鲚、凤鲚等多种 grenadier anchovy

垍 jì ㄐㄧˋ 坚土 hard clod

洎 jì ㄐㄧˋ 到，及 up till：自古～今 *from ancient times to the present*

迹（*跡、*蹟） jì ㄐㄧˋ 脚印(㊀踪－) footprint：足～ *footprint* | 兽蹄鸟～ *footprints of all types of animals* ⓘ①物体遗留下的印痕（㊀痕－）trace：～象 *indication* | 事～ *deed* | 轨～ *trajectory; track* ②前人遗留下的事物（多指建筑、器物等）remains：古～ *place of historical interest* | 陈～ *thing of the past*

既 jì ㄐㄧˋ ❶终了，尽 to finish：言未～ *before one can finish speaking* ❷副词，已经 (adverb) already：霜露～降 *after the onset of frost* | ～往不咎 *forgive and forget* | 保持～有的荣誉 *retain one's laurels* [既而] 连词，后来，表示经过一段时间以后 (conjunction) then：起初不信，～将信将疑，最后完全折服 *refusing to believe first, then half believing and half doubting, but totally convinced in the end* ❸连词，既然，后面常与"就""则"相应，表示先提出前提，而后加以推论 (conjunction) since (often followed by 就 or 则 to indicate reasoning)：～要做，就要做好。*If you are going to do it, do it well.* ❹副词，常跟"且""又"连用，表示两者并列 (adverb) often used with 且 or 又 to indicate coordination：～高且大 *big and tall* | ～快又好 *fast and good*

塈 jì ㄐㄧˋ ❶用泥涂屋顶 to plaster (a roof) with mud ❷休息 to rest ❸取 to fetch

暨 jì ㄐㄧˋ 与，及，和 and

鱀(鱭) jì ㄐㄧˋ [白鱀豚] 哺乳动物，又叫白鳍豚，身体纺锤形，上部浅蓝灰色，下部白色，有背鳍。生活在淡水中，是我国特有的珍贵动物 Yangtze River dolphin (also called 白鳍豚)

勣(勣) jì ㄐㄧˋ 用于人名 used in given names

⇨ 勣 see also 绩 on p. 293

绩(績、❷△*勣) jì ㄐㄧˋ ❶把麻搓(cuō)捻成线或绳 to twist hempen thread：纺～ *twist hempen thread* ❷功业，成果 achievement：成～ *result* | 战～ *military exploits* | 功～ *contribution and achievement*

⇨ 勣 see also 勣 on p.293

觊(覬) jì ㄐㄧˋ 希望，希图 to covet [觊觎] (－yú) 非分地希望或企图 to covet

继(繼) jì ㄐㄧˋ 连续，接着 (㊀－续) to continue：～任 *succeed someone (as sth)* | ～往开来 *carry forward a cause and forge ahead into the future* | 前仆后～。*As one man falls, another steps into the breach.* [继承] 1 接受遗产 to inherit (sth from someone deceased) 2 继续前人的事业 to carry on (a cause)

偈 jì ㄐㄧˋ 佛经中的唱词 (in Buddhism) gatha (metrical chant)

⇨ see also jié on p.318

徛 jì ㄐㄧˋ 〈方 dialect〉站立 to stand

寄 jì ㄐㄧˋ ❶托付，寄托 to entrust：～放 *leave (sth somewhere or with sb)* | ～希望于未来 *pin one's hopes on the future* ❷依靠，依附 depend on：～居 *live far away from home or as a guest* | ～生 *lead a parasitic existence* | ～宿 *to lodge; (of students) to board* ❸托人传送，特指由邮局传递 to post：～信 *send a letter* | ～钱 *remit money* | ～包裹 *send a parcel*

J

by post

祭 jì ㄐㄧˋ ❶对死者表示追悼、敬意（㊥—奠）to hold a memorial ceremony for：公～烈士 *hold a memorial ceremony for the martyrs* ❷用供品供奉祖宗或鬼神等（㊥—祀）to make sacrificial offerings to：～神 *offer sacrifices to gods* | ～天 *worship Heaven*

漈 jì ㄐㄧˋ ❶水边 waterside ❷用于地名 used in place names：大～（在浙江省景宁）*Daji (in Jingning, Zhejiang Province)*

穄 jì ㄐㄧˋ （—子）一种谷物，又叫糜（méi）子，跟黍子相似，但不黏 non-glutinous proso millet (also called 糜 méi 子)

鰶（鰶） jì ㄐㄧˋ 鱼名，身体侧扁，长约 20 厘米，银灰色，生活在海里 gizzard shad

寂 jì ㄐㄧˋ 静，没有声音（㊥—静）silent：～然无声 *absolutely silent*［寂寞］（—mò）清静，孤独 lonely

惎 jì ㄐㄧˋ ❶毒害 to poison ❷忌恨 be jealous and resentful

蓟（薊） jì ㄐㄧˋ 草本植物，茎多刺，花紫色，可入药 Japanese thistle

稷 jì ㄐㄧˋ ❶古代一种粮食作物，有的书说是黍属，有的书说是粟（谷子）(ancient) non-glutinous millet ❷古代以稷为百谷之长，因此帝王奉祀为谷神 (ancient) god of grains［社稷］土神和谷神 god of the earth and god of grains ㊕古代指国家 (ancient) country：捍卫～ *defend one's country* | 以～为重 *put the country first*

鲫（鯽） jì ㄐㄧˋ 鱼名，像鲤鱼，没有须，背脊隆起，生活在淡水中 crucian carp

髻 jì ㄐㄧˋ 梳在头顶或脑后的发结（fàjié）bun (hairstyle)：发～ *bun* | 高～ *high bun*

冀 jì ㄐㄧˋ ❶希望（㊥希—）to hope：～其成功 *hope it will be successful* ❷河北省的别称 another name for Hebei Province

骥（驥） jì ㄐㄧˋ 好马 thoroughbred horse：按图索～ *stick rigidly to regulations; search by following clues*

罽 jì ㄐㄧˋ 用毛做成的毡子一类的东西 felt

濈 jì ㄐㄧˋ 泉水涌出的样子 (of a spring) gushing

檵 jì ㄐㄧˋ 檵木，常绿灌木或小乔木，叶椭圆形，花淡黄色。枝叶可提制栲胶，种子可榨油，叶可入药 Chinese witch hazel

JIA ㄐㄧㄚ

加 jiā ㄐㄧㄚ ❶增多，几种事物合起来（㊥增—）to add; to increase：～价 *raise prices* | 三个数相～ *add three numbers together*［加工］把原料制成成品或使粗制物品精良 to process［加油儿］㊗努力，加劲儿 make an all-out effort ❷施以某种动作 used to introduce an action：希～注意。*Please take note.* | ～以保护 *put sth under protection* ❸把本来没有的添上去（㊥添—）to add：～上

J

引号 *put quotation marks*

伽 jiā ㄐㄧㄚ ［伽倻］（—yē）伽倻琴，朝鲜族弦乐器 gayageum (string instrument used by Korean ethnic group)［伽利略］意大利天文学家、物理学家 Galileo (Galilei)

⇨ see also gā on p.193, qié on p.535

茄 jiā ㄐㄧㄚ 〈古 ancient〉荷茎 stem of a lotus flower
［雪茄］（外 *loanword*）一种较粗较长用烟叶卷成的卷烟 cigar

⇨ see also qié on p.535

迦 jiā ㄐㄧㄚ 迦河，水名，分东迦、西迦两支，均源于山东省，至江苏省汇合，流入大运河 Jiahe River

迦 jiā ㄐㄧㄚ 译音用字 used in transliteration

珈 jiā ㄐㄧㄚ 古代妇女的一种首饰 (ancient) ornament for women

枷 jiā ㄐㄧㄚ 旧时一种套在脖子上的刑具 (old) cangue［枷锁］喻束缚人的习俗、观念、制度等 fetter：砸碎封建～ *throw off the yoke of feudalism*

痂 jiā ㄐㄧㄚ 伤口或疮口表面血液、淋巴液等凝结成的东西 crust

笳 jiā ㄐㄧㄚ 胡笳，我国古代北方民族的一种乐器，类似笛子 (ancient) flute-like instrument (of northern nomadic tribes)

袈 jiā ㄐㄧㄚ ［袈裟］（—shā）和尚披在外面的一种法衣 (in Buddhism) kasaya (the monk's robe)

跏 jiā ㄐㄧㄚ ［跏趺］（—fū）佛教徒的一种坐姿 (in Buddhism) crossed-legged sitting posture

嘉 jiā ㄐㄧㄚ ❶美好 good：～宾 *distinguished guest* ❷赞美 to praise：～许 *approve of*｜精神可～。*The spirit is commendable.*

夹（夾） jiā ㄐㄧㄚ ❶从东西的两旁钳住 to press from both sides：～菜 *pick up food with chopsticks*｜用镊（niè）子～邮票 *pick up stamps with a pair of tweezers* 引①处在两者之间，两旁有东西限制住 to be between：书里～着一张纸。*There is a piece of paper between the pages of the book.*｜～道 *narrow lane; line up on both sides of the road*｜两山～一水。*The river flows between the mountains.* ②从两面来的 from two sides：～攻 *attack from two sides* ❷胳膊向胁部用力，使腋下放着的东西不掉下 carry under one's arm：～着书包 *carry one's schoolbag under one's arm* ❸掺杂（连—杂）to mix：～七杂八 *incoherent (in speaking)*｜～生 *not fully cooked* ❹（—子、—儿）夹东西的器具 clip; binder：文件～ *(document) folder*｜皮～儿 *leather wallet*

⇨ see also gā on p.193, jiá on p.296

浃（浹） jiā ㄐㄧㄚ 湿透，遍及 to be soaked：汗流～背 *be drenched in sweat*

梜（梜） jiā ㄐㄧㄚ 〈古 ancient〉❶护书的夹板 book

casing ❷筷子 chopsticks

佳 jiā ㄐㄧㄚ 美，好的 good：～音（好消息）*good news*｜～句 *beautiful line*｜～作 *excellent work*

家（❶傢） jiā ㄐㄧㄚ ❶家庭，人家 family：勤俭持～ *manage one's household with thrift and industry*｜张～有五口人。*The Zhangs are a family of five.* 谦辞，用于对别人称自己亲属中比自己年纪大或辈分高的 (humble speech) used to refer to one's more senior family members：～兄 *my older brother*｜～父 *my father* (傢 is the elaborate form of 家 in 家伙，家具 and 家什.)［家常］家庭日常生活 daily family life：～便饭 *simple meal; home cooking*｜叙～ *chat idly*［家畜］（-chù）由人喂养的兽类，如马、牛、羊、狗、猪等 livestock［家伙］（-huo）1 一般的用具、工具 tool 2 指武器 weapon 3 指牲畜或人（轻视或玩笑）farm animal; rogue (contemptuous or humorous)［家具］家庭用具，主要指床、柜、桌、椅等 furniture［家什］（-shi）用具，器物 furniture; utensil：厨房里的～擦洗得干干净净。*The kitchen utensils were scrubbed spotless.* ❷ 家庭的住所 home：回～ *go home*｜这儿就是我的～。*This is my home.* ❸指经营某种行业或有某种身份的人家 family in a certain trade or of a certain status：农～ *farmer*｜酒～ *pub* ❹掌握某种专门学识或有丰富实践经验以及从事某种专门活动的人 specialist：科学～ *scientist*｜水稻专～ *expert in rice growing*｜政治～ *politician*｜阴谋～ *schemer* ❺学术流派 school (of thought)：儒～ *Confucian School*｜道～ *Daoist School*｜百～争鸣。*One hundred schools of thought contend with each other.* ❻指相对各方中的一方 side：对～ *partner; the other party in a proposed marriage*｜上～ *(in a game) sb who precedes one in play; supplier*｜下～ *(in a game) sb next in turn to play; client* ❼（jia）词尾，指一类的人（多按年龄或性别分）(suffix) used to refer to a certain type of people, usually based on age group or gender：孩子～ *children*｜姑娘～ *girls* ❽量词，用于家庭或企业 (measure word) used for a family or a business：一～人家 *a family*｜两～饭馆 *two restaurants*

⇨ see also jie on p.321

镓（鎵） jiā ㄐㄧㄚ 金属元素，符号 Ga，银白色，质软，可用来制半导体和光学玻璃等 gallium (Ga)

葭 jiā ㄐㄧㄚ 初生的芦苇 young reed shoot

［葭莩］（-fú）苇子里的薄膜 membrane inside a reed stem ⓨ 关系疏远的亲戚 distant relative

豭 jiā ㄐㄧㄚ 公猪 boar

夹（夾、*裌、△*袷） jiá ㄐㄧㄚˊ 两层的（衣被等）double-layered (clothing or beddings,

J

etc.)：～裤 *lined trousers* | ～被 *lined quilt*

⇨ see also gā on p.193, jiā on p.295

⇨ 袷 see also qiā on p.524

郏(郟) jiá ㄐㄧㄚˊ 郏县，在河南省 Jiaxian (in Henan Province)

荚(莢) jiá ㄐㄧㄚˊ 豆类植物的长形的果实 pod：豆～（豆角）*bean pod* | 皂～ *Chinese honey locust* | 槐树～ *black locust legume*

铗(鋏) jiá ㄐㄧㄚˊ ❶冶铸用的钳 furnace tongs ❷剑 sword ❸剑柄 hilt

颊(頰) jiá ㄐㄧㄚˊ 脸的两侧 cheek：两～绯红。*Both cheeks are red.* (see picture of 头 on page 660)

蛱(蛺) jiá ㄐㄧㄚˊ ［蛱蝶］(— dié) 蝴蝶的一类，翅有鲜艳的色斑，前足退化或短小，触角锤状 checkerspots

恝 jiá ㄐㄧㄚˊ 无忧愁，淡然 carefree［恝置］不在意，置之不理 to ignore

戛(*戞) jiá ㄐㄧㄚˊ 打击 to knock lightly：～齿（上下齿叩击）*click one's teeth*

［戛然］1 形容嘹亮的鸟鸣声 (of bird cries) loud：～长鸣 *loud squawk* 2 形容声音突然中止 (of sound) stopping abruptly：鼓声～而止。*The drumming suddenly stopped.*

［戛戛］形容困难 difficult：～乎难哉！*How difficult it is!*

⇨ see also gā on p.193

甲 jiǎ ㄐㄧㄚˇ ❶天干的第一位，用作顺序的第一 *jia* (the first of the ten Heavenly Stems, a system used in the Chinese calendar); first：～等 *first rate* ㊀居首位，超过所有其他的 to top：桂林山水～天下。*Guilin's scenery is without equal anywhere in the world.*［甲子］我国纪日、纪年或计算岁数的一种方法，把十干和十二支按顺序配合，六十组干支字轮一周叫一个甲子 *Jiazi* (cycle of sixty years in traditional Chinese chronology) ❷古代军人打仗穿的护身衣服，用皮革或金属做成 (ancient) armour：盔～ *armour* ❸动物身上有保护功能的硬壳 shell：龟～ *tortoise shell* | ～虫 *beetle* | ～骨文 *oracle bone inscription* ❹手指或脚趾上的角质硬壳 nail：指～ *finger nail* ❺现代用金属做成的有保护功用的装备 armour (protective equipment made of metal)：装～汽车 *armoured vehicle* ❻旧时户口的一种编制 (old) unit of civil administration (see 保 ❸ on page 22 for reference)

岬 jiǎ ㄐㄧㄚˇ ❶岬角，突入海中的尖形的陆地，多用于地名 headland (often in place names)：野柳～（在台湾省台北）*Yeliujia Cape (in Taipei, Taiwan Province)* ❷两山之间 narrow pass between mountains

胛 jiǎ ㄐㄧㄚˇ 肩胛，肩膀后方的部位 scapula［肩胛骨］肩胛上部左右两块三角形的扁平骨头 scapula (see picture of 人体骨

骼 on page 220)

钾(鉀) jiǎ ㄐㄧㄚˇ 金属元素，符号K，银白色，蜡状。它的化合物用途很广，有的是重要肥料 potassium (K)

贾(賈) jiǎ ㄐㄧㄚˇ ❶姓 (surname) Jia ❷古多用于人名 ancient, often used in given names

〈古 ancient〉 also same as 价(價)(jià)

⇨ see also gǔ on p.220

槚(檟) jiǎ ㄐㄧㄚˇ ❶楸(qiū)树的别名 another name for Manchurian walnut ❷茶树的古名 ancient name for tea plant

假(❷△*叚) jiǎ ㄐㄧㄚˇ ❶不真实的，不是本来的，跟"真"相对 false (opposite of 真)：～发 *wig* | ～话 *lie* [假如] [假使] 连词，如果 (conjunction) if ❷借用，利用(㊥一借) make use of：～手于人 *use sb else for one's own ends* | ～公济私 *use public office for private gain* ❸据理推断，有待验证的 hypothetical：～设 *to suppose; hypothesis* | ～说 *hypothesis*

⇨ see also jià on p.299

⇨ 叚 see also xiá on p.703

嘏 jiǎ ㄐㄧㄚˇ (又) see gǔ on page 219

瘕 jiǎ ㄐㄧㄚˇ 肚子里结块的病 abdominal mass

斝 jiǎ ㄐㄧㄚˇ 古代一种盛酒的器皿 (ancient) a type of wine vessel

价(價) jià ㄐㄧㄚˋ 价钱，商品所值的钱数 price：～格 *price* | ～值 *value* | ～目 *marked price* | 物～ *price* | 减～ *cut the price*

⇨ see also jiè on p.319, jie on p.320

驾(駕) jià ㄐㄧㄚˋ ❶把车套在牲口身上 to harness：～辕 *pull (a cart or carriage) between the shafts* | ～轻就熟（喻做熟悉、容易的事）*handle sth with ease and familiarity* ❷古代车乘的总称。敬辞，称对方 (ancient) carriage; (polite speech) you：劳～。*Excuse me.* | 大～光临 *grace sb with one's presence* ❸特指帝王的车，借指帝王 (specifically) emperor's carriage; emperor：～崩（帝王死去）*(of an emperor) to die* ❹操纵，使开动 to operate：～飞机 *pilot a plane* | ～驶 *to drive* [驾驭]（-yù）驱使车马行进或停止 to drive ㊀管理，控制，支配 to control：～时局 *handle the current political situation* | 提高～语言的能力 *improve one's language skills*

架 jià ㄐㄧㄚˋ ❶(-子、-儿) 用作支承的东西 supporting framework：书～儿 *shelf* | 葡萄～ *grape trellis* | 笔～儿 *brush stand* | 房～子 *structural carcass (of a building)* | 车～子 *car frame* [担架] 医院或军队中抬送病人、伤员的用具 stretcher ❷支承 to support ①支撑，搭起 prop up; to erect：把枪～住 *mount a gun* | ～桥 *build a bridge* ②搀扶 to support by the arm：他受伤了，～着他走。*He is injured. Give him a hand*

J

and help him walk. ③ 抵挡，禁（jīn）受 fend off; to bear：招～ *to withstand* | 这么重的负担，他～得住吗？ *How can he possibly cope with such a heavy burden?* ❸用强力把人劫走 to kidnap：绑～ *to kidnap* | 被几个人～走了 *been strong-armed away by several people* ❹互相殴打或争吵的事 a fight：打了一～ *had a fight* | 劝～ *try to stop people fighting* ❺量词，多用于有机械或有支柱的东西 measure word for machinery or sth with a prop：五～飞机 *five planes* | 一～机器 *a machine* | 一～葡萄 *a trellis of grapes* [架次] 量词，一架飞机出动或出现一次叫一架次。如飞机出现三次，第一次五架，第二次十架，第三次十五架，共三十架次 (measure word) sortie

假 jià ㄐㄧㄚˋ 照规定或经过批准暂时离开工作、学习场所的时间 holiday; leave：放～ *be on holiday* | 寒～ *winter holiday* | ～期 *holiday* | 请～ *ask for leave*

⇨ see also jiǎ on p.298

嫁 jià ㄐㄧㄚˋ ❶女子到男方家成亲，也泛指女子结婚，跟"娶"相对 (of a woman) to marry (opposite of 娶)：出～ *(of a woman) get married* | ～娶 *to marry* [嫁接] 把要繁殖的植物的芽或枝接在另一种植物上，以达到提高品种质量等目的 to graft ❷把祸害、怨恨推到别人身上 to shift (sth bad or resentment, etc.)：转～ *to shift* | ～怨 *divert resentment away from oneself* | ～祸于人 *push disaster onto sb else*

稼 jià ㄐㄧㄚˋ 种田 to till [稼穑]（-sè）种谷和收谷，农事的总称 farm work [庄稼]（-jia）五谷，农作物 crops：种～ *grow crops*

JIAN ㄐㄧㄢ

戋（戔）jiān ㄐㄧㄢ 小，少㊣ small; few：所得～～ *be poorly rewarded*

浅（淺）jiān ㄐㄧㄢ [浅浅] 形容流水声 used to indicate the sound of flowing water

⇨ see also qiǎn on p.528

笺（箋、❷*牋、❷*椾）jiān ㄐㄧㄢ ❶注释 annotation ❷小幅的纸 small sheet of paper：便～ *memo pad* | 信～ *notepaper* ㊀书信 letter：华～ *your honourable letter*

溅（濺）jiān ㄐㄧㄢ [溅溅] same as "浅浅(jiān-)"

⇨ see also jiàn on p.305

钱（錢）jiān ㄐㄧㄢ 姓 (surname) Jian

尖 jiān ㄐㄧㄢ ❶（-儿）物体锐利的末端或细小的部分 sharp end：笔～儿 *nib* | 刀～儿 *knifepoint* | 针～儿 *needle tip* | 塔～儿 *pinnacle of a tower* [尖锐] 1 刺耳的 shrill：～的声音 *piercing sound* 2 锋利的，深刻的 incisive：～的批评 *scathing criticism* 3 激烈 intense：～的思想斗争 *intense mental struggle* | 矛盾～化 *inten-*

sification of conflict ❷末端极细小 (of the end) sharp：把铅笔削～了 *sharpened the pencil* ❸感觉锐敏 (of senses) sharp：眼～ *have a sharp eye* | 耳朵～ *have keen ears* ❹声音高而细 (of a sound) sharp：～声 ～气 *squeaking* ❺出类拔萃的人或物品 cream of the crop：～儿货 *(of sth) pick of the bunch* | ～子生 *top student*

奸(❸*姦) jiān ㄐㄧㄢ ❶虚伪，狡诈（㊥一狡、一诈）wily：～雄 *senior politician who advances their position through unscrupulous machinations* | ～笑 *give a sinister smile* | 不藏～，不耍滑 *exert oneself and never dodge work or responsibilities* ❷叛国的人 traitor：汉～ *traitor to the Chinese people* | 锄～ *eliminate traitors* [奸细] 替敌人刺探消息的人 spy ❸男女发生不正当的性行为 have an illicit sexual relationship：通～ *commit adultery* | ～污 *to rape or seduce*

歼(殲) jiān ㄐㄧㄢ 消灭（㊥一灭）to annihilate：围～ *surround and destroy* | 全～入侵之敌 *wipe out the enemy invaders*

坚(堅) jiān ㄐㄧㄢ ❶结实，硬，不容易破坏（㊥一固、一硬）hard; solid：～冰 *hard ice* | ～不可摧 *indestructible* ㊀不动摇 steadfast：～定 *steadfast; to make steadfast* | ～强 *strong; to make strong* | ～决 *resolute* | ～持 *to insist* | ～守 *stick to* [中坚] 骨干 mainstay：社会～ *pillar of society* | ～分子 *backbone* ❷坚固的东西或阵地 stronghold：攻～战 *storming of a fortified position* | 无～不摧 *invincible*

鲣(鰹) jiān ㄐㄧㄢ 鱼名，身体纺锤形，大部分无鳞，生活在海洋里 skipjack tuna

间(間、*閒) jiān ㄐㄧㄢ ❶中间，两段时间或两种事物相接的地方 middle：课～操 *setting-up exercises between classes* | 彼此～有差别。*There is a difference between them.* ❷在一定的地方、时间或人群的范围之内 in a certain place, time or group of people：田～ *field* | 晚～ *evening* | 人～ *this world* ❸房间，屋子 room：车～ *workshop* | 衣帽～ *cloakroom* | 卫生～ *toilet* ❹量词，用于房屋 measure word for rooms：一～房 *a room* | 广厦千～ *a good number of spacious rooms*

⇨ see also jiàn on p.304
⇨ 閒 see also jiàn 间 on p.304, xián 闲 on p.707

肩 jiān ㄐㄧㄢ ❶肩膀，脖子旁边胳膊上边的部分 shoulder：双～ *both shoulders* (see picture of 人体 on page 647) ❷担负 to shoulder：身～重任 *take on heavy responsibilities*

艰(艱) jiān ㄐㄧㄢ 困难（㊥一难）difficult; hard：～辛 *arduous* | ～苦 *hard* | 文字～深 *abstruse writing*

监(監) jiān ㄐㄧㄢ ❶督察 to supervise：～察 *to supervise (government officials)* |

～工 *to oversee; overseer* | ～考 *to invigilate; invigilator* ❷牢，狱(㊀一牢、一狱) prison：收～ *put in prison* | 探～ *visit a prisoner* [监禁] 把人押起来，限制他的自由 to imprison

⇨ see also jiàn on p.306

兼 jiān ㄐㄧㄢ ❶加倍，把两份并在一起 to double：～旬(二十天) *twenty days* | ～程(用加倍的速度赶路) *travel at twice the speed* | ～并 *to merger* ❷所涉及的或所具有的不只一方面 to double up as：～任 *serve concurrently as* | 德才～备 *have both talent and moral integrity*

搛 jiān ㄐㄧㄢ 用筷子夹 to pick up with chopsticks：～菜 *pick up food with chopsticks*

蒹 jiān ㄐㄧㄢ 没长(zhǎng)穗的芦苇 (young) spikeless reed

缣(縑) jiān ㄐㄧㄢ 多根丝线并在一起织成的丝织品 fine silk fabric

鹣(鶼) jiān ㄐㄧㄢ 鹣鹣，比翼鸟，古代传说中的一种鸟 (in Chinese legend) love birds

鳒(鰜) jiān ㄐㄧㄢ 鱼名，两只眼都在身体的一侧，有眼的一面黄褐色，无眼的一面白色，主要产于我国的南海 tropical halibut

菅 jiān ㄐㄧㄢ 草本植物，叶细长，根很坚韧，可做炊帚、刷子等 silky kangaroo grass [草菅] ㊇轻视 to belittle：～人命 *treat human life as if it was worth nothing*

渐(漸) jiān ㄐㄧㄢ ❶浸 to soak：～染 *be imperceptibly influenced by long exposure* ❷流入 to flow into：东～于海 *flow east into the sea*

⇨ see also jiàn on p.306

犍 jiān ㄐㄧㄢ 阉割过的公牛 ox; bullock

⇨ see also qián on p.528

鞬 jiān ㄐㄧㄢ 马上盛弓箭的器具 arrow quiver on horseback

湔 jiān ㄐㄧㄢ 洗 to wash

煎 jiān ㄐㄧㄢ ❶熬(áo) to simmer in water：～药 *decoct medicinal herbs* ❷把食物放在少量的热油里弄熟 to shallow fry：～鱼 *fry fish* | ～豆腐 *fry tofu* ❸量词，熬中药的次数 (measure word for the number of times of decocting herbal medicine) decoction：头～药 *first decoction* | 二～ *second decoction*

缄(緘) jiān ㄐㄧㄢ 封，闭 to seal：～口 *hold one's tongue* [缄默] 闭口不言 maintain silence

瑊 jiān ㄐㄧㄢ [瑊石] 一种像玉的美石 a type of jade-like stone

鞯(韉) jiān ㄐㄧㄢ 垫马鞍的东西 saddle pad：鞍～ *saddle with a blanket*

櫼 jiān ㄐㄧㄢ 木楔子(xiēzi) wooden wedge

囝 jiǎn ㄐㄧㄢˇ 〈方 dialect〉儿子 son

⇨ see also nān on p.469

J

拣(揀) jiǎn ㄐㄧㄢˇ ❶挑选(㊀挑一) to choose: ～好的苹果送给奶奶 *pick out some good apples and give them to granny* | 挑肥～瘦 *pick what is to one's personal advantage* ❷ same as "捡"

枧(梘) jiǎn ㄐㄧㄢˇ 〈方 dialect〉肥皂 soap: 香～ *toilet soap*

笕(筧) jiǎn ㄐㄧㄢˇ 横安在屋檐或田间引水的长竹管 bamboo water pipe

茧(繭、❶*蠒、❶絸)** jiǎn ㄐㄧㄢˇ ❶(一子、一儿)某些昆虫的幼虫在变成蛹之前吐丝做成的壳。家蚕的茧是缫(sāo)丝的原料 cocoon ❷手、脚上因摩擦而生的硬皮 callus: 老～ *callus* | 脚底磨出了～子 *have got calluses on the soles of one's feet from rubbing* 也作"趼"(also written as 趼)

柬 jiǎn ㄐㄧㄢˇ 信件、名片、帖子等的泛称 letter; card; note: 请～(请客的帖子) *invitation card*

暕 jiǎn ㄐㄧㄢˇ 明亮 bright

俭(儉) jiǎn ㄐㄧㄢˇ 节省,不浪费 thrifty: ～朴 *thrifty and simple* | 勤～ *industrious and frugal* | 省吃～用 *scrimp and save*

捡(撿) jiǎn ㄐㄧㄢˇ 拾取 to pick; to gather: ～柴 *gather firewood* | 把笔～起来 *pick up the pen* | ～了一张画片 *picked up an illustrated card*

检(檢) jiǎn ㄐㄧㄢˇ 查(㊀一查) to examine; to check: ～字 *look up a word in a dictionary* | ～验 *to test* | ～阅 *to inspect* | ～察 *investigate and check* | ～讨 *to self-examine* [检点] 1 仔细检查 check carefully 2 注意约束(言行) be discreet: 失于～ *be indiscreet* [检举] 告发坏人、坏事 inform on (an offender/offensive deed)

硷(鹼、*鹻) jiǎn ㄐㄧㄢˇ (old) same as "碱"

睑(瞼) jiǎn ㄐㄧㄢˇ 眼睑,眼皮 eyelid (see picture of 人的眼睛 on page 753)

趼 jiǎn ㄐㄧㄢˇ (一子) same as "茧"

减(*減) jiǎn ㄐㄧㄢˇ ❶由全体中去掉一部分 to subtract: ～价 *cut the price* | 三～二是一。*Three minus two is one.* ❷降低程度,衰退 to reduce; to decrease: ～肥 *lose weight* | ～灾 *alleviate natural disasters* | ～色 *(of an effect, etc.) to diminish* | 热情不～ *have undamped enthusiasm*

碱(*堿) jiǎn ㄐㄧㄢˇ ❶含有10个分子结晶水的碳酸钠,性滑,味涩 soda ❷化学上称能在水溶液中电离而生成氢氧根的化合物 alkali ❸被碱质侵蚀 to be corroded by alkali: 好好的罐子,怎么～了? *How come the nice pot has been corroded?* | 那堵墙全～了。*The wall was covered in alkali.*

J

剪 jiǎn ㄐㄧㄢˇ ❶（～子）剪刀，一种铰东西的用具 scissors ❷像剪子的器具 sth like scissors：火～ *fire tongs* | 夹～ *tweezers* ❸用剪子使东西断开 to cut with scissors：～断 *cut with a pair of scissors* | ～开 *cut open with scissors* [剪影] 按人影或物体的轮廓剪成的图形 paper-cut silhouette ⑩事物的一部分或概况 sketch ❹除掉 to eliminate：～灭 *wipe out* | ～除 *to exterminate*

谫（譾、**譾） jiǎn ㄐㄧㄢˇ 浅薄 superficial：学识～陋 *have little learning*

翦 jiǎn ㄐㄧㄢˇ ❶same as "剪" ❷姓 (surname) Jian

锏（鐧） jiǎn ㄐㄧㄢˇ 古代的一种兵器，像鞭，四棱 (ancient) four-sided heavy mace

⇨ see also jiàn on p.304

裥（襇） jiǎn ㄐㄧㄢˇ 衣服上打的褶子 pleat

简（簡） jiǎn ㄐㄧㄢˇ ❶古时用来写字的竹片或木片 (ancient) bamboo slip; wood slip ⑭书信 letter：书～ *letter* ❷简单，简化，跟"繁"相对 simple; simplify (opposite of 繁)：～写 *write Chinese characters in a simplified form* | 删繁就～ *prune (a piece of writing) to make it as concise as possible* | 精兵～政 *consolidate staffing and streamline administration* [简直] 副词，实在是，完全是 (adverb) simply; totally：你若不提这件事，我～就忘了。*It would have simply slipped from my mind if you hadn't mentioned it.* ❸简选，选择（人才）to select (a talent)：～拔 *to select*

戬 jiǎn ㄐㄧㄢˇ ❶剪除，剪灭 to wipe out ❷福 good fortune

蹇 jiǎn ㄐㄧㄢˇ ❶跛，行走困难 to limp; lame ❷迟钝，不顺利 retarded; difficulty：～涩 *(of writing) ponderous* | ～滞 *straitened* | 命运多～ *be ill-starred* ❸指驽马，也指驴 inferior horse; (also) donkey

謇 jiǎn ㄐㄧㄢˇ ❶口吃，言辞不顺畅 to stammer ❷正直 upright

瀽 jiǎn ㄐㄧㄢˇ 泼（水），倾倒（液体）to pour

见（見） jiàn ㄐㄧㄢˋ ❶看到 to see：眼～是实。*Seeing is believing.* ⑪接触，遇到 to come into contact with：这种病怕～风。*People with this illness should avoid exposure to wind.* | 胶卷不能～光。*Film should not be exposed to light.* ❷看得出，显现出 to seem; to appear：病已～好 *have started to recover from the illness* | ～分晓 *know the outcome* | ～效 *become effective* ❸（文字等）出现在某处，可参考 (of a text, etc.) to refer to; to see：～上 *see above* | ～下 *see below* | ～《史记·陈涉世家》*see* Records of the Grand Historian: The Hereditary Biography of Chen She ❹会见，会面 to meet (someone)：接～ *receive (someone)* | 看望多年未～的老战友 *visit a long-lost fellow soldier* ❺对于事物的看法

(㊥一识) view; opinion: ～地 *understanding* | 远～ *vision* | 固执己～ *arbitrary and stubborn* ❻助词 auxiliary word ①用在动词前面表示被动 used before a verb to form the passive voice: ～笑 *be ridiculed* | ～疑 *come under suspicion* ②用在动词前面表示对说话人怎么样 used before a verb to refer to sth done to the speaker: ～谅 *forgive me* | ～告 *keep me informed* | ～教 *instruct me* ❼用在"听""看""闻"等动词后，表示结果 used after verbs like 听, 看 and 闻 to indicate the result: 看～ *to see* | 听不～ *can not hear* ❽姓 (surname) Jian

⇨ see also xiàn on p.709

舰(艦) jiàn ㄐㄧㄢˋ 军舰，战船 warship: ～队 *fleet* | 巡洋～ *cruiser*

件 jiàn ㄐㄧㄢˋ ❶量词，用于个体事物 (measure word for individual objects) item: 一～事 *one thing* | 两～衣服 *two pieces of clothing* ❷(一儿) 指可以一一计算的事物 item: 零～儿 *parts* ❸指文书等 document: 文～ *file; document* | 来～ *post received*

牮 jiàn ㄐㄧㄢˋ ❶斜着支撑 to support with a slanting prop: 打～拨正(房屋倾斜，用柱子支起弄正) *support and right (a leaning building)* ❷用土石挡水 to hold back water with earth and stone

间(間、*閒) jiàn ㄐㄧㄢˋ ❶(一儿) 空隙 interspace; opening: 当～儿 *middle* ㊀嫌隙，隔阂 discord: 亲密无～ *(of people) inseparable* ❷不连接，隔开 separated; divided: ～断 *be interrupted* | ～隔 *interval* | 黑白相～ *black and white* | 晴～多云 *sunny with occasional cloud* [间或] 副词，偶尔 (adverb) occasionally: 他～也来一两次。*He would come over once in a while.* [间接] 通过第三者发生关系的，跟"直接"相对 indirect (opposite of 直接): ～经验 *indirect experience* ❸挑拨使人不和 to sow discord: 离～ *drive a wedge between* | 反～计 *scheme of sowing discord among one's enemies*

⇨ see also jiān on p.300

⇨ 閒 see also jiān 间 on p.300, xián 闲 on p.707

涧(澗) jiàn ㄐㄧㄢˋ 夹在两山间的水沟 mountain stream

锏(鐧) jiàn ㄐㄧㄢˋ 嵌在车轴上的铁条，可以保护车轴并减少摩擦力 iron protector for the axle

⇨ see also jiǎn on p.303

谫(譾) jiàn ㄐㄧㄢˋ [谫谫] 1 能言善辩 eloquent: ～之辞 *eloquent words* 2 浅薄 superficial: ～俗子 *shallow vulgar person*

饯(餞) jiàn ㄐㄧㄢˋ ❶饯行，饯别，设酒食送行 to give a farewell dinner ❷用蜜或糖浸渍(果品) to preserve (fruit) in honey or sugar: 蜜～ *preserved fruit*

贱(賤) jiàn ㄐㄧㄢˋ ❶价钱低，跟“贵”相对 cheap (opposite of 贵)：这布真～。*The cloth is really cheap.* ❷指地位卑下，跟“贵”相对(㊀卑－) lowly (opposite of 贵)：贫～ *poor and lowly* 谦辞，称有关自己的事物 (polite) used to refer to things related to oneself：～姓 *my humble family name* | ～恙 *my illness* ❸卑鄙 despicable：下～ *base*

践(踐) jiàn ㄐㄧㄢˋ ❶踩，踏(㊀－踏) to step on; to trample ❷履行，实行 to carry out; to fulfil：～约 *keep a promise* | ～言 *keep one's word* | 实～ *put into practice*

溅(濺) jiàn ㄐㄧㄢˋ 液体受冲激向四外飞射 to splash：～了一脸水。*One's face was splattered with water.* | 水花四～。*Water splashed in all directions.*

⇨ see also jiān on p.299

建 jiàn ㄐㄧㄢˋ 立，设立，成立(㊀－立) to establish：八一～军节 *1st August, the People's Liberation Army Day* | ～都 *make (a place) the capital* | ～筑 *to build; building* | ～设 *to construct* [建议] 向有关方面提出建设性的意见 to propose

健 jiàn ㄐㄧㄢˋ ❶强壮，身体好(㊀－康、强－) (of people) strong; healthy：～儿 *strong and vigorous person* | ～步 *vigorous strides* | 保～ *maintain health* [健全] 1（身体）健康而无缺陷 (physically) healthy 2（组织、制度等）完备无缺欠或使完备 (of an organization, system, etc.) perfect; to perfect：制度很～ *have a sophisticated system in place* | ～组织 *improve the organization* ❷善于 to be good at：～谈 *talkative* [健忘] 容易忘，记忆力不强 forgetful

楗 jiàn ㄐㄧㄢˋ 竖插在门闩上使门拨不开的木棍 wooden catch (for a door bolt)

毽 jiàn ㄐㄧㄢˋ （－子、－儿）一种用脚踢的玩具，多用布等把铜钱或金属片包扎好，装上鸡毛做成 shuttlecock

腱 jiàn ㄐㄧㄢˋ 肌腱，连接肌肉和骨骼的一种组织，白色，质地坚韧 tendon

键(鍵) jiàn ㄐㄧㄢˋ ❶即辖，车轴头上穿着的铁棍，可使轮不脱落 linchpin (same as 辖) ❷机器上钢制的长方形零件，用来连接并固定轴和齿轮等 shaft key ❸插在门上关锁门户的金属棍子 (of a door) metal bolt [关键] ㊕事物的紧要部分，对于情势有决定作用的部分 (of things) key ❹某些乐器或机器上使用时按动的部分 (of a musical instrument or machine) key：～盘 *keyboard*

踺 jiàn ㄐㄧㄢˋ 踺子（－zi），体操运动等的一种翻身动作 somersault

荐(薦) jiàn ㄐㄧㄢˋ ❶推举，介绍(㊀举－、推－) to recommend：～人 *recommend people* | 毛遂自～ *put oneself for-*

ward ❷草，又指草席 grass; (also) grass mat

剑(劍、*劒) jiàn ㄐㄧㄢˋ 古代的一种兵器，长条形，两面有刃，安有短柄 sword

监(監) jiàn ㄐㄧㄢˋ ❶帝王时代的官名或官府名 imperial office (or bureau)：太～ *eunuch* | 国子～ *State Academy Directorate* | 钦天～（掌管天文历法的官府）*Astronomical Bureau* ❷姓 (surname) Jian

⇨ see also jiān on p.300

槛(檻) jiàn ㄐㄧㄢˋ ❶栏杆 balustrade ❷圈（juān）兽类的栅栏 cage

⇨ see also kǎn on p.350

鉴(鑒、*鑑、*鍳) jiàn ㄐㄧㄢˋ ❶镜子 mirror 引可以作为警戒或引为教训的事 warning：前车之覆，后车之～。*An overturned cart ahead should be a warning to those behind.* | 引以为～ *take as a warning* [鉴戒] 可以使人警惕的事情 warning ❷照 to mirror：光可～人 *as shiny and glossy as a mirror* ❸观看，审察 to scrutinize：～定 *to appraise; evaluation* | ～赏 *to appreciate* | ～别 *to distinguish; to discern* | 某某先生台～（书信用语）*Dear Mr so-and-so, may I draw your attention to... (used in letter writing)* [鉴于] 看到，觉察到 considering：～旧的工作方法不能适应需要，于是创造了新的工作方法。*The old methods were no longer adequate and as a result, new methods were developed.*

渐(漸) jiàn ㄐㄧㄢˋ 副词，慢慢地，一点一点地 ⑧ (adverb) gradually：循序～进 *progress step by step* | ～入佳境 *become better and better* | 他的病～～好了。*Gradually, he is recovering from his illness.*

⇨ see also jiān on p.301

谏(諫) jiàn ㄐㄧㄢˋ 旧时称规劝君主、尊长，使改正错误 (old) to remonstrate (with an emperor or one's senior)

僭 jiàn ㄐㄧㄢˋ 超越本分，古时指地位在下的冒用在上的名义或礼仪、器物等 to transgress (one's place)：～越 *transgress one's place*

箭 jiàn ㄐㄧㄢˋ ❶用弓发射到远处的兵器，箭杆前端装有金属尖头 arrow ❷形状或功能像箭的东西 sth like an arrow (in shape or in function)：令～ *flag used as a symbol of military orders in ancient China* | 火～ *rocket*

JIANG ㄐㄧㄤ

江 jiāng ㄐㄧㄤ ❶大河的通称 river：黑龙～ *Heilongjiang River* | 珠～ *Pearl River* | 雅鲁藏布～ *Yarlung Tsangpo River* ❷专指长江，我国最大的河流，发源于青海省，流入东海 Yangtze River

茳 jiāng ㄐㄧㄤ [茳芏]（－dù）草本植物，茎三棱形，可用来编席 *Cyperus malaccensis*

J

豇 jiāng ㄐㄧㄤ ［豇豆］草本植物，果实为长荚，嫩荚和种子都可用作蔬菜 cowpea

将（將） jiāng ㄐㄧㄤ ❶副词，将要，快要 (adverb) about to：天～明。*Dawn is breaking.*｜后日～返京 *will return to Beijing the day after tomorrow* ❷介词，把 (preposition) used to introduce an object：～革命进行到底 *carry the revolution through to its end* ❸下象棋时攻击对方的“将”或“帅” (in Chinese chess) to check：～军（也比喻使人为难）*to check; (figurative) put sb on the spot* ❹用言语刺激 to provoke; dare sb：别把他～急了。*Stop teasing him. He'll get angry.* ❺带，领，扶助 to bring; to support：～雏 *bring one's young children*｜扶～ *support by the arm* ❻保养 to take care of one's health：～养 *rest and recuperate*｜～息 *rest and recuperate* ❼〈方 dialect〉兽类生子 (of animals) to give birth to：～驹 *give birth to a foal*｜～小猪 *give birth to piglets* ❽助词，用在动词和“出来”“起来”“上去”等的中间 (auxiliary word) used between a verb and words like 出来，起来，上去，etc.：走～出来 *walk out*｜叫～起来 *start screaming*｜赶～上去 *catch up* ❾姓 (surname) Jiang

［将就］（－jiu）勉强适应，凑合 to make do：～着用 *make do with sth*

⇨ see also jiàng on p.308

浆（漿） jiāng ㄐㄧㄤ ❶比较浓的液体 thick liquid：纸～ *(wood) pulp*｜豆～ *soy milk*｜泥～ *slurry* ❷用米汤或粉浆等浸润纱、布、衣服等，使干后发硬变挺 to starch (fabric)：～衣裳 *starch clothes*

⇨ see also jiàng on p.308

鳉（鱂） jiāng ㄐㄧㄤ 鱼名，头扁平，腹部突出，口小。生活在淡水中 *Atheriniformes*; silverside

姜（❶薑） jiāng ㄐㄧㄤ ❶草本植物，地下茎黄色，味辣，可供调味用，也可入药 ginger ❷姓 (surname) Jiang

僵（❶*殭） jiāng ㄐㄧㄤ ❶直挺挺，不灵活 stiff：～尸 *stiffened corpse*｜～硬 *stiff*｜手冻～了。*One's hands are numb with cold.* ❷双方相持不下，两种意见不能调和 deadlocked：闹～了 *have a strained relationship*｜～局 *stalemate*｜～持不下 *reach a deadlock*

缰（繮、*韁） jiāng ㄐㄧㄤ 缰绳，拴牲口的绳子 rein：信马由～ *keep a loose rein and let the horse go where it pleases; (figuratively) go with the flow*

礓 jiāng ㄐㄧㄤ ［砂礓］同“砂姜”，沙土中的不规则石灰质硬块，可用作建筑材料 (same as 砂姜) irregular lime concretions

［礓䃰儿］（－cār）台阶 step; stair

疆 jiāng ㄐㄧㄤ 边界，疆界 border：～土 *territory*｜～域 *territory*｜边～ *frontier* ⓘ界限 boundary：万寿无～ *live an infinitely long life* ［疆场］（－chǎng）战

J

场 battlefield [疆場] (—yì) 边界 field side; borderland

讲(講) jiǎng ㄐㄧㄤˇ ❶说，谈 to say; to talk: ～话 *to talk; to lecture* | 他对你～了没有？ *Has he told you?* ❷解释(㊥—解) to explain: ～书 *explain a text* | 这个字有三种～法。*This character has three meanings.* ❸谋求，顾到 to stress; pay attention to: ～卫生 *pay attention to hygiene* [讲究] (—jiu) 1 讲求，注重 to stress: ～质量 *put a premium on quality* 2 精美 exquisite: 这房子盖得真～。*This house is beautifully built.* 3 (—儿) 一定的方法或道理，惯例 convention; particular method: 写春联有写春联的～儿。*The writing of Spring Festival Couplets has its own conventions.* ❹商量 to discuss: ～价儿 *to bargain*

奖(獎、*奬) jiǎng ㄐㄧㄤˇ ❶奖励，夸奖(㊥褒—) to reward; to praise: ～状 *certificate (of distinction)* | ～金 *prize money* | ～给他一万元 *award him a prize of ten thousand yuan* ❷为了鼓励或表扬而给予的荣誉或财物等 prize; award: 得～ *win a prize* | 发～ *present an award* ❸指彩金 lottery prize: ～券 *lottery ticket* | 中～ *win a lottery prize*

桨(槳) jiǎng ㄐㄧㄤˇ 划船的用具，常装置在船的两旁 oar; paddle

蒋(蔣) jiǎng ㄐㄧㄤˇ 姓 (surname) Jiang

耩 jiǎng ㄐㄧㄤˇ 用耧播种(zhòng) to plough and sow: ～地 *plough and seed the field* | ～棉花 *plough and sow cotton seeds*

膙 jiǎng ㄐㄧㄤˇ (—子) 茧子 callus

匠 jiàng ㄐㄧㄤˋ ❶有专门手艺的人 craftsman: 木～ *carpenter* | 瓦～ *bricklayer* | 能工巧～ *masterful craftsman* ❷灵巧，巧妙 skilful: ～心 *ingenuity* ❸指在某方面有很深造诣的人 master: 文学巨～ *literary master*

降 jiàng ㄐㄧㄤˋ ❶下落，落下(㊥—落) to fall: ～雨 *rain* | 温度下～。*The temperature drops.* | ～落伞 *parachute* ❷使下落 to lower: ～级 *to relegate* | ～格 *lower a standard* | ～低物价 *reduce prices* ❸姓 (surname) Jiang

⇨ see also xiáng on p.713

洚 jiàng ㄐㄧㄤˋ 大水泛滥 to flood: ～水(洪水) *flood*

绛(絳) jiàng ㄐㄧㄤˋ 深红色 crimson

虹 jiàng ㄐㄧㄤˋ 义同"虹"(hóng)，限于单用 same in meaning as 虹 (hóng), used alone

⇨ see also hóng on p.254

将(將) jiàng ㄐㄧㄤˋ ❶军衔名，在校级之上 general [将领] 高级军官 high-ranking military officers ❷统率指挥 to command: ～兵 *command troops*

⇨ see also jiāng on p.307

浆(漿) jiàng ㄐㄧㄤˋ [浆糊] (—hu) same as "糨糊" [浆子] (—zi) same as "糨子"

⇨ see also jiāng on p.307

酱(醬) jiàng ㄐㄧㄤˋ ❶用发酵后的豆、麦等做成的一种调味品，有黄酱、甜面酱、豆瓣酱等 thick sauce (made from soy beans, flour, etc.) ❷用酱或酱油腌制 to preserve in sauce：把萝卜～一～ *pickle the mooli in soy sauce* ❸像酱的糊状食品 sauce：芝麻～ *sesame sauce* | 果～ *jam* | 虾～ *salted shrimp paste*

弶 jiàng ㄐㄧㄤˋ ❶一种捕捉鸟兽的工具 snare ❷用弶捕捉 to snare

强(*強、*彊) jiàng ㄐㄧㄤˋ ❶强(qiáng)硬不屈 unyielding：倔～ *unyielding* ❷固执己见，不服劝导 stubborn：你别～嘴。*Stop talking back.*

⇨ see also qiáng on p.531, qiǎng on p.532

犟(**勥) jiàng ㄐㄧㄤˋ same as "强(jiàng)"

糨(**糡) jiàng ㄐㄧㄤˋ 稠，浓 (of pastes, sauces, etc.) thick：粥太～了。*The rice porridge is too thick.* [糨糊](-hu) [糨子](-zi) 用面等做成的可以粘贴东西的糊状物品 paste; glue

JIAO ㄐㄧㄠ

艽 jiāo ㄐㄧㄠ [秦艽]草本植物，叶阔而长，花紫色，根可入药 large leaf gentian

交 jiāo ㄐㄧㄠ ❶付托，付给 to hand over：这事～给我办。*Leave the task to me.* | 货已经～齐了。*The goods have all been delivered.* [交代] 1 把经手的事务移交给接替的人 to hand over (one's work)：～工作 *hand over work to another person* 2 把事情或意见向有关的人说明 to explain：把事情～清楚 *explain the issue clearly* ❷相连，接合 to meet; to adjoin：～界 *be bounded (on sth)* | 目不～睫(jié) *not sleep a wink* | ～叉 *to intersect; to overlap* ㊀相交处 intersection：春夏之～ *at the turn of spring and summer* ❸互相来往联系 to contact; to befriend：结～ *make friends (with sb)* | ～朋友 *make friends* | ～流 *to exchange* | ～际 *to socialize* | ～涉 *to negotiate* | ～换 *to exchange* | ～易 *make a deal* | 打～道 *deal with sb* ❹交情，友谊 friendship：我和他没有深～。*I'm not close friends with him.* | 一面之～ *nodding acquaintance* ❺一齐，同时 simultaneously：风雨～加 *strong wind and driving rain* | 饥寒～迫 *be afflicted with hunger and cold* ❻ same as "跤(jiāo)"

郊 jiāo ㄐㄧㄠ 城外 suburb：西～ *western suburb* | 近～ *inner suburb* | 市～ *suburbs* | ～游 *go on an excursion*

茭 jiāo ㄐㄧㄠ [茭白]菰经黑粉菌寄生后膨大的嫩茎，可用作蔬菜 edible stem of the Machurian wild rice

峧 jiāo ㄐㄧㄠ 用于地名 used in place names：～头（在浙江省舟山市）*Jiaotou (in Zhoushan,*

Zhejiang Province)

姣 jiāo ㄐㄧㄠ 形容相貌美 beautiful：～好 *beautiful*

胶(膠) jiāo ㄐㄧㄠ ❶黏性物质，有用动物的皮、角等熬制成的，也有植物分泌的或人工合成的 glue; gum; adhesive：鹿角～ *deer-horn glue* | 鳔（biào）～ *isinglass* | 桃～ *peach gum* | 万能～ *contact adhesive* ❷指橡胶 rubber：～鞋 *rubber shoes* | ～皮 *rubber* ❸有黏性、像胶的 sticky; adhesive：～泥 *clay* ❹黏着，黏合 to stick with glue：～着状态 *stalemate* | ～柱鼓瑟（喻拘泥不知变通）*be stuck in a groove*

鸡(鵁) jiāo ㄐㄧㄠ [鸡鶄]（-jīng）古书上说的一种水鸟，腿长，头上有红毛冠 a type of waterbird in ancient Chinese texts

蛟 jiāo ㄐㄧㄠ 蛟龙，古代传说中能发洪水的一种龙 (in Chinese legend) flood dragon

跤 jiāo ㄐㄧㄠ 跟头（tou）fall; tumble：跌了一～ *had a fall* | 摔～ *have a fall*

鲛(鮫) jiāo ㄐㄧㄠ 鲨鱼 shark (see 鲨 shā on page 575)

浇(澆) jiāo ㄐㄧㄠ ❶灌溉 to irrigate; to water：～地 *irrigate the field* ❷淋 to spatter; to pour：～了一身水 *be drenched* ❸把液汁倒入模型 to cast; to mould：～版 *plate casting* | ～铸 *to cast* ❹刻薄（㊂-薄）mean; harsh

娇(嬌) jiāo ㄐㄧㄠ ❶美好可爱 delicate：～娆 *delicately beautiful* | ～小 *petite* ❷爱怜过甚 to pamper; to overindulge：～生惯养 *grow up pampered and spoiled* | 小孩子别太～了。*Don't spoil the child.* ❸脆弱，不坚强 (of people) feeble; fragile：～气 *frail*

骄(驕) jiāo ㄐㄧㄠ ❶自满，自高自大 proud; arrogant：戒～戒躁 *guard against arrogance and rashness* | ～兵必败。*Pride comes before a fall.* [骄傲] 1 自高自大，看不起别人 arrogant：～自满是一定要失败的。*Arrogance and complacency can only end in failure.* 2 自豪 proud (of sth)：我们为祖国的成就而～。*We are proud of our country's achievements.* | 光荣的历史传统是值得我们～的。*We should be proud of glorious historical traditions.* ❷猛烈 intense; fierce：～阳似火。*The scorching sun is beating down.*

教 jiāo ㄐㄧㄠ 传授 to teach：～书 *to teach* | 我～历史。*I'm a history teacher.* | 我～给你做。*Let me show you how to do it.*

⇨ see also jiào on p.313

椒 jiāo ㄐㄧㄠ 植物名 plant name ①花椒，落叶灌木，枝上有刺，果实红色，种子黑色，可供药用或调味 Chinese prickly ash ②胡椒，常绿灌木，种子味辛香，可供药用或调味 pepper ③番椒，辣椒，秦椒，草本植物，花白色，有的果实味辣，可用作蔬菜，又可供调味用 sweet pepper; chilli pepper

焦 jiāo ㄐㄧㄠ ❶火候过大或火力过猛，使东西烧成炭样 to burn; to be burned：饭烧～了。*The rice has been burned.* | 衣服烧～了。*The clothes are scorched.* | ～头烂额（形容十分狼狈）*be rushed off one's feet* ❷焦炭 coke：煤～ *coal* | 炼～ *coking* ❸酥，脆 crisp; crunchy：麻花炸得真～。*The fried dough twist is really crisp.* ❹着急，烦躁（㊀一躁）worried; agitated：心～ *worried* | ～急 *worried* | ～灼 *be racked with anxiety* ❺能量、功、热等单位名焦耳的简称，符号 J。joule (short for 焦耳, J)

僬 jiāo ㄐㄧㄠ ［僬侥］(－yáo）古代传说中的矮人 (in Chinese legend) dwarf

蕉 jiāo ㄐㄧㄠ 植物名 plant name ①香蕉，又叫甘蕉，形状像芭蕉，果实长形，稍弯，果肉软而甜 banana (also called 甘蕉) ② see 芭蕉 (bā－) at 芭 on page 10

燋 jiāo ㄐㄧㄠ〈古 ancient〉用来点火的引火物 tinder

礁 jiāo ㄐㄧㄠ 海洋或河湖里接近水面的岩石 reef: 暗～ *reef*

鹪(鷦) jiāo ㄐㄧㄠ ［鹪鹩］(－liáo）鸟名，又叫巧妇鸟，身体小，头部浅棕色，有黄色眉纹，尾短。做的窝很精巧 wren (also called 巧妇鸟)

矫(矯) jiáo ㄐㄧㄠˊ ［矫情］(－qing)〈方 dialect〉指强词夺理 (of people) unreasonable; contentious：瞎～ *be unreasonable*

⇨ see also jiǎo on p.312

嚼 jiáo ㄐㄧㄠˊ 用牙齿磨碎食物 to chew ［嚼舌］信口胡说，搬弄是非 to gossip

⇨ see also jiào on p.314, jué on p.344

角 jiǎo ㄐㄧㄠˇ ❶牛、羊、鹿等头上长出的坚硬的东西 horn; antler ❷形状像角的东西 sth like a horn：菱～ *water caltrop* | 皂～ *Chinese honeylocust* ❸几何学上指自一点引两条射线所成的形状 angle：直～ *right angle* | 锐～ *acute angle* ❹(－儿）物体边沿相接的地方 corner：桌子～儿 *corner of a desk* | 墙～儿 *corner of walls* ❺突入海中的尖形的陆地，多用于地名 headland (often used in place names)：成山～(在山东省荣成) *Chengshanjiao (in Rongcheng, Shandong Province)* ❻星宿名，二十八宿之一 *jiao* (one of the twenty-eight constellations in ancient Chinese astronomy) ❼货币单位，一圆钱的十分之一 *jiao* (currency unit, equal to 0.1 yuan) ❽量词，从整块划分成角形的 (measure word) wedge; triangle-shaped part：一～饼 *a slice of pancake*

⇨ see also jué on p.343

侥(僥、*儌) jiǎo ㄐㄧㄠˇ ［侥幸］(*儌倖）由于偶然的原因获得利益或免去不幸 by luck; by a fluke：～心理 *readiness to leave sth to chance* | ～赢了一个球 *be fortunate to win by one goal*

⇨ see also yáo on p.760

佼 jiǎo ㄐㄧㄠˇ 美好beautiful［佼佼］胜过一般的 outstanding：～者 *one that stands out*

狡 jiǎo ㄐㄧㄠˇ 狡猾，诡诈 wily; crafty：奸～ *sly*｜～辩 *make a specious argument*

饺(餃) jiǎo ㄐㄧㄠˇ （一子、一儿）包成半圆形的有馅的面食 *jiaozi*; dumpling

恔 jiǎo ㄐㄧㄠˇ 聪慧 intelligent

⇨ see also xiào on p.718

绞(絞) jiǎo ㄐㄧㄠˇ ❶拧，扭紧 to twist;to wring：～干毛巾 *wring out a towel* ❷用绳子把人勒死 to hang：～刑 *execution by hanging*｜～索 *hang man's noose* ❸量词，用于纱、毛线等 (measure word for yarn) skein：一～毛线 *a skein of woollen yarn*

铰(鉸) jiǎo ㄐㄧㄠˇ ❶用剪刀剪 to cut with scissors：把绳子～开 *cut the rope with scissors* ❷机械工业上的一种切削法，使工件上原有的孔提高精度 to ream：～孔 *ream (a hole)*｜～刀 *reamer*

皎 jiǎo ㄐㄧㄠˇ 洁白明亮㊀white and bright：～～白驹 *white foal*｜～洁的月亮 *bright silver moon*

挢(撟) jiǎo ㄐㄧㄠˇ ❶举，翘 to raise; to lift：舌～不下（形容惊讶得说不出话来）*dumbfounded* ❷纠正 to rectify：～邪防非 *prevent and rectify evil practices*

矫(矯) jiǎo ㄐㄧㄠˇ ❶纠正，把弯曲的弄直 to put right; to straighten out：～正 *rectify*｜～枉过正 *to overcorrect*｜～揉造作（喻故意做作）*affected and artificial*［矫情］故意违反常情，表示与众不同 to affect eccentricity ❷假托 to pretend; to counterfeit：～命 *forge an order* ❸强健，勇武（㊀一健）strong; valiant：～捷 *strong and agile* ❹(ancient) same as "挢"

⇨ see also jiáo on p.311

脚(*腳) jiǎo ㄐㄧㄠˇ ❶人和某些动物身体最下部接触地面的部分 (of human and some animals) foot (see picture of 人体 on page 647) ❷最下部 (of things) foot：山～ *foot of a mountain*｜墙～ *base of a wall*

⇨ see also jué on p.344

搅(攪) jiǎo ㄐㄧㄠˇ ❶扰乱（㊀一扰）to disturb; to upset：～乱 *throw into confusion*｜打～ *to disturb*｜不要胡～。*Don't mess around.* ❷拌 to stir：把锅～一～ *stir the food in the pot*｜～匀了 *stir well*

湫 jiǎo ㄐㄧㄠˇ 低洼 low-lying［湫隘］低湿狭小 low, wet and cramped

⇨ see also qiū on p.544

敫 jiǎo ㄐㄧㄠˇ 姓 (surname) Jiao

徼 jiǎo ㄐㄧㄠˇ ［徼倖］(old) same as "侥幸"

⇨ see also jiào on p.314

缴(繳) jiǎo ㄐㄧㄠˇ ❶交纳，交出（多指履行义务或被迫）to pay;to hand over (often when one has no option)：～税

J

pay tax | ～枪投降 *hand over one's gun and surrender* ❷迫使交出 to force to hand over (weapons): ～了敌人的械 *disarm the enemy*

⇨ see also zhuó on p.879

璬 jiǎo ㄐㄧㄠˇ 古书上说的一种玉佩 a type of ornamental jade piece in ancient Chinese texts

皦 jiǎo ㄐㄧㄠˇ ❶纯白，明亮 pure white; bright ❷清白，清晰 clear

剿（*勦、*勦）jiǎo ㄐㄧㄠˇ 讨伐，消灭 to quell; to suppress: ～匪 *stamp out bandits* | 围～ *surround and suppress*

⇨ see also chāo on p.71

叫（*呌）jiào ㄐㄧㄠˋ ❶呼喊（㊀—喊）to shout; to yell: 大～一声 *let out a yell* ❷动物发出声音 (of animals) to cry: 鸡～ *chicken crows* ❸称呼，称为 to name; to be called: 他～什么名字？*What is his name?* | 这～宇宙飞船。*This is called a spaceship.* ❹召唤 to call; to send for: ～他明天来 *ask him to come tomorrow* | 请你把他～来。*Please ask him to come over.* ❺使，令，让 to let; to make: 这件事应该～他知道。*He should be told about this.* | ～人不容易懂 *hard to understand* ❻介词，被（后面必须说出主动者）(preposition) used as a sign of passive voice and to introduce the doer of an action: 敌人～我们打得落花流水。*The enemy were heavily defeated by us.*

峤（嶠）jiào ㄐㄧㄠˋ 山道 mountain path

⇨ see also qiáo on p.533

轿（轎）jiào ㄐㄧㄠˋ （—子）旧式交通工具，由人抬着走 sedan chair

觉（覺）jiào ㄐㄧㄠˋ 睡眠 sleep

⇨ see also jué on p.343

校 jiào ㄐㄧㄠˋ ❶比较 to compare: ～场（旧时演习武术的地方）*(old) drill ground* ❷订正 to collate; to proofread: ～订 *to collate* | ～稿子 *proofread a manuscript*

⇨ see also xiào on p.718

较（較）jiào ㄐㄧㄠˋ ❶比（㊀比—）to compare: ～量 *have a contest* | 两者相～，截然不同。*The two are radically different when compared.* | 斤斤计～ *care too much about petty gains and losses* ㊁副词，表示对比着显得更进一层 (adverb) comparatively; relatively: 中国应当对于人类有～大的贡献。*China should make greater contributions to mankind.* | 成绩～好。*Results are relatively good.* ❷明显 obvious; manifest: 彰明～著 *manifest* | 两者～然不同。*The two are manifestly different.*

教 jiào ㄐㄧㄠˋ ❶指导，教诲（㊀—导）to teach: ～育 *to educate* | 施～ *to instruct* | 受～ *be instructed* | 指～ *to instruct* ❷使，令，让 to let; to make: 风能～船走。*Wind can propel boats.* | ～人为难 *put sb in a difficult situation*

J

❸宗教 religion：佛～ *Buddhism*|道～ *Taoism*|～会 *church* ❹姓 (surname) Jiao

➩ see also jiāo on p.310

滘 jiào ㄐㄧㄠˋ same as "滘"[东滘]地名，在广东省广州 Dongjiao (a place in Guangzhou, Guangdong Province)

酵 jiào ㄐㄧㄠˋ 发酵，有机物由于某些真菌或酶而分解，能使有机物发酵的真菌叫酵母菌 to ferment (the fungus that causes fermentation is called 酵母菌)

窖 jiào ㄐㄧㄠˋ ❶收藏东西的地洞 cellar：地～ *cellar*|白菜～ *cellar for storing Chinese cabbage* ❷把东西藏在窖里 to store in a cellar：～萝卜 *store mooli in a cellar*

滘 jiào ㄐㄧㄠˋ 〈方 dialect〉分支的河道，多用于地名 tributary (often used in place names)：双～（在广东省阳春）*Shuangjiao (in Yangchun, Guangdong Province)*|沙～（在广东省顺德）*Shajiao (in Shunde, Guangdong Province)*

斠 jiào ㄐㄧㄠˋ ❶古时平斗斛的器具 (ancient) strickle ❷校订 to collate

噍 jiào ㄐㄧㄠˋ 嚼，吃东西 to chew; to eat [倒噍]（dǎo－）same as "倒嚼" (see 嚼 jiào on page 314 for reference)

醮 jiào ㄐㄧㄠˋ ❶古代婚娶时用酒祭神的礼 (ancient) libation at a wedding ceremony：再～（再嫁）*(of a woman) remarry* ❷道士设坛祭神 (of a Taoist priest) to perform a sacrificial ritual：打～ *perform a sacrificial ritual*

徼 jiào ㄐㄧㄠˋ ❶边界 borderland ❷巡察 to patrol

➩ see also jiǎo on p.312

藠 jiào ㄐㄧㄠˋ （－子、－头）same as "薤 (xiè)"

嚼 jiào ㄐㄧㄠˋ [倒嚼]（dǎo－）反刍 (of an animal) to ruminate

➩ see also jiáo on p.311, jué on p.344

爝 jiào ㄐㄧㄠˋ（又）see jué on page 344

皭 jiào ㄐㄧㄠˋ 洁白，干净 pure-white; clean

JIE ㄐㄧㄝ

节(節) jiē ㄐㄧㄝ [节骨眼儿]（－gu－）〈方 dialect〉㖄紧要的、能起决定作用的环节或时机 critical link/juncture; vital moment

➩ see also jié on p.316

疖(癤) jiē ㄐㄧㄝ （－子）小疮 boil; furuncle

阶(階、*堦) jiē ㄐㄧㄝ 台阶，建筑物中为了便于上下，用砖、石等砌成的、分层的东西 (of buildings) step：～梯 *steps* (see picture of 房屋的构造 on page 170) ㊉①等级 rank; grade：军～ *military rank*|～级 *class*|～层 *social stratum* ②事物发展的段落 (in the process of development) stage：～段 *stage*

皆 jiē ㄐㄧㄝ 副词，全，都 (adverb) all：～大欢喜。*Every-*

one is happy. | 人人～知 *be known to all*

喈 jiē ㄐㄧㄝ ㊀ ①形容敲击钟、铃等的声音 used to describe the sound of bells, etc.: 钟鼓～～ *booming drums and bells* ② 形容鸟鸣声 (of birds) to chirp: 鸡鸣～～。*The hens and roosters are clucking and crowing.*

湝 jiē ㄐㄧㄝ ㊀形容水流动的样子 used to describe the flowing of water: 淮水～～。*The Huaihe River is flowing.*

楷 jiē ㄐㄧㄝ 楷树，落叶乔木，又叫黄连木，果实长圆形，红色，种子可榨油，木材黄色，可用来制器具 Chinese pistache (also called 黄连木)

⇨ see also kǎi on p.349

结(結) jiē ㄐㄧㄝ 植物长(zhǎng)(果实) to bear (fruit): 树上～了许多苹果。*The trees are laden with apples.* [结实] 1 植物长(zhǎng)果实 to fruit: 开花～ *to flower and bear fruit* 2 (－shi) 坚固耐用 (of sth) sturdy; solid: 这双鞋很～。*This is a very sturdy pair of shoes.* 3 (－shi) 健壮 (of people) strong: 他的身体很～。*He's very strong.*

⇨ see also jié on p.317

秸(*稭) jiē ㄐㄧㄝ 农作物去穗或脱粒后剩下的茎 grain stalk (after threshing): 麦～ *wheat straw* | 秫～ *sorghum stalk* | 豆～ *beanstalk*

接 jiē ㄐㄧㄝ ❶连接 to connect; to join: ～电线 *connect electrical wires* | ～纱头 *join thrums* ❷继续，连续 to continue: ～着往下讲 *go on talking* ❸接替 to take over (one's job or shift): 谁～你的班? *Who is taking over from you?* ❹接触，挨近 to contact: ～洽 *reach out and discuss* | 交头～耳 *whisper to each other* ❺收，取 to receive: ～到一封信 *receive a letter* | ～受 *to accept* | ～纳 *to admit (into an organization)* ❻迎 to meet: ～待 *to receive (sb)* | 到车站～人 *meet someone at the station* ❼托住，承受 to catch; to hold: ～球 *catch a ball* | 把包～住 *catch the bag*

痎 jiē ㄐㄧㄝ 古书上说的一种疟疾 a kind of malaria (in ancient Chinese texts)

揭 jiē ㄐㄧㄝ ❶把盖在上面的东西拿起或把黏合着的东西分开 to uncover; to tear off: ～锅盖 *lift the lid off a pot* | 把这张膏药～下来 *peel off the herbal plaster* ❷使隐瞒的事物显露 to expose: ～短 *expose one's shortcomings* | ～发 *to expose* | ～露 *to reveal* | ～穿阴谋 *uncover a plot* ❸高举 to raise: ～竿而起 (指民众起义) *rise up in arms; rise in rebellion*

嗟 jiē ㄐㄧㄝ 文言叹词 exclamation in classical Chinese: ～，来食! *Hey, come and eat!* | ～叹 *to sigh* | ～乎 *alas*

街 jiē ㄐㄧㄝ 两边有房屋的比较宽阔的道路，通常指开设商店的地方 street [街坊] (－fang) 邻居 neighbour

J

孑 jié ㄐㄧㄝˊ 单独，孤单 alone; lonely：～立 *isolated* | ～然一身 *all alone in this wide world*

节（節） jié ㄐㄧㄝˊ ❶（一儿）植物学上称茎上长叶的部位 node ❷（一儿）物体的分段或两段之间连接的地方 section; joint：骨～ *a joint* | 两～火车 *two railway coaches* ❸段落 paragraph; stage：季～ *season* | 时～ *time* | ～气 *solar term; one of the 24 seasonal devision points in traditional Chinese calendar* | 章～ *chapter* ❹节日，纪念日或庆祝的日子 festival：春～ *Spring Festival* | 清明～ *Tomb Sweeping Day* | 端午～ *Dragon Boat Festival* | 中秋～ *Mid-Autumn Festival* | 国庆～ *National Day* ❺礼度 formality：礼～ *courtesy* ❻音调高低缓急的限度 rhythm：～奏 *rhythm* | ～拍 *metre* ❼省减，限制（㊣一省、一约）to economize; to restrain：～制 *to restrain* | 开源～流 *open up new avenues of income and reduce expenditure* | ～衣缩食 *scrimp and save* ㊞扼要摘取 to excerpt：～录 *excerption* | ～译 *abridged translation* ❽操守（㊣一操）moral fibre：保持晚～ *maintain one's moral integrity in later years* | 守～（封建礼教称夫死不再嫁人）*not remarry after becoming a widow (in feudal times)* ❾事项 item; affair：情～ *plot; story line* | 细～ *detail* ❿古代出使外国所持的凭证 (ancient) tally (issued to an envoy as credentials) [使节] 派到外国的外交官员 diplomatic envoy ⓫航海速度单位，符号 kn，每小时航行 1 海里为 1 节 knot (kn)

⇨ see also jiē on p.314

讦（訐） jié ㄐㄧㄝˊ 揭发别人的阴私 expose sb's dirty secrets：攻～ *expose and attack sb's past misconduct*

劫（*刦、*刧、*刼） jié ㄐㄧㄝˊ ❶强取，掠夺（㊣抢一）to rob：趁火打～ *plunder a burning house; profit from someone else's misfortunes* ❷威逼，胁迫 to force; to coerce：～持 *to hijack* ❸灾难 disaster：浩～ *catastrophe* | ～数 *doom*

蜐 jié ㄐㄧㄝˊ [石蜐] 甲壳动物，即龟足，外形像龟的脚，有石灰质的壳，生活在海边的岩石缝里 Japanese goose barnacle (same as 龟足)

岊 jié ㄐㄧㄝˊ ❶山的转弯处 bend (in a mountain) ❷用于地名 used in place names：白～（在陕西省神木）*Baijie (in Shenmu, Shaanxi Province)*

劼 jié ㄐㄧㄝˊ ❶坚固 (of things) sturdy; solid ❷谨慎 cautious ❸勤勉 diligent; conscientious

诘（詰） jié ㄐㄧㄝˊ 追问 to interrogate：反～ *ask in retort* | 盘～ *to interrogate*

⇨ see also jí on p.287

拮 jié ㄐㄧㄝˊ [拮据]（一jū）经济境况不好，困窘 hard up; in straightened circumstances

洁（潔） jié ㄐㄧㄝˊ 干净（㊣一净）clean：街道清～

street cleaning | ～白 *pure white* ⓦ清白，不贪污 pure; uncorrupted: 贞～ *chaste* | 廉～ *honest and clean*

结(結) jié ㄐㄧㄝˊ ❶系(jì)，绾(wǎn) to tie: ～网 *weave a net* | ～绳 *tie a knot in a rope* | 张灯～彩 *be decked out in lanterns and coloured silk streamers* [结构] 1 各组成部分的搭配和排列 structure: 文章的～ *structure of the article* 2 建筑上指承重的部分 (in construction) structure: 钢筋混凝土～ *reinforced concrete structure* ❷(－子)用绳、线或布条等绾成的扣 (tied) knot: 打～ *tie a knot* | 活～ *slip knot* ❸聚，合 to come together ①凝聚 to concentrate; to congeal: ～冰 *to freeze* | ～晶 *to crystallize* ②联合，发生关系 to be connected: ～婚 *to marry* | ～交 *make friends* | 集会～社 *gather and form an association* ❹结束，完了(liǎo) to conclude; to finish: ～账 *settle a bill* | ～局 *the end* | ～论 *conclusion* ❺一种保证负责的字据 written guarantee: 具～ *sign a written undertaking*

➪ see also jiē on p.315

桔 jié ㄐㄧㄝˊ ❶[桔梗](－gěng)草本植物，花紫色，根可入药 balloon flower ❷[桔槔](－gāo)一种利用杠杆原理汲水的工具 shadoof (a counter-balanced lever used to lift water)

➪ see also jú on p.337

袺 jié ㄐㄧㄝˊ 用衣襟兜东西 to carry in the front panel of one's garment

颉(頡) jié ㄐㄧㄝˊ [仓颉]上古人名，传说是黄帝的史官，汉字的创造者(ancient) Cangjie (name of the inventor of Chinese characters)

➪ see also xié on p.721

鲒(鮚) jié ㄐㄧㄝˊ 古书上说的一种蚌 a kind of clam (in ancient Chinese texts)

杰(*傑) jié ㄐㄧㄝˊ ❶才能出众的人(ⓛ俊－) outstanding person: 英～ *hero* | 豪～ *hero* ❷特异的，超过一般的 outstanding; extraordinary: ～作 *masterpiece* | ～出 *outstanding*

桀 jié ㄐㄧㄝˊ ❶凶暴 cruel ❷古人名，夏朝末代的君主，相传是暴君 Jie (last ruler of the Xia Dynasty, traditionally considered a tyrant) ❸古代指鸡栖的小木桩 (ancient) small wooden post on which chickens roost ❹ (ancient) same as "杰(傑)"

絜 jié ㄐㄧㄝˊ 同"洁"，多用于人名 same as 洁, often used in given names

絜 jié ㄐㄧㄝˊ ❶〈古 ancient〉same as "洁" ❷姓 (surname) Jie

➪ see also xié on p.720

捷(*㨗) jié ㄐㄧㄝˊ ❶战胜 to defeat; to win: 我军大～。*Our army has won a resounding victory.* | ～报 *news of victory* ❷快，速(ⓛ敏－) quick; prompt: 快～ *fast and nimble* | ～径(近路) *shortcut* | ～足先登(行动敏捷，先达到目的)。*The swift-footed arrives first.*

J

寁 jié ㄐㄧㄝˊ(又) see zǎn on page 818

婕 jié ㄐㄧㄝˊ [婕妤](-yú) 汉代宫中女官名 (in the Han Dynasty) title of a female official

睫 jié ㄐㄧㄝˊ 睫毛，眼睑边缘上生的细毛 eyelash：目不交～ *not sleep a wink* (see picture of 人的眼睛 on page 753)

偈 jié ㄐㄧㄝˊ ❶勇武 valiant; valorous ❷跑得快 swift-footed

⇨ see also jì on p.293

楬 jié ㄐㄧㄝˊ 用作标志的小木桩 stake (used as a marker)

碣 jié ㄐㄧㄝˊ 圆顶的石碑 round-topped stone tablet：～石 *tombstone* | 残碑断～ *crumbling monuments and tombstones*

竭 jié ㄐㄧㄝˊ 尽，用尽 to use up; to exhaust：～力 *do one's utmost* | ～诚 *whole-heartedly* | 声嘶力～ *shout oneself hoarse* | 取之不尽，用之不～ *inexhaustible*

羯 jié ㄐㄧㄝˊ ❶公羊，特指阉割过的 ram (especially neutered) ❷我国古代北方的民族 Jie (ancient ethnic group in the North of China)

截 jié ㄐㄧㄝˊ ❶割断，弄断 to cut; to sever：～开这根木料 *cut the log* | ～长补短 *take from the long to add to the short; use one person's strengths to compensate for the weaknesses of another* [截然] 副词，分明地，显然地 (adverb) distinctly：～不同 *distinctly different* ❷(-子、-儿) 量词，段 (measure word) section：上半～儿 *upper half* | 一～儿木头 *a log* | 一～路 *a stretch of road* ❸阻拦 to intercept：～住他 *stop him* [截止] 到期停止 to close; to terminate：～报名 *closing of registration* | 到月底～。*The closing date is the end of this month.*

姐 jiě ㄐㄧㄝˇ ❶称同父母比自己年纪大的女子 ㊀elder sister ❷对比自己年纪大的同辈女性的称呼 used to address an older woman of one's own generation：表～ *(elder female) cousin (daughter of one's father's sisters or mother's brothers or sisters)* | 刘～ *Sister Liu*

解(觧)** jiě ㄐㄧㄝˇ ❶剖开，分开(㊀分-) to cut open：～剖 *to dissect* | 难～难分 *in (a) stalemate; sentimentally attached* | 瓦～ *to disintegrate* ❷把束缚着、系(jì)着的东西打开 to untie：～扣 *to unbutton* | ～衣服 *to unbutton one's clothes* [解放] 1 推翻反动政权，使广大人民群众脱离压迫，获得自由 to liberate 2 解除束缚，得到自由或发展 to remove the restrictions on; to free：～生产力 *liberate productive forces* ❸除去 to remove ①消除 to get rid of：～恨 *give vent to one's hatred* | ～渴 *quench one's thirst* ②废除，停止 to terminate; to stop：～职 *dismiss from office* | ～约 *terminate an agreement* ❹讲明白，分析说明(㊀-释、注-) to explain：～答 *to explain* | ～劝 *to soothe by explaining / analyzing* ❺

懂，明白 to understand：令人不～ *puzzling* | 通俗易～ *accessible and easy to understand* ❻代数方程中未知数的值 (of equation) solution ❼演算 to solve：～方程 *solve an equation* ❽解手儿，大小便 to go to the toilet; to relieve oneself：大～ *empty one's bowels* | 小～ *pass water*

⇨ see also jiè on p.320, xiè on p.722

檞 jiě ㄐㄧㄝˇ 檞树，一种木质像松的树 a kind of tree similar to pines

介 jiè ㄐㄧㄝˋ ❶在两者中间 to be in between：～乎两者之间 *be between the two* | ～绍 *to introduce* | 媒～ *medium* | 中～ *agent* [介词] 用在名词、代词或名词性词组前，合起来表示对象、方向等的词，如"从、向、在、以、对于"等 preposition ❷放在心里 to care; to mind：～意 *to mind* | ～怀 *be upset* ❸正直 righteous; upright：耿～ *upright and honest* ❹甲 armour ①古代军人穿的护身衣服 (ancient) armour：～胄在身 *in one's armour* ②动物身上的甲壳 (of animals) shell：～虫 *crustacean* ❺量词，个（用于人，多表示微贱，只与数词"一"搭配）measure word for people, usually to indicate humbleness and only used with 一：一～书生 *a mere learner* ❻旧戏曲脚本里指示演员的动作、表情时的用语 (old) used to indicate action or emotion in a play：打～ *fighting* | 饮酒～ *drinking*

价 jiè ㄐㄧㄝˋ 旧时称被派遣传送东西或传达事情的人 (old) errand boy

⇨ see also jià on p.298, jie on p.320

芥 jiè ㄐㄧㄝˋ 芥菜，草本植物，花黄色，茎叶和块根可以吃，种子味辛辣，研成细末叫芥末，可供调味用 brown mustard

⇨ see also gài on p.195

玠 jiè ㄐㄧㄝˋ 古代的一种礼器，即大圭 ceremonial jade object (same as 大圭)

界 jiè ㄐㄧㄝˋ ❶相交的地方 border：～碑 *boundary marker* | 边～ *boundary; frontier* | 国～ *national boundaries* | 省～ *provincial boundaries* ❷范围 scope; extent：眼～ *vision* | 管～ *jurisdiction* 特指按职业或性别等所划的范围 circles：教育～ *educational circles* | 科学～ *scientific circles* | 妇女～ *women's circles* ❸生物分类中的最高一级单位，其下为"门" kingdom (the highest category in taxonomic classification)：动物～ *animal kingdom* | 植物～ *plant kingdom* ❹地层系统分类的第二级，在"宇"之下、"系"（xì）之上，是在地质年代"代"的时期内形成的地层 erathem (the subdivision of eonothem in stratigraphic classification)：古生～ *Paleozoic Erathem* | 中生～ *Mesozoic Erathem* | 新生～ *Cenozoic Erathem*

疥 jiè ㄐㄧㄝˋ 疥疮，皮肤病，因疥虫寄生而引起，非常刺痒 scabies

蚧 jiè ㄐㄧㄝ see 蛤蚧 (gé—) at 蛤 on page 205

骱 jiè ㄐㄧㄝ 骨节与骨节衔接的地方 (of bones) joint：脱～（脱臼）*(of bones) dislocation*

戒 jiè ㄐㄧㄝ ❶防备 to be on guard：～心 *wariness* | ～备 *be on the alert* [戒严] 非常时期在全国或一地所采取的增设警戒、限制交通等措施 to impose martial law ❷警惕着不要做或不要犯 to guard against：～骄～躁 *guard against arrogance and rashness* ❸革除嗜好 to give up (a habit)：～酒 *give up drinking* | 把烟～了 *quit smoking* ❹佛教约束教徒的条规 Buddhist precepts：五～ *Five Precepts* | 清规～律 *Buddhist precepts; straitjacket of disciplines and regulations*

诫(誡) jiè ㄐㄧㄝ 警告，劝人警惕 to warn; to admonish：告～ *to warn* | 训～ *to admonish* | 劝～ *to exhort*

悈 jiè ㄐㄧㄝ 警戒，警惕 to be wary

届(*屆) jiè ㄐㄧㄝ ❶到 to arrive：～时 *when the time arrives* | ～期 *when the time comes* ❷量词，次，期 (measure word for conference, graduates, etc.) time; term：第一～ *first term* | 上～ *the previous term* | 应（yīng）～ *current (class of graduates)* | 本～ *current (government, class of graduates, etc.)*

借(❸❹△藉) jiè ㄐㄧㄝ ❶暂时使用别人的财物等 to borrow：～钱 *borrow money* | ～车 *borrow a car* | ～用 *to borrow* [借光] 请人让路或问事的客气话 excuse me (when asking others to make way or about sth) ❷暂时把财物等给别人使用 to lend：～给他几块钱 *lend him a few* yuan ❸假托 to use as a pretext：～端 *on the pretext of* | ～故 *on an excuse* | ～口 *under the pretext of* | ～题发挥 *seize on sth and grind one's axe* ❹凭借，依靠 to make use of：～助 *with the help of*

⇨ 藉 see also jí on p.289, jiè on p.320

喈 jiè ㄐㄧㄝ 赞叹 to praise

藉 jiè ㄐㄧㄝ ❶垫在下面的东西 mat; pad ❷垫衬 cushion; lining：枕～ *pillow and cushion; lie about in disarray* ❸ see 借 on page 320

⇨ see also jí on p.289

解(觧)** jiè ㄐㄧㄝ 指押送财物或犯人 to escort (property or a criminal)：～款 *transported cash* | 起～ *(of a criminal, etc.) be escorted somewhere*

⇨ see also jiě on p.318, xiè on p.722

犗 jiè ㄐㄧㄝ 阉割过的牛 bullock

褯 jiè ㄐㄧㄝ （—子）尿布 nappy

价(價) jie ·ㄐㄧㄝ 助词 auxiliary word used as a suffix：震天～响 *deafening* | 成天～闹 *making much noise all day* long

⇨ see also jià on p.298, jiè on p.319

家 jie ·ㄐㄧㄝ 助词 auxiliary word used as a suffix：整天～ *all day* | 成年～ *all year round*

⇨ see also jiā on p.296

JIN ㄐㄧㄣ

巾 jīn ㄐㄧㄣ 擦东西或包裹、覆盖东西用的纺织品 towel; cloth：手～ *towel* | 头～ *scarf*

斤(❶* **觔**) jīn ㄐㄧㄣ ❶市制重量单位，1斤是10两（旧制16两），合0.5千克 *jin*, a traditional Chinese unit for measuring weight, equal to 0.5 kilograms. There are 10 两 (formerly 16 两) in 1 斤. ❷古代砍伐树木的工具 (ancient) axe：斧～ *axe*

[斤斤] 过分看重微小的利害 to care too much about petty gains and losses：～计较 *care too much about petty gains and losses*

釿(**釿**) jīn ㄐㄧㄣ ❶ (ancient) same as "斤❷" ❷古代金属重量单位，也是货币单位 unit for measuring the weight of metal as well as monetary unit in ancient times

今 jīn ㄐㄧㄣ ❶现在，现代，跟"古"相对 now; modern (opposite of 古)：～昔 *past and present* | 博古通～ *well-versed in matters past and present* ❷当前 now; present：～天 *today* | ～年 *this year*

衿 jīn ㄐㄧㄣ ❶襟 front of a garment：青～（旧时念书人穿的衣服）*(old) scholar's garment* ❷系（jì）上衣襟的带子 belt; girdle

矜 jīn ㄐㄧㄣ ❶怜悯，怜惜 to feel compassion for ❷自尊自大，自夸 to brag：自～其功 *blow one's own trumpet* ❸慎重，拘谨 to be cautious：～持 *restrained*

⇨ see also guān on p.226, qín on p.538

金 jīn ㄐㄧㄣ ❶金属元素，通称金子，符号Au，黄赤色，质软，是贵重的金属 (usually known as 金子) gold (Au) ㊖尊贵，珍贵 honoured; precious：～榜 *list of successful candidates in imperial examinations* | ～玉良言 *invaluable advice* | ～科玉律 *unchangeable rules and laws* ❷金属，指金、银、铜、铁等，具有光泽和延展性，容易传热和导电 metal (referring to gold, silver, copper, iron, etc.)：五～ *hardware* | 合～ *alloy* ❸钱 money：现～ *cash* | 奖～ *prize money* | 基～ *fund* ❹像金子的颜色 golden：～发碧眼 *golden hair and blue eyes* ❺朝代名，女真族完颜阿骨打所建立（公元1115—1234年）Jin Dynasty (1115—1234, founded by Wanyan Aguda of the Jurchens)

津 jīn ㄐㄧㄣ ❶渡口，过江河的地方 ferry (crossing)：问～（打听渡口，泛指探问）*make enquiries* [津梁] 桥 bridge ㊖做引导用的事物 bridge (to sth else) ❷口液，唾液 saliva：～液

saliva [津津] 形容有滋味，有趣味 interesting：～有味 *with keen pleasure* | ～乐道 *talk about with relish* ❸滋润 to moisten [津贴] 1 用财物补助 to pay (sb) an allowance 2 正式工资以外的补助费，也指供给制人员的生活零用钱 allowance ❹指天津 Tianjin

琎 jīn ㄐㄧㄣ 一种玉 a type of jade

筋(*觔) jīn ㄐㄧㄣ ❶肌肉的旧称 (former name for 肌肉) muscle：～骨 *bones and muscles* ❷俗称皮下可以看见的静脉血管 (informal) blue veins：青～ *blue veins* ❸俗称肌腱或骨头上的韧带 (informal) tendon; sinew; ligament：扭了～ *tore a tendon* | 牛蹄～ *beef tendon* ❹像筋的东西 sth like a tendon：钢～ *steel bar* | 橡皮～儿 *rubber band*

禁 jīn ㄐㄧㄣ ❶禁受，受得住，耐(用) to bear; to endure：～得起考验 *can stand the test* | 这种布～穿。*This type of cloth is hard-wearing.* ❷忍耐 to contain oneself: 他不～(忍不住)笑起来。*He couldn't help but laugh.*

⇨ see also jìn on p.325

襟 jīn ㄐㄧㄣ 衣服胸前或背后的部分 (of a garment) front; back：大～ *front (of a Chinese garment)* | 小～ *inner piece (of a Chinese garment)* | 底～ *inner piece (of a Chinese garment)* | 对～ *front-closure pieces (of a Chinese garment)* | 后～ *back (of a garment)* (see picture of 上衣 on page 767) [襟怀] 胸怀 (breadth of) mind：～坦荡 *broad-minded and honest*

仅(僅) jǐn ㄐㄧㄣˇ 副词，只 ⓐ (adverb) only：小水电站～～三个月就建成了。*The small hydropower plant was completed in no more than three months.* | ～写过两篇短文 *have written only two short essays* | 这些意见～供参考。*These opinions are just for reference.*

⇨ see also jìn on p.323

尽(儘) jǐn ㄐㄧㄣˇ ❶极，最 utmost：～底下 *the very bottom* | ～里头 *furthest end* | ～先录用 *have priority when being recruited* ❷有多少用多少 as much as possible：～量 *to the best of one's ability; as far as possible* | ～着力气做 *do one's best* [尽管] 1 连词，纵然，即使 (conjunction) although; though：～他不接受这个意见，我还是要向他提。*I'm going to voice my opinion, even if he doesn't accept it.* 2 只管，不必顾虑 without hesitation：有话～说吧！*Feel free to speak your mind!* ❸放在最先 to give priority to：座位先～着请来的客人坐。*Seats should be given to the invited guests first.* | 先～着旧衣服穿 *wear the old clothes first*

⇨ see also jìn on p.323

卺 jǐn ㄐㄧㄣˇ 瓢，古代结婚时用作酒器 drinking gourd; ladle (used as a wine vessel during a wedding ceremony in ancient times) [合卺] 旧时夫妇成婚的

J

一种仪式 sharing a drink from the marriage gourds (part of a wedding ceremony in ancient times)

紧(緊、*緊、*緊) jǐn ㄐㄧㄣˇ ❶密切合拢，跟"松"相对 tight (opposite of 松)：捆～ *tie (sth) tight* ㊀靠得极近 very close：～邻 *next-door neighbour* | ～靠着 *be very close to* ❷物体受到几方面的拉力以后所呈现的紧张状态 taut; stretched tightly：鼓面绷得非常～。*The drumhead is stretched taut.* [紧张] 不松弛，不缓和 tense; strained：精神～ *feel tense* | 工作～ *be very busy at work* ❸使紧 to tighten：把弦～一～ *tighten the string a bit* | ～一～腰带 *tighten one's belt* ❹事情密切接连着，时间急促没有空隙 hard-pressed (for time)：功课很～ *be very busy at school* | 抓～时间 *make the best use of time* ㊀因时间短促而加快 quicken; speed up (due to lack of time)：～走 *quicken one's steps* | 手～点儿就能多出活儿 *work faster and one will be more productive* ❺形势严重或关系重要 critical; crucial：～要 *crucial* | ～急 *urgent* ❻生活不宽裕 hard up：日子过得很～ *struggle to make ends meet*

堇 jǐn ㄐㄧㄣˇ ❶堇菜，草本植物，花白色，带紫色条纹，全草可入药 (of plant) viola ❷紫堇，草本植物，花紫色，全草味苦，可入药 corydalis

谨(謹) jǐn ㄐㄧㄣˇ ❶慎重，小心（㊥一慎）cautious; circumspect：～守规程 *meticulously comply with regulations* ❷郑重，恭敬 respectful：～启 *yours respectfully* | ～向您表示祝贺。*I'd like to extend my most sincere congratulations to you.*

馑(饉) jǐn ㄐㄧㄣˇ 荒年（㊥饥一）famine year

廑 jǐn ㄐㄧㄣˇ ❶古书上指小屋 hut (in ancient Chinese texts) ❷ (old) same as "仅"

⇨ see also qín 勤 on p.538

瑾 jǐn ㄐㄧㄣˇ 美玉 beautiful jade

槿 jǐn ㄐㄧㄣˇ 木槿，落叶灌木，花有红、白、紫等颜色，茎皮纤维可用来造纸，树皮和花可入药 rose of Sharon

锦(錦) jǐn ㄐㄧㄣˇ ❶有彩色花纹的丝织品 brocade：～缎 *brocade* | 蜀～ *brocade from Sichuan* | ～上添花 *be the icing on the cake (literally means 'add flowers to the brocade')* ❷鲜明美丽 splendid; glorious：～霞 *splendid clouds* | ～鸡 *golden pheasant*

仅(僅) jìn ㄐㄧㄣˋ 将近，几乎（多见于唐人诗文）nearly (often used in literary works from the Tang Dynasty)：山城～百层。*Nearly one hundred storeys above the hilltop did the city soar.* | 士卒～万人。*There were approximately ten thousand soldiers.*

⇨ see also jǐn on p.322

尽(盡) jìn ㄐㄧㄣˋ ❶完毕 to complete：用～力气 *with all one's strength* | 说不～的

好处 *innumerable benefits* ㊀达到极端 to push (sth) to the limit：～善～美 *be the acme of perfection* | ～头 *end* [自尽] 自杀 to commit suicide ❷全部用出 to use up; to exhaust：～心 *to do (sth) with all one's heart* | ～力 *do one's best* | 仁至义～ *do one's utmost to help* ㊀竭力做到 to do one's best to perform：～职 *fulfil one's duty* ❸都，全 completely：他说的～是些废话。*Everything he said is a load of crap.*

⇨ see also jǐn on p.322

荩(藎) jìn ㄐㄧㄣˋ ❶荩草，草本植物，茎很细，花灰绿色或带紫色，茎和叶可做黄色染料，纤维是造纸原料 small carpetgrass ❷忠诚 loyal：～臣 *loyal official*

浕(濜) jìn ㄐㄧㄣˋ 浕水，古水名，在湖北省枣阳，今称沙河 Jinshui River (ancient river name, in Zaoyang, Hubei Province, now called 沙河)

赆(贐) jìn ㄐㄧㄣˋ 临别时赠的礼物 farewell present：～仪 *farewell present*

烬(燼) jìn ㄐㄧㄣˋ 物体燃烧后剩下的东西（㊇灰一）ash; cinder：化为灰～ *be reduced to ashes* | 烛～ *candle ash*

进(進) jìn ㄐㄧㄣˋ ❶向前移动，跟"退"相对 to move forward (opposite of 退)：前～ *to advance* | ～军 *(of troops) to march; advance* | 更～一层 *go one step further* | ～一步提高产品质量 *further improve the quality of a product* [进步] 1 向前发展，比原来好 to progress; to improve：时代又～了。*Once again, the times have moved forward.* 2 适合时代要求，对社会发展起促进作用的 progressive：思想很～ *think in a progressive way* [进化] 事物由简单到复杂、由低级到高级的发展过程 to evolve ❷跟"出"相对 to enter; to go into (opposite of 出) ①入，往里面去 to enter：～工厂 *enter a factory* | ～学校 *go into a school* ②收入或买入 to receive; to buy：～款 *income* | ～项 *income* | ～货 *(of a store) buy stock* ❸量词，用于旧式建筑房院前后的层次 (measure word for the number of courtyards in a traditional-style residential compound) layer：这房子是两～院子。*The house has two layers of courtyards.* ❹奉呈 to submit：～献 *present respectfully* | ～言 *offer one's advice (for peers or seniors)*

琎(璡) jìn ㄐㄧㄣˋ 一种像玉的石头 jade-like stone

近 jìn ㄐㄧㄣˋ ❶跟"远"相对 near; close (opposite of 远) ①距离短 (of distance) close, near：～郊 *environs (of a city)* | 路很～。*It's a very short journey.* | 天津离北京很～。*Tianjin is very close to Beijing.* ②现在以前不久的时间 recent：～几天 *the last few days* | ～来 *recently* ❷亲密，关系密切 (of relationship) close：亲～ *intimate; close* | ～亲 *close relative* ❸接近，差别小，差不多 to approach; to be close to：

相～ *be similar; be close* | ～似 *be similar* | 年～五十 *be getting on for fifty* ❹浅近 (of language, etc.) accessible：言～旨远 *profound truth couched in simple language*

靳 jìn ㄐㄧㄣˋ 〈古 ancient〉吝惜，不肯给予 parsimonious; stingy

妗 jìn ㄐㄧㄣˋ ❶舅母 wife of one's mother's brother ❷（－子）妻兄、妻弟的妻子 wife of one's wife's brother：大～子 *wife of one's wife's elder brother* | 小～子 *wife of one's wife's younger brother*

劲（勁） jìn ㄐㄧㄣˋ（－儿）力气，力量 strength; energy：有多大～使多大～ *use every ounce of one's strength* ㊟ ①效力，作用 potency; efficacy：酒～儿 *influence of alcohol* | 药～ *efficacy of a drug* ②精神、情绪、兴趣等 vigour; spirit：干活儿起～ *work with vigour* | 一股子～头儿 *full of drive* | 一个～儿地做 *keep on working hard* | 老玩儿这个真没～。*It's so boring playing this over and over again.* ③指属性的程度 degree (of a quality)：你瞧这块布这个白～儿。*Look how white this piece of cloth is.* | 咸～儿 *salty kick* | 高兴～儿 *joy*

⇨ see also jìng on p.329

晋（*晉） jìn ㄐㄧㄣˋ ❶进，向前 to move forward; to advance：～见 *have an audience with* | ～级 *be promoted* ❷周代诸侯国名，在今山西省和河北省南部，河南省北部，陕西省东部 Jin (a state in the Zhou Dynasty) ❸山西省的别称 another name for Shanxi Province ❹朝代名 name of dynasties ①晋武帝司马炎所建立（公元 265—420 年）Jin Dynasty (265—420, founded by Sima Yan, Emperor Wu) ②五代之一，石敬瑭所建立（公元 936—947 年），史称后晋 Later Jin Dynasty (936—947, one of the Five Dynasties, founded by Shi Jingtang)

搢（搢）** jìn ㄐㄧㄣˋ 插 to insert

［搢绅］same as "缙绅"

溍 jìn ㄐㄧㄣˋ 古水名 Jin (ancient river name)

缙（縉、縉）** jìn ㄐㄧㄣˋ 浅红色的帛 pale red silk fabric

［缙绅］古代称官僚或做过官的人，也作"搢绅" (ancient) official; retired official (also written as 搢绅)

瑨 jìn ㄐㄧㄣˋ 一种像玉的石头 jade-like stone

浸 jìn ㄐㄧㄣˋ ❶泡，使渗透 to soak; to immerse：～透 *to soak* | ～入 *to immerse* | 把种子放在水里～一～ *soak the seeds in water for a while* ❷逐渐 gradually：～渐 *gradually* | 交往～密 *gradually become closer to each other*

祲 jìn ㄐㄧㄣˋ 古人指不祥之气 (ancient) sinister atmosphere

禁 jìn ㄐㄧㄣˋ ❶不许，制止 to ban; to prohibit：～止 *to ban* | ～赛 *ban (someone) from a match* |

J

查～ *check and prohibit* ❷法律或习惯上制止的事 prohibition; taboo：入国问～。*On entering a new country, learn about its bans and taboos.* | 犯～ *violate a ban* ❸拘押 to detain; to imprison：～闭 *place someone in confinement* | 监～ *to imprison* ❹旧时称皇帝居住的地方 (old) forbidden court (where an emperor lives)：～中 *forbidden courts* | 紫～城 *Forbidden City* ㊁ 不能随便通行的（地方）restricted (area)：～地 *out-of-bounds area* | ～区 *restricted area* ❺避忌 taboo：～忌 *taboo*

⇨ see also jīn on p.322

噤 jìn ㄐㄧㄣˋ 闭口，不作声 to keep quiet：～若寒蝉 *keep quiet out of fear (literally means 'as silent as a cicada in cold weather')*

墐 jìn ㄐㄧㄣˋ ❶用泥涂塞 to fill with mud ❷ same as "殣❶"

觐(覲) jìn ㄐㄧㄣˋ 朝见君主或朝拜圣地 to have an audience with (an emperor); to visit (a holy place)：～见 *have an audience with* | 朝～ *have an audience with the emperor; hajj*

殣 jìn ㄐㄧㄣˋ ❶掩埋 to bury ❷饿死 to starve to death

JING ㄐㄧㄥ

茎(莖) jīng ㄐㄧㄥ ❶通常指植物的主干。能起支撑作用，又是养料和水分运输的通道。有些植物有地下茎，作用是储藏养料和进行无性繁殖 stem; tuber ❷量词，用于长条形的东西 (measure word) stalk：数～小草 *a few stalks of grass* | 数～白发 *several white hairs*

泾(涇) jīng ㄐㄧㄥ 泾河，发源于宁夏回族自治区，流至陕西省入渭河 Jinghe River (originating in Ningxia Hui Autonomous Region) [泾渭分明] 泾河水清，渭河水浊，两河汇流处清浊不混。The waters of the Jinghe River and the Weihe River are easily distinguishable. ㊂ 两种事物界限清楚 readily distinguishable

经(經) jīng ㄐㄧㄥ ❶经线，织布时拴在机器上的竖纱，编织物的纵线，跟"纬"相对 the warp (opposite of 纬) ❷地理学上假定的沿地球表面连接南北两极并跟赤道垂直的线，从通过英国格林尼治天文台原址的经线起，以东称"东经"，以西称"西经"，各为180° longitude ❸持久不变的，正常 constant; normal：～常 *often* | 不～之谈 *egregious nonsense* ㊁ 指义理，法则 law; rule：离～叛道 *rebel against orthodoxy* | 天～地义 *unalterable truth* ❹尊为典范的著作或宗教的典籍 classic (work); scripture：～典 *classic* | 佛～ *Buddhist scripture* | 圣～ *holy book* | 古兰～ *Koran* ❺治理，管理 to manage; to administer：～商 *be in business* | ～纪 *manage (a business)* | ～营 *run (a business)* | ～理 *manager* [经济] 1 通常指一个国家的国民经济或国民经济的某一部门，例如工业、农业、

商业、财政、金融等 economy 2 指经济基础，即一定历史时期的社会生产关系，它是政治和意识形态等上层建筑的基础 economic basis 3 指国家或个人的收支状况 (government) revenue; (personal) income：～富裕 *rich* 4 耗费少而收益大 economical：这样做不～。*It's not good value for money.* ❻ 经受，禁（jīn）受 to go through：～风雨，见世面 *broaden one's mind through trials and tribulations* ❼ 经过，通过 to pass：途～上海 *go via Shanghai* | ～他一说我才明白。*It only dawned on me after his explanation.* | 久～考验 *time-tested* [经验] 由实践得来的知识或技能 experience ❽中医称人体内的脉络 (of traditional Chinese medicine) channel：～络 *channel* ❾月经，妇女每月周期性子宫出血 menstruation：～期 *menstrual period* | 停～ *menopause* ❿缢死 to hang; to string up：自～ *hang oneself*

京 jīng ㄐㄧㄥ ❶京城，国家的首都。特指我国首都北京 capital (of a country); (specifically) Beijing：～广铁路 *Beijing–Guangzhou railway* | ～剧 *Peking Opera* ❷古代数目名，指一千万 (ancient) ten million

[京族] 1 我国少数民族，参看附录 四 the Gin People (one of the ethnic groups in China. See Appendix Ⅳ.) 2 越南的主要民族 the Gin people (major ethnic group in Vietnam)

猄 jīng ㄐㄧㄥ [黄猄]一种鹿，即黄麂，背部棕黄色 Chinese muntjac (same as 黄麂)

惊(驚) jīng ㄐㄧㄥ ❶骡、马等因为害怕而狂奔起来不受控制 (of mule, horse, etc.) to shy; to stampede：马～了。*The horse shied.* ❷精神突然受到刺激而紧张或不安 to be surprised; to be startled：受～ *be frightened* | 吃～ *be surprised* | ～喜 *be pleasantly surprised* | 处变不～ *remain unperturbed in a crisis* | ～心动魄 *heart-stopping* | ～慌 *to panic* ❸惊动 to alert：打草～蛇 *act rashly and alert one's enemy*

鲸(鯨) jīng ㄐㄧㄥ 哺乳动物，外形像鱼，胎生，用肺呼吸，俗叫鲸鱼，最大的长达 30 米，小的只 1 米左右。生活在海洋里 whale (informal 鲸鱼) [鲸吞] 吞并，常指强国对弱国的侵略行为 to annex (the territory of another country)

麖 jīng ㄐㄧㄥ 古书上说的一种鹿，一说是水鹿 a type of deer in ancient Chinese texts; (also) sambar

荆 jīng ㄐㄧㄥ ❶落叶灌木，叶掌状分裂，花蓝紫色，枝条可用来编筐、篮等，古时用荆条做刑具 chaste tree：负～请罪（向人认错）*make a humble and sincere apology* [荆棘]（-jí）泛指丛生多刺的灌木 thorn (bush) ㊕障碍和困难 difficulties ❷春秋时楚国也称荆 Jing (another name for the state of Chu during the Spring and Autumn Period)

菁 jīng ㄐㄧㄥ ㊟草木茂盛 lush; luxuriant

[菁华] 最精美的部分 essence

腈 jīng ㄐㄧㄥ 有机化合物的一类，无色液体或固体，有特殊气味，遇酸或碱就分解 nitrile

睛 jīng ㄐㄧㄥ 眼球，眼珠 eyeball：目不转～ *eyes are glued to sth* | 画龙点～ *add the magic finishing touches*

鶄（鶄） jīng ㄐㄧㄥ see 䴔鶄 (jiāo—) at 䴔 on page 310

精 jīng ㄐㄧㄥ ❶细密的 refined; careful：～制 *made with care* | ～选 *select carefully* | ～打细算 *plan and budget very carefully* ❷聪明，思想周密 intelligent; smart：这孩子真～。*The kid is really smart.* | ～明强干 *smart and capable* ❸精华，物质中最纯粹的部分，提炼出来的东西 essence：麦～ *malt extract* | 酒～ *ethanol* | 炭～ *charcoal product* [精神] 1 即主观世界，包括思想、作风等，是客观世界的反映 mind; spirit：物质可以变成～，～可以变成物质。*Matter can be transformed into consciousness and consciousness into matter.* 2 内容实质 gist：领会文件～ *get the gist of the document* 3（—shen）指人表现出来的活力 vigour; spirits：振作～ *rouse one's spirits* ❹完美，最好 perfect; wonderful：～美 *exquisite* | ～彩 *wonderful* | ～装 *hardback* | ～益求～ *keep honing and perfecting sth* ❺精液，男子和雄性动物生殖腺分泌的含有精子的液体 semen ❻专一，深入 well-versed; proficient：博而不～ *be a jack of all trades* | ～通 *be well-versed in* | 他～于针灸。*He is an excellent acupuncturist.* ❼很，极 extremely：～湿 *dripping wet* | ～瘦 *skinny* | ～光 *with nothing left* ❽迷信的人以为多年老物变成的妖怪 goblin; spirit：妖～ *evil spirit* | 狐狸～ *fox demon; seductive woman*

鼱 jīng ㄐㄧㄥ see 鼩鼱 (qú—) at 鼩 on page 547

旌 jīng ㄐㄧㄥ ❶古代用羽毛装饰的旗子，又指普通的旗子 (ancient) plume-decorated flag; flag ❷表扬 to commend：～表 *to commend*

晶 jīng ㄐㄧㄥ 形容光亮 ㊟brilliant; dazzling：～莹 *sparkling and crystal-clear* | 亮～～的 *shiny* [晶体] 原子、离子、分子按一定的空间位置排列而成，且具有规则外形的固体 crystal [结晶] 1 由液体或气体变成许多有一定形状的小颗粒的现象 to crystallize 2 晶体 crystal ㊞ 成果 achievement：这本著作是他多年研究的～。*This book is the fruit of his many years of research.*

粳（*杭、*粳） jīng ㄐㄧㄥ 粳稻，稻的一种，米粒短而粗 japonica rice

兢 jīng ㄐㄧㄥ [兢兢] 小心，谨慎 cautious：战战～ *gingerly* | ～业业 *circumspect and conscientious*

井 jǐng ㄐㄧㄥˇ ❶从地面向下挖成的能取出水的深洞，洞壁

多砌上砖石 well ❷形状跟井相像的物体 sth like a well：天～ *courtyard* | 盐～ *salt well* | 矿～ *mine shaft* ❸整齐，有秩序 ⑧ in good order; orderly：～～有条 *shipshape; methodical* | 秩序～然 *orderly* ❹星宿名，二十八宿之一 *jing* (one of the twenty-eight constellations in ancient Chinese astronomy)

阱(*穽) jǐng ㄐㄧㄥˇ 陷阱，捕野兽用的陷坑 trap; snare

汫 jǐng ㄐㄧㄥˇ 用于地名 used in place names：～洲（在广东省饶平）*Jingzhou (in Raoping, Guangdong Province)*

肼 jǐng ㄐㄧㄥˇ 有机化合物，无色油状液体，有剧毒。可用来制药等 hydrazine

刭(剄) jǐng ㄐㄧㄥˇ 用刀割脖子 to cut one's throat：自～ *cut one's own throat*

颈(頸) jǐng ㄐㄧㄥˇ 脖子，头和躯干相连接的部分 neck (see picture of 人体 on page 647)

⇨ see also gěng on p.210

景 jǐng ㄐㄧㄥˇ ❶风景，风光 scenery; view：良辰美～ *pleasing scenery and beautiful day* | ～致 *scenery* | ～色 *landscape; scene* ❷景象，情况 scene; state：盛～ *grand view* | 晚～ *evening scene; life in old age* | 远～ *long-term prospects* ❸戏剧、电影等中的场面和景物 (of plays, films, etc.) scenery：布～ *stage scenery* | 内～ *indoor scenery* | 外～ *outdoor setting* ❹佩服，敬慕 to esteem; to admire：～仰 *to revere* | ～慕 *to esteem* ❺指日光 sunlight：春和～明。*The spring is clement and the sunshine bright.*

[景颇族] 我国少数民族，参看附录四 the Jingpo people (one of the ethnic groups in China. See Appendix Ⅳ.)

〈古 ancient〉also same as 影 (yǐng)

憬 jǐng ㄐㄧㄥˇ 醒悟 to wake up to sth：闻之～然 *be awakened on hearing sth*

璟 jǐng ㄐㄧㄥˇ 玉的光彩 (of jade) lustre

儆 jǐng ㄐㄧㄥˇ 使人警醒，不犯过错 to warn; to admonish：～戒 *to admonish* | 惩（chéng）一～百 *make an example by punishing one person to warn others*

璥 jǐng ㄐㄧㄥˇ 一种玉 a type of jade

警 jǐng ㄐㄧㄥˇ ❶注意可能发生的危险 to be on guard; to be alert：～戒 *be on guard* | ～惕 *be wary of* | ～备 *be on the alert* | ～告（提醒人注意）*to warn* ❷需要戒备的危险事件或消息 alarm：火～ *fire alarm* | 告～ *report an emergency* | ～报 *alarm* ❸感觉敏锐 alert; keen：～觉 *vigilance* | ～醒 *esaily awoken; be alerted*

劲(勁) jìng ㄐㄧㄥˋ 坚强有力 powerful; forceful：～旅 *crack troops* | ～敌 *formidable opponent* | 刚～ *bold and powerful* | 疾风知～草。*Adversity is the touchstone of character.*

⇨ see also jìn on p.325

径(徑、❶❸△*逕) jìng ㄐㄧㄥˋ ❶小路 path：山～ *mountain trail* ㊟达到目的的方法 path (to a goal)：捷～ *shortcut* | 门～ *way (to achieve sth)* [径赛] 各种赛跑和竞走项目比赛的总称 track events [径庭] ㊟相差太远 drastically different：大相～ *be poles apart* ❷直径，两端以圆周为界，通过圆心的线段 diameter：半～ *radius* | 口～ *(of tubes, etc.) calibre* ❸副词，表示直接前往某处或直接做某件事 (adverb) straight, directly：事毕～返北京 *upon completion, return directly to Beijing* | ～行办理 *handle sth directly* | ～与有关单位联系 *contact relevant departments directly*

⇨ 逕 see also 迳 on p.330

迳(逕) jìng ㄐㄧㄥˋ 用于地名 used in place names：～头（在广东省佛冈）*Jingtou (in Fogang, Guangdong Province)*

⇨ 逕 see also 径 on p.330

胫(脛、*踁) jìng ㄐㄧㄥˋ 小腿 shin

痉(痙) jìng ㄐㄧㄥˋ 痉挛（luán），俗叫抽筋，症状是肌肉收缩，手脚抽搐（chù）spasm (informal 抽筋)

净(*浄) jìng ㄐㄧㄥˋ ❶干净，清洁 clean：～水 *clean water* | 脸要洗～。*Face must be washed clean.* ❷洗，使干净 to wash; to clean：～面 *wash one's face* | ～手 *wash one's hands* ❸什么也没有，空，光 empty; used up：钱用～了。*There is not a penny left.* ❹纯，纯粹的 net; pure：～利 *net profit* | ～重 *net weight* ❺副词 adverb ①单，只，仅 only：好的都挑完了，～剩下次的了。*All the good ones are chosen, and only the inferior ones are left.* ②全（没有别的）all：秋风一刮，满地～是树叶。*As soon as the autumn wind blew, the ground was left covered in leaves.* ❻传统戏曲里称花脸 (in traditional Chinese opera) painted-face role

竫 jìng ㄐㄧㄥˋ ❶安静 quiet ❷编造 to fabricate

静 jìng ㄐㄧㄥˋ ❶停止的，跟"动"相对 still (opposite of 动)：～止 *still* | 风平浪～ *(of an expanse of water) calm and tranquil* ❷没有声音 silent; quiet：清～ *quiet* | 更（gēng）深夜～ *time is late and the night still* | ～悄悄 *quiet*

倞 jìng ㄐㄧㄥˋ 强，强劲 strong; powerful

⇨ see also liàng on p.400

竞(競) jìng ㄐㄧㄥˋ 比赛，互相争胜（㊖-赛）to compete：～走 *race walking* | ～渡 *compete in a boat race* [竞争] 为了自己或本集团的利益而跟人争胜 to compete

竟 jìng ㄐㄧㄥˋ ❶终了（liǎo），完毕 to finish; to end：读～ *finish reading* | 继承先烈未～的事业 *carry on the unfinished work of the martyrs* ㊞ ①到底，终于 in the end：有志者事～成。*Where*

J

there's a will, there's a way. ② 整，从头到尾 from beginning to end：～日 *throughout the day* | ～夜 *all night long* ❷副词，居然，表示出乎意料 (adverb, indicating surprise) unexpectedly：这样巨大的工程，～在短短半年中就完成了。*To people's surprise, such a huge project was completed in just half a year.*

境 jìng ㄐㄧㄥˋ ❶疆界(㊀边－) border; boundary：国～ *national boundary* | 入～ *enter a country* ❷地方，处所 place：如入无人之～ *sweep all before one as if there's no resistance* ㊀ ①品行学业的程度 (academic or moral) state：学有进～ *make progress in one's studies* ②环境，遭遇到的情况 circumstances; situation：家～ *family circumstances* | 处～ *situation one finds oneself in* | 事过～迁。*Things have passed and the situation has changed.*

獍 jìng ㄐㄧㄥˋ 古书上说的一种像虎豹的兽，生下来就吃生它的母兽 tiger-like beast in ancient Chinese texts which eats its mother after birth

镜(鏡) jìng ㄐㄧㄥˋ ❶(－子)用来反映形象的器具，古代用铜磨制，现代用玻璃制成 mirror ❷利用光学原理特制的各种器具 lens：显微～ *microscope* | 望远～ *telescope* | 眼～ *glasses* | 凸透～ *convex lens* | 三棱～ *triangular prism*

婧 jìng ㄐㄧㄥˋ 女子有才能 (of a woman) talented

靓(靚) jìng ㄐㄧㄥˋ 妆饰，打扮 to make up; to dress up

⇨ see also liàng on p.401

靖 jìng ㄐㄧㄥˋ ❶安静，平安 peaceful ❷旧指平定，使秩序安定 (old) to pacify (see 绥❶ on page 626 for reference)

敬 jìng ㄐㄧㄥˋ ❶尊重，有礼貌地对待(㊀尊－) to respect：～客 *treat guests respectfully* | ～之以礼 *respect someone in accordance with the rites* | ～赠 *present respectfully* | ～献 *offer respectfully* ❷恭敬 respectful：～请指教。*Please kindly offer (me) some advice.* | 毕恭毕～ *be very respectful* ❸有礼貌地送上去 to offer politely：～酒 *propose a toast* | ～茶 *serve tea respectfully*

JIONG ㄐㄩㄥ

坰 jiōng ㄐㄩㄥ 离城市很远的郊野 outer suburb

駉(駉) jiōng ㄐㄩㄥ ❶马肥壮 ㊂(of a horse) stout and strong：～～牡马 *strong stallion* ❷骏马 steed

扃 jiōng ㄐㄩㄥ 从外面关门的闩(shuān)、钩等 bolt / hook (used to shut a door from the outside) ㊁ ①门 door ②上闩，关门 to bolt (the door)

冏 jiǒng ㄐㄩㄥˇ ❶光 light ❷明亮 bright

迥(*逈) jiǒng ㄐㄩㄥˇ 远 distant; far：～异(相差很远) *markedly different* [迥

然］显然，清清楚楚地 distinctly：～不同 *be distinctly different*

泂 jiǒng ㄐㄩㄥˇ 远 remote

䌹（絅、褧）** jiǒng ㄐㄩㄥˇ 古代称罩在外面的单衣 (ancient) unlined outer garment

炯（*烱） jiǒng ㄐㄩㄥˇ 光明，明亮 ⓐbright：目光～～ *gleaming and penetrating eyes*

炅 jiǒng ㄐㄩㄥˇ 火光 firelight ⇨ see also guì on p.232

煚 jiǒng ㄐㄩㄥˇ ❶火 fire ❷日光 sunlight

颎（熲） jiǒng ㄐㄩㄥˇ 火光 firelight

窘 jiǒng ㄐㄩㄥˇ ❶穷困 in straitened circumstances：～迫 *poverty-stricken* | 生活很～ *live a hard life* ❷为难，难堪 embarrassed：～相 *embarrassed look* | 他一时答不上来，显得很～。*He was unable to answer the question straight away and looked rather embarrassed.* ❸使为难 to embarrass：大家一再追问，～得他满脸通红。*He blushed with embarrassment when they all pressed him for an answer.*

JIU ㄐㄧㄡ

纠（糾、*糺） jiū ㄐㄧㄡ ❶缠绕(㊟一缠) to entangle［纠纷］牵连不清的争执 dispute ❷矫正 to rectify：～正 *to correct* | ～偏 *to rectify*［纠察］在群众活动中维持秩序 to maintain order at a public gathering ❸集合（多含贬义）to gang up (often disapproving)：～合 *gang up* | ～集 *gang together* | ～结 *be entangled*

赳 jiū ㄐㄧㄡ ［赳赳］健壮威武的样子 robust and valiant：雄～ *valiant* | ～武夫 *robust and valiant soldiers*

鸠（鳩） jiū ㄐㄧㄡ ❶鸽子一类的鸟，常见的有斑鸠、山鸠等 turtledove ❷聚集（多含贬义）to flock (often disapproving)：～聚 *gang up*

究 jiū ㄐㄧㄡ (formerly pronounced jiù) 推求，追查 to investigate; to probe into：～办 *investigate and deal with* | 追～ *get to the bottom of* | 推～ *examine and explore* | 必须深～ *must get to the bottom of (sth)*［究竟］1 副词，到底，表示追问 (adverb) on earth：～是怎么回事？ *What on earth is this all about?* 2 结果 outcome; truth：大家都想知道个～。*Everyone wants to know exactly what happened.*［终究］副词，到底 (adverb) eventually：问题～会弄清楚的。*The problem will be clarified in the end.*

阄（鬮） jiū ㄐㄧㄡ （～儿）抓阄时用的纸团等 lot［抓阄儿］为了赌胜负或决定事情而各自抓取做好记号的纸团等 to draw lots

揪 jiū ㄐㄧㄡ 用手抓住或拉住 to grab; to pull：赶快～住他！ *Quick! Catch him!* | ～断了

J

绳子 *pulled and snapped the rope* | ～下一块面 *pinch off a piece of dough*

啾 jiū ㄐㄧㄡ ［啾啾］多形容动物的细小的叫声 often used to describe quiet sounds made by animals

鬏 jiū ㄐㄧㄡ （－儿）头发盘成的结 (of hair) bun：梳了个抓～儿 *wear double buns*

九 jiǔ ㄐㄧㄡˇ 数目字 (number) nine ［数九］（shǔ－）从冬至日起始的八十一天，每九天为一个单位，从"一九"数到"九九"to count the Nines (referring to the nine nine-day periods starting from the winter solstice)：～寒天 *coldest time of the year* ㊂表示多次或多数 many：～死一生 *escape from the jaws of death many times* | ～霄 *highest heaven*

氿 jiǔ ㄐㄧㄡˇ 湖名，在江苏省宜兴，分东氿、西氿 Lake Jiu (in Yixing, Jiangsu Province)

⇨ see also guǐ on p.231

久 jiǔ ㄐㄧㄡˇ ❶时间长，跟"暂"相对（㊈长－）(of time) long (opposite of 暂)：年深日～ *with the passage of time* | 很～没有见面了 *have not seen sb for a long time* ❷时间的长短 (of time) length：你来了多～了？*How long have you been here?* | 离别两年之～ *have been parted for two years*

玖 jiǔ ㄐㄧㄡˇ ❶一种像玉的浅黑色石头 blackish jade-like stone ❷"九"字的大写 (elaborate form of 九, used in commercial or financial context) nine

灸 jiǔ ㄐㄧㄡˇ 烧，多指用艾叶等烧灼或熏烤身体某一部分的治疗方法 to treat with moxibustion：针～ *acupuncture and moxibustion*

韭（*韮） jiǔ ㄐㄧㄡˇ 韭菜，草本植物，叶细长而扁，花白色，叶和花嫩时可用作蔬菜 Chinese chives

酒 jiǔ ㄐㄧㄡˇ 用高粱、米、麦或葡萄等发酵制成的含乙醇的饮料，有刺激性，多喝对身体有害 alcoholic drink

旧（舊） jiù ㄐㄧㄡˋ ❶跟"新"相对 old (opposite of 新) ①过去的，过时的 outdated：～俗 *antiquated customs* | ～脑筋 *old way of thinking* | ～社会 *old society* ②因经过长时间而变了样子 old and worn：衣服～了。*The clothes are old now.* ❷指交情，有交情的人 friendship; acquaintance：有～ *have an old friendship/love (with sb)* | 故～ *old friends and acquaintances*

臼 jiù ㄐㄧㄡˋ ❶舂米的器具，一般用石头制成，样子像盆 mortar ❷像臼的 used to refer to things which resemble a mortar：～齿 *molar*

桕 jiù ㄐㄧㄡˋ 乌桕树，落叶乔木，叶秋天变红，花黄色。种子外面包着一层白色脂肪叫桕脂，可制蜡烛和肥皂。种子可榨油 Chinese tallow tree

舅 jiù ㄐㄧㄡˋ ❶母亲的弟兄㊀ uncle (brother of one's mother) ❷（－子）妻子的弟兄 brother-in-law (brother of one's wife): 妻～ *brother-in-law (brother of one's wife)* | 小～子 *brother-in-law (younger brother of one's wife)* ❸古代称丈夫的父亲 (ancient) father-in-law (one's husband's father): ～姑(公婆) *(of a woman) father- and mother-in-law*

咎 jiù ㄐㄧㄡˋ ❶过失，罪 blame; culpability: ～由自取 *have only oneself to blame* ❷怪罪，处分 to blame: 既往不～ *let bygones be bygones* ❸凶 misfortune: 休～(吉凶) *fortune and misfortune*

疚 jiù ㄐㄧㄡˋ 长期生病 chronically ill ㊕对自己的过失感到不安、痛苦 guilty; remorseful: 负～ *conscience-stricken* | 内～ *guilty*

柩 jiù ㄐㄧㄡˋ 装着尸体的棺材 coffin with a corpse inside: 灵～ *coffin containing a corpse*

救(*捄) jiù ㄐㄧㄡˋ 帮助，使脱离困难或危险 to save: ～济 *relieve (poverty)* | ～援 *to rescue* | ～命 *save one's life* | ～火(帮助灭火) *fight a fire* | ～生圈 *lifebuoy* | 求～ *ask sb to come to the rescue*

厩(*廄、*廐) jiù ㄐㄧㄡˋ 马棚，泛指牲口棚 stable; (generally) livestock shed: ～肥 *farmyard manure*

就 jiù ㄐㄧㄡˋ ❶凑近，靠近 to approach: ～着灯光看书 *read by lamplight* | 避重～轻 *avoid the important and dwell on the trivial* ❷从事，开始进入 to engage in; to begin: ～学 *go to school* | ～业 *employment* ❸依照现有情况，趁着 according to: ～近上学 *go to a school nearby* | ～地取材 *make use of local resources* ❹随同着吃、喝下去 to have (a food or drink) with (another food or drink): 小米粥～咸菜 *have millet porridge with pickles* | 花生米～酒 *have peanuts with wine* ❺完成 to accomplish: 造～人才 *train talent* ❻副词 adverb ①加强肯定语气 used as an affirmative intensifier: 这么一来～好办了。*This makes it so much easier.* ②在选择句中跟否定词相应，表示肯定语气 corresponding to the negator in an alternative sentence to indicate the affirmative mode: 不是你去，～是我去。*Either you go or I will.* ❼副词，立刻，不用经过很多时间 (adverb) immediately: 他一来，我～走。*I'll leave the minute he arrives.* | 他～要参军了。*He is joining the army soon.* ❽连词，就是，即使，表示假定 (conjunction) even if, even though: 天～再冷我们也不怕。*We won't be deterred no matter how cold it gets.* | 你～送来，我也不要。*I wouldn't take it even if you brought it to me.* ❾副词，单，只，偏偏 (adverb) only: 他～爱看书。*He loves nothing but reading.* | 怎么～我不能去? *Why am I the only one not allowed to go?*

僦 jiù ㄐㄧㄡˋ 租赁 to rent: ～屋 *rent a house*

J

岆 jiù ㄐㄧㄡˋ 用于地名 used in place names：～峪（在陕西省周至）*Jiuyu (in Zhouzhi, Shaanxi Province)*

鹫(鷲) jiù ㄐㄧㄡˋ 鸟名，身体大，有的颈部无毛。性凶猛，吃动物尸体，也捕食小动物。种类较多，如秃鹫、兀鹫 vulture

JU ㄐㄩ

车(車) jū ㄐㄩ 象棋棋子的一种 (in Chinese chess) chariot

⇨ see also chē on p.72

且 jū ㄐㄩ ❶文言助词，相当于"啊" auxiliary word in classical Chinese, similar to 啊：狂童之狂也～！ *Ah,how foolish the foolish youth!* ❷用于人名 used in given names

⇨ see also qiě on p.535

苴 jū ㄐㄩ 大麻的雌株，开花后能结果实 female hemp plant

岨 jū ㄐㄩ qū ㄑㄩ(又) 带土的石山 earth-covered rocky hill

狙 jū ㄐㄩ 古书里指一种猴子 a type of monkey in ancient Chinese texts

[狙击] 乘人不备，突然出击 to ambush

砠 jū ㄐㄩ 带土的石山 earth-covered rocky hill

疽 jū ㄐㄩ 中医指一种毒疮，局部肿胀坚硬，皮肤颜色不变 (in traditional Chinese medicine) abscess：痈～ *abscess*

趄 jū ㄐㄩ see 趑趄 (zī—) at 趑 on page 880

⇨ see also qiè on p.537

雎 jū ㄐㄩ 雎鸠，古书上说的一种鸟，又叫王雎 a type of bird in ancient Chinese texts (also called 王雎)

拘 jū ㄐㄩ ❶逮捕或扣押(㊊—捕、—押) to arrest; to detain：～票 *arrest warrant* | ～留 *detain* | ～禁 *take into custody* ❷限，限制 to restrain：～管 *restrain* | 不～多少 *no matter how many* ❸拘束，不变通 to restrain; to be inflexible：～谨 *overcautious* | ～泥(nì)成法 *adhere rigidly to established laws and regulations*

沟 jū ㄐㄩ 泃河，水名，发源于河北省东北部，流经北京市东部和天津市北部 Juhe River (originating in the north-east of Hebei Province and flowing through eastern Beijing and northern Tianjin)

驹(駒) jū ㄐㄩ ❶少壮的马 youthful horse：千里～ *winged steed; promising young man* ❷(—子)小马 (of a horse) foal：马～子 *foal* 又指小驴、骡等 (of a donkey, mule, etc.) foal：驴～子 *foal*

鮈(鮈) jū ㄐㄩ 鱼名，身体小，侧扁或近圆筒形，有一对须，背鳍一般没有硬刺。生活在温带淡水中 gudgeon

居 jū ㄐㄩ ❶住 to dwell; to reside：分～ *(of a married cou-*

J

ple) live separately | 久～乡间 *dwell in the countryside for a long time* ❷住处 residence：新～ *new home* | 故～ *former home* ❸站在，处于 to be in (a certain position)：～中 *be in the middle* | ～高临下 *be in a commanding position* | ～间(jiān)调停（在双方中间调解）*mediate between two parties* ❹当，任 to act as：以前辈自～ *assume the airs of a senior* ❺安放 to place：是何～心？*What are you up to?* ❻积蓄，储存 to save：奇货可～ *sth rare that is worth hoarding* | 囤积～奇 *hoard and corner the market* ❼停留 to stop：岁月不～。*Time waits for no one.* | 变动不～ *constantly changing*

[居然] 副词，竟，出乎意外地 (adverb) unexpectedly：没想到他会来，他～来了。*Against all expectations, he turned up.*

据 jū ㄐㄩ see 拮据 (jié—) at 拮 on page 316

⇨ see also jù on p.339

崌 jū ㄐㄩ see 岍崌山 (lì——) at 岍 on page 392

琚 jū ㄐㄩ 古人佩带的一种玉 (ancient) a type of jade ornament

椐 jū ㄐㄩ 古书上说的一种树，枝节肿大，可以做拐杖 a type of tree in ancient Chinese texts

腒 jū ㄐㄩ 干腌的鸟类肉 dried and preserved bird meat

锯(鋸) jū ㄐㄩ same as "锔(jū)"

⇨ see also jù on p.340

裾 jū ㄐㄩ 衣服的大襟 front of a traditional Chinese gown 引衣服的前后部分 front and back of a garment

俱 jū ㄐㄩ 姓 (surname) Ju

⇨ see also jù on p.339

掬 jū ㄐㄩ 用两手捧 to scoop with both hands：以手～水 *scoop water with both hands* | 笑容可～（形容笑得明显）*beam broadly*

鞠 jū ㄐㄩ ❶养育，抚养 to rear; to raise ❷古代的一种皮球 (ancient) a type of leather ball：蹴(cù)～（踢球）cuju, *ancient Chinese sport similar to football*

[鞠躬] 弯腰表示恭敬谨慎，现指弯身行礼 to bow

娵 jū ㄐㄩ ❶[娵隅]（—yú）古代南方少数民族称鱼为娵隅 fish (term used by ethnic groups in southern China in ancient times) ❷姓 (surname) Ju

锔(鋦) jū ㄐㄩ 用锔子（一种两脚钉）连合破裂的器物 to mend (broken items) with clamps：～盆 *mend a basin with clamps* | ～缸 *mend a large cauldron with clamps* | ～锅 *mend a wok with clamps* | ～碗 *mend a bowl with clamps*

⇨ see also jú on p.337

鞫 jū ㄐㄩ ❶审问 to interrogate; to question：～讯 *to interrogate* | ～审 *(of the police) to question* ❷穷困 poverty-stricken

局(❼❽*跼、❽*侷) jú ㄐㄩˊ

J

❶部分 part：～部 *part* ❷机关及团体组织分工办事的单位 (government) bureau：教育～ *bureau of education* | 公安～ *public security bureau* ❸某些商店或办理某些业务的机构的名称 store; organization: 书～ *bookshop* | 邮～ *post office* ❹棋盘 chessboard ❺着棋的形势 situation on the chessboard ⓨ事情的形势、情况 situation：结～ *ending* | 大～ *bigger picture* | 时～ *current political situation* | ～面 *situation* | 搅～ *stir things up* ❻量词，下棋或其他比赛一次叫一局 (measure word) game (in chess and other games) ❼弯曲 bent ❽拘束，拘谨 constrained [局促] 1 狭小 confined; cramped 2 拘谨不自然 constrained：他在生人面前有些～。*He is a bit awkward with strangers.*

焗 jú ㄐㄩˊ 〈方 dialect〉烹饪方法，利用蒸气使密封容器中的食物变熟 to steam (food)：盐～鸡 *salted steamed chicken* [焗油] 一种染发、养发、护发方法。在头发上抹油后，用特制机具蒸气加热，待冷却后用清水冲洗干净 to treat hair with oil

锔 (鋦) jú ㄐㄩˊ 人造的放射性金属元素，符号 Cm。curium (Cm)

⇨ see also jū on p.336

桔 jú ㄐㄩˊ informal written form for 橘

⇨ see also jié on p.317

菊 jú ㄐㄩˊ 菊花，草本植物，秋天开花，颜色、形状各异，供观赏。种类很多，有的花可入药 chrysanthemum

湨 jú ㄐㄩˊ 湨河，水名，在河南省济源 Juhe River (in Jiyuan, Henan Province)

鶪 (鶪) jú ㄐㄩˊ 古书上说的一种鸟，即伯劳，嘴坚硬而锐利，捕食鱼、虫、小鸟等，是益鸟 shrike (in ancient Chinese texts, same as 伯劳)

橘 jú ㄐㄩˊ 橘树，常绿乔木，果实叫橘子，扁球形，味甜酸。果皮红黄色，可入药 mandarin (its fruit is called 橘子)

弆 jǔ ㄐㄩˇ 收藏，保藏 to keep; to preserve：藏～ *collect*

柜 jǔ ㄐㄩˇ 柜柳，落叶乔木，即枫杨，羽状复叶，性耐湿、耐碱，可固沙。枝韧，可以编筐 Chinese wingnut (same as 枫杨)

⇨ see also guì on p.232

矩 (*榘) jǔ ㄐㄩˇ ❶画方形的工具 (carpentry) square：～尺 (曲尺) *carpentry square* | 不以规～不能成方圆。*Nothing can be accomplished without proper rules and regulations (literally means 'without a compass or square, one will not be able to draw a circle or square').* ❷法则，规则 regulation：循规蹈～ *be stuck in a groove*

咀 jǔ ㄐㄩˇ 含在嘴里细细玩味 to chew：含英～华 (喻读书吸取精华) *absorb the essence (of a book)* [咀嚼] (－jué) 嚼 (jiáo) to chew ⓨ体味 to chew over

⇨ see also zuǐ on p.889

沮 jǔ ㄐㄩˇ ❶阻止 to prevent ❷坏，败坏 to feel gloomy [沮

丧］（－sàng）失意，懊丧 feel dejected

⇨ see also jù on p.339

龃（齟）jǔ ㄐㄩˇ ［龃龉］（－yǔ）牙齿上下对不上 malocclusion 喻 意见不合 to disagree

莒 jǔ ㄐㄩˇ 周代诸侯国名，在今山东省莒南一带 Ju (a state in the Zhou Dynasty, in today's Junan, Shandong Province)

筥 jǔ ㄐㄩˇ 圆形的竹筐 round bamboo basket

枸 jǔ ㄐㄩˇ ［枸橼］（－yuán）常绿乔木，又叫香橼，花白色。果实有香气，味酸 citron (also called 香橼)

⇨ see also gōu on p.215, gǒu on p.215

蒟 jǔ ㄐㄩˇ 植物名 plant name ①蒟蒻（ruò），草本植物，又叫魔芋，地下茎扁球形，生吃有毒，可入药 devil's tongue (also called 魔芋) ②蒟酱，藤本植物，又叫蒌叶，花绿色。果实有辣味，可制调味品 betel pepper (also called 蒌叶)

举（舉、*擧）jǔ ㄐㄩˇ ❶向上抬，向上托 to raise：～手 *raise one's hands*｜高～红旗 *hold aloft the red flag* 引①动作行为 behaviour：～止 *bearing*｜一～一动 *every move* ②发起，兴起 to initiate：～义 *start an uprising*｜～事 *rise up in arms*｜～办 *hold (an event)* ❷提出 to cite：～证 *cite as evidence*｜～例 *give an example*｜～出一件事实来 *cite a fact* ❸推选，推荐 to elect：大家～他做代表。*He was elected as representative.* ❹全 all：～国 *throughout the country*｜～世 *the whole world* ❺举人的简称 a successful candidate in the imperial examinations at the provincial level in the Ming and Qing dynasties (short for 举人)：中（zhòng）～ *be a successful candidate in the imperial civil service examination at the provincial level (in the Ming and Qing dynasties)*｜武～ *successful candidate in the military imperial examination*

榉（櫸）jǔ ㄐㄩˇ ❶榉树，落叶乔木，和榆相似。木材耐水，可造船 Chinese zelkova ❷山毛榉，落叶乔木，花淡黄绿色，树皮像鳞片。木质很坚硬，可用来制枕木、家具等 south Chinese beech

踽 jǔ ㄐㄩˇ ［踽踽］形容独自走路孤零零的样子 (of walking) solitary：～独行 *walking alone*

巨（❶△*鉅）jù ㄐㄩˋ ❶大 huge：～浪 *huge wave*｜～型飞机 *large aircraft*｜～款 *huge sums of money* ❷姓 (surname) Ju

⇨ 鉅 see also 钜 on p.339

讵（詎）jù ㄐㄩˋ 岂，怎 how come：～料 *who would have expected*｜～知 *who would have known*

拒 jù ㄐㄩˋ 抵挡，抵抗（连 抗－）to resist：～敌 *repel the enemy*｜～捕 *resist arrest*｜～腐蚀，永不沾 *resist corruption and never be contaminated* 引不接受

to refuse: ～绝 *turn down* | ～聘 *turn down a job offer*

苣 jù ㄐㄩˋ see 莴苣 (wōju) at 莴 on page 687

⇨ see also qǔ on p.548

岠 jù ㄐㄩˋ ❶大山 mountain ❷东岠岛、西岠岛，岛名，都在浙江省舟山市 Dongju Island, Xiju Island (both in Zhoushan, Zhejiang Province)

炬 jù ㄐㄩˋ 火把 (flaming) torch: 火～ *torch*

钜(鉅) jù ㄐㄩˋ ❶用于地名 used in place names: ～桥镇（在河南省鹤壁）*Juqiaozhen (in Hebi, Henan Province)* ❷姓 (surname) Ju

⇨ 鉅 see also 巨 on p.338

秬 jù ㄐㄩˋ 黑黍子 black millet

距 jù ㄐㄩˋ ❶距离，离开 be away from: 相～数里 *be several miles apart* | ～今已数年 *already several years ago* ㊀两者相离的长度 distance: 株～ *plant spacing* ❷雄鸡爪后面突出像脚趾的部分 (rooster) spur ❸ (ancient) same as "拒"

句 jù ㄐㄩˋ （－子）由词和词组组成的能表示一个完整意思的话 sentence

⇨ see also gōu on p.214

具 jù ㄐㄩˋ ❶器具，器物 tool: 工～ *tool* | 家～ *furniture* | 文～ *stationery* | 农～ *farming tools* ❷备，备有 to have: ～备 *to have* | 略～规模 *begin to take shape* [具体] 1 明确，不抽象，不笼统 concrete: 这个计划定得很～。*This is a very detailed plan.* 2 特定的 specific: ～的人 *specific person* | ～的工作 *specific work*

俱 jù ㄐㄩˋ 全，都 all: 父母～存。*Both one's parents are alive.* | 面面～到 *touch upon everything*

⇨ see also jū on p.336

惧(懼) jù ㄐㄩˋ 害怕 (㊥恐－) to fear: 临危不～ *remain calm in the face of danger*

犋 jù ㄐㄩˋ 畜力单位名，能拉动一辆车、一张犁、一张耙等的一头或几头牲口叫一犋，多指两头 unit of animal power (enough to pull a cart, etc., often refers to two draught animals)

飓(颶) jù ㄐㄩˋ 飓风，发生在大西洋西部和西印度群岛一带热带海洋上的风暴，风力常达12级以上，同时有暴雨 hurricane

沮 jù ㄐㄩˋ [沮洳] (－rù) 低湿的地带 swamp

⇨ see also jǔ on p.337

倨 jù ㄐㄩˋ 傲慢 supercilious: 前～后恭 *supercilious first and then ingratiating* | ～傲 *haughty*

剧(劇) jù ㄐㄩˋ ❶厉害，猛烈 drastic; violent: ～痛 *severe pain* | 加～ *to aggravate* | ～烈 *strenuous* ❷戏剧，文艺的一种形式，作家把剧本编写出来，利用舞台由演员化装演出 drama

据(據、*摅) jù ㄐㄩˋ ❶凭依，倚仗 to rely on ❷介词，依据 (prepo-

J

sition) according to：～理力争 *argue strongly based on principle* | ～我看问题不大。*As far as I can see, it's not a big problem.* ❸占（㊀占一）to seize：～守 *to defend* | ～为己有 *to appropriate (sth) as one's own* ❹可以用作证明的事物，凭证（㊀凭一、证一）evidence：收～ *receipt* | 字～ *written pledge* | 票～ *bonds and securities; receipt* | 真凭实～ *conclusive evidence* | 无凭无～ *groundless*

⇨ see also jū on p.336

锯（鋸） jù ㄐㄩˋ ❶用薄钢片制成的器具，有尖齿，可以拉（lá）开木料、石料等 saw：拉～ *use a saw* | 手～ *handsaw* | 电～ *electric saw* ❷用锯拉（lá）to saw：～木头 *saw logs* | ～树 *saw a tree*

⇨ see also jū on p.336

踞 jù ㄐㄩˋ ❶蹲或坐 to squat; to sit：龙蟠（pán）虎～（形容地势险要）*(of a strategic location) forbidding and inaccessible* | 箕～（古人席地而坐，把两腿像八字形分开，是一种不拘礼节、傲慢不敬的坐姿）*sit on the floor with splayed legs* ❷占据 to occupy：盘～ *occupy illegally*

聚 jù ㄐㄩˋ 会合，集合（㊀一集）to gather; to come together：大家～在一起谈话。*People gathered around and chatted.* | ～少成多。*Many small amounts build up to make a large amount.* | 欢～ *have a happy reunion*

窭（窶） jù ㄐㄩˋ 贫穷 poor

屦（屨） jù ㄐㄩˋ 古代的一种鞋，用麻、葛等制成 (ancient) a type of shoe (made from flax or vines)

遽 jù ㄐㄩˋ ❶急，仓猝 hasty; rushed：不敢～下断语 *unwilling to jump to a hasty conclusion* ❷遂，就 then

澽 jù ㄐㄩˋ 澽水，水名，在陕西省 Jushui River (in Shaanxi Province)

醵 jù ㄐㄩˋ ❶凑钱喝酒 pool money to buy drinks ❷聚集，凑（钱）to pool (money)：～资 *pool money*

JUAN ㄐㄩㄢ

捐 juān ㄐㄩㄢ ❶捐助或献出 to donate：～钱 *donate money* | ～棉衣 *donate cotton padded coats* | ～献 *make a donation* | 募～ *ask for donations* ❷赋税的一种 levy; tax：房～ *property tax* | 车～ *vehicle tax* ❸舍弃（㊀一弃）to give up：为国～躯 *lay down one's life for one's country*

涓 juān ㄐㄩㄢ 细小的流水 streamlet［涓滴］极小量的水 tiny droplets of water ㊀极少量的钱或物 tiny amount (of money, etc.)：～归公。*Every public penny should go to the public purse.*

娟 juān ㄐㄩㄢ 秀丽，美好 elegant：～秀 *graceful*

焆 juān ㄐㄩㄢ 明亮 bright

鹃（鵑） juān ㄐㄩㄢ see 杜鹃 at 杜 on page 148

圈 juān ㄐㄩㄢ 关闭起来，用栅栏等围起来 to pen up：把小鸡～起来 *pen up the chicks*

⇨ see also juàn on p.341, quān on p.549

朘 juān ㄐㄩㄢ 缩，减 to contract; to decrease

镌(鐫、鎸)** juān ㄐㄩㄢ 雕刻 to carve：～刻图章 *carve a seal* | ～碑 *engrave a stone tablet*

蠲 juān ㄐㄩㄢ 免除（㊀一除、一免）to waive

卷(捲) juǎn ㄐㄩㄢˇ ❶把东西弯转裹成圆筒形 to roll：～行李 *roll up one's luggage* | ～帘子 *draw up the curtains* ❷一种大的力量把东西撮（cuō）起或裹住 sweep up：风～着雨点劈面打来。*The wind whipped up the rain and lashed it against one's face.* | ～入旋涡（喻被牵连到不利的事件中）*be sucked into a whirlpool (referring to a negative situation)* ❸（一儿）弯转裹成的筒形的东西 roll：烟～儿 *cigarette* | 行李～儿 *bedding roll* | 纸～儿 *paper roll* ❹（一儿）量词，用于成卷儿的东西 (measure word) roll：一～胶布 *a roll of tape* | 两～纸 *two rolls of paper*

⇨ see also juàn on p.341

锩(錈) juǎn ㄐㄩㄢˇ 刀剑卷刃 (of the edge of a knife or sword) to turn

卷 juàn ㄐㄩㄢˋ ❶可以舒卷（juǎn）的书画 scroll：手～ *hand scroll* | 长～ *long scroll* ❷书籍的册本或篇章 volume：第一～ *volume one* | 上～ *part one* | ～二 *volume two* ❸（一子、一儿）考试写答案的纸 exam paper：试～ *exam paper* | 交～ *hand in an exam paper* | 历史～子 *history exam paper* ❹案卷，机关里分类汇存的档案、文件 dossier; archive：～宗 *dossier; folder* | 查一查底～ *have a look at the original archives*

⇨ see also juǎn on p.341

倦(*勌) juàn ㄐㄩㄢˋ 疲乏，懈怠（㊀疲一）tired：诲人不～ *never weary of teaching* | 厌～ *be tired of*

圈 juàn ㄐㄩㄢˋ 养家畜等的栅栏 pen; fold：猪～ *pigsty* | 羊～ *sheepfold*

⇨ see also juān on p.341, quān on p.549

桊 juàn ㄐㄩㄢˋ 穿在牛鼻上的小铁环或小木棍儿 (of cattle) nose ring; nose stick：牛鼻～儿 *(of cattle) nose ring*

眷(❶*睠) juàn ㄐㄩㄢˋ ❶顾念，爱恋 to have tender feelings for：～顾 *show concern for* | ～恋 *be emotionally attached to* ❷亲属 kin：～属 *family members; (specifically) couple* | 家～ *wife and children (sometimes referring specifically to wife)* | 亲～ *relatives*

隽(*雋) juàn ㄐㄩㄢˋ 肥肉 fatty meat

［隽永］（言论、文章）意味深长 (of words or articles) profound

⇨ see also jùn on p.346

狷(*獧) juàn ㄐㄩㄢˋ ❶胸襟狭窄，急躁 narrow-minded; impatient：～急 *irascible* ❷耿直 upright

绢(絹) juàn ㄐㄩㄢˋ 一种薄的丝织物 thin silk fabric［手绢］手帕 handkerchief

罥 juàn ㄐㄩㄢˋ 挂 to hang

鄄 juàn ㄐㄩㄢˋ 鄄城，地名，在山东省 Juancheng (a place in Shandong Province)

JUE ㄐㄩㄝ

屩(屫、*蹻) juē ㄐㄩㄝ 草鞋 straw sandals

⇨ 蹻 see also qiāo 跷 on p.533

撅 juē ㄐㄩㄝ ❶翘起 stick up：～着尾巴 *stick up its tail*｜小辫儿～着。*One's pigtails are sticking up.* ❷折（zhé）to snap：把竿子～断了 *snapped the bamboo pole*

噘 juē ㄐㄩㄝ 翘起（嘴唇）to pout：～嘴 *to pout*

孓 jué ㄐㄩㄝˊ ［孑孓］（jié－）蚊子的幼虫 wriggler

决(*決) jué ㄐㄩㄝˊ ❶原义为疏导水流，后转为堤岸被水冲开口子 (originally) channel a flow; (later) (of a dam) to burst：～口 *(of a dam) to burst; breach*［决裂］破裂（指感情、关系、商谈等）break up：谈判～。*Negotiations break down.* ❷决定，拿定主意 to decide：～心 *determination; be determined*｜迟疑不～ *remain hesitant*［决议］经过会议讨论决定的事项 resolution (by a committee, council, etc.) ⑤副词，一定，必定 (adverb) definitely; absolutely：他～不会失败。*There is no way that he can fail.* ❸决定最后胜负 decide the outcome：～赛 *final*｜～战 *decisive battle* ❹执行死刑 to execute：枪～ *execute by firing squad*

诀(訣) jué ㄐㄩㄝˊ ❶诀窍，高明的方法 trick; knack：秘～ *secret of success*｜妙～ *ingenious method* ❷用事物的主要内容编成的顺口的便于记忆的词句 mnemonic formula：口～ *mnemonic formula*｜歌～ *versified mnemonic formula* ❸辞别，多指不再相见的分别（㊀－别）bid farewell (usually forever)：永～ *bid farewell forever*

抉 jué ㄐㄩㄝˊ 剔出 pick out［抉择］挑选，选择 to choose

驶(駃) jué ㄐㄩㄝˊ ［驶騠］（－tí）1 驴骡，由公马和母驴交配所生 hinny 2 古书上说的一种骏马 a kind of steed (in ancient Chinese texts)

玦 jué ㄐㄩㄝˊ 环形有缺口的佩玉 penannular jade ring

砄 jué ㄐㄩㄝˊ ❶石头 stone ❷用于地名 used in place names：石～（在吉林省集安）*Shijue (in Ji'an, Jilin Province)*

鴃(鴂) jué ㄐㄩㄝˊ 古书上说的一种鸟，即伯劳，嘴坚硬而锐利，捕食鱼、虫、小鸟等，是益鸟 shrike (in ancient Chinese texts, same as 伯劳)

觖 jué ㄐㄩㄝˊ 不满 discontented [觖望] 因不满而怨恨 feel bitter and discontented

角 jué ㄐㄩㄝˊ ❶竞争，争胜 to compete; to contend：～斗 *to wrestle* | ～逐 *to contend* | 口～(吵嘴) *to quarrel* ❷(一儿) 演员，角色 actor; actress; role：主～ *lead (in a film or play)* | 他演什么～儿？ *What role did he play?* [角色] (*脚色) 1 戏曲演员按所扮演人物的性别和性格等分的类型。又叫行当。如京剧的"生、旦、净、丑" (also called 行当) role (in traditional Chinese opera) 2 戏剧或电影里演员所扮演的剧中人物 character (in a play or film) ❸古代五音"宫、商、角、徵(zhǐ)、羽"之一 *jue*, one of the five notes in the ancient Chinese pentatonic scale ❹古代形状像爵的酒器 (ancient) a type of wine vessel ❺姓 (surname) Jue

⇨ see also jiǎo on p.311

桷 jué ㄐㄩㄝˊ 方形的椽(chuán)子 square rafter

珏 jué ㄐㄩㄝˊ 合在一起的两块玉 two jade pieces joined together

觉(覺) jué ㄐㄩㄝˊ ❶(人或动物的器官) 对刺激的感受和辨别 to sense; to perceive：视～ *vision* | 听～ *hearing* | ～得 *to feel; to think* | 不知不～ *without one's being aware of it* ❷睡醒，醒悟 wake up：如梦初～ *as if waking up from a dream* | ～醒 *wake up (to reality)* | ～悟 *come to realize; political awareness*

⇨ see also jiào on p.313

绝(絕) jué ㄐㄩㄝˊ ❶断 to sever：～望 *lose all hope* | 络绎不～ *in an endless stream* [绝句] 我国旧体诗的一种，每首四句，每句五字或七字，有一定的平仄和押韵的限制 *jueju* (a form of classical Chinese poetry consisting of four lines, and with five or seven characters in each line) ❷尽，穷尽 to exhaust：气～ *breathe one's last* | 法子都想～了 *cannot think of any more methods* [绝境] 没有希望、没有出路的情况 hopeless situation ❸极，极端的 extreme：～妙 *marvellous* | ～密 *top-secret* ㊀独一无二的，无人能及的 unique; unrivalled：～技 *unique skill* | 这幅画真叫～了。*This painting is absolutely stunning.* [绝顶] 1 山的最高峰 summit：泰山～ *summit of Mount Tai* 2 副词，极端，非常 (adverb) extremely：～聪明 *extremely clever* ❹副词，一定，无论如何 (adverb) on any account：～不允许这样的事再次发生。*This must never be allowed to happen again.* [绝对] 1 副词，一定，肯定 (adverb) absolutely：～可以取胜 *can definitely win* | ～能够办到 *can definitely do it* 2 无条件，无限制，不依存于任何事物的，跟"相对"相对 absolute (opposite of 相对)：物质世界的存在是～的。*The existence of the material world is absolute.*

倔 jué ㄐㄩㄝˊ 义同"倔"(juè)，只用于"倔强" same in mean-

J

ing as 倔 (juè) (only used in 倔强)
[倔强]（－jiàng）（性情）刚强不屈，固执 stubborn：性格～。*The character is stubborn.*

⇨ see also juè on p.345

掘 jué ㄐㄩㄝˊ 挖，刨 to dig：～地 *to dig* | 临渴～井 *not prepare until it's too late*

崛 jué ㄐㄩㄝˊ 高起，突起 to rise high：～起 *rise to prominence*

脚(*腳) jué ㄐㄩㄝˊ （－儿）(old) same as "角 (jué) ❷"

⇨ see also jiǎo on p.312

厥 jué ㄐㄩㄝˊ ❶气闭，昏倒 to pass out; to faint：晕～ *pass out* | 痰～ *phlegm syncope* ❷文言代词，其，他的，那个的 (pronoun in classical Chinese) his; her; that of：～父 *his/her father* | ～后 *their offspring; after that* | 大放～词 *to rant*

劂 jué ㄐㄩㄝˊ see 剞劂 (jī－) at 剞 on page 283

蕨 jué ㄐㄩㄝˊ 草本植物，野生，用孢子繁殖。嫩叶叫蕨菜，可以吃，地下茎可制淀粉 fern (its tender leaves are called 蕨菜)

獗 jué ㄐㄩㄝˊ see 猖獗 (chāng－) at 猖 on page 68

潏 jué ㄐㄩㄝˊ 潏水，水名，在湖北省随州，涢（yún）水支流 Jueshui River (in Suizhou, Hubei Province, branch of Yunshui River)

橛(*橜) jué ㄐㄩㄝˊ （－子、－儿）小木桩 wooden peg

镢(鐝) jué ㄐㄩㄝˊ〈方 dialect〉（－头）刨地用的农具 digging hoe

蹶(**蹷) jué ㄐㄩㄝˊ 跌倒 to fall; to trip (up) ⓔ挫折，失败 suffer a setback：一～不振 *unable to bounce back after a setback*

⇨ see also juě on p.345

傕 jué ㄐㄩㄝˊ 用于人名。李傕，东汉末人 Jue (used in given names, e.g. Li Jue, in the late Eastern Han Dynasty)

谲(譎) jué ㄐㄩㄝˊ 欺诈，玩弄手段 be crafty：诡～ *treacherous*

镭(鐍) jué ㄐㄩㄝˊ 箱子上安锁的环状物 ring on a trunk (for installing a lock)

噱 jué ㄐㄩㄝˊ 大笑 laugh out loud

⇨ see also xué on p.741

爵 jué ㄐㄩㄝˊ ❶古代的酒器 (ancient) a type of wine vessel ❷爵位，君主国家贵族封号的等级 rank of nobility：侯～ *marquess* | 封～ *confer a title of nobility*

嚼 jué ㄐㄩㄝˊ 义同"嚼"（jiáo），用于书面语复合词 same in meaning as 嚼 (jiáo) (in compounds in written Chinese)：咀（jǔ）～ *to chew; (figurative) to contemplate*

⇨ see also jiáo on p.311, jiào on p.314

爝 jué ㄐㄩㄝˊ jiào ㄐㄧㄠˋ（又）火把 (flaming) torch

矍 jué ㄐㄩㄝˊ [矍铄]（－shuò）形容老年人精神好

hale and hearty

攫 jué ㄐㄩㄝˊ 用爪抓取 (of a bird of prey) seize (sth) with its talons ㊀夺取（㊥一夺、一取）to seize

玃 jué ㄐㄩㄝˊ 古书上指一种较大的猴子 a type of large monkey in ancient Chinese texts

钁（鐝） jué ㄐㄩㄝˊ ❶（一头）刨土的农具 pickaxe ❷用锄掘地 dig with a pickaxe

蹶 juě ㄐㄩㄝˇ ［尥蹶子］(liào-zi) 骡马等跳起来用后腿向后踢 (of a mule or horse) kick with its back legs

⇨ see also jué on p.344

倔 juè ㄐㄩㄝˋ 言语直，态度生硬 surly; brusque：那老头子真～。*That old man is so brusque.*

⇨ see also jué on p.343

JUN ㄐㄩㄣ

军（軍） jūn ㄐㄩㄣ ❶武装部队 armed forces：～队 *armed forces* | 解放～ *Chinese People's Liberation Army* | 海～ *navy* ❷军队的编制单位，是师的上一级 (military unit) army, corps ❸泛指有组织的集体 (generally) army (of people)：劳动大～ *army of workers*

皲（皸） jūn ㄐㄩㄣ 皮肤因寒冷或干燥而破裂 (of skin) to chap：手脚～裂 *chapped hands and feet* 也作"龟" (jūn) (also written as 龟 jūn)

均 jūn ㄐㄩㄣ ❶平，匀（yún）（㊥一匀、平一）even; equal：～分 *distribute evenly* | 平～数 *average* | 势～力敌 *be evenly matched* ❷都（dōu），皆 all：老小～安。*The family are all doing well.* | ～已布置就绪。*Everything has been set up.*

〈古 ancient〉also same as 韵 (yùn)

钧（鈞） jūn ㄐㄩㄣ ❶古代重量单位，合三十斤 *jun* (an ancient Chinese unit for measuring weight, equal to 30 斤)：千～一发（喻极其危险的事态）*be in imminent danger* ❷制陶器所用的转轮 potter's wheel：陶～（喻造就人才）*nurture talents* ❸敬辞（对尊长或上级）(polite speech, addressing one's senior) you, your：～命 *your order* | ～安 *your good health* | ～鉴 *your attention*

筠 jūn ㄐㄩㄣ ［筠连］地名，在四川省 Junlian (a place in Sichuan Province)

⇨ see also yún on p.812

龟（龜） jūn ㄐㄩㄣ same as "皲"

⇨ see also guī on p.231, qiū on p.543

君 jūn ㄐㄩㄣ ❶封建时代指帝王、诸侯等 monarch, lord (in feudal times) ❷敬辞 used as a polite speech：张～ *Mr Zhang* ［君子］古指有地位的人，后又指品行好的人 gentleman

莙 jūn ㄐㄩㄣ ［莙荙菜］（一dá一）甜菜的变种，又叫厚皮菜、牛皮菜，叶大而肥厚，可用作蔬菜 chard (also called 厚皮菜, 牛皮菜)

J

鲪(鮶) jūn ㄐㄩㄣ 鱼名，身体侧扁而长，口大而斜，尾鳍圆形。生活在海里 marine rockfish

菌 jūn ㄐㄩㄣ 低等生物名 name of lower life forms ①真菌，不开花，没有茎和叶子，不含叶绿素，不能自己制造养料，以寄生方式生活，种类很多 fungus ②细菌，一大类单细胞的微生物，特指能使人生病的病原细菌 bacteria; (specifically) pathogenic bacteria

⇨ see also jùn on p.346

麇 jūn ㄐㄩㄣ 古书里指獐子 Chinese water deer (in ancient Chinese texts)

⇨ see also qún on p.554

俊(❶*儁、❶*雋) jùn ㄐㄩㄣˋ ❶才智过人的 very talented: ～杰 *person of outstanding talent*｜～士 *person of outstanding talent* ❷容貌美丽 beautiful: 那姑娘真～。*That girl is really beautiful.*｜～俏 *pretty*

峻 jùn ㄐㄩㄣˋ 山高而陡 precipitous: ～峭 *precipitous*｜陡～ *steep*｜崇山～岭 *soaring mountains and precipitous peaks* ㊐喻 严厉苛刻 harsh: 严刑～法 *harsh punishments and draconian laws*

馂(餕) jùn ㄐㄩㄣˋ 吃剩下的食物 leftovers

浚(*濬) jùn ㄐㄩㄣˋ 疏通，挖深（㊐连疏一）to dredge: ～井 *dredge a well*｜～河 *dredge a river*

⇨ see also xùn on p.744

骏(駿) jùn ㄐㄩㄣˋ 好马 steed

晙 jùn ㄐㄩㄣˋ ❶早晨 morning ❷明亮 bright

焌 jùn ㄐㄩㄣˋ 用火烧 to burn

⇨ see also qū on p.547

葰 jùn ㄐㄩㄣˋ 大 large

⇨ see also suǒ on p.630

畯 jùn ㄐㄩㄣˋ 指西周管奴隶耕种的官 government official in charge of slave agriculture (in the Western Zhou Dynasty)

竣 jùn ㄐㄩㄣˋ 事情完毕 to complete: ～工 *(of a project) be completed*｜大工告～。*Mission accomplished.*

郡 jùn ㄐㄩㄣˋ 古代行政区域，秦以前比县小，从秦代起比县大 (ancient) prefecture

捃 jùn ㄐㄩㄣˋ 拾取 to pick up: ～摭（zhí）（搜集）*to collect*

珺 jùn ㄐㄩㄣˋ 一种美玉 a type of fine jade

隽(*雋) jùn ㄐㄩㄣˋ same as "俊❶"

⇨ see also juàn on p.341

菌 jùn ㄐㄩㄣˋ 就是蕈（xùn）(same as 蕈 xùn) mushroom

⇨ see also jūn on p.346

䐃 jùn ㄐㄩㄣˋ 〈古 ancient〉❶肌肉突起处 protuberance of muscle ❷腹内或肠间的脂肪 fat in the abdomen or intestines

J

K ㄎ

KA ㄎㄚ

咔 kā ㄎㄚ 形容器物清脆的撞击声或断裂声 click：～，门锁撞上了。*The door locked with a click.* [咔嚓]（－chā）形容树枝等折断的声音 crack; snap

⇨ see also kǎ on p.347

咖 kā ㄎㄚ [咖啡]（－fēi）（外 loanword）常绿灌木或小乔木，生长在热带，花白色，果实红色，种子可制饮料。也指这种饮料 coffee (plant or drink)

⇨ see also gā on p.193

喀 kā ㄎㄚ ❶形容呕吐、咳嗽等的声音 used to describe the choking sound of vomiting or coughing ❷ same as "咔 (kā)"

揢 kā ㄎㄚ 用刀子刮 to scrape with a blade

卡 kǎ ㄎㄚˇ（外 loanword）❶卡车，载重的大汽车 lorry; truck：十轮～ *10 wheeler truck* ❷卡片，小的纸片（一般是比较硬的纸）card：资料～ *data card* | 贺年～ *New Year card* ❸卡路里的简称，热量的非法定计量单位，符号 cal，1 克纯水的温度升高 1 摄氏度所需的热量为 1 卡，合 4.186 8 焦 cal; (gram) calorie

[卡通]（外 loanword）1 动画片 animated cartoon 2 漫画 cartoon

⇨ see also qiǎ on p.524

佧 kǎ ㄎㄚˇ [佧佤族]（－wǎ－）佤族的旧称 old name for 佤族

咔 kǎ ㄎㄚˇ [咔叽]（－jī）（外 loanword）一种很厚的斜纹布 khaki (cloth)

⇨ see also kā on p.347

胩 kǎ ㄎㄚˇ 有机化合物的一类，异腈（jīng）的旧称，无色液体，有恶臭，剧毒 carbylamine (old name of 异腈 jīng)

咯 kǎ ㄎㄚˇ 用力使东西从食道或气管里出来 to cough up：把鱼刺～出来 *cough up a fishbone* | ～血 *cough up blood* | ～痰 *cough up phlegm*

⇨ see also gē on p.203, lo on p.414

KAI ㄎㄞ

开（開） kāi ㄎㄞ ❶把关闭的东西打开 to open; to turn on：～门 *open a door* | ～抽屉 *pull open a drawer* | ～口说话 *start to talk* 引 ①收拢的东西放散 to open out：～花 *(of flowers) bloom* | ～颜（笑）*to smile* ②把整体的东西划分成部分的 to divide into parts：三十二～本 *32 mo* ③凝结的东西融化 to thaw out：～冻 *to thaw* | ～河（河水化冻）*(of a river) thaw out and be navigable*

[开交] 分解，脱离（多用于否

定式）(often used in the negative) to disentangle; to break free：忙得不可～ *have one's hands full*｜闹得不可～ *kick up a blazing row* ❷通，使通 to open up; to clear out：想不～ *take things too hard*｜～路先锋 *trailblazer*［开通］（－tong）思想不守旧，容易接受新事物 open-minded; enlightened ❸使显露出来 to uncover：～采 *to mine*｜～发 *to develop; open up; to exploit*｜～矿 *open a mine* ❹扩大，发展 to extend; to develop：～拓（tuò）*open up; to explore*｜～源节流 *tap new sources and regulate outflow*｜～展 *to launch; carry out* ❺发动，操纵 to start up; to operate：～车 *drive a vehicle*｜～船 *sail a ship*｜～炮 *fire a cannon*｜～动脑筋 *use one's brains*［开火］指发生军事冲突 to open fire; to engage in battle ㊀两方面冲突 to start a conflict ❻起始 to begin：～端 *beginning*｜～春 *(of spring) begin*｜～学 *(of a semester) begin*｜～工 *go into operation; begin construction*｜～演 *(of play, film) to start*｜刚～了个头儿 *just started* ❼设置，建立 set up; to establish：～医院 *establish a hospital*［开国］建立新的国家 to found a new state ❽支付 to pay：～支 *to spend; expenditure*｜～销 *to pay; expense* ❾沸，滚 to boil：～水 *boiled water*｜水～了。*The water is boiling.* ❿举行 to hold (a convention,etc.)：～会 *hold a meeting* ⓫写 to write out：～发票 *make out an invoice*｜～药方 *write a prescription* ⓬放在动词后面，表示趋向或结果 used after a verb to indicate direction or result ①表示分开或扩展 to spread; to extend：睁～眼 *open one's eyes*｜张～嘴 *open up one's mouth*｜打～窗户 *open the window*｜消息传～了。*The news has spread widely.* ②表示开始并继续下去 to begin and continue：雨下～了。*The rain has started falling.*｜唱～了 *start to sing* ③表示容下 to hold; to contain：屋子小，坐不～。*The room is too small for so many people.* ⓭（外 loanword）黄金的纯度单位（以二十四开为纯金）carat：十八～金 *18-carat gold* ⓮热力学温度单位名开尔文的简称，符号 K。Kelvin (K)

锎（鐦） kāi ㄎㄞ 人造的放射性金属元素，符号 Cf。californium (Cf)

揩 kāi ㄎㄞ 擦，抹 to wipe：～鼻涕 *wipe a runny nose*｜～背 *wipe one's back*｜～油（喻占便宜 piányi）*get petty advantages (at the expense of other people/ the state)*

剀（剴） kǎi ㄎㄞˇ［剀切］（－qiè）1 符合事理 true and pertinent：～中（zhòng）理 *be true and pertinent* 2 切实 earnest and sincere：～教导 *earnestly teach*

凯（凱） kǎi ㄎㄞˇ 军队得胜回来奏的乐曲 strains of triumph：～歌 *song of triumph*｜奏～（指取得胜利）*win a victory*｜～旋（得胜回还）*make a*

K

triumphant return

垲(塏) kǎi ㄎㄞˇ 地势高而干燥 (of topography) high and arid

闿(闓) kǎi ㄎㄞˇ 开 to open

恺(愷) kǎi ㄎㄞˇ 快乐，和乐 happy; joyful

铠(鎧) kǎi ㄎㄞˇ 铠甲，古代的战衣，上面缀有金属薄片，可以保护身体 (a suit of) armour

莰 kǎi ㄎㄞˇ 莰烷，有机化合物，是莰（kǎn）的同分异构体，天然的莰尚未发现 carane

楷 kǎi ㄎㄞˇ ❶法式，模范（㊥—模）model; pattern ❷楷书，现在通行的一种汉字字体，是由隶书演变而来的 regular script in Chinese calligraphy：小～ *regular script in small characters* | 正～ *regular script*

⇨ see also jiē on p.315

锴(鍇) kǎi ㄎㄞˇ 好铁，多用于人名 (often used in given names) quality iron

慨(❷*嘅) kǎi ㄎㄞˇ ❶愤激 indignant：愤～ *be indignant* ❷感慨 to sigh with emotion：～叹 *lament with sighs* ❸慷慨，不吝啬 generous：～允 *kindly consent; generously promise* | ～然相赠 *give generously*

忾(愾) kài ㄎㄞˋ 愤怒，恨 anger; hatred：同仇敌～（大家一致痛恨敌人）*share righteous hatred against a common foe*

炌 kài ㄎㄞˋ 明火 a burning fire

欬 kài ㄎㄞˋ see 謦欬 (qǐng—) at 謦 on page 542

⇨ see also ké 咳 on p.355

KAN ㄎㄢ

刊(*栞) kān ㄎㄢ ❶刻 to carve：～石 *carve in stone* | ～印 *compose and print* ㊒排印出版 to print; to publish：～行 *print and publish* | 停～ *stop publication* [刊物] 杂志等出版物，也省称刊 periodical; publication：周～ *weekly (publication)* | 月～ *monthly (publication)* ❷削除，修改 to delete; to correct：不～之论（指至理名言）*unalterable statement* | ～误表 *errata*

看 kān ㄎㄢ 守护 to look after; to take care of; to tend：～门 *act as doorkeeper* | ～家 *look after the house* | ～守 *to watch; to guard; gaoler* ㊒监视 to keep under surveillance：把他～起来 *place him under surveillance*

⇨ see also kàn on p.350

勘 kān ㄎㄢ ❶校对，复看核定（㊥校—）to proofread：～误 *correct errors in publication* | ～正 *proofread and correct* ❷细查，审查 to investigate; to survey：～探 *to prospect; to explore* | ～验 *conduct an inquest* | ～测 *to survey* | 实地～查 *carry out an on-the-spot survey*

堪 kān ㄎㄢ ❶可以，能，足以 may; can：～以告慰 *may*

K

serve as a consolation | 不～设想 *be unbearable to imagine* ❷忍受，能支持 to bear; to endure：难～ *unbearable* | 狼狈不～ *be in an awkward predicament*

嵁 kān ㄎㄢ ［嵁岩］高峻的山岩 towering rock

戡 kān ㄎㄢ 平定（叛乱）to suppress (a rebellion)：～乱 *put down a rebellion*

龛（龕） kān ㄎㄢ 供奉佛像、神位等的小阁子 shrine：神～ *shrine for idols or ancestral tablets*

坎（❷*埳） kǎn ㄎㄢˇ ❶高出地面的埂状突起 ridge：沟沟～～ *setbacks; barriers* | 越过一道～ *pass over an obstacle* ❷低陷不平的地方，坑穴 pit ❸八卦之一，符号是"☵"，代表水 *kan* (one of the Eight Trigrams used in ancient divination, symbol ☵, representing water) ❹发光强度单位名坎德拉的简称，符号 cd。candela (cd)

［坎坷］（－kě）1 道路不平的样子 (of road) bumpy; rough 2 形容不顺利，不得志 (of life) full of frustrations

砍 kǎn ㄎㄢˇ 用刀、斧等猛剁，用力劈 to chop; to hack; to cut (down/off)：～柴 *cut firewood* | 把树枝～下来 *lop off a branch*

莰 kǎn ㄎㄢˇ 莰烷，有机化合物，白色晶体，有樟脑的香味，易挥发 bornane

侃 kǎn ㄎㄢˇ 闲谈，聊天 to chat：他真能～。*He is a real chatterbox.* | ～大山 *chew the fat*

［侃侃］理直气壮、从容不迫的样子 confident and composed：～而谈 *talk with ease and assurance*

槛（檻） kǎn ㄎㄢˇ 门槛，门限 threshold (see picture of 房屋的构造 on page 170)

⇨ see also jiàn on p.306

顑（顲） kǎn ㄎㄢˇ ［顑颔］（－hàn）面黄肌瘦 pale and thin

看 kàn ㄎㄢˋ ❶用眼睛感受外界事物 to look; to see; to read：～书 *read a book* | ～电影 *watch a movie* ❷观察（㊎察－）to examine; to observe：～脉 *(of a doctor) take/feel sb's pulse* | ～透了他的心思 *see through his thoughts* ㊋诊治 to treat (an illness or patient)：～病 *treat an illness* | 大夫把我的病～好了。*The doctor cured my illness.* ❸访问，拜望（㊎－望）to call on; to visit：到医院里去～病人 *visit a patient in hospital* ❹看待，照应，对待 to look upon; to regard; to look after：另眼相～ *look at with quite different eyes* | ～重 *regard as important* | 照～ *attend to* ❺想，以为 to think：我～应该这么办。*I think that's the way to go.* ❻先试试以观察它的结果 to try and see：问一声～ *try asking* | 做做～ *have a try* ❼提防，小心 to mind; to watch out：别跑，～摔着。*Don't run, lest you fall.*

⇨ see also kān on p.349

衎 kàn ㄎㄢˋ ❶快乐 jovial ❷刚直 upright; righteous

坎 kàn ㄎㄢˋ ［赤坎］地名，在台湾省 Chikan (a place in Taiwan Province)

墈 kàn ㄎㄢˋ 〈方 dialect〉高的堤岸，多用于地名 (often used in place names) high bank：～上（在江西省乐平）*Kanshang (a place in Leping, Jiangxi Province)*

磡 kàn ㄎㄢˋ 山崖 cliff

阚（闞） kàn ㄎㄢˋ 姓 (surname) Kan

⇨ see also hǎn on p.241

瞰（*矙） kàn ㄎㄢˋ 望，俯视，向下看 to look down from a height; to overlook［鸟瞰］1 从高处向下看 to get a bird's-eye view 2 事物的概括描写 overview：世界大势～ *an overview of the world trend*

KANG ㄎㄤ

闶（閌） kāng ㄎㄤ ［闶阆］(—láng）〈方 dialect〉建筑物中空旷的部分，又叫闶阆子 open space in a building (also called 闶阆子)

⇨ see also kàng on p.352

康 kāng ㄎㄤ ❶安宁 peaceful：身体健～ *in good health*｜～乐 *peaceful and happy* ❷富裕，丰盛 plentiful; abundant：～年 *year of abundance*｜小～ *comparatively well-off* ❸ same as "糠"

［康庄大道］四通八达的大路，比喻光明美好的前途 a broad road extending in all directions; (figurative) bright future

塃 kāng ㄎㄤ 用于地名 used in place names：盛～（在湖北省谷城）*Shengkang (in Gucheng, Hubei Province)*

慷（**忼） kāng ㄎㄤ ［慷慨］（—kǎi）1 情绪激昂 fervent; impassioned：～陈词 *speak passionately* 2 待人热诚，肯用财物帮助人 generous：他待人很～。*He is generous to others.*｜～解囊 *help generously with money*

糠（*穅、*粇） kāng ㄎㄤ ❶从稻、麦、谷子等籽实上脱下来的皮或壳 chaff ❷空，空虚 spongy：萝卜～了。*The radish has gone spongy.*

鱇（鱇） kāng ㄎㄤ see 鮟鱇 (ān—) at 鮟 on page 5

扛 káng ㄎㄤˊ 用肩膀承担 to carry on the shoulder：～粮食 *carry grains*｜～着一杆枪 *with a gun resting on one's shoulder*［扛活］旧时指做长工 (old) to work as a regular farm labourer

⇨ see also gāng on p.200

亢 kàng ㄎㄤˋ ❶高（㊀高—）high ㊁高傲 arrogant：不卑不～ *neither humble nor haughty* ❷过甚，极 excessive; extreme：～奋 *excessively excited*｜～旱 *extremely dry* ❸星宿名，二十八宿之一 kang (one of the twenty-eight constellations in ancient Chinese astronomy)

伉 kàng ㄎㄤˋ ❶对等，相称（chèn）to match; to be

K

equal to [伉俪]（-lì）配偶，夫妇 married couple; husband and wife ❷正直 upright and outspoken：～直 *upright and unyielding*

抗 kàng ㄎㄤˋ ❶抵御（㊀抵-）to resist; to combat：～战 *fight a war against aggression; war of resistance* | ～旱 *fight against drought* | ～洪 *combat a flood* ㊁ ①不妥协 be unyielding：～辩 *to refute; to demur* ②拒绝，不接受（㊀-拒）to defy; to refuse：～命 *defy an order* | ～税 *refuse to pay taxes* [抗议] 声明不同意，同时谴责对方的行动 to protest ❷匹敌，相当 to be a match for; to rival：～衡（不相上下，抵得过）*to rival; to equal* | 分庭～礼（行平等的礼节，转指势均力敌，也指相互对立）*stand up to sb as an equal; be an equal rival*

闶（閌） kàng ㄎㄤˋ 高大 tall and big

⇨ see also kāng on p.351

炕（❶*匟） kàng ㄎㄤˋ ❶北方用砖、坯等砌成的睡觉的台，下面有洞，连通烟囱，可以烧火取暖 *kang*, heatable brick or adobe bed (common in northern China) ❷〈方 dialect〉烤 to bake or dry by the heat of a fire：把湿衣服放在火边～一～ *dry wet clothes by the fire*

钪（鈧） kàng ㄎㄤˋ 金属元素，符号 Sc，银白色，质软。可用来制特殊玻璃、合金等 scandium (Sc)

KAO ㄎㄠ

尻 kāo ㄎㄠ 屁股 buttocks

考（❶-❸*攷） kǎo ㄎㄠˇ ❶测试，测验（㊀-试）to examine; to carry out or undergo an examination：期～ *end-of-term examination* | ～语文 *take a language test* ❷检查（㊀-察、查-）to inspect; to check：～勤 *check attendance* | ～绩 *assess one's professional performance; test scores* | ～核 *examine; appraise* [考验] 通过具体行动、困难环境等来检验（是否坚定、正确）to test; to try ❸推求，研究 to study; to investigate：～古 *engage in archaeological studies; archaeology* | ～证 *to investigate and check; make textual criticism* [考虑] 斟酌，思索 to think over; to consider：～一下再决定 *think it over before deciding* | ～问题 *consider a matter* [考究]（-jiu）1 考查，研究 to investigate; to observe and study：～问题 *probe into an issue* 2 讲究 tasteful; exquisite：衣着～ *elegantly dressed* ❹老，年纪大（㊀寿-）aged ❺原指父亲，后称已死的父亲 (originally referring to a father) deceased father：如丧～妣 *grieved as if bereaved of parents* | 先～ *deceased father*

拷 kǎo ㄎㄠˇ 打（㊀-打）to beat; to torture：～问 *interrogate with torture*

[拷贝]（外 loanword）1 复制 to

K

copy; to replicate 2 复制本，电影方面指用拍摄成的电影底片洗印出来的胶片 copy (of film)

洘 kǎo ㄎㄠˇ 用于地名 used in place names：～溪（在广东省揭西）*Kaoxi (in Jiexi, Guangdong Province)*

栲 kǎo ㄎㄠˇ 栲树，常绿乔木，木质坚硬，用于建筑等。树皮含鞣酸，可制栲胶，又可制染料 *Castanopsis fargesii Franch* (an evergreen tree used for construction)

[栲栳]（－lǎo）一种用竹子或柳条编的盛东西的器具，又叫笆斗 wicker basket (also called 笆斗)

烤 kǎo ㄎㄠˇ ❶把东西放在火的周围使干或使熟 to bake; to roast; to toast：～烟叶子 *flue-cured tobacco leaf* | ～白薯 *baked sweet potato* | ～箱 *oven; toaster* ❷向着火取暖 to warm by the fire：～手 *warm one's hands by the fire* | 围炉～火 *warm oneself by a stove*

铐(銬) kào ㄎㄠˋ ❶（－子）手铐子，束缚犯人手的刑具 handcuffs ❷用手铐束缚 to handcuff：把犯人～起来。*Handcuff the criminal.*

犒 kào ㄎㄠˋ 指用酒食或财物慰劳 to reward with food and drink or bounties：～劳 *reward with food and drink* | ～赏 *reward with food or bounties*

靠 kào ㄎㄠˋ ❶倚着，挨近（㊀倚－）to lean against/on; to be near to; to get close to：～墙站着 *lean against a wall* | 船～岸了。*The boat has docked.* ❷依靠，依赖 to rely on; to depend on：～集体的力量战胜灾害 *overcome a disaster through collective strength* | ～劳动致富 *become better off by working* [靠山] ㊉所依赖的人或集体 patron; backing ❸信赖 to trust：可～ *reliable; trustworthy* | ～得住 *dependable* [牢靠] 1 稳固 firm; stable 2 稳妥可信赖 dependable; reliable：这人做事最～。*This person is most dependable.*

熇 kào ㄎㄠˋ 用微火使鱼、肉等菜肴的汤汁变浓或耗干 to thicken a broth through simmering

KE ㄎㄜ

坷 kē ㄎㄜ [坷垃]（－la）土块 clod

➪ see also kě on p.356

苛 kē ㄎㄜ ❶苛刻，过分 exacting; excessive：～求 *make excessive demands* | ～责 *criticize too severely* ❷苛细，繁重，使人难于忍受 excessively detailed; too harsh to bear：～政 *harsh government* | ～捐杂税 *exorbitant taxes and levies*

珂 kē ㄎㄜ ❶玉名 a kind of jade ❷马笼头上的装饰 ornament on a bridle：玉～ *jade ornament on a bridle; (figurative) high officials and nobles*

柯 kē ㄎㄜ ❶斧子的柄 axe-handle; helve ❷草木的枝茎 stalk; branch

[柯尔克孜族] 我国少数民族，参看附录四 the Kirgiz (Khalkhas)

K

people (one of the ethnic groups in China. See Appendix Ⅳ.)

轲(軻) kē ㄎㄜ 用于人名。孟子，名轲，战国时人 used in given names, e.g. Mencius of the Warring States Period was named Ke

牁 kē ㄎㄜ [牂牁](zāng－) 1 古水名 Zangke (an ancient river) 2 古地名 Zangke (an ancient place)

钶(鈳) kē ㄎㄜ 金属元素铌(ní)的旧称 columbium (Cb) (old name of 铌 ní)

疴(*痾) kē ㄎㄜ (formerly pronounced ē) 病 illness：沉～(重病) *severe illness* | 染～ *contract an illness*

匼 kē ㄎㄜ 古代的一种头巾 a kerchief in ancient times

[匼河] 地名，在山西省芮城 Kehe (a place in Ruicheng, Shanxi Province)

科 kē ㄎㄜ ❶分门别类用的名称 a classification division ①生物的分类单位之一，在"目"之下、"属"之上 family (a category in taxonomic classification)：狮子属于食肉类的猫～。*The lion is a carnivore of the cat family.* | 槐树是豆～植物。*The pagoda tree is a plant of the pea family.* ②机关内部组织划分的部门 division or subdivision of an administrative unit; section; department：财务～ *finance section* | 总务～ *general affairs section* ③学术或业务的类别 branch of academic or vocational study：文～ *liberal arts* | 理～ *the sciences* | 内～ *internal medicine; department of medicine* | 外～ *surgery; surgical department*

[科学] 1 反映自然、社会、思维的客观规律的分科的知识体系 science 2 合乎科学的 scientific：这种做法不～。*This is not a scientific method.* ❷法律条文 legal clauses：～文 *legal clauses* | 作奸犯～ *violate the law and commit crimes* | 金～玉律 *golden laws and esteemed rules; infallible doctrine* ❸判定 to sentence：～以徒刑 *sentence to imprisonment* | ～以罚金 *impose a fine* ❹旧戏曲脚本里指示角色表演动作时的用语 stage directions in classical Chinese opera：叹～ *sighing* | 饮酒～ *drinking wine*

蝌 kē ㄎㄜ [蝌蚪](－dǒu) 蛙或蟾蜍等的幼体，黑色，身体椭圆，有长尾，生活在水中，逐渐长出后脚、前脚，尾巴消失，最后变成蛙或蟾蜍等 tadpole

棵 kē ㄎㄜ 量词，用于植物 measure word for plants：一～树 *a tree*

稞 kē ㄎㄜ 青稞，大麦的一种，产在西藏、青海等地，可做糌粑(zānba)，也可酿酒 highland barley (grown in Tibet and Qinghai, etc.)

窠 kē ㄎㄜ 鸟兽的巢穴 nest; burrow [窠臼] ㊗现成的格式或老套子 set pattern; stereotype

颗(顆) kē ㄎㄜ 量词，多用于圆形或粒状的东西 measure word, often for things

small and round：一～珠子 *a pearl* | 一～心 *a heart* | 两～钉子 *two nails*

髁 kē ㄎㄜ 骨头上的突起，多长在骨头的两端 condyle

颏(頦) kē ㄎㄜ 下巴颏儿，脸的最下部分，在两腮和嘴的下面 chin

⇨ see also ké on p.355

搕 kē ㄎㄜ 敲，碰 to knock：～烟袋锅子 *knock the ashes out of a pipe*

榼 kē ㄎㄜ 古时盛酒或水的器皿 an ancient vessel for wine or water

磕 kē ㄎㄜ 碰撞在硬东西上 to knock (against sth hard)：～破了头 *get a cut from bumping the head* | 碗～掉一块。*The bowl has been chipped.* | ～头（旧时的跪拜礼）*kowtow*

瞌 kē ㄎㄜ ［瞌睡］困倦想睡或进入半睡眠状态 to doze; to drowse：打～ *doze off*

壳(殼) ké ㄎㄜˊ （一儿）坚硬的外皮 shell：核桃～儿 *walnut shell* | 鸡蛋～儿 *egg shell* | 贝～儿 *sea shell*

⇨ see also qiào on p.534

咳(△*欬) ké ㄎㄜˊ 咳嗽，呼吸器官受刺激而迅速吸气，又猛烈呼出，声带振动发声 to cough

⇨ see also hāi on p.238
⇨ 欬 see also kài on p.349

颏(頦) ké ㄎㄜˊ 鸟名 a kind of bird：红点～ *Siberian rubythroat* | 蓝点～ *bluethroat*

⇨ see also kē on p.355

揢 ké ㄎㄜˊ 〈方 dialect〉❶卡（qiǎ）住 to get stuck; to be jammed：抽屉～住了，拉不开。*The drawer got stuck and won't open.* | 鞋小了～脚。*These shoes are too small and pinch (my) feet.* ❷刁难 to make life difficult for; to give a hard time to：～人 *give sb a hard time* | 你别拿这事来～我。*Don't try to baffle me with that.*

可 kě ㄎㄜˇ ❶是，对，表示准许 to approve：许～ *allow; permit* | 认～ *approve* | 不置～否 *not to say yes or no; be noncommittal* ［可以］1 表示允许 can; may：～，你去吧！*Alright, you may go!* 2 适宜，能 to suit; to fit：现在～穿棉衣了。*People can wear cotton-padded clothes now.* | 马铃薯～当饭吃。*Potatoes are a fitting staple food.* 3 过甚，程度深 rather：这几天冷得真～。*It's been rather cold these past few days.* 4 还好，差不多 passable; not bad：这篇文章还～。*This article is not bad.* ❷能够 can：牢不～破的友谊 *unbreakable friendship* | ～大～小 *can be big or small* ［可能］能够，有实现的条件 possible; probable：这个计划～提前实现。*The plan can be completed ahead of schedule.* ❸值得，够得上（用在动词前）(used before a verb) to be worth：～怜 *pitiable* | ～爱 *lovable* | ～恶（wù）*detestable* ❹适合 to suit; to fit：～心 *satisfying* | 饭菜～口。*The food is tasty.* ㊀尽（jǐn），就某

K

种范围不加增减 within the limits of: ～着钱花 *spend within one's budget* | ～着这块布料做件衣服 *make a garment with the full length of the cloth* ❺连词，可是，但，却 (conjunction) but; however; yet: 大家很累（lèi），～都很愉快。*Everybody was tired, yet all were happy.* ❻副词 adverb ①加强语气 used for emphasis: 这工具使着～得劲了。*This tool is rather handy.* | 他写字～快了。*He writes quite fast.* | 这篇文章～写完了。*This article is finally done.* ②表示疑问 used to question: 你～知道？ *Do you know?* | 这话～是真的？ *Is it true?* ③和"岂"字义近 similar to 岂: ～不是吗！ *Isn't it!* | ～不就糟了吗？ *That would be bad, wouldn't it?* ④大约 about: 年～三十许 *about thirty years of age* | 长～六米 *around six metres in length* ❼ same in meaning as 可以 2: 根～食。*The root is edible.* ❽ same in meaning as 可以 4: 尚～ *acceptable; not bad*

⇨ see also kè on p.356

坷 kě ㄎㄜˇ see 坎坷 (kǎn—) at 坎 on page 350

⇨ see also kē on p.353

K

岢 kě ㄎㄜˇ ［岢岚］（—lán）地名，在山西省 Kelan (a place in Shanxi Province)

炣 kě ㄎㄜˇ 火 fire

渴 kě ㄎㄜˇ 口干想喝水 thirsty: 我～了。*I am thirsty.* ⑩迫切 thirstily; eagerly; yearningly: ～望 *crave/long for; aspire to* | ～求 *hanker after; aspire to*

可 kè ㄎㄜˋ ［可汗］（—hán）古代鲜卑、突厥、回纥、蒙古等族君主的称号 khan

⇨ see also kě on p.355

克（❷–❺△剋、❷–❺*尅）kè ㄎㄜˋ ❶能 can; to be able to: 不～分身 *can't get away* | ～勤～俭 *be industrious and frugal* ❷战胜 to defeat; to win: ～敌制胜 *defeat an enemy and win a victory* ⑪战胜而取得据点 to capture (a stronghold): 攻无不～ *ever-victorious* | 连～数城 *capture one city after another* ［克复］战胜而收回失地 to retake; to recapture (lost land) ❸克服，克制，制伏 to restrain; to subdue: ～己奉公 *work selflessly for the public interest* | 以柔～刚 *overcome the hard with the soft* ❹严格限定 to strictly limit: ～期 *within a time limit* | ～日完成 *complete by a fixed date* ❺消化 to digest: ～食 *help digestion* ❻（藏 Tibetan）容量单位，1 克青稞约重 25 市斤。也是地积单位，播种 1 克种子的土地称为 1 克地，1 克约合 1 市亩 unit of volume, 1 克 of qingke barley equal to about 25 斤; also unit of land area, equal to about one 亩 ❼（外 loanword）质量单位，符号 g，1 克等于 1 千克的千分之一 gram (g)

［克隆］（外 loanword）1 生物体通过体细胞进行无性繁殖，复制出遗传性状完全相同的生命物质或生命体 clone 2 借指复制 to clone; to replicate

⇨ 剋(*尅) see also kēi on p.358

氪 kè ㄎㄜˋ 气体元素，符号Kr，无色、无味、无臭，不易跟其他元素化合 krypton (Kr)

刻 kè ㄎㄜˋ ❶雕，用刀子挖（㊄雕－）to carve; to engrave; to inscribe：～图章 *engrave a seal* [深刻] 深入，对事理能进一层分析 penetrating; profound：～地领会 *thoroughly understand* | 描写得很～。*It is an in-depth depiction.* ❷十五分钟为一刻 quarter (of an hour) ❸时间 moment：即～ *this moment* | 顷～（极短的时间）*in a flash* ❹不厚道（㊄－薄）mean; unkind：尖～ *acrimonious* | 苛～ *harsh* [刻苦] 不怕难，肯吃苦 assiduous; painstaking：～用功 *hardworking* | 生活很～ *lead a simple and frugal life* ❺ same as "克❹"

恪 kè ㄎㄜˋ 恭敬，谨慎 respectful and scrupulous：～遵 *scrupulously obey* | ～守 *strictly abide by*

客 kè ㄎㄜˋ ❶客人，跟"主"相对（㊄宾－）guest; visitor (opposite of 主)：来～了。*Here comes a guest.* | 请～ *treat guests* | 会～ *receive a visitor* [客观] 1 离开意识独立存在的，跟"主观"相对 objective (opposite of 主观)：人类意识属于主观，物质世界属于～。*Human consciousness is subjective, and the material world objective.* 2 依据外界事物而做观察的，没有成见的 impersonal; unbiased：他看问题很～。*He has an unbiased way of looking at things.* [客家] 古代移住闽、粤等地的中原汉族人的后裔 Hakkas [客气] 谦让，有礼貌 polite; courteous ❷出门在外的 away from home：～居 *live as a traveller or guest* | ～籍 *province into which a settler has moved; settler from another province* | ～商 *travelling merchant; foreign businessman* ❸指奔走他方，从事某种活动的人 person engaged in some particular pursuit：说～ *person sent to persuade; lobbyist* | 侠～ *knight errant* ❹旅客，顾客 traveller; passenger：～车 *passenger train/coach* | ～满 *(of theatre, hotel, etc.) be full up* | 乘～ *passenger*

课(課) kè ㄎㄜˋ ❶功课，有计划的分段教学 class; lesson：上～ *give/attend a class* | 今天没～。*There is no class today.* [课题] 研究、讨论的主要问题或需要解决的重大事项 subject of study ❷旧指教书 (old) to teach：～徒 *teach students* | ～读 *to teach; learn* ❸古赋税的一种 (old) tax ❹使交纳捐税 to levy; to collect：～以重税 *levy a heavy tax* ❺旧指某些机关学校等行政上的单位 (old) section; department：会计～ *accounting section* | 教务～ *dean's office* ❻占卜的一种 a kind of divination：起～ *practise divination*

骒(騍) kè ㄎㄜˋ 雌性的，指骡、马等 (of horse, mule, etc.) female

锞(錁) kè ㄎㄜˋ （－子）小块的金锭或银锭

small ingot of gold or silver

缂(緙) kè ㄎㄜˋ 缂丝(也作"刻丝"),我国特有的一种丝织的手工艺品。织纬线时,留下要补织图画的地方,然后用各种颜色的丝线补上,织出后好像是刻出的图画 (also written as 刻丝) a technique in, and product of, Chinese silk tapestry

嗑 kè ㄎㄜˋ 上下门牙对咬有壳的或硬的东西 to crack sth between the teeth: ~瓜子 *crack melon seeds*

溘 kè ㄎㄜˋ 忽然 abruptly; suddenly: ~逝(称人突然死亡) *die suddenly*

KEI ㄎㄟ

剋(*尅) kēi ㄎㄟ 〈方 dialect〉❶打(人) to beat (sb) ❷申斥 to scold: 狠狠地~了他一顿 *gave him a good scolding*

⇨ see also kè 克 on p.356

KEN ㄎㄣ

肯(❷*肎) kěn ㄎㄣˇ ❶许可,愿意 to agree; to consent; to be willing to: 他不~来。*He does not want to come.* | 只要你~做就能成功。*You will succeed if you are willing to do it.* | 首~(点头答应) *nod agreement* [肯定] 1 正面承认 to affirm; to approve; to confirm: ~成绩,指出缺点 *point out weaknesses while affirming achievements* 2 确定不移 definite; sure; affirmative: 我们的计划~能超额完成。*We will definitely overfulfil our plan.* ❷骨头上附着的肉 meat/flesh attached to the bone [肯綮](-qìng) 筋骨结合的地方 joint between a tendon and a bone ㊑ 事物的关键 crux; key point [中肯](zhòng-) ㊑ 抓住重点,切中要害 pertinent; to the point: 说话~ *speak pertinently*

啃 kěn ㄎㄣˇ 用力从较硬的东西上一点一点地咬下来 to bite; to gnaw; to nibble: ~老玉米 *nibble at an ear of corn* | 老鼠把抽屉~坏了。*The rats have gnawed the drawer.*

垦(墾) kěn ㄎㄣˇ ❶用力翻土 to cultivate (land): ~地 *cultivate the soil* ❷开垦,开辟荒地 to reclaim (marshland etc.): ~荒 *reclaim wasteland* | ~殖 *reclaim and cultivate wasteland*

恳(懇) kěn ㄎㄣˇ 诚恳,真诚 sincere; earnest: ~求 *to entreat* | ~托 *make a sincere request* | ~谈 *have a frank discussion*

龈(齦) kěn ㄎㄣˇ same as "啃"

⇨ see also yín on p.781

掯 kèn ㄎㄣˋ 〈方 dialect〉❶按,压 to press; to push down: ~住牛脖子 *pin a cow by the neck* ❷刁难 to make things difficult: 勒(lēi)~ *force; extort*

裉(**褃) kèn ㄎㄣˋ 衣服腋下前后相连的部分 armpit (of clothing): 杀~(把裉缝上) *sew a sleeve onto the*

K

body of a jacket | 抬～（称衣服从肩到腋下的宽度）*measurement from the shoulder to the armpit* (see picture of 上衣 on page 767)

KENG ㄎㄥ

坑(*阬) kēng ㄎㄥ ❶（－子、－ル）洼下去的地方 hole; pit：水～ *water hole* | 泥～ *mud puddle* ❷把人活埋 to bury alive：～杀 *bury alive* ❸坑害，设计（jì）使人受到损害 to entrap; to frame：～人 *entrap* ❹地洞，地道 tunnel; pit：～道 *gallery; adit* | 矿～ *mine pit*

吭 kēng ㄎㄥ 出声，发言 to utter (a sound or word)：不～声 *not utter a sound/word* | 一声也不～ *say nothing at all*

⇨ see also háng on p.243

硁(硜、䃘)** kēng ㄎㄥ 形容敲打石头的声音 clang (of stones)

铿(鏗) kēng ㄎㄥ 金石等敲打、撞击的响声 clang; clatter［铿锵］（－qiāng）声音响亮而有节奏 rhythmic and sonorous：～悦耳 *sonorous and pleasant to the ear*

KONG ㄎㄨㄥ

空 kōng ㄎㄨㄥ ❶里面没有东西或没有内容 empty; hollow; vacant：～房子 *empty / vacant house* | ～碗 *empty bowel* ㉃不合实际的 unrealistic：～话 *empty talk; lip service* | ～想 *daydream* | ～谈 *indulge in empty talk; empty talk*［空洞］没有内容的 devoid of content：他说的话很～。*His words are vague and too general.*［空头］不发生作用的，有名无实的 nominal; ineffective：～支票 *bad cheque*［凭空］无根据 groundless：～捏造 *fabricate stories out of thin air* ❷无着落，无成效，无结果 in vain; for nothing：～跑了一趟 *made a trip for nothing* | ～忙一阵 *make fruitless efforts* | 落～ *come to nothing* | 扑了个～ *fail to catch/meet sb* ❸天空 sky：～军 *air force* | 航～ *aviation*［空间］一切物质存在和运动所占的地方 space; room［空气］包围在地球表面，充满空间的气体，是氮、氧和少量惰性气体及其他气体的混合物 air ㊄情势 atmosphere：～紧张 *in a tense atmosphere* ❹姓 (surname) Kong

⇨ see also kòng on p.360

埪 kōng ㄎㄨㄥ 用于地名 used in place names：裴家～（在陕西省西安）*Peijiakong (in Xi'an, Shaanxi Province)*

崆 kōng ㄎㄨㄥ［崆峒］（－tóng）1 山名，在甘肃省平凉 Kongtong (a mountain in Pingliang, Gansu Province) 2 岛名，在山东省烟台 Kongtong (an island in Yantai, Shandong Province)

硿 kōng ㄎㄨㄥ 形容石头撞击声 clang of stones

⇨ see also kòng on p.360

箜 kōng ㄎㄨㄥ［箜篌］（－hóu）古代的一种弦乐器，

像瑟而比较小 a harp-like ancient Chinese string instrument

孔 kǒng ㄎㄨㄥˇ ❶小洞，窟窿 hole; opening：鼻～ *nostril* | 针～ *pinhole* ❷量词，用于窑洞、隧道等 measure word for cave, tunnel, etc.：一～土窑 *a cave dwelling*

恐 kǒng ㄎㄨㄥˇ ❶害怕，心里慌张不安（㊀一惧、一怖）to fear; to dread; to be afraid：唯～ *fear only* | 惊～ *panic-stricken and terrified* | 有恃（shì）无～ *be emboldened by sb's support* [恐吓]（一hè）吓（xià）唬，威吓（hè）to intimidate; to frighten [恐慌] 1 慌张害怕 panic-stricken 2 危机，使人感觉不安的现象 crisis：经济～ *economic panic* ❷副词，恐怕，表示疑虑不定或推测，有"或者""大概"的意思 (adverb, used to indicate supposition or conjecture) perhaps; maybe：～不可信。*It may not be reliable.* | ～事出有因。*I suppose it did not happen for nothing.*

倥 kǒng ㄎㄨㄥˇ [倥偬]（一zǒng）1 事情紧迫匆促 pressing; urgent：戎马～（形容军务繁忙）*be busy with military duties* 2 穷困 impoverished

空 kòng ㄎㄨㄥˋ ❶使空（kōng），腾出来 to vacate; to leave empty：～一个格 *leave a blank space* | ～出一间房子 *vacate a room* | 想法～出一些时间来 *try to squeeze out some time* ❷闲着的，没被利用的 unused; unoccupied：～房 *vacant room* | ～地 *open ground; vacant lot* ❸（一儿、一子）没被占用的时间或地方 free time; open space：有～儿再来。*Come again when you have time.* | 会场里挤得连一点儿～儿都没有。*The conference hall was packed.*

⇨ see also kōng on p.359

控 kòng ㄎㄨㄥˋ ❶告状，告发罪恶（㊀一告）to accuse; to charge：指～ *to accuse* | 被～ *be charged* | ～诉 *to denounce; to accuse* ❷节制，驾驭 to control; to operate：遥～ *control remotely; command from a distance* | 掌～ *have under control; be in charge* | ～制 *to control; to dominate* ❸倒悬瓶、罐等，使其中的液体流净 to turn a liquid container upside down to empty it out

硿 kòng ㄎㄨㄥˋ 用于地名 used in place names：～南（在广东省五华）*Kongnan (in Wuhua, Guangdong Province)*

⇨ see also kōng on p.359

鞚 kòng ㄎㄨㄥˋ 带嚼子的马笼头 headstall

KOU ㄎㄡ

抠(摳) kōu ㄎㄡ ❶用手指或细小的东西挖 to dig (out) with a finger or sth pointed：～了个小洞 *scratched a small hole* | 把掉在砖缝里的豆粒～出来 *pick out the beans from brick joints* ㊀向狭窄的方面深求 to delve into：～字眼 *split hairs about wording* | 死～书本 *delve mechanically into books* ❷雕刻

K

（花纹）to carve; to cut ❸〈方 dialect〉吝啬，小气 stingy; miserly：～门儿 *stingy; miserly* | 这人真～。*This person is so stingy.*

抠(摳) kōu ㄎㄡ 弓弩两端系弦的地方 notch on either side of a bow (to fasten the bowstring)

眍(瞘) kōu ㄎㄡ ［眍䁖］（-lou）眼睛深陷 (of eyes) to sink in: 他病了一场，眼睛都～了。*His eyes are sunken following his illness.*

芤 kōu ㄎㄡ ❶古时葱的别名 (ancient) another name for spring onion ❷芤脉，中医指按起来中空无力的脉象，好像按葱管的感觉 (in traditional Chinese medicine) hollow pulse

口 kǒu ㄎㄡˇ ❶人和动物吃东西的器官，有的也是发音器官的一部分 mouth (see picture of 头 on page 660)［口舌］1 因说话引起的误会或纠纷 quarrel 2 劝说、交涉或搬弄是非时说的话 talking：费尽～ *do a lot of talking*［口吻］从语气间表现出来的意思 tone ❷容器通外面的部分 (of containers) mouth; rim：缸～ *mouth of an urn* | 碗～ *rim of a bowl* | 瓶～ *mouth of a bottle* ❸（-儿）出入通过的地方 opening; entrance：门～ *doorway; gate* | 胡同～儿 *entrance of an alley* | 河～ *mouth of a river* | 海～ *seaport* | 关～ *strategic pass; juncture* 特指长城的某些关口 (specifically) certain gateways of the Great Wall：～北 *(generally) area north of the Great Wall* | ～蘑 *St. George's mushroom (special local product of Zhangjiakou)* | ～马 *horse breed from north of the Great Wall* 特指港口 (specifically) seaport：～岸 *port* | 出～ *(of ships) leave from port; to export* | 转（zhuǎn）～ *(of goods) to transit* ❹（-子、-儿）破裂的地方 cut; hole：衣服撕了个～儿。*The clothes are torn.* | 伤～ *wound* | 决～ *(of a dyke, etc.) be breached; levee breach* ❺锋刃 edge of a knife：刀还没有开～。*The knife has not been sharpened.* ❻骡马等的年龄（骡马等的年龄可以由牙齿的多少和磨损的程度看出来）age of a draught animal (as shown by the number and degree of wear of its teeth)：这匹马～还轻。*The horse is still young.* | 六岁～ *(of horses, mules, etc.) six years of age* ❼量词 measure word ①用于人 for people：一家五～ *a family of five* ②用于牲畜 for livestock：一～猪 *a pig* ③用于器物 for utensils：一～锅 *a pot* | 一～钟 *a clock*

叩(❶*敂) kòu ㄎㄡˋ ❶敲打 to knock; to tap：～门 *knock on the door* ❷叩头（首），磕头，一种旧时代的礼节 to kowtow：～拜 *to kowtow* | ～谢 *thank earnestly (literally means 'express thanks by kowtowing')* ❸询问，打听 to ask; to enquire：～问 *make enquiries*

扣(❷*釦) kòu ㄎㄡˋ ❶用圈、环等东西套住或拢住 to button up; to buck-

K

le：把门～上 *bolt the door* | 把扣子～好 *do up the buttons* ❷（－子、－儿）衣纽 button：衣～ *button* ❸（－子、－儿）绳结 knot; buckle：活～儿 *slip knot* ❹把器物口朝下放或覆盖东西 to place a cup, bowl etc. upside down：把碗～在桌上 *place the bowl bottom up on a table* | 用盆把剩菜～上 *cover a left-over dish with a basin* ㊞ 使相合 to relate; to match：这句话～在题上了。*This sentence is relevant to the title.* ❺扣留，关押 to detain; to arrest：驾驶证被～了 *driving licence is taken (by police)* | 他被～了起来。*He is detained.* ❻从中减除 to deduct; to subtract：九～（减到原数的百分之九十）*10 per cent deduction* | 七折八～（喻一再减除）*(make) various deductions*［克扣］私行扣减，暗中剥削 to embezzle; to pocket：～工资 *pocket one's salary* ❼螺纹 screw thread：螺丝～ *screw thread* | 套～ *buckle threads using a screw die* ㊞ 螺纹的一圈叫一扣 circle of thread (on a screw)：拧上两～就行。*Drive in the screw with two twists and it should be fine.*

筘（**簆）kòu ㄎㄡˋ 织布机上的一种机件，经线从筘齿间通过，它的作用是把纬线推到织口 reed (a part on a weaving machine)

寇（*寇）kòu ㄎㄡˋ ❶盗匪，侵略者 bandit; invader：敌～ *(invading) enemy* ❷敌人来侵略 (of enemy) to invade：～边 *harass a border area*

蔻 kòu ㄎㄡˋ［豆蔻］草本植物，形状像芭蕉，种子扁圆形，暗棕色，有香味，可入药 *Myristica fragrans* (an evergreen tree widely grown across tropical regions of China)
［豆蔻年华］指女子十三四岁的年龄 (of girls) in early teens

鷇（鷇）kòu ㄎㄡˋ 初生的小鸟 fledgling; young bird

KU ㄎㄨ

矻 kū ㄎㄨ［矻矻］努力、勤劳的样子 diligent; industrious

刳 kū ㄎㄨ 从中间破开再挖空 to hollow out：～木为舟 *hollow a canoe out of a tree trunk*

枯 kū ㄎㄨ 水分全没有了，干（㊀－干、干－）withered; dried up：～树 *dead tree* | ～草 *withered grass* | ～井 *dry well* ㊇ 肌肉干瘪 skinny：～瘦的手 *skinny hand*［枯燥］没趣味 dull; uninteresting：～乏味 *dull and boring* | 这种游戏太～。*This game is too boring.*

骷 kū ㄎㄨ［骷髅］（－lóu）没有皮肉毛发的尸骨或头骨 human skeleton; human skull

哭 kū ㄎㄨ 因痛苦悲哀等而流泪发声 to cry; to weep：痛～流涕 *shed bitter tears* | ～～啼啼 *weeping and wailing*

圐（**啰）kū ㄎㄨ［圐圙］（－lüè）（蒙 *Mongolian*）围起来的草场，多用于地名 (often used in place names)

K

pasture; meadow：薛～（在山西省山阴）*Xueku (a place in Shanyin, Shanxi Province)*

窟 kū ㄎㄨ ❶洞穴 hole; cave：石～ *rock cave; grotto* | 狡兔三～（喻有多个藏身的地方）。*A wily hare has three burrows. (figuratively means 'A crafty person has several hideouts.')* [窟窿]（－long）孔，洞 hole; cavity ⓔ 亏空，债务 deficit; debt：拉～（借债）*borrow money* ❷某种人聚集的地方 den：贫民～ *slum* | 魔～ *monsters' den*

苦 kǔ ㄎㄨˇ ❶像胆汁或黄连的味道，跟"甜""甘"相对 bitter (opposite of 甜 or 甘)：～胆 *gall bladder* | 良药～口利于病。*Bitter medicine has blessed effects.* ❷感觉难受的，困苦的 painful; hard：～境 *plight* | ～日子 *hard life* | 吃～耐劳 *endure hardships and stand hard work* [苦主] 被害人的家属 family of the victim in a criminal case ❸为某种事物所苦 to suffer from：～夏 *lose appetite and weight in summer* | ～于不懂英文 *be handicapped due to lack of English* ❹有耐心地，尽力地 painstakingly; assiduously：～劝 *earnestly persuade* | ～学 *study hard* | ～战 *fight a bitter battle* | ～求 *beg assiduously* ❺使受苦 to cause sb to suffer：这件事～了他。*This matter really made him suffer.*

库（庫） kù ㄎㄨˋ ❶贮存东西的房屋或地方（连仓－）warehouse; storehouse：入～ *put in storage* | 水～ *reservoir* ❷电荷量单位名库仑的简称，符号 C。coulomb (C)

裤（褲、*袴） kù ㄎㄨˋ 裤子 trousers; pants (see picture of 裤子 on page 767)

绔（絝） kù ㄎㄨˋ ❶旧同"裤"，古指套裤 (old) same as 裤; (ancient) trousers ❷ see 纨绔 (wán－) at 纨 on page 672

喾（嚳） kù ㄎㄨˋ 传说中上古帝王名 name of a ruler in remote antiquity in Chinese legend

酷 kù ㄎㄨˋ ❶残酷，暴虐、残忍的 cruel; brutal：～刑 *cruel punishment* ❷极，表示程度深 extreme：～暑 *intense heat of summer* | ～似 *be the exact image of* | ～爱 *ardently love* ❸（外 loanword）形容人潇洒英俊或表情冷峻 (of personal appearance) cool

KUA ㄎㄨㄚ

夸（誇） kuā ㄎㄨㄚ ❶说大话 to brag; to talk big：～口 *to boast* | ～大 *to exaggerate* | ～～其谈 *(of talking or writing) high-sounding but meaningless* [夸张] 1 说得不切实际，说得过火 to exaggerate; to overstate 2 一种修辞手法，用夸大的词句来形容事物 hyperbole ❷夸奖，用话赞扬 to praise; to commend：人人都～他进步快。*Everyone praises his quick progress.*

姱 kuā ㄎㄨㄚ 美好 gorgeous

K

侉(**咵) kuǎ ㄎㄨㄚˇ ❶口音与本地语音不同（多含轻蔑意）(often derisive) having an accent：他说话有点儿～。*He talks with an accent.* ❷土气 rustic：这身衣服真～。*Those clothes look so countrified.*

垮 kuǎ ㄎㄨㄚˇ 倒塌，坍塌 to collapse; to fall：房子被大水冲～了。*The house was washed down by flood waters.* ㊀完全破坏 to break down：别把身体累～了。*Don't let your overworking cause a health breakdown.* [垮台] 崩溃瓦解 to collapse; fall from power

挎 kuà ㄎㄨㄚˋ ❶胳膊弯起来挂着东西 to carry on one's arm：他胳膊上～着篮子。*He is carrying a basket on his arm.* ❷把东西挂在肩头上或挂在腰里 to carry over one's shoulder or at one's side：肩上～着文件包 *have a suitcase slung over one's shoulder*

胯 kuà ㄎㄨㄚˋ 腰和大腿之间的部分 hip：～骨 *hip bone* | ～下 *crotch*

跨 kuà ㄎㄨㄚˋ ❶抬起一条腿向前或旁边移动 to step; to stride：一步～过 *cross in one stride* | ～着大步 *in big strides* ❷骑，两脚分在器物的两边坐着或立着 to bestride; to straddle：～在马上 *sit astride on horseback* | 小孩～着门槛。*The child straddled the threshold.* ❸超越时间或地区之间的界限 to cut across; to go beyond：～年度 *going beyond the year* | ～省 *trans-provincial* ❹附在旁边 attached：～院 *side house; side compound* | 旁边～着一行（háng）小字。*Attached beside is a row of small-sized characters.*

KUAI ㄎㄨㄞ

扻(**擓**) kuǎi ㄎㄨㄞˇ ❶搔，轻抓 to scratch：～痒痒 *scratch an itch* ❷用胳膊挎着 to carry on one's arm：～着篮子 *with a basket on one's arm*

蒯 kuǎi ㄎㄨㄞˇ 蒯草，草本植物，丛生在水边，叶条形，可用来织席或造纸 wool grass

会(**會**) kuài ㄎㄨㄞˋ 总计 to total [会计] 1 管理和计算财务的工作 accounting 2 管理和计算财务的人 accountant

⇨ see also huì on p.274

侩(**儈**) kuài ㄎㄨㄞˋ 旧指以拉拢买卖、从中取利为职业的人 (old) middleman [市侩] 唯利是图、庸俗可厌的人 sordid merchant; vulgarian

郐(**鄶**) kuài ㄎㄨㄞˋ 周代诸侯国名，在今河南省新密 Kuai (a feudal state in the Zhou Dynasty, in today's Xinmi, Henan Province)

哙(**噲**) kuài ㄎㄨㄞˋ 咽下去 to swallow

狯(**獪**) kuài ㄎㄨㄞˋ 狡猾 sly; cunning：狡～ *deceitful*

浍(**澮**) kuài ㄎㄨㄞˋ 田间水沟 field ditch

⇨ see also huì on p.275

脍(**膾**) kuài ㄎㄨㄞˋ 细切的肉 finely chopped

K

meat：～炙人口（喻诗文等被人传诵）*(of a piece of good writing, etc.) oft-quoted and widely loved*

脍（膾） kuài ㄎㄨㄞˋ 鱼名，即鳓（lè）鱼 Chinese herring (same as 鳓 lè 鱼)

块（塊） kuài ㄎㄨㄞˋ ❶（一儿）成疙瘩或成团的东西 lump; chunk：糖～儿 *sweets; lumps of sugar*｜土～ *clods*｜～根 *root tuber*｜～茎 *tuber* ❷量词 measure word ①用于块状或某些片状的东西 for things lumpy or flat：一～地 *a piece of land*｜一～布 *a piece of cloth*｜一～肥皂 *a cake of soap* ②用于货币 for currency：十～钱 *ten yuan*

快 kuài ㄎㄨㄞˋ ❶速度高，跟"慢"相对 fast (opposite of 慢)：～车 *express train/bus*｜进步很～ *rapid progress* ❷赶紧，从速 hurriedly：～上学吧！ *Hurry up to school!*｜～回去吧！ *Hurry back now!* ❸副词，将，就要，接近 (adverb) soon：天～亮了。*The day is breaking.*｜他～五十岁了。*He is going on 50.*｜我～毕业了。*I will soon graduate.* ❹敏捷 nimble; agile：脑子～ *quick-witted*｜手疾眼～ *deft of hand and quick of eye* ❺锋利，跟"钝"相对 sharp (opposite of 钝)：刀不～了，该磨一磨。*The knife needs sharpening.*｜～刀斩乱麻（喻迅速果断地解决复杂的问题）*take resolute and effective measures to solve a complicated problem (literally means 'cut a tangled skein of jute with a sharp knife')* ❻爽快，直截了当 straightforward; forthright：～人～语 *forthright in character*｜心直口～ *be frank and outspoken* ❼高兴，舒服 pleased; happy：～乐 *happy*｜～活 *merry; cheerful*｜～事 *delightful event*｜大～人心 *to the people's great satisfaction*｜身子不～ *not feel well*

筷 kuài ㄎㄨㄞˋ（一子）用竹、木、金属等制的夹饭菜或其他东西用的细棍儿 chopsticks

KUAN ㄎㄨㄢ

宽（寬） kuān ㄎㄨㄢ ❶阔大，跟"窄"相对（㊀一广、一阔）wide; broad (opposite of 窄)：马路很～。*The road is very wide.*［宽绰］（一chuo）1 宽阔 spacious 2 富裕 well-off ❷物体横的方面的距离，长方形多指短的一边 width：长方形的面积是长乘以～。*The area of a rectangle is the length multiplied by the width.* ❸放宽，使松缓 to relax; to extend：～限 *extend a time limit*｜～心 *feel relieved; be relaxed* ㊁ ①解除，脱 to remove; to relieve：请～了大衣吧。*Please take off your overcoat.* ②延展 to extend：～限几天 *extend a deadline by a few days* ③宽大，不严 lenient：～容 *to tolerate*｜从～处理 *treat leniently* ❹宽裕，富裕 well-off：手头不～ *have no money to spare*

髋（髖） kuān ㄎㄨㄢ 髋骨，通称胯骨，组成骨盆的大骨，左右各一，是由髂骨、

K

坐骨、耻骨合成的 hip bone

款(*欵) kuǎn ㄎㄨㄢˇ ❶法令、规定、条文里下分的项目 section (of an article in a legal document); paragraph：第几条第几～ *certain section of certain article* ❷（一子）经费，钱财（㊥一项）fund：存～ *deposit; bank savings* | 拨～ *allocate funds; appropriation* ❸器物上刻的字 inscription：钟鼎～识（zhì） *bronze inscription* ㊀（一儿）书画、信件头尾上的名字 names of the sender or recipient on paintings, letters, etc.：上～ *name of recipient* | 下～ *name of painter, calligrapher, or sender* | 落～（题写名字） *write name of the sender or recipient* [款式] 格式，样子 style; design ❹诚恳 sincere：～待 *treat cordially; to entertain* | ～留 *cordially urge (a guest) to stay* ❺敲打，叩 to knock：～门 *knock at the door* | ～关而入 *knock at the door and enter* ❻缓，慢 leisurely：～步 *walk with deliberate steps* | 点水蜻蜓～～飞。*The dragonflies touch the water and fly leisurely.*

窾 kuǎn ㄎㄨㄢˇ 空 empty

K

KUANG ㄎㄨㄤ

匡 kuāng ㄎㄨㄤ ❶纠正 to correct; to rectify：～谬（miù） *correct mistakes* | ～正 *to rectify* ❷救，帮助 to save; to help：～救 *to rescue* | ～助 *to assist* ❸〈方 dialect〉粗略计算，估算 to estimate：～算～算 *give a rough calculation*

劻 kuāng ㄎㄨㄤ [劻勷]（一ráng）急促不安 anxious

诓(誆) kuāng ㄎㄨㄤ 骗，欺骗（㊥一骗）to deceive; to cheat：别～人。*Don't play hoaxes.*

哐 kuāng ㄎㄨㄤ 形容物体撞击震动声 crash; bang：～啷（lāng） *crash; bang* | ～的一声脸盆掉在地上了。*The basin fell to the ground with a crash.*

洭 kuāng ㄎㄨㄤ 洭水，古水名，在今广东省 Kuangshui River (an ancient river name, in today's Guangdong Province)

筐 kuāng ㄎㄨㄤ（一子、一儿）竹子或柳条等编的盛东西的器具 basket

狂 kuáng ㄎㄨㄤˊ ❶疯癫，精神失常（㊥疯一、癫一）crazy; mad：～人 *madman; person with extreme arrogance* | 发～ *go mad; be out of one's mind* ❷任情地做，不用理智约束感情 unrestrained：～放不拘 *totally unconventional and untrammelled* | ～喜 *wild with joy* | ～欢 *rejoice with wild excitement* [狂妄] 极端自高自大 wildly arrogant; presumptuous ❸猛烈的，声势大的 violent：～风暴雨 *furious storm* | ～澜（大浪头）*raging wave; (figuratively) turbulent situation; violent trend* | ～飙（急骤的大风）*hurricane; (figuratively) violent power*

诳(誑) kuáng ㄎㄨㄤˊ 欺骗，瞒哄 to deceive; to cheat：～语 *a lie*

鵟(鵟) kuáng ㄎㄨㄤˊ 鸟名，外形像老鹰，尾部羽毛不分叉，吃鼠类等，是益鸟 buteo

夼 kuǎng ㄎㄨㄤˇ 〈方 dialect〉两山间的大沟，多用于地名 (often used in place names) valley; low-lying land：刘家～（在山东省烟台）*Liujiakuang (a place in Yantai, Shandong Province)* | 马草～（在山东省荣成）*Macaokuang (a place in Rongcheng, Shandong Province)*

邝(鄺) kuàng ㄎㄨㄤˋ 姓 (surname) Kuang

圹(壙) kuàng ㄎㄨㄤˋ ❶墓穴 grave; coffin pit ❷旷野 open country; wilderness [圹埌]（-làng）形容原野一望无际的样子 (of open country) boundless; vast

纩(纊) kuàng ㄎㄨㄤˋ 丝绵絮 silk floss

旷(曠) kuàng ㄎㄨㄤˋ ❶空阔（㊀空一）open and vast：～野 *open country* | 地～人稀 *vast land and sparse population* [旷世] 当代没有能够相比的 unequalled by contemporaries; outstanding：～功勋 *outstanding deeds* ❷心境阔大 free from worries and petty ideas：心～神怡 *elated and blissful* | ～达 *broad-minded* ❸荒废，耽搁 to waste; to neglect：～工 *not show up at work without leave* | ～课 *play truant* | ～日持久 *long-drawn-out*

矿(礦、*鑛) kuàng ㄎㄨㄤˋ (formerly pronounced gǒng) ❶矿物，蕴藏在地层中的自然物质 mineral：铁～ *iron ore* | 煤～ *coal mine* | 油～ *oil deposit* ❷开采矿物的场所 mine：～井 *(underground) mine* | ～坑 *pit* | 下～ *go work in a mine*

况(*況) kuàng ㄎㄨㄤˋ ❶情形（㊀情一）condition; situation：近～ *recent developments* | 实～ *live scene; what is actually happening on the spot* ❷比，譬 to compare：以古～今 *draw parallels from history* ❸文言连词，表示更进一层 (conjunction in classical Chinese) used to express a higher degree ①相当于"况且" equivalent to 况且：～仓卒吐言，安能皆是？*Moreover, since these words were uttered offhand, how can they be all correct?* ②相当于"何况" equivalent to 何况：此事成人尚不能为，～幼童乎？*Even an adult cannot do it, much less a child.* [况且] 连词，表示更进一层 (conjunction) moreover; in addition：这本书内容很好，～也很便宜，买一本吧。*This book is good in contents, and inexpensive. Why not get a copy?* [何况] 连词，表示反问 (conjunction) much less; let alone：小孩都能办到，～我呢？*Even a child can do it, let alone me.*

K

贶(貺) kuàng ㄎㄨㄤˋ 赐，赠 to give; to grant

框 kuàng ㄎㄨㄤˋ ❶门框，安门的架子 doorframe (see picture of 房屋的构造 on page 170) ❷(一子、一儿)镶在器物外围有支撑作用或保护作用的东西 frame; case: 镜～儿 *picture frame* | 眼镜～子 *rims of spectacles* ❸(一儿)周围的圈儿 frame; circle 喻 原有的范围，固有的格式 restriction; convention; set pattern: 不要有～～儿。*Don't be limited by any restrictions.* ❹加框 to draw a frame around: 把这几个字～起来 *frame these words* ❺限制，约束 to restrain; to restrict: 不要～得太严，要有灵活性。*Don't be too restrictive; rather, allow some flexibility.*

眶 kuàng ㄎㄨㄤˋ (一子、一儿)眼眶，眼的四周 eye socket: 眼泪夺～而出 *tears gushing from the eyes*

KUI ㄎㄨㄟ

亏(虧) kuī ㄎㄨㄟ ❶缺损，折(shé)耗 to lose (money, etc.); to have a deficit: 月有盈～(圆和缺)。*The moon waxes and wanes.* | 气衰血～ *dual depletion of energy and blood* | ～本 *lose money (in business)* 引 ①缺少，缺，欠 to be short of; to lack: 功～一篑 *fall short of success for lack of a final effort (literally means 'fail to build a mound for want of one final basket of earth')* | ～秤 *cheat in weights (on a scale); (of goods) lose weight* | 理～ *be in the wrong* ②损失 loss: 吃～(受损失) *suffer losses* [亏空](一kong)所欠的钱物 debt; deficit: 弥补～ *make up a deficit* ❷亏负，对不起 to treat unfairly: ～心 *having a guilty conscience* | 人不～地，地不～人。*Cheat not the land, and it will not cheat you.* ❸多亏，幸而 fortunately; thanks to: ～了你提醒我，我才想起来。*Thanks to your reminder, I recalled it.* ❹表示讥讽 even (used in irony): ～你还学过算术，连这么简单的账都不会算。*You have even learnt math, and you can't do such simple calculation.*

刲 kuī ㄎㄨㄟ 割 to cut

岿(巋) kuī ㄎㄨㄟ 高大 towering; lofty: ～然不动 *stand tall and steadfast*

悝 kuī ㄎㄨㄟ 用于人名，李悝，战国时政治家 used in given names, e.g., Li Kui, a politician in the Warring States Period

盔 kuī ㄎㄨㄟ ❶作战时用来保护头的帽子，多用金属制成 helmet: ～甲 *suit of armour* | 钢～ *steel helmet* ❷盆子一类的器皿 basin-like containers: 瓦～ *basin-like pottery container*

窥(窺、*闚) kuī ㄎㄨㄟ 从小孔、缝隙或隐蔽处偷看 to peep; to spy on: ～探 *spy on* | ～伺 *lie in wait for* | ～见真相 *detect the truth* | 管～蠡测(从竹管里看天，用瓢

K

量海水，形容见识浅陋）*restricted in vision and shallow in understanding (literally means 'look at the sky through a bamboo tube and measure the sea with a calabash')*

奎 kuí ㄎㄨㄟˊ 星宿名，二十八宿之一 *kui* (one of the twenty-eight constellations in ancient Chinese astronomy)

喹 kuí ㄎㄨㄟˊ [喹啉]（一lín）有机化合物，无色油状液体，有特殊臭味，可用来制药和制染料 quinoline

蝰 kuí ㄎㄨㄟˊ 蝰蛇，一种毒蛇，生活在森林或草地里 Russell's viper

逵 kuí ㄎㄨㄟˊ 通各方的道路 thoroughfare; road

馗 kuí ㄎㄨㄟˊ same as "逵"

隗 kuí ㄎㄨㄟˊ 姓 (surname) Kui ⇨ see also wěi on p.681

魁 kuí ㄎㄨㄟˊ ❶为首的人或事物（㊇一首）chief; head：罪～祸首 *arch-criminal* ❷大 big：身～力壮 *of stalwart build* [魁梧] [魁伟] 高大（指身体）of big stature ❸魁星，北斗七星中第一星，又第一星至第四星的总称 first star of the Plough; collectively the first four stars of the Plough

櫆 kuí ㄎㄨㄟˊ 北斗星 the Plough

揆 kuí ㄎㄨㄟˊ ❶揣测（㊇一度duó、一测）to conjecture; to guess：～情度理 *measure or weigh by reason and common practice* ❷道理，准则 principle; standard ❸掌管 to manage; to administrate：以～百事 *have sb take care of everything* ㊀ 旧称总揽政务的人，如宰相、内阁总理等 (old) prime minister or any official of similar rank：阁～ *prime minister*

葵 kuí ㄎㄨㄟˊ 植物名 plant name ①向日葵，又叫葵花，草本植物，花序盘状，花常朝向太阳，种子叫葵花子，可以吃，又可榨油 common sunflower (also called 葵花) ②蒲葵，常绿乔木，叶片大，可做蒲扇 Chinese fan palm

骙(騤) kuí ㄎㄨㄟˊ [骙骙] 形容马强壮 (of a horse) strong

睽 kuí ㄎㄨㄟˊ 隔离（㊇一违、一离）to separate

戣 kuí ㄎㄨㄟˊ 古代戟一类的兵器 (ancient) halberd-like weaponry

暌 kuí ㄎㄨㄟˊ ❶违背不合 to violate; to run counter to ❷same as "睽"

[睽睽] 张大眼睛注视 to stare; to gaze：众目～ *under so many watchful eyes*

夔 kuí ㄎㄨㄟˊ ❶古代传说中一种奇异的动物，似龙，一足 a one-legged dragon-like monster in ancient Chinese legend ❷夔州，古地名，今重庆市奉节 Kuizhou (ancient name of today's Fengjie, Chongqing Municipality)

頍(頍) kuǐ ㄎㄨㄟˇ 古代的一种发饰，用来束发并固定帽子 an ancient hair ornament

傀 kuǐ ㄎㄨㄟˇ [傀儡]（一lěi）木偶戏里的木头人 puppet ㊖ 徒有虚名，无自主权，受

K

人操纵的人或组织 puppet (person or organization)：～政府 *puppet government*

跬 kuǐ ㄎㄨㄟˇ 古代称半步，一只脚迈出的距离，相当于今天的一步 half a step (in ancient times, equivalent to one step of today)：～步不离 *follow closely*

煃 kuǐ ㄎㄨㄟˇ 火燃烧的样子 blazing; glowing

匮（匱） kuì ㄎㄨㄟˋ 缺乏（㊀—乏）deficient; short (of supplies)

〈古 ancient〉 also same as 柜 (guì)

蒉（蕢） kuì ㄎㄨㄟˋ 古时用草编的筐子 a straw basket in ancient times

馈（饋、*餽） kuì ㄎㄨㄟˋ 馈赠，赠送 to present with (a gift)

溃（潰） kuì ㄎㄨㄟˋ ❶溃决，大水冲开堤岸 (of a dyke or dam) to burst [溃围] 突破包围 to break through an encirclement ❷散乱，垮台 to collapse：～散 *(of troops) be routed and disperse in disorder* | ～败 *(of troops) be defeated/routed* | ～不成军 *be utterly routed* | 崩～ *to collapse* ❸肌肉组织腐烂 to fester; to ulcerate：～烂 *to fester* | ～疡 (yáng) *ulcer*

⇨ see also huì on p.276

愦（憒） kuì ㄎㄨㄟˋ 昏乱，糊涂（㊀昏—）muddle-headed

襀（繢） kuì ㄎㄨㄟˋ 〈方 dialect〉 ❶（—儿）用绳子、带子等拴成的结 knot：活～儿 *slip-knot* | 死～儿 *fast knot* ❷拴，系 (jì) to tie; to fasten：～个襀儿 *tie a knot* | 把牲口～上 *tie up a draught animal*

聩（聵） kuì ㄎㄨㄟˋ 耳聋 deaf; hard of hearing: 昏～（喻不明事理）*decrepit and muddle-headed* | 发聋振～（喻用语言文字等方式唤醒愚昧麻木的人）*to enlighten the ignorant and the benighted (literally means 'rouse the deaf and awaken the unhearing')*

篑（簣） kuì ㄎㄨㄟˋ 古时盛土的筐子 (ancient) basket for holding earth：功亏一～ *fall short of success for lack of a final effort (literally means 'fail to build a mound for want of one final basket of earth')*

喟 kuì ㄎㄨㄟˋ 叹气 to sigh：感～ *sigh with feeling* | ～叹 *sigh with deep feeling*

愧（*媿） kuì ㄎㄨㄟˋ 羞惭（㊀惭—、羞—）ashamed：问心无～ *have a clear conscience* | 他真不～是劳动模范。*He has proven himself a model worker.*

KUN ㄎㄨㄣ

坤（△*堃） kūn ㄎㄨㄣ ❶八卦之一，符号是"☷"，代表地 *kun* (one of the Eight Trigrams used in ancient divination, symbol ☷, representing earth) ❷称女性的 female; feminine：～包 *lady's handbag* |

～车 *lady's bicycle*

昆(❹*崑、❹*崐) kūn ㄎㄨㄣ ❶众多 many [昆虫] 节肢动物的一类，身体分头、胸、腹三部分，有三对足，如蜂、蝶、跳蚤、蝗虫等 insect ❷子孙，后嗣 offspring：后～ *descendant* ❸哥哥 elder brother：～弟 *brothers* | ～仲 *(used of other people) brothers* ❹[昆仑] 山脉名，西起帕米尔高原，分三支向东分布 Kunlun Mountains

婫 kūn ㄎㄨㄣ 人名用字 used in given names

琨 kūn ㄎㄨㄣ 一种玉 a kind of jade

焜 kūn ㄎㄨㄣ 明亮 bright

鹍(鵾、**鶤) kūn ㄎㄨㄣ [鹍鸡] 古书上说的一种像鹤的鸟 (in ancient Chinese texts) a crane-like bird

锟(錕) kūn ㄎㄨㄣ [锟铻] (-wú) 宝刀和宝剑名 name of precious knives and swords

醌 kūn ㄎㄨㄣ 有机化合物的一类，是芳香族母核的两个氢原子各由一个氧原子所代替而成的 quinone

鲲(鯤) kūn ㄎㄨㄣ 传说中的一种大鱼 (in Chinese legend) an enormous fish

堃 kūn ㄎㄨㄣ ❶ see 坤 on page 370 ❷用于人名 used in given names ❸姓 (surname) Kun

裈(褌) kūn ㄎㄨㄣ 古代称有裆裤或内裤 (ancient) trousers; underpants

髡(**髨) kūn ㄎㄨㄣ 古代剃去头发的刑罚 to shave off all the hair (a punishment in ancient times)

捆(*綑) kǔn ㄎㄨㄣˇ ❶用绳等缠紧、打结 to tie up; to bundle up：把行李～上 *tie up the baggage* ❷(-子、-儿) 量词，用于捆在一起的东西 (measure word) bundle：一～儿柴火 *a bundle of firewood* | 一～儿竹竿 *a bundle of bamboo poles* | 一～报纸 *a bundle of newspapers*

阃(閫) kǔn ㄎㄨㄣˇ ❶门槛 threshold ❷妇女居住的内室 boudoir

悃 kǔn ㄎㄨㄣˇ 诚实，诚心 sincere; sincerity

壸(壼) kǔn ㄎㄨㄣˇ 宫里面的路 alley in a palace

困(❸❹睏) kùn ㄎㄨㄣˋ ❶陷在艰难痛苦里面 to be stranded：为病所～ *be afflicted with illness* ㊀包围住 to surround：把敌人～在城里 *bottle up the enemy inside city walls* ❷穷苦，艰难 poverty-stricken; hard-pressed：～难 *difficulty; difficult; poverty-stricken* | ～境 *predicament* ❸疲乏，困倦 tired; sleepy：孩子～了，该睡觉了。*The child is tired. It's time for bed.* ❹〈方 dialect〉睡 to sleep：～觉 *to sleep*

KUO ㄎㄨㄛ

扩(擴) kuò ㄎㄨㄛˋ 放大，张大 to expand; to en-

K

large：～音器 *megaphone* | ～充 *expand and strengthen* | ～大 *to expand; to extend* | ～容 *enlarge capacity; to expand*

括（*搭）kuò ㄎㄨㄛˋ ❶扎，束 to draw together; to tie (up)：～发（fà）*tie up one's hair* | ～约肌（在肛门、尿道等靠近开口的地方，能收缩、扩张的环状肌肉）*sphincter* ❷包容（㊣包－）to include：总～ *sum up*

⇨ see also guā on p.223

适 kuò ㄎㄨㄛˋ (ancient) same as "逜"

⇨ see also shì on p.603

蛞 kuò ㄎㄨㄛˋ ［蛞蝼］（－lóu）蝼蛄 mole cricket［蛞蝓］（－yú）软体动物，像蜗牛而没有壳，吃蔬菜或瓜果的叶子，对农作物有害 slug

逜 kuò ㄎㄨㄛˋ 疾速，多用于人名 (often used in given names) fast; rapid

阔（闊、*濶）kuò ㄎㄨㄛˋ ❶面积或范围宽广（㊣广－）wide; vast; broad：宽～ *vast; (of mind, knowledge, etc.) broad* | 高谈～论 *indulge in loud and empty talk* ㊀时间长或距离远 long in time or distance：～别 *be long separated* ❷钱财多，生活奢侈 wealthy; rich：摆～ *flaunt one's wealth* | ～气 *luxurious; showily rich* | ～人 *rich person; the rich*

廓 kuò ㄎㄨㄛˋ ❶物体的外缘 outline：轮～ *outline; profile* | 耳～ *auricle* ❷空阔 open and vast：寥～ *boundless; vast* ❸扩大 to extend; to expand

［廓清］肃清，清除 to clean up; to sweep away：～道路上的障碍 *clear away all obstacles on the road* | 残匪已经～。*The remnants of the outlaw band have been cleared out.*

L ㄌ

LA ㄌㄚ

垃 lā ㄌㄚ [垃圾](—jī)脏土或扔掉的破烂东西 rubbish; garbage

拉 lā ㄌㄚ ❶牵，扯，拽 to pull; to drag; to draw: ～车 *pull a cart* | 把渔网～上来 *draw in a fishing net* 引①使延长 drag out; draw out: ～长声儿 *to drawl* ②拉拢，联络 to solicit; draw in: ～关系 *build connections* [拉倒](—dǎo)算了，作罢 drop it: 他不来～。*If he won't come, then let him be.* ❷排泄粪便 empty one's bowels: ～屎 *to shit* ❸用车运 transport (by vehicle): ～货 *transport goods* | ～肥料 *haul fertilizer* ❹帮助 to help: 他有困难，应该～他一把。*We should give him a helping hand now that he has difficulties.* ❺牵累，牵扯 to implicate; to involve: 一人做事一人当，不要～上别人。*One should take responsibility for one's action and not drag others into it.* ❻拉动乐器的某部分，使乐器发出声音 to play (bowed instruments and accordions etc.): ～二胡 *play the erhu* | ～手风琴 *play the accordion* ❼闲谈 to chat: ～话 *have a chat* | ～家常 *to chit-chat*

[拉祜族](—hù—)我国少数民族，参看附录四 the Lahu people (one of the ethnic groups in China. See Appendix Ⅳ.)

⇨ see also lá on p.373

啦 lā ㄌㄚ [呼啦][哇啦][叽哩呱啦] 拟声词 onomatopoeia

⇨ see also la on p.374

邋 lā ㄌㄚ [邋遢](—ta)不利落，不整洁 sloppy: 他收拾得很整齐，不像过去那样～了。*He is all tidied up, no longer his former sloppy self.*

旯 lá ㄌㄚˊ see 旮旯(gā—) at 旮 on page 193

拉 lá ㄌㄚˊ 割，用刀把东西切开一道缝或切断 to cut; to slit: ～了一个口子 *got a cut* | ～下一块肉 *cut off a piece of flesh*

⇨ see also lā on p.373

砬(**磖) lá ㄌㄚˊ 〈方 dialect〉砬子，大石块。多用于地名 (often used in place names) rock

剌 lá ㄌㄚˊ same as "拉(lá)"

⇨ see also là on p.374

喇 lǎ ㄌㄚˇ [喇叭](—ba) 1 一种管乐器 a woodwind instrument; trumpet; horn 2 像喇叭的东西 loudspeaker; horn (of a vehicle): 汽车～ *car horn* | 扩音～ *loudspeaker*

[喇嘛](—ma)(藏 *Tibetan*)藏传佛教的僧侣，原为尊称，意思是

"上人" (originally an honorific speech meaning 'spiritual master') *lama* (in Tibetan Buddhism)

剌 là ㄌㄚˋ 〈古 ancient〉违背常情、事理，乖张 perverse; disagreeable：乖～ *contrary to reason; perverse* | ～谬 *ridiculous*

⇨ see also lá on p.373

瘌 là ㄌㄚˋ ［瘌痢］（—lì）〈方 dialect〉秃疮，生在人头上的皮肤病 favus (of the scalp)

蝲 là ㄌㄚˋ ［蝲蛄］（—gǔ）甲壳动物，外形像龙虾而小。生活在淡水中，是肺吸虫的中间宿主 crayfish［蝲蝲蛄］（——gǔ）same as "蝼蛄"

鯻（鰊） là ㄌㄚˋ 鱼名，身体侧扁，灰白色，有黑色纵条纹，口小。生活在热带和亚热带海里 grunt

鬎 là ㄌㄚˋ ［鬎鬁］（—lì）same as "瘌痢"

落 là ㄌㄚˋ 丢下，遗漏 leave out; be missing; fall behind：丢三～四 *miss this and that* | ～了一个字 *missed out a character* | 大家走得快，把他～下了。*Everyone walked fast, leaving him behind.*

⇨ see also lào on p.383, luò on p.429

腊（臘、❶*臈） là ㄌㄚˋ ❶古代在农历十二月举行的一种祭祀 ancient sacrificial rite performed in the twelfth month of the lunar year ㊕农历十二月 the twelfth month of the lunar year：～八（农历十二月初八）*the eighth day of the twelfth lunar month* | ～肉（腊月或冬天腌制后风干或熏干的肉）*cured meat* ❷姓 (surname) La

⇨ see also xī on p.697

蜡（蠟） là ㄌㄚˋ ❶动物、植物或矿物所产生的某些油质，具有可塑性，易熔化，不溶于水，如蜂蜡、白蜡、石蜡等 wax ❷蜡烛，用蜡或其他油脂制成的照明的东西，多为圆柱形，中心有捻，可以燃点 candle

⇨ see also zhà on p.828

辣（*辢） là ㄌㄚˋ ❶姜、蒜、辣椒等的味道 peppery; spicy; hot ㊖凶狠，刻毒 cruel; ruthless：毒～ *sinister* | 心狠手～ *cruel and merciless* ❷辣味刺激 (of smell or taste) to burn; to sting：～眼睛 *sting the eyes*

镴（鑞） là ㄌㄚˋ 锡和铅的合金，又叫白镴、锡镴，可用来焊接金属器物 solder (also called 白镴，锡镴)

啦 la ·ㄌㄚ 助词，"了"（le）、"啊"（a）合音，作用大致和"了（le）❷"接近，但感情较为强烈 auxiliary word, fusion of 了 (le) and 啊 (a), similar in function to 了 (le) ❷, but stronger in tone：他已经来～。*He has already arrived.* | 他早就走～。*He left a long time ago.*

⇨ see also lā on p.373

鞡 la ·ㄌㄚ see 靰鞡 (wù—) at 靰 on page 692

LAI ㄌㄞ

来（來） lái ㄌㄞˊ ❶从别的地方到说话人所在的地

方，由另一方面到这一方面，跟“去”相对 to come (opposite of 去)：我～北京三年了。*It's been three years since I came to Beijing.*|～信 *send a letter here; incoming letter*|～源 *source; to originate* [来往]交际 have dealings (with) ❷表示时间的经过 ever since; up to now ①某一个时间以后 since：自古以～ *since ancient times*|从～ *has always*|向～ *all along*|这一年～他的进步很大。*He has made great strides in the past year.* ②现在以后 from now on：未～ *future*|～年（明年）*next year* ❸表示约略估计的数目，将近或略超过某一数目 approximately：十～个 *ten or so*|三米～长 *around three metres*|五十～岁 *about fifty years of age* ❹做某一动作（代替前面的动词）to do (used in place of a more specific verb mentioned before)：再～一个！ *Encore!*|这样可～不得！ *One can't do it that way!*|我办不了，你～吧！ *I can't do it. Suppose you give it a try?* ❺在动词前，表示要做某事 used before a verb to introduce an action：我～问你。*Let me ask you.*|大家～想想办法。*Let's work out a solution.*|我～念一遍吧！ *I will read it out.* ❻在动词后，表示曾经做过。也说“来着”（-zhe）used after a verb to indicate a completed action (also 来着 -zhe)：昨天开会你跟谁辩论～？ *Who was it that you debated with at yesterday's meeting?*|这话我哪儿说～？ *Whenever did I say that?* ❼在动词后，表示动作的趋向 used after a verb to indicate direction：一只燕子飞过～。*A swallow flew over here.*|大哥托人捎～了一封信。*Elder brother had someone bring me a letter.*|拿～ *bring over here*|进～ *come in*|上～ *come up* ❽表示发生，出现 to happen; to appear：房屋失修，夏天一下暴雨，麻烦就～了。*With the house out of repair, a summer storm will bring trouble.*|问题～了。*Problems are coming up.*|困难～了。*Difficulties are showing up.* ❾助词，在数词“一”“二”“三”后，表示列举 auxiliary word, used after 一, 二 and 三 to indicate listing：一～领导正确，二～自己努力，所以能胜利地完成任务。*Thanks to sound leadership, and to my own efforts, I was able to successfully complete the mission.* ❿在诗歌等中用作衬字 used as a syllable filler in ballads：正月里～是新春。*Spring comes with the first month of the year.*

俫(**倈**) lái ㄌㄞˊ 用于地名 used in place names：大～庄（在山东省潍坊）*Dalaizhuang (in Weifang, Shandong Province)*

莱(**萊**) lái ㄌㄞˊ 藜 lamb's quarters

崃(**崍**) lái ㄌㄞˊ see 邛崃 (qióng－) at 邛 on page 542

徕(**徠**) lái ㄌㄞˊ [招徕]把人招来 to solicit：～顾客 *solicit customers*

L

涞(淶) lái ㄌㄞˊ 涞水，古水名，即今拒马河。今河北省涞源县和涞水县都从涞水得名 Laishui River (ancient name of today's Jumahe River, wherefrom Laiyuan and Laishui, both of Hebei Province, got their names)

梾(棶) lái ㄌㄞˊ [梾木] 落叶乔木，花黄白色，核果椭圆形。木质坚硬细致，种子可榨油 large-leaved dogwood

铼(錸) lái ㄌㄞˊ 金属元素，符号 Re，质硬，电阻高。可用来制电灯灯丝等，也用作催化剂 rhenium (Re)

赉(賚) lài ㄌㄞˋ 赐，给 to grant; to bestow: 赏～ *grant a reward; reward*

睐(睞) lài ㄌㄞˋ ❶瞳仁不正 cock-eyed ❷看，向旁边看 look at; to glance; to squint: 青～（指喜欢或重视）*to favour*

赖(賴、*頼) lài ㄌㄞˋ ❶依赖，仗恃，倚靠 rely on; depend on: 倚～ *rely on* | 任务的提前完成有～于大家的共同努力。*The early completion of the job depended on the concerted efforts of all.* ❷抵赖，不承认以前的事 to deny; to go back on one's word: ～账 *repudiate a debt* | 事实俱在，～是～不掉的。*The facts are plain to see—there is no repudiating it.* ❸诬赖，硬说别人有过错 to falsely accuse: 自己做错了，不能～别人。*One should not blame others for one's own fault.* ❹怪罪，责备 to blame; to reprimand: 学习不进步只能～自己不努力。*You have only your own lack of effort to blame if you are not making progress in your studies.* ❺不好，劣，坏 bad; poor: 今年庄稼长得真不～。*The crops are not bad at all this year.* ❻留在某处不肯离开 drag on one's stay in a place: ～着不走 *linger on* | 每天～在家里，什么也不干 *stay at home every day doing nothing*

濑(瀨) lài ㄌㄞˋ 流得很急的水 rapids

癞(癩) lài ㄌㄞˋ ❶中医指麻风病 (in traditional Chinese medicine) leprosy ❷〈方 dialect〉癞痢 favus (of the scalp) ❸像生了癞的 favus-like ①因生癣疥等皮肤病而毛发脱落的 mangy: ～狗 *mangy dog* ②表皮凹凸不平或有斑点的 (of skin) pitted; spotty: ～蛤蟆 *toad* | ～瓜 *bitter gourd*

籁(籟) lài ㄌㄞˋ 古代的一种箫 a type of ancient flute ⑤孔穴里发出的声音，泛指声音 sound emitted by a hole; (generally) sound: 天～ *sounds of nature* | 万～俱寂。*Silence reigns.*

LAN ㄌㄢ

兰(蘭) lán ㄌㄢˊ 植物名 name of plants ①兰花，草本植物，丛生，叶细长，花味清香。有草兰、建兰等多种 orchid ②兰草，草本植物，叶卵形，边缘锯齿形。秋天开花，有香味，

可供观赏 fragrant thoroughwort

拦(攔) lán ㄌㄢˊ 遮拦，阻挡，阻止(㊀—挡、阻—) to bar; to block; to obstruct: ～住他，不要让他进来。*Stop him from coming in.*

栏(欄) lán ㄌㄢˊ ❶遮拦的东西 fence; railing; hurdle: 木～ *wood fence* | 花～ *fenced flowerbed* [栏杆] 用竹、木、金属或石头等制成的遮拦物 fence; railing; balustrade (also written as 阑干): 桥～ *bridge railings* ❷养家畜的圈(juàn) fold; sty: 牛～ *cattle pen* ❸书刊报章在每版或每页上用线条或空白分成的各个部分 column (in a book, newspaper or magazine): ～目 *column* | 新闻～ *news column* | 广告～ *advertisement column* | 每页分两～。*Each page is divided into two columns.* ❹表格中分项的格子 field (in a form): 前三～ *the first three fields* | 备注～ *note field* ❺专门用来张贴布告、报纸等的地方 board (for putting up notices, etc.): 报～ *newspaper board* | 宣传～ *publicity board*

岚(嵐) lán ㄌㄢˊ 山中的雾气 mountain haze

婪 lán ㄌㄢˊ 贪爱财物(㊀贪—) greedy

阑(闌) lán ㄌㄢˊ ❶ same as "栏❶" [阑干] 1 纵横交错，参差错落 crisscross: 星斗～ *(the sky is) dotted with stars* 2 same as "栏杆" ❷ same as "拦" ❸尽，晚 (of time) late; coming to an end: 夜～人静。*All is quiet in the dead of night.* [阑珊] 衰落，衰残 coming to an end; waning [阑入] 进入不应进去的地方，混进 sneak in; enter (a forbidden place) without permission

谰(讕) lán ㄌㄢˊ 抵赖，诬陷 to slander; to deny: ～言(诬赖的话) *slander*

澜(瀾) lán ㄌㄢˊ 大波浪，波浪(㊀波—) billows; waves: 力挽狂～ *save a critical situation* | 推波助～ *add fuel to the flame*

斓(斕) lán ㄌㄢˊ see 斑斓 (bān —) at 斑 on page17

镧(鑭) lán ㄌㄢˊ 金属元素，符号 La，银白色，质软。它的化合物可制光学玻璃、高温超导体等 lanthanum (La)

襕(襴) lán ㄌㄢˊ 古代上下衣相连的长袍在下摆所加的横幅 horizontal strip on an ancient gown

蓝(藍) lán ㄌㄢˊ ❶蓼(liǎo)蓝，草本植物，叶长椭圆形。从叶子中提制的靛青可做染料，叶可入药 indigo plant ❷用靛青染成的颜色，像晴天天空的颜色 blue [蓝本] 著作所根据的原本 source (of a literary work) [蓝领] 一般指从事生产、维修等体力劳动的工人 blue-collar worker

褴(襤) lán ㄌㄢˊ [褴褛] (*蓝缕)(—lǚ) 衣服破烂 tattered

篮(籃) lán ㄌㄢˊ (—子、—儿) 用藤、竹、柳条等

编的盛东西的器具，上面有提梁 basket：菜～子 *shopping basket* | 网～ *netted basket*

礛(礛) lán ㄌㄢˊ 用于地名 used in place names：干～（在浙江省舟山市）*Ganlan (in Zhoushan, Zhejiang Province)*

览(覽) lǎn ㄌㄢˇ 看，阅（㊐阅一）to look; to read; to see：游～ *go sightseeing* | 博～群书 *widely read* | 一～表 *list; chart*

揽(攬) lǎn ㄌㄢˇ ❶把持 take hold of; to grasp; to monopolize：大权独～ *arrogate all powers to oneself* ❷拉到自己这方面或自己身上来 take on; take upon oneself：包～ *undertake the whole thing* | ～生意 *solicit business* | 推功～过 *decline all credit but take on any blame* ❸搂，捆 pull into one's arms; hold in one's arms：母亲把孩子～在怀里。*The mother held her child in her arms.* | 用绳子把柴火～上点儿。*Pull a rope around the firewood.*

缆(纜) lǎn ㄌㄢˇ ❶系船用的粗绳子或铁索 cable; mooring rope：～绳 *cable twisted rope line* | 解～（开船）*cast off; set sail* ㊀许多股绞成的粗绳 thick rope; cable：钢～ *steel cable* | 电～ *electric cable* | 光～ *optical cable* ❷用绳子拴（船）to moor：～舟 *moor a boat*

榄(欖) lǎn ㄌㄢˇ see 橄榄(gǎn —) at 橄 on page 198

罱 lǎn ㄌㄢˇ ❶捕鱼或捞水草、河泥的工具 dredger ❷用罱捞 to dredge up：～河泥肥田 *dredge sludge from a river to fertilize fields*

漤 lǎn ㄌㄢˇ ❶把柿子放在热水或石灰水里泡几天，去掉涩味 steep persimmons in hot water or limewash to remove the puckery taste ❷用盐腌（菜），除去生味 to salt (vegetables)

懒(懶、*嬾) lǎn ㄌㄢˇ ❶怠惰，不喜欢工作，跟"勤"相对（㊐一惰）lazy; indolent; slothful (opposite of 勤)：～汉 *lazybones* | 好（hào）吃～做 *be gluttonous and lazy* [懒得]（—de）不愿意，厌烦 not feel like; not in the mood：我都～说了。*I don't feel like commenting.* ❷疲惫，困乏 sluggish; listless：浑身发～ *feel listless all over*

烂(爛) làn ㄌㄢˋ ❶因过熟而变得松软 mushy; soft：稀粥～饭 *thin gruel and pulpy rice* | 蚕豆煮得真～。*The broad beans have really been boiled to a mush.* ㊀程度极深的 thoroughly; utterly：～醉 *dead drunk* | 台词背得～熟。*One has memorized one's lines thoroughly.* ❷东西腐坏（㊐腐一）to rot; to decay：桃和葡萄容易～。*Peaches and grapes go bad easily.* ㊁崩溃，败坏 to collapse; to worsen：敌人一天天～下去，我们一天天好起来。*Day by day the enemy declines while we thrive.* ❸破碎（㊐破一）torn; worn out：破铜～铁 *waste metal* | ～纸 *waste paper* | 衣服穿～了。*The clothes are worn out.* ❹头绪乱 messy：～摊子 *shambles*

L

[烂漫]（*烂熳、*烂缦）1 色彩鲜明美丽 bright-coloured; brilliant：山花～ *bright mountain flowers in full bloom* 2 坦率自然，毫不做作 unaffected：天真～ *innocent and artless*

滥(濫) làn ㄌㄢˋ ❶流水漫溢 to overflow; to flood：泛～ *to overflow; spread unchecked* [滥觞]（—shāng）㊕事物的起源 source ❷不加选择，不加节制 excessive; unrestrained; indiscriminate：～交朋友 *make friends indiscriminately* | ～用 *to abuse* | 粗制～造 *crudely made* | 宁缺毋～ *rather go without than have sth shoddy* ㊀浮泛不合实际 superficial and unrealistic：陈词～调 *hackneyed and stereotyped words*

LANG ㄌㄤ

啷 lāng ㄌㄤ see 当啷 (dāng—) at 当 on page 117

郎 láng ㄌㄤˊ ❶对年轻男子的称呼 term of address for a young man：～才女貌 *talented young man and beautiful young woman; (figurative) (of a couple) perfectly matched* ㊀对某种人的称呼 a form of address for people engaged in a particular profession：货～ *street vendor* | 放牛～ *cowherd* ❷女子称情人或丈夫 used by a woman in addressing her husband or lover：情～ *lover* | ～君 *my husband* ❸古官名 minister (in imperial times)：侍～ *deputy minister* [郎中] 1〈方 dialect〉医生 doctor 2 古官名 gentleman of the interior (ancient official title) ❹姓 (surname) Lang

⇨ see also làng on p.380

廊 láng ㄌㄤˊ ❶（—子）走廊，有顶的过道 corridor; veranda; porch：游～ *covered corridor* | 长～ *gallery* ❷（—子）廊檐，房屋前檐伸出的部分，可避风雨，遮太阳 eaves (of a veranda)

嫏 láng ㄌㄤˊ [嫏嬛]（—huán）same as "琅嬛"

榔 láng ㄌㄤˊ [榔头]（—tou）锤子 hammer

鎯(鋃) láng ㄌㄤˊ [鎯头] (old) same as "榔头"

螂(*蜋) láng ㄌㄤˊ see 螳螂 (táng—) at 螳 on page 640, 蜣螂 (qiāng—) at 蜣 on page 530, 蟑螂 (zhāng—) at 蟑 on page 833, and 蚂螂 (mālang) at 蚂 on page 431

狼 láng ㄌㄤˊ 兽名，像狗，嘴长而尖，耳直立，尾下垂。性狡猾凶狠，昼伏夜出 wolf [狼狈] 1 倒霉或受窘的样子 in an awkward situation; in a dilemma; in a tight corner：～不堪 *in an extremely awkward position* 2 勾结起来（共同做坏事）work hand in glove：～为奸 *collude in doing evil* [狼烟] 古代在白天报警的烽火，据说用狼粪燃烧 smoke of burning wolf dung (used as a daytime alarm signal in ancient times) ㊀战火 war：～四起 *war breaking out all around*

阆(閬) láng ㄌㄤˊ see 闶阆 (kāng—) at 闶 on page

351

⇨ see also làng on p.380

琅(*瑯) láng ㄌㄤˊ 一种玉石 a kind of jade [琅玕](—gān)像珠子的美石 pearl-like stone [琅琅]形容金石相击的声音或响亮的读书声 tinkle; jingle; sound of reading aloud：书声～ *ringing sound of reading aloud*

[琅嬛](—huán)神话中天帝藏书的地方。也作"嫏嬛" legendary library of the God of Heaven (also written as 嫏嬛)

桹 láng ㄌㄤˊ [桹桹]形容木头相撞击的声音 sound of wood striking wood

锒(鋃) láng ㄌㄤˊ [锒铛](—dāng) 1 铁锁链 iron chains：～入狱 *be chained and put in prison* 2 形容金属撞击的声音 clank; clang

稂 láng ㄌㄤˊ 古书上指狼尾草 (in ancient Chinese texts) Chinese pennisetum

筤 láng ㄌㄤˊ 幼竹 young bamboo

朗 lǎng ㄌㄤˇ ❶明朗，明亮，光线充足 light; bright：晴～ *sunny and cloudless* | 豁(huò)然开～ *be suddenly enlightened* | 天～气清 *clear and fresh air under a blue sky* ❷声音清楚、响亮 loud and clear：～诵 *read aloud with expression* | ～读 *read aloud*

蓢 lǎng ㄌㄤˇ 用于地名 used in place names：～底(在广东省恩平) *Langdi (in Enping, Guangdong Province)* | 南～(在广东省中山) *Nanlang (in Zhongshan, Guangdong Province)*

塱(**㙟) lǎng ㄌㄤˇ 用于地名 used in place names：河～(在广东省阳春) *Helang (in Yangchun, Guangdong Province)*

㮾 lǎng ㄌㄤˇ [㮾梨]地名，在湖南省长沙县 Langli (a place in Changsha County, Hunan Province)

烺 lǎng ㄌㄤˇ 明朗 bright

郎 làng ㄌㄤˋ [屎壳郎]蜣螂(qiāngláng)的俗称 dung beetle (informal name for 蜣螂)

⇨ see also láng on p.379

埌 làng ㄌㄤˋ see 圹埌(kuàng—) at 圹 on page 367

莨 làng ㄌㄤˋ [莨菪](—dàng)草本植物，花黄色微紫，全株有黏性腺毛，并有特殊臭味。有毒。根、茎、叶可入药 henbane

崀 làng ㄌㄤˋ [崀山]地名，在湖南省新宁 Langshan (a place in Xinning, Hunan Province)

阆(閬) làng ㄌㄤˋ [阆中]地名，在四川省 Langzhong (a place in Sichuan Province)

⇨ see also láng on p.379

浪 làng ㄌㄤˋ ❶大波(㊀波—、—涛) big wave：海～ *sea wave* | 兴风作～ *make trouble* ❷像波浪起伏的东西 things resembling waves：声～ *sound wave* | 麦～ *rippling wheat* ❸放纵 to indulge：～游 *loaf around* | ～费 *to waste*

L

眼 làng ㄌㄤˋ 〈方 dialect〉晾晒 to air-dry; to sun-dry

蒗 làng ㄌㄤˋ [宁蒗](níng—) 彝族自治县，在云南省 Ninglang (a Yi autonomous county in Yunnan Province)

LAO ㄌㄠ

捞(撈) lāo ㄌㄠ ❶从液体里面取东西 lift out (of a liquid): ～鱼 *catch fish* | ～面 *get noodles (from boiling water)* | 打～ *get out of water* ❷用不正当的手段取得 get by improper means: ～一把 *reap some profit* | ～好处 *fish for personal gains*

劳(勞) láo ㄌㄠˊ ❶劳动，人类创造物质或精神财富的活动 to work; to labour: 按～分配 *to allocate according to work done* | 不～而获 *reap without sowing* ❷疲劳，辛苦 fatigued; hard-working: 任～任怨 *bear hardship without complaint* ❸烦劳 to bother [劳驾] 请人帮助的客气话 (polite expression used when asking for help) will you please: ～开门。*Would you open the door please?* ❹慰劳，用言语或实物慰问 express appreciation; reward: ～军 *reward troops* ❺功勋 meritorious service: 汗马之～ *achievements in battle; (generally) extraordinary service*

塝(壈) láo ㄌㄠˊ see 圪塝 (gē—) at 圪 on page 203

唠(嘮) láo ㄌㄠˊ [唠叨] (—dao) 没完没了地说，絮叨 to chatter; to nag: 人老了就爱～。*People tend to get garrulous when they get old.*

⇨ see also lào on p.383

崂(嶗) láo ㄌㄠˊ 崂山，山名，在山东省青岛。也作"劳山" Laoshan Mountain (also written as 劳山, in Qingdao, Shandong Province)

铹(鐒) láo ㄌㄠˊ 人造的放射性金属元素，符号 Lr。lawrencium (Lr)

痨(癆) láo ㄌㄠˊ 痨病，中医指结核病，通常指肺结核 (in traditional Chinese medicine) consumptive disease; (usually) pulmonary tuberculosis

牢 láo ㄌㄠˊ ❶养牲畜的圈 (juàn) pen; fold: 亡羊补～ (喻事后补救) *mend the fold after the sheep is lost; (figurative) remedy a situation after the fact* ㊕古代称做祭品的牲畜 (ancient) sacrificial animal: 太～(牛) *sacrificial ox* | 少～(羊) *sacrificial sheep* ❷监禁犯人的地方 (㊣监—、—狱) prison; jail: 坐～ *be in prison* ❸结实，坚固 firm; durable; fast: ～不可破 *indestructible* | ～记党的教导 *keep in mind the Party's teachings*

[牢骚] (—sao) 烦闷不满的情绪 dissatisfaction: 发～ *to grumble* | ～满腹 *full of complaints*

醪 láo ㄌㄠˊ 汁渣混合的酒，浊酒。也泛称酒 unstrained wine; (generally) wine [醪糟] 江米酒 fermented glutinous rice

老 lǎo ㄌㄠˇ ❶年岁大，时间长 old; aged ①跟"少""幼"

相对 aged (opposite of 少 or 幼)：～人 *the aged* 敬辞 polite speech used after a surname：吴～ *the venerable Wu* | 范～ *the venerable Fan* ②陈旧的 old; outdated：～房子 *old house* | ～观念 *outdated idea* ③经历长，有经验 experienced; veteran：～手 *old hand* | ～干部 *veteran cadre* ④跟“嫩”相对 tough (opposite of 嫩)：～笋 *tough bamboo shoots* | 菠菜～了。*The spinach has grown tough.* | ～绿 *deep green* ⑤副词，长久 (adverb) for a long time：～没见面了 *have not seen sb for ages* ⑥副词，经常，总是 (adverb) always; often; all the time：你怎么～迟到呢？*Why are you always late?* ⑦原来的 original：～家 *old home (distinct from one's present home); hometown* | ～脾气 *original temperament* | ～地方 *same old place* ❷副词，极，很 (adverb) very; extremely：～早 *very early* | ～远 *far away* ❸排行（háng）在末了的 youngest (among siblings)：～儿子 *youngest son* | ～妹子 *youngest sister* ❹词头 prefix ①加在称呼上 used before forms of address to indicate respect or intimacy：～弟 *young man; buddy* | ～师 *teacher* | ～张 *old Zhang* ②加在兄弟姊妹次序上 used to indicate order of birth：～大 *eldest child* | ～二 *second born* ③加在某些动植物名词上 used in the names of certain animals and plants：～虎 *tiger* | ～鼠 *mouse* | ～玉米 *corn on the cob*

佬 lǎo ㄌㄠˇ 成年男子（含轻视意）(derisive) guy：阔～ *rich guy* | 乡巴～ *country bumpkin*

荖 lǎo ㄌㄠˇ 荖浓溪，水名，在台湾省 Laonongxi River (in Taiwan Province)

姥 lǎo ㄌㄠˇ ［姥姥］［老老］（－lao）1 外祖母 (maternal) grandmother 2 旧时接生的女人 (old) midwife

⇨ see also mǔ on p.464

栳 lǎo ㄌㄠˇ see 栲栳 (kǎo－) at 栲 on page 353

铑(銠) lǎo ㄌㄠˇ 金属元素，符号 Rh，银白色，质硬，耐腐蚀。铂铑合金可制热电偶等 rhodium (Rh)

潦 lǎo ㄌㄠˇ ❶雨水大 (of rain) heavy ❷路上的流水，积水 stream/puddle (on the road)

⇨ see also liáo on p.402

络(絡) lào ㄌㄠˋ 义同“络（luò）❶”，用于一些口语词 (in some spoken words) same in meaning as 络 (luò) ❶［络子］（－zi）1 用线绳结成的网状袋子 string bag 2 绕线等的器具 spindle

⇨ see also luò on p.429

烙 lào ㄌㄠˋ ❶用器物烫、熨 to brand; to iron：～铁（tie）*iron; soldering iron* | ～衣服 *iron clothes*［烙印］在器物上烧成的做标记的印文 brand; stamp ⑩不易磨灭的痕迹 indelible mark：时代～ *marks of time* ❷放在铛（chēng）或锅里加热使熟 to bake (in a pan)：～饼 *pan-baked bread*

L

➪ see also luò on p.429

落 lào ㄌㄠˋ 义同“落”（luò），用于一些口语词语，如“落炕、落枕、落不是、落埋怨”等 (in some spoken words, such as 落炕，落枕，落不是，落埋怨，etc.) same in meaning as 落 (luò)

➪ see also là on p.374, luò on p.429

酪 lào ㄌㄠˋ ❶用动物的乳汁做成的半凝固食品 junket：奶～ *cheese* ❷用果实做的糊状食品 sweet paste made from crushed nuts or fruits：杏仁～ *almond cream* | 核桃～ *walnut paste*

唠（嘮） lào ㄌㄠˋ〈方 dialect〉说话，闲谈 to chat：来，咱们～一～。*Come on, let's have a chat.*

➪ see also láo on p.381

涝（澇） lào ㄌㄠˋ 雨水过多，被水淹，跟“旱”相对 be waterlogged; be inundated (opposite of 旱)：排～ *drain excess water* | 防旱防～ *prevent drought and waterlogging*

耢（耮） lào ㄌㄠˋ ❶功用和耙 (bà) 相似的农具，用荆条等编成。又叫耱 (mò)、盖或盖擦 leveller (a farm tool used to level land, also called 耱 mò, 盖 or 盖擦) ❷用耢平整土地 to level (with a leveller)

嫪 lào ㄌㄠˋ 姓 (surname) Lao

LE ㄌㄜ

肋 lē ㄌㄜ [肋脦]（-de）（-te）（又）衣裳肥大，不整洁 sloppy; slovenly：瞧你穿得这个～！*Look how sloppily dressed you are!*

➪ see also lèi on p.386

仂 lè ㄌㄜˋ〈古 ancient〉余数 remainder

叻 lè ㄌㄜˋ [石叻] 我国侨民称新加坡。又叫叻埠 (used by overseas Chinese, also called 叻埠) Singapore

泐 lè ㄌㄜˋ ❶石头被水冲击而成的纹理 patterns made by waves eroding rocks ❷ same as “勒 (lè) ❹”：手～（亲手写，旧时书信用语）(old, used in letter correspondence) hand written by

勒 lè ㄌㄜˋ ❶套在牲畜头上带嚼子的笼头 headstall; halter ❷收住缰绳不使前进 to rein in; to halt：悬崖～马 *rein in on the brink of the precipice* ❸强制 to force; to compel：～令 *to compel (by legal authority)* | ～索 *to extort* ❹ 刻 to carve; to engrave; to inscribe：～石 *inscribe on a stone* | ～碑 *carve on a stone tablet*

➪ see also lēi on p.384

竻 lè ㄌㄜˋ [竻竹] 一种枝上有硬刺的竹子 thorny bamboo

鳓（鰳） lè ㄌㄜˋ 鱼名，又叫鲙（kuài）鱼、曹白鱼，背青灰色，腹银白色。生活在海里 (also called 鲙 kuài 鱼，曹白鱼) slender shad

乐（樂） lè ㄌㄜˋ ❶快乐，欢喜，快活 happy; joyful：～趣 *delight* | ～事 *pleasure* | ～而忘返 *have so much fun that one forgets to leave* ❷乐于 to

L

enjoy：～此不疲 *never get bored with it* [乐得] 正好，正合心愿 be only glad to：～这样做 *would readily do it* ❸（一子、一儿）使人快乐的事情 pleasure; fun：取～ *have fun* | 逗～儿 *crack jokes* ❹ 笑 to laugh：可～ *funny* | 把一屋子人都逗～了 *made the whole room laugh* | 你～什么？ *What are you laughing about?* ❺ 姓 (surname) Le

⇨ see also yuè on p.810

了 le ·ㄌㄜ 助词 auxiliary ① 放在动词或形容词后，表示动作或变化已经完成 used after a verb or adjective to indicate completion：买～一本书 *bought a book* | 水位低～一米 *water level has dropped by one metre* ②用在句子末尾或句中停顿的地方，表示变化或出现新的情况 used at the end of a sentence or phrase to indicate a change or a new situation 1 指明已经出现或将要出现某种情况 used to indicate a situation that has already occurred or is about to occur：下雨～。*It's raining.* | 明天就是星期日～。*It will be Sunday tomorrow.* 2 认识、想法、主张、行动等有变化 used to indicate a change in understanding, idea or plan：我现在明白他的意思～。*Now I know what he means.* | 他今年暑假不回家～。*He is not going home for this summer break.* | 我本来没打算去，后来还是去～。*I had not planned to go, but went after all.* 3 随假设的条件转移 used to indicate a conditional possibility：你早来一天就见着他～。*If you had come one day earlier, you would have seen him.* 4 催促或劝止 used to express a tone of persuasion or dissuasion：走～，走～，不能再等～！ *It's time to go. We can't wait any longer!* | 算～，不要老说这些事～！ *Forget it, don't keep bringing up such things!*

⇨ see also liǎo on p.402

饹(餎) le ·ㄌㄜ see 饸饹 (hé—) at 饸 on page 247

LEI ㄌㄟ

勒 lēi ㄌㄟ 用绳子等捆住或套住，再用力拉紧 to tighten (with a rope, etc.)：把行李～紧点儿 *tie the baggage tight* | ～住缰绳 *hold the reins tightly*

⇨ see also lè on p.383

累(纍) léi ㄌㄟˊ ❶连缀或捆 to bind; to tie [累累] 连续成串 in clusters：果实～ *fruit hanging in clusters* [累赘]（—zhui）多余的负担，麻烦 burden; cumbersome：孩子小，成了～。*A child is young, and has became a bother.* | 这事多～。*This matter is a real burden.* ❷ (ancient) same as "缧"

⇨ see also lěi on p.385, lèi on p.386

嫘 léi ㄌㄟˊ [嫘祖] 人名，传说是黄帝的妃，发明了养蚕 Leizu (in legend, wife of the Yellow Emperor, and inventor of sericulture)

L

缧(縲) léi ㄌㄟˊ [缧绁](—xiè) 捆绑犯人的绳索。借指牢狱 rope (for tying up prisoners); prison

雷 léi ㄌㄟˊ ❶云层放电时发出的巨大声音 thunder：打～ *to thunder* | 春～ *spring thunder* | ～阵雨 *thunder shower* [雷霆] 震耳的雷声 thunderclap ㊐怒气或威力 rage; power：大发～ *fly into a rage* | ～万钧 *crushing blow* [雷同] 打雷时，许多东西同时响应，比喻随声附和，不该相同而相同 echo what others have said; identical ❷军事上用的爆炸武器 mine：地～ *landmine* | 鱼～ *torpedo*

擂 léi ㄌㄟˊ ❶研磨 to pestle; to pound：～钵（研东西的钵）*mortar and pestle* ❷打 to beat; to hit：～鼓 *beat the drum* | 自吹自～（喻自我吹嘘）*sing one's own praises*

⇨ see also lèi on p.386

檑 léi ㄌㄟˊ 滚木，古代守城用的圆柱形的大木头，从城上推下打击攻城的人 log (thrown from city walls against attackers)

礌 léi ㄌㄟˊ 礌石，古代守城用的石头，从城上推下打击攻城的人 stones (thrown from city walls against attackers)

镭(鐳) léi ㄌㄟˊ 放射性金属元素，符号 Ra，银白色，质软。医学上用镭治疗癌症和皮肤病 radium (Ra)

羸 léi ㄌㄟˊ 瘦 thin; skinny：身体～弱。*(His) physique is thin and weak.*

罍 léi ㄌㄟˊ 古代一种形状像壶的容器，多用来盛酒 an ancient urn-shaped vessel, often used for wine

耒 lěi ㄌㄟˇ ❶古代一种农具，形状像木叉 a fork-shaped agricultural tool ❷耒耜上的木把（bà）wooden handle of such a tool [耒耜]（—sì）古代一种耕地用的农具，形状像犁 (ancient) plough-like agricultural tool

诔(誄) lěi ㄌㄟˇ ❶古时叙述死者生平，表示哀悼（多用于上对下）(ancient) make a memorial speech (senior to junior) ❷这类表示哀悼的文章，即诔文 memorial speech (same as 诔文)

垒(壘) lěi ㄌㄟˇ ❶古代军中用作防守的墙壁或工事（㊥壁—）(in ancient military use) rampart; wall：堡～ *fort* | 两军对～ *two armies confront each other* | 深沟高～ *dig deep trenches and build high walls* ❷把砖、石等重叠砌起来 to build by piling up bricks, stones, etc.：～墙 *build a wall* | 把井口～高一些 *build the mouth of the well higher*

累(❶纍) lěi ㄌㄟˇ ❶重叠，堆积 pile up; to accumulate：危如～卵 *as precarious as a stack of eggs* | 积年～月 *for years and months* [累累] 1 屡屡 again and again; many times 2 形容累积得多 innumerable; countless：罪行～ *have a long criminal record* [累进] 照原数目多少而递增，如 2、4、8、16 等，

L

原数越大，增加的数也越大 progression：～率 *graduated rates*｜～税 *progressive taxation* ❷连累 to involve; to implicate：～及 *to implicate*｜受～ *be dragged in*｜牵～ *tie down; to involve (in trouble)*｜～你操心 *make you worry*

⇨ see also léi on p.384, lèi on p.386

磊 lěi ㄌㄟˇ 石头多㊀(of stones) heaped; piled：怪石～～ *heaps of strange stones*

［磊落］心地光明坦白 open and upright

蕾 lěi ㄌㄟˇ 花骨朵，含苞未放的花 flower bud：蓓～ *buds*｜花～ *flower bud*

瘤 lěi ㄌㄟˇ 中医指皮肤上起的小疙瘩 (in traditional Chinese medicine) pimples on the skin

儡 lěi ㄌㄟˇ see 傀儡 (kuǐ—) at 傀 on page 369

藟 lěi ㄌㄟˇ ❶藤 vine：葛～ *creeping grape* ❷缠绕 to twine; to bind ❸ same as "蕾"

肋 lèi ㄌㄟˋ 胸部的两旁 costal region：两～ *both sides of the chest*｜～骨 *rib*

⇨ see also lē on p.383

泪(*淚) lèi ㄌㄟˋ 眼泪 tear

类(類) lèi ㄌㄟˋ ❶种(zhǒng)，好多相似事物的综合(㊀种—) class; category; type：分～ *to classify*｜～型 *type*｜以此～推 *deduce the rest from this* ❷类似，好像 to resemble; be similar to：画虎～犬 *try to draw a tiger and make it look like a dog; (figurative) to imitate poorly*

纇(纇) lèi ㄌㄟˋ 缺点，毛病 flaw; defect

累 lèi ㄌㄟˋ ❶疲乏，过劳 tired; fatigued：今天干活儿～了。*I am tired out from work today.* ❷使疲劳 tire out; wear out：别～着他。*Don't tire him out.*

⇨ see also léi on p.384, lěi on p.385

酹 lèi ㄌㄟˋ 把酒洒在地上表示祭奠 pour a libation

擂 lèi ㄌㄟˋ 擂台，古时候比武的台子 platform for martial arts contest; arena：摆～ *throw down the gauntlet*｜打～ *take up the challenge*

⇨ see also léi on p.385

嘞 lei ·ㄌㄟ 助词，跟"喽"(lou)相似 auxiliary word, similar to 喽 (lou)：雨不下了，走～！*Let's get going now the rain has stopped.*

LENG ㄌㄥ

塄 léng ㄌㄥˊ 田地边上的坡子，又叫地塄 bank on a field edge (also called 地塄)

楞 léng ㄌㄥˊ same as "棱"

崚 léng ㄌㄥˊ líng ㄌㄧㄥˊ(又)［崚嶒］(—céng)形容山高 (of peaks) towering and steep

棱(*稜) léng ㄌㄥˊ (—子、—儿) ❶物体上不同方向的两个平面接连的部分 edge; arris：见～见角 *be angulated; (of a person) be of character* ❷物体表面上的条状突起部分 ridge; corrugation：瓦～ *rows of tiles on a roof*｜搓板的～儿 *ridges*

of a washboard

⇨ see also líng on p.410

冷 lěng ㄌㄥˇ ❶温度低，跟"热"相对（㊉寒一）cold; chilly (opposite of 热)：昨天下了雪，今天真～。*It snowed yesterday, and today it's really cold.* ❷寂静，不热闹 desolate：～清清 *cold and dreary* | ～落 *unfrequented; give sb the cold shoulder* ❸生僻，少见的（㊉一僻）uncommon; rare：～字 *rare character* | ～货（不流行或不畅销的货物）*low-selling goods* ❹不热情，不温和 (of one's manner) cold; frosty：～脸子 *frosty look* | ～言～语 *sarcastic remarks* | ～笑 *to sneer* | ～酷 *callous; cold-hearted* [冷静] 不感情用事 sober; cool：头脑～ *sober-minded* ❺突然，意料以外的 sudden; unexpected：～不防 *suddenly* | ～枪 *sniper's shot*

堎 lèng ㄌㄥˋ [长堎] 地名，在江西省新建 Changleng (a place in Xinjian, Jiangxi Province)

睖 lèng ㄌㄥˋ [睖睁]（一zheng）眼睛发直，发愣 stare blankly; be in a daze

愣 lèng ㄌㄥˋ ❶呆，失神 distracted; stupefied; absent-minded：两眼发～ *have a distracted look in one's eyes* | 吓得他一～。*He was struck dumb.* ❷鲁莽，说话做事不考虑对不对 rash; reckless：～头～脑 *rash; impetuous* | 他说话做事太～。*He is too reckless in his speech and actions.* ㊈蛮，硬，不管行得通行不通 obstinate：～干 *act obstinately* | 明知不对，他～那么说。*Knowing full well they were wrong, he sticks obstinately to those words.*

LI ㄌㄧ

哩 lī ㄌㄧ [哩哩啦啦] 形容零零散散或断断续续的样子 scattered; on and off：瓶子漏了，水～地洒了一地。*The bottle got a leak and water dripped all over the ground.* | 雨～下了一天。*It rained on and off for a whole day.*

⇨ see also lǐ on p.390, li on p.395

丽（麗） lí ㄌㄧˊ [高丽] 1 我国古族名，古国名。又叫高句（gōu）丽 Gaoli (also called 高句 gōu 丽, an ancient ethnic group, and state, in China) 2 朝鲜半岛历史上的王朝，即王氏高丽 Goryeo (a historical kingdom on the Korean Peninsula) [丽水] 地名，在浙江省 Lishui (a place in Zhejiang Province)

⇨ see also lì on p.393

骊（驪） lí ㄌㄧˊ 纯黑色的马 pure black horse

缡（纚） lí ㄌㄧˊ see 綝缡 (lín 一) at 綝 on page 406

鹂（鸝） lí ㄌㄧˊ [黄鹂] 鸟名，又叫黄莺，羽毛黄色，从眼边到头后部有黑色斑纹，叫声悦耳 oriole (also called 黄莺)

鲡（鱺） lí ㄌㄧˊ see 鳗鲡 (mán 一) at 鳗 on page 435

厘（△*釐） lí ㄌㄧˊ ❶法定计量单位中十进分数单位词头之一，表示 10^{-2}，符号 c。(suffix) centi- (c) ❷计量单

L

位名，10厘是1分 measurement unit, equal to 1/10 of a 分①市制长度，1厘约合0.333毫米 unit for length, equal to 0.333 millimetres ②市制地积，1厘约合6.667平方米 unit for area, equal to 6.667 square metres ③市制重量，1厘合50毫克 unit for weight, equal to 50 milligrams ❸利率，年利率1厘按百分之一计，月利率1厘按千分之一计 for interest rates, equal to an annual rate of 1%, or a monthly rate of 0.1% ❹治理，整理 to regulate; to rectify; to administer：～正 *to correct* | ～定 *to collate and stipulate (rules and regulations)*

⇨ 釐 see also xī on p.699

喱 lí ㄌㄧˊ see 咖喱 (gā－) at 咖 on page 193, and 啫喱(zhě－) at 啫 on page 840

狸(*貍) lí ㄌㄧˊ (－子)哺乳动物，又叫山猫，毛棕黄色，有黑色斑纹 leopard cat (also called 山猫)

离(離) lí ㄌㄧˊ ❶相距，隔开(㊀距－) be apart from; be at a distance from：北京～天津一百多公里。*Beijing is over 100 km from Tianjin.* | ～国庆节很近了。*National Day is drawing near.* ❷离开，分开，分别 to leave; part from：～家 *be away from home* | ～婚 *to divorce* | ～散(sàn) *(of family members) to disperse; discrete* [离间](－jiàn)从中挑拨，使人不团结 sow discord; drive a wedge between [离子]原子或原子团失去或得到电子后叫作离子 ion ❸缺少 be without：发展工业～不了钢铁。*Steel is indispensable for industrial development.* ❹八卦之一，符号是"☲"，代表火 *li*, one of the Eight Trigrams used in ancient divination, symbol ☲, representing fire [离奇]奇怪的，出乎意料的 strange; odd; weird

蓠(蘺) lí ㄌㄧˊ [江蓠]红藻的一种，暗红色，分枝不规则，生长在浅海湾中。可用来制琼脂 *Gracilaria confervoides* (a red alga found in shallow bays, can be used to make agar)

漓(❷灕) lí ㄌㄧˊ ❶ see 淋漓(lín－) at 淋 on page 406 ❷漓江，水名，在广西壮族自治区桂林 Lijiang River (in Guilin, Guangxi Zhuang Autonomous Region)

缡(縭、褵)** lí ㄌㄧˊ 古时妇女的围裙 (ancient) apron (worn by women)：结～(古时指女子出嫁) *(ancient, of a woman) get married*

篱(籬) lí ㄌㄧˊ 篱笆，用竹、苇、树枝等编成的障蔽物 bamboo/twig fence：竹～茅舍 *thatched cottage with a bamboo fence*

醨 lí ㄌㄧˊ 味淡的酒 light wine

梨(*棃) lí ㄌㄧˊ 梨树，落叶乔木，花五瓣，白色，果实叫梨，味甜多汁。种类很多 pear tree; pear

犁(*犂) lí ㄌㄧˊ ❶耕地的农具 plough ❷用犁耕

L

to plough：用新式犁～地 *plough the field with a new-style plough*

嫠 lí ㄌㄧˊ 寡妇 widow：～妇 *widow*

黎 lí ㄌㄧˊ 众 multitudinous; numerous：～民 *common people*｜～庶 *common people*

［黎明］天刚亮的时候 daybreak

［黎族］我国少数民族，参看附录四 the Li people (one of the ethnic groups in China. See Appendix Ⅳ.)

藜（❷*蔾） lí ㄌㄧˊ ❶草本植物，花黄绿色，嫩叶可以吃。茎长（zhǎng）老了可做拐杖 lamb's quarters［藜藿］藜和藿都是野菜，泛指粗劣的食物 (generally) coarse food ❷ see 蒺藜 (jíli) at 蒺 on page 288

檬 lí ㄌㄧˊ ［檬檬］常绿小乔木，又叫广东柠檬，枝有刺，叶椭圆形，花紫红色，主要用作果树的砧木 mandarin lime (also called 广东柠檬)

黧 lí ㄌㄧˊ 黑里带黄的颜色 sallow black

罹 lí ㄌㄧˊ ❶遭受灾难或不幸 suffer from：～难（nàn）*die in a disaster or an accident*｜～祸 *fall victim to a disaster* ❷忧患，苦难 misery; suffering

蠡 lí ㄌㄧˊ 贝壳做的瓢 shell serving as a dipper：以～测海（喻见识浅薄）*measure the sea with a dipper; (figurative) have a shallow understanding*

⇨ see also lǐ on p.391

劙 lí ㄌㄧˊ 割开 to cut; to pierce

礼（禮） lǐ ㄌㄧˇ ❶由一定社会的道德观念和风俗习惯形成的为大家共同遵行的仪节 ceremony; rite; ritual：典～ *formal ceremony*｜婚～ *wedding* ❷表示尊敬的态度或动作 courtesy; etiquette; manners：敬～ *to salute*｜～貌 *courtesy; politeness* ㊀以礼相待 treat sb with due respect; receive sb with courtesy：～贤下士 *(of people in a high position) treat talented people with courtesy* ❸礼物，用来表示庆贺或敬意 present; gift：献～ *present a gift*｜一份～ *a present*｜大～包 *big package of gift*

李 lǐ ㄌㄧˇ 李（子）树，落叶乔木，花白色。果实叫李子，熟时黄色或紫红色，可以吃 plum tree (its fruit is called 李子)

里（❹❺裏、❹❺*裡） lǐ ㄌㄧˇ ❶市制长度单位，1 里是 150 丈，合 500 米 a traditional Chinese unit for measuring length, equal to 500 metres.There are 150 丈 in 1 里. ❷居住的地方 where one lives：故～ *native place*｜返～ *return to one's hometown*｜同～（现在指同乡）*sb from the same place* ❸街坊（古代五家为邻，五邻为里）neighbour (in ancient China, every 5 families formed a 邻, and every 5 邻 a 里)：邻～ *neighbourhood; neighbours*｜～弄（lòng）*lanes and alleys* ❹（一子、一儿）衣物的内层，跟"表""面"相对 lining; liner; inside (opposite of 表 or 面)：衣裳～儿 *lining of a* *garment* | 被～*inner side of a quilt* | 鞋～子 *liner of a shoe* | 箱子～儿 *suitcase lining* ❺里面，内部，跟"外"相对 inside (opposite of 外)：屋子～*inside the room* | 手～*in one's hand* | 碗～*in a bowl* | 箱子～面 *inside the chest* 引一定范围以内 within a certain range：夜～*during the night* | 这～*here* | 哪～*where* [里手] 1 (～儿) 靠里的一边，靠左边 inner side; left-hand side 2〈方 dialect〉内行 expert; old hand

俚 lǐ ㄌㄧˇ 民间的，通俗的 popular; rustic：～歌 *folk song* | ～语 *slang*

哩 lǐ ㄌㄧˇ 又读 yīnglǐ，现写作"英里"，英美制长度单位，1 哩等于 5280 呎，合 1609 米 mile (also pronounced yīnglǐ, now written as 英里)

⇨ see also lī on p.387, li on p.395

浬 lǐ ㄌㄧˇ 又读 hǎilǐ，现写作"海里"，计量海洋上距离的长度单位，1 浬合 1852 米，只用于船只航行的路程 nautical mile (also pronounced hǎilǐ, now written as 海里)

娌 lǐ ㄌㄧˇ see 妯娌 (zhóuli) at 妯 on page 864

理 lǐ ㄌㄧˇ ❶物质组织的条纹 texture; grain：肌～*texture* | 木～*wood grain* ❷道理，事物的规律 reason; logic：讲～*reason with sb; reasonable* | 合～*reasonable* 特指自然科学 (specifically) natural sciences：～科 *science (as a branch of learning)* | ～学院 *science school* [理论] 1 人们从实践中概括出来又在实践中证明了的关于自然界和人类社会的规律性的系统的认识 theory; principle：基础～*basic theory* 2 据理争论 reason with; to debate：跟他～一番 *argue it out with him* [理念] 思想，观念 idea; concept：投资～*investment philosophy* | 营销～*marketing concept* [理性] 把握了事物内在联系的认识阶段，也指判断和推理的能力 reason; rationality ❸管理，办 to manage; to administer：～家 *manage household affairs* | ～财 *manage money matters* | 当家～事 *be in charge of family affairs* 引整理，使整齐 put in order; tidy up：～发 *get/give a haircut* | 把书～一～*sort out and tidy up the books* ❹对别人的言语行动表示态度 pay attention to; to heed：答～*to respond* | ～睬 *pay attention to* | ～会 *understand; pay attention to* | 置之不～*ignore it*

锂(鋰) lǐ ㄌㄧˇ 金属元素，符号 Li，银白色，质软，是金属元素中最轻的。可用来制合金、电池等 lithium (Li)

鲤(鯉) lǐ ㄌㄧˇ 鱼名，身体侧扁，嘴边有长短须各一对，生活在淡水中 carp

逦(邐) lǐ ㄌㄧˇ see 迤逦 (yǐ—) at 迤 on page 772

澧 lǐ ㄌㄧˇ 澧水，水名，在湖南省北部，流入洞庭湖 Lishui River (in northern Hunan Province, flowing into Dongting Lake)

醴 lǐ ㄌㄧˇ 甜酒 sweet wine

L

鳢（鱧） lǐ ㄌㄧˇ 乌鳢，鱼名，又叫黑鱼，身体圆筒形，头扁，背鳍和臀鳍很长，性凶猛，生活在淡水中 Northern snakehead (also called 黑鱼)

蠡 lǐ ㄌㄧˇ 蠡县，地名，在河北省 Lixian (a place in Hebei Province)

⇨ see also lí on p.389

力 lì ㄌㄧˋ ❶力量，力气，动物肌肉的效能 physical strength：身强～壮 *robust and strong* 㓞 ①身体器官的效能 capacity (of an organ)：目～ *vision* | 脑～ *brainpower* ②一切事物的效能 power; force：电～ *electrical power* | 药～ *efficacy of a medicine* | 浮～ *buoyancy force* | 说服～ *persuasiveness* | 生产～ *productive force* ❷用极大的力量，尽力 with all might and main：纠正不～ *fail to rectify thoroughly* | ～战 *fight hard* | 据理～争 *fight for one's point of view on just grounds* ❸改变物体运动状态的作用叫力。力有三个要素，即力的大小、方向和作用点 force (in physics)

朸 lì ㄌㄧˋ ❶古县名，西汉置，约在今山东省商河县东北 an ancient county set up in the Western Han Dynasty, in the northeast of today's Shanghe County, Shandong Province ❷姓 (surname) Li

荔（*茘） lì ㄌㄧˋ ［荔枝］常绿乔木，果实也叫荔枝。外壳紫红色，有疙瘩，果肉色白多汁，味甜美 lychee

珕 lì ㄌㄧˋ 蚌、蛤等一类动物，古人用其壳做刀剑鞘上的装饰 shellfish (used as scabbard ornaments in ancient times)

历（歷、❹曆、❹*厤） lì ㄌㄧˋ ❶经历，经过 pass through; to undergo; to experience：～尽甘苦 *have experienced the sweetnesses and pains of life* | ～时十年 *have taken 10 years* ❷经过了的 previous：～年 *over the years* | ～代 *in past ages; for generations* | ～史 *history* ［历来］副词，从来，一向 (adverb) always; constantly; all along：中国人民～就是勤劳勇敢的。*The Chinese people have always been industrious and courageous.* ［历历］一个一个很清楚的 distinct and clear：～在目 *come clear and vivid before the eyes* | ～可数 *so distinct that each can be counted* ❸遍，逐一 all; one by one：～览 *see/read/visit all* | ～访名家 *visit all the established figures* ❹历法，推算年、月、日和节气的方法 calendric system：阴～ *lunar calendar* | 阳～ *solar calendar* 㓞 记录年、月、日、节气的书、表、册页 calendar; almanac：日～ *calendar* | ～书 *almanac*

坜（壢） lì ㄌㄧˋ 坑。多用于地名 hole (often used in place names)：中～（在台湾省）*Zhongli (in Taiwan Province)*

苈（藶） lì ㄌㄧˋ see 葶苈 (tíng－) at 葶 on page 655

呖（嚦） lì ㄌㄧˋ ［呖呖］鸟类清脆的叫声 chirping：～莺声 *warbling of the oriole*

屴(㟯) lì ㄌㄧˋ [屴崌山](-jū-)山名，在江西省乐平 Lijushan Mountain (in Leping, Jiangxi Province)

沥(瀝) lì ㄌㄧˋ ❶液体一滴一滴地落下 to drip; to trickle: 滴～ *drip and trickle* [呕心沥血]形容费尽心思 make painstaking efforts: 为培养下一代～ *work with might and main to educate the next generation* ❷液体渗出来的点滴 drop: 余～ *heeltap; small share of the profits*

枥(櫪) lì ㄌㄧˋ 马槽 manger: 老骥伏～，志在千里。*An old steed in the stable still aspires to heroic exploits. (figurative) Old people may still cherish high aspirations.*

疬(癧) lì ㄌㄧˋ see 瘰疬 (luǒ -) at 瘰 on page 428

雳(靂) lì ㄌㄧˋ see 霹雳 (pī -) at 霹 on page 500

厉(厲) lì ㄌㄧˋ ❶严格，切实 strict; rigorous: ～行节约 *practice strict economy* | ～禁 *strictly forbid* ❷严厉，严肃 stern; severe: 正言～色 *with a harsh voice and stern countenance* ❸凶猛 fierce; severe [厉害][利害](-hai) 1 凶猛 ferocious: 老虎很～。*The tiger is a ferocious animal.* 2 过甚，很 serious; terrible: 疼得～ *terribly painful* | 闹得～ *make a terrible scene* ❹(ancient) same as "砺": 秣马～兵 *make active preparations for war*

励(勵) lì ㄌㄧˋ 劝勉，奋勉 to encourage; exert oneself: ～志 *exert oneself and concentrate on realizing one's aspiration* | 奖～ *to award*

砺(礪) lì ㄌㄧˋ ❶粗磨刀石 coarse whetstone ❷磨(mó) to sharpen; to whet: 砥～ *whetstone; toughen up; to encourage*

蛎(蠣) lì ㄌㄧˋ 牡蛎，软体动物，又叫蚝(háo)，身体长卵圆形，有两面壳，生活在浅海泥沙中。可入药 oyster (also called 蚝 háo)

粝(糲) lì ㄌㄧˋ 粗糙的米 brown rice

疠(癘) lì ㄌㄧˋ ❶瘟疫 plague; pestilence ❷恶疮 sore

立 lì ㄌㄧˋ ❶站 to stand: ～正 *stand at attention* ㊀竖着，竖起来 standing; stand sth up: ～柜 *wardrobe* | 把伞～在门后头。*Stand the umbrella behind the door.* [立场]认识和处理问题时所处的地位和所抱的态度，也特指阶级立场 standpoint; position; (also specifically) class standpoint: ～坚定 *be firm in one's stand* ❷做出，定出 set up; to establish ①建立，设立 set up: ～碑 *erect a monument* ②建树 to achieve: ～功 *render meritorious service* ③制定 draw up: ～合同 *enter into a contract* | ～规矩 *draw up a set of rules* ④决定 to determine: ～志 *be determined to* ❸存在，生存 to exist; to live: 自～ *stand on one's own feet* | 独～ *stand alone; (be) independent* ❹立刻，立时，马上，即刻 immediately;

right away：～奏奇效 *have immediate and marked effect* | 当机～断 *act decisively at the crucial moment*

莅（*蒞、*涖） lì ㄌㄧˋ 到（㊤—临）be present; to arrive：～会 *attend a meeting*

笠 lì ㄌㄧˋ 斗笠，用竹篾等编制的遮阳挡雨的帽子 bamboo hat

粒 lì ㄌㄧˋ ❶（—儿）成颗的东西，细小的固体 granule; grain：米～儿 *grains of rice* | 豆～儿 *beans* | 盐～儿 *grains of salt* [粒子] 构成物体的比原子核更简单的物质，包括电子、质子、中子、光子、介子、超子和各种反粒子等 particle ❷量词，多用于粒状的东西 measure word for grain-like things：一～米 *a grain of rice* | 两～丸药 *two pills* | 三～子弹 *three bullets*

吏 lì ㄌㄧˋ 旧时代的官员 (old) official：贪官污～ *corrupt officials*

丽（麗） lì ㄌㄧˋ ❶好看，漂亮 beautiful; pretty：美～ *beautiful* | 秀～ *delicate and graceful* | 壮～ *magnificent; glorious* | 富～ *extravagant; lavish* | 风和日～ *warm and sunny* ❷附着（㊤附—）attach to; adhere to

⇨ see also lí on p.387

郦（酈） lì ㄌㄧˋ 姓 (surname) Li

俪（儷） lì ㄌㄧˋ 相并的，对偶的 paired; parallel：～词 *literary style marked by antitheses* | ～句（对偶的文辞）*parallel sentences* ㊫指属于夫妇的 of a couple：～影（夫妇的合影）*photograph of a couple*

利 lì ㄌㄧˋ ❶好处，跟“害”“弊”相对（㊤—益）benefit; advantage (opposite of 害 or 弊)：这件事对人民有～。*This is beneficial to the people.* | 兴～除弊 *promote the beneficial and dispel the harmful* ❷使得到好处 to benefit：毫不～己，专门～人 *utter devotion to others without any thought of oneself* [利用] 发挥人或事物的作用，使其对自己方面有利 make use of：废物～ *turn scrap material to good use* | ～他的长处 *make use of his strengths* | ～这个机会 *take this opportunity* ❸顺利，与主观的愿望相合 favourable; smooth：吉～ *auspicious* | 敌军屡战不～。*The enemy was defeated in several battles.* ❹利息，贷款或储蓄所得的子金 interest：本～两清 *principal and interest all paid up* | 高～贷 *usury* ❺利润 profit：暴～ *huge profit (gained by illegitimate means)* | 薄～多销 *low margin high volume* ❻工具、武器等锋利，尖锐，跟“钝”相对 sharp (opposite of 钝)：～刃 *sharp knife* | ～剑 *sharp sword* | ～口（指善辩的口才）*glib tongue* [利害] 1（—hài）利益和损害 advantage and disadvantage; gains and losses：不计～ *regardless of gains and losses* 2（—hai）same as “厉害” [利落]（—luo）[利索]（—suo）1 爽快，敏捷 nimble; agile：他做事很～。*He handles*

L

things very effectively. 2 整齐 neat and tidy：东西收拾～了。*Things have been tidied up.*

俐 lì ㄌㄧˋ see 伶俐 (líng－) at 伶 on page 408

莉 lì ㄌㄧˋ see 茉莉 (mòli) at 茉 on page 460

猁 lì ㄌㄧˋ see 猞猁 (shē－) at 猞 on page 585

浰 lì ㄌㄧˋ 浰江，水名，在广东省和平县，东江支流 Lijiang River (in Heping County, Guangdong Province, tributary to Dongjiang River)

⇨ see also liàn on p.398

痢 lì ㄌㄧˋ ❶痢疾，传染病，症状是发热、腹痛，粪便中有血液、脓或黏液 dysentery ❷ see 瘌痢 (là－) at 瘌 on page 374

鬁 lì ㄌㄧˋ see 鬎鬁 (là－) at 鬎 on page 374

例 lì ㄌㄧˋ ❶（－子）可以做依据的事物 example; instance; precedent：惯～ *convention; precedent* | 举一个～子 *give an example* | 史无前～ *unprecedented* ❷规定，体例 regulation; rule; statute：条～ *regulations* | 发凡起～ *explain the general content and format (of a book)* [例外] 在一般的规律、规定之外 exception：全体参加，没有一个～。*All attended without exception.* | 遇到～的事就得灵活处理。*Flexibility must be exercised in dealing with exceptional cases.* ❸合于某种条件的事例 case：病～ *case (of illness)* | 案～ *case* ❹按条例规定的，照成规进行的 regular; routine：～会 *regular meeting* | ～假 *official holiday; (euphemism) menstrual period* | ～行公事 *a matter of routine*

戾 lì ㄌㄧˋ ❶罪过 crime; sin ❷乖张，不顺从 perverse; unreasonable：乖～ *disagreeable* | 暴～ *ruthless and tyrannical* ❸〈古 ancient〉至 arrive at：鸢（yuān）飞～天，鱼跃于渊。*Hawks fly into the sky, and fishes leap in the water.(figurative) Everything is in its proper place.*

唳 lì ㄌㄧˋ 鸟鸣 (of birds) to cry：鹤～ *crane cries*

隶（隷、*隸、*𨽻） lì ㄌㄧˋ ❶附属，属于（㊥－属）be subordinate to：直～中央 *directly under central authority* ❷封建时代的衙役 runner in government offices in imperial China：～卒 *runner in government offices in imperial China* ❸隶书，汉字的一种字体，由篆书简化演变而成 clerical script (a style of Chinese calligraphy) ❹旧时地位低下而被奴役的人 (old) servant; slave：奴～ *slave* | 仆～ *servant*

珎（瓅） lì ㄌㄧˋ see 玓珎(dì－) at 玓 on page 130

栎（櫟） lì ㄌㄧˋ 落叶乔木，俗叫柞（zuò）树或麻栎，花黄褐色，果实叫橡子或橡斗。木质坚硬，可制家具或供建筑用，叶可喂柞蚕。另有栓皮栎，树皮质地轻软，是制造软木器物的主要原料 sawtooth oak (informal 柞 zuò 树 or 麻栎，its fruit is called 橡子 or 橡斗)

L

➪ see also yuè on p.810

轹（轢） lì ㄌㄧˋ 车轮碾轧 (of a cart or carriage) to run over 喻 欺压 to bully and oppress

砾（礫） lì ㄌㄧˋ 小石，碎石 gravel：砂～ *sand gravel* | 瓦～ *rubble*

跞（躒） lì ㄌㄧˋ 走，跨越 to walk; to leap：骐骥一～，不能千里。*Even a fine steed can't cover a thousand* li *in one leap.*

➪ see also luò on p.428

鬲（**䰛） lì ㄌㄧˋ 古代炊具，形状像鼎而足部中空 an ancient type of cookware with three hollow legs

➪ see also gé on p.205

栗（❷*慄） lì ㄌㄧˋ ❶栗（子）树，落叶乔木，果实叫栗子，果仁味甜，可以吃。木质坚实，可供建筑和制器具用，树皮可供鞣皮及染色用，叶子可喂栗蚕 Chinese chestnut tree (its fruit is called 栗子) ❷发抖，因害怕或寒冷而身体颤动 to shiver; to tremble：不寒而～ *tremble with fear*

傈 lì ㄌㄧˋ ［傈僳族］（－sù－）我国少数民族，参看附录四 the Lisu people (one of the ethnic groups in China. See Appendix Ⅳ.)

溧 lì ㄌㄧˋ 寒冷 cold：～冽（非常寒冷）*bitterly cold*

溧 lì ㄌㄧˋ ［溧水］［溧阳］地名，都在江苏省 Lishui; Liyang (both in Jiangsu Province)

篥 lì ㄌㄧˋ see 觱篥 (bì－) at 觱 on page 37

詈 lì ㄌㄧˋ 骂 to scold; to curse：～骂 *to scold* | ～辞（骂人的话）*abusive language*

哩 li ·ㄌㄧ 助词，同"呢"（ne）auxiliary word, same as 呢 (ne)

➪ see also lī on p.387, lǐ on p.390

蜊 li ·ㄌㄧ 蛤蜊 clam (see 蛤 gé on page 205 for reference)

璃（*瓈） li ·ㄌㄧ see 玻璃 (bō－) at 玻 on page 47, and 琉璃 (liú－) at 琉 on page 413

LIA ㄌㄧㄚ

俩（倆） liǎ ㄌㄧㄚˇ 两个（"俩"字后面不能再用"个"字或其他量词）two (not to be followed by 个 or other measure words)：夫妇～ *husband and wife* | 买～馒头 *buy two steamed buns* | 仨瓜～枣 *(figurative) mere trifles*

➪ see also liǎng on p.400

LIAN ㄌㄧㄢ

奁（奩、*匳、*匲、*籢）

lián ㄌㄧㄢˊ 女子梳妆用的镜匣 (woman's) case toiletry［妆奁］嫁妆 dowry

连（連） lián ㄌㄧㄢˊ ❶相接，连续（⊜－接）to link; to connect; to join：天～水，水～天。*The sky and water seem to merge into one.* | 骨肉相～ *as closely linked as flesh and blood* | ～成一片 *joined together* | 接～不断 *continuously* | ～年 *for years on end*［连词］连接词、词组或句子的词，如"和""或者""但是"等 conjunction, like 和, 或者,

L

但是, etc. [连枷] 打谷用的农具 flail [连绵] (*联绵) 接续不断 continuous; uninterrupted ❷ 带，加上(连一带) including; adding; with：～说带笑 *both talking and laughing* | ～根拔 *root out* | ～我一共三个人。*There are three people including me.* ❸介词，就是，即使(后边常用"都""也"跟它相应) (preposition) even：他从前～字都不认得，现在会写信了。*Before, he couldn't read a single character, and now he can write letters.* | 精耕细作，～荒地也能变成良田。*With intensive farming, even wasteland can be turned into fertile fields.* ❹军队的编制单位，是排的上一级 (military) company

莲(蓮) lián ㄌㄧㄢˊ 草本植物，又叫荷，生长在浅水中。叶叫荷叶、莲叶，大而圆，花主要为粉红、白色两种。种子叫莲子，包在倒圆锥形的花托内，合称莲蓬。地下茎叫藕。种子和地下茎都可以吃 lotus (also called 荷)

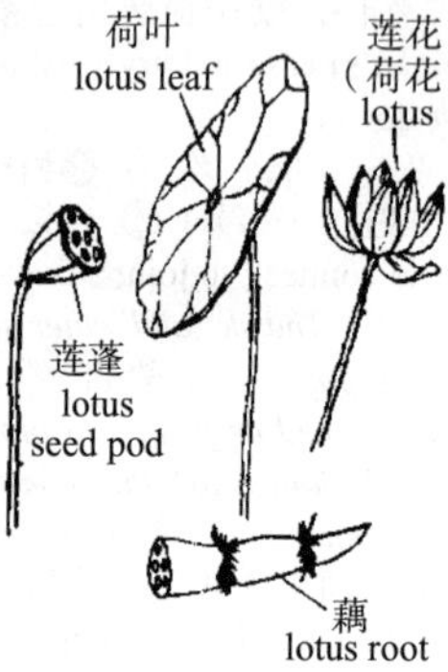

莲 lotus

涟(漣) lián ㄌㄧㄢˊ ❶水面被风吹起的波纹 ripples：～漪(yī) *ripples; wavelet* ❷泪流不止 (叠)(of tears) continually falling：泪～～ *teary-faced* [涟洏] (-ér) 形容涕泪交流 (of tears) flowing continuously

梿(槤) lián ㄌㄧㄢˊ [梿枷] (-jiā) same as "连枷"

鲢(鰱) lián ㄌㄧㄢˊ 鱼名，又叫白鲢，身体侧扁，鳞细，腹部白色，生活在淡水中 silver carp (also called 白鲢)

怜(憐) lián ㄌㄧㄢˊ ❶可怜，同情(连一悯) sympathize with; to pity：同病相～。*Fellow sufferers feel sympathy for each other.* | ～惜 *take pity on* ❷爱 to love：爱～ *love tenderly*

帘(❷簾) lián ㄌㄧㄢˊ (-子、-儿) ❶旧时店铺挂在门前，用布制成的标志 (old) shop banner ❷用布、竹、苇等做的遮蔽门窗的东西 curtain

联(聯) lián ㄌㄧㄢˊ ❶联结，结合 to unite; to join; ally with：～盟 *alliance; coalition* | ～席会议 *joint conference* [联络] 接洽，彼此交接 to contact ❷(-儿) 对联，对子 antithetical couplet：上～ *the first line of a couplet* | 下～ *the second line of a couplet* | 挽～ *elegiac couplet* | 春～ *Chinese New Year couplet*

廉(*亷、*廉) lián ㄌㄧㄢˊ ❶品行正，不贪污 honest and clean：～洁 *incorruptible* | 清～ *honest and upright* ❷便宜，价钱低(连低-)

inexpensive：～价 *cheap*

濂 lián ㄌㄧㄢˊ 濂江，水名，在江西省南部 Lianjiang River (in southern Jiangxi Province)

臁 lián ㄌㄧㄢˊ 小腿的两侧 shank：～骨 *shin bone* | ～疮 *chronic shank ulcer*

镰（鐮、*鎌、*鐮）lián ㄌㄧㄢˊ 镰刀，用来收割谷物和割草的农具 sickle

蠊 lián ㄌㄧㄢˊ see 蜚蠊 (fěi—) at 蜚 on page 174

磏 lián ㄌㄧㄢˊ 一种磨刀石 a type of sharpening stone

⇨ see also qiān on p.526

琏（璉）liǎn ㄌㄧㄢˇ 古代宗庙盛黍稷的器皿 (ancient) container to hold grain offerings in an ancestral temple

敛（斂、*歛）liǎn ㄌㄧㄢˇ ❶收拢，聚集（㊀收一）hold back; to collect：～足（收住脚步，不往前进）*hang back* | ～钱 *collect money* ❷约束，检束 to restrain：～迹 *lie low; retire from public life*

脸（臉）liǎn ㄌㄧㄢˇ（一儿）面孔，头的前部，从额到下巴 face ㊀①物体的前部 front (of objects)：鞋～儿 *upper of a shoe* | 门～儿 *shop front; shop* ②体面，面子，颜面（㊀一面）feelings; face; dignity：丢～ *lose face* | 不要～（骂人的话）*shameless (in name calling)*

裣（襝）liǎn ㄌㄧㄢˇ ［裣衽］（—rèn）旧时指妇女行礼 (old) (of ladies) to salute

蔹（蘞）liǎn ㄌㄧㄢˇ 藤本植物，叶多而细，有白蔹、赤蔹等 ampelopsis

练（練）liàn ㄌㄧㄢˋ ❶白绢 white silk：江平如～。*The river lies as smooth as silk.* ❷把生丝煮熟，使柔软洁白 boil and scour raw silk ❸练习，反复学习，多次地操作 to practise; to drill：～兵 *drill soldiers; to train* | ～本领 *practice one's skills* ❹经验多，精熟 experienced; skilled：～达 *experienced and skilful* | 老～ *seasoned* | 熟～ *skilful* | 干（gàn）～ *capable and experienced*

炼（煉、*鍊）liàn ㄌㄧㄢˋ ❶用火烧制 to smelt; to refine：～钢 *smelt steel* | ～焦 *coking* | 真金不怕火～。*The genuine article can stand up to tests.* ❷用心琢磨使精练 to polish：～字 *search for the best word* | ～句 *polish a sentence* ❸烹熬炮（páo）制 to extract：～乳 *condensed milk*

恋（戀）liàn ㄌㄧㄢˋ ❶想念不忘，不忍舍弃，不想分开 long for; feel attached to：留～ *be reluctant to leave* | ～家 *be tied to home* | ～～不舍 *be reluctant to bid farewell* ［恋栈］马舍不得离开马棚，比喻贪恋禄位 the horse is reluctant to leave the stable; (figurative) cling to an official post when one should leave ❷恋爱 to love; be in love：初～ *first love; have just fallen in love* | 婚～ *love and marriage* | 失～ *be disappointed in love; be jilted*

浰 liàn ㄌㄧㄢ 用于地名 used in place names：汫(píng)～(在江苏省宜兴) *Pinglian (in Yixing, Jiangsu Province)*

⇨ see also lì on p.394

殓(殮) liàn ㄌㄧㄢ 装殓，把死人装入棺材里 to encoffin：入～ *put a corpse in a coffin*｜大～ *encoffining ceremony*

潋(瀲) liàn ㄌㄧㄢ [潋滟](-yàn)水波相连的样子 rippling and glistening：水光～ *water shimmers*

链(鏈、*鍊) liàn ㄌㄧㄢ ❶(-子、-儿)多指用金属环连套而成的索子 chain：表～ *watch chain*｜铁～ *iron chain* ❷英美制长度单位，1链合20.1168米 chain (an imperial and American unit of length, equal to 20.1168 metres) ❸计量海洋上距离的长度单位，1链是1海里的十分之一，合185.2米 cable length, equal to 185.2 metres

琏 liàn ㄌㄧㄢ 一种玉 a kind of jade

楝 liàn ㄌㄧㄢ 落叶乔木，花淡紫色，果实椭圆形，种子、树皮都可入药 chinaberry tree

鰊(鰊) liàn ㄌㄧㄢ same as "鲱(fēi)"

裢(褳) lian ·ㄌㄧㄢ see 褡裢(dā-) at 褡 on page 107

LIANG ㄌㄧㄤ

良 liáng ㄌㄧㄤ ❶好(㊀-好、优-、善-) good; fine：～药 *good medicine*｜～田 *fertile land*｜消化不～ *dyspepsia; indigestion* ❷很 very：～久 *a good while*｜获益～多 *have benefited a lot*｜用心～苦 *have taken great pains*

俍 liáng ㄌㄧㄤ 完美，良好 perfect

粮(糧) liáng ㄌㄧㄤ ❶可吃的谷类、豆类等 grain; food; provisions：食～ *food*｜杂～ *coarse cereals* ❷旧指作为农业税的粮食 (old) tax in the form of grains; farm tax：纳～ *pay farm tax*｜交公～ *deliver tax grain to the state*

踉 liáng ㄌㄧㄤ [跳踉]跳跃 to jump; to leap

⇨ see also liàng on p.401

凉(*涼) liáng ㄌㄧㄤ 温度低(若指天气，比"冷"的程度浅) cool; cold：饭～了。*The food has gone cold.*｜立秋之后天气～了。*After the beginning of Autumn, the weather has turned cold.* ㊥灰心或失望 disheartened; disappointed：听到这消息，我心里就～了。*At hearing the news, I got quite disheartened.* [凉快](-kuai) 1 清凉爽快 nice and cool 2 乘凉 enjoy the cool：到外头～～去 *go outside to cool off*

⇨ see also liàng on p.400

综(綜) liáng ㄌㄧㄤ 古代用来系帽子的丝带 (ancient) silk hat strap

椋 liáng ㄌㄧㄤ 古书上说的一种叶像柿叶的树，又叫椋子木 a large-leaved dogwood in ancient Chinese texts (also called 椋子木)

辌(輬) liáng ㄌㄧㄤˊ see 辒辌 (wēn—) at 辒 on page 685

梁(❶-❹*樑) liáng ㄌㄧㄤˊ ❶房梁，架在墙上或柱子上支撑屋顶的横木 beam：大～ *summer beam* | 上～ *upper beam* (see picture of 房屋的构造 on page 170) ❷桥（㊥桥—）bridge：石～ *rock bridge* | 津～ *bridge cover a ferry crossing; (figurative) guide* ❸（—子、—儿）器物上面便于提携的弓形物 arch-shaped handle：茶壶～儿 *teapot handle* | 篮子的提～儿坏了。*The basket handle is broken.* ❹（—子、—儿）中间高起的部分 ridge：山～ *mountain ridge* | 鼻～ *bridge of the nose* ❺朝代名 Liang (dynasty name) ①南朝之一，萧衍所建立（公元 502—557 年）Liang Dynasty (502—557, one of the Southern Dynasties, founded by Xiao Yan) ②五代之一，朱温所建立（公元 907—923 年），史称后梁 Liang Dynasty (907—923, known as Later Liang Dynasty, one of the Five Dynasties, founded by Zhu Wen)

粱 liáng ㄌㄧㄤˊ 谷子的优良品种的统称 fine millet [高粱]（gāoliang）谷类作物，茎高，籽实可供食用，又可以酿酒 sorghum

墚 liáng ㄌㄧㄤˊ 我国西北地区称条状的黄土山岗 loess hillock (in north-western China)

量 liáng ㄌㄧㄤˊ ❶用器物计算东西的多少或长短 to measure：用斗～米 *measure rice with a dou* | 用尺～布 *measure cloth with a ruler* | 车载斗～ *plentiful* ❷估量 to estimate：思～（liang）*to consider* | 打～（liang）*size up; to think*

⇨ see also liàng on p.401

两(兩) liǎng ㄌㄧㄤˇ ❶数目，一般用于量词和"半、千、万、亿"前 two (often used before a measure word or 半，千，万，亿)：～本书 *two books* | ～匹马 *two horses* | ～个月 *two months* | ～半 *two halves* | ～万 *twenty thousand* [In terms of usage, 两 and 二 are used differently in some cases. For numbers, such as "一，二，三，四" or "二，四，六，八"，for decimal and fractional numbers, such as 零点二 (0.2), 三分之二，二分之一，as well as for ordinal numbers, such as 第二 and 二哥，only 二 is used; whereas before a measure word, usually 两 is used, such as in 两个人用两种方法 (two people adopt two methods) and 两条路通两个地方 (the two roads lead to two places). Both 两 and 二 can be used before traditional measurement units, with 二 used more frequently (though 二两 cannot be 两两). Before new measurement units, though, usually 两 is used, such as in 两吨 or 两公里. In multi-digit numbers, 二 but not 两 is used in hundreds place, tens place and unit place, such as

二百二十二; however, before 千, 万 and 亿, both 两 and 二 can be used, though in such instances as 三万二千, 两亿二千万, as well as where 千 follows 万 or 亿, 二 is used more often.] ❷双方 both; either: ～便 *beneficial/convenient for both* | ～可 *both/either will do* | ～全 *suit both* | ～相情愿 *by mutual consent* ❸表示不定的数目（十以内的）some; a few (under 10): 过～天再说吧。*Let's deal with it in a couple of days.* | 他真有～下子。*He really knows his tricks.* ❹市制重量单位，1 斤是 10 两（旧制 16 两），1 两合 50 克。*liang* [a traditional Chinese unit for measuring weight, equal to 50 grams. There are 10 两 (16 in the old system) in 1 斤.]

俩(倆) liǎng ㄌㄧㄤˇ [伎俩]（jì—）手段，花招 tricks; intrigue

⇨ see also liǎ on p.395

両(兩) liǎng ㄌㄧㄤˇ 〈方 dialect〉靠近水的平缓高地，多用于地名 smooth high ground near water (often used in place names): ～塘 *Liangtang* | 沙～圩（都在广东省罗定）*Shaliangxu (both places in Luoding, Guangdong Province)*

唡(啢) liǎng ㄌㄧㄤˇ 又读 yīngliǎng，现写作"英两"，英美制重量单位，常衡 1 唡是 1 磅的 1/16，约合 28.35 克。现用"盎司" ounce (also pronounced yīngliǎng, now written as 英两; now replaced with 盎司)

裲(緉) liǎng ㄌㄧㄤˇ 一双，古时计算鞋、袜的单位 (ancient) pair (for shoes or socks)

魉(魎) liǎng ㄌㄧㄤˇ see 魍魉 (wǎng—) at 魍 on page 676

亮 liàng ㄌㄧㄤˋ ❶明，有光 bright; light: 天～了。*It's daybreak.* | 敞～ *light and spacious* | 刀磨得真～。*The knife has been sharpened until it gleams.* ❷（～儿）光线 light: 屋里一点～儿也没有。*There is hardly any light in the room.* ㊀灯烛等照明物 lamp, candle, etc.: 拿个～儿来 *bring over a light* ❸明摆出来 to show; to reveal: ～相 *strike a stage pose; show up* | 把牌一～ *lay one's cards on the table* | 有本事～几手。*Show your tricks if you are so good.* ❹明朗，清楚 clear; enlightened: 你这一说，我心里头就～了。*As soon as you said that, everything became clear to me.* | 打开窗子说～话 *frankly speaking* ❺声音响 loud and clear: 洪～ *sonorous*

倞 liàng ㄌㄧㄤˋ 求索 to ask; to demand

⇨ see also jìng on p.330

凉(*涼) liàng ㄌㄧㄤˋ 放一会儿，使温度降低 to let cool down: ～一杯开水 *let a cup of boiled water cool off*

⇨ see also liáng on p.398

谅(諒) liàng ㄌㄧㄤˋ ❶原谅 to understand; to forgive: 体～（体察其情而加以原谅）*show consideration for* | 敬希见～。*I hope you will excuse me.*

L

[谅解]由了解而消除意见 to come to an understanding ❷信实 trustworthy：～哉斯言。*These are honest remarks.* ❸推想 to suppose; to presume; to expect：～他不敢胡来。*I don't think he would dare to act recklessly.*

晾 liàng ㄌㄧㄤˋ ❶把衣物放在太阳下面晒或放在通风透气的地方使干 to dry (clothes, etc., in the sun or air)：～衣服 *dry clothes* ❷冷落，不理睬 to cold-shoulder：把他～在一边。*He is left in the cold.* ❸ same as "凉 (liàng)"

悢 liàng ㄌㄧㄤˋ 悲伤，惆怅 sad; sorrowful：～然 *sorrowful*

踉 liàng ㄌㄧㄤˋ [踉跄]（-qiàng）走路不稳 to stagger

➪ see also liáng on p.398

辆（輛）liàng ㄌㄧㄤˋ 量词，用于车 (measure word for vehicles)：一～汽车 *a car*

靓（靚）liàng ㄌㄧㄤˋ〈方 dialect〉漂亮，好看 pretty; good-looking：～女 *pretty girl*

➪ see also jìng on p.331

量 liàng ㄌㄧㄤˋ ❶旧指测量东西多少的器物，如斗、升等 (old) measure equipment (such as 斗 or 升) [量词]表示事物或行动单位的词，如"张、条、个、只、遍"等 measure word (such as 张，条，个，只，遍，etc.) ❷限度 capacity：酒～ *capacity for liquor*｜气～ *tolerance*｜饭～ *appetite*｜胆～ *courage* ❸数量，数的多少 quantity; amount：质～并重 *give equal consideration to quality and quantity*｜大～ *in large quantities*[分量]（fènliang）重量 weight：不够～ *short measure (in weight)*｜称称～ *weigh up* ❹估计，审度（duó）to estimate; to measure：～力而行 *act according to one's ability*｜～入为出 *live within one's means*

➪ see also liáng on p.399

LIAO ㄌㄧㄠ

撩 liāo ㄌㄧㄠ ❶提，掀起 to lift up; to hold up：～起长衫 *lift up the bottom of a long gown*｜把帘子～起来 *lift up the curtain* ❷用手洒水 to sprinkle with one's hand：先～上点水再扫 *sprinkle some water on the floor before sweeping*

➪ see also liáo on p.402

蹽 liāo ㄌㄧㄠ〈方 dialect〉跑，走 to run; to dash：他一气～了二里地。*He ran two* li *in one dash.*

辽（遼）liáo ㄌㄧㄠˊ ❶远（㊥-远）vast; distant：～阔 *vast; extensive* ❷朝代名，契丹族耶律阿保机建立（公元907—1125年）Liao Dynasty (907—1125, founded by Yelv Abaoji of the Khitan people)

疗（療）liáo ㄌㄧㄠˊ 医治（㊥医-、治-）to cure; to treat：～病 *treat an illness*｜诊～ *diagnose and treat* ㊣解除痛苦或困难 to relieve (pain or suffering)：～饥 *alleviate one's hunger*｜～贫 *relieve poverty*

窌 liáo ㄌㄧㄠˊ 针灸穴位名 *liao* (an acupoint)

L

聊 liáo ㄌㄧㄠ ❶姑且，略 merely; just：～以自慰 *just to console oneself* | ～胜一筹 *slightly better* | ～胜于无 *better than nothing* ❷依赖 to rely on：百无～赖 *bored stiff* | 民不～生(无法生活)。*The masses have nothing to live on.* [无聊] 1 没有兴趣 boring; bored 2 没有意义 meaningless ❸聊天，闲谈 to chat：别～啦，赶快干吧！*Stop chewing the rag and get on with work!*

僚 liáo ㄌㄧㄠ ❶官 official [官僚] 指旧时各级政府里的官吏。现在把脱离人民群众，不深入实际的领导作风和工作作风叫官僚主义 bureaucrat (官僚主义 bureaucracy) ❷旧时指在一块做官的人 (old) colleague in office：同～ *colleague*

撩 liáo ㄌㄧㄠ 挑弄，引逗 to tease; to provoke：～拨 *tease* | 景色～人。*The scenery is intoxicating.*

⇨ see also liāo on p.401

嘹 liáo ㄌㄧㄠ [嘹亮] 声音响亮 loud and clear

獠 liáo ㄌㄧㄠ 面貌凶恶 fierce-looking; fiendish：～面 *fiendish features* [獠牙] 露在嘴外面的长牙 tusk; bucktooth

潦 liáo ㄌㄧㄠ [潦倒] (－dǎo) 颓丧，不得意 dejected; down and out：穷困～ *be penniless and frustrated* [潦草] 草率，不精细 sloppy：工作不能～。*One should not be perfunctory with work.* | 字写得太～。*The handwriting is too sloppy.*

⇨ see also lǎo on p.382

寮 liáo ㄌㄧㄠ 小屋 hut; shack：竹～ *bamboo shed* | 茶～ *teahouse*

嫽 liáo ㄌㄧㄠ 美好 fine; charming

缭(繚) liáo ㄌㄧㄠ ❶缠绕 to entangle; to twine：～乱 *confused; tangled* | ～绕 *coil; wind around* ❷用针线缝缀 to sew with slanting stitches：～缝(fèng) *stitch a seam* | ～贴边 *stitch the hem*

橑 liáo ㄌㄧㄠ ❶屋檐 eaves ❷用于地名 used in place names：太平～(在福建省连城) *Taipingliao (in Liancheng, Fujian Province)*

燎 liáo ㄌㄧㄠ 延烧 (of fire) to spread; to burn：星星之火，可以～原。*A single spark can start a prairie fire.*

⇨ see also liǎo on p.403

鹩(鷯) liáo ㄌㄧㄠ see 鹪鹩 (jiāo－) at 鹪 on page 311

簝 liáo ㄌㄧㄠ 古代祭祀时盛肉的竹器 an ancient bamboo basket to hold meat offerings

漻 liáo ㄌㄧㄠ 水清而深 (of water) clear and deep

寥 liáo ㄌㄧㄠ ❶稀疏 ⓐscanty; sparse：～若晨星 *as few as morning stars* | ～～无几 *very few* ❷空旷，静寂 open and spacious; silent：～廓 *boundless* | 寂～ *silent and lonely*

髎 liáo ㄌㄧㄠ same as "窌 (liáo)"

了(❶△瞭) liǎo ㄌㄧㄠ ❶明白 to understand;

to be clear about: 明～*understand*|～ 解 *acquire an understanding*|一目～然 *understand at a glance*|不甚～～ *not know much (about sth)* ❷完了，结束 to finish; to settle: 事情已经～了（le）。*It's all settled.*|话犹未～ *before one can finish speaking*|不～～之 *settle sth by leaving it unsettled*|没完没～ *endlessly*|敷衍～事 *do things in a perfunctory manner* [直截了当] 言语行动简单爽快 straightforward ❸在动词后，跟"不""得"连用，表示不可能或可能 used with 不 or 得 after a verb to express possibility: 这本书我看不～。*This book is beyond me.*|这事你办得～。*You are able to handle it.*

⇨ see also le on p.384

⇨ 瞭 see also liào on p.404

钌（釕） liǎo ㄌㄧㄠˇ 金属元素，符号Ru，银灰色，质硬而脆。可用来制合金等，也用来制催化剂 ruthenium (Ru)

⇨ see also liào on p.403

蓼 liǎo ㄌㄧㄠˇ 草本植物，生长在水边，花白色或浅红色，种类很多 knotweed

憭 liǎo ㄌㄧㄠˇ 明白；明了 clear; apparent

燎 liǎo ㄌㄧㄠˇ 挨近了火而烧焦 to singe; to scorch: 烟熏火～ *choked by smoke and scorched by flame*|把头发～了 *singed one's hair*

⇨ see also liáo on p.402

尥 liào ㄌㄧㄠˋ ［尥蹶子］（－juězi）骡马等跳起来用后腿向后踢 (of mules, horses, etc.) to kick backward

钌（釕） liào ㄌㄧㄠˋ ［钌铞ル］（－diàor）钉在门窗上可以把门窗扣住的东西 hasp and staple: 门～ *hasp and staple on a door*

⇨ see also liǎo on p.403

料 liào ㄌㄧㄠˋ ❶料想，估计，猜想 to expect; to predict: 预～ *predict; anticipate*|不出所～ *as was expected*|～事如神 *foretell like a prophet* ❷处理，照管 to deal with; to attend to: ～理 *manage; handle*|照～ *take care of* ❸（－子、－ル）材料，可供制造其他东西的物质 material; stuff: 原～ *raw material*|木～ *timber*|衣裳～子 *clothing material*|肥～ *fertilizer*|燃～ *fuel* ❹喂牲口用的谷物 feed; fodder: ～豆ル *bean fodder*|草～ *hay*|牲口得喂～才能肥。*Livestock must be given fodder in order to be fattened up.* ❺烧料，一种熔点较低的类似玻璃的物质，用来制造器皿或手工艺品 a kind of glass-like material (used to make utensils or handcrafts): ～器 *opaque coloured glassware* ❻量词，中药配方全份叫一料（多用于配制丸药）(measure word in Chinese medicine) one prescription

撂 liào ㄌㄧㄠˋ 放下，搁置 to put down; to drop: 把碗～在桌子上 *put the bowl on the table*|～下工作不管 *leave a job unattended*

廖 liào ㄌㄧㄠˋ 用于地名 used in place names: 圪（gē）～乡

L

（在山西省宁武）Geliaoxiang (in Ningwu, Shanxi Province)

廖 liào ㄌㄧㄠ 姓 (surname) Liao

瞭 liào ㄌㄧㄠ 瞭望，远远地望 to watch from a height or a distance：你在远处～着点儿。*Go keep watch at a distance.* | ～望台 *watch tower*

⇨ see also liǎo 了 on p.402

镣（鐐） liào ㄌㄧㄠ 脚镣，套在脚腕上使不能快走的刑具 fetters; shackles

LIE ㄌㄧㄝ

咧 liē ㄌㄧㄝ ［咧咧］（—lie）〈方 dialect〉1 乱说，乱讲 to blabber; to gossip：瞎～ *talk nonsense* 2 小孩儿哭 (of a child) to cry：这孩子一～起来就没完。*This child cries non-stop once he/she gets started.*

⇨ see also liě on p.404, lie on p.405

咧 liě ㄌㄧㄝˇ 嘴向旁边斜着张开 to grin：～嘴 *grin* | ～着嘴笑 *give a broad smile*

⇨ see also liē on p.404, lie on p.405

裂 liě ㄌㄧㄝˇ 〈方 dialect〉东西的两部分向两旁分开 to part in the middle; to split open：衣服没扣好，～着怀 *shirt unbuttoned, one's chest lays bare*

⇨ see also liè on p.405

列 liè ㄌㄧㄝˋ ❶行（háng）列，排成的行 row; rank：队～ *queue; formation* | 出～ *come out of the rank; fall out* | 前～ *the front rank* ❷陈列，排列，摆出 to line up; to display：姓名～后 *names are listed behind* | ～队 *line up* | 开～账目 *draw up an accounts list* ㊞①归类 to classify：～入甲等 *put in the first class* ②类 kind; category：不在讨论之～ *not on the list for discussion* ［列席］参加会议，而没有表决权 to attend (a meeting) without voting rights ❸众多，各 each and every; various：～国 *various states or countries* | ～位 *all of you; ladies and gentlemen* ❹量词，用于成行列的事物 measure word for things in a row：一～火车 *a train*

冽 liè ㄌㄧㄝˋ 寒冷（㊈凛—）cold; chilly：山高风～ *high mountain and piercing wind*

峛 liè ㄌㄧㄝˋ 用于地名 used in place names：～屿（在福建省云霄）*Lieyu (in Yunxiao, Fujian Province)*

洌 liè ㄌㄧㄝˋ ❶水清 (of water) clear：山泉清～。*The spring water is crystal clear.* ❷酒清 (of liquor) limpid

烈 liè ㄌㄧㄝˋ ❶猛烈，厉害 fierce; intense：～火 *raging fire* | ～日 *scorching sun* ❷气势盛大 ㊇ momentous：轰轰～～ *on a grand and spectacular scale* ❸刚直，有高贵品格的，为正义、人民、国家而死难的 staunch; upright：刚～ *upright and unyielding* | 先～ *martyr* | ～士 *martyr*

䴕（鴷） liè ㄌㄧㄝˋ 鸟名，即啄木鸟，嘴坚硬，尖

而直，舌细长，能啄食树中的虫，是益鸟 woodpecker (same as 啄木鸟)

裂 liè ㄌㄧㄝ 破开，开了缝(fèng) to break open; to crack: ～痕 *crack; rift* | ～缝 *crack; crevice* | 手冻～了 *hands have got chapped in the cold* | 破～ *break* | 四分五～ *break into pieces*

⇨ see also liě on p.404

趔 liè ㄌㄧㄝ [趔趄] (－qie) 身体歪斜，脚步不稳，要摔倒的样子 to stagger; to stumble

劣 liè ㄌㄧㄝ 恶，不好，跟"优"相对 (㊀恶－) bad; of low quality (opposite of 优): 不分优～ *regardless of quality* | 土豪～绅 *local tycoons and wicked gentry*

埒 liè ㄌㄧㄝ ❶矮墙 low wall ❷同等 to equal: 财力相～ *have equal financial capacity*

脟 liè ㄌㄧㄝ 〈古 ancient〉肋骨上的肉 spare rib meat

捩 liè ㄌㄧㄝ 扭转 to twist; to turn: 转～点(转折点) *turning point*

猎(獵) liè ㄌㄧㄝ ❶打猎，捕捉禽兽 to hunt: 狩～ *hunt* | 渔～ *fishing and hunting* | ～人 *hunter* | ～狗 *hunting dog* ❷搜寻 to seek: ～奇 *hunt for novelty*

躐 liè ㄌㄧㄝ ❶超越 to pass over; to go beyond: ～等(越级) *bypass one's immediate superiors* | ～进 (不依照次序前进) *advance by skipping necessary steps* ❷踩，践踏 to trample upon

鱲(鱲) liè ㄌㄧㄝ 鱼名，又叫桃花鱼，身体侧扁，两侧银白色，雄鱼带红色，有蓝色斑纹，生殖季节色泽鲜艳。种类较多，生活在淡水中 kissing gourami (also 桃花鱼)

鬣 liè ㄌㄧㄝ 兽类颈上的长毛 mane: 马～ *mane of a horse*

咧 lie ·ㄌㄧㄝ 〈方 dialect〉助词，意思相当于"了""啦" auxiliary word, equivalent in meaning to 了 or 啦: 好～。*Alright then.* | 他来～。*Here he comes.*

⇨ see also liē on p.404, liě on p.404

LIN ㄌㄧㄣ

拎 līn ㄌㄧㄣ 〈方 dialect〉提 to lift; to carry: ～着一篮子菜 *carrying a basket of vegetables*

邻(鄰、*隣) lín ㄌㄧㄣˊ ❶住处接近的人家 neighbour: 东～ *neighbour to the east* | 四～ *near neighbours* ❷邻近，接近，附近 neighbouring; adjacent: ～国 *neighbouring country* | ～居 *neighbour* | ～舍 *neighbour house* ❸古代五家为邻 a five-family neighbourhood in ancient China

林 lín ㄌㄧㄣˊ ❶长在土地上的许多树木或竹子 forest; woods: 树～ *woods* | 竹～ *bamboo grove* | 防护～ *shelter forest* | ～立(像树林一样密集排列) *stand in great numbers* ㊟聚集在一起的同类的人或事物 group of similar things; circles: 学～ *academic circles* | 艺～

L

art circles| 民族之～ *nations of the world* | 著作之～ *forest of books* ❷ 林业 forestry：农～牧副渔 *farming, forestry, animal husbandry, sideline production and fishery*

啉 lín ㄌㄧㄣˊ see 喹啉 (kuí—) at 喹 on page 369

淋 lín ㄌㄧㄣˊ 水或其他液体洒落在物体上 to sprinkle; to pour：风吹雨～ *exposed to the elements*| 花蔫了，～上点ₗ水吧。*Shall we give the plant some water? The flower is drooping.*

[淋漓] (—lí) 湿淋淋往下滴落 dripping wet：墨迹～ *dripping with ink* | 大汗～ *dripping with sweat* ㊕畅达 free from inhibition：～尽致 *(of a description, etc.) thorough and hearty*| 痛快～ *hearty and unrestrained*

⇨ see also lìn on p.408

綝(綝) lín ㄌㄧㄣˊ [綝纚] (—lí) 衣裳、羽毛等下垂的样子。也作"綝缡" (of clothing, feathers, etc.) drooping (also written as 綝缡)

⇨ see also chēn on p.73

琳 lín ㄌㄧㄣˊ 美玉 fine jade [琳琅] (—láng) 1 珠玉一类的东西 beautiful jade, pearl, etc.：～满目(形容美好的东西很多) *a dazzling array of beautiful objects* 2 形容玉撞击的声音 clink; jingle (of jade)

箖 lín ㄌㄧㄣˊ ❶古书上指一种竹子 (in ancient Chinese texts) a kind of bamboo ❷用于地名 used in place names：～投围(在广东省陆丰) *Lintouwei (in Lufeng, Guangdong Province)*

霖 lín ㄌㄧㄣˊ 久下不停的雨 continuous heavy rain [甘霖] 对农作物有益的雨 timely rainfall：大旱逢～。*A long drought is broken by timely rain.* ㊕恩泽 bounty; favour

临(臨) lín ㄌㄧㄣˊ ❶到，来 to arrive; to be present：光～ *presence (of a guest, etc.)*| 莅～ *arrive; be present* | 喜事～门。*A blessing descends upon the house.*| 身～其境 *be personally on the scene* ㊀遭遇，碰到 to encounter; to be faced with：～渴掘井 *start digging a well only when thirsty; (figurative) start acting too late* [临时] 1 到时候，当时 when the time comes; at the last moment：事先有准备，～就不会忙乱。*If you come prepared, you won't be in a rush when the time comes.* 2 暂时，非长期的 temporary; provisional：你先～代理一下。*You will be the acting agent.*| ～政府 *interim government* ❷ 挨着，靠近 to be close to; to overlook ①指地点，多指较高的靠近较低的 to overlook：～河 *be close to the river* | ～街 *overlook a street* ②指时间。将要，快要 about to; just before：～走 *before leaving* | ～别 *before parting* [临床] 医学上称医生给人诊治疾病 clinical [临盆] 孕妇快要生小孩ₗ to be about to give birth ❸ 照着字、画模仿 to copy：～帖 *practice calligraphy through copying a model* | ～摹 *copy (a model of* *painting, calligraphy, etc.)*

粼 lín ㄌㄧㄣˊ ［粼粼］形容水清澈 (of water) clear; crystalline：～碧波 *clear, blue ripples* | 清～的河水 *crystal clear river*

嶙 lín ㄌㄧㄣˊ ［嶙峋］(－xún) 山石一层层的重叠不平 (of mountain rocks) jagged; rugged

遴 lín ㄌㄧㄣˊ 谨慎选择(㊀－选) to select carefully：～选人才 *select talented people*

〈古 ancient〉also same as 吝(lìn)

潾 lín ㄌㄧㄣˊ ［潾潾］形容水清 (of water) clear; transparent：～的水波 *clear ripples* | 春水～ *crystal clear spring waters*

驎(驎) lín ㄌㄧㄣˊ 毛色斑驳似鱼鳞的马 piebald horse

璘 lín ㄌㄧㄣˊ 玉的光彩 lustre of jade

辚(轔) lín ㄌㄧㄣˊ ［辚辚］形容车行走的声音 (of a carriage) rattle：车～，马萧萧 *chariots rattling and horses neighing*

磷(*燐、*粦) lín ㄌㄧㄣˊ 非金属元素，符号P，常见的有黄磷（又叫白磷）和红磷。黄磷有毒，燃烧时生浓烟，军事上可制烟幕弹和燃烧弹；红磷无毒，可制安全火柴 phosphorus (P)

瞵 lín ㄌㄧㄣˊ 注视，瞪着眼睛看 to gaze：鹰～鹗视 *eye fiercely*

鏻(鏻) lín ㄌㄧㄣˊ 一类具有特定结构的含磷有机化合物 phosphonium

翷 lín ㄌㄧㄣˊ 飞翔的样子 soaring

鳞(鱗) lín ㄌㄧㄣˊ ❶鱼类、爬行动物等身体表面长的角质或骨质的小薄片 (of fish, reptile, etc.) scale ❷ 像鱼鳞的 scalelike：～茎 *bulb (of a plant)* | 芽～ *bud scale* | 遍体～伤（伤痕密得像鱼鳞似的）*covered with cuts and bruises*

麟(*麐) lín ㄌㄧㄣˊ 麒麟，古代传说中的一种动物，像鹿而大，有角，有鳞甲 *qilin* (an animal in ancient Chinese legend, with horns and scales)：凤毛～角（喻罕见而珍贵的东西）*rare and precious objects or persons*

凛(**凜) lǐn ㄌㄧㄣˇ ❶寒冷（㊀－冽）cold; chilly ❷严肃，严厉 ㊂stern; austere：威风～～ *majestic looking* | 大义～然 *awe-inspiring righteousness* ❸ (ancient) same as "懔"

廪(**廩) lǐn ㄌㄧㄣˇ ❶粮仓（㊀仓－）granary; warehouse ❷ 指粮食 food supplies

懔(**懍) lǐn ㄌㄧㄣˇ 畏惧 fearful

檩(**檁) lǐn ㄌㄧㄣˇ 屋架或山墙上托住椽子的横木 purlin (see picture of 房屋的构造 on page 170)

吝(*悋) lìn ㄌㄧㄣˋ 过分爱惜自己的财物等，当用的舍不得用，当给的舍不得给（㊀－啬）stingy; miserly：～惜 *to grudge; to stint*

赁（賃） lìn ㄌㄧㄣˋ 租(㊥租—) to rent; to lease: ～房 *rent housing* | ～车 *lease a car* | 出～ *to let; for rent*

淋 lìn ㄌㄧㄣˋ ❶过滤 to filter; to strain: ～盐 *desalinate* | ～硝 *filter saltpetre* ❷淋病，性病，又叫白浊，病人尿道红肿溃烂，严重的尿里带脓血 gonorrhoea (also called 白浊)

⇨ see also lín on p.406

蔺（藺） lìn ㄌㄧㄣˋ ［马蔺］草本植物，又叫马莲，根状茎粗，叶条形，花蓝紫色。叶坚韧，可捆扎东西，又可造纸。根可制刷子 Chinese small iris (also called 马莲)

躏（躪） lìn ㄌㄧㄣˋ see 蹂躏 (róu —) at 蹂 on page 563

膦 lìn ㄌㄧㄣˋ 有机化合物的一类，是磷化氢的氢原子部分或全部被烃基取代而成的衍生物 phosphine

LING ㄌㄧㄥ

〇 líng ㄌㄧㄥˊ 数的空位，用于数字中 zero: 三～六号 *number 306* | 二～一一年 *the year 2011*

伶 líng ㄌㄧㄥˊ 伶人，旧称以唱戏为职业的人(㊥优—)(old) actor/actress: 坤(女的)～ *actress* | 名～ *famous actor/actress*

［伶仃］(*零丁)(—dīng) 形容孤独 lonely; alone: 孤苦～ *alone and uncared for*

［伶俐］(—lì) 聪明，灵活 clever; bright: ～的孩子 *bright kid* | 口齿很～ *clever and eloquent*

［伶俜］(—pīng) 形容孤独 lonely; alone: ～无依 *alone and helpless*

玲 líng ㄌㄧㄥˊ 用于地名 used in place names: ～头(在广东省潮安) *Lingtou (in Chao'an, Guangdong Province)*

苓 líng ㄌㄧㄥˊ ❶指茯(fú)苓 hoelen ❷苓耳，古书上说的一种植物 a plant in ancient Chinese texts, now called rough cocklebur

囹 líng ㄌㄧㄥˊ ［囹圄］(*囹圉)(—yǔ) 古代称监狱 (ancient) gaol; prison: 身陷～ *be behind bars*

泠 líng ㄌㄧㄥˊ 清凉 clear and cool: ～风 *cool air; breeze* ［泠泠］1 形容清凉 cool 2 声音清越 (of sound) clear and far-reaching

姈 líng ㄌㄧㄥˊ 女子聪敏伶俐 (of a woman) smart and dexterous

玲 líng ㄌㄧㄥˊ 形容玉碰击的声音 ㊇tinkle (of jade): ～～盈耳 *tinkling sounds fill one's ears* ［玲珑］(—lóng) 1 金玉声 jingle (of metal and jade) 2 器物细致精巧 (of things) exquisite: 小巧～ *small and exquisite* 3 灵活敏捷 clever and nimble: ～活泼 *nimble and sprightly*

柃 líng ㄌㄧㄥˊ 柃木，常绿灌木或小乔木，叶椭圆形或披针形，花白色，浆果球形，枝叶可入药 East Asian eurya

昤 líng ㄌㄧㄥˊ ［昤昽］(—lóng) 古代指日光 (ancient) sunlight

瓴 líng ㄌㄧㄥˊ 古代一种盛（chéng）水的瓶子 (ancient) water jar：高屋建～（从房顶上往下泻水，比喻居高临下的形势）*operate from a strategically advantageous position*

铃(鈴) líng ㄌㄧㄥˊ ❶（－儿）铃铛，用金属做成的响器 bell：摇～ *ring a bell*｜车～儿 *bicycle bell*｜电～儿 *electric bell* ❷形状像铃的东西 bell-shaped things：杠～ *barbell*｜哑～ *dumbbell*

鸰(鴒) líng ㄌㄧㄥˊ see 鹡鸰 (jí－) at 鹡 on page 289

聆 líng ㄌㄧㄥˊ 听（㊣－听）to listen：～教 *listen to your words of wisdom*

蛉 líng ㄌㄧㄥˊ ［白蛉］昆虫，俗叫白蛉子，比蚊子小，雄的吸植物汁液，雌的吸人、畜的血，能传染黑热病等 sandfly (informal 白蛉子)

舲 líng ㄌㄧㄥˊ ❶有窗户的船 houseboat (with windows)：～船 *a small houseboat with lookout windows* ❷小船 small boat ❸用于地名 used in place names：～舫（fǎng）乡（在湖南省茶陵）*Lingfangxiang (in Chaling, Hunan Province)*

翎 líng ㄌㄧㄥˊ 鸟的翅和尾上的长羽毛 plume; tail feather：雁～ *wild goose feather*｜野鸡～ *pheasant feather*

羚 líng ㄌㄧㄥˊ 羚羊，哺乳动物，像山羊，腿细长，行动轻捷，种类较多 antelope

零 líng ㄌㄧㄥˊ ❶落 to fall; to drop ①植物凋谢（㊣－落、凋－）(of leaves, flowers, etc.) to wither and fall ②液体滴落 (of liquid) to drop：感激涕～ *so grateful as to shed tears* ❷零头，放在整数后表示附有零数 a little extra; odd：一千挂～儿 *a thousand odd*｜一年～三天 *one year and three days* ❸部分的，细碎的，跟“整”相对（㊣－碎）fractional; odd (opposite of 整)：～件 *part; component*｜～钱 *(of money) change*｜～用 *incidental expense*｜～活儿（零碎工作）*odd job* ❹数学上把数字符号“0”读作零 zero：一减一得～。*One minus one is zero.* ㊀没有，无 naught：他的计划等于～。*His plans are as good as nothing.*｜～距离 *zero distance*｜～污染 *zero pollution* ❺某些量度的计算起点 starting point for some measurements：～点十分 *ten past midnight*｜～下5摄氏度 *minus 5 degrees centigrade*

龄(齡) líng ㄌㄧㄥˊ ❶岁数（㊣年－）age; years：高～ *advanced in years* ❷年数 length of time：工～ *years of service*｜党～ *party standing* ❸某些生物体发育过程中的不同阶段。如昆虫的幼虫第一次蜕皮前叫一龄虫 instar

澪 líng ㄌㄧㄥˊ ❶古水名 Ling (an ancient river) ❷用于地名 used in place names：浒（xǔ）～（在江苏省如东）*Xuling (in Rudong, Jiangsu Province)*

灵(靈) líng ㄌㄧㄥˊ ❶有效验（㊣－验）effective：这种药吃下去很～。*This medicine is very effective.* ❷聪明，

L

机敏（㊀连—敏）clever; quick-witted：心～手巧 *clever and deft*｜耳朵很～ *have sharp ears* ❸活动迅速，灵巧 nimble; agile：这辆车的刹车不～。*The car's brakes don't work well.* ❹旧时称神仙或关于神仙的 (old) deity; god：神～ *divine spirits* ❺灵魂，精神 spirit; soul：在天之～ *soul of the deceased*｜英～ *spirit of the brave departed*｜～感 *inspiration*｜～性 *sagacity* ❻属于死人的 of the dead：～柩 *coffin containing a corpse*｜～床 *bier* ㊀转装着死人的棺材 coffin containing a corpse：移～ *relocate a coffin*

棂（欞、櫺）** líng ㄌㄧㄥˊ 窗棂（子），窗户上构成窗格子的木条或铁条 window lattice; lattice work

凌 líng ㄌㄧㄥˊ ❶冰 icicle：冰～ *ice*｜黄河～汛 *jumble ice on the Yellow River*｜滴水成～ *dripping water turning into ice* ❷欺凌，侵犯，欺压 to bully; to insult：～辱 *bully and humiliate*｜盛气～人 *be domineering* ❸升，高出 to rise high; to soar：～云 *soar above the clouds*｜～空而过 *streak across the sky* ❹迫近 to draw near：～晨 *early morning; before dawn*

陵 líng ㄌㄧㄥˊ ❶大土山（㊀连丘—）hill; mound ❷高大的坟墓 mausoleum; imperial tomb：黄帝～ *Mausoleum of the Yellow Emperor*｜中山～ *Sun Yat-sen Mausoleum*

菱（*蔆） líng ㄌㄧㄥˊ 草本植物，生长在池沼中，叶略呈三角形，花白色。果实有硬壳，大都有角，叫菱或菱角，可以吃 water caltrop

崚 líng ㄌㄧㄥˊ（又）see léng on page 386

淩 líng ㄌㄧㄥˊ same as “凌❷❸❹”

棱 líng ㄌㄧㄥˊ ❶哀怜 to pity; to sympathize with ❷惊恐 fearful

绫（綾） líng ㄌㄧㄥˊ（—子）一种很薄的丝织品，一面光，像缎子 damask silk：～罗绸缎 *silks and brocades*

棱 líng ㄌㄧㄥˊ［穆棱］地名，在黑龙江省 Muling (a place in Heilongjiang Province)

⇨ see also léng on p.386

祾 líng ㄌㄧㄥˊ〈古 ancient〉福 blessing; happiness

鲮（鯪） líng ㄌㄧㄥˊ 鱼名，又叫土鲮鱼，背部青灰色，性怕冷，生活在淡水中 dace (also called 土鲮鱼)［鲮鲤］哺乳动物，即穿山甲，全身有角质的鳞片，爪善掘土，吃蚂蚁 pangolin (same as 穿山甲)

酃 líng ㄌㄧㄥˊ 酃县，旧县名，在今湖南省衡阳东，现叫炎陵县 Lingxian (old name of today's Yanling County, in east of Hengyang, Hunan Province)

醽 líng ㄌㄧㄥˊ［醽醁］（—lù）古代的一种美酒 a fine wine in ancient times

令 lǐng ㄌㄧㄥˇ（外 *loanword*）量词，原张的纸 500 张为 1 令 (measure word for paper) ream

⇨ see also lìng on p.411

L

岭(嶺) lǐng ㄌㄧㄥˇ 山脉 mountain; ridge: 五～ *the Five Ridges* | 秦～ *Qinling Mountains* | 翻山越～ *cross mountain after mountain*

领(領) lǐng ㄌㄧㄥˇ ❶颈, 脖子 neck: ～巾 *scarf* | ～带 *tie* | 引～而望 *crane one's neck for a look* ❷(一子、一儿)衣服围绕脖子的部分 collar; neckband (see picture of 上衣 on page 767) ㊞事物的纲要 outline; main point; gist: 纲～ *programme; guiding principle; platform (of a party etc.)* | 要～ *main point* [领袖] ㊕国家、政治团体、群众组织等的高级领导人 leader ❸带, 引, 率(㊟带一、率一) to lead; to usher; to guide: ～队 *lead a group; team leader* | ～头 *take the lead* ❹领有的, 管辖的 territorial: ～土 *territory* | ～海 *territorial waters* | ～空 *territorial air space* ❺接受, 取得 to accept; to take: ～教 *thanks for your advice/instruction/performance* | ～款 *draw money* ❻了解, 明白 to understand; to grasp: ～会(对别人的意思理解并有所体会) *to grasp* | ～悟 *to comprehend* ❼量词 measure word ①用于衣服 used for robes: 一～青衫 *a blue-green robe* ②用于席、箔等 used for mats, screens, etc.: 一～席 *a mat* | 一～箔 *a screen*

另 lìng ㄌㄧㄥˋ 另外, 别的 other; another: ～买一个 *buy another* | 那是～一件事。*That's another matter.*

令 lìng ㄌㄧㄥˋ ❶上级对下级的指示 order; command: 下～ *give an order* | 明～规定 *explicitly decreed* | 法～ *laws and decrees* ❷上级指示下级(㊟命一) to order; to command: 责～ *to order* | ～全体官兵遵照执行 *order all officers and men to comply* ❸古代官名 magistrate (in ancient times): 县～ *county magistrate* ❹使, 使得 to cause; to make: ～人起敬 *fill one with respect* | ～人兴奋 *exhilarating* | 利～智昏 *be blinded by lust for gain* ❺时令, 时节 season: 月～ *monthly climate* | 夏～ *summertime* ❻美好, 善 good: ～名 *good reputation* 敬辞 polite speech your: ～兄 *your elder brother* | ～尊(称对方的父亲) *your father* ❼词之短小者叫令 short lyric: 调笑～ *teasing song* | 十六字～ *a sixteen-character lyric*

⇨ see also lǐng on p.410

呤 lìng ㄌㄧㄥˋ see 嘌呤 (piào—) at 嘌 on page 506

LIU ㄌㄧㄡ

溜 liū ㄌㄧㄡ ❶滑行 to slide; to glide: ～冰 *to skate* | 从滑梯上～下来 *go down the slide* ㊞滑溜, 平滑, 无阻碍 slippery; smooth; sleek: 光～(liu) *smooth; glossy* ❷溜走, 趁人不见走开 to sneak away; to slip off: 一眼不见他就～了。*He slipped away as soon as he had a chance.* ❸沿着, 顺着 along: ～边儿 *along the* edge | ～着墙根儿走 *walk along the wall* ❹ same as "熘"

[溜达] (*蹓跶) 散步，随便走走 to stroll; to saunter

⇨ see also liù on p.414

熘 liū ㄌㄧㄡ 烹饪方法，跟炒相似，作料里掺淀粉 to sauté;to quick-fry：～肉片 *sauté pork slices* 也作"溜" also written as 溜

蹓 liū ㄌㄧㄡ ❶滑行 to slide：～冰 *to skate* ❷悄悄走开 to sneak off; to slip away

⇨ see also liù on p.414

刘(劉) liú ㄌㄧㄡˊ 姓 (surname) Liu

浏(瀏) liú ㄌㄧㄡˊ 清亮 clear; limpid

[浏览] 泛泛地看 to browse; to glance over

留(*畱、*䨓、*畄) liú ㄌㄧㄡˊ ❶停止在某一个地方(㊎停一) to remain; to stay：他～在天津了。*He is staying in Tianjin.* | ～学(留居外国求学) *study abroad* ㊀注意力放在某人或事物上面 to concentrate on：～心 *be careful* | ～神 *take care* ❷不让别人离开 to ask sb to stay; to keep sb from leaving：～客 *ask a guest to stay* | 挽～ *persuade to stay* | 他一定要走，我～不住他。*He is bent on leaving, and I cannot keep him.*

[留难] (一nàn) 故意与人为难(nán) to make things difficult for; to frustrate ❸接受，收容(㊎收一) to accept; to take：把礼物～下 *accept a gift* ❹保留 to reserve; to keep：～余地 *leave some leeway* | ～胡子 *grow a beard* | 今天我回来晚，请给我～饭。*I will be late today, please save me some food.* ❺遗留 to leave behind：祖先～下了丰富的文化遗产。*Our ancestors have left a rich cultural heritage.*

馏(餾) liú ㄌㄧㄡˊ 蒸馏，加热使液体变成蒸气后再凝成纯净的液体 to distil

⇨ see also liù on p.414

骝(騮) liú ㄌㄧㄡˊ 古书上指黑鬣黑尾巴的红马 (in ancient Chinese texts) red horse with black mane and tail

榴 liú ㄌㄧㄡˊ 石榴，落叶灌木，又叫安石榴，花多为红色，果实也叫石榴，球形，内有很多种子，种子上的肉可吃。根、皮可入药 pomegranate tree; pomegranate (also called 安石榴)

飗(飀) liú ㄌㄧㄡˊ [飗飗] 微风吹动的样子 breezy

镏(鎦) liú ㄌㄧㄡˊ 一种镀金方法，把溶解在水银里的金子涂在器物表面做装饰，所镏的金层经久不退 to gild

⇨ see also liù on p.414

鹠(鶹) liú ㄌㄧㄡˊ [鸺鹠] (xiū一) 鸟名，像猫头鹰，捕食鼠、兔等，对农业有益 collared owlet

瘤(*癅) liú ㄌㄧㄡˊ (一子) 生物体的组织细胞不正常增生而成的疙瘩 tumour：肉～ *sarcoma* | 骨～ *osteoma; bone tumour*

流 liú ㄌㄧㄡˊ ❶液体移动 to flow：水往低处～。*Water flows*

L

downwards. | ～水不腐。*Running water never becomes putrid.* | ～汗 *to sweat* | ～血 *to bleed* [流浪] 生活无着，漂泊不定 live a vagrant life [流利] 说话、书写等灵活顺畅 fluent：他说一口～的普通话。*He speaks fluent putonghua (Mandarin).* | 他的钢笔字写得很～。*He writes smoothly with a fountain pen.* ❷像水那样流动 to circulate; to flow：～通 *circulation* | 空气对～ *air convection* ㊀ ①移动不定 to drift; to move：～星 *meteor; shooting star* ②运转不停 running：～光 *passing time* | ～年 *fleeting time* ③不知来路，意外地射来的 erratic; stray：～矢 *stray arrow* | ～弹 *stray bullet* ④传播或相沿下来 to spread; to pass down：～行 *popular* | ～传 *spread* ❸流动的液体、气体等 flowing liquid，air, current, etc.：河～ *river* | 电～ *electric current* | 寒～ *cold current* | 气～ *air current* 也指像水一样流动的人或物 people or things that flow like water：人～ *stream of people* | 车～ *stream of vehicles* | 物～ *logistics* ❹趋向坏的方面 to degenerate; to change for the worse：～于形式 *become a mere formality* | 放任自～ *let things drift; let people do as they like* ❺品类 class ①派别 school：九～ *the nine schools of thoughts* ②等级 grade：第一～产品 *first rate products* ❻旧时的一种刑罚，把人送到荒远的地方去，充军 to banish; to exile：～放 *send into exile*

琉(*瑠、*璢) liú ㄌㄧㄡˊ [琉璃] (-li) 用铝和钠的硅酸化合物烧制成的釉料 coloured glaze：～瓦 *glazed tile*

硫 liú ㄌㄧㄡˊ 非金属元素，符号 S，通称硫黄，淡黄色，质硬而脆。可用来制硫酸、药物等 sulphur (S) (usually known as 硫黄)

旒 liú ㄌㄧㄡˊ ❶旗子上面的飘带 streamer ❷古代皇帝礼帽前后下垂的玉串 (ancient) fringes of jade beads hanging from the front and back of the Emperor's ceremonial hat

鎏 liú ㄌㄧㄡˊ 古代帝王冠冕前后悬垂的玉串 (ancient) fringes of jade beads hanging from the front and back of the Emperor's ceremonial hat

鎏 liú ㄌㄧㄡˊ ❶成色好的金子 fine gold ❷ same as "镏 (liú)"

畱 liú ㄌㄧㄡˊ 用于地名 used in place names：后～（在江苏省金坛）*Houliu (in Jintan, Jiangsu Province)*

镠(鏐) liú ㄌㄧㄡˊ 成色好的金子 fine gold

珋 liǔ ㄌㄧㄡˇ 一种有光的美石 a fine lustrous stone

柳(*栁、*桺) liǔ ㄌㄧㄡˇ ❶柳树，落叶乔木，枝细长，叶狭长，花黄绿色。种子上有白色毛状物，成熟后随风飞散，叫柳絮 willow ❷星宿名，二十八宿之一 *liu* (one of the twenty-eight constellations in ancient Chinese astronomy)

L

绺(綹) liǔ ㄌㄧㄡˇ (—儿)量词，用于成束的理顺了的丝、线、须、发等 (measure word for hair, thread, etc.) tress; lock; skein：两～儿线 *two strands of thread* | 五～儿须 *goatee beard in five tufts* | 一～儿头发 *a lock of hair*

锍(鋶) liǔ ㄌㄧㄡˇ 有色金属冶炼过程中产生的各种金属硫化物的互熔体 matte

罶(罚)** liǔ ㄌㄧㄡˇ 捕鱼的竹篓子，鱼进去就出不来 bamboo fish trap

六 liù ㄌㄧㄡˋ 数目字 (number) six

陆(陸) liù ㄌㄧㄡˋ "六"字的大写 elaborate form of 六 (six), used in commercial or financial context

⇨ see also lù on p.420

碌(*磟) liù ㄌㄧㄡˋ [碌碡](—zhou)用来轧脱谷粒或轧平场院的农具，圆柱形，用石头做成 stone roller (for threshing grain, levelling a threshing floor, etc.)

⇨ see also lù on p.421

遛 liù ㄌㄧㄡˋ ❶散步，慢慢走，随便走走 to stroll; to saunter：～大街 *saunter along the streets* | 吃完饭出去～～ *go for a stroll after dinner* ❷牵着牲畜或带着鸟慢慢走 to walk (an animal)：～马 *walk a horse* | ～鸟 *go for a walk carrying a bird*

馏(餾) liù ㄌㄧㄡˋ 把凉了的熟食品再蒸热 reheat by steaming：把馒头～一～ *heat up buns by steaming*

⇨ see also liú on p.412

溜(❷❸霤)** liù ㄌㄧㄡˋ ❶急流 swift current; turbulent flow：大～ *torrent* | 今天河水～很大。*The river is flowing fast today.* ❷顺房檐滴下来的水 water dripping from the eaves：檐～ *water dripping from the eaves* ❸屋檐上安的接雨水用的长水槽 rain gutter：水～ *rain gutter* ❹(—儿)量词，用于成行(háng)列的事物 (measure word) row; line：一～三间房 *a row of three rooms*

⇨ see also liū on p.411

镏(鎦) liù ㄌㄧㄡˋ [镏子]〈方 dialect〉戒指 ring：金～ *gold ring*

⇨ see also liú on p.412

蹓 liù ㄌㄧㄡˋ same as "遛❶"

⇨ see also liū on p.412

鹨(鷚) liù ㄌㄧㄡˋ 鸟名，身体小，嘴细长。吃害虫，种类较多，是益鸟 pipit

LO ㄌㄛ

咯 lo ·ㄌㄛ 助词 auxiliary word：那倒好～！ *That would've been good.*

⇨ see also gē on p.203, kǎ on p.347

LONG ㄌㄨㄥ

龙(龍) lóng ㄌㄨㄥˊ ❶我国古代传说中的一种动物，身体长，有鳞，有角，能走、能飞、能游泳。近代古生物学上指一些有脚有尾的爬

行动物 Chinese dragon; huge extinct reptile：恐～ *dinosaur* | 翼手～ *pterodactyl* ❷古代指帝王 (ancient) emperor; imperial：真～天子 *emperor* | ～体 *emperor's health* | ～颜 *countenance of an emperor* | ～袍 *imperial robe* | ～床 *imperial bed* ❸形状像龙的或有龙的图案的东西 objects resembling a Chinese dragon,or decorated with dragon imagery：～灯 *dragon lantern* | ～舟 *dragon boat*

〈古 ancient〉 also same as 垄 (lǒng)

茏(蘢) lóng ㄌㄨㄥˊ [茏葱] [葱茏] 草木茂盛的样子 verdant; lush

咙(嚨) lóng ㄌㄨㄥˊ 喉咙，咽喉 throat (see 喉 hóu on page 255 for reference)

泷(瀧) lóng ㄌㄨㄥˊ 急流的水 rapids

➪ see also shuāng on p.613

珑(瓏) lóng ㄌㄨㄥˊ see 玲珑 (líng－) at 玲 on page 408

栊(櫳) lóng ㄌㄨㄥˊ ❶窗户 window ❷围养禽兽的栅栏 cage; pen

昽(曨) lóng ㄌㄨㄥˊ see 昤昽 (líng－) at 昤 on page 408, 曚昽 (méng－) at 曚 on page 446, and 曈昽 (tóng－) at 曈 on page 658

胧(朧) lóng ㄌㄨㄥˊ see 朦胧 (méng－) at 朦 on page 446

砻(礱) lóng ㄌㄨㄥˊ ❶用来去掉稻壳的器具，形状像磨 rice huller ❷用砻去掉稻壳 to hull (rice with a huller)：～谷舂米 *hull grain and pound rice*

眬(矓) lóng ㄌㄨㄥˊ see 蒙眬 (méng－) at 蒙 on page 446

聋(聾) lóng ㄌㄨㄥˊ 耳朵听不见声音，通常也指听觉迟钝 deaf; hard of hearing：他耳朵～了。*He is deaf now.*

笼(籠) lóng ㄌㄨㄥˊ ❶(－子、－儿)养鸟、虫的器具，用竹、木条或金属丝等编插而成 cage; coop：鸟～子 *birdcage* | 鸡～ *chicken coop* | 蝈蝈～ *katydid cage* ㊀旧时囚禁犯人的东西 (old) cage for prisoners：囚～ *prisoner's cage* | 牢～ *bonds; trap* ❷用竹、木等材料制成的有盖的蒸东西的器具 steamer (for cooking)：蒸～ *food steamer* | ～屉 *food steamer*

➪ see also lǒng on p.416

隆 lóng ㄌㄨㄥˊ ❶盛大，厚，程度深 grand; deep; intense：～冬 *depths of winter* | ～恩 *great favour* | ～重 *solemn; ceremonious* ❷兴盛（㊀－盛、兴－）prosperous; flourishing ❸高出，使高出 to bulge; to swell up：～起 *to bulge* | ～胸 *enlarge one's breasts*

漋 lóng ㄌㄨㄥˊ 用于地名 used in place names：永～（在湖北省京山县）*Yonglong (in Jingshan County, Hubei Province)*

癃 lóng ㄌㄨㄥˊ ❶古书上指年老衰弱多病 (in ancient Chinese texts) infirmity ❷癃闭，中医指小便不通的病 (in traditional Chinese medicine) retention of urine

L

窿 lóng ㄌㄨㄥˊ ❶〈方 dialect〉煤矿坑道 coal mine tunnel ❷ see 窟窿 (kūlong) at 窟 on page 363

陇(隴) lǒng ㄌㄨㄥˇ ❶陇山，山名，位于陕西、甘肃两省交界的地方 Mount Longshan (on the border between Shaanxi and Gansu provinces) ❷甘肃省的别称 Long (another name of Gansu Province)：～海铁路 *Lanzhou-Lianyungang Railway*

拢(攏) lǒng ㄌㄨㄥˇ ❶凑起，总合 to add up; to sum up：～共 *altogether* | ～总 *in all* ❷靠近，船只靠岸（㊀靠－）to approach; to reach：～岸 *draw alongside the shore* | 拉～ *draw sb over to one's side; cosy up to; rope in* | 他们俩总谈不～。*The two of them can never come to an agreement.* ❸收束使不松散 to hold together; to gather up：～紧 *hold tight* | 用绳子把柴火～住 *pull a rope around the firewood* | ～不住人心 *cannot muster up support* ❹梳，用梳子整理头发 to comb：～一～头发 *comb one's hair* ❺合上，聚拢 to close; to shut：笑得嘴都合不～了 *smile from ear to ear*

垄(壟、 **壠)** lǒng ㄌㄨㄥˇ ❶田地分界的埂子 ridge (between fields) ❷农作物的行（háng）或行与行间的空地 row of crops; space between rows of crops：～沟 *furrow* | 宽～密植 *wide spacing and dense planting* | 缺苗断～ *poor germination of crop seeds* ❸像田埂的东西 objects resembling ridges：瓦～ *tile ridge*

［垄断］操纵市场，把持权柄，独占利益 to monopolize; monopoly

笼(籠) lǒng ㄌㄨㄥˇ ❶遮盖，罩住 to envelop; to cover; to veil：黑云～罩着天空。*Black clouds are covering the sky.*

［笼络］用手段拉拢人 to win sb over (often by improper means)：～人心 *buy people's support* ❷比较大的箱子 large trunk or case：箱～ *suitcase*

［笼统］（-tǒng）概括而不分明，不具体 general; sweeping：话说得太～了。*These remarks are too general.*

⇨ see also lóng on p.415

箢(簢) lǒng ㄌㄨㄥˇ 用于地名 used in place names：织～（在广东省阳西）*Zhilong (in Yangxi, Guangdong Province)*

弄 lòng ㄌㄨㄥˋ〈方 dialect〉弄堂，小巷，小胡同 lane; alley

⇨ see also nòng on p.483

哢 lòng ㄌㄨㄥˋ ❶鸟叫 to chirp ❷用于地名 used in place names：～村（在广东省潮安）*Longcun (in Chao'an, Guangdong Province)*

崠 lòng ㄌㄨㄥˋ（壮 *Zhuang*）石山间的平地 small area of flat ground between rocky hills

LOU ㄌㄡ

搂(摟) lōu ㄌㄡ ❶用手或工具把东西聚集起来 to gather up：～柴火 *gather firewood*

㊐ 搜刮 to extort money：～钱 *extort money* ❷向着自己的方向拨 to pull：～枪机 *pull the trigger*

⇨ see also lǒu on p.417

瞜（瞜） lōu ㄌㄡ〈方 dialect〉看 to look：让我～一～。*Let me have a look.*

剅（剅）** lóu ㄌㄡˊ〈方 dialect〉堤坝下面的水口，水道 sluiceway：～口 *sluice valve*｜～嘴 *sluice valve*

娄（婁） lóu ㄌㄡˊ ❶星宿名，二十八宿之一 *lou* (one of the twenty-eight constellations in ancient Chinese astronomy) ❷〈方 dialect〉（某些瓜类）过熟而变质 (of melons) overripe and unfit to eat：瓜～了。*The melon is overripe.*

偻（僂） lóu ㄌㄡˊ ❶［偻啰］（—luo）(old) same as "喽啰" ❷ see 佝偻 (gōu—) at 佝 on page 215

⇨ see also lǚ on p.423

塿（塿） lóu ㄌㄡˊ ［塿土］褐土的一种，因长期施用粪肥而在原耕作层上形成的上下两层土壤 a kind of brown soil, formed by long-term manuring

蒌（蔞） lóu ㄌㄡˊ ［蒌蒿］（—hāo）草本植物，花淡黄色，可入药 common mugwort

喽（嘍） lóu ㄌㄡˊ ［喽啰］（*偻啰）（—luo）旧时称盗贼的部下，现在多比喻追随恶人的人 (old) foot soldier; (in an outlaw band) lackey

⇨ see also lou on p.418

溇（漊） lóu ㄌㄡˊ 溇水，水名，在湖南省 Loushui River (in Hunan Province)

楼（樓） lóu ㄌㄡˊ ❶两层以上的房屋 storeyed building：～房 *storeyed building*｜大～ *big building* ❷楼房的一层 storey; floor：一～ *ground floor (British); first floor (American)*｜三～ *second floor (British); third floor (American)*

膢（膢） lóu ㄌㄡˊ lǘ ㄌㄩˊ（又）古代一种祭祀方式 an ancient sacrificial ritual

耧（耬） lóu ㄌㄡˊ 用来开沟并播种（zhǒng）的农具 seed plough; drill

蝼（螻） lóu ㄌㄡˊ 蝼蛄（gū），昆虫，又叫蝲蝲蛄、土狗子，背褐色，有翅，前足铲状，能掘土，咬食农作物的根、茎 mole cricket (also called 蝲蝲蛄，土狗子)

髅（髏） lóu ㄌㄡˊ see 骷髅 (kū—) at 骷 on page 362, and 髑髅 (dú—) at 髑 on page 147

搂（摟） lǒu ㄌㄡˇ ❶两臂合抱，用手臂拢着（㊀—抱）to hug; to embrace; to cuddle：把孩子～在怀里 *cuddle a child in one's arms* ❷量词，用于两臂合抱的东西 (measure word) armful：抱来一～柴禾 *bring over an armful of firewood*

⇨ see also lōu on p.416

嵝（嶁） lǒu ㄌㄡˇ see 岣嵝 (gǒu—) at 岣 on page 215

篓（簍） lǒu ㄌㄡˇ （—子、—儿）盛东西的器具，

用竹、荆条等编成 basket：字纸～儿 *wastepaper basket* | 油～ *lined oil basket*

陋 lòu ㄌㄡˋ ❶丑的，坏的，不文明的 ugly; uncultured：丑～ *ugly* | ～规 *objectionable practice* | ～习 *bad habit; vulgar custom* ❷狭小 narrow：～室 *cramped room* | ～巷 *narrow alley* ❸少，简略 scanty; limited; shallow：学识浅～ *have little learning* | 因～就简 *make do with what is available* | 孤～寡闻（见闻少）*ignorant and ill-informed*

镂(鏤) lòu ㄌㄡˋ 雕刻 to engrave; to carve：～花 *engrave designs* | ～骨铭心（喻永远不忘）*(of memories) engraved on one's heart*

瘘(瘻、瘺)** lòu ㄌㄡˋ 瘘管，体内因发生病变向外溃破而形成的管道，病灶里的分泌物可以由瘘管里流出来 fistula

漏 lòu ㄌㄡˋ ❶物体由孔缝透过或滴下 to leak：水壶～了 *kettle is leaking* | 油箱～了 *gas tank is leaking* [漏洞] 比喻做事的破绽，不周密的地方 leak; flaw; loophole：堵塞～ *plug a leak* ❷泄漏，泄露 to divulge; to disclose; to leak：～了风声 *leak word* | 走～消息 *leak information* ❸遗落 to leave out; to miss：这一项可千万不能～掉。*Don't ever leave this item out.* ❹漏壶，古代计时的器具，用铜制成。壶上下分好几层，上层底有小孔，可以滴水，层层下注，以底层蓄水多少计算时间 water clock; clepsydra

露 lòu ㄌㄡˋ 义同"露(lù)❸"，用于一些口语词语，如"露怯、露脸、露马脚"等 same in meaning as 露 (lù) ❸ , used in some spoken words such as 露怯 , 露脸 , 露马脚 , etc.

⇨ see also lù on p.422

喽(嘍) lou ·ㄌㄡ 助词，意思相当于"啦" auxiliary word, equivalent in meaning to 啦：下雪～！ *It's snowing!* | 看，他们来～！ *Look, here they are!*

⇨ see also lóu on p.417

LU ㄌㄨ

撸(擼) lū ㄌㄨ 〈方 dialect〉 ❶ 捋 (luō) to strip; to roll up：～袖子 *roll up one's sleeves* | ～树叶 *strip off leaves* ❷撤职 to dismiss sb from a post; to strip sb of power：他的职务被～了。*He has been dismissed from his post.* ❸责备，训斥 to reprimand; to scold：他被～了一顿。*He was taken to task.*

噜(嚕) lū ㄌㄨ [噜苏] (－su) 〈方 dialect〉 啰唆 to talk endlessly; wordy; troublesome

卢(盧) lú ㄌㄨˊ 姓 (surname) Lu

垆(壚、❷鑪)** lú ㄌㄨˊ ❶黑色坚硬的土 black hard earth ❷旧时酒店里安放酒瓮的土台子。也指酒店 (old) adobe table (in an old wine shop); wine shop

泸(瀘) lú ㄌㄨˊ [泸州]地名，在四川省 Luzhou (a place in Sichuan Province)

栌(櫨) lú ㄌㄨˊ [黄栌]落叶小乔木，叶卵形，秋天变成红色。木材黄色，可制器具，也可做染料 smoke tree

胪(臚) lú ㄌㄨˊ 陈列，陈述 to set out; to display; to narrate：～列 *to enumerate; to list* | ～情（陈述心情）*describe one's emotions*

鸬(鸕) lú ㄌㄨˊ [鸬鹚]（－cí）鸟名，俗叫鱼鹰，羽毛黑色，闪绿光，能游泳，善于捕食鱼类。渔人常用来帮助捕鱼 cormorant (informal 鱼鹰)

铲(鑪) lú ㄌㄨˊ 人造的放射性金属元素，符号 Rf。rutherfordium (Rf)

⇨ 鑪 see also 炉 on p.419

颅(顱) lú ㄌㄨˊ 头的上部，包括头骨和脑，也指头 skull; head：～骨 *skull*

舻(艫) lú ㄌㄨˊ see 舳舻 (zhú －) at 舳 on page 867

鲈(鱸) lú ㄌㄨˊ 鱼名，身体侧扁，嘴大，鳞细，银灰色，背部和背鳍上有黑斑，性凶猛 bass; perch

芦(蘆) lú ㄌㄨˊ 芦苇，草本植物，生长在浅水里，茎中空。可用来造纸、编席等，根状茎可入药 reed

庐(廬) lú ㄌㄨˊ 房舍 hut; cottage：茅～ *thatched cottage*

炉(爐、^△*鑪) lú ㄌㄨˊ（－子）取暖、做饭或冶炼用的设备 stove; oven; furnace：电～ *electric stove* | 煤气～ *gas stove* | 炼钢～ *steelmaking furnace*

⇨ 鑪 see also 铲 on p.419

卤(鹵、滷) lǔ ㄌㄨˇ ❶制盐时剩下的黑色汁液，又叫盐卤，是氯化镁、硫酸镁、溴化镁及氯化钠等的混合物，味苦有毒 bittern (also called 盐卤) ❷浓汁 thick stock; thick gravy：茶～ *strong tea* | 打～面 *noodles with meat and gravy* ❸用盐水、酱油等浓汁制作食品 to stew in seasoned sauce：～鸡 *pot-stewed chicken* | ～煮豆腐 *stewed tofu*

硇(磠) lǔ ㄌㄨˇ [硇砂] same as "硇(náo)砂"

虏(虜、*虜) lǔ ㄌㄨˇ ❶俘获（㊥俘－）to capture; to take prisoner：～获甚众 *have captured many* ❷打仗时捉住的敌人（㊥俘－）captive

掳(擄) lǔ ㄌㄨˇ 抢取（㊥－掠）to pillage; to loot

鲁(魯) lǔ ㄌㄨˇ ❶愚钝，莽撞 dull-witted; imprudent; impetuous：粗～ *coarse; rude* | 愚～ *uncouth* [鲁莽]（*卤莽）不仔细考虑事理，冒失 reckless; imprudent ❷周代诸侯国名，在今山东省南部一带 Lu (a state during the Zhou Dynasty, in today's southern Shandong Province) ❸山东省的别称 Lu (another name of Shandong Province)

L

滷(滷) lǔ ㄌㄨˇ 用于地名 used in place names：～港（在安徽省芜湖）*Lugang (in Wuhu, Anhui Province)*

橹(櫓、*樐、*艣、*艪) lǔ ㄌㄨˇ 拨水使船前进的器具 oar; scull：摇～ *row the boat*

镥(鑥) lǔ ㄌㄨˇ 金属元素，符号 Lu，银白色，质软。可用于核工业 lutetium (Lu)

甪 lù ㄌㄨˋ ［甪直］地名，在江苏省苏州 Luzhi (a place in Suzhou, Jiangsu Province)

陆(陸) lù ㄌㄨˋ ❶陆地，高出水面的土地 land：登～ *landing* | ～路 *land route* | ～军 *army* ❷姓 (surname) Lu

［陆离］形容色彩繁杂 riotously colourful：光怪～ *grotesque and diversified*

［陆续］副词，接连不断 (adverb) in succession：开会的人～地到了。*The attendees arrived one after another.*

⇨ see also liù on p.414

录(録) lù ㄌㄨˋ ❶录制，记录，抄写，记载 to record; to copy; to write down：～像 *video; take a video* | ～音 *audio recording; record audio* | 把这份公文～下来 *copy down this document* ❷记载言行或事物的书刊 record book; register; catalogue：语～ *quotation* | 备忘～ *memorandum* | 回忆～ *memoirs* ❸采取，任用 to select; to employ; to hire：收～ *to collect* | ～用 *to employ* | ～取 *to enrol; to recruit*

菉 lù ㄌㄨˋ 用于地名 used in place names：梅～（在广东省吴川）*Meilu (in Wuchuan, Guangdong Province)*

崬 lù ㄌㄨˋ（壮 *Zhuang*）土山间的平地 small area of flat ground between earth hills

渌 lù ㄌㄨˋ 渌水，水名，在湖南省株洲 Lushui River (in Zhuzhou, Hunan Province)

逯 lù ㄌㄨˋ 姓 (surname) Lu

騄(騄) lù ㄌㄨˋ ［騄駬］（-ěr）古代骏马名。也作"騄耳" an ancient steed (also written as 騄耳)

绿(綠) lù ㄌㄨˋ same in meaning as 绿 (lǜ) ［绿林］1 原指西汉末年聚集在绿林山（在今湖北省大洪山一带）的农民起义军，后来泛指聚集山林、反抗封建统治者的人们 (originally referring to a peasant revolt around Lulinshan, i.e., today's Dahongshan in Hubei Province) heroes of the bush; heroes of the Robin Hood type 2 旧指上山为匪、抢劫财物的集团 (old) bandits ［鸭绿江］水名。是中国和朝鲜两国的界河。源出吉林省东南中朝边境的长白山，西南流到辽宁省丹东入黄海 Yalujiang River (boundary river between China and North Korea, originating from Mount Changbaishan on the border in the southeast of Jilin Province and flowing south-westward into the Yellow Sea at Dandong, Liaoning Province)

⇨ see also lǜ on p.424

琭 lù ㄌㄨˋ 一种玉 a kind of jade

禄 lù ㄌㄨˋ 古代官吏的俸给（㊀俸－）(ancient) official salary：高官厚～ *high office with a handsome salary*

碌 lù ㄌㄨˋ ❶平凡 commonplace; mediocre：庸～ *mediocre and unambitious* [碌碌] 平庸，无所作为 commonplace; mediocre：庸庸～ *mediocre and unambitious* ❷繁忙 busy：忙～ *busy*

⇨ see also liù on p.414

盝 lù ㄌㄨˋ ❶古代的一种盒子 a kind of box in ancient times ❷漉，过滤 to seep through; to filter

箓(籙) lù ㄌㄨˋ ❶簿子，册子 account book; register; record book ❷符箓，道士画的驱使鬼神的符号，是一种迷信骗人的东西 symbols drawn by Daoist priests to invoke or expel spirits

醁 lù ㄌㄨˋ see 醽醁 (líng－) at 醽 on page 410

辂(輅) lù ㄌㄨˋ ❶古代车辕上用来牵引车子的横木 horizontal drawbar (on the shaft of an ancient chariot) ❷古代的大车 (ancient) carriage

赂(賂) lù ㄌㄨˋ ❶贿赂，用财物买通别人 to bribe ❷财物，特指赠送的财物 money or goods (specifically gifted)

鹿 lù ㄌㄨˋ 哺乳动物，反刍类，腿细长，尾短，毛黄褐色，有的有花斑，性情温驯，有的雄鹿有树枝状的角。种类很多 deer

漉 lù ㄌㄨˋ 液体往下渗，过滤 to seep through; to filter：～网 *mesh screening* | ～酒 *filter rice wine* [湿漉漉] 物体潮湿的样子 wet; damp

辘(轆) lù ㄌㄨˋ [辘轳] (－lu) 1 安在井上绞起汲水斗的器具 well-pulley 2 机械上的绞盘 windlass; winch

簏 lù ㄌㄨˋ 竹箱等竹编的盛物器具 woven bamboo trunk

麓 lù ㄌㄨˋ 山脚下 foot of a hill or mountain：泰山之～ *at the foot of Mount Tai*

路 lù ㄌㄨˋ ❶道，往来通行的地方（㊀－途、－径、道－）road; path; way：公～ *highway* | 水～ *waterway* | 高架～ *elevated road* ㊁思想或行动的方向、途径 sequence; line; logic：思～ *train of thought* | 生～ *means of livelihood; way out* ❷方面，地区 region; side：各～人马 *people from all sides* | 南～货 *southern goods* ❸种类 kind：两～货 *two different kinds* | 他俩是一～人。*The two of them are of the same type.*

蕗 lù ㄌㄨˋ 甘草的别名 another name of 甘草

潞 lù ㄌㄨˋ ❶潞水，水名，即今山西省的浊漳河 Lushui River (today's Zhuozhang River in Shanxi Province) ❷潞江，水名，即云南省的怒江 Lujiang River (also known as Nujiang River in Yunnan Province)

璐 lù ㄌㄨˋ 美玉 fine jade

鹭(鷺) lù ㄌㄨˋ 鸟名，翼大尾短，颈和腿很长，常见的有白鹭、苍鹭、绿鹭等 heron [鹭鸶]（—sī）鸟名，即白鹭，羽毛纯白色，顶有细长的白羽，捕食小鱼 egret (same as 白鹭)

露 lù ㄌㄨˋ ❶露水，靠近地面的水蒸气夜间遇冷凝结成的小水珠 dew：～珠 *dew drop* | 甘～ *sweet dew* ㉆露天，没有遮蔽，在屋外的 open-air; outdoors：风餐～宿 *endure the rigours of living in the wilderness* | ～营 *camp out; go camping* ❷用药料、果汁等制成的饮料 beverage distilled from herbs, fruits, etc.：枇杷～ *loquat syrup* | 果子～ *fruit juice* | 玫瑰～ *rose water* ❸显出来，现出来（㊀显—）to reveal; to expose; to show：～骨 *explicit; undisguised* | 暴～ *to expose* | 揭～ *to reveal* | 不～声色 *not betray one's feeling or intentions* | 面～笑容 *with a smile on one's face*

⇨ see also lòu on p.418

稑 lù ㄌㄨˋ 古代指后种而先熟的谷物 (ancient) early-maturing cereals

僇 lù ㄌㄨˋ ❶侮辱 to humiliate; to insult ❷ same as "戮"

勠 lù ㄌㄨˋ 并，合 to unite; to join [勠力] 合力，并力 to join efforts; to join forces：～同心 *unite in a concerted effort*

戮(❶*剹) lù ㄌㄨˋ ❶杀（㊀杀—、屠—）to kill; to slay ❷ (old) same as "勠"

轳(轤) lu ·ㄌㄨ see 辘轳(lù—) at 辘 on page 421

氇(氌) lu ·ㄌㄨ see 氆氇(pǔ—) at 氆 on page 514

LÜ ㄌㄩ

驴(驢) lǘ ㄌㄩˊ 家畜，像马而小，耳朵长。可以驮东西、拉车或供人骑 donkey

闾(閭) lǘ ㄌㄩˊ ❶里门，巷口的门 inner gate; gate of an alley ❷古代二十五家为一闾 neighbourhood of 25 families in ancient China

榈(櫚) lǘ ㄌㄩˊ see 栟榈(bīng—) at 栟 on page 45, and 棕榈(zōng—) at 棕 on page 885

膢(膢) lǘ ㄌㄩˊ(又) see lóu on page 417

吕 lǚ ㄌㄩˇ 我国古代音乐十二律中的阴律，有六种，总称六吕 six even-numbered notes in the ancient Chinese 12-pitch musical scale

侣 lǚ ㄌㄩˇ 同伴（㊀伴—）companion; partner：情～ *lovers*

梠 lǚ ㄌㄩˇ 〈古 ancient〉屋檐 eaves

铝(鋁) lǚ ㄌㄩˇ 金属元素，符号 Al，银白色，质轻。是重要的工业原料 aluminium (Al)

稆(穭)** lǚ ㄌㄩˇ 谷物等不种自生的 self-sown：～生 *self-grow* 也作"旅" also written as 旅

捋 lǚ ㄌㄩˇ 用手指顺着抹过去，整理 to stroke; to smooth out:

L

～胡子 *stroke one's beard* | ～头发 *smooth one's hair*

➪ see also luō on p.427

旅 lǚ ㄌㄩˇ ❶出行，在外作客 to travel; to stay away from home：～行 *to travel* | ～馆 *hotel* | ～途 *journey; trip* | ～居 *reside away from home* | ～客 *traveller; passenger* | ～美华侨 *overseas Chinese residing in the US* ❷军队的编制单位，是团的上一级 (military) brigade ❸指军队 troops：军～ *troops* | 强兵劲～ *powerful army* ❹共同 together; jointly：～进～退 *move forward and backward jointly* ❺same as "稆"：～生 *self-grow* | ～葵 *Chinese mallow*

膂 lǚ ㄌㄩˇ 脊梁骨 backbone [膂力] 体力 physical strength：～过人 *possessing extraordinary physical strength*

偻(僂) lǚ ㄌㄩˇ ❶脊背弯曲 hunchbacked：伛(yǔ)～ *hunchbacked* ❷迅速 instantly; at once：不能～指（不能迅速指出来）*unable to point out right away*

➪ see also lóu on p.417

屡(屢) lǚ ㄌㄩˇ 副词，屡次，接连着，不止一次 (adverb) repeatedly; time and again：～见不鲜 *often seen* | ～战～胜 *score one victory after another*

缕(縷) lǚ ㄌㄩˇ ❶线 thread：一丝一～ *every thread* ❷一条一条地 in fine detail：～述 *state in detail* | ～析 *analyse in detail* ❸量词，股 (measure word) wisp; skein; strand：一～炊烟 *a wisp of cooking smoke* | 两～线 *two strands of thread*

褛(褸) lǚ ㄌㄩˇ see 褴褛 (lán –) at 褴 on page 377

履 lǚ ㄌㄩˇ ❶鞋 shoe：革～ *leather shoes* | 削足适～（喻不合理地迁就现有条件）*cut one's feet to fit the shoes;(figurative) mechanically copy and apply regardless of specific conditions* ❷踩在上面，走过 to walk on; to tread on：如～薄冰 *be very careful (as if treading on thin ice)* ㉖履行，实行 to fulfil; to carry out; to honour：～约 *honour an agreement* [履历] 个人的经历 personal biography; curriculum vitae ❸脚步 footstep：步～轻盈 *nimble-footed*

垏 lǜ ㄌㄩˋ 土埂 earth ridge between fields

律 lǜ ㄌㄩˋ ❶法则，规章 rule; statute; regulation [律诗] 我国旧体诗的一种，有一定的格律和字数，分五言、七言两种 regulated eight-lined classical poetry forms, with five or seven equal numbers of characters to each line [规律] 事物之间的内在的必然的联系，又叫法则，是不以人的主观意志为转移的 law; regular pattern (also called 法则) [一律] 同样，没有例外 same; without exception ❷约束 to restrain; to keep under control：严于～己 *be strict with oneself* | 自～ *autonomy* | 他～ *heteronomy* ❸我国古代审定乐音高低的标准，把乐音分为六律（阳律）和六吕（阴律），

合称十二律 six odd-numbered notes (阳律) in the ancient Chinese 12-pitch musical scale (十二律) the other six are the even-numbered notes (阴律)

葎 lù ㄌㄩˋ 葎草，草本植物，茎有倒生的刺，花黄绿色，全草可入药 wild hop

虑(慮) lù ㄌㄩˋ ❶思考，寻思 to consider; to ponder; to think：思～ *to deliberate* | 考～ *to consider* | 深思远～ *think deeply and plan carefully* ❷ 担忧 to concern; to worry：忧～ *to worry* | 过～ *worry too much* [顾虑]有所顾忌，担心，不肯或不敢行动 to have misgivings; to be hesitant：～重重 *be full of misgivings* | 打消～ *dispel misgivings*

滤(濾) lù ㄌㄩˋ 使液体、气体经过纱布、木炭、沙子等物，除去其中所含的杂质、毒气而变纯净 to filter; to strain

率 lù ㄌㄩˋ 两个相关的数在一定条件下的比值 ratio; rate; proportion：利～ *interest rate* | 速～ *speed; rate* | 增长～ *growth rate* | 出勤～ *attendance rate*

⇨ see also shuài on p.612

绿(綠) lù ㄌㄩˋ 一般草和树叶的颜色，蓝和黄合成的颜色 green：红花～叶 *red flowers with green leaves* | ～地 *green; lawn* [绿色]㊕无公害、无污染的 environment-friendly; green：～食品 *green foods*

⇨ see also lù on p.420

氯 lù ㄌㄩˋ 气体元素，符号 Cl，黄绿色，味臭，有毒，能损伤呼吸器官。可用来漂白、消毒 chlorine (Cl)

LUAN ㄌㄨㄢ

峦(巒) luán ㄌㄨㄢˊ ❶小而尖的山 low and pointed hill ❷连着的山 mountains in a range：山～起伏 *undulating hills* | 峰～ *ridges and peaks*

孪(孿) luán ㄌㄨㄢˊ 双生，一胎两个 twin：～生兄弟 *twin brothers*

娈(孌) luán ㄌㄨㄢˊ 美好 pretty; handsome

栾(欒) luán ㄌㄨㄢˊ 栾树，落叶乔木，花黄色。叶可做青色染料。花可入药，又可做黄色染料。木材可制器具，种子可榨油 golden rain tree

挛(攣) luán ㄌㄨㄢˊ 手脚蜷曲不能伸开 contracture：痉～ *spasm; convulsions*

鸾(鸞) luán ㄌㄨㄢˊ 传说中凤凰一类的鸟 mythical phoenix-like bird：～凤和鸣（喻夫妻和美）*happily married couple*

脔(臠) luán ㄌㄨㄢˊ 切成小块的肉 small slice of meat：～割（分割）*cut up; carve up*

滦(灤) luán ㄌㄨㄢˊ 滦河，水名，在河北省东北部 Luanhe River (in the northeast of Hebei Province)

銮(鑾) luán ㄌㄨㄢˊ 一种铃铛 a kind of bell

卵 luǎn ㄌㄨㄢˇ 动植物的雌性生殖细胞，特指动物的蛋

ovum; egg; spawn：鸟～ *bird's egg* | 鸡～ *chicken egg* | ～生 *oviparity*

乱（亂）luàn ㄌㄨㄢˋ ❶没有秩序（㊟纷－）disorderly; in a mess：杂～ *in a jumble* | 这篇稿子写得太～。*This article is in a muddle.* ❷战争，武装骚扰 chaos; riot; turmoil：叛～ *mutiny* | 战～ *chaos of war* | 避～ *run away from social upheaval* ❸混淆（xiáo）to mix up; to confuse：以假～真 *create confusion by passing off the fake with the real one* ❹任意，随便 arbitrary; random：～吃 *eat without discrimination* | ～跑 *run about unchecked* ❺男女关系不正当 promiscuous; licentious：淫～ *promiscuous*

LÜE ㄌㄩㄝ

䂮 lüè ㄌㄩㄝˋ 锋利 sharp

掠 lüè ㄌㄩㄝˋ ❶夺取（㊟－夺）to rob; to plunder; to pillage：～取 *to rob; to plunder* | ～人之美（把别人的好处说成是自己的）*claim credit due to others* ❷轻轻擦过 to brush past; to skim over：燕子～檐而过。*The swallow swept past the eaves.*

略（*畧）lüè ㄌㄩㄝˋ ❶大致，简单，不详细，跟"详"相对 general; sketchy; outline (opposite of 详)：～图 *sketch map; schematic diagram* | ～表 *summary list* | ～知一二 *know just a little* | ～述大意 *give a general idea* | 叙述过～。*The narration is too general.* | 粗～计算 *rough calculation* ❷省去，简化 to omit; to leave out：～去不计 *leave out of consideration* | 过程从～ *leave out the process* ❸简要的叙述 summary：史～ *outlined history* | 要～ *outline* ❹计谋 strategy; scheme; plan：方～ *overall plan* | 策～ *tactics* | 战～ *strategy* | 雄才大～ *(of a person) great talent and bold strategy* ❺抢，掠夺 to capture; to seize：侵～ *to invade* | 攻城～地 *attack cities and seize territory*

锊（鋝）lüè ㄌㄩㄝˋ 古代重量单位，约合旧制六两 ancient unit for weight, equal to about six 两 in the old system

圙（**啗）lüè ㄌㄩㄝˋ see 圐圙 (kū－) at 圐 on page 362

LUN ㄌㄨㄣ

抡（掄）lūn ㄌㄨㄣ 手臂用力挥动 to brandish; to swing; to wield：～刀 *brandish a sword* | ～拳 *swing one's fist*

⇨ see also lún on p.426

仑（侖、❷*崙、❷*崘）lún ㄌㄨㄣˊ ❶条理，伦次 logical sequence; coherence ❷ see 昆仑 at 昆 on page 371

伦（倫）lún ㄌㄨㄣˊ ❶辈，类 the like; the same kind; peer：无与～比 *peerless* ❷条理，次序 logical sequence; order：语

无～次 *talk incoherently* ❸人伦，指人与人之间的关系，特指长幼尊卑之间的关系 human relations; ethics：天～之乐 *family happiness* | ～常 *(traditional) ethics in human relationships*

论(論) lún ㄌㄨㄣˊ 《论语》，古书名，主要记载孔子及其门人的言行 *Analects of Confucius*

⇨ see also lùn on p.426

抡(掄) lún ㄌㄨㄣˊ 选择，选拔 to select; to choose：～材 *select suitable material*

⇨ see also lūn on p.425

囵(圇) lún ㄌㄨㄣˊ see 囫囵 (hú—) at 囫 on page 258

沦(淪) lún ㄌㄨㄣˊ ❶水上的波纹 ripple ❷沉没（mò），陷落（㊣—陷、沉—）to sink; to decline; to fall：～亡 *(of a country) perish* | ～于海底 *sink to the bottom of the sea*

纶(綸) lún ㄌㄨㄣˊ ❶钓鱼用的线 fishing line：垂～ *go fishing* ❷指某些合成纤维 synthetic fibre：锦～ *nylon* | 涤～ *terylene*

⇨ see also guān on p.226

轮(輪) lún ㄌㄨㄣˊ ❶（—子、—儿）车轮，车轱辘 wheel (on a vehicle)：三～车 *tricycle* ㊀安在机器上能旋转并促使机器动作的圆形部件 wheel (on a machine)：齿～儿 *cogwheel* | 飞～儿 *flywheel* | 偏心～儿 *eccentric wheel* ❷像车轮的东西 wheel-like objects：日～ *the Sun* | 年～ *annual ring* [轮廓]（—kuò）1 物体的外围 profile; outline 2 事情的大概情形 rough idea; overview ❸轮船 ship; boat (mechanically propelled)：海～ *ocean going vessel* | 油～ *oil tanker* ❹轮流，依照次第转 to take turns：～班 *be on duty in turns; to rotate* | ～值 *take turns to be on duty* | 这回～到我了。*It's my turn now.* ❺量词，用于圆形物或循环的事物、动作 (measure word for circular things) round：一～红日 *a red sun* | 他比我大两～（十二岁为一轮）。*He is two cycles my senior (a cycle being twelve years).*

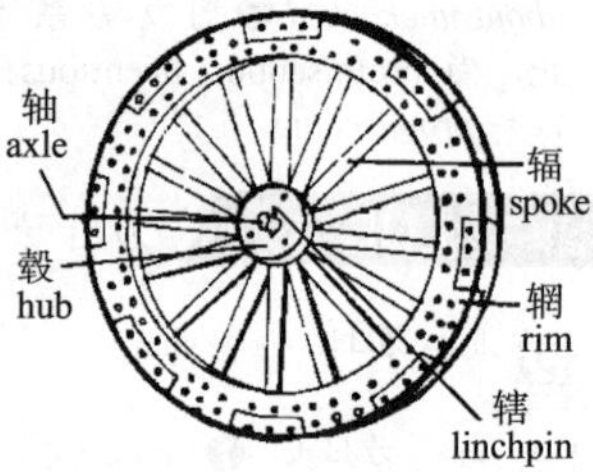

旧式车轮 an old-style wheel

锍(錀) lún ㄌㄨㄣˊ 人造的放射性金属元素，符号 Rg。roentgenium (Rg)

埨(埨) lǔn ㄌㄨㄣˇ 〈方 dialect〉田地中的土垄 earth ridge in a field

论(論) lùn ㄌㄨㄣˋ ❶分析、判断事物的道理（㊣评—、议—）to discuss; to reason; to comment：不能一概而～ *should not treat them all alike* | 讨～ *to discuss* ❷分析、阐明事物道理

的文章、理论和言论 theory; view; opinion：实践～ *theory of practice* | 唯物～ *materialism* | 社～ *editorial* | 舆～ *public opinion* ❸按照某种单位或类别说 by; according to：～件 *by the piece* | ～天 *by the day* | 买西瓜～斤还是～个儿？ *Are the watermelons sold by the* jin *or by the piece?* ❹衡量，评定 to weigh; to decide on：按质～价 *set prices according to quality* | ～功行赏 *give rewards on the basis of merit*

⇨ see also lún on p.426

LUO ㄌㄨㄛ

捋 luō ㄌㄨㄛ 用手握着东西，顺着东西移动 to rub one's palm along：～榆钱儿 *strip elm samaras off the twig* | ～虎须（喻冒险）*stroke a tiger's whiskers; (figurative) do sth very daring*

⇨ see also lǚ on p.422

啰（囉） luō ㄌㄨㄛ ［啰唆］［啰嗦］（－suo）1 说话絮絮叨叨 long-winded; garrulous 2 办事使人感觉麻烦 troublesome; overelaborate

⇨ see also luó on p.427, luo on p.430

罗（羅） luó ㄌㄨㄛˊ ❶捕鸟的网（㊀－网）net for catching birds：天～地网 *nets above and snares below; tight encirclement* ❷张网捕捉 to catch with a net：门可～雀 *having very few visitors (literally means 'One can net sparrows at the door.')* ㊁搜集 to gather; to collect：网～ *search and gather* | 搜～ *seek and collect; scout for* ［罗致］招请（人才）to recruit; to enlist the service of ❸散布，陈列 to scatter; to display：星～棋布 *scattered all around* | ～列 *spread out; to enumerate* ❹过滤流质或筛细粉末用的器具，用木或铁片做成圆框，蒙上粗绢或马尾（yǐ）网、铁丝网制成 sieve; sifter ❺用罗筛东西 to sieve; to sift：～面 *sift flour* ❻轻软有稀孔的丝织品 silk gauze：～衣 *thin silk garment* | ～扇 *silk gauze fan* ❼（外 *loanword*）量词，十二打（dá）叫一罗 (measure word) twelve dozen; gross ❽ same as "脶 (luó)"

［罗汉］梵语音译"阿罗汉"的省称，佛教对某种"得道者"的称呼 arhat

［罗盘］测定方向的仪器，又叫罗盘针。把磁针装置在圆盘中央，盘上刻着度数和方位。是我国古代四大发明之一 compass (also called 罗盘针, one of the Four Great Inventions in ancient China)

萝（蘿） luó ㄌㄨㄛˊ 莪蒿。通常指某些能爬蔓的植物 creeper：茑～ *cypress vine* | 女～ *Usnea*

［萝卜］(－bo)草本植物，种类很多。块根也叫萝卜，可用作蔬菜，种子可入药 turnip; radish

啰（囉） luó ㄌㄨㄛˊ ［啰唣］（－zào）吵闹 to make noise

⇨ see also luō on p.427, luo on p.430

逻（邏） luó ㄌㄨㄛˊ 巡逻，巡察 to patrol

L

[逻辑]（外 *loanword*）1 思维的规律 logic (mode of reasoning)：这几句话不合～。*These few sentences are illogical.* 2 研究思维的形式和规律的科学。又叫论理学 logic (as a science of reasoning, also called 论理学) 3 客观的规律性 objective law: 符合事物发展的～ *follow natural logic*

猡（玀）luó ㄌㄨㄛˊ〈方 dialect〉猪猡，猪 pig

椤（欏）luó ㄌㄨㄛˊ see 桫椤 (suō—) at 桫 on page 628

锣（鑼）luó ㄌㄨㄛˊ 一种打击乐器，形状像铜盘，用槌子敲打，发出声音 gong：铜～ *copper gong* | 鸣～开道 *sound the gong to clear the way* | ～鼓喧天 *deafening sound of gongs and drums*

箩（籮）luó ㄌㄨㄛˊ 用竹子编的底方上圆的器具 bamboo basket (with a square bottom and round mouth)

觇（覼、**覶）luó ㄌㄨㄛˊ [觇缕]（—lǚ）逐条详尽地陈述 to state one by one in full detail

脶（腡）luó ㄌㄨㄛˊ 手指纹 fingerprint

骡（騾、*蠃）luó ㄌㄨㄛˊ（—子）家畜，由驴、马交配而生。鬃短，尾巴略扁，生命力强，一般没有生育能力。可以驮东西、拉车或供人骑 mule

螺 luó ㄌㄨㄛˊ ❶软体动物，有硬壳，壳上有旋纹，种类很多 spiral shell; snail：～蛳 *freshwater snail* | 田～ *field snail* | 海～ *sea snail* | 钉～ Oncomelania hupensis [螺丝] 应用螺旋原理做成的使物体固定或把两个物体连接起来的东西，有螺钉和螺母 screw [螺旋] 1 简单机械，圆柱体表面或物体孔眼里有像螺蛳壳纹理的螺纹 spiral; helix 2 螺旋形的 spiral：～桨 *propeller* ❷ same as “脶 (luó)”

倮 luǒ ㄌㄨㄛˇ same as “裸”

裸（*躶、*蠃）luǒ ㄌㄨㄛˇ 光着身子 naked; nude：～体 *nude; naked* | 赤～～ *stark-naked; undisguised* ⑤引没有东西包着的 bare; exposed：～线（没有外皮的电线）*bare wire* | ～子植物 *gymnosperm*

蓏 luǒ ㄌㄨㄛˇ 古书上指瓜类植物的果实 (in ancient Chinese texts) melon

瘰 luǒ ㄌㄨㄛˇ [瘰疬]（—lì）病名，由结核菌侵入淋巴结而引起，多发生在颈部或腋部，症状是出现硬块，溃烂后不易愈合 cervical scrofula

嬴 luǒ ㄌㄨㄛˇ see 蜾嬴 (guǒ—) at 蜾 on page 235

泺（濼）luò ㄌㄨㄛˋ 泺水，古水名，在今山东省济南 Luoshui (an ancient river, in today's Jinan, Shandong Province) [泺口] 地名，在山东省济南 Luokou (a place in Jinan, Shandong Province)

⇨ see also pō on p.510

跞（躒）luò ㄌㄨㄛˋ [卓跞] [卓荦] 卓绝 unsur-

L

passed; extraordinary：才华～ *with outstanding talent*

⇨ see also lì on p.395

荦(犖) luò ㄌㄨㄛˋ [荦荦]明显，分明 conspicuous; prominent：～大端 *major items; salient point*

洛 luò ㄌㄨㄛˋ ❶洛河，水名，在陕西省北部。又叫北洛河 Luohe River (also called 北洛河, in northern Shaanxi Province) ❷洛河，水名，发源于陕西省南部，流至河南省西部入黄河。古作"雒" Luohe River (originating from southern Shaanxi Province, flowing into Yellow River in western Henan Province, written as 雒 in ancient times) ❸姓 (surname) Luo

骆(駱) luò ㄌㄨㄛˋ 古书上指黑鬃的白马 (in ancient Chinese texts) black-maned white horse

[骆驼] (－tuo) 哺乳动物，反刍类，身体高大，背上有肉峰。能耐饥渴，适于负重物在沙漠中远行 camel

络(絡) luò ㄌㄨㄛˋ ❶像网子那样的东西 net-like objects：脉～ *arteries and veins; train of thought* | 橘～ *tangerine pith* | 丝瓜～ *loofah* ❷用网状物兜住，笼罩 to hold in place with a net; to enmesh：用络(lào)子～住 *hold in place with a string bag* ❸缠绕 to wind; to twist; to twine：～纱 *winding (in textile)* | ～线 *winding (in textile)*

[络绎] (－yì) 连续不断 in an endless stream：参观的人～不绝。*There is an endless stream of visitors.*

⇨ see also lào on p.382

珞 luò ㄌㄨㄛˋ see 瓔珞 (yīng－) at 瓔 on page 784

[珞巴族] 我国少数民族，参看附录四 the Lhoba people (one of the ethnic groups in China. See Appendix Ⅳ.)

烙 luò ㄌㄨㄛˋ see 炮烙 (páo－) at 炮 on page 494

⇨ see also lào on p.382

硌 luò ㄌㄨㄛˋ 山上的大石 large rock (on a mountain)

⇨ see also gè on p.207

落 luò ㄌㄨㄛˋ ❶掉下来，往下降 to fall; to drop; to descend：～泪 *shed tears* | 降～ *to fall; to land* | 太阳～山了。*The sun has set behind the hills.* ❷衰败 to decline; to be on the wane：没(mò)～ *declining* | 破～户 *impoverished household* ❸遗留在后面 to fall behind：～后 *fall/lag behind* | ～伍 *fall behind the ranks; out of date* | ～选 *fail to be chosen; lose an election* ❹停留 to stay; to stop over：安家～户 *(of people) settle down* | ～脚 *stop over; to stay* 引留下 to leave behind：不～痕迹 *leave no trace behind* ❺停留或聚居的地方 whereabouts; settlement：村～ *village* | 下～ *whereabouts* | 着～ *whereabouts* ❻归属 to fall to; to rest with：今天政权～在人民手里了。*Today, political power has fallen into the hands of the people.* ❼古代指庆祝建筑物完工的祭礼，后来建筑物完工称为落成 (ancient) construction completion ceremony (hence the term 落成 for the completion of a construction) ❽写下 to write down：～款 *names of the sender and the recipient written on a painting, gift, letter, etc.; write down such names* | ～账 *enter an item in account*

[落泊](－bó)[落魄](－pò)[落拓](－tuò) 1 潦倒失意 dejected; down and out 2 豪迈，不拘束 bold and generous; unconstrained

⇨ see also là on p.374, lào on p.383

雒 luò ㄌㄨㄛˋ ❶ same as "洛❷" ❷姓 (surname) Luo

摞 luò ㄌㄨㄛˋ ❶把东西重叠地往上放 to stack up; to pile up：把书～起来 *stack up books* ❷量词，用于重叠着放起来的东西 (measure word) stack; pile：一～砖 *a stack of bricks* | 一～碗 *a pile of bowls*

漯 luò ㄌㄨㄛˋ [漯河] 地名，在河南省 Luohe (a place in Henan Province)

⇨ see also tà on p.633

啰(囉) luo ·ㄌㄨㄛ see 偻啰 (lóu－) at 偻 on page 417

啰(囉) luo ·ㄌㄨㄛ ❶助词，作用大致和"了(le)❷"一样 auxiliary word, same in function as 了 (le)❷：你去就成～。*It will be fine if you are there.* ❷ see 喽啰 (lóu－) at 喽 on page 417

⇨ see also luō on p.427, luó on p.427

M ㄇ

M ㄇ

呒(嘸) ḿ ㄇ́ 〈方 dialect〉没有 none

呣 ḿ ㄇ́ （单纯的双唇鼻音）叹词，表示疑问 (exclamation) used to indicate query or doubt：～，你说什么？ *Mm? What did you say?*

呣 m̀ ㄇ̀ 叹词，表示答应 (exclamation) used in responses：～，我知道了。*Mm, I see.*

MA ㄇㄚ

孖 mā ㄇㄚ 〈方 dialect〉相连成对 joint pair：～仔（zǎi）（双胞胎）*twins*

⇨ see also zī on p.879

妈(媽) mā ㄇㄚ ❶称呼母亲 ㊂ mom; mum ❷对跟母亲同辈或年长的已婚女性的称呼 term of address for a married woman of one's mother's generation; elderly married woman：大～ *auntie (wife of father's elder brother; polite form of address for an elderly woman)* | 姑～ *aunt (father's married sister)*

蚂(螞) mā ㄇㄚ ［蚂螂］（－lang）〈方 dialect〉蜻蜓 dragonfly

⇨ see also mǎ on p.432, mà on p.433

抹 mā ㄇㄚ ❶擦 to wipe：～桌子 *wipe a table* ❷用手按着并向下移动 press and slide one's hand downwards：把帽子～下来 *slip off one's hat* | ～不下脸来（指碍于情面）*be unable or unwilling to do sth for fear of hurting sb's feelings*

⇨ see also mǒ on p.459, mò on p.460

摩 mā ㄇㄚ ［摩挲］（－sa）用手轻轻按着一下一下地移动 to rub gently：～孩子的头 *stroke the child's head*

⇨ see also mó on p.459

吗(嗎) má ㄇㄚˊ 〈方 dialect〉什么 what; something：干～呀？ *What are you doing?* | 该吃点～儿了。*It's time to eat something.*

⇨ see also mǎ on p.432, ma on p.433

麻(❶*蔴) má ㄇㄚˊ ❶草本植物，种类很多，有大麻、苎麻、苘（qǐng）麻、亚麻等等。茎皮纤维也叫麻，可用来制绳索、织布等 general term for hemp, flax, jute, ramie, etc. ［麻烦］（－fan）烦琐，费事 troublesome：这事真～。*This matter is really troublesome.* ❷像腿、臂被压后的那种不舒服的感觉 numb; tingling：腿～了。*The leg is numb.* | 手发～。*The hand* *has become numb.* ❸感觉不灵或全部丧失（㊥一木）insensible (to sth)［麻痹］1 身体的一部分因为神经系统的病变而发生知觉或运动的障碍 paralysis 2 失去警惕性 to let down one's guard：～大意 *careless; negligent*［麻醉］用药物或针刺使全身或局部暂时失去知觉 to anaesthetize ㊥用手段使人思想认识模糊，不能明辨是非 lull sb into a confused state ❹表面粗糙 (of surface) rough：这张纸一面光一面～。*This piece of paper is glossy on one side and matte on the other.*

马(馬) mǎ ㄇㄚˇ 家畜，头小，脸长，颈上有鬃，尾有长毛。供人骑或拉东西等 horse［马脚］指破绽（zhàn），漏洞 flaw; loophole：露出～来了 *showed the cloven hoof; exposed the flaw*［马上］副词，立刻 (adverb) immediately：我～就到。*I will be there right away.*

［马虎］（-hu）不认真 careless; slapdash：这事可不能～。*One mustn't be careless in this matter.*

吗(嗎) mǎ ㄇㄚˇ ［吗啡］（-fēi）（外 *loanword*）有机化合物，白色粉末，味苦，用鸦片制成。医药上用作镇痛剂 morphine

⇨ see also má on p.431, ma on p.433

犸(獁) mǎ ㄇㄚˇ ［猛犸］古脊椎动物，又叫毛象，像现代的象，全身有长毛，已绝种 mammoth (also called 毛象)

玛(瑪) mǎ ㄇㄚˇ ［玛瑙］（-nǎo）矿物名，质硬耐磨，颜色美丽，可做轴承、研钵、装饰品等 agate

码(碼) mǎ ㄇㄚˇ ❶（-子、-儿）代表数目的符号 sign indicating a number：数～ *numeral; number; digital* | 号～ *number* | 苏州～子（〡、〢、〣、〤、〨等）*Suzhou numerals (traditional number notation used by Chinese shopkeepers)* | 明～儿售货（在商品上标明价码出售）*sell sth with price clearly marked* ❷（-子）计算数目的用具，如砝码、筹码等 counting tool (such as weights, counters, chips) ❸量词，用于一件事或一类事 (measure word for things or kinds)：这是两～事。*These are two different issues.* ❹（外 *loanword*）英美制长度单位，1 码等于 3 英尺，合 0.914 4 米 (unit of measurement) yard ❺〈方 dialect〉摞（luò）起，垒起 to pile up：～砖头 *stack bricks up* | 小孩儿～积木。*Children play with toy blocks.*

蚂(螞) mǎ ㄇㄚˇ ［蚂蟥］（-huáng）"蛭"的俗称 leech (informal name for 蛭)［蚂蚁］（-yǐ）昆虫，身体小而长，多为黑色或褐色，在地下做窝，成群穴居 ant

⇨ see also mā on p.431, mà on p.433

杩(榪) mà ㄇㄚˋ ［杩头］床两头或门扇上下两端的横木 wooden head and foot board of a bed; crosspieces at top

M

and bottom of a door

祃(禡) mà ㄇㄚˋ 古代行军时，在军队驻扎的地方举行的祭礼 (in ancient times) sacrificial ritual held at a military camp

蚂(螞) mà ㄇㄚˋ [蚂蚱] (—zha) 蝗虫 locust (see 蝗 huáng on page 270 for reference)

⇨ see also mā on p.431, mǎ on p.432

骂(罵、*罵、*傌) mà ㄇㄚˋ ❶用粗野的话侮辱人 to curse; to swear at：不要～人。*Do not insult people.* ❷〈方 dialect〉斥责 to scold

么(△麽) ma ·ㄇㄚ same as "吗(ma)"

⇨ see also me on p.441, yāo on p.759

⇨ 麽 see also me 么 on p.441, mó on p.459

吗(嗎) ma ·ㄇㄚ 助词 auxiliary word ①表疑问或反问 used to express doubt or a rhetorical question：你听明白了～？*Do you understand what you've been told?* | 还要你来教我～？*Do you think I need you to tell me that?* ②用在句中停顿处 used to indicate a pause in a sentence：天要下雨～，我就坐车去。*If it rains, I'll take a bus.*

⇨ see also má on p.431, mǎ on p.432

嘛 ma ·ㄇㄚ 助词，表示很明显，事理就是如此（有时有提示意）(auxiliary word) used to indicate an obvious fact; sometimes used as a prompt：有意见就提～。*Do tell us your opinion if you disagree.* | 不会不要紧，边干边学～。*It's all right if you don't know how because you'll learn on the job.*

蟆(*蟇) ma ·ㄇㄚ see 蛤蟆 (há—) at 蛤 on page 237

MAI ㄇㄞ

埋 mái ㄇㄞˊ 把东西放在坑里用土盖上 to bury：掩～ *to bury* | ～地雷 *lay landmines* ㊀隐藏，使不显露 to hide：隐姓～名 *withdraw from public view by concealing one's identity* [埋伏] 在敌人将要经过的地方布置下军队，准备袭击 lie in ambush [埋没] (—mò) 使人才、功绩、作用等显露不出来 to stifle (sb's talent); to conceal (sb's achievement and role)：不要～人才 *do not stifle people's talents* [埋头] ㊀专心，下工夫 focus or work diligently on sth：～苦干 *keep one's nose to the grindstone*

⇨ see also mán on p.434

霾 mái ㄇㄞˊ 阴霾，空气中因悬浮着大量的烟、尘等微粒而形成的混浊现象 haze

买(買) mǎi ㄇㄞˇ 拿钱换东西，跟"卖"相对(㊈购—) to buy (opposite of 卖)：～戏票 *buy theatre tickets* | ～了一台电脑 *bought a computer* ㊀贿赂 to bribe：～通 *to bribe* [买办] 1

M

采购货物的人 (of goods) buyer 2 殖民地、半殖民地国家里替外国资本家在本国市场上经管商业、银行业、工矿业、运输业等等的中间人和经纪人 comprador [买卖]（—mai）生意，商业 business; commerce：做～ *engage in business* ㉠铺子 shop

荬(藚) mǎi ㄇㄞˇ see 苣荬菜 (qǔmai—) at 苣 on page 548

劢(勱) mài ㄇㄞˋ 努力 to strive

迈(邁) mài ㄇㄞˋ ❶抬起腿来跨步 to take a step; to stride: ～过去 *step over it* | ～了一大步 *took a big stride* | 向前～进 *march forward* ❷老（㊀老—）old：年～ *elderly* ❸（外 *loanword*）英里，用于机动车行驶速度。现也把千米（公里）说成迈 (for vehicle speed) mile (kilometre is also called 迈 now)

麦(麥) mài ㄇㄞˋ （—子）谷类作物，分大麦、小麦、燕麦等多种，籽实磨面供食用。通常专指小麦 cereal crop (barley, wheat, oats, etc., usually specifically refers to wheat)

唛(嘜) mài ㄇㄞˋ 译音用字。商标，进出口货物的包装上所做的标记 (transliterated loanword) brand mark; trademark

鿏(鿏) mài ㄇㄞˋ 人造的放射性金属元素，符号 Mt。meitnerium (Mt)

卖(賣) mài ㄇㄞˋ ❶拿东西换钱，跟"买"相对 to sell (opposite of 买)：～菜 *sell vegetables* ㉠出卖国家、民族或别人的利益 to betray：叛～ *to betray* | ～国贼 *traitor (to one's country)* ❷尽量使出（力气）put in one's all (effort, etc.)：～力 *spare no effort* | ～劲儿 *push oneself* ❸卖弄，显示、表现自己 to show off：～功 *show off one's merits* | ～乖 *show off one's cleverness* | ～弄才能 *show off one's talents*

脉(*脈、*衇、*衂) mài ㄇㄞˋ ❶分布在人和动物全身的血管 veins and arteries：动～ *artery* | 静～ *vein* ❷脉搏，动脉的跳动 pulse：诊～ *take one's pulse* ❸像血管那样分布的东西 sth that spreads out like blood vessels：山～ *mountain range* | 矿～ *(mineral) vein* | 叶～ *(leaf) vein, nerve*

⇨ see also mò on p.461

霢 mài ㄇㄞˋ [霢霂]（—mù）小雨 light rain; drizzle

MAN ㄇㄢ

嫚 mān ㄇㄢ 〈方 dialect〉女孩子 girl

⇨ see also màn on p.436

颟(顢) mān ㄇㄢ [颟顸]（—han）1 不明事理 muddle-headed：糊涂～ *muddle-headed* 2 漫不经心 careless：那人太～，做事靠不住。*That person is too careless to rely on.*

埋 mán ㄇㄢˊ [埋怨] 因为事情不如意而对人或事物表示不满，责怪 to blame：他自己不小心，还～别人。*It's his own fault for being careless, but he's blaming others.*

⇨ see also mái on p.433

蛮(蠻) mán ㄇㄢˊ ❶粗野，不通情理（㊟野－）rough; unreasonable: ～横(hèng) *rude and unreasonable* | ～不讲理 *being unreasonable* | 胡搅～缠 *pester sb with unreasonable demands* ㊂愣，强悍 rash; reckless: ～劲 *brute strength* | ～干 *act rashly* ❷我国古代称南方的民族 (ancient) non-Han ethnic groups in the south of China ❸〈方 dialect〉副词，很 (adverb) very: ～好 *quite good* | ～快 *quite fast*

谩(謾) mán ㄇㄢˊ 欺骗，蒙蔽 to deceive; to hide the truth from sb

⇨ see also màn on p.436

蔓 mán ㄇㄢˊ [蔓菁](－jing)草本植物，即芜菁，叶狭长，花黄色，块根扁圆形。块根也叫蔓菁，可以吃 turnip (same as 芜菁); turnip root (also 蔓菁)

⇨ see also màn on p.436, wàn on p.675

馒(饅) mán ㄇㄢˊ [馒头](－tou)一种用发面蒸成的食品，无馅 *mantou* (a steamed paste with no filling)

鳗(鰻) mán ㄇㄢˊ [鳗鲡](－lí)鱼名，又叫白鳝，身体前圆后扁，背鳍、臀鳍和尾鳍连在一起。生活在淡水中，到海里产卵 European eel (also called 白鳝)

鬘 mán ㄇㄢˊ 形容头发美 (of a person's hair) beautiful

瞒(瞞) mán ㄇㄢˊ 隐瞒；隐藏实情，不让别人知道 to conceal facts from sb: 这事不必～他。*There's no need to keep this matter from him.*

鞔 mán ㄇㄢˊ ❶把皮革固定在鼓框的周围，做成鼓面 to cover a drum with leather: 牛皮可以～鼓。*Cowhide can be used for making drums.* ❷把布蒙在鞋帮上 to cover the upper of a shoe with cloth: ～鞋 *fix a piece of cloth on a shoe upper*

满(滿) mǎn ㄇㄢˇ ❶全部充实，没有余地 full: 会场里人都～了。*The venue is full of people.* | ～地都是绿油油的庄稼。*The entire land is covered with bright green crops.* | ～口答应 *grant the request without hesitation* [满意]愿望满足或符合自己的意见 satisfied; pleased: 这样办，他很～。*He's very pleased that it's been done this way.* [满足] 1 觉得够了 satisfied: 他并不～于现有的成绩。*He's not satisfied with the current results.* 2 使人觉得在所需求的方面不缺什么了 to satisfy: ～人民的需要 *satisfy the needs of the people* [自满]不虚心，骄傲 complacent; proud ❷到了一定的限度 to reach a certain limit: 假期已～。*The holidays are over.* | ～了一年。*It has been a whole year.* ❸(斟酒)使满 to fill (a cup or glass with liquor): ～上一杯 *fill a cup* ❹副词，十分，

完全 (adverb) very; totally：积极性～高 *very enthusiastic* | ～以为不错 *really believe that it was quite good* | ～不在乎 *totally unconcerned*
[满族] 我国少数民族，参看附录四 the Manchu people (one of the ethnic groups in China. See Appendix Ⅳ.)

螨(蟎) mǎn ㄇㄢˇ 节肢动物，身体小，多为圆形或卵形。种类很多，有的传染疾病，危害农作物 mite

蔄(蔄) màn ㄇㄢˋ ❶用于地名 used in place names：～山镇（在山东省文登）*Manshanzhen (in Wendeng, Shandong Province)* ❷姓 (surname) Man

曼 màn ㄇㄢˋ ❶延长 to prolong; to stretch：～声而歌 *to sing long-drawn-out notes* ❷柔美 graceful：轻歌～舞 *soft singing and graceful dancing*

谩(謾) màn ㄇㄢˋ 轻慢，没有礼貌 to slight (sb); rude：～骂 *hurl abuse (at sb)*
⇨ see also mán on p.435

墁 màn ㄇㄢˋ 用砖或石块铺地面 to lay the floor/ground with tiles or stones：花砖～地 *lay the floor with patterned tiles*

蔓 màn ㄇㄢˋ 义同"蔓"（wàn），多用于合成词，如蔓草、蔓延等 same in meaning as 蔓 (wàn), often used in compounds, e.g. 蔓草，蔓延 [蔓延] 形容像蔓草一样地不断扩展滋生 to spread (like weeds)
⇨ see also mán on p.435, wàn on p.675

幔 màn ㄇㄢˋ （－子）悬挂起来用作遮挡的布、绸子等 curtain：布～ *cloth curtain* | 窗～ *(window) curtain*

漫 màn ㄇㄢˋ ❶水过满，漾出来 (of liquid) to overflow：河水～出来了。*The river overflowed its banks.* ㊞淹没 to flood：水不深，只～到脚面。*The water isn't deep; it only comes up to the feet.* | 大水～过房子了。*The floodwater has covered the houses.* ❷满，遍 all over：～山遍野 *all over the mountains and plains; (figurative) many* | 大雾～天。*The sky is shrouded in heavy fog.* ❸没有限制，没有约束 unlimited; unrestrained：～谈 *talk randomly* | ～不经心 *careless; negligent* | ～无边际 *boundless; without limit* [漫长] 时间长或路程远 (of time or journey) long：～的岁月 *a long period of time* | ～的道路 *long road* ❹莫，不要 do not：～说 *do not say* | ～道 *do not say*

慢 màn ㄇㄢˋ ❶迟缓，速度低，跟"快"相对 slow (opposite of 快)：～车 *slow train/bus* | ～～地走 *walk slowly* | 我的表～五分钟。*My watch is five minutes slow.* ❷态度冷淡，不热情 (of attitude) cold：怠～ *give sb the cold shoulder; (polite expression) neglect a guest* | 傲～ *arrogant*

嫚 màn ㄇㄢˋ 侮辱，怠慢 to insult; to despise
⇨ see also mān on p.434

缦(縵) màn ㄇㄢˋ 没有彩色花纹的丝织品 plain

M

silk fabric

熳 màn ㄇㄢˋ [烂熳] see 烂漫 at 烂 on page 378

镘（鏝） màn ㄇㄢˋ 抹（mò）墙用的工具 trowel

MANG ㄇㄤ

牤（犆）** māng ㄇㄤ 〈方 dialect〉牤牛，公牛 bull

邙 máng ㄇㄤˊ [邙山] 山名，在河南省西北部 Mount Mangshan (in northwestern Henan Province)

芒 máng ㄇㄤˊ ❶某些禾本科植物籽实壳上的细刺 prickles on the seeds of certain plants ❷像芒的东西 prickle-like things: 光～ *rays of light; brilliance* | 锋～ *(of a knife or weapon) tip; cutting edge; (figurative) vigour and talent displayed* ❸草本植物，秋天开花，黄褐色。叶细长有尖，可用来造纸、编鞋 Chinese silver grass

忙 máng ㄇㄤˊ ❶事情多，没空闲 busy: 工作～ *busy with work* | ～碌 *busy* ❷急（㊥急一）urgently; quickly: 不慌不～ *take one's time* | 先别～着下结论。*Don't jump to a conclusion.* ❸急速地做 do sth quickly: 大家都在～生产。*All of us are busy with production.*

杧 máng ㄇㄤˊ [杧果] 常绿乔木，生长在热带。果实也叫杧果，形状像肾，可以吃。也作"芒果" mango (also written as 芒果); mango tree

盲 máng ㄇㄤˊ 瞎，看不见东西 blind; visually impaired: ～人 *visually impaired person* | ～道 *tactile paving for the visually impaired* | 夜～ *nyctalopia; night blindness* ㊑对某种事物不能辨认的人 a person who is ignorant of sth: 文～ *illiterate* | 色～ *achromatopsia; color blindness* | 计算机～ *computer illiterate* | 扫～ *eradicate illiteracy* [盲从] 自己没有原则，没有见地，盲目随着别人 to follow blindly [盲目] ㊑对事情认识不清楚 uninformed, aimless: ～的行动是不会有好结果的。*Blind actions will not have good consequences.*

氓 máng ㄇㄤˊ [流氓] 原指无业游民，后来指品质恶劣，不务正业，为非作歹的坏人 (originally referring to an unemployed vagrant) hooligan

⇨ see also méng on p.445

茫 máng ㄇㄤˊ ❶对事理全无所知，找不到头绪 totally ignorant; directionless: 迷～ *confused; directionless* | ～然无知 *ignorant* | ～无头绪 *be at a loss; not know where to begin* ❷形容水势浩渺 (of body of water) vast [茫茫] 面积大，看不清边沿 vast; boundless: 大海～ *the vast sea* | 雾气～ *boundless fog*

硭 máng ㄇㄤˊ [硭硝] 矿物，现作"芒硝"，成分是硫酸钠，无色或白色晶体。可用来制玻璃、造纸等，医药上用作泻剂 mirabilite; crystalized sodium sulfate (now written as 芒硝)

M

铓(鋩) máng ㄇㄤˊ ❶刀、剑等的尖端 (of knives, swords, etc.) tip; point ❷ 铓锣，一种民间打击乐器，流行于云南省傣族和景颇族地区 a percussion instrument popular among the Dai and Jingpo peoples in Yunnan Province

尨 máng ㄇㄤˊ ❶毛多而长的狗 a dog with long, thick coat ❷ 杂色 mottled

⇨ see also méng on p.445

庬 máng ㄇㄤˊ ❶大，厚重 big; hefty ❷姓 (surname) Mang

牻 máng ㄇㄤˊ 毛色黑白相间的牛 black and white piebald cow

莽 mǎng ㄇㄤˇ ❶密生的草 thick grass：草～ *uncultivated land; (old, figurative) common people* ❷ 粗鲁，冒失 uncouth; rash：～汉 *boorish fellow* | ～撞 *careless and rash* | 鲁～ *rash; hot- headed*

漭 mǎng ㄇㄤˇ ［漭漭］形容水广阔无边 (of a body of water) boundless

蟒 mǎng ㄇㄤˇ 一种蛇，又叫蚺蛇，无毒，身体大，背有黄褐色斑纹，腹白色，常生活在近水的森林里 python (also called 蚺蛇)

MAO ㄇㄠ

猫(*貓) māo ㄇㄠ 哺乳动物，面呈圆形，身体长，瞳孔随光线强弱而缩小放大，脚有利爪，善跳跃，会捉老鼠 cat

⇨ see also máo on p.439

毛 máo ㄇㄠˊ ❶动植物的皮上所生的丝状物 (on animals and plants) hair ❷像毛的东西 hair-like object ① 指谷物等 plants; (especially) crops：不～（未开垦不长庄稼）之地 *uncultivatable land* ② 衣物等上长的霉菌 mould (on clothes, etc.)：老没见太阳，东西都长～了。*The sun hasn't come out for a long time and everything's gone mouldy.* ❸ 粗糙，没有加工的 rough; unprocessed：～坯 *semi-finished product; blank* ❹ 不是纯净的 gross：～重 *gross weight* | ～利 *gross profit* ❺ 小 small：～孩子 *small child* | ～～雨 *drizzle* ❻ 行动慌忙 hurried; impetuous：～手～脚 *impetuous* ❼ 惊慌失措 out of one's wits：把他吓～了。*He was shocked out of his wits.* | 心里发～ *very scared* ❽ 货币贬值 (of currency) devaluation：钱～了。*Money is worth less.* ❾ 角，一圆钱的十分之一 mao (one-tenth of 1 *yuan*)

［毛南族］我国少数民族，参看附录四 the Maonan people (one of the ethnic groups in China. See Appendix Ⅳ.)

牦(*犛、*氂) máo ㄇㄠˊ ［牦牛］一种牛，身体两旁和四肢外侧有长毛，尾毛很长。产于我国青藏高原地区，当地人用来拉犁、驮运货物 domestic yak

旄 máo ㄇㄠˊ 古代用牦（máo）牛尾装饰的旗子 (ancient) flag adorned with yak's tail

〈古 ancient〉also same as 耄 (mào)

酕 máo ㄇㄠˊ [酕醄](—táo) 大醉的样子 blind drunk

髦 máo ㄇㄠˊ 古代称幼儿垂在前额的短头发 (ancient) fringe (on a child's forehead) [时髦] 时兴的 trendy; fashionable

矛 máo ㄇㄠˊ 古代兵器，在长柄的一端装有金属枪头 (ancient weapon) spear [矛盾] ㊕ 1 言语或行为前后抵触，对立的事物互相排斥 contradiction (disagreement between statements, actions, facts, etc.) 2 指事物内部各个对立面之间的互相依赖又互相排斥的关系 contradiction (unity of opposites)

茅 máo ㄇㄠˊ 茅草，草本植物，又叫白茅，叶条形。可用来覆盖屋顶或制绳索 cogongrass (also called 白茅)

蝥 máo ㄇㄠˊ [斑蝥] 昆虫，腿细长，鞘翅上有黄黑色斑纹。可入药 blister beetle

蟊 máo ㄇㄠˊ 吃苗根的害虫 plant pest (that feeds on the roots of seedlings) [蟊贼] ㊙ 对人民有害的人 social vermin

茆 máo ㄇㄠˊ same as "茅"

猫(*貓) máo ㄇㄠˊ [猫腰] 弯腰 bend one's back

⇨ see also māo on p.438

锚(錨) máo ㄇㄠˊ 铁制的停船器具，有钩爪，用铁链连在船上，抛到水底，可以使船停稳 anchor

冇 mǎo ㄇㄠˇ 〈方 dialect〉没有 not to do; not to have

卯(*夘、*戼) mǎo ㄇㄠˇ ❶ 地支的第四位 *mao* (the fourth of the twelve Earthly Branches, a system used in the Chinese calendar) ❷ 卯时，指早晨五点到七点 *mao* (the period from 5 a.m. to 7 a.m.) ❸ (一子、一儿) 器物接榫(sǔn)的地方凹入的部分 mortise：对～眼 *fit into the mortise* | 凿个～儿 *chisel a mortise*

峁 mǎo ㄇㄠˇ 〈方 dialect〉小山包 hillock：下了一道坡，又上一道～ *went down the slope and then up the hillock again*

泖 mǎo ㄇㄠˇ 水面平静的小湖 small, calm lake [泖湖] 古湖名，在今上海市松江西部 Maohu Lake (an ancient lake, in the west of today's Songjiang, Shanghai Municipality) [泖桥] 地名，在上海市 Maoqiao (a place in Shanghai Municipality)

昴 mǎo ㄇㄠˇ 星宿名，二十八宿之一 *mao* (one of the twenty-eight constellations in ancient Chinese astronomy)

铆(鉚) mǎo ㄇㄠˇ 用钉子把金属物连在一起 (of metals) to rivet：～钉 *a rivet* | ～接 *rivet bonding* | ～工 *riveting; riveter (worker)*

芼 mào ㄇㄠˋ 拔取(菜、草) to pull up (vegetables or grass)

眊 mào ㄇㄠˋ 眼睛看不清楚 poor eyesight

耄 mào ㄇㄠˋ 年老，八九十岁的年纪 elderly (in one's

eighties or nineties)：～耋（dié）之年 *advanced age*

皃 mào ㄇㄠˋ 〈古 ancient〉same as "貌"

貌 mào ㄇㄠˋ ❶相貌，长（zhǎng）相（㊀容—）appearance; features：美～ *good looks* | 不能以～取人 *cannot judge a person by his/her appearance* ❷外表，表面 appearance; exterior：～合神离 *apparent congeniality belying real differences* | ～似强大 *appear strong and powerful* ㊀样子 appearance：全～ *overall view; whole picture* | 概～ *general picture* | 原～ *original appearance* ❸古书注解里表示状态用的字，如"飘飘：飞貌"等 used in annotations in ancient books to indicate state or condition

茂 mào ㄇㄠˋ 茂盛（shèng），草木旺盛 luxuriant：～密 *thick and luxuriant* | 繁～ *lush* | 根深叶～ *to have deep roots and lush foliage; (figurative) be well established and thriving* ㊀丰富而美好 abundant and good：图文并～ *with excellent texts and illustrations* | 声情并～ *with rich vocals and emotions*

冒（*冐） mào ㄇㄠˋ ❶向外透，往上升 to emit; to rise：～泡 *to bubble* | ～烟 *emit smoke* | ～火 *be furious* | ～尖 *go over the brim; over (a round figure); (figurative) be conspicuous; emerge* | ～头ㄦ *emerge; over (a round figure)* ❷不顾（恶劣的环境或危险等）to disregard bad conditions, danger, etc.：～雨 *brave the rain* | ～险 *take risk* ❸不加小心，鲁莽，冲撞 careless; rash：～进 *make a premature advance* | ～昧 *(humble speech) be presumptuous* | ～犯 *to offend*［冒失］鲁莽，轻率 rash; hasty ❹用假的充当真的，假托 to forge; to fake：～牌 *(of brands and trademarks) fake; (figurative) impostor* | ～名 *assume another person's name* ❺姓 (surname) Mao

⇨ see also mò on p.461

帽（*帽） mào ㄇㄠˋ ❶帽子 hat; cap ❷（～ㄦ）作用或形状像帽子的东西 sth that resembles a cap in usage or appearance：螺丝～ㄦ *screw head* | 笔～ㄦ *pen cap*

瑁 mào ㄇㄠˋ see 玳瑁 (dài—) at 玳 on page 112

贸（貿） mào ㄇㄠˋ ❶交换财物 to trade：抱布～丝 *carry money to buy silk (from a girl in order to strike up a conversation) (布 here refers to ancient Chinese cash.)*［贸易］商业活动 trade：国际～ *international trade* ❷冒冒失失或轻率的样子 ㊀rash; hasty：～然参加 *take part without thinking* | ～～然来 *arrive without warning*

袤 mào ㄇㄠˋ 南北距离的长度 distance between north and south：广～数千里。*The length and breadth measure several thousand li.*

楙 mào ㄇㄠˋ ❶即木瓜 papaya; pawpaw (same as 木瓜) ❷(ancient) same as "茂"

瞀 mào ㄇㄠˋ ❶目眩，看不清楚 with blurred vision ❷精神昏乱（㊣—乱）dazed and confused

懋 mào ㄇㄠˋ ❶努力，勉励 to work hard; to encourage ❷盛大 grand

鄚 mào ㄇㄠˋ (formerly pronounced mò)［鄚州］地名，在河北省任丘 Maozhou (a place in Renqiu, Hebei Province)

ME ㄇㄜ

么(△麽) me ·ㄇㄜ ❶词尾 suffix: 怎～ *how; what; however* | 那～ *then* | 多～ *how; how very* | 这～ *so; like that; this way* | 什～ *what* ❷助词，用在句中停顿处 (auxiliary word) used as a mid-sentence pause: 不让你去～，你又偏要去。*I do not want you to go, but you still insist on going.*

⇨ see also ma on p.433, yāo on p.759

⇨ 麽 see also ma 么 on p.433, mó on p.459

MEI ㄇㄟ

没 méi ㄇㄟˊ ❶没有，无 not to have: 他～哥哥。*He does not have an older brother.* | 我～那本书。*I do not have that book.* ㊉表示估量或比较，不够，不如 (for estimate or comparison) not as: 他～（不够）一米八高。*He is shorter than 1.8 metres.* | 汽车～（不如）飞机快。*A car is not as fast as a plane.* ❷副词，没有，不曾，未 (adverb) not; not yet: 事情～处理完。*The work is not finished.* | 衣服～干。*The clothes are not dried.*

⇨ see also mò on p.460

玫 méi ㄇㄟˊ ［玫瑰］(—gui) 落叶灌木，枝上有刺。花有紫红色、白色等多种，香味浓，可以做香料，花和根可入药 beach rose

枚 méi ㄇㄟˊ ❶树干 (of trees) branch: 伐其条～ *cut down the branches and slender stems* ❷古代士兵衔于口中以禁喧声的用具 (ancient) a gag (soldiers put in their mouths to keep quiet): 衔～疾走 *forced march with gags in their mouths* ❸量词，相当于"个" (measure word) equivalent to 个: 三～勋章 *three medals* ［枚举］一件一件地举出来 to enumerate: 不胜～ *too many to enumerate*

眉 méi ㄇㄟˊ ❶眉毛，眼上额下的毛 eyebrow: ～飞色舞 *beam with delight* | ～开眼笑 *beam with joy* (see picture of 头 on page 660)［眉目］借指事情的头绪或事物的条理 (figurative) thread of sth complicated; the logic of a matter: 有点儿～了 *begin to see a little light* | ～不清楚。*The logic is unclear.* ❷书眉，书页上端的空白 (of pages) top margin: ～批 *marginalia at the top of a page*

郿 méi ㄇㄟˊ 郿县，在陕西省。今作"眉县" Meixian (in Shaanxi Province, now written as

眉县)

嵋 méi ㄇㄟˊ see 峨嵋 (é—) at 峨 on page 157

猸 méi ㄇㄟˊ (一子)哺乳动物，即鼬獾，又叫白猸，像猫而小，身体棕灰色，脸上有白斑 Chinese ferret-badger (same as 鼬獾，also called 白猸)

湄 méi ㄇㄟˊ 河岸，水滨 river bank; waterside

瑂 méi ㄇㄟˊ 一种像玉的美石 a jade-like stone

楣 méi ㄇㄟˊ 门框上边的横木 lintel (see picture of 房屋的构造 on page 170)

镅(鎇) méi ㄇㄟˊ 人造的放射性金属元素，符号 Am。americium (Am)

鹛(鶥) méi ㄇㄟˊ 鸟名，通常指画眉，羽毛多为棕褐色，翅短，嘴尖，尾巴长，叫的声音好听 melodious laughingthrush

莓 méi ㄇㄟˊ 指某些果实很小、聚生在球形花托上的植物，常见的是草莓 berry

梅(*楳、*槑) méi ㄇㄟˊ 落叶乔木，初春开花，有白、红等颜色，分五瓣，香味浓，果实味酸 Chinese plum

脢 méi ㄇㄟˊ (一子)〈方 dialect〉猪、牛等脊椎两旁的条状瘦肉，即里脊 tenderloin (same as 里脊)

酶 méi ㄇㄟˊ 有机化合物的一大类，对生物化学变化起催化作用，消化食物、发酵就是靠酶的作用 enzyme

霉(❷黴) méi ㄇㄟˊ ❶衣物、食品等受了潮热长霉菌 to go mouldy: ～烂 *be spoiled by mildew* | 发～ *go mouldy* ❷霉菌，真菌的一类，常寄生或腐生在食物或衣物的表面，呈细丝状，有曲霉、青霉等 mould (a fungus)

媒 méi ㄇㄟˊ 撮合男女婚事的人(㊀一妁 shuò) matchmaker ㊂ 使双方发生关系的人或物 go-between; intermedium: ～介 *medium; intermedium* | ～质 *medium* | 传～ *media; intermedium* [媒体]指传播信息的工具，如报刊、广播、电视等 the media

煤 méi ㄇㄟˊ ❶又叫煤炭，黑色或黑褐色固体，成分以碳为主，是古代植物压埋在地下，在缺氧高压条件下，年久变化而成的，是重要的燃料和化工原料 coal (also called 煤炭) ❷〈方 dialect〉(一子)烟气凝结的黑灰 soot: 锅～子 *soot on the bottom of a pot*

糜(穈)** méi ㄇㄟˊ (一子)即穄 broomcorn millet (same as 穄) (see 穄 jì on page 294 for reference)

⇨ see also mí on p.448

每 měi ㄇㄟˇ ❶指全体中的任何一个或一组 each; every: ～人 *each person* | ～回 *each time* | ～次 *each time* | ～三天 *every three days* | ～一分钱 *each cent* ❷指反复的动作中的任何一次或一组 every: ～战必胜 *victorious in every battle* | ～逢十五日出版 *be published on the fifteenth of each*

month [每每]副词，常常 (adverb) always：他工作很忙，～干到深夜。*He is very busy at work and he always works until late at night.*

美 měi ㄇㄟˇ ❶好，善 good：～德 *virtue* | ～意 *goodwill* | ～貌 *(of a person) beautiful (appearance)* | ～景 *beautiful scenery* | 尽善尽～ *flawless* | 物～价廉 *good products at low prices* ❷赞美，称赞，以为好 to praise：～称 *laudatory title* | ～言 *put in a good word; fine words* ❸使美、好看 to make attractive; to beautify：～容 *have beauty treatment* | ～发（fà）*have one's hair done* ❹〈方 dialect〉得意，高兴 be complacent; be happy：～滋滋的 *be pleased with oneself* | 得了个满分，瞧把他～的。*He got full marks; see how pleased he is with himself.* ❺指美洲，包括北美洲和南美洲，世界七大洲中的两个洲 the Americas

渼 měi ㄇㄟˇ ❶波纹 ripple ❷用于地名 used in place names：～陂（bēi）村（在江西省吉安）*Meibeicun (in Ji'an, Jiangxi Province)*

媄 měi ㄇㄟˇ 女子貌美 (of women) beautiful

镁(鎂) měi ㄇㄟˇ 金属元素，符号 Mg，银白色，燃烧时能发强光。镁铝合金可制飞机、宇宙飞船等 magnesium (Mg)

浼 měi ㄇㄟˇ ❶污染 to contaminate ❷恳托 to request; ask a favour of sb

妹 mèi ㄇㄟˋ ❶（一子）称同父母比自己年纪小的女子 ㊀ younger sister ❷对比自己年纪小的同辈女性的称呼 sister (used to address younger female of one's generation)：表～ *younger female first cousin*

昧 mèi ㄇㄟˋ ❶昏，糊涂，不明白 muddle-headed; ignorant：愚～ *uneducated; ignorant* | 蒙～ *uncivilized; ignorant* | 冒～ *(often humble speech) be presumptuous* ❷隐藏，隐瞒 to hide; to conceal：拾金不～ *not pocket money one picks up*

寐 mèi ㄇㄟˋ 睡着（zháo）to fall asleep：假～ *take a catnap* | 夜不能～ *cannot fall asleep at night* | 梦～以求 *crave sth day and night*

魅 mèi ㄇㄟˋ 传说中的鬼怪 (in Chinese legend) ghost and monster：鬼～ *ghosts and monsters* [魅力] 很能吸引人的力量 charm; glamour

袂 mèi ㄇㄟˋ 衣袖 (of garment) sleeve：联～（结伴）赴津 *go to Tianjin together* [分袂] 离别 to part; to separate

媚 mèi ㄇㄟˋ ❶巴结，逢迎 to curry favour with; to fawn on：～俗 *appeal to vulgar taste* | 献～ *ingratiate oneself with sb* | 奴颜～骨 *obsequious* ❷美好，可爱 lovely：妩～ *lovely; charming* | 春光明～ *beautiful and bright spring day*

MEN ㄇㄣ

闷(悶) mēn ㄇㄣ ❶因气压低或空气不流通而

引起的不舒服的感觉 stuffy：天气～热。*The weather is hot and stuffy.* | 这屋子矮，又没有窗子，太～了。*This low and windowless house is too stuffy.* ❷呆在屋里不出门 to stay indoors and not go out：别总～在家里，多出去走走。*You should go out more instead of staying at home all the time.* ❸密闭 to cover tightly：茶刚泡上，～一会儿再喝。*The tea has just been made; let it steep a while before drinking it.* ❹〈方 dialect〉声音不响亮 (of voice) low; soft：这人说话～声～气。*This person speaks so softly.*

⇨ see also mèn on p.445

门（門） mén ㄇㄣˊ ❶（～儿）建筑物、车船等的出入口。又指安在出入口上能开关的装置 door; gate：防盗～ *security door* | ～镜 *peephole* ⊛门径，诀窍 approach; way：摸不着～儿 *cannot find the right approach* | 窍～儿 *key (to a complicated problem); tactic* ❷（～儿）形状或作用像门的东西 sth that resembles a door in usage or appearance：电～ *electric switch* | 闸～ *sluice gate; valve* | 球～ *goal* ❸家族或家族的一支 family; branch of a family：一～老小 *the whole family* | 长（zhǎng）～长子 *the eldest son of the eldest branch of the family* ❹一般事物的分类 category：分～别类 *group into categories* ❺生物的分类单位之一，在"界"之下、"纲"之上 phylum：被子植物～ *angiospermae* | 脊索动物～ *chordata* ❻学术思想或宗教的派别 school of academic thought or religion：儒～ *Confucianism* | 佛～ *Buddhism* ❼量词，用于炮、功课、技术和亲戚、婚姻等 (measure word) used for cannons, subjects, skills, relatives, marriages, etc.：一～炮 *a cannon* | 一～手艺 *a skill* | 一～功课 *a subject* | 两～亲戚 *two groups of relatives* ❽事件，多指负面的事件 (often of scandals) case：学历～ *qualifications scandal* | 考试～ *exam scandal*

［门巴族］我国少数民族，参看附录四 the Monba people (one of the ethnic groups in China. See Appendix Ⅳ.)

扪（捫） mén ㄇㄣˊ 按，摸 to press; to touch：～心自问（反省）*search one's soul*

钔（鍆） mén ㄇㄣˊ 人造的放射性金属元素，符号 Md。mendelevium (Md)

璊（璊） mén ㄇㄣˊ 赤色的玉 red jade

亹 mén ㄇㄣˊ ［亹源］回族自治县，在青海省。今作"门源" Menyuan, a Hui Autonomous County (in Qinghai Province, now written as 门源)

⇨ see also wěi on p.682

闷 mèn ㄇㄣˋ ❶〈方 dialect〉水从地下冒出 (of water) to emerge from beneath the ground ❷用于地名 used in place names：～塘（在广西壮族自治区宾阳）*Mentang (in Binyang, Guangxi Zhuang Autonomous Region)*

⇨ see also qǐ on p.521

M

闷(悶) mèn ㄇㄣˋ ❶心烦，不痛快 depressed; bored：～得慌 *feel bored and restless* | ～～不乐 *unhappy* ❷密闭，不透气 airtight：～子车 *boxcar*

⇨ see also mēn on p.443

焖(燜) mèn ㄇㄣˋ 盖紧锅盖，用微火把饭菜煮熟 to cook (slowly in a covered pot)：～饭 *cook rice over a slow fire*

懑(懣) mèn ㄇㄣˋ ❶烦闷 unhappy ❷愤慨，生气 angry：愤～ *resentful*

们(們) men ·ㄇㄣ 词尾，表人的复数 (suffix) used to indicate more than one person：你～ *you* | 咱～ *we; us* | 他～ *they; them* | 学生～ *students* | 师徒～ *masters and apprentices*

MENG ㄇㄥ

蒙(❶❷矇) mēng ㄇㄥ ❶欺骗(㊣－骗) to cheat; to lie：别～人。*Don't lie.* | 谁也～不住他。*Nobody can pull the wool over his eyes.* ❷胡乱猜测 to make a wild guess：这回叫你～对了。*You've guessed correctly this time.* ❸昏迷 to lose consciousness：他被球打～了。*He was knocked out by the ball.*

⇨ see also méng on p.446, měng on p.447

尨 méng ㄇㄥˊ [尨茸]（－róng）蓬松 fluffy

⇨ see also máng on p.438

氓(**甿) méng ㄇㄥˊ〈古 ancient〉民（特指外来的）。也作"萌" common people (specifically from other places)(also written as 萌)

⇨ see also máng on p.437

虻(*蝱) méng ㄇㄥˊ 昆虫，身体灰黑色，翅透明，生活在野草丛里，雄的吸植物汁液，雌的吸人、畜的血。种类很多 horsefly：牛～ *horsefly; gadfly*

郿(鄳) méng ㄇㄥˊ 古地名，在今河南省罗山一带 Meng (an ancient place, in today's Luoshan, Henan Province)

萌 méng ㄇㄥˊ 萌芽，植物生芽 to germinate; to sprout ㊐开始发生 to begin to happen：知者（有见识的人）见于未～。*A wise man foresees something before it happens.* | 故态复～(多用于贬义) *back to the old state (often disapproving)*

〈古 ancient〉also same as 氓 (méng)

盟 méng ㄇㄥˊ ❶旧时指宣誓缔约，现多指团体和团体、阶级和阶级或国和国的联合 (old) to swear alliance; (now) alliance：联～ *alliance; coalition* | 同～ *to ally; alliance* | ～国 *allied country* ❷发（誓）to swear (an oath)：～个誓 *swear an oath* ❸内蒙古自治区的行政区划单位。包括若干旗、县、市 league (an administrative division in Inner Mongolia Autonomous Region)

蒙(❹濛、❺矇、❻懞) méng ㄇㄥˊ ❶没有知识，愚昧 ignorant：启～ *impart rudimentary knowledge; to enlighten* | 发～ *teach a child to read and write* | ～昧 *uncivilized; ignorant* ❷覆盖 to cover：～头盖脑 *cover one's head* | ～上一张纸 *cover with a piece of paper* [蒙蔽] 隐瞒事实，欺骗 conceal the truth; to deceive ❸受 to be subjected to：～难（nàn）*(of famous, high-status people) suffer a catastrophe* | 承～招待，感谢之至。*Thank you very much for hosting.* ❹形容雨点细小㊀used to describe very light rain：～～细雨 *light drizzling rain* [空蒙] 形容景色迷茫 used to describe a blurry scene：山色～ *indistinct mountainous scenery* ❺眼睛失明 blind [蒙眬] 目不明 bleary：睡眼～ *sleepy-eyed* ❻朴实敦厚 simple and honest ❼姓 (surname) Meng

⇨ see also mēng on p.445, měng on p.447

嵘 méng ㄇㄥˊ 山名 name of a mountain

幪 méng ㄇㄥˊ see 帡幪 (píng—) at 帡 on page 509

檬 méng ㄇㄥˊ see 柠檬 (níng—) at 柠 on page 481

曚 méng ㄇㄥˊ [曚昽]（—lóng）日光不明 (of sunlight) not bright; dim

朦 méng ㄇㄥˊ [朦胧]（—lóng）1 月光不明 (of moonlight) not bright; hazy 2 不清楚，模糊 unclear; indistinct：烟雾～ *hazy smog*

鹲(鸏) méng ㄇㄥˊ 鸟名，身体大，嘴大而直，灰色或白色，尾部有长羽毛，生活在热带海洋上，捕食鱼类 tropicbird

礞 méng ㄇㄥˊ [礞石] 岩石名，有青礞石和金礞石两种，可入药 schist (including chlorite schist and mica-schist, can be used in traditional Chinese medicine)

艨 méng ㄇㄥˊ [艨艟]（—chōng）古代的一种战船 a kind of warship in ancient times

甍 méng ㄇㄥˊ 屋脊 roof ridge：碧瓦飞～ *green roof tiles and curved roofs* | 雕～ *carved roof ridge*

瞢 méng ㄇㄥˊ ❶日月昏暗无光 (of the sun and moon) dim ❷目不明 bleary

勐 měng ㄇㄥˇ ❶勇敢 brave ❷云南省西双版纳傣族地区称小块的平地。多用于地名 (often used in place names) used by the Dai people of Xishuangbanna, Yunnan Province to refer to a small piece of flat land

猛 měng ㄇㄥˇ ❶气势壮，力量大 powerful; strong; fierce：～虎 *fierce tiger* | 勇～ *full of courage and strength* | 用力过～ *use too much force* | 药力～ *strong medicinal effect* | 火力～ *intense fire power* ❷忽然，突然 suddenly：～然惊醒 *wake up suddenly* | ～地摔倒 *trip and fall suddenly*

锰(錳) měng ㄇㄥˇ 金属元素，符号Mn，银白色，质硬而脆。锰铁合金叫锰钢，用

于工业 manganese (Mn)

蜢 měng ㄇㄥˇ see 蚱蜢 (zhà－) at 蚱 on page 828

艋 měng ㄇㄥˇ ［舴艋］（zé－）小船 small boat

蒙 měng ㄇㄥˇ ［蒙古族］1 我国少数民族，参看附录四 the Mongol people (one of the ethnic groups in China. See Appendix Ⅳ.) 2 蒙古国的主要民族 the main ethnic group in Mongolia ［内蒙古］我国少数民族自治区，1947 年 5 月建立 Inner Mongolia Autonomous Region

⇨ see also mēng on p.445, méng on p.446

獴 měng ㄇㄥˇ 哺乳动物，身体长，脚短，嘴尖，耳朵小，捕食蛇、蟹等。如蛇獴、蟹獴 mongoose

蠓 měng ㄇㄥˇ 蠓虫，昆虫，比蚊子小，褐色或黑色，雌的吸人、畜的血，能传染疾病 biting midge

懵（**懞） měng ㄇㄥˇ ［懵懂］（－dǒng）糊涂，不明白事理 muddle-headed; ignorant

孟 mèng ㄇㄥˋ ❶旧时兄弟姊妹排行（háng）有时用孟、仲、叔、季做次序，孟是老大 (old) eldest among siblings (孟，仲，叔，季 were sometimes used to indicate the birth order)：～兄 *eldest brother* | ～孙 *eldest grandchild* ❷指农历一季中月份在开头的 (in traditional Chinese calendar) the first month of the season：～春（春季第一月）*the first month of spring* | ～冬（冬季第一月）*the first month of winter* ［孟浪］鲁莽，考虑不周到 rash; careless：此事不可～。*(We) mustn't act rashly in this matter.*

梦（夢） mèng ㄇㄥˋ ❶睡眠时体内体外各种刺激或残留在大脑里的外界刺激引起的影像活动 dream ❷做梦 to dream：～游 *to sleepwalk; travel in one's dream* | ～见 *dream of (sth/sb)* ❸比喻空想，幻想 pipedream; fantasy：～想 *to vainly hope; to dream of; dream* | 以前的打算最后只成了一场～。*All our previously made plans have become just a dream.* ❹愿望，理想 wish; vision：儿时的～终于实现了。*My childhood dream has finally come true.*

MI ㄇㄧ

咪 mī ㄇㄧ 形容猫叫声㊟ miaow

眯（*瞇） mī ㄇㄧ ❶眼皮微微合拢 to narrow one's eyes：～缝（feng）*narrow one's eyes until they are slits* | ～着眼笑 *smile with one's eyes narrowed into slits* ❷〈方 dialect〉小睡 to nap：～一会儿 *take a nap*

⇨ see also mí on p.448

弥（彌、❶瀰） mí ㄇㄧˊ ❶满，遍 full; throughout：～月（小孩儿满月）*complete the first month of a baby's life* | ～天大罪 *colossal crime* ［弥漫］1 水满 (of water) full 2 到处都是，充满 to be filled with：

硝烟～ *filled with the smoke of gunpowder* ❷补，合（㊀–补）to repair; to remedy ❸更加 even more：老而～坚 *stronger with age*｜欲盖～彰。*The more one tries to hide, the more is revealed.*

祢（禰） mí ㄇㄧˊ (formerly pronounced nǐ) 姓 (surname) Mi

猕（獼） mí ㄇㄧˊ ［猕猴］一种猴，面部红色无毛，有颊囊，尾短，臀疣显著 Rhesus Monkey

迷 mí ㄇㄧˊ ❶分辨不清，失去了辨别、判断的能力 to lose ability to differentiate and make judgment：～了路 *lost one's way* ［迷彩］使人迷惑不易分辨的色彩 camouflage：～服 *camouflage clothing* ［迷信］盲目地信仰和崇拜。特指信仰神仙鬼怪等。blindly trust; (specifically) hold superstitious beliefs ❷醉心于某种事物，发生特殊的爱好（hào）become fascinated by sth：入～ *fascinated; enchanted*｜～恋 *infatuated with* ❸沉醉于某种事物的人 aficionado; fan：棋～ *chess enthusiast*｜球～ *football fan*｜戏～ *traditional Chinese opera aficionado* ❹使人陶醉 enchanting：景色～人 *enchanting scenery*

眯（*瞇） mí ㄇㄧˊ 尘土入眼，不能睁开看东西 unable to open one's eyes (due to dust falling into them)

⇨ see also mī on p.447

谜（謎） mí ㄇㄧˊ ❶谜语，影射事物或文字的隐语 riddle：灯～ *lantern riddle*｜～底 *solution of a riddle; truth*｜猜～ *guess a riddle; to guess* ❷比喻还没有弄明白的或难以理解的事物 (figurative) sth that is still unknown or hard to understand：那件事的真相至今还是个～。*The truth of the matter is still unknown to this day.*

醚 mí ㄇㄧˊ 有机化合物的一类，由一个氧原子连接两个烃基而成。乙醚是医药上常用的麻醉剂 ether

糜 mí ㄇㄧˊ ❶粥 rice gruel; porridge ❷烂（㊀–烂）rotten; pulverized ❸浪费 to waste：～财妨农 *squander wealth and impede agricultural development growth of crops* ❹姓 (surname) Mi

⇨ see also méi on p.442

縻 mí ㄇㄧˊ ❶牛缰绳 halter (for an ox or cow) ❷系（jì），捆，拴 to tie up; to harness ［羁縻］㊃牵制，笼络 to bridle; to restrain

靡 mí ㄇㄧˊ 浪费（㊀奢–）to waste：不要～费钱财。*Do not waste money.*

⇨ see also mǐ on p.449

蘼 mí ㄇㄧˊ ［蘼芜］（–wú）古书上指芎䓖（xiōngqióng）的苗 (in ancient Chinese texts) Sichuan lovage shoot

醾 mí ㄇㄧˊ ［酴醾］（tú–）重（chóng）酿的酒 twice-brewed liquor

麋 mí ㄇㄧˊ 麋鹿，哺乳动物，又叫四不像，头像马，身像驴，蹄像牛，角像鹿，身体灰褐色。原产于我国，是珍贵的动物 Pere

M

David's deer (also called 四不像)

米 mǐ ㄇㄧˇ ❶去了壳的谷类或其他植物的籽实 husked seed：小～ *millet* | 花生～ *shelled peanut* 特指去了壳的稻的籽实 (specifically) husked rice：买一袋～ *buy a bag of rice* ❷（外 *loan-word*）长度单位，符号 m，1 米等于 10 分米 metre(m)

洣 mǐ ㄇㄧˇ 洣水，水名，在湖南省东南部 Mishui River (in southeastern Hunan Province)

脒 mǐ ㄇㄧˇ 有机化合物的一类，如磺胺脒 amidine

敉 mǐ ㄇㄧˇ 安抚，安定 to pacify; to stabilize：～平 *to quash (rebellion, etc.)*

芈 mǐ ㄇㄧˇ 姓 (surname) Mi

弭 mǐ ㄇㄧˇ 止，息 to stop：水患消～。*The flooding has been averted.* | ～乱（平息战乱）*cease war turmoil*

靡 mǐ ㄇㄧˇ ❶无，没有 without; not have：～日不思 *not a day goes by without thinking of sth/sb* ❷倒下 to fall：望风披～ *be frightened into flight*

[靡靡之音] 颓废、趣味低级的乐曲、歌曲 decadent music

⇨ see also mí on p.448

汨 mì ㄇㄧˋ 汨罗江，水名，在湖南省岳阳 Miluojiang River (in Yueyang, Hunan Province)

觅(覓、*覔) mì ㄇㄧˋ 找，寻求（㊥寻—）to seek; to look for：～食 *look for food* | ～路 *look for a way*

泌 mì ㄇㄧˋ 分泌，从生物体里产生出某种物质 to secrete：～尿 *urinate*

⇨ see also bì on p.33

宓 mì ㄇㄧˋ 安，静 tranquil

祕 mì ㄇㄧˋ ❶ see 秘 on page 449 ❷姓 (surname) Mi

⇨ see also bì 秘 on p.34

秘(△*祕) mì ㄇㄧˋ (formerly pronounced bì) 不公开的，不让大家知道的（㊥—密）secret; concealed：～方 *secret formula* | ～诀 *secret (of success)* | ～不示人 *keep sth a secret*

⇨ see also bì on p.34

密 mì ㄇㄧˋ ❶事物间距离短，空隙小，跟"稀""疏"相对（㊥稠—）(opposite of 稀，疏) close together; thick：～植 *apply close planting* | ～云不雨 *very cloudy but no rain; (figurative) Conditions are ripe for sth to happen but nothing has happened yet.* | 枪声越来越～。*The gunshots are getting more and more frequent.* ㊀精致，细致 intricate; detailed：精～ *precise* | 细～ *(of texture) fine; detailed* ❷关系近，感情好（㊥亲—）(of relationship) close：～友 *intimate friend* | ～切 *close; to make close* ❸不公开 secret; concealed：～谋 *to plot* | ～谈 *have a confidential talk* | ～码电报 *coded telegram* ㊀秘密的事物 secret：保～ *keep a secret* | 泄～ *leak a secret* | 告～ *inform against sb*

谧(謐) mì ㄇㄧˋ 安静（㊥安—）tranquil

M

嘧 mì ㄇㄧˋ ［嘧啶］（— dìng）有机化合物，无色晶体，有刺激性气味，溶于水、乙醇和乙醚。可用来制药等 pyrimidine

蜜 mì ㄇㄧˋ ❶蜂蜜，蜜蜂采取花的甜汁酿成的东西 honey ［蜜饯］用蜜、糖浸渍果品。又指用蜜、糖浸渍的果品 to crystallize fruit using honey and sugar; candied fruit ❷甜美 sweet：～月 *honeymoon* | 甜言～语 *sweet talk; honeyed words*

幂（*冪） mì ㄇㄧˋ ❶覆盖东西的巾 cloth cover ❷覆盖，遮盖 to cover; to conceal ❸表示一个数自乘若干次的形式叫幂。如 t 自乘 n 次的幂为 t^n。(mathematics) power

蓂 mì ㄇㄧˋ see 菥蓂 (xī—) at 菥 on page 697

⇨ see also míng on p.457

MIAN ㄇㄧㄢ

眠 mián ㄇㄧㄢˊ ❶睡觉（㊀睡—）to sleep：安～ *sleep peacefully* | 失～ *(suffer from) insomnia* | 长～（婉指人死）*eternal rest (euphemism for sb's death)* ❷某些动物在一个较长时间内不吃不动的生理现象 to hibernate：冬～ *winter hibernation* | 蚕三～了。*The silkworms have exuviated three times.*

绵（緜、*縣） mián ㄇㄧㄢˊ ❶丝绵，蚕丝结成的片或团，可用来絮衣被等 silk floss ❷性质像丝绵的 with the quality of silk floss ①软弱，单薄 soft; insubstantial：～薄 *meagre strength* ②延续不断 continuous：～延 *extend over a period (or a distance)*

棉 mián ㄇㄧㄢˊ ❶棉花，草本植物，叶掌状分裂，果实桃形。种子外有白色的絮，也叫棉花，供纺织及絮衣被用。种子可以榨油 cotton; cotton plant ❷棉絮 cotton fibre; cotton wadding：～衣 *cotton-padded clothing* | ～线 *cotton thread*

丏 miǎn ㄇㄧㄢˇ 遮蔽，看不见 to cover; to be invisible

沔 miǎn ㄇㄧㄢˇ 沔水，水名，汉江的上游河段，在陕西省南部 Mianshui River (in the upper reaches of the Hanjiang River, in southern Shaanxi Province)

免 miǎn ㄇㄧㄢˇ ❶去掉，除掉 to remove：～冠 *take off one's hat in salutation; be bareheaded* | ～职 *relieve sb of his/her post* | ～费 *free of charge* ❷避免 to avoid：～疫 *be immune to* | 做好准备，以～临时抓瞎。*Be prepared to avoid being at a loss when the time comes.* ❸勿，不可 do not; not be allowed：闲人～进。*Off limits to unauthorized persons.*

勉 miǎn ㄇㄧㄢˇ ❶勉力，力量不够还尽力做 to do one's utmost：～为其难（nán）*try to do what is beyond one's power* ［勉强］（—qiǎng）1 尽力 do one's best：～支持下去 *do one's best to hold out* 2 刚刚够，不充足 barely enough：这种说法很～（理由不充足）。*This argument is unconvincing.* |

M

勉勉强强及格 *barely pass (the exam)* 3 不是心甘情愿的 reluctant：～答应 *reluctantly agree* 4 让人去做不愿做的事 force sb to do sth：不要～他。*Don't force him.* ❷勉励，使人努力 to encourage; to urge：互～ *encourage one another* | 有则改之，无则加～。*If a criticism is valid, correct the mistake; if it isn't, use it to urge yourself not to make that mistake.*

娩 miǎn ㄇㄧㄢˇ 分娩，妇女生孩子 to give birth

冕 miǎn ㄇㄧㄢˇ 古代大（dà）夫以上的官戴的礼帽。后来专指帝王的礼帽 (ancient) ceremonial hat worn by senior officials; (later and specifically) crowns of emperors and kings：加～ *to crown*

鮸（鮸） miǎn ㄇㄧㄢˇ 鱼名，身体侧扁而长，棕褐色，生活在海里 (fish) miiuy croaker

劻 miǎn ㄇㄧㄢˇ 勉力，勤勉 industrious; diligent

偭 miǎn ㄇㄧㄢˇ ❶向，面向 to face ❷违背 to transgress; to violate：～规越矩（违背正常的法度）*violate normal rules and regulations*

湎 miǎn ㄇㄧㄢˇ 沉迷（多指喝酒）to indulge in (often liquor)：沉～于酒色 *indulge in wine and women*

愐 miǎn ㄇㄧㄢˇ ❶思，想 to think ❷勤勉 diligent

缅（緬） miǎn ㄇㄧㄢˇ 遥远 faraway; remote：～怀 *to reminisce* | ～想 *to reminisce*

觍（靦） miǎn ㄇㄧㄢˇ ［觍觍］（－tiǎn）(old) same as "腼腆"

⇨ see also tiǎn on p.650

腼 miǎn ㄇㄧㄢˇ ［腼腆］（－tiǎn）害羞，不敢见生人 shy：这孩子太～。*This child is too shy.*

渑（澠） miǎn ㄇㄧㄢˇ ［渑池］地名，在河南省三门峡市 Mianchi (a place in Sanmenxia, Henan Province)

⇨ see also shéng on p.593

面（❽—⓫麵、❽—⓫*麪、❶—❼靣）** miàn ㄇㄧㄢˋ ❶面孔，脸，头的前部（㊥脸－、颜－）face：～前 *in front (of sb)* | ～带笑容 *have/wear a smile on one's face* ［面子］（－zi）1 体面 dignity; face：爱～ *care about one's reputation* | 丢～ *lose face* 2 情面 personal feelings：大公无私，不讲～ *impartial without considering others' personal feelings* ❷用脸对着，向着 to face：背山～水 *with mountains behind and water in front* ❸当面，直接接头的 face to face; directly：～谈 *speak to sb face to face* | ～议 *negotiate face to face* ❹（－子、－儿）事物的外表，跟"里"相对 surface (opposite of 里)：地～ *the earth's surface* | 水～ *water surface* | 被～儿 *quilt cover* ❺几何学上指线移动所生成的图形，有长有宽，没有厚 (in geometry) surface：平～ *plane* | ～积

M

area ❻ 方面，边，部 aspect; direction; part of: 正～ *façade; right side* | 反～ *reverse side; back* | 上～ *above; top part* | 下～ *below; bottom part* | ～～俱到 *attend to every aspect of a matter* ❼量词，用于扁平的物体 measure word for flat objects: 一～旗 *a flag* | 一～镜子 *a mirror* | 一～锣 *a cymbal* ❽粮食磨成的粉 flour: 小米～ *millet flour* | 玉米～ *cornmeal* 特指小麦磨成的粉 (specifically) wheat flour: 一袋～ *a bag of flour* ❾（一子、一儿）粉末 powder: 药～儿 *medicinal powder* | 粉笔～儿 *chalk dust* ❿面条 noodles: 挂～ *a kind of dried noodle* | 炸酱～ *noodles served with fried bean sauce* | 方便～ *instant noodles* | 一碗～ *a bowl of noodles* ⓫食物含纤维少而柔软 (of food) soft and doughy: 这种瓜很～。*This gourd is mushy.*

眄 miàn ㄇㄧㄢˋ 斜着眼睛看 to look askance: 顾～ *look round*

MIAO ㄇㄧㄠ

喵 miāo ㄇㄧㄠ 形容猫叫的声音 miaow

苗 miáo ㄇㄧㄠˊ ❶（一儿）指幼小的植株 seedling; young plant: 麦～ *wheat seedling* | 树～ *sapling* [苗条] 人的身材细长、好看 (of a person) slim ❷（一儿）形状像苗的 (of sth) resembling a seedling: 笤帚～儿 *small whisk broom* | 火～儿 *tongue of flame* ❸某些初生的饲养的动物 newborn of certain reared animals: 鱼～ *(of fish) fry* ❹子孙后代（㊣一裔）descendant ❺疫苗，能使机体产生免疫力的微生物制剂 vaccine: 卡介～ *Bacillus Calmette-Guérin (BCG) vaccine*

[苗族] 我国少数民族，参看附录四 the Miao people (one of the ethnic groups in China. See Appendix Ⅳ.)

描 miáo ㄇㄧㄠˊ 依照原样摹画或重复地画（㊣一摹）(for drawings) to trace: ～图 *trace a design* | ～花 *trace a flower pattern*

[描写] 依照事物的情状，用语言或线条、颜色表现出来 to describe; to portray: 他很会～景物。*He is good at portraying scenery.*

鹋（鶓） miáo ㄇㄧㄠˊ see 鸸鹋 (ér—) at 鸸 on page 161

瞄 miáo ㄇㄧㄠˊ 把视力集中在一点上，注意看 to take aim at; to focus: 枪～得准。*The gun's aim is good.* | 眼光～向未来。*Set your sights on the future.*

杪 miǎo ㄇㄧㄠˇ 树枝的细梢 tip of a twig ㊀ 末尾 end: 岁～ *year's end* | 月～ *end of a month*

眇（*玅） miǎo ㄇㄧㄠˇ ❶瞎了一只眼睛。后也泛指瞎了眼睛 blind in one eye; (later and generally) blind ❷细小 tiny

秒 miǎo ㄇㄧㄠˇ ❶谷物种子壳上的芒 awn of cereals ❷计量单位 unit of measurement ①圆周的一分的六十分之一 (of angles) second ②经纬度的一分的六十

分之一 (of longitude and latitude) second ③时间的一分钟的六十分之一 (of time) second

渺(❷△*淼) miǎo ㄇㄧㄠˇ ❶微小 tiny: ～小 *tiny* | ～不足道 *insignificantly small* ❷水势辽远 (of body of water) endless; vast: 浩～ *(of water) extending to the distance* [渺茫] 离得太远看不清楚 remote and vague ⑩看不见前途的或没有把握的 uncertain (of one's future); indefinite: 这件事～得很。*This matter is quite unpromising.*

缈(緲) miǎo ㄇㄧㄠˇ see 缥缈 (piāo—) at 缥 on page 505

淼 miǎo ㄇㄧㄠˇ ❶ see 渺 on page 453 ❷用于人名 used in given names ❸用于地名 used in place names: ～泉(在江苏省常熟) *Miaoquan (in Changshu, Jiangsu Province)* ❹姓 (surname) Miao

藐 miǎo ㄇㄧㄠˇ 小(㊦—小) small: ～视 *to despise*

邈 miǎo ㄇㄧㄠˇ 远 far

妙(*玅) miào ㄇㄧㄠˋ ❶美，好 good: ～品 *fine work of art* | ～不可言 *too wonderful for words* ❷奇巧，神奇(㊦巧—) ingenious; magical: ～计 *brilliant scheme; ingenious plan* | ～诀 *clever way (of doing sth)* | ～用 *wonderful effect*

庙(廟) miào ㄇㄧㄠˋ ❶旧时供祖宗神位的地方 (old) temple (in ancient times for honouring one's ancestors): 家～ *ancestral temple* | 宗～ *ancestral temple of a ruling family* ❷供神佛或历史上有名人物的地方 temple (for worshipping deities or honouring famous historical figures); shrine: 龙王～ *temple of the Dragon King* | 孔～ *temple of Confucius* ❸庙会，设在寺庙里或附近的集市 temple fair; fair: 赶～ *go to a temple fair*

缪(繆) miào ㄇㄧㄠˋ 姓 (surname) Miao

⇨ see also miù on p.458, móu on p.463

MIE ㄇㄧㄝ

乜 miē ㄇㄧㄝ [乜斜](—xie) 1 眼睛因困倦而眯成一条缝 (of tired eyes) to be half closed: ～的睡眼 *half-closed sleepy eyes* 2 眼睛略眯而斜着看，多指不满意或看不起的神情 look askance with narrowed eyes (often refers to a look of dissatisfaction or disdain)

⇨ see also niè on p.479

咩(*哶、*哶) miē ㄇㄧㄝ 形容羊叫的声音 baa

灭(滅) miè ㄇㄧㄝˋ ❶火熄，使火熄(㊦熄—) (of a flame) to go out; to extinguish: ～火器 *fire extinguisher* | ～灯 *turn off a light* | 火～了。*The fire has gone out.* ❷完，尽，使不存在(㊦消—) to die out; to put sth out of existence: ～亡 *become*

extinct | 磨～ *to obliterate* | 自生自～ *(of sth) emerge and perish of itself* | 长自己的志气，～敌人的威风 *emphasize one's spirited resolve to make the enemy less intimidating* ❸被水漫过 covered by water：～顶之灾（致命的灾祸）*(figurative) fatal disaster*

蔑(❸衊) miè ㄇㄧㄝ ❶无，没有 without：～以复加 *be in the extreme* ❷小 small：～视（看不起，轻视）*to despise* ❸涂染 to stain［诬蔑］［污蔑］造谣毁坏别人的名誉 to slander; to smear (sb's reputation)

篾 miè ㄇㄧㄝ （一子、一儿）劈成条的竹片 thin bamboo strip：竹～子 *bamboo splint* 泛指劈成条的芦苇、高粱等茎皮 (generally) splints cut from stalks of reeds, sorghum, etc.：苇～儿 *reed splint*

蠛 miè ㄇㄧㄝ ［蠛蠓］（一měng）古书上指蠓 midge (in ancient Chinese texts) (see 蠓 on page 447 for reference)

MIN ㄇㄧㄣ

民 mín ㄇㄧㄣˊ ❶人民 people：为国为～ *for one's nation and people* | 以～为本。*The people are the foundation (of a state).*［民主］1 指人民有管理国家和自由发表意见的权利 (of politics) democracy 2 根据大多数群众意见处理问题的工作方式 (of working style) democratic：作风～ *have a democratic style*［民生］人民的生计 people's livelihood：关注～ *be concerned about people's livelihood*［公民］在一国内有国籍，享受法律上规定的公民权利并履行公民义务的人 citizen［国民］指具有某国国籍的人 national (citizen of a country) ❷指人或人群 person or people［民族］历史上形成的稳定的人群共同体，其特征是有共同语言、共同地域、共同经济生活和表现于共同文化上的共同心理素质 nation; ethnic group［居民］在一个地区内较长时期固定居住的人 resident ❸民间的 of the common people; folk：～俗 *folk custom* | ～歌 *folk song* ❹指从事某种职业或具有某种身份、特征的人 used to indicate people with certain occupations or identities：农～ *farmer* | 牧～ *herdsman* | 渔～ *fisherman* | 灾～ *disaster victims* | 侨～ *national of a particular country residing abroad* | 股～ *stock investor* | 网～ *netizen* ❺非军事的 civil; non-military：～用 *civil* | ～航 *civil aviation* ❻ same as "苠"

苠 mín ㄇㄧㄣˊ 庄稼生长期较长，成熟期较晚 (of crops) having a longer growing period and late maturation：～穇子（cǎnzi）*finger millet with longer growing period* | ～高粱 *sorghum with longer growing period* | 黄谷子比白谷子～。*Yellow foxtail millet takes a longer time to grow and mature than white foxtail millet.*

岷 mín ㄇㄧㄣˊ 岷山，山名，在四川省北部，绵延于四川、甘肃两省边境 Minshan Mountain

(in northern Sichuan Province, straddling the border of Sichuan and Gansu provinces)

珉 mín ㄇㄧㄣˊ 像玉的石头 jade-like stone

缗(緡) mín ㄇㄧㄣˊ ❶古代穿铜钱用的绳 (ancient) string for stringing coins together ❷钓鱼用的绳 fishing line

玟 mín ㄇㄧㄣˊ same as "珉"
⇨ see also wén on p.686

旻 mín ㄇㄧㄣˊ ❶天，天空 sky：～天 *sky*｜苍～ *the heavens* ❷秋天 autumn

忞 mín ㄇㄧㄣˊ 勉力 to do one's best

皿 mǐn ㄇㄧㄣˇ 器皿，盘、盂一类的东西 household utensil (such as plate, basin, etc.)

闵(閔) mǐn ㄇㄧㄣˇ ❶ same as "悯" ❷姓 (surname) Min

悯(憫) mǐn ㄇㄧㄣˇ ❶哀怜(㊤怜－) to feel (pity) for：其情可～。*This case deserves sympathy.*｜悲天～人 *bemoan the state of the world and feel pity for mankind* ❷忧愁。也作"愍" sad; worried (also written as 愍)

闽(閩) mǐn ㄇㄧㄣˇ 福建省的别称 Min (another name of Fujian Province)

抿 mǐn ㄇㄧㄣˇ ❶刷，抹 to brush; to wipe：～了～头发 *smoothed one's hair (with a slightly wet hairbrush)* ❷收敛 to close lightly; to tuck; to furl：～着嘴笑 *smile with closed lips*｜水鸟一～翅，一头扎进水里。*The water fowl tucked its wings and plunged into the water.* ㊇收敛嘴唇，少量沾取 to sip：他真不喝酒，连～都不～。*He really doesn't drink, not even a drop.*

泯 mǐn ㄇㄧㄣˇ 消灭(㊤－灭) to get rid of; to vanish：童心未～ *still a child at heart*

湣 mǐn ㄇㄧㄣˇ 古谥号用字 Min (used in posthumous titles in ancient times)

愍(惽)** mǐn ㄇㄧㄣˇ same as "悯"

黾(黽) mǐn ㄇㄧㄣˇ [黾勉](－miǎn)努力，勉力 to work hard; to do one's best：～从事 *exert oneself in doing sth*

敏 mǐn ㄇㄧㄣˇ ❶有智慧，反应迅速，灵活(㊤－捷、灵－) intelligent; quick; nimble：～感 *sensitive*｜～锐 *perceptive; sharp*｜机～ *alert and resourceful*｜敬谢不～(婉转表示不愿意做) *perhaps not (a tactful way of saying one doesn't want to do sth)* ❷努力 work hard：～行不怠 *make unremitting efforts at self-cultivation*

鳘(鰵) mǐn ㄇㄧㄣˇ 鱼名，即鳕鱼 cod (same as 鳕鱼)

MING ㄇㄧㄥ

名 míng ㄇㄧㄥˊ ❶(－儿)名字，人或事物的称谓 name：人～ *a person's name*｜国～ *a country's name*｜起个～儿 *give sb/sth a name* [名词]表示人、地、事、物的名称的词，如"学生、北京、戏剧、

M

桌子”等 noun ❷叫出，说出 to say; to articulate：无以～之 *cannot be described* | 莫～其妙 *cannot make any sense (of sth)* ❸名誉，声誉 reputation：有～ *famous* | 出～ *famous* | 不为～，不为利 *not for fame or fortune* ㊀有声誉的，大家都知道的 well-known; reputable：～医 *famous doctor* | ～将 *famous general* | ～胜 *a famous place of scenic beauty or historical significance* | ～言 *famous saying* | ～产 *famous product* ❹量词 measure word ①用于人 used to indicate people：学生四～ *four students* ②用于名次 used to indicate order：第二～ *second place*

茗 míng ㄇㄧㄥˊ ❶茶树的嫩芽 tender tea leaves ❷茶 tea：香～ *fine tea* | 品～ *enjoy fine tea*

洺 míng ㄇㄧㄥˊ 洺河，水名，在河北省南部 Minghe River (in southern Hebei Province)

铭（銘）míng ㄇㄧㄥˊ ❶刻在器物上记述生平、事业或用来警惕、勉励自己的文字 inscription：墓志～ *epitaph* | 座右～ *motto* ❷在器物上刻字 to inscribe ㊕形容牢记 to memorize：～记 *engrave in one's mind* | 刻骨～心 *(of memory) deep and lasting (literally means 'be engraved on one's bone and heart')* | ～诸肺腑 *be engraved on one's mind*

明 míng ㄇㄧㄥˊ ❶亮，跟“暗”相对 bright (opposite of 暗)：～亮 *bright and shiny* | 天～了。*Day is breaking.* | ～晃晃的刺刀 *a gleaming bayonet* ❷明白，清楚 comprehensible; clear：说～ *explain* | 表～ *make clear* | 黑白分～ *sharp contrast between black and white; clear distinction between right and wrong* | 情况不～。*The situation is unclear.* | ～～是他搞的。*Clearly, it's his responsibility.* ㊀懂得，了解 to know; to understand：深～大义 *understand the important principles thoroughly* | 知书～理 *educated and cultivated* ❸公开，不秘密，不隐蔽，跟“暗”相对 open; not secret (opposite of 暗)：～讲 *openly say sth* | 有话～说 *say sth out in the open* | ～码售货 *sell goods at marked price* | ～枪易躲，暗箭难防。*It is easy to dodge an open attack but hard to defend against a secret assault.* ❹视觉，眼力 sight：失～ *lose one's sight* ❺视觉灵敏，能看清事物 clear-sighted：英～ *wise* | 精～ *shrewd* | 耳聪目～ *have good ears and eyes; have a sharp wit* | 眼～手快 *very observant and dexterous* ❻神明，迷信称神灵 deity［明器］［冥器］殉葬用的器物 funerary object ❼次（指日或年）(for day or year) next：～日 *tomorrow; next day* | ～年 *next year* ❽朝代名，明太祖朱元璋所建立（公元1368—1644年）Ming Dynasty (1368—1644, founded by Zhu Yuanzhang, Emperor Taizu)

鸣（鳴）míng ㄇㄧㄥˊ ❶鸟兽或昆虫叫 (of birds, animals or insects) to call：鸟～ *birdcall* | 驴～ *braying* | 蝉～

chirping of a cicada ❷发出声音，使发出声音 to make a sound; to cause sth to make a sound: 自～钟 *chiming clock* | 孤掌难～。*It's difficult to achieve sth without help. (literally means 'You can never clap with one hand.')* | ～炮 *gun salute* ❸表达，发表(情感、意见、主张) to express; to articulate (emotions, views, suggestions): ～谢 *express formal thanks* | ～不平 *complain of unfairness* | 百家争～ *contention of a hundred schools of thought*

冥(*寘、*冥) míng ㄇㄧㄥˊ ❶昏暗 dim ㊀ 愚昧 ignorant; uneducated: ～顽不灵 *ignorant and stubborn* ❷深奥，深沉 deep; profound: ～想 *be deep in thought* | ～思苦想 *cudgel one's brains* ❸迷信的人称人死以后进入的世界 the netherworld

[冥蒙] [溟濛] (-méng) 形容烟雾弥漫 foggy; misty

蓂 míng ㄇㄧㄥˊ [蓂荚] (-jiá) 传说中尧时的一种瑞草 (in Chinese legend) a herbaceous plant that augured well during the reign of the sage-king Yao

⇨ see also mì on p.450

溟 míng ㄇㄧㄥˊ 海 the sea: 北～有鱼。*There is a fish in the north sea.*

暝 míng ㄇㄧㄥˊ ❶日落，天黑 (of the sun) to set; (of the sky) to become dark ❷黄昏 dusk; evening: ～色 *twilight*

瞑 míng ㄇㄧㄥˊ 闭眼 to close one's eyes: ～目(多指人死时心中无牵挂) *close one's eyes (often of people dying peacefully)*

螟 míng ㄇㄧㄥˊ 螟虫，昆虫，即螟蛾的幼虫。种类很多，如三化螟、二化螟、大螟、玉米螟等，危害农作物 larva of pyralid moths

[螟蛉] (-líng) 一种绿色小虫 larva of corn earworm ㊕ 义子，抱养的孩子。又叫螟蛉子 adopted child (also called 螟蛉子) (see 蜾蠃 guǒluǒ at 蜾 on page 235 for reference)

酩 mǐng ㄇㄧㄥˇ [酩酊] (-dǐng) 醉得迷迷糊糊的 in a drunken stupor: ～大醉 *be dead drunk*

命(*슮) mìng ㄇㄧㄥˋ ❶生命，动物、植物的生活能力，也就是跟矿物、水等所以有区别的地方 life: 性～ *life* | 救～ *save sb's life* | 拼～ *risk one's life* ❷迷信的人认为生来就注定的贫富、寿数等 fate: 算～ *tell sb's fortune* | ～该如此 *be predestined* ❸上级指示下级(㊥-令) to command; to order: ～你前往。*I command you to go.* | ～大军火速前进 *order the troops to speedily advance* ❹上级对下级的指示 command; order: 奉～ *act under orders* | 遵～ *obey an order* | 恭敬不如从～。*Obedience is better than courtesy.* ❺给予(名称等) to give (a name, etc.): ～名 *give a name* | ～题 *assign a topic* [命中] (-zhòng) 射中或击中目标 hit the target ❻指派，使用 to designate; to use: ～驾 *give the order* *to start (a carriage); set out* | ～笔 *take up one's pen (or paint brush)*

MIU ㄇㄧㄡ

谬(謬) miù ㄇㄧㄡˋ ❶错误的，不合情理的 wrong; absurd：～论 *fallacy* | 荒～ *absurd* ❷差错 discrepancy：失之毫厘，～以千里。*A small error leads to a big discrepancy.*

缪(繆) miù ㄇㄧㄡˋ see 纰缪(pī—) at 纰 on page 499
⇨ see also miào on p.453, móu on p.463

MO ㄇㄛ

摸 mō ㄇㄛ ❶用手接触或轻轻抚摩 to touch; to caress：～小孩儿的头 *touch a child's head* | ～～多光滑。*Touch this and see how smooth it is.* ❷用手探取 to fish for sth (with one's hands)：～鱼 *catch fish with one's hands* | 从口袋里～出一张钞票来 *fish out a banknote from the pocket* ㉇①揣测，试探 to guess; to probe：～底 *(get to) know the real situation* | 我～准了他的脾气。*I've got a handle on his temperament.* | ～不清他是什么意思。*(I) don't get what he means.* ②在黑暗中行动，在认不清的道路上行走 to grope in the dark：～营 *attack enemy's camp under cover of darkness* | ～黑 *grope in the dark* | ～了半夜才到家。*(I) finally got back after half a night of finding my way home.* [摸索] 多方面探求、寻找 to try to find out：～经验 *gain experience by feeling one's way*

谟(謨、*謩) mó ㄇㄛˊ 计谋，计划 strategy; plan：宏～ *grand plan*

馍(饃、*饝) mó ㄇㄛˊ 〈方 dialect〉面制食品，通常指馒头 ㊣ steamed bun (usually refers to *mantou*)

嫫 mó ㄇㄛˊ [嫫母] 传说中的丑妇 Momu (an ugly woman in Chinese legend)

摹 mó ㄇㄛˊ 仿效，照着样子做 to copy：临～ *copy (a painting or a piece of calligraphy)* | 描～ *to trace (a drawing)* | 把这个字～下来。*Copy this character.*

模 mó ㄇㄛˊ ❶法式，规范 model; standard：～式 *pattern* | 楷～ *role model* [模型] 依照原物或计划中的事物（如建筑）的形式做成的物品 (of objects) model ❷仿效（㊣一仿、一拟）to copy; to imitate ❸模范 an exemplary person or thing：劳～ *model worker* | 英～ *heroic model*

[模糊]（—hu）不分明，不清楚 unclear; blurry

[模特儿]（外 loanword）写生、雕塑时的描摹对象或参考对象，有时也指某些示范表演者 model (in life drawing or sculpture, etc.)：时装～ *fashion model*
⇨ see also mú on p.463

膜 mó ㄇㄛˊ ❶（—儿）动植物体内像薄皮的组织 membrane：肋～ *pleura* | 耳～ *eardrum* |

M

苇～ *reed membrane* ❷（一儿）像膜的薄皮 thin, membrane-like film：面～ *face mask* | 塑料薄～儿 *plastic film*

麽 mó ㄇㄛˊ ❶[幺麽]（yāo－）微小 petty; insignificant：～小丑 *petty villain* ❷姓 (surname) Mo

⇨ see also ma 么 on p.433, me 么 on p.441

嬷 mó ㄇㄛˊ [嬷嬷]（－mo）1 旧时称奶妈为嬷嬷 (old) wet nurse 2〈方 dialect〉称呼老年妇女 elderly woman

摩 mó ㄇㄛˊ ❶摩擦，蹭（cèng）to rub：～拳擦掌 *be eager to get into action (literally means 'rub one's hands and clench one's fists in eager anticipation')* ❷抚摩，摸 to caress; to touch：～弄 *to fondle* | 按～ *to massage* [摩挲]（－suō）用手抚摩 to caress; to stroke ❸研究切磋 to study; to exchange views [观摩] 观察之后，加以研究，吸收别人的优点 to observe and emulate：～教学 *teaching demonstration* ❹物质的量的单位名摩尔的简称，符号 mol。(short for 摩尔, a unit of measure) mole (mol)

⇨ see also mā on p.431

蘑 mó ㄇㄛˊ [萝藦]草本植物，蔓生，叶心脏形，花白色带淡紫色斑纹，全草入药 *metaplexis japonica*

磨 mó ㄇㄛˊ ❶摩擦 to rub：～刀 *grind/sharpen a knife* | ～墨 *(in Chinese calligraphy) grind an ink slab on an ink stone to produce ink* [磨合] 新组装的机器经过一定时期的使用，把摩擦面上的加工痕迹磨光而变得更加密合 (of machinery) to break in ㊕ 彼此在合作过程中逐渐适应和协调 to get to know each other; to adapt to each other [磨炼] [磨练] 在艰苦环境中锻炼 to temper oneself ❷阻碍，困难（㊟－难、折－）obstruction; difficulty：好（hǎo）事多～。*The road to success is strewn with setbacks.* ㊀ 纠缠 to pester; to plague：小孩子～人。*Children pester you.* ❸拖延，耗时间 to take time; to waste time：～工夫 *take too much time to do sth* ❹逐渐消失，消灭 to sink into oblivion; to obliterate：百世不～ *go on forever* | ～灭 *to obliterate* [消磨] 1 使精力等逐渐消失 fritter away; idle away：～志气 *fritter away one's aspirations* 2 消耗 idle away：不再用打牌～时光 *no longer kill time by playing cards*

⇨ see also mò on p.462

蘑 mó ㄇㄛˊ 蘑菇，某些可以吃的蕈（xùn）类，如口蘑、松蘑 mushroom

魔 mó ㄇㄛˊ ❶宗教或神话中指害人性命、迷惑人的恶鬼 demon; devil：妖～鬼怪 *evil spirits of every description* | 恶～ *demon* ❷不平常，奇异 unusual; strange：～力 *magical power* | ～术 *magic*

劘 mó ㄇㄛˊ 切削 to cut; to chip

抹 mǒ ㄇㄛˇ ❶涂（㊟涂－）to smear; to apply：伤口上～

上点儿药。*Apply some medication to the wound.* ❷揩，擦 to rub; to wipe：～眼泪 *wipe away tears* | 一～一手黑 *blacken one's hand with a single wipe* ❸除去 to remove：～零儿（不计算尾数）*(of numbers) round off* | ～掉几个字 *erase a few words* [抹杀] [抹煞] 一概不计，勾销 to negate; to obliterate：一笔～ *totally negate*

⇨ see also mā on p.431, mò on p.460

万 mò ㄇㄛˋ [万俟]（－qí）复姓 (two-character surname) Moqi

⇨ see also wàn on p.674

末 mò ㄇㄛˋ ❶梢，尖端，跟"本"相对 tip (opposite of 本)：～梢 *end* | 本～倒置 *take what's incidental for what's fundamental* | 秋毫之～ *the minutest thing* | 细枝～节（喻事情不重要的部分）*unimportant detail (literally means 'small twigs and knots of a tree')* ❷最后，终了（liǎo），跟"始"相对（㊌－尾）final; the end (opposite of 始)：～代 *the last reign of a dynasty* | 周～ *weekend* | 十二月三十一日是一年的最～一天。*31 December is the last day of the year.* ❸（－子、－儿）碎屑（㊌粉－）powder; dust：粉笔～儿 *chalk dust* | 茶叶～儿 *tea dust* | 把药材研成～儿。*Grind the medicinal ingredients into powder.* ❹传统戏曲里扮演中年男子的角色 *mo* (middle-aged male role in traditional Chinese opera)

抹 mò ㄇㄛˋ 涂抹，泥（nì）to smear：他正在往墙上～石灰。*He is smearing lime on the wall.*

⇨ see also mā on p.431, mǒ on p.459

茉 mò ㄇㄛˋ [茉莉]（－li）1 常绿灌木，花白色，香味浓，可用来熏制茶叶 jasmine 2 紫茉莉，草本植物，又叫草茉莉，花有红、白、黄、紫等颜色，胚乳粉质，可用作化妆粉 Marvel of Peru; Four O'clock Flower (also called 草茉莉)

沫 mò ㄇㄛˋ （－子、－儿）液体形成的许多细泡（㊌泡－）foam：肥皂～儿 *soap suds* | 唾～（tuòmo）*spittle*

妺 mò ㄇㄛˋ 古人名用字 used in given names in ancient times

秣 mò ㄇㄛˋ ❶牲口的饲料 fodder：粮～ *grain and fodder* ❷喂牲口 to feed animals：～马厉兵（喂马、磨兵器，指做战斗准备）*feed the horses and sharpen the weapons (to prepare for battle)*

靺 mò ㄇㄛˋ [靺鞨]（－hé）我国古代东北方的民族 the Mohe people (an ethnic group in northeastern China in ancient times)

没 mò ㄇㄛˋ ❶隐在水中 to sink; to submerge：沉～ *to sink* | ～入水中 *sink into the water* ㊀隐藏 to hide：神出鬼～ *appear and disappear mysteriously* | 出～无常 *appear and disappear erratically* [没落] 衰落，趋向灭亡 to decline; to wane; to decay：～阶级 *declining social class* ❷漫过，高过 to rise beyond; to be higher than：水～了头顶。*The water covered* *the top of (his) head.* | 庄稼都长得～人了。*The crops have grown taller than people.* ❸把财物扣下 to confiscate: ～收 *confiscate* | 罚～ *fine and confiscate* ❹ 终，尽 the end：～世（指终身，一辈子）*one's whole life* ❺ same as "殁"

➪ see also méi on p.441

殁 mò ㄇㄛˋ 死 to die：病～ *die of an illness* | ～于异乡 *die in a foreign land* (also written as 没)

陌 mò ㄇㄛˋ 田间的小路（㊣阡－）footpath between fields：～头杨柳 *willows along the road; (figurative) spring scenery* [陌生] 生疏，不熟悉 unfamiliar; strange

貊 mò ㄇㄛˋ 我国古代称东北方的民族 (ancient) Mo (name for ethnic groups living in the northeast of China)

冒 mò ㄇㄛˋ [冒顿]（－dú）汉初匈奴的一个首领名 Modu (the name of a leader of the Xiongnu people in the early Han Dynasty)

➪ see also mào on p.440

脉（*脈、**脈）mò ㄇㄛˋ [脉脉] 形容用眼神表达爱慕的情意 (of the look in one's eyes) affectionate：～含情 *look (at sb) amorously*

➪ see also mài on p.434

莫 mò ㄇㄛˋ ❶不要 do not：闲人～入 *no entry for unauthorized persons* ❷表示没有谁或没有哪一种东西 no one; nothing：～不欣喜。*There was no one who was not overjoyed.* | ～大的光荣 *greatest honour* [莫非] 副词，难道 (adverb) could it be; is it possible that：～是他回来了吗？ *Could it be that he has returned?* [莫逆] 朋友之间感情非常好 close relationship between friends：～之交 *close friends* [莫须有] 也许有吧。后用来表示凭空捏造 perhaps there is/are; fabricated; groundless ❸ 不 no; not：变化～测 *change unpredictably* | 爱～能助 *be willing to help but not in a position to do so*
[莫邪]（－yé）古宝剑名 Moye (name of an ancient sword)

〈古 ancient〉also same as 暮(mù)

蓦（驀）mò ㄇㄛˋ 突然，忽然 suddenly：他～地站起来。*He suddenly stood up.* | ～然回首 *suddenly turn around*

漠 mò ㄇㄛˋ ❶地面为沙石覆盖，缺乏流水，气候干燥，植物稀少的地区 desert：沙～ *desert* [广漠] 广大，看不到边际 vast and bare ❷冷淡地，不经心地 indifferent：～视 *to disregard* | ～不关心 *indifferent* [漠然] 不关心的样子 indifferent; unconcerned

寞 mò ㄇㄛˋ 寂静，清静（㊣寂－）solitary; quiet：～～ *silent* | ～然 *lonely*

镆（鏌）mò ㄇㄛˋ [镆铘]（－yé）same as "莫邪"

瘼 mò ㄇㄛˋ 病 illness：民～（人民的痛苦）*the suffering of the masses*

貘 mò ㄇㄛˋ 哺乳动物，像猪而略大，鼻子圆而长，能伸缩，善游泳，产于热带 tapir

嘿 mò ㄇㄛˋ same as “默”

⇨ see also hēi on p.250

墨 mò ㄇㄛˋ ❶写字绘画用的黑色颜料 Chinese ink：一锭～ *a slab of Chinese ink* | ～汁 *prepared Chinese ink* ❷写字、绘画或印刷用的各色颜料(coloured) ink：～水 *ink* | 油～ *printing ink* ❸名家写的字或画的画 calligraphic works or paintings by famous artists：～宝 *precious calligraphy/painting* ❹黑色或近于黑色的 black; near-black：～晶（黑色的水晶）*black crystal* | ～菊 *dark Chrysanthemum* ❺贪污 corruption：贪～ *take bribes* | ～吏 *corrupt official* ❻古代在犯人脸上刺刻涂墨的刑罚 (ancient punishment) facial tattoo in ink

默 mò ㄇㄛˋ 不说话，不出声㊊ not to speak; to remain silent：沉～ *reticent* | ～～不语 *remain silent* | ～读 *read silently* | ～写（凭记忆写出）*write from memory* | ～认（心里承认而不表示出来）*give tacit acknowledgement/agreement*

缧(纆) mò ㄇㄛˋ 绳索 rope

磨 mò ㄇㄛˋ ❶把粮食弄碎的工具 mill; grinder：石～ *millstone* | 电～ *electric grinder* ❷用磨把粮食弄碎 to mill; to grind：～豆腐 *mill soya beans to make beancurd* | ～面 *mill flour* ❸〈方 dialect〉掉转（多用于狭窄的空间）(often in tight spaces) turn around：～车 *turn the car around (in a tight spot)* | ～不开身 *too narrow for sb to turn around*

⇨ see also mó on p.459

礳 mò ㄇㄛˋ ［礳石渠］地名，在山西省阳城 Moshiqu (a place in Yangcheng, Shanxi Province)

耱 mò ㄇㄛˋ 耢（lào）farm tool used for flattening earth

MOU ㄇㄡ

哞 mōu ㄇㄡ 形容牛叫的声音 moo

牟 móu ㄇㄡˊ ❶谋取 to strive for：～利 *seek profit* ❷姓 (surname) Mou

⇨ see also mù on p.464

侔 móu ㄇㄡˊ 相等，齐 to equal to; to match：超五帝，～三王 *surpass the Five Emperors and equal to the Three Kings*

眸 móu ㄇㄡˊ （一子）眼中瞳仁，泛指眼睛 (of eye) pupil; (generally) eye：凝～远望 *gaze into the distance*

蛑 móu ㄇㄡˊ see 蝤蛑 (yóu—) at 蝤 on page 793

谋(謀) móu ㄇㄡˊ ❶计划，计策，主意（㊃—略、计—）plan; scheme; idea：阴～ *conspiracy* | 有勇无～ *brave but not resourceful* ❷设法寻求 to seek：～职 *seek employment* | 另～出路 *find another way out* | 为人民～幸福 *work for the happiness of the people* ❸商议 to discuss：不～而合 *agree without prior con-*

sultaion | 与虎～皮 *fool's errand (literally means 'asking a tiger for its skin')*

缪(繆) móu ㄇㄡˊ [绸缪] (chóu－) 1 修缮 to repair：未雨～（喻事先做好准备）*make preparations beforehand (literally means 'repair the house before it rains')* 2 缠绵 sentimentally attached：情意～ *be deep in love*

⇨ see also miào on p.453, miù on p.458

鍪 móu ㄇㄡˊ 古代的一种锅 (ancient) a kind of cooking pot [兜鍪] 古代打仗时戴的盔 (ancient) war helmet

某 mǒu ㄇㄡˇ 代词，代替不明确指出的人、地、事、物等 (pronoun) certain：～人 *a certain person* |～国 *a certain country* |～日 *a certain day* | 张～ *a person with the surname Zhang* |～～学校 *a certain school*

MU ㄇㄨ

毪 mú ㄇㄨˊ 毪子，西藏产的一种氆氇（pǔlu）woolen fabric from Tibet

模 mú ㄇㄨˊ （－儿）模子 mould：～具 *mould* | 字～儿 *(in printing) matrix* | 铜～儿 *copper matrix* [模子]（－zi）用压制或浇灌的方法制造物品的工具 mould [模样] 形状，容貌 appearance

⇨ see also mó on p.458

母 mǔ ㄇㄨˇ ❶母亲，妈妈，娘 mother：～系 *matrilineal* | ～性 *maternal instinct* ❷ 对女性长辈的称呼 one's female elders：姑～ *aunt (father's sister)* | 舅～ *aunt (wife of mother's brother)* | 祖～ *grandmother (father's mother)* ❸ 雌性的 female (bird and animal)：～鸡 *hen* | 这口猪是～的。*This pig is a sow.* ❹ 事物所从产生出来的 origin：～校 *alma mater* | ～株 *(in botany) female parent* | 工作～机 *machine tool* | 失败为成功之～。*Failure is the mother of success.* ㊞一套东西中间可以包含其他部分的 sth that contains other parts nesting within it：子～环 *master link sub assembly* | 子～扣 *snap fastener* | 螺丝～ *(hardware device) nut*

拇 mǔ ㄇㄨˇ 拇指，手和脚的大指 thumb; big toe

姆 mǔ ㄇㄨˇ 保姆，负责照管儿童或料理家务的女工 nanny

钴(鈷) mǔ ㄇㄨˇ [钴钴]（gǔ－）古书上指熨斗 clothes iron (in ancient Chinese texts)

踇 mǔ ㄇㄨˇ 脚的拇指，大脚趾 big toe：～外翻 *bunion*

牡 mǔ ㄇㄨˇ 雄性的（鸟兽），跟"牝"相对 (of birds and animals) male (opposite of 牝)：～牛 *bull* 又指植物的雄株 (in botany) male plant：～麻 *male hemp*

亩(畝、*畆、*畮、*畒、*畂、*畋) mǔ ㄇㄨˇ 市制地积单位，1亩是10分，约合666.7平方米 *mu* (a traditional

Chinese unit for measuring area, equal to 666.7 square metres. There are 10 分 in 1 亩.)

姥 mǔ ㄇㄨˇ 年老的妇人 elderly woman

⇨ see also lǎo on p.382

木 mù ㄇㄨˋ ❶树木，树类植物的通称 tree：乔～ *arbour*｜灌～ *shrub* [木本植物] 具有木质茎的植物，如松、柏、玫瑰等 woody plant ❷木头，供制造器物或建筑用的木料 wood：～材 *timber*｜枣～ *jujube wood*｜杉～ *Chinese fir wood*｜～器 *wooden object* ❸棺材 coffin：棺～ *coffin*｜行将就～ *have one foot in the grave* ❹感觉不灵敏 not sensitive/perceptive：～头～脑 *blockheaded*｜这人太～，怎么说他也不明白。*This person is stupid; he can't get it however much one explains.* ㊀失去知觉(㊈麻－) numb：手脚麻～。*Limbs become numb.*｜舌头发～ *feel numb in the tongue*

沐 mù ㄇㄨˋ 洗头 wash one's hair：栉(zhì)风～雨(形容奔波辛苦) *be exposed to the elements as one travels about (literally means 'be combed by the wind and washed by the rain')* [沐浴] 洗澡 to bathe ㊉受润泽 to be nourished：～在阳光雨露下 *bathe in sunlight and rain*

霂 mù ㄇㄨˋ see 霢霂 (mài－) at 霢 on page 434

目 mù ㄇㄨˋ ❶眼睛 eye：～瞪口呆 *be stunned speechless*｜历历在～ *come clearly into view*｜～空一切(自高自大) *haughty* [目标] 1 射击、攻击或寻求的对象 target：对准～射击。*Aim and shoot at the target.*｜不要暴露～。*Do not expose your position.* 2 想达到的境地 goal; objective：这是我们奋斗的～。*This is the goal of our struggle.* [目前] [目下] 眼前，现在 present moment; now ❷看 to see：一～了然 *be clear at a single glance* ❸大项中再分的小项 sub-category：大纲细～ *outline and details* ❹目录 list; catalogue：剧～ *list of plays*｜书～ *book list* ❺生物的分类单位之一，在“纲”之下、“科”之上 (in taxonomic classification) order：鸽形～ *Columbiformes*｜银耳～ *Tremellales* ❻计算围棋比赛输赢的单位 eye (unit of score in the game of *weiqi*/go)

苜 mù ㄇㄨˋ [苜蓿] (－xu) 草本植物，叶长圆形，花紫色，可以喂牲口、做肥料 alfalfa; lucerne

钼(鉬) mù ㄇㄨˋ 金属元素，符号 Mo，银白色，可用来制合金钢，也用于制作电器元件 molybdenum (Mo)

仫 mù ㄇㄨˋ [仫佬族] (－lǎo－) 我国少数民族，参看附录四 the Mulam people (one of the ethnic groups in China. See Appendix Ⅳ.)

牟 mù ㄇㄨˋ ❶用于地名 used in place names：～平(在山东省烟台) *Muping (in Yantai, Shandong Province)* ❷姓 (surname) Mu

⇨ see also móu on p.462

牧 mù ㄇㄨˋ 放养牲口 to herd：～羊 *herd goats/sheep* | ～童 *shepherd boy; herder* | ～场 *grazing land; livestock farm* | 畜～业 *animal husbandry* | 游～ *rove about as a nomad* [牧师] 基督教负责管理教堂及礼拜等事务的专职人员 pastor

募 mù ㄇㄨˋ 广泛征求 to solicit extensively：～捐 *raise money* | 招～ *to recruit* | ～了一笔款 *raised a sum of money*

墓 mù ㄇㄨˋ 埋死人的地方（㊟坟－）burial ground; grave：公～ *public cemetery* | 烈士～ *martyr's grave* | ～碑 *gravestone* | 扫～ *sweep a grave; pay respects to the dead at their graves*

幕（*幙） mù ㄇㄨˋ ❶帐 tent; curtain ①覆盖在上面的（㊟帐－）canopy ②垂挂着的 curtain; screen：银～ *silver screen; cinema* | 开～ *(of events) to open* [黑幕] 暗中作弊捣鬼的事情 shady dealings; inside story [内幕] 内部的实际情形（多指隐秘的事）inside story; what goes on behind the scenes ❷古代将帅办公的地方 (ancient) work place of a military commander：～府 *office of a military commander; (in Japan) the Shogun* ❸话剧或歌剧的较完整的段落 (in plays or operas) an act：独～剧 *one-act play*

〈古 ancient〉also same as 漠 in 沙漠

慕 mù ㄇㄨˋ ❶羡慕，仰慕 to envy; to admire：～名 *admire a famous person* ❷思念 to yearn; to think of：思～ *think of sb with respect*

暮 mù ㄇㄨˋ ❶傍晚，太阳落的时候 evening; dusk：朝（zhāo）～ *dawn and dusk; day and night* [暮气] ㊖不振作的精神，不求进取的作风 lethargy; apathy：～沉沉 *lethargic* ❷晚，将尽 late; soon to end：～春 *late spring* | ～年 *old age* | 天寒岁～ *wintry cold at the end of the year*

睦 mù ㄇㄨˋ 和好，亲近（㊟和－）harmonious; peaceful：婆媳不～ *conflict between mother-in-law and daughter-in-law* | ～邻（同邻家或邻国和好相处）*(of people and nations) have good relations with neighbours*

穆 mù ㄇㄨˋ ❶温和 temperate; mild ❷恭敬，严肃（㊟肃－）reverent; solemn：静～ *solemn and quiet*

M

N ㄋ

N ㄋ

唔 ń ㄋ́（又）same as “嗯 (ń)”
⇨ see also ńg on p.474, wú on p.690

嗯 ń ㄋ́（又） see ńg on page 474

嗯（**呒） ň ㄋ̌（又） see ňg on page 474

嗯（**叽） ǹ ㄋ̀（又） see ǹg on page 474

NA ㄋㄚ

那 nā ㄋㄚ 姓 (surname) Na
⇨ see also nà on p.467, nèi on p.473

拿（*舒） ná ㄋㄚ́ ❶用手取，握在手里 to take; to hold：～笔 *hold a pen* | ～枪 *hold a gun* | ～张纸来 *fetch a piece of paper* | ～着镰刀割麦子 *cut wheat with a sickle* ❷掌握，把握 to be sure of; to have a firm grasp of：～主意 *make a decision* | 做好做不好，我可～不稳。*I'm not sure whether it can be done well.* [拿手] 擅长 to be good at：～好戏 *(of operas or dramas) the part an actor/actress plays best; one's speciality* | 组织文娱活动，他很～。*He is very good at organizing recreational activities.* ❸故意做出 to pretend; to affect：～架子 *put on airs* | ～腔～调 *talk in an affected tone* ❹刁难，挟 (xié) 制 to make difficulties for sb; to corner sb：你不干有人干，你～不住人。*You can't corner me with this, because if you won't do it, someone else will.* ❺侵蚀，侵害 to cause damage to sth：这块木头让药水～白了。*The wood was bleached by the chemical solution.* ❻逮捕，捉（㊥ 捉～）to catch; to capture; to arrest：～获 *to capture; to arrest* | 猫～老鼠。*The cat catches the mouse.* ❼介词 preposition ①把 used to introduce the object of the following verb：我～你当朋友看待。*I see you as a friend.* ②用 with：～这笔钱买身衣服。*Buy some clothes with this money.*

镎（**鎿**） ná ㄋㄚ́ 放射性金属元素，符号 Np。neptunium (Np)

乸 nǎ ㄋㄚ̌ 〈方 dialect〉雌，母的 female：鸡～（母鸡）*hen*

哪 nǎ ㄋㄚ̌ 代词 pronoun ①表示疑问，后面跟量词或数量词，要求在所问范围中有所确定 (used before measure words or numbers) which; what：你喜欢读～种书？*What type of books do you like to read?* [哪儿] [哪

里]什么地方 where：你在～住？*Where do you live?* | ～有困难，就到～去。*Go wherever there are difficulties.* ㊕用于反问句 (used in rhetorical questions) how could; not at all：我～知道？（我不知道）*How should I know?* | 他～笨啊？（他不笨）*He is not dumb at all.* ②表示反问 (used to indicate a rhetorical question) how can; how could：没有耕耘，～有收获？*No pain, no gain. (literally means 'If you haven't worked on your land, how could you bring in the harvest?')*

⇨ see also na on p.468, né on p.472, něi on p.473

那 nà ㄋㄚˋ 代词，指较远的时间、地方或事物，跟"这"相对 (pronoun, opposite of 这) that：～时 *then; at that time; in those days* | ～里 *there; at/in that place* | ～个 *that; that one* | ～样 *that kind; so; such; like that* | ～些 *those* [那么]（*那末）（－me）1 代词，那样 (pronoun) that; that kind of：就～办吧 *do it that way* | 要不了～多 *do not need that much* | ～个人 *that kind of person* | ～个脾气 *a temper like that* 2 连词，跟前面"如果""若是"等相应，表示申说应有的结果或做出判断 (conjunction, used as a pattern together with 如果 or 若是) then; in that case：如果敌人不投降，～就消灭他。*If the enemy won't surrender, then kill him.*

⇨ see also nā on p.466, nèi on p.473

蒳 nà ㄋㄚˋ 用于地名 used in place names：～拔林（在台湾省）*Nabalin (in Taiwan Province)*

⇨ see also nuó on p.485

娜 nà ㄋㄚˋ 用于人名 (used in given names) Na

⇨ see also nuó on p.485

呐 nà ㄋㄚˋ [呐喊]大声叫喊 to shout; to yell; to cry out：摇旗～*(in ancient battles) wave flags and make battle cries; voice one's support* | ～助威 *cheer on*

纳(納) nà ㄋㄚˋ ❶收入，放进 to receive; to take in：出～*cashier; receive and pay out money; receive and lend books, etc.* | 吐故～新 *get rid of the old and take in the new* ㊊①接受 to accept：采～*adopt (a suggestion or plan)* | ～谏 *take advice* ②享受 to enjoy：～凉 *enjoy the cool* ❷缴付（㊎缴－）to pay; to turn in：～税 *pay taxes* ❸补缀，缝补，现在多指密密地缝 to sew and mend; (now often) to sew close stitches：～鞋底 *stitch soles of cloth shoes* ❹（外 loanword）法定计量单位中十进分数单位词头之一，表示 10^{-9}，符号 n。nano- (n) [纳西族]我国少数民族，参看附录四 the Naxi people (one of the ethnic groups in China. See Appendix Ⅳ.)

肭 nà ㄋㄚˋ see 腽肭兽(wà－－) at 腽 on page 671

钠(鈉) nà ㄋㄚˋ 金属元素，符号 Na，银白色，质软，燃烧时能发强光。是重要的工业原料 sodium (Na)

衲 nà ㄋㄚˋ ❶僧衣 Buddhist monk's robe㊕僧人 Buddhist monk：老～ *eldly monk (also used by an elderly monk to refer to himself)* ❷ same as "纳❸"：百～衣 *monk's robe made of patches; patchwork clothing*

捺 nà ㄋㄚˋ ❶用手按 to press down ❷（一儿）汉字从上向右斜下的一种笔形（㇏）(in a Chinese character) right falling stroke："人"字是一撇一～。*The Chinese character 人 is written with a left falling stroke followed by a right falling stroke.*

哪 na ·ㄋㄚ 助词，"啊"受到前一字韵母 n 收音的影响而发生的变音 (auxiliary word) a variation of 啊，used after words ending with the consonant "n"：同志们，加油干～！*Comrades, work harder!*

⇨ see also nǎ on p.466, né on p.472, něi on p.473

NAI ㄋㄞ

乃（△*廼、*迺）nǎi ㄋㄞˇ ❶文言代词，你，你的 (pronoun in classical Chinese) you; your：～父 *your father* | ～兄 *your brother* ❷副词，才，就 (adverb) just; only：吾求之久矣，今～得之。*I've been looking for it long, but have only got it now.* | 知己知彼，胜～不殆。*Know the enemy and know yourself. Only then will you never lose your battle.* ❸是，就是 to be：失败～成功之母。*Failure is the mother of success.*

［乃至］1 甚至 even：全班～全校都行动起来了。*The whole class and even the whole school have taken action.* 2 以至于 so as to; as a result：平日疏于管理，～如此。*This is the result of daily negligence of management.*

艿 nǎi ㄋㄞˇ ［芋艿］即芋头。也作"芋奶" taro (also written as 芋奶)

奶（*嬭）nǎi ㄋㄞˇ ❶乳房，哺乳的器官 breast ❷乳汁 milk：牛～ *milk; cow's milk* | ～油 *cream* | ～粉 *milk powder* ❸用自己的乳汁喂孩子 to breastfeed：～孩子 *breastfeed a baby*

［奶奶］1 祖母 (paternal) grandmother 2 对老年妇人的尊称 (honorific term) old lady：邻居老～ *the old lady from the next door*

氖 nǎi ㄋㄞˇ 气体元素，符号 Ne，无色、无臭，不易与其他元素化合。把氖装入真空管中通电，能发红光，可做霓虹灯 neon (Ne)

迺（*廼）nǎi ㄋㄞˇ ❶see 乃 on page 468 ❷用于地名 used in place names：～子街村（在吉林省永吉）*Naizijiecun (in Yongji, Jilin Province)* ❸姓 (surname) Nai

奈 nài ㄋㄞˋ 奈何，怎样，如何 how; however：无～ *not know what to do; unfortunately* | 怎～ *but; however* | 无～何（无可奈何，没有办法可想）*feel/be*

N

helpless; can do nothing

柰 nài ㄋㄞˋ （一子）落叶小乔木，花白色，果实小。可做苹果砧木 crab apple

萘 nài ㄋㄞˋ 有机化合物，无色晶体，有特殊气味，易升华。过去用的卫生球就是萘制成的，现已禁用 naphthalene

佴 nài ㄋㄞˋ 姓 (surname) Nai

⇨ see also èr on p.162

耐 nài ㄋㄞˋ 受得住，禁（jīn）得起 to be able to bear/stand：～劳 *able to endure hard work* | ～用 *durable* | ～烦 *patient* | ～火砖 *firebrick* | 忍～ *to bear; to restrain* | 俗不可～ *unbearably vulgar* [耐心] 不急躁，不厌烦 patient：～说服 *persuade sb patiently*

耏 nài ㄋㄞˋ 古代一种剃除面颊上胡须的刑罚 to shave off the beard (a form of punishment in ancient times)

⇨ see also ér on p.161

鼐 nài ㄋㄞˋ 大鼎 big cauldron

褦 nài ㄋㄞˋ [褦襶]（-dài）不晓事，不懂事 thoughtless; foolish

NAN ㄋㄢ

囝 nān ㄋㄢ 〈方 dialect〉same as "囡"

⇨ see also jiǎn on p.301

囡 nān ㄋㄢ 〈方 dialect〉小孩儿 child

男 nán ㄋㄢˊ ❶男性，男子，男人 man; male：～女平等 *gender equality* | ～学生 *male student* ❷儿子 son：长（zhǎng）～ *eldest son* ❸古代五等爵位（公、侯、伯、子、男）的第五等 baron (the fifth of the five ranks of nobility in ancient China)：～爵 *baron*

南 nán ㄋㄢˊ 方向，早晨面对太阳右手的一边，跟"北"相对 (opposite of 北) south：～方 *the south; the southern region* | 指～针 *compass*

莔 nán ㄋㄢˊ 一种草 a type of grass

喃 nán ㄋㄢˊ [喃喃] 小声叨唠 to murmur; to mutter：～自语 *mutter to oneself*

楠（*枏、*柟）nán ㄋㄢˊ 楠木，常绿乔木，木质坚固，是贵重的建筑材料，又可用来造船、制器物等 *Phoebe zhennan* (an evergreen tree, can be used as valuable material for boat building and woodwork)

难（難）nán ㄋㄢˊ ❶不容易（㊀艰-）difficult; hard：～事 *difficulty* | ～题 *difficult question; thorny problem* | ～写 *difficult to write* | ～产 *have a difficult delivery; (of plans) be difficult to realize* | ～得 *hard to get; rare* | ～免 *inevitable* | ～保 *cannot guarantee; cannot say for sure that* [难道] 副词，加强反问语气 (adverb, used in a rhetoric question for emphasis) how can; why not：河水～会倒流吗？ *How can a river run backward?* | 他们能完成

任务，～我们就不能吗？*If they can complete the task, shall we not?* ❷使人不好办 to baffle; to frustrate：这可真～住他了。*He was completely baffled.*［难为］（—wei）1 令人为难 to put sb in a difficult situation：他不会跳舞，就别～他了。*He can't dance, so don't press him to.* 2 亏得，表示感谢 (used to express gratitude) it is kind of sb：这么冷的天，～你还来看我。*It is nice of you to visit me on such a cold day.*｜～你把机器修好了。*It is very kind of you to fix the machine.* ❸不好 unpleasant; bad：～听 *unpleasant to the ear; harsh; disreputable*｜～看 *unsightly; (of look or expression) unpleasant; embarassing*

〈古 ancient〉also same as 傩 (nuó)

⇨ see also nàn on p.470

赧 nǎn ㄋㄢˇ 因羞惭而脸红 to blush with shame：～然 *blushing*｜～颜 *blush with shame*

腩 nǎn ㄋㄢˇ 〈方 dialect〉牛、鱼等腹部松软的肉 belly meat; flank steak：牛～*flank steak*｜鱼～*fish belly*

蝻 nǎn ㄋㄢˇ （—子、—儿）仅有翅芽还没生成翅膀的蝗虫 nymph of a locust

难(難) nàn ㄋㄢˋ ❶灾患，困苦（㊀灾—、患—）disaster; trouble; calamity：～民 *refugee*｜遭～*be hit by a disaster*｜逃～*flee from a calamity; be a refugee*｜大～临头 *be faced with looming calamity* ❷诘责 to blame; to reproach：非～*find fault with*｜责～*to blame; to censure*｜刁～*make sth difficult for sb*｜问～*question closely; to query*

⇨ see also nán on p.469

婻 nàn ㄋㄢˋ ❶容貌美丽 beautiful ❷微胖 plump

NANG ㄋㄤ

囊 nāng ㄋㄤ ［囊膪］（—chuài）see 膪 on page 90

⇨ see also náng on p.470

囔 nāng ㄋㄤ ［囔囔］（—nang）小声说话 to mumble; to murmur

囊 náng ㄋㄤˊ 口袋 bag; sack; pocket：探～取物（喻极容易）*a piece of cake; as easy as falling off a log (literally means 'take something out of one's pocket')*［囊括］全部包罗 to include; to embrace：～四海 *bring the whole country under imperial rule*｜～本次比赛全部金牌 *sweep all the gold medals at the competition*

⇨ see also nāng on p.470

馕(饢) náng ㄋㄤˊ （维 *Uygur*）一种烤制成的面饼，是维吾尔、哈萨克等民族的主食 *nang*; flatbread (a staple food of the Uygur and Kazak ethnic groups)

⇨ see also nǎng on p.471

曩 nǎng ㄋㄤˇ 从前的，过去的 past; former：～日 *in the past; in the olden days*｜～者（从前）*in the past; formerly*

攮 nǎng ㄋㄤˇ 用刀刺 to stab：～了一刀 *made a stab with a knife* | ～子（短而尖的刀）*dagger*

馕（饢） nǎng ㄋㄤˇ 拼命地往嘴里塞食物 to cram (food into the mouth)

⇨ see also náng on p.470

儾 nàng ㄋㄤˋ ❶软弱 weak; feeble ❷ same as "齉"

齉 nàng ㄋㄤˋ 鼻子堵住，发音不清 blocked (nose)：～鼻儿 *nasal; sb who speaks nasally*

NAO ㄋㄠ

孬 nāo ㄋㄠ 〈方 dialect〉❶不好，坏 bad：人品～ *be a bad character* ❷怯懦，没有勇气 cowardly：这人太～。*He is a stinking coward.* | ～种 *coward*

呶 náo ㄋㄠˊ 喧哗㊀to clamour; to chatter：～～不休 *babble on; chatter away*

挠（撓） náo ㄋㄠˊ ❶扰乱，使事情不能顺利进行 to hinder：阻～ *to hinder; to obstruct* ❷弯曲 to yield; to bend：不屈不～（喻不屈服）*unyielding; dauntless* | 百折不～（喻有毅力）*unflinching; persevering* ❸搔，抓 to scratch：～痒痒 *to scratch*

铙（鐃） náo ㄋㄠˊ ❶铜质圆形的打击乐器，比钹大 *nao* (big cymbal) ❷古代的一种军中乐器，像铃铛，但没有中间的锤 tongueless bell (an ancient musical instrument used in the army)

蛲（蟯） náo ㄋㄠˊ 蛲虫，寄生虫，像线头，白色，寄生在人的肠内，雌虫夜里爬到肛门处产卵 pinworm

峱（嶩）** náo ㄋㄠˊ 古山名，在今山东省临淄附近 (ancient) Nao Mountain (near today's Linzi, Shandong Province)

硇（硵）** náo ㄋㄠˊ [硇砂] 矿物名，就是天然出产的氯化铵，可入药 sal ammoniac [硇洲] 岛名，在广东省湛江市东南海中 Naozhou (an island, to the south-east of Zhanjiang, Guangdong Province)

猱 náo ㄋㄠˊ 古书上说的一种猴子 a kind of monkey (in ancient Chinese texts)

嶩 náo ㄋㄠˊ 同"峱"。用于人名 (used in given names) same as 峱

垴 nǎo ㄋㄠˇ 〈方 dialect〉山岗、丘陵较平的顶部。多用于地名 flat hilltop (often used in place names)

恼（惱） nǎo ㄋㄠˇ ❶发怒，使发怒 to be angry; to irritate：～怒 *get angry; lose one's temper* | ～火 *annoyed; irritated* | 惹～了他 *provoked him* | ～羞成怒 *be humiliated into anger* | 你别～我。*Do not make me angry.* ❷烦闷，苦闷（㊀烦一、苦一）annoyed; upset：懊～ *annoyed; upset with regret*

脑（腦） nǎo ㄋㄠˇ ❶（一子）人和高等动物神经系

N

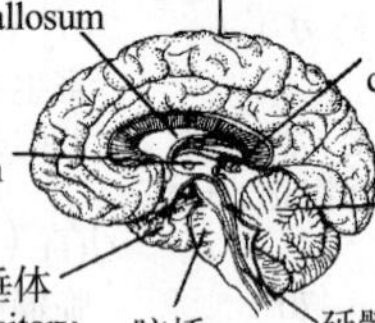

人的脑 Human Brain

统的主要部分，在颅腔里，分大脑、小脑和脑干等部分，主管全身知觉、运动和思维、记忆等活动 brain［脑筋］［脑子］㊉指思考、记忆等能力 brain; mind：开动～ *think hard; use one's brain* ❷（一儿）形状或颜色像脑子的东西 (resembling brain in form or colour) jelly; cream：豆腐～儿 *jellied bean curd*

瑙 nǎo ㄋㄠˇ see 玛瑙 (mǎ—) at 玛 on page 432

闹（鬧、*閙） nào ㄋㄠˋ ❶ 不安静 noisy; loud ①人多声音杂 noisy：～市 *busy street* ②喧哗，搅扰 to clamour; to disturb：不要～了！ *Stop the noise!* | 孙悟空大～天宫。 *The Monkey King wreaked havoc in Heaven.* ㊊戏耍，耍笑 to play a joke (on sb); to tease：～着玩儿 *play a joke* ❷发生（病、灾等不好的事）to suffer from; to be troubled by：～病 *fall ill* | ～嗓子 *have a sore throat* | ～水灾 *suffer from floods* | ～蝗虫 *suffer from locust plagues* | ～笑话 *make a fool of oneself* ❸发泄，发作 to give vent to：～情绪 *be in a bad mood* | ～脾气 *vent one's anger* ❹搞，弄 to do; to be engaged in：～生产 *be engaged in production* | ～革命 *carry out the revolution* | 把问题～清楚 *get to the bottom of the problem*

淖 nào ㄋㄠˋ 烂泥 deep mud; mire：泥～ *bog; mire; morass*

［淖尔］（蒙 *Mongolian*）湖泊 nor (Mongolian word for "lake")：达里～（就是达里泊，在内蒙古自治区）*Dali Nor (i.e. Dali Lake, in the Inner Mongolia Autonomous Region)* | 库库～（就是青海湖）*Koko Nor (i.e. Qinghai Lake)* | 罗布～（就是罗布泊，在新疆维吾尔自治区）*Lop Nor (i.e. Lop Lake, in the Xinjiang Uygur Autonomous Region)*

臑 nào ㄋㄠˋ 牲畜前肢的下半截 shank (lower half of the forelimbs of a livestock)

NE ㄋㄜ

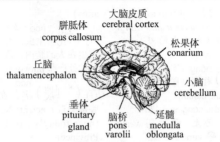

哪 né ㄋㄜˊ ［哪吒］（一zhā）神话里神的名字 *Nezha*

(a deity in Chinese mythology)

⇨ see also nǎ on p.466, na on p.468, něi on p.473

讷(訥) nè ㄋㄜˋ 语言迟钝，不善讲话 inarticulate; slow of speech：口～ *slow of speech* | 木～ *of simple manners and few words*

呢 ne ·ㄋㄜ 助词 auxiliary word ①表示疑问（句中含有疑问词）used to indicate a question：你到哪儿去～？*Where are you going?* | 怎么办～？*Now what?* ②表示确定的语气 used to convey certainty：早着～ *still too early* | 还没有来～ *haven't arrived yet* ③表示动作正在进行 used to indicate a continuous action：他睡觉～。*He is sleeping.* ④用在句中表示停顿 used to indicate a pause：喜欢～，就买下；不喜欢～，就不买。*If you like it, just buy it. If you don't, then don't buy it.*

⇨ see also ní on p.475

NEI ㄋㄟ

哪 něi ㄋㄟˇ "哪"（nǎ）和"一"的合音，但指数量时不限于一 (combined pronunciation of 哪 and 一) which; what：～个 *which one* | ～些 *which ones* | ～年 *which year* | ～几年 *which years*

⇨ see also nǎ on p.466, na on p.468, né on p.472

馁(餒) něi ㄋㄟˇ ❶饥饿 hungry; famished：冻～ *suffer from cold and hunger* ㊀没有勇气 discouraged：气～ *discouraged* | 胜不骄，败不～。*No arrogance in victory, and no despair in defeat.* ❷古称鱼腐烂为馁 (ancient) (of fish) rotten

内 nèi ㄋㄟˋ ❶里面，跟"外"相对 inner; inside; within (opposite of 外)：～室 *inner room* | ～衣 *underwear* | ～情 *inside information/story* | 国～ *domestic; the inner of a country* | 党～ *within the party* 特指体内或内心 (of organs) internal; (mentally) inside：～伤 *internal damage* | ～功 *(of* qigong*) exercises to strengthen internal organs; internal power* | ～科 *internal medicine; general medicine* | ～疚 *guilty; conscience-stricken* | ～省（xǐng）*to introspect; be critical of oneself* [内行]（－háng）对于某种事情有经验 (an) expert; (a) professional [内务] 1 集体生活中室内的日常事务 (of dormitories or barracks) routine cleaning：整理～ *tidy up the barracks* 2 指国内事务（多指民政）internal affairs：～部 *Ministry of Internal Affairs* ❷指妻子或妻子的亲属 wife; wife's relative：～人 *wife* | ～兄 *wife's elder brother* | ～侄 *son of wife's brother*

〈古 ancient〉also same as 纳(nà)

那 nèi ㄋㄟˋ "那"（nà）和"一"的合音，但指数量时不限于一 (combined pronunciation of 那 and 一) that; those：～个 *that* | ～些 *those* | ～年 *that year* | ～三年 *those three years*

⇨ see also nā on p.466, nà on p.467

N

NEN ㄋㄣ

恁 nèn ㄋㄣˋ 〈方 dialect〉代词 pronoun ①那么，这么 so; such：～大 *so big* | ～高 *so tall; so high* | 要不了～些 *not need that much* ②那 that; those：～时 *at that time* | ～时节 *at that time*

嫩 nèn ㄋㄣˋ 〈古 ancient〉same as "嫩"

⇨ see also ruǎn on p.566

嫩(*嫰) nèn ㄋㄣˋ ❶初生而柔弱，娇嫩，跟"老"相对 tender; delicate (opposite of 老)：～芽 *sprout* | 肉皮～ *have delicate skin* 引①经火力烧制的时间短 (of cooked food) tender; under-done：鸡蛋煮得～。*The eggs are soft-boiled.* ②阅历浅，不老练 inexperienced; immature：他担任主编还～了点儿。*He is not experienced enough to be the editor-in-chief.* ❷淡，浅 (of colour) light; pale：～黄 *pale yellow* | ～绿 *light green*

NENG ㄋㄥ

能 néng ㄋㄥˊ ❶能力，才干，本事 ability; capacity; competence：各尽其～ *to the best of their ability* | 无～ *incompetent* | 才～ *talent* ❷有才干的 able; capable：～人 *talented person; able person* | ～者多劳。*An able person is always busy.* | ～手 *expert; dab hand* ❸能够，胜任 to be able to; to be qualified for：他～开车。*He can drive.* | ～完成任务 *be able to complete the task* | ～说会道 *be eloquent; have the gift of the gab* [能动] 自觉努力，积极活动的 self-motivated; active：主观～性 *subjective activity* | ～地学习 *learn actively* ❹会（表示可能性）can; may (used to indicate possibility)：他还～来吗？*Will he come?* ❺应，该 should：你不～这样不负责任。*You shouldn't be as irresponsible as this.* ❻能量，度量物质运动的一种物理量 energy：电～ *electric energy* | 核～ *nuclear energy*

NG ㄫ

唔 ńg ㄫˊ ń ㄋˊ (又) same as "嗯 (ńg)"

⇨ see also ń on p.466, wú on p.690

嗯 ńg ㄫˊ ń ㄋˊ (又) 叹词，表示疑问 (exclamation, used to indicate inquiry) eh：～？你说什么？*Eh? What did you say?*

嗯(㕶)** ňg ㄫˇ ň ㄋˇ (又) 叹词，表示不以为然或出乎意外 (exclamation, used to indicate disagreement or surprise) well; hey：～！我看不一定是那么回事。*Well, I don't think so.* | ～！你怎么还没去？*Hey! Why are you still here?*

嗯(叿)** ǹg ㄫˋ ǹ ㄋˋ (又) 叹词，表示答应 (exclamation, used to indicate consent) OK：～，就这么办吧。*OK, let's do it like this.*

N

NI ㄋㄧ

妮 nī ㄋㄧ （一子、一儿）女孩子 girl

尼 ní ㄋㄧˊ 梵语音译"比丘尼"的省称。佛教指出家修行的女子。通常叫尼姑 (short for 比丘尼， from Sanskrit, usually called 尼姑) bhikkhuni; Buddhist nun

伲 ní ㄋㄧˊ 姓 (surname) Ni

⇨ see also nì on p.476

坭 ní ㄋㄧˊ ❶ same as "泥 (ní)" ❷ 用于地名 used in place names：白～（在广东省佛山市）*Baini (in Foshan, Guangdong Province)*

呢 ní ㄋㄧˊ （一子）一种毛织物 (often heavy) woolen fabric

[呢喃]（一nán）形容燕子的叫声 (of swallows) twitter; chirrup

⇨ see also ne on p.473

泥 ní ㄋㄧˊ ❶土和水合成的东西 mud ❷像泥的东西 paste; pulp; mash：印～（印色）*(used for stamp seal) ink paste; inkpad* | 枣～ *date paste* | 山药～ *mashed yam*

⇨ see also nì on p.476

怩 ní ㄋㄧˊ see 忸怩 (niǔ一) at 忸 on page 482

铌(鈮) ní ㄋㄧˊ 金属元素，旧叫钶（kē），符号 Nb，钢灰色，质硬。可用来制合金钢、电子管和超导材料 niobium (Nb) (formerly called 钶 kē)

倪 ní ㄋㄧˊ 端，边际 end; extremity [端倪] 头绪 clue：事情已略有～。*Some clues have been found.*

猊 ní ㄋㄧˊ see 狻猊 (suān一) at 狻 on page 625

輗(輗) ní ㄋㄧˊ 古代大车辕端连接、固定横木或车轭的部件 (of an ancient carriage) brace; joint (between the ends of shafts and the singletree or yoke for connection and reinforcement)

霓(*蜺) ní ㄋㄧˊ see 虹 on page 254

齯(齯) ní ㄋㄧˊ 老年人牙齿落尽后又长出的小牙，古时作为长寿的象征 new tooth (of an elderly person after total tooth loss, symbol of longevity in ancient China)

鲵(鯢) ní ㄋㄧˊ 两栖动物，有大鲵和小鲵两种。大鲵俗叫娃娃鱼，眼小，口大，四肢短，尾巴扁，叫声像小孩哭，生活在溪水中 (Asiatic and giant) salamander (the giant salamander is informally called 娃娃鱼)

麑 ní ㄋㄧˊ 小鹿 fawn

拟(擬) nǐ ㄋㄧˇ ❶打算 to plan to; to intend to：～往上海 *plan to head for Shanghai* ❷初步设计编制，起草 to draft; to draw up：～稿 *draw up a draft* | ～议 *proposal; to draft* | ～定计划 *work out a plan* ❸仿照（㊀模一）to imitate; to mimic：～作 *imitation (of a literary work)* [拟声词] 模拟事物声音的词，如"咚、砰、叮当、哐啷"等 onomatopoeic word

N

你 nǐ ㄋㄧˇ 代词，指称对方 (pronoun) you

旎 nǐ ㄋㄧˇ see 旖旎 (yǐ—) at 旖 on page 773

薿 nǐ ㄋㄧˇ ㊂形容茂盛 flourishing; luxuriant; lush: 黍稷~~ *crops growing luxuriantly*

伲 nì ㄋㄧˋ 〈方 dialect〉代词，我，我们 (pronoun) I; we

⇨ see also ní on p.475

泥 nì ㄋㄧˋ ❶涂抹 to plaster; to daub; to smear: ~墙 *plaster a wall* | ~炉子 *cover a stove with daub* ❷固执，死板（㊀拘—）stubborn; rigid; inflexible

⇨ see also ní on p.475

昵(*暱) nì ㄋㄧˋ 亲近（㊀亲—）intimate: ~称 *pet name*

逆 nì ㄋㄧˋ ❶向着相反的方向，跟"顺"相对 contrary; counter; against (opposite of 顺): ~风 *against the wind; upwind* | ~水行舟 *sail against the current* | 倒行~施 *go against historical trends; act in defiance of reason and common sense* ㊁不顺利 adverse; difficult: ~境 *adversity; unfavorable circumstances* ❷抵触，不顺从 to go against; to disobey: ~反心理 *rebellious psychology* | 忠言~耳。*Sincere advice is often unpleasant to the ear.* ❸背叛者或背叛者的 traitor; traitorous: ~产 *traitor's property* ❹迎接 to greet; to meet: ~战 *battle the enemy head-on* ㊁预先 in advance; beforehand: ~料 *to predict; to anticipate*

匿 nì ㄋㄧˋ 隐藏，躲避（㊀隐—、藏—）to hide; to conceal: ~名信 *anonymous letter* | 销声~迹 *disappear from the scene (literally means 'keep silent and lie low')*

陧 nì ㄋㄧˋ [埤陧]（pì—）〈古 ancient〉same as "埤堄"

堄 nì ㄋㄧˋ see 埤堄 (pì—) at 埤 on page 502

睨 nì ㄋㄧˋ 斜着眼睛看 to cast a sidelong glance: ~视 *to cast an oblique look*

腻(膩) nì ㄋㄧˋ ❶食物油脂过多 oily; greasy: 油~ *greasy* | 肥~ *fatty and greasy* [细腻] 1 光滑 smooth; fine: 质地~ *of a fine texture* 2 细致 delicate; exquisite; subtle: 描写~ *describe with subtlety* ❷腻烦，因过多而厌烦 to be bored with; to be fed up with; to be tired of: 玩~了 *be bored with playing* | 听~了 *have heard too much of sth* ❸积污，污垢 soot; grime: 尘~ *dirt*

溺 nì ㄋㄧˋ ❶淹没 to drown; to be submerged in: ~死 *be drowned* | ~水 *sink in water* ❷沉迷不悟，过分 to be addicted to; to be hooked on: ~信 *believe too firmly in* | ~爱 *to spoil; to pamper*

⇨ see also niào on p.479

NIAN ㄋㄧㄢ

拈 niān ㄋㄧㄢ 用手指搓捏或拿东西 to pick up (with the thumb and one or two fingers); to pinch: ~须 *finger one's beard* | ~花 *pick/pluck a flower* | ~阄（抓

阄儿）*draw lots* | 信手～来 *have words or material at one's fingertips and write with facility (literally means 'pick up at random')*

蔫 niān ㄋㄧㄢ 植物因失去水分而萎缩 (of plants) to wither; to wilt：花～了。*The flower has wilted.* | 菜～了。*The vegetable has shrivelled up.* ㊀ 精神不振，不活泼 to be listless; to be languid

年（*秊） nián ㄋㄧㄢˊ ❶地球绕太阳一周的时间。公历规定平年365天，闰年366天 year ㊀ ①年节，一年的开始 New Year; Spring Festival; Chinese New Year：过～ *celebrate the Spring Festival* | ～画 *New Year picture* ②时期 (in history) period; time：光绪～间 *during the reign of Emperor Guangxu* | 民国初～ *the early years of the Republic of China* [年头儿] 1 全年的时间 one year：看看已是三个～ *three years have passed* 2 时代 times; ages：那～穷人可真苦哇。*The poor lived a miserable life back then.* 3 庄稼的收成 harvest：今年～真好，比去年多收一倍。*We had a good harvest this year, which doubled that of the last.* ❷每年的 annual; yearly：～会 *annual meeting* | ～产量 *annual output; annual yield* ❸年纪，岁数（㊁一龄、一岁）age：～老 *old* | ～轻 *young* ㊀ 人一生所经年岁的分期 period/stage (in one's life)：青～ *youth* | 壮～ *prime of life* ❹年景，年成，收成 harvest：丰～ *rich harvest; good year*

粘 nián ㄋㄧㄢˊ ❶same as "黏" ❷姓 (surname) Nian

⇨ see also zhān on p.830

鲇（鮎、**鯰） nián ㄋㄧㄢˊ 鱼名，头大，口宽，皮上有黏液，无鳞。生活在淡水中 Amur catfish

黏 nián ㄋㄧㄢˊ 像胶水或糨糊所具有的能使物体粘（zhān）合的性质 sticky; gluey; adhesive：～液 *slime; mucus* | 这江米很～。*The glutinous rice is very sticky.*

捻 niǎn ㄋㄧㄢˇ ❶用手指搓转（zhuàn）to twist (with the fingers)：～线 *twist yarn* | ～麻绳 *make a cord by twisting hemp fibre* ❷（一子、一儿）用纸、布条等搓成的像线绳样的东西 twist (a thin cord made by twisting paper, cloth, etc.)：纸～儿 *spill (a twist of paper for lighting a fire)* | 药～儿 *fuse (for igniting explosive)* | 灯～儿 *lampwick*

辇（輦） niǎn ㄋㄧㄢˇ (formerly pronounced liǎn) 古时用人拉着走的车，后来多指皇帝、皇后坐的车 (ancient) man-drawn carriage; imperial carriage

撵（攆） niǎn ㄋㄧㄢˇ ❶驱逐，赶走 to drive away; to banish; to expel：～走 *send off* | ～出去 *drive out* ❷追赶 to catch up with; to chase：他～不上我。*He couldn't catch up with me.*

碾 niǎn ㄋㄧㄢˇ ❶（一子）把东西轧（yà）碎或压平的器具 roller (for crushing or pressing)：石～ *stone roller* | 汽～ *steam*

N

roller ❷轧，滚压 to grind (with a roller)：～米 *husk rice*｜～药 *grind (traditional) medicine with a roller*

蹍 niǎn ㄋㄧㄢˇ 〈方 dialect〉踩 to step on; to tread

廿 niàn ㄋㄧㄢˋ 二十 twenty：～四史 *the Twenty-Four Histories*

念(❸❹*唸) niàn ㄋㄧㄢˋ ❶惦记，常常地想(㊥惦一) to miss; to often think of：思～ *to miss; remember fondly*｜想～ *to miss; long to see*｜不～旧恶 *not bear a grudge*｜怀～革命先烈 *cherish the memory of revolutionary martyrs* ❷想法(一头) thought; idea：杂～ *distracting thought*｜一～之差 *a momentary slip (often resulting in serious consequences)* ❸诵读 to read aloud：～书 *read a book*｜～诗 *chant a poem* ❹指上学 to go to/attend (school)：～高中 *go to senior high school* ❺"廿"的大写 (elaborate form of 廿) twenty

埝 niàn ㄋㄧㄢˋ 用土筑成的小堤或副堤 low bank between fields or shallow waters

NIANG ㄋㄧㄤ

娘(*孃) niáng ㄋㄧㄤˊ ❶对年轻女子的称呼 young woman; girl：渔～ *fisher girl*｜新～ *bride* [娘子] 1 尊称青年或中年妇女(多见于早期白话) (honorific speech, term of address for young or middle-aged woman, often used in early vernacular Chinese) you; your 2 旧称妻 (old) wife [姑娘](-niang) 1 未婚女子的通称 unmarried woman; maiden 2 女儿 daughter ❷母亲 mother ❸称长(zhǎng)一辈或年长的已婚妇女 term of address for an elderly married woman：大～ *aunt (term of address for the wife of one's father's elder brother or an elderly married woman)*｜婶～ *aunt (term of address for the wife of one's father's younger brother or a woman of that age)*｜师～ *madam (term of address for the wife of one's teacher or master)*

酿(釀) niàng ㄋㄧㄤˋ ❶利用发酵作用制造 to brew; to ferment：～酒 *make wine; brew beer*｜～造 *to make (wine, vinegar, etc.); to brew* ㊇ ①蜜蜂做蜜 (of bees) to make (honey)：～蜜 *make honey* ②逐渐形成 to lead to; to bring about：～成大祸 *brew big trouble* ❷指酒 alcoholic drink：佳～ *good liquor; vintage wine*

NIAO ㄋㄧㄠ

鸟(鳥) niǎo ㄋㄧㄠˇ 脊椎动物的一类，温血卵生，用肺呼吸，全身有羽毛，后肢能行走，一般前肢变为翅能飞 bird

茑(蔦) niǎo ㄋㄧㄠˇ 一种小灌木，茎能攀缘其他树木 a kind of climbing shrub [茑萝] 蔓草，花红色或白色 cypress vine

袅(裊、*嬝、*嫋、*褭) niǎo ㄋㄧㄠˇ [袅袅] 1 烟气缭

绕上腾的样子 (of smoke/vapour) curling upward：炊烟～ *smoke spiralling from kitchens* 2 细长柔软的东西随风摆动的样子 (of sth slender and flexible) flowing with the wind：垂杨～。*The weeping willows wave in the wind.* 3 声音绵延不绝 (of sound) lingering：余音～。*The lingering sound seems still in the air.* [袅娜] (－nuó) 1 形容草木柔软细长 (of plants) slender and flexible 2 形容女子姿态优美 (of a woman) graceful

嬲 niǎo ㄋㄧㄠˇ 戏弄，纠缠 to tease; to pester

尿 niào ㄋㄧㄠˋ ❶小便，从肾脏滤出、由尿道排泄出来的液体 urine ❷排泄小便 to urinate; to pee; to piss

⇨ see also suī on p.625

脲 niào ㄋㄧㄠˋ 尿素，有机化合物，无色晶体。广泛用于塑料、药剂和农业等生产中 urea; carbamide

溺 niào ㄋㄧㄠˋ same as "尿 (niào)"

⇨ see also nì on p.476

NIE ㄋㄧㄝ

捏(*揑) niē ㄋㄧㄝ ❶用拇指和其他手指夹住 to pinch; to hold (between the thumb and other fingers)：～着一粒豆 *hold a bean in one's fingers* ❷用手指把软的东西做成一定的形状 to mould with one's fingers：～饺子 *make dumplings* | ～泥人儿 *mould clay figurines* ❸假造，虚构 to make up; to forge; to fabricate：～造 *to make up* | ～报 *to misreport*

苶 nié ㄋㄧㄝˊ 〈方 dialect〉❶疲倦，精神不振 tired; listless; languid：发～ *look tired* | ～呆呆的 *look listless* ❷呆，傻 stupid：～子 *fool*

乜 niè ㄋㄧㄝˋ 姓 (surname) Nie

⇨ see also miē on p.453

陧 niè ㄋㄧㄝˋ see 杌陧 (wù－) at 杌 on page 692

涅(*湼) niè ㄋㄧㄝˋ ❶可做黑色染料的矾石 graphite ❷染黑 to dye sth black：～齿 *dye one's teeth black* [涅白] 不透明的白色 opaque white

[涅槃] 梵语音译，佛教代指佛或僧人死亡 nirvana

聂(聶) niè ㄋㄧㄝˋ 姓 (surname) Nie

嗫(囁) niè ㄋㄧㄝˋ [嗫嚅] (－rú) 口动，吞吞吐吐，想说又停止 to mumble; to hum and haw

镊(鑷) niè ㄋㄧㄝˋ 镊子，夹取毛发、细刺及其他细小东西的器具 tweezers

颞(顳) niè ㄋㄧㄝˋ [颞颥] (－rú) 头颅两侧靠近耳朵上方的部分 temple (of one's head)

蹑(躡) niè ㄋㄧㄝˋ ❶踩 to step on; to tread：～足其间（指参加到里面去）*join in (literally means 'put one's feet in')* [蹑手蹑脚] 行动很轻的样子 walking on tiptoe ❷追随 to follow：～踪 *to track; to trail*

臬 niè ㄋㄧㄝ ❶箭靶子的中心 bullseye; centre of a target ❷古代测日影的标杆 gnomon ❸标准，法式 criterion; standard: 圭～ *criterion; standard*

嵲 niè ㄋㄧㄝ see 嵽嵲 (dié—) at 嵽 on page 138

闑(闑) niè ㄋㄧㄝ 〈古 ancient〉 ❶在两扇门相交处所竖的短木 short wooden stake (between the two leaves of a door/gate) ❷指门 door; gate

镍(鎳) niè ㄋㄧㄝ 金属元素，符号Ni，银白色。可用于制合金钢、铸币、电镀等 nickel (Ni)

菍 niè ㄋㄧㄝ [地菍]草本植物，叶倒卵形或椭圆形，花紫红色，全草入药 *Melastoma dodecandrum Lour* (a medicinal herb)

啮(嚙、*齧、*囓) niè ㄋㄧㄝ 咬 to gnaw; to nibble: 虫咬鼠～。*Insects bite and mice nibble.*

孽(*孼) niè ㄋㄧㄝ ❶邪恶，也指邪恶的人 evil; wicked; villain: ～党 *clique of traitors* | 妖～ *monster; fiend* ❷恶因，恶事 sin; evil; crime: 造～ *do evil; commit a sin* | 罪～ *sin* ❸不忠或不孝 disloyal; unfilial: ～臣 *treacherous vassal* | ～子 *unfilial son*

蘖(**櫱) niè ㄋㄧㄝ 树木砍去后又长出来的芽子 sprout (from the base of a tree); tiller: 萌～ *sprout; bud* [分蘖]稻、麦等农作物的种子生出幼苗后，在接近地面主茎的地方分枝 (of rice, wheat, etc.) to tiller

蘖(**糵) niè ㄋㄧㄝ 酒曲 starter (for making liquor)

NIN ㄋㄧㄣ

您 nín ㄋㄧㄣ 代词，"你"的敬称 (pronoun, polite speech) you

NING ㄋㄧㄥ

宁(寧、❶-❸△*甯、*寍)

níng ㄋㄧㄥ ❶安宁 calm; peaceful: ～静 *peaceful* | 鸡犬不～ *general disturbance (literally means 'even fowls and dogs are left no peace')* [归宁]旧时女子出嫁后回娘家看望父母 (old, of a married woman) go back home to visit one's parents ❷使安宁 to appease; to calm; to pacify: 息事～人 *appease a quarrel; make concessions to avoid trouble* ❸江苏省南京的别称 Ning (another name for Nanjing, Jiangsu Province) ❹姓 (surname) Ning

⇨ see also nìng on p.481

⇨ 甯 see also nìng on p.481

拧(擰) níng ㄋㄧㄥ 握住物体的两端向相反的方向用力 to wring; to twist: ～毛巾 *wring a towel* | ～绳子 *twist a rope*

⇨ see also nǐng on p.481, nìng on p.481

苧(薴) níng ㄋㄧㄥ 有机化合物，无色液体，有香味，存在于柑橘类的果皮中，可用来制香料 limonene

⇨ see also zhù 苎 on p.868

咛(嚀) níng ㄋㄧㄥˊ see 叮咛 at 叮 on page 139

狞(獰) níng ㄋㄧㄥˊ 凶恶 fierce; ferocious：～笑 *to grin malevolently* (see 狰狞 zhēng－ at 狰 on page 847 for reference)

柠(檸) níng ㄋㄧㄥˊ ［柠檬］（－méng）常绿小乔木，生长在热带、亚热带，果实也叫柠檬，椭圆形，两端尖，淡黄色，味酸，可制饮料 lemon

聍(聹) níng ㄋㄧㄥˊ see 耵聍 (dīng－) at 耵 on page 139

凝 níng ㄋㄧㄥˊ ❶凝结，液体遇冷变成固体，气体因温度降低或压力增加变成液体 to condense; to curdle; to solidify：～固 *solidify* | 油～住了。*The oil congealed.* ❷聚集，集中 to concentrate; to focus：～神 *concentrate all attention* | ～视 *to gaze* | 独坐～思 *sit all alone in meditation*

拧(擰) nǐng ㄋㄧㄥˇ ❶扭转，控制住东西的一部分而绞转（zhuàn）to screw：～螺丝钉 *drive a screw* | ～墨水瓶盖 *screw/unscrew the cap of an ink bottle* ❷相反，颠倒，错 contrary; upside down; wrong：我弄～了。*I got it wrong.* | 意思满～。*The meaning is totally wrong.* ⓘ抵触 to differ; to disagree：两人越说越～。*The more they talk, the more the two of them differ.*

⇨ see also níng on p.480, nìng on p.481

宁(寧、△*甯、*寗) nìng ㄋㄧㄥˋ 副词，宁可，表示比较后做出的选择，情愿 (adverb) would rather... (than)：～死不屈 *would rather die than surrender* | ～缺毋滥 *would rather go without than make a poor choice*

⇨ see also níng on p.480

拧(擰) nìng ㄋㄧㄥˋ 倔强，别扭，不驯服 stubborn; obstinate; unbending：～脾气 *stubbornness*

⇨ see also níng on p.480, nǐng on p.481

泞(濘) nìng ㄋㄧㄥˋ 烂泥 mud; slush; mire ［泥泞］1 有烂泥难走 muddy; slushy：道路～。*The roads are muddy.* 2 淤积的烂泥 ooze; bog; sludge：陷入～ *get bogged down in mud*

佞 nìng ㄋㄧㄥˋ ❶有才智 intelligent; talented：不～（旧时谦称自己）*(old,humble speech) I* ❷善辩，巧言谄媚 eloquent; given to flattery：～口 *evil tongue* | ～人（有口才而不正派的人）*sycophant*

甯 nìng ㄋㄧㄥˋ ❶ see 宁 on page 481 ❷姓 (surname) Ning

⇨ see also níng 宁 on p.480

NIU ㄋㄧㄡ

妞 niū ㄋㄧㄡ （－儿）女孩子 girl

牛 niú ㄋㄧㄡˊ ❶家畜，反刍类，头上有角，力量大，可以耕田或拉车，常见的有黄牛、

N

水牛、牦牛等 ox; cattle ❷形容固执或骄傲 stubborn; headstrong; proud：～脾气 *stubbornness* | 自打当了经理，就～起来了。*He has been acting like a big shot ever since he became the manager.* ❸星宿名，二十八宿之一 *Niu* (one of the twenty-eight constellations in ancient Chinese astronomy) ❹ 力的单位名牛顿的简称，符号N。(a unit of force, short for 牛顿) newton (N)

扭 niǔ ㄋㄧㄡˇ 转动一部分 to turn; to twist; to wrench：～过脸来 *turn one's face* | ～转身子 *turn one's body* 引 ①走路时身体摇摆转动 (of walking gait) to sway; to swing：～秧歌 *do the* yangge *dance* | 一～一～地走 *walk with swaying hips* ②拧伤筋骨 to sprain; to wrench：～了筋 *get one's tendon wrenched* | ～了腰 *sprained one's waist* ③扳转，转变情势 to change (circumstances); to reverse (a situation)：～转局面 *turn the tide*

狃 niǔ ㄋㄧㄡˇ 因袭，拘泥 to follow closely; to stick to：～于习俗 *stick to conventions* | ～于成见 *prejudiced*

忸 niǔ ㄋㄧㄡˇ [忸怩] (—ní) 不好意思、不大方的样子 timid; bashful; coy：～作态 *be affectedly bashful*

纽(紐) niǔ ㄋㄧㄡˇ ❶器物上可以提起或系挂的部分 handle; knob：秤～ *lifting cord of a steelyard* | 印～ *seal top engraved in the likeness of animals, with a hole for a tassel* ❷ (—子) 纽扣，可以扣合衣物的球状物或片状物 button ❸ 枢纽 hub; pivot：～带 *link*

杻 niǔ ㄋㄧㄡˇ 古书上说的一种树 a kind of tree in ancient Chinese texts

⇨ see also chǒu on p.86

钮(鈕) niǔ ㄋㄧㄡˇ ❶器物上用手开关或调节的部件 knob; button; switch：按～ *push button* | 旋～ *knob* ❷ same as "纽❷"

拗(*抝) niù ㄋㄧㄡˋ 固执，不驯顺 stubborn; obstinate：执～ *stubborn* | 脾气很～ *being a stubborn person*

⇨ see also ǎo on p.8, ào on p.8

NONG ㄋㄨㄥ

农(農、*辳) nóng ㄋㄨㄥˊ ❶种庄稼 agriculture; farming：务～ *be engaged in farming* | ～业 *agriculture* | ～机 *agricultural machinery* | ～谚 *farmer's saying* ❷ 农民 farmer; peasant：菜～ *vegetable grower* | 老～ *old farmer* | 工～联盟 *worker peasant alliance*

侬(儂) nóng ㄋㄨㄥˊ 代词 pronoun ①〈方 dialect〉你 you ②我(多见于旧诗文)(often in classical poetry) I; me; my

哝(噥) nóng ㄋㄨㄥˊ [哝哝] (—nong) 小声说话 to murmur; to whisper

浓(濃) nóng ㄋㄨㄥˊ ❶含某种成分多，跟"淡"

相对 thick; heavy; dense; concentrated (opposite of 淡): ～茶 *strong tea* | ～烟 *thick smoke* ❷深厚，不淡薄 deep; strong: 兴趣正～ *deeply interested* | ～厚 *(of interest, emotion, etc.) deep; strong*

脓(膿) nóng ㄋㄨㄥˊ 化脓性炎症病变所形成的黄白色汁液，是死亡的白细胞、细菌及脂肪等的混合物 pus

秾(穠) nóng ㄋㄨㄥˊ 花木繁盛 (of plants) luxuriant; flourishing: ～艳 *(of plants) bright-coloured*

酞(醲) nóng ㄋㄨㄥˊ 酒味浓厚 (of alcoholic drink) mellow; rich

弄(*挵) nòng ㄋㄨㄥˋ (formerly pronounced lòng) ❶拿着玩，戏耍(㊥玩一、戏一) to play with; to fiddle with: 不要～火。*Don't play with fire.* ❷搞，做 to do; to make; to get: 这件事一定要～好。*This must be duly done.* | ～点儿水喝 *get some water to drink* | ～饭 *to cook* ❸搅扰 to disturb; to upset: 这消息～得人心不安。*This news caused much anxiety among the people.* ❹要，炫耀 to manipulate; to show off: ～权 *manipulate power* | ～手段 *play tricks* | 舞文～墨 *juggle with words*

⇨ see also lòng on p.416

NOU ㄋㄡ

耨(鎒)** nòu ㄋㄡˋ ❶古代一种锄草的农具 (ancient) hoe (used for weeding) ❷锄草 to weed with a hoe: 深耕易～ *plough deeply and weed thoroughly*

NU ㄋㄨ

奴 nú ㄋㄨˊ 旧社会中受剥削阶级压迫、剥削、役使的没有自由的人 slave: ～隶 *slave* | 农～ *serf* | 家～ *house slave* ㊥为了支付贷款等而不得不拼命工作的人 those enslaved by mortgage loans, etc.: 房～ *mortgage slave* | 车～ *slave of the car (sb enslaved by the expenses of keeping a car)* [奴役] 把人当作奴隶使用 to enslave [奴才] 1 旧时奴仆对主人的自称 (old) I; me (used by servants to refer to themselves) 2 指甘心供人驱使、帮助作恶的坏人 a servile follower; lackey

孥 nú ㄋㄨˊ 儿子，或指妻和子 son; wife and children: 妻～ *wife and children*

驽(駑) nú ㄋㄨˊ 驽马，劣马，走不快的马 jade (horse); inferior horse ㊝愚钝无能 incompetent: ～钝 *slow-witted*

笯 nú ㄋㄨˊ 用于地名 used in place names: 黄～(在江西省高安) *Huangnu (in Gao'an, Jiangxi Province)*

努(❷拟)** nǔ ㄋㄨˇ ❶尽量地使出(力量) to exert oneself: ～力 *make an effort* ❷突出 to protrude: ～嘴 *pout one's lips* ❸〈方 dialect〉因用力太过，身体内部受伤 to sprain;

to strain：扛太重的东西容易～着腰。*Carrying too heavy a load can sprain your back.*

弩 nǔ ㄋㄨˇ 一种利用机械力量射箭的弓 crossbow

砮 nǔ ㄋㄨˇ ❶可做箭镞的石头 sharp stone (that can be made into an arrowhead) ❷石制箭头 stone arrowhead

胬 nǔ ㄋㄨˇ ［胬肉］中医指眼球结膜增生而突起的肉状物 pterygium

怒 nù ㄋㄨˋ ❶生气，气愤（㊀恼－）angry; furious：发～ *lose one's temper* | ～发(fà)冲冠（形容盛怒）*bristle with anger (literally means 'become so angry that one's hair raises his hat')* | ～容满面 *look very angry* ❷气势盛 flourishing; of great momentum：～涛 *raging wave* | ～潮 *surging tide* | 鲜花～放。*Flowers burst into full bloom.*

［怒族］我国少数民族，参看附录四 the Nu people (one of the ethnic groups in China. See Appendix Ⅳ.)

傉 nù ㄋㄨˋ 用于人名。秃发傉檀，东晋时南凉国君 Nu (used in given names, e.g. Tufa Nutan, king of the Southern Liang Kingdom in the Eastern Jin Dynasty)

NÜ ㄋㄩ

女 nǚ ㄋㄩˇ ❶女性，女子，女人，妇女 woman; female; girl：～士 *madam* | ～工 *female worker* | 男～平等 *gender equality* ❷女儿 daughter：一儿一～ *one son and one daughter* ❸星宿名，二十八宿之一 *Nü* (one of the twenty-eight constellations in ancient Chinese astronomy)

〈古 ancient〉also same as 汝(rǔ)

钕(釹) nǚ ㄋㄩˇ 金属元素，符号Nd，银白色。可用来制合金、激光材料等，也用作催化剂 neodymium (Nd)

恧 nǜ ㄋㄩˋ 惭愧 to be ashamed

衄(*衂、*䶊) nǜ ㄋㄩˋ 鼻衄，鼻子流血 to have a nosebleed

朒 nǜ ㄋㄩˋ 亏缺，不足 to be lacking in; to be deficient in

NUAN ㄋㄨㄢ

暖(*煖、*暝、*煗) nuǎn ㄋㄨㄢˇ 暖和(huo)，不冷（㊀温－）warm：风和日～ *warm and sunny* | ～洋洋 *warm* ㊀使温和(huo) to warm：～一～手 *warm your hands*

NÜE ㄋㄩㄝ

疟(瘧) nüè ㄋㄩㄝˋ 疟疾(ji)，传染病，又叫疟子(yàozi)，症状是周期性地发冷发热，热后大量出汗，全身无力 malaria (also 疟子 yàozi)

⇨ see also yào on p.762

虐 nüè ㄋㄩㄝˋ 残暴（㊀暴－）cruel; tyrannical：～待 *to maltreat ; to abuse*

NUO ㄋㄨㄛ

挪 nuó ㄋㄨㄛˊ 移动 to move; to shift：把桌子～一～ *move the table* | ～用款项 *divert money; embezzle funds*

郍 nuó ㄋㄨㄛˊ 用于地名 used in place names：～溪（在湖南省洞口县）*Nuoxi (in Dongkou County, Hunan Province)*

⇨ see also nà on p.467

娜 nuó ㄋㄨㄛˊ see 袅娜 (niǎo —) at 袅 on page 478

⇨ see also nà on p.467

傩（儺） nuó ㄋㄨㄛˊ 旧指驱逐瘟疫的迎神赛会 (old) religious ceremony to drive away plague

诺（諾） nuò ㄋㄨㄛˋ ❶答应的声音，表示同意 ㊂yes; OK：～～连声 *say yes over and again* ❷ 应允 to promise; to consent：～言 *a promise* | 慨～ *consent readily*

喏 nuò ㄋㄨㄛˋ ❶〈方 dialect〉叹词，表示让人注意自己所指示的事物 (exclamation, used to call attention) hey; well：～，这不就是你的那把伞？*Hey, isn't this your umbrella?* ❷ same as "诺"

⇨ see also rě on p.557

锘（鍩） nuò ㄋㄨㄛˋ 人造的放射性金属元素，符号 No。nobelium (No)

搦 nuò ㄋㄨㄛˋ ❶握，持，拿着 to hold; to grasp：～管（握着笔）*to wield a brush* ❷挑（tiǎo），惹 to provoke：～战 *challenge (sb) to a battle*

懦 nuò ㄋㄨㄛˋ 怯懦，软弱无能（㊀—弱）cowardly; timid：～夫 *coward*

糯（*稬、*稉） nuò ㄋㄨㄛˋ 糯稻，稻的一种，米粒富于黏性 (unhusked) glutinous rice：～米 *(threshed and polished) glutinous rice*

O ㄛ

O ㄛ

噢 ō ㄛ 叹词，表示了解 (exclamation, used to show realization) oh：～，就是他！*Oh, it's him!*｜～，我懂了。*Oh, I see.*

哦 ó ㄛ́ 叹词，表示疑问、惊奇等 (exclamation, used to show doubt, surprise,etc.) oh：～，是这样的吗？*Oh, is that so?*｜～，是那么一回事。*Oh, so that's it.*

⇨ see also é on p.157, ò on p.486

嚄 ǒ ㄛ̌ 叹词，表示惊讶 (exclamation, used to show surprise) oh：～，这是怎么搞的？*Oh, how is this?*

⇨ see also huō on p.278

哦 ò ㄛ̀ 叹词，表示领会、醒悟 (exclamation, used to show understanding or realization) oh：～，我明白了。*Oh, I see.*

⇨ see also é on p.157, ó on p.486

OU ㄡ

区(區) ōu ㄡ 姓 (surname) Ou

⇨ see also qū on p.545

讴(謳) ōu ㄡ 歌唱 to sing [讴歌] 歌颂，赞美 sing the praises of; to eulogize

沤(漚) ōu ㄡ 水泡 froth：浮～ *froth; (figurative) transience of human life*

⇨ see also òu on p.487

瓯(甌) ōu ㄡ ❶小盆 bowl ❷杯 cup：茶～ *tea cup*｜酒～ *wine bowl* ❸瓯江，水名，在浙江省南部 Oujiang River (in the south of Zhejiang Province) ❹浙江省温州的别称 Ou (another name for Wenzhou, a city in Zhejiang Province)

欧(歐) ōu ㄡ ❶姓 (surname) Ou ❷指欧洲，世界七大洲之一 Europe ❸电阻单位名欧姆的简称，符号 Ω。(short for 欧姆) ohm

殴(毆) ōu ㄡ 打人(㊀一打) to beat up; to hit：～伤 *beat and injure*｜斗～ *to scuffle*

鸥(鷗) ōu ㄡ 鸟名，羽毛多为白色，翅长而尖，生活在湖海上，捕食鱼、螺等 gull

㺍 ǒu ㄡ̌ 㺍山，山名，又地名，都在安徽省枞(zōng)阳 Oushan (a mountain as well as a place name, both in Zongyang, Anhui Province)

呕(嘔) ǒu ㄡ̌ 吐(tù)(㊀一吐) to vomit：～血(xuè) *vomit blood* [作呕](zuò－) 恶心，形容非常厌恶(wù) feel like vomiting; (figurative) dislike very much

O

炈（熰） ǒu ㄡˇ ❶烧火时柴草等没有充分燃烧而产生大量的烟 to give off a lot of smoke as a result of poor burning：～了一屋子烟。*The room was full of smoke.* ❷使柴草等不起火苗只冒烟地烧 to smoulder：把灶里的柴火～了。*Burn off the firewood in the stove.* ❸用燃烧艾草等的烟驱蚊蝇 to smoke out (mosquitoes and flies)：～蚊子 *smoke out mosquitoes*

偶 ǒu ㄡˇ ❶偶像，用木头或泥土等制成的人形 idol (made of wood, clay, etc.) ❷双，成双或成对，跟"奇"（jī）相对 even; in pairs (opposite of 奇)：～数 *even number* | 无独有～。*It is not unique, but has its counterpart.* [对偶] 文字作品中音调谐和、意义相对、字数相等的语句，骈体文的基本形式 (in writing) parallelism (pair of lines with corresponding tones, meanings and same number of characters) ❸偶然 occasionally; accidental：～发事件 *chance occurrence* [偶然] 不经常，不是必然的 occassionally; accidental：～去一次 *visit occasionally* | 这些成就的取得绝不是～的。*These achievements were by no means accidental.*

耦 ǒu ㄡˇ ❶古代称两个人在一起耕地 (ancient) (of two persons) to plough side by side ❷ same as "偶❷"

藕 ǒu ㄡˇ 莲的地下茎，长圆形，肥大有节，中间有许多管状小孔，可以吃 lotus root (see picture of 莲 on page 396) [藕荷] [藕合] 淡紫色 pale pinkish purple

沤（漚） òu ㄡˋ 长时间地浸泡 to soak for a long time：～麻 *ret flax*

⇨ see also ōu on p.486

怄（慪） òu ㄡˋ 故意惹人恼怒，或使人发笑，逗弄 to annoy; to tease; to amuse：你别～人了。*Stop annoying me.* | ～得他直冒火。*He was very much annoyed.* [怄气] 闹别扭，生闷气 to sulk：不要为这点儿小事～。*Don't sulk over such a small thing.*

O

P 夂

PA 夂丫

趴 pā 夂丫 ❶肚子向下卧倒 to lie on one's stomach：～在地上射击 *lie face down on the ground shooting* ❷身体向前靠在东西上 to bend over：～在桌子上写字 *bend over the desk writing*

舥 pā 夂丫 古书上说的一种船 a kind of ship in ancient Chinese texts

葩 pā 夂丫 花 flower：奇～ *exotic and beautiful flower*

啪 pā 夂丫 形容放枪、拍掌或东西撞击等的声音 bang

扒 pá 夂丫́ ❶用耙（pá）搂（lōu），聚拢 to rake together：～草 *rake up the straw*｜～土 *rake the soil smooth* ❷扒窃 to pick sb's pocket：～手（小偷）*pickpocket* ❸炖烂，煨烂 to braise：～猪头 *stewed pighead*

⇨ see also bā on p.10

杷 pá 夂丫́ see 枇杷 (pípɑ) at 枇 on page 501

爬 pá 夂丫́ ❶手和脚一齐着地前行，虫类向前移动 to crawl; to creep：～行 *to crawl; (figurative) work slowly by following conventions*｜连滚带～ *roll and crawl*｜小孩子会～了。*The baby can crawl now.*｜不要吃苍蝇～过的东西。*Don't eat anything that flies have crawled over.*［爬虫］爬行动物的旧称，行走时多用腹面贴地，如龟、鳖、蛇等 (former name for 爬行动物) reptile ❷攀登 to climb：～山 *climb a mountain*｜～树 *climb a tree*｜猴子～竿。*A monkey is climbing a pole.*

钯（鈀） pá 夂丫́ same as "耙 (pá)"

⇨ see also bǎ on p.12

耙 pá 夂丫́ ❶（一子）聚拢谷物或平土地的用具 rake ❷用耙子平整土地或聚拢、散开柴草、谷物等 to level (the ground) with a rake; to rake (straw)：～地 *level the ground with a rake*

⇨ see also bà on p.13

筢 pá 夂丫́（一子）搂（lōu）柴草的竹制器具 bamboo rake

琶 pá 夂丫́ see 琵琶 (pípɑ) at 琵 on page 501

潖 pá 夂丫́［潖江口］地名，在广东省清远 Pajiangkou (a place in Qingyuan, Guangdong Province)

掱 pá 夂丫́［掱手］从别人身上窃取财物的小偷儿，现作"扒手" (now written as 扒手) pickpocket

帕 pà 夂丫̀ ❶（一子）包头或擦手脸用的布或绸 handkerchief; kerchief：首～ *kerchief*｜手～ *handkerchief* ❷压强单位名帕斯卡的简称，符号 Pa，天气预报

中常用“百帕”(short for 帕斯卡) Pascal (Pa)

怕 pà ㄆㄚˋ ❶害怕 to fear; to be afraid of：老鼠～猫。*A mouse is afraid of a cat.* ❷副词，恐怕，或许，表示猜想或疑虑 (adverb, used to express concern) perhaps：他～是不会来了。*I'm afraid he will not come.*｜不提前预防～要出大问题。*Lack of precautions could well give rise to great trouble.*

PAI ㄆㄞ

拍 pāi ㄆㄞ ❶用手掌或片状物打 to pat：～球 *bounce a ball*｜～手 *to clap* ㊀（－子）乐曲的节奏（㊥节－）beat：这首歌每节有四～。*The song is in four-four time.* ❷（－子、－儿）拍打东西的用具 bat; racket：蝇～儿 *flyswatter*｜球～子 *bat (for tennis, badminton, etc.)* ❸拍马屁 to flatter：吹吹～～ *fawn on* ❹摄影（㊥－摄）to take (a picture)：～照片 *take a photo*｜～电影 *shoot a film* ❺发 to wire：～电报 *send a telegram* ❻（外 loanword）法定计量单位中十进倍数单位词头之一，表示10^{15}，符号 P。peta- (P)

俳 pái ㄆㄞˊ 古代指杂戏、滑稽戏，也指演这种戏的人 (ancient) farce; comedian in a farce：～优 *comedian in a variety show* ㊕诙谐，玩笑 humorous：～谐 *farcical*

排 pái ㄆㄞˊ ❶摆成行（háng）列（㊥－列）to put in order; to line up：～队 *queue (up)*｜～行 *seniority among siblings*｜论资～辈 *arrange in order of seniority* [排场]（－chang）铺张的场面 ostentation and extravagance：不讲～ *not go in for ostentation and extravagance* ❷排成的行列 row：并～ *side by side*｜坐在前～ *sit in the front row* ❸木筏或竹筏，也指为便于水上运送而扎成排的木材或竹材 raft; rows of logs or bamboos transported by water ❹军队的编制单位，是班的上一级 platoon ❺量词，用于成行列的 (measure word for things in rows) line; row：一～椅子 *a row of chairs* ❻除去，推开 to remove; to expel; to push：～水 *drain water*｜～山倒海（形容力量大）*great in momentum and irresistible (literally means 'topple mountains and overturn seas')*｜～难（nàn）*overcome difficulties* [排泄]生物把体内的废物如汗、尿、屎等排出体外 to excrete ❼排演，练习演戏 to rehearse：～戏 *rehearse a play*｜彩～ *dress rehearsal*

⇨ see also pǎi on p.490

徘 pái ㄆㄞˊ [徘徊]（－huái）来回地走 to wander around; to pace up and down：他在那里～很久。*He wandered around there for a long time.* ㊀犹疑不决 to hesitate：～观望 *wait and see*｜左右～ *hesitate between two alternatives*

棑 pái ㄆㄞˊ same as “簰”

牌 pái ㄆㄞˊ ❶（－子、－儿）用木板或其他材料做的标志

或凭信物 board; sign：招～ *shop sign; (figurative) reputation; brand name* | 指路～ *signpost* | 存车～儿 *parking ticket* ㊀商标 brand; make：名～ *famous brand* | 冒～ *fake* | 解放～汽车 *Jiefang brand motor vehicle* ❷古代兵士作战时用来遮护身体的东西 shield：挡箭～ *shield; (figurative) excuse* | 藤～ *cane shield* ❸娱乐或赌博用的东西 cards; dominoes：打～ *play cards* | 扑克～ *(playing) cards* ❹词或曲的曲调的名称 title of the tunes of *ci* or *qu*：词～ *title of the tunes to which* ci *poems are composed* | 曲～ *title of the tunes to which* qu *songs are composed*

簰(**簿) pái ㄆㄞˊ ❶ same as "排❸" ❷用于地名 used in place names：～洲（在湖北省嘉鱼）*Paizhou (in Jiayu, Hubei Province)*

迫(*廹) pǎi ㄆㄞˇ ［迫击炮］从炮口装弹，以曲射为主的火炮 mortar

⇨ see also pò on p.511

排 pǎi ㄆㄞˇ ［排子车］〈方 dialect〉用人拉的一种搬运东西的车 handcart

⇨ see also pái on p.489

哌 pài ㄆㄞˋ ［哌嗪］（－qín）有机化合物，白色晶体，易溶于水，有驱除蛔虫等作用 piperazine

派 pài ㄆㄞˋ ❶水的支流 tributary ❷一个系统的分支（㊀－系）faction; branch：流～ *school; set* | ～生 *to derive* ❸派别，政党和学术、宗教团体等内部因主张不同而形成的分支 sect; faction ❹作风，风度 style：～头 *style* | 正～ *upright* | 气～ *bearing; grandeur* ㊕有气派，有风度 to be imposing：他这身打扮可真～！*The way he dresses is really stylish.* ❺分配，指定 to appoint; to assign：分～ *to assign* | ～人去办 *send someone to do it*

蒎 pài ㄆㄞˋ ［蒎烯］（－xī）有机化合物，无色液体，是松节油的主要成分 pinene

湃 pài ㄆㄞˋ see 澎湃 (péng－) at 澎 on page 498

PAN ㄆㄢ

番 pān ㄆㄢ ［番禺］（－yú）地名，在广东省广州 Panyu (a place in Guangzhou, Guangdong Province)

⇨ see also fān on p.165

潘 pān ㄆㄢ 姓 (surname) Pan

攀 pān ㄆㄢ ❶抓住别的东西向上爬 to climb：～登 *to climb* | ～树 *climb a tree* | ～岩 *rock climbing* ❷拉拢，拉扯（㊀－扯）to involve：～谈 *engage in small talk* | ～亲道故 *claim to be sb's relative or friend*

爿 pán ㄆㄢˊ 〈方 dialect〉❶劈开的成片的木柴 strip of chopped wood：柴～ *chopped firewood* ❷量词，用于商店等 measure word for shops：一～水果店 *a fruit shop*

胖 pán ㄆㄢˊ 安泰舒适 easy and comfortable：心广体～ *be*

carefree and contented

⇨ see also pàng on p.493

盘(盤) pán ㄆㄢˊ ❶(–子、–儿)盛放物品的扁而浅的用具，多为圆形 plate; tray：托～ *serving tray* | 茶～儿 *tea tray* | 和～托出(喻全部说出) *lay all one's cards on the table* [通盘]全面 overall：～打算 *take the overall situation into account* ❷(–儿)形状像盘或有盘的功用的物品 sth in the shape or with the function of a plate：脸～儿 *face* | 磨(mò)～ *millstone* | 棋～ *chessboard* | 算～ *abacus* ❸回旋地绕 to coil; to twist：～香 *incense coil* | ～杠子(在杠子上旋转运动) *exercise on a horizontal bar* | 把绳子～起来 *coil up the rope* | ～山公路 *winding mountain road* | ～根错节 *interwoven roots and stems; (figurative) be complicated and intricate* [盘剥]利上加利地剥削 to exploit [盘旋]绕着圈地走或飞 to circle ❹垒，砌(炕、灶) to build (a *kang* or a cooking stove)：～炕 *build a kang* | ～灶 *build a cooking stove* ❺盘查，仔细查究 to check：～账 *check accounts* | ～货 *take stock* | ～问 *to cross-examine; to question* | ～算(细心打算) *to calculate* ❻(–儿)指市场上成交的价格 market price：开～ *open a quotation* | 收～ *close a quotation* | 平～ *steady trading; (of stock price) flat* ❼量词，用于形状像盘子的东西或某些棋类、球类比赛等 measure word for things shaped like a plate or for chess and ball games：一～机器 *a machine* | 一～磨(mò) *a set of millstones* | 一～棋 *a game of chess* | 打了一～乒乓球 *played a game of table tennis*

[盘费](–fei) [盘缠](–chan)旅途上的费用 travel expenses

[盘桓](–huán)1 回环旋绕 wind round and round 2 留恋在一个地方，逗留 to linger

槃 pán ㄆㄢˊ same as "盘❶❸"

磐 pán ㄆㄢˊ 大石头 huge rock：安如～石 *be as solid as a rock*

磻 pán ㄆㄢˊ 磻溪，古水名，在今陕西省宝鸡东南 Panxi (an ancient river, in the south-east of today's Baoji, Shaanxi Province)

蟠 pán ㄆㄢˊ 屈曲，环绕 to curl：虎踞龙～ *forbidding strategic point (literally means 'like a coiling dragon and a crouching tiger')*

蹒(蹣) pán ㄆㄢˊ [蹒跚](*盘跚)(–shān)腿脚不灵便，走路缓慢、摇摆的样子 staggering：步履～ *to stagger*

判 pàn ㄆㄢˋ ❶分辨，断定(㊟–断) to distinguish; to judge：～别是非 *distinguish between right and wrong* ㊊评定 to judge; to grade：裁～ *judge; referee; to judge; to referee* | ～卷子 *mark examination papers* [批判]分析、批驳错误的思想、观点和行为 to criticize ❷分开 to separate ㊣截然不同 obviously different：～若两人 *be no longer one's former self* ❸

P

判决，司法机关对案件做出决定 to judge (a case)：～案 *judge a case* | ～处徒刑 *to sentence (sb) to imprisonment*

泮 pàn ㄆㄢˋ ❶融解，分散 to dissolve; to thaw ❷泮池，旧时学宫前的水池 (old) pond in front of a school

叛 pàn ㄆㄢˋ 背叛，叛离 to betray：～徒 *traitor* | ～国投敌 *betray one's country and defect to the enemy*

畔 pàn ㄆㄢˋ ❶田地的界限 boundary of a field ⓘ边 side; bank：河～ *river bank* | 篱～ *side of the hedge* ❷ (ancient) same as "叛"

袢 pàn ㄆㄢˋ same as "襻"

拚 pàn ㄆㄢˋ 〈方 dialect〉舍弃，豁出去 to give up：～命 *risk one's life*

盼 pàn ㄆㄢˋ ❶盼望，想望 to look forward to ❷看(ⓛ顾－) to look：左顾右～ *look around*

鋬 pàn ㄆㄢˋ 〈古 ancient〉器物上的提梁 handle of a utensil

襻 pàn ㄆㄢˋ ❶（－儿）扣襻，扣住纽扣的套 button loop ❷（－儿）功用或形状像襻的东西 loop-like thing：鞋～儿 *shoe strap* ❸扣住，使分开的东西连在一起 to fasten：～上几针（缝住）*sew it up with a few stitches*

PANG ㄆㄤ

乓 pāng ㄆㄤ 形容枪声、东西撞击声 bang：～的一声枪响 *the crack of a gun*

雱 pāng ㄆㄤ 雪下得很大 to snow heavily

滂 pāng ㄆㄤ 水涌出的样子 (of water) overflowing; gushing ［滂湃］（－pài）水势盛大 (of water) roaring and rushing ［滂沱］（－tuó）雨下得很大 pouring：大雨～ *torrential rain* ⓜ泪流得很多 full of tears：涕泗～ *tears streaming down one's cheeks*

膀(胮)** pāng ㄆㄤ 浮肿 to swell：他肾脏有病，脸有点儿～。*He had kidney trouble and his face was a little swollen.*

⇨ see also bǎng on p.19, páng on p.493

彷(徬)** páng ㄆㄤˊ ［彷徨］（*旁皇）（－huáng）游移不定，不知道往哪里走好 to pace up and down; to waver：～歧途 *hesitate at the crossroads*

⇨ see also fǎng on p.171

庞(龐) páng ㄆㄤˊ ❶大（指形体或数量）colossal (in size or number)：数字～大 *a huge number* | ～然大物 *colossus* ❷杂乱（ⓛ－杂）numerous and disorderly ❸面庞，脸盘 face

逄 páng ㄆㄤˊ 姓 (surname) Pang

旁 páng ㄆㄤˊ ❶旁边，左右两侧 side：～观 *look on* | ～若无人 *be natural or overweening (literally means 'have no regard for the presence of other people')* | 两～都是大楼。*There are tall buildings*

P

on both sides. ❷其他，另外 other：～人 *other people* | ～的话就不说了。*(I) won't say anything else.* ❸汉字的偏旁 graphic component of a Chinese character："枯"是"木"字～。*The graphic component of 枯 is 木.*

〈古 ancient〉also same as 傍(bàng)

膀 páng ㄆㄤˊ［膀胱］(－guāng)俗叫尿脬(suīpāo)，暂存尿液的囊状体，在骨盆腔内 (informal 尿脬 suīpāo) urinary bladder (see picture of 人体内脏 on page 819)

⇨ see also bǎng on p.19, pāng on p.492

磅 páng ㄆㄤˊ［磅礴］(－bó)1 广大无边际 boundless：大气～ *grand and magnificent* 2 扩展，充满 to permeate; to fill：正义之气，～宇内。*Boundless justice permeates the universe.*

⇨ see also bàng on p.20

螃 páng ㄆㄤˊ［螃蟹］(－xiè) see 蟹 on page 723

鳑(鰟) páng ㄆㄤˊ［鳑鲏］(－pí)鱼名，身体侧扁，形状像鲫鱼，卵圆形，生活在淡水中，卵产在蚌壳里 bitterling

嗙 pǎng ㄆㄤˇ〈方 dialect〉夸大，吹牛，信口开河 to boast; to brag：你别听他瞎～。*Don't believe him, he is all bragging.* | 胡吹乱～ *shoot one's mouth off*

耪 pǎng ㄆㄤˇ 用锄翻松地，锄 to hoe：～地 *hoe the field*

胖(肨)** pàng ㄆㄤˋ 人体内含脂肪多，跟"瘦"相对 fat (opposite of 瘦)：他长得很～。*He is quite fat.*

⇨ see also pán on p.490

PAO ㄆㄠ

抛(拋)** pāo ㄆㄠ ❶扔，投 to throw; to cast：～球 *toss a ball* | ～砖引玉 *make some introductory remarks to induce others to come up with valuable opinions*［抛锚］把锚投入水底，使船停稳 drop anchor ㊕①汽车等因发生故障，中途停止行驶 (of cars) break down ②进行中的事情因故停止 be suspended［抛售］为争夺市场牟取利润，压价出卖大批商品 to dump; to undersell ❷丢下(㊐－弃) to abandon; to leave behind：～开自己的事不管 *leave one's own business unattended* | 把对手～在了后头 *leave one's rival behind*

泡 pāo ㄆㄠ ❶(－儿)鼓起而松软的东西 puffy and soft thing：豆腐～儿 *bean curd puff* ❷虚而松软，不坚硬 spongy; puffy and soft：这块木料发～。*This piece of wood is rather spongy.* ❸量词，用于屎尿 measure word for the times of excretions：一～尿 *a piss*

⇨ see also pào on p.494

脬 pāo ㄆㄠ ❶尿(suī)脬，膀胱(pángguāng) urinary bladder ❷ same as "泡(pāo)❸"

刨 páo ㄆㄠˊ ❶挖掘 to dig：～花生 *dig peanuts* | ～坑 *dig a hole* ❷减，除去 to exclude：

P

～去他还有俩人。*There are two people, not counting him.* | 十五天～去五天，只剩下十天了。*With five days gone in the fifteen days, there remain only ten days.*

⇨ see also bào on p.23

咆 páo ㄆㄠˊ［咆哮］(－xiào）猛兽怒吼 (of beasts) to roar ㊟江河奔腾轰鸣或人暴怒叫喊 (of people) to bellow; (of rivers) to roar：黄河在～。*The Yellow River roars past.* | ～如雷 *roar with rage*

狍（** 麅）páo ㄆㄠˊ（－子）一种鹿，毛夏季栗红色，冬季棕褐色，雄的有树枝状的角 roe deer

庖 páo ㄆㄠˊ 庖厨，厨房 kitchen：～人（古代称厨师）*(ancient) cook*［庖代］［代庖］㊕替人处理事情或代做别人分内的工作 act in sb's place; work on behalf of sb

炮 páo ㄆㄠˊ 烧 to burn［炮烙］(－luò, formerly pronounced －gé)［炮格］古代的一种酷刑 bind sb to a hot bronze pillar as a kind of cruel torture in ancient times［炮制］用烘、炒等方法把原料加工制成中药 prepare medicinal herbs by parching, roasting, etc. ㊂指编造，制作（多含贬义）(often disapproving) cook up：如法～ *follow a set pattern; follow suit* | ～假新闻 *create fake news*

⇨ see also bāo on p.21, pào on p.495

袍 páo ㄆㄠˊ（－子、－儿）长衣 robe：棉～儿 *cotton gown* | ～笏（hù）登场（登台演戏，比喻上台做官）*dress up and go on stage; (figurative) assume an official post*

匏 páo ㄆㄠˊ 匏瓜，葫芦的一种，俗叫瓢葫芦，果实比葫芦大，对半剖开可以做水瓢 (informal 瓢葫芦) a kind of bottle gourd

跑 páo ㄆㄠˊ 走兽用脚刨地 to paw the earth：～槽（牲口刨槽根）*paw at the base of the trough* | 虎～泉（在浙江省杭州）*Hupao Spring (in Hangzhou, Zhejiang Province)*

⇨ see also pǎo on p.494

跑 pǎo ㄆㄠˇ ❶奔，两只脚或四条腿交互向前跃进 to run：赛～ *to race* | ～步 *to jog; march at the double* ㊂物体离开原地，很快地移动 to move fast：汽车在公路上飞～。*The car is racing down the road.* | 纱巾被风刮～了。*The gauze scarf was blown away by the wind.* ❷逃跑，逃走 to escape; to run away：别让犯人～了。*Don't let the prisoners run away.* ㊟泄漏，挥发 to leak; to evaporate：～电 *leak electricity* | ～油 *leak oil* | ～气 *leak gas* ❸为某种事务而奔走 to run errands：～外 *work as a travelling salesperson* | ～买卖 *travel around doing business* | ～材料 *rush about getting materials*

⇨ see also páo on p.494

奅 pào ㄆㄠˋ 虚大 large

泡 pào ㄆㄠˋ ❶（－儿）气体在液体内使液体鼓起来形成的球状或半球状体（㊝－沫）

P

bubble：冒～儿 *rise in bubbles* ❷（～儿）像泡一样的东西 bubble-shaped thing：脚上起了一个～ *get a blister on one's foot* | 电灯～儿 *light bulb* ❸用液体浸物品 to soak：～茶 *make tea* | ～饭 *thick gruel; cooked rice simmered/soaked in soup or water* ㊞长时间地待在某处消磨时光或做某事 to kill time; to dawdle：～吧 *hang out in a bar* | ～蘑菇（故意纠缠，拖延时间）*to dawdle*

⇨ see also pāo on p.493

炮（*砲、*礮）pào ㄆㄠˋ ❶武器的一类，有迫击炮、高射炮、火箭炮等 cannon ❷爆竹 firecracker：鞭～ *firecrackers* | ～仗（zhang）*firecracker*

⇨ see also bāo on p.21, páo on p.494

疱（*皰）pào ㄆㄠˋ 皮肤上长的像水泡的小疙瘩，也作"泡" blister (also written as 泡)

PEI ㄆㄟ

呸 pēi ㄆㄟ 叹词，表示斥责或唾弃 (exclamation, used to express censure or contempt) pah：～！胡说八道。*Bah! That's nonsense.*

胚（*肧）pēi ㄆㄟ 初期发育的生物体 embryo [胚胎] 初期发育的动物体 embryo ㊞事情的开始 embryonic stage

衃 pēi ㄆㄟ 凝聚的血 congealed blood

醅 pēi ㄆㄟ 没过滤的酒 unfiltered wine/liquor

陪 péi ㄆㄟˊ 随同，在旁边做伴（㊀—伴）to accompany：～同 *to accompany* | ～读 *serve as a companion for sb in study; a companion in study* | ～练 *accompany sb in training; training partner* | 我～你去。*I will go with you.* | ～客人 *accompany a guest* [陪衬] 从旁衬托 to set sth/sb off

培 péi ㄆㄟˊ 为保护植物或墙堤等，在根基部分加土 to bank up (with earth)：～土 *bank up with earth* [培养] 1 训练教育 to train：～干部 *train cadres* 2 使繁殖 to cultivate：～真菌 *incubate fungus* [培育] 培养幼小的生物，使它发育成长 to cultivate：～树苗 *grow saplings*

赔（賠）péi ㄆㄟˊ ❶补还损失（㊀—偿）to compensate：～款 *pay an indemnity; (of a defeated nation) pay reparations; indemnity; reparations* | ～礼（道歉）*make an apology* | ～偿 *to compensate; reparation* ❷亏损，跟"赚"相对 to lose money in business (opposite of 赚)：～钱 *lose money in business* | ～本 *lose money in business*

锫（錇）péi ㄆㄟˊ 人造的放射性金属元素，符号 Bk。berkelium (Bk)

裴 péi ㄆㄟˊ 姓 (surname) Pei

沛 pèi ㄆㄟˋ 盛（shèng），大 abundant：充～ *abundant* | 丰～ *plentiful*

旆 pèi ㄆㄟˋ 古时接在旗子末端形状像燕尾的装饰，泛指旌旗 (ancient) swallow-tailed pennant; (generally) banner

霈 pèi ㄆㄟˋ ❶大雨 heavy rain ❷雨多的样子 (of rain) heavy：油然作云，～然下雨。*Thick clouds gather and a heavy rain pours down.*

帔 pèi ㄆㄟˋ 古代披在肩背上的服饰 (ancient) short embroidered cape over one's shoulders：凤冠霞～ *phoenix coronet and embroidered tasselled cape*

佩（❸**珮） pèi ㄆㄟˋ ❶佩带，挂 to wear：～戴勋章 *wear a medal* | 腰间～着一支手枪 *wear a pistol in one's belt* ❷佩服，心悦诚服 to admire; to revere：可敬可～ *honorable and admirable* | 钦～ *to admire* | 赞～ *to admire* ❸古代衣带上佩带的玉饰 a kind of jade ornament worn at the waist in ancient times：环～ *(jade) pendant*

配 pèi ㄆㄟˋ ❶两性结合 to mate; to join in marriage ①男女结婚 to marry：婚～ *to marry* ②使牲畜交合 to mate：～种 *to breed* | ～猪 *mate pigs* [配偶] 指夫或妻 spouse：已有～ *have a spouse already* ❷用适当的标准加以调和 to mix：～颜色 *match up colours* | ～药 *make up a prescription* ㊀相当，合适 to match：夫妻俩很相～。*The couple are a good match.* | 上衣跟裤子不太～。*The suit does not go very well with the trousers.* ❸有计划地分派，安排 to apportion：分～ *to distribute* | ～备人力 *provide manpower* ❹流放 to exile：发～ *banish sb into exile* ❺把缺少的补足 to find sth to fit or replace sth else：～零件 *replace parts* | ～把钥匙 *have a duplicate key cut* | ～一块玻璃 *replace a piece of glass* [配套] 把若干相关的事物组合成一整套 to form a complete set ❻衬托，陪衬 to set off; to foil：红花～绿叶 *green leaves setting off red flowers* | ～角(jué) *supporting role; minor role* ❼够得上 to deserve：他～称为先进工作者。*He deserves to be named a model worker.*

辔（轡） pèi ㄆㄟˋ 驾驭牲口的嚼子和缰绳 bridle：鞍～ *saddle and bridle* [辔头] 辔 bridle

PEN ㄆㄣ

喷（噴） pēn ㄆㄣ 散着射出 to spray; to spurt：～壶 *watering can* | ～泉 *fountain* | ～气式飞机 *jet plane* | 火山～火。*The volcano erupted.* [喷嚏] (—tì) 因鼻黏膜受刺激而引起的一种猛烈带声的喷气现象。又叫嚏喷 (tìpen) sneeze (also called 嚏喷 tìpen)

⇨ see also pèn on p.497

盆 pén ㄆㄣˊ (—子、—儿) 盛放或洗涤东西的用具，通常是圆形，口大，底小，不太深 basin：花～ *flower pot* | 脸～ *washbasin* [盆地] 被山或高地围绕着

P

的平地 basin：四川～ *Sichuan Basin* | 塔里木～ *Tarim Basin*

湓 pén ㄆㄣˊ 湓水，水名，在江西省西北部 Penshui River (in the north-west of Jiangxi Province)

喷(噴) pèn ㄆㄣˋ ❶香气扑鼻 delicious-smelling; fragrant：～香 *delicious-smelling* | ～鼻儿香 *delicious-smelling* ❷（一儿）蔬菜、鱼虾、瓜果等上市正盛的时期 (of vegetables, shrimps, fruits etc.) in season：西瓜～儿 *watermelon season* | 对虾正在～儿上。*Prawns are in season.* ❸（一儿）开花结实的次数或成熟收割的次数 used to express the number of times of flowering, or harvesting：头～棉花 *first crop of cotton* | 二～棉花 *second crop of cotton* | 绿豆结二～角了。*The mung beans are bearing their second crop of pods.*

⇨ see also pēn on p.496

PENG ㄆㄥ

抨 pēng ㄆㄥ 抨击，攻击对方的短处 to attack by words; to censure

怦 pēng ㄆㄥ 形容心跳声 ⓐ thump：紧张得心～～跳 *one's heart fluttered with nervousness*

砰 pēng ㄆㄥ 形容撞击声、重物落地声 bang：～的一声，枪响了。*The shot rang out with a crack.*

烹 pēng ㄆㄥ ❶煮 to boil; to cook：～调（tiáo）*to cook (dishes)* [烹饪]（一rèn）做饭做菜 to cook ❷烹饪方法，用热油略炒之后，再加入液体调味品，迅速翻炒 to fry quickly in hot oil and stir in sauce：～对虾 *quick-fried prawns in brown sauce*

嘭 pēng ㄆㄥ 形容敲门声等 ⓐ bang：～～的敲门声 *the sound of banging on the door*

澎 pēng ㄆㄥ 〈方 dialect〉溅 to splash：～了一身水 *be splashed all over with water*

⇨ see also péng on p.498

芃 péng ㄆㄥˊ [芃芃]形容草木茂盛 (of plants) luxuriant

朋 péng ㄆㄥˊ 彼此友好的人（ⓔ一友）friend：亲～好友 *one's relatives and friends* | 宾～满座 *packed with guests and friends*

堋 péng ㄆㄥˊ 我国战国时期科学家李冰在修建都江堰时所创造的一种分水堤 a kind of bifurcation dyke created in the Warring States period by Li Bing

淜 péng ㄆㄥˊ 用于地名 used in place names：普～（在云南省祥云）*Pupeng (in Xiangyun, Yunnan Province)*

弸 péng ㄆㄥˊ 充满 to fill; to be full

棚 péng ㄆㄥˊ （一子、一儿）❶把席、布等搭架支张起来遮蔽风雨或日光的东西 canopy of reed mats, cloth, etc.：天～ *ceiling; canopy* | 凉～ *canopy; awning* ❷简易的或临时性的建筑物 shed; shack：牲口～ *barn* | 工～ *builders'*

P

shed | 防震～ *earthquake shelter*

硼 péng ㄆㄥˊ 非金属元素，符号B，有晶体硼和无定形硼两种形态，可用来制合金钢，也用于核工业 boron (B)

鹏(鵬) péng ㄆㄥˊ 传说中最大的鸟 (in Chinese legend) bird of the largest size; roc [鹏程万里] 形容前途远大 have a bright future

彭 péng ㄆㄥˊ 姓 (surname) Peng

澎 péng ㄆㄥˊ [澎湃]（—pài）大浪相激 (of waves) to surge

[澎湖] 我国岛屿，在台湾海峡东南部，与其附近岛屿共有64个，总称“澎湖列岛” Penghu (one of the islands of Penghu Islands in People's Republic of China, made up of 64 islands in the south-east of the Taiwan Strait)

⇨ see also pēng on p.497

膨 péng ㄆㄥˊ 胀大 to balloon; to expand [膨脝]（—hēng）1 肚子胀的样子 potbellied 2 物体庞大笨重 bulky [膨胀]（—zhàng）物体的体积或长度增加 to expand：空气遇热～。*The air expands when heated.* ㊀ 数量增加 to increase in quantity：通货～ *inflation*

蟛 péng ㄆㄥˊ [蟛蜞]（—qí）一种螃蟹，身体小，生活在水边，对农作物有害 sesarmid crab

搒 péng ㄆㄥˊ 用棍子或竹板子打 to beat with a rod

⇨ see also bàng on p.20

蓬 péng ㄆㄥˊ ❶飞蓬，草本植物，叶像柳叶，籽实有毛，随风飞扬 blue fleabane ❷散乱 ㊂ unkempt; dishevelled：～头散发 *shock-headed* | 乱～～的茅草 *tangled reeds* [蓬松] 松散（指毛发或茅草等）fluffy

[蓬勃]（—bó）旺盛 flourishing：～发展 *develop vigorously* | 朝气～ *be full of youthful spirit*

篷 péng ㄆㄥˊ ❶张盖在上面，遮蔽日光、风、雨的东西，用竹篾、苇席、布等做成 awning; covering：船～ *awning of a boat* ❷船帆 sail：扯起～来 *hoist the sails*

捧 pěng ㄆㄥˇ ❶两手托着 to hold sth in both hands：手～鲜花 *hold flowers in one's hands* | ～着一个坛子 *hold a jar in one's hands* [捧腹] 捧着肚子，形容大笑 split one's sides (with laughter)：令人～ *make people burst out laughing* ❷奉承或代人吹嘘 to flatter; to boost：吹～ *to flatter* | 用好话～他 *flatter him with praise* | ～场（chǎng）*support an activity by being present* ❸量词，用于两手能捧起的东西 (measure word for things can be held with both hands) double handful：一～花生 *a double handful of peanuts*

椪 pèng ㄆㄥˋ [椪柑] 常绿小乔木，又叫芦柑，叶椭圆形，花白色，果实大，皮橙黄色，汁多味甜 Ponkan Mandarin (a kind of mandarin orange, also called 芦柑)

碰(*掽、*踫) pèng ㄆㄥˋ ❶撞击 to

knock：～杯（表示祝贺）*clink glasses*｜～破了皮 *get a graze*｜～钉子 *meet with a rebuff*｜～壁（喻事情做不通）*suffer setbacks; be rebuffed (literally means 'bash one's head against a wall')* ❷相遇 to bump into：我在半路上～见他。*I bumped into him on the way.* ❸没有把握地试探 to try one's luck：～一～机会 *take a chance*

PI ㄆㄧ

丕 pī ㄆㄧ 大 big great：～业 *great cause*｜～变 *immense change*

伾 pī ㄆㄧ ［伾伾］有力的样子 strong

邳 pī ㄆㄧ ［邳州］地名，在江苏省 Pizhou (a place in Jiangsu Province)

坯 pī ㄆㄧ ❶没有烧过的砖瓦、陶器等 (of brick, pottery, etc.) base：砖～ *unbaked brick* 特指砌墙用的土坯 (specifically) adobe：打～ *make an adobe*｜脱～ *mould adobe blocks* ❷（－子、－儿）半成品 semi-finished product：钢～ *steel billet*｜酱～子 *semi-finished sauce*｜面～儿 *cooked noodles before being served with sauce and trimmings*

狉 pī ㄆㄧ ［狉狉］野兽蠢动的样子 (of wild animals) roam about：鹿豕～。*Deer and boar are roaming from place to place.*

驲（駓） pī ㄆㄧ 古代指毛色黄白相间的马 (ancient) yellow and white horse

批 pī ㄆㄧ ❶用手掌打 to slap ❷写上字句，判定是非、优劣、可否 to write comments (on a report from a subordinate, etc.)：～示 *write comments or instructions; comments or instructions (on a report from a subordinate)*｜～准 *to ratify*｜～改作文 *correct compositions* ❸（－儿）附注的意见或注意之点 comment：眉～（写在书眉上的批语、批注）*comments at the top of a page*｜在文后加了一条小～儿 *added a note at the end of the article* ❹批评，批判 to criticise：～驳 *to criticise*｜挨了一通～ *be criticised* ❺量词，用于大宗的货物或同时行动的许多人 (measure word for large quantity of goods or people acting at the same time) batch; group：一～货 *a batch of goods*｜一～人 *a bunch of people* ［批发］大宗发售货物 to wholesale

纰（紕） pī ㄆㄧ 布帛、丝缕等破坏散开 (of cloth, thread, etc.) to come apart ［纰漏］因疏忽而引起的错误 careless mistake ［纰缪］（－miù）错误 error

砒 pī ㄆㄧ ❶ former name for 砷 (shēn) ❷砒霜，砷的氧化物，有剧毒，可做杀虫剂 white arsenic

钋（鈚） pī ㄆㄧ 钋箭，古代的一种箭 a kind of arrow in ancient times

披 pī ㄆㄧ ❶覆盖在肩背上 to drape over one's shoulder：～

P

红 *drape a length of red cloth over the shoulders* | ～着大衣 *draping an overcoat over one's shoulders* | ～星戴月（形容起早贪黑辛勤劳动或昼夜赶路）*work/travel from before dawn till after dusk* ❷打开 to unroll：～襟 *loosen one's jacket* | ～卷（juàn）*open a book and read* | ～肝沥胆（喻竭诚效忠）*be loyal and faithful* [披露]（－lù）发表 to announce; to reveal [披靡]（－mǐ）草木随风散倒 (of plants) be windswept ㊗敌军溃散 (of an enemy) be defeated and dispersed：所向～ *be invincible* ❸裂开 to split (open)：竹竿～了。*The bamboo pole has split.* | 指甲～了。*The finger nail split.* ❹劈开，劈去 to cleave; to chop：～荆斩棘（喻克服创业中的种种艰难）*overcome difficulties (literally means 'break through brambles and thorns')*

劈 pī ㄆㄧ ❶用刀斧等破开 to chop：～木头 *chop wood* ❷冲着，正对着 right against：～脸 *right in the face* | 大雨～头浇下来。*The rain came pelting down on our heads.* ❸雷电毁坏或击毙 (of thunder) to strike：大树让雷～了。*The big tree was struck by lightning.* ❹尖劈，简单机械，由两斜面合成，刀、斧等都属于这一类 wedge

[劈啪] 形容拍打声、爆裂声 crack

⇨ see also pǐ on p.502

噼 pī ㄆㄧ [噼啪] same as "劈啪"

霹 pī ㄆㄧ [霹雳]（－lì）响声很大的雷，是云和地面之间强烈的雷电现象 thunderbolt

皮 pí ㄆㄧˊ ❶人和动植物体表面的一层组织 skin; peel：牛～ *cowhide; oxhide* | 树～ *bark* | 荞麦～ *buckwheat husk* | 碰破了点儿～ *grazed one's skin* ❷皮革 hide; leather：～包 *leather case* | ～箱 *leather suitcase* | ～鞋 *leather shoes* ❸表面 surface：地～ *ground* | 水～儿 *surface of water* ❹包在外面的东西 wrapper; cover：书～ *dust jacket* | 封～ *(of a book) cover; envelope* ❺薄片状的东西 thin sheet：铅～ *lead sheet* | 粉～ *sheet jelly made from bean or sweet potato starch* | 海蜇～ *jellyfish skin* ❻韧性大，不松脆 soggy; sticky：～糖 *sticky candy* | 饼～了。*The pan cake has become soggy.* ❼顽皮，淘气 naughty：这孩子真～。*The kid is so naughty.* ❽（外loanword）法定计量单位中十进分数单位词头之一，表示 10^{-12}，符号 p。pico- (p)

陂 pí ㄆㄧˊ [黄陂] 地名，在湖北省武汉 Huangpi (a place in Wuhan, Hubei Province)

⇨ see also bēi on p.25, pō on p.509

铍（鈹）pí ㄆㄧˊ 金属元素，符号 Be，钢灰色，铍铝合金质硬而轻。可用来制飞机机件等，也用于核工业 beryllium (Be)

疲 pí ㄆㄧˊ 身体感觉劳累（㊟－乏、－倦、－惫）exhausted; tired：精～力尽 *be worn out* | ～于奔命 *be kept constantly on the run*

[疲癃]（－lóng）衰老多病 ageing and ailing [疲沓] (*疲塌) (—tɑ) 懈怠，不起劲 slack：作风～ *be slack in one's style* | 工作～ *be slack in one's work*

鲏(鮍) pí ㄆㄧˊ see 鳑鲏 (páng—) at 鳑 on page 493

芘 pí ㄆㄧˊ [芘芣] (—fú) 古书上指锦葵 mallow (in ancient Chinese texts)

⇨ see also bǐ on p.32

枇 pí ㄆㄧˊ [枇杷] (—pɑ) 常绿乔木，叶长椭圆形，花白色。果实也叫枇杷，圆球形，黄色，味甜。叶可入药 loquat

毗(*毘) pí ㄆㄧˊ ❶辅佐 to assist ❷接连 to be adjacent to：～连 *be adjacent to* | ～邻 *border on*

蚍 pí ㄆㄧˊ [蚍蜉] (—fú) 大蚂蚁 big ant

琵 pí ㄆㄧˊ [琵琶] (—pɑ) 弦乐器，用木做成，下部长圆形，上有长柄，有四根弦 *pipa* (a Chinese stringed instrument with four strings)

貔 pí ㄆㄧˊ 传说中的一种野兽，似熊 a bear-like wild animal in Chinese legend [貔貅] (—xiū) 传说中的一种猛兽 *pixiu* (a fierce wild animal in Chinese legend) ㊀勇猛的军队 powerful army

郫 pí ㄆㄧˊ 郫县，地名，在四川省 Pixian (a place in Sichuan Province)

陴 pí ㄆㄧˊ 城墙上呈⊓⊓形的矮墙 parapet (of city wall)

埤 pí ㄆㄧˊ 〈古 ancient〉增加 to increase：～益 *increase/ improve greatly*

⇨ see also pì on p.502

啤 pí ㄆㄧˊ [啤酒] 用大麦做主要原料制成的酒 beer

脾 pí ㄆㄧˊ 脾脏，人和高等动物的内脏之一，椭圆形，赤褐色，是个淋巴器官，也是血库 spleen (see picture of 人体内脏 on page 819) [脾气] (—qi) 1 性情 temperament：～好 *good-tempered* 2 容易发怒的性情 bad temper：有～ *have a temper* | 发～ *lose one's temper* [脾胃] 借指对事物喜好的习性 taste; liking：不合他的～。*It does not suit his temperament.* | 两人～相投。*They have similar likes and dislikes.*

裨 pí ㄆㄧˊ 副，辅佐的 (㊁偏—) subordinate：～将 *lower-ranking general*

⇨ see also bì on p.35

蜱 pí ㄆㄧˊ 节肢动物，身体扁平，种类很多，大部分以吸血为生。对人畜和农作物有害 tick (a small creature that feeds on blood)

鼙 pí ㄆㄧˊ 古代军中用的一种鼓 a kind of drum used in the army in ancient times：～鼓（古代军队中用的小鼓） *small army drum in ancient times*

罴(羆) pí ㄆㄧˊ 熊的一种，即棕熊，又叫马熊，毛棕褐色，能爬树，会游泳 (same as 棕熊, also called 马熊) brown bear

匹(❶*疋) pǐ ㄆㄧˇ ❶量词 measure word ①用于骡、马等 for mules, horses, etc.：三～马 *three horses* ②用

P

于整卷的布或绸缎等 for rolls of cloth, silk, etc.：一～红布 *a bolt of red cloth* ❷相当，相敌，比得上 to be a match for; to rival［匹敌］彼此相等 be equal to［匹配］1 婚配 to marry 2（元器件等）配合 (of components) to be matching

苉 pǐ ㄆㄧˇ 有机化合物，存在于煤焦油中 picene

庀 pǐ ㄆㄧˇ ❶具备 to possess ❷治理 to administer

圮 pǐ ㄆㄧˇ 坍塌，倒塌 to collapse; to fall apart：倾～ *to collapse*

仳 pǐ ㄆㄧˇ［仳离］夫妻离散 (of husband and wife) to be separated

否 pǐ ㄆㄧˇ ❶恶，坏 wicked; bad：～极泰来（坏的到了尽头，好的就来了。否和泰都是《周易》六十四卦中的卦名，分别代表坏和好的事情）。*Extreme adversity marks the beginning of fortune.* ❷贬斥 to censure：臧（zāng）～人物（评论人物的优劣）*pass judgement on sb*

⇨ see also fǒu on p.181

痞 pǐ ㄆㄧˇ ❶痞块，中医指肚子里可以摸得到的硬块 (in traditional Chinese medicine) mass in abdomen ❷（一子）流氓，无赖 scoundrel：地～ *local bullies and loafers*｜～棍 *ruffian*

嚭（** 噽）pǐ ㄆㄧˇ 大 big; large

劈 pǐ ㄆㄧˇ 分开 to divide; to cut：～柴 *firewood*｜～成两份儿 *divide into two parts*｜～一半给你。*(I'll) give you half.*

⇨ see also pī on p.500

擗 pǐ ㄆㄧˇ 分裂，使从原物体上分开 to break off：～棒子（玉米）*pick corncobs*

癖 pǐ ㄆㄧˇ 对事物的特别爱好 addiction; craving：烟～ *addiction to smoking*｜洁～ *mysophobia*｜怪～ *curious habit*｜嗜酒成～ *be addicted to alcohol*

屁 pì ㄆㄧˋ 从肛门排出的臭气 fart

媲 pì ㄆㄧˋ 并，比 to be a match for：～美 *compare well with*

埤 pì ㄆㄧˋ［埤堄］（－nì）〈古 ancient〉城上矮墙。也作"埤院" battlements (also written as 埤院)

⇨ see also pí on p.501

睥 pì ㄆㄧˋ bì ㄅㄧˋ（又）［睥睨］（－nì）眼睛斜着看 to look askance at ㊂看不起 to look down on sb/sth：～一切 *treat everything with disdain*

淠 pì ㄆㄧˋ 淠河，水名，在安徽省西部 Pihe River (in the west of Anhui Province)

辟（❶–❸闢）pì ㄆㄧˋ ❶开辟，从无到有地开发建设 to open up：开天～地 *the dawn of creation; the beginning of time*｜这一带将～为开发区。*The area will be opened up as a development zone.* ❷驳斥，排除 to refute：～谣 *deny a rumour*｜～邪说 *refute heresy* ❸透彻 incisive：精～ *sharp* ❹法，法律 law［大辟］古代指死刑 (ancient) death penalty

⇨ see also bì on p.36

僻 pì ㄆㄧˋ ❶偏僻，距离中心地区远的 remote; out-of-the-way：～静 *secluded* | 穷乡～壤 *poor backwater* ❷不常见的 rare：冷～ *desolate; unfamiliar* | 生～字 *rare Chinese character* ❸性情古怪，不合群（㊥乖—）eccentric：孤～ *unsociable and eccentric* | 怪～ *eccentric*

澼 pì ㄆㄧˋ see 洴澼 (píng—) at 洴 on page 509

甓 pì ㄆㄧˋ 砖 brick

䴙（鷿） pì ㄆㄧˋ ［䴙䴘］（—tī）鸟名，略像鸭而小，羽毛黄褐色 grebe

譬 pì ㄆㄧˋ 打比方（㊥—喻、—如）to make an analogy

PIAN ㄆㄧㄢ

片 piān ㄆㄧㄢ （—子、—儿）same as "片 (piàn) ❶", used in 相片儿，画片儿，唱片儿，电影片儿, etc.

⇨ see also piàn on p.504

扁 piān ㄆㄧㄢ ［扁舟］小船 small boat：一叶～ *a small boat*

⇨ see also biǎn on p.38

偏 piān ㄆㄧㄢ ❶歪，不在中间 slanting; inclined to one side：镜子挂～了。*The mirror has been hung askew.* | 太阳～西了。*The sun slanted to the west.* ㊀不全面，不正确 partial：～于一端 *be partial* | ～听～信 *listen only to one side* | ～差（chā）*deviation; error* ［偏向］1 无原则地支持，袒护 be partial to ; to favour：妈妈总是～弟弟。*Mum always favours my younger brother.* 2 不正确的倾向 deviation：纠正～ *correct a deviation* ❷副词，表示跟愿望、预料或一般情况不相同 ㊇ (adverb, used to express sth different from expectations, hopes, etc.) wilfully：不让他干，他～干。*He was told not to do it, but he did it all the same.* | 我去看他，～～他没在家。*He happened to be out when I went to visit him.*

犏 piān ㄆㄧㄢ 犏牛，牦牛和黄牛杂交生的牛 dzo (male)/ dzomo (female) (hybrid between domestic cattle and yak)

篇 piān ㄆㄧㄢ ❶首尾完整的文章（㊥—章）piece of writing：名～ *famous piece of writing* ❷（—儿）量词 measure word ①用于文章 for articles：一～论文 *a thesis* ②用于纸张、书页（一篇是两页）(for paper, page of a book, etc.) sheet ［篇幅］文章的长短，书籍报刊篇页的数量 (of articles) length; (of books, newspapers and magazines) space：～不长 *(of articles) not long* | ～太大 *(of articles) too long*

翩 piān ㄆㄧㄢ 很快地飞 to flutter swiftly ［翩翩］轻快地飞舞的样子 light; brisk：舞姿～ *dance lightly* 形容风流潇洒 genteel：风度～ *graceful bearing* ［翩跹］（—xiān）形容轻快地跳舞 (to dance) lightly：～起舞 *dance with quick, light steps*

便 pián ㄆㄧㄢˊ ［便便］肚子肥大的样子 bulging：大腹～ *with a big belly* ［便宜］（—yi）物价较低 low-priced：这些花布

P

都很～。*The patterned cloth is very low-priced.* ㊀小利，私利 unearned gains：不要占～。*Don't profit at another's expense.* (see also biànyí at 便 biàn on page 39)

⇨ see also biàn on p.39

媥 pián ㄆㄧㄢˊ ［媥娟］1 美好的样子 beautiful 2 回环曲折的样子 winding

楩 pián ㄆㄧㄢˊ ❶古书上说的一种树 a kind of tree in ancient Chinese texts ❷用于地名 used in place names：～树岔（在福建省福鼎）*Pianshucha (in Fuding, Fujian Province)*

骈（駢） pián ㄆㄧㄢˊ 两物并列成双的，对偶的（㊀一俪）parallel：～句 *parallel sentences* ［骈文］旧时的一种文体，文中用对偶的句子，讲究声韵和谐，辞藻华丽 (old) parallel prose

胼 pián ㄆㄧㄢˊ ［胼胝］（－zhī）俗叫膙（jiǎng）子。手上、脚上因摩擦而生成的硬皮 (informal 膙 jiǎng 子) callus

蹁 pián ㄆㄧㄢˊ ［蹁跹］（－xiān）形容旋转舞动 whirling about (in dancing)

谝（諞） piǎn ㄆㄧㄢˇ 显示，夸耀 to show off; to display：～能 *show off one's skills*

塄 piǎn ㄆㄧㄢˇ 用于地名 used in place names：长河～（在四川省安岳）*Changhepian (in Anyue, Sichuan Province)*

片 piàn ㄆㄧㄢˋ ❶（－子、－儿）平而薄的物体 flat, thin piece：明信～ *postcard* | 铁～ *piece of iron* | 玻璃～ *sheet of glass* | 肉～ *slice of meat* ❷切削成薄片 to slice：～肉片 *slice meat* | 把豆腐干～一～。*Slice the dried bean curds.* ❸少，零星 brief; fragmentary：～言（几句话）*a few words* | ～纸只（zhī）字 *fragment of writing* | ～刻（短时间）*an instant* ［片面］不全面，偏于一面的 one-sided; partisan：观点～ *biased view* | 不要～看问题。*Do not take a one-sided approach to problems.* ❹指较大地区内划分的较小地区 part of a place：分～儿开会 *hold a meeting in each part of an area* ❺量词 measure word ①用于地面、水面或成片的东西等 for land, water, or thin, flat things, etc.：一大～绿油油的庄稼 *a vast stretch of green crops* | 一～汪洋 *a wide expanse of water* | 两～儿药 *two tablets* ②用于景色、气象、声音、语言、心意等（前面用"一"字）for scenery, atmosphere, voice, feeling, etc. (preceded by 一)：一～好心 *well meaning* | 一～欢呼声 *a great cheer*

⇨ see also piān on p.503

骗（騙） piàn ㄆㄧㄢˋ ❶欺蒙（㊀欺－）to cheat; to deceive：～人 *pull sb's leg; deceive sb* | 诈～ *to swindle* ❷用欺蒙的手段谋得（㊀诓－）to cheat sb (out) of sth：～钱 *cheat sb out of their money* | ～取信任 *gain the trust of sb by fraudulent means* ❸侧身抬腿跨上 to leap into the saddle：一～腿骑上自行车 *leap onto*

P

a bike

PIAO ㄆㄧㄠ

剽 piāo ㄆㄧㄠ ❶抢劫，掠夺（㊜－掠）to rob; to loot［剽窃］抄袭他人著作 to plagiarise ❷轻快而敏捷 nimble：～悍 *quick and fierce*

漂 piāo ㄆㄧㄠ 浮在液体上面不沉下去 to float：树叶在水上～着。*Leaves are floating on the water.*［漂泊］（－bó）㊙为了生活、职业而流浪奔走 lead a wandering life：～在外 *roam about*

⇨ see also piǎo on p.505, piào on p.506

慓 piāo ㄆㄧㄠ same as "剽❷"

缥(縹) piāo ㄆㄧㄠ［缥缈］［飘渺］（－miǎo）形容隐隐约约，若有若无 dimly discernible：山在虚无～间。*The mountains were dimly discernible.*

⇨ see also piǎo on p.505

飘(飄、*飃) piāo ㄆㄧㄠ 随风飞动或摆动 to flutter (in the wind)：～雪花 *snowflakes swirling*｜～起了炊烟 *smoke rising from kitchen chimneys*｜～扬 *to flutter*｜红旗～～ *fluttering red flags*［飘零］花、树叶等坠落 (of flowers, leaves, etc.) to fade and fall ㊙流落在外，无依无靠 to wander：～异乡 *roam through a foreign land*｜半世～ *be adrift half of one's life*［飘摇］（*飘飖）（－yáo）随风摆动 sway in the wind：烟云～上升。*Clouds of smoke were curling upward.*

薸 piāo ㄆㄧㄠ（又）see piáo on page 505

螵 piāo ㄆㄧㄠ［螵蛸］（－xiāo）螳螂的卵块 mantis egg-case

朴 piáo ㄆㄧㄠˊ 姓 (surname) Piao

⇨ see also pō on p.509, pò on p.510, pǔ on p.513

嫖(闝)** piáo ㄆㄧㄠˊ 男子玩弄妓女 to visit prostitutes：～娼 *visit prostitutes*

瓢 piáo ㄆㄧㄠˊ（－儿）舀（yǎo）水或取东西的用具，多用瓢葫芦或木头制成 gourd/wooden ladle

薸 piáo ㄆㄧㄠˊ piāo ㄆㄧㄠ（又）［大薸］水草，又叫水浮莲，叶子可用作猪饲料 water lettuce (also called 水浮莲)

莩 piǎo ㄆㄧㄠˇ same as "殍"

⇨ see also fú on p.185

殍 piǎo ㄆㄧㄠˇ 饿死的人 person who starved to death：饿～ *bodies of those who died of hunger* 也作"莩" also written as 莩

漂 piǎo ㄆㄧㄠˇ ❶用水加药品使东西退去颜色或变白 to bleach：～白 *to bleach; to launder money* ❷用水淘去杂质 to rinse：用水～一～。*Rinse it in water.*｜～朱砂 *rinse the cinnabar*

⇨ see also piāo on p.505, piào on p.506

缥(縹) piǎo ㄆㄧㄠˇ ❶青白色 pale-green ❷青白色丝织品 pale-green silk

⇨ see also piāo on p.505

P

瞟 piǎo ㄆㄧㄠˇ 斜着眼看一下 to cast a sidelong glance at: ～了他一眼 *gave him a sidelong glance*

票 piào ㄆㄧㄠˋ ❶（一子、一儿）钞票，纸币 banknote ❷印的或写的凭证 ticket: 车～ *bus/train ticket* | 股～ *shares* | 选～ *ballot* ❸称非职业的演戏 amateur performance: ～友 *amateur performer* | 玩儿～ *do an amateur performance; (generally) do a job as a sideline* ❹被绑匪挟持借以勒取赎金的人质 hostage: 绑～儿 *kidnap (for ransom)* | 撕～儿（指杀死人质）*kill a hostage*

蔈 piào ㄆㄧㄠˋ 用于地名 used in place names: ～草乡（在重庆市云阳）*Piaocaoxiang (in Yunyang, Chongqing Municipality)*

嘌 piào ㄆㄧㄠˋ [嘌呤]（一lìng）有机化合物，无色晶体，易溶于水，在人体内嘌呤氧化而变成尿酸 purine

漂 piào ㄆㄧㄠˋ [漂亮]（一liang）1 美，好看 beautiful 2 出色 remarkable: 活儿干得很～。*The work is well done.*

⇨ see also piāo on p.505, piǎo on p.505

骠（驃） piào ㄆㄧㄠˋ ❶勇猛 valiant: ～勇 *valiant* ❷马快跑的样子 (of a horse) galloping fast [骠骑] 古代将军的名号 title of a high-ranking general of the cavalry in ancient times: ～将军 *cavalry general*

⇨ see also biāo on p.40

PIE ㄆㄧㄝ

氕 piē ㄆㄧㄝ 氢的同位素之一，符号 ^{1}H，质量数 1，是氢的主要成分 protium (^{1}H)

撇 piē ㄆㄧㄝ ❶丢开，抛弃 to cast aside; to discard: ～开 *cast aside* | ～弃 *to abandon* [撇脱]〈方 dialect〉1 简便 simple and convenient 2 爽快，洒脱 frank; candid ❷由液体表面舀取 to skim: ～油 *skim off the fat*

⇨ see also piě on p.506

瞥 piē ㄆㄧㄝ 很快地大略看一下 to shoot a glance at: 朝他～了一眼 *shot a glance at him*

苤 piě ㄆㄧㄝˇ [苤蓝]（一lan）草本植物，甘蓝的一种，叶有长柄。茎扁球形，也叫苤蓝，可用作蔬菜 kohlrabi

撇 piě ㄆㄧㄝˇ ❶平着向前扔 to fling; to throw: ～砖头 *throw a brick* | ～球 *throw a ball* ❷（一儿）汉字从上向左斜下写的一种笔形（丿）(in a Chinese character) left-falling wedge-shaped stroke: 八字先写一～儿。*The character* 八 *begins with a left-falling stroke.* ❸（一儿）量词，用于像汉字的撇形的东西 measure word for things resembling a left-falling stroke: 两～儿胡子 *two wisps of a moustache*

⇨ see also piē on p.506

锹（鐅） piě ㄆㄧㄝˇ 烧盐用的敞口锅。用于地名 (used in place names) cauldron for boiling salt: 曹～（在江苏省东台）*Caopie (a place in Dongtai,*

Jiangsu Province)

PIN ㄆㄧㄣ

拼 pīn ㄆㄧㄣ ❶连合，凑合（㊀—凑）to piece together：～音 *combine sounds into syllables*｜东～西凑 *scrape together*｜把两块板子～起来 *join two boards together* ❷不顾一切地干，豁（huō）出去 to go all out：～命 *risk one's life*｜～到底 *fight to the finish*

姘 pīn ㄆㄧㄣ 一方或双方已婚的、非夫妻关系的男女非法同居 to have illicit sexual relations with：～夫 *illicit male lover*｜～妇 *mistress*

玭 pín ㄆㄧㄣˊ 珍珠 pearl

贫（貧） pín ㄆㄧㄣˊ ❶穷，收入少，生活困难，跟"富"相对（㊀—穷）poor (opposite of 富)：～困 *impoverished*｜清～ *poor (often of scholars in old times)* ❷缺乏，不足（㊀—乏）to lack：～血 *anaemia* ❸絮烦可厌 talkative; garrulous：他的嘴太～。*He's really got a mouth on him.*

频（頻） pín ㄆㄧㄣˊ 屡次，连次（㊀—繁、—数 shuò）㊂ repeatedly：～～招手 *wave one's hand again and again*｜捷报～传。*Good news keeps pouring in.* [频率]（—lǜ）在一定的时间或范围内事物重复出现的次数 frequency

蘋（蘋） pín ㄆㄧㄣˊ 蕨类植物，又叫田字草，茎横卧在浅水的泥中，四片小叶，像"田"字 four-leaf clover (also called 田字草)

➪ 蘋 see also píng 苹 on p.508

颦（顰） pín ㄆㄧㄣˊ 皱眉头 to frown [效颦]㊕模仿他人而不得当 imitate with ludicrous effect

嫔（嬪） pín ㄆㄧㄣˊ 封建时代皇宫里的女官 female court attendant

品 pǐn ㄆㄧㄣˇ ❶物品，物件 article; product：～名 *name of an article*｜商～ *commodity*｜赠～ *complimentary gift*｜非卖～ *goods not for sale* [品牌]产品的牌子。特指知名产品的牌子 brand name; (specifically) famous brand：～效应 *brand effect* ❷等级，种类 grade：上～ *top grade*｜下～ *lowest grade; poor quality*｜精～ *fine works; quality goods* ❸性质 character; quality：人～ *moral quality*｜～质 *character* ❹辨别好坏、优劣等 to savour; to appraise：～茶 *sip tea and assess its flavour and quality*｜我～出他的为人来了。*I have found out what sort of person he is.*

榀 pǐn ㄆㄧㄣˇ 量词，房架一个叫一榀 measure word for frame of a house

牝 pìn ㄆㄧㄣˋ 雌性的（鸟兽），跟"牡"相对 (of birds and animals) female (opposite of 牡)：～马 *mare*｜～鸡 *hen*

聘 pìn ㄆㄧㄣˋ ❶请人担任工作 to employ：～书 *letter of appointment*｜～请 *to employ*｜～他当编辑 *engage him as an editor* ❷

P

指女子订婚或出嫁 (of women) to betroth; to get married: 行～ *deliver betrothal gifts* | 出～ *(of a girl) get married*

PING ㄆㄧㄥ

乒 pīng ㄆㄧㄥ ❶形容枪声或物体撞击声 bang; crack: ～的一声枪响 *crack of a gun* ❷指乒乓球 ping-pong; table tennis: ～协 *table tennis association* | ～坛 *table tennis world* [乒乓] (－pāng) 1 形容物体撞击声 rattling: 雹子打在玻璃上～乱响。*Hailstones were rattling against the glass.* 2 指乒乓球 ping-pong; table tennis

俜 pīng ㄆㄧㄥ see 伶俜 at 伶 on page 408

涄 pīng ㄆㄧㄥ 水流的样子 (of water) flowing

娉 pīng ㄆㄧㄥ [娉婷] (－tíng) 形容女子姿态美好的样子 (of a woman) slender and elegant

平 píng ㄆㄧㄥˊ ❶不倾斜，无凹凸，像静止的水面那样 level; flat: ～地 *level ground* | 把纸铺～了。*Spread out the paper.* ㊀均等 equal: ～分 *share out equally* | 公～ *fair* ❷使平 to level; to make even: 把地～一～ *level the ground* ❸安定，安静 calm: ～心静气 *dispassionately* | 风～浪静 *calm and tranquil* ❹经常的，一般的 ordinary: ～日 *normal days; peacetime* | ～淡 *prosaic; pedestrian* ❺平声，汉语四声之一。普通话的平声分阴平和阳平两类：阴平调子高而平，符号作"－"；阳平调子向高扬起，符号作"ˊ"。level tone (one of the four tones in Mandarin Chinese pronunciation)

评(評) píng ㄆㄧㄥˊ 议论或评判(㊐－论、－议) to comment on; to appraise: ～语 *comment* | ～理 *reason things out* | ～比 *appraise through comparison* | ～阅 *read and appraise* ㊀指评论的话或文章 comment; commentary: 书～ *book review* | 短～ *short commentary* [评价] 对事物估定价值 to evaluate: 客观～ *objective evaluation* | 予以新的～ *make a new evaluation* [评介] 评论介绍 review [评判] 判定胜负或优劣 to judge [批评] 1 指出工作、思想、作风上的错误或缺点 to criticise: ～与自我～ *criticism and self-criticism* | ～了保守思想 *criticised conservative ideas* 2 评论 criticism; commentary: 文学～ *literary criticism*

坪 píng ㄆㄧㄥˊ 平坦的场地 level ground: 草～ *lawn* | ～坝 *open and flat space* | 停机～ *apron; aircraft parking space*

苹(△蘋) píng ㄆㄧㄥˊ [苹果] 落叶乔木，叶椭圆形，花白色，果实也叫苹果，球形，红色、青色或黄色，味甜 apple

⇨ 蘋 see also pín 蘋 on p.507

泙 píng ㄆㄧㄥˊ ❶河谷 river valley ❷姓 (surname) Ping

玶 píng ㄆㄧㄥˊ 一种玉 a kind of jade

枰 píng ㄆㄧㄥˊ 棋盘 chessboard: 棋～ *chessboard* | 推～认

输 *admit defeat in a chess game by pushing the chessboard forward*

萍 píng ㄆㄧㄥˊ 浮萍，草本植物，浮生在水面，茎扁平像叶子，根垂在水里 common duckweed：～踪（喻漂泊不定的行踪）*uncertain whereabouts* | ～水相逢（喻偶然遇见）*meet by chance*

蚲 píng ㄆㄧㄥˊ 古书上指米中的小黑虫 small black insect in rice (in ancient Chinese texts)

鲆（鮃） píng ㄆㄧㄥˊ 鱼名，身体侧扁，两眼都在身体的左侧，有眼的一侧灰褐色或深褐色，无眼的一侧白色。常见的有牙鲆、斑鲆等 lefteye flounder

凭（憑、*凴） píng ㄆㄧㄥˊ ❶靠着 to lean on：～栏 *lean on a railing* | ～几（jī）*lean on a desk* ❷依靠，仗恃 to rely on; to depend on：劳动人民～着双手创造世界。*The working people create the world with their hands.* | 光～武器不能打胜仗。*One cannot win a war by weapons alone.* ❸证据（㊀—证、—据）proof：真～实据 *concrete evidence* | 口说无～。*Verbal statements are no guarantee.* ❹介词，根据 (preposition) on the basis of; according to：～票入场。*Admission by ticket.* | ～大家的意见做出决定。*Make decision according to general opinion.* ❺连词，任凭，无论 (conjunction) no matter (how, what, where, when, etc.)：～你怎么说，我也不信。*No matter what you say, I won't believe it.*

苹 píng ㄆㄧㄥˊ 古书上指马蔺（一种草本植物）white flowered iris (in ancient Chinese texts)

帡 píng ㄆㄧㄥˊ [帡幪]（—méng）古代称覆盖用的东西，指帐幕等 (ancient) canopy, tent or similar cover

洴 píng ㄆㄧㄥˊ [洴澼]（—pì）漂洗（丝绵）to rinse (silk)

屏 píng ㄆㄧㄥˊ ❶遮挡，遮挡物 (to) shield; (to) screen：～藩 *screen and fence; (figuratively) border area* | ～蔽 *to shield; protective screen* | ～障 *protective screen* | ～风（挡风或阻隔视线用的家具）*screen* | 围～ *folding screen* ❷字画的条幅，通常以四幅或八幅为一组 set of vertical scrolls：四扇～ *a set of four scrolls*

⇨ see also bǐng on p.46

瓶（*缾） píng ㄆㄧㄥˊ（—子、—儿）口小腹大的器皿，多为瓷或玻璃做成，通常用来盛液体 bottle：酒～子 *wine bottle* | 花～儿 *vase* | 一～子油 *a bottle of oil*

PO ㄆㄛ

朴 pō ㄆㄛ [朴刀]旧式兵器，刀身狭长，刀柄略长，双手使用 (old) knife with a long blade

⇨ see also piáo on p.505, pò on p.510, pǔ on p.513

钋（釙） pō ㄆㄛ 放射性金属元素，符号 Po。polonium (Po)

陂 pō ㄆㄛ [陂陀]（—tuó）不平坦 uneven

P

⇨ see also bēi on p.25, pí on p.500

坡 pō ㄆㄛ（～子、～儿）倾斜的地方 slope：山～ *mountain slope* | 高～ *high slope* | 上～ *go up a slope* | 下～ *go down a slope* [坡度] 斜面与地平面所成的角度 gradient

颇(頗) pō ㄆㄛ ❶偏，不正 oblique：偏～ *biased* ❷副词，很，相当地 (adverb) rather：离别～久 *be away for quite some time* | ～为不易 *be quite difficult*

泊 pō ㄆㄛ 湖 lake：湖～ *lake* | 血～（一大摊血）*a pool of blood*

⇨ see also bó on p.48

泺(濼) pō ㄆㄛ 同"泊"（pō），湖泊 (same as 泊 pō) lake

⇨ see also luò on p.428

泼(潑) pō ㄆㄛ ❶猛力倒水使散开 to splash：～水 *sprinkle water* | ～街 *sprinkle water on the streets* ❷野蛮，不讲理 uncouth：撒（sā）～ *be shrewish and make a scene* [泼辣] 凶悍 fierce and tough ㊕有魄力，不怕困难 daring and resolute：他做事很～。*He is bold and resolute in action.*

钹(鏺) pō ㄆㄛ 〈方 dialect〉❶用镰刀、钐（shàn）刀等抡开来割（草、谷物等）to cut or reap (grass, crop, etc.) with a sickle ❷一种镰刀 a kind of sickle

酦(醱) pō ㄆㄛ 在原酒的基础上再酿（酒）to remake (wine); to rebrew (beer)

婆 pó ㄆㄛˊ 年老的妇人 ㊂ old woman：老太～ *old woman* | 苦口～心 *(admonish) with patience and sincerity* ㊀①丈夫的母亲 ㊂ husband's mother ②祖母 ㊂ granny [婆娑]（－suō）1 盘旋舞蹈的样子 whirling (in dancing)：～起舞 *start dancing* 2 树枝纷披的样子 (of twigs) swaying：杨柳～ *swaying willows* 3 泪水下滴的样子 tearful：泪眼～ *tearful eyes*

鄱 pó ㄆㄛˊ [鄱阳] 1 湖名，在江西省北部 Poyang Lake (in the north of Jiangxi Province) 2 地名，在江西省 Poyang (a place in Jiangxi Province)

皤 pó ㄆㄛˊ 形容白色 white：须发～然 *white-haired*

繁 pó ㄆㄛˊ 姓 (surname) Po

⇨ see also fán on p.166

叵 pǒ ㄆㄛˇ 不可 impossibly：～信 *unreliable* | 居心～测 *be up to no good; have a sinister design*

钷(鉕) pǒ ㄆㄛˇ 人造的放射性金属元素，符号 Pm。promethium (Pm)

笸 pǒ ㄆㄛˇ [笸箩]（－luo）盛谷物等的一种器具，用柳条或篾条编成 shallow basket

朴 pò ㄆㄛˋ 朴树，落叶乔木，花淡黄色。木材可制家具 Chinese hackberry [厚朴] 落叶乔木，树皮厚，花白色。树皮可入药 houpu magnolia; magnolia-bark

⇨ see also piáo on p.505, pō on p.509, pǔ on p.513

P

迫(*廹) pò ㄆㄛˋ ❶用强力压制，硬逼(㊖逼一) to force; to compel：～害 *to persecute* | 饥寒交～ *suffer from cold and hunger* | 被～同意 *be forced to agree* ❷急促(㊖急一) urgent：～切 *pressing* | 从容不～ *leisurely* | ～不及待 *be unable to hold oneself back* ❸接近 to approach：～近 *to approach*

➪ see also pǎi on p.490

珀 pò ㄆㄛˋ see 琥珀(hǔ一) at 琥 on page 260

粕 pò ㄆㄛˋ 米渣滓 dregs of rice (see 糟❶[糟粕] on page 820 for reference)

魄 pò ㄆㄛˋ ❶迷信指依附形体而存在的精神(㊖魂一) soul：失魂落～ *be panic-stricken* ❷精神，精力 vigour：气～ *boldness of vision; impressive manner* | 体～ *physique and vigour* | ～力 *boldness*

破 pò ㄆㄛˋ ❶碎，不完整 broken; torn：碗打～了。*The bowl was broken.* | 衣服～了。*The clothes were worn out.* | 手～了。*(I) have cut my hand.* | 牢不可～ *unbreakable* [破绽](一zhàn) 衣服的裂口，比喻做事或说话露出的漏洞 burst seam; (figurative) flaw：他话里有～。*What he said was flawed.* ❷分裂(㊖一裂) to cut：势如～竹 *with crushing force* | 一～两半 *be cut in two* ㊔化整为零 to break a banknote into small changes：一元的票子～成两张五角的。*Break a one* yuan *note into two five* jiao *notes.* ❸使损坏(㊖一坏) to destroy：～釜沉舟 *cut off all means of retreat to show one's determination to press ahead (literally means 'break the cauldrons and sink the boats')* ㊕破除，批判 to abolish; to criticize：～旧立新 *destroy the old and establish the new* | 不～不立。*Without destruction there can be no construction.* ❹超出 to break through：～例 *make an exception* | ～格 *break a rule* | 打～纪录 *break a record* | 突～定额 *exceed the quota* ❺冲开，打败 to defeat：～阵 *break a battle array* | 大～敌军 *rout the enemy* ❻揭穿 to expose：～案 *crack a case* | 说～ *to reveal* | ～除迷信 *banish all blind faith* ❼花费，耗费 to spend：～费 *spend money/time* | ～工夫 *spend time* [破产] 企业或个人处于资不抵债的状态 bankruptcy ㊔丧失全部财产 to go bankrupt ㊕失败，破灭 come to nothing：敌人的阴谋～了。*The enemy's scheme fell through.* ❽不好的，令人鄙视的 poor; lousy：～戏 *lousy play* | ～货 *shoddy goods; loose woman* | 这样的～差事谁也不愿意干。*Nobody would care to do such a troublesome job.*

桲 po ·ㄆㄛ see 榅桲(wēn一) at 榅 on page 685

POU ㄆㄡ

剖 pōu ㄆㄡ ❶破开(㊖解一) to cut open：把瓜～开 *cut open a melon* [剖面] 东西切开后现出的平面 section：横～ *cross* *section* | 纵 ～ *longitudinal section* ❷分析，分辨 to dissect; to analyse：～析 *analyse* | ～明事理 *analyse the whys and wherefores of a matter*

抔 póu ㄆㄡˊ ❶用手捧东西 to hold with cupped hands：～饮（两手捧起而饮）*scoop up with cupped hands and drink* ❷量词，把，捧 (measure word) double handful：一～土 *a double handful of earth*

裒 póu ㄆㄡˊ ❶聚 to gather ❷减少 to draw out：～多益寡（减有余补不足）*take from the fat to pad the lean*

掊 pǒu ㄆㄡˇ 掊击，抨击 to attack

PU ㄆㄨ

仆 pū ㄆㄨ 向前跌倒 to fall forward：前～后继。*As those in front fall, those behind take up their positions.*

⇨ see also pú on p.512

扑(撲) pū ㄆㄨ ❶轻打，拍 to dab; to pat：～粉 *to dab powder* | ～打～打衣服上的土 *dust off one's clothes* ❷冲 to throw oneself at; to pounce on：向敌人猛～ *pounce on the enemy* | 香气～鼻。*A sweet smell assails one's nostrils.*

［扑哧］形容笑声或水、气挤出来的声音 sound of laughing, blowing air or spurting water

铺(鋪) pū ㄆㄨ 把东西散开放置，平摆 to spread：～轨 *lay a railway track* | 平～直叙（说话作文简单直接地叙述，没有精彩处）*speak or write in a simple, straightforward style* | ～平道路 *pave the way* ［铺张］为了在形式上好看而多用人力物力 extravagant：反对～浪费 *oppose extravagance and waste*

⇨ see also pù on p.514

噗 pū ㄆㄨ 形容水或气喷出的声音 sound of squeezing out water/air：～的一声吹灭了蜡烛 *blew out the candle with a puff* ［噗嗤］（－chī）same as "扑哧"

潽 pū ㄆㄨ 液体沸腾溢出 to boil over：牛奶～出来了。*The milk is boiling over.*

仆(僕) pú ㄆㄨˊ ❶被雇到家里做杂事、供役使的人 servant：～人 *servant* | 女～ *maid servant* ［仆从］旧时指跟随在身边的仆人 (old) footman ㊖ 受人控制并追随别人的 servile：～国 *vassal country* ❷旧时男子谦称自己 (old) (humble speech for men) I

⇨ see also pū on p.512

匍 pú ㄆㄨˊ ［匍匐］（－fú）爬，手足并行 to crawl (also 匍伏)：～前进 *crawl forward*

葡 pú ㄆㄨˊ ［葡萄］（－tɑo）藤本植物，茎有卷须，叶掌状分裂，花黄绿色，果实也叫葡萄，圆形或椭圆形，可以吃，也可酿酒 grape (vine)

莆 pú ㄆㄨˊ ［莆田］地名，在福建省 Putian (a place in Fujian Province)

脯 pú ㄆㄨˊ （一子、一儿）胸脯，胸部 breast：鸡～子 *chicken breast*

⇨ see also fǔ on p.188

蒲 pú ㄆㄨˊ see 摴蒱 (chū一) at 摴 on page 87

蒲 pú ㄆㄨˊ 香蒲，草本植物，生长在浅水或池沼中，叶长而尖。可用来编席、蒲包和扇子 bulrush：～扇 *bulrush leaf fan*

酺 pú ㄆㄨˊ 〈古 ancient〉朝廷特许的聚会饮酒，也泛指聚会饮酒 drinking party approved by the government; (generally) drinking party

菩 pú ㄆㄨˊ ［菩萨］（一sà）梵语音译"菩提萨埵（duǒ）"的省称。佛教中指地位仅次于佛的人。泛指佛和某些神 (short for 菩提萨埵 duǒ, from Sanskrit) Bodhisattva; (generally) Buddha; deity

墣 pú ㄆㄨˊ 土块 lump of soil

璞 pú ㄆㄨˊ 含玉的石头或没有雕琢过的玉石 uncut jade：～玉浑金（喻品质好）*simple and pure character (literally means 'uncut jade and unrefined gold')*

镤（鏷） pú ㄆㄨˊ 放射性金属元素，符号 Pa。protactinium (Pa)

穙 pú ㄆㄨˊ ❶谷类作物堆积 (of cereal crops) to heap up ❷禾或草等稠密 (of seedlings or grass) dense

濮 pú ㄆㄨˊ ［濮阳］地名，在河南省 Puyang (a place in Henan Province)

朴（樸） pǔ ㄆㄨˇ 没有细加工的木料 rough timber ⓨ朴实，朴素 simple：俭～ *thrifty*｜质～ *simple and unadorned*

⇨ see also piáo on p.505, pō on p.509, pò on p.510

埔 pǔ ㄆㄨˇ ［黄埔］地名，在广东省广州 Huangpu (a place in Guangzhou, Guangdong Province)

⇨ see also bù on p.53

圃 pǔ ㄆㄨˇ 种植蔬菜、花草、瓜果的园子 garden：花～ *flower garden*｜苗～ *nursery garden*

浦 pǔ ㄆㄨˇ 水边或河流入海的地区 riverside or river estuary

溥 pǔ ㄆㄨˇ ❶广大 vast ❷普遍 universal

普 pǔ ㄆㄨˇ 普遍，全，全面 general; universal：～天同庆。*Everybody joins in the celebration.*｜～查 *conduct a general survey* ［普及］传布和推广到各方面 to popularise：～教育 *make education universal* ［普通］通常，一般 ordinary：～人 *the common people*｜～读物 *general reader* ［普米族］我国少数民族，参看附录四 the Pumi people (one of the ethnic groups in China. See Appendix Ⅳ.)

谱（譜） pǔ ㄆㄨˇ ❶依照事物的类别、系统编制的表册 record; register：年～ *chronological life*｜家～（记载家族世系的表册）*family tree*｜食～ *recipe* ❷记录音乐、棋局等的符号或图形 (of music) score; (of chess games) manual：歌～ *music*

P

score for a song | 乐(yuè)～ *music score* | 棋～ *chess manual* ❸编写歌谱 to set to music：～曲 *put to music* ❹（一儿）大致的准则，把握 grasp：他做事有～儿。*He has a basic grasp of what he does.*

氆 pǔ ㄆㄨˇ ［氆氇］（—lu）（藏 *Tibetan*）藏族地区出产的一种毛织品 a kind of woolen fabric produced in Tibet

镨(鐠) pǔ ㄆㄨˇ 金属元素，符号 Pr，淡黄色。它的化合物多呈绿色，可用作颜料等 praseodymium (Pr)

蹼 pǔ ㄆㄨˇ 青蛙、乌龟、鸭子、水獭等动物脚趾中间的膜。也指像蹼的用具 (of ducks, frogs, etc.) web; web-shaped thing：脚～ *flippers* | ～泳 *finswimming*

铺(鋪、*舖) pù ㄆㄨˋ ❶(一子、一儿）商店 shop; store：饭～ *small restaurant*| 杂货～*grocery*❷床(㊀床一）plank bed：上下～ *bunk bed* | 临时搭～ *make a temporary bed* ❸旧时的驿站，现在用于地名 (old) courier station (now used in place names)：三十里～ *Sanshilipu (a place)*

⇨ see also pū on p.512

堡 pù ㄆㄨˋ 旧时的驿站，现多用于地名 (old) courier station (now often used in place names)：十里～ *Shilipu (a place)*

⇨ see also bǎo on p.23, bǔ on p.52

暴 pù ㄆㄨˋ 晒，晒干。后作“曝”（pù）。to expose to the sun (later written as 曝 pù)

⇨ see also bào on p.24

瀑 pù ㄆㄨˋ 瀑布，水从高山上陡直地流下来，远看好像垂挂着的白布 waterfall

⇨ see also bào on p.24

曝 pù ㄆㄨˋ 晒 to expose to the sun：一～十寒（喻没有恒心）*work in fits and starts (literally means 'sun for one day and chill for ten days')*

⇨ see also bào on p.24

Q ㄑ

QI ㄑㄧ

七 qī ㄑㄧ 数目字 seven

柒 qī ㄑㄧ “七”字的大写 (elaborate form of 七, used in commercial or financial context) seven

沏 qī ㄑㄧ 用开水冲茶叶或其他东西 to steep; to infuse (tea etc.) in hot water：～茶 *make tea*

妻 qī ㄑㄧ （一子）男子的配偶，跟“夫”“丈夫（一fu）”相对 wife (opposite of 夫 or 丈夫一fu)

⇨ see also qì on p.523

郪 qī ㄑㄧ 郪江，水名，在四川省东部，涪（fú）江支流 Qijiang River (in the east of Sichuan Province, a branch of Fujiang River)

凄（❶❸*淒、❷*悽）qī ㄑㄧ ❶寒凉 chilly; cold：～风苦雨 *chilly wind and driving rain; (figurative) miserable conditions* ❷悲伤（㊥一惨）sad; wretched ❸冷落寂静 desolate; dreary：～清 *bleak; distressing* | ～凉 *desolate; miserable*

萋 qī ㄑㄧ ［萋萋］形容草生长得茂盛 (of grass) lush; flourishing：芳草～。*The grass is very lush.*

栖（*棲）qī ㄑㄧ 鸟停留在树上 (of birds) to perch; to rest ㊀居住，停留 to dwell; to stay：两～ *amphibious* | ～身之处 *a place to stay* ［栖霞］地名，在山东省 Qixia (a place in Shandong Province)

⇨ see also xī on p.695

桤（榿）qī ㄑㄧ 桤木，落叶乔木，木质轻软，可制器具，嫩枝叶可入药 alder

戚（❷*慼、❷*慽）qī ㄑㄧ ❶亲戚，因婚姻联成的关系 relative (by marriage) ❷忧愁，悲哀 sadness; sorrow：休～相关 *be bound together by common interests* ［戚戚］忧愁的样子 worried; distressed：君子坦荡荡，小人常～～。*A gentleman is open and calm, but a person of low position is often distressed and fretful.*

嘁 qī ㄑㄧ ［嘁嘁喳喳］形容细碎的说话声 (of speech) chattering; babbling：～地说个不停 *chatter away*

期 qī ㄑㄧ ❶规定的时间或一段时间 appointed date; scheduled time：定～ *set a time limit; periodic* | 分～ *by stages* | 过～ *be overdue* | 学～ *semester* | ～中 *midterm* | ～限 *time limit* ㊀刊物出版的号数 (of publications) issue number ❷约定时日 appoint a time：不～而遇 *meet by chance* [期货交易]一种非现金、非现货的买卖。双方按约定的条件、时间交割货物、外汇或有价证券等 futures trading ❸盼望，希望(㊟-望) to expect; to hope for：～盼 *look forward to* | ～待 *to anticipate* | ～许 *have high expectations* | 反复试验，以～得到良好的效果 *make repeated experiments in the hope of obtaining good results*

⇨ see also jī on p.285

欺 qī ㄑㄧ ❶欺骗，蒙混 to cheat; to deceive：自～～人 *deceive oneself as well as others* [欺世盗名]欺骗世人，窃取名誉 gain fame by deception ❷欺负，压迫，侮辱(㊟-侮) to bully; to insult：仗势～人 *take advantage of one's power to bully others*

攲 qī ㄑㄧ same as "敧 (qī)"

敧 qī ㄑㄧ 倾斜，歪向一边 to lean; to slant; to tilt：～侧 *lean to one side* | ～倾 *tilt sideways*

⇨ see also yī on p.768

缉(緝) qī ㄑㄧ 一针对一针地缝 sew in close stitches：～鞋口 *hem the top edge of a shoe*

⇨ see also jī on p.285

漆 qī ㄑㄧ ❶黏液状涂料的统称。可分为天然漆和人造漆两类 paint; varnish; lacquer ❷用漆涂 to paint; to varnish

蹊 qī ㄑㄧ [蹊跷](-qiāo)奇怪，可疑 strange; suspicious：这事有点儿～。*This smells a bit fishy.* 也说"跷蹊"(qiāoqi)(also 跷蹊 qiāoqi)

⇨ see also xī on p.698

㬤 qī ㄑㄧ 〈方 dialect〉❶东西湿了之后要干未干 to be drying; to be almost dry：雨过天晴，路上渐渐～了。*After the rain, the sun came out and the road gradually dried up.* ❷用沙土等吸收水分 absorb water using sand, soil, etc.：地上有水，铺上点儿沙子～一～。*Cover the puddles on the road with sand to soak up the water.*

亓 qí ㄑㄧˊ 姓 (surname) Qi

郊 qí ㄑㄧˊ ❶古地名，在今陕西省岐山县东北 Qi (an ancient place name, in the north-east of today's Qishan County, Shaanxi Province) ❷姓 (surname) Qi

岐 qí ㄑㄧˊ ❶岐山，山名，又地名，在陕西省 (mountain name) Qishan Mountain; (place name) Qishan (both in Shaanxi Province) ❷ same as "歧"

歧 qí ㄑㄧˊ ❶岔道，大路分出的小路 branch road; forked road：～路亡羊 *lose a sheep at the fork in the road; (figurative) take the wrong path in complicated situations* [歧途]比喻错误的道路 wrong path：误入～ *go astray* ❷不相同，不一致 different; discrepant：～视 *discriminate against* | ～义 *ambiguity*

跂 qí ㄑㄧˊ 多生出的脚趾 extra toe

⇨ see also qǐ on p.522

齐(齊) qí ㄑㄧˊ ❶整齐，东西一头平或排成

一条直线 even; neat：参差不～ *irregular* | 庄稼长得很～。*The crops are all the same height.* | 纸叠得很～。*The paper is folded neatly.* ❷达到，跟什么一般平 to reach; be on the same level as：河水～腰深。*The river is waist-deep.* ❸同时，同样，一起 identical; simultaneous：～心 *be of one mind* | ～声高唱 *sing loudly in chorus* | 百花～放，推陈出新。*Let a hundred flowers bloom, and weed out the old to bring forth the new.* | 一～用力 *pull together* ❹全，完全（㊟一全）all; all complete：材料都预备～了。*All the materials are ready now.* | 代表都到～了。*All the representatives are here.* ❺周代诸侯国名，在今山东省北部、东部和河北省东南部 Qi (a state in the Zhou Dynasty, in the north and the east of today's Shandong Province and the south-east of today's Hebei Province) ❻朝代名 (name of a dynasty) Qi ①南朝之一，萧道成所建立（公元 479—502 年）Southern Qi Dynasty (479—502, one of the Southern Dynasties, founded by Xiao Daocheng) ②北朝之一，高洋所建立（公元 550—577 年），史称北齐 Northern Qi Dynasty (550—577, one of the Northern Dynasties, founded by Gao Yang)

〈古 ancient〉also same as 斋 (zhāi) in 斋戒

荠(薺) qí ㄑㄧˊ see 荸荠 (bíqi) at 荸 on page 31

⇨ see also jì on p.292

脐(臍) qí ㄑㄧˊ ❶肚脐，胎儿肚子中间有一条管子，跟母体的胎盘连着，这个管子叫脐带，出生以后，脐带脱落的地方就是肚脐 navel; belly button ❷螃蟹腹部下面的甲壳 abdomen of a crab：公蟹为尖～，母蟹为团～。*Male crabs have a narrow, triangular abdomen, whereas females have a broad, round one.*

蛴(蠐) qí ㄑㄧˊ ［蛴螬］（— cáo）金龟子的幼虫，约 3 厘米长，圆筒形，白色，身上有褐色毛，生活在土里，吃农作物的根和茎 white grub

祁 qí ㄑㄧˊ 盛大 grand; magnificent：～寒（严寒，极冷）*extremely cold*

圻 qí ㄑㄧˊ 地的边界 (of land) boundary

〈古 ancient〉also same as 垠 (yín)

祈 qí ㄑㄧˊ 向神求福（㊟一祷）to pray ㊂请求 beg for; plead for：敬～照准 *beg to have my request granted*

颀(頎) qí ㄑㄧˊ 身子高㊢(of stature) tall：～长 *tall*

旂 qí ㄑㄧˊ ❶古代指有铃铛的旗子 (ancient) flag/banner with bells ❷ see 旗 on page 518

蕲(蘄) qí ㄑㄧˊ ❶祈求，请求 to pray for; beg for ❷用于地名 used in place names：～春（在湖北省）*Qichun (in Hubei Province)*

芪 qí ㄑㄧˊ 黄芪，草本植物，茎横卧在地面上，花淡黄色，根可入药 milkvetch root

轵(軝) qí ㄑㄧˊ 古代车毂(gǔ)上的装饰 (ancient) decoration on a wheel hub

祇 qí ㄑㄧˊ 古代称地神 (ancient) god of the earth：神～ *gods and goddesses; deities*

⇨ see also zhǐ 只 on p.854

其 qí ㄑㄧˊ ❶代词 pronoun ①他，他们 he/she/it; they; him/her/it; them：不能任～自流 *cannot let events take their own course*｜劝～努力学习。*Advise one/them to study harder.* ②他的，他们的 his/her/its; their：各得～所 *each in his/her proper place*｜人尽～才，物尽～用。*Put one's talents to full use and make the most of things.* ❷那，那个，那些 that; those：～他 *(of people or things) other*｜～次 *secondly; secondarily*｜本无～事。*There wasn't such a thing.*｜～中有个原因。*There is a reason for that.* [其实] 实在的，事实上 actually; in fact：他说不懂，～早就懂了。*He says he doesn't understand, but actually he has long understood it.* ❸文言副词 adverb in classical Chinese ①表示揣测、反诘 used to indicate conjecture or to form a rhetorical question：岂～然乎? *Is it really the truth?*｜～奈我何? *What can they do to me?* ②表示命令、劝勉 used to indicate command or persuasion：子～勉之! *You must exert yourself for it!* ❹词尾 suffix：极～快乐 *extremely happy*｜尤～伟大 *especially great*

萁 qí ㄑㄧˊ 〈方 dialect〉豆茎 beanstalk

淇 qí ㄑㄧˊ 淇河，源出河南省林州，流入卫河 Qihe River (originating from Linzhou, Henan Province, and flowing into Weihe River)

骐(騏) qí ㄑㄧˊ 有青黑色纹理的马 striped black horse

琪 qí ㄑㄧˊ ❶一种玉 a kind of jade ❷珍异 rare：～花瑶草 *exotic flowers and rare herbs*

棋(*棊、*碁) qí ㄑㄧˊ 文娱用品名，有象棋、围棋等 board game (like chess)

祺 qí ㄑㄧˊ 吉祥，福气 good luck; blessing

綦 qí ㄑㄧˊ ❶青黑色 bluish black：～巾 *bluish white dress* ❷极 extremely; exceedingly：～难 *extremely difficult*｜言之～详 *describe in great detail*

蜞 qí ㄑㄧˊ see 蟛蜞 (péng－) at 蟛 on page 498

旗(❶△*旂) qí ㄑㄧˊ ❶(－子、－儿)用布、纸、绸子或其他材料做成的标志，多半是长方形或方形 flag; banner: 国～ *national flag*｜校～ *school flag* ❷清代满族的军队编制和户口编制，共分八旗。后又建立蒙古八旗、汉军八旗 the 'Eight Banners' system (the military and administrative organization of the Manchu people in the Qing Dynasty, later Mongolian and Han Eight Banners were also set up) ㊀属于八旗的，特指属于满族的 of the Eight Banners; (specifically)

Q

Manchurian：～人 *banner person (member of one of the Eight Banners); (specifically) Manchu* | ～袍 qipao; *cheongsam* | ～装 *Manchu clothing* ❸内蒙古自治区的行政区划单位，相当于县 banner (an administrative division at county level in the Inner Mongolia Autonomous Region)

鲯(鯕) qí ㄑㄧˊ ［鲯鳅］鱼名，体长而侧扁，头大，眼小，黑褐色，生活在海洋里 mahi-mahi; dolphinfish

璂 qí ㄑㄧˊ 古代弁（帽子）上的玉饰 (ancient) jade ornament (on a hat)

麒 qí ㄑㄧˊ ［麒麟］see 麟 on page 407

奇 qí ㄑㄧˊ ❶特殊的，稀罕，不常见的 rare; unusual：～事 *strange affair* | ～闻 *fantastic story* | ～冷 *unusually cold* | ～丑 *incredibly ugly* ㊁出人意料的，令人不测的 unexpected; unpredictable：～兵 *troops suddenly appearing from nowhere* | ～计 *ingenious strategy* | ～袭 *launch a surprise attack* | 出～制胜 *defeat one's opponent by a surprise move* ❷惊异，引以为奇 wonder at; be astonished by：世人～之。*The world wondered at it.* ❸姓 (surname) Qi

⇨ see also jī on p.283

埼(碕)** qí ㄑㄧˊ 弯曲的岸 meandering coast

萕 qí ㄑㄧˊ ［萕莱主山］山名，在台湾省 Qilaizhushan Mountain (in Taiwan Province)

崎 qí ㄑㄧˊ ［崎岖］（－qū）形容山路不平 (of mountain path) rugged; bumpy

骑(騎) qí ㄑㄧˊ ❶跨坐在牲畜或其他东西上 to ride; sit (on a horse, etc.)：～马 *ride a horse* | ～自行车 *ride a bicycle* ㊁兼跨两边 exist on both sides; to straddle：～缝盖章 *stamp a document across the edges of all pages* ❷ (formerly pronounced jì) 骑兵，也泛指骑马的人 cavalryman; (generally) horse rider：车～ *(especially) chariots and horses* | 轻～ *light cavalry; standard motorcycle* | 铁～ *armoured cavalry* ❸ (formerly pronounced jì) 骑的马 mount; steed：坐～ *mount*

琦 qí ㄑㄧˊ 美玉 fine jade ㊈珍奇 rare and precious

锜(錡) qí ㄑㄧˊ ❶古代一种带三足的锅 (ancient) a type of three-legged cooking pot ❷古代的一种凿子 (ancient) a type of chisel

俟 qí ㄑㄧˊ ［万俟］（mò－）复姓 (surname) Moqi

⇨ see also sì on p.619

耆 qí ㄑㄧˊ 年老，六十岁以上的人 old; person aged sixty and above：～年 *advanced in age*

愭 qí ㄑㄧˊ ❶恭顺 respectful and submissive ❷畏惧 afraid; fearful

鳍(鰭) qí ㄑㄧˊ 鱼类和其他水生脊椎动物的运动器官，由薄膜、柔软分节的鳍条和坚硬不分节的鳍棘组成 fin

Q

鬐 qí ㄑㄧˊ 马脖子上部的长毛。又叫马鬃、马鬣 (of a horse) mane (also called 马鬃，马鬣)

畦 qí ㄑㄧˊ 田园中分成的小区 small plot of field divided by ridges：种一～菜 *grow a bed of vegetables*

乞 qǐ ㄑㄧˇ 乞求，向人讨、要、求 beg for; to request：～怜 *beg for pity* | ～恕 *beg for forgiveness* | ～食 *beg for food* | 行～ *beg one's bread*

芑 qǐ ㄑㄧˇ 古书上说的一种植物 a type of plant in ancient Chinese texts

屺 qǐ ㄑㄧˇ 没有草木的山 bare hill

岂(豈) qǐ ㄑㄧˇ 副词，表示反诘 (adverb) used to indicate a rhetorical question ①哪里，怎么 how could：～敢！*How dare I?* | ～有此理？*Outrageous!* ②难道 isn't it：～非怪事？*Isn't it odd?*

〈古 ancient〉also same as 恺 (kǎi) and 凯 (kǎi)

玘 qǐ ㄑㄧˇ 古代佩带的玉 (ancient) jade ornament

杞 qǐ ㄑㄧˇ ❶植物名 plant name ①即枸（gǒu）杞 barbary wolfberry fruit ②杞柳，落叶灌木，生长在水边，叶长椭圆形，枝条可编箱、笼、筐、篮等器物 *Salix integra* (a species of willow) ❷周代诸侯国名，在今河南省杞县 Qi (a state in the Zhou Dynasty, in today's Qi County of Henan Province)：～人忧天（指不必要的忧虑）*unnecessarily worried (literally means 'a man in Qi state worried that the sky might fall')*

起 qǐ ㄑㄧˇ ❶由躺而坐或由坐而立等 sit up; stand up：～床 *get out of bed* | ～立 *rise to one's feet* ㊀离开原来的位置 change position ①移开，搬开 to move; to leave：～身 *start off; get out of bed; rise to one's feet* | ～运 *ship off* ②拔出，取出 to remove; draw out：～钉子 *pull out a nail* | ～货 *unload the cargo* [起居] 日常生活 daily life：～有恒 *lead a regular life* ❷由下向上升，由小往大里涨 to rise; grow in size：一～一落 *rise and fall* | ～劲 *vigorous; zealous* | 面～了。*The dough has risen.* [起色] 好转的形势，转机 improvement; sign of recovery：病有～。*The patient shows signs of recovery.* ❸长出 to get; to have：～燎泡 *have a blister* | ～痱子 *get miliaria* ❹开始 to start; to begin：～笔 *start writing (character, article, etc.); first stroke (of a Chinese character)* | ～点 *starting point* | 从今天～ *from today on* [起码] 最低限度，最低的 at least; at a minimum：～要十天才能完工。*This work will take at least ten days to complete.* ❺发生，发动 to initiate; to launch：～疑 *become suspicious* | ～意 *conceive an (evil) design* | ～火 *light the fire to cook a meal; (of fire) break out* | ～风 *the wind starts to blow* | ～兵 *send an army* [起义] 发动武装革命，也指脱离反革命集团投入革命

Q

阵营 to rise up; rise up in revolt and cross over to the revolutionary camp ❻ 拟定 to draft; work out: ～草 *draw up* ❼ 建造，建立 to build; set up: ～房子 *build a house* | 白手～家 *rise from rags to riches* ❽〈方 dialect〉介词，从 (preposition) from: ～南到北 *from south to north* | ～这里剪开 *cut it open from here* ❾ 量词 measure word ① 批，群 group; batch: 一～人走了，又来一～。*One group of people left, and then another group came.* ② 件，宗 instance; case: 三～案件 *three cases* | 两～事故 *two accidents* ❿ 在动词后，表示动作的趋向、关涉等 up (used after a verb, to describe the direction, effect, etc. of the action): 抱～ *lift up* | 拿～ *pick up* | 扛～大旗 *carry the big flag; (figurative) lead a team forward* | 提～精神 *brace oneself* | 引～大家注意 *draw public attention* | 想不～什么地方见过他。*I cannot think where I've met him before.* ⓫在动词后，跟"来"连用，表示动作开始 begin/start to (used after a verb, followed by 来, to indicate the commencement of an action): 大声念～来 *start to read aloud* | 唱～歌来 *start to sing* ⓬ 在动词后，常跟"不""得"连用 used after a verb, and often preceded by 不 or 得①表示力量够得上或够不上 used to indicate capability or incapability: 买不～ *cannot afford*| 经得～考验 *be able to stand the test* ②表示够不够格，达到没达到某种标准 used to indicate being up to standard or not: 看不～ *look down upon* | 瞧得～ *think highly of*

企 qǐ ㄑㄧˇ ❶踮着脚跟 stand on tiptoe: ～踵 *stand on tiptoe* | ～足而待 *await on tiptoe* ❷ 希望，盼望 hope for; to expect: ～望 *look forward to* | ～盼 *expect anxiously* [企图] 图谋，打算（多含贬义）(disapproving) (to) attempt; (to) design: ～逃跑 *attempt to escape* | 政治～ *political attempt*

[企业] 从事生产、运输、贸易等经济活动的部门，如工厂、矿山、铁路、贸易公司等 enterprise; business

杏 qǐ ㄑㄧˇ 〈古 ancient〉明星 bright star

⇨ see also mèn on p.444

启(**啓**、***啟**、***棨**) qǐ ㄑㄧˇ ❶打开 to open: ～封 *break the seal; open a sealed envelope* | ～门 *open the door* ㊀开导 to enlighten; to awaken: ～蒙 (méng) *to enlighten* | ～发 *to inspire* | ～示 *to reveal; enlightenment* ❷ 开始 to start; to begin: ～用 *start using* ❸ 陈述 to state; to inform: 敬～者 *I wish to inform you; to whom it may concern* [启事] 向群众说明事情的文字，现在多登在报纸上 notice: 寻人～ *missing person notice* | 征婚～ *marriage-seeking notice* ❹ 书信 letter; written message: 书～ *letter* | 小～ *note*

棨 qǐ ㄑㄧˇ ❶古时用木头做的一种通行证 (ancient) a type of pass (made of wood)：～信 *token* ❷古代官吏出行时用作前导的一种仪仗，用木头做成，略如戟形 wooden halberd of honour (preceding an official's carriage in ancient times)

䏿 qǐ ㄑㄧˇ 〈古 ancient〉腓肠肌（小腿肚子）calf muscle; gastrocnemius

跂 qǐ ㄑㄧˇ 踮着脚站着 stand on tiptoe：～望 *look forward to*

⇨ see also qí on p.516

婍 qǐ ㄑㄧˇ 容貌美丽 beautiful

绮(綺) qǐ ㄑㄧˇ ❶有花纹或图案的丝织品 patterned silk fabric：～罗 *patterned silk fabric* ❷美丽 beautiful：～丽 *(often of scenery) gorgeous* | ～思 *(of writing) fanciful thoughts*

稽 qǐ ㄑㄧˇ 稽首，古时跪下叩头的礼节 (ancient) to kowtow

⇨ see also jī on p.285

气(氣) qì ㄑㄧˋ ❶没有一定的形状、体积，能自由流动的物体 gas：煤～ *coal gas*| 蒸～ *vapour* 特指空气 (specifically) air：～压 *air pressure* | 给自行车打～。*Pump up the tyres of the bicycle.* ❷（～儿）气息，呼吸 breath; breathing：没～儿了 *stop breathing* | 上～不接下～ *be out of breath* ❸自然界寒、暖、阴、晴等现象 weather; natural phenomenon related to weather：天～ *weather* | 节～ *solar term (one of the twenty-four periods that match the major seasonal changes in a year)* ❹（～儿）鼻子闻到的味儿 smell; odour：香～ *fragrance; scent* | 臭～ *stink* | 烟～ *smoky smell* ❺人的精神状态 spirit; morale：勇～ *courage* | 朝～蓬勃 *be full of youthful spirit* [气势]（人和事物）表现出的某种力量和态势 momentum; imposing presence ❻作风，习气 style; habit：官～ *bureaucratic style* | 俗～ *vulgar* | 骄娇二～ *arrogant and delicate ways* ❼怒或使人发怒 be angry; make sb angry：他生～了。*He was angry.* | 别～我了。*Stop annoying me.* ❽欺压 to bully; to insult：受～ *be bullied* ❾中医指能使人体器官正常发挥功能的原动力 *qi* (the vital energy in the human body according to traditional Chinese medicine)：～血 *qi and blood* | ～虚 *qi deficiency*| 元～ *primordial qi* ❿中医指某种症象 symptom in traditional Chinese medicine：湿～ *eczema* | 脚～ *common name of* 脚癣 *tinea pedis; beriberi* | 痰～ *psychosis; apoplexy*

汽 qì ㄑㄧˋ 液体或某些固体变成的气体，特指水蒸气 steam; water vapour：～船 *steamboat*

讫(訖) qì ㄑㄧˋ ❶完结，终了 finished; settled：收～ *(of a payment) received* | 付～ *(of a bill) paid* | 验～ *checked (for acceptance)* ❷截止 to end：起～ *the beginning and the end*

迄 qì ㄑㄧˋ ❶到 up to; till: ～今未至 *so far have not arrived yet* ❷始终 all along: ～未成功 *have not achieved success yet*

汔 qì ㄑㄧˋ 庶几，差不多 perhaps; maybe

弃(*棄) qì ㄑㄧˋ 舍(shě)去，扔掉 to abandon; to forsake: 抛～ *cast off* | 丢～ *throw away* | 遗～ *to discard* | ～权 *abstain from voting; waive one's right (to play in a sport)* | 前功尽～ *waste all the previous efforts*

妻 qì ㄑㄧˋ 〈古 ancient〉以女嫁人 to marry a girl/woman to sb

⇨ see also qī on p.515

炁 qì ㄑㄧˋ same as "气" [坎炁](kǎn－)中药上指干燥的脐带 dried umbilical cord (in traditional Chinese medicine)

泣 qì ㄑㄧˋ ❶无声或小声哭 to sob; to whimper: 抽～ *to sob* | 啜(chuò)～ *to whimper* | ～不成声 *choke with sobs* ❷眼泪 tears: ～下如雨。*Tears stream down one's face.*

亟 qì ㄑㄧˋ 屡次 repeatedly; again and again: ～来问讯 *come to pay one's respects frequently*

⇨ see also jí on p.287

契(栔)** qì ㄑㄧˋ ❶用刀雕刻 to carve; to engrave ❷刻的文字 carved inscription: 书～ *written language* ❸契约，证明买卖、抵押、租赁等关系的合同、文书、字据 contract; deed: 地～ *title deed for land* | 房～ *title deed for a house* | 卖身～ *contract for selling oneself/someone* ❹相合，情意相投 agree with each other; be compatible: 默～ *well-coordinated; secret agreement* | 相～ *get along well with each other* | ～友 *close friend*

[契丹]我国古代东北地区的一个民族，曾建立辽国 *Qidan* (also called Khitan, an ancient ethnic group in Northeast China, who founded the Liao Dynasty)

⇨ see also xiè on p.722

碶 qì ㄑㄧˋ 用石头砌的水闸 water gate made of stone

砌 qì ㄑㄧˋ 建筑时垒砖石，用泥灰黏合 to build (by laying bricks or stones): ～墙 *build a wall* | ～炕 *build a* kang *(heatable brick bed)*

湆 qì ㄑㄧˋ 古水名，在今甘肃省 Qi (an ancient river, in today's Gansu Province)

葺 qì ㄑㄧˋ 用茅草覆盖房子 to thatch: 修～(修补)房屋 *repair a house*

碛(磧) qì ㄑㄧˋ 浅水中的沙石 gravel (in shallow water) [沙碛]沙漠 desert

槭 qì ㄑㄧˋ 落叶小乔木，叶掌状分裂，秋季变成红色或黄色。种类很多 maple

礤 qì ㄑㄧˋ 用于地名 used in place names: 黄～(在广东省新丰) *Huangqi (in Xinfeng, Guangdong Province)*

器(噐)** qì ㄑㄧˋ ❶用具的总称 tool; utensil: 武～ *weapon* | 容～ *container*

Q

［器官］生物体中具有某种独立生理机能的部分，如耳、眼、花、叶等 (of a living organism) organ：消化～ *digestive organ* | 生殖～ *genital organ* ❷人的度量、才干 tolerance; talent：～量 *tolerance* | 成～ *grow up to be a useful person* ❸器重，看重，看得起 think highly of

憩(*憇) qì ㄑㄧˋ 休息（㊀休一）take a rest：小～ *take a little rest*

QIA ㄑㄧㄚ

掐 qiā ㄑㄧㄚ ❶用手指用力捏，用指甲按或截断 to pinch; to nip：～掉豆芽菜的根 *nip the roots off the bean sprouts* ㊀割断，截去 cut off：～电线 *cut off the wire* ❷用手的虎口及手指紧紧握住 to clutch; to grip：一把～住 *clutch sth/sb tightly* ❸（一子、一儿）量词，拇指和食指或中指相对握着的数量 (measure word) pinch; handful：一小～儿韭菜 *a pinch of Chinese chives* | 一～子青菜 *a handful of vegetables*

袷 qiā ㄑㄧㄚ ［袷袢］（一pàn）（维 *Uygur*）维吾尔、塔吉克等民族所穿的对襟长袍 traditional Uygur or Tajik robe that buttons down the front

⇨ see also jiá 夹 on p.296

葜 qiā ㄑㄧㄚ see 菝葜 (bá一) at 菝 on page 11

拤 qiá ㄑㄧㄚˊ 用两手掐住 grip with both hands

卡 qiǎ ㄑㄧㄚˇ ❶（一子）在交通要道设置的检查或收税的地方 checkpoint; customs pass：关～ *check-post* ❷（一子）夹东西的器具 clip; fastener：头发～子 *hairpin* ❸夹在中间，堵塞 be stuck in：鱼刺～在嗓子里。*A fish bone is stuck in one's throat.* | 纸～在打印机里拿不出来了。*The paper is jammed inside the printer and cannot be removed.*

⇨ see also kǎ on p.347

洽 qià ㄑㄧㄚˋ ❶跟人联系，商量（事情）to consult; to discuss：接～ *contact sb and arrange a matter* | ～谈 *to negotiate* | 商～ *discuss (a matter) with sb* ❷谐和 be in harmony/agreement：融～ *harmonious*

恰 qià ㄑㄧㄚˋ ❶正巧，刚刚 just; exactly：～巧 *by chance* | ～到好处 *be just right for the purpose* | ～如其分（fèn）*be just to the proper extent* | ～好 *just right* ❷合适，适当 proper; appropriate：～当 *appropriate*

髂 qià ㄑㄧㄚˋ ［髂骨］腰部下面腹部两侧的骨，下缘与耻骨、坐骨联成髋（kuān）骨 ilium (see picture of 人体骨骼 on page 220)

QIAN ㄑㄧㄢ

千(❷韆) qiān ㄑㄧㄢ ❶数目，十个一百 thousand ㊀表示极多，常跟“万”“百”连用 thousands of; a great number of (often used with

万 or 百)：～言万语 *innumerable words* | ～军万马 *tens of thousands of troops; vast army* | ～锤百炼 *thoroughly seasoned* [千万] 副词，务必 (adverb) by all means：～不要铺张浪费。*Be sure to avoid extravagance and waste.* ❷ see 秋千 at 秋 on page 544 ❸法定计量单位中十进倍数单位词头之一，表示 10^3，符号 k。kilo (k)

仟 qiān ㄑ丨ㄢ "千"字的大写 thousand (elaborate form of 千，used in commercial or financial context)

阡 qiān ㄑ丨ㄢ ❶田间的小路（㊀一陌 mò） footpath (between fields) ❷通往坟墓的道路 path leading to a grave

圩 qiān ㄑ丨ㄢ 用于地名 used in place names：清～ *Qingqian* | 平～ *Pingqian*（都在安徽省青阳）*(both in Qingyang, Anhui Province)*

扦 qiān ㄑ丨ㄢ ❶（一子、一儿）用金属或竹、木制成的像针的东西 skewer ❷插，插进去 to skewer; stick in：～花 *arrange flowers (in a vase)* | 用针～住 *fasten sth with a needle*

芊 qiān ㄑ丨ㄢ 草木茂盛㊂(of grass and trees) lush; flourishing：郁郁～～ *luxuriantly green* [芊绵] [芊眠] 草木茂密繁盛 (of vegetation) thick and lush

迁(遷) qiān ㄑ丨ㄢ ❶机关、住所等另换地点（㊀一移）(of institutions and residences) to move：～都（dū）*move the capital to another place* | ～居 *move house* [迁就] 不坚持自己的意见，凑合别人 accommodate oneself to; to compromise：不能～ *do not give in* | ～应该是有原则的。*Compromise should be based on certain principles.* [迁延] 拖延 to delay; to postpone：已经～了一个多月了。*It has been postponed for over a month.* ❷变动，改变（㊀变一）to change; become different：事过境～。*It's all past, and circumstances are different now.*

杄 qiān ㄑ丨ㄢ ❶青杄、白杄等的统称，常绿乔木，木材可供建筑用 spruce ❷用于地名 used in place names：～树底（在河北省涞源）*Qianshudi (in Laiyuan, Hebei Province)* | ～木沟（在山西省宁武）*Qianmugou (in Ningwu, Shanxi Province)*

瓩 qiānwǎ ㄑ丨ㄢㄨㄚˇ 现写作"千瓦"，功率单位，1 瓩等于 1 000 瓦 (now written as 千瓦) kilowatt (kW)

钎(釺) qiān ㄑ丨ㄢ（一子）一头尖的长钢棍，多用来在岩石上打洞 drill rod：打～ *hammer the drill rod* | 扶～ *hold the drill rod* | 钢～ *drill steel*

岍 qiān ㄑ丨ㄢ 岍山，山名，在陕西省宝鸡。今作"千山"(now written as 千山) Qianshan Mountain (in Baoji, Shaanxi Province)

汧 qiān ㄑ丨ㄢ [汧阳] 地名，在陕西省。今作"千阳" (now written as 千阳) Qianyang (a place in Shaanxi Province)

佥(僉) qiān ㄑ丨ㄢ 〈古 ancient〉全，都 all; the whole

Q

签(簽、❸-❻籤) qiān ㄑㄧㄢ ❶亲自写上姓名或画上符号 to sign (by writing)：～名 *sign one's name; signature* | 请你～个字。*Please sign your name.* ❷简要地写出（意见）write brief comments：～注 *write comments and suggestions (on a book/document)* ❸（－子、－儿）用竹木等物做成的细棍或片状物 small stick; slip (made of wood, bamboo, etc.)：牙～儿 *toothpick* | 竹～儿 *bamboo slip* ❹（－儿）书册里做标志的纸片或其他物件上做标志的东西 mark; label; tag：书～ *bookmark* | 标～ *label* | 浮～ *note pasted on the margin of a page* ❺粗粗地缝合 to tack (in sewing)：～上花边 *tack the lace on* ❻旧时用于占卜或赌博的细长竹片或细棍 (old) bamboo slips/sticks used for divination or gamble

牵(牽) qiān ㄑㄧㄢ ❶拉，引领向前 to pull; lead along：～着一头牛 *be leading an ox* | ～牲口 *lead the cattle* | 手～着手 *be hand in hand* ❷连带，带累（㊖－连）to involve; to implicate：～扯 *drag in* | ～涉 *to involve* | ～累 *tie down; to implicate* | ～制 *to contain (an opposing force)* [牵强]（－qiǎng）勉强把两件无关或关系很远的事物拉在一起 far-fetched; forced：这话太～。*This remark is too far-fetched.* | ～附会 *draw a forced analogy* ❸缠连，挂念 care about; be concerned about：～挂 *be concerned about* | ～记 *worry about* | 意惹情～ *get one's heart entangled*

铅(鉛) qiān ㄑㄧㄢ ❶金属元素，符号Pb，银灰色，质软，熔点低，有毒。可用来制合金、蓄电池等 lead (Pb) ❷石墨制的铅笔芯 pencil core (made of graphite)：～笔 *pencil*

⇨ see also yán on p.751

悭(慳) qiān ㄑㄧㄢ 吝啬(㊖－吝) stingy

谦(謙) qiān ㄑㄧㄢ 虚心，不自高自大 modest; humble：～虚 *modest* | ～让 *modestly decline* | 满招损，～受益。*Pride leads to losses whereas modesty brings benefits.*

磏 qiān ㄑㄧㄢ 用于地名 used in place names：大～（在贵州省遵义）*Daqian (in Zunyi, Guizhou Province)*

⇨ see also lián on p.397

愆(*諐) qiān ㄑㄧㄢ ❶罪过，过失 sin; mistake：～尤 *fault* | 罪～ *sin* ❷错过，耽误 to miss (a deadline); to delay：～期 *miss a deadline*

鹐(鵮) qiān ㄑㄧㄢ 尖嘴的家禽或鸟啄东西 (of birds) to peck：鸡～麦穗。*The chickens are pecking at the heads of wheat.* | 乌鸦把瓜～了。*The crows have pecked some holes in the melon.*

骞(騫) qiān ㄑㄧㄢ 高举。多用于人名，如西汉有张骞 to hold high up (often used in given names, e.g. Zhang Qian of the Western Han Dynasty)

Q

搴 qiān ㄑㄧㄢ ❶拔取 pull out; to uproot：斩将～旗 *kill enemy generals and grab their flags* ❷ same as "褰"

褰 qiān ㄑㄧㄢ 把衣服提起来 lift up (a garment)：～裳 *lift up a skirt*

荨(蕁、藙)** qián ㄑㄧㄢ［荨麻］草本植物，茎叶生细毛，皮肤接触时会引起刺痛。茎皮纤维可做纺织原料 nettle

⇨ see also xún on p.743

钤(鈐) qián ㄑㄧㄢ ❶印章 seal; stamp［钤记］旧时印的一种 (old) a kind of official seal ❷盖印章 to seal sth：～印 *use a seal*｜～章 *use an official seal*

黔 qián ㄑㄧㄢ ❶黑色 black：～首（古代称老百姓）*(ancient) the common people* ❷贵州省的别称 Qian (another name for Guizhou Province)

前 qián ㄑㄧㄢ ❶跟"后"相对 front (opposite of 后) ①指空间，人脸所向的一面，在正面的 (of spatial position) front; anterior: ～面 *in front (of)*｜向～走 *go forward*｜天安门～ *in front of Tian'anmen*｜楼～ *in front of the building*｜床～ *in front of the bed* ②指时间，往日的，过去的 (of time) former; earlier：～天 *the day before yesterday*｜史无～例 *unprecedented* ③指次序，靠头里的 (of sequence) first; top：～五名 *top five* ❷向前行进 go forward：勇往直～ *march forward courageously*｜畏缩不～ *hang back in fear* ❸未来的（用于展望）future; prospective：～景 *prospect*｜向～看 *look ahead*

虔 qián ㄑㄧㄢ 恭敬 pious; devout：～诚 *pious*｜～心 *devotion; pious*

钱(錢) qián ㄑㄧㄢ ❶货币 money; coin; cash：铜～ *copper coin* 🄯 费用 fee; cost：车～ *fare*｜饭～ *cost of a meal* ❷圆形像钱的东西 coin-shaped object：纸～ *paper money (as an offering to the dead)*｜榆～儿 *seed pod of an elm tree* ❸财物 wealth; riches：有～有势 *be both rich and powerful* ❹市制重量单位，1两的十分之一，合5克 a traditional Chinese unit for measuring weight, equal to 5 grams. (There are 10 钱 in 1 两.)

钳(鉗、箝、❶**拑)** qián ㄑㄧㄢ ❶用东西夹住 to clamp; to grip (with pincers)［钳制］用强力限制 clamp down on ❷(－子) 夹东西的用具 pliers; pincers：火～ *fire tongs*｜老虎～ *bench vice; pliers*

掮 qián ㄑㄧㄢ 用肩扛(káng)东西 carry on the shoulder［掮客］〈方 dialect〉指替买卖货物的双方介绍交易，从中取得佣钱的人 broker

乾 qián ㄑㄧㄢ ❶八卦之一，符号是☰，代表天 *qian* (one of the Eight Trigrams used in ancient divination, symbol ☰, representing heaven) ❷乾县，在陕西省 Qianxian (a place in Shaanxi

Province)

⇨ see also gān 干 on p.196

墘 qián ㄑㄧㄢˊ 用于地名 used in place names：车路～（在台湾省）*Cheluqian (in Taiwan Province)* | 田～（在广东省汕尾）*Tianqian (in Shanwei, Guangdong Province)*

軒 qián ㄑㄧㄢˊ 骊靬（lí－），古代县名，在今甘肃省永昌 Liqian (an ancient county name, in today's Yongchang, Gansu Province)

犍 qián ㄑㄧㄢˊ ［犍为］（－wéi）地名，在四川省 Qianwei (a place in Sichuan Province)

⇨ see also jiān on p.301

潛（*濳） qián ㄑㄧㄢˊ ❶隐在水面下活动 to dive; go underwater：～水艇 *submarine*| 鱼～鸟飞。*Fish are diving deep in the river and birds are flying high in the sky.* ❷隐藏，隐蔽 to hide; to lurk：～伏 *to lurk* | ～藏 *to hide* | ～力 *potential* | ～移默化 *influence imperceptibly* ［潜心］十分专心而深入 be wholly devoted to sth：～研究 *be devoted to academic study* ❸秘密地，不声张 secretly; stealthily：～行 *move secretly* | ～逃 *(often of suspected offender) run away in secret*

肷（膁）** qiǎn ㄑㄧㄢˇ 身体两旁肋骨和胯骨之间的部分（多指兽类的）(often of animals) loin (the part between ribs and hips)：～窝 *loin*

浅（淺） qiǎn ㄑㄧㄢˇ ❶从表面到底或从外面到里面距离小，跟"深"相对（❸❹同）shallow; of short distance in depth or length (opposite of 深, also ❸ ❹)：这条河很～。*This river is very shallow.* | 这个院子太～。*This courtyard is too short.* ❷不久，时间短 not long in time; recent：年代～ *recent in years* | 相处的日子还～ *have not known each other for a long time* ❸程度不深 superficial：～见 *(often humble speech) superficial view* | 阅历～ *have little experience* | 交情～ *have no deep friendship* | 这篇文章很～。*This article is very simple.* | ～近 *easy to understand* ❹颜色淡 (of colour) light; pale：～红 *pale red* | ～绿 *light green*

⇨ see also jiān on p.299

遣 qiǎn ㄑㄧㄢˇ ❶派，差(chāi)，打发（㊣派－、差－）to send; to dispatch：特～ *send on a special mission* | ～送 *send back* ❷排解，发泄 to dispel; to give vent to：～闷（mèn）*relieve boredom*| 消～ *entertain oneself*

谴（譴） qiǎn ㄑㄧㄢˇ 责备(㊣－责）to reproach; to condemn

缱（繾） qiǎn ㄑㄧㄢˇ ［缱绻］（－quǎn）情意缠绵，感情好得离不开 deeply attached (to sb)

嗛 qiǎn ㄑㄧㄢˇ 颊囊，猴子等嘴里两腮上暂时贮存食物的地方 cheek pouch

〈古 ancient〉 also same as 谦 (qiān) and 歉 (qiàn)

欠 qiàn ㄑㄧㄢˋ ❶借别人的财物还（hái）没归还（huán）to owe; be in debt：～债 *be in debt*｜我～他十块钱。*I owe him ten yuan.* ❷缺乏，不够（㊀－缺）be short of; be lacking in：文章～通。*The writing is not logical.*｜身体～安 *not feel very well* ❸身体稍稍向上移动 raise slightly (a part of the body)：～身 *half rise from one's seat*｜～脚 *slightly raise one's heels* ❹哈欠（qian），疲倦时张口出气 to yawn：～伸 *stretch and yawn*｜打哈～ *give a yawn*

芡 qiàn ㄑㄧㄢˋ ❶草本植物，又叫鸡头，生长在水中，茎叶都有刺，花紫色。果实叫芡实。种仁可以吃，也可制淀粉 prickly water lily; cordon euryale (also called 鸡头) ❷烹饪时用淀粉调成的浓汁 starch (in cooking)：勾～ *thicken the sauce with starch*｜汤里加点儿～ *add starch to the soup*

嵌 qiàn ㄑㄧㄢˋ 把东西卡在空隙里 to insert; to imbed; to inlay：镶～ *to inlay*｜～入 *to imbed*｜匣子上～着象牙雕的花。*The box is inlaid with ivory flowers.*

伣（俔） qiàn ㄑㄧㄢˋ ❶譬如，如同 as if; like ❷古代船上用来观测风向的羽毛 feather wind vane (used on ships in ancient times)

纤（縴） qiàn ㄑㄧㄢˋ 拉船的绳 tow-rope [纤手] 给人介绍买卖并从中取利的人 broker; go-between [拉纤] 1 拉着纤绳使船前进 tow a boat along a river bank 2 给人介绍买卖以从中取利 act as a go-between

➩ see also xiān on p.706

茜 qiàn ㄑㄧㄢˋ ❶茜草，草本植物，茎有刺毛，秋天开花，黄色。根红色，可做染料，也可入药 madder ❷红色 red

➩ see also xī on p.695

倩 qiàn ㄑㄧㄢˋ ❶美好 beautiful; attractive：～影 *beautiful figure (of a woman)* ❷请人代做 ask sb to do sth on one's behalf：～人代笔 *ask sb to write on one's behalf*

绮（綪） qiàn ㄑㄧㄢˋ 青赤色丝织品 bluish red silk fabric

蒨 qiàn ㄑㄧㄢˋ ❶同"茜"（qiàn）。多用于人名 same as 茜 (qiàn) (often used in given names) ❷姓 (surname) Qian

堑（塹） qiàn ㄑㄧㄢˋ 防御用的壕沟 moat; trench：天～（天然的壕沟，指险要）*natural barrier* ⓔ挫折 setback; frustration：吃一～，长一智。*A fall into a pit, a gain in your wit.*

椠（槧） qiàn ㄑㄧㄢˋ ❶古代写字用的木板 (ancient) wooden tablet for writing ❷古书的雕版，版本 wood-block edition of ancient books：古～ *ancient edition*｜宋～ *Song Dynasty edition*

慊 qiàn ㄑㄧㄢˋ 不满，怨恨 dissatisfied; resentful

➩ see also qiè on p.537

歉 qiàn ㄑㄧㄢˋ ❶觉得对不住人 feel one has let sb down：

抱～ *apologetic* | 道～ *to apologize* | 深致～意。*Express my deep regret.* ❷收成不好 poor harvest：～收 *have a bad harvest* | ～年 *a lean year (of harvest)*

QIANG ㄑㄧㄤ

抢(搶) qiāng ㄑㄧㄤ same as "戗(qiāng)❶"

⇨ see also qiǎng on p.531

呛(嗆) qiāng ㄑㄧㄤ ❶水或食物进入气管而引起不适或咳嗽 to choke (on water or food)：喝水～着了 *choke on water while drinking* | 吃饭吃～了 *choke on food while eating* ❷〈方 dialect〉咳嗽 to cough

⇨ see also qiàng on p.532

玱(瑲) qiāng ㄑㄧㄤ 玉相击声 jingling (sound of two pieces of jade hitting each other)

枪(槍、*鎗) qiāng ㄑㄧㄤ ❶刺击用的长矛 spear; lance：长～ *lance* | 红缨～ *red-tasselled spear* ❷发射子弹的武器 gun; firearm：手～ *pistol* | 机关～ *machine gun* ❸形状或性能像枪的器具 gun-like instrument/tool：焊～ *welding gun* | 水～ *hydraulic monitor; water gun*

戗(戧) qiāng ㄑㄧㄤ ❶逆，反方向 be in an opposite direction：～风 *go against the wind* | ～水 *go against the current* ❷（言语）冲突 come into verbal conflict：说～了。*The talk ended in a quarrel.*

⇨ see also qiàng on p.532

羌(*羗、*羌) qiāng ㄑㄧㄤ 我国古代西部的民族 Qiang (one of the ethnic groups in western China in ancient times)

[羌族] 我国少数民族，参看附录四 the Qiang people (one of the ethnic groups in China. See Appendix Ⅳ.)

蜣 qiāng ㄑㄧㄤ [蜣螂]（-láng）昆虫，俗叫屎壳郎（shǐkelàng），全身黑色，有光泽，会飞，吃粪尿或动物的尸体 (informal 屎壳郎) dung beetle

戕 qiāng ㄑㄧㄤ 杀害 to kill：自～ *commit suicide* [戕贼] 摧残，伤害 to injure; to harm：～身体 *ruin one's health*

斨 qiāng ㄑㄧㄤ 古代一种斧子 (ancient) a kind of axe

腔 qiāng ㄑㄧㄤ ❶（-子）动物身体中空的部分 (of animal bodies) cavity; chamber：胸～ *thoracic cavity* | 口～ *oral cavity* ㉛器物中空的部分 (of appliances) cavity; chamber：炉～ *chamber of a furnace* | 锅台～子 *stove cavity* ❷（-儿）说话的语调，乐曲的调子 (of speech) tone, accent; (of music) tune：开～（说话）*begin to speak* | 南～北调 *speak with a mixed accent; people speaking all kinds of accents* | 离～走板 *be out of tune; (figurative) go out of bounds* | 梆子～ *clapper tune; clapper opera (a kind of local operas performed to the accompaniment of wooden clappers)* [京腔] 北京语音 Beijing accent：一口～ *speak*

Q

in a thick Beijing accent

锖(錆) qiāng ㄑㄧㄤ ［锖色］某些矿物表面因氧化作用而形成的薄膜所呈现的色彩，常跟矿物固有的颜色不同 tarnish

锵(鏘) qiāng ㄑㄧㄤ 形容金属或玉石的撞击声 ㊧ clang (sound of metal or jade objects hitting each other)：锣声～～ *the clang of gongs*

跄(蹌) qiāng ㄑㄧㄤ ［跄跄］形容行走合乎礼节 (of walking) according to protocol/etiquette

⇨ see also qiàng on p.532

镪(鏹) qiāng ㄑㄧㄤ ［镪水］强酸的俗称 (informal name for 强酸) strong acid：硝～ *nitric acid*

⇨ see also qiǎng on p.532

强(*強、*彊) qiáng ㄑㄧㄤˊ ❶健壮，有力，跟"弱"相对（㊥一壮、一健）strong; powerful (opposite of 弱)：～大 *powerful* | 身～力壮 *be healthy and strong* ㊂有余 slightly more than：四分之一～ *a little more than one quarter* ［强调］特别重视，用坚决的口气提出 to emphasize; to stress ［强梁］强横不讲理 brutal ❷程度高 strong; high in degree：责任心很～ *have a strong sense of responsibility* ❸好 superior; better：要～ *be anxious to outdo others* | 他写的字比你的～。*His handwriting is better than yours.* ❹使用强力 by force; by violence：～制 *to force* | ～占 *seize by force* | ～索财物 *extort money and property from others* ❺使强大或强壮 to strengthen; to enhance：～身之道 *the method of body building* | 富国～兵 *enrich a country and strengthen its military power* ❻姓 (surname) Qiang

⇨ see also jiàng on p.309, qiǎng on p.532

蔃 qiáng ㄑㄧㄤˊ 用于地名 used in place names：黄～（在广东省阳春）*Huangqiang (in Yangchun, Guangdong Province)*

墙(墻、*牆) qiáng ㄑㄧㄤˊ 用砖、石等砌成承架房顶或隔开内外的建筑物（㊥一壁）wall：砖～ *brick wall* | 城～ *city wall* | 院～ *walls surrounding a yard*

蔷(薔) qiáng ㄑㄧㄤˊ ［蔷薇］（-wēi）落叶或常绿灌木，茎上多刺，花有红、黄、白等颜色。可制香料，也可入药 rose

嫱(嬙) qiáng ㄑㄧㄤˊ 古时宫廷里的女官名 an official title for women serving at the imperial palace：妃～ *imperial concubines*

樯(檣、*艢) qiáng ㄑㄧㄤˊ 帆船上挂风帆的桅杆 (of a sailboat) mast

抢(搶) qiǎng ㄑㄧㄤˇ ❶夺，硬拿（㊥一夺）to rob; to snatch; to grab：～球 *fight for the ball* | ～劫 *to rob* | 他把我的相片～去了。*He snatched away my photograph.* ❷赶在前头，争先 rush/hurry to do sth：～着把活儿做

Q

了 *rush to have the work done* | ～修河堤 *make urgent repairs to the river embankment* ❸刮，擦（去掉表面的一层）to scratch; to scrape：磨剪子～菜刀 *hone the scissors and sharpen the kitchen knives* | 摔了一跤，把膝盖上的皮～去一块 *fell and scratched one's knees*

⇨ see also qiāng on p.530

羟（羥）qiǎng ㄑㄧㄤˇ 羟基，又叫氢氧基，有机化合物中含有氢和氧的基 hydroxyl radical (also called 氢氧基)

强（*強、*彊）qiǎng ㄑㄧㄤˇ ❶硬要，迫使 to force; to compel：～迫 *to force* | ～词夺理 *use lame arguments; be unreasonable in arguing* | ～人所难 *make sb do sth against his/her will* ❷勉强 try to do what's beyond one's power：牵～ *far-fetched* | ～颜欢笑 *force a smile*

⇨ see also jiàng on p.309, qiáng on p.531

Q

镪（鏹）qiǎng ㄑㄧㄤˇ〈古 ancient〉指成串的钱 a string of copper coins［白镪］银子 silver

⇨ see also qiāng on p.531

襁（*繦）qiǎng ㄑㄧㄤˇ［襁褓］（－bǎo）包婴儿的被、毯等 swaddling clothes：在～中 *in one's infancy*

呛（嗆）qiàng ㄑㄧㄤˋ 有刺激性的气体使鼻子、嗓子等器官感到不舒服 (of irritating gas) to irritate; to sting (the respiratory tract)：烟～嗓子。*The smoke irritates the throat.* | 辣椒味～得难受。*The smell of chilli pepper is very irritating.*
［够呛］形容十分厉害，很难支持 unbearable; terrible：这一阵子忙得真～ *have been terribly busy recently* | 他病得～。*He is seriously ill.* (also written as 够戗)

⇨ see also qiāng on p.530

戗（戧）qiàng ㄑㄧㄤˋ 支持，支撑 prop up; to support：墙要倒，拿杠子～住。*The wall is about to fall, so let's prop it up with a log.*［够戗］same as "够呛"

⇨ see also qiāng on p.530

炝（熗）qiàng ㄑㄧㄤˋ 烹饪方法 cooking methods ①油锅热后，放主菜前先放入葱等急炒一下，使有香味 fry aromatic ingredients in hot oil to release flavour before putting in the main ingredients：～锅 *quickly fry aromatic ingredients in hot oil to release flavour* ②把原料放在沸水中焯（chāo）一下，取出后再用香油等调料拌 blanch ingredients first and then dress them with sesame oil, etc.：～豆芽 *blanched bean sprouts*

跄（蹌）qiàng ㄑㄧㄤˋ see 踉跄 (liàng－) at 踉 on page 401

跻（蹡）qiàng ㄑㄧㄤˋ［踉蹡］（liàng－）same as "踉跄"

⇨ see also qiāng on p.531

QIAO ㄑㄧㄠ

悄 qiāo ㄑㄧㄠ［悄悄］没有声音或声音很低 quietly;

making little sound：静～ *very quiet* | 部队～地出动。*The army set out without being noticed.*

⇨ see also qiǎo on p.534

硗(磽) qiāo ㄑㄧㄠ 地坚硬不肥沃(㊀—薄、—瘠、—确) (of land) hard and infertile：地有肥～。*Some land is fertile and some is barren.*

跷(蹺、*蹻) qiāo ㄑㄧㄠ ❶脚向上抬 lift up (one's feet)：～脚 *stand on tiptoe* | ～腿 *lift up one's legs* ❷竖起(指头) hold up (a finger)：～起大拇指称赞 *stick up one's thumb in approval*

[跷蹊] (—qi) see 蹊跷 (qīqiāo) at 蹊 on page 516

⇨ 蹻 see also juē 屩 on p.342

雀 qiāo ㄑㄧㄠ 雀子，雀(què)斑 freckle

⇨ see also qiǎo on p.534, què on p.553

锹(鍬、*鍫) qiāo ㄑㄧㄠ 挖土或铲其他东西的器具 shovel; spade：铁～ *spade*

劁 qiāo ㄑㄧㄠ 骟(shàn)，割去牲畜的睾丸或卵巢 to castrate; to geld (livestock)：～猪 *castrate a piglet* | ～羊 *castrate a lamb*

敲 qiāo ㄑㄧㄠ ❶打，击 to knock; to strike：～锣 *beat a gong* | ～边鼓(喻从旁帮人说话) *(figurative) speak/act to back sb up on the side* ❷敲竹杠，讹诈财物或抬高价格 to blackmail; to overcharge：～诈 *to blackmail* | 被人～了一笔 *be overcharged*

橇 qiāo ㄑㄧㄠ ❶古代在泥路上行走所乘的用具 (ancient) sled for travelling over muddy roads ❷雪橇，在冰雪上滑行的工具 sleigh

缲(繰、幧)** qiāo ㄑㄧㄠ 做衣服边儿或带子时藏着针脚的缝法 sew with invisible stitches：～一根带子 *make a ribbon with invisible stitches* | ～边 *hem with slip stitches*

⇨ see also sāo on p.572

乔(喬) qiáo ㄑㄧㄠˊ ❶高 tall [乔木] 树干和树枝有明显区别的大树，如松、柏、杨、柳等 tree (e.g. 松，柏，杨 and 柳) [乔迁] 称人迁居的客气话 (polite expression) move house ❷作假，装 pretend to be; disguise oneself as [乔装] [乔妆] 改变服装面貌，掩蔽身份 disguise oneself as someone else：～打扮 *dress up*

侨(僑) qiáo ㄑㄧㄠˊ ❶寄居在国外(从前也指寄居在外乡) to live abroad; (formerly) to live far away from one's home：～居 *live abroad* ❷寄居在祖国以外的人 person living abroad：华～ *overseas Chinese*

荞(蕎、△*荍) qiáo ㄑㄧㄠˊ 荞麦，谷类作物，茎紫红色，叶三角形，花白色。籽实黑色，磨成粉供食用 buckwheat

峤(嶠) qiáo ㄑㄧㄠˊ 山尖而高 (of mountains) high and pointed

⇨ see also jiào on p.313

Q

桥(橋) qiáo ㄑㄧㄠˊ 架在水上（或空中）便于通行的建筑物 bridge：拱～ *arch bridge* | 天～ *over-bridge; overpass* | 独木～ *single-plank bridge* | 立交～ *flyover* | 长江大～ *Yangtze River bridge*

硚(礄) qiáo ㄑㄧㄠˊ [硚口] 地名，在湖北省武汉 Qiaokou (a place in Wuhan, Hubei Province)

鞒(鞽) qiáo ㄑㄧㄠˊ 马鞍拱起的地方 saddle-bow：鞍～ *saddle-bow*

荍 qiáo ㄑㄧㄠˊ ❶草本植物，即锦葵，叶掌状，花紫色或白色，可供观赏 mallow (same as 锦葵) ❷ see 荞 on page 533

翘(翹) qiáo ㄑㄧㄠˊ ❶举起，抬起，向上 to raise; hold up：～首 *raise one's head* | ～望 *raise one's head to look at; look forward eagerly to* ❷翘棱（leng），板状物体因由湿变干而弯曲不平 curl up; become warped：桌面～棱了。*The table top is warped.*

⇨ see also qiào on p.535

谯(譙) qiáo ㄑㄧㄠˊ 谯楼，古代城门上建筑的瞭望楼 (ancient) watchtower over a city gate

憔(*顦) qiáo ㄑㄧㄠˊ [憔悴]（-cuì）黄瘦，脸色不好 haggard; withered：面容～ *look haggard and worn out*

樵 qiáo ㄑㄧㄠˊ ❶〈方 dialect〉柴 firewood：砍～ *cut firewood* ❷打柴 gather firewood：～夫 *woodcutter*

瞧 qiáo ㄑㄧㄠˊ 看 to look at; to watch; to see：～见 *catch sight of* | ～得起 *think highly of* | ～不起 *look down upon*

巧 qiǎo ㄑㄧㄠˇ ❶技巧，技术 skill; technique ❷灵巧，灵敏，手的技能好 clever/skillful with one's hands：心灵手～ *be clever and handy* | 他很～。*He is very skillful with his hands.* ❸虚浮不实（指话）glib; artful：花言～语 *sweet talk* | ～取豪夺 *take away by trickery or force* ❹恰好，正遇在某种机会上 coincidental; lucky：～合 *coincidental* | ～遇 *run into sb by chance* | 凑～ *lucky* | 碰～ *by chance* | 赶～ *as it happens*

悄 qiǎo ㄑㄧㄠˇ ❶忧愁 ㊟ sad; worried：忧心～～ *deeply worried* ❷寂静无声或声音很低 silent; quiet：～然无声 *all quiet* | 低声～语 *speak in a whisper*

⇨ see also qiāo on p.532

雀 qiǎo ㄑㄧㄠˇ 义同"雀"（què），用于"家雀儿"等口语词 same in meaning as 雀 (què)(used in spoken language, e.g. 家雀儿)

⇨ see also qiāo on p.533, què on p.553

愀 qiǎo ㄑㄧㄠˇ 脸色改变 change one's expression：～然作色 *put on a stern face*

壳(殼) qiào ㄑㄧㄠˋ 坚硬的外皮 shell; hull; crust：甲～ *crusta* | 地～ *Earth's crust*

⇨ see also ké on p.355

Q

俏 qiào ㄑㄧㄠˋ ❶漂亮，相貌美好 pretty; good-looking：俊～ *good-looking* ❷货物的销路好 selling well：～货 *goods in great demand* | 走～ *popular; best-selling* | 紧～ *short of demand* ❸〈方 dialect〉烹饪方法，做菜时为增加滋味、色泽，加上少量的青蒜、香菜、木耳之类 (in cooking) to season (with green onion, coriander, etc.)

诮（**誚**）qiào ㄑㄧㄠˋ 责备，讥讽 to blame; to ridicule：～责 *to reproach* | 讥～ *mock at*

峭（*__陗__）qiào ㄑㄧㄠˋ 山又高又陡（㊥陡－）high and steep; precipitous：～壁 *cliff* ㊑严峻 serious; severe：～直（严峻刚直）*serious and upright*

鞘 qiào ㄑㄧㄠˋ 装刀、剑的套子 sheath; scabbard：刀～ *knife sheath*

⇨ see also shāo on p.583

窍（**竅**）qiào ㄑㄧㄠˋ ❶窟窿，孔洞 hole; opening; aperture：七～（耳、目、口、鼻）*seven apertures of the head (i.e. ears, eyes, mouth and nose)* | 一～不通（喻一点儿也不懂）*(figurative) be utterly ignorant of* ❷（－儿）事情的关键 the key to sth：诀～儿 *secret of success* | ～门儿 *knack* | 开～儿 *begin to understand*

翘（**翹**、**__蹺__）qiào ㄑㄧㄠˋ 一头向上仰起 stick up one end：板凳～起来了。*One end of the bench tilted up.* [翘尾巴] ㊑傲慢或自鸣得意 be cocky

⇨ see also qiáo on p.534

撬 qiào ㄑㄧㄠˋ 用棍、棒等拨、挑（tiǎo）东西 prise open：把门～开。*Prise the door open.*

QIE ㄑㄧㄝ

切 qiē ㄑㄧㄝ ❶用刀从上往下割 to cut; to chop; to slice：～成片 *cut into slices* | 把瓜～开 *cut up a melon* [切磋]（－cuō）㊑在业务、思想等方面互相研究讨论，取长补短 learn from each other through discussion ❷几何学上指直线与弧线或两个弧线相接于一点 (in geometry) be tangent to：～线 *tangent line* | ～点 *point of tangency* | 两圆相～。*These two circles are in tangential contact.*

⇨ see also qiè on p.536

伽 qié ㄑㄧㄝˊ [伽蓝] 梵语音译"僧伽蓝摩"的省称，指僧众所住的园林，后指佛寺 Buddhist monastery; Buddhist temple (short for 僧伽蓝摩, from Sanskrit)

⇨ see also gā on p.193, jiā on p.295

茄 qié ㄑㄧㄝˊ （－子）草本植物，花紫色。果实也叫茄子，紫色，也有白色或绿色的，可用作蔬菜 aubergine; eggplant

⇨ see also jiā on p.295

且 qiě ㄑㄧㄝˇ ❶连词，表示并列或进一层 (conjunction) and：既高～大 *both tall and big* ❷连词，尚且，表示让步 (conjunction) even (used to indi-

Q

cate concession)：死～不怕，还怕困难吗？*If we are not even afraid of death, are we still afraid of difficulties?* ❸副词，表示暂时 (adverb) for a moment; for the time being：～慢 *wait a moment* | ～住 *stop for a while* ❹文言副词，将要 (adverb in classical Chinese) nearly; almost：年～九十 *almost ninety years old* ❺且……且……，表示两个动作同时进行 while; as (“且……且……” used as a pattern to indicate that two actions happen at the same time.)：～走～说 *talk and walk at the same time* | ～行～想 *think about it while walking* ❻副词，且……呢，表示经久 (adverb) for a long time (“且……呢” used as a pattern)：这双鞋～穿呢。*This pair of shoes will last a long time.* ❼姓 (surname) Qie

⇨ see also jū on p.335

Q

切 qiè ㄑㄧㄝ ❶密合，贴近 correspond to; conform with：～身利害 *personal interest* | 不～实际 *be unrealistic* [切齿] 咬牙表示痛恨 gnash one's teeth in hatred ❷紧急 urgent; eager; anxious：急～ *anxious; hurried* | 迫～ *urgent* | 回国心～ *be eager to return to one's homeland* ❸切实，实在，着实 by all means; be sure to; must：～记 *be sure to keep in mind* | ～忌 *avoid by all means* | 恳～ *earnest and eager* ❹旧时汉语标音的一种方法，取上一字的声母与下一字的韵母和声调，拼成一个音，又叫反切，如“同”字是徒红切 *qie* (an old form of Chinese phonetic notation, in which the initial consonant of the first character and the vowel of the second character are combined together to form a new sound with the same tone of the second character, e.g. 同 is the *qie* of 徒 and 红)(also called 反切)

⇨ see also qiē on p.535

窃(竊) qiè ㄑㄧㄝ ❶偷盗 to steal; to pilfer：～案 *case of theft* | 行～ *to steal* ㊃用不合法不合理的手段取得 to usurp; to seize：～位 *usurp a high post* | ～国 *usurp state power* ❷私自，暗中 secretly; stealthily：～听 *to eavesdrop* | ～笑 *to snicker* 旧时用作谦辞 (old) (humble speech) I：～谓 *I venture to argue* | ～以为 *in my humble opinion*

郄 qiè ㄑㄧㄝ 姓 (surname) Qie 〈古 ancient〉 also same as 郤 (xì)

妾 qiè ㄑㄧㄝ ❶旧时男子在正妻以外娶的女子 concubine：纳～ *take a concubine* ❷谦辞，旧时女人自称 (humble speech used by women in old times) I; me

怯 qiè ㄑㄧㄝ ❶胆小，没勇气（㊜－懦）timid; cowardly：胆～ *timid* | ～场 *have stage fright* ❷〈方 dialect〉俗气，见识不广，不合时宜 vulgar; ignorant; inappropriate：露～ *make a fool of oneself* | 衣服的颜色有点儿～。*The colour of the dress is a little tacky.*

朅 qiè ㄑㄧㄝ ❶离去 to leave; go away ❷勇武 brave

挈 qiè ㄑㄧㄝ ❶用手提着 to lift; hold with hands: 提纲～领(喻简明扼要地把问题提示出来) *bring out the central points* ❷带，领 bring along: ～眷 *take one's family along*

锲(鍥) qiè ㄑㄧㄝ 用刀子刻 to carve; to engrave: 镂金～玉 *engrave the gold and carve the jade* | ～而不舍(喻做事坚持不懈，有恒心，有毅力) *carry on with perseverance*

惬(愜、*慝) qiè ㄑㄧㄝ 满足，畅快 satisfied; pleased: ～意 *pleased* | ～心 *contented* [惬当] (－dàng) 恰当 appropriate

箧(篋) qiè ㄑㄧㄝ 箱子一类的东西 suitcase; trunk: 箱～ *trunks and suitcases* | 书～ *trunks for holding books*

趄 qiè ㄑㄧㄝ 倾斜 to slant; to lean: ～着身子 *lean sideways*

⇨ see also jū on p.335

慊 qiè ㄑㄧㄝ 满足，满意 satisfied; contented: 不～(不满) *dissatisfied*

⇨ see also qiàn on p.529

QIN ㄑㄧㄣ

钦(欽) qīn ㄑㄧㄣ ❶恭敬 to respect; to admire: ～佩 *hold in esteem* | ～仰 *regard with admiration* ❷封建时代指有关皇帝的 of/by the emperor: ～定 *be written or approved by the emperor himself* | ～赐 *granted by the emperor himself* | ～差(chāi)大臣 *government inspector*

嵚(嶔) qīn ㄑㄧㄣ [嵚崟] (－yín) 山高的样子 (of mountains) high

侵 qīn ㄑㄧㄣ ❶侵犯，夺取别人的权利 to invade; infringe upon: ～略 *to invade* | ～害 *to damage* | ～吞 *to embezzle (money); to annex (land)* ❷渐近 approaching: ～晨 *just before dawn*

骎(駸) qīn ㄑㄧㄣ [骎骎] 马跑得很快的样子 (of horses) galloping ⑤|渐行渐进的样子 rapidly approaching: ～日上 *make rapid progress daily*

亲(親) qīn ㄑㄧㄣ ❶有血统或夫妻关系的 related by blood or marriage: ～人 *family member* | ～兄弟 *blood brothers* 特指父母 (specifically) parent: 双～ *both parents* | 养～ *take care of one's parents* ❷婚姻 marriage; matrimony: 定～ *get engaged* | ～事 *marriage* ❸特指新妇 (specifically) bride: 娶～ *(of a man) get married* ❹亲戚，因婚姻联成的亲属关系 relative by marriage: 姑表～ *cousinship (relationship between children of a brother and a sister)* ❺本身，自己的 personal; of one's own: ～笔信 *autograph letter* | ～眼见的 *be seen with one's own eyes* | ～手做的 *be made with one's own hands* ❻感情好，关系密切 close; intimate: ～密 *intimate* | 兄弟相～。*Brothers are close to each other.* ❼用嘴唇接触，表示喜爱 to kiss: 他～了～孩子的小脸蛋。*He kissed the child's*

Q

little cheeks.

⇨ see also qìng on p.542

衾 qīn ㄑㄧㄣ 被子 quilt：～枕 *bedding*

芹 qín ㄑㄧㄣˊ 芹菜，草本植物，羽状复叶，叶柄肥大，茎、叶可用作蔬菜 celery

芩 qín ㄑㄧㄣˊ 植物名 plant name ①古书上指芦苇一类的植物 a kind of reed (in ancient Chinese texts) ②黄芩，草本植物，花淡紫色，根黄色，可入药 baical skullcap

矜(**獾) qín ㄑㄧㄣˊ 〈古 ancient〉矛、戟的柄 handle of a lance/halberd

⇨ see also guān on p.226, jīn on p.321

梣 qín ㄑㄧㄣˊ(又) see chén on page 74

琴(*栞) qín ㄑㄧㄣˊ ❶古琴，一种弦乐器，用梧桐等木料做成，有五根弦，后来增加为七根 *qin* (a plucked musical instrument with five, and later seven, strings) ❷某些乐器的统称，如风琴、钢琴、胡琴等 the general term for certain musical instruments, e.g. 风琴，钢琴 and 胡琴

秦 qín ㄑㄧㄣˊ ❶周代诸侯国名，在今陕西省和甘肃省一带 Qin (a state in the Zhou Dynasty, in today's Shaanxi and Gansu Provinces) ❷朝代名，秦始皇嬴政所建立（公元前 221—公元前 206 年），建都咸阳（在今陕西省咸阳东）。秦是我国历史上第一个统一的中央集权的封建王朝 Qin Dynasty (221 BC—206 BC, founded by Ying Zheng, Emperor Qinshihuang–First Emperor of Qin Dynasty) ❸陕西省的别称 Qin (another name for Shaanxi Province)

嗪 qín ㄑㄧㄣˊ see 哌嗪 (pài－) at 哌 on page 490

溱 qín ㄑㄧㄣˊ ［溱潼］（－tóng）地名，在江苏省泰州 Qintong (a place in Taizhou, Jiangsu Province)

⇨ see also zhēn on p.843

螓 qín ㄑㄧㄣˊ 一种形体较小的蝉 a kind of small cicada

覃 qín ㄑㄧㄣˊ 姓 (surname) Qin

⇨ see also tán on p.636

禽 qín ㄑㄧㄣˊ ❶鸟类的总称 (general term) birds：家～ *poultry*｜飞～ *birds* ❷〈古 ancient〉鸟兽的总称 bird and beast ❸ (ancient) same as “擒”

擒 qín ㄑㄧㄣˊ 捕捉 to catch; to capture：～获 *to capture*｜束手就～ *be seized without fighting*｜～贼先～王。*To catch a gang of bandits, first catch their leader.*

噙 qín ㄑㄧㄣˊ 含在里面 to hold (in one's mouth, eyes, etc.)：嘴里～了一口水 *hold some water in one's mouth*｜眼里～着泪水 *one's eyes brimming with tears*

檎 qín ㄑㄧㄣˊ ［林檎］落叶小乔木，即花红，花粉红色，果实像苹果而小，可以吃 crab-apple (same as 花红)

勤(❹*懃、❶△**廑) qín ㄑㄧㄣˊ ❶做事尽力，不偷懒，跟“懒”“惰”

相对 hard-working; diligent (opposite of 懒 or 惰): ～快 *diligent* | ～劳 *industrious* | ～学苦练 *study hard and train vigorously* ㊀经常，次数多 often; frequently: ～洗澡 *bathe regularly* | 夏天雨～。*It rains often in summer.* | 房子要～打扫。*The house needs to be cleaned frequently.* ❷按规定时间上班的工作 attendance (at school, work, etc.): 出～ *turn up for* | 缺～ *be absent from work* | 考～ *check on attendance* ❸勤务，公家分派的公共事务 work; duty; service: 内～ *internal/office work* | 外～ *field work* ❹ see 殷勤 at 殷 on page 780

⇨ 廑 see also jǐn on p.323

懄 qín ㄑㄧㄣˊ 勇敢 brave; courageous

梫 qǐn ㄑㄧㄣˇ 古书上指肉桂 cassia bark (in ancient Chinese texts) (see 桂 on page 233 for reference)

锓(鋟) qǐn ㄑㄧㄣˇ 雕刻 to carve; to engrave: ～版 *printing block*

寝(寢、*寑) qǐn ㄑㄧㄣˇ ❶睡觉 to sleep: ～室 *dormitory* | 废～忘食 *(to be so absorbed or occupied as to) forget food and sleep* ❷睡觉的地方 bedroom: 就～ *go to bed* | 寿终正～ *(old) die a natural death in one's home* ❸停止进行 to stop; to cease: 事～。*The matter died down.* ❹面貌难看 ugly: 貌～ *looking ugly*

吣(唚、**𠹠)** qìn ㄑㄧㄣˋ 猫狗呕吐 (of dogs or cats) to vomit ⑩用脏话骂人 to curse; to abuse: 满嘴胡～ *talk rubbish*

沁 qìn ㄑㄧㄣˋ ❶渗入，浸润 seep into; to permeate: 香气～人心脾。*The fragrance permeated one's whole body.* ❷〈方 dialect〉纳入水中 to soak; immerse in water ❸〈方 dialect〉头向下垂 to lower (one's head): ～着头 *lower one's head*

揿(撳、*搇) qìn ㄑㄧㄣˋ 〈方 dialect〉用手按 to press; to push (with hands): ～电铃 *ring the bell*

QING ㄑㄧㄥ

青 qīng ㄑㄧㄥ ❶颜色 a kind of colour ①绿色 green: ～草 *green grass* ②蓝色 blue: ～天 *blue sky* ③黑色 black: ～布 *black cloth* | ～线 *black thread* ❷青草或没有成熟的庄稼 green grass; unripe crops: 看(kān)～ *keep watch over the ripening crops* | 踏～ *go for an outing in spring* | ～黄不接(陈粮已经吃完，新庄稼还没有成熟) *temporary shortage (before the new harvest comes in)* ❸青年 young people: 共～团 *the Communist Youth League of China* | 老中～相结合 *integrate the old, the middle-aged and the young in one team*

[青史] 原指竹简上的记事，后指史书 historical records (originally referring to records on bamboo slips): ～留名 *leave one's name in history*

Q

圊 qīng ㄑㄧㄥ 厕所 pit toilet; latrine: ～土 *night soil* | ～肥 *stable manure*

清 qīng ㄑㄧㄥ ❶纯净透明，没有混杂的东西，跟“浊”相对 clear; pure (opposite of 浊): ～水 *clear water* | 天朗气～。*The sky is blue and the air is clear.* ㉁①单纯地 purely; simply: ～唱（不化装的戏曲演唱） *sing (traditional opera or songs) without make-up or musical accompaniment* ②安静（㊣－静）quiet; peaceful: ～夜 *a peaceful night* ❷明白，不混乱 clear; lucid: 分～ *to distinguish* | ～楚 *clear; distinct* | 说不～ *cannot explain clearly* ❸一点儿不留，净尽 completely; thoroughly: ～除 *to eliminate* ❹清除不纯成分以纯洁组织 to purge (an organization); to purify: ～党 *purge a party* ❺查点（清楚）to sort and count: ～仓 *make an inventory of the storage* ❻公正廉明 honest and just: ～官 *honest and upright official* ❼朝代名（公元 1616—1911 年），公元 1616 年女真族首领爱新觉罗·努尔哈赤建立后金，1636 年国号改为清，1644 年建都北京 Qing Dynasty (1616—1911, founded by Nurhaci, a leader of the Manchu people)

蜻 qīng ㄑㄧㄥ ［蜻蜓］（－tíng）昆虫，俗叫蚂螂（mālang），胸部有翅两对，腹部细长，常在水边捕食蚊子等，是益虫 dragonfly

鲭（鯖） qīng ㄑㄧㄥ 鱼名，身体呈梭形，头尖，口大。种类很多 mackerel

轻（輕） qīng ㄑㄧㄥ ❶分量小，跟“重”相对 (of weight) light (opposite of 重): 这块木头很～。*This piece of wood is very light.* ❷程度浅 (of degree) mild; minor: 口～（味淡）*(of food) not salty; liking bland food* | ～伤 *minor injury* ❸数量少 (of quantity) little/few; light: 年纪～ *be young* | 他的工作很～。*His workload is very light.* ❹用力小 soft; gentle: 物品易碎，注意～放。*Fragile! Handle with care.* | 手～一点儿。*Handle gently.* ❺认为没价值，不以为重要 make light of; to belittle: ～视 *look down upon* | ～敌 *underestimate the enemy* | 人皆～之。*Everyone looked down upon him/her/it.* ❻随便，不庄重 rash; careless: ～薄（bó）*frivolous* | ～率（shuài）*indiscreet* | ～举妄动 *act rashly and blindly* ［轻易］随便 easy; effortless; easily; effortlessly: 不要～下结论。*Don't draw hasty conclusions.*

氢（氫） qīng ㄑㄧㄥ 气体元素，符号 H，是已知元素中最轻的，无色、无味、无臭，跟氧化合成水。工业上用途很广 hydrogen (H)

倾（傾） qīng ㄑㄧㄥ ❶歪，斜（㊣－斜）to incline; to slant: 身体稍向前～ *lean forward slightly* ❷倾向，趋向 tendency; inclination: 左～ *left leaning; radical* | 右～ *right leaning; conservative* ［倾心］一心

向往，爱慕 to admire; fall in love with ❸倒塌 to collapse; to topple：～颓 *fall apart* [倾轧]（-yà）互相排挤 engage in internal strife ❹使器物反转或歪斜，倒（dào）出里面的东西 to empty; to dump：～盆大雨 *rain cats and dogs* | ～箱倒箧 *empty out all trunks and chests; (figurative) try one's best* ⑤尽数拿出，毫无保留 to exhaust; use up (all one's resources)：～吐（tǔ）*pour out; vent* [倾销] 一种以低于成本的价格大量抛售商品的不正当竞争手段 dump at a very low price

卿 qīng ㄑㄧㄥ ❶古时高级官名 (ancient) minister; high official：上～ *high-ranking official* | 三公九～ *high officials; (specifically) the three councillors of state and the nine ministers in ancient times* ❷古代用作称呼，君称臣，夫称妻或夫妻对称 (ancient) you (term of address by an emperor to his officials, or between husband and wife)

勍 qíng ㄑㄧㄥˊ 强 strong; powerful：～敌 *strong opponent*

黥（**剠）qíng ㄑㄧㄥˊ 古代在犯人脸上刺刻涂墨的刑罚。又叫墨刑 to brand sb's face (a form of punishment in ancient times)(also called 墨刑)

情 qíng ㄑㄧㄥˊ ❶感情，情绪，外界事物所引起的爱、憎、愉快、不愉快、惧怕等的心理状态 feeling; emotion：无～ *heartless; merciless* | 温～ *tender feelings* ❷爱情 love; romance：谈～说爱 *engage in a romantic relationship* ❸情面，情分 favour; mercy：说～ *ask for a favour* | 求～ *plead for mercy* ❹状况 situation; circumstance：实～ *the truth* | 真～ *the facts* | 军～ *military intelligence* | ～况 *circumstances; development* | ～形 *situation* [情报] 关于各种情况的报告（多带机密性质）information

晴 qíng ㄑㄧㄥˊ 天空中没有云或云量很少，跟"阴"相对 sunny; clear (opposite of 阴)：～天 *sunny day* | 天～了。*The sky has cleared (up).*

赗（賵）qíng ㄑㄧㄥˊ 承受财产等（㊀-受）to inherit (money, property, etc.)

氰 qíng ㄑㄧㄥˊ 碳与氮的化合物，无色气体，有杏仁味，有剧毒，燃烧时发桃红色火焰 cyanogen

檠（**橄）qíng ㄑㄧㄥˊ ❶灯架。也指灯 lampstand; lamp ❷矫正弓弩的器具 device for holding a crossbow in position

擎 qíng ㄑㄧㄥˊ 向上托，举 to lift; hold up：～天柱 *mainstay; (in legends) pillars of heaven* | 众～易举。*Many hands make light work.*

苘（**檾、**蘔）qǐng ㄑㄧㄥˇ 苘麻，草本植物，茎直立，茎皮纤维可制绳索 Chinese jute

顷（頃）qǐng ㄑㄧㄥˇ ❶市制地积单位，1 顷是

100亩，约合6.666 7公顷(66 666.7平方米) *qing* (a traditional Chinese unit for measuring area, equal to around 6.666 7 hectares. There are 100 亩 in 1 顷.) ❷短时间 a little while：有～ *after a while* | 俄～ *in very short time* | ～刻 *in a moment* 引刚才，不久以前 just now：～闻 *just heard* | ～接来信。*I have just received your letter.*

〈古 ancient〉also same as 倾 (qīng)

庼(廎、高)** qǐng ㄑㄧㄥˇ 小厅堂 small hall

请(請) qǐng ㄑㄧㄥˇ ❶求(连—求) ask for; request for：～假 *ask for leave* | ～示 *request instructions* 敬辞(放在动词前面)(polite speech) please (used before a verb)：～坐 *please take a seat* | ～教 *to consult* | ～问 *may I ask* | ～进来。*Please come in.* ❷延聘，邀，约人来 to invite：～医生 *call for a doctor* | ～专家做报告 *invite an expert to deliver a lecture*

謦 qǐng ㄑㄧㄥˇ 咳嗽 to cough [謦欬](—kài) 指谈笑 make light conversation：亲聆～ *listen with reverence to sb talk*

庆(慶) qìng ㄑㄧㄥˋ ❶祝贺(连—贺) to celebrate：～功 *celebrate an achievement/a victory* | ～祝 *to celebrate* ❷可祝贺的事 occasion for celebration：国～ *National Day* | 大～ *grand celebration; birthday (of an elderly person)*

亲(親) qìng ㄑㄧㄥˋ [亲家] 夫妻双方的父母彼此的关系和称呼 (both relationship and term of address) in-law; parent of one's son/daughter-in-law

⇨ see also qīn on p.537

碃 qìng ㄑㄧㄥˋ 用于地名 used in place names：大金～ *Dajinqing* | 西金～ *Xijinqing* (都在山东省海阳) *(both in Haiyang, Shandong Province)*

箐 qìng ㄑㄧㄥˋ 〈方 dialect〉山间的大竹林，泛指树木丛生的山谷 bamboo grove; (generally) wooded valley

綮 qìng ㄑㄧㄥˋ 相结合的地方 joint; junction (see 肯綮 at 肯❷ on page 358 for reference)

磬 qìng ㄑㄧㄥˋ ❶古代的一种打击乐器，用玉或石做成，悬在架上，形略如曲尺 chime stone (a percussion instrument in ancient China, made of jade or stone) ❷和尚敲的铜铁铸的钵状物 a bowl-shaped Buddhist percussion instrument, made of metal

罄 qìng ㄑㄧㄥˋ 器皿已空，尽，用尽 use up; to exhaust：告～ *run out (of sth)* | 售～ *sell out* | ～竹难书(诉说不完，多指罪恶) *(of misdeeds) too numerous to record*

QIONG ㄑㄩㄥ

邛 qióng ㄑㄩㄥˊ [邛崃](—lái) 山名，在四川省。又叫崃山 Mount Qionglai (in Sichuan Province) (also called 崃山)

Q

筇 qióng ㄑㄩㄥˊ 古书上说的一种竹子，可以做手杖 a kind of bamboo mentioned in ancient Chinese texts：～杖 *bamboo walking stick*

穷（窮）qióng ㄑㄩㄥˊ ❶缺乏财物，跟"富"相对（㊟贫一）poor; poverty-stricken (opposite of 富)：～人 *poor people* | 他过去很～。*He was once very poor.* ❷到尽头，没有出路 run out; have no way out：理屈辞～ *find oneself in the wrong and out of words* | 日暮途～ *the sun has set and the road has ended; (figurative) be close to one's end* ❸达到极点 extremely; to the last degree：～凶极恶 *extremely brutal and wicked* ❹推究到极限 to exhaust; examine thoroughly：～物之理 *thoroughly study the whys and wherefores of things* | ～原竟委 *get to the bottom of a matter*

䓖（藭）qióng ㄑㄩㄥˊ see 芎䓖 (xiōng—) at 芎 on page 730

茕（煢、**惸）qióng ㄑㄩㄥˊ ❶没有弟兄，孤独 lonely; having no brother ❷忧愁 sad; depressed

穹 qióng ㄑㄩㄥˊ 高起成拱形的，隆起 arched：～苍（苍天）*the vault of heaven; the sky*

琼（瓊）qióng ㄑㄩㄥˊ ❶美玉 fine jade ㊥美好，精美 fine; exquisite：～浆（美酒）*good wine* | ～楼玉宇（华丽的建筑）*magnificent buildings* ❷海南省的别称 Qiong (another name for Hainan Province)

蛩 qióng ㄑㄩㄥˊ 〈古 ancient〉❶蟋蟀 cricket ❷蝗虫 locust; grasshopper

跫 qióng ㄑㄩㄥˊ 形容脚踏地的声音 (of sound of footsteps) tap-tap-tap; tapping：足音～然 *excite to hear footsteps when living in a desolate place; (figurative) rare guest*

銎 qióng ㄑㄩㄥˊ 斧子上安柄的孔 eye of an axe (for installing handle)

QIU ㄑㄧㄡ

丘（❸*坵）qiū ㄑㄧㄡ ❶土山，土堆 mound; hummock：土～ *knoll* | 沙～ *sand dune* | ～陵 *hill* ❷坟墓（㊟一墓）grave; tomb ❸〈方 dialect〉量词，用于水田分隔开的块 (measure word for paddy fields) plot; parcel：一～五亩大的稻田 *a paddy field with an area of five* mu ❹用砖石封闭有尸体的棺材，浮厝（cuò）build a vault with bricks and stones to enclose a coffin (with a corpse in it)

邱 qiū ㄑㄧㄡ ❶same as "丘❶" ❷姓。古也作"丘" (surname) Qiu (also written as 丘 in ancient times)

蚯 qiū ㄑㄧㄡ ［蚯蚓］（—yǐn）环节动物，身体圆而长，生活在土壤里，能翻松土壤，对农作物有益 earthworm

龟（龜）qiū ㄑㄧㄡ ［龟兹］（—cí）汉代西域国名，

Q

在今新疆维吾尔自治区库车一带 Qiuci (an ancient state in the Western Regions of the Han Dynasty, in today's Kuqa County, Xinjiang Uygur Autonomous Region)

⇨ see also guī on p.231, jūn on p.345

秋(❺鞦、❶–❹*烁、❶–❹*穐) qiū ㄑㄧㄡ ❶四季中的第三季 autumn; fall [三秋] 1 秋收、秋耕、秋播的合称 the three autumn tasks (i.e. autumn harvesting, ploughing and sowing) 2 指三年 three years: 一日不见，如隔～。*A single day apart seems like three years.* ❷庄稼成熟的时期 harvest season: 麦～ *wheat harvest season* ❸年 year: 千～万代 *thousands of years* ❹指某个时期(多指不好的) (often negative) certain period of time: 多事之～ *troubled times* ❺[秋千] 运动和游戏用具，架子上系(jì)两根长绳，绳端拴一块板，人在板上前后摆动 swing

萩 qiū ㄑㄧㄡ 古书上说的一种蒿类植物 a kind of wormwood in ancient Chinese texts

湫 qiū ㄑㄧㄡ 水池 pond; pool: 大龙～(瀑布名，在浙江省北雁荡山) *Dalongqiu (the name of a waterfall, in Yandangshan Mountain, Zhejiang Province)*

⇨ see also jiǎo on p.312

楸 qiū ㄑㄧㄡ 楸树，落叶乔木，树干高，叶大，木质致密，耐湿，可用来造船，也可做器具 Manchurian catalpa

鹙(鶖) qiū ㄑㄧㄡ 秃鹙，古书上说的一种水鸟，头颈上没有毛，性贪暴，好吃蛇 a kind of bald water bird in ancient Chinese texts

鳅(鰍) qiū ㄑㄧㄡ 泥鳅，鱼名，身体圆，尾侧扁，口小，有须，皮上有黏液，常钻在泥里 pond loach

鰌(鰌) qiū ㄑㄧㄡ same as "鳅"

鞧(**鞦) qiū ㄑㄧㄡ ❶后鞧，套车时拴在驾辕牲口屁股上的皮带子 leather hip strap for a shaft horse ❷〈方 dialect〉收缩 to contract: ～着眉头 *knit one's brows* | 大辕马～着屁股向后退。*The shaft horse contracted its hind muscles and backed up.*

仇 qiú ㄑㄧㄡˊ 姓 (surname) Qiu

⇨ see also chóu on p.85

犰 qiú ㄑㄧㄡˊ [犰狳] (－yú) 哺乳动物，头尾、躯干和四肢有鳞片，腹部有毛，爪锐利，穴居土中，吃杂食。产于南美洲等地 armadillo

訄 qiú ㄑㄧㄡˊ 逼迫 to force; to compel

鼽 qiú ㄑㄧㄡˊ 鼻子堵塞不通 stuffy nose; nasal congestion

囚 qiú ㄑㄧㄡˊ ❶拘禁(㊀－禁) to imprison; take into custody: ～犯 *prisoner* | ～在牢里 *put in jail* ❷被拘禁的人 prisoner; captive: 死～ *prisoner sentenced to death* | 阶下～ *captive; prisoner of war*

泅 qiú ㄑㄧㄡˊ 游泳 to swim

Q

求 qiú ㄑㄧㄡˊ ❶设法得到 to seek; to pursue: 不～名，不～利 *seek neither fame nor fortune* | ～学 *go to school; seek knowledge* | ～出百分比 *calculate a percentage* ❷恳请，乞助 ask for; beg for: ～教（jiào）*ask for advice* | ～人 *ask others for help* ❸需要 demand: 供～ *supply and demand*

俅 qiú ㄑㄧㄡˊ ❶恭顺的样子 ㊀ subservient ❷俅人，我国少数民族独龙族的旧称 the Qiu people (former name for 独龙族，i.e. the Dulong people, one of the ethnic groups in China)

逑 qiú ㄑㄧㄡˊ 匹配，配偶 mate; life companion

球（❷*毬）qiú ㄑㄧㄡˊ ❶（一儿）圆形的立体物 sphere; globe: ～体 *sphere* ❷（一儿）指某些球形的体育用品，也指球类运动 ball; ball game: 足～ *football* | 乒乓～儿 *table tennis; table tennis ball* | ～赛 *match (of a ball game)* | ～迷 *fan (of a ball game)* ❸指地球，也泛指星体 the Earth; (generally) star, planet: 全～ *the whole world* | 北半～ *northern hemisphere* | 星～ *star* | 月～ *moon*

赇（賕）qiú ㄑㄧㄡˊ 贿赂 bribery: 枉法受～ *bend the law and take bribes*

銶（銶）qiú ㄑㄧㄡˊ 古代的一种凿子 a kind of chisel in ancient times

裘 qiú ㄑㄧㄡˊ 皮衣 fur coat: 集腋成～（喻积少成多）。*Collect fur under the foxes' forelegs, and you can make a fur coat.; (figurative) Many small amounts accumulate to a large sum.*

虬（*虯）qiú ㄑㄧㄡˊ ❶虬龙，传说中的一种龙 a kind of dragon in legends ❷蜷曲的 curly: ～须 *curly beard* | ～髯 *curly whiskers*

酋 qiú ㄑㄧㄡˊ ❶酋长，部落的首领 chief of a tribe; chieftain ❷（盗匪、侵略者的）头子 leader; chief (of bandits, invaders, etc.): 匪～ *bandit leader* | 敌～ *chief of enemy troops*

遒 qiú ㄑㄧㄡˊ 强健，有力（㊀一劲、一健）strong; vigourous

蝤 qiú ㄑㄧㄡˊ [蝤蛴]（一qí）天牛的幼虫，身长足短，白色 larva of a longhorn beetle

⇨ see also yóu on p.793

巯（巰）qiú ㄑㄧㄡˊ 巯基，有机化合物中含硫和氢的基 hydrosulfide group

璆 qiú ㄑㄧㄡˊ 美玉 fine jade

糗 qiǔ ㄑㄧㄡˇ ❶干粮，炒米粉或炒面 dry food ❷〈方 dialect〉饭或面食粘（zhān）连成块状或糊状 (of rice or wheat foods) stick together: 面条儿～了。*The noodles have stuck together.*

QU ㄑㄩ

区（區）qū ㄑㄩ ❶分别（㊀一别、一分）distinguish between ❷地域 zone; region; area: 山～ *mountain area* | 工业～ *industrial zone* | 开

发～*development zone*｜自然保护～*nature reserve* ❸行政区划单位，有跟省平级的自治区和比市低一级的市辖区等 (of administrative division) region; district

[区区] 小，细微 trivial; petty：～小事 *a petty matter*

⇨ see also ōu on p.486

坂(墟) qū ㄑㄩ 用于地名 used in place names：邹～（在江苏省常州）*Zouqu (in Changzhou, Jiangsu Province)*

岖(嶇) qū ㄑㄩ see 崎岖 (qí—) at 崎 on page 519

驱(驅、*敺、*駈) qū ㄑㄩ ❶赶牲口 to drive (a horse, an ox, etc.)：～马前进 *urge the horse on* ㊀赶走（㊊—逐）to expel; to banish：～散 *to disperse*｜～除 *get rid of* [驱使] 差遣，支使别人为自己奔走 order about ❷快跑（㊊驰—）to gallop：并驾齐～ *drive/run abreast of one another*｜长～直入 *march straight in*

躯(軀) qū ㄑㄩ 身体（㊊身—）body：七尺之～ *a human adult body (esp. man)*｜为国捐～ *lay down one's life for one's country*

曲(❹麯、❹△*麴) qū ㄑㄩ ❶弯，跟“直”相对（㊊弯—）winding; curved; bent (opposite of 直)：～线 *curve*｜～径通幽。*A winding path leads to a secluded place.*｜山间小路～～弯弯。*The mountain path is full of twists and turns.* ㊃不公正，不合理 wrong; unjust：～解 *to misinterpret*｜是非～直 *rights and wrongs* ❷弯曲的地方 bend; turn：河～ *meander* ❸偏僻的地方 remote place：乡～ *remote village* ❹酿酒或制酱时引起发酵的块状物，用某种霉菌和大麦、大豆、麸皮等制成 yeast：酒～ *distiller's yeast* ❺姓 (surname) Qu

⇨ see also qǔ on p.548

⇨ 麴 see also 麴 on p.547

岫 qū ㄑㄩ 用于地名 used in place names：岞(zuò)～(在河南省内乡) *Zuoqu (in Neixiang, Henan Province)*

蛐 qū ㄑㄩ [蛐蛐儿]（—qur）〈方 dialect〉蟋蟀 cricket

诎(詘) qū ㄑㄩ ❶缩短 to shorten ❷嘴笨 inarticulate; slow of speech ❸屈服，折服 to yield; to give in

屈 qū ㄑㄩ ❶使弯曲，跟“伸”相对 to bend; to fold (opposite of 伸)：～指可数 *so few that can be counted on the fingers* ❷低头，使屈服 to yield; to submit：宁死不～ *rather die than surrender*｜威武不能～ *shall not be subdued by force* ❸委屈 unfair treatment：受～ *be treated unfairly* ㊀冤枉（㊊冤—）wrong; injustice：叫～ *complain of being wronged*

䓛 qū ㄑㄩ 有机化合物，白色或带银灰色晶体，有毒，在紫外线照射下可发荧光 chrysene

坥 qū ㄑㄩ 混杂蚯蚓排泄物的土 soil mixed with earthworm

casting

岨 qū ㄑㄩ（又） see jū on page 335

蛆 qū ㄑㄩ 苍蝇的幼虫，白色，身体柔软，有环节，多生在不洁净的地方 maggot

袪 qū ㄑㄩ 古代放在驴背上驮东西用的木板 (ancient) board on a donkey's back for carrying things

胠 qū ㄑㄩ ❶从旁边撬开 prise open from one side：～箧（偷东西） *to steal* ❷腋下 armpit

祛 qū ㄑㄩ 除去，驱逐 to dispel; to remove：～疑 *remove suspicion* | ～暑 *reduce summer heat* | ～痰剂 *phlegm-expelling formula*

袪 qū ㄑㄩ 袖口 cuff (of a sleeve)

焌 qū ㄑㄩ ❶把燃烧着的东西弄灭 extinguish a fire ❷用不带火苗的火烧烫 burn with non-flaming fire ❸烹饪方法，在热锅里加油，油热后先放作料，然后放菜 a cooking method that involves frying the aromatic ingredients in hot oil first before putting in the main ingredients：～锅儿 *release the flavour of aromatics in hot oil*

⇨ see also jùn on p.346

黢 qū ㄑㄩ 形容黑 black; dark：～黑的头发 *very black hair* | 屋子里黑～～的，什么也看不见。*It was very dark in the room and nothing could be seen.*

趋（趨） qū ㄑㄩ ❶快走 to hasten; to hurry：～而迎之 *hurry to meet sb* ㊀迎合 cater to; pander to：～奉 *toady to* | ～炎附势 *pander to those in power* ❷情势向着某方面发展、进行 tend to：～势 *trend* | 大势所～ *it is the general trend* | 意见～于一致。*The opinions tend to be the same.*

〈古 ancient〉also same as 促 (cù)

麴（麯） qū ㄑㄩ 姓(surname) Qu

⇨ 麯 see also qū 曲 on p.546

劬 qú ㄑㄩˊ 劳累（㊔－劳） tired; fatigued

朐 qú ㄑㄩˊ ［临朐］地名，在山东省 Linqu (a place in Shandong Province)

鸲（鴝） qú ㄑㄩˊ 鸟名，身体小，尾巴长，嘴短而尖，羽毛美丽 bush robin［鸲鹆］（－yù）鸟名，又叫八哥儿，全身黑色，头和背部微呈绿色光泽，能模仿人说话 crested myna (also called 八哥儿)

鼩 qú ㄑㄩˊ ［鼩鼱］（－jīng）哺乳动物，像老鼠，嘴长而尖，头部和背部棕褐色。多生活在山林中 shrew

渠（❸**佢） qú ㄑㄩˊ ❶水道，特指人工开的河道、水沟 canal; ditch; channel：沟～ *ditches and canals* | 水到～成。*When water flows here, there will naturally be a canal.; (figurative) When the right time comes, success will naturally follow.* | 挖一条～ *dig a ditch* ❷大 great：～帅 *leader* | ～魁 *chief* ❸〈方 dialect〉他 he; him：不知～为何人。*I don't know who he is.*

Q

蕖 qú ㄑㄩˊ [芙蕖](fú–) 荷花的别名 lotus (another name for 荷花)

磲 qú ㄑㄩˊ see 砗磲 (chē–) at 砗 on page 73

璩 qú ㄑㄩˊ 〈古 ancient〉耳环 earrings

蘧 qú ㄑㄩˊ ❶[蘧麦]草本植物，叶子狭披针形，花淡红色或白色。全草可入药 lilac pink herb ❷[蘧然]惊喜的样子 pleasantly surprised ❸姓 (surname) Qu

籧 qú ㄑㄩˊ [籧篨](–chú)古代指用竹子或苇子编的粗席 (ancient) coarse mat made of bamboo or reed

瞿 qú ㄑㄩˊ 姓 (surname) Qu

灈 qú ㄑㄩˊ 用于地名 used in place names：～阳(在河南省遂平) *Quyang (in Suiping, Henan Province)*

氍 qú ㄑㄩˊ [氍毹](–shū)毛织的地毯。古代演剧多在地毯上，因此又用氍毹代指舞台 wool carpet; stage (because plays were often performed on carpets in ancient times)

臞 qú ㄑㄩˊ same as "癯"

癯 qú ㄑㄩˊ 瘦 thin; lean：清～ *lean*

衢 qú ㄑㄩˊ 大路，四通八达的道路 broad road; main road：通～ *roads that extend to all directions*

蠼(**蠷) qú ㄑㄩˊ [蠼螋](–sōu)昆虫，身体扁平狭长，黑褐色，腹端有铗状尾须一对，生活在潮湿的地方，危害家蚕等 earwig

曲 qǔ ㄑㄩˇ (–子、–儿)❶歌，能唱的文辞(㊀歌–) song; verse for singing：戏～ *traditional Chinese opera* | 小～儿 *ditty* | 唱～儿 *sing traditional opera/songs* ❷歌的乐调(yuèdiào) tune; melody：这支歌是他作的～。*The melody of the song was written by him.* ❸元代盛行的一种韵文体裁，可以入乐 *qu* (a type of verse popular in the Yuan Dynasty, which can be sung along with a melody)

⇨ see also qū on p.546

苣 qǔ ㄑㄩˇ [苣荬菜](–mai–)草本植物，叶长椭圆披针形，花黄色。茎叶嫩时可以吃 field sow-thistle

⇨ see also jù on p.339

取 qǔ ㄑㄩˇ ❶拿到手里 to get; to fetch：～书 *fetch the books* | 到银行～款 *go to the bank and withdraw some cash* ❷获得，招致 to gain; bring about：～暖 *warm oneself* | ～笑(开玩笑) *make fun of* | ～保就医 *release on bail for medical treatment* | 自～灭亡 *bring about one's own destruction* ❸挑选，采用 to adopt; to choose：～材 *select materials from* | ～景 *find a view to paint or photograph* | 录～ *to recruit* | ～个名儿 *give a name* | ～道天津 *go via Tianjin* | 听～意见 *listen to suggestions* | 吸～经验 *draw lessons* [取消]废除，撤销 to cancel; to

Q

abolish：～参赛资格 *disqualify sb from the competition*

娶 qǔ ㄑㄩˇ 把女子接过来成亲，跟“嫁”相对 take a wife (opposite of 嫁)：～妻 *marry a woman*

竘 qǔ ㄑㄩˇ 雄健，雄壮 robust; masculine

龋(齲) qǔ ㄑㄩˇ [龋齿]俗叫虫牙，因口腔里的食物渣滓发酵，产生酸类，侵蚀牙齿的釉质而形成空洞，这样的牙齿叫作龋齿 dental caries

去 qù ㄑㄩˋ ❶离开所在的地方到别处，由自己一方到另一方，跟“来”相对 go to; leave for (opposite of 来)：我要～工厂。*I want to go to the factory.*｜马上就～ *go right now*｜给他～封信 *send him a letter* ❷距离，差别 be away from; be different from：相～不远 *be slightly different* ❸已过的。特指刚过去的一年 past; (specifically) last (year)：～年 *last year*｜～冬今春 *last winter and this spring* ❹除掉，减掉 to remove; get rid of：～皮 *peel off the skin*｜～病 *cure a disease*｜太长了，～一段。*Cut off a paragraph/part because it is too long.* ❺扮演（戏曲里的角色）to play/act (a part in a Chinese opera)：他在《西游记》里～孙悟空。*He played the part of the Monkey King in* A Journey to the West. ❻在动词后，表示趋向 used after a verb to indicate direction：上～ *go up*｜进～ *go in* ❼在动词后，表示持续 used after a verb to indicate continuity：信步走～ *to stroll*｜让他说～。*Just let him babble on.* ❽去声，汉语四声之一。普通话去声的调子是下降的，符号作“ˋ”。falling tone (one of the four tones in Mandarin Chinese pronunciation, symbol ‘ˋ’)

阒(闃) qù ㄑㄩˋ 形容寂静 quiet; silent：～无一人。*All is quiet and not a soul is to be seen.*

趣 qù ㄑㄩˋ ❶意向 inclination; intention：旨～ *main purpose*｜志～ *aspiration* ❷趣味，兴味 interest; delight：有～ *interesting*｜～事 *amusing episode*｜自讨没～（自寻不愉快、没意思）*bring contempt upon oneself*

〈古 ancient〉also same as 促 (cù)

觑(覷、**覰、**覻) qù ㄑㄩˋ 看，窥探 to look; to peek：偷～ *steal a glance at*｜面面相～ *stare at each other in bewilderment* [小觑] 小看，轻视 to underestimate：后生不可～。*Don't underestimate young people.*

QUAN ㄑㄩㄢ

悛 quān ㄑㄩㄢ 悔改 to repent; mend one's way：怙(hù)恶不～（坚持作恶，不肯悔改）*stick to one's vile ways and refuse to change*

圈 quān ㄑㄩㄢ ❶（一子、一儿）环形，环形的东西 circle; ring：画一个～儿 *draw a circle*｜铁～ *iron ring* ㊀①周，周

遭 surrounding area：跑了一～儿 *ran a lap* | 兜了个大～子 *took a roundabout course* ② 范围 range; scope：这话说得出～儿了。*This remark has gone too far.* ❷画环形 draw a circle：～阅 *circle one's name after reading a document submitted for approval* | ～个红圈当记号 *mark with a red circle* ❸包围 to enclose; to pen：打一道墙把这块地～起来。*Build a wall to enclose this plot of land.*

⇨ see also juān on p.341, juàn on p.341

棬 quān ㄑㄩㄢ 曲木制成的饮器 a kind of wooden cup

鄄 quān ㄑㄩㄢ 用于地名 used in place names：柳树～（在河北省唐山）*Liushuquan (in Tangshan, Hebei Province)* | 蒙～（在天津市蓟县）*Mengquan (in Jixian, Tianjin)*

权(權) quán ㄑㄩㄢˊ ❶权力，权柄，职责范围内支配和指挥的力量 power; authority：政～ *political power; regime* | 掌～ *come to power* | 有～处理这件事 *have the authority to deal with this matter* ❷权利 right; entitlement：选举～ *suffrage; the right to vote* | 人～ *human rights* | 版～ *copyright* ❸势力，有利形势 influence; advantageous position：主动～ *right to take the initiative* | 制海～ *command of the sea* ❹变通，不依常规 be flexible：～变 *adapt one's tactics according to the situation* | ～且如此 *let it be so for the time being* ❺衡量，估计 to weigh; to measure：～衡 *to balance* | ～其轻重 *weigh up the matter carefully* ❻〈古 ancient〉秤锤 weight (of a steelyard)

全 quán ㄑㄩㄢˊ ❶完备，齐备，完整，不缺少（㊀齐一）complete：百货公司的货很～。*The department store sells a full range of products.* | 这部书不～了。*This book is no longer complete.* ❷整个，遍 whole; entire：～国 *the whole country* | ～校 *the whole school* | ～力以赴 *do one's very best* [全面] 顾到各方面的，不片面 comprehensive; all-round：～规划 *map out an overall plan* | 看问题要～。*(We) should take an all-round view of things.* ❸保全，成全，使不受损伤 make complete; keep intact：两～其美 *gratify both sides* ❹副词，都 (adverb) all; completely：代表们～来了。*All the representatives have come.*

佺 quán ㄑㄩㄢˊ 用于人名 (used in given names) Quan

诠(詮) quán ㄑㄩㄢˊ ❶解释（㊀一释）to explain; to interpret ❷事物的理 reason; logic：真～ *true meaning*

荃 quán ㄑㄩㄢˊ 古书上说的一种香草 a kind of aromatic plant in ancient Chinese texts

辁(輇) quán ㄑㄩㄢˊ ❶古代指木制的没有辐条的小车轮 (ancient) wooden wheel without spokes ❷小，浅薄 little; superficial; shallow：～才 *man of limited ability*

Q

牷 quán ㄑㄩㄢˊ 古指供祭祀用的毛色纯的牛 (ancient) cow of uniform colour (for sacrifice)

铨（銓） quán ㄑㄩㄢˊ ❶衡量轻重 to weigh ❷旧时称量才授官，选拔官吏 (old) to select (officials) by qualifications：～选 *select by qualifications*

痊 quán ㄑㄩㄢˊ 病好了，恢复健康（㊀－愈）to heal; fully recover

筌 quán ㄑㄩㄢˊ 捕鱼的竹器 bamboo fish trap：得鱼忘～（喻达到目的后就忘了原来凭借的东西）*forget the trap as soon as the fish is caught; (figurative) be ungrateful*

醛 quán ㄑㄩㄢˊ 有机化合物的一类，由醛基和烃基（或氢原子）连接而成 aldehyde

泉 quán ㄑㄩㄢˊ ❶泉水 spring; fountain：清～ *clear spring* | 甘～ *sweet spring water* ❷水源（㊀源－）water source; headwater［黄泉］［九泉］称人死后所在的地方 the nether world; Hades ❸钱币的古称 (ancient) money; coin

琭 quán ㄑㄩㄢˊ 一种玉 a kind of jade

鳈（鰁） quán ㄑㄩㄢˊ 鱼名，体长十几厘米，深棕色，有斑纹，口小，生活在淡水中。种类较多 Chinese lake gudgeon

拳 quán ㄑㄩㄢˊ ❶（－头）屈指卷握起来的手 fist：双手握～ *clench both fists* | 赤手空～ *be bare-handed* ❷拳术，一种徒手的武术 bare-handed exercises; Chinese boxing：打～ *practise Chinese boxing* | 太极～ taijiquan *(shadow boxing)* ❸肢体弯曲 (of limbs) to bend; to cross：～腿坐在炕上 *sit on* kang *with both legs crossed*

［拳拳］形容恳切 sincere：情意～ *show sincere feelings*

婘 quán ㄑㄩㄢˊ 美好的样子 beautiful

蜷（踡）** quán ㄑㄩㄢˊ 身体弯曲 curl one's body：～缩 *huddle up* | 身体～作一团。*The body is curled up.*

鬈 quán ㄑㄩㄢˊ ❶头发美好 (of hair) beautiful ❷头发卷曲 (of hair) curly; wavy

颧（顴） quán ㄑㄩㄢˊ 眼睛下面、两腮上面突出的部分 cheekbone (see picture of 头 on page 660)

犬 quǎn ㄑㄩㄢˇ 狗 dog：家～ *dog* | 警～ *police dog* | 牧羊～ *shepherd dog*

畎 quǎn ㄑㄩㄢˇ 田地中间的小沟 small ditch in a field［畎亩］田间 fields

绻（綣） quǎn ㄑㄩㄢˇ see 缱绻 (qiǎn－) at 缱 on page 528

劝（勸） quàn ㄑㄩㄢˋ ❶劝说，讲明事理使人听从 to exhort; to advise：规～ *to exhort* | 好言相～ *advise sb with kind words* | ～他不要喝酒 *advise him not to drink wine* ❷勉励（㊀－勉）encourage sb to make more effort：～学 *encourage one to study hard* | 惩恶～善 *punish evildoer and encourage virtue*

券 quàn ㄑㄩㄢˋ ❶票据或用作凭证的纸片 ticket; certificate; voucher：债～ *government bond* | 入场～ *admission ticket* ❷"拱券"的"券"(xuàn)的又音 another pronunciation for 券 (xuàn) in 拱券

⇨ see also xuàn on p.739

QUE ㄑㄩㄝ

炔 quē ㄑㄩㄝ 炔烃(tīng)，有机化合物的一类，分子中含有三键结构。乙炔是重要的工业原料 alkyne

缺 quē ㄑㄩㄝ ❶短少，不够(㊥一乏、一少) be short of; to lack：东西齐全，什么也不～。*All materials are ready and nothing is lacking.* ❷残破(㊥残一) broken and incomplete：～口 *notch; shortage* | 完整无～ *intact; complete* [缺点] 工作或行为中不完美、不完备的地方 shortcoming; weakness [缺陷] 残损或不圆满的地方 defect ❸该到未到 fail to attend; be absent from：～席 *be absent (from a meeting, a class, etc.)* | ～勤 *be absent from work* | ～考 *miss an examination* ❹空额(指职位) vacancy：补～ *fill a vacancy* | 肥～ *vacancy of lucrative post*

阙(闕) quē ㄑㄩㄝ ❶古代用作"缺"字 (ancient) same as "缺" [阙如] 空缺 be lacking; be deficient：尚付～ *be still wanting* [阙疑] 有怀疑的事情暂时不下断语，留待查考 leave a difficult question open ❷过错 fault; error：～失 *mistake* ❸姓 (surname) Que

⇨ see also què on p.553

瘸 qué ㄑㄩㄝˊ 腿脚有毛病，走路时身体不平衡 to limp; to hobble：一～一拐 *hobble along* | 他是摔～的。*He became lame after a fall.*

却(*卻、*郤) què ㄑㄩㄝˋ ❶后退(㊥退一) to step back; to flinch：望而～步 *step back at the sight of sth* ❷退还，不受 to decline; to refuse：盛情难～。*Such kindness is difficult to decline.* ❸和"去""掉"用法相近 be off (similar to 去 and 掉)：失～力量 *lose power* | 了～一件心事 *take a load off one's mind* ❹副词，表示转折 (adverb) but; however: 这个道理大家都明白，他～不知道。*Everybody understands this, but he doesn't.*

埆 què ㄑㄩㄝˋ 土地不肥沃 (of land) barren; infertile

确(❶—❸確、❶—❸塙、❶—❸**碻)** què ㄑㄩㄝˋ ❶符合事实的，真实(㊥一实) true; authentic：千真万～ *absolutely true* | 正～ *correct* [确切] 1 准确，恰当 exact; precise 2 真实可靠 true; reliable ❷副词，的确，确实 (adverb) really; indeed：～有其事。*There is really such a thing.* | ～系实情。*It is indeed the truth.* ❸坚固，固定 firm; determined：～定不移 *uncontestable* | ～保丰收 *guarantee a good harvest* ❹ same as "埆"

Q

埆(**碏**) què ㄑㄩㄝ 大石多的山，也指大石头，多用于地名 rocky mountain; boulder (often used in place names)：～石（在广东省汕头）*Queshi (a place in Shantou, Guangdong Province)*

悫(**愨**、**慤) què ㄑㄩㄝ 诚实，谨慎（㊀一诚）honest and discreet

雀 què ㄑㄩㄝ 鸟名，身体小，翅膀长，雌雄羽毛颜色多不相同，吃粮食粒和昆虫。种类很多，特指麻雀，泛指小鸟 (specifically) sparrow; (generally) small bird [雀跃]㊃高兴得像麻雀那样跳跃 jump for joy

⇨ see also qiāo on p.533, qiǎo on p.534

阕(**闋**) què ㄑㄩㄝ ❶停止，终了 to end; to finish：乐～（奏乐终了）。*The music ended.* ❷量词，用于词或歌曲 (measure word for songs and *ci*) piece; stanza

阙(**闕**) què ㄑㄩㄝ〈古 ancient〉❶皇宫门前两边的楼 watchtower on either side of a palace gate：宫～ *imperial palace* ❷墓道外所立的石牌坊 stone memorial archway (along the path leading to a grave)

⇨ see also quē on p.552

搉 què ㄑㄩㄝ ❶敲击 to knock ❷ see 榷 on page 553

榷(^△*搉、*榷) què ㄑㄩㄝ ❶专利，专卖 to monopolize：～盐 *monopoly on salt* | ～茶 *monopoly on tea* ❷商讨（㊀商一）to discuss; to consult

鹊(**鵲**) què ㄑㄩㄝ 喜鹊，鸟名，背部黑褐色，肩、颈、腹等部白色，翅有大白斑，尾长。民间传说听见喜鹊叫，将有喜事来临 magpie

碏 què ㄑㄩㄝ ❶用于人名，石碏，春秋时卫国大夫 Que (used in given names, e.g. Shi Que, a senior official of the Wei State during the Spring and Autumn Period) ❷用于地名 used in place names：～下（在浙江省仙居）*Quexia (in Xianju, Zhejiang Province)*

QUN ㄑㄩㄣ

囷 qūn ㄑㄩㄣ 古代一种圆形的谷仓 (ancient) round granary

逡 qūn ㄑㄩㄣ 退 step back; to retreat [逡巡] 有所顾虑而徘徊或退却 to hesitate; hang back

裙(*帬、*裠) qún ㄑㄩㄣˊ（一子、一儿）一种围在下身的服装 skirt; dress：连衣～ *dress*

群(*羣) qún ㄑㄩㄣˊ ❶聚集在一起的人或物 a group of people, animals, etc.：人～ *crowd* | 羊～ *a flock of sheep* | 楼～ *a cluster of buildings* | 成～结队 *gather in groups* ㊀众多的 a great amount of; numerous：～岛 *archipelago* | ～山 *chain of mountains* | ～居 *live in groups; gather in groups* | ～集 *assemble in large numbers* | 博览～书 *read extensively* ❷众人 the masses; many people：～策～力 *pool the wisdom and efforts of everyone* | ～起而攻之。*Many people rise up against sb/sth.* ❸量词，用于成群的人或物 (measure word) group; herd; flock：一～娃娃 *a group of kids* | 一～牛 *a herd of cattle*

麇(** 麏) qún ㄑㄩㄣˊ 成群 to flock together; to swarm [麇集] 许多人或物聚集在一起 to gather; to assemble：记者～会场。*The reporters gathered together at the conference.*

⇨ see also jūn on p.346

Q

R ㄖ

RAN ㄖㄢ

蚺 rán ㄖㄢˊ ［蚺蛇］即蟒蛇 python (same as 蟒蛇)

髯（*髥） rán ㄖㄢˊ 两颊上的胡子，泛指胡子 (of a man) whisker; beard

然 rán ㄖㄢˊ ❶是，对 right; correct：不以为～ *consider sth not so* ❷代词，这样，如此 (pronoun) such; that; so：不尽～ *be not exactly so* | 知其～，不知其所以～ *know the hows but not the whys* ［然后］连词，以后（表示两件事前后承接）(conjunction) then：先研究一下，～再决定 *have a closer look at it before making a decision* ［然则］连词，既然这样，那么……(conjunction) in that case; then：是进亦忧，退亦忧，～何时而乐耶？ *(He) is worried both in court and in exile. When can (he) enjoy happiness then?* ［然而］连词，但是（表示转折）(conjunction) but; however：他虽然失败了多次，～并不灰心。*He failed over and again, but never lost heart.* ❸词尾，表示状态 suffix to indicate a kind of state：突～ *suddenly* | 忽～ *all of a sudden* | 显～ *obviously* | 欣～ *readily* ❹ (ancient) same as "燃"

燃 rán ㄖㄢˊ ❶烧起火焰（㊀一烧）to burn; to flame：～料 *fuel* | 自～ *autoignition; spontaneous ignition* ❷引火点着（zháo）to ignite; to light：～灯 *light a lamp* | ～放花炮 *set off firecrackers*

冉（*冄） rǎn ㄖㄢˇ 姓 (surname) Ran

［冉冉］慢慢地 slowly; gradually：红旗～上升。*The red flag rose slowly.*

苒 rǎn ㄖㄢˇ ［荏苒］（rěn－）时间不知不觉地过去 (of time) to slip by：光阴～。*Time flies.*

䎃 rǎn ㄖㄢˇ 鸟翅膀下的细毛，绒羽 (of a bird) down

染 rǎn ㄖㄢˇ ❶用染料使东西着色 to dye：～布 *dye cloth* | ～色 *to dye* | ～头发 *dye one's hair* ❷感受疾病或沾上坏习惯 to catch (an illness); to fall into (a bad habit)：传～ *to infect* | ～病 *catch an illness* | 一尘不～ *spotlessly clean* ［染指］指从中分取非分的利益或插手本分以外的事情 get an unearned share of; interfere in

RANG ㄖㄤ

嚷 rāng ㄖㄤ ［嚷嚷］（－rang）1 吵闹 to shout; to yell：大家别乱～。*Stop yelling, everyone.* 2 声张 to disclose; to make public：这事先别～出去。*Keep this a se-*

cret for the time being.

⇨ see also rǎng on p.556

儴 ráng ㄖㄤˊ 因循，沿袭 to follow; to abide by

勷 ráng ㄖㄤˊ see 劻勷（kuāng —）at 劻 on page 366

蘘 ráng ㄖㄤˊ ［蘘荷］草本植物，花白色或淡黄色，花穗和嫩芽可以吃，根状茎可入药 myoga ginger

瀼 ráng ㄖㄤˊ 瀼河，水名，又地名，都在河南省鲁山县 Ranghe (name of a river and a place in Lushan County, Henan Province)

⇨ see also ràng on p.557

禳 ráng ㄖㄤˊ 迷信的人祈祷消除灾殃 to expel (a disaster or misfortune) by prayers：～灾 *ward off disaster*

穰 ráng ㄖㄤˊ ❶庄稼的茎秆 (of crops) stalk ❷丰盛 ㊣ abundant; plentiful：五谷蕃熟，～～满家。*A bountiful harvest of all crops filled up the granary.* ❸ same as "瓤"

瓤 ráng ㄖㄤˊ ❶(－子、－儿)瓜、橘等内部包着种子的肉、瓣 flesh; pulp：西瓜～儿 *watermelon pulp*｜橘子～儿 *tangerine segments* ㊀东西的内部 inside; interior：秫秸～儿 *pulp of sorghum stalks*｜信～儿 *letter (in an envelope)* ❷〈方 dialect〉身体软弱，技术差 (of body or skills) weak：病了一场，身子骨～了 *became weak after the illness*｜你修车的技术真不～。*You are really good at fixing cars.*

欀 ráng ㄖㄤˊ 衣服脏 (of clothes) dirty

壤 rǎng ㄖㄤˇ ❶松软的土 soil［土壤］陆地表面的一层疏松物质，有养分，能生长植物 soil ❷地 earth; land：天～之别 *worlds apart; a world of difference*

攘 rǎng ㄖㄤˇ ❶侵夺(㊣－夺) to seize; to snatch ❷排斥 to resist; to reject：～除 *get rid of* ❸窃取 to steal; to grab：～取 *to grab*｜～窃 *to steal*

［攘攘］纷乱的样子 disorderly; chaotic：熙熙～ *hustling and bustling*

嚷 rǎng ㄖㄤˇ 大声喊叫 to shout; to yell：大～大叫 *shout out loudly*｜你别～了，大家都睡觉了。*Stop yelling. Everyone is sleeping.*

⇨ see also rāng on p.555

让（讓）ràng ㄖㄤˋ ❶不争，尽（jǐn）着别人 to concede; to give way：～步 *to compromise*｜谦～ *modestly decline* ㊀①请 to invite; to offer：把他～进屋里来 *invite him into the room* ②避开 to make way：～开 *step aside*｜～路 *make way* ❷索取一定代价，把东西给人 to sell; to transfer：出～ *to sell*｜转～ *to transfer (at a price)* ❸许，使 to allow; to let：不～他来 *not let him come*｜～他去取 *let him fetch it* ㊀任凭 to leave alone; to let go unchecked：～他闹去。*Just let him do his own monkey business.* ❹介词，被 (preposition) by：那个碗～他摔坏了。*That bowl was broken by him.*

瀼 ràng ㄖㄤˋ 瀼渡河，水名，在重庆 Rangduhe River (in Chongqing)

⇨ see also ráng on p.556

RAO ㄖㄠ

荛(蕘) ráo ㄖㄠˊ 柴草 dried grass (used as fuel)：薪～ *firewood*

饶(饒) ráo ㄖㄠˊ ❶富足，多(㊀富－) rich; abundant; plentiful：丰～ *abundant* | ～舌(多话) *talkative* ❷额外增添 to add some extra for nothing：～上一个 *take/give one extra* ❸宽恕，免除处罚(㊀－恕) to spare; to have mercy on：不依不～ *be hard on sb* | ～了他吧。*Please let him off.* | 不能轻～ *not able to let off lightly* ❹〈方 dialect〉尽管 in spite of; despite：～这么检查还有漏洞呢。*Despite all this checking, there are still loopholes.*

娆(嬈) ráo ㄖㄠˊ [妖娆][娇娆]娇艳，美好 charming; enchanting：花枝～ *be as pretty as flowers* | 妆容～ *be gorgeously dressed*

⇨ see also rǎo on p.557

桡(橈) ráo ㄖㄠˊ 〈方 dialect〉船桨 oar [桡骨]前臂靠拇指一侧的骨头 radius (see picture of 人体骨骼 on page 220)

扰(擾) rǎo ㄖㄠˇ 扰乱，打搅(㊀搅－) to trouble; to disturb

娆(嬈) rǎo ㄖㄠˇ 烦扰，扰乱 to bother; to annoy

⇨ see also ráo on p.557

绕(繞、❷❸*遶) rào ㄖㄠˋ ❶缠 to wind; to coil：～线 *wind thread* ㊀纠缠，弄迷糊 to confuse; to baffle：这句话一下子把他～住了。*This remark confused him all of a sudden.* ❷走弯曲、迂回的路 to detour; to go round：～远 *take a detour* | ～过暗礁 *bypass the submerged rocks* | ～了一个大圈子 *take a long way round; (figurative) beat about the bush* ❸围着转 to circle; to move round：鸟～着树飞。*The birds circled over the tree.* | ～场一周 *do a lap around the stadium*

RE ㄖㄜ

喏 rě ㄖㄜˇ 古代表示敬意的呼喊 (polite greeting) here; here I am：唱～(对人作揖，同时出声致敬) *to greet (while bowing with hands folded in front)*

⇨ see also nuò on p.485

惹 rě ㄖㄜˇ 招引，挑逗(㊀招－) to provoke; to invite; to tease：～事 *cause trouble* | ～人注意 *draw attention*

热(熱) rè ㄖㄜˋ ❶物理学上把能使物体的温度升高的那种能叫"热" heat ❷温度高，跟"冷"相对 hot (opposite of 冷)：炎～ *scorching; burning hot* | 天～。*The weather is hot.* | ～水 *hot water* ❸使热(多指食物) to heat up; to warm up：把菜～一～ *heat up the dish* ❹情

R

意深 (of feelings) deep; warm: 亲～ *affectionate; show affection for* | ～情 *enthusiasm* | ～心 *warm-hearted* ❺衷心羡慕 envious; keen: 眼～ *envious* | ～衷 *be keen on* ❻受人欢迎 popular; in great demand: ～门儿 *popular* | ～货 *goods in high demand* ❼指某种事物风行，形成热潮 craze; fever; rush: 旅游～ *tourist boom* | 集邮～ *stamp-collecting craze*

REN ㄖㄣ

人 rén ㄖㄣˊ ❶能制造工具并能使用工具进行劳动的高等动物 human being; human [人口] 1 人的数目 population: ～普查 *census* 2 泛指人 human; person: 拐卖～ *human trafficking* [人类] 人的总称 mankind; humanity; human race: 造福～ *benefit mankind* [人手] 指参加某项工作的人 manpower: 缺～ *short of manpower* | ～齐全 *be fully staffed* ❷指某种人 person (of a particular activity or group): 工～ *worker* | 客～ *guest* | 商～ *business person* | 媒体～ *media worker* ❸别人 others; another person: ～云亦云 *repeat what others say* | 助～为乐 *enjoy helping others* ❹指人的品质、性情 character; personality: 老张～不错。*Mr Zhang is a nice man.* ㊀人格或面子 dignity; reputation: 丢～ *lose face* ❺指人的身体或意识 the state of one's health or mind: 我今天～不大舒服。*I am out of sorts today.*

壬 rén ㄖㄣˊ 天干的第九位，用作顺序的第九 ren (the ninth of the ten Heavenly Stems, a system used in the Chinese calendar); ninth

任 rén ㄖㄣˊ 姓 (surname) Ren [任县] [任丘] 地名，都在河北省 Renxian; Renqiu (place names, both in Hebei Province)

⇨ see also rèn on p.559

仁 rén ㄖㄣˊ ❶同情，友爱 benevolence; compassion: ～慈 *benevolent* | ～厚 *benevolent and generous* | ～心 *benevolence* | ～至义尽 *do one's best to help* ❷敬辞，用于对对方的尊称 (polite speech) you; your: ～兄 *my brother; my dear friend (address to a man older than the speaker)* | ～弟 *my brother; my dear friend (address to a man younger than the speaker)* ❸(～儿) 果核的最里面的部分 kernel; stone: 杏～儿 *apricot kernel*

[不仁] 1 不仁慈，无仁德 heartless; merciless: ～不义 *be neither virtuous nor righteous* 2 手足丧失感觉，不能运动 numb: 麻木～ *indifferent* | 四体～ *numbness in the limbs*

忍 rěn ㄖㄣˇ ❶耐，把感觉或感情压住不表现出来(㊥－耐) to bear; to endure; to tolerate: ～痛 *bear the pain; (do sth) reluctantly* | ～受 *to bear* | 容～ *put up with* [忍俊不禁] (－－－jīn) 忍不住笑 cannot hold back a smile ❷狠心，残酷 (㊥残－) to have the heart to: ～心 *be hardhearted enough to*

荏 rěn ㄖㄣˇ ❶草本植物，即白苏，叶卵圆形，花白色。种子可入药 perilla (same as 白苏) ❷软弱 weak; timid: 色厉内～(外貌刚强，内心懦弱) *tough outwardly but timid inwardly*

稔 rěn ㄖㄣˇ ❶庄稼成熟 (of crops) to ripen ㊕年 year: 离家凡五～ *have been away from home for five years* ❷熟悉 to be familiar with; to know well: ～知 *know very well* | 素～ *have always been familiar with*

刃 rèn ㄖㄣˋ ❶(－儿) 刀剑等锋利的部分 blade; knife-edge: 刀～儿 *blade; (figurative) crucial point* ❷刀 knife; sword: 利～ *sharp knife/sword* | 白～战 *hand-to-hand combat; bayonet fighting* ❸用刀杀 to kill with sword or knife: 若遇此贼，必手～之。*If (I) should ever see this evil man, (I) would kill him with my own sword.*

仞 rèn ㄖㄣˋ 古时以八尺或七尺为一仞 traditional Chinese unit for measuring length, equal to seven or eight 尺

讱(訒) rèn ㄖㄣˋ 言语迟钝 (of speech) slow; inarticulate

纫(紉) rèn ㄖㄣˋ ❶引线穿针 to thread a needle: ～针 *thread a needle* ❷缝缀 to sew; to stitch: 缝～ *to sew*

韧(韌、*靭、*韌、*靱) rèn ㄖㄣˋ 又柔软又结实，不易折断，跟"脆"相对 tough; supple but strong (opposite of 脆): ～性 *pliability; (figurative) tenacity* | 坚～ *tenacious* | 柔～ *supple*

轫(軔、*軔) rèn ㄖㄣˋ 支住车轮不让它转动的木头 log used to stop a wheel [发轫] ㊑事业开始 to commence; to start: 新文学运动～于五四时期。*The New Literature Movement started from the May 4th period.*

牣 rèn ㄖㄣˋ 充满 (㊌充－) to fill up; to be full of

认(認) rèn ㄖㄣˋ ❶分辨，识别 (㊌－识) to tell; to recognize; to identify: ～字 *know/learn how to read* | ～明 *to identify* | ～不出 *cannot recognize* [认真] 仔细，不马虎 careful; earnest; serious ❷承认，表示同意 to admit; to accept: ～可 *to approve of; to accept* | ～错 *admit one's mistake* | 公～ *generally acknowledge* | 否～ *to deny* ❸跟本来没有关系的人建立某种关系 to establish a certain relationship with: ～老师 *formally acknowledge sb as one's master* | ～了一门干亲 *established a nominal kinship*

任 rèn ㄖㄣˋ ❶相信，依赖 (㊌信－) to trust; to rely on ❷任命，使用，给予职务 to appoint; to assign: ～用 *to assign (sb to a post)* | 委～ *to appoint* ❸负担或担当 (㊌担－) to assume; to take up: ～课 *give classes* | 连选连～ *win a re-election* | ～劳～怨 *work hard and not be upset by criticism* ❹职务，任务 official post; duty:

R

到～ *assume office* | 重～ *important task* | 一身而二～ *hold two posts concurrently* ❺由着，听凭 to let; to allow：～意 *at will; arbitrarily* | ～性 *wayward; capricious* | 放～ *not to interfere* | 不能～其自然发展 *must not let it develop by itself* ❻连词，不论 (conjunction) no matter：～谁说也不听 *listen to nobody at all* | ～什么都不懂 *know nothing whatsoever* ㊀任何，无论什么 any; every：～人皆知。*Everybody knows it.* ❼量词，用于任同一官职的前后次序或次数 (measure word) term (of office)：首～大使 *the first ambassador* | 为官一～，造福一方。*Wherever holding the office, bring benefits to the region.*

⇨ see also rén on p.558

R

饪(飪、*餁) rèn ㄖㄣˋ 烹饪，做饭做菜 to cook

妊(*姙) rèn ㄖㄣˋ 妊娠(shēn)，怀孕 to be pregnant：～妇 *pregnant woman*

纴(紝、**絍) rèn ㄖㄣˋ〈古 ancient〉❶织布帛的丝缕 thread; silk：抽茧作～ *reel off raw silk from cocoons* ❷纺织(㊥一织) weaving

衽(*袵) rèn ㄖㄣˋ〈古 ancient〉❶衣襟 front part of a gown ❷衽席，睡觉用的席子 sleeping mat

葚 rèn ㄖㄣˋ [桑葚儿]桑树结的果实，用于口语 mulberry (used in spoken Chinese)

⇨ see also shèn on p.591

RENG ㄖㄥ

扔 rēng ㄖㄥ ❶抛，投掷 to throw; to toss：～球 *toss a ball* | ～砖 *throw a brick* ❷丢弃，舍(shě)弃 to throw away; to get rid of：把这些破烂东西～了吧。*Please throw away the junk.*

仍 réng ㄖㄥˊ 副词，仍然，依然，还，照旧 (adverb) still; yet：吃了几服(fù)药，病～不见好。*After taking medicine several times, there was still no sign of improvement.* | 他虽然忙，～每天坚持学习。*He was very busy, but still found time to study every day.*

礽 réng ㄖㄥˊ 福 happiness; blessing; good fortune

RI ㄖ

日 rì ㄖˋ ❶太阳 sun：～光 *sunlight* [日食] (*日蚀) 月亮运行到太阳和地球的中间，遮住太阳照到地球上的光，致使部分或完全看不见太阳的现象 solar eclipse ❷白天，跟"夜"相对 day; daytime (opposite of 夜)：～班 *day shift* | ～场 *day show* ❸天，一昼夜 day; a single day and night：阳历平年一年三百六十五～。*A usual Gregorian year consists of 365 days.* ㊀某一天 a specific day：纪念～ *anniversary* | 生～ *birthday* [日子] (-zi) 1 天 day：这些～工作很忙 *have been very busy with work these days* 2 指某一天 a specific day：今天是喜庆的～。*Today is a day of cele-*

bration. 3 生活 life：如今过上了好～。*Now (we are) living a happy life.* ❹一天天，每天 day by day; every day：～益强大 *increasingly powerful* | ～新月异 *change rapidly* | ～理万机 *attend to numerous affairs of state every day* ❺时候 time; period：春～ *spring* | 往～ *the past* | 来～方长。*There will be ample time.*

驲（馹） rì ㄖ ❶古代驿站用的马车 (ancient) post chaise ❷用于地名 used in place names：～面（在广西壮族自治区灵山县）*Rimian (in Lingshan County, the Guangxi Zhuang Autonomous Region)*

RONG ㄖㄨㄥ

戎 róng ㄖㄨㄥˊ ❶武器 weapon; arms ❷军队，军事 troops; military affairs：从～ *join the army* | ～装 *military uniform* ❸我国古代称西部的民族 general name for ethnic groups in the west of ancient China

狨 róng ㄖㄨㄥˊ 古书上指金丝猴 (in ancient Chinese texts) snub-nosed monkey

绒（絨、*羢、*毧） róng ㄖㄨㄥˊ ❶柔软细小的毛 down; fine hair; fluff：～毛 *down* | 驼～ *camel hair* | 鸭～被 *duck down quilt* ❷带绒毛的纺织品 flannel; velvet：丝～ *silk velvet* | 天鹅～ *velvet*

肜 róng ㄖㄨㄥˊ ❶古代指在祭祀后的第二天又进行的祭祀 sacrifice of the second day (in ancient Chinese worshipping rituals) ❷姓 (surname) Rong

茸 róng ㄖㄨㄥˊ ❶草初生纤细柔嫩的样子 (of young grass) delicate; fine：绿～～的草地 *soft green meadow* ❷鹿茸，带细毛的才生出来的鹿角，可入药 pilose antler

荣（榮） róng ㄖㄨㄥˊ ❶草木茂盛 luxuriant; flourishing：欣欣向～ *thriving; flourishing* ㊀兴盛 to thrive：繁～ *to prosper* ❷光荣，跟"辱"相对 glory; honour; credit (opposite of 辱)：～誉 *honour; (of a title) honorary* | ～耀 *glory* | ～获冠军 *win the championship*

嵘（嶸） róng ㄖㄨㄥˊ see 峥嵘 (zhēng－) at 峥 on page 847

蝾（蠑） róng ㄖㄨㄥˊ ［蝾螈］(－yuán)两栖动物，像蜥蜴 newt; salamander

容 róng ㄖㄨㄥˊ ❶容纳，包含 to hold; to contain：～器 *container* | ～量 *volume* | 屋子小，～不下。*The room is small and cannot accommodate so many.* ❷对人度量大，不计较 to tolerate; to forgive：宽～ *to tolerate* | ～忍 *put up with* | 大度～人 *generous and tolerant* ❸让，允许 to let; to allow：～许 *to permit* | 不～人说话 *not give others a chance to speak* | 不～他胡来 *not let him make trouble* ❹相貌，仪表（㊀－貌）appearance; look：笑～ *smile* | 面～ *countenance* ㊀样子 appearance; image：军～

soldier's appearance and bearing | 市～ *the look of a city* ❺或许，也许（㊟－或）perhaps; probably; possibly：～有异同 *possibly with variations*

蓉 róng ㄖㄨㄥˊ ❶用瓜果豆类等制成的粉状物，常用来做糕点馅儿 paste; mash：椰～ *mashed coconut stuffing* | 莲～ *lotus seed paste* | 豆～ *bean mash* ❷四川省成都的别称 Rong (another name for Chengdu, capital city of Sichuan Province)

溶 róng ㄖㄨㄥˊ 在水或其他液体中化开（㊟－化）to dissolve: 樟脑～于酒精而不～于水。*Camphor dissolves in alcohol but not in water.*

瑢 róng ㄖㄨㄥˊ see 瑽瑢(cōng－) at 瑽 on page 99

榕 róng ㄖㄨㄥˊ ❶榕树，常绿乔木，生长在热带和亚热带，树冠大，有气根，叶和气根可入药 Chinese banyan ❷福建省福州的别称 Rong (another name for Fuzhou, capital city of Fujian Province)

熔 róng ㄖㄨㄥˊ 固体受热到一定温度时变成液体（㊟－化）to melt; to fuse：～炼 *to smelt; (figurative) to temper* | ～炉 *furnace*

镕（鎔）róng ㄖㄨㄥˊ ❶铸造用的模型 casting mould ㊕陶冶（思想品质）to mould (one's character)：习礼仪，～气质 *learn about etiquette and cultivate one's temperament* ❷ (old) same as "熔"

融（*螎）róng ㄖㄨㄥˊ ❶固体受热变软或变为流体（㊟－化）to thaw; to melt：太阳一晒，雪就～了。*As soon as the sun shone, the snow melted.* ❷融合，调和 to blend; to intermingle：～洽 *harmonious* | 通～ *make an exception for sb; accommodate sb with a short-time loan* | 水乳交～ *in perfect harmony*［融会贯通］参合多方面的道理而得到全面透彻的领悟 to achieve thorough understanding of sth through mastery of all relevant material ❸流通 to circulate ［金融］货币的流通，即汇兑、借贷、储蓄等经济活动的总称 finance

冗（*宂）rǒng ㄖㄨㄥˇ ❶闲散的，多余无用的 redundant; superfluous：～员 *superfluous staff* | 文辞～长 *lengthy and tedious writing* ❷繁忙，繁忙的事 busy; busy schedule：～务缠身 *get bogged down in miscellaneous duties* | 拨～（客套话，从繁忙的事务中抽出时间）*(polite expression) find time to do sth* ❸烦琐 trivial and tedious：～杂 *miscellaneous*

氄（**毴）rǒng ㄖㄨㄥˇ 鸟兽细软的毛 (of a bird) down; (of a mammal) underfur

ROU ㄖㄡ

柔 róu ㄖㄡˊ ❶软，不硬（㊟－软）soft; supple：～枝 *slender branch* | ～嫩 *tender* ❷柔和，

跟“刚”相对 gentle; mild (opposite of 刚): 温～ *gentle* | ～情 *tender feelings* | 刚～相济 *temper force with mercy* | 以～克刚 *use a soft approach to overcome a tough one*

揉 róu ㄖㄡˊ ❶用手来回搓 to rub; to massage: ～一～腿 *massage the legs* | 沙子到眼里可别～。*Don't rub your eyes when sand gets into them.* ❷团弄 to knead; to crumple: ～面 *knead dough* | ～馒头 *knead dough for steamed buns* ❸使东西弯曲 to bend: ～以为轮 *bend it into a wheel*

辋(輮) róu ㄖㄡˊ ❶车轮的外周 (of a wheel) rim ❷使弯曲 to bend

煣 róu ㄖㄡˊ 用火烤木材使弯曲 to apply heat to bend wood

糅 róu ㄖㄡˊ 混杂 to mix; to mingle: ～合 *mix together* | 真伪杂～ *truth mixed with lies*

蹂 róu ㄖㄡˊ [蹂躏] (－lìn) 践踏，踩 to trample on; to step on ⑩用暴力欺压、侮辱、侵害 to bully; to ravage: 惨遭～ *be ravaged*

鞣 róu ㄖㄡˊ 制造皮革时，用栲胶、鱼油等使兽皮柔软 to tan (animal skins): ～皮子 *tan hides*

肉 ròu ㄖㄡˋ ❶人或动物体内红色、柔软的物质。某些动物的肉可以吃 flesh; meat [肉搏] 徒手或用短兵器搏斗 to fight hand-to-hand: 跟敌人～ *engage in hand-to-hand combat with the enemy* ❷果肉，果实中可以吃的部分 (of fruits) flesh; pulp: 桂圆～ *longan flesh* ❸〈方 dialect〉果实不脆，不酥 (of fruits) soft: ～瓤西瓜 *soft watermelon* ❹〈方 dialect〉行动迟缓，性子慢 slow: 做事真～ *be a slow mover* | ～脾气 *slow temper*

RU ㄖㄨ

如 rú ㄖㄨˊ ❶依照 in accordance with; following: ～法炮(páo)制 *follow suit* | ～期完成 *complete on time* ❷像，如，同 like; as: ～此 *such; so; in that way* | 坚强～钢 *as strong as iron* | 整旧～新 *make sth old look brand new* [如今] 现在，现代 nowadays; now; these days ❸及，比得上（只用于否定式，表示比较）(used only in negation to denote comparison) to be as good as; to be like: 我不～他。*I'm not as good as he is.* | 自以为不～ *consider oneself inferior* | 与其这样，不～那样 *rather that than this* ❹到，往 to go to: ～厕 *go to the toilet* ❺连词，如果，假使 (conjunction) if; in case: ～不同意，可提意见。*If you disagree, you can make your own suggestion.* ❻词尾，表示状态 suffix to indicate a kind of state: 空空～也 *all empty* | 突～其来 *out of the blue* ❼表示举例 such as; for example: 他兴趣广泛，～游泳、集邮、书法等他都喜欢。*He is a man of many interests, such as swimming, stamp collecting and calligraphy.*

R

茹 rú ㄖㄨˊ 吃 to eat：～素 *eat a vegetarian diet* | ～毛饮血 *eat raw meat and drink blood; (figurative) live a primitive life* ㊖ 忍 to bear; to endure：～痛 *bear the pain* | 含辛～苦 *endure all kinds of hardships*

铷(鉫) rú ㄖㄨˊ 金属元素，符号 Rb，银白色，质软。可用来制光电管等 rubidium (Rb)

儒 rú ㄖㄨˊ ❶旧时指读书的人 (old) scholar; learned man：～生 *Confucian scholar* | ～商 *scholarly business person* | 腐～（迂腐的书生）*pedant* ❷儒家，春秋战国时代以孔子、孟子为代表的一个学派。提倡以仁为中心的道德观念，主张德治 the Confucian school：～学 *Confucianism*| ～术 *Confucian teachings*

薷 rú ㄖㄨˊ ［香薷］草本植物，茎四棱形，紫色，叶卵形，花粉红色，果实棕色。茎和叶可提取芳香油 Vietnamese Balm

嚅 rú ㄖㄨˊ see 嗫嚅 (niè—) at 嗫 on page 479

濡 rú ㄖㄨˊ ❶沾湿，润泽 to moisten; to dip in liquid：～笔 *dip a writing brush in ink* | 耳～目染（由于听得多、看得多，无形中受到影响）*be imperceptibly influenced by what one constantly sees and hears* ❷停留，迟滞 to linger; to lag：～滞 *to stay; to dawdle* ❸容忍 to endure; to tolerate：～忍 *put up with*

孺 rú ㄖㄨˊ 小孩子，幼儿 child; young kid：～子 *child* | 妇～ *women and children*

嬬 rú ㄖㄨˊ 柔弱的样子 delicate; feeble

襦 rú ㄖㄨˊ 短衣，短袄 short jacket

颥(顬) rú ㄖㄨˊ see 颞颥 (niè—) at 颞 on page 479

蠕(*蝡) rú ㄖㄨˊ (formerly pronounced ruǎn) 像蚯蚓那样慢慢地行动 to wriggle; to creep：～动 *to wriggle*

汝 rǔ ㄖㄨˇ 文言代词，你 (pronoun in classical Chinese) you; your：～等 *you (people)* | ～将何往？*Where are you going?*

乳 rǔ ㄖㄨˇ ❶乳房，分泌奶汁的器官 breast ❷乳房中分泌出来的白色奶汁 milk：母～ *breast milk* ❸像乳汁的东西 milk-like liquid：豆～ *soy milk* ❹生，繁殖 to multiply; to reproduce：孳（zī）～ *to breed; (generally) to derive* ❺初生的，幼小的 newborn; young：～燕 *young swallow*| ～鸭 *duckling* | ～猪 *piglet*

辱 rǔ ㄖㄨˇ ❶羞耻，跟"荣"相对 shame; disgrace; dishonour (opposite of 荣)：屈～ *humiliation* | 奇耻大～ *great humiliation* ❷使受到羞耻 to insult; to humiliate：中国人民不可～。*Chinese people are never to be insulted.* | 丧权～国 *forfeit sovereign rights and bring humiliation to one's nation* ❸玷辱 to disgrace; to dishonour：～命 *fail to accomplish a mission* ❹谦辞，表示承蒙 (humble speech) to feel honoured by: ～承 *have the honour of* | ～蒙 *be indebted to*

擩 rǔ ㄖㄨˇ 〈方 dialect〉插，塞 to put in: 一脚～进泥里 *step in the mud* | 把钱～给他 *slip some money to him*

入 rù ㄖㄨˋ ❶跟“出”相对 to enter (opposite of 出) ①从外面进到里面 to enter; to go in: ～场 *to enter (a stadium, theatre, etc.)* | ～夜 *at nightfall* | 纳～轨道 *direct sth into the orbit of* ②收进，进款 income: 量～为出 *make two ends meet* | ～不敷出 *live beyond one's means* ❷参加 to join: ～学 *start school* | ～会 *become a member (of an association, etc.)* ❸合乎，合于 to agree with; to conform to: ～时 *fashionable; trendy* | ～情～理 *fair and reasonable* ❹入声，古汉语四声之一。普通话没有入声。有的方言有入声，发音一般比较短促 entering tone (one of the four tones in classical Chinese pronunciation, still retained in certain dialects now)

洳 rù ㄖㄨˋ see 沮洳 (jù—) at 沮 on page 339

蓐 rù ㄖㄨˋ 草席，草垫子 straw mat [坐蓐] 临产 in labour

溽 rù ㄖㄨˋ 湿 humid; damp: ～暑（夏天潮湿闷热的气候）*sultry summer*

缛(縟) rù ㄖㄨˋ 繁多，烦琐 elaborate; cumbersome: ～礼 *overelaborate formalities* | 繁文～节 *bureaucracy; unnecessary and overelaborate procedures*

褥 rù ㄖㄨˋ （—子）装着棉絮铺在床上的东西 cotton-padded mattress: 被～ *bedding*

RUA ㄖㄨㄚ

挼 ruá ㄖㄨㄚˊ 〈方 dialect〉❶（纸、布等）折皱，不平展 creased; crumpled: 纸～了。*The paper is crumpled.* ❷（布）快要磨破 (of cloth) soon to wear out: 裤子穿了好多年，都～了。*After many years of service, this pair of trousers will soon wear out.*

⇨ see also ruó on p.567

RUAN ㄖㄨㄢ

堧(壖)** ruán ㄖㄨㄢˊ ❶城郭旁、宫殿庙宇外或河边的空地 empty space outside a city wall, palace, temple, or by the river ❷用于地名 used in place names: 坑～（在江西省万年）*Kengruan (in Wannian, Jiangxi Province)*

阮 ruǎn ㄖㄨㄢˇ ❶一种弦乐器，四根弦。西晋阮咸善弹此乐器，故名阮咸，简称阮 (short for 阮咸) a Chinese stringed instrument with four strings ❷姓 (surname) Ruan

朊 ruǎn ㄖㄨㄢˇ 蛋白质的旧称 protein (former name for 蛋白质)

软(軟、*輭) ruǎn ㄖㄨㄢˇ ❶物体组织疏松，容易改变形状，跟“硬”相对（㊟柔—）soft; supple (opposite of 硬)：绸子比布～。*Silk is softer than cloth.* [软件] 1 与计算机系统的运行有关的程序、文件、数据等的统称，是计算机系统的组成部分 software 2 借指生产、科研、经营等过程中的人员素质、管理水平、服务质量等 quality of staff, management and services, etc. ❷ 柔和 gentle; mild：～风 *breeze* | ～语 *soft words* ❸ 懦弱(㊀－弱) (of character) weak; feeble：欺～怕硬 *bully the weak and fear the strong* ㊁ ①容易被感动或动摇 to be easily moved or influenced：心～ *be soft-hearted* | 耳朵～ *be credulous* ②不用强硬的手段进行 soft：～磨(mó) *wear down using soft tactics* | ～求 *to plead* ❹ 没有气力 (of physical strength) feeble; weak：两腿发～ *be weak at the knees* ❺质量差的，不高明的 poor (in quality, etc.)：功夫～ *have weak skills*

媆 ruǎn ㄖㄨㄢˇ 柔美的样子 gentle and graceful

⇨ see also nèn on p.474

瑌 ruǎn ㄖㄨㄢˇ 一种次于玉的美石 a kind of nephrite, inferior to jade

RUI ㄖㄨㄟ

蕤 ruí ㄖㄨㄟˊ see 葳蕤 (wēi－) at 葳 on page 677

蕊(*蘂、*橤、△*繠) ruǐ ㄖㄨㄟˇ 花蕊，种子植物有性生殖器官的一部分。分雄蕊和雌蕊两种 stamen; pistil

繠 ruǐ ㄖㄨㄟˇ ❶下垂的样子 drooping; sagging ❷ see 蕊 on page 566

芮 ruì ㄖㄨㄟˋ 周代诸侯国名，在今陕西省大荔东南 Rui (a state in the Zhou Dynasty, in the south-east of today's Dali, Shaanxi Province)

汭 ruì ㄖㄨㄟˋ 河流汇合的地方，河流弯曲的地方 confluence; river bend

枘 ruì ㄖㄨㄟˋ 〈古 ancient〉榫(sǔn) tenon [枘凿](－záo) 方枘圆凿，比喻意见不合 disagree with each other (literally means 'a square tenon in a round mortise')

蚋 ruì ㄖㄨㄟˋ 昆虫，略像蝇而较小，黑色，胸背隆起，雌的吸人畜的血，能传播疾病 black fly

锐(鋭) ruì ㄖㄨㄟˋ ❶快或尖(指刀枪的锋刃)，跟"钝"相对(㊀－利、尖－) sharp; keen (opposite of 钝)：其锋甚～ *with a very sharp blade* ❷感觉灵敏 sharp; keen; perceptive：敏～ *perceptive* | 眼光～利 *have sharp eyes* ❸锐气，勇往直前的气势 spirit; vigour; morale：～不可当 *be irresistable* | 养精蓄～ *build up one's strength* ❹骤，急剧 rapidly; dramatically：～减 *to slump; to plummet* | ～增 *increase rapidly*

瑞 ruì ㄖㄨㄟˋ 吉祥，好预兆 lucky; auspicious; propitious：～雪兆丰年。*A timely snow promises a good harvest.* | 祥～ *auspicious*

sign

睿(*叡) ruì ㄖㄨㄟ 通达，看得深远 far-sighted; insightful：～智 *wise and prescient*

RUN ㄖㄨㄣ

闰(閏) rùn ㄖㄨㄣ 地球公转一周的时间为365天5时48分46秒。公历规定一年365天，所余的时间约每四年积累成一天，加在二月里。农历规定一年354天或355天，所余的时间约每三年积累成一个月，加在某一年里。这样的办法在历法上叫作闰 leap; intercalary; bissextile：～年 *leap year* | ～月 *leap month*

润(潤) rùn ㄖㄨㄣ ❶湿，不干枯 moist; wet; damp：湿～ *moist; damp* | ～泽 *moist and shiny* ❷加油或水，使不干枯 to lubricate; to moisten：～肠 *lubricate the intestines* | ～～嗓子 *moisten the throat* ❸细腻光滑 smooth：珠圆玉～ *(of songs or writing) elegant and polished (literally means 'round as pearls and smooth as jade')* | 皮肤光～ *silky smooth skin* ❹使有光彩，修饰文字（㊀一饰）to polish; to touch up：～色 *to polish (a piece of writing)* ❺利益 profit; benefit：分～ *share profits* | 利～ *profit*

RUO ㄖㄨㄛ

挼 ruó ㄖㄨㄛˊ 揉搓（㊀一搓）to crumple; to knead; to rub：把纸条～成团 *crumple the note up into a ball*

⇨ see also ruá on p.565

若 ruò ㄖㄨㄛˋ ❶连词。若是，如果，假如 (conjunction) if; supposing：～不努力，就要落后。*If you don't work hard, you will be left behind.* ❷如，像 as if; like：～无其事 *as if nothing has happened* | 旁～无人 *as if nobody is around; (figurative) very self-assured* | 年相～ *similar in age* | ～有～无 *faintly discernible* ❸文言代词，你 (pronoun in classical Chinese) you; your：～辈 *you (people)*

[若干]（-gān）代词，多少（问数量或指不定量）(pronoun) how many; how much; a certain number/amount of：价值～？*How much is it?* | 关于农业的～问题 *several questions on agriculture*

鄀 ruò ㄖㄨㄛˋ ❶春秋时楚国的都城，在今湖北省宜城东南 Ruo (an ancient place name, the capital city of Chu State in the Spring and Autumn Period, in the south-east of today's Yicheng, Hubei Province) ❷用于地名 used in place names：～太（在广西壮族自治区武鸣）*Ruotai (in Wuming, the Guangxi Zhuang Autonomous Region)*

偌 ruò ㄖㄨㄛˋ 这么，那么 such; so：～大年纪 *so advanced in years*

婼 ruò ㄖㄨㄛˋ [婼羌]（-qiāng）地名，在新疆维吾尔自治区。今作“若羌” Ruoqiang

(a place in the Xinjiang Uygur Autonomous Region) (now written as 若羌)

箬(*篛) ruò ㄖㄨㄛˋ ❶箬竹，竹子的一种，叶大而宽，可编竹笠，又可用来包粽子 large-leafed bamboo ❷箬竹的叶子 leaves of large-leafed bamboo

弱 ruò ㄖㄨㄛˋ ❶力气小，势力差，跟"强"相对 weak; feeble (opposite of 强)：身体～ *physically weak* | ～小 *weak and small* | ～势群体 *the disadvantaged* | 不甘示～ *be unwilling to be outdone/outshone* ㊀不够，差一点儿 a little less than：三分之二～ *a little less than two thirds* ❷年纪小 young：老～病残 *the old, the young, the sick and the disabled* ❸丧失（指人死）lose by death：又～一个 *another person died*

蒻 ruò ㄖㄨㄛˋ 古书上指嫩的香蒲，也指用这种草编的席子 (in ancient Chinese texts) young cattail; grass mat

爇 ruò ㄖㄨㄛˋ 点燃，焚烧 to burn; to light; to ignite：焚香～烛 *burn incense and light candles*

R

S ㄙ

SA ㄙㄚ

仨 sā ㄙㄚ 三个（本字后面不能再用"个"字或其他量词）three (not to be followed by 个 or any other measure word)：他们哥儿～ *those three brothers*

撒 sā ㄙㄚ ❶放，放开 to release; to let go：～网 *cast a net* | ～手 *let go; give up* | ～腿就跑 *run off in a flash* ❷尽量施展或表现出来（多含贬义）(often disapproving) to show or express sth to the maximum effect：～娇 *behave like a spoilt child; charm by being coquettish* | ～泼 *be unreasonable and make a scene*

［撒拉族］我国少数民族，参看附录四 the Salar people (one of the ethnic groups in China. See Appendix Ⅳ.)

➪ see also sǎ on p.569

洒（灑）sǎ ㄙㄚˇ ❶把水散布在地上 to sprinkle/splash water on the ground：扫地先～些水。*Wet the floor a little before sweeping it.* ❷东西散落 to fall and scatter：～了一地粮食。*Grains were scattered all over the ground.*

［洒脱］（－tuo）言谈、举止自然，不拘束 unaffected and uninhibited (in speech and manner)：这个人很～。*This man has a natural way about him.*

靸 sǎ ㄙㄚˇ 〈方 dialect〉把布鞋后帮踩在脚后跟下，穿（拖鞋）(when wearing shoes) to stand on the backs of one's shoes; to wear (slippers)：～着鞋 *squashing the back of the shoes with one's heels*

撒 sǎ ㄙㄚˇ ❶散播，散布 to spread; to disseminate：～种 *sow seeds* ❷散落，洒 to fall and scatter; to spill：小心点，别把汤～了。*Be careful. Don't spill the soup.*

➪ see also sā on p.569

潵 sǎ ㄙㄚˇ 潵河，水名，在河北省迁西、兴隆一带 Sahe River (in the region of Qianxi and Xinglong in Hebei Province)

卅 sà ㄙㄚˋ 三十 thirty：五～运动 *the May Thirtieth Movement*

挲（攃）sà ㄙㄚˋ 侧手击 to throw a side punch

脎 sà ㄙㄚˋ 有机化合物的一类，由同一个分子内的两个羰基和两个分子的苯肼缩合而成 osazone

飒（颯、*颾）sà ㄙㄚˋ 形容风声叠 (of sound) soughing; rustling：秋风～～。*The autumn wind soughs.* ［飒爽］豪迈而矫健 bold and vigorous：～英姿 *heroic bearing*

萨(薩) sà ㄙㄚˋ 姓(surname) Sa

挲(*抄) sa ·ㄙㄚ see 摩挲(mā—) at 摩 on page 431

⇨ see also shā on p.576, suō on p.628

SAI ㄙㄞ

揌(**攓) sāi ㄙㄞ same as "塞(sāi)❶"

腮(*顋) sāi ㄙㄞ 两颊的下半部 lower part of the cheek：尖嘴猴～ *with pointed mouth and sunken cheeks*

鳃(鰓) sāi ㄙㄞ 鱼的呼吸器官，在头部两边 gills

塞 sāi ㄙㄞ ❶堵，填入 to stuff; to fill：把窟窿～住 *fill in the hole*｜往书包里～了一本书 *stuffed a book into the schoolbag* ❷(－子、－儿)堵住器物口的东西 stopper; plug：瓶～儿 *bottle stopper*｜软木～儿 *cork*

⇨ see also sài on p.570, sè on p.573

噻 sāi ㄙㄞ [噻唑](－zuò)有机化合物，无色液体，易挥发。可用来制药物和染料 thiazole

塞 sài ㄙㄞˋ 边界上的险要地方 strategic location at the border：要～ *strategic pass; fortress*｜～外 *area beyond the Great Wall*

⇨ see also sāi on p.570, sè on p.573

赛(賽) sài ㄙㄞˋ ❶比较好坏、强弱 to compete; to contest：～跑 *running race*｜～歌会 *singing competition*｜田径～ *track and field competition* ❷胜似 to be better than：一个～一个 *each better than the last* ㊕比得上 comparable to：小玩意儿～真的。*This little toy is just like the real thing.*｜那人足智多谋，人称～诸葛。*That man, wise and full of strategies, is known as a 'veritable Zhuge Liang'. (Zhuge Liang was a famous strategist and statesman during the Three Kingdoms Period.)* ❸旧时举行祭典酬报神灵 (old) thanksgiving ritual：～神 *thanksgiving ritual for the gods*｜～会 *religious festival with parades and floats*

SAN ㄙㄢ

三 sān ㄙㄢ 数目字(number) three ㊀表示再三、多次 repeated; multiple：～令五申 *repeated orders and warnings*｜～番五次 *multiple times*

弎 sān ㄙㄢ same as "三"

叁 sān ㄙㄢ "三"字的大写 (elaborate form of 三, used in commercial or financial context) three

毵(毿) sān ㄙㄢ [毵毵] 毛发、枝条等细长的样子 (of hair, twigs, etc.) long and thin：柳枝～。*The weeping willow branches are long and thin.*

伞(繖、*傘、❶*繖) sǎn ㄙㄢˇ ❶挡雨或遮太阳的用具，可张可收 umbrella; parasol：雨～ *umbrella* | 阳～ *parasol* ❷像伞的东西 sth like an umbrella：灯～ *lampshade* | 降落～ *parachute* | 滑翔～ *paraglider*

散(*散) sǎn ㄙㄢˇ ❶没有约束，松开 unrestrained; to loosen：披～着头发 *let one's hair down* | 绳子～了。*The rope is loose.* [散漫]随随便便，不守纪律 slack undisciplined：自由～ *unrestrained* | 生活～ *undisciplined lifestyle* [散文]文体的名称，对"韵文"而言，不用韵，字句不求整齐。现多指杂文、随笔、特写等文学作品 prose; essay (opposite of 韵文) ❷零碎的，不集中的 scattered：～装 *unpackaged; in bulk* | ～居 *live in different locations* | 零零～～ *scattered* ❸药末(多用于中药名)(often in names of traditional Chinese medicine) powdered medicine：丸～膏丹 *pill, powder, ointment and tablet (the four types of traditional Chinese medicinal preparation)* | 健胃～ *stomach powders*

⇨ see also sàn on p.571

馓(饊) sǎn ㄙㄢˇ 馓子，一种油炸食品 a kind of deep-fried food

糁(糝) sǎn ㄙㄢˇ 〈方 dialect〉米粒(指煮熟的)(cooked) grains of rice

⇨ see also shēn on p.589

散(*散) sàn ㄙㄢˋ ❶分开，由聚集而分离 to disperse; to separate：～会 *meeting is over* | 云彩～了。*The clouds have dispersed.* ❷分布，分给 to distribute：～传单 *distribute handbills* | 撒种(zhǒng)～粪 *sow seeds and spread fertiliser* ❸排遣 to dispel; to drive away：～心 *relieve boredom* | ～闷 *relieve boredom*

⇨ see also sǎn on p.571

SANG ㄙㄤ

丧(喪、**丧) sāng ㄙㄤ 跟死了人有关的事 funeral; mourning：～事 *funeral* | 治～ *make funeral arrangements*

⇨ see also sàng on p.571

桑(*桒) sāng ㄙㄤ 落叶乔木，叶卵形，花黄绿色。果实叫桑葚，味甜可吃。叶可喂蚕，木材可制器具，皮可造纸 mulberry

搡 sǎng ㄙㄤˇ 猛推 to shove; to thrust：连推带～ *push and shove* | 把他～一个跟头 *pushed him to the ground*

嗓 sǎng ㄙㄤˇ ❶(一子)喉咙 throat ❷(一儿)发音器官的声带及发出的声音 voice：～门儿 *voice* | 哑～儿 *hoarse voice*

磉 sǎng ㄙㄤˇ 柱子底下的石礅 (of a column) plinth

颡(顙) sǎng ㄙㄤˇ 额，脑门子 forehead

丧(喪、**丧) sàng ㄙㄤˋ 丢掉，失

去（㊈—失）to lose：～命 *to die*｜～失立场 *lose one's standpoint* ［丧气］1 情绪低落 low spirits：灰心～ *discouraged and disheartened* 2（—qi）不吉利，倒霉 unlucky：钱包丢了，真～！*(I) was unfortunate enough to lose (my) wallet.*

➪ see also sāng on p.571

SAO ㄙㄠ

搔 sāo ㄙㄠ 用指甲挠 to scratch (with one's fingernails)：～痒 *scratch an itch*

溞 sāo ㄙㄠ 水蚤 water flea

骚（騷）sāo ㄙㄠ ❶扰乱，不安定（㊈—扰）to disturb; to upset：～动 *disturbance; commotion*｜～乱 *riot* ❷ same as "臊(sāo)" ❸指屈原著的《离骚》short for《离骚》(a long poem by Qu Yuan) ［骚人］诗人 poet ［风骚］1 泛指文学 (generally) literature 2 妇女举止轻佻 (of a woman) coquettish; vampish

缫（繅）sāo ㄙㄠ 把蚕茧浸在滚水里抽丝 to reel (silk from cocoons)：～丝 *reel silk*｜～车（缫丝用的器具）*reeling machine*

缲（繰）sāo ㄙㄠ same as "缫"

➪ see also qiāo on p.533

臊 sāo ㄙㄠ 像尿那样难闻的气味 sharp, fetid smell (like urine)：尿～气 *stench of urine*｜狐～ *body odour*

➪ see also sào on p.572

扫（掃）sǎo ㄙㄠˇ ❶拿笤帚等除去尘土 to sweep; to clean up：～地 *sweep the floor* ❷像扫一样的动作或作用 sweeping motion or effect ①消除 to eliminate：～兴（xìng）*have one's spirits dampened*｜～雷 *remove mines*｜～盲 *eliminate illiteracy* ②左右快速移动 to move quickly from side to side：～射 *spray gunfire*｜眼睛四下里一～ *glanced all around* ③全，所有的 all; total：～数归还 *return in full*

➪ see also sào on p.572

嫂 sǎo ㄙㄠˇ（—子）哥哥的妻子 ㊂ wife of older brother：二～ *wife of second oldest brother*｜～夫人 *(polite speech) your wife*

扫（掃）sào ㄙㄠˋ ［扫帚］（—zhou）一种用竹枝等做的扫地用具 broom

➪ see also sǎo on p.572

埽 sào ㄙㄠˋ ❶治理河道的工程上用的材料，以竹木为框架，用树枝、石子、土填实其中，做成柱形，用以堵水 fascine ❷用许多埽修成的临时性堤坝或护堤 fascine embankment

瘙 sào ㄙㄠˋ ［瘙痒］皮肤发痒 itch

臊 sào ㄙㄠˋ 难为情，害羞 shy; embarrassed：害～ *shy*｜～得脸通红 *blush with embarrassment*｜不知羞～ *shameless*

➪ see also sāo on p.572

S

SE ㄙㄜ

色 sè ㄙㄜ ❶颜色，由物体发射、反射的光通过视觉而产生的印象 colour：日光有七～。*Sunlight has seven colours.*｜红～ *red* ❷脸色，脸上表现出的神情、样子 countenance; expression：和颜悦～ *have a kind face*｜喜形于～ *be radiant with joy* ❸情景，景象 view; scene：行～匆匆 *set out in haste* ❹种类 kind; sort：各～用品 *all types of articles for use*｜货～齐全 *comprehensive range of goods and products* ❺成色，品质，质量 quality：足～纹银 *the purest fine silver*｜成～ *purity* ❻妇女的容貌 woman's appearance：姿～ *(of a woman) good looks* ❼指情欲 lust; sexual desire：～情 *pornographic*｜好～ *lecherous*｜贪～ *given to lust*

⇨ see also shǎi on p.576

铯(銫) sè ㄙㄜ 金属元素，符号 Cs，银白色，质软。用于制光电池和火箭推进器等 caesium (Cs)

涩(澀、*澁、*濇) sè ㄙㄜ ❶不光滑，不滑溜 rough; unsmooth：轮轴发～，该上点儿油了。*The axle is not turning smoothly; it needs lubricating.* ❷一种使舌头感到不滑润不好受的味道 (taste) astringent：这柿子很～。*This persimmon has a very astringent taste.* ❸文章难读难懂 (of writing) abstruse：文字艰～ *abstruse writing*

啬(嗇) sè ㄙㄜ 小气，当用的财物舍不得用（㊀吝－）stingy; penny-pinching

穑(穡) sè ㄙㄜ 收割庄稼 to harvest

瑟 sè ㄙㄜ 古代的一种弦乐器，通常有二十五根弦 an ancient stringed musical instrument, usually with 25 strings［瑟瑟］1 形容轻微的声音 used to describe soft sounds：秋风～ *autumn wind soughs* 2 形容颤抖 used to describe trembling：～发抖 *be trembling*

璱 sè ㄙㄜ 玉色鲜明洁净 (of jadeite) bright and clear

塞 sè ㄙㄜ 义同"塞(sāi)❶"，用于某些合成词或成语中，如"闭塞、堵塞、阻塞、塞责、闭目塞听"等 same in meaning as 塞 (sāi) ❶, used in certain compounds or idioms like 闭塞，堵塞，阻塞，塞责，闭目塞听，etc.

⇨ see also sāi on p.570, sài on p.570

SEN ㄙㄣ

森 sēn ㄙㄣ 树木众多 thickly wooded：～林 forest［森森］形容树木众多，深密 (of trees) dense; thick：林木～ *dense forest* ㊑气氛寂静可怕 gloomy; gruesome：阴～的 *gloomy and horrid*

［森严］整齐严肃，防备严密 stringent：戒备～ *heavyly guarded*

S

SENG ㄙㄥ

僧 sēng ㄙㄥ 梵语音译"僧伽"的省称。佛教指出家修行的男人，和尚 (short for 僧伽, from Sanskrit) Buddhist monk

SHA ㄕㄚ

杀(殺) shā ㄕㄚ ❶使人或动物失去生命 to kill：～敌立功 *render meritorious service by killing enemies* | ～虫药 *insecticide* | ～鸡焉用牛刀。*Why use a hammer to break an egg? (literally means 'Why use a cow knife to kill a chicken?')* ❷战斗 to go into battle; to fight：厮～ *to fight at close quarters* | 搏～ *to fight and kill* | ～出重（chóng）围 *break out of a heavy siege* ❸消减 to reduce：～价 *force down the price sharply* | ～暑气 *(in hot weather) cool down* | 拿别人～气 *vent one's anger on others* ❹〈方 dialect〉药物等刺激身体感觉疼痛 to sting; to smart (from the effects of medicine, etc.)：这药上在疮口上～得慌。*This medicine is causing the open sore to sting badly.* ❺收束 to bring to a close：～尾 *signal the end* | ～账 *close the account* ❻勒紧，扣紧 to fasten tightly：～车（把车上装载的东西用绳勒紧）*secure the cargo on a vehicle tightly with rope* | ～一～腰带 *tighten the belt* ❼在动词或形容词后，表示程度深 used after verb or adjective to indicate intensity：气～ *very annoyed* | 急～ *very anxious* | 笑～人 *very funny*

刹 shā ㄕㄚ 止住（车、机器等）to brake (vehicles, machines, etc.)：～车 *brake; to brake*

➪ see also chà on p.64

铩(鎩) shā ㄕㄚ ❶古代一种兵器，长柄，锋端有双刃 ancient weapon with a long handle and two blades on its tip ❷摧残，伤害 to harm; to wrench：～羽之鸟（伤了翅膀的鸟，喻失意的人）*bird with an injured wing; (figuratively) a person with frustrated hopes and ambitions*

杉 shā ㄕㄚ 义同"杉"(shān)，用于"杉木、杉篙"等 same in meaning as 杉 (shān), used in 杉木, 杉篙, etc.

➪ see also shān on p.576

沙 shā ㄕㄚ ❶（一子）非常细碎的石粒 sand：～土 *sandy soil* | ～滩 *beach* ❷像沙子的东西 sth like sand：蚕～（桑蚕的粪）*silkworm excrement* | 豆～ *sweetened bean paste* | ～瓤西瓜 *watermelon with grainy pulp* ❸声音不清脆不响亮 (of sound) hoarse：～哑 *hoarse* ❹姓 (surname) Sha

➪ see also shà on p.575

莎 shā ㄕㄚ 多用于人名、地名 often used in given names or place names [莎车] 地名，在新疆维吾尔自治区 Shache (a place in Xinjiang Uygur Autonomous Region)

➪ see also suō on p.628

S

痧 shā ㄕㄚ 中医指霍乱、中暑、肠炎等急性病 (in traditional Chinese medicine) acute diseases such as cholera, sunstroke, enteritis, etc.: 发～ *suffer from heatstroke or other acute diseases* | 绞肠～ *cholera* | 刮～ *(in traditional Chinese medicine) scraping therapy*

裟 shā ㄕㄚ see 袈裟 (jiā—) at 袈 on page 295

鲨 (鯊) shā ㄕㄚ 鱼名，又叫鲛，身体近纺锤形，性凶猛，捕食其他鱼类，生活在海洋里。种类很多。鳍制成的食物叫鱼翅。肝可制鱼肝油 shark (also called 鲛)

纱 (紗) shā ㄕㄚ ❶用棉花、麻等纺成的细缕，可以用它捻成线或织成布 yarn: 纺～ *spinning yarn* ❷经纬线稀疏或有小孔的织品 gauze; voile: 羽～ *camlet* | ～布 *gauze* ㊀像纱布的制品 products that resemble gauze: 铁～ *wire gauze* | 塑料窗～ *plastic window screen*

砂 shā ㄕㄚ same as "沙 (shā) ❶❷"

煞 shā ㄕㄚ ❶same as "杀❸❺❻❼" ❷same as "刹 (shā)"

⇨ see also shà on p.575

啥 shá ㄕㄚˊ 〈方 dialect〉代词，什么 (pronoun) what: 干～? *What are (you) doing?* | 你姓～? *What is your surname?* | 他是～地方人? *Where is he from?*

傻 (**儍) shǎ ㄕㄚˇ ❶愚蠢，糊涂 foolish; muddle-headed: 说～话 *say foolish things* | 吓～了 *be scared stiff* ❷死心眼 stubborn: 这样好的事你都不干，真～。*How foolish of you to refuse to do such a good thing.*

沙 shà ㄕㄚˋ 经过摇动把东西里的杂物集中，以便清除 to shake (to gather the unwanted bits together in sth for easy disposal): 把小米里的沙子～一～。*Shake the millet to gather the sand together.*

⇨ see also shā on p.574

唼 shà ㄕㄚˋ [唼喋] (—zhá) 形容鱼、鸟等吃东西的声音 used to describe the sound of fish, birds, etc. eating

厦 (*廈) shà ㄕㄚˋ ❶大屋子 big house: 广～ *large building* | 高楼大～ *tall buildings* ❷房子后面突出的部分 back veranda: 前廊后～ *front and rear verandas*

⇨ see also xià on p.705

嗄 shà ㄕㄚˋ 嗓音嘶哑 (of voice) hoarse

⇨ see also á on p.1

歃 shà ㄕㄚˋ 用嘴吸取 to suck [歃血] 古人盟会时饮牲畜的血，表示诚意 solemnize an oath by drinking animal blood in ancient times

煞 shà ㄕㄚˋ ❶极，很 extremely; very: ～费苦心 *make a painstaking effort* | 脸色～白 *extremely pale face* ❷迷信的人指凶神 (in superstition) wrathful spirit: ～气 *an air of evil* | 凶～ *fierce demon*

⇨ see also shā on p.575

S

箑 shà ㄕㄚˋ 扇子 fan (cooling device)

霎 shà ㄕㄚˋ 小雨。也指轻微的风雨声 drizzle; light rain; faint sound of wind and rain

[霎时] 极短的时间，一会ㄦ an instant

挲(*挱) sha ·ㄕㄚ see 挓挲 (zhā—) at 挓 on page 825

⇨ see also sɑ on p.570, suō on p.628

SHAI ㄕㄞ

筛(篩) shāi ㄕㄞ ❶（一子）用竹子等做成的一种有孔的器具，可以把细的东西漏下去，粗的留下 sieve; sift ❷用筛子过东西 to sieve; to sift：～米 *sieve rice* | ～煤 *sieve coal* ⓨ挑选后淘汰 select and then eliminate：把不合格的人～出去 *screen out unqualified people* ❸敲（锣）to beat (a gong)：～了三下锣 *beat the gong three times*

[筛酒] 1 斟酒 to pour liquor 2 把酒弄热 to heat up liquor

酾(釃) shāi ㄕㄞ（又）see shī on page 596

色 shǎi ㄕㄞˇ （一ㄦ）义同"色"（sè），用于一些口语词 (used in some spoken expressions) same in meaning as 色 (sè)：落（lào）～ㄦ *fading of colour* | 掉～ *lose colour* | 不变～ㄦ *colour does not change*

⇨ see also sè on p.573

晒(曬) shài ㄕㄞˋ ❶把东西放在太阳光下使它干燥，人或物在阳光下吸收光和热 to sun：～衣服 *put the clothes out in the sun* | ～太阳 *bask in the sun* ⓨ对人置之不理 to ignore sb：把来访者～在一旁 *ignore one's visitors* ❷（外 *loanword*）展示，多指在网络上公开透露（自己的信息）to display (usually one's own information online)：～工资 *show off one's salary* | ～隐私 *reveal private matters*

SHAN ㄕㄢ

山 shān ㄕㄢ ❶地面上由土石构成的高起的部分 mountain; hill：爬～ *climb mountain* | ～高水深 *high mountains and deep waters* | 人～人海（形容人多）*very crowded* ❷蚕蔟 bundle of straw for silkworms to spin cocoons on：蚕上～了。*The silkworms have nested in the straw bundle.* ❸山墙，房屋两头的墙 gable walls：房～ *gable of a house*

舢 shān ㄕㄢ [舢板]（*舢舨）一种用桨划的小船 sampan

芟 shān ㄕㄢ 割草 to cut (grass)：～草 *cut grass* ⓨ除去 to remove：～剪繁枝 *prune excess branches*

杉 shān ㄕㄢ 常绿乔木，树干高而直，叶呈针状，果实球形。木材供建筑和制器具用 China fir

⇨ see also shā on p.574

钐(釤) shān ㄕㄢ 放射性金属元素，符号 Sm，银白色，质硬。可用来制激光材料，也用于核工业、陶瓷工

业 samarium (Sm)

⇨ see also shàn on p.578

衫 shān ㄕㄢ 上衣，单褂 shirt; unlined upper garment：长～ *long tunic worn by men* | 衬～ *shirt*

删（*刪）shān ㄕㄢ 除去，去掉文字中不妥当的部分 to delete (words)：～改 *make deletions and changes (to texts)* | ～除 *to delete* | 这个字应～去。*This character should be deleted.*

姗（*姍）shān ㄕㄢ ［姗姗］形容走路缓慢从容 (walk) with an unhurried and calm gait：～来迟 *arrive late yet unflustered*

珊（*珊）shān ㄕㄢ ［珊瑚］一种腔肠动物所分泌的石灰质的东西，形状像树枝，有红、白等色，可以做装饰品。这种腔肠动物叫珊瑚虫 coral

栅（*柵）shān ㄕㄢ ［栅极］电子管靠阴极的一个电极 grid (of an electrode)

⇨ see also zhà on p.828

跚 shān ㄕㄢ see 蹒跚 (pán－) at 蹒 on page 491

苫 shān ㄕㄢ 草帘子，草垫子 reed curtain; reed mat：草～子 *reed mat*

⇨ see also shàn on p.578

痁 shān ㄕㄢ 〈古 ancient〉疟疾 malaria

埏 shān ㄕㄢ 用水和（huó）泥 to knead a mixture of clay and water

⇨ see also yán on p.750

烻 shān ㄕㄢ 闪光的样子 shining

⇨ see also yàn on p.755

扇（❶❷**搧）shān ㄕㄢ ❶摇动扇子或其他东西，使空气加速流动生风 to fan：～扇子 *wave a fan* ❷用手掌打 to slap：～了他一耳光 *slapped his face* ❸ same as "煽❷"

⇨ see also shàn on p.579

煽 shān ㄕㄢ ❶ same as "扇 (shān) ❶" ❷鼓动（别人做不应该做的事）to instigate; to incite：～动 *to instigate* | ～惑 *to incite and lure*

潸（**潸）shān ㄕㄢ 流泪的样子 ㊀ in tears; tearful：不禁（jīn）～～ *cannot help but shed tears* | ～然泪下 *shed tears*

膻（*羶、*羴）shān ㄕㄢ 像羊肉的气味 (of smell) goatish; hircine：～气 *hircine odour* | ～味儿 *muttony smell; muttony taste*

闪（閃）shǎn ㄕㄢˇ ❶天空的电光 lightning：打～ *(of lightning) to flash* ❷突然显现或忽明忽暗 to appear suddenly; to flash：灯光一～ *light flashes* | ～念 *a flash of thought* | 山后～出一条小路来。*Behind the mountain a small path suddenly appears.* | ～得眼发花 *flash so much that one's eyes are dazzled* ❸光辉闪耀 to shimmer; to shine：～金光 *shimmering golden light* | 电～雷鸣 *lightning flashes and thunder roars* ❹侧转身体躲避 to dodge:

～开 *get out of the way* ❺ 因动作过猛，筋肉扭伤而疼痛 to sprain：～了腰 *sprained one's lower back*

陕(陝) shǎn ㄕㄢˇ 陕西省的简称 short for Shaanxi Province

睒(**䀹) shǎn ㄕㄢˇ 眨，眼睛很快地开闭 to blink：飞机一～眼就不见了。*The aircraft disappeared in the blink of an eye.*

睒 shǎn ㄕㄢˇ ❶闪电 lightning ❷晶莹的样子 crystal-clear

讪(訕) shàn ㄕㄢˋ ❶讥笑 to sneer：～笑 *to ridicule; to mock* ❷难为情的样子 embarrassed：脸上发～ *look embarrassed* | 他～～地走了。*He walked away, embarrassed.* [搭讪] 为了想跟人接近或把尴尬的局面敷衍过去而找话说 to make small talk (to get close to sb or smooth over an awkward situation)

汕 shàn ㄕㄢˋ [汕头] 地名，在广东省 Shantou (a place in Guangdong Province)

疝 shàn ㄕㄢˋ 疝气，病名，指某一脏器通过周围组织较薄弱的地方鼓起来。种类很多，通常指小肠疝气 hernia

赸 shàn ㄕㄢˋ ❶躲开，走开 to avoid; to leave ❷ same as "讪❷"

苫 shàn ㄕㄢˋ 用席、布等遮盖 to cover (with a mat, cloth, etc.)：拿席～上点儿。*Cover it with a mat.*

⇨ see also shān on p.577

钐(釤、**鐥、**鐥) shàn ㄕㄢˋ 抡开镰刀或钐镰割 to cut (with a sickle or a scythe)：～草 *cut the grass* | ～麦 *cut the wheat* [钐镰] [钐刀] 一种把儿很长的大镰刀 scythe

⇨ see also shān on p.576

单(單) shàn ㄕㄢˋ ❶单县，在山东省 Shanxian (in Shandong Province) ❷姓 (surname) Shan

⇨ see also chán on p.65, dān on p.114

墠(墠) shàn ㄕㄢˋ 古代祭祀用的平地 flat ground used for making religious offerings in ancient times

掸(撣) shàn ㄕㄢˋ ❶我国史书上对傣族的一种称呼 Shan (a name for the Dai people in Chinese historical writings) ❷掸族，缅甸民族之一，大部分居住在掸邦（缅甸自治邦之一）the Shan people (one of the ethnic groups in Myanmar mostly living in Myanmar's Shan State)

⇨ see also dǎn on p.115

禅(禪) shàn ㄕㄢˋ 禅让，指古代帝王让位给别人，如尧让位给舜，舜让位给禹 to abdicate the throne in favour of another person

⇨ see also chán on p.66

剡 shàn ㄕㄢˋ 剡溪，水名，在浙江省东北部 Shanxi (a river in the northeast of Zhejiang Province)

S

⇨ see also yǎn on p.753

掞 shàn ㄕㄢˋ 舒展，铺张 to spread out

⇨ see also yàn on p.755

扇 shàn ㄕㄢˋ ❶（—子）摇动、转动以生风取凉或换气的用具 fan (for cooling or ventilation)：折～ *folding fan* | 蒲～ *palm-leaf fan* | 电～ *electric fan* ❷量词，用于门窗等 measure word for doors, windows, etc.：一～门 *a door* | 两～窗户 *two windows* | 一～磨（mò）*a millstone*

⇨ see also shān on p.577

骟（騸） shàn ㄕㄢˋ 割掉牲畜的睾丸或卵巢 to neuter; to spay：～马 *spayed horse; gelding* | ～猪 *barrow; spayed sow*

善 shàn ㄕㄢˋ ❶善良，品质或言行好 kind; good-natured; well-mannered：心～ *kind-hearted* | ～举 *charitable act* | ～事 *good deeds; charity* ❷好的事情、行为、品质，跟"恶"相对 good; moral (opposite of 恶)：行～ *do good deeds* | 劝～规过 *advocate good deeds and warn against wrongdoing* ❸交好，和好 amiable; friendly：友～ *friendly* | 相～ *be friendly to each other* ㊀熟习 familiar：面～ *look familiar* ❹高明的，良好的 clever; wise：～策 *clever plan* [善后] 妥善地料理和解决事故、事件发生以后的问题 to resolve problems arising from an accident/incident ❺长(cháng)于，能做好 to be good at：勇敢～战 *brave and good at fighting* | ～辞令（长于讲话）*be eloquent* ㊀好好地 in a good way; well：～待 *treat sb/sth well* | ～为说辞 *put in a good word for sb* ❻爱，容易 be inclined to; easily：～变 *capricious* | ～疑 *get suspicious easily*

鄯 shàn ㄕㄢˋ [鄯善] 1 古代西域国名 Shanshan (ancient kingdom in the Western Regions) 2 地名，在新疆维吾尔自治区 Shanshan (a place in Xinjiang Uygur Autonomous Region)

墡 shàn ㄕㄢˋ 白色黏土 white clay

缮（繕） shàn ㄕㄢˋ ❶修缮，修补，整治 to repair; to mend ❷抄写 (in writing) to copy：～写 *(in writing) to copy*

膳（*饍） shàn ㄕㄢˋ 饭食 meal：晚～ *dinner* | ～费 *meal expenses*

蟮 shàn ㄕㄢˋ [曲蟮]（qū—）蚯蚓，也作"蛐蟮" earthworm (also written as 蛐蟮)

鳝（鱔、*鱓） shàn ㄕㄢˋ 鱼名，通常指黄鳝，外形像蛇，身体黄色有黑斑 Asian swamp eel

擅 shàn ㄕㄢˋ ❶超越职权，独断独行 to overstep one's authority; to act in a dictatorial manner：专～ *dictatorial* | ～自 *act on one's own accord* | ～离职守 *leave one's post without permission* ❷专于某种学术或技能 be specialised：～长数学 *be good at mathematics* | 不～辞令 *be ineloquent*

嬗 shàn ㄕㄢˋ 更替，变迁 to evolve; to change：～变

transmutation; evolution

嶦 shàn ㄕㄢˋ 山坡 (of a mountain) slope

赡(贍) shàn ㄕㄢˋ ❶供给人财物 to provide for：～养父母 *provide for one's parents* ❷富足，足够 affluent; sufficient：家道颇～ *have quite a wealthy family*

SHANG ㄕㄤ

伤(傷) shāng ㄕㄤ ❶身体受损坏的地方 injury：腿上有块～。*There's an injury on one's leg.* | 内～ *internal injury* | 外～ *external injury* ❷损害 to injure：～了筋骨 *injured one's bones and muscles* | ～脑筋（费思索）*knotty; troublesome* ❸因某种致病因素而得病 to get sick due to sth：～风 *catch a cold* | ～寒 *(in traditional Chinese medicine) illness caused by cold temperatures; (in modern medicine) typhoid fever* ❹因过度而感到厌烦 to be fed up with sth：吃糖吃～了 *be sick of eating sweets* ❺妨碍 to hinder; to spoil：无～大雅 *involve no major principle* ❻悲哀(㊥悲－) sadness：～感 *sentimental* | ～心 *be sad* ❼得罪 to offend：～众 *offend many people* | 开口～人 *offend sb with one's words*

汤(湯) shāng ㄕㄤ ［汤汤］水流大而急 (of water) gushing：浩浩～～，横无际涯。*The vast surging waters stretch endlessly into the distance.*

⇨ see also tāng on p.638

殇(殤) shāng ㄕㄤ ❶还没到成年就死了 to die before reaching maturity ❷指战死者 those who die in battle (esp. for their country)：国～ *national martyr*

觞(觴) shāng ㄕㄤ 古代喝酒用的器物 a type of wine cup in ancient times：举～称贺 *lift a cup in congratulation*

商 shāng ㄕㄤ ❶商量，两个以上的人在一起计划，讨论 to discuss：面～ *discuss face-to-face* | 有事相～ *have something to discuss* ❷生意，买卖 business; trade：～业 *commerce* | ～品 *merchandise* | 通～ *have trade relations* | 经～ *engage in business* ［商标］企业用来使自己的产品或服务与其他企业的产品或服务相区别的具有明显特征的标志 trademark ❸商人，做买卖的人 trader; business person：布～ *cloth trader* | 富～ *rich business person* ❹商数，除法运算的得数 quotient：八被二除～数是四。*The quotient of eight divided by two is four.* ❺用某数做商 (a number) to be the quotient：二除八～四。*Eight divided by two yields four.* ❻商代，成汤所建立（公元前 1600—公元前 1046 年），盘庚迁殷后，又称殷代（公元前 1300—公元前 1046 年）Shang Dynasty (1600—1046 BC, founded by Cheng Tang; also known as Yin Dynasty after Pan Geng moved the capital to Yin in 1300 BC) ❼古代五音“宫、

商、角（jué）、徵（zhǐ）、羽”之一 *shang* (one of the five notes in the ancient Chinese pentatonic scale) ❽星宿名，即心宿，二十八宿之一 *shang* (one of the twenty-eight constellations in ancient Chinese astronomy)

墒（**暘）shāng ㄕㄤ 田地里土壤的湿度 moisture (in soil)：抢～ *rush to plant sth when the soil is damp* | 保～ *lock the moisture in the soil* | 底～ *moisture of the soil before sowing* | ～情 *moisture status of the soil*

熵 shāng ㄕㄤ 为了衡量热力体系中不能利用的热能，用温度除热能所得的商 (in thermodynamics) entropy

上 shǎng ㄕㄤˇ “上声”（shàng —）的“上”的又音 another pronunciation of 上 in 上声 (shàng—) (see 上 shàng ❿ on page 581)

垧 shǎng ㄕㄤˇ 旧时地积单位，各地不同。在东北地区1垧一般合15亩 a traditional Chinese unit for measuring area that varies by region (1 垧 equals 15 亩 in northeastern China.)

晌 shǎng ㄕㄤˇ ❶一天内的一段时间，一会儿a period in a day; a while：工作了半～ *worked for a long while* | 停了一～ *stopped for a moment* ❷晌午（wu），正午 noon：睡～觉 *take an afternoon nap* | 歇～ *take an afternoon nap/rest*

赏（賞）shǎng ㄕㄤˇ ❶指地位高的人或长辈给地位低的人或晚辈财物（㊀—赐）to grant; to bestow (when a senior or socially superior person gives sth to their junior or social inferior)：～给他一匹马 *reward him with a horse* ❷敬辞 polite speech：～光（请对方接受自己的邀请）*please accept my invitation* | ～脸 *honour sb (by being present or accepting the gift)* ❸奖励（㊀奖—）to reward：～罚分明 *be impartial in reward and punishment* ❹奖赏的东西 reward：领～ *receive one's reward* | 悬～ *offer a reward* ❺玩赏，因爱好（hào）某种东西而观看 to enjoy; take delight in：欣～ *to appreciate* | 鉴～ *to appreciate (art, etc.)* | 雅俗共～ *enjoyed by both highbrows and lowbrows* [赏识] 认识到别人的才能或作品的价值而予以重视或赞扬 recognize the worth of ; think highly of

上 shàng ㄕㄤˋ ❶位置在高处的，跟“下”相对 up; above (opposite of 下)：山～ *up on the mountain* | ～面 *above* ㊁①次序在前的 previous：～篇 *previous section* | ～卷 *the previous volumn* | ～星期 *last week* ②等级高的 (of class/grade) high：～等 *high grade* | ～级 *one's superior* ③质量高的，好的 (of quality) high; top：～策 *the best plan* | ～等货 *high quality goods* ❷由低处到高处 to go up：～山 *go up the mountain* | ～楼 *go upstairs* ㊁①去，到 to go：你～哪儿？～北京。*Where are you going? I'm going to Beijing.* | ～街去 *go shopping;*

S

take to the street ②向前进 to advance：同志们快～啊！ *Charge, comrades!* ③进呈 to submit; to present：～书 *submit a written statement*｜谨～ *(used at the end of a letter) Respectfully yours, ...* ❸增加 to increase ①添补 to fill; to replenish：～水 *add water*｜～货 *buy more goods; increase inventory* ②安装 to install：～刺刀 *fix a bayonet*｜～螺丝 *tighten the screw* ③涂上 to smear; to apply：～颜色 *apply colour*｜～药 *apply medicine* ④登载，记上 to be published; to be recorded：～报 *appear in a newspaper*｜～光荣榜 *be on an honours list*｜～账 *enter in an account* ❹按规定时间进行某种活动 to do sth according to a fixed schedule：～课 *attend class*｜～班 *go to work* ❺拧紧发条 to tighten; to wind：～弦 *wind up (a clock, watch, etc.)*｜表该～了。*The watch needs winding up.* ❻放在名词后 used after a noun ①表示在某一物体的表面 on：地～ *on the floor/ground*｜墙～ *on the wall*｜桌子～ *on the table* ②表示在中间 in the middle：半路～ *on the way*｜心～ *in one's heart* ③表示在某一事物的范围内 within; during：会～ *during a meeting*｜书～ *in a book* ④表示方面 in terms of; with respect to：组织～ *in terms of an organisation*｜思想～ *ideologically*｜理论～ *theoretically* ❼在动词后，表示完成 used after a verb to indicate completion：选～代表 *be chosen as a representative*｜排～队 *line* ❽在动词后 used after a verb ①跟"来""去"连用，表示趋向 used with 来 or 去 to indicate inclination/direction：骑～去 *mount up*｜爬～来 *climb up* ②表示要求达到目标或已达到目标 indicating a wish to reach a goal, or that a goal has been reached：锁～锁 *lock up*｜沏～茶 *brew tea*｜考～大学 *gained admission to a university* ❾达到一定程度或数量 to reach a certain extent or quantity：～档次 *reach a high grade*｜成千～万 *thousands upon thousands* ❿（又 shǎng）上声，汉语四声之一。普通话上声的调子是拐弯的，先降低再升高，符号作"ˇ" one of the four tones in Chinese. In Putonghua, it falls and then rises (ˇ).

尚 shàng ㄕㄤˋ ❶还（hái）still：年纪～小 *still young*｜～不可知 *still unknown*［尚且］连词，常跟"何况"连用，表示进一层的意思 (conjunction, often used with 何况) even：你～不行，何况是我。*Even you can't do it, let alone me.*｜细心～难免出错，何况粗枝大叶。*Even a careful person makes mistakes, let alone a careless one.* ❷尊崇，注重 to venerate; to attach importance to：～武 *venerate martial matters*｜崇～ *to advocate; to uphold*［高尚］崇高 noble; lofty ❸风气习惯 customs; conventions：时～ *trend; fashion*｜风～ *prevailing custom*

绱（緔、**鞝）shàng ㄕㄤˋ 把鞋帮、

鞋底缝合成鞋 to make a shoe (by sewing the upper to the sole)：～鞋 *sew a shoe*

裳 shang ·ㄕㄤ ［衣裳］衣服 clothes

⇨ see also cháng on p.70

SHAO ㄕㄠ

捎 shāo ㄕㄠ 捎带，顺便给别人带东西 deliver sth in passing：～封信去 *deliver a letter on one's way*

梢 shāo ㄕㄠ （一儿）树枝的末端 tip (of a tree branch)：树～ *tree top* ㊀末尾 end; tip：眉～ *tip of one's eyebrow*

稍 shāo ㄕㄠ 副词，略微（㊀一微）(adverb) slightly：～有不同 *slightly different* | 请～等一下。*Please wait a moment.*

⇨ see also shào on p.584

蛸 shāo ㄕㄠ see 蠨蛸 (xiāo—) at 蠨 on page 717, and 虷 (bā) 蛸岛 at 虷 on page 11

⇨ see also xiāo on p.716

筲（*籍） shāo ㄕㄠ ❶一种竹器 a type of bamboo container ❷桶 pail; bucket：水～ *water bucket* | 一～水 *a bucket of water*

艄 shāo ㄕㄠ ❶船尾 stern (of a boat) ❷舵 rudder; helm：掌～ *take the helm* ［艄公］掌舵的人，泛指船夫 helmsman; (generally) boatman

鞘 shāo ㄕㄠ 鞭鞘，拴在鞭子头上的细皮条 (of a whip) thong

［乌鞘岭］岭名，在甘肃省天祝 Wushaoling (a mountain range in Tianzhu, Gansu Province)

⇨ see also qiào on p.535

烧（燒） shāo ㄕㄠ ❶使东西着火（㊀燃一、焚一）to burn; to set sth on fire ❷用火或发热的东西使物品受热起变化 to heat：～水 *boil water* | ～砖 *fire tiles* | ～炭 *light charcoal* ❸烹饪方法，先用油炸再加入汤汁炒或炖，或先煮熟再炸 to stew after frying; to fry after stewing：～茄子 *braised aubergine* | ～羊肉 *braised mutton* ❹发烧，体温增高 to have a fever：打完针就不～了。*The fever will be gone after the injection.* ㊀比正常体温高的体温 fever：～退了。*The fever has come down.* ❺施肥过多，使植物枯萎、死亡 to damage; to hurt (due to over-fertilisation) ❻因富有而忘乎所以 to grow arrogant from wealth：有俩钱，看把他～的。*He's only got a couple of quid, and look at how bigheaded he's become.*

勺 sháo ㄕㄠ ❶（一子、一儿）一种有柄的可以舀（yǎo）取东西的器具 ladle; spoon：饭～ *rice ladle* | 铁～ *metal ladle* ❷市制容量单位，1升的百分之一 a traditional Chinese unit for measuring volume (There are 100 勺 in 1 升.)

芍 sháo ㄕㄠ ［芍药］（一yao）草本植物，花像牡丹，供观赏，根可入药 common garden peony

杓 sháo ㄕㄠˊ same as "勺❶"
➪ see also biāo on p.40

苕 sháo ㄕㄠˊ 〈方 dialect〉红苕，即甘薯 sweet potato (same as 甘薯)
➪ see also tiáo on p.651

玿 sháo ㄕㄠˊ 一种美玉 a type of fine jade

柖 sháo ㄕㄠˊ ❶树摇动的样子 (of trees) swaying ❷箭靶 archery target

韶 sháo ㄕㄠˊ ❶古代的乐曲名 name of a piece of music in ancient times ❷美 beautiful: ～光 *beautiful times (usually spring)*| ～华（指青年时代）*glorious youth*

S

少 shǎo ㄕㄠˇ ❶跟"多"相对 (opposite of 多) ①数量小的 few; in small quantity: ～数 *small number; minority* | ～有 *uncommon*| ～见 *seldom seen* | 稀～ *rare* ②缺（㊎缺－）short of; lacking: 文娱活动～不了他。*Entertainment activities can't happen without him.* ❷短暂 a little while; a moment: ～等 *wait a moment* | ～待 *wait a moment* ❸丢，遗失 to lose; to be missing: 屋里～了东西。*Things are missing in the room.*
➪ see also shào on p.584

少 shào ㄕㄠˋ 年纪轻，跟"老"相对 young (opposite of 老): 年～ *young* | ～年 *youth* | ～女 *teenage girl* | 男女老～ *men and women, young and old*
➪ see also shǎo on p.584

召 shào ㄕㄠˋ ❶周代诸侯国名，在陕西省凤翔一带 Shao (a state in the Zhou Dynasty, near Fengxiang of today's Shaanxi Province) ❷姓 (surname) Shao
➪ see also zhào on p.837

卲 shào ㄕㄠˋ same as "劭❷"

邵 shào ㄕㄠˋ 姓 (surname) Shao

劭 shào ㄕㄠˋ ❶劝勉 to encourage ❷美好 good: 年高德～ *aged and virtuous*

绍(紹) shào ㄕㄠˋ 接续，继续 to continue

哨 shào ㄕㄠˋ ❶巡逻，侦察 to patrol; to reconnoitre: ～探 *to inquire; to scout* ❷警戒防守的岗位 sentry post: 放～ *guard a sentry post* | ～兵 *sentry* | 观察～ *observation post* ❸（－子、－儿）一种小笛 whistle: 吹～集合。*Gather when the whistle is blown.* ❹鸟叫 (of a bird) to chirp: 黄莺～得真好听。*The black-naped oriole's chirping is so pleasant.*

睄 shào ㄕㄠˋ 〈方 dialect〉略看一眼 to glance

稍 shào ㄕㄠˋ ［稍息］军事或体操的口令，命令队伍从立正姿势变为休息的姿势 (military command) at ease
➪ see also shāo on p.583

潲 shào ㄕㄠˋ ❶雨点被风吹得斜洒 (of rain) to slant: 雨往南～。*The rain is blown towards the south.* ㊀洒水 to spray; to sprinkle: 马路上～些水。*Spray some water on the road.* ❷〈方 dialect〉泔水 slops; swill: ～水 *slops* | 猪～ *pigswill*

SHE ㄕㄜ

畲(畬) shē ㄕㄜ 同“畲”。多用于地名 (often used in place names) same as 畲

奢 shē ㄕㄜ ❶挥霍财物，过分享受（㊣－侈）luxurious; profligate：～华 *opulent* | ～靡 *extravagant* | 穷～极欲 *extreme hedonism* ❷过分的 excessive：～望 *unrealistic hope*

赊(賒) shē ㄕㄜ ❶买卖货物时延期付款或延期收款 to buy on credit; to sell on credit：～账 *buy on credit; sell on credit* | ～购 *buy on credit* ❷远 far：江山蜀道～。*Rivers, mountains: the road to Shu is long.* ❸ (ancient) same as “奢❶”

畲 shē ㄕㄜ [畲族] 我国少数民族，参看附录四 the She people (one of the ethnic groups in China. See Appendix Ⅳ.)

畲 shē ㄕㄜ 焚烧田地里的草木，用草木灰做肥料耕种 to slash and burn

⇨ see also yú on p.798

猞 shē ㄕㄜ [猞猁]（－lì）哺乳动物，像狸猫，毛多棕黄色，有灰褐色斑点。四肢粗长，善爬树，性凶猛 lynx

舌 shé ㄕㄜˊ ❶舌头，人和动物嘴里辨别滋味、帮助咀嚼和发音的器官 tongue [舌战] 激烈辩论 intense debate ❷像舌头的东西 sth like a tongue：帽～ *(of a cap) visor* | 火～ *tongues of fire* ❸铃或铎（duó）中的锤 (of a bell) clapper

折 shé ㄕㄜˊ ❶断 to break; to snap：绳子～了。*The rope has snapped.* | 棍子～了。*The long stick is broken.* ❷亏损 to suffer a loss：～本 *lose one's capital* [折耗] 损耗，损失 (of goods) to suffer damage and loss (during transit, storage, etc.)：青菜～太大。*The green vegetables suffered too much damage.* ❸姓 (surname) She

⇨ see also zhē on p.838, zhé on p.838

佘 shé ㄕㄜˊ 姓 (surname) She

蛇(*虵) shé ㄕㄜˊ 爬行动物，俗叫长虫（chong），身体细长，有鳞，没有四肢，种类很多，有的有毒，捕食蛙等小动物 snake (informal 长虫)

⇨ see also yí on p.770

阇(闍) shé ㄕㄜˊ [阇梨] 梵语音译“阿阇梨”的省称。佛教指高僧，泛指僧 (short for 阿阇梨, from Sanskrit) senior (Buddhist) monk; (Buddhist) monk

⇨ see also dū on p.146

舍(捨) shě ㄕㄜˇ ❶放弃，不要了 to abandon; to give up：～己为人 *give up one's own interest for the sake of others* | ～近求远 *seek far and wide for what lies close at hand* | 四～五入 *(mathematics) round to the nearest whole number* ❷施舍 to give alms; to dispense charity：～粥 *distribute porridge (to the needy)* | ～药 *distribute medicine (to the* *needy)*

⇨ see also shè on p.586

厍(厙) shè ㄕㄜˋ 〈方 dialect〉村庄（多用于村庄名）village (often used in village names)

设(設) shè ㄕㄜˋ ❶布置，安置 to arrange; to place：～岗 *post a sentry* | 办事处～在北京。*The office is located in Beijing.* [设备] 为某一目的而配置的建筑与器物等 equipment：车间里～很完善。*The workshop is fully equipped.* ❷筹划 to plan：～法 *make an attempt to* [设计] 根据一定的目的要求预先制定方法、程序、图样等 to design ❸假定 to assume：～ *x=a assuming that x=a,...* ❹假使（㊄一若）if; supposing

社 shè ㄕㄜˋ ❶古代指祭祀土地神的地方 (ancient) site for making offerings to earth deities [社火] 民间在节日扮演的各种杂戏 folk theatre (performed during festivals) ❷指某些团体或机构 organisation; association：合作～ *cooperative* | 通讯～ *news agency* | 集会结～ *assembly and association* [社会] 1 指由一定的经济基础和上层建筑构成的整体 society：封建～ *feudal society* | 社会主义～ *socialist society* 2 指由于共同的物质条件和生活方式而联系起来的人群 group of people with common material conditions and lifestyles：上层～ *upper-class society* | ～思潮 *social trend* [社交] 指社会上人与人的交际往来 social intercourse [社区] 社会上有一定区域、人群、组织形式、生活服务设施等的居住区 community

舍 shè ㄕㄜˋ ❶居住的房子 residence：旅～ *hotel* | 宿～ *dormitory* ❷养家畜的圈 pen (for farm animals)：猪～ *pigpen* | 牛～ *cow pen* ❸古代行军三十里叫一舍 unit for measuring distance in ancient military manoeuvres (There are 30 里 in 1 舍.)：退避三～（喻对人让步）*retreat by a distance of ninety* li*; (figurative) give ground* ❹谦辞，用于对别人称自己的亲戚或年纪小辈分低的亲属 (humble speech) my (used when describing one's relations, especially younger relations, to a third party)：～亲 *my relatives* | ～弟 *my younger brother* | ～侄 *my nephew* ❺姓 (surname) She

⇨ see also shě on p.585

拾 shè ㄕㄜˋ 轻步而上 to step up lightly：～级（逐步登上梯级）*climb up the stairs one step at a time*

⇨ see also shí on p.598

射(*䠶) shè ㄕㄜˋ ❶放箭，用推力或弹（tán）力送出子弹等 to shoot (arrows, bullets, etc.)：～箭 *shoot an arrow* | 扫～ *spray gunfire* | 高～炮 *anti-aircraft gun* ❷液体受到压力迅速挤出 (of liquids) to shoot out; to spray：喷～ *to spray; to spurt* | 注～ *to inject* ❸放出光、热等 (of light, heat, etc.) to emit; to radiate：反～ *to reflect* | 光芒四～ *light* *shines in all directions* ❹有所指 to refer to：暗～ *hint at* | 影～ *obliquely insinuate*

麝 shè ㄕㄜˋ 哺乳动物，又叫香獐子，像鹿而小，没有角，有獠牙。雄的脐部有香腺，能分泌麝香 musk deer (also called 香獐子)

涉 shè ㄕㄜˋ ❶蹚着水走，泛指渡水 to wade：跋山～水 *make an arduous journey across mountains and rivers* | 远～重洋 *travel great distances across the seas* ❷经历 to experience：～险 *go through dangers* | ～世 *experience the world* ❸牵连，关联（㊀牵—）to implicate; to be connected with：～案 *connected with a criminal case* | ～嫌 *be suspected of involvement* | ～外 *concern foreign affairs* | ～及 *to involve; to related to*

赦 shè ㄕㄜˋ 免除刑罚 (of a crime) to pardon：大～ *amnesty* | ～免 *to pardon; to remit (a punishment)* | ～罪 *absolve from sin; to pardon*

摄（攝） shè ㄕㄜˋ ❶吸取 to absorb：～取养分 *absorb nutrients* | ～食 *(of animals) to feed* ❷摄影 to take a photograph; to shoot a film：～制 *to produce (TV or film)* | 这组照片～于南沙群岛。*These photographs were taken in the Nansha Islands.* ❸保养 to conserve one's health; to maintain：珍～ *take care of one's body* ❹代理（多指统治权）(often of the authority to rule) act on behalf of：～政 *act as regent* | ～位 *act as regent*

滠（灄） shè ㄕㄜˋ 滠水，水名，在湖北省 Sheshui River (in Hubei Province)

慑（懾、*慴） shè ㄕㄜˋ 恐惧，害怕 to fear; to be afraid：～服 *submit out of fear* | 震～ *to overawe* [威慑] 用武力或威势使对方感到恐惧 to terrorise with military force

歙 shè ㄕㄜˋ 歙县，在安徽省 Shexian (in Anhui Province)

⇨ see also xī on p.698

SHEI ㄕㄟ

谁（誰） shéi ㄕㄟˊ shuí ㄕㄨㄟˊ（又）代词 pronoun ①表示问人 who：～来啦？*Who came?* ②任指，表示任何人，无论什么人 anyone：～都可以做。*Anyone can do it.*

SHEN ㄕㄣ

申 shēn ㄕㄣ ❶地支的第九位 *shen* (the ninth of the twelve Earthly Branches, a system used in the Chinese calendar) ❷申时，指下午三点到五点 the period from 3 p.m. to 5 p.m. ❸陈述，说明 give an account; to explain：～请 *to apply* | ～辩 *defend oneself* | ～冤 *(plead for) redressing a wrong* | 重～ *to reiterate* | 三令五～ *repeatedly order and warning* [申斥] 斥责 to rebuke; to denounce ❹上海的别称 another name for Shanghai

伸 shēn ㄕㄣ ❶舒展开，跟"屈"相对 to extend (opposite of 屈)：～手 *extend one's hand* | ～缩 *extend and withdraw; be flexible* ❷表白 to argue one's case; to explain oneself：～冤 *(plead for) redressing a wrong*

呻 shēn ㄕㄣ 吟诵 to intone [呻吟] (–yín) 哼哼，病痛时发出声音 to moan (in pain)：无病～ *moan when one is not sick; (figurative) indulge in empty sentimentality*

绅(紳) shēn ㄕㄣ ❶古代士大夫束在腰间的大带子 (ancient) thick belt worn by literati-officials ❷绅士，旧称地方上有势力、有地位的人，一般是地主或退职官僚 (old) local gentry：乡～ *country gentleman* | 土豪劣～ *local tyrants and wicked gentry* | 开明士～ *enlightened gentry* [绅士] 1 same as "绅❷" 2 称有教养、有风度的男子。也指男子有教养，有风度 gentleman; gentlemanly

珅 shēn ㄕㄣ 一种玉 a type of jade

砷 shēn ㄕㄣ 非金属元素，旧叫砒（pī），符号 As，有黄、灰、黑褐三种颜色，有金属光泽，质脆有毒。可用来制合金，它的化合物可做杀菌剂和杀虫剂 (formerly called 砒 pī) arsenic (As)

屾 shēn ㄕㄣ 并立的两山 two mountains side by side

身 shēn ㄕㄣ ❶人、动物的躯体（㊣–体、–躯）(of humans and animals) body：全～ *the whole body* | 上～ *the upper body* | 半～不遂 *hemiplegia* | 人～自由 *personal freedom* ㊀物体的主要部分 main part of an object：船～ *(of a ship) hull* | 河～ *river bed* | 树～ *(of a tree) trunk* ❷指生命 life：以～殉职 *die in the line of duty* | 舍～炸碉堡 *sacrifice one's life to blow up a blockhouse* ❸亲身，亲自，本人 in person：～临其境 *visit in person* | ～体力行（亲身努力去做）*practise what one preaches* | 以～作则 *set an example with one's actions* ❹指人的地位 status：～败名裂 *lose one's standing and reputation* [身份] [身分]（–fen）1 指在社会上及法律上的地位 identity: 验明～ *prove sb's identity* 2 特指受人尊敬的地位 (specifically) high status; dignity：有失～ *beneath one's dignity* | 这是位有～的人。*This is a person of high social status.* ❺（–儿）量词，用于衣服 measure word for clothing：我做了一～儿新衣服。*I got a new outfit made.*

侁 shēn ㄕㄣ ❶[侁侁] 形容众多 many ❷姓 (surname) Shen

诜(詵) shēn ㄕㄣ ❶[诜诜] 形容众多 many ❷姓 (surname) Shen

骁(駪) shēn ㄕㄣ [骁骁] 形容众多 many

参(參、❷*葠、❷*蓡) shēn ㄕㄣ ❶星宿名，二十八宿之一 *shen* (one of the twenty-eight constellations in ancient Chinese astronomy) [参商] 参和商都是二十八宿之一，两者不同时在天空出现 two of the twenty-eight constellations in ancient Chinese astronomy that appear at different times ㊀①分离不得相见 to be parted ② 不和睦 not harmonious ❷人参，草本植物。根肥大，肉质，略像人形，可入药 ginseng

⇨ see also cān on p.57, cēn on p.61

糁(糝、**粁) shēn ㄕㄣ (一儿) 谷类制成的小渣 ground grains：玉米～儿 *ground maize*

⇨ see also sǎn on p.571

鲹(鰺) shēn ㄕㄣ 鱼名，身体侧扁，呈卵圆形，鳞细，生活在海洋里 scad

莘 shēn ㄕㄣ ❶莘县，在山东省 Shenxian (in Shandong Province) ❷姓 (surname) Shen

[莘莘] 形容众多 many：～学子 *many students*

⇨ see also xīn on p.724

甡 shēn ㄕㄣ ❶[甡甡] 形容众多 many ❷姓 (surname) Shen

娠 shēn ㄕㄣ 胎儿在母体中微动。泛指怀孕 foetal movements; (generally) pregnancy：妊～ *pregnancy*

深(*湥) shēn ㄕㄣ ❶从上到下或从外面到里面距离大，跟"浅"相对（❹❺同）deep (opposite of 浅, also ❹ and ❺)：～水 *deep water* | 这条河很～。*This river is very deep.* | ～山 *deep mountains* | 这个院子很～。*This courtyard is very deep.* ❷从上到下或从外面到里面的距离，深度 depth：水～一米。*The water is one metre deep.* [深浅] 1 深度 depth 2 说话的分寸 (of speech) sense of propriety：他说话不知道～。*He doesn't have any boundaries when he speaks.* ❸久，时间长 long; late：～秋 *late autumn* | ～更半夜 *the dead of night* | 年～日久 *with the passing of the days and years* ❹程度高的 deep; of high level：～信 *deeply believe* | ～知 *be fully aware of* | ～谋远虑 *think deeply and plan carefully* | 情谊很～ *deep friendship between people* | 这本书内容太～。*The contents of this book are really profound.* | ～入浅出 *explain sth profound in a simple way* ❺(颜色)重 (of colour) deep：～红 *deep red* | 颜色太～。*The colour is too deep.*

棽 shēn ㄕㄣ chēn ㄔㄣ (又) [棽棽] 形容繁盛茂密 verdant; lush

燊 shēn ㄕㄣ 旺盛 flourishing; prosperous

什 shén ㄕㄣˊ [什么] (一me) 代词 pronoun ①表示疑问 what (indicating a question)：想～？*What are you thinking of?* | ～人？*Who is it?* ②指不确定的或任何事物 something; anything：我想吃点儿～。*I want to eat something.* | ～事都难不住他。*There is nothing that he cannot overcome.* ③表示惊讶或不满 what

S

(indicating surprise or dissatisfaction)：～！明天就走？*What! We're leaving tomorrow?* | 这是～话！ *What kind of talk is this!*

⇨ see also shí on p.596

甚 shén ㄕㄣˊ same as "什(shén)"

⇨ see also shèn on p.591

神 shén ㄕㄣˊ ❶宗教指天地万物的创造者和统治者，迷信的人指神仙或被他们崇拜的人死后的精灵 god; deity; spirit：无～论 *atheism* | 不信鬼～ *do not believe in ghosts and spirits* ⓘ①不平凡的，特别高超的 extraordinary; exceptional：～力 *exceptional physical strength* | ～医 *highly-skilled doctor* ②不可思议的，特别稀奇的（㊎－秘）unfathomable; exceptionally strange：这事真是越说越～了。*The more it is talked about, the more miraculous it becomes.* [神通] 特殊的手段或本领 special powers; immense capabilities：大显～ *give full play to one's abilities* | ～广大 *be extremely resourceful* ❷心力，心思，注意力 thoughts; concentration：劳～ *taxing on one's mind* | 留～ *be alert* | 看得出了～ *look at sth until one is transfixed* | 聚精会～ *to concentrate* ❸（－儿）神气，表情 facial expression：你瞧他这个～儿，有点儿不对劲儿。*Look at his expression; something is wrong.* | ～色 *expression*

钟（鉀） shén ㄕㄣˊ 一类具有特定结构的含砷的有机化合物 arsonium

沈（❶❷瀋） shěn ㄕㄣˇ ❶汁 liquid extract：墨～未干。*The ink has yet to dry.* ❷沈阳，地名，在辽宁省 Shenyang (a place in Liaoning Province) ❸姓 (surname) Shen

⇨ see also chén on p.74

审（審） shěn ㄕㄣˇ ❶详细，周密 detailed; thorough：～慎 *cautious* | 精～ *accurate and careful* ⓘ仔细思考，反复分析、推究 to think carefully; to study closely：～查 *to inspect; to examine* | ～核 *examine and verify* | 这份稿子～完了。*This manuscript has been checked.* [审计] 专设机关对国家各级政府、金融机构、企业事业组织的财务收支情况进行监督、审查并提出意见 to audit ❷审问，讯问案件 to interrogate：～案 *try a case* | ～判 *put to trial* | 公～ *public trial* ❸知道 to know：不～近况何如？ *How have things been lately?*(also written as 谂) ❹的确，果然 indeed：～如其言。*What he says is indeed true.*

婶（嬸） shěn ㄕㄣˇ ❶（－子、－儿）叔叔的妻子 ㊀ aunt (wife of one's father's younger brother) ❷称呼跟母亲同辈而年纪较小、没有亲属关系的已婚妇女 auntie (term of address for an unrelated married woman younger than one's mother)：张大～儿 *Auntie Zhang*

哂 shěn ㄕㄣˇ 微笑 to smile：～存 *please accept (this small gift)* | ～纳 *please accept (this small gift)* |

聊博一～ *for your entertainment*

矧 shěn ㄕㄣˇ 文言连词，况，况且 (conjunction in classical Chinese) moreover; besides

谂(諗) shěn ㄕㄣˇ ❶ same as “审❸” ❷劝告 to advise; to urge

瞫 shěn ㄕㄣˇ 往深处看 to look into the depths

肾(腎) shèn ㄕㄣˋ 肾脏，俗叫腰子，人和高等动物的排泄器官之一，能滤出尿液 kidney (informal 腰子)

甚 shèn ㄕㄣˋ ❶很，极 very; extremely：进步～快 *progress rapidly* | 他说得未免过～。*Surely he's exaggerating.* [甚至] [甚至于] 连词，表示更进一层 (conjunction) even：不学习就会落后，～会犯错误。*If you don't study, you'll fall behind. You may even make mistakes.* | 这件事扰乱了他的生活，～影响了他的工作。*This matter has disrupted his daily life; it has even affected his work.* ❷超过，胜过 to exceed; to surpass：更有～者 *what is more* | 日～一日 *get worse/better by the day* ❸〈方 dialect〉代词，什么 (pronoun) what：要它做～? *What do (you) want it for?* | 姓～名谁? *What is (your) name?*

⇨ see also shén on p.590

葚 shèn ㄕㄣˋ [桑葚] 桑树结的果实 mulberry fruit

⇨ see also rèn on p.560

椹 shèn ㄕㄣˋ same as “葚(shèn)”

⇨ see also zhēn on p.843

昚 shèn ㄕㄣˋ ❶see 慎 on page 591 ❷用于人名。赵昚，南宋孝宗 used in given names, e.g. Zhao Shen, Emperor Xiaozong of the Southern Song Dynasty

胂 shèn ㄕㄣˋ 有机化合物的一类，是砷化氢分子中的氢被烃基替换而成的。多有剧毒 arsine

渗(滲) shèn ㄕㄣˋ 液体慢慢地透入或漏出 to seep; to ooze：水～到土里去了。*The water has seeped into the soil.* | 天很热，汗～透了衣服。*The weather is so hot that sweat has soaked through (my) clothes.*

瘆(瘮) shèn ㄕㄣˋ 使人害怕 frightening：～人 *scary* | 夜里走山路，有点儿～得慌。*It's quite scary to travel along a mountain path at night.*

蜃 shèn ㄕㄣˋ 大蛤蜊 large clam [蜃景] 又叫海市蜃楼，光线通过密度不同的空气层时，由于折射作用，把远处景物反映在天空或地面而形成的幻景。在沿海或沙漠地带有时能看到。古人误认为是蜃吐气而成 mirage (also called 海市蜃楼)

慎(△*昚) shèn ㄕㄣˋ 小心，加小心(㊀谨－) careful; cautious：不～ *careless* | ～重 *cautious*

SHENG ㄕㄥ

升(❸❹△*昇、❹△*陞) shēng ㄕㄥ ❶容积单位，符号

L（1），1 升等于 1 000 毫升。litre (l) ❷量粮食的器具，容量为 1 斗的十分之一 tool for measuring grain (capacity equals one-tenth of 1 斗) ❸向上移动，使向上移动 to rise; to raise：～旗 *raise the flag* | 太阳～起来了。*The sun has risen.* ❹提高 to elevate：～级 *to promote; to escalate*

昇 shēng ㄕㄥ ❶ see 升 on page 591 ❷用于人名。毕昇，宋代人，首创活字版印刷术 used in given names, e.g. Bi Sheng, inventor of the first movable type printing ❸姓 (surname) Sheng

陞 shēng ㄕㄥ ❶ see 升 on page 591 ❷ 姓 (surname) Sheng

生 shēng ㄕㄥ ❶出生，诞生 to be born; to give birth：～辰 *birthday* | 孙中山～于公元 1866 年。*Sun Yat-sen was born in 1866.* ❷可以发育的物体在一定的条件下发展长大 to grow：种子～芽。*The seed is sprouting.* | ～根 *take root* ⓘ发生，产生 to occur; to cause：～病 *fall sick* | ～疮 *get an abscess* | ～事 *make trouble* [生产] 1 人们使用工具来创造各种生产资料和生活资料 to produce 2 生小孩儿 to give birth ❸活，跟“死”相对 to be alive (opposite of 死)：～老病死 *birth, old age, illness and death (the inevitable stages of life)* | 贪～怕死 *crave for life and fear death* | 苟且偷～ *live out a dishonourable existence* ⓘ ① 生计 living：谋～ *earn one's living* | 营～ *earn one's living; job* ②生命 life：杀～ *take the life of sentient beings* | 丧～ *lose one's life; to die* | 众～ *all sentient beings* ③ 有生命力的 alive; living：～物 *living things* | ～龙活虎 *vigorous and full of life* ④整个生活阶段 one's life：平～ *all one's life* | 一～ *all one's life* ❹使柴、煤等燃烧起来 to ignite; to light：～火 *start a fire* | ～炉子 *light a stove* ❺没有经过烧煮的或烧煮没有熟的 raw; uncooked：夹～饭 *half-cooked rice; (figurative) sloppy work* | ～肉 *raw meat* | 不喝～水 *do not drink unboiled water* ❻植物果实没有成长到熟的程度 unripe：～瓜 *unripe melon* ❼不常见的，不熟悉的(ⓔ—疏) unfamiliar：陌～ *unfamiliar* | ～人 *stranger* | ～字 *new character* ❽不熟练 not skilful：～手 *beginner* ❾没有经过炼制的 untreated; unprocessed：～皮子 *pelt* | ～药 *unprocessed medicinal herbs* ❿ 生硬，硬，强 (qiǎng) rigid; tough：～拉硬拽 *drag sb forcefully; draw a forced analogy* | ～不承认 *adamantly refuse to admit* ⓫表示程度深 very; much：～疼 *very painful* | ～怕 *deeply afraid* ⓬指正在学习的人 learner：学～ *student* | 师～ *teachers and students* | 实习～ *intern; trainee* 旧时又指读书人 (old) scholar; intellectual：书～ *scholar* ⓭传统戏曲里扮演男子的一种角色 a kind of male role in traditional Chinese opera：老～ *role of an older man* | 小～ *role of a younger man* ⓮词尾 suffix：好～ *very; quite* | 怎～是

好？ *What is to be done now?*

牲 shēng ㄕㄥ 牲口，普通指牛、马、驴、骡等家畜。古代特指供宴飨祭祀用的牛、羊、猪 draught animal; (specifically) sacrificial cow, goat or pig offered to deities in ancient times

胜 shēng ㄕㄥ former name for 肽 (tài)

➪ see also shèng on p.594

笙 shēng ㄕㄥ 管乐器，用若干根长短不同的簧管制成，用口吹奏 wind instrument made of reed pipes of varying lengths

甥 shēng ㄕㄥ ❶外甥，姊妹的儿子 nephew (son of one's sister) ❷〈方 dialect〉外甥，女儿的儿子 grandson (son of one's daughter)

声（聲） shēng ㄕㄥ ❶声音，物体振动时所产生的能引起听觉的波 sound; voice：～如洪钟 *have a booming voice* | 大～说话 *speak loudly* ❷声母，字音开头的辅音，如"报(bào)告(gào)""丰(fēng)收(shōu)"里的 b、g、f、sh 都是声母 initial consonant (of a Chinese syllable) ❸声调（diào），字音的高低升降 tone (see "调 diào" ❹ on page 136 for reference) ❹说出来使人知道，扬言 to announce; to state：～明 *to declare; declaration* | ～讨 *to denounce; to condemn* | ～张 *make public; to disclose* | ～东击西 *make a feint attack* ❺名誉 fame; reputation：名～ *reputation* | ～望 *prestige* ❻量词，用于声音 measure word for sound：一～巨响 *a huge bang* | 喊了两～ *gave two shouts*

渑（澠） shéng ㄕㄥˊ 古水名，在今山东省淄博一带 name of an ancient river; in today's Zibo, Shandong Province

➪ see also miǎn on p.451

绳（繩） shéng ㄕㄥˊ ❶（一子）用两股以上的棉、麻纤维或棕、草等拧成的条状物 rope; cord [绳墨] 木工取直用的器具 (in carpentry) line marker ㊕规矩，法度 regulation; law ❷约束，制裁 to restrict; to punish：～之以法 *punish according to the law*

省 shěng ㄕㄥˇ ❶行政区划单位，直属中央 province ❷节约，耗费少，跟"费"相对 to economise; to save (opposite of 费)：～钱 *save money* | ～时间 *save time* | ～事 *save the trouble* ❸简略（㊀一略）to abbreviate：～称 *abbreviation; short for* | ～写 *to abbreviate*

➪ see also xǐng on p.728

眚 shěng ㄕㄥˇ ❶眼睛生翳（yì）cataract (in the eye) ❷灾祸 disaster; calamity ❸过错 mistake

圣（聖） shèng ㄕㄥˋ ❶最崇高的，最有智慧的 holy; sacred：～火 *sacred fire* | ～地 *holy land* | ～明 *insightful and wise* [圣人] 旧时称具有最高智慧和道德的人 (old) sage ❷称学问、技术有特殊成就的人 guru; master (a person who has achieved great things in their fields)：诗～ *the*

S

sage of poetry | 棋～ *the sage of chess* ❸封建时代尊称帝王 (in feudal times) king; emperor: ～上 *Your Majesty; His Majesty* | ～旨 *imperial edict*

胜(勝) shèng ㄕㄥˋ ❶赢，胜利，跟"败""负"相对 to win (opposite of 败 or 负): 打～仗 *win the battle* | 得～ *score a victory* ❷打败（对方）to defeat (sb): 以少～多 *defeat a numerically superior force* ❸超过 to exceed; to surpass: 今～于昔 *the present is better than the past* | 一个～似一个 *each one is better than the last* ❹优美的 beautiful: ～地 *famous scenic location* | ～景 *beautiful scenery* ㊁优美的地方或境界 beautiful place or state: 名～ *scenic place; historical site* | 引人入～ *captivating* ❺ (formerly pronounced shēng) 能担任，能承受 be able to take responsibility; be able to bear: ～任 *be qualified for; be competent in* | 不～其烦 *be bored beyond endurance* ❻ (formerly pronounced shēng) 尽 exhaustively: 不～感激 *be immensely grateful* | 不～枚举 *too numerous to be listed one by one*

⇨ see also shēng on p.593

晟 shèng ㄕㄥˋ ❶光明 light; bright ❷旺盛，兴盛 prosperous; bustling

盛 shèng ㄕㄥˋ ❶兴旺 flourishing ; bustling: 旺～ *vigorous; vibrant* | 茂～ *lush; exuberant* | 繁荣昌～ *thriving and prosperous* | 梅花～开。*Plums are in full bloom.* ❷炽烈 blazing; flaming: 年轻气～ *young and full of fire* | 火势很～。*The fire is blazing.* ❸丰富，华美 abundant; resplendent: ～宴 *lavish banquet* | ～装 *resplendent dress* ❹热烈，大规模的 grand; large-scale: ～会 *grand gathering* | ～况 *grand occasion* ❺深厚 deep; profound: ～意 *great kindness; generosity* | ～情 *great kindness; kind hospitality* ❻姓 (surname) Sheng

⇨ see also chéng on p.77

乘 shèng ㄕㄥˋ ❶春秋时晋国的史书叫乘，后因称一般的史书为乘 historical records (originally referring to the history books of the State of Jin during the Spring and Autumn Period): 史～ *historical works* ❷量词，古代称一辆四匹马拉的兵车为一乘 measure word for war chariots pulled by four horses in ancient times: 千～之国 *state with a thousand war chariots*

⇨ see also chéng on p.78

剩(*賸) shèng ㄕㄥˋ 多余，余留下来(㊀－余) to have (sb/sth) left; (of sb/sth) be surplus: ～饭 *leftover meal* | ～货 *surplus goods*

嵊 shèng ㄕㄥˋ [嵊州] 地名，在浙江省 Shengzhou (a place in Zhejiang Province)

SHI ㄕ

尸(❶*屍) shī ㄕ ❶尸体，人或动物死后的身体 corpse ❷古代祭祀时代表死者受祭的人 (ancient) person representing the dead to whom offerings were made ❸ 不做事情，空占职位 to occupy (a position) without doing anything：～位 *occupy a position without doing anything*

鸤(鳲) shī ㄕ [鸤鸠] (— jiū) 古书上指布谷鸟 cuckoo (in ancient Chinese texts)

失 shī ㄕ ❶丢（㊥遗—）to lose：～物招领 *lost and found*｜机不可～。*The chance cannot be missed.*｜～而复得 *find sth that was lost* ㊂ ① 违背 to breach; to violate：～信 *break one's promise*｜～约 *violate a contract; break one's promise* ② 找不着 to get lost：～踪 *be missing*｜～群之雁 *wild goose separated from its flock*｜迷～ *be lost* ❷没有掌握住 to fail to hold on to：～足 *to trip; take a wrong turn in life*｜～言 *make an indiscreet remark*｜～火 *catch fire* ❸没有达到目的 fail to reach a goal：～意 *be frustrated*｜～望 *be disappointed*｜～策 *to misjudge* [失败] 1 被打败 be defeated 2 计划或希望没能实现 (of plans or hopes) to fail ❹错误，疏忽 error; negligence：千虑一～。*Even the most careful person will make mistakes.* ❺改变常态 to change (from the norm)：～色 *turn pale; lose lustre*｜～声痛哭 *weep loudly*

师(師) shī ㄕ ❶老师，传授知识技能的人 teacher ㊂榜样 example; model：前事不忘，后事之～。*Remember the past, for it teaches the future.* [师傅] 1 传授技艺的老师 master (teacher of skills) 2 对有实践经验的工人的尊称 honorific term for an experienced worker ❷由师徒关系而产生的 involving a master-apprentice relationship：～兄 *fellow apprentice (male, and who entered the apprenticeship before oneself)* ❸掌握专门学术或技艺的人 person with specialised knowledge or skill：工程～ *engineer*｜医～ *doctor; physician*｜律～ *lawyer*｜理发～ *barber* ❹仿效 to imitate; to follow：～法 *to follow the style, knowledge or technique (of a great master)* ❺ 军队 army; troops：誓～ *pledge resolution before going to war*｜百万雄～ *powerful army of a million soldiers* ❻军队的编制单位，是团的上一级 (of military) a division

狮(獅) shī ㄕ 狮子，兽名，毛黄褐色，雄的颈上有长鬣，性凶猛，有兽王之称。多生活在非洲和亚洲西部 lion

浉(溮) shī ㄕ 浉河，在河南省信阳，入淮河 Shihe River (in Xinyang, Henan Province)

鲺(鰤) shī ㄕ 鱼名，身体纺锤形，稍侧扁，背部蓝褐色，鳞小而圆，尾鳍分叉。生活在海里 (fish) yellowtail

䴓(鳾) shī ㄕ 鸟名，背部青灰色，腹部淡褐色，嘴长而尖，脚短爪硬，生活在树林中 Eurasian nuthatch

邿 shī ㄕ 用于地名 used in place names：大～城（在山东省济阳）*Dashicheng (in Jiyang, Shandong Province)*

诗（詩） shī ㄕ 一种文体，形式很多，多用韵，可以歌咏朗诵 poetry

虱（*蝨） shī ㄕ （一子）昆虫，身体小，寄生在人畜身上，吸食血液，能传染疾病 louse

鲺（鯴） shī ㄕ 节肢动物，身体扁圆形，像臭虫，头上有一对吸盘。寄生在鱼类身体的表面 fish louse

施 shī ㄕ ❶实行 to carry out：～工 *to construct* | 无计可～ *at one's wit's end* | 倒行逆～ *go against the flow* [施展] 发挥能力 give full play to ❷用上，加上 to use; to add：～肥 *to fertilise* | ～粉 *apply powder* ❸给予 to give：～礼 *to salute* | ～恩 *do a kindness* ❹施舍，把财物送给穷人或出家人 to give alms：～主 *alms giver* | 布～ *give alms*

湿（濕、*溼） shī ㄕ 沾了水或是含的水分多，跟"干"相对 wet; damp (opposite of 干)：地很～。*The floor is very wet.* | 手～了。*(My) hands are wet.*

蓍 shī ㄕ 蓍草，草本植物，俗叫蚰蜒草或锯齿草，茎直立，花白色。全草可入药，也可制香料 *Achillea wilsoniana* (informal 蚰蜒草 or 锯齿草)

酾（釃） shī ㄕ shāi ㄕㄞ（又）❶滤酒 to sieve wine ❷斟酒 to pour wine ❸疏导河渠 to dredge a river

嘘 shī ㄕ 叹词，表示反对、制止、驱逐等 (exclamation) shush; shoo：～，小点儿声！*Shush, be quiet!*

⇨ see also xū on p.734

十 shí ㄕˊ ❶数目字 (number) ten ⓘ表示达到顶点 used to indicate completeness：～足 *sheer; hundred-percent* | ～分 *very; fully* | ～全～美 *perfect in every way* ❷法定计量单位中十进倍数单位词头之一，表示10^1，符号da。deka- (da)

什 shí ㄕˊ ❶同"十❶"（多用于分数或倍数）same as 十❶ (often in fractions or multiples)：～一（十分之一）*one-tenth* | ～百（十倍或百倍）*ten times; a hundred times* ❷各种的，杂样的 various; miscellaneous：～物 *odds and ends* | 家～（家用杂物）*odds and ends for home use* [什锦] 各种各样东西凑成的（多指食品）(often of food) assorted; mixture：～糖 *assortment of candy* | 素～ *mixed vegetarian dish*

⇨ see also shén on p.589

石 shí ㄕˊ ❶（一头）构成地壳的坚硬物质，是由矿物集合而成的 stone; rock：花岗～ *granite* | ～磨 *stone mill* | ～砚 *inkstone* ❷指石刻 stone engraving：金～ *inscriptions on ancient bronzes and stone tablests* ❸古代容量单位，一石为十斗 an ancient Chinese unit for measuring volume, equal to 10 斗 ❹古代重

量单位，一石为一百二十斤 an ancient Chinese unit for measuring weight, equal to 120 斤 ❺姓 (surname) Shi

⇨ see also dàn on p.115

炻 shí 𠂆 [炻器]介于陶器和瓷器之间的陶瓷制品，如水缸、砂锅等 ceramic product with qualities between porcelain and pottery

祏 shí 𠂆 古时宗庙中藏神主的石匣 stone box containing ancestor's spirit tablet in ancestral temples of ruling houses in ancient times

鼫 shí 𠂆 古书上指鼯（wú）鼠一类的动物 an animal related to the flying squirrel in ancient Chinese texts

时(時、*旹) shí 𠂆 ❶时间，一切物质不断变化或发展所经历的过程 time ❷时间的一段 period of time ①比较长期的（㊀—代）era; epoch：古～ *ancient times* | 唐～ *the Tang period* | 盛极一～ *very popular for a time* ②一年中的一季 season：四～ *the four seasons* ③时辰，一昼夜的十二分之一 one of the twelve periods a day was divided into in ancient China：子～ *the* zi *period (from 11 pm to 1 am)* ④小时，一昼夜的二十四分之一 hour ⑤时候 (a certain) time：平～ *on usual days* | 到～叫我一声。*Give me a call when the time comes.* ⑥钟点 o'clock：八～上班 *start work at eight o'clock* [不时] 1 不定时 at times：～之需 *a rainy day* 2 常常 often：联欢会上～爆发出笑声和掌声。*There were frequent bursts of laughter and applause at the gathering.* ❸时机 opportunity; chance：待～而动 *bide one's time* ❹规定的时间 scheduled time：准～起飞 *take off on time* ❺现在的，当时的 contemporary; current：～髦 *trendy* | ～事 *current affairs* [时装] 式样最新的服装，当代流行的服装 fashion ❻时常，常常 ㊂ often; always：学而～习之 *constantly review what you learn* | ～～帮助他人 *always help others* ❼有时候 sometimes：天气～阴～晴。*The weather is cloudy with sunny intervals.* | 身体～好～坏。*One's health is good at times, but sometimes it takes a turn for the worse.*

埘(塒) shí 𠂆 古代称在墙壁上挖洞做成的鸡窝 (ancient) chicken nest that was dug into a wall

鲥(鰣) shí 𠂆 鱼名，背部黑绿色，腹部银白色，鳞下多脂肪。肉味鲜美 Reeves shad

识(識) shí 𠂆 ❶知道，认得，能辨别 to know; to recognize：～货 *know what's what* | ～字 *be literate* | ～别真假 *distinguish between genuine and fake* ❷知识，所知道的道理 knowledge：常～ *general knowledge* | 学～ *academic knowledge* ❸见识，辨别是非的能力 insight; discernment：卓～ *remarkable in-*

S

sight | 有～之士 *insightful person*

⇨ see also zhì on p.857

实(實、❶❷△*寔) shí ㄕ ❶充满 filled; full: 虚～ *the empty and the solid; the abstract and the concrete* | ～心球 *medicine ball* | ～足年龄 *actual age* ❷真，真诚，跟“虚”相对 genuine; sincere (opposite of 虚): ～心～意 *honest and sincere* | ～话～说 *not beat about the bush* | ～事求是 *seek truth from facts; be realistic and truthful* [实词] 能够单独用来回答问题，有比较实在意义的词，跟“虚词”相对，如名词、动词等 content word (e.g. noun, verb, etc.) (opposite of 虚词) [实践] 1 实行(自己的主张)，履行(自己的诺言) to carry out; to implement 2 人们改造自然和改造社会的有意识的活动 practice [实在] 1 真，的确 really; indeed: ～好 *really good* 2 (－zɑi) 不虚 solid; practical: 他的学问很～。*His knowledge is solid.* | 话说得挺～。*What (he) said was rather practical.* ❸种子，果子 seed; fruit: 开花结～ *bloom and bear fruit*

拾 shí ㄕ ❶捡，从地下拿起来 to pick up: ～麦子 *pick wheat grains* | ～了一支笔 *picked up a pen* ❷“十”字的大写 (elaborate form of 十, used in commercial or financial context) ten [拾掇] (－duo) 1 整理 tidy up: 把屋子～一下 *tidy up the room* | 把院子～～ *tidy up the yard* 2 修理 to repair: ～钟表 *repair clocks and watches* | ～机器 *repair a machine* | ～房子 *renovate a house*

⇨ see also shè on p.586

食 shí ㄕ ❶吃 to eat: ～肉 *eat meat* [食言] 指失信 to break one's promise: 决不～ *never break one's promise* ❷吃的东西 food: 素～ *vegetarian food* | 零～ *snack* | 面～ *food made of wheat* | 丰衣足～ *have ample food and clothing* ❸日月亏缺或完全看不见的现象 eclipse: 日～ *solar eclipse* | 月～ *lunar eclipse*

⇨ see also sì on p.619

蚀(蝕) shí ㄕ ❶损伤，亏缺 to damage; to be damaged: 侵～ *to corrode; to erode* | 腐～ *to corrode; to corrupt* ❷ (old) same as “食 (shí) ❸”

湜 shí ㄕ 形容水清见底 ㊀ (of water) crystal clear

寔 shí ㄕ ❶放置 to place; to lay ❷ see 实 on page 598

史 shǐ ㄕˇ ❶历史，自然或社会以往发展的过程。也指记载历史的文字和研究历史的学科 history ❷古代掌管记载史事的官 (ancient) official historian

驶(駛) shǐ ㄕˇ ❶车马快跑 (of vehicles) to speed; (of horses) to gallop ❷开动交通工具(多指有发动机的)，使行动 to drive (wheeled vehicles); to sail (boats, ships, etc.): 驾～ *to drive* | 轮船～入港口。*The ship sailed into the port.*

矢 shǐ ㄕˇ ❶箭 arrow: 有的(dì)放～ *have a specific target in view* ❷发誓 to take an oath: ～口

抵赖 *adamantly deny* ❸ (ancient) same as "屎"：遗～ *to defecate*

豕 shǐ ㄕˇ 猪 pig

使 shǐ ㄕˇ ❶用 to use：～劲 *use one's strength*｜～拖拉机耕种 *use a tractor to farm*｜这支笔很好～。*This pen writes smoothly.* ❷派，差（chāi）遣 to send：支～ *order about; send on an errand*｜～人前往 *send sb to go* ❸让，令，叫 to make; to cause：～人高兴 *make one happy*｜迫～ *to compel* ❹假若，假使 if; suppose ❺驻外国的外交长官 senior diplomat：大～ *ambassador*｜公～ *(of diplomatic rank) minister*［使命］奉命去完成的某种任务。泛指重大的任务 task; mission：历史～ *historical mission*｜外交～ *diplomatic mission*

始 shǐ ㄕˇ ❶开始，起头，最初，跟"末""终"相对 beginning (opposite of 末 or 终)：～祖 *first ancestor*｜不知～于何时。*It is not known when it started.*｜自～至终 *from beginning to end*｜原～社会 *primitive society*［未始］未尝，本来没有 not; never：这样做～不可。*It is not inconceivable that it could be done this way.* ❷才 only：参观至下午五时～毕。*The visit didn't end until 5 pm.*

屎 shǐ ㄕˇ 大便，粪 faeces ㊀眼、耳等的分泌物 (from eyes, ears, etc.) secretion：眼～ *gum in the eyes*｜耳～ *ear wax*

士 shì ㄕˋ ❶古代介于卿大夫和庶民之间的一个阶层 a class of people between senior officials and commoners in ancient times ❷古代指未婚的男子，泛指男子 (ancient) bachelor; (generally) man：～女 *men and women* ❸指读书人 intellectual：学～ *(academic degree) bachelor*｜～农工商 *intellectuals, farmers, artisans and merchants* ❹对人的美称 complimentary title for a person：志～ *person of ideals and integrity*｜壮～ *heroic man*｜烈～ *martyr* ❺军人的一级，在尉以下，也泛指军人 (military rank) sergeant and corporal; (generally) soldier：上～ *staff sergeant*｜中～ *sergeant*｜～气 *morale* ❻称某些专业人员 part of certain professional titles：护～ *nurse*｜助产～ *midwife*

仕 shì ㄕˋ 旧称做官 (old) become an official：出～ *become an official*｜～途 *official career*［仕女］1 宫女 palace maid 2 传统绘画中的美女 beautiful women in traditional Chinese paintings

氏 shì ㄕˋ ❶姓。古代姓和氏有区别，氏从姓分出，后来姓和氏不分了，姓、氏可以混用 surname (in ancient times, 姓 and 氏 were differentiated; both words are used interchangeably now) ❷旧时称已婚的妇女，通常在夫姓后再加父姓，父姓后加"氏" (old) née (氏 was added after her maiden name)：张王～（夫姓张，父姓王）*Mrs Zhang, née Wang* ❸后世对有影响的人的称呼 used as a respectful form of address for fig-

S

ures who had a great influence on later generations: 神农～ *Shennong*| 太史～ *The Grand Historian (Sima Qian)* | 摄～温度 *temperature in Celsius*

⇨ see also zhī on p.851

舐 shì ㄕˋ 舔 to lick: 老牛～犊（喻人疼爱儿女）*the old cow licks the calf; (figurative) parents love their children*

示 shì ㄕˋ 表明，把事物拿出来或指出来使别人知道 to show; to indicate: ～众 *show the public* | ～威 *to demonstrate (at a protest)* | 表～ *to express* | 暗～ *hint at* | ～范 *to demonstrate (to show how sth is done)* | 以目～意 *express one's intentions with one's eyes*

胨 shì ㄕˋ 有机化合物，溶于水，遇热不凝固，是食物蛋白和蛋白胨的中间产物 proteose

世(****丗**) shì ㄕˋ ❶一个时代 era: 近～ *current times* ❷一辈一辈相传的 hereditary; passed down from one generation to the next: ～袭 *hereditary*| ～医 *doctor from a long line of doctors* ❸人的一生 one's life: 一～为人 *live a life as a person* | 今生今～ *in this lifetime* ❹指从先辈起就有交往、友谊的 of people who maintain good family friendship: ～伯 *uncle (family friend of one's father's generation)* | ～兄 *elder brother (family friend of one's own generation)* ❺世界，宇宙，全球 world; universe: ～上 *in the world* | ～人 *people of the world*

贳(**貰**) shì ㄕˋ ❶出赁，出借 to rent out; to lend ❷赊欠 to buy or sell on credit ❸宽纵，赦免 to indulge; to pardon

市 shì ㄕˋ ❶做买卖或集中做买卖的地方 market: 开～ *(of a business) to open* | 菜～ *produce market* | 牲口～ *livestock market* [超市] 超级市场的简称。一种任顾客自选商品的综合性零售商店 supermarket (short for 超级市场) ❷买 to buy: ～恩 *try to win sb's favour* | 沽酒～脯(fǔ) *buy wine and meat* ❸卖 to sell: 转以～人 *to re-sell* ❹人口密集的行政中心或工商业、文化发达的地方 city: 城～ *city*| 都～ *metropolis* ❺行政区划单位，有直辖市和省(或自治区)辖市等 municipality; city (including province-level municipalities, prefectural-level cities, etc.): 北京～ *Beijing Municipality* | 唐山～ *Tangshan City* ❻属于我国度量衡市用制的 used for traditional Chinese units of measurement: ～尺 chi, *a traditional unit of length that equals 1/3 metre* | ～升 sheng, *a traditional primary unit of dry measure for grain that equals 1 litre* | ～斤 jin, *a traditional unit of weight that equals 0.5 kilogram*

柿(***柹**) shì ㄕˋ 柿树，落叶乔木，花黄白色。果实叫柿子，扁圆形，红黄色，可以吃。木材可用来制器具 persimmon

铈(**鈰**) shì ㄕˋ 金属元素，符号 Ce，铁灰色，

质软。可用来制合金 cerium (Ce)

式 shì ㄕ ❶物体外形的样子 type; style: 新～ *new style* [形式] 事物的外表 external form ❷特定的规格 specifications: 格～ *format* | 程～ *form; programme* ❸仪式，典礼 ceremony: 开幕～ *opening ceremony* | 阅兵～ *military parade* ❹自然科学中表明某些规律的一组符号 formula: 公～ *formula* | 方程～ *equation* | 分子～ *molecular formula*

试(試) shì ㄕ ❶按照预定想法非正式地做 to try; to attempt: ～验 *experiment* | ～用 *try out* | ～一～看 *give it a try* ❷考，测验(㊟考一、测一) examination; test: ～题 *examination question* | 口～ *oral test* | ～金石 *touchstone*

拭 shì ㄕ 擦 to wipe: ～泪 *wipe away tears* | ～目以待(形容殷切期待) *wait and see*

栻 shì ㄕ 古代占卜用的器具 a tool used for divination in ancient times

轼(軾) shì ㄕ 古代车厢前面用作扶手的横木 horizontal wooden hand rail in front of carriages in ancient times

弑 shì ㄕ 古时候指臣杀君、子杀父母等行为 (ancient) to kill (one's ruler, parent, etc.): ～君 *regicide* | ～父 *patricide*

似 shì ㄕ [似的][是的](-de)助词，表示跟某种事物或情况相似 (auxiliary word) similar to: 肤色像雪～那么白 *complexion as white as snow* | 瓢泼～大雨 *raining cats and dogs*

⇨ see also sì on p.619

势(勢) shì ㄕ ❶势力，权力，威力 power; influence: 倚～欺人 *abuse power to bully others* ❷表现出来的情况，样子 situation; form ①属于自然界的 used for natural states: 地～ *terrain* | 山～险峻 *precipitous mountain* ②属于动作的 used for actions: 姿～ *posture* | 手～ *hand gesture* ③属于政治、军事或其他方面的 used for political, military, etc. situations: 时～ *trend of the times* | 大～所趋 *general course of development* | 乘～追击 *push on while the going is good* ❸雄性生殖器 male genitalia: 去～ *to castrate*

事 shì ㄕ ❶(-儿)事情，自然界和社会中的一切现象和活动 matter; thing [事变] 突然发生的重大政治、军事性事件 incident (of political or military significance): 七七～ *the July 7 Incident* [事态] 形势或局面 situation: ～严重 *the situation is serious* ❷职业 occupation; job: 谋～ *look for a job* | 他现在做什么～? *What is his job now?* ❸关系或责任 involvement; responsibility: 你回去吧，没有你的～了。*Please go back. You're not involved anymore.* | 这件案子里还有他的～呢。*This case also contains matters connected to him.* ❹变故，事故 accident: 出～ *have an accident* | 平安无～ *safe and*

S

sound [事故] 出于某种原因而发生的不幸事情，如工作中的死伤等 accident ❺做，治 to do; to be engaged in：大～宣扬 *widely publicise* | 不～生产 *not engaged in production* ❻旧指侍奉 (old) to wait upon：～亲 *attend to one's parents*

侍 shì ㄕˋ 服侍，伺候，在旁边陪着 to serve; to wait upon：～立 *(of servants, attendants, etc.) attend*

峙 shì ㄕˋ [繁峙] 地名，在山西省 Fanshi (a place in Shanxi Province)

⇨ see also zhì on p.858

恃 shì ㄕˋ 依赖，仗着 to depend on：有～无恐 *be emboldened with strong backing*

饰(飾) shì ㄕˋ ❶修饰，装饰，装点得好看 to decorate：油～门窗 *paint the doors and windows* ㊀假托，遮掩 to cover up：～辞 *embellishing words* | 文过～非 *gloss over one's mistakes* ❷装饰用的东西 decoration：首～ *jewellery* | 窗～ *window decoration* ❸装扮，扮演角色 to play a part (in films, plays, etc.)

视(視、*眎、*眡) shì ㄕˋ ❶看 to view; to see：～点 *viewpoint* | 近～眼 *myopia* | ～而不见 *look but do not see* ❷视察，观察 to inspect; to observe：巡～一周 *make a round of inspection* | 监～ *to monitor* ❸看待 to regard：重～ *treat sth as important* | ～死如归 *face death fearlessly* | 一～同仁 *treat all equally*

昰 shì ㄕˋ ❶ see 是 on page 602 ❷用于人名。赵昰，南宋端宗 used in given names, e.g. Zhao Shi, Emperor Duanzong of the Southern Song Dynasty

是(△*昰) shì ㄕˋ ❶表示判断 to be (used to indicate judgement)：他～工人。*He is a worker.* | 这朵花～红的。*This flower is red.* ❷表示存在 used to indicate existence：满身～汗 *covered in sweat* | 山上全～树。*The mountain is covered by trees.* ❸表示让步，先承认所说的，再转入正意 used to indicate a concession before making one's main point：东西旧～旧，可是还能用。*It is certainly old, but it is still usable.* | 话～说得很对，可是得 (děi) 认真去做。*What (you) said is true, but you must do it carefully.* ❹表示适合 used to indicate aptness：来的～时候 *arrive at an opportune time* | 放的～地方 *has been put in the right place* ❺表示凡是，任何 any; all：～重活儿他都抢着干。*He always volunteers first to do any heavy work.* ❻用于选择问句 used in alternative questions：你～坐轮船～坐火车？ *Are you taking a boat or a train?* ❼加重语气 used for emphasis：～谁告诉你的？ *Who was it that told you?* | 天气～冷。*The weather is indeed cold.* ❽对，合理，跟“非”相对 right; reasonable (opposite of 非)：懂得～非 *know the difference be-*

tween right and wrong｜他说的～。*What he said is right.* ⑤认为对 to believe to be right：～其所是 *affirm what one thinks is right*［是非］1 正确和错误 right and wrong：辨明～ *discern between right and wrong* 2 纠纷，争执 conflict：挑拨～ *provoke a conflict*｜惹～ *get involved in a conflict* ❾ 文言代词，这，此 (pronoun in classical Chinese) this：如～ *like so*｜～日天气晴朗。*It is fine and sunny on this day.*［国是］国家大计 state affairs：共商～ *discuss state affairs together*

谥(諡) shì ㄕˋ 订正 to correct; to amend

媞 shì ㄕˋ 聪慧 intelligent

适(適) shì ㄕˋ ❶切合，相合（⑳一合）suitable; proper：～宜 *suitable*｜～意 *agreeable; comfortable*｜～用 *be applicable* ❷舒服 comfortable：安～ *peaceful and comfortable*｜稍觉不～ *feel slightly uncomfortable* ❸刚巧 to happen to：～逢其会 *come just at the right time* ❹刚才，方才 just now：～从何处来？*Where did (you) just come from?* ❺往，到 towards; to：无所～从 *not know what course to take* ⑤旧指女子出嫁 (old, for a woman) to marry：～人 *to marry*

⇨ see also kuò on p.372

室 shì ㄕˋ ❶屋子 house; room：～内 *indoor*｜教～ *classroom* ⑤①妻子 wife：妻～ *wife*｜继～ *second wife (after the first one dies)* ②家，家族 family：皇～ *imperial family*｜十～九空 *nine out of ten houses are deserted* ❷机关团体内的工作单位 office：会计～ *accounts office* ❸星宿名，二十八宿之一 shi (one of the twenty-eight constellations in ancient Chinese astronomy)

逝 shì ㄕˋ ❶过去 to pass：光阴易～ *time passes quickly* ❷死，多用于表示对死者的敬意 (often to show respect to the deceased) to die：～世 *pass away*｜不幸病～ *unfortunately passed away after an illness*

誓 shì ㄕˋ ❶当众表示，决心依照说的话实行 to publicly pledge：～不两立 *be irreconcilable*｜～为共产主义奋斗终身 *pledge to devote one's whole life to fighting for communism* ❷表示决心的话 oath：宣～ *take an oath*｜发～ *to vow*｜～言 *oath; pledge*

莳(蒔) shì ㄕˋ 移栽植物 (in agriculture) to transplant：～秧 *transplant seedlings*

释(釋) shì ㄕˋ ❶说明，解说（⑳解一、注一）to explain：解～字句 *explain words and sentences*｜古诗浅～ *simplified explanations of ancient poems* ❷消散 to dissipate：冰～（喻怀疑、误会等完全消除）*(figurative) to dispel (doubt or misunderstanding)*｜～疑 *dispel doubts; clear up difficulties* ❸放开，放下 to let go; to put down：～放 *to release*｜手不～卷 *always have a book in one's hand*｜如～重负 *a great load* *off one's mind* ❹把坐监服刑的人释放 (for prisoners) to release：保～ *release on bail* | 开～ *release a prisoner* ❺佛教创始人“释迦牟尼”的省称，泛指佛教 Sakyamuni (short for 释迦牟尼); (generally) Buddhism：～氏（佛家）*Buddhist* | ～子（和尚）*Buddhist monk* | ～教 *Buddhism*

谥(謚、*諡) shì ㄕˋ 我国古代，在最高统治者或其他有地位的人死后，依其生前事迹给予的称号，如“武”帝、“哀”公等。又叫谥号 posthumous epithet of a ruler or important person in ancient times based on his life (also called 谥号)

嗜 shì ㄕˋ 喜爱，特别爱好 to love; to be addicted to：～学 *love to study* | ～睡 *hypersomnia* [嗜好]（－hào）对于某种东西特别爱好，爱好成癖。也指特殊的爱好 hobby; addiction

筮 shì ㄕˋ 古代用蓍草占卦（迷信）(ancient superstition) divination using the yarrow plant

噬 shì ㄕˋ 咬 to bite：吞～ *to devour* | ～脐莫及（喻后悔无及）*too late for regrets*

奭 shì ㄕˋ 盛大 grand

襫 shì ㄕˋ see 袯襫 (bó－) at 袯 on page 49

螫 shì ㄕˋ 有毒腺的虫子刺人或牲畜 (of poisonous insects) to sting

匙 shi ·ㄕ see 钥匙 (yào－) at 钥 on page 763

⇨ see also chí on p.80

殖 shi ·ㄕ [骨殖]（gǔ－）尸骨 bones of the dead

⇨ see also zhí on p.853

SHOU ㄕㄡ

收(**収) shōu ㄕㄡ ❶接到，接受，跟“发”相对 to receive (opposite of 发)：～发 *receive and dispatch* | ～信 *receive a letter* | ～条 *receipt* | 接～ *to receive; take over* | 招～ *to recruit* | ～账（受款记账）*enter received payments into the accounts* ❷藏或放置妥当 to put away; to keep：这是重要东西，要～好了。*This is an important thing and must be kept properly.* ❸割取成熟的农作物 to harvest; to reap：秋～ *autumn harvest* | ～麦子 *harvest wheat* ❹获得（经济利益）to earn (profit)：～益 *earnings; profit* | ～支相抵 *break even* ❺招回 to recall; to call back：～兵 *withdraw troops* ❻聚，合拢 to gather; to close：疮～口了。*The wound has closed.* ❼结束 to end：～尾 *wind up (a project); to end* | ～工 *stop work* | ～场 *ending* ❽控制，收敛 to control; to restrain：～住脚步 *stop in one's tracks* | 把心～一～ *settle down and concentrate on one's work/study again* ❾逮捕拘禁 to arrest; to take into custody：～监 *to imprison*

熟 shóu ㄕㄡˊ 义同“熟”(shú)，用于口语 (spoken) same in meaning as 熟 (shú)

⇨ see also shú on p.608

手 shǒu ㄕㄡˇ ❶人体上肢前端能拿东西的部分 hand (see picture of 人体 on page 647) [手足] 比喻兄弟 (figurative) brothers ❷拿着 to hold：人～一册 *a copy in everyone's hand* ❸（一儿）量词，用于技能、本领等 measure word for skill, talent, etc.：有两～儿 *be rather skilful* ❹亲手 with one's own hands; in person：～书 *letter written in one's own hand; handwriting* | ～植 *plant by hand* ❺做某种事情或擅长某种技能的人 used to refer to a person skilled in a certain area, or who performs a certain role：选～ *contestant* | 生产能～ *production expert* | 水～ *sailor* | 神枪～ *sharpshooter* ❻小巧易拿的 handy; portable：～机 *mobile phone* | ～包 *handbag* | ～册 *handbook*

守 shǒu ㄕㄡˇ ❶防卫，守卫，跟"攻"相对 to defend (opposite of 攻)：～城 *defend a city* | 坚～阵地 *hold fast to one's position* [墨守] 依照老法子不肯改进 stick to (old ways)：～成规 *stick to conventions* ❷看守，看护 to keep watch; to guard：～门 *guard the door* | ～着病人 *stay by the patient's side* ❸遵守，依照 abide by：因循～旧 *stick to the old ways and refuse to innovate* | ～时间 *be on time* | ～纪律 *be disciplined* | ～法 *abide by the law* ❹靠近，依傍 near; adjacent to：～着水的地方，要多种稻子。*Plant more rice in the areas near water.*

首 shǒu ㄕㄡˇ ❶头，脑袋 head：昂～ *hold one's head high* | ～饰 *jewellery* [首领] 某些团体的领导人 leader ❷领导人，带头的 leader：～长 *head official; senior official* ❸第一，最高的 first; highest：～要 *top priority* | ～席 *seat of honour; first place* ❹最先，最早 earliest：～次 *first time* | ～创 *to pioneer; to originate* | ～播 *initial broadcast* ❺出头告发 to report (an offender)：自～ *surrender oneself (to the police, justice, etc.)* | 出～ *inform on a criminal; surrender oneself* ❻量词，用于诗歌、乐曲等 measure word for poems, music, etc.：一～诗 *a poem* | 一～歌 *a song*

艏 shǒu ㄕㄡˇ 船体的前部 prow

寿(壽) shòu ㄕㄡˋ ❶活得岁数大 advanced age：人～年丰。*The people enjoy long lives and bountiful annual harvests.* ❷年岁，生命 age; life：长～ *long life* | ～命 *lifespan* ❸寿辰，生日 birthday：祝～ *congratulate sb on their birthday* | ～礼 *birthday present (for an elderly person)* ❹婉辞，装殓死人的 (euphemism) used for items related to a corpse or coffin：～材 *coffin prepared before one's death* | ～衣 *clothing for a corpse*

受 shòu ㄕㄡˋ ❶接纳，接受 to accept; to receive：～贿 *take bribes* | ～教育 *receive education* ❷忍耐某种遭遇（㊀忍一）to

S

endure：～不了 *cannot bear* | ～罪 *endure hardship* ❸遭到 to encounter; to suffer (usually unfortunate events or bad things)：～批评 *be criticised* | ～害 *suffer injury; be killed* | ～风 *catch a cold* ❹适合 to suit; to be agreeable：～听（听着入耳）*pleasant to hear* | ～看（看着舒服）*pleasant to look at*

授 shòu ㄕㄡˋ ❶给，与 to give; to confer：～旗 *present a flag* | ～奖 *present an award* | ～意（把自己的意思告诉别人让别人照着办）*to inspire (sb to do sth)* ❷传授 to teach：～课 *give lessons*

绶(綬) shòu ㄕㄡˋ 一种丝质带子，古代常用来拴在印纽上 silk ribbon (often tied to seals in ancient times)：～带 *ribbon tied to a seal or medal* | 印～ *a seal and the silk ribbon on it*

狩 shòu ㄕㄡˋ 打猎，古代指冬天打猎 to hunt; to hunt in winter in ancient times：～猎 *hunting*

售 shòu ㄕㄡˋ 卖 to sell：～票 *sell tickets* | 零～ *to retail* | 销～ *to market; to sell* ㊀施展 carry out：以～其奸 *in order to carry out one's evil plans*

兽(獸) shòu ㄕㄡˋ ❶哺乳动物的通称，一般指有四条腿、全身生毛的哺乳动物 mammal ❷形容野蛮，下流 barbaric; indecent：～欲 *animal lust* | ～行 *brutal act*

瘦 shòu ㄕㄡˋ ❶含脂肪少，跟"胖""肥"相对 thin; lean (opposite of 胖 or 肥)：～肉 *lean meat* | 身体很～。*The body is very thin.* ❷衣服鞋袜等窄小，跟"肥"相对 (of clothing, shoes, etc.) tight (opposite of 肥)：这件衣裳穿着～了。*This piece of clothing has gotten tight.* ❸土地瘠薄 (of land) barren：～田 *barren field* ❹笔画细 (of calligraphic strokes) thin：～硬 *thin and strong* | 钟书体～ *thin calligraphic style of Zhong Yao (?—230)* | ～金体 *thin calligraphic style created by Zhao Ji (1082—1135), Emperor Huizong of the Northern Song Dynasty*

SHU ㄕㄨ

殳 shū ㄕㄨ 古代一种竹、木制成的兵器，顶端有棱无刃。有的在顶端装有刺球和矛 (ancient) a type of weapon made of bamboo or wood

书(書) shū ㄕㄨ ❶成本儿的著作 book：读～ *read a book* | 著～ *write a book; book* ❷信（㊜—信）letter：家～ *family letter* | ～札 *letter* | 来～已悉。*I have received your letter.* ❸文件 document：证明～ *certificate* | 申请～ *application letter* ❹写字（㊜—写）to write：～法 *calligraphy* ㊕字体 calligraphy style：楷～ *regular script (a style of Chinese calligraphy)* | 隶～ *official script (a style of Chinese calligraphy)*

抒 shū ㄕㄨ 抒发，尽量表达 to express; to convey：～情 *express emotions* | 各～己见。*Everyone expresses their own opinion.*

纾(紓) shū ㄕㄨ 缓和，解除 to relieve; to extricate：～难（nàn）*provide relief in a disaster*

舒 shū ㄕㄨ ❶展开，伸展 to spread; to open up：～眉展眼 *look contented* [舒服] [舒坦] 身心愉快 comfortable ❷从容，缓慢 leisurely

枢(樞) shū ㄕㄨ ❶门上的转轴 door hinge：户～不蠹。*A door hinge is never worm-eaten; (figurative) Regular activity keeps one healthy.* ❷指重要的或中心的部分 pivot [枢纽] 重要的部分，事物相互联系的中心环节 hub：交通～ *transportation hub* [中枢] 中心，中央 centre：神经～ *nerve centre*

叔 shū ㄕㄨ ❶兄弟排行常用伯、仲、叔、季为次序，叔是老三 third eldest among brothers (伯，仲，叔，季 are often used to indicate the birth order of brothers) ❷叔父，父亲的弟弟。又称跟父亲同辈而年纪较小、没有亲属关系的男子 ㊊ uncle (father's younger brother); unrelated man who is of one's father's generation and younger than one's father：大～ *uncle (unrelated man of one's father's generation)* ❸（－子）丈夫的弟弟 brother-in-law (one's husband's younger brother)：小～子 *brother-in-law*

菽(尗)** shū ㄕㄨ 豆类的总称 beans

淑 shū ㄕㄨ 善，美 good; graceful：贤～ *virtuous* | ～女 *gentle and virtuous woman*

陎 shū ㄕㄨ 姓 (surname) Shu

姝 shū ㄕㄨ 美丽，美好。也指美女 beautiful; beautiful woman：名～ *famous beautiful woman*

殊 shū ㄕㄨ ❶不同 different：特～情况 *special circumstances* | ～途同归 *reach the same goal via different routes* ❷特别突出 outstanding; exceptional：～荣 *exceptional honour* | ～勋 *exceptional exploits* ❸极，很 extremely：～佳 *extremely good* | ～可钦佩 *especially worthy of admiration* ❹断，绝 to break; to sever [殊死] 1 古代指斩首的死刑 (ancient) beheading 2 拼着性命 to risk one's life：～战斗 *fight fearlessly and desperately*

倏(*倐、*儵) shū ㄕㄨ 极快地，忽然 very quickly; suddenly：～忽 *in an instant* | ～尔而逝 *disappear in the blink of an eye*

梳 shū ㄕㄨ ❶（－子）整理头发的用具，又叫拢子 comb (also called 拢子) ❷用梳子整理头发 to comb：～头 *comb one's hair*

疏(❶-❹*疎) shū ㄕㄨ ❶清除阻塞，使畅通（㊄－通）to dredge; to unblock：～导 *to dredge; clear the way* ❷分散 to scatter：～散 *to evacuate; to disperse* ❸事物间距离大，空隙大，跟"密"相对（㊄稀－）sparse (opposite of 密)：～林 *sparse woodland* | ～密不均 *of uneven density* ㊀①不亲

密，关系远的 (of relationships) distant：亲～ *close and distant* | ～远 *(become) distant* ②不细密，粗心 careless：～神 *careless* | ～忽 *carelessness* ❹空虚 empty; void：志大才～ *have great ambition but little talent* ❺粗 coarse; rough：～食 *rough food* ❻不熟悉 unfamiliar：生～ *unfamiliar* | 人生地～ *not familiar with either place or people* ❼分条说明的文字 text that explains different points：上～ *present a memorial (to a monarch)* | 奏～（封建时代臣下向皇帝陈述事情的文章）*(present a) memorial to a monarch* ❽对古书旧有注文做的阐释 annotations (on existing commentary in old books)：注～ *notes and commentaries*

蔬 shū ㄕㄨ 蔬菜，可以做菜的植物（多属草本）vegetable：～食 *vegetarian food*

鄃 shū ㄕㄨ 古县名，在今山东省夏津附近 Shu (an ancient county near today's Xiajin, Shandong Province)

输(輸) shū ㄕㄨ ❶从一个地方运送到另一个地方（㊣运一）to transport：～出 *to export* | ～血 *transfuse blood* ❷送给，捐献 to give; to donate：捐～ *to donate* | ～财助学 *donate money to education* ❸败，负，跟"赢"相对 to lose; to be defeated (opposite of 赢)：认～ *admit defeat* | ～了官司 *lost a lawsuit* | ～了两个球 *lost by two goals*

毹 shū ㄕㄨ see 氍毹 (qú—) at 氍 on page 548

摅(攄) shū ㄕㄨ 发表或表示出来 to express：各～己见。*Everyone expresses their own opinion.*

秫 shú ㄕㄨˊ 高粱，多指黏高粱 sorghum (often glutinous sorghum)：～米 *glutinous sorghum; millet grains* | ～秸（高粱秆）*sorghum stalk*

孰 shú ㄕㄨˊ 文言代词 pronoun in classical Chinese ①谁 who：～谓不可？*Who says it is not possible?* ②什么 what：是（这个）可忍，～不可忍？*If this can be tolerated, what cannot?* ③哪个 which：～胜～负，尚未可知。*It is still not known which side will win and which side will lose.*

塾 shú ㄕㄨˊ 旧时私人设立的教学的地方 (old) private school：私～ *(old) private school* | 村～ *village private school*

熟 shú ㄕㄨˊ ❶食物烧煮到可吃的程度 cooked：饭～了。*The rice is cooked.* | ～菜 *cooked food* ❷成熟，植物的果实或种子长成 ripe：麦子～了。*The wheat is ripe.* ❸程度深 profound; deep：深思～虑 *ponder deeply* | ～睡 *sleep soundly* ❹因常接触而知道得清楚 familiar：～悉 *familiar* | ～人 *familiar person* | 这条路我～。*I know this road well.* ❺熟练，对某种工作精通而有经验 skilled：～手 *skilled person* | 纯～ *skilful; practised* | ～能生巧 *practice makes perfect* ❻经过加工或炼制的 processed; refined：～铁 *wrought iron* | ～皮子

S

tanned leather

⇨ see also shóu on p.604

姝 shú ㄕㄨˊ 宫廷女官名 female palace official

赎(贖) shú ㄕㄨˊ ❶用财物换回抵押品 to redeem (a pawned item or sth offered as a collateral)：～当（dàng）*redeem a pawned item* | 把东西～回来 *redeem sth and get it back* ❷用行动抵消、弥补罪过（旧时特指用财物减免刑罚）to atone for; (old) to pay a fine in lieu of punishment：自～ *atone for one's crime* | 立功～罪 *perform meritorious service to atone for one's crime*

暑 shǔ ㄕㄨˇ 热 heat：中（zhòng）～ *get heatstroke* | ～天 *hot summer day*

署 shǔ ㄕㄨˇ ❶办公的处所 office：海关总～ *General Administration of Customs* ❷布置 to arrange; to prepare：部～ *to deploy; deployment* ❸签名，题字 to sign; to inscribe：签～ *sign one's name* | ～名 *put one's signature to* ❹暂代 to replace temporarily：～理 *acting*

薯(*藷) shǔ ㄕㄨˇ 植物名 plant name ①甘薯，草本植物，又叫白薯、红薯或番薯，茎细长，块根可以吃 sweet potato (also called 白薯，红薯 or 番薯) ②马铃薯，草本植物，又叫土豆、山药蛋，块茎可以吃 potato (also called 土豆 or 山药蛋) ③[薯蓣]（-yù）草本植物，又叫山药，块根圆柱形，可以吃，也可入药 Chinese yam (also called 山药)

曙 shǔ ㄕㄨˇ 天刚亮 daybreak：～色 *light of early dawn* | ～光 *morning twilight*

黍 shǔ ㄕㄨˇ （-子）谷类作物，籽实碾成米叫黄米，性黏，可以吃，也可酿酒 proso millet

属(屬) shǔ ㄕㄨˇ ❶同一家族的成员 family member：家～ *family member* | 眷～ *family dependant* | 亲～ *(family) relative* ❷类别 category：金～ *metal* ❸生物的分类单位之一，在"科"之下、"种"之上 genus (a category in taxonomic classification)：梨～ *Pyrus* | 狐～ *Vulpes* ❹有管辖关系，也指有管辖关系的人或单位（㊥隶一）subordinate to; (of a person or organisation) subordinate：直～ *directly under* | ～局 *subordinate bureau* | ～员 *subordinate (under sb's authority)* | 下～ *subordinate* ❺归类 to classify：～于自然科学 *classed as natural science* ❻为某人或某方所有 to belong to：这本书现在～你了。*This book is yours now.* | 胜利终～甲队。*In the end, the victory was Team A's.* ❼是 to be：查明～实 *prove to be true* ❽用属相记生年（用干支纪年，十二支配合十二种动物，人生在哪年，就属哪种动物叫"属相"）(of Chinese zodiac animals) to be born in the year of：甲子、丙子等子年生的都～鼠。*Those who were born in zi years like the* jiazi *and* bingzi *years were born in the Year of the Rat.*

⇨ see also zhǔ on p.868

S

蜀 shǔ ㄕㄨˇ ❶古国名 name of ancient states ①周代诸侯国名，在今四川省成都一带 Shu (a state in the Zhou Dynasty, around today's Chengdu, Sichuan Province) ②蜀汉，三国之一，刘备所建立（公元221—263年），在今四川省，后来扩展到贵州省、云南省和陕西省汉中一带 Shu Han (one of the Three Kingdoms founded by Liu Bei) ❷四川省的别称 another name for Sichuan Province

鼠 shǔ ㄕㄨˇ 老鼠，哺乳动物，俗叫耗子，体小尾长，门齿发达，繁殖力强，能传染疾病 rat; mouse (informal 耗子)

数(數) shǔ ㄕㄨˇ ❶一个一个地计算 to count: ～一～ *count up* ㊀比较起来最突出 to be the best: 就～他有本领。*He is the most capable.* ❷责备，列举过错 to scold; to blame: ～落 (luo) *scold sb by listing their wrongdoings* | ～说 *to scold*

⇨ see also shù on p.611, shuò on p.616

术(術) shù ㄕㄨˋ ❶技艺，学问 skill; knowledge: 武～ *martial arts* | 技～ *skill* | 美～ *art* | 不学无～ *have neither learning nor skill* [术语] 学术和各种工艺上的专门用语 terminology; jargon ❷方法 method: 战～ *military tactic* | 防御之～ *defensive tactic*

⇨ see also zhú on p.866

述 shù ㄕㄨˋ 讲说，陈说（㊀叙一、陈一、一说）to narrate: 口～ *give an oral account*

沭 shù ㄕㄨˋ 沭河，发源于山东省，流至江苏省入新沂河 Shuhe River (originates in Shandong Province and flows into Xinyi River in Jiangsu Province)

钵(鉥) shù ㄕㄨˋ ❶长针 long needle ❷刺 to prick

戍 shù ㄕㄨˋ 军队防守 military defence: 卫～ *garrison* | ～边 *garrison the frontier*

束 shù ㄕㄨˋ ❶捆住 to bind; to tie: ～发 (fà) *tie up one's hair* | ～手～脚 *be tied down by many things; over-cautious* [束缚] (-fù) 捆绑 tie up ㊁使受到限制 to restrict; to stifle: 不要～群众的创造性。*Do not stifle the creativity of the masses.* ❷成捆ル或成条的东西 bundle; beam: 花～ *bouquet of flowers* | 光～ *light beam* ❸量词，捆ル (measure word) bundle; bouquet: 一～鲜花 *a bundle of fresh flowers* ❹控制(㊀约一) to control: 拘～ *restrained; be ill at ease* | 管～ *to check; to control* | ～身自爱 *restrain and care for oneself*

树(樹) shù ㄕㄨˋ ❶木本植物的通称 tree ❷种植，栽培 to plant; to cultivate ❸立，建立（㊀一立）to establish: ～雄心，立壮志 *set lofty ambitions and ideals*

竖(豎、*豎) shù ㄕㄨˋ ❶直立，跟地面垂直的，跟"横"相对 to stand vertical; to erect (opposite of 横)：把棍子～起来。*Stand the pole up vertically.* ❷从上到下的或从前到后的，跟“横”相对 vertical; from front to back (opposite of 横)：～着写 *write from top to bottom* | ～着挖道沟 *dig a drain from front to back* ❸直，汉字自上往下写的一种笔形（丨）(in a Chinese character) vertical stroke：“十”字是一横一～。*The character 十 is written with a horizontal stroke followed by a vertical stroke.* ❹竖子，古时指未成年的仆人，也用于对人的一种蔑称 (ancient) underage servant; (also) a derogatory form of address

俞 shù ㄕㄨˋ same as “腧”

⇨ see also yú on p.799

隃 shù ㄕㄨˋ 古地名，在今山西省代县西北 an ancient place name, in northwest of today's Daixian County, Shanxi Province

腧 shù ㄕㄨˋ 腧穴，人体上的穴道 acupuncture point; acupoint：肺～ *lung acupoint* | 胃～ *stomach acupoint*

恕 shù ㄕㄨˋ 宽恕，原谅 to forgive：饶～ *to pardon* | ～罪 *pardon an offence* | ～我直言。*Pardon me for being direct.*

庶(*庻) shù ㄕㄨˋ ❶众多 many：～民（旧指老百姓）*(old) the common people* | 富～ *be rich and populous* ❷庶几（jī），将近，差不多 almost; around：～乎可行。*It is perhaps doable.* ❸宗法制度下指家庭的旁支 minor branch of the family under the patriarchal system：～出 *born of a concubine*

裋 shù ㄕㄨˋ 古代仆役穿的一种粗布衣服 (ancient) coarse servant clothes

数(數) shù ㄕㄨˋ ❶数目，划分或计算出来的量 number：基～ *cardinal number* | 序～ *ordinal number* | 岁～ *age* | 次～ *number of times* | 人～ *number of people* [数词] 表示数目的词，如“一、九、千、万”等 numeral ❷几，几个 a few：～次 *several times* | ～日 *a few days* | ～人 *several people* ❸（迷信）劫数，命运 fate; destiny：在～难逃 *cannot escape one's fate* | 气～已尽 *one's days are numbered*

⇨ see also shǔ on p.610, shuò on p.616

墅 shù ㄕㄨˋ 别墅，住宅以外供游玩休养的园林房屋 villa

漱(*潄) shù ㄕㄨˋ 含水荡洗口腔 to gargle：～口 *rinse one's mouth* | 洗～ *clean one's face and mouth* ㊀ 洗涤，冲刷 to cleanse; to scour：悬泉瀑布，飞～其间。*Cascades and waterfalls spray mists through the air.*

澍 shù ㄕㄨˋ 及时的雨 timely rain

SHUA ㄕㄨㄚ

刷 shuā ㄕㄨㄚ ❶（一子、一儿）用成束的毛、棕等制成的清除东西或涂抹东西的用具 brush ❷用刷子或类似刷子的用具来清除或涂抹 to brush：～牙 *brush teeth*｜～鞋 *clean shoes*｜～锅 *scour a pot*｜用石灰～墙 *whitewash the wall* ㊀淘汰 to eliminate; to knock out：第一轮比赛就被～掉了 *be eliminated in the first round of competition* ❸ same as "唰"

⇨ see also shuà on p.612

唰 shuā ㄕㄨㄚ 形容迅速擦过去的声音 swooshing; swishing：小雨～～地下起来了。*The light rain came rustling down.*

耍 shuǎ ㄕㄨㄚˇ ❶〈方 dialect〉玩（㊥玩一）to play：孩子们在院子里～。*The children are playing in the garden.* ❷玩弄，表演 to play with; to perform：～猴 *monkey performance*｜～大刀 *perform with a broad sword* ❸戏弄 to make fun of：别～人。*Don't make fun of people.* ❹弄，施展 to demonstrate：～手艺 *demonstrate skills*｜～威风 *display power and prestige*｜～手腕（指使用不正当的方法）*use tricks*

刷 shuà ㄕㄨㄚˋ ［刷白］色白而略微发青 white with a green tinge

⇨ see also shuā on p.611

SHUAI ㄕㄨㄞ

衰 shuāi ㄕㄨㄞ 事物发展转向微弱（㊥一微）to decline; to weaken：～败 *to decline*｜～老 *old and feeble*｜～弱 *weak*［衰变］指放射性元素放射出粒子后变成另一种元素 (of radioactive elements) decay

⇨ see also cuī on p.102

摔（❹**踤）shuāi ㄕㄨㄞ ❶用力往下扔 throw down with force：把帽子往床上一～就走了 *threw the hat down on the bed and left* ❷很快地掉下 to fall quickly：从树上～了下来 *fell from the tree* ❸因掉下而毁坏 drop and break：把碗～了 *dropped the bowl and broke it* ❹跌跤 to trip and fall：他～倒了。*He tripped and fell.*｜～了一跤 *tripped and fell*

甩 shuǎi ㄕㄨㄞˇ ❶抡，扔 to swing; to fling：～袖子 *wave one's sleeves*｜～手榴弹 *throw a grenade* ❷抛开，抛弃 throw off; to abandon：～车（使列车的车厢与机车分开）*uncouple a carriage*｜被～在后面 *be left behind*｜～掉了跟踪的特务 *gave the secret agent who was following one the slip*

帅（帥）shuài ㄕㄨㄞˋ ❶军队中最高一级的指挥官 commander-in-chief：元～ *marshal*｜统～ *commander-in-chief* ❷英俊，潇洒，漂亮 handsome; cool：这个小伙儿很～。*This boy is very handsome.*｜他的动作～极了。*His movements are so cool.*｜字写得～。*The words are beautifully written.*

率 shuài ㄕㄨㄞˋ ❶带领，统领（㊥一领）to lead; to command：～队 *lead troops*｜～师出征 *lead the troops on a military campaign* ❷轻易地，不细想，

不慎重（㊣轻一、草一）hastily; careless carelessly：粗～ *rough and careless* ❸爽直坦白（㊣直一）frank ❹大率，大概，大略 generally; roughly：～皆如此 *mostly so* ❺遵循 to abide by; to follow：～由旧章 *abide by the old ways* ❻模范 model：表～ *example; model*

⇨ see also lǜ on p.424

蟀 shuài ㄕㄨㄞˋ see 蟋蟀（xī一）at 蟋 on page 698

SHUAN ㄕㄨㄢ

闩（閂、**櫦）shuān ㄕㄨㄢ ❶门闩，横插在门后使门推不开的棍子 door bolt ❷用闩插上门 to bolt a door：把门～上 *bolt the door*

拴 shuān ㄕㄨㄢ 用绳子系（jì）上 to fasten with rope：～马 *tie a horse* | ～车 *hired vehicle* ㊥被事物缠住而不能自由行动 to be tied down：被琐事～住了 *be tied down by trivial matters* | 能～住他的人，却～不住他的心。*(She) might have snared him, but (she) couldn't capture his heart.*

栓 shuān ㄕㄨㄢ ❶器物上可以开关的机件 bolt; switch：枪～ *bolt of a gun* | 消火～ *fire hydrant* ❷塞子或作用跟塞子相仿的东西 stopper; plug：～塞 *embolism* | ～剂 *suppository* | 血～ *thrombus*

涮 shuàn ㄕㄨㄢˋ ❶放在水中摆动，略微洗洗 to rinse：～～手 *rinse one's hands* | 把毛笔～一～ *wash the writing brush* ❷把水放在器物中摇动，冲洗 to swill sth out：～瓶子 *swill a bottle with water* ❸把肉片等在滚水里放一下就取出来（蘸作料吃）to scald (meat slices) in boiling water; to dip-boil：～锅子 *dip-boil food in a hotpot* | ～羊肉 *dip-boiled mutton slices* ❹〈方 dialect〉耍弄，骗 to make a fool of; to trick：被人～了 *be tricked by sb*

腨 shuàn ㄕㄨㄢˋ 腿肚子 (of a leg) calf

SHUANG ㄕㄨㄤ

双（雙、**雙）shuāng ㄕㄨㄤ ❶两个，一对，跟"单"相对 pair; dual (opposite of 单)：～管齐下 *execute two actions at the same time* | 好事成～ *good things come in twos* ❷量词，用于成对的东西 (measure word) pair：一～鞋 *a pair of shoes* | 两～筷子 *two pairs of chopsticks* ❸偶数的 (of a number) even：～数（二、四、六、八等）*even number* ❹加倍的 double：～份 *double portion* | ～料 *of extra quality; with double qualifications*

泷（瀧）shuāng ㄕㄨㄤ 泷水，水名，在广东省 Shuangshui River (in Guangdong Province)

⇨ see also lóng on p.415

漴 shuāng ㄕㄨㄤ 用于地名 used in place names：～缺

（在上海市奉贤）*Shuangque (in Fengxian, Shanghai Municipality)*

⇨ see also chóng on p.84

霜 shuāng ㄕㄨㄤ ❶附着在地面或靠近地面的物体上的白色微细冰粒，是接近地面的水蒸气降至0°C以下凝结而成的 frost ⓔ白色 white：～鬓 *white hair on one's temples* ❷像霜的东西 sth like frost：柿～ *white powder produced in the making of dried persimmons* | 盐～ *salt efflorescence*

孀 shuāng ㄕㄨㄤ 寡妇，死了丈夫的妇人 widow：遗～ *widow* | ～居 *live as a widow*

骦（驦） shuāng ㄕㄨㄤ see 骕骦 (sù－) at 骕 on page 623

礵 shuāng ㄕㄨㄤ 北礵岛，岛名，在福建省霞浦 Beishuang Island (in Xiapu, Fujian Province)

鹴（鸘） shuāng ㄕㄨㄤ see 鹔鹴 (sù－) at 鹔 on page 623

爽 shuǎng ㄕㄨㄤˇ ❶明朗，清亮 bright and clear：秋高气～ *clear and crisp autumn day* | ～目 *pleasant to the eye* ❷清凉，清洁 cool; clean：凉～ *nice and cool* | 清～ *fresh and clean* ❸痛快，率直 frank; straightforward：豪～ *forthright* | 直～ *frank* | ～快 *straightforward* [爽性] 索性，干脆 might as well：既然晚了，～不去吧。*Since it's late, we might as well not go.* ❹舒适，畅快 well; comfortable：身体不～ *feel uncomfortable* | 人逢喜事精神～。*One is always in high spirits on happy occasions.* ❺不合，违背 to miss; to deviate：～约 *fail to keep an appointment* | 毫厘不～ *extremely precise*

SHUI ㄕㄨㄟ

谁（誰） shuí ㄕㄨㄟˊ（又）see shéi on page 587

水 shuǐ ㄕㄨㄟˇ ❶一种无色无味无臭透明的液体，化学成分是H_2O。water：雨～ *rainwater* | 喝～ *drink water* ❷河流 river：赤～ *Chishui River* | 汉～ *Hanshui River* ❸江、河、湖、海的通称 general term for rivers, lakes and the sea water：～产 *aquatic product* | ～陆交通 *land and water transport* | ～旱码头 *a centre accessible by both land and water* [水平] 1 静水的平面 horizontal 2 达到的程度 standard; level：文化～ *education level; level of cultural refinement* ❹汁液 liquid; juice：药～ *liquid medicine* | 橘子～ *tangerine juice* ❺额外附加的费用 additional charge：贴～ *agio; top-up payment* ❻量词，衣服洗的次数 (measure word for laundry) wash：这衣服不禁（jīn）穿，洗了两～就破了。*This piece of clothing is not durable; it came apart after only two washes.*

[水族] 我国少数民族，参看附录四 the Sui people (one of the ethnic groups in China. See Appendix Ⅳ.)

说（說） shuì ㄕㄨㄟˋ 用话劝说别人，使他听从自己的意见 to persuade：游～ *to*

lobby

⇨ see also shuō on p.615, yuè on p.811

帨 shuì ㄕㄨㄟˋ 古代的佩巾 (ancient) handkerchief

税 shuì ㄕㄨㄟˋ 政府依法向纳税人征收的货币或实物 tax：纳～ *pay tax* | 营业～ *business tax* | 个人所得～ *personal income tax*

睡 shuì ㄕㄨㄟˋ 闭目安息，大脑皮质处于休息状态（㊥一眠）to sleep：～着（zháo）了 *have fallen asleep* | ～午觉 *take an afternoon nap*

SHUN ㄕㄨㄣ

吮 shǔn ㄕㄨㄣˇ 聚拢嘴唇来吸（㊥一吸）to suck：～乳 *suck on mother's breast*

楯 shǔn ㄕㄨㄣˇ 栏干 balustrade

⇨ see also dùn on p.154

顺（順） shùn ㄕㄨㄣˋ ❶向着同一个方向，跟"逆"相对 in the same direction as (opposite of 逆)：～风 *have a favourable wind* | ～水 *go with the current* | 通～ *clear and coherent* ❷沿，循 along：～河边走 *walk along the river's bank* ㊀依次往上往下或依次往后 in sequence; along：～着楼梯 *go up (or down) the staircase* | ～着台阶 *go up (or down) the stairs* | ～着坡 *go up (or down) the slope* | 遇雨～延 *will be postponed if it rains* ❸随，趁便 to act at one's convenience; in passing：～手关门。*Close the door behind you.* | ～口说出来 *said it offhandedly* ❹整理，理顺 to arrange; to put in order：～一～头发 *smoothen one's hair* | 文章太乱，得～一～。*The essay is too messy; it needs to be made more coherent.* ❺服从，不违背 to obey：～从 *to obey* | 归～ *come over and pledge allegiance to* ❻适合，不别扭 to suit; to please：～心 *to one's satisfaction* | ～眼 *pleasant to the eye* | ～耳 *pleasant to the ear*

舜 shùn ㄕㄨㄣˋ 传说中上古帝王名 Shun (a legendary ruler in ancient times)

瞬 shùn ㄕㄨㄣˋ 一眨（zhǎ）眼，转眼 blink of an eye：～息万变（形容在极短时间内变化极多）*undergo many changes in a short period of time* | 转～即逝 *vanish in the blink of an eye*

SHUO ㄕㄨㄛ

说（說） shuō ㄕㄨㄛ ❶用话来表达自己的意思 to talk; to say ❷解释 to explain：～明 *to explain; explanation* | 解～ *to explain* ❸说合，介绍 to bring two or more parties together; to introduce：～亲 *act as matchmaker* ❹言论，主张 theory; ideas：学～ *theory* | 著书立～ *write a book to propose a theory* ❺责备 to reprimand：他挨～了。*He was scolded.* | ～了他一顿。*He was given a dressing-down.*

⇨ see also shuì on p.614, yuè on p.811

S

妁 shuò ㄕㄨㄛˋ 旧指媒人 (old) matchmaker

烁(爍) shuò ㄕㄨㄛˋ 光亮的样子 bright：闪～ *to flicker*

铄(鑠) shuò ㄕㄨㄛˋ ❶熔化金属 to melt (metal)：～金 *melt metal* | ～石流金（形容天气极热）*melt rocks and metals; (figurative) bakingly hot* ❷销毁，消损 to destroy; to weaken ❸ same as "烁"

朔 shuò ㄕㄨㄛˋ ❶农历每月初一日 the first day of each month in the traditional Chinese calendar ❷北 north：～风 *north wind* | ～方 *the north*

S

搠 shuò ㄕㄨㄛˋ 扎，刺 to prick; to stab

蒴 shuò ㄕㄨㄛˋ 蒴果，果实的一种，由两个以上的心皮构成，成熟后裂开，内含许多种子，如芝麻、棉花、百合等的果实 (of fruit type) capsule

槊 shuò ㄕㄨㄛˋ 长矛，古代的一种兵器 long spear

硕(碩) shuò ㄕㄨㄛˋ 大 big; large：～果 *large fruit; (figurative) great achievement* | ～大无朋（形容无比的大）*gigantic*
[硕士] 学位名，在学士之上，博士之下 (academic degree) master

数(數) shuò ㄕㄨㄛˋ 屡次（连频～）repeatedly：～见不鲜（xiān）*be a familiar sight*

⇨ see also shǔ on p.610, shù on p.611

SI ㄙ

厶 sī ㄙ ancient character form for 私

私 sī ㄙ ❶属于个人的或为了个人的，跟"公"相对 personal; private (opposite of 公)：～事 *private matter* | ～信 *private letter* 引为自己的 selfish：～心 *selfish motive* | 自～ *selfish* | 假公济～ *use an official position for private gain* | 大公无～ *impartial; selfless* ❷秘密而不公开，不合法，也指不合法的货物 secret; illicit; (also) illegal goods：～货 *smuggled goods* | ～自 *privately; without permission* | 走～ *to smuggle* | 缉～ *crack down on smuggling* ❸暗地里，偷偷地 secretly：～语 *to whisper; private talk*

司 sī ㄙ ❶主管，主持，经办 to manage; to take charge of: 各～其职 *everyone has their own task* | ～令 *commander* | ～法 *judiciary* ❷中央各部中所设立的分工办事的单位 department (under a ministry)：外交部礼宾～ *Protocol Department of Ministry of Foreign Affairs* | ～长 *director of a department*

峒 sī ㄙ 峒峿（wú），地名，在江苏省新沂 Siwu (a place in Xinyi, Jiangsu Province)

丝(絲) sī ㄙ ❶蚕吐出的像线的东西，是织绸缎等的原料 silk 喻细微，极少 minuscule; tiny amount：纹～不动 *stay absolutely still* ❷（～儿）像丝的东西 sth like silk：铁～

iron wire | 萝卜～儿 *shredded radish* ❸计量单位名，10 忽是 1 丝，10 丝是 1 毫 measuring unit (There are 10 忽 in 1 丝, and 10 丝 in 1 毫.) [丝毫] 极少，极小，一点（多和否定词连用）tiny amount; very small (often used in negative phrases)：～不错 *not the least bit wrong* ❹量词，表示极少、极小的量 measure word indicating a small amount or degree：一～笑容 *a faint smile* | 一～风也没有 *not even a puff of wind*

咝 (噝) sī ㄙ 形容枪弹等很快地在空中飞过的声音 ㊀ whizz (sound made by a bullet travelling through the air)：子弹～～地从身旁飞过。*Bullets were whizzing past (me).*

鸶 (鷥) sī ㄙ see 鹭鸶 (lù—) at 鹭 on page 422

思 sī ㄙ ❶想，考虑，动脑筋（㊥—想）to think; to consider：事要三～ *think twice before one does sth* | 不假～索 *without thinking* | ～前想后 *ponder over* [思维] 在表象、概念的基础上进行分析、综合、判断、推理等认识活动的过程 thought; thinking ❷想念，挂念 to miss; to pine for：相～ *yearning between lovers* | ～家心切 *be very homesick* | ～念 *to miss; long for* ❸思路，想法 line of thought：文～ *train of thought in writing* | 构～ *plan and organize (a writing)*

偲 sī ㄙ [偲偲] 互相切磋，互相督促 learn from and encourage each other

⇨ see also cāi on p.55

缌 (緦) sī ㄙ 细的麻布 fine linen

楒 sī ㄙ 用于地名 used in place names：～栗（在重庆市）*Sili (in Chongqing Municipality)*

飔 (颸) sī ㄙ 凉风 cool wind

罳 sī ㄙ see 罘罳 (fú—) at 罘 on page 184

锶 (鍶) sī ㄙ 金属元素，符号 Sr，银白色，质软。可用来制合金、光电管、烟火、药品等 strontium (Sr)

虒 sī ㄙ [虒亭] 地名，在山西省襄垣 Siting (a place in Xiangyuan, Shanxi Province)

斯 sī ㄙ ❶文言代词，这，这个，这里 (pronoun in classical Chinese) this; here：～人 *this person* | ～时 *this time* | 生于～，长于～ *was born and grew up here* ❷文言连词，乃，就 (conjunction in classical Chinese) then; thus：有备～可以无患矣。*If one is prepared, then there is no worry.*

厮 (*廝) sī ㄙ ❶旧时对服杂役的男子的蔑称 (old) derisive form of address for a male servant：小～ *boy-servant* ㊁对人轻慢的称呼（宋以来的小说中常用）derisive form of address for a person (often used in novels from the Song Dynasty onwards)：这～ *this knave* | 那～ *that knave* ❷互相 mutual; together：～守 *stay together* | ～打 *to fight* | ～混（hùn）*play around together; mix with*

澌 sī ㄙ 随水流动的冰 floating ice

撕 sī ㄙ 扯开，用手使分开 to tear; to rip：把布～成两块 *tear the cloth in two*

嘶 sī ㄙ ❶马叫 to neigh：人喊马～ *people shout and horses neigh* ❷声音哑 hoarse：～哑 *hoarse* | 声～力竭 *be hoarse and exhausted*

凘 sī ㄙ 尽 to terminate; to die：～灭 *to die out; to vanish*

蛳(螄) sī ㄙ ［螺蛳］(luó—) 淡水螺的通称 freshwater snail

漦 sī ㄙ chí ㄔ(又) 口水，涎沫 saliva

死 sǐ ㄙˇ ❶生物失去生命，跟"活"相对(㊀—亡) to die (opposite of 活) ㊁①不顾性命，拼死 to the death：～守 *defend to the death; obstinately cling to* | ～战 *battle to the death* ②至死，表示坚决 until death; resolutely：～不认账 *stubbornly refuse to admit what one has said or done* ③表示达到极点 extremely：乐～了 *extremely fun* | 笑～人 *extremely funny* ❷不可调和的 irreconcilable：～敌 *implacable foe* ❸不活动，不灵活 stagnant; fixed; inflexible：～水 *stagnant water* | ～心眼 *one-track mind; stubborn* | 把门钉～了 *nailed the door closed* ［死机］计算机等在运行中因程序错误等原因，显示屏上图像静止不动，无法继续操作 (of computers) to crash ㊕不通的 stopped up; not open：～胡同 *dead end* | 把洞堵～了 *plugged the hole up*

巳(巳)** sì ㄙˋ ❶地支的第六位 *si* (the sixth of the twelve Earthly Branches, a system used in the Chinese calendar) ❷巳时，指上午九点到十一点 *si* (the period from 9 a.m. to 11 a.m.)

汜 sì ㄙˋ 汜河，水名，在河南省郑州 Sihe River (in Zhengzhou, Henan Province)

祀(*禩) sì ㄙˋ ❶祭祀 to offer sacrifice (to deities or ancestors) ❷〈古 ancient〉殷代人指年 (during the Yin Dynasty) year：十有三～ *thirteen years*

四 sì ㄙˋ 数目字 (number) four

泗 sì ㄙˋ ❶鼻涕 nasal mucus：涕～(眼泪和鼻涕) *tears and snot* ❷泗河，水名，在山东省济宁 Sihe River (in Jining, Shandong Province)

驷(駟) sì ㄙˋ 古代同驾一辆车的四匹马，或者套着四匹马的车 (ancient) the four horses pulling a carriage; a carriage pulled by four horses：一言既出，～马难追(喻话说出后无法再收回) *what is said cannot be taken back; a promise must be kept*

寺 sì ㄙˋ ❶古代官署名 (ancient) court (government department)：太常～ *Court of Imperial Sacrifices* ❷寺院，佛教出家人居住的地方 Buddhist temple; Buddhist monastery ❸伊斯兰教徒礼拜、讲经的地方 mosque：清真～ *mosque*

似（△*佀）sì ㄙˋ ❶像，相类（⊜类一）to resemble; to look like：相～ *similar* | ～是而非 *apparently true but actually false; specious* ❷副词，似乎，好像，表示不确定 (adverb) seemingly; maybe：～应再行研究。*Perhaps more studies should be done.* | 这个建议～欠妥当。*This suggestion seems unsuitable.* ❸介词，表示比较，有超过的意思 (preposition) more than：一个高～一个 *each taller than the last* | 生活一天好～一天。*Life is getting better day by day.*

⇨ see also shì on p.601

姒 sì ㄙˋ 古代称丈夫的嫂子 (ancient) sister-in-law (husband's elder brother's wife)：娣～（妯娌）*sisters-in-law (women whose husbands are brothers)*

兕 sì ㄙˋ 古书上指雌的犀牛 female rhinoceros (in ancient Chinese texts)

佀 sì ㄙˋ ❶ see 似 on page 619 ❷姓 (surname) Si

耜 sì ㄙˋ ❶古代的一种农具，形状像锹 (ancient) a shovel-shaped farming tool ❷耒下端的起土部分，类似铧 (ancient) plough blade

伺 sì ㄙˋ 守候，观察 to wait; to observe：窥～ *wait and watch from the shadows* | ～机而动 *wait for an opportune time to act*

⇨ see also cì on p.98

饲（飼、*飤）sì ㄙˋ 喂养 to feed; to raise：～鸡 *raise chickens* | ～蚕 *raise silkworms* | ～养 *feed and raise* | ～料 *animal feed* | 鼻～ *nasal feed*

觇（覗）sì ㄙˋ 窥视 to spy on

笥 sì ㄙˋ 盛饭或盛衣物的方形竹器 square bamboo container (for rice or clothing)

嗣 sì ㄙˋ ❶接续，继承 to succeed to; to inherit：～位 *succeed to the throne* ❷子孙 descendants：后～ *descendants*

俟（*竢）sì ㄙˋ 等待 to wait：～机 *wait for opportunity* | ～该书出版后即寄去。*Wait for the book to be published and then send it immediately.*

⇨ see also qí on p.519

涘 sì ㄙˋ 水边 water side

食 sì ㄙˋ 拿东西给人吃 to feed; to bring sb food

⇨ see also shí on p.598

肆 sì ㄙˋ ❶不顾一切，任意去做 without restraint; wilfully：放～ *unrestrained; presumptuous* | ～无忌惮 *without scruple* | ～意妄为 *do wrong without scruple* ❷旧时指铺子，商店 (old) shop：茶坊酒～ *teahouses and wine shops* ❸"四"字的大写 (elaborate form of 四, used in commercial or financial context) four

SONG ㄙㄨㄥ

忪 sōng ㄙㄨㄥ see 惺忪 (xīng—) at 惺 on page 726

⇨ see also zhōng on p.861

松(❷-❺鬆) sōng ㄙㄨㄥ ❶常绿乔木，树皮多鳞片状，叶针形。种类很多，木材用途很广 pine tree ❷松散，不紧密，不靠拢，跟"紧"相对 loose (opposite of 紧)：捆得太～ *tied too loosely* | 土质～ *soil is loose* ❸宽，不紧张，不严格 lax; slack; loose：规矩太～ *the regulations are too lenient* | ～懈 *relaxed; slack* ❹放开，使松散 to loosen：～手 *loosen one's grip* | ～绑 *untie sb* | ～一～马肚带 *loosen the girth of the saddle* ❺用瘦肉做成的茸毛状或碎末状的食品 (meat) floss：肉～ *meat floss*

凇 sōng ㄙㄨㄥ [雾凇]通称"树挂"，寒冷天水汽在树枝上结成的白色松散冰晶 rime (ice tufts on branches, usually known as 树挂)

菘 sōng ㄙㄨㄥ 〈方 dialect〉菘菜，草本植物，即大白菜 Chinese cabbage (same as 大白菜)

崧 sōng ㄙㄨㄥ ❶ (old) same as "嵩" ❷用于地名 used in place names：～厦镇（在浙江省上虞）*Songxiazhen (in Shangyu, Zhejiang Province)*

淞 sōng ㄙㄨㄥ 吴淞江，发源于太湖，到上海市与黄浦江汇合流入长江 Wusong River (originates from Taihu Lake and converges with Huangpu River at Shanghai before flowing into the Yangtze River)

娀 sōng ㄙㄨㄥ 有娀，古国名，在今山西省运城一带 Yousong (an ancient state in today's Yuncheng, Shanxi Province)

嵩 sōng ㄙㄨㄥ ❶嵩山，又叫嵩高，五岳中的中岳，在河南省 Mount Songshan (also called 嵩高; the central mountain of the Five Great Mountains, in Henan Province) ❷高 tall

㧐(摗) sǒng ㄙㄨㄥˇ ❶挺立 to stand upright ❷〈方 dialect〉推 to push

怂(慫) sǒng ㄙㄨㄥˇ ❶惊惧 to fear ❷鼓动 to incite [怂恿]（-yǒng）鼓动别人去做 to incite

耸(聳) sǒng ㄙㄨㄥˇ ❶高起，直立 to raise; to stand erect：高～ *stand tall and erect* | ～立 *to tower* ❷耸动，惊动 to stir up; to excite：～人听闻（故意说夸大或吓人的话使人震惊）*deliberately try to create a sensation*

悚 sǒng ㄙㄨㄥˇ 害怕，恐惧 be afraid：毛骨～然 *be petrified*

竦 sǒng ㄙㄨㄥˇ ❶恭敬，肃敬 respectful ❷ same as "悚"

讼(訟) sòng ㄙㄨㄥˋ ❶在法庭争辩是非曲直，打官司 to bring a case to court：诉～ *to litigate; litigation* | ～事 *lawsuit* ❷争辩是非 to debate; to argue：聚～纷纭 *profuse debate without agreement*

颂(頌) sòng ㄙㄨㄥˋ ❶颂扬，赞扬别人的好处 to praise：歌～ *sing in praise* ❷祝颂，祝愿 to express good wishes：敬～时绥 *(in correspondence)*

best wishes ❸古代祭祀时用的舞曲 (ancient) dance music played when offering sacrifices to deities or ancestors：周～ *(in* Book of Songs*)* Eulogies of Zhou | 鲁～ *(in* Book of Songs*)* Eulogies of Lu ❹以颂扬为内容的文章或诗歌 ode

宋 sòng ㄙㄨㄥˋ ❶周代诸侯国名，在今河南省商丘一带 Song (a state in the Zhou Dynasty, in today's Shangqiu, Henan Province) ❷朝代名 name of dynasties ①南朝之一，刘裕所建立（公元420—479年） Liu Song Dynasty (420—479, one of the Southern Dynasties, founded by Liu Yu) ②宋太祖赵匡胤所建立（公元960—1279年） Song Dynasty (960—1279, founded by Zhao Kuangyin, Emperor Taizu) ❸指宋刊本或宋体字 books of the Song Dynasty; Song typeface：影～ *traced copy of a printed book from the Song Dynasty* | 老～ *original Song Dynasty typeface* | 仿～ *Imitation Song typeface*

送 sòng ㄙㄨㄥˋ ❶把东西从甲地运到乙地 to send; to deliver：～信 *send a letter* | ～货 *deliver goods* ❷赠给 to give as a gift; to offer：他～了我一支钢笔。*He gave me a fountain pen as a present.* ❸送行，陪伴人到某一地点 to see sb off; to accompany：～孩子上学 *take the child to school* | 把客人～到门口 *see the guest to the door* | 欢～ *send off* ❹丢掉，丧失 to lose：～命 *lose one's life* | 断～ *to ruin* | 葬～ *to ruin*

诵(誦) sòng ㄙㄨㄥˋ ❶用有高低抑扬的腔调念 to read out; to declaim：朗～ *to read aloud* | ～诗 *read out a poem* ❷背诵，凭记忆读出 to recite：熟读成～ *read until one knows it by heart* ❸称述，述说 to state; to narrate：传～ *be on everyone's lips*

SOU ㄙㄡ

鄋 sōu ㄙㄡ ［鄋瞒］春秋时小国，也称长狄，在今山东省济南北。一说在今山东省高青 (also called 长狄) Souman (a small state during the Spring and Autumn Period, in the north of today's Jinan or Gaoqing, Shandong Province)

搜(❶△*蒐) sōu ㄙㄡ ❶寻求，寻找 to look for; to search：～集 *to collect* | ～罗 *to gather* | ～救 *search and rescue* ❷搜索检查 to search and check：～身 *do a body search*

嗖 sōu ㄙㄡ 形容迅速通过的声音 whoosh; whizz：标枪～的一声过去了。*The javelin flew past with a whoosh.* | 子弹～～地飞过。*Bullets whizzed past.*

馊(餿) sōu ㄙㄡ 食物等因受潮热引起质变而发出酸臭味 (of food, etc.) to go rancid：饭～了。*The rice is rancid.* ㊂坏 bad：～主意 *bad idea*

廋 sōu ㄙㄡ 隐藏，藏匿 to hide

溲 sōu ㄙㄡ 排泄大小便。特指排泄小便 to excrete; (specifically) to urinate

飕(颼) sōu ㄙㄡ ❶风吹（使变干或变冷）to dry or cool sth by wind：洗的衣服被风～干了。*The laundry has been dried by the wind.* ❷ same as "嗖"

锼(鎪) sōu ㄙㄡ 镂刻，用钢丝锯挖刻木头 to carve (wood with a wire saw)：椅背的花是～出来的。*The patterns on the back of the chair are carved.*

螋 sōu ㄙㄡ see 蠼螋 (qú—) at 蠼 on page 548

艘 sōu ㄙㄡ 量词，用于船只 measure word for ships, boats, etc.：大船五～ *five large ships* | 军舰十～ *ten warships*

蒐 sōu ㄙㄡ ❶草名，即茜草 Indian madder (same as 茜草) ❷春天打猎 to hunt (in spring) ❸ see 搜 on page 621

叟 sǒu ㄙㄡˇ 老头ㄦ elderly man：童～无欺。*(We) do not cheat anyone, from children to the elderly.*

瞍 sǒu ㄙㄡˇ ❶眼睛没有瞳仁 eye without a pupil ❷盲人 blind person

嗾 sǒu ㄙㄡˇ ❶指使狗时发出的声音 sound used to command a dog ❷教唆指使 to entice; to instigate：～使 *egg sb on*

擞(擻) sǒu ㄙㄡˇ ［抖擞］振作，振奋 to invigorate; to rouse：～精神 *rouse one's spirits* | 精神～ *high spirits*

⇨ see also sòu on p.622

薮(藪) sǒu ㄙㄡˇ ❶生长着很多草的湖泽 overgrown lake/marsh ❷人或物聚集的地方 gathering place：渊～ *gathering place*

嗽(*嗽) sòu ㄙㄡˋ 咳嗽 to cough (see 咳 ké on page 355 for reference)

擞(擻) sòu ㄙㄡˋ 用通条插到火炉里，把灰抖掉 to remove ash from a stove with a poker：把炉子～一～ *give the stove a poking*

⇨ see also sǒu on p.622

SU ㄙㄨ

苏(❶–❹蘇、❺囌、❷△*甦、❶–❹*蘓) sū ㄙㄨ ❶植物名 plant name ①紫苏，草本植物，叶紫黑色，花紫红色，叶和种子可入药 purple common perilla ②白苏，草本植物，茎四棱形，花白色，茎、叶、种子可入药 common perilla ❷假死后再活过来 to regain consciousness：～醒 *to resuscitate; wake up* | 死而复～ *die and come back to life* ❸指江苏或江苏苏州 Su (refers to Jiangsu Province or Suzhou, Jiangsu Province)：～剧 *Suzhou opera* | ～绣 *Suzhou embroidery* ❹（外 *loanword*）苏维埃，苏联国家权力机关。我国第二次国内革命战争时期曾把工农民主政权也叫苏维埃 Soviet; workers' and peasants' political power established during

China's Second Revolutionary Civil War: ～区 *Soviet area* ❺ see 噜苏 (lūsu) at 噜 on page 418

甦 sū ㄙㄨ ❶ see 苏❷ on page 622 ❷用于人名 used in given names

酥 sū ㄙㄨ ❶酪，用牛羊奶凝成的薄皮制成的食物 curd (made from cow's or goat's milk) ❷松脆，多指食物 (often of food) crispy; flaky: ～糖 *crunchy sweet* ❸含油多而松脆的点心 puff pastry: 桃～ *walnut biscuit* ❹软弱无力 weak; feeble: ～软 *limp; soft* | 站了一天，腿都～了。*(My) legs have gone weak after standing up all day.*

稣(穌) sū ㄙㄨ same as "苏❷"

窣 sū ㄙㄨ see 窸窣 (xī－) at 窸 on page 698

俗 sú ㄙㄨˊ ❶风俗，社会上长期形成的风气、习惯等 custom; convention: 移风易～ *change prevailing habits and customs* ❷大众化的，最通行的，习见的 popular; common: ～语 *popular saying* | 通～ *popular; common* ❸趣味低，不高雅 vulgar; boorish: ～不可耐 *unbearably low-brow* | 这张画儿画得太～。*This painting is in rather poor taste.* [庸俗] 平庸，鄙俗 philistine ❹指没出家的人，区别于出家的佛教徒等 secular person; layperson: 僧～ *monks and laypersons*

夙 sù ㄙㄨˋ ❶早 early: ～兴夜寐（早起晚睡）*sleep late and rise early* ❷一向有的，旧有的 long-standing: ～愿 *long-cherished wish* | ～志 *long-cherished ambition*

诉(訴、△*愬) sù ㄙㄨˋ ❶叙说（㊀－说）to tell; to narrate: 告～ *to tell* | ～苦 *air one's grievances* ❷控告（㊀控－）to accuse; to sue: ～讼 *to litigate; litigation* | 起～ *to prosecute; to bring a lawsuit against* | 上～ *to appeal* | 公～ *public prosecution* [投诉] 公民或单位认为其合法权益遭受侵犯，向有关部门请求依法处理 to lodge a complaint

肃(肅) sù ㄙㄨˋ ❶恭敬 respectful: ～立 *stand at attention in respect* | ～然起敬 *filled with deep respect* ❷严正，认真 stern; serious: 严～ *serious* | ～穆 *solemn and respectful* ❸清除 to eliminate: ～反 *suppress counter-revolutionaries* | ～贪 *wipe out corruption* [肃清] 彻底清除 to eradicate: ～流毒 *eradicate harmful influences* | ～土匪 *eradicate bandits*

骕(驌) sù ㄙㄨˋ [骕骦] (－shuāng) 古书上说的一种良马 an excellent breed of horse in ancient Chinese texts

鹔(鷫) sù ㄙㄨˋ [鹔鹴] (－shuāng) 古书上说的一种水鸟 a type of aquatic bird in ancient Chinese texts

素 sù ㄙㄨˋ ❶本色，白色 natural colour; white: ～服 *white mourning clothes* | ～丝 *white silk* ㊁颜色单纯，不艳丽 (of colour)

S

plain; simple: ～雅 *simple and elegant* | 这块布花色很～。*This fabric is very simple in design and colour.* ❷本来的 original: ～质 *quality* | ～性 *disposition* ⓘ事物的基本成分 basic ingredient: 色～ *pigment* | 毒～ *toxin* | 因～ *factor* ❸蔬菜类的食物，跟"荤"相对 vegetarian food (opposite of 荤): ～食 *vegetarian food* | 吃～ *eat vegetarian food; be a vegetarian* ❹平素，向来 usually: ～日 *usually*| ～不相识 *have not met sb before* ❺古代指洁白的生绢 (ancient) pure white silk: 尺～（写在绢帛上的信）*letter written on silk*

傃 sù ㄙㄨˋ ❶面向，向着 to face ❷平常，平素 usually

嗉（❶**膆）sù ㄙㄨˋ ❶（－子）嗉囊，鸟类食管下储存食物的地方 (of a bird) crop: 鸡～子 *crop of a chicken* ❷（－子）装酒的小壶 small wine flask

愫 sù ㄙㄨˋ 情愫，真实的心情 genuine feelings

速 sù ㄙㄨˋ ❶快（㊀迅－）fast: ～成 *achieve by quick methods* | ～冻 *quick-freeze* | 火～ *at top speed* [速度] 运动的物体在单位时间内所通过的距离 velocity; speed [速记] 用简便的符号快速记录话语 shorthand ❷邀请 to invite: 不～之客 *uninvited guest*

𫗧（餗）sù ㄙㄨˋ 鼎中的食物 food contained in a *ding* vessel

涑 sù ㄙㄨˋ 涑水河，水名，在山西省西南部 Sushuihe River (in southwestern Shanxi Province)

觫 sù ㄙㄨˋ see 觳觫 (hú－) at 觳 on page 259

宿（*宿）sù ㄙㄨˋ ❶住，过夜，夜里睡觉 to stay for the night: 住～ *accommodation* | ～舍 *dormitory* ❷年老的，长久从事某种工作的 elderly; experienced; veteran: ～将（经历多、老练的指挥官）*experienced commander* ❸旧有的，素有的 long-standing; from before: ～疾 *old illness* | ～愿得偿 *a long-held wish has been fulfilled* ❹姓 (surname) Su

⇨ see also xiǔ on p.731, xiù on p.732

缩（縮）sù ㄙㄨˋ [缩砂密] 草本植物，花白色，种子可入药，叫砂仁 *Amomum villosum* (its seed is called 砂仁)

⇨ see also suō on p.629

蹜 sù ㄙㄨˋ [蹜蹜] 小步快走 to scuttle

粟 sù ㄙㄨˋ 谷子，见"谷❸"旧时泛称谷类 millet (see 谷❸); (old) grains

僳 sù ㄙㄨˋ see 傈僳族 (lì－－) at 傈 on page 395

谡（謖）sù ㄙㄨˋ 起，起来 to rise up

塑 sù ㄙㄨˋ 用泥土等做成人物的形象 to sculpt: ～像 *sculpture* | 泥～木雕 *(motionless like a) statue* [塑料] 具有可塑性的高分子化合物的统称 plastic

溯（*泝、*遡）sù ㄙㄨˋ 逆着水流的方向走 to go up stream: ～河而

上 *go upstream along a river* ㊀追求根源或回想 to trace back; to recall：推本～源 *trace the origins* | 回～ *to recall* | 追～ *trace back to*

愬 sù ㄙㄨˋ ❶ see 诉 on page 623 ❷用于人名。李愬，唐代人 used in given names (e.g. Li Su of the Tang Dynasty)

蔌 sù ㄙㄨˋ 菜肴，野菜 cooked food; edible wild plants：山肴野～ *mountain game and edible wild plants*

簌 sù ㄙㄨˋ [簌簌] 1 形容风吹叶子等的声音 rustle：忽然听见芦苇里～地响。*Suddenly there came rustling sounds from the reeds.* 2 纷纷落下的样子 falling down：泪珠～地往下落 *tears streaming down*

SUAN ㄙㄨㄢ

狻 suān ㄙㄨㄢ [狻猊]（-ní）传说中的一种猛兽 *suanni* (legendary ferocious beast)

酸（❸**痠）suān ㄙㄨㄢ ❶化学上称能在水溶液中产生氢离子的物质，分为无机酸、有机酸两类 acid：盐～ *hydrochloric acid* | 硝～ *nitric acid* | 醋～ *acetic acid* | ～雨 *acid rain* ❷像醋的气味或味道 sour：～菜 *pickled Chinese cabbage* | 这个梨真～。*This pear is really sour.* ❸微痛无力 ache; sore：腰～腿痛 *aching back and sore legs* | 腰有点儿发～。*There's a slight ache in (my) lower back.* ❹悲痛，伤心 grieved; sad：心～ *feel sad* | 十分悲～ *very sad* ❺讥讽读书人的迂腐 pedantic：～秀才 *pedantic scholar* [寒酸] 指文人的贫苦或不大方的样子 (of a scholar) poor and shabby

蒜 suàn ㄙㄨㄢˋ 大蒜，草本植物，花白色，叶和花轴（蒜薹）嫩时可以吃。地下茎通常分瓣，味辣，可供调味用 garlic

筭 suàn ㄙㄨㄢˋ ❶计算用的筹码 counter; chip (for performing calculations) ❷ same as "算"

算（**祘）suàn ㄙㄨㄢˋ ❶核计，计数 to calculate; to count：～～多少钱 *calculate how much it costs* | ～账 *work out the accounts; get even with sb* ❷打算，计划 to plan; to project：失～ *to misjudge* ㊀推测 to infer：我～着他今天该来。*I'm guessing that he should come today.* ❸作为，当作 to count as; to regard as：这个～我的。*Count this one as mine.* ㊀算数，承认 to hold; to admit：不能说了不～ *cannot renege on one's words* ❹作罢，不再提起 to let it go; to give up：～了，不要再啰唆了。*Forget it and stop nagging.* ❺副词，总算 (adverb) finally：今天～把问题弄清楚了 *finally sorted out the problem today*

SUI ㄙㄨㄟ

尿 suī ㄙㄨㄟ same in meaning as 尿 (niào) ❶：尿（niào）～ *to urinate*

⇨ see also niào on p.479

虽(雖) suī ㄙㄨㄟ 连词，虽然，用在上半句，表示"即使""纵然"的意思，下半句多有"可是""但是"相应 (conjunction) although：为人民而死，～死犹生。*When one dies for the people, one's spirit lives on despite one's death.* | 工作～忙，可是学习也没有放松。*Although (he) is busy with work, (he) never lets up in (his) learning.*

荽 suī ㄙㄨㄟ ［胡荽］即芫荽（yánsui），俗叫香菜 coriander (same as 芫荽 yánsui, informal 香菜)

眭 suī ㄙㄨㄟ 〈古 ancient〉目光紧紧注视 to stare

S

睢 suī ㄙㄨㄟ 睢县，在河南省 Suixian (in Henan Province)

濉 suī ㄙㄨㄟ 濉河，水名，在安徽省北部 Suihe River (in northern Anhui Province)

绥(綏) suí ㄙㄨㄟˊ ❶安抚 to placate; to soothe：～靖 *to pacify* ❷平安 safe and sound：顺颂台～（书信用语。台，敬称对方）*(in correspondence) wish you are well*

隋 suí ㄙㄨㄟˊ 朝代名，隋文帝杨坚所建立（公元581—618年）Sui Dynasty (581—618, founded by Yang Jian, Emperor Wen)

随(隨) suí ㄙㄨㄟˊ ❶跟着 to follow：～说～记 *record at the same time as it is spoken* | 我～着大家走。*I will go along with all of you.* ［随即］副词，立刻 (adverb) immediately ❷顺从，任凭，由 to let sb (do as they like)：～意 *as one likes* | ～他的便 *do as he likes* ❸顺便，就着 in passing; at one's convenience：～手关门 *close the door hehind you* ❹〈方 dialect〉像 to look like：他长（zhǎng）得～他父亲。*He looks like his father.*

遂 suí ㄙㄨㄟˊ 义同"遂（suì）❶"，用于"半身不遂"（身体一侧发生瘫痪）same in meaning as 遂 (suì) ❶, used in 半身不遂 (hemiplegia)

⇨ see also suì on p.627

髓 suǐ ㄙㄨㄟˇ ❶骨髓，骨头里的像脂肪的物质 bone marrow：敲骨吸～（喻残酷地剥削）*break the bone and suck the marrow; (figurative) exploit mercilessly*［精髓］事物精要的部分 core; essence ❷像髓的东西 sth like marrow：脑～ *brain matter*

岁(歲、*嵗、嵗)** suì ㄙㄨㄟˋ ❶量词，计算年龄的单位，一年为一岁 (measure word) years old：三～的孩子 *three-year-old child* ❷年 year：去～ *last year* | ～月 *years* ❸年成 the year's harvest：歉～ *lean year* | 富～ *bumper year*

谇(誶) suì ㄙㄨㄟˋ ❶责骂 to scold ❷问 to ask ❸直言规劝 to remonstrate frankly

碎 suì ㄙㄨㄟˋ ❶完整的东西破坏成零片零块，使变碎 to break into pieces：粉～ *break into smithereens; to smash* | 碗打～了。*The bowl was smashed to pieces.* |

～纸机 *shredder* ❷零星，不完整 fragmentary; scattered: ～布 *fabric scraps* | 琐～ *trivial* ❸说话唠叨 garrulous: 嘴～ *garrulous*

祟 suì ㄙㄨㄟˋ 迷信说法指鬼神带给人的灾祸 misfortune (brought on by spirits or ghosts) [鬼祟] 行为不光明，常说"鬼鬼祟祟" furtive (often 鬼鬼祟祟): 行动～ *furtive behaviour* [作祟] 暗中捣鬼 to secretly make mischief: 从中～ *secretly cause trouble*

遂 suì ㄙㄨㄟˋ ❶顺，如意 to satisfy; to fulfill: ～心 *to one's liking* | ～愿 *have one's wish fulfilled* ❷成功，实现 to succeed: 未～ *fail to accomplish* | 所谋不～ *fail in an attempt* ❸于是，就 then; thereupon: 服药后腹痛～止。*The stomach pains stopped after medication.*

⇨ see also suí on p.626

隧 suì ㄙㄨㄟˋ 隧道，在山中或地下开凿而成的通路 tunnel

璲 suì ㄙㄨㄟˋ 一种玉制的信物 jade token

䍁(䍁) suì ㄙㄨㄟˋ 古书上说的一种车饰 a kind of carriage ornament in ancient Chinese texts

燧 suì ㄙㄨㄟˋ ❶上古取火的器具 flint ❷古代告警燃点的烟火 (ancient) fire and smoke signal

镃(鐩) suì ㄙㄨㄟˋ 古代利用日光取火的凹镜 (ancient) concave glass used for starting fires

穟 suì ㄙㄨㄟˋ same as "穗❶"

邃 suì ㄙㄨㄟˋ 深远 deep; profound ①指空间(㊥深～) (of physical space) deep ②指时间 (of time) far back: ～古 *ancient times* ③指程度 of high degree: 精～ *deep; profound* | ～密 *deep; profound*

襚 suì ㄙㄨㄟˋ 古代指赠死者的衣被 (ancient) clothing and blankets given to the dead

旞 suì ㄙㄨㄟˋ 古代导车的旗杆顶上用完整彩色羽毛做装饰的旗子 (ancient) flag with feather ornaments for guiding carriages

穗(❷繐)** suì ㄙㄨㄟˋ ❶(～儿)谷类植物聚生在一起的花或果实 ear of grain: 高粱～儿 *ear of sorghum* | 麦～儿 *ear of wheat* ❷(～子、～儿)用丝线、布条或纸条等结扎成的装饰品 tassel: 大红旗上挂着金黄的～子。*A golden tassel hangs from the big red flag.* ❸广东省广州的别称 Sui (another name for Guangzhou, Guangdong Province)

SUN ㄙㄨㄣ

孙(孫) sūn ㄙㄨㄣ ❶(～子)儿子的儿子 grandson (son of one's son) [子孙] 后代 descendant ❷孙子以后的各代 descendant of one's grandson: 玄～ *great-great-grandson* ❸跟孙子同辈的亲属 relative who is of the same generation as one's grandson: 外～ *grandson (son of*

one's daughter) | 侄～ *great-nephew (grandson of one's brother)* ❹ 植物再生的 (of plants) regrown: 稻～ *new rice shoot grown from old stalk* | ～竹 *branch grown from the tip of a bamboo*

〈古 ancient〉 also same as 逊 (xùn)

荪(蓀) sūn ㄙㄨㄣ 古书上说的一种香草 a kind of aromatic herb in ancient Chinese texts

狲(猻) sūn ㄙㄨㄣ see 猢狲 (hú—) at 猢 on page 258

飧(*飱) sūn ㄙㄨㄣ 晚饭 evening meal

损(損) sǔn ㄙㄨㄣˇ ❶ 减少 to reduce: ～失 *lose sth; loss* | ～益 *profit and loss* | 增～ *increase and decrease* ❷ 损坏，伤害 to damage; to harm: 破～ *damage* | 完好无～ *intact* | ～伤 *to injure; injury* | ～人利己 *harm others for one's own gain* ❸ 用刻薄话挖苦人 to mock; to ridicule: 别～人啦！ *Stop mocking others!* ❹ 刻薄，毒辣 mean; sarcastic: 说话太～ *speak in a really vicious manner* | 这法子真～。 *This plan is really vicious.*

笋(*筍) sǔn ㄙㄨㄣˇ 竹子刚从土里长出的嫩芽，可用作蔬菜 bamboo shoot ㊀ 幼嫩的 young and tender: ～鸡 *young chicken*

隼 sǔn ㄙㄨㄣˇ 鸟名，又叫鹘 (hú)，一般为灰褐色，性凶猛，捕食鼠、兔和鸟类。种类很多 falcon (also called 鹘 hú)

榫 sǔn ㄙㄨㄣˇ （一子、一儿、一头）器物两部分利用凹凸相接的凸出的部分 tenon

SUO ㄙㄨㄛ

莎 suō ㄙㄨㄛ 莎草，草本植物，茎三棱形，花黄褐色。地下的块茎叫香附子，黑褐色，可入药 sedge

⇨ see also shā on p.574

娑 suō ㄙㄨㄛ see 婆娑 (pó—) at 婆 on page 510

桫 suō ㄙㄨㄛ [桫椤] (—luó) 蕨类植物，木本，茎高而直，叶片大，羽状分裂 flying spider-monkey tree fern

挲(*挱) suō ㄙㄨㄛ see 摩挲 (mó—) at 摩 on page 459

⇨ see also sɑ on p.570, shɑ on p.576

唆 suō ㄙㄨㄛ 调唆，挑动别人去做坏事 to incite; to instigate: ～使 *to abet* | ～讼 *incite sb to begin litigation* | 教 (jiào) ～ *to abet*

梭 suō ㄙㄨㄛ （一子）织布时牵引纬线（横线）的工具，两头尖，中间粗，像枣核的形状 (weaver's) shuttle

睃 suō ㄙㄨㄛ 斜着眼睛看 to give a sidelong glance

羧 suō ㄙㄨㄛ 羧基，有机化合物中含碳、氧和氢的基 carboxyl

蓑(*簑) suō ㄙㄨㄛ 蓑衣，用草或棕毛制成的

雨衣 rain cape made of straw or palm fibre

嗍 suō ㄙㄨㄛ 用唇舌裹食，吮吸 to suck

趖 suō ㄙㄨㄛ 〈方 dialect〉移动 to move：日头～西。*The sun moves to the west.*

缩(縮) suō ㄙㄨㄛ ❶向后退 to retreat：畏～ *recoil in fear* | 退～ *to cower; shrink back* ❷由大变小，由长变短，由多变少 to contract; to shrink：热胀冷～ *expand when hot and contract when cold* | ～了半尺 *shrank by half a foot* | ～短 *to shorten* | 节衣～食 *skimp on clothing and food* | 紧～开支 *reduce one's outgoings* [缩影] 比喻可以代表同一类型的具体而微的人或事物 microcosm

⇨ see also sù on p.624

所(所)** suǒ ㄙㄨㄛˇ ❶处所，地方 place; site：住～ *residence* | 各得其～。*Everyone is properly placed or provided for.* ❷机关或其他办事的地方 organisation; office：研究～ *research institute* | 派出～ *local police station* | 诊疗～ *clinic* ❸明代驻兵防边的地点，因大小不同有千户所、百户所。现在多用于地名 frontier garrison in the Ming Dynasty (now often used in place names)：海阳～（在山东省乳山市）*Haiyangsuo (a place in Rushan City, Shandong Province)* ❹量词 measure word ①用于房屋 used for houses：两～房子 *two houses* ②用于学校等 used for schools, etc.：一～学校 *a school* | 两～医院 *two hospitals* ❺助词，放在动词前，代表接受动作的事物 auxiliary word placed in front of a verb to indicate the recipient of an action ①动词后不再用表事物的词 with no words denoting a thing used after the verb：耳～闻，目～见 *what the ears hear and the eyes see* | 我们对人民要有～贡献。*We must make some contributions to the people.* | 各尽～能，按劳分配。*From each according to his ability; to each according to his labour.* ②动词后再用"者"或"的"字代表事物 with 者 or 的 used after the verb to denote a thing：吾家～寡有者 *the things that my house is short of* | 这是我们～反对的。*This is what we are opposed to.* ③动词后再用表事物的词 with words denoting a thing used after a verb：他～提的意见 *the views given by him* ❻助词，放在动词前，跟前面"为"字相应，表示被动 auxiliary word that indicates passive voice when placed before the verb and preceded by 为：为人～笑 *laughed at by people* [所以] 连词，表因果关系，常跟"因为"相应 (conjunction, often paired with 因为) therefore; and so：他有要紧的事，～不能等你了。*He had an urgent matter to attend to, and so he couldn't wait for you.* | 他～进步得这样快，是因为能刻苦学习。*He improved so quickly because he worked very hard.*

索 suǒ ㄙㄨㄛˇ ❶（－子）大绳子 thick rope：绳～ *rope*| 船～ *ship's rope* | 铁～桥 *simple wire suspension bridge* ❷ 搜寻，寻求（㊎搜－）to search for; to seek：按图～骥 *search for a fine steed using a painting of it; (figurative) cling rigidly to set methods*| 遍～不得 *search everywhere in vain*［索引］把书籍或报刊里边的要项摘出来，按一定次序排列，标明页数，以便查检的资料 index ❸讨取，要 to demand; to ask for：～钱 *demand money* | ～价 *state the asking price* | ～赔 *claim indemnity* ❹尽，空 void; empty：～然无味 *dull* ❺单独 alone：离群～居 *live in solitude*

［索性］副词，直截了当，干脆 (adverb) simply; just：发现对方毫无诚意，他～走了。*He simply left when he found that the other party was not interested at all.*

溹 suǒ ㄙㄨㄛˇ 溹泸河，即索泸河，水名，在河北省东南部，清凉江支流 Suoluhe River (same as 索泸河，tributary of Qingliang River, in southeastern Hebei Province)

唢（嗩） suǒ ㄙㄨㄛˇ ［唢呐］（－nà）管乐器，形状像喇叭 Chinese musical instrument shaped like a trumpet

琐（瑣、*瑣） suǒ ㄙㄨㄛˇ ❶ 细小，零碎（㊎－碎）small; fragmentary：～事 *trivial matter* | ～闻 *trivial news* | 繁～ *tedious and overdetailed* ❷ 卑微 lowly; humble：猥～ *(of appearance) wretched*

锁（鎖、*鎻） suǒ ㄙㄨㄛˇ ❶加在门、箱等上面使人不能随便打开的器具 lock：门上上～ *put a lock on the door* ❷用锁关住 to lock：把门～上 *lock the door* | 拿锁～上箱子 *lock the box with a padlock* ❸链子 chain：枷～ *cangue and shackles* | ～镣 *fetters* ❹一种缝纫法，多用在衣物边沿上，针脚很密，线斜交或钩连 to lock stitching：～扣眼 *lock stitch a buttonhole* | ～边 *lock stitch a hem*

葰 suǒ ㄙㄨㄛˇ 姓 (surname) Suo ⇨ see also jùn on p.346

嗦 suo ·ㄙㄨㄛ see 哆嗦 (duō－) at 哆 on page 155, and 啰唆 (luō－) at 啰 on page 427

S

T 去

TA 去丫

他 tā 去丫 代词 pronoun ❶称你、我以外的第三人，一般指男性，有时泛指，不分性别 (usually used for men, sometimes used for both men and women) he; him; his ❷别的 other; another：～人 *other people* | ～乡 *a place far from one's hometown* [其他] 别的 other; another ❸虚指（用于动词和数量词之间）used between a verb and a quantifier as a meaningless form word：睡～一觉 *have a sleep* | 干～一场 *have a big go at it* ❹指另外的地方 other place：久已～往 *have long been to other places*

她 tā 去丫 代词，称你、我以外的女性第三人。也用以代称祖国、国旗等令人敬爱、珍爱的事物 (pronoun, used for women or something one treasures such as one's motherland) she; her; hers

它(*牠) tā 去丫 代词，专指人以外的事物 (pronoun, used specifically for things) it; its [其它] 同"其他"（用于事物）same as 其他 (used for things)

铊(鉈) tā 去丫 金属元素，符号Tl，银白色，质软。可用来制合金等。铊的化合物有毒 thallium (Tl)

➪ see also tuó on p.668

趿 tā 去丫 趿拉（la），穿鞋只套上脚的前半部 to wear shoes with the heels exposed：～拉着一双旧布鞋 *wearing a pair of old cloth shoes with the backs trodden down* | ～拉着木板鞋 *wearing wooden slippers*

塌 tā 去丫 ❶倒（dǎo），下陷 to collapse; to sink：墙～了。*The wall fell in.* | 房顶子～了。*The roof sagged.* | 人瘦得两腮都～下去了。*He/she was so thin that his/her cheeks had sunk in.* ❷下垂 to droop：这棵花晒得～秧了。*The flower has drooped in the sun.* ❸安定，镇定 to calm down; to settle down：～下心来 *settle down one's mind*

溻 tā 去丫 出汗把衣服、被褥等弄湿 to become soaked with sweat：天太热，我的衣服都～了。*It was so hot that my clothes were all drenched in sweat.*

禢 tā 去丫 〈方 dialect〉在衣物上缝缀花边 to hem (clothes) with lace or ribbons：～一道绦（tāo）子 *hem with lace* [汗禢儿] 贴身衬衣 undershirt

踏 tā 去丫 [踏实]（-shi）1 切实，不浮躁 steady; dependable：他工作很～。*He is steady in his work.* 2（情绪）安定，

安稳 free from anxiety; at peace: 事情办完就～了。*One will feel at peace once the matter is settled.*

⇨ see also tà on p.632

础(磋) tǎ ㄊㄚˇ 用于地名 used in place names: ～石(在浙江省龙泉市) *Tashi (in Longquan, Zhejiang Province)*

⇨ see also dá on p.108

塔(*墖) tǎ ㄊㄚˇ ❶佛教特有的建筑物，尖顶，有很多层 pagoda ❷像塔形的建筑物 tower: 水～ *water tower* | 灯～ *lighthouse* | 纪念～ *memorial tower; monument*

[塔吉克族] 1 我国少数民族，参看附录四 the Tajik People (one of the ethnic groups in China. See Appendix Ⅳ.) 2 塔吉克斯坦的主要民族 the Tajik People (the major ethnic group in Tajikistan)

[塔塔尔族] 我国少数民族，参看附录四 the Tatar People (one of the ethnic groups in China. See Appendix Ⅳ.)

溚 tǎ ㄊㄚˇ (外 *loanword*) 焦油的旧称，用煤或木材制得的一种黏稠液体，黑褐色，是化学工业上的重要原料 (former name for 焦油) tar

獭(獺) tǎ ㄊㄚˇ 水獭，哺乳动物，毛棕色，穴居水边，能游泳，捕食鱼类等。另有旱獭，生活在陆地上，善掘土 otter; marmot

鳎(鰨) tǎ ㄊㄚˇ 鱼名，又叫鳎目鱼，身体形状像舌头，两眼都在身体的一侧，有眼的一侧褐色。生活在海洋里，种类很多 sole (a kind of fish, also called 鳎目鱼)

拓(*搨) tà ㄊㄚˋ 在刻铸文字、图像的器物上，蒙一层纸，捶打后使凹凸分明，涂上墨，显出文字、图像来 to make a rubbing (from inscriptions, pictures on stone tablets or bronze vessels): ～本 *book of rubbings* | ～片 *a piece of rubbing*

⇨ see also tuò on p.669

沓 tà ㄊㄚˋ 多，重复 numerous; repeated: 杂～ *numerous and disorderly* | 纷至～来 *come thick and fast*

⇨ see also dá on p.108

踏 tà ㄊㄚˋ 踩 to tread; to stamp: ～步 *mark time* | 一脚～空了 *missed one's step* ⓘ亲自到现场去 to investigate on site: ～看 *conduct an on-the-spot investigation* | ～勘 *conduct a field survey*

⇨ see also tā on p.631

闼(闥) tà ㄊㄚˋ see 佻闼(tiāo —) at 佻 on page 650

挞(撻) tà ㄊㄚˋ 打，用鞭、棍等打人 to flog; to whip; to lash: 鞭～ *flog; (figurative) castigate*

闼(闥) tà ㄊㄚˋ 门，小门 small door: 排～直入(推开门就进去) *push the door open and go straight in*

嗒 tà ㄊㄚˋ 失意的样子 dejected; despondent: ～丧 *despondent* | ～然若失 *deeply despondent*

⇨ see also dā on p.107

鞳 tà ㄊㄚˋ [镗鞳] (tāng—) 〈古 ancient〉形容钟鼓声 clinking and drumming

遝 tà ㄊㄚˋ ❶趁着 taking advantage of ❷纷多 numerous: ～集 *(a group of people) get together with no particular order* [杂遝]行人很多，拥挤纷乱。现作"杂沓" numerous and disorderly (now written as 杂沓)

阘(闒) tà ㄊㄚˋ [阘茸](－róng)卑贱，低劣 mean and low

榻 tà ㄊㄚˋ 狭长而低的床 long, narrow and low bed; couch [下榻]寄居，住宿 to stay (in a hotel, inn, or at someone's house)

蹋 tà ㄊㄚˋ ❶踏，踩 to tread; to stamp ❷踢 to kick

漯 tà ㄊㄚˋ 漯河，古水名，在今山东省 Tahe River (an ancient river in today's Shandong Province)

⇨ see also luò on p.430

遢 ta ・ㄊㄚ see 邋遢(lā－) at 邋 on page 373

TAI ㄊㄞ

台 tāi ㄊㄞ [天台]山名，在浙江省东部 Mount Tiantai (in the east of Zhejiang Province)

⇨ see also tái on p.633

苔 tāi ㄊㄞ [舌苔]舌头上面的垢腻，由衰死的上皮细胞和黏液等形成，观察它的颜色可以帮助诊断病症 tongue coating

⇨ see also tái on p.634

胎 tāi ㄊㄞ ❶人或其他哺乳动物母体内的幼体 foetus: 怀～ *be pregnant* | ～儿 *foetus* | ～生 *viviparous* ㊀事情的开始，根源 source; root: 祸～ *root of the trouble* ❷器物的粗坯或衬在内部的东西 roughcast; padding: 这个帽子是软～儿的。*This hat is soft-padded.* | 泥～ *unpainted clay statue* | 铜～(塑像、做漆器等用) *bronze roughcast* ❸轮胎 tyre: 内～ *inner tube* | 外～ *tyre*

台(❶❸❹❻臺、❹檯、❺颱) tái ㄊㄞˊ ❶高而平的建筑物 platform; stage; terrace: 戏～ *stage* | 讲～ *dais* | 主席～ *rostrum* | 楼阁亭～ *pavilions, terraces and towers (traditional Chinese architecture)* ㊀①(－儿)像台的东西 platform-shaped thing: 井～ *well platform* | 窗～儿 *windowsill; window ledge* ②器物的座子 stand: 灯～ *lamp stand* | 蜡～ *candlestick* ❷敬辞 (polite speech) you: ～鉴 *please read my letter (used in an old-fashioned letter right after the name of the addressee in the salutation)* | ～启 *please open my letter (used after the name of the addressee on an envelope)* | 兄～ *you (male friend older than oneself)* ❸量词，用于整场演出的节目或机器、仪器等 measure word for machinery, apparatus, etc. or a whole set of items performed on a single occasion: 唱一～戏 *put on a play* | 一～机器 *a machine* ❹桌子，案子 table: 写字～ *writing desk* | 柜～ *counter* ❺台风，发生在太平洋西部热带海洋上的一种极猛烈的风暴，

中心附近风力达 12 级以上，同时有暴雨 typhoon ❻指台湾省 Taiwan Province：～商 *Taiwanese businessman* | 港～ *Hong Kong and Taiwan*

⇨ see also tāi on p.633

邰 tái ㄊㄞˊ 姓 (surname) Tai

抬(**擡) tái ㄊㄞˊ ❶举，提高 to lift; to raise: ～手 *lift up one's hand* | ～脚 *lift up one's foot* | ～起头来 *raise one's head* ㊀使上升 to raise: ～价 *raise prices* [抬头] 1 (一ル) 信函上另起一行或空格书写，表示尊敬 to begin a new line or insert a space (in letter-writing to show respect) 2 发票、收据上写的户头 name of a buyer, payer or receiver (on receipts, bills, etc.) ❷共同用手或肩搬运东西 to carry: 一个人搬不动两个人～。*Two people will carry it if one person cannot.* | 把桌子～过来 *move the table over* [抬杠] ㊕争辩 to argue for the sake of arguing

苔 tái ㄊㄞˊ 隐花植物的一类，根、茎、叶的区别不明显，绿色，生长在阴湿的地方 liverwort

⇨ see also tāi on p.633

骀(駘) tái ㄊㄞˊ 劣马 inferior horse [驽骀] (nú一) 劣马 inferior horse ㊕庸才 mediocre person

⇨ see also dài on p.112

炱 tái ㄊㄞˊ 烟气凝积而成的黑灰，俗叫烟子或煤子 (informal 烟子 or 煤子) soot: 煤～ *coal soot* | 松～ (松烟) *pine soot*

跆 tái ㄊㄞˊ 用脚踩踏 to tread [跆拳道] 一种拳脚并用的搏击运动 tae kwon do

鲐(鮐) tái ㄊㄞˊ 鱼名，俗叫鲐巴鱼，身体纺锤形，背部青蓝色，腹部淡黄色，生活在海里 chub mackerel (informal 鲐巴鱼)

薹 tái ㄊㄞˊ ❶草本植物，生长在水田里，茎扁三棱形，叶扁平而长，可用来制蓑衣等 sedge ❷韭菜、油菜、蒜等蔬菜长出的花莛 (tíng) bolt (of leek, rape, garlic, etc.)

太 tài ㄊㄞˋ ❶副词，过于 (adverb) too: ～长 *too long* | ～热 *too hot* ❷副词，极端，最 (adverb) extremely: ～好 *extremely good* | 人民的事业～伟大了。*The cause of the people is supreme.* [太古] 最古的时代 remote antiquity [太平] 平安无事 peaceful ❸对大两辈的尊长的称呼所加的字 senior; great- (in generational hierarchy): ～老伯 *great-uncle* ❹高，大 highest; greatest: ～空 *outer space* | ～学 *imperial college* ❺(外 loanword) 法定计量单位中十进倍数单位词头之一，表示10^{12}，符号 T。tera (T)

汰 tài ㄊㄞˋ 淘汰，除去没有用的成分 to discard; to eliminate; to weed: 优胜劣～ *survival of the fittest*

态(態) tài ㄊㄞˋ 形状，样子 (㊉形一、状一、姿一) appearance; shape; form: 丑～ *ugly appearance or perfor-*

mance | 变～ *metamorphose* ㊄情况 state; condition：事～ *state of affairs* [态度] 1 指人的举止神情 manner：～大方 *have an easy manner* 2 对于事情采取的立场或看法 attitude：～鲜明 *the attitude is clear-cut* | 表明～ *make one's attitude clear*

肽 tài ㄊㄞˋ 有机化合物，旧叫胜（shēng），由氨基酸脱水而成，含有羧基和氨基 peptide (formerly called 胜 shēng)

钛（鈦） tài ㄊㄞˋ 金属元素，符号 Ti，银灰色，质硬而轻，耐腐蚀，熔点高。钛合金可用于航空、航天和航海工业 titanium (Ti)

酞 tài ㄊㄞˋ 有机化合物的一类，由一个分子的邻苯（běn）二酸酐（gān）与两个分子的酚（fēn）缩合而成，如酚酞 phthalein

泰 tài ㄊㄞˋ ❶平安，安定 safe; peaceful：国～民丰。*The country is prosperous and the people are living in affluence.* | ～然处之 *take it calmly* ❷极 extreme：～西（旧指欧洲）*(old) Europe*

[泰山] 五岳中的东岳，在山东省中部 Mount Tai (the eastern mountain of the Five Great Mountains, in the middle of Shandong Province) ㊇称岳父 father-in-law (wife's father)

TAN ㄊㄢ

坍 tān ㄊㄢ 崖岸、建筑物或堆起的东西倒塌，从基部崩坏（㊅—塌）to collapse：墙～了。*The wall fell down.*

贪（貪） tān ㄊㄢ ❶贪图，求多，不知足 to have an insatiable desire：～玩 *be excessively fond of fun* | ～便宜（piányi）*be keen on gaining petty advantages* | ～得无厌 *have an insatiable greed* ❷爱财 to hanker after (money)：～财 *be greedy for money* | ～墨（贪污）*corrupt* [贪污] 利用职权非法地取得财物 to embezzle

怹 tān ㄊㄢ 〈方 dialect〉"他"的敬称 he (polite speech of 他)

啴（嘽） tān ㄊㄢ [啴啴] 形容牲畜喘息的样子 wheezing (of a farm animal)

⇨ see also chǎn on p.67

摊（攤） tān ㄊㄢ ❶摆开，展开 to spread out：～场（cháng）（把庄稼晾在场上）*spread grain that has just been gathered on a threshing ground* | 把问题～到桌面上来 *put all issues on the table* ㊄烹饪方法，把糊状物放在锅上使成薄片 to spread out and fry：～鸡蛋 *make omelettes* | ～煎饼 *make pancakes* ❷（—子、—儿）摆在地上或用席、板等摆设的售货处 stall; stand; booth：～位 *stall* | 地～儿 *roadside stall* | 水果～儿 *fruit stand* ❸量词，用于摊开的糊状物 measure word for spread-out paste：一～泥 *a mud puddle* ❹分担财物 to share; to take a share in：～派 *apportion* | 每人～五元。*Each will contribute*

5 yuan. ❺遇到，碰上 to befall：他一向爱躲清静，这件事偏偏让他～上了。*He has been seeking a peaceful and quiet life, but this thing happened to him of all people.*

滩(灘) tān ㄊㄢ ❶河海边淤积成的平地或水中的沙洲 beach; sandbank：～地 *beach land* ❷水浅多石而水流很急的地方 shoal：险～ *dangerous shoals*

瘫(癱) tān ㄊㄢ 瘫痪(huàn)，神经功能发生障碍，肢体不能活动 to be paralysed

坛(❶❷壇、❸罎、❸*壜、❸*罈) tán ㄊㄢˊ ❶古代举行祭祀、誓师等大典用的土、石等筑的高台 altar：天～ *Temple of Heaven* | 先农～ *Altar of Agriculture* ⓘ指文艺界、体育界或舆论阵地 circles (of literature, art, sports or public opinions)：文～ *literary world* | 乒～ *table tennis world* | 论～ *forum* ❷用土堆成的平台，多在上面种花 raised bed：花～ *raised flower bed* ❸(－子)一种口小肚大的陶器 round earthenware container with a small mouth

昙(曇) tán ㄊㄢˊ 云彩密布，多云 cloudy; overcast

[昙花] 灌木状常绿植物，花大，白色，开的时间很短 broad-leaved epiphyllum

[昙花一现] 比喻事物一出现很快就消失 like a flash in the pan

倓 tán ㄊㄢˊ 安然不疑。多用于人名 (often used in given names) calm; peaceful

郯 tán ㄊㄢˊ [郯城] 地名，在山东省 Tancheng (a place in Shandong Province)

谈(談) tán ㄊㄢˊ ❶说，对话 to talk; to speak：面～ *talk with sb face to face* | 请你来～一～。*You are invited to come and talk about it.* | ～天(闲谈) *chat* ❷言论 remark：奇～ *strange tale* | 无稽之～ *unfounded rumour*

惔 tán ㄊㄢˊ 燃烧 to burn

锬(錟) tán ㄊㄢˊ 长矛 spear

痰 tán ㄊㄢˊ 肺泡、支气管和气管分泌的黏液 phlegm

弹(彈) tán ㄊㄢˊ ❶被其他手指压住的手指用力伸开 to flick：用手指～他一下 *flick him with one's finger* | 把帽子上的土～下去 *flick the dust off the cap* ❷使弦振动 to pluck; to play (a stringed musical instrument)：～弦子 *play the* xianzi | ～琵琶 *pluck the* pipa | ～棉花 *fluff cotton* ❸利用一个物体的弹性把另一个物体放射出去 to catapult：～射 *shoot out* [弹性] 物体因受外力暂变形状，外力一去即恢复原状的性质 elasticity ⓘ事物的伸缩性 flexibility ❹指检举违法失职的官吏(㊟－劾) to impeach (a public official)

⇨ see also dàn on p.116

覃 tán ㄊㄢˊ ❶深 profound：～思 *be deep in thought* ❷延伸 to extend：葛之～兮！*Oh, the long kudzu vines!* ❸姓 (surname)

Tan

⇨ see also qín on p.538

谭(譚) tán ㄊㄢˊ ❶ same as "谈" ❷姓 (surname) Tan

潭 tán ㄊㄢˊ 深水池，深水坑 deep pool：清～ *clear pool* | 泥～ *mire* ㊀ 深 deep：～渊 *abyss*

磹 tán ㄊㄢˊ 用于地名 used in place names：～口（在福建省华安）*Tankou (in Hua'an, Fujian Province)*

镡(鐔) tán ㄊㄢˊ 姓(surname) Tan

⇨ see also chán on p.66, xín on p.725

橝 tán ㄊㄢˊ 〈方 dialect〉坑，水塘。多用于地名 (often used in place names) pool; pond

澹 tán ㄊㄢˊ ［澹台］（－tái）复姓 (two-character surname) Tantai

⇨ see also dàn on p.117

檀 tán ㄊㄢˊ 植物名 plant name ①檀香，常绿乔木，生长在热带和亚热带。木质坚硬，有香味，可制器物及香料，又可入药 white sandalwood ②紫檀，常绿乔木，生长在热带和亚热带。木质坚硬，可做器具 red sandalwood ③黄檀，落叶乔木，果实豆荚状，木质坚硬 rosewood ④青檀，落叶乔木，果实有翅，木质坚硬 wingceltis

忐 tǎn ㄊㄢˇ ［忐忑］（－tè）心神不定 perturbed：～不安 *uneasy*

坦 tǎn ㄊㄢˇ ❶平坦，宽而平 broad and level：～途 *smooth road* ❷心地平静 calm：～然 *calm* ❸ 直率 straightforward：～诚 *open and sincere*［坦白］1 直爽，没有隐私 straightforward：襟怀～ *open hearted* 2 如实地说出（自己的错误或罪行）to confess

钽(鉭) tǎn ㄊㄢˇ 金属元素，符号 Ta，钢灰色，质硬，耐腐蚀，熔点高。可用于航天工业及核工业等 tantalum (Ta)

袒(*襢) tǎn ㄊㄢˇ ❶脱去或敞开上衣，露出身体的一部分 to be stripped to the waist：～胸露臂 *bare one's chest and expose one's arms* ❷ 袒护，不公正地维护一方面 to shield：左～ *take sides; partial* | 偏～ *be biased towards*

菼 tǎn ㄊㄢˇ 古书上指荻 a kind of reed in ancient Chinese texts

毯 tǎn ㄊㄢˇ （－子）厚实有毛绒的织品 blanket; carpet：地～ *carpet* | 毛～ *woollen blanket*

璮 tǎn ㄊㄢˇ 一种玉 a kind of jade

叹(嘆、*歎) tàn ㄊㄢˋ ❶ 吟咏 to chant：一唱三～ *one sang and the other three joined in* ❷因忧闷悲痛而呼出长气 to sigh in lament：～了一口气 *heaved a sigh* | 仰天长～ *look up to heaven and sigh heavily* | ～息 *heave a sigh* ❸因高兴而发出长声 to exclaim in joy：赞～ *gasp in admiration* | ～为观止 *acclaim sth to be the best*［叹词］表示喜、怒、哀、乐各种情感以及应答、招呼的词，如"嗯、喂、哎呀"等 exclamation (such as 嗯,喂,哎呀,

etc.)

炭 tàn ㄊㄢˋ ❶木炭，把木材和空气隔绝，加高热烧成的黑色燃料。燃烧时无烟 charcoal ❷像炭的东西 items resembling coal：山楂～（中药）*hawthorn charcoal (used in Chinese medicine)* ❸〈方 dialect〉煤 coal：挖～ *dig for coal*

碳 tàn ㄊㄢˋ 非金属元素，符号 C，无定形碳有焦炭、木炭等，晶体碳有金刚石、石墨等。碳是构成有机物的主要成分。碳和它的化合物在工业和医药上用途极广 carbon (C)

探 tàn ㄊㄢˋ ❶寻求，探索 to try to find out; to explore：～源 *trace to its source* ❷探测 to examine; to survey; to probe：～矿 *prospect (for mineral deposit)* ❸侦察，暗中考察 to investigate：～案 *investigate a case* | ～听 *snoop around* ❹试探 to sound out：先～一～口气 *sound things out first* ❺做侦察工作的人 detective：密～ *secret agent* ❻探望，访问 to visit：～亲 *go home to see one's relatives (especially the parents or spouse)* | ～视 *visit* ❼（头或上体）伸出 (of one's head or upper body) to stretch forward：～出头来 *stick one's head out* | 车行时不要～身车外。*Don't lean out of the vehicle when it is moving.*

TANG ㄊㄤ

汤（湯） tāng ㄊㄤ ❶热水 boiling water：赴～蹈火 *defy all difficulties and dangers (literally means 'jump into the boiling water and step on the fire')* ❷煮东西的汁液 water in which sth has been boiled：米～ *rice water* | 鸡～ *chicken consommé* | ～药 *Chinese medicine decoction* ❸烹调后汁特别多的副食 soup：白菜～ *Chinese cabbage soup* ❹姓 (surname) Tang

⇨ see also shāng on p.580

铴（鐋） tāng ㄊㄤ 铴锣，小铜锣 small brass gong

𨱎（盪） tāng ㄊㄤ（又）多用于人名 (often used in given names) see dàng on page120

耥 tāng ㄊㄤ tǎng ㄊㄤˇ（又）用耥耙弄平田地、清除杂草 to weed and loosen the soil (with a harrow) [耥耙]（－bà）清除杂草、弄平田地的农具 paddy-field harrow

趟 tāng ㄊㄤ (old) same as "蹚"

⇨ see also tàng on p.641

嘡 tāng ㄊㄤ 形容打钟、敲锣、放枪等的声音 clang：～的一声，锣响了。*The gong sounded with a clang.*

镗（鏜） tāng ㄊㄤ same as "嘡"

⇨ see also táng on p.640

蹚（*踼） tāng ㄊㄤ ❶从有水、草等的地方走过去 to paddle; to wade：他～着水过去了。*He waded across the water.* ❷用犁、锄等把土翻开，把草锄去 to turn the soil and dig up weeds (with a hoe, etc.)：～地 *turn the soil*

羰 tāng ㄊㄤ 羰基，有机化合物中含碳和氧的基 carbonyl

唐 táng ㄊㄤˊ ❶夸大，虚夸 boastful; exaggerative：荒～ *absurd* | ～大无验 *sheer bragging* ❷空，徒然 futile; in vain：～捐（白费）*in vain* ❸朝代名 name of dynasty ①唐高祖李渊所建立（公元 618—907 年）Tang Dynasty (618—907, founded by Li Yuan, Emperor Gaozu) ②五代之一，李存勖所建立（公元 923—936 年），史称后唐 Later Tang Dynasty (923—936, one of the Five Dynasties, founded by Li Cunxu)

[唐突] 1 冲撞，冒犯 to offend：～尊长 *offend one's elders and betters* 2 莽撞，冒失 offensive; abrupt; curt

鄌 táng ㄊㄤˊ [鄌郚]（－wú）地名，在山东省昌乐 Tangwu (a place in Changle, Shandong Province)

塘 táng ㄊㄤˊ ❶堤岸，堤防 embankment：河～ *river embankment* | 海～ *seawall* ❷水池（㊀池－）pond：水～ *pond* | 荷～ *lotus pond* | 苇～ *reed pond* ❸浴池 common bathing pool：澡～ *bathhouse*

搪 táng ㄊㄤˊ ❶挡，抵拒 to keep out (sb/sth)：～饥 *allay one's hunger* ❷敷衍，应付 to do sth perfunctorily：～差事（敷衍了事）*muddle through one's work*

[搪塞]（－sè）敷衍塞（sè）责 do sth perfunctorily：做事情要认真，不要～。*When doing things, one should put one's heart into it instead of just going through the motions.* ❸用泥土或涂料抹上或涂上 to apply (clay, paint, or coating)：～炉子 *line a stove with clay* | ～瓷（一种用石英、长石等制成的像釉子的物质）*enamel*

溏 táng ㄊㄤˊ 泥浆 mud ㊀不凝结半流动的 viscous：～心鸡蛋 *soft-boiled egg*

瑭 táng ㄊㄤˊ 古书上指一种玉 a kind of jade in ancient Chinese texts

螗 táng ㄊㄤˊ 古书上指一种较小的蝉 a kind of small cicada in ancient Chinese texts

糖（❶* 餹、❷** 醣）táng ㄊㄤˊ ❶从甘蔗、甜菜、米、麦等提制出来的甜的东西 sugar ❷有机化合物的一类，又叫碳水化合物，是人体内产生热能的主要物质，如蔗糖、淀粉等 carbohydrate (also called 碳水化合物)

赯 táng ㄊㄤˊ 赤色（指人的脸色）ruddy (of one's complexion)：紫～脸 *purplish complexion*

堂 táng ㄊㄤˊ ❶正房，高大的屋子 main room of a traditional courtyard house：～屋 *central room (of a one-storey traditional Chinese house)* | 礼～ *auditorium* [令堂] 对对方母亲的尊称 (honorific speech) your mother ❷专供某种用途的房屋 room for a specific purpose：课～ *classroom* ❸过去官吏审案办事的地方 courtroom in a *yamen*：大～ *courtroom in a* yamen | 过～ *stand trial in a court* ❹指同宗但不是嫡亲的（亲属）(relationship between cousins, etc.) of the same paternal grandfather or great-grandfather：～兄弟 *cousins (sons of one's father's brothers)* ❺量词，用于分节的课程、审案的次数等 measure word for classes, trials, etc.：一～课 *one class*｜审过两～ *have been tried twice in court*

[堂皇]盛大，大方 magnificent：冠冕～ *dignified or impressive on the surface*｜富丽～ *palatial*

[堂堂]仪容端正，有威严 dignified; impressive：相貌～ *dignified appearance*

T

棠 táng ㄊㄤˊ 植物名 plant name ①棠梨树，即杜树 birch leaf pear (same as 杜树) ②海棠树，落叶小乔木，花白色或粉红色。果实也叫海棠，球形，黄色或红色，味酸甜 crab-apple

鄌 táng ㄊㄤˊ 古地名，在今江苏省六合 Tang (an ancient place name, in today's Liuhe, Jiangsu Province)

樘 táng ㄊㄤˊ ❶门框或窗框 frame (of a door or window)：门～ *door frame*｜窗～ *window frame* ❷量词，用于一套门（窗）框和门（窗）扇 measure word for a door or window and its frame：一～玻璃门 *a glass door*

⇨ see also chēng on p.76

膛 táng ㄊㄤˊ ❶体腔 body cavity：胸～ *chest*｜开～ *cut open the chest and abdomen* ❷（一儿）某些器物中空的部分 chamber：炉～ *stove chamber*｜枪～ *gun bore*

镗(鏜) táng ㄊㄤˊ 加工切削机器零件上已有的钻孔 to bore：～床 *boring machine*

⇨ see also tāng on p.638

螳 táng ㄊㄤˊ 螳螂，昆虫，俗叫刀螂，头三角形，触角呈丝状，前足发达，像镰刀 mantis (informal 刀螂)：～臂当（dāng）车（喻做事不自量力必然失败）*overestimate one's own strength (literally means 'a mantis tries to stop a cart')*

帑 tǎng ㄊㄤˇ 古时指收藏钱财的府库和府库里的钱财 (old) state treasury funds

〈古 ancient〉also same as 孥 (nú)

倘 tǎng ㄊㄤˇ 连词，假使，如果 (conjunction) if：～若 *if*｜～能努力，定可成功。*One is sure to succeed if one works hard.*

⇨ see also cháng on p.69

埫 tǎng ㄊㄤˇ 〈方 dialect〉山间平地，平坦的地，多用于地名 (often used in place names) flat land：贾～（在宁夏回族自治区海原）*Jiatang (a place in Haiyuan, Ningxia Hui Autonomous Region)*｜都家～（在陕西省安康）*Dujiatang (a place in Ankang, Shaanxi Province)*

淌 tǎng ㄊㄤˇ 流 to drip; to trickle：～眼泪 *shed tears*｜汗珠直往下～ *sweat dripped down*｜流～ *flow*

惝 tǎng ㄊㄤˇ（又）see chǎng on page 70

耥 tǎng ㄊㄤˇ（又）see tāng on page 638

躺 tǎng ㄊㄤˇ 身体横倒，也指车辆、器具等倒在地上 (of body, vehicles, or other objects)

to lie; to recline: ～在床上 *lie in bed*| 一棵大树～在路边。*A big tree lay on the roadside.*

傥(儻) tǎng ㄊㄤˇ ❶same as "倘 (tǎng)" ❷see 倜傥 (tì—) at 倜 on page 648

镋(钂) tǎng ㄊㄤˇ 古代一种兵器，跟叉相似 a kind of fork-shaped weapon in ancient time

烫(燙) tàng ㄊㄤˋ ❶温度高，皮肤接触温度高的物体感觉疼痛或受伤 to scald; to burn: 开水很～ *the boiling water is very hot* | ～手 *thorny (literally means 'hot to touch')* | ～伤 *scald; burn* | 小心～着！*Be careful not to get scalded!* ❷用热的物体使另外的物体起变化 to warm; to heat; to iron: ～酒（使热）*heat wine* | ～衣服（使平）*iron clothes* ❸烫头发 to perm (hair): 电～ *electric perm*

趟 tàng ㄊㄤˋ 量词 measure word ①来往的次数 (used for trips) time: 他来了一～。*He has been here once.* | 这～火车去上海。*This train is going to Shanghai.* ②（一儿）用于成行的东西 used for things in a row: 屋里摆着两～桌子。*There are two rows of tables in the room.* | 用线把这件衣服缝上一～ *sew a row of stitches onto the clothes with thread*

⇨ see also tāng on p.638

TAO ㄊㄠ

叨 tāo ㄊㄠ 受到（好处）to get the benefit of; to receive (favour): ～光 *be much obliged to you* | ～教（jiào）*have the benefit of your instruction* [叨扰] 谢人款待的客套话 (polite expression) thank you for your hospitality

⇨ see also dāo on p.120

弢 tāo ㄊㄠ ❶see 韬 on page 642 ❷用于人名 used in given names

涛(濤) tāo ㄊㄠ 大波浪（㊥波一、浪一）great wave

焘(燾) tāo ㄊㄠ（又）多用于人名 (often used in given names) see dào on page 122

绦(縧、*絛、*縚) tāo ㄊㄠ （一子）用丝线编织成的花边或扁平的带子，可以装饰衣物 silk ribbon [绦虫] 寄生在人或家畜、家禽、鱼等动物肠道内的虫子，身体长而扁，像绦子，由节片组成 tapeworm

掏(*搯) tāo ㄊㄠ ❶挖 to dig: 在墙上～一个洞 *make a hole in the wall* ❷伸进去取 to (reach in and) take out: 把口袋里的钱～出来 *take the money in the pocket out* | ～耳朵 *pick one's ears*

滔 tāo ㄊㄠ 漫，充满 to flood; to inundate: 波浪～天 *waves running high* | 罪恶～天 *be guilty of the most heinous crimes* [滔滔] 1 大水漫流 torrential: 海水～ *seawater surges* 2 话语连续不断 incessant: ～不绝 *talk nineteen to the dozen* | 议论～ *discussion is heated*

慆 tāo ㄊㄠ 喜悦 happy

韬(韜、△**弢) tāo ㄊㄠ ❶弓或剑的套子 (of a bow) case; (of a sword) sheath [韬略] 指六韬、三略，古代的兵书 *Liutao* and *Sanlue* (two ancient works of military strategy) ㊕用兵的计谋 military strategy ❷隐藏，隐蔽（多指才能）to hide (often one's talents)：～晦 *lie low*

饕 tāo ㄊㄠ 贪婪，贪食 to be gluttonous：老～（贪吃的人）*glutton; voracious eater* [饕餮]（－tiè）传说中一种凶恶的兽，古代铜器上多刻它的头部形状做装饰 *taotie* (a kind of ferocious animal in Chinese legend) ㊖1 凶恶的人 fierce person 2 贪吃的人 voracious eater

咷 táo ㄊㄠ 哭 to wail; to cry [号咷]（háo－）same as "号啕"

逃(**迯) táo ㄊㄠ ❶逃跑，逃走 to run away; to escape：～脱 *run away*｜望风而～ *flee at the mere sight of an oncoming force*｜追歼～敌 *pursue and wipe out the fleeing enemy* ❷逃避，避开 to evade：～荒 *flee from famine*｜～难 *flee from a calamity*｜在劫难～ *there is no escaping fate*

洮 táo ㄊㄠ 洮河，水名，在甘肃省南部 Taohe River (in the south of Gansu Province)

桃 táo ㄊㄠ ❶桃树，落叶乔木，花白色或红色，果实叫桃子或桃儿，略呈球形，有绒毛，味甜，可以吃 peach tree ❷（－儿）形状像桃子的东西 peach-shaped thing：棉～儿 *cotton boll* ❸核桃 walnut：～仁 *walnut kernel*｜～酥 *walnut shortbread*

鼗 táo ㄊㄠ 长柄的摇鼓，俗叫拨浪鼓 pellet drum (informal 拨浪鼓)

陶 táo ㄊㄠ ❶用黏土烧制的器物 earthenware ❷制造陶器 to make pottery：～铸 *mould*｜～冶（制陶器和炼金属，喻造就良好的品格、情操等）*make pottery and smelt metal; (figurative) mould (character, etc.)* ❸陶然，快乐的样子 contented; happy：～醉 *be drunk with* ❹姓 (surname) Tao

⇨ see also yáo on p.761

萄 táo ㄊㄠ see 葡萄 (pú－) at 葡 on page 512

啕 táo ㄊㄠ see 号啕 (háo－) at 号 on page 243

淘 táo ㄊㄠ ❶洗去杂质 to rinse out (gravel, sand, etc.)：～米 *wash rice*｜～金 *pan for gold; (figurative) try to make high profits* [淘汰] 去坏的留好的，去不合适的留合适的 to eliminate through selection/competition：自然～ *natural selection* ❷消除泥沙、渣滓等，挖浚 to dredge：～井 *dredge a well*｜～缸 *clean a tank* ❸淘气，顽皮 mischievous：这孩子真～。*This child is really naughty.*

騊(騊) táo ㄊㄠ [騊駼]（－tú）古代良马名 name of a fine horse in ancient times

绹(綯) táo ㄊㄠˊ ❶绳索 rope ❷〈方 dialect〉用绳索捆 to tie with a rope

醄 táo ㄊㄠˊ see 酕醄 (máo—) at 酕 on page 439

梼(檮) táo ㄊㄠˊ [梼杌] (—wù) 1 古代传说中的恶兽，恶人 (in Chinese legend) fierce beast; fierce person 2 春秋时楚国史书名 title of the history of the state of Chu in the Spring and Autumn Period

讨(討) tǎo ㄊㄠˇ ❶查究，处治 to punish; to investigate and ascertain ㊟征伐，发动攻击 to send armed forces to suppress：南征北～ *fight up and down the country* [声讨] 宣布罪行而加以抨击 to denounce ❷研究，推求 to discuss：～论 *to discuss* | 研～ *study and discuss* ❸索取 to ask for; to demand：～债 *demand the payment of a debt* ❹求，请求 to beg for; to ask for：～饶 *beg for mercy* | ～教 (jiào) *seek advice* ❺招惹 to provoke; to cause：～厌 *annoying* | ～人欢喜 *lovable*

套 tào ㄊㄠˋ ❶ (—子、—儿) 罩在外面的东西 case; cover：褥～ *mattress cover* | 外～儿 *overcoat* | 手～儿 *glove* | 书～ *slipcover for a book* [河套] 地域名，被黄河三面环绕，在内蒙古自治区和宁夏回族自治区境内 Hetao (a district name, in Inner Mongolia Autonomous Region and Ningxia Hui Autonomous Region) ❷加罩 to cover with：～鞋 *overshoes* | ～上一件毛背心 *put on a woolen vest* ❸ (—子、—儿) 装在衣物里的棉絮 cotton padding：被～ *cotton padding of a quilt* | 袄～ *padded lining of a traditional Chinese padding* | 棉花～子 *cotton wadding* ❹事物配合成的整体 set：～餐 *set meal; combo; (figurative) package service* | ～装 *suit; a set (of goods)* | 成～ *set* ❺量词，同类事物合成的一组 (measure word for a group of similar things) set：一～制服 *a uniform* | 一～茶具 *a tea set* ❻模拟，照做 to model sth on; to copy：这是从那篇文章上～下来的。*This is copied from that article.* [套语] [套话] 1 客套话，如"劳驾、借光、慢走、留步"等 conventional phrase, such as 劳驾，借光，慢走，留步，etc. 2 行文、说话中的一些不解决实际问题的现成的、公式化的语句 formulaic phrase ❼ (—儿) 用绳子等做成的环 knot：双～结 *double knot* | 活～儿 *slip knot* | 牲口～ *harness for a draught animal* [圈套] 陷害人的诡计 trick; trap：他不小心上了～。*He was so careless that he was caught in a trap.* | 那是敌人的～。*That is a trick of the enemy.* ❽用套拴系 to harness：～车 (把车上的套拴在牲口身上) *harness a draught animal to a cart* ㊂用计骗取 to coax sth out of sb：用话～他 *worm the secret out of him* | ～出他的话来 *coax the word out of him* ❾互相衔接或重叠 to overlap：～耕 *make* *deep furrows in the soil with two ploughs, one following the other* | ～种 *interplant* ❿拉拢，表示亲近 to cosy up to：～交情 *get in with sb unfamiliar* | ～近乎 *cotton up to sb unfamiliar*

TE ㄊㄜ

忑 tè ㄊㄜˋ see 忐忑 (tǎn—) at 忐 on page 637

忒 tè ㄊㄜˋ 差错 error：差～ *error*

⇨ see also tuī on p.665

铽(鋱) tè ㄊㄜˋ 金属元素，符号 Tb，银灰色，质软。可用来制荧光物质及某些元件等 terbium (Tb)

特 tè ㄊㄜˋ ❶特殊，不平常的，超出一般的 special; unusual：～色 *characteristic* | ～效 *special effect* | ～产 *speciality* ㉪ 格外，非常 particularly：身体～棒 *health is excellent* | 天气～冷 *weather is particularly cold* [特别] 1 特殊，与众不同 special：样式很～ *style is very special* 2 副词，尤其 (adverb) especially：～聪明 *very clever* | ～是数学学得好 *do well in mathematics in particular* ❷专，单一 specially; specifically：～为 *specially* | ～设 *set up for a special purpose* | ～意来看你 *came specially to see you* ❸只，但 only, just：不～此也。*There is more to it than that.*

慝 tè ㄊㄜˋ 奸邪，罪恶 wickedness; evil：隐～（别人不知道的罪恶）*hidden crime*

脦 te ·ㄊㄜ（又）see de on page 124

TENG ㄊㄥ

熥 tēng ㄊㄥ 把熟的食物蒸热 to heat up by steaming：～馒头 *heat up steamed buns by steaming*

鼟 tēng ㄊㄥ 形容敲鼓声 drumbeat

疼 téng ㄊㄥˊ ❶人、动物因病、刺激或创伤而引起的难受的感觉（㊥一痛）to be in pain：肚子～ *have a stomachache* | 腿摔～了 *one's leg hurts after the fall* ❷喜爱，爱惜（㊥一爱）to dote on; to love dearly：他奶奶最～他。*His grandmother loves him most.*

腾(騰) téng ㄊㄥˊ ❶奔跑，跳跃（㊥奔一）to jump：欢～ *jump for joy* | 龙～虎跃 *hustle and bustle about* ❷上升 to soar：～空 *rise high into the air* | 蒸～ *(of steam) rise swiftly* | ～云驾雾 *mount the clouds and ride the mist; (figurative) feel giddy* [腾腾] 形容气势旺盛 vigorous; steaming：雾气～ *misty* | 热气～ *steaming hot* ❸空出来，挪移 to clear out; to vacate：～出两间房来 *vacate two rooms* | ～不出空来 *cannot find the time/space* ❹(teng) 词尾（在动词后，表示动作的反复连续）used after verbs to express repeated actions：倒～ *move about; trade in* | 翻～ *turn sth over and over; toss* *about* | 折（zhē）～ *be restless* | 闹～ *wrangle; laugh and joke noisily*

誊（謄） téng ㄊㄥˊ 照原稿抄写 to copy out：～写 *copy out* | ～清 *make a clean copy* | 这稿子太乱，要～一遍。*The manuscript is so untidy that you need to make a clean copy of it.*

滕 téng ㄊㄥˊ 周代诸侯国名，在今山东省滕州 Teng (a state of the Zhou Dynasty, in today's Tengzhou, Shandong Province)

螣 téng ㄊㄥˊ 螣蛇，古书上说的一种能飞的蛇 a kind of flying snake in ancient Chinese texts

縢 téng ㄊㄥˊ ❶封闭，约束 to seal off; to restrain ❷绳子 rope

藤（*籐） téng ㄊㄥˊ ❶植物名 plant name ①紫藤，藤本植物，俗叫藤萝，花紫色 wisteria (informal 藤萝) ②白藤，木本植物，俗叫藤子，茎细长，柔软而坚韧，可用来编篮、椅、箱等 rattan (informal 藤子) ❷蔓 vine：葡萄～ *grape vine* | 顺～摸瓜 *follow the clues to track sth/sb down (literally means 'follow the vine to get the melon')*

螣（䲢） téng ㄊㄥˊ 鱼名，身体近圆筒形，青灰色，有褐色网状斑纹，头大眼小，常生活在海底 stargazer

TI ㄊㄧ

体（體） tī ㄊㄧ ［体己］［梯己］（－ji）1 家庭成员个人积蓄的财物 private savings 2 亲近的 intimate：～话 *words spoken in confidence*

⇨ see also tǐ on p.647

剔 tī ㄊㄧ ❶把肉从骨头上刮下来 to pick meat from bones：～骨肉 *meat removed from the bones* | 把肉～得干干净净 *pick the bones clean* ⓘ从缝隙或孔洞里往外挑（tiǎo）拨东西 to pick (from a crack or fissure)：～牙 *pick one's teeth* | ～指甲 *clean one's fingernails* ❷把不好的挑（tiāo）出来（ⓔ－除）to weed out：把有伤的果子～出去 *pick out the bruised fruits* | ～庄（旧指挑出有缺点的货品廉价出卖）*(old) pick out the inferior goods to sell at reduced prices*

踢 tī ㄊㄧ 用脚撞击 to kick：～球 *kick a ball* | ～毽子 *kick a shuttlecock* | 一脚～开 *kick away*

梯 tī ㄊㄧ ❶（－子）登高用的器具或设备 ladder：楼～ *staircase* | 软～ *rope ladder* | 电～ *lift; elevator* ❷像梯子的 ladder-shaped：～形 *trapezium* ［梯田］在山坡上开辟的一层一层像阶梯的田地 terraced fields

䏲 tī ㄊㄧ 化合物的一类，是锑化氢中的氢原子部分或全部被烃基取代而成，大多有毒 stibine

锑（銻） tī ㄊㄧ 金属元素，符号 Sb，银白色，有光泽，质硬而脆，有毒。用于工业和医药中 stibium (Sb)

䴘（鷉） tī ㄊㄧ see 䴙䴘 (pì－) at 䴙 on page 503

T

擿 tī ㄊㄧ 揭发 to expose：发奸～伏（揭发奸邪，使无可隐藏）*expose sb's evil deeds*

⇨ see also zhì on p.860

荑 tí ㄊㄧˊ ❶草木初生的叶芽 sprout ❷稗子一类的草 tare

⇨ see also yí on p.769

绨（綈） tí ㄊㄧˊ 光滑厚实的丝织品 thick silk

⇨ see also tì on p.648

鹈（鵜） tí ㄊㄧˊ ［鹈鹕］（－hú）鸟名，俗叫淘河、塘鹅，体大嘴长，嘴下有皮囊可以伸缩，捕食鱼类 pelican (informal 淘河，塘鹅）

提 tí ㄊㄧˊ ❶垂手拿着（有环、柄或绳套的东西）to carry (things with a ring or handle) in one's hand (with arm hanging down)：～着一壶水 *carrying a kettle of water*｜～着一个篮子 *carrying a basket*｜～心吊胆（形容担心或害怕）*have one's heart in one's mouth*｜～纲挈（qiè）领（喻扼要提出）*bring out the essentials* ❷使事物由低往高、由后往前移动 to lift：～升 *promote*｜～高 *raise*｜～前 *ahead of time*｜～早 *in advance* ❸舀取油、酒等液体的工具 ladle; dipper：油～ *oil-dipper*｜醋～ *vinegar-dipper* ❹说起，举出 to put forward; to mention：经他一～，大家都想起来了。*Everyone recalled it at his mention.*｜～意见 *offer an opinion*｜～供 *provide* ❺取出（㊟－取）to extract：把款～出来 *withdraw money* ㊂把被关押的人带出来 to summon for interrogation：～审 *bring to trial*｜～犯人 *bring a prisoner to trial* ❻汉字的一种笔形（㇀），即“挑”（tiǎo）(in a Chinese character, same as 挑 tiǎo) rising stroke ❼姓 (surname) Ti

⇨ see also dī on p.127

騠（騠） tí ㄊㄧˊ see 駃騠 (jué－) at 駃 on page 342

缇（緹） tí ㄊㄧˊ 橘红色 orange-red

瑅 tí ㄊㄧˊ 一种玉 a kind of jade

题（題） tí ㄊㄧˊ ❶古指额头 (ancient) forehead ❷题目，写作或讲演内容的总名目 subject; topic：命～ *set a question; assign a topic*｜出～ *assign a topic; set an exam paper*｜难～（喻不容易做的事情）*thorny issue*｜离～太远 *stray far away from the subject* ㊂练习或考试时要求解答的问题 question：试～ *examination item*｜算～ *arithmetic problem*｜出两道～ *set two questions*｜问答～ *essay question* ［题材］写作内容的主要材料 subject matter ❸写上，签署 to inscribe：～名 *to autograph*｜～字 *to inscribe*｜～词 *write words of commemoration, encouragement or appreciation; dedication*

醍 tí ㄊㄧˊ ［醍醐］（－hú）精制的奶酪 finest cream

鳀（鯷） tí ㄊㄧˊ 鱼名，身体侧扁，长 10—13 厘米，眼和口都大，趋光性强，生活在海里 anchovy

啼（*嗁） tí ㄊㄧˊ ❶哭，出声地哭（㊟－哭）

to cry：悲～ *cry with despair* | 用不着哭哭～～ *no need to cry* ❷某些鸟兽叫 (of certain birds and animals) to cry：鸡～ *cocks crow* | 猿～ *apes cry*

遆 tí ㄊㄧˊ ❶用于地名 used in place names：北～（在山西省临汾）*Beiti (in Linfen, Shanxi Province)* ❷姓 (surname) Ti

蹄（*蹏）tí ㄊㄧˊ（－子、－儿）马、牛、羊等生在趾端的角质保护物。又指有角质保护物的脚 hoof：马不停～ *without pause*

体（體）tǐ ㄊㄧˇ ❶人、动物的全身（(连)身－）body：～重 *weight* | ～温（身体的温度）*body temperature* (引)身体的一部分 part of the body：四～ *four limbs* | 上～ *upper part of the body* | 肢～ *limbs* [体面]（－mian）1 身份 dignity：有失～ *be an affront to one's dignity* 2 光彩，光荣 honourable：张口骂人很不～。*It is disgraceful to swear at people.* 3 好看 good-looking：长得～ *have good looks* [体育] 指锻炼身体增强体质的教育 physical education：～课 *physical education class* | 发展～运动，增强人民体质 *promote physical exercise and enhance the people's health* ❷事物的本身或全部 mass：物～ *object* | 全～ *whole* | 个～ *individual* | ～积 *bulk; volume* ❸形式，规格 style; form：字～ *typeface; style of calligraphy* | 得～（合宜）*appropriate* ❹作品的体裁 style：文～ *literary form* | 骚～ *poetry in the style of* Li Sao | 骈～ *parallel style* | 古～ *ancient-style (poetry)* ❺亲身，设身处地 to experience sth personally：～验 *learn through personal experience* | ～会 *learn from experience* | ～味 *to savour* | ～谅 *give sympathetic consideration to* [体贴] 揣度（duó）别人的处境和心情，给予关心、照顾 to be considerate：～入微 *be extremely consid-*

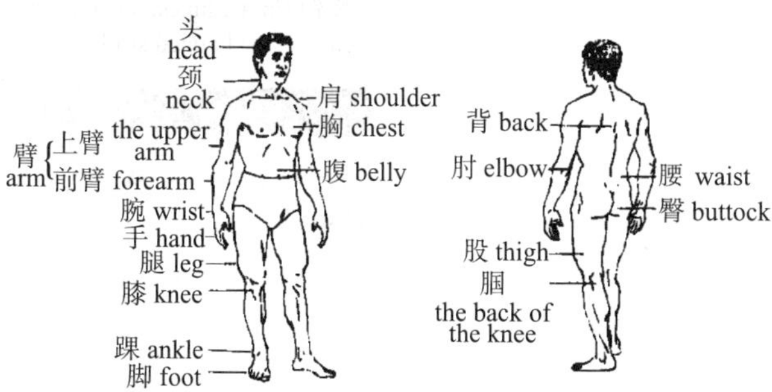

人 体
human body

erate

⇨ see also tī on p.645

屉(**屜) tì ㄊㄧˋ 器物中可以随意拿出的盛放东西的部分，常常是匣形或是分层的格架 drawer：抽～ *drawer*｜笼～ *food steamer*

剃(*鬀、△*薙) tì ㄊㄧˋ 用特制的刀刮去毛发 to shave：～头 *have one's hair shaved*｜～光 *have one's head shaved clean*

涕 tì ㄊㄧˋ ❶眼泪 tear ❷鼻涕，鼻子里分泌的液体 (nasal) mucus

悌 tì ㄊㄧˋ 指弟弟敬爱哥哥 (of a younger brother) to love and respect one's elder brother：孝～ *filial piety and fraternal love*

绨(綈) tì ㄊㄧˋ 比绸子厚实、粗糙的纺织品，用丝做经，棉线做纬 blended silk and cotton fabric

⇨ see also tí on p.646

俶 tì ㄊㄧˋ ［俶傥］（－tǎng）same as "倜傥"

⇨ see also chù on p.89

倜 tì ㄊㄧˋ ［倜傥］（－tǎng）洒脱，不拘束 unconstrained：风流～ *unconventional and romantic*

逖(**逷) tì ㄊㄧˋ 远 far away

惕 tì ㄊㄧˋ 小心谨慎 cautious; watchful ［警惕］对可能发生的危险情况或错误倾向保持警觉 to be alert：提高～，保卫祖国 *sharpen the vigilance and defend the motherland*｜～贪图享乐思想的侵蚀 *guard against the corrosive influence of hedonistic ideas*

裼 tì ㄊㄧˋ 婴儿的包被 swaddling clothes

⇨ see also xī on p.698

替 tì ㄊㄧˋ ❶代，代理(㊥－代、代－) to take the place of; to replace：～班 *take sb else's place in a work shift*｜我～你洗衣服。*I will do the laundry for you.* ❷介词，为（wèi），给 for：大家都～他高兴。*Everybody was happy for him.* ❸衰废 decline; fall：兴～ *rise and fall*｜隆～ *rise and fall*

殢(殢) tì ㄊㄧˋ ❶困倦 to be tired and sleepy ❷滞留 to be held up ❸困扰，纠缠 to be perplexed and pestered

薙 tì ㄊㄧˋ ❶除去野草 to remove weeds ❷ see 剃 on page 648

嚏 tì ㄊㄧˋ ［嚏喷］（－pen）see 喷嚏 on page 496

趯 tì ㄊㄧˋ ❶跳跃 to jump ❷汉字的一种笔形（亅），今称钩 (in a Chinese character, now called 钩) hooked stroke

TIAN ㄊㄧㄢ

天 tiān ㄊㄧㄢ ❶在地面以上的高空 sky ㊞在上的 top：～头（书页上部空白部分）*top margin*｜～桥（架在空中的高桥，桥下可以通行）*overpass*［天文］日月星辰等天体在宇宙间分布、运行等现象 astronomy ❷自然的，天生的 natural; inborn：～生 *inborn*｜～性 *nature; natural in-*

stinct | ～险 *natural barrier* | ～然 *natural* ❸日，一昼夜，或专指昼间 day; (specifically) daytime：今～ *today* | 一整～ *all day* | 白～黑夜 *day and night* ⓘ一日之内的某一段时间 time of a day：～不早了。*It is getting late.* ❹气候 weather：～冷 *weather is cold* | 阴～ *overcast day* [天气] 1 冷、热、阴、晴等现象 weather：～要变。*The weather is changing.* 2 时间 time of day：～不早了。*It's getting late.* ❺季节，时节 season：春～ *spring* | 热～ *hot season* ❻迷信的人指神佛仙人或他们所住的地方 heaven：～堂 *heaven* | 老～爷 *god* [天子] 古代指统治天下的帝王 (ancient) the emperor

添 tiān ㄊㄧㄢ 增加 (㊞增－) to add：再～几台机器 *get several more machines* | 锦上～花 *embellish what is already beautiful (literally means 'add flowers to brocade')*

黇 tiān ㄊㄧㄢ [黇鹿] 一种鹿，角的上部扁平或呈掌状，尾略长，性温顺 fallow deer

田 tián ㄊㄧㄢˊ ❶种植农作物的土地 field：水～ *watered field* | 稻～ *paddy field* | 种～ *work the land* ⓘ和农业有关的 agricultural：～家 *farming family* [田地] 1 same as "田❶" 2 地步，境遇（多指坏的）situation (often negative)：怎么弄到这步～了？*How come things have turned out as bad as this?* [田赛] 田径运动中各种跳跃、投掷项目比赛的总称 field event competition ❷指可供开采的蕴藏矿物的地带 field (containing natural resources)：煤～ *coalfield* | 油～ *oilfield* | 气～ *gas field* ❸ same as "畋"

佃 tián ㄊㄧㄢˊ 佃作，耕种田地 to cultivate

⇨ see also diàn on p.134

沺 tián ㄊㄧㄢˊ 用于地名 used in place names：～泾镇（在江苏省苏州）*Tianjingzhen (in Suzhou, Jiangsu Province)*

畋 tián ㄊㄧㄢˊ 打猎 to go hunting

畑 tián ㄊㄧㄢˊ （外 *loanword*）日本人姓名用字 used in Japanese names

钿(鈿) tián ㄊㄧㄢˊ 〈方dialect〉钱，硬币 money：铜～ *copper coin; money* | 洋～ *silver dollar*

⇨ see also diàn on p.134

盷 tián ㄊㄧㄢˊ 眼珠转动 (of eyeballs) to rotate

恬 tián ㄊㄧㄢˊ 安静（㊞－静）tranquil ⓘ安然，坦然，不在乎 indifferent; unperturbed：～不知耻 *be devoid of all sense of shame* | ～不为怪 *be not surprised at all*

甜 tián ㄊㄧㄢˊ 像糖或蜜的味道，跟"苦"相对 sweet (opposite of 苦)：～食 *dessert* ⓜ使人感觉舒服的 pleasant：～美 *sweet* | ～言蜜语 *sweet talk* | 睡得真～ *sleep really well*

湉 tián ㄊㄧㄢˊ [湉湉] 形容水面平静 (of water) peaceful

填 tián ㄊㄧㄢˊ ❶把空缺的地方塞满或补满 to fill：～平洼地

level up low-lying land ❷ 填写，在空白表格上按照项目写 to fill out：～志愿书 *fill out an application form* | ～表 *fill out a form*

阗(闐) tián ㄊㄧㄢˊ 充满 to be filled with：喧～ *noisy and crowded*

[和阗] 地名，在新疆维吾尔自治区。今作"和田" Hetian (a place in Xinjiang Uygur Autonomous Region)(now written as 和田)

忝 tiǎn ㄊㄧㄢˇ 辱没(mò)。谦辞 (humble speech) to be unworthy of the honour：～属知己 *have the honour to be a friend of yours* | ～列门墙(愧在师门) *have the honour to be a student of sb's*

舔 tiǎn ㄊㄧㄢˇ 用舌头接触东西或取东西 to lick; to lap

殄 tiǎn ㄊㄧㄢˇ 尽，绝 to exterminate：暴～天物(任意糟蹋东西) *waste nature's produce mindlessly*

掭 tiǎn ㄊㄧㄢˇ ❶撑，推 to support; to push ❷拨 to stir; to turn

⇨ see also chēn on p.73

淟 tiǎn ㄊㄧㄢˇ 污浊，肮脏 filthy; dirty

惧 tiǎn ㄊㄧㄢˇ 惭愧 ashamed

晪 tiǎn ㄊㄧㄢˇ 明亮 bright

觍(覥) tiǎn ㄊㄧㄢˇ ❶形容惭愧 ashamed：～颜 *be shamefaced* ❷厚着脸皮 to be brazen：～着脸(不知羞) *brazen it out* ❸ see 靦觍 (miǎn—) at 靦 on page 451

腆 tiǎn ㄊㄧㄢˇ ❶丰厚 sumptuous ❷胸部或腹部挺起 (of chest or belly) to bulge：～胸脯 *stick out one's chest* | ～着个大肚子 *with one's big belly hanging out* ❸ see 腼腆 (miǎn—) at 腼 on page 451

靦(靦) tiǎn ㄊㄧㄢˇ ❶ same as "觍" ❷形容人脸的样子 used to describe a person's face：～然人面 *pretend to be a person of some worth while hiding shame inside*

⇨ see also miǎn on p.451

掭 tiàn ㄊㄧㄢˋ 用毛笔蘸墨汁在砚台上弄均匀 to dip a writing brush in ink and shape it properly on an ink stone：～笔 *dip a writing brush in ink and shape it properly on an ink stone*

瑱 tiàn ㄊㄧㄢˋ 古时冠冕两侧垂到耳旁的玉饰，可以用来塞耳 (ancient) jade ornament hanging from both sides of a royal crown

⇨ see also zhèn on p.845

TIAO ㄊㄧㄠ

佻 tiāo ㄊㄧㄠ 轻薄，不庄重 frivolous [佻仫](—tà) 轻佻 frivolous

挑 tiāo ㄊㄧㄠ ❶用肩担着 to shoulder：～水 *carry water on the shoulder* | 别人～一担，他～两担。*Others carried one load while he carried two.* ❷(—子、—儿) 挑、担的东西 shoulder pole and its load; load carried on a shoulder pole：挑着空～子 *carrying a shoulder pole without any load* ❸（一儿）量词，用于成挑儿的东西 measure word for things carried on a shoulder pole：一～儿水 *a pair of buckets of water carried on a shoulder pole* | 两～儿粪 *two pairs of baskets of manure carried on a shoulder pole* ❹选，拣（㊥一选、一拣）to select：～好的送给他 *pick out the best and give them to him*| ～错 *find fault (with)*| ～毛病 *pick holes* [挑剔] 过于严格地指摘细微差错 to nit-pick

⇨ see also tiǎo on p.652

祧 tiāo ㄊㄧㄠ 古代称远祖的庙，在封建宗法制度中指承继先代 (ancient) temple for remote ancestors; to inherit from previous generations：承～ *be heir to*

条（條） tiáo ㄊㄧㄠ ❶（一子、一儿）植物的细长枝 twig: 柳～儿 *willow twig* | 荆～ *twig of the chaste tree* ❷（一子、一儿）狭长的东西 strip：面～儿 *noodles* | 布～儿 *strip of cloth* | 纸～儿 *slip of paper* ❸细长的形状 stripe：～纹 *stripe* | 花～儿布 *striped cloth* | ～绒 *corduroy* ❹项目，分项目的 item：宪法第一～ *article one of the constitution* | ～例 *regulation* [条件] 1 双方规定应遵守的事项 terms; requirement 2 事物产生或存在的因素 condition：自然～ *natural conditions* | 有利～ *favourable conditions* | 一切事物都依着～、地点和时间起变化。*Everything changes according to conditions, place and time.* ❺条理，秩序，层次 order：井井有～ *shipshape* | 有～不紊 *in perfect order* ❻量词 measure word ①用于长形的东西 for sth long：一～河 *a river* | 两～大街 *two streets* | 三～绳 *three ropes* | 四～鱼 *four fish* | 两～腿 *two legs* ②用于分项目的事物 for things that can be listed item by item：这一版上有五～新闻。*There were five pieces of news on this page.*

鲦（鰷） tiáo ㄊㄧㄠ 鱼名，身体小，呈条状，银白色，生活在淡水中 sharpbelly

苕 tiáo ㄊㄧㄠ ❶古书上指凌霄花，藤本植物，又叫紫葳，花红色 Chinese trumpet creeper (also called 紫葳, in ancient Chinese texts) ❷苕子，草本植物，花紫色，可用作绿肥 vetch ❸苇子的花 reed flower

⇨ see also sháo on p.584

岧 tiáo ㄊㄧㄠ [岧峣]（—yáo）山高 (of mountains) high

迢 tiáo ㄊㄧㄠ 远㊂ remote：千里～～ *from afar*

笤 tiáo ㄊㄧㄠ [笤帚]（—zhou）扫除尘土的用具，用脱去籽粒的高粱穗、黍子穗或棕等做成 broom

龆（齠） tiáo ㄊㄧㄠ 儿童换牙 (of children) to lose one's milk teeth：～年（童年）*early childhood*

髫 tiáo ㄊㄧㄠ 古时小孩子头上扎起来的下垂的短发 (ancient) child's hanging hair：垂～ *early childhood* | ～年（指幼

年）*childhood*

调(調) tiáo ㄊㄧㄠˊ ❶配合均匀 to mix：～色 *blend colours* | ～味 *to season* | 风～雨顺 *favourable weather* ㊀使和谐 to mediate：～剂 *adjust* | ～解 *mediate* | ～整 *adjust* [调停] 使争端平息 to mediate ❷挑拨；挑逗(㊥—唆) to incite; to tease：～嘴弄舌 *tittle-tattle* | ～笑 *make fun of* | ～戏 *take liberties with*

[调皮] 好开玩笑，顽皮 naughty

⇨ see also diào on p.136

蜩 tiáo ㄊㄧㄠˊ 古书上指蝉 cicada (in ancient Chinese texts)

蓨 tiáo ㄊㄧㄠˊ 草本植物，即羊蹄草，叶子椭圆形。根茎叶浸出的汁液，可防治棉蚜、红蜘蛛、菜青虫等 sowthistle tasselflower herb (same as 羊蹄草)

挑 tiǎo ㄊㄧㄠˇ ❶用竿子等把东西举起或支起 to lift up with a pole：～起帘子来 *raise the curtain* | 把旗子～起来 *lift the flag up with a pole* ❷用条状物或有尖的东西拨开或弄出 to poke：把火～开 *poke the fire* | ～了～灯心 *trimmed the lamp wick* | ～刺 *pick out a splinter* ❸一种刺绣方法 to cross-stitch：～花 *cross-stitch work* ❹拨弄，引动(㊥—拨) to provoke; to incite：～衅 *provoke* | ～动 *arouse; instigate* | ～起矛盾 *sow discord* [挑战] 1 激怒敌人出来打仗 throw down the gauntlet 2 鼓动对方和自己竞赛 challenge (to a contest)：甲乙两队互相～。*Team A and Team B challenged each other.* ❺汉字由下斜着向上写的一种笔形（㇀）(in a Chinese character) rising stroke

⇨ see also tiāo on p.650

朓 tiǎo ㄊㄧㄠˇ 古代称农历月底月亮在西方出现。多用于人名 (often used in given names, ancient)(of the moon) to appear in the west at the end of a lunar month

窕 tiǎo ㄊㄧㄠˇ see 窈窕 (yǎo—) at 窈 on page 762

嬥 tiǎo ㄊㄧㄠˇ 身材匀称美好 (of one's figure) fine

眺(*覜) tiào ㄊㄧㄠˋ 眺望，往远处看 to look into the distance (from a high place)：登高远～ *ascend a height to enjoy a distant view*

跳 tiào ㄊㄧㄠˋ ❶用力使脚离地，全身向上或向前(㊥—跃) to jump：～高 *high jump* | ～远 *long jump* | ～绳 *skip rope* ㊀越过 to skip：～级 *skip a year* | 这一课书～过去不学。*This lesson is skipped.* [跳板] 1 一头搭在车、船上的长板，便于上下 gangplank ㊂作为过渡的途径、工具 springboard; sth that leads to one's goal 2 供游泳跳水的长板 divingboard ❷一起一伏地动 to throb：心～ *heart beats* | 眼～ *eyelid twitches*

粜(糶) tiào ㄊㄧㄠˋ 卖粮食，跟"籴"相对 to sell (grain)(opposite of 籴)

TIE ㄊㄧㄝ

帖 tiē ㄊㄧㄝ ❶妥当，合适 well-placed：妥～ *fitting* | 安～

be at ease ❷ 顺从，驯服 to be submissive：～伏 *be obedient* | 俯首～耳（含贬义）*(disapproving) be docile and obedient*

⇨ see also tiě on p.653, tiè on p.653

怗 tiē ㄊㄧㄝ 平定，安宁 to suppress; to pacify

贴（貼） tiē ㄊㄧㄝ ❶ 粘（zhān），把一种薄片状的东西粘在另一种东西上（㊀粘一）to paste：～布告 *put up a notice* | ～邮票 *affix a stamp* ❷靠近，紧挨 to keep close to：～身 *figure-hugging; nicely-fitting* | ～着墙走 *walk along the wall*［贴切］恰当，确切 apt; appropriate ❸添补，补助（㊀一补）to give financial assistance：房～ *housing allowance* | 每月～给他一些钱 *give him a monthly allowance* ❹ same as "帖 (tiē)" ❺量词，用于膏药 (measure word for medicated plaster) piece

萜 tiē ㄊㄧㄝ 有机化合物的一类，多为有香味的液体 terpene

帖 tiě ㄊㄧㄝˇ ❶（～儿）便条 brief note：字～儿 *note; notice* ❷（～子）邀请客人的纸片 invitation：请～ *invitation (card)* | 喜～ *wedding invitation* ❸旧时写着生辰八字等内容的纸片 (old) card containing details of a person's name, age, birthplace, etc.：庚～ *age card* | 换～ *exchange age cards and become sworn brothers*

⇨ see also tiē on p.652, tiè on p.653

铁（鐵、銕）** tiě ㄊㄧㄝˇ 金属元素，符号 Fe，纯铁灰白色，质硬，在潮湿空气中易生锈。是重要的工业原料，用途极广 iron (Fe) ㊃ ①坚硬 hard：～蚕豆 *roasted broad bean* | ～拳 *iron fist* ②意志坚定 unyielding; hard：～人 *iron man/woman* | ～姑娘队 *iron girls' team* ③确定不移 ironclad：～的纪律 *iron discipline* | ～案如山 *ironclad case* ④残暴或精锐 ruthless; elite：～蹄 *iron heel (of tyranny)* | ～骑 *strong cavalry* ⑤借指兵器 arms：手无寸～ *completely unarmed*

帖 tiè ㄊㄧㄝˋ 学习写字时模仿的样本 calligraphy copybook：碑～ *book of stele rubbings* | 字～ *calligraphy copybook*

⇨ see also tiē on p.652, tiě on p.653

餮 tiè ㄊㄧㄝˋ see 饕餮 (tāo－) at 饕 on page 642

TING ㄊㄧㄥ

厅（廳） tīng ㄊㄧㄥ ❶聚会或招待客人用的大房间 hall：客～ *living room* | 餐～ *dining hall* ❷政府机关的办事单位 government department：办公～ *general office*

汀 tīng ㄊㄧㄥ 水边平地，小洲 low, level land along a river; islet［汀线］海岸被海水侵蚀而成的线状的痕迹 line track (of a seashore)

听（聽） tīng ㄊㄧㄥ ❶用耳朵接受声音 to listen：

～广播 *listen to the radio* | 你～～外面有什么响声。*Listen and see what that noise outside is.* ❷顺从，接受意见 to heed：行动～指挥 *act in accordance with instructions* | 我告诉他了，他不～。*I told him about it but he wouldn't listen.* ❸ (formerly pronounced tìng) 任凭，随 to allow：～其自然 *let nature take its course* | ～便 *do as one pleases* | ～凭 *allow* ❹治理，判断 to administer：～政（指封建帝王临朝处理政事）*hold court* ❺（外 *loanword*）马口铁筒 tin：～装啤酒 *tinned beer* | 一～饼干 *a tin of biscuits*

烃(烴) tīng ㄊㄧㄥ 碳氢化合物 hydrocarbon

绽(綎) tīng ㄊㄧㄥ 用来系佩玉的绶带 ribbon (attached to jade)

桯 tīng ㄊㄧㄥ ❶锥子等中间的杆子 awl shaft：锥～子 *awl shaft* ❷古代放在床前的小桌子 (ancient) small bedside table

鞓 tīng ㄊㄧㄥ 皮革制的腰带 leather belt

廷 tíng ㄊㄧㄥˊ 朝廷，封建时代君主受朝问政的地方 imperial court［宫廷］1 帝王的住所 palace 2 由帝王及其大臣构成的统治集团 imperial court

莛 tíng ㄊㄧㄥˊ （一儿）某些草本植物的茎 stem：麦～儿 *wheat stem* | 油菜～儿 *rape stalk*

庭 tíng ㄊㄧㄥˊ ❶正房前的院子 front yard：～院 *front courtyard* | 前～ *front yard*［家庭］以婚姻和血统关系为基础的社会单位，包括父母、子女和其他共同生活的亲属 family ❷厅堂 hall：大～广众 *public place with a large crowd* ❸法庭，审判案件的处所或机构 law court：开～ *open a court session* | ～长 *president of a law court of tribunal*

蜓 tíng ㄊㄧㄥˊ see 蜻蜓(qīng－) at 蜻 on page540, and 蝘蜓(yǎn－) at 蝘 on page753

霆 tíng ㄊㄧㄥˊ 霹雷，霹雳 thunderbolt：雷～ *thunderclap*

蜓 tíng ㄊㄧㄥˊ 古无脊椎动物，又叫纺锤虫，长 3—6 毫米，外壳多呈纺锤形。生活在海洋里，现已灭绝 *fusulinida* (also called 纺锤虫)

亭 tíng ㄊㄧㄥˊ ❶（一子）有顶无墙、供休息用的建筑物，多建筑在路旁或花园里 pavilion ㉄建筑得比较简单的小房子 kiosk：书～ *book stall* | 邮～ *postal kiosk* ❷适中，均匀 well-balanced：～匀 *well-balanced* | ～午（正午，中午）*noon*

［亭亭］1 形容高耸 towering 2 美好 graceful and erect：～玉立 *(of a woman) tall, slim and graceful* (also written as 婷婷)

停 tíng ㄊㄧㄥˊ ❶止住，中止不动（㊀－顿、－止）to stop：一辆汽车～在门口。*A car stops at the gate.* | 钟～了。*The clock has stopped.* ❷停留 to stop over：我去天津，在北京～了两天。*On my way to Tianjin, I stopped over in Beijing for two days.* ❸妥当 settled：～妥 *in (good) order*［停当］（－dang）齐备，妥当 ready ❹

（一儿）总数分成几份，其中一份叫一停儿 portion：三～儿中的两～儿 *two portions out of three portions* | 十～儿有九～儿是好的。*Nine out of ten of them are good.*

葶 tíng ㄊㄧㄥˊ ［葶苈］（—lì）草本植物，花黄色，种子可入药 *Draba nemorosa* woolly whitlowgrass

渟 tíng ㄊㄧㄥˊ 水停止不动 (of water) to stagnate：渊～ *deep stagnant pool*

婷 tíng ㄊㄧㄥˊ ㊀美好 graceful and erect

圢 tǐng ㄊㄧㄥˇ 用于地名 used in place names：上～坂（在山西省垣曲）*Shangtingban (in Yuanqu, Shanxi Province)* | 南～坂（在山西省垣曲）*Nantingban (in Yuanqu, Shanxi Province)*

町 tǐng ㄊㄧㄥˇ 〈古 ancient〉❶田界 raised path as border between fields ❷田地 farmland

⇨ see also dīng on p.139

侹 tǐng ㄊㄧㄥˇ 平直 level and straight

挺 tǐng ㄊㄧㄥˇ ❶笔直 upright; straight: 笔～ *erect* | ～进（勇往直前）*press onward* | 直～～地躺着不动 *lying stiff and still* ［挺拔］1 直立而高耸 tall and straight 2 坚强有力 steady and forceful：笔力～ *vigorous brush strokes* ❷撑直或凸出 to stick out：～起腰来 *straighten one's back* | ～胸抬头 *puff one's chest out and lift one's chin* | ～身而出 *step forward bravely* ㊀勉强支撑 to endure：有病早治，不能硬～着。*When ill, one should see a doctor as soon as possible; one cannot afford to stick it out.* ❸副词，很 (adverb) pretty; very：～好 *pretty good* | ～和气 *very friendly* | ～爱学习 *very fond of study* | 这花～香。*This flower is really fragrant.* ❹量词，用于机枪 measure word for machine guns

珽 tǐng ㄊㄧㄥˇ 古代天子所持的玉笏（hù）jade tablet (held by an emperor in ancient times)

梃 tǐng ㄊㄧㄥˇ 棍棒 club; stick

⇨ see also tìng on p.655

烶 tǐng ㄊㄧㄥˇ 火焰燃烧的样子 flaming

铤（鋌） tǐng ㄊㄧㄥˇ 快步跑 to run fast：～而走险（指走投无路而采取冒险行动）*make a reckless move in desperation*

颋（頲） tǐng ㄊㄧㄥˇ 正直，直 upright

艇 tǐng ㄊㄧㄥˇ 轻便的小船，小型的军用船只 light boat; naval vessel：游～ *yacht* | 汽～ *steamboat* | 赛～ *racing boat* | 舰～ *naval vessel* | 潜～ *submarine*

梃 tìng ㄊㄧㄥˋ ❶梃猪，杀猪后，在猪腿上割一个口子，用铁棍贴着腿皮往里捅 to poke a pointed iron rod between the leg shin and flesh of a slaughtered pig in order to pump up the skin for dehairing and cleansing ❷梃猪用的铁棍 iron rod used for the above purpose

⇨ see also tǐng on p.655

TONG ㄊㄨㄥ

恫（**痌）tōng ㄊㄨㄥ 病痛 sickness：～瘝（guān）在抱（把人民的疾苦放在心里）*take the hardships of the people to heart*

⇨ see also dòng on p.143

通 tōng ㄊㄨㄥ ❶没有阻碍，可以穿过，能够达到 to be open; to lead to：～行 *pass through* | 条条大路～北京。*All roads lead to Beijing.* | 四～八达 *extend in all directions* | ～车 *be open to traffic* | ～风 *ventilate* ㉄ ①顺，指文章合语法，合事理 coherent ②彻底明了（liǎo），懂得 to know well：精～业务 *be expert at one's trade* | 他～三种语言。*He is fluent in three languages.* ③四通八达的，不闭塞的 open; accessible：～都大邑 *metropolitan city* [通过] 1 穿过去，走过去 to pass (through)：火车～南京长江大桥。*The train crosses the Nanjing Yangtze River Bridge.* 2 介词，经过 (preposition) through：～学习提高了认识 *improved one's understanding through study* 3（提案）经过讨论大家同意 (of a motion) to pass (after discussion)：～一项议案 *pass a motion* [通货] 在社会经济活动中作为流通手段的货币 currency：～膨胀 *inflation* [通融] 破例迁就 to bend the rules ㉄ 临时借用 to borrow money short term：购房款不够，只得向亲戚～几万。*One has to borrow tens of thousands of dollars from relatives as one did not have enough money for the house.* ❷传达 to tell：～报 *circulate a notice* | ～告 *announce* | ～信 *correspond; communicate* ❸往来交接 to connect; to exchange：～商 *have trading relations* | 互～情报 *exchange information* ❹普遍，全 general：～病 *common fault* | ～共 *altogether* | ～盘计划 *overall plan* | ～力合作 *make a concerted effort* [通俗] 浅显的，适合于一般文化程度的 common; popular：～读物 *popular literature* ❺量词，用于电报、电话等 measure word for letters, telegrams, etc.：发一～电报 *send a telegram* | 打一～电话 *make a call* ❻姓 (surname) Tong

⇨ see also tòng on p.659

嗵 tōng ㄊㄨㄥ 形容脚步声、心跳声等 thud (of footsteps, heartbeats, etc.)：心～～地跳 *heart thumps*

樋 tōng ㄊㄨㄥ 古书上说的一种树 a kind of tree in ancient Chinese texts

仝 tóng ㄊㄨㄥˊ ❶ see 同 on page 656 ❷姓 (surname) Tong

砼 tóng ㄊㄨㄥˊ 混凝土 concrete

同（△*仝）tóng ㄊㄨㄥˊ ❶一样，没有差异 similar; same：～等 *equal* | ～岁 *be the same age* | ～感 *have the same feeling* | 大～小异 *alike except for minor differences* [同化] 使不同的事物变成相同或相近的事物 to assimilate [同时] 1 在同一个时候 same time 2 表示进一层，并且 furthermore：修好淮河可以防止水灾，～还可以防止旱灾。*Harnessing the Huaihe River prevents not only floods but also droughts.* [同志] 一般指志同道合的人，为共同的理想、事业而奋斗的人。特指同一个政党的成员 comrade ❷跟……相同 to be the same as：～上 *as above* | ～前 *as above* | 情～手足 *feel as close as kin* ❸共同 together：会～ *be in conjunction with* | 陪～ *accompany* ❹副词，同，一起 (adverb) together：～吃～住～劳动 *eat, live and work together* | 一路～行 *be together all the way* ❺介词，跟 (preposition) with：他～哥哥一样勤奋。*He is as diligent as his brother.* | ～坏人做斗争 *fight against bad people* ❻连词，和 (conjunction) and：我～你都去。*Both you and I will go there.*

⇨ see also tòng on p.659

侗 tóng ㄊㄨㄥˊ 旧指童蒙无知 (old) childish and ignorant

⇨ see also dòng on p.143, tǒng on p.658

诇(詷) tóng ㄊㄨㄥˊ 共同 together

垌 tóng ㄊㄨㄥˊ [垌冢] (－zhǒng) 地名，在湖北省汉川 Tongzhong (a place in Hanchuan, Hubei Province)

⇨ see also dòng on p.143

茼 tóng ㄊㄨㄥˊ [茼蒿] (－hāo) 草本植物，花黄色或白色，茎、叶有特殊香味，嫩时可吃 crowndaisy

哃 tóng ㄊㄨㄥˊ 用于地名 used in place names：响～（在上海市崇明）*Xiangtong (in Chongming, Shanghai)*

峒(*峝) tóng ㄊㄨㄥˊ see 崆峒 (kōng－) at 崆 on page 359

⇨ see also dòng on p.143

桐 tóng ㄊㄨㄥˊ 植物名 plant name ①泡（pāo）桐，落叶乔木，花白色或紫色，生长快，是较好的固沙防风树木。木质疏松，可做琴、箱、船模等物 paulownia ②油桐，落叶乔木，又叫桐油树，花白色，有红色斑点，果实近球形。种子榨的油叫桐油，可用作涂料 tung oil tree (also called 桐油树) ③梧桐 phoenix tree

烔 tóng ㄊㄨㄥˊ [烔炀] (－yáng) 地名，在安徽省巢湖市 Tongyang (a place in Chaohu, Anhui Province)

铜(銅) tóng ㄊㄨㄥˊ 金属元素，符号 Cu，淡紫红色，在潮湿空气中易生锈，遇醋起化学作用生乙酸铜，有毒。是重要的工业原料，用途很广 copper (Cu)

酮 tóng ㄊㄨㄥˊ 有机化合物的一类，由羰基和两个烃基连接而成 ketone

鲖(鮦) tóng ㄊㄨㄥˊ [鲖城] 地名，在安徽省临泉县 Tongcheng (a place in Linquan County, Anhui Province)

佟 tóng ㄊㄨㄥˊ 姓 (surname) Tong

T

峂 tóng ㄊㄨㄥˊ ［峂峪］地名，在北京市海淀 Tongyu (a place in Haidian, Beijing)

彤 tóng ㄊㄨㄥˊ 红色 red

童 tóng ㄊㄨㄥˊ ❶儿童，小孩子 child：～谣 *nursery rhyme* ㊀①未长成的，幼 young; immature：～牛（没有生角的小牛）*calf without horns* ②未有过性生活的 virgin：～男 *virgin boy* | ～女 *virgin girl* ③秃的 bare：～山（没有草木的山）*bare hill* ［童话］专给儿童编写的故事 children's fairy tale ❷旧时指未成年的男仆 (old) boy servant：家～ *page-boy* | 书～ *boy servant waiting on a scholar*

僮 tóng ㄊㄨㄥˊ (ancient) same as "童❷"

⇨ see also zhuàng on p.874

潼 tóng ㄊㄨㄥˊ ［潼关］地名，在陕西省 Tongguan (a place in Shaanxi Province)

橦 tóng ㄊㄨㄥˊ 古书上指木棉树 kapok tree (in ancient Chinese texts)

曈 tóng ㄊㄨㄥˊ ［曈昽］（-lóng）天将亮的样子 (of the sky) brightening

瞳 tóng ㄊㄨㄥˊ 瞳孔，俗叫瞳仁，眼球中央的小孔，可以随着光线的强弱缩小或扩大 pupil (informal 瞳仁，see picture of 人的眼睛 on page 753)

穜 tóng ㄊㄨㄥˊ 古代指早种晚熟的谷类 (ancient) late-maturing cereal

翧 tóng ㄊㄨㄥˊ 飞翔的样子 flying; soaring

侗 tǒng ㄊㄨㄥˇ ［优侗］(lǒng-) same as "笼统"

⇨ see also dòng on p.143, tóng on p.657

筒（*筩） tǒng ㄊㄨㄥˇ 粗大的竹管 section of thick bamboo ㊀①较粗的中空而高的器物 thick tube-shaped object：烟～（tong）*chimney* | 邮～ *mailbox* | 笔～ *brush pot* ②（-儿）衣服等的筒状部分 tube-shaped part of an article of clothing, etc.：袖～ *sleeve* | 袜～ *leg of a stocking* | 靴～ *leg of a boot*

统（統） tǒng ㄊㄨㄥˇ ❶总括，总起来 all; together：～率 *command* | ～一 *unify* | ～筹 *make overall plans* ❷事物的连续关系（㊥系-）interconnected system：血～ *blood relationship* | 传～ *tradition*

捅（摓）** tǒng ㄊㄨㄥˇ 戳，刺，碰 to poke; to stab：把窗户～破了 *poked a hole in the window* | ～马蜂窝（喻惹祸）*stir up a hornet's nest* ㊑揭露 to give away：把问题全～出来了 *disclosed all the problems*

㛚 tǒng ㄊㄨㄥˇ 用于地名 used in place names：黄～铺（在江西省德安）*Huangtongpu (in De'an, Jiangxi Province)*

桶 tǒng ㄊㄨㄥˇ 盛水或其他东西的器具，深度较大 bucket：水～ *water pail* | 煤油～ *coal oil tank* ［皮桶子］做皮衣用的成件的毛皮 semi-finished fur lining

T

同（* **衕**） tòng ㄊㄨㄥˋ ［胡同］巷，较窄的街道 lane

⇨ see also tóng on p.656

恸（**慟**） tòng ㄊㄨㄥˋ ❶极悲哀 feel deep sorrow：～泣 *to wail* | ～切 *deepest sorrow* ❷指痛哭 to wail; cry bitterly：悲极而～ *wail with deep sorrow*

通 tòng ㄊㄨㄥˋ 量词，用于某些动作 measure word for some actions：打了三～鼓 *beat the drum three times* | 详详细细说了一～ *gave a detailed account*

⇨ see also tōng on p.656

痛 tòng ㄊㄨㄥˋ ❶疼（㊥疼－）painful：头～ *headache* | 不～不痒 *superficial; scratching the surface* | ～定思～ *draw a lesson from a bitter experience* ［痛苦］身体或精神感到非常难受 painful ❷悲伤（㊥悲－、哀－）be sad：～心 *be terribly distressed* | ～不欲生 *be so overwhelmed with grief as to wish one were dead* ❸极，尽情地，深切地，彻底地 deeply; thoroughly：～恨 *hate bitterly* | ～饮 *drink one's fill* | ～惜 *deeply regret* | ～改前非 *make a clean break with one's past errors* ［痛快］（－kuai）1 爽快，爽利 candid：他是个～人。*He is a straightforward man.* 2 尽兴，舒畅，高兴 to one's heart's content; happy：这活儿干得真～。*Doing the work really gives one much satisfaction.* | 看他的样子好像有点儿不～。*Judging by his look, he seems a little bit unhappy.*

TOU ㄊㄡ

偷（❸* **媮**） tōu ㄊㄡ ❶窃取，趁人不知道拿人东西据为己有 to steal［小偷］偷东西的人 thief ❷行动瞒着人 ㊇ stealthily：～看 *steal a glance* | ～拍 *take a sneaky photo* | ～～地走了 *sneaked away* | ～懒（趁人不知道少做事）*be lazy when others' backs are turned* ❸苟且 think only of the present：～安 *seek temporary ease* | ～生 *drag out an ignoble existence* ❹抽出（时间）find (time)：～空（kòng）*grab a moment* | ～闲 *snatch some time off*

头（**頭**） tóu ㄊㄡˊ ❶脑袋，人身体的最上部分或动物身体的最前面的部分（㊥－颅）head ㊦头发 hair：剃～ *have a haircut* | 分～ *parted hair* ［头脑］1 脑筋，思想 head; mind：他～清楚。*He has a clear mind.* | 不要被胜利冲昏～。*Don't get dizzy with success.* 2 要领，门路 main gist：这事我摸不着～。*I cannot make head nor tail of this matter.* ❷（－儿）事情的起点或终点 beginning or end：开～儿 *to begin; make a beginning; beginning* | 从～儿说起 *start from the beginning* | 什么时候才是个～儿呀！ *When on earth will it come to an end?* ❸物体的顶端 end; tip (of objects)：山～ *hilltop* | 笔～ *brush tip; nib; (figurative) writing skill* ㊦（－儿）物品的残余部分 end; remnant：烟～儿 *cigarette end* |

T

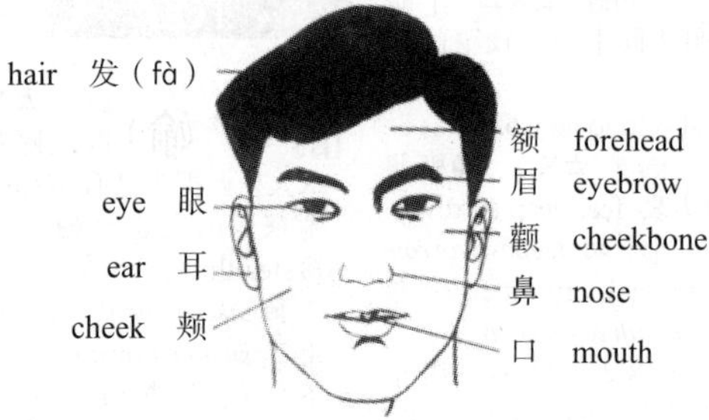

头 head

蜡～儿 *candle end* | 布～儿 *cloth remnant* [头绪] 条理，处理事物的门径 main threads：我找不出～来。*I cannot straighten things out.* ❹以前，在前面的 last; previous：～两年 *last two years* | 我在～里走。*I walked in front.* ❺次序在最前，第一 first：～等 *first-class* |～号 *number one; best* |～班 *first flight/bus/train* ❻ 接近，临 before：～睡觉最好洗洗脚。*It's better to wash one's feet before going to bed.* ❼（一子、一儿）首领（"头子"含贬义）chief; head (头子 is derogatory.)：特务～子 *spy-master* | 选他当～儿 *elect him as the chief* ❽（一儿）方面 side：他们两个是一～儿的。*The two of them are on the same side.* ❾ 量词 measure word ①用于牛驴等牲畜 for domestic animals：一～牛 *a head of cattle* | 两～驴 *two donkeys* ②用于像头的东西 for head-shaped things：两～蒜 *two bulbs of garlic* ❿表示约计、不定数量的词 used to express an indefinite number or quantity：三～五百 *about three hundred to five hundred* | 十～八块 *about eight or ten yuan* ⓫（tou）名词词尾 noun suffix ①放在名词性语素后 used after a noun: 木～ *wood*| 石～ *stone*| 拳～ *fist* ②放在形容词性语素后 used after an adjective: 甜～儿 *sweet taste; benefit*| 苦～儿 *bitter taste, suffering* ③放在动词性语素后 used after a verb：有听～儿 *worth listening* | 没个看～儿 *nothing worth seeing* ⓬（tou）方位词词尾 suffix used after a word of location: 前～ *front*| 上～ *higher place* | 外～ *outside*

投 tóu ㄊㄡˊ ❶抛，掷，扔（多指有目标的）to hurl (often at a target)：～石 *hurl a stone* |～入江中 *throw into the river* 引①跳进去 throw oneself into：～河 *throw oneself into a river (to drown oneself)* |～井 *throw oneself into a well* |～火 *throw oneself into the fire* ②放进去 to drop：～放 *throw in;to invest; to launch (a product)*

[投资] 在生产等事业上投入资金，也指投入的资金 to invest; investment ❷ 投射 to cast：影子～在窗户上。*A shadow fell on the window.* ❸ 走向，进入 to go to：～宿 *stay for the night* | 弃暗～明 *forsake darkness for light; (figurative) break away from evil and embrace justice* | ～入新战斗 *go into a new battle* [投奔] (-bèn) 归向，前去依靠 go to sb seek refuge：～亲友 *go to one's relatives and friends for help/shelter* | ～祖国 *go to one's motherland* ❹ 寄，递送 (㊀-递) to send：～书 *send a letter; the letter one sends* | ～稿 *submit a piece of writing for publication* ❺ 合 to fit ①相合 to fit with：情～意合 *be compatible in heart and mind* ② 迎合 cater to：～其所好 (hào) *cater to sb's tastes* [投机] 1 意见相合 agreeable：他俩一见就很～。*They hit it off the moment they met.* 2 利用时机，谋取私利 to speculate; seek private gain by hook or by crook：～取巧 *be opportunistic* | ～分子 *opportunist* ❻ 临近，在……以前 before：～明(天亮前) *before dawn* | ～暮(天黑前) *towards dusk*

骰 tóu ㄊㄡˊ 骰子，一般叫色 (shǎi) 子，游戏用具或赌具 dice (usually called 色 shǎi 子)

钭(斜) tǒu ㄊㄡˇ dǒu ㄉㄡˇ(又) 姓 (surname) Tou

敨 tǒu ㄊㄡˇ 〈方 dialect〉❶ 把包着或卷着的东西打开 to unfold; to open ❷抖搂 (尘土等) to shake off (dust, etc.)

透 tòu ㄊㄡˋ ❶穿通，通过 to penetrate：钉～了 *nail has gone through* | 这种纸厚，扎不～。*This kind of paper is too thick to pierce through.* | ～光 *transparent* | ～气 *to air; get a breath of fresh air* | ～过现象看本质 *see through appearances to get to the essence* ㊅ ①很通达，极明白 clear：～彻 *thorough* | 理讲～了 *principle has been explained thoroughly* ②泄漏 to reveal：～露 *to reveal; to display* | ～底 *reveal the ins and outs* | ～个信儿 *disclose a piece of information* [透支] 支款超过存款的数目 to overdraw ❷极度 extremely：恨～了 *hate bitterly* ❸显露 to show：他～着很老实。*He looks very honest.* | 这朵花白里～红。*This flower is white touched with red.* ❹达到饱满的、充分的程度 complete; thorough：雨下～了。*This rain is a real good soaker.*

TU ㄊㄨ

凸 tū ㄊㄨ 高出，跟"凹"(āo)相对 protruding (opposite of 凹 āo)：～出 *protrude* | ～透镜 *convex lens*

秃 tū ㄊㄨ ❶没有头发 bald：～顶 *go bald; bald head* ❷(树木)没有枝叶，(山)没有树木 (of trees, mountains) bare：～树 *leafless tree* | 山是～的。*The mountain is bare.* ❸羽毛等脱落，物体失去尖端 (of birds,etc.) featherless; (of pointed objects) blunt：～尾巴

鸡 *bare-tailed chicken* | ～针 *blunt needle* ❹表示不圆满，不周全 unsatisfactory; incomplete：这篇文章写得有点ㄦ～。*The article is a little bit too sketchy.*

突 tū ㄊㄨ ❶忽然 suddenly：～变 *change suddenly; quantum leap* | ～发 *happen suddenly* | ～击 *attack suddenly; rush to finish* [突然] 急速而出乎意外 sudden：～事件 *unexpected event* | 来得很～ *happened suddenly* | ～停止 *suddenly stop* ❷超出，冲破 to break through：～出 *to break through* | ～破纪录 *break a record* | ～围 *break out from encirclement* ❸古时灶旁的出烟口，相当于今天的烟筒 chimney (in ancient times)：灶～ *chimney* | 曲～徙(xǐ)薪（喻防患未然）*bend the chimney and remove the firewood to prevent a possible fire; (figurative) guard against all eventualities*

葖 tū ㄊㄨ see 菁葖(gū－) at 菁 on page 218

瑹 tū ㄊㄨ [瑹玗](－fú) 一种玉 a kind of jade

图(圖) tú ㄊㄨˊ ❶用绘画表现出来的形象 picture：～画 *drawing* | ～解 *to illustrate; to diagram* | 地～ *map* | 蓝～ *blueprint* | 插～ *illustration* ❷画 to draw; to paint：画影～形 *draw sb's picture* ❸计谋，计划 plan：良～ *well-designed plan; great vision* | 宏～ *great plan* ❹谋取，希望得到（㊀－谋）to seek; to plan for：唯利是～ *be intent on nothing but profit*

[图腾]（外 loanword）原始社会的人用动物、植物或其他自然物作为其氏族血统的标志，并把它当作祖先来崇拜，这种被崇拜的对象叫图腾 totem

荼 tú ㄊㄨˊ ❶古书上说的一种苦菜 a kind of bitter edible plant in ancient Chinese texts [荼毒] 毒害 torment：百姓惨遭～。*The people were brutally tormented.* ❷古书上指茅草的白花 white reed flower (in ancient Chinese texts)：如火如～ *like a raging fire; thriving; intense*

途 tú ㄊㄨˊ 道路(㊀－径、道－、路－、－程) road：坦～ *smooth road* | 道听～说 *hearsay* | 半～而废 *give up half way* [前途] ㊁未来的境地，发展的前景 prospect; future

涂(❶－❹塗、❺**凃) tú ㄊㄨˊ ❶使颜色、油漆等附着(zhuó)在物体上 to apply (dye, paint, etc.)：～上一层油 *apply a coat of oil* ❷用笔等抹上或抹去 to cross out; to scribble：～写 *to scribble* | 乱～乱画 *to scribble* | 写错了可以～掉。*Misspellings can be crossed out.* | ～改 *to alter* [涂鸦] 比喻书法拙劣或胡乱写作 to scrawl ❸泥泞 mud [涂炭] 比喻极为困苦的境地 utter misery：生灵～ *the people are plunged into an abyss of misery* ❹ same as "途" ❺姓 (surname) Tu

駼(駼) tú ㄊㄨˊ see 騊駼(táo－) at 騊 on page 642

梌 tú ㄊㄨˊ 用于地名 used in place names：～圩（xū）村（在广东省惠东）*Tuxucun (in Huidong, Guangdong Province)*

稌 tú ㄊㄨˊ 稻子 rice

酴 tú ㄊㄨˊ ❶酒曲 distiller's yeast ❷酴酒，重（chóng）酿的酒 double-fermented wine

徒 tú ㄊㄨˊ ❶步行(不用车、马) travel on foot：～行 *be on foot* ❷空 bare：～手 *bare-handed* 引徒然，白白地 in vain：～劳往返 *hurry back and forth for nothing*｜～劳无益 *work to no avail* ❸只，仅仅 merely：～托空言 *make empty promises*｜不～无益，反而有害 *not just useless but actually harmful* ❹徒弟 disciple; apprentice：学～ *apprentice; work as an apprentice* ❺同一派系或信仰同一宗教的人 religious follower：教～ *religious follower* ❻人（今多指坏人）person (now often refers to a type of bad person)：匪～ *bandit*｜不法之～ *lawbreaker* ❼徒刑，剥夺犯人自由的刑罚，分有期徒刑和无期徒刑两种 imprisonment

菟 tú ㄊㄨˊ ［於菟］（wū－）〈古 ancient〉老虎的别称 tiger (another name for 老虎)

⇨ see also tù on p.664

屠 tú ㄊㄨˊ ❶宰杀牲畜（连－宰）to slaughter (domestic animals)：～狗 *butcher a dog*｜～户 *butcher* ❷残杀人 to massacre (people)：～杀 *massacre*｜～城 *massacre the inhabitants of a conquered city*

腯 tú ㄊㄨˊ 肥（指猪）(of a pig) fat

土 tǔ ㄊㄨˇ ❶地面上的沙、泥等混合物（连－壤）earth; soil：沙～ *sandy soil*｜黏～ *clay*｜～山 *mound* ❷土地 land：国～ *territory*｜领～ *territory* ❸本地的 native; local：～产 *local produce; local*｜～话 *local dialect* ❹指民间生产的，出自民间的 home-made：～布 *hand-woven cloth*｜～专家 *self-taught expert* ❺不开通，不时兴 unrefined：～里～气 *countrified*｜～头～脑 *countrified*

［土家族］［土族］都是我国少数民族，参看附录四 the Tujia people; the Tu people (both ethnic groups in China. See Appendix Ⅳ.)

吐 tǔ ㄊㄨˇ 使东西从嘴里出来 to spit：不要随地～痰。*No spitting.*｜～唾沫 *to spit* 引①说出 to tell：～露（lù）*to reveal*｜坚不～实 *refuse to tell the truth* ②露出，放出 put forth：高粱～穗了。*The sorghum has produced ears.*｜蚕～丝 *silkworms spin silk*

⇨ see also tù on p.663

钍(釷) tǔ ㄊㄨˇ 放射性金属元素，符号 Th，银灰色，质软，可作为核燃料用于核工业中 thorium (Th)

吐 tù ㄊㄨˋ 消化道或呼吸道里的东西从嘴里涌出（连呕－）to throw up; to vomit：上～下泻 *suffer from both vomiting and diarrhoea*｜～血 *spit blood* 喻退还（侵吞的财物）give up (embezzled property)：～出赃款 *return embezzled/stolen money*

⇨ see also tǔ on p.663

兔(*兎、*兔) tù ㄊㄨˋ (一子、一儿) 哺乳动物，耳长，尾短，上唇中间裂开，后腿较长，跑得快 rabbit

堍 tù ㄊㄨˋ 桥两头靠近平地的地方 ramp (of a bridge)：桥～ *bridge ramp*

菟 tù ㄊㄨˋ 植物名 plant name ①菟丝子，寄生的蔓草，茎细长，常缠绕在别的植物上，对农作物有害。籽实可入药 Chinese dodder ②菟葵，草本植物，花淡紫红色，多生长在山地树丛里 hellebore

⇨ see also tú on p.663

TUAN ㄊㄨㄢ

猯 tuān ㄊㄨㄢ 用于地名 used in place names：～卧梁（在陕西省米脂）*Tuanwoliang (in Mizhi, Shaanxi Province)*

湍 tuān ㄊㄨㄢ 水流得很急，也指急流的水 fast-flowing; rapids

煓 tuān ㄊㄨㄢ 火势旺盛的样子 flaming

团(團、❸糰) tuán ㄊㄨㄢˊ ❶圆形 ㊢ round：～扇 *moon-shaped fan* | 雌蟹是～脐的。*Female crabs have round abdomens.* ❷(一子、一儿) 圆形或球形的东西 objects shaped like a ball：纸～ *paper crumpled up into a ball* | 云～ *cloud cluster* | 蒲～ *cattail hassock* ❸指球形的食品 foodstuff shaped like a ball：饭～儿 *rice ball* | 菜～子 *vegetable ball* ㉑量词，用于成团的东西或抽象的事物 measure word for things in a ball or sth abstract：一～线 *a ball of thread* | 两～废纸 *two balls of waste paper* | 一～和气 *(originally) genial; keep on the right side of everyone (often at the expense of principle)* | 一～糟 *a complete mess* ❹把东西揉弄成球形 roll sth into a ball：～泥球 *make mud balls* | ～饭团子 *make rice balls* ❺会合在一起 to assemble：～聚 *have a reunion; to unite and gather* | ～圆 *have a reunion* [团结] 为了实现共同理想或完成共同任务而联合或结合 to unite：～起来，争取胜利！ *Unite and seize victory!* ❻工作或活动的集体组织 group：文工～ *song and dance ensemble* | 代表～ *delegation* | ～体 *organization* ❼在我国特指共产主义青年团 (specifically) Communist Youth League of China ❽军队的编制单位，是营的上一级 regiment

抟(摶) tuán ㄊㄨㄢˊ same as "团❹"

疃 tuǎn ㄊㄨㄢˇ ❶禽兽践踏的地方 ground trampled by animals ❷村庄，屯。多用于地名 (often used in place names) village

彖 tuàn ㄊㄨㄢˋ 论断，推断 to infer：～凶吉 *judge whether the omens are poor or auspicious* [彖辞]《易经》中总括一卦含义的言辞 commentary on the meaning of trigram combinations in the *Book of Changes*

TUI ㄊㄨㄟ

忒 tuī ㄊㄨㄟ 〈方 dialect〉副词，太 (adverb) too：风～大 *wind is too strong* | 路～滑 *road is too slippery*

⇨ see also tè on p.644

推 tuī ㄊㄨㄟ ❶用力使物体顺着用力的方向移动 to push：～车 *push a cart* | ～了他一把 *gave him a push* | ～磨 *turn a millstone* ㊀使工具向前移动进行工作 to pare：用刨子～光 *smooth it out with a plane* | ～头（理发）*cut sb's hair (with clippers); have a haircut* [推敲] ㊟斟酌文章字句 to deliberate：仔细～ *deliberate carefully* | 一字费～ *consider every word carefully* ❷使事情开展 push forward：～广 *to popularize* | ～销 *promote sales* | ～动 *to push forward* ❸进一步想，由已知推断其余 to infer：～求 *to inquire* | ～测 *to infer* | ～理 *to reason* | ～算 *to reckon* | 类～ *reason by analogy* ❹辞让，推卸 to decline; to shirk ①辞退，让给 to decline：～辞 *to decline* | ～让 *decline out of modesty* ②推卸责任，托辞 refuse on a certain pretext：～诿 *pass the buck* | ～三阻四 *decline with all sorts of excuses* | ～病不来 *plead illness and not come* ❺往后挪动（时间）to postpone：再往后～几天 *postpone for a few more days* ❻举荐，选举 to elect：公～一个人做代表 *elect one representative by public vote* ❼指出某人某物的优点 to praise highly：～许（称赞）*to commend* | ～重（重视、钦佩）*have a high regard for* | ～崇 *praise highly*

隤（隤） tuí ㄊㄨㄟˊ ❶same as "颓" ❷[虺隤]（huī－）same as "虺隤"

尵（尵） tuí ㄊㄨㄟˊ see 虺尵 (huī－) at 虺 on page 272

颓（頹、*穨） tuí ㄊㄨㄟˊ ❶崩坏，倒塌 to collapse：～垣断壁 *crumbling walls and ruined buildings* [颓废] 1 建筑物倒坏 collapsed 2 精神萎靡不振 in low spirit ❷败坏 decadent：～风败俗 *degenerate practice and depraved customs* [颓唐] 精神不振，情绪低落 dejected

魋 tuí ㄊㄨㄟˊ ❶古书上说的一种兽，像小熊 a kind of bear-like beast in ancient Chinese texts ❷姓 (surname) Tui

腿（❶*骽） tuǐ ㄊㄨㄟˇ ❶人和动物用来支持身体和行走的部分 leg：大～ *thigh* | 后～ *hind leg* (see picture of 人体 on page 647) [火腿] 用盐腌制的猪腿 ham ❷（－儿）器物下部像腿的部分 leg-shaped support：桌子～儿 *table leg* | 凳子～儿 *chair leg*

退 tuì ㄊㄨㄟˋ ❶向后移动，跟"进"相对 move backwards (opposite of 进)：败～ *retreat in defeat* | 敌人已经～了。*The enemy has retreated.* [退步] 1 逐渐向下，落后 fall behind：学习不

T

努力，成绩怎能不～？ *If you do not study hard, how can you expect not to fall behind in your grades?* 2 后退的余地 leeway：话没有说死，留了～。*What one said was not final, with some leeway left.* ❷使向后移动 cause to move back：～兵 *force the enemy to retreat* | ～敌 *drive the enemy back* ❸离开，辞去 withdraw from：～席 *leave a banquet or meeting* | ～职 *leave office* ❹送还，不接受，撤销 to return; to cancel：～货 *return goods* | ～票 *cancel a ticket* | ～钱 *to refund* | ～婚 *break off an engagement* ❺减退，下降 to recede：～色 *to fade* | ～烧 *sooth a fever*

煺（**燵、**攙） tuì ㄊㄨㄟˋ 已宰杀的猪、鸡等用滚水烫后去掉毛 remove the hair or feathers from a slaughtered animal

褪 tuì ㄊㄨㄟˋ 脱落，脱去 shed hairs：兔子正～毛。*The rabbit is shedding its hairs.* [褪色] 退色，颜色变淡或消失 to fade

⇨ see also tùn on p.667

蜕 tuì ㄊㄨㄟˋ ❶蛇、蝉等脱下来的皮 slough (of snakes, cicadas, etc.) ❷蛇、蝉等动物脱皮 (of snakes, cicadas, etc.) to slough [蜕化] ㊕变质，腐化堕落 to degenerate

TUN ㄊㄨㄣ

吞 tūn ㄊㄨㄣ 不经咀嚼，整个咽到肚子里 to swallow：囫囵～枣 *swallow a date without chewing; (figurative) read without understanding* | 狼～虎咽 *eat voraciously* ㊆①忍受不发作出来 suffer in silence：忍气～声（不敢作声）*swallow one's pride* ②兼并，侵占 to seize; to annex：～没 *to embezzle; to engulf* | ～并 *to seize; to annex*

焞 tūn ㄊㄨㄣ 光明 bright

暾 tūn ㄊㄨㄣ 刚出来的太阳 newly-risen sun：朝～ *early morning sun*

屯 tún ㄊㄨㄣˊ ❶聚集，储存 store up：～粮 *store up grain* ㊆（军队）驻扎 to station (troops)：～兵 *to station (troops)* ❷（一子、一儿）村庄，多用于地名 (often used in place names) village：皇姑～（在辽宁省沈阳）*Huanggutun (a place in Shenyang, Liaoning Province)*

⇨ see also zhūn on p.876

坉 tún ㄊㄨㄣˊ 寨子，多用于地名 (often used in place names) village：大～（在广东省吴川）*Datun (a place in Wuchuan, Guangdong Province)*

囤 tún ㄊㄨㄣˊ 囤积，积存，存储货物、粮食 store up (goods, food)：～货 *store up goods*

⇨ see also dùn on p.153

饨（**飩**） tún ㄊㄨㄣˊ see 馄饨 (húntun) at 馄 on page 277

忳 tún ㄊㄨㄣˊ 忧伤，烦闷 distressed

鲀（**魨**） tún ㄊㄨㄣˊ 河豚，鱼名，头圆形，口小，生活在海里，有些也进入淡水。

种类很多。肉味鲜美，但血液和内脏有剧毒 pufferfish

豚 tún ㄊㄨㄣˊ 小猪，也泛指猪 suckling pig; (generally) pig

臀（*臋）tún ㄊㄨㄣˊ 屁股 buttocks：～部 *buttocks* (see picture of 人体 on page 647)

氽 tǔn ㄊㄨㄣˇ 〈方 dialect〉❶漂浮 to float：木头在水上～ *wood floats on water* ❷用油炸 to deep-fry：油～花生米 *deep-fried peanuts*

褪 tùn ㄊㄨㄣˋ 使穿着、套着的东西脱离 slip out of sth：把袖子～下来 *slip one's arms out of one's sleeves* | 狗～了套跑了。*The dog slipped the lead and ran away.* ㊀向内移动而藏起来 to hide：把手～在袖子里 *hide one's hands in one's sleeves* | 袖子里～着一封信。*There is a letter hidden in one of the sleeves.*

⇨ see also tuì on p.666

TUO ㄊㄨㄛ

乇 tuō ㄊㄨㄛ 用于地名 used in place names：黎～（在湖南省长沙）*Lituo (in Changsha, Hunan Province)*

托（❹–❻*託）tuō ㄊㄨㄛ ❶用手掌向上承受着东西 hold (sth) in the palm：～着枪 *holding the gun in one's hand* ❷衬，垫 set off：烘云～月 *paint clouds to set off the moon* ❸（～儿）承托器物的东西 something serving as a support：茶～儿 *saucer* | 花～儿 *flower receptacle* ❹（～儿）帮行骗者诱人上当的人 shill：当～儿 *serve as a shill* | 医～儿 *quack doctor's shill* ❺寄，暂放 to entrust：～儿所 *nursery* ❻请别人代办(㊟委～) to entrust; ask sb to do sth：～你买本书 *ask you to buy a book* ❼推托，借故推诿或躲闪 give as a pretext：～病 *plead illness* | ～故 *find an excuse* ❽（外 loanword）压强的非法定计量单位，1托合133.322帕 Torr

饦（飥）tuō ㄊㄨㄛ see 馎饦 (bó–) at 馎 on page 50

侂 tuō ㄊㄨㄛ 委托，寄托 to entrust

拖（*拕）tuō ㄊㄨㄛ ❶牵引，拉，拽 to drag; to pull：～车 *trailer* | ～泥带水（形容做事不爽利）*sloppy* | ～拉机 *tractor* ❷拖延，拉长时间 to delay：～沓 *sluggish* | ～腔 *draw out a word (when singing) ; a word that has been drawn out (when singing)* | 这件事应赶快结束，不能再～。*This matter should be settled as soon as possible and cannot be put off any longer.*

脱 tuō ㄊㄨㄛ ❶离开，落掉 come off：～节 *come apart* | ～逃 *run away* | 走～ *to escape* | ～皮 *shed skin* ㊁遗漏（文字）leave out (words)：～误 *omissions and errors* | 这中间～去了几个字。*There are several characters missing in the middle.* ❷取下，去掉 take off：～衣裳 *take off one's*

clothes | ～帽 *take off one's hat*

驮(馱、*䭾) tuó ㄊㄨㄛˊ 用背（多指牲口）负载人或物 to carry (on the back of a farm animal)：那匹马～着两袋粮食。*The horse is carrying two bags of grain on its back.*

⇨ see also duò on p.156

佗 tuó ㄊㄨㄛˊ 负荷 to load [华佗] 东汉末名医 Hua Tuo (famous doctor at the end of the Eastern Han Dynasty)

陀 tuó ㄊㄨㄛˊ 山冈 hill [陀螺]（-luó）1 一种儿童玩具，呈圆锥形，用绳绕上后抽拉或用鞭子抽打，可以在地上旋转 spinning top 2 陀螺仪的简称，测量运动物体角速度和角位移的装置。用于飞机、舰船等的控制 (short for 陀螺仪) gyroscope

坨 tuó ㄊㄨㄛˊ ❶（-子、-儿）成块或成堆的东西 lump：泥～子 *lump of mud* ❷面食煮熟后黏结在一起 (of cooked food) stick together：饺子～了。*The dumplings have stuck together.* ❸露天盐堆 pile of salt in the open

沱 tuó ㄊㄨㄛˊ ❶〈方 dialect〉可以停放船的水湾。多用于地名 (often used in place names) small bay in a river ❷沱江，长江的支流，在四川省东部 Tuojiang River (in the east of Sichuan Province)

驼(駝、*駞) tuó ㄊㄨㄛˊ ❶骆驼 camel：～绒 *camel hair* | ～峰 *camel hump* ❷身体向前曲，背脊突起 be hunchbacked：～背 *be hunchbacked* | 背都～了 *one's back has become bent*

柁 tuó ㄊㄨㄛˊ 房柁，屋架前后两个柱子之间的大横梁 beam

⇨ see also duò on p.156

砣 tuó ㄊㄨㄛˊ ❶秤锤 steelyard weight ❷碾砣，碾子上的碾子 stone roller

铊(鉈) tuó ㄊㄨㄛˊ same as "砣❶"

⇨ see also tā on p.631

鸵(鴕) tuó ㄊㄨㄛˊ 鸵鸟，鸟名，现代鸟类中最大的鸟，颈长，翅膀小，不能飞，腿长，走得很快，生活在沙漠中 ostrich

酡 tuó ㄊㄨㄛˊ 喝了酒，脸色发红 flushed with drinking：～颜 *face flushed from drinking*

跎 tuó ㄊㄨㄛˊ see 蹉跎 (cuō-) at 蹉 on page 104

鮀(鮀) tuó ㄊㄨㄛˊ 生活在淡水中的小型鱼类。也用于地名 small fish (also used in place names)：～莲（在广东省汕头）*Tuolian (a place in Shantou, Guangdong Province)*

鼧 tuó ㄊㄨㄛˊ [鼧鼥]（-bá）哺乳动物，即旱獭，俗叫土拨鼠，耳短，毛灰黄色，爪善掘土 marmot (same as 旱獭, informal 土拨鼠)

橐(**槖) tuó ㄊㄨㄛˊ 一种口袋 a kind of bag

鼍(鼉) tuó ㄊㄨㄛˊ 鼍龙，一种鳄，即扬子鳄，俗叫猪婆龙，是我国特有的动物 Chinese alligator (same as 扬子鳄,

informal 猪婆龙)

妥 tuǒ ㄊㄨㄛˇ ❶适当，合适（㊇—当）appropriate：已经商量～了。*An agreement has been made through discussion.* | ～为保存 *take good care of* | 这样做不～。*Acting like this is not appropriate.* [妥协] 在发生争执或斗争时，一方让步或双方让步 to compromise：在原则性问题上决不能～。*On questions of principle there can never be any compromise.* ❷齐备，完毕 ready：事已办～。*The matter has been settled.*

庹 tuǒ ㄊㄨㄛˇ 成人两臂左右伸直的长度（约 5 尺）arm spread (about 5 尺 , around 1.67 m)

椭（橢） tuǒ ㄊㄨㄛˇ 椭圆，长圆形，把一个圆柱体或正圆锥体斜着用一个平面截开，所成的截口就是椭圆形 oval

拓 tuò ㄊㄨㄛˋ ❶开辟，扩充 open up ❷姓 (surname) Tuo ❸ see 落拓 (luò—) at 落 on page 429

⇨ see also tà on p.632

柝（欜）** tuò ㄊㄨㄛˋ 〈古 ancient〉打更用的梆子 watchman's clapper

跅 tuò ㄊㄨㄛˋ [跅弛]（—chí）放荡 dissolute

萚（蘀） tuò ㄊㄨㄛˋ 草木脱落的皮或叶 fallen bark; fallen leaves

箨（籜） tuò ㄊㄨㄛˋ 竹笋上一片一片的皮 sheaths (of a bamboo shoot)

唾 tuò ㄊㄨㄛˋ ❶唾液，通称唾沫，口腔里分泌的液体，有湿润口腔、帮助消化等作用 saliva (usually known as 唾沫) ❷啐（cuì），从嘴里吐（tǔ）出来 to spit：～手可得（形容极容易得到）*can be obtained with ease* | ～弃（轻视、鄙弃）*to loathe*

W ㄨ

WA ㄨㄚ

坬 wā ㄨㄚ 用于地名 used in place names：朱家～（在陕西省佳县）*Zhujiawa (in Jiaxian, Shaanxi Province)*｜王～子（在陕西省吴起）*Wangwazi (in Wuqi, Shaanxi Province)*

呱 wā ㄨㄚ 用于地名 used in place names：～底（在山西省闻喜）*Wadi (in Wenxi, Shanxi Province)*

窊 wā ㄨㄚ 同“洼”，用于地名 same as 洼，used in place names：薛家～（在山西省宁武）*Xuejiawa (in Ningwu, Shanxi Province)*

挖（**穵）wā ㄨㄚ 掘，掏 to dig; to excavate：～个坑 *dig a hole*｜～战壕 *dig a trench*｜～潜力 *tap potential*

［挖苦］（-ku）用尖刻的话讥笑人 to deride; to speak sarcastically：你别～人。*Don't you start digging at others.*

哇 wā ㄨㄚ 形容哭叫声、呕吐声等 sound of crying or vomiting：哭得～～的 *wail loudly*｜～的一声吐了一地 *vomited all over the ground with a retching noise*

⇨ see also wa on p.671

洼（窪）wā ㄨㄚ ❶（-儿）凹陷的地方 low-lying area; hollow：水～儿 *puddle*｜山～儿 *mountain valley* ❷低凹，深陷 low-lying; sunken：～地 *low-lying land*｜这地太～。*This piece of land is too low-lying.*｜眼眶～进去 *eyes are sunken*

蛙（*鼃）wā ㄨㄚ 两栖动物，卵孵化后为蝌蚪，逐渐变化成蛙。种类很多，青蛙是常见的一种，捕食害虫，对农作物有益 frog

娲（媧）wā ㄨㄚ ［女娲］神话中的女神，传说她曾经炼五色石补天 Nüwa (goddess in Chinese mythology credited with smelting coloured stones and repairing the sky)

娃 wá ㄨㄚˊ ❶（-子、-儿）小孩子 child; baby：女～儿 *baby girl*｜胖～～ *chubby baby* ❷旧称美女 (old) pretty girl：娇～ *cute young girl* ❸〈方 dialect〉某些幼小的动物 some newborn animals：猪～ *piglet*｜鸡～ *chick*

瓦 wǎ ㄨㄚˇ ❶用陶土烧成的 earthen：～盆 *earthen basin*｜～器 *earthenware* ❷用陶土烧成的覆盖房顶的东西 tile：～房 *tile-roofed house*［瓦解］㊀溃散 disintegrate; collapse：土崩～ *crumble like plow-cloven clods or broken tiles* ❸（外 loanword）功率单位名瓦特的简称，符号 W。watt (W)

⇨ see also wà on p.671

佤 wǎ ㄨㄚˇ [佤族] 我国少数民族，参看附录四 the Va people (one of the ethnic groups in China. See Appendix Ⅳ.)

瓦 wà ㄨㄚˋ 盖（瓦）to tile (a roof)：～瓦（wǎ）*put tiles on a roof* [瓦刀] 瓦工用来砍断砖瓦并涂抹泥灰的工具 tile cleaver

⇨ see also wǎ on p.670

袜（襪、*韈、*韤）wà ㄨㄚˋ （-子）穿在脚上、不直接着（zháo）地的东西，一般用布、纱线等制成 socks

腽 wà ㄨㄚˋ [腽肭兽]（-nà-）哺乳动物，即海狗。生活在海洋里。阴茎和睾丸叫腽肭脐，可入药 fur seal; ursine seal (same as 海狗)

哇 wa ·ㄨㄚ 助词（前面紧挨着的音一定是 u、ao、ou 等结尾的）auxiliary word following vowels such as u, ao, ou, etc.：你别哭～。*Don't you cry.* | 多好～！*How marvellous!* | 快走～！*Hurry up!*

⇨ see also wā on p.670

WAI ㄨㄞ

歪 wāi ㄨㄞ ❶不正，偏斜 askew; slanting：～着头 *with one's head tilted* | 这张画挂～了。*The picture is hung askew.* [歪曲] 故意颠倒是非 to distort; to misrepresent：～事实 *distort the facts* ❷不正当的，不正派的 devious; crooked：～门邪道 *crooked ways* | ～风 *unhealthy trend*

崴（❷**踒）wǎi ㄨㄞˇ ❶〈方 dialect〉（-子）山、水弯曲处。多用于地名 bend in a river or mountain range (often used in place names)：三道～子（在吉林省靖宇）*Sandaowaizi (a place in Jingyu, Jilin Province)* ❷（脚）扭伤 to sprain (ankle) ❸山路不平 (of mountain paths) rugged

⇨ see also wēi on p.677

外 wài ㄨㄞˋ ❶外面，外部，跟"内""里"相对 outside; outer (opposite of 内 or 里)：国～ *abroad* | ～伤 *wound* [外行]（-háng）对某种业务或事情不懂，缺乏经验 layman; non-professional ❷不是自己这方面的 other：～国 *foreign country* | ～乡 *other parts of the country* | ～人 *outsider* ❸指外国 foreign：对～贸易 *foreign trade* | 古今中～ *past and present, in China and abroad* | ～宾 *foreign guest* ❹关系疏远的 not closely related：这里没～人。*There are no outsiders here.* | 见～ *stand on formality* ❺称母亲、姐妹或女儿方面的亲戚 (of relatives) on the side of one's mother, sister, or daughter：～祖母 *maternal grandmother* | ～甥 *nephew (one's sister's son)* | ～孙 *grandson (one's daughter's son)* ❻（除此）另外，以外 additional; extra：～加 *plus* | 此～ *in addition* ❼非正式的 informal; unofficial：～号 *nickname* | ～史 *unofficial history* ❽旧时戏曲角色名，多演老年男

子 role of an old man in traditional Chinese opera

WAN ㄨㄢ

弯(彎) wān ㄨㄢ ❶屈曲不直(㊀一曲) curved; bent: ～路 *winding road* ❷使弯曲 to bend: ～腰 *bend down* ❸(一子、一儿)曲折的部分 turn; curve: 转～抹角 *beat about the bush* | 这根竹竿有个～儿。*There is a curve in this bamboo pole.* ❹拉(弓) to draw (a bow): ～弓 *draw a bow*

塆(壪) wān ㄨㄢ 山沟里的小块平地。多用于地名 a plot of flat land in a gully (often used in place names)

湾(灣) wān ㄨㄢ ❶水流弯曲的地方 bend in a river: 汾河～ *Fenhe river bend* ❷海湾，海洋伸入陆地的部分 gulf; bay: 胶州～ *Jiaozhou Bay*| 港～ *harbour* ❸使船停住 to moor: 把船～在那边。*Moor the boat over there.*

剜 wān ㄨㄢ 用刀挖，挖去 to cut out; to scoop out: ～肉补疮(喻只顾眼前，不惜用有害的方法来救急) *cut out a piece of flesh to cure a boil; (figurative) resort to a remedy worse than the ailment*

帵 wān ㄨㄢ 〈方 dialect〉(一子)裁衣服剩下的大片布料 leftover cloth (after a garment is cut out)

蜿 wān ㄨㄢ [蜿蜒](一yán) 蛇爬行的样子 (of snakes etc.) wriggling ㊀弯弯曲曲 winding; meandering: 一条～的小路 *a winding path*

豌 wān ㄨㄢ [豌豆] 草本植物，花白色或紫色，种子和嫩茎、叶都可用作蔬菜 pea

婠 wān ㄨㄢ 美丽，美好 beautiful

丸 wán ㄨㄢˊ ❶(一子、一儿)小而圆的东西 ball; pellet: 弹～ *pellet* | 药～儿*pill* | 肉～子 *meatball* ❷专指丸药 pill of Chinese medicine: ～散膏丹 *pill, powder, ointment, and pellet (the four forms of Chinese medicine)* ❸量词，用于丸药 (measure word for Chinese medicine) pill

芄 wán ㄨㄢˊ 芄兰，多年生蔓(màn)草，叶对生，心脏形，花白色，有紫红色斑点。茎、叶和种子可入药 butterfly weed

汍 wán ㄨㄢˊ [汍澜](一lán) 流泪的样子 tearful

纨(紈) wán ㄨㄢˊ 白色的细绢 fine white silk [纨绔](一kù)古代贵族子弟的华美衣着(zhuó) fine clothing worn by rich men's sons in ancient times: ～子弟(指专讲吃喝玩乐的富家子弟) *profligate sons of the rich; playboy*

完 wán ㄨㄢˊ ❶齐全(㊀一整) intact; whole: ～美*perfect* | ～善 *perfect* ❷尽，没有了 to finish; to use up: 用～了 *all used up* | 卖～了 *sold out* | 事情做～了 *job done* ❸做成，了结 to complete: ～成任务 *accomplish a mission* | ～工 *work completed* | ～婚 *get married*

❹交纳 to pay：～粮 *pay farm tax by delivering grain* | ～税 *pay taxes*

玩(❸-❺*翫) wán ㄨㄢˊ ❶（一儿）游戏，做某种游戏（㊟一耍）to play; to have fun：出去～ *go out and have fun* | ～皮球 *play with a ball* [玩弄] 1 摆弄着玩 to play with：上课不要～手机。*Do not play with mobile phones in class.* 2 耍弄，搬弄 to play with; to resort to (tricks, etc.)：～手段 *play tricks* | ～辞藻 *play with words* 3 戏弄 to play around with; to flirt with：～女性 *play around with women* [玩意儿] 1 玩具 toy; plaything 2〈方 dialect〉指杂技、曲艺，如魔术、大鼓等 performances such as acrobatics, cross talks, ballad singing, magic, etc. 3 指东西、事物 thing ❷（一儿）耍弄，使用 to play (tricks etc.); to use：～花招儿 *play tricks* ❸观赏 to appreciate; to enjoy：游～ *go sightseeing* | ～物丧志 *sap one's spirit by seeking pleasures* ❹可供观赏、把玩的东西 object for appreciation：古～ *curio; antique* ❺轻视，用不严肃的态度来对待（㊟一忽）to treat lightly; to make fun of：～世不恭 *be cynical* | ～视（忽视）*overlook; ignore*（❸❹❺ formerly pronounced wàn）

顽(頑) wán ㄨㄢˊ ❶愚蠢无知 stupid; thick-headed：～钝 *dull and obtuse* | 愚～ *ignorant and stubborn* ❷固执，不容易变化 stubborn; obstinate：～梗 *very obstinate* | ～疾 *chronic disease* [顽固] 1 思想保守，不愿意接受新鲜事物 stubbornly conservative; diehard 2 坚持自己的错误观点或做法，不加改变 obstinate; stubborn [顽强] 坚强，不屈服 indomitable; tenacious：～地工作着 *work tenaciously* | 他很～，没有被困难吓倒。*He is tenacious, and undaunted by difficulties.* ❸顽皮，小孩淘气 mischievous; naughty：～童 *naughty child* ❹ same as "玩❶❷"

烷 wán ㄨㄢˊ 烷烃（tīng），有机化合物的一类，分子中只含有单键结构。烷系化合物是构成石油的主要成分 alkane

宛 wǎn ㄨㄢˇ ❶曲折 winding; tortuous [宛转] 1 辗转 to toss about; to turn back and forth 2 same as "婉转" ❷宛然，仿佛 seemingly; as if：音容～在 *(of the deceased) as if their voice and face were still there*

菀 wǎn ㄨㄢˇ 紫菀，草本植物，叶子椭圆状披针形，花蓝紫色。根和根状茎可入药 tatarinow's aster

⇨ see also yù on p.803

惋 wǎn ㄨㄢˇ 叹惜 to sigh：～惜 *feel sorry for; regret*

婉 wǎn ㄨㄢˇ ❶和顺，温和 mild; gentle：～言 *tactful words* | 委～ *euphemistic* [婉转] [宛转] 说话温和而曲折，但不失本意 mild and indirect; tactful：措辞～ *put it tactfully* ❷美好 beautiful; graceful

琬 wǎn ㄨㄢˇ 美玉 fine jade [琬圭] 上端浑圆、没有棱角的圭 round-topped jade tablet

W

椀 wǎn ㄨㄢˇ ❶用于科技术语 used in scientific and technical terminology：橡～（橡树果实的碗状外壳）*acorn shell* ❷ see also 碗 on page 674

碗（*盌、△*椀、瓮）wǎn ㄨㄢˇ 盛饮食的器皿 bowl

畹 wǎn ㄨㄢˇ 古代地积单位，三十亩（一说十二亩）为一畹 (ancient) land measurement unit, 1 畹 equals 30 (or 12) 亩

［畹町］（－dīng）地名，在云南省瑞丽 Wanding (a place in Ruili, Yunnan Province)

挽（❸*輓）wǎn ㄨㄢˇ ❶拉 to draw; to hold (arm or hand)：～弓 *draw a bow*｜手～着手 *hand in hand* ❷设法使局势好转或恢复原状 to reverse; to retrieve：～救 *rescue*｜力～狂澜 *save a desperate situation* ❸追悼死人 to lament (a death)：～歌 *elegy*｜～联 *elegiac couplet* ❹卷 to roll up：～起袖子 *roll up one's sleeves*

晚 wǎn ㄨㄢˇ ❶太阳落了的时候 evening; night：从早到～ *from dawn to dusk*｜～饭 *supper*｜～会 *evening party* ㊀夜间 night：昨～没睡好 *did not sleep well last night* ❷时间靠后的，比合适的时间居后 late; later：～年（老年）*old age*｜～秋 *late in autumn*｜来～了 *came late*｜赶快努力还不～。*It's not too late to make an effort.* ❸后来的 junior; younger：～辈 *younger generation* ❹晚辈对长辈的自称（多用于书信）your humble junior (often in letters)

莞 wǎn ㄨㄢˇ ［莞尔］微笑的样子 smiling：～而笑 *give a soft smile*

⇨ see also guǎn on p.226

脘 wǎn ㄨㄢˇ 胃脘，中医指胃的内部 (in traditional Chinese medicine) gastral cavity

皖 wǎn ㄨㄢˇ 安徽省的别称 (another name for Anhui Province) Wan

绾（綰）wǎn ㄨㄢˇ 把长条形的东西盘绕起来打成结 to coil up; to tie up：～结 *tie a knot*｜～个扣儿 *tie a knot*｜把头发～起来 *coil up one's hair*

万（萬）wàn ㄨㄢˋ ❶数目，十个一千 ten thousand ㊀表示极多 a very great number; all：～物 *all nature*｜气象～千 *majestic in all its variety*｜～能胶 *all-purpose glue* ［万岁］千秋万代永远存在（祝颂语）long live：人民～！*Long live the people!*｜祖国～！*Long live our motherland!* ［万一］㊁意外，意外地 just in case：以防～ *be prepared for the unexpected*｜～下雨也不要紧，我带着伞呢。*Even if it does happen to rain, it's no problem: I have brought an umbrella.* ❷极，很，绝对 extremely; absolutely：～难 *extremely difficult*｜～全 *foolproof*｜～不得已 *have no alternative* ❸姓 (surname) Wan

⇨ see also mò on p.460

沥（澫）wàn ㄨㄢˋ 用于地名 used in place names：～尾（在广西壮族自治区东兴）

Wanwei (in Dongxing, Guangxi Zhuang Autonomous Region)

婠 wàn ㄨㄢˋ 形容女子美好 (of women) attractive; beautiful

⇨ see also yuán on p.806

腕 wàn ㄨㄢˋ （～子）胳膊下端跟手掌，或小腿跟脚相连的部分 wrist (see picture of 人体 on page 647)

蔓 wàn ㄨㄢˋ （～儿）细长能缠绕的茎 tendrilled vine：瓜～儿 *melon vine*

⇨ see also mán on p.435, màn on p.436

WANG ㄨㄤ

尢 wāng ㄨㄤ same as "尪"

⇨ see also yóu on p.791

尪（**尫） wāng ㄨㄤ ❶胫、脊或胸部弯曲的病 bent calves, back or chest ❷瘦弱 thin and weak; frail

汪 wāng ㄨㄤ ❶深广 (of a body of water) deep and vast：～洋大海 *boundless ocean* ❷液体聚集在一个地方 (of liquid) to accumulate：地上～着水 *with a puddle on the ground* [汪汪] 1 充满水或眼泪的样子 tearful; watery：水～ *watery* | 泪～ *tearful* 2 形容狗叫声 woof ❸量词，用于液体 (measure word for water body) pool：一～水 *a pool of water*

亡（*亾） wáng ㄨㄤˊ ❶逃（㊀逃－）to flee; to escape：～命 *to flee* | 流～ *go into exile* ㊁失去 to lose; to be missing：～羊补牢（喻事后补救）*remedy a situation after the fact* | 唇～齿寒（喻利害相关）*if the lips are gone, the teeth will feel the cold; (figurative) share a common lot* ❷死（㊀死－）to die：伤～ *casualties* ㊁死去的 dead：～弟 *deceased younger brother* ❸灭（㊀灭－）to perish; to fall：～国 *subjugate a nation* | 兴～ *rise and fall*

⇨ see also wú on p.690

王 wáng ㄨㄤˊ ❶古代指帝王或最高的爵位 (ancient) king; monarch ❷一族或一类中的首领 chief; leader：兽～ *king of beasts* | 蜂～ *queen bee* | 花中之～ *king of flowers* ❸大，辈分高 grand; great：～父（祖父）*grandfather* | ～母（祖母）*grandmother* ❹姓 (surname) Wang

⇨ see also wàng on p.676

网（網） wǎng ㄨㄤˇ ❶用绳线等结成的捕鱼捉鸟的器具 net：渔～ *fishing net* [网罗] 搜求，设法招致 to gather; to enlist：～人才 *enlist able men* ❷用网捕捉 to catch with a net：～鱼 *net fish* | ～鸟 *net birds* ❸像网的东西 sth like a net：～兜儿 *string bag* | 铁丝～ *wire netting* ❹像网样的组织或系统 network：通信～ *communication network* | 宣传～ *publicity network* 特指互联网 internet：～页 *web page* | ～站 *website* | 上～ *go on the internet*

罔（*図） wǎng ㄨㄤˇ ❶蒙蔽，诬 to deceive; to libel：欺～ *cheat* ❷无，没有 no; not：置若～闻（放在一边不管，好像没听见一样）*turn a deaf ear*

W

惘 wǎng ㄨㄤˇ 不得意(㊀怅一) frustrated; disappointed: ～然 *disappointed*

辋(輞) wǎng ㄨㄤˇ 车轮外周的框子 rim (of a wheel) (see picture of 旧式车轮 on page 426)

魍 wǎng ㄨㄤˇ [魍魉](－liǎng)传说山林中的一种怪物 monster found in mountains and forests in Chinese legend

枉 wǎng ㄨㄤˇ ❶曲，不直 bent; crooked: 矫～过正 *overcorrect* ❷使歪曲 to distort: ～法 *pervert the law* ❸受屈，冤屈(㊀冤一、屈一) to be treated unjustly; to be wronged ❹徒然，白白地 in vain; to no avail: ～然 *in vain* | ～费心机 *rack one's brains in vain*

往(*徃) wǎng ㄨㄤˇ ❶去，到 to go; to head for: 来～ *come and go* | ～返 *make a return trip* | 一个～东，一个～西 *one goes east, and the other goes west* ❷过去(㊀一昔) past; previous: ～年 *former years* | ～事 *past events* ❸介词，朝，向 (preposition) toward; in the direction of: ～东走 *head east* | ～前看 *look forward* | 此车开～上海。*This train is bound for Shanghai.*

[往往] 副词，常常 (adverb) often; usually: 这些小事情～被人忽略。*These trifles tend to get neglected.*

王 wàng ㄨㄤˋ ❶统一天下 to rule over the world: 以德行仁者～。*He who practices benevolence by means of virtue shall rule the world.* ❷统治 to rule: ～此大邦 *govern this big state*

⇨ see also wáng on p.675

旺 wàng ㄨㄤˋ 盛，兴盛(㊀一盛、兴一) prosperous; flourishing: 火很～ *fire burns robustly* | ～季 *peak period*

望(*朢) wàng ㄨㄤˋ ❶看，往远处看 to look into the distance: 登高远～ *climb high and look into the distance* | ～尘莫及 *too far behind to catch up* ❷探访问候(㊀看一) to call on; to visit: 拜～ *call on* ❸希图，盼(㊀盼一、希一) to expect; to hope: ～子成龙 *long to see one's son to succeed in life* | 喜出～外 *be overjoyed (at unexpected good news, etc.)* | 丰收有～。*A bumper harvest is in sight.* ❹怨恨，责怪 to resent; to hate ❺名望，声誉 reputation; prestige: 德高～重 *be of noble character and high prestige* | 威～ *prestige* ❻农历每月十五日 the 15th day of a lunar month ❼介词，向 (preposition) toward: ～东走 *head east* | ～上瞧 *look upward*

妄 wàng ㄨㄤˋ 乱，荒诞不合理 absurd; reckless: ～动 *take rash action* | ～想 *wishful thinking* | 勿～言。*Don't talk recklessly.*

忘 wàng ㄨㄤˋ 忘记，不记得，遗漏 to forget: 别～了拿书。*Don't forget to get the book.* | 喝水不～掘井人。*When you drink the water, think of those who dug the well.*

WEI ㄨㄟ

危 wēi ㄨㄟ ❶不安全，跟“安”相对（㊜—险）dangerous; perilous (opposite of 安)：～急 *critical; in grave danger* | ～重 *critically ill* | 转～为安 *tide over a crisis* [危言耸听] 故意说吓人的话使听的人吃惊 to say sth shocking to provoke a reaction [临危] 将死，面临生命危险 facing death; facing deadly peril ❷损害（㊜—害）to endanger：～及家国 *put one's family and country in harm's way* ❸高的，陡的 high; steep：～楼 *high building* ❹端正 proper; upright：正襟～坐 *sit up properly* ❺星宿名，二十八宿之一 *wei* (one of the twenty-eight constellations in ancient Chinese astronomy)

委 wēi ㄨㄟ [委蛇]（—yí）1 周旋，应付 to accede to superficially：虚与～（假意敷衍）*deal with sb courteously but without sincerity* 2 same as “逶迤”

⇨ see also wěi on p.681

逶 wēi ㄨㄟ [逶迤]（—yí）道路、河道等弯曲而长 winding; meandering：山路～ *mountain path winds on*

巍 wēi ㄨㄟ 高大 ㊕ towering; lofty：～峨 *lofty* | ～～高山 *towering mountain*

威 wēi ㄨㄟ ❶使人敬畏的气魄 power; might：示～ *demonstrate strength; hold a demonstration* | ～力 *power* | ～望 *prestige* | 权～ *authority* | 狐假虎～ *borrow power to do evil* ❷凭借力量或势力 with power or force：～胁 *threaten* | ～逼 *coerce*

葳 wēi ㄨㄟ [葳蕤]（—ruí）草木茂盛的样子 luxuriant; lush

崴 wēi ㄨㄟ [崴嵬]（—wéi）山高的样子 (of a mountain) lofty; towering

⇨ see also wǎi on p.671

偎 wēi ㄨㄟ 紧挨着，亲密地靠着 to snuggle up to; to lean close to：小孩ㄦ～在母亲的怀里。*The child snuggled up to his/her mother.*

隈 wēi ㄨㄟ 山、水等弯曲的地方 bend (in rivers, mountains, etc.)

煨 wēi ㄨㄟ ❶在带火的灰里把东西烧熟 to roast in fresh cinders：～白薯 *roast sweet potato* ❷用微火慢慢地煮 to stew; to simmer：～鸡 *stew chicken* | ～肉 *stew meat*

鳂（鰃） wēi ㄨㄟ 鱼名，身体侧扁，眼大，口大而斜，多为红色。生活在热带海洋里 squirrelfish

微 wēi ㄨㄟ ❶小，细小（㊜细—）minute; tiny：防～杜渐 *guard against gradual creeping corruption* ❷轻微，稍（㊜稍—）㊕ slight：～感不适 *feel slightly unwell* | ～～一笑 *smile faintly* ❸衰落，低下 to decline：衰～ *decline* ❹精深，精妙 profound; subtle：～妙 *subtle* ❺法定计量单位中十进分数单位词头之一，表示10^{-6}，符号μ。micro- (μ)

W

溦 wēi ㄨㄟ 小雨 light rain

薇 wēi ㄨㄟ 草本植物，又叫巢菜、野豌豆，花紫红色，是优良饲料，可入药 bush vetch (also called 巢菜，野豌豆)

韦(韋) wéi ㄨㄟˊ 熟皮子，去毛加工鞣制的兽皮 leather

违(違) wéi ㄨㄟˊ ❶背(bèi)，反，不遵守(㊀-背、-反) to disobey; to violate: ～法 *break the law* | ～章 *break rules and regulations* | 阳奉阴～ *obey in appearance but oppose in private* ❷不见面，离别 to be separated; to leave: 久～。*It's been long since we last met.*

围(圍) wéi ㄨㄟˊ ❶环绕，四周拦挡起来 to enclose; to surround: ～巾 *scarf* | ～墙 *enclosure; enclosing wall* | 包～ *encircle* ❷四周 all sides; periphery: 四～ *all around* | 周～ *vicinity* ❸(-子)圈起来用作拦阻或遮挡的东西 defensive wall; curtain: 土～子 *village fortification* | 床～子 *bed curtain* ❹量词 measure word ①两只手的拇指和食指合拢起来的长度 length of the circle formed when one's thumbs and index fingers are brought together: 腰大十～ *a waist of ten hand spans* ②两只胳膊合拢起来的长度 length of the circle formed when one brings one's hands together at arm's length: 树大十～ *a tree trunk ten arm spans around*

帏(幃) wéi ㄨㄟˊ 帐子，幔幕 curtain

闱(闈) wéi ㄨㄟˊ ❶古代宫室的旁门 side gate of an imperial palace: 宫～(宫殿里边) *palace chambers* ❷科举时代称考试或考场 imperial examination; imperial examination hall: 秋～ *autumn imperial examination* | 入～ *enter the imperial examination hall*

沩(潙) wéi ㄨㄟˊ 用于地名 used in place names: ～源口(在湖北省阳新) *Weiyuankou (in Yangxin, Hubei Province)*

涠(潿) wéi ㄨㄟˊ [涠洲] 岛名，在广西壮族自治区北海市南部海域 Weizhou (an island south of Beihai City, Guangxi Zhuang Autonomous Region)

为(爲、為)** wéi ㄨㄟˊ ❶做，行 to do; to act: 事在人～。*The success of the matter depends on one's efforts.* | 所作所～ *all one's actions* ㊀作为，做事的能力 ability: 年轻有～ *young and capable* ❷做，当 to serve as: 他被选～人大代表。*He is elected deputy to the National People's Congress.* | 拜他～师 *take him as one's teacher* ❸成为，变成 to become: 一分～二 *divide one into two* | 高岸～谷，深谷～陵。*High banks become valleys, and deep valleys hills; (figurative) things can turn to the opposite.* ❹是 to be: 十二

个～一打。*Twelve is a dozen.* ❺介词，被 (preposition) by：～人所笑 *get laughed at by others* ❻文言助词，常跟“何”相应，表疑问 auxiliary word in classical Chinese, often used in conjunction with 何 to form a question：何以家～？*What do I need a family for?* ❼附于单音形容词后，构成表示程度、范围的副词 following a monosyllabic adjective to make an adverb of degree or extent：大～增色 *add lots of lustre* | 广～传播 *widely spread* ❽附于表程度的单音副词后，加强语气 following a monosyllabic adverb of degree to add emphasis：极～重要 *extremely important* | 尤～出色 *particularly outstanding*

⇨ see also wèi on p.682

沩(溈、**潙) wéi ㄨㄟˊ 沩水，水名，在湖南省长沙 Weishui River (a river in Changsha, Hunan Province)

圩 wéi ㄨㄟˊ ❶低洼地区周围防水的堤 dyke; embankment ❷有圩围住的地区 diked marsh：～田 *polder* | 盐～ *salt pan* ❸（一子）围绕村落四周的障碍物 protective embankments surrounding a village：土～子 *village fortification* | 树～子 *tree grill* (also written as 围子)

⇨ see also xū on p.732

峗 wéi ㄨㄟˊ 用于地名 used in place names：～家湾（在四川省乐至）*Weijiawan (in Lezhi, Sichuan Province)*

涠 wéi ㄨㄟˊ 涠水，水名，在湖北省南部，松滋河支流 Weishui River (a river in southern Hubei Province, tributary to the Songzihe River)

桅 wéi ㄨㄟˊ 桅杆，船上挂帆的杆子 mast

鮠(鮠) wéi ㄨㄟˊ 鱼名，身体前部扁平，后部侧扁，有四对须，无鳞。生活在淡水中 *leiocassis*

硙(磑) wéi ㄨㄟˊ ［硙硙］形容很高的样子 high; lofty

⇨ see also wèi on p.683

唯 wéi ㄨㄟˊ ❶单单，只 only：～有 *only* | ～恐 *only fear that* | ～利是图 *seek nothing but profit* ❷文言叹词，表示答应 (exclamation in classical Chinese) used to indicate consent［唯唯诺诺］形容一味顺从别人的意见 abjectly compliant

帷 wéi ㄨㄟˊ （一子）围在四周的帐幕 curtain：车～子 *vehicle curtain* | 运筹～幄 *devise strategies within the command tent*

惟 wéi ㄨㄟˊ ❶ same as “唯❶” ❷但是 but：雨虽止，～路途仍甚泥泞。*Although the rain has stopped, the road is still quite muddy.* ❸文言助词，用在句首，有加强语气的作用 (auxiliary word in classical Chinese) used at the start of a sentence as an intensifier：～二月既望 *on the 16th day of the second lunar month* ❹思，想。“思惟”通常写作“思维” to think (思惟 is usually written as 思维)

W

维(維) wéi ㄨㄟˊ ❶连接(㊀—系) to tie up; to hold together [维护] 保全, 保护 to safeguard; to defend [维持] 设法使继续存在 to maintain ❷文言助词 auxiliary word in classical Chinese: 步履～艰 *hard to move one's feet* ❸思考 to think: 思～ *thinking*

[维吾尔族] 我国少数民族, 参看附录四 the Uygur people (one of the ethnic groups in China. See Appendix Ⅳ.)

琟 wéi ㄨㄟˊ 古代指一种像玉的石头 (ancient) a jade-like stone

潍(濰) wéi ㄨㄟˊ 潍河, 水名, 在山东省潍坊 Weihe River (in Weifang, Shandong Province)

嵬 wéi ㄨㄟˊ 高大耸立 lofty; towering

伟(偉) wěi ㄨㄟˇ 大(㊀—大) great; big: 魁～ *big and tall* | ～人(对人民有大功绩的人) *great personage* | 宏～ *magnificent* | ～业 *great cause*

苇(葦) wěi ㄨㄟˇ (—子) 芦苇 reed (see 芦 on page 419 for reference)

纬(緯) wěi ㄨㄟˇ ❶纬线, 织布时用梭穿织的横纱, 编织物的横线, 跟"经"相对 weft; woof (opposite of 经) ❷地理学上假定的沿地球表面跟赤道平行的线, 从赤道起, 以北称北纬, 以南称南纬, 各为 90°。latitude ❸指纬书(东汉神学迷信附会儒家经义的一类书) augury book (of Eastern Han Dynasty)

玮(瑋) wěi ㄨㄟˇ 玉名 a kind of jade

晖(暐) wěi ㄨㄟˇ 形容光很盛 bright; brilliant

炜(煒) wěi ㄨㄟˇ 光明 bright

韡(韡) wěi ㄨㄟˇ ㊂盛, 光明 brilliant; bright

韪(韙) wěi ㄨㄟˇ 是, 对(常和否定词连用) right (often used with a negative word): 冒天下之大不～ *in defiance of world opinion*

伪(僞、偽)** wěi ㄨㄟˇ ❶假, 不真实 false; fake: 去～存真 *get rid of the false and keep the true* | ～造 *forge* | ～装 *disguise* ❷不合法的 illegal: ～政府 *puppet government*

芀(蔿、蒍)** wěi ㄨㄟˇ 姓 (surname) Wei

尾 wěi ㄨㄟˇ ❶(—巴)鸟、兽、虫、鱼等身体末端突出的部分 tail: 虎头蛇～ *fine start and poor finish* ❷末端 end: 排～ *at the end* ❸尾随, 在后面跟 to follow: ～其后 *follow sb* ❹量词, 用于鱼 measure word for fish ❺星宿名, 二十八宿之一 *wei* (one of the twenty-eight constellations in ancient Chinese astronomy)

⇨ see also yǐ on p.772

娓 wěi ㄨㄟˇ [娓娓] 形容谈论不倦或说话动听 (of someone talking) tireless; pleasing to the ear: ～道来 *recount in a vivid and pleasing manner* | ～动听 *(of* *speech) interesting and pleasing to the ear*

艉 wěi ㄨㄟˇ 船体的尾部 stern (of a vessel)

委 wěi ㄨㄟˇ ❶任，派，把事交给人办（㊀一任）to appoint; to entrust: ～以重任 *entrust with an important task* ❷抛弃，舍弃（㊀一弃）to throw away; to cast aside: ～之于地 *cast sth to the ground* ❸推诿 to shift: ～罪 *shift blame* ❹曲折，婉转 indirect; roundabout: 话说得很～婉 *remarks made tactfully* [委屈]（一qu）含冤受屈或心里苦闷 wronged; upset: 心里有～，又不肯说。*One is feeling wronged and upset, but is not willing to talk about it.* ❺末，尾 end: 原～ *the whole story* ❻确实 indeed; actually: ～系实情 *indeed the true story* | ～实 *indeed* ❼委员或委员会的简称 short for 委员 or 委员会: 编～ *editorial board* | 体～ *physical culture and sports commission* | 市～ *municipal committee (of the Communist Party of China)*

⇨ see also wēi on p.677

诿（諉）wěi ㄨㄟˇ 推托，推卸 to shift: ～过 *shift blame* | 推～ *pass the buck*

萎 wěi ㄨㄟˇ 干枯衰落 to wither; to wilt: 枯～ *wither* | ～谢 *wither* | 气～ *disheartened* [萎缩] 1 体积缩小，表面变皱 to shrink; to shrivel: 肌肉～ *muscular atrophy* 2 衰退 to decline: 经济～ *recession* [萎靡] [委靡]（一mǐ）颓丧，不振作 dejected; dispirited: 精神～ *spirits are downcast*

痿 wěi ㄨㄟˇ 中医指身体某部分萎缩或丧失功能的病 (in traditional Chinese medicine) flaccid paralysis: 阳～ *impotence*

洧 wěi ㄨㄟˇ [洧川] 地名，在河南省尉氏 Weichuan (a place in Weishi, Henan Province)

痏 wěi ㄨㄟˇ ❶瘢痕 sore; scar ❷创伤 wound

鲔（鮪）wěi ㄨㄟˇ ❶古书上指鲟（xún）鱼 (in ancient Chinese texts) sturgeon ❷鱼名，身体纺锤形，背部蓝黑色，生活在海洋里 mackerel tuna

隗 wěi ㄨㄟˇ 姓 (surname) Wei

⇨ see also kuí on p.369

廆 wěi ㄨㄟˇ 用于人名。慕容廆，西晋末年鲜卑族的首领 used in given names, e.g., Murong Wei, chief of the Xianbei people toward the end of Western Jin Dynasty

⇨ see also guī on p.231

頠（頠）wěi ㄨㄟˇ 安静 quiet

猥 wěi ㄨㄟˇ ❶鄙陋，下流 obscene; base: ～辞 *obscene language* [猥亵]（一xiè）1 淫秽，下流 lewd; obscene: 言辞～。*One's language is obscene.* 2 做下流的动作 to molest; to harass: ～妇女 *harass a woman* ❷杂，多 numerous; multifarious: ～杂 *multifarious*

薳 wěi ㄨㄟˇ ❶草名 narrow-leaved polygala ❷姓 (surname) Wei

亹 wěi ㄨㄟˇ [亹亹] 1 形容勤勉不倦 diligent; assiduous 2 形容向前推移、行进 moving forward

⇨ see also mén on p.444

卫(衛、**衞) wèi ㄨㄟˋ ❶保护，防护(㊥保一) to defend; to guard: 保家～国 *protect one's home and defend one's country* | 自～ *self-defence* [卫生] 有益于身体的健康，能预防疾病 hygienic; sanitary: 院内不太～。*The sanitary conditions are less than ideal in the courtyard.* 也指合乎卫生的情况 hygiene; sanitation: 讲～ *pay attention to hygiene* | 环境～ *environmental sanitation* ❷防护人员 guard: 警～ *security guard* | 后～ *rear guard* ❸明代驻兵的地点 troop station in the Ming Dynasty: ～所 *troop station* ❹周代诸侯国名，在今河南省北部和河北省南部一带 Wei (a state in the Zhou Dynasty, in today's northern Henan and southern Hebei provinces)

为(爲、**為) wèi ㄨㄟˋ ❶介词，表示行为的对象 (preposition) for: ～人民服务 *serve the people* ❷介词，表示原因、目的(可以和“了”连用) (preposition) for the purpose of; for the sake of (can be used with 了): 别～一点儿小事而争吵。*Don't fight over such trifles.* | ～了美好的明天而努力 *work hard for a bright tomorrow* ❸介词，对，向 (preposition) to: 且～诸君言之 *just to tell you gentlemen* ❹帮助，卫护 to support; to help

⇨ see also wéi on p.678

未 wèi ㄨㄟˋ ❶地支的第八位 *wei* (the eighth of the twelve Earthly Branches, a system used in the Chinese calendar) ❷未时，指下午一点到三点 the period from 1 p.m. to 3 p.m. ❸副词，表示否定 (adverb) used to indicate the negative ①不 not: ～知可否 *not know if it is all right* ②没有，不曾 not yet: ～成年 *under age* | 此人～来。*This person has not arrived.* ❹放在句末，表示疑问 placed at the end of a sentence to form a question: 君知其意～? *Do you know what that means?*

味 wèi ㄨㄟˋ ❶(一儿)味道，滋味，舌头尝东西所得到的感觉 taste; flavour: 五～ *the five flavours* | 带甜～儿 *with a sweet taste* | ～同嚼蜡 *taste no better than wax* ❷(一儿)气味，鼻子闻东西所得到的感觉 smell; odour: 香～儿 *sweet smell* | 臭～儿 *bad smell* ❸指某些菜肴、食物 used to refer to certain types of dish food: 海～ *seafood* | 野～ *food made of wild animals* ❹(一儿)意味，情趣 significance; taste: 趣～ *interest* | 意～深长 *of profound significance* ❺体会，研究 to understand; to ponder: 细～其言 *ponder the remarks* | 体～ *appreciate; savour* ❻量词，用于中药的种类 (measure word for Chinese medicine prescription) ingredient：这个方子一共七～药。*The prescription is made up of seven different herbs.*

位 wèi ㄨㄟˋ ❶位置，所在的地方 place; location：座～ *seat* | 到～ *come in place* | 就～ *take one's place* ❷职位，地位 position; status ❸特指皇位 throne：即～ *ascend the throne* | 在～ *on the throne* | 篡～ *usurp the throne* ❹一个数中，每个数码所占的位置 place (in a multi-digit number); figure：个～ *unit's place* | 十～ *ten's place* ❺量词，用于人（含敬意）measure word for people (polite speech)：诸～同志 *you comrades* | 三～客人 *three guests*

畏 wèi ㄨㄟˋ ❶怕（㊀—惧）to fear：大无～ *fearless* | 不～艰险 *fear no danger nor difficulty* | ～首～尾 *be overcautious* ❷敬佩 respect：后生可～。*Youngsters are to be revered.*

喂（❷❸*餵、❷❸*餧）wèi ㄨㄟˋ ❶叹词，打招呼时用 (exclamation) hello; hey：～，是谁？*Hello, who is this?* | ～，快来呀！*Hey, hurry over!* ❷把食物送进人嘴里 to feed (sb)：～小孩儿 *feed a child* ❸给动物东西吃 to feed (animals)：～牲口 *feed live stock* ㊀畜（xù）养 to raise (animals)：～鸡 *raise chickens* | ～猪 *raise pigs*

硙 wèi ㄨㄟˋ 〈方 dialect〉石磨（mò）stone mill

碨（磑）wèi ㄨㄟˋ same as "硙"

⇨ see also wéi on p.679

胃 wèi ㄨㄟˋ ❶胃脏，人和高等动物消化器官之一，能分泌胃液、消化食物 stomach (see picture of 人体内脏 on page 819) ❷星宿名，二十八宿之一 *wei* (one of the twenty-eight constellations in ancient Chinese astronomy)

谓（謂）wèi ㄨㄟˋ ❶说 to say：可～恰到好处 *can be said to be just right* | 勿～言之不预。*Don't say I didn't forewarn you.* ❷称，叫作 to call; to name：称～ *appellation* | 何～人工呼吸法？*What is meant by artificial respiration?* [所谓] 所说的 so-called：～分析，就是分析事物的矛盾。*The so-called analysis is the analysing of the contradictions of things.* [无谓] 没意义，说不出道理 meaningless：这种争论太～了。*This kind of dispute is quite pointless.*

猬（*蝟）wèi ㄨㄟˋ 刺猬，哺乳动物，嘴很尖，身上长着硬刺，昼伏夜出，捕食昆虫、鼠、蛇等 hedgehog

渭 wèi ㄨㄟˋ 渭河，发源于甘肃省，横贯陕西省入黄河 Weihe River (originating in Gansu Province, flowing eastward across Shaanxi Province and into the Yellow River)

煟 wèi ㄨㄟˋ ❶光明 bright ❷旺盛 exuberant; vigorous

尉 wèi ㄨㄟˋ ❶古官名 (ancient) officer：太～ *supreme government official in charge of military*

W

affairs ❷军衔名，在校级之下 (military rank) junior officer：上～ *captain*
［尉氏］地名，在河南省 Weishi (a place in Henan Province)

⇨ see also yù on p.804

蔚 wèi ㄨㄟˋ ❶草木茂盛 exuberant; lush 㓁 盛大 magnificent; grand：～为大观 *make a splendid sight* ［蔚蓝］晴天天空的颜色 bright blue; azure：～的天空 *bright blue sky* ❷云气弥漫 (of clouds) to spread：云蒸霞～ *colourful clouds slowly rising*

⇨ see also yù on p.804

慰 wèi ㄨㄟˋ ❶使人心里安适 to console; to comfort：安～ *comfort* | ～问 *visit to extend sympathy/gratitude* | ～劳 *bring gifts or entertainment in recognition of services rendered* ［慰藉］（一jiè）安慰，抚慰 to comfort ❷心安 to feel relieved：欣～ *pleased* | 甚～ *very pleased*

螱 wèi ㄨㄟˋ 昆虫，即白蚁，外形像蚂蚁，蛀食木材 termite (same as 白蚁)

霨 wèi ㄨㄟˋ 形容云起的样子 (of clouds) rising

鳚(鰃) wèi ㄨㄟˋ 鱼名，身体小而侧扁，无鳞，生活在近海 blenny

遗(遺) wèi ㄨㄟˋ 赠与 to present to：～之千金 *make sb a handsome gift (in money)*

⇨ see also yí on p.770

䥝(䥝) wèi ㄨㄟˋ huì ㄏㄨㄟˋ（又）古代的一种鼎 a kind of tripod in ancient times

魏 wèi ㄨㄟˋ ❶古国名 name of ancient states ①战国国名，在今河南省北部，山西省西南部一带 State of Wei (one of the Warring States, in today's northern Henan and southwestern Shanxi provinces) ②三国之一，曹丕所建立（公元 220—265 年），在今黄河流域甘肃省以下各省和湖北、安徽、江苏三省北部及辽宁省南部 Kingdom of Wei (220—265 AD, founded by Cao Pi, one of the Three Kingdoms) ❷北魏，北朝之一，鲜卑族拓跋珪所建立（公元 386—534 年），后分裂为东魏和西魏 Northern Wei Dynasty (386—534 AD, founded by Tuoba Gui of the Xianbei ethnic group, later to break up into Eastern Wei and Western Wei)

WEN ㄨㄣ

温 wēn ㄨㄣ ❶不冷不热（㊀一暖）warm：～水 *warm water* ［温饱］衣食充足 warm and well-fed ❷温度，冷热的程度 temperature：气～ *air temperature* | 低～ *low temperature* | 体～ *body temperature* ❸性情柔和（㊀一柔、一和）gentle; mild ❹使东西热 to warm up：～酒 *warm up wine* ❺复习 review：～课 *review lessons* | ～故知新 *review the old and learn the new* ❻中医指温热病 (in traditional Chinese medicine) warm heat disease：春～ *spring fever* | 冬～ *winter fever* ❼ same as "瘟"

榅 wēn ㄨㄣ ［榅桲］（－po）落叶灌木或小乔木，叶椭圆形，花淡红色或白色。果实也叫榅桲，有香气，味酸，可制蜜饯，也可入药 quince

辒（轀） wēn ㄨㄣ ［辒辌］（－liáng）古代可以卧的车，也用作丧车 sleeping carriage in ancient times (also used as a hearse)

瘟 wēn ㄨㄣ 瘟疫，流行性急性传染病 plague; acute communicable disease：～病 *seasonal febrile disease* | 春～ *spring fever* | 鸡～ *fowl plague* | 猪～ *swine fever*

薀 wēn ㄨㄣ ［薀草］〈方 dialect〉指水中生长的杂草，可用作肥料 water weeds

鳁（鰮） wēn ㄨㄣ ［鳁鲸］鲸的一种，体长可达18米，背部黑色，腹部白色 sei whale

文 wén ㄨㄣˊ ❶事物错综所成的纹理或形象 certain noteworthy natural phenomenon：天～ *astronomy* | 水～ *hydrology* ❷在身上、脸上刺画字或花纹 to tattoo：断发～身 *cut one's hair and tattoo one's body* ❸文字，记录语言的符号 script; character：甲骨～ *oracle bone script* | 外～ *foreign language* | ～盲 *illiterate* ［文言］以古汉语为基础的书面语，跟"白话"相对 classical Chinese writing (opposite of 白话)：半～半白 *mixed literary and vernacular styles* ❹文章，用文字写成的有条理的篇章 literary composition：作～ *composition* | 古～ *classical prose* | 应用～ *practical writing* ❺旧时指礼节仪式 (old) formal ritual：虚～ *empty formality* | 繁～缛节 *unnecessary and over-elaborate formalities* ［文化］1 人类在社会历史发展过程中所创造的物质财富和精神财富的总和，特指精神财富，如哲学、科学、教育、文学、艺术等 culture 2 考古学用语，指同一个历史时期的不依分布地点为转移的遗迹、遗物的综合体。同样的工具、用具，同样的制作技术等，是同一种文化的特征，如仰韶文化等 (in archaeology) culture 3 运用文字的能力和一般知识 education; literacy：～水平 *educational level* | 学～ *learn to read and write* ❻非军事的，非武力的，跟"武"相对 civilian; civil (opposite of 武)：～职 *civilian post* | 能～能武 *able with both the pen and the sword* | ～臣武将 *civil officials and military officers* ㊟柔和 gentle; mild：～雅 *refined; cultured* | ～绉绉 *genteel* ［文火］不猛烈的火 slow fire; low heat ❼量词，用于旧时的铜钱 measure word for copper coins in old times：一～钱 *one coin* | 一～不值 *worthless* ❽ (formerly pronounced wèn) 文饰，掩饰 to cover up; to paint over：～过饰非 *gloss over mistakes*

芠 wén ㄨㄣˊ 古代指一种草 (ancient) a kind of grass

驳（駇） wén ㄨㄣˊ 赤鬣白身黄目的马 white horse with a red mane and yellow eyes

纹(紋) wén ㄨㄣˊ 条纹(㊀—理) lines; vein: 水～ *ripple* | 指～ *fingerprint* | 有一道～儿 *there is a line*

⇨ see also wèn on p.687

玟 wén ㄨㄣˊ 玉的纹理 patterning in jade

⇨ see also mín on p.455

炆 wén ㄨㄣˊ 〈方 dialect〉用微火焖食物 to simmer; to cook over a slow fire

蚊(*螡、*蟁) wén ㄨㄣˊ (一子) 昆虫，幼虫叫孑孓，生活在水里。成虫身体细长，雄的吸植物汁液，雌的吸人畜的血。能传染疟疾、流行性乙型脑炎等。种类很多 mosquito

雯 wén ㄨㄣˊ 有花纹的云彩 patterned cloud

闻(聞) wén ㄨㄣˊ ❶听见 to hear: 风～ *get wind of* | 耳～不如目见。*Hearsay is no equal to witnessing.* ❷听见的事情，消息 news; hearsay: 新～ *news* | 奇～ *anecdote* ❸ (formerly pronounced wèn) 出名，有名望 well-known; famous: ～人 *celebrity* | 默默无～ *unknown to the public* ❹名声 reputation: 令～ *good reputation* | 丑～ *scandal* ❺用鼻子嗅气味 to smell: 你～～这是什么味? *Have a smell and see what it is.* | 我～见香味了。*I smelt the fragrance.*

阌(閿) wén ㄨㄣˊ [阌乡] 地名，在河南省灵宝 Wenxiang (a place in Lingbao, Henan Province)

刎 wěn ㄨㄣˇ 割脖子 to cut one's throat: ～颈 *cut one's throat* | 自～ *commit suicide by cutting one's throat*

吻(*脗) wěn ㄨㄣˇ ❶嘴唇(㊀唇—) lip: 接～ *to kiss on the mouth* [吻合] 相合 to fit; to tally ❷用嘴唇接触表示喜爱 to kiss ❸动物的嘴 mouth (of an animal)

抆 wěn ㄨㄣˇ 擦 to wipe: ～泪 *wipe tears*

紊 wěn ㄨㄣˇ (formerly pronounced wèn) 乱(㊀—乱) disorderly; confused: 有条不～ *in good order*

稳(穩) wěn ㄨㄣˇ ❶稳固，安定 steady; stable: 站～ *stand firm* | ～步前进 *forge ahead steadily* ㊗沉着，不轻浮 steady; sedate: ～重 *steady* ❷使稳定 to stabilize; to steady: ～住局势 *stabilize the situation* ❸准确，可靠 reliable; certain: 十拿九～ *quite certain*

问(問) wèn ㄨㄣˋ ❶有不知道或不明白的请人解答 to ask; to enquire: ～事处 *information desk* | ～一道题 *ask about a problem* ❷慰问 to extend sympathy/greetings: ～候 *greet* ❸审讯，追究 to examine; to interrogate: ～口供 *question for testimony/confession* ㊊问罪，惩办 to punish; to condemn: 胁从不～。*Those who took part under duress will not be punished.* ❹管，干预 to care; to bother: 概不过～ *no questions asked*

汶 wèn ㄨㄣˋ 汶河，水名，在山东省。汶川，地名，在四川省 Wenhe River (a river in Shandong Province); Wenchuan (a place in Sichuan Province)

纹（紋） wèn ㄨㄣˋ same as "璺"

⇨ see also wén on p.686

揾 wèn ㄨㄣˋ ❶用手指按住 to press down with fingers ❷擦 to wipe：～泪 *wipe off tears*

璺 wèn ㄨㄣˋ 器物上的裂痕 crack (in utensils)：这个碗有一道～。*This bowl has a crack in it.* | 打破砂锅～（谐"问"）到底 *get to the bottom of things*

WENG ㄨㄥ

翁 wēng ㄨㄥ ❶老头儿 old man：渔～ *old fisherman* | 老～ *old man* ❷父亲 father ❸丈夫的父亲或妻子的父亲 father-in-law：～姑（公婆）*parents-in-law (one's husband's parents)* | ～婿 *father-in-law and son-in-law*

嗡 wēng ㄨㄥ 形容昆虫飞动等声音 ㊀ buzz：蜜蜂～～地飞。*Bees are buzzing around.* | 飞机～～响。*An aeroplane makes a droning noise.*

滃 wēng ㄨㄥ 滃江，水名，在广东省北部 Wengjiang River (in northern Guangdong Province)

⇨ see also wěng on p.687

鎓（鎓） wēng ㄨㄥ ［鎓盐］在水溶液中离解出有机正离子的含氧、氮或硫的盐类 onium salt

鹟（鶲） wēng ㄨㄥ 鸟名，身体小，嘴稍扁平，吃害虫，是益鸟 flycatcher

蓊 wěng ㄨㄥˇ 形容草木茂盛 (of vegetation) lush：～郁 *lush* | ～茸 *lush and thick*

滃 wěng ㄨㄥˇ ❶形容水盛 (of water) gushing ❷形容云起 (of clouds) rising

⇨ see also wēng on p.687

瓮（*甕、*罋） wèng ㄨㄥˋ 一种盛水、酒等的陶器 urn; earthen jar

蕹 wèng ㄨㄥˋ 蕹菜，草本植物，俗叫空心菜，茎中空，叶心脏形，叶柄长，花白色，漏斗状。嫩茎叶可用作蔬菜 water spinach (informal 空心菜)

齆 wèng ㄨㄥˋ 鼻子堵塞不通气 (of nose) blocked; stuffy：～鼻 *stuffy nose*

WO ㄨㄛ

挝（撾） wō ㄨㄛ ［老挝］国名，在中南半岛 Laos (a country in Indochina)

⇨ see also zhuā on p.871

莴（萵） wō ㄨㄛ ［莴苣］（-ju）草本植物，叶多长形，花黄色，分叶用和茎用两种。叶用的叫莴苣菜或生菜，茎用的叫莴笋，都可用作蔬菜 lettuce

涡（渦） wō ㄨㄛ 旋涡，水流旋转形成的中间低洼的地方 whirlpool：卷入旋～（喻被牵入纠纷里）*get dragged into disputes*

⇨ see also guō on p.234

窝(窩) wō ㄨㄛ ❶(—儿) 禽兽或其他动物的巢穴 nest; lair：鸡～ *hencoop* | 马蜂～ *hornets' nest* | 狼～ *wolves' den* ⓪人的安身处，人或物所占的位置 place：安乐～ *cosy nest* | 挪个～儿 *move to another place* ❷藏匿犯法的人或东西 to harbour; to shelter (criminals or illegal things)：～贼 *harbour a thief* | ～赃 *hide the spoils* | ～藏 *harbour* ❸坏人聚集之处 (of evil-doers) lair; den：贼～ *thieves' lair* ❹(—儿) 洼陷的地方 pit; hollow：山～ *remote mountain area* | 酒～儿 *dimple* ❺弄弯 to bend：把铁丝～个圆圈 *bend the iron wire into a circle* ❻郁积不得发作或发挥 to hold in; to suppress：～火 *choke with anger* | ～心 *depressed (due to being wronged/offended)* [窝工] 因调配不好，工作人员没有充分发挥作用 (of manpower) lie idle due to poor organization ❼量词，用于一胎所生或一次孵出的动物 (measure word for newborn animals) brood; litter：一～小猪 *a litter of piglets*

蜗(蝸) wō ㄨㄛ 蜗牛，软体动物，有螺旋形扁圆的硬壳，头部有两对触角，吃嫩叶，对农作物有害 snail [蜗居] ⓪窄小的住所。也指在窄小的处所居住 narrow abode; to live in a humble dwelling：～斗室 *live in a small room*

倭 wō ㄨㄛ 古代称日本 (ancient) Japan

踒 wō ㄨㄛ （手、脚等）猛折而筋骨受伤 to sprain (wrist or ankle)：手～了 *wrist is sprained*

喔 wō ㄨㄛ 形容公鸡的叫声 cock-a-doodle-doo; crow

我 wǒ ㄨㄛˇ 代词，自称，自己 (pronoun) I; me; my：～国 *my country* | 自～批评 *self criticism* | 忘～ *oblivious of oneself*

肟 wò ㄨㄛˋ 有机化合物的一类，由羟胺与醛或酮缩合而成 oxime

沃 wò ㄨㄛˋ ❶土地肥(⊜肥—) (of land or soil) fertile：～土 *fertile soil* | ～野 *fertile land* ❷灌溉，浇 to irrigate; to water：雪～大地 *snow waters the land* | ～灌 *irrigate*

卧(**臥) wò ㄨㄛˋ ❶睡倒，躺或趴 to lie down：仰～ *lie down on one's back* | ～倒 *drop to the ground* | ～病 *be bed-ridden* ❷睡觉用的 for sleeping in：～室 *bedroom* | ～铺 *sleeping berth* ❸趴伏（指动物）(of animals) to crouch; to sit：鸡～在窝里 *chicken sits in the coop* | 藏龙～虎 *hidden dragon and crouching tiger*

偓 wò ㄨㄛˋ 用于人名。偓佺（quán），古代传说中的仙人 used in given names, e.g., Wo Quan, an immortal in ancient legend

握 wò ㄨㄛˋ 攥（zuàn），手指弯曲合拢来拿 to clench (the fist)：～手 *shake hands*

幄 wò ㄨㄛˋ 帐幕 curtain：帷～ *army tent*

渥 wò ㄨㄛˋ ❶沾湿，沾润 to wet; to moisten ❷厚，重 thick; heavy：优～（优厚）*generous (payment/conditions)*

龌(齷) wò ㄨㄛˋ ［龌龊］（—chuò）肮脏，不干净 dirty; filthy ㊥人的品质恶劣 (of character) despicable

涴 wò ㄨㄛˋ 〈方 dialect〉弄脏，泥、油等沾在衣服、器物上 to get (clothes, items, etc.) dirty

⇨ see also yuān on p.805

硪 wò ㄨㄛˋ （—子）一种砸实地基的工具 punner

斡 wò ㄨㄛˋ 转，旋 to revolve; to rotate ［斡旋］居中调停，把弄僵了的局面扭转过来 to mediate：从中～ *mediate between parties*

WU ㄨ

乌(烏) wū ㄨ ❶乌鸦，鸟名，有的地区叫老鸹（gua）、老鸦，羽毛黑色，嘴大而直 crow; raven (also called 老鸹 gua or 老鸦 in some regions) ［乌合］㊥无组织地聚集 to assemble in a disorderly fashion：～之众 *motley crew* ❷黑色 black; dark: ～云 *dark cloud* | ～木 *ebony* ❸文言代词，表示疑问，哪，何 (pronoun in classical Chinese) where; how：～足道哉？*Don't mention it.* ❹姓 (surname) Wu

［乌呼］same as "呜呼 1"

［乌孜别克族］我国少数民族，参看附录四 the Uzbek people (one of the ethnic groups in China. See Appendix Ⅳ.)

⇨ see also wù on p.693

邬(鄔) wū ㄨ 姓 (surname) Wu

呜(嗚) wū ㄨ 拟声词 ㊀ (onomatopoeia) hoot; toot：工厂汽笛～～地叫。*The factory's siren hoots.*

［呜呼］1 文言叹词，旧时祭文常用"呜呼"表示叹息 (exclamation in classical Chinese) alas 2 借指死亡 to die：一命～ *a life sadly lost*

钨(鎢) wū ㄨ 金属元素，符号 W，灰黑色，质硬而脆，熔点高。钨丝可以做电灯泡中的细丝，含钨的钢叫钨钢，可制机器、钢甲等 tungsten

圬(杇)** wū ㄨ ❶泥瓦工人用的抹（mǒ）子 trowel ❷抹（mò）墙 to plaster

污(*汙、*汚) wū ㄨ ❶肮脏（㊤—秽）dirty; filthy：～泥 *sludge* ㊥不廉洁 corrupted：贪～ *embezzle* ❷弄脏 to defile; to dirty：玷～ *to defile* | ～染 *pollute* ［污辱］用无理的言行给人以难堪 to insult; to humiliate

巫 wū ㄨ 专以祈祷求神骗取财物的人 witch; wizard

诬(誣) wū ㄨ 硬说别人做了某种坏事（㊤—赖）to accuse falsely：～告 *lodge a false accusation* | ～蔑 *slander; defame* | ～陷 *frame sb*

於 wū ㄨ 文言叹词 (exclamation in classical Chincse) alas ［於乎］［於戏］（—hū）same

W

as "呜呼 1"

⇨ see also yū on p.796, yú on p.798

洿 wū ㄨ ❶低洼的地方 low-lying land; depression: ～池 *pool* ❷掘成水池 to dig a pool

屋 wū ㄨ ❶房(㊀房－) house ㊁〈方 dialect〉家 home ❷房间 room: 他俩住一～。*The two of them share a room.*

恶(惡) wū ㄨ ❶(ancient) same as "乌(wū)❸" ❷文言叹词，表示惊讶 (exclamation in classical Chinese) oh: ～，是何言也！*Oh, what is this talk?!*

⇨ see also ě on p.158, è on p.158, wù on p.693

亡 wú ㄨˊ (ancient) same as "无"

⇨ see also wáng on p.675

无(無) wú ㄨˊ ❶没有，跟"有"相对 to not have; to be without (opposite of 有): ～限 *infinite* | 从～到有 *grow out of nothing* ❷不 not: ～须 *no need* | ～论 *no matter what* | ～妨 *might as well* [无非] 不过是，不外如此 nothing but; simply: 他批评你，～是想帮助你进步。*He was simply trying to help you move forward when he criticized you.* [无论] 连词，不拘，不管，常跟"都"连用 (conjunction) no matter (often used with 都): ～是谁都要遵守纪律。*Everybody has to observe disciplines; no matter who.*

芜(蕪) wú ㄨˊ 长满乱草(㊀荒－) overgrown with weeds; shaggy: ～城 *deserted city* ㊂杂乱 mixed and disorderly: ～杂 *mixed and disorderly* | ～词 *superfluous words*

毋 wú ㄨˊ 文言副词，不要，不可以 (adverb in classical Chinese) do not; cannot: 宁缺～滥 *rather go without than have sth shoddy*

吾 wú ㄨˊ 文言代词，我，我的 (pronoun in classical Chinese) I, my: ～爱～师。*I love my mentor.*

郚 wú ㄨˊ see 郿郚 (táng－) at 郿 on page 639

唔 wú ㄨˊ see 咿唔 (yī－) at 咿 on page 767

⇨ see also ń on p.466, ńg on p.474

峿 wú ㄨˊ see 峒峿 (sī－) at 峒 on page 616

浯 wú ㄨˊ 浯河，水名，在山东省东部 Wuhe River (in eastern Shandong Province)

珸 wú ㄨˊ [琨珸] (kūn－) 一种次于玉的美石 a kind of jade-like stone

梧 wú ㄨˊ 梧桐，落叶乔木，树干很直，叶掌状分裂，木质坚韧而轻，可用来制乐器或器具 Chinese parasol tree

铻(鋙) wú ㄨˊ see 锟铻 (kūn－) at 锟 on page 371

鼯 wú ㄨˊ 鼯鼠，哺乳动物，像松鼠，前后肢之间有薄膜，能从树上滑翔下来。住在树洞中，昼伏夜出 flying squirrel

吴 wú ㄨˊ ❶古国名 name of ancient states ①周代诸侯国

名，在今江苏省南部和浙江省北部，后来扩展到淮河下游一带 Wu (a state in the Zhou Dynasty, in today's southern Jiangsu and northern Zhejiang provinces, later extending to the lower reaches of the Huaihe River) ②三国之一，孙权所建立(公元 222—280 年)，在今长江中下游和东南沿海一带 one of the Three Kingdoms (222—280 AD, founded by Sun Quan, in today's middle and lower reaches of the Yangtze River and south-eastern coast) ❷指江苏省南部和浙江省北部一带 southern Jiangsu and northern Zhejiang provinces

蜈 wú ㄨˊ [蜈蚣](— gong) 节肢动物，身体长而扁，由许多环节构成，每节有脚一对，头部的脚像钩子，能分泌毒液。捕食小昆虫，可入药 centipede

鹀(鵐) wú ㄨˊ 鸟名，像麻雀，雄鸟羽毛颜色较鲜艳，吃种子和昆虫 bunting

五 wǔ ㄨˇ 数目字 five

伍 wǔ ㄨˇ ❶古代军队的编制，五个人为一伍 ancient military unit (of five soldiers)㊀军队 army：入～ *enlist in the army* ❷一伙 company：相与为～ *keep company with* ❸"五"字的大写 (elaborate form of 五， used in commercial or financial context) five

午 wǔ ㄨˇ ❶地支的第七位 *wu* (the seventh of the twelve Earthly Branches, a system used in the Chinese calendar) ❷午时，指白天十一点到一点 *wu* (the period from 11 a.m. to 1 p.m.)：～饭 *lunch* 特指白天十二点 noon：～前 *before noon* | 下～ *afternoon* [午夜] 半夜 midnight

仵 wǔ ㄨˇ 仵作，旧时官署中负责检验死伤的人员 (old) coroner

迕 wǔ ㄨˇ ❶相遇 to meet; to come across ❷逆，违背 to disobey; to defy：违～ *disobey*

忤(*啎) wǔ ㄨˇ 逆，不顺从 disobedient：～逆 *disobey (one's parents)*

旿 wǔ ㄨˇ 光明 bright

庑(廡) wǔ ㄨˇ 古代堂下周围的屋子 (ancient) side room in a traditional compound house

沅(潕) wǔ ㄨˇ 沅水，水名，在湖南省 Wushui River (in Hunan Province)

怃(憮) wǔ ㄨˇ 怃然，失意的样子 disappointed

妩(嫵、娬)** wǔ ㄨˇ [妩媚] (女子) 姿态美好 (of a woman) lovely; charming：～多姿 *charming and graceful*

武 wǔ ㄨˇ ❶关于军事或技击的，跟"文"相对 relating to the military or to martial arts (opposite of 文)：～装 *arms; military equipment* | ～术 *martial arts* | 动～ *use force* | 文～双全 *versed in both civil and martial arts* ❷勇

猛 valiant; fierce: 英～ *valiant* [武断] 只凭主观判断 to make an arbitrary assertion; arbitrary: 你这种看法太～。*Your opinion is quite arbitrary.* ❸半步 half a step: 行不数～ *before a few steps are taken* 泛指脚步 (generally) step: 步～整齐 *march in step*

珷 wǔ ㄨˇ [珷玞] (－fū) 一种像玉的石块 a kind of jade-like stone

鹉(鵡) wǔ ㄨˇ see 鹦鹉 (yīng－) at 鹦 on page 784

侮 wǔ ㄨˇ 欺负, 轻慢 (㊀－辱、欺－) to bully; to insult; to humiliate: 中国人民是不可～的。*The Chinese people are not to be bullied.* | 抵御外～ *fight against foreign aggression*

捂(摀)** wǔ ㄨˇ 严密地遮盖住或封闭起来 to cover; to seal: 用手～着嘴 *muffle one's mouth with one's hand* | 放在罐子里～起来免得走味儿 *seal it in a jar to keep its flavour*

牾 wǔ ㄨˇ 抵触, 冲突, 不顺从 to conflict with; to go against: 抵～ *conflict with*

舞 wǔ ㄨˇ ❶按一定的节奏转动身体表演各种姿势 to dance: 手～足蹈 *dance for joy* | ～剑 *perform a sword-dance* | 秧歌～ *Yangko dance* [鼓舞] 激励, 使人奋发振作 to inspire;to encourage: ～人心 *fill people with enthusiasm* ❷耍弄 to play tricks: ～弊 *to cheat* | ～文弄墨 *engage in phrase-mongering*

潕 wǔ ㄨˇ 潕阳河, 水名, 发源于贵州, 流到湖南叫沅水 Wuyanghe River (originating in Guizhou Province, flowing to Hunan Province where it is called 沅水)

兀 wù ㄨˋ ❶高而上平 tall and level on top ❷高耸特出 towering; lofty: 突～ *lofty*

屼 wù ㄨˋ 形容山秃 (of mountains) bare

杌 wù ㄨˋ 杌凳, 较矮的凳子 stool

[杌陧] (－niè) (局势、心情等) 不安 (of a situation or state of mind) unsettled

靰 wù ㄨˋ [靰鞡] (－la) 东北地区冬天穿的一种用皮革做的鞋, 里面垫着靰鞡草。也作"乌拉" leather boots lined with *wula* sedge, worn in winter in north-eastern China (also written as 乌拉)

勿 wù ㄨˋ 副词, 别, 不要 (adverb) do not: 请～动手! *No touching!* | 闻声～惊。*Don't be alarmed at the sound.*

芴 wù ㄨˋ 有机化合物, 白色片状晶体, 存在于煤焦油中。可用来制染料和药物等 fluorene

物 wù ㄨˋ ❶东西 thing: ～价 *prices* | 万～ *all things* | 事～ *things* ㊀具体内容 content; substance: 言之有～ *speak or write with substance* [物质] 1 独立于人们意识之外, 能为人们的意识所反映的客观存在 matter: ～不灭 *conservation of matter* | ～是可以被认识的。*Matter can be known.*

2 指金钱，供吃、穿、用的东西等 material：～丰富 *material supplies are abundant* ❷"我"以外的人或环境，多指众人 outside world (as distinct from oneself)：～我两忘 *oblivious to oneself and the outside world* | 待人接～ *the way one gets along with people*

乌（烏） wù ㄨˋ ［乌拉］（-la）same as "靰鞡"

⇨ see also wū on p.689

坞（塢、*隖） wù ㄨˋ ❶小障蔽物，防卫用的小堡 small fortification ❷四面高中间凹下的地方 hollow：山～ *col* | 花～ *sunken flowerbed* ［船坞］在水边建筑的停船或修造船只的地方 dock; dockyard

戊 wù ㄨˋ 天干的第五位，用作顺序的第五 *wu* (the fifth of the ten Heavenly Stems, a system used in the Chinese calendar); fifth

务（務） wù ㄨˋ ❶事情（㊀事－）affair：任～ *task* | 公～ *official business* | 医～室 *clinic* ❷从事，致力 to be engaged in：～农 *be a farmer* ❸追求 to pursue：～实 *be practical* | 不～虚名 *not pursue empty fame* ❹务必，必须，一定 must; be sure to：～请准时出席 *be sure to attend on time* | 除恶～尽 *one must remove evil to its roots*

雾（霧） wù ㄨˋ ❶接近地面的水蒸气，遇冷凝结后飘浮在空气中的微小水珠 fog; mist ❷像雾的东西 sth like mist：喷～器 *sprayer*

误（誤、**悮） wù ㄨˋ ❶错（㊀错－）wrong; mistake：～解 *misunderstand* | 讹～ *error* ❷耽误，耽搁 to hinder：～事 *cause a delay* | ～点 *be late* | 生产学习两不～ *keep up in both work and study* ❸因自己做错而使人受害 to hinder; to impede：～人子弟 *(of a teacher) mislead youngsters* ❹不是故意而做错事 mistakenly; accidentally：～伤 *injure by mistake* | ～入歧途 *go astray*

恶（惡） wù ㄨˋ 讨厌，憎恨 to loathe; to hate：可～ *detestable; loathsome* | 深～痛绝 *detest bitterly*

⇨ see also ě on p.158, è on p.158, wū on p.690

悟 wù ㄨˋ 理解，明白，觉醒（㊀醒－）to realize; to understand; to awaken：领～ *comprehend* | 恍然大～ *be suddenly enlightened* ［觉悟］1 由迷惑而明白 to realize; to become aware 2 指政治认识 political consciousness：提高～ *heighten political consciousness*

晤 wù ㄨˋ 遇，见面 to meet; to interview：～面 *meet* | ～谈 *meet and talk; interview* | 会～ *meet*

焐 wù ㄨˋ 用热的东西接触凉的东西，使它变暖 to warm up：用热水袋～一～手 *warm one's hands with a hot-water bottle*

痦（**瘑） wù ㄨˋ ［痦子］突起的痣 protruding mole

寤 wù ㄨˋ 睡醒 to wake up

婺 wù ㄨˋ 婺水，古水名，在江西省东北部 Wushui River (an ancient river in north-eastern Jiangxi Province)

骛（騖） wù ㄨˋ ❶乱跑 to run about：驰～ *gallop* ❷追求，致力 to strive for; to go after：好（hào）高～远 *reach for what is beyond one's grasp; aim too high* | 旁～ *be distracted by other pursuits*

鹜（鶩） wù ㄨˋ 鸭子 duck：趋之若～（像鸭子一样成群地跑过去，形容很多人争着去，含贬义）*(disapproving) rush to sth like a flock of ducks*

鋈 wù ㄨˋ ❶白色金属 copper-nickel alloy ❷镀 to plate

X T

XI T丨

夕 xī T丨 ❶日落的时候 sunset：朝（zhāo）～ *morning and evening* | ～照 *evening glow* ❷夜 evening; night：除～ *New Year's Eve* | 风雨之～ *stormy night*

汐 xī T丨 夜间的海潮 evening tide：潮～ *morning and evening tides*

矽 xī T丨 非金属元素硅（guī）的旧称 silicon (former name for the non-metallic element 硅)

穸 xī T丨 ［窀穸］（zhūn－）墓穴 grave; tomb

兮 xī T丨 文言助词，相当于现代的"啊" auxiliary word in classical Chinese, equivalent to 啊 in modern Chinese：大风起～云飞扬。*A great gale sweeps and the clouds fly across the sky.* | 魂～归来！*May the soul of the deceased return to us!*

西 xī T丨 ❶方向，太阳落下的一边，跟"东"相对 west (opposite of 东)：由～往东 *from west to east* | ～房 *west room* | ～南角 *southwest corner* ❷事物的样式或方法属于西方（多指欧、美两洲）的 Western：～餐 *Western food* | ～服 *Western suit*

茜 xī T丨 多用于人名（人名中也有读 qiàn 的）often used in given names (sometimes pronounced as qiàn in given names)

⇨ see also qiàn on p.529

恓 xī T丨 ［恓惶］（－huáng）惊慌烦恼的样子 vexed; upset

栖 xī T丨 ［栖栖］忙碌不安定的样子 restless; fidgety

⇨ see also qī on p.515

牺（犧） xī T丨 古代指用作祭品的毛色纯一的牲畜 (ancient) a beast of a uniform colour for sacrifice; sacrifice：～牛 *sacrificial ox* ［牺牲］古代为祭祀宰杀的牲畜 beast slaughtered for sacrifice in ancient times ㊕ 1 为人民、为正义事业而献出自己的生命 to sacrifice one's life 2 泛指为某种目的舍弃权利或利益等 (generally) to sacrifice one's rights or interests for a certain purpose; to give up

硒 xī T丨 非金属元素，符号 Se，灰色晶体或红色粉末，导电能力随光的照射强度的增减而改变。可用来制晶体管和光电管等 selenium (Se)

舾 xī T丨 船舶装备品 equipment and installations on a ship ［舾装］1 船舶装置和舱室设备（如锚、舵、缆、桅杆、救生设备、航行仪器、管路、电路等）的统称 out fitting (of a ship) 2 船体下水后，装备上述设备和刷油漆等工作 to out fit (a ship)

粞 xī ㄒㄧ 碎米 crushed rice：糠～ *bran and crushed rice*

吸 xī ㄒㄧ ❶从口或鼻把气体引入体内，跟“呼”相对 to inhale; to breathe in (opposite of 呼)：～气 *to inhale* | ～烟 *smoke a cigarette* ❷引取液体、固体 to absorb; to attract：棉花能～水。*Cotton absorbs water.* | ～墨纸 *blotting paper* | ～铁石 *magnet* | ～尘器 *vacuum cleaner* [吸收] 摄取，采纳 to absorb; to take in：植物由根～养分。*Plants absorb nutrients by way of their roots.* | ～先进经验 *assimilate good experiences from others*

希 xī ㄒㄧ ❶少 rare; scarce; uncommon：物以～为贵。*What is scarce is precious.* ❷盼望(㊜－望) to hope：～准时出席。*Please be present on time.* | ～早日归来。*I look forward to your early return.*

俙 xī ㄒㄧ 当面对质 to confront (in a law court)

郗 xī ㄒㄧ (formerly pronounced chī) 姓 (surname) Xi

唏 xī ㄒㄧ 叹息 to whimper; to sob [唏嘘] [嘘唏] 抽搭，哭泣后不自主地急促呼吸 to sob; to whimper

浠 xī ㄒㄧ 浠河，水名，在湖北省黄冈 Xihe River (in Huanggang, Hubei Province)

晞 xī ㄒㄧ ❶干，干燥 dry; arid：晨露未～。*The morning dew has not dried yet.* ❷破晓，天亮 daybreak：东方未～ *before the day has dawned*

欷 xī ㄒㄧ [欷歔] (－xū) same as “唏嘘”

烯 xī ㄒㄧ 烯烃，有机化合物的一类，分子中含有双键结构 alkene; olefin

睎 xī ㄒㄧ ❶瞭望 to keep a lookout ❷仰慕 to admire

稀 xī ㄒㄧ ❶事物间距离远、空隙大，跟“密”相对(㊜－疏) sparse; thinly scattered (opposite of 密)：棉花种得太～了。*The cotton seeds were sown too thinly.* | ～客 *rare visitor* ❷浓度小，含水分多的，跟“稠”相对(㊜－薄) thin; watery (opposite of 浓)：～饭 *porridge; rice or millet gruel* | ～米汤 *thin millet gruel* | ～泥 *watery mud* | ～释 *to dilute* ❸少(㊜－少、－罕) rare; scarce; uncommon：～有金属 *rare metal*

豨 xī ㄒㄧ 古书上指猪 (in ancient Chinese texts) pig

[豨莶] (－xiān) 草本植物，茎上有灰白的毛，花黄色。全草可入药 common St. Paul's wort

昔 xī ㄒㄧ 从前 former times; the past：～日 *former days* | 今～ *the present and the past*

惜 xī ㄒㄧ ❶爱惜，重视，不随便丢弃 to cherish; to treasure：～阴(爱惜时间) *value every moment* | ～墨如金 *be scrupulous and succinct in writing or painting* [怜惜] 爱惜，同情 feel tender sympathy for; have pity on ❷舍不得(㊜吝－) to spare; to grudge：～别 *be reluctant to part* | 不～牺牲 *spare no sacrifice* | ～指失掌(喻因小失大) *spare a finger only to lose the whole hand* | 在所不～ *balk at nothing* ❸可惜，

感到遗憾 to regret; to deplore: 痛～ *deeply regret* | ～未成功 *feel pity for the failure*

腊 xī ㄒㄧ 干肉 dried meat
⇨ see also là on p.374

析 xī ㄒㄧ 分开 to divide; to slice: 条分缕～ *make a careful and detailed analysis* | 分崩离～ *fall to pieces* ㊀解释 to explain; to analyse: ～疑 *resolve doubts* | 分～ *to analyse; analysis*

菥 xī ㄒㄧ [菥蓂] (－mì) 草本植物，又叫遏蓝菜，叶匙形，花白色，果实扁圆形。叶可用作蔬菜，种子可榨油，全草可入药 Boor's mustard herb (also called 遏蓝菜)

淅 xī ㄒㄧ 淘米 to wash rice [淅沥] (－lì) 形容轻微的风雨声或落叶声等 (of rain) to patter; (of wind or falling leaves) to rustle

晰(*晳) xī ㄒㄧ 明白，清楚 clear; distinct: 清～ *distinct* | 明～ *lucid*

晳 xī ㄒㄧ 人的皮肤白 fair-skinned: 白～ *light-complexioned*

蜥 xī ㄒㄧ [蜥蜴] (－yì) 爬行动物，俗叫四脚蛇，身上有细鳞，尾巴很长，脚上有钩爪，生活在草丛里 lizard (informal 四脚蛇)

肸 xī ㄒㄧ 用于人名。羊舌肸，春秋时晋国大夫 used in given names, e.g. Yangshe Xi, a senior official in the State of Jin in the Spring and Autumn Period

饻(餏) xī ㄒㄧ 老解放区一种计算工资的单位，一饻等于几种实物价格的总和 a monetary unit in the communist-ruled areas (liberated areas) before 1949

息 xī ㄒㄧ ❶呼吸时进出的气 breath: 鼻～ *breathing* | 喘～ *to pant* | 叹～ *to sigh* ❷停止，歇 to stop; to rest: ～怒 *calm one's anger* | 经久不～ *prolonged; lasting* | 按时作～ *work and rest on schedule* ❸消息 news: 信～ *message* | 声～ *sound* ❹利钱 interest: 年～ *annual interest rate* | 无～贷款 *interest-free loan* ❺儿女 one's children: 子～ *children (of sb)* ❻繁殖，滋生 to grow; to multiply: 生～ *to grow* | 蕃～ *multiply greatly*

熄 xī ㄒㄧ 火灭，使灭(㊥－灭) (of fire, etc.) to die out; to put out: 炉火已～。*The stove fire has died out.* | ～灯 *turn off the light*

螅 xī ㄒㄧ [水螅] 腔肠动物，身体圆筒形，上端有小触手，附着 (zhuó) 在池沼、水沟中的水草上 hydra

奚 xī ㄒㄧ ❶古代指奴隶 (ancient) slave ❷文言代词，表示疑问，相当于"何" (pronoun in classical Chinese, equivalent to 何) why; what; how; where
[奚落] 讥诮，嘲笑 to scoff at

傒 xī ㄒㄧ [傒倖] (－xìng) 烦恼，焦躁 to be vexed; restless with anxiety

徯 xī ㄒㄧ ❶等待 to wait ❷same as "蹊"

溪(△*谿) xī ㄒㄧ 山里的小河沟 brook

蹊 xī ㄒㄧ 小路（㊀—径）footpath

⇨ see also qī on p.516

谿 xī ㄒㄧ ❶ see 溪 on page 697 ❷姓 (surname) Xi

鸂（鸂） xī ㄒㄧ ［鸂鶒］（—chì）古书上指像鸳鸯的一种水鸟 (in ancient Chinese texts) a kind of water bird similar to mandarin duck

鼷 xī ㄒㄧ ［鼷鼠］小家鼠 house mouse

悉 xī ㄒㄧ ❶知道 to know; to learn：获～ *get to know* | 熟～此事 *know the matter well* ❷尽，全 entire; total：～心 *with utmost care* | ～数捐献 *donate all* | ～听尊便。*It's all up to you.*

窸 xī ㄒㄧ ［窸窣］（—sū）形容细小的摩擦声 to rustle

蟋 xī ㄒㄧ ［蟋蟀］（—shuài）昆虫，身体黑褐色，雄的好斗，两翅摩擦能发声 cricket

翕 xī ㄒㄧ ❶合，收敛 to furl; to shut：～动 *close and open* | ～张 *furl and unfurl* ❷和顺 amiable and compliant

［翕忽］迅速的样子 fast; speedy

噏 xī ㄒㄧ same as "吸"

歙 xī ㄒㄧ 吸气 to sniff; to inhale

⇨ see also shè on p.587

熻 xī ㄒㄧ ❶燃烧 to burn; to ignite ❷火光，光亮 flare; blaze

犀 xī ㄒㄧ ❶犀牛，哺乳动物，略像牛，皮粗厚多皱纹，几乎无毛，鼻子上长一个角或两个角，产于亚洲和非洲 rhinoceros ❷坚固 stable; solid：～利（锐利）*sharp*

樨 xī ㄒㄧ ［木樨］即桂花 same as 桂花

锡（錫） xī ㄒㄧ ❶金属元素，符号 Sn，银白色，质软，在空气中不易起变化。可用来制合金或焊接金属等 tin (Sn) ❷赏赐 to bestow

［锡伯族］（—bó—）我国少数民族，参看附录四 the Xibe people (one of the ethnic groups in China. See Appendix Ⅳ.)

裼 xī ㄒㄧ 敞开或脱去上衣，露出身体的一部分（㊀袒—）unbutton or remove one's upper garment and bare one's chest or upper body

⇨ see also tì on p.648

熙（*熈、*煕） xī ㄒㄧ ❶光明 bright ❷和乐 ㊂ harmonious and happy：众人～～ *everyone happy and gay* ❸ (ancient) same as "嬉"

［熙攘］（—rǎng）形容人来人往，非常热闹 boisterous; bustling with activity：熙熙攘攘 *hustle and bustle*

僖 xī ㄒㄧ 快乐 joyful

嘻 xī ㄒㄧ 喜笑的样子或声音 ㊂ to giggle：笑～～ *giggling* | ～～哈哈 *laughing and joking*

嬉 xī ㄒㄧ 游戏，玩耍 to play：～闹 *laugh and frolic* | ～皮笑脸 *grin cheekily; be comically cheerful*

熹 xī ㄒㄧ 光明 bright ［熹微］日光微明 (of sunlight at dawn) faint

嘻 xī ㄒㄧ 炽热 blazing hot

嶲 xī ㄒㄧ ［越嶲］地名，在四川省。今作“越西”Yuexi (a place in Sichuan Province, now written as 越西)

酅 xī ㄒㄧ ❶古地名。春秋时纪国乡邑，在今山东省临淄东。又，春秋时齐国属地，在今山东省东阿南 Xi (an ancient town of state Ji, also a colony of state Qi, in the Spring and Autumn Period, both in today's Shandong Province) ❷姓 (surname) Xi

觿 xī ㄒㄧ 古代用骨头等制的解绳结的锥子 an ancient tool made of bone for untying a knot of a rope

膝(*厀) xī ㄒㄧ 膝盖，大腿和小腿相连的关节的前部 knee (see picture of 人体 on page 647)

羲 xī ㄒㄧ 姓 (surname) Xi

曦 xī ㄒㄧ 阳光 sunlight：晨～ *early morning sunlight*

爔 xī ㄒㄧ same as “曦”

釐 xī ㄒㄧ ❶〈古 ancient〉same as “僖” ❷姓 (surname) Xi

⇨ see also lí 厘 on p.387

醯 xī ㄒㄧ ❶醋 vinegar ❷ former name for 酰 (xiān)

巇 xī ㄒㄧ ［险巇］形容山险 precipitous; steep ㊀道路艰难 (of road) treacherous

习(習) xí ㄒㄧˊ ❶学过后再温熟，反复地学使熟练 to study; to learn; to review; to practise：自～ *study by oneself* | 复～ *review (lessons)* | ～字 *practise penmanship* | ～作 *do exercise in composition; exercise in composition, drawing, etc.* ❷对某事熟悉 to be accustomed to; to be familiar with：～兵（熟于军事）*knowledgeable in military affairs* ㊀常常 often：～见 *commonly seen* | ～闻 *often hear of* ❸习惯，长期重复地做，逐渐养成的不自觉的行为 habit; usual practice：积～ *old habit* | ～气 *bad practice* | 恶～ *bad habit* | 相沿成～ *become customary through long-term practice*

嶍 xí ㄒㄧˊ ［嶍峨］(－é)山名，在云南省玉溪 Xi'e (a mountain in Yuxi, Yunnan Province)

鳛(鰼) xí ㄒㄧˊ ❶古书上指泥鳅 (in ancient Chinese texts) loach ❷鳛水，地名，在贵州省。今作“习水”Xishui (now written as 习水, a place in Guizhou Province)

席(❶*蓆) xí ㄒㄧˊ ❶(－子)用草或苇子等编成的东西，通常用来铺(pū)床或炕 mat ❷座位 seat; place：出～(到场) *be present;to attend* | 缺～(不到场) *be absent* | 入～ *take one's place* ❸特指议会中的席位，表示当选的人数 seat (in a legislative assembly) ❹酒席，成桌的饭菜 feast; banquet; dinner：摆了两桌～ *give a banquet of two tables*

觋(覡) xí ㄒㄧˊ 男巫 sorcerer

袭(襲) xí ㄒㄧˊ ❶袭击，趁敌人不备给以攻击

to raid; to make a surprise attack (on): *夜～ night raid* | *空～ air raid* ❷照样做，照样继续下去 to follow the pattern; to copy; to imitate: *因～ carry on (old customs, rules, etc.)* | *沿～ carry on as before* | *世～ hereditary; inherit* ❸量词，用于成套的衣服 (measure word for clothing) suit: *衣一～ a suit of clothes*

郋 xí ㄒㄧˊ 姓 (surname) Xi

媳 xí ㄒㄧˊ 儿媳，儿子的妻子 daughter-in-law［媳妇］儿子的妻子 daughter-in-law［媳妇儿（-fur）］1 妻子 wife: *兄弟～ brother's wife; sister-in-law* 2 已婚的年轻妇女 married young woman: *新～ newly married young woman*

骽(騱) xí ㄒㄧˊ 前足全白的马 horse with white front hoofs

隰 xí ㄒㄧˊ ❶低湿的地方 damp low-lying land ❷新开垦的田地 newly cultivated land

檄 xí ㄒㄧˊ 檄文，古代用于征召或声讨等的文书 (ancient) official call to arms; denunciation of the enemy

洗 xǐ ㄒㄧˇ ❶用水去掉污垢（㊀-涤）to wash: *～衣服 wash clothes* | *～脸 wash one's face*［洗礼］1 基督教接受人入教时所举行的一种仪式 the rite of baptism 2 指经受的锻炼和考验 severe test; ordeal: *战斗的～ test of battle*［洗手］比喻盗贼等不再偷抢 wash one's hands of sth; (figurative) give up (a vocation, hobby, etc.) ❷清除干净 to clear away; to eliminate: *清～ to purge; to rinse* ❸冲洗，照相的显影定影 to develop photos: *～相片 develop photos* ❹洗雪 to redress; to clear (of charges, etc.): *～冤 redress a wrong* ❺如水洗一样抢光，杀光 to kill and loot; to sack: *～城 massacre the inhabitants and rob everything of a captured city* | *～劫一空 loot everything* ❻掺和整理 to shuffle (cards, etc.): *～牌 shuffle cards*

⇨ see also xiǎn on p.708

铣(銑) xǐ ㄒㄧˇ 用能旋转的多刃刀具切削加工金属工件 to mill: *～床 milling machine* | *～刀 milling cutter*

⇨ see also xiǎn on p.708

枲 xǐ ㄒㄧˇ 枲麻，大麻的雄株，只开花，不结果实 male hemp plant

玺(璽) xǐ ㄒㄧˇ 印，自秦代以后专指皇帝的印 seal; royal seal (since the Qin Dynasty): *玉～ imperial jade seal*

徙 xǐ ㄒㄧˇ 迁移（㊀迁-）to move; to migrate

蓰 xǐ ㄒㄧˇ 五倍 five fold: *倍～（数倍）multiplied*

屣 xǐ ㄒㄧˇ 鞋 shoe

喜 xǐ ㄒㄧˇ ❶高兴，快乐（㊀-欢、欢-）to be happy; to be joyous: *～出望外 overjoyed* ❷可庆贺的，特指关于结婚的 joyful; relating to wedding: *要节约办～事 should economize on wedding* ❸妇

女怀孕叫"有喜"pregnancy (called "有喜") ❹爱好 to like: ～闻乐见 *love to see and hear* ❺适于 suitable: 海带～荤。*Kelp goes well with meat.* | 植物一般都～光。*Most plants are photophilic.*

憙 xǐ ㄒㄧˇ ❶喜悦 joyful ❷喜好 to like; to love

禧 xǐ ㄒㄧˇ ❶ (formerly pronounced xī) 福, 吉祥 auspiciousness ❷ 喜庆 festivity; joyous event: 新～ *happy in the new year*

饎(饎) xǐ ㄒㄧˇ 人造的放射性金属元素，符号 Sg。seaborgium (Sg)

蟢 xǐ ㄒㄧˇ 蟢子（也作"喜子"），又叫喜蛛、蟏蛸（xiāoshāo），一种长（cháng）腿的小蜘蛛 a long-legged spider (also written as 喜子 and called 喜蛛，蟏蛸 xiāoshāo)

鱚(鱚) xǐ ㄒㄧˇ 鱼名，又叫沙钻（zuàn），身体近圆筒形，银灰色，嘴尖，眼大。生活在近海沙底 sand borer (also called 沙钻 zuàn)

葸 xǐ ㄒㄧˇ 害怕，畏惧 to be scared; to fear: 畏～不前 *be too frightened to go forward*

戏(戲、*戯) xì ㄒㄧˋ ❶玩耍 to play: 游～ *game; to play* | 儿～ *be hasty and responsible; trifling matter* ❷嘲弄，开玩笑 to make fun of; to play a joke on: ～言 *joke* | ～弄 *play tricks on;to tease* ❸戏剧，也指杂技 drama; show: 一出～ *a play* | 唱～ *perform an opera* | 听～ *go to the theatre* | 马～ *circus show* | 皮影～ *shadow play*

⇨ see also hū on p.257

饩(餼) xì ㄒㄧˋ ❶古代指赠送人的粮食 (ancient) grain as gift ❷赠送（谷物、饲料、牲畜等）to present (grains, fodder or livestock) as gift

系(❸❺係、❸❹❻繫) xì ㄒㄧˋ ❶系统，有连属关系的 system; series: ～列 *series* | 水～ *river system* | 世～ *bloodline; genealogy* ❷高等学校中按学科分的教学单位 department; faculty: 中文～ *department of Chinese* | 化学～ *department of chemistry* ❸关联 to relate to; to bear on: 干～ *connection; implication* ❹联结，拴 to tie; to fasten: ～马 *tether a horse* ㊂ 牵挂 to be concerned: ～念 *feel concerned about* | 情～于民 *be concerned about the people* [联系] 联络，接头 to contact: 时常和他～ *keep in touch with him* ❺是 to be: 确～实情 *be indeed the truth* ❻把人或东西捆住往上提或向下送 to fasten and lift or lower with a rope: 从房上把东西～下来 *lower sth down from the roof* ❼地层系统分类的第三级，在"界"之下，是在地质年代"纪"的时期内形成的地层 system (the subdivision of erathem in stratigraphic classification): 第四～ *the Quaternary system* | 侏罗～ *the Jurassic system* | 寒武～ *the Cambrian system*

⇨ see also jì on p.291

屃(屓、屭)** xì ㄒㄧˋ see 赑屃(bì—) at 赑 on page 36

细(細) xì ㄒㄧˋ ❶跟"粗"相对 thin; fine (opposite of 粗) ①颗粒小的 fine; in small particles: ～沙 *fine sand* | ～末 *fine dust* ②长条东西直径小的 thin; slender: ～竹竿 *thin bamboo pole* | ～铅丝 *thin lead wire* ③精细 fine; exquisite: 江西～瓷 *fine porcelain from Jiangxi* | 这块布真～。*This is an exquisite piece of cloth.* ④声音小 (of sound) thin and soft: 嗓音～ *a thin voice* ⑤周密 careful; meticulous: 胆大心～ *brave and cautious* | 精打～算 *be meticulous in reckoning* | 深耕～作 *deep ploughing and intensive cultivation* ❷细小的，不重要的 trifle: ～节 *detail* | 事无巨～ *all matters, big or small*

盻 xì ㄒㄧˋ 怒视 to glare at: 瞋目～之 *glare at sb*

咥 xì ㄒㄧˋ 大笑的样子 laughing
⇨ see also dié on p.137

郤 xì ㄒㄧˋ ❶ same as "隙" ❷姓 (surname) Xi

绤(綌) xì ㄒㄧˋ 粗葛布 coarse linen

阋(鬩) xì ㄒㄧˋ 争吵 to quarrel [阋墙] 弟兄们在家里互相争吵 (of brothers) quarrel at home ㊗内部不和 internal strife

舄 xì ㄒㄧˋ 鞋 shoe

潟 xì ㄒㄧˋ 咸水浸渍的土地 land impregnated with salt: ～卤(盐碱地) *saline-alkaline soil*

隙 xì ㄒㄧˋ ❶裂缝(㊥缝－) crack; crevice: 墙～ *crack in a wall* | 门～ *narrow opening of a door* ㊗①感情上的裂痕 discord; rift: 嫌～ *grudge* ②空(kòng)子，机会 loophole; opportunity: 乘～ *take advantage of an opportunity* ❷空(kòng)，没有东西的 open; empty: ～地 *unoccupied place; vacant plot*

禊 xì ㄒㄧˋ 古代春秋两季在水边举行的意在除去所谓不祥的祭祀 ancient cleansing ritual held in spring and autumn on water's edge

滃 xì ㄒㄧˋ 水急流的声音 gushing (of water)

XIA ㄒㄧㄚ

呷 xiā ㄒㄧㄚ 小口儿地喝 to sip: ～茶 *sip tea* | ～一口酒 *take a sip of wine*

虾(蝦) xiā ㄒㄧㄚ 节肢动物，身体长，有壳，腹部有很多环节，生活在水里。种类很多 shrimp; prawn
⇨ see also há on p.237

瞎 xiā ㄒㄧㄚ ❶眼睛看不见东西 to be blind; blind ❷副词，胡乱地，没来由地 (adverb) blindly; aimlessly: ～忙 *be busy for nothing* | ～说八道 *talk nonsense* ❸〈方 dialect〉乱 tangled: 把线弄～了 *tangled up the yarn* ❹〈方 dialect〉农作物籽粒不饱满 (of grain) blind: ～穗 *blind wheatear* | ～高粱 *blind sorghum plant*

匣 xiá ㄒㄧㄚˊ （一子、一儿）收藏东西的器具，通常指小型的，有盖可以开合 small box [话匣子] 1 留声机的俗称 (informal name for 留声机) gramophone 2 指话多的人（含讽刺义）chatterbox

狎 xiá ㄒㄧㄚˊ 亲近而态度不庄重 to be improperly familiar with: ～昵 *be improperly familiar with* | ～侮 *to slight*

柙 xiá ㄒㄧㄚˊ 关猛兽的木笼。旧时也指押解犯人的囚笼或囚车 wooden cage (to lock up beasts or prisoners)

翈 xiá ㄒㄧㄚˊ 羽毛主干两侧的部分 barb of a feather

侠(俠) xiá ㄒㄧㄚˊ 旧称依仗个人力量帮助被欺侮者的人或行为 (old) chivalrous person or deed: 武～ *swordsman; knight-errant* | ～客 *knight-errant* | ～义 *chivalry* | ～骨 *chivalry* | ～肝义胆 *chivalry and loyalty*

峡(峽) xiá ㄒㄧㄚˊ 两山夹水的地方 gorge: ～谷 *canyon* | 长江三～ *the Three Gorges on the Yangtze River* [地峡] 海洋中连接两块陆地的狭窄陆地 isthmus [海峡] 两块陆地之间连接两个海域的狭窄水道 strait: 台湾～ *the Taiwan Straits*

狭(狹、*陿) xiá ㄒㄧㄚˊ 窄，不宽阔（㊀一窄、一隘）narrow: 地方太～ *too narrow a space* | ～路相逢（指仇敌相遇）*(of adversaries) come into unavoidable confrontation*

硖(硤) xiá ㄒㄧㄚˊ [硖石] 地名，在浙江省海宁 Xiashi (a place in Haining, Zhejiang Province)

叚 xiá ㄒㄧㄚˊ 姓 (surname) Xia ⇨ see also jiǎ 假 on p.298

遐 xiá ㄒㄧㄚˊ ❶远 far; distant: ～迩（远近）*far and near* | ～方 *remote place* | ～想 *daydream* ❷长久 lasting: ～龄（高龄）*advanced age*

瑕 xiá ㄒㄧㄚˊ 玉上面的斑点 flaw in a piece of jade; blemish ㊉ 缺点（㊀一疵）flaw; shortcoming; imperfection: ～瑜互见 *have both strong and weak points* | 纯洁无～ *pure and unblemished* | ～不掩瑜 *one flaw does not mar a piece of good jade*

暇 xiá ㄒㄧㄚˊ 空（kòng）闲，没有事的时候 leisure; free time: 得～ *have free time* | 无～ *have no time* | 自顾不～（连自己都顾不过来）*unable even to fend for oneself (let alone others)*

霞 xiá ㄒㄧㄚˊ 因受日光斜照而呈现红、橙、黄等颜色的云 rosy clouds; morning or evening glow: ～光 *rays of morning or evening sunlight* | 朝（zhāo）～ *morning glow* | 晚～ *evening glow*

辖(轄、❶鎋、❶**舝)** xiá ㄒㄧㄚˊ ❶车轴头上穿着的小铁棍，可使轮不脱落 linchpin (see picture of 旧式车轮 on page 426) ❷管理（㊀管一）to administer; to govern: 直～ *directly under the jurisdiction of* | 统～ *have*

X

under one's command | ～区 *area under one's jurisdiction*

黠 xiá ㄒㄧㄚˊ 聪明而狡猾 crafty; cunning：狡～ *sly* | 慧～ *shrewd; clever and artful*

下 xià ㄒㄧㄚˋ ❶位置在低处的，跟"上"相对 below; down; under (opposite of 上)：～面 *under; below* | 楼～ *downstairs* | 山～ *at the foot of the mountain* ㉄①次序靠后的 next; latter：～篇 *next chapter* | ～卷 *the last volume (of a two or three-volume book)* | ～月 *next month* ②等级低的 lower in rank：～级服从上级。*Lower ranks are subordinate to higher ones.* 谦辞 (humble speech) I; me; my：正中（zhòng）～怀（正合自己的心意）*suit me just right* ③质量低的 lower in quality：～品 *low grade item* | ～策 *the worse (of two or three) plan/strategy/measure; stupid move* ❷由高处到低处 to descend：～山 *go down the mountain* | ～楼 *go downstairs* ㉄①进 to go in：～水游泳 *jump in water to swim* ②离开 to leave：～班 *go off work* | ～课 *finish class* ③往……去 to go to：～乡 *go down to the country side* | ～江南 *go on a tour to Jiangnan (typically area south of the lower reaches of the Yangtze River)* ④投送，颁布 to issue; to deliver：～书 *deliver a letter* | ～令 *issue orders* ⑤向下面 downward：～达 *make known to lower levels* | 权力～放 *transfer powers to a lower level* ⑥降落 (of rain, snow, etc.) to fall：～雨 *to rain* | ～雪 *to snow* ❸方面，方位 side; direction：两～里都同意 *both parties agree* | 向四～一看 *look all around* ❹减除 to take off ①卸掉 to unload; to take off：～货 *unload goods* ②除去 to get rid of：～火 *dampen (bodily) fire (a concept in traditional Chinese medicine, sometimes taken as akin to inflammation)* | ～泥 *rub off dirt (on the skin)* ❺用 to apply：～工夫 *make efforts* ❻攻克，攻陷 to capture：连～数城 *capture several cities in succession* | 攻～ *to capture* ❼退让 to give in; to yield：各不相～ *neither would yield* ❽用在名词后 used after a noun ①表示在里面 inside：言～ *the implied* | 意～ *intention* | 都～（京城之内）*within the capital city* ②表示当某个时节 at (a point in time)：年～ *around New Year's day* | 节～ *period before or around a major festival* ❾用在动词后 used after a verb ①表示属于一定范围、情况、条件等 within a certain extent, under certain conditions, etc.：属～ *subordinate* | 鼓舞～ *encouraged by* | 在老师指导～ *under the teacher's guidance* ②表示动作的完成或结果 indicating completion or result of an action：打～基础 *lay foundations* | 准备～材料 *prepare the materials* ③跟"来""去"连用表示趋向或继续 used with 来 or 去 to indicate a tendency or continuation：滑～去 *slip down* | 慢慢停～来 *gradually slow down* |

念～去 *continue reading* ❿（－子、－儿）量词，指动作的次数 (measure word) time：打十～ *hit ten times* | 轮子转了两～子。*The wheel turned a few turns.* ⓫（动物）生产 (of animals) to give birth to：猫～小猫了。*The cat gave birth to kittens.* | 鸡～蛋。*A hen lays eggs.* ⓬少于（某数）fewer than：不～三百人 *no fewer than three hundred people*

吓(嚇) xià ㄒㄧㄚˋ 使害怕 to frighten; to intimidate：困难～不倒英雄汉。*Real heroes will not be scared of difficulties.* [吓唬]（－hu）使人害怕，威胁 to threaten; to intimidate：你别～人。*Don't you try to scare people.*

⇨ see also hè on p.249

夏 xià ㄒㄧㄚˋ ❶四季中的第二季，气候最热 summer ❷华夏，中国的古名 Huaxia (ancient name for China) ❸朝代名 Xia Dynasty ①夏代，传说是禹（一说启）建立的（约公元前 2070—公元前 1600 年）Xia Dynasty (2070—1600 BC, founded by Yu, some say Qi, according to legend) ②西夏，党项族元昊建立（公元 1038—1227 年）Western Xia Dynasty (1038—1227, founded by Yuan Hao of the Dangxiang ethnic group)

厦(*廈) xià ㄒㄧㄚˋ [厦门] 地名，在福建省 Xiamen (a place in Fujian Province)

⇨ see also shà on p.575

唬 xià ㄒㄧㄚˋ same as "吓"

⇨ see also hǔ on p.259

罅 xià ㄒㄧㄚˋ 裂缝 crack; rift：云～ *rift in the clouds*

XIAN ㄒㄧㄢ

仙(*僊) xiān ㄒㄧㄢ 神话中称有特殊能力，可以长生不死的人 celestial being; immortal; fairy

氙 xiān ㄒㄧㄢ 气体元素，符号 Xe，无色、无味、无臭，不易跟其他元素化合。把氙装入真空管中通电，能发蓝色的光 xenon (Xe)

籼(*秈) xiān ㄒㄧㄢ 籼稻，水稻的一种，米粒细而长 long-grain rice

先 xiān ㄒㄧㄢ ❶时间在前的，次序在前的 earlier; first：占～ *take the lead* | 首～ *first of all* | 领～ *be in the lead* | 争～恐后 *strive to be the first and fear to lag behind* [先进] 进步快，水平高，值得推广和学习的 advanced ❷副词，暂时 (adverb) for the moment：这件事～放一放，以后再考虑。*Let's put the matter off for now. We can consider it later.* ❸祖先，上代 ancestor; older generation：～人 *ancestor; forefather* | ～辈 *forefather; older generation* ❹对死去的人的尊称 the late：～父 *my late father* | ～烈 *martyr*

酰 xiān ㄒㄧㄢ 酰基，由含氧酸的分子失去一个羟基而成的原子团 acyl

X

纤(纖) xiān ㄒㄧㄢ 细小 fine; tiny; slim [纤尘] 细小的灰尘 fine dust: ～不染 *be spotlessly clean; maintain one's purity* [纤维] 细长像丝的物质。一般分成天然纤维和合成纤维两大类 fibre

⇨ see also qiàn on p.529

跹(蹮) xiān ㄒㄧㄢ see 蹁跹 (pián－) at 蹁 on page 504

忺 xiān ㄒㄧㄢ 高兴，适意 happy; enjoyable

掀 xiān ㄒㄧㄢ 揭起，打开 to lift (a cover, etc.); to open up: ～锅盖 *take the lid off the pot* | ～帘子 *lift the curtain* ⓘ翻动，兴起 to cause to surge; to start: 白浪～天 *white waves surge up high* | ～起生产热潮 *set off a new surge in production*

锨(鍁、**杴、**枕) xiān ㄒㄧㄢ 铲东西用的一种工具，用钢铁或木头制成板状的头，后面安把儿 shovel: 木～ *wooden shovel* | 铁～ *iron shovel*

祆 xiān ㄒㄧㄢ [祆教] 拜火教，公元前 6 世纪波斯人创立，崇拜火，南北朝时传入我国 Zoroastrianism (started in Persia in the 6th century BC, spread to China during the Northern and Southern dynasties)

莶(薟) xiān ㄒㄧㄢ see 豨莶 (xī－) at 豨 on page 696

妗(嬐) xiān ㄒㄧㄢ ❶敏捷快速 brisk; sprightly ❷庄重恭敬 solemn and respectful

铦(銛) xiān ㄒㄧㄢ ❶古代一种兵器 a kind of weapon in ancient times ❷锋利 sharp

鲜(鮮、❶-❹*鱻) xiān ㄒㄧㄢ ❶新的，不陈的，不干枯的(连新－) fresh: ～果 *fresh fruit* | ～花 *fresh flower* | ～肉 *fresh meat* | ～血 *blood* ❷滋味美好(连－美) fresh and delicious; tasty: 这汤真～。*The soup is so delicious.* ❸有光彩的 brightly coloured: ～红 *bright red* | ～艳 *brightly coloured* | ～明 *clear-cut* ❹新鲜的食物 fresh and delicious food: 尝～ *taste a fresh delicacy* ❺姓 (surname) Xian

[鲜卑族] (－bēi－) 我国古代北方民族 the Xianbei people (an ancient ethnic group in northern China)

⇨ see also xiǎn on p.709

暹 xiān ㄒㄧㄢ [暹罗] 泰国的旧称 former name for 泰国

骞(騫) xiān ㄒㄧㄢ 高飞的样子 flying high

孅 xiān ㄒㄧㄢ 〈古 ancient〉细小 tiny

伭 xián ㄒㄧㄢˊ xuán ㄒㄩㄢˊ(又) 姓 (surname) Xian; Xuan

弦(❶❹*絃) xián ㄒㄧㄢˊ ❶弓上发箭的绳状物 bowstring ❷月亮半圆 crescent: 上～ *the first quarter of the moon* | 下～ *the last quarter of the moon* ❸数学名词 mathematical term ①连接圆周上任意两点的线段 chord ②我国古代称不等腰直角三角形中的斜边 (ancient) hypotenuse ❹(－儿) 乐器上发

声的线 (of a musical instrument) string ❺ 钟表等的发条 (of a clock) spring：表～断了。*The watch spring broke.*

玹 xián ㄒㄧㄢˊ 姓 (surname) Xian
⇨ see also xuán on p.738, xuàn on p.739

舷 xián ㄒㄧㄢˊ 船、飞机等左右两侧的边儿 side of a ship or aircraft

闲（閑、❶–❸*閒）xián ㄒㄧㄢˊ ❶没有事情做（㊥一暇）not busy; idle：没有～工夫 *have no time to spare* ㊀ 放着，不使用 not in use; unoccupied：～房 *vacant room or house* | 机器别～着。*Don't let the machine lie idle.* ❷没有事情做的时候 spare time; leisure：农～ *slack season in farming* | 忙里偷～ *snatch a little leisure from a busy life* ❸与正事无关的 irrelevant; digressive：～谈 *chitchat* | ～人免进。*No admittance. Staff only.* [闲话] 与正事无关的话，背后不负责的议论 chitchat; gossip：讲别人的～ *to gossip* ❹栅栏 railings; fence ❺防御 to defend：防～ *guard and hinder*
⇨ 閒 see also jiān 间 on p.300, jiàn 间 on p.304

娴（嫻、*嫺）xián ㄒㄧㄢˊ ❶熟练（㊥一熟）adept; skilled：～于辞令 *have a silver tongue* ❷文雅 refined; elegant：～静 *gentle and refined* | ～雅 *refined and elegant*

痫（癇）xián ㄒㄧㄢˊ 癫痫，俗叫羊痫风或羊角风，一种时犯时愈的暂时性大脑功能紊乱的病，病发时突然昏倒，口吐泡沫，手足痉挛 epilepsy (informal 羊痫风 or 羊角风)

鹇（鷳）xián ㄒㄧㄢˊ 白鹇，鸟名，尾巴长，雄的背部白色，有黑纹，腹部黑蓝色，雌的全身棕绿色 silver pheasant

贤（賢）xián ㄒㄧㄢˊ ❶有道德的，有才能的，也指有道德、有才能的人 virtuous and able; worthy; person of such quality：～明 *wise and able; sagacious* | 选～与能 *recommend virtuous and talented people* | 任人唯～ *employ sb on merit* ❷敬辞，用于平辈或晚辈 polite speech, address for a younger person：～弟 *my worthy brother* | ～侄 *my good nephew*

挦（撏）xián ㄒㄧㄢˊ 扯，拔（毛发）to pull (hair); to pluck (feather)：～鸡毛 *pluck a chicken (of its feathers)*

咸（❷鹹）xián ㄒㄧㄢˊ ❶全，都 all：少（shào）长（zhǎng）～集。*Young and old are all gathered together.* | ～知其不可。*All know it can't be done.* ❷像盐的味道，含盐分多，跟"淡"相对 salty; salted (opposite of 淡)

诚（諴）xián ㄒㄧㄢˊ ❶和洽，和谐 congenial; harmonious ❷诚恳，真诚 sincere

涎（*次）xián ㄒㄧㄢˊ 口水 saliva：流～ *to drool* | 垂～三尺（形容羡慕，很想得到）*drool with greed*

衔(銜、❶❷*啣、*衘) xián ㄒㄧㄢˊ ❶马嚼子 snaffle bit ❷用嘴含，用嘴叼 to hold in the mouth：燕子～泥。*Swallows carry bits of earth in their bills.* ㊀ ① 心里怀着 to cherish; to harbour (feelings or thoughts)：～恨 *harbour resentment* | ～冤 *nurse a bitter sense of wrong* ②奉，接受 to follow; to accept (orders, etc.)：～命 *follow/accept orders* [衔接] 互相连接 to link up; to join ❸（一儿）职务和级别的名号 rank; title：职～ *title* | 军～ *military rank* | 授～ *confer title*

嫌 xián ㄒㄧㄢˊ ❶嫌疑，可疑之点 suspicion：避～ *avoid suspicion* ❷厌恶（wù），不满意 to dislike; to loathe：讨人～ *be a nuisance* | 这种布很结实，就是～太厚。*The cloth is quite sturdy, but just a little too thick.* ❸怨恨 ill will; grudge：前～ *previous grudge* | 夙无仇～ *never have any grudges (between two parties)* | 挟～报复 *bear resentment against sb and retaliate*

狝(獮) xiǎn ㄒㄧㄢˇ 古代指秋天打猎 (ancient) to hunt in autumn

冼 xiǎn ㄒㄧㄢˇ 姓 (surname) Xian

洗 xiǎn ㄒㄧㄢˇ same as "冼"
⇨ see also xǐ on p.700

铣(銑) xiǎn ㄒㄧㄢˇ 有光泽的金属 shiny metal [铣铁] 铸铁的旧称 former name for 铸铁

⇨ see also xǐ on p.700

筅(**筅) xiǎn ㄒㄧㄢˇ〈方 dialect〉筅帚，炊帚，用竹子等做成的刷锅、碗的用具 pot-scouring brush (also 炊帚)

跣 xiǎn ㄒㄧㄢˇ 光着脚 barefooted：～足 *barefoot*

显(顯) xiǎn ㄒㄧㄢˇ ❶露在外面容易看出来 apparent; obvious：明～ *obvious* | ～而易见 *obviously* | 道理很～然。*The logic is apparent.* ❷表现，露出 to show; to appear：～示 *to show* | ～微镜 *microscope* | 没有高山，不～平地。*Without high mountains, flatland does not show.* ❸有名声、地位、权势的 prominent：～贵 *eminent person* | ～宦 *official of high rank* ❹敬辞（称先人）(polite speech) my late (parent or ancestor)：～考 *my late father* | ～妣 *my late mother*

险(險) xiǎn ㄒㄧㄢˇ ❶可能遭受的灾难（㊥危一）danger; risk：冒～ *take a risk; to venture* | 保～ *insure; guarantee* | 脱～ *escape danger* ❷可能发生灾难的 dangerous; perilous：～症 *dangerous illness* | ～境 *dangerous situation* | 好～。*That was close.* ❸要隘，不易通过的地方 narrow pass; perilous place：天～ *natural barrier* ❹存心狠毒 sinister; vicious：阴～ *sinister* | ～诈 *sinister and crafty* ❺几乎，差一点儿 by a hair's breadth; nearly：～遭不幸 *come within an inch of death* | ～些掉在河里 *almost fall in the river*

崄（嶮） xiǎn ㄒㄧㄢˇ see 㟜崄 (yào—) at 㟜 on page 763

猃（獫） xiǎn ㄒㄧㄢˇ 古指长（cháng）嘴的狗 (ancient) long-snouted dog

［猃狁］（—yǔn）我国古代北方的民族，战国后称匈奴 Xianyun (an ancient ethnic group in northern China, called 匈奴 after the Warring States Period)

蚬（蜆） xiǎn ㄒㄧㄢˇ 软体动物，介壳形状像心脏，有环状纹，生活在淡水软泥里 freshwater clam

𤞤（玁） xiǎn ㄒㄧㄢˇ ［𤞤狁］（—yǔn）same as "猃狁"

𥙬 xiǎn ㄒㄧㄢˇ 祭祀剩余的肉 leftover sacrificial meat

㬎 xiǎn ㄒㄧㄢˇ ❶ same as "显❶" ❷用于人名。赵㬎，南宋恭帝 used in given names, e.g. Zhao Xian, Emperor Gong of the Southern Song Dynasty

鲜（鮮、*尠、*尟） xiǎn ㄒㄧㄢˇ 少 rare; few：～见 *rarely seen* | ～有 *rare* | 寡廉～耻 *shameless*

⇨ see also xiān on p.706

藓（蘚） xiǎn ㄒㄧㄢˇ 隐花植物的一类，茎叶很小，没有真根，生长在阴湿的地方 moss

燹 xiǎn ㄒㄧㄢˇ 火，野火 wild fire ［兵燹］指战乱所造成的焚烧毁坏等灾害 flames of war

櫶 xiǎn ㄒㄧㄢˇ 常绿乔木，又叫蚬木，叶椭圆卵形，花白色，果实椭圆形，木质坚实细致，是我国珍贵的树种 *Euryodendron excelsum* (also called 蚬木)

见（見） xiàn ㄒㄧㄢˋ same as "现❶"

⇨ see also jiàn on p.303

苋（莧） xiàn ㄒㄧㄢˋ 苋菜，草本植物，茎细长，叶椭圆形，茎叶可用作蔬菜 edible amaranth

岘（峴） xiàn ㄒㄧㄢˋ 岘山，山名，在湖北省 Mount Xian (in Hubei Province)

现（現） xiàn ㄒㄧㄢˋ ❶显露 to show; to emerge：出～ *to appear* | ～了原形 *reveal one's true nature* ［现象］事物的表面状态 appearance; phenomenon ❷现在，目前 present; current：～况 *current situation* | ～代 *modern times; modern* ㊀当时 offhand; extempore：～趸～卖 *teach what one has just learned (literally means 'sell what one has purchased in bulk')* | ～成的 *ready-made* ❸实有的，当时就有的 available; ready：～金 *cash* | ～钱 *cash* | ～货 *goods in stock* ❹现款 ready money; cash：兑～ *cash (a cheque, etc.); fulfil (promise, etc.)* | 贴～ *discount*

晛（晛） xiàn ㄒㄧㄢˋ 太阳出现 (of the sun) to appear

睍（睍） xiàn ㄒㄧㄢˋ 用于人名。嵬名（嵬名，复姓）睍，西夏末帝 used in given names, e.g. Weiming Xian, last Emperor of the Western Xia Dynasty

县(縣) xiàn ㄒㄧㄢˋ 行政区划单位，由直辖市、地级市、自治州等领导 county
〈古 ancient〉also same as 悬(xuán)

限 xiàn ㄒㄧㄢˋ ❶指定的范围 limit; bound: 以三天为～ *a deadline of three days* ❷限制(范围) to set limit; to place restrictions: ～三天完工 *set a limit of three days to complete the job* | 作文不～字数。*There is no limit of length to the composition.* [限制] 规定范围，不许超过。也指规定的范围 to restrict; to limit; limit ❸〈古 ancient〉门槛 threshold: 门～ *threshold* | 户～ *threshold*

线(綫、△*線) xiàn ㄒㄧㄢˋ ❶用丝、金属、棉或麻等制成的细长的东西 thread; wire: 棉～ *cotton thread* | 电～ *electric wire* | 毛～ *yarn* [一线] 1 表示极少 little; very thin: ～光明 *a glimmer of light* | ～希望 *a faint gleam of hope* 2 指战争的最前线或直接从事生产、教学等工作的岗位 front line: 在～作战 *fight on the front line* | 深入生产～ *go to the front line of production* [线索] 喻事物发展的脉络或据以解决问题的头绪 clue; thread: 那件事情有了～。*There is a lead on that matter now.* ❷几何学上指点移动所生成的图形，有长，没有宽和厚 (geometry) line: 直～ *straight line* | 曲～ *curve* ❸像线的东西 sth like a line: 光～ *ray* | 紫外～ *ultraviolet ray* | 航～ *air route* | 京广～ *Beijing-Guangzhou railway line* | 战～ *battlefront* | 生命～ *lifeline* ❹边缘交界处 border: 防～ *line of defence* | 国境～ *boundary line*
⇨ 線 see also 线 on p.711

宪(憲) xiàn ㄒㄧㄢˋ ❶法令 statute; decree: ～令 *statute* ❷指宪法 constitution: ～章 *charter* | 立～ *formulate a constitution* | 违～ *violate the constitution* | 修～ *revise the constitution* [宪法] 国家的根本法。具有最高的法律效力，是其他立法工作的根据。通常规定一个国家的社会制度、国家制度、国家机构和公民的基本权利和义务等 constitution

陷 xiàn ㄒㄧㄢˋ ❶掉进，坠入，沉下 to get bogged down; to entrap; to cave in: ～到泥里去了 *get stuck in the mud* | 地～下去了。*The ground sank.* [陷阱] 为捉野兽或敌人而挖的坑 trap; pitfall 喻害人的阴谋 trap; trick ❷凹进 to sink: 两眼深～ *eyes deep-set* ❸设计害人 to frame (sb): ～害 *fabricate a charge* | 诬～ *make a false charge against* ❹被攻破，被占领 (of a town, etc.) to be captured: 失～ *fall into enemy hands* | ～落 *be lost to the enemy* ❺缺点 shortcoming; defect: 缺～ *defect*

馅(餡) xiàn ㄒㄧㄢˋ (一子、一儿) 包在面食、点心等食物里面的肉、菜、糖等东西 (of food) filling; stuffing: 饺子～儿 *the filling of dumplings*

羡 xiàn ㄒㄧㄢˋ ❶羡慕，因喜爱而希望得到 to admire; to envy: 艳～(十分羡慕) *keenly*

admire/envy ❷ 多余的 surplus：～余 *surplus*

缐(線) xiàn ㄒㄧㄢˋ 姓 (surname) Xian

⇨ 線 see also 线 on p.710

腺 xiàn ㄒㄧㄢˋ 生物体内由腺细胞组成的能分泌某些化学物质的组织 gland：汗～ *sweat gland* | 泪～ *tear gland* | 乳～ *mammary gland* | 蜜～ *nectary*

缐(線) xiàn ㄒㄧㄢˋ 金属线 metal wire

献(獻) xiàn ㄒㄧㄢˋ 恭敬庄严地送给 to offer; to present; to dedicate：～花 *present flowers* | ～礼 *offer a present* | 把青春～给祖国 *dedicate one's youth to one's country* ㊀表现出来给人看 to show：～技 *show skills* | ～殷勤 *ingratiate oneself*

霰 xiàn ㄒㄧㄢˋ 水蒸气在高空中遇冷凝结成的白色小冰粒，在下雪花以前往往先下霰 graupel

XIANG ㄒㄧㄤ

乡(鄉) xiāng ㄒㄧㄤ ❶城市外的区域 rural area; country side：下～ *go to the countryside* | 城～交流 *circulation between town and country* ❷自己生长的地方或祖籍 native place; home village：故～ *hometown* | 还～ *return to hometown* | 同～ *person from the same village/town* | 背井离～ *leave one's native place* [老乡] 生长在同一地方的人 person from one's village or town ❸行政区划单位，由县或区等领导 township

芗(薌) xiāng ㄒㄧㄤ ❶古书上指用以调味的香草 fragrant herb used as seasoning (in ancient Chinese texts) ❷芳香 fragrance

相 xiāng ㄒㄧㄤ ❶交互，动作由双方来（㊜互一、一互）mutually; reciprocally; each other：～助 *mutual assistance* | ～亲～爱 *love each other* | 言行～符 *match words to deeds* ㊀加在动词前面，表示一方对另一方的动作 added in front of a verb to indicate the action of one party on another：～信 *to believe* | 好言～劝 *advise sb with kind words* [相当] 1 对等，等于 to equal; to match：年纪～ *of about the same age* 2 合适 appropriate; suitable：找个～的人 *find a suitable person* 3 副词，表示有一定的程度 (adverb) considerably; quite：这首诗写得～好。*The poem is very well written.* [相对] 依靠一定条件而存在，随着一定条件而变化的，跟"绝对"相对 relative; comparative (opposite of 绝对) ❷看 to evaluate by seeing：～中 *take a fancy to* | 左～右看 *check up and down*

⇨ see also xiàng on p.714

厢(*廂) xiāng ㄒㄧㄤ ❶厢房，正房前面两旁的房屋 wing (of a house)：东～ *east wing* | 西～ *west wing* ㊀边，方面 side; aspect：这～ *this side* | 两～ *both sides* ❷靠近城的地区 vicinity of a city：城～ *city proper*

and surrounding area | 关～ *neighbourhood outside a city gate* ❸ 包厢，戏院里特设的单间座位 (theatre) box ❹车厢，车里容纳人或东西的地方 (railway) carriage

葙 xiāng ㄒㄧㄤ ［青葙］草本植物，叶卵形至披针形，花淡红色。种子叫青葙子，可入药 plumed cockscomb

湘 xiāng ㄒㄧㄤ ❶湘江，源出广西壮族自治区，流至湖南省入洞庭湖 Xiangjiang River (originating in Guangxi Zhuang Autonomous Region, flowing through Hunan Province into Dongting Lake) ❷湖南省的别称 (another name for Hunan Province) Xiang

缃(緗) xiāng ㄒㄧㄤ 浅黄色 light yellow

箱 xiāng ㄒㄧㄤ ❶（一子）收藏衣物等的方形器具，通常是上面有盖儿扣住 chest; box ❷像箱子的东西 sth like a box: 信～ *mail box* | 风～ *bellows*

香 xiāng ㄒㄧㄤ ❶气味好闻，跟"臭"相对 fragrant; sweet-smelling (opposite of 臭): ～花 *fragrant flower* ㊗①舒服 comfortable: 睡得～ *sleep soundly* | 吃得真～ *eat with relish* ②受欢迎 popular; favoured: 这种货物在农村～得很。*The merchandise is very popular in the countryside.* ❷味道好 savoury; delicious: 饭～。*The food is appetizing.* ❸称一些天然有香味的东西 perfume; spice: 檀～ *sandalwood* 特指用香料做成的细条 incense: 线～ *joss-stick* | 蚊～ *mosquito-repellent incense*

襄 xiāng ㄒㄧㄤ 帮助 to assist; to help: ～办 *help manage* | ～理 *assistant manager*

骧(驤) xiāng ㄒㄧㄤ 马抬着头快跑 (of a horse) to gallop

纕(纕) xiāng ㄒㄧㄤ 佩带 to wear (a badge, sword, etc.)

瓖 xiāng ㄒㄧㄤ same as "镶"

镶(鑲) xiāng ㄒㄧㄤ 把东西嵌进去或在外围加边 to inlay; to mount: ～牙 *put in a false tooth* | 在衣服上～一道红边 *edge a garment with a red border* | 金～玉嵌 *inlaid with gold and jade*

详(詳) xiáng ㄒㄧㄤˊ ❶细密，完备，跟"略"相对（㊥一细）detailed; comprehensive (opposite of 略): ～谈 *have a detailed discussion* | ～情 *details* | 不厌其～ *go into minute detail* ❷清楚地知道 to know clearly: 内容不～ *not clear about the details* ❸说明，细说 to give details; to elaborate on: 余容再～。*More details to come.* | 内～。*(on envelope) Details enclosed.* ❹（仪态）从容稳重 calm and sedate: 安～ *composed; serene* | 举止～雅 *have a serene and elegant manner*

庠 xiáng ㄒㄧㄤˊ 庠序，古代的乡学，也泛指学校 local school in ancient times; (generally) school

祥 xiáng ㄒㄧㄤˊ ❶吉利（㊥吉一）auspicious; lucky: ～瑞

propitious omen | 不～ *ominous* ⓩ 和善，友善 kindly; amiable：慈～ *loving; benign* | ～和 *peaceful and auspicious* ❷指吉凶的预兆（迷信）omen

降 xiáng ㄒㄧㄤˊ ❶投降，归顺 to surrender; to capitulate：宁死不～ *rather die than surrender* ❷降服，使驯服 to subdue; to tame：～龙伏虎 *subdue the dragon and tame the tiger; (figurative) overcome formidable adversaries*

⇨ see also jiàng on p.308

翔 xiáng ㄒㄧㄤˊ 盘旋地飞而不扇动翅膀 to circle in the air; to fly：滑～ *to glide*

[翔实] [详实] 详细而确实 detailed and accurate

享（*亯）xiǎng ㄒㄧㄤˇ 享受，受用 to enjoy：～福 *live in ease and comfort* | 久～盛誉 *have long enjoyed high reputation* | 资源共～ *share resources*

响（響）xiǎng ㄒㄧㄤˇ ❶（一儿）声音 sound; noise：听不见～儿了。*Sound can no longer be heard.* ❷发出声音 to make a sound; to ring：大炮～了。*The cannons roared.* | 钟～了。*The bell rang.* | 一声不～ *not utter a sound* ❸响亮，声音高，声音大 loud; noisy：这个铃真～。*This bell is very loud.* ❹回声 echo：如～斯应（形容反应迅速）*prompt in response* [响应]（-yìng）回声相应。比喻用言语、行动表示赞同 to answer; to respond (often positively)：～祖国的号召 *answer the call of one's country*

饷（餉、*饟）xiǎng ㄒㄧㄤˇ ❶过去指军警的薪给（jǐ）(old) pay (for soldiers, policemen, etc.)：领～ *receive pay* | 关～ *get paid* ❷用酒食等款待 to entertain with food and drink

鲞（鯗）xiǎng ㄒㄧㄤˇ 鲞虫，即知声虫，又叫地蛹 larva; grub (same as 知声虫, also called 地蛹)

飨（饗）xiǎng ㄒㄧㄤˇ ❶用酒食款待 to entertain with food and drink：以～读者（用来满足读者的需要）*gratify the reader* ❷ same as "享"

想 xiǎng ㄒㄧㄤˇ ❶动脑筋，思索 to think; to consider：我～出一个办法来了。*I have thought of a way.* ⓨ①推测，认为 to suppose; to assume：我～他不会来了。*I guess he is not coming after all.* | 我～这么做才好。*I suppose this is the way to go.* ②希望，打算 to want to; to feel like (doing sth)：他～去学习。*He wants to go and study.* | 要～学习好，就得努力。*Good learning comes from hard work.* ❷怀念，惦记 to miss; to yearn for：～家 *long for home* | 时常～着前方的战士 *often think of the soldiers on the frontline*

鲞（鮝、**鯗）xiǎng ㄒㄧㄤˇ 剖开晾干的鱼 dried fish

向（❶❸❹❻嚮、❻*曏）xiàng ㄒㄧㄤˋ ❶对着，朝着，特指脸部或胸部对着，跟"背"

相对 to face; to turn towards (opposite of 背): 这间房子～东。*This room faces east.* [向导]引路的人 guide ❷介词，表示动作的方向或对象 (preposition) towards: ～前看 *look forward* | ～雷锋同志学习。*Learn from Comrade Lei Feng.* ❸方向 direction: 我转(zhuàn)～(认错了方向)了。*I got lost.* ㊀意志所趋 inclination; preference: 志～ *aspiration* | 意～ *intention* ❹近，临 to be near: ～晚 *close to evening* | ～晓雨停。*Rain stopped early in the morning.* ❺偏袒，袒护 to side with; to be partial to: 偏～ *be partial to* ❻从前 past: ～日 *in the old days* | ～者 *in the past* ㊀从开始到现在 until now; all along: 本处～无此人。*There has never been such a person here.* [向来][一向]副词，从来，表示从很早到现在 (adverb) all along: 他～不喝酒。*He never drinks.*

珦 xiàng ㄒㄧㄤˋ 一种玉 a kind of jade

项(項) xiàng ㄒㄧㄤˋ ❶颈的后部 nape of the neck ❷事物的种类或条目 item: 事～ *item; matter* | ～目 *item; event* | 义～ *(in a dictionary) an item of an entry; subentry* | 强～ *forte* ㊕钱，经费(㊥款－) sum of money: 用～ *items of expenditure* | 进～ *income* | 欠～ *debt* ❸量词，用于分项目的事物 (measure word) item: 两～任务 *two tasks* | 三大纪律八～注意 *Three Rules of Disciplines and Eight Points for Attention* ❹代数中不用加号、减号连接的单式，如$4a^2b$，ax^3。(algebra) term

巷 xiàng ㄒㄧㄤˋ 较窄的街道 lane; alley: 大街小～ *big streets and small alleys*

⇨ see also hàng on p.243

相 xiàng ㄒㄧㄤˋ ❶(－儿)样子，容貌(㊥－貌) looks; appearance: 长(zhǎng)得很喜～(xiang) *have a happy appearance* | 狼狈～ *embarrassed look* | 照～ *have a picture taken* ❷察看 to appraise by looking: ～马 *look at a horse to judge its worth* | ～机行事 *act when the time is opportune* | 人不可以貌～ *never judge a person by appearances* ❸辅助，也指辅佐的人，古代特指最高级的官 to assist; assistant; (ancient) highest official: 吉人天～。*Heaven helps a virtuous person.* | 宰～ *prime minister* ❹姓 (surname) Xiang

⇨ see also xiāng on p.711

象 xiàng ㄒㄧㄤˋ ❶哺乳动物，耳朵大，鼻子圆筒形，可以伸卷。多有一对特长的门牙，突出唇外。多产于亚洲的印度、非洲等热带地方 elephant ❷形状，样子(㊥形－) appearance; shape; image: 景～ *scene* | 万～更新。*All things take on a new aspect.* [象征]用具体的东西表现事物的某种意义，例如鸽子象征和平 to symbolize; to stand for; symbol; emblem

像 xiàng ㄒㄧㄤˋ ❶相似 to resemble; to take after: 他很～他母亲。*He takes after his mother.*

[好像] 1 相似 to be like; to resemble 2 似乎，仿佛 to seem; to look as if：我～见过他。*I seem to have met him before.* ❷比照人物做成的图形 portrait; picture：画～ *portrait* | 塑～ *statue* ❸比如，比方 such as; for example：这件事很多人不知道，～我就是一个。*Many people don't know about it, I for one.*

橡 xiàng ㄒㄧㄤˋ ❶橡树，即栎树 oak (same as 栎树) ❷橡胶树，常绿乔木，花白色，树的乳状汁液可制橡胶 rubber tree

XIAO ㄒㄧㄠ

肖 xiāo ㄒㄧㄠ 姓 (surname) Xiao

⇨ see also xiào on p.718

削 xiāo ㄒㄧㄠ 用刀平着或斜着去掉物体外面的一层 to peel with a knife; to pare：～铅笔 *sharpen a pencil* | 把梨皮～掉 *peel a pear*

⇨ see also xuē on p.740

逍 xiāo ㄒㄧㄠ [逍遥] (－yáo) 自由自在，无拘无束 free and unfettered：～自在 *be leisurely and carefree*

消 xiāo ㄒㄧㄠ ❶溶化，散失 (㊥－溶) to disappear; to dissolve：冰～ *ice melts* | 烟～火灭。*Smoke disperses as fire die out.* [消化] 胃肠等器官把食物变成可以吸收的养料 to digest ㊐理解、吸收所学的知识 to understand and absorb (knowledge); to digest ❷灭掉，除去 (㊥－灭) to eliminate; to dispel：～毒 *to disinfect* | ～炎 *alleviate inflammation* [消费] 为了满足生产、生活的需要而消耗物质财富 to consume [消极] 起反面作用的，不求进取的，跟"积极"相对 passive; negative (opposite of 积极)：～因素 *negative factor* | 态度～ *take a passive attitude* [消息] 音信，新闻 news ❸消遣，把时间度过去 to pass away time：～夜 *night snack; have a night snack* | ～夏 *pass the summer in leisure* ❹〈方 dialect〉需要 to need：不～说 *needless to say*

宵 xiāo ㄒㄧㄠ 夜 night：通～ *all night through* | ～禁 *curfew* [元宵] 1 元宵节，农历正月十五日晚上 Lantern Festival (the 15th of the first month in lunar calendar) 2 一种江米（糯米）面做成的球形有馅儿食品，多在元宵节吃 sweet dumpling made of glutinous rice flour

绡(綃) xiāo ㄒㄧㄠ 生丝 raw silk 又指用生丝织的东西 raw silk fabric

硝 xiāo ㄒㄧㄠ ❶矿物名 name of a mineral ①硝石，无色或白色晶体，成分是硝酸钾或硝酸钠，可制肥料或炸药 nitre; saltpetre ②芒硝，无色透明晶体，成分是硫酸钠，是工业原料，也可做泻剂 mirabilite ❷用芒硝加黄米面等处理毛皮，使皮板儿柔软 to taw; to tan：～皮子 *tan hide*

销(銷) xiāo ㄒㄧㄠ ❶熔化金属 to melt (metal)[销毁] 毁灭，常指烧掉 to destroy (usually by burning) ❷

去掉 to cancel; to annul：～假（jià）*report back after leave of absence*| 报～ *submit an expense account; get reimbursed* | 撤～ *to cancel;to rescind* ❸卖出（货物）to sell：一天～了不少的货。*A lot of goods have been sold in one day.*| 供（gōng）～ *supply and marketing*| 脱～ *sold out* | ～路 *sale; market* ❹开支，花费 to expend; to spend：花～ *expense; cost* | 开～ *expenditure* ❺（－子）机器上像钉子的零件 pin; dowel ❻把机器上的销子或门窗上的插销推上 to fasten with a pin

蛸 xiāo ㄒㄧㄠ ［蟏蛸］（piāo－）螳螂的卵块 egg capsule of a mantis

⇨ see also shāo on p.583

霄 xiāo ㄒㄧㄠ ❶云（㊥云－）cloud ❷天空 sky：重（chóng）～ *the highest heavens* | 九～ *the highest of heavens* | ～壤之别（形容相去很远）*the difference between heaven and earth*

魈 xiāo ㄒㄧㄠ ［山魈］1 一种猴，脸蓝色，鼻子红色，嘴上有白须，全身毛黑褐色，腹部白色，尾巴很短 mandrill 2 传说中山里的鬼怪 mountain ghost

枭（梟） xiāo ㄒㄧㄠ ❶ same as "鸮 (xiāo)" ❷勇健（常有不驯顺的意思）valiant; fierce and reckless：～将 *intrepid general* | ～雄 *person of valour and ambition* ❸魁首，首领 chief; head：毒～ *drug baron* ❹〈古 ancient〉悬挂（砍下的人头）to hang up (cut-off head) for display：～首 *expose a cut-off head to public view* | ～示 *hang up a cut-off head for public view*

枵 xiāo ㄒㄧㄠ ❶空虚 empty; hollow：～腹从公 *attend to one's duties on an empty stomach* ❷布的丝缕稀而薄 (of fabric) sheer; very thin：～薄 *sheer*

鸮（鴞） xiāo ㄒㄧㄠ 猫头鹰一类的鸟 owl and similar birds

哓（嘵） xiāo ㄒㄧㄠ ［哓哓］形容争辩声或鸟类因恐惧而发出的鸣叫声 noisy bickering; frightened cries of birds

骁（驍） xiāo ㄒㄧㄠ ❶好马 fine horse ❷勇健（㊥－勇）valiant; intrepid：～将 *valiant general*

虓 xiāo ㄒㄧㄠ 猛虎怒吼 (of a tiger) to roar

猇 xiāo ㄒㄧㄠ ❶same as "虓" ❷猇亭，地名，在湖北省宜昌 Xiaoting (a place in Yichang, Hubei Province)

萧（蕭） xiāo ㄒㄧㄠ ❶冷落、没有生气的样子 dreary; desolate：～然 *desolate; deserted* | ～瑟 *bleak; desolate* | ～索 *dreary* ［萧条］寂寞冷落 desolate; bleak：晚景～ *alone and dreary in old age* ㊞不兴旺 in a depression/slump：经济～ *economic depression* ❷姓 (surname) Xiao

［萧萧］形容马叫声或风声 to neigh; to whinny

潇（瀟） xiāo ㄒㄧㄠ 水清而深 (of water) deep and clear

[潇洒]（－sǎ）行动举止自然大方，不呆板，不拘束 natural and unrestrained

蟏(蠨) xiāo ㄒㄧㄠ [蟏蛸]（－shāo）same as 蟢子

箫(簫) xiāo ㄒㄧㄠ 管乐器。古代的排箫是许多管子排在一起的，后世用一根管子做成，竖着吹的叫洞箫 a wind instrument, the ancient 排箫 consisted of many pipes in a row; later it became a single pipe called 洞箫

翛 xiāo ㄒㄧㄠ 〈古 ancient〉无拘无束，自由自在 unrestrained：～然 *carefree*

[翛翛]羽毛残破的样子 (of feathers) broken

嚣(囂) xiāo ㄒㄧㄠ 喧哗 to clamour; to make a noise：叫～ *to clamour* [嚣张]放肆，邪恶势力上升 rampant; arrogant：气焰～ *behave with unbearable insolence*

洨 xiáo ㄒㄧㄠˊ 洨河，水名，在河北省西南部 Xiaohe River (in southwestern Hebei Province)

崤 xiáo ㄒㄧㄠˊ 崤山，山名，在河南省西部。又叫崤陵 Xiaoshan (also called 崤陵, a mountain in western Henan Province)

淆(△*殽) xiáo ㄒㄧㄠˊ 混淆，错杂，混乱 confused; mixed：～乱 *mixed and disorderly; confused* | 混～不清 *confused*

殽 xiáo ㄒㄧㄠˊ ❶see 淆 on page 717 ❷同"崤"，用于古地名 same as 崤, used in ancient place names：～之战 *the battle of Xiao*

小 xiǎo ㄒㄧㄠˇ ❶跟"大"相对 small; little (opposite of 大) ①面积少的，体积占空间少的，容量少的 small; little：～山 *hill* | 地方～ *small space* ②数量少的 few; little：数目～ *small in quantity* | 一～半 *less than half* ③程度浅的 low in degree：学问～ *with little learning* | ～学 *primary school* ④声音低的 low in sound volume：～声说话 *speak in a low voice* ⑤年幼，排行最末的 young; youngest：他比你～。*He is younger than you.* | 他是我的～弟弟。*He is my youngest brother.* ⑥年幼的人 the young：一家老～ *the whole family, old and young* ⑦谦辞 humble speech：～弟 *I; me* | ～店 *my store* [小看]轻视，看不起 to look down upon：别～人。*Don't look down on people.* ❷时间短 short in time：～坐 *sit for a short while* | ～住 *stay for a few days* ❸稍微 a little; slightly：牛刀～试 *a modest display of one's talent* ❹略微少于，将近 a little less than; close to：这里离石家庄有～三百里。*It is close to 300 li from here to Shijiazhuang.*

晓(曉) xiǎo ㄒㄧㄠˇ ❶天刚亮的时候 dawn; daybreak：～行夜宿 *travel by day and rest by night* | 鸡鸣报～。*Cocks crow at dawn.* ❷晓得，知道，懂得（㊀知－）to know; to understand：家喻户～ *widely known* |

通～ *thoroughly understand* ❸使人知道 to let know; to tell：～以利害 *warn sb of the consequence*

谀(謏) xiǎo ㄒㄧㄠˇ 小 small; a little：～才 *somewhat talented* | ～闻（小有名声）*enjoy a little fame*

筱(篠)** xiǎo ㄒㄧㄠˇ ❶小竹子 thin bamboo ❷同"小"。多用于人名 (often used in given names) same as 小

皛 xiǎo ㄒㄧㄠˇ ❶明亮 bright ❷用于地名 used in place names：～店（在河南省中牟）*Xiaodian (in Zhongmu, Henan Province)*

孝 xiào ㄒㄧㄠˋ ❶指尊敬、奉养父母 filial duty; filial piety：～顺 *show filial obedience; perform filial duty* | ～敬 *show filial respect* ❷指居丧的礼俗 mourning：守～ *observe mourning* ❸丧服 mourning dress：戴～ *wear mourning dress*

哮 xiào ㄒㄧㄠˋ 吼叫 to howl; to roar：咆～ *roar*

[哮喘] 呼吸急促困难的症状 asthma

涍 xiào ㄒㄧㄠˋ ❶古水名，在今河南省 Xiao (an ancient name for a river, in today's Henan Province) ❷姓 (surname) Xiao

肖 xiào ㄒㄧㄠˋ 像，相似 to resemble; to be like：子～其父。*The son takes after his father.* [肖像] 画像，相片 portrait; portraiture

⇨ see also xiāo on p.715

恔 xiào ㄒㄧㄠˋ 畅快，满意 contented; gratified

⇨ see also jiǎo on p.312

校 xiào ㄒㄧㄠˋ ❶学校 school ❷军衔名，在尉和将之间 field officer

⇨ see also jiào on p.313

效(❶*傚、❸*効) xiào ㄒㄧㄠˋ ❶模仿（㊥－法、仿－）to imitate; to follow：上行下～。*Subordinates follow the example of superiors.* ❷效验，功用，成果 effect; result：这药吃了很见～。*The drug did have effect.* | ～果 *effect; result* | 无～ *invalid; ineffective* [效率] 1 物理学上指有用的功在总功中所占的百分比 (of physics) efficiency 2 单位时间内所完成的工作量 productiveness：生产～ *productivity* | 工作～ *work efficiency* ❸尽，献出 to devote; to render (service)：～力 *to serve* | ～劳 *work for*

滧 xiào ㄒㄧㄠˋ 用于地名 used in place names：五～（在上海市崇明）*Wuxiao (in Chongming, Shanghai Municipality)*

笑(*咲) xiào ㄒㄧㄠˋ ❶露出愉快的表情，发出欢喜的声音 to laugh; to smile：逗～ *make people laugh* | 眉开眼～ *be all smiles* | 啼～皆非 *not know whether to laugh or cry* [笑话] (－hua) 1 (－－儿) 能使人发笑的话或事 joke 2 轻视，讥讽 to laugh at：别～人。*Don't laugh at others.* ❷讥笑，嘲笑 to laugh at; to sneer at：见～ *incur ridicule* | 耻～ *sneer at* | 五十步～百步 *the pot calls the kettle black*

啸(嘯) xiào ㄒㄧㄠˋ ❶人撮口发出长而清脆的声音，打口哨 to whistle：长～一声，山鸣谷应。*A long whistle echoes from mountains and valleys.* ❷ 禽兽拉长声音叫 to howl; to roar：虎～ *the roar of a tiger* | 猿～ *the cry of an ape* ❸自然界发出的或飞机、子弹等飞掠而过的声音 (of a bullet, plane, etc.) to whirr; to whiz：海～ *seismic sea wave; tsunami* | 子弹尖～着掠过头上。*A bullet whizzed past over (his) head.*

斅(斆) xiào ㄒㄧㄠˋ 教导，使觉悟 to teach; to enlighten

XIE ㄒㄧㄝ

些 xiē ㄒㄧㄝ ❶量词，表示不定的数量 (measure word) a few; some：有～工人 *a few workers* | 炉子里要添～煤。*We need to add some coal to the stove.* | 看～书 *read some books* | 长(zhǎng)～见识 *gain some experience* ❷ 跟"好""这么"连用表示很多 (used with 好，这么) quite a few; so many：好～人 *many people* | 这么～天 *so many days* | 制造出这么～个机器 *produced so many machines* ❸用在形容词后表示略微 (following an adjective) somewhat：病轻～了 *got a bit better from illness* | 学习认真～，理解就深刻～。*The more efforts in studying, the better understanding.* [些微] 略微 slightly

揳 xiē ㄒㄧㄝ 捶，打。特指把钉、橛等捶打到其他东西里面去 to punch; to hit (esp. to drive a nail or wedge)：在墙上～钉子 *drive a nail into the wall* | 把桌子～一～ *wedge the table a little*

楔 xiē ㄒㄧㄝ （一儿）填充器物的空隙使其牢固的木橛、木片等 wedge：这个板凳腿活动了，加个～儿吧。*The leg of this stool has come loose. Let's put a wedge in it.* [楔子] (-zi) 1 义同"楔" same in meaning as 楔 2 杂剧里加在第一折前头或插在两折之间的小段，近代小说的引子 prologue (in a novel or a play)

歇 xiē ㄒㄧㄝ ❶休息 to rest; to take a rest：坐下～一会儿 *sit down and take a break* ❷停止 to stop：～工 *stop work* | ～业 *close business* | ～枝（果树在一定年限内停止结果或结果很少）*(of fruit tree) bear less fruit (after a productive year)* ❸〈方 dialect〉很短的一段时间，一会儿 a little while; a short time：过了一～ *after a while*
[歇斯底里]（外 *loanword*）即癔(yì)病 hysteria ⑩情绪激动，举止失常 hysterical

蝎(*蠍) xiē ㄒㄧㄝ （一子）节肢动物，卵胎生。口部两侧有螯，胸脚四对，后腹狭长，末端有毒钩，用来防敌和捕虫。干制后可入药 scorpion

叶 xié ㄒㄧㄝˊ 和洽，合 concordance; rhyme：～韵 *to rhyme (by temporarily shifting pronunciation of a character)*

⇨ see also yè on p.765

X

协(協) xié ㄒㄧㄝˊ ❶共同合作，辅助 to cooperate; to make joint efforts：～商 *to consult; to negotiate* | ～办 *assist in doing sth* | ～查 *assist in an investigation* ❷调和，和谐 harmonious; coordinated：～调 *to coordinate* | ～和 *to harmonize*

胁(脅、*脇) xié ㄒㄧㄝˊ ❶从腋下到腰的部分 (of human body) flank：～下 *flank* ❷逼迫恐吓(hè) to coerce; to force：威～ *to threaten* | ～制 *enforce obedience* [胁从] 被胁迫而随从别人做坏事 to be an accomplice under duress ❸收敛 to shrink：～肩谄笑（谄媚人的丑态）*cringe and smile obsequiously*

邪(*衺) xié ㄒㄧㄝˊ ❶不正当 evil; heretical：歪风～气 *unhealthy trends and evil practices* | 改～归正 *mend one's ways* ㊀奇怪，不正常 strange; eerie：～门 *odd; strange* | 一股～劲 *an abnormal eruption or venting of mental or physical force* ❷中医指引起疾病的环境因素 pathogenic; unhealthy environmental factor：风～ *wind pathogen* | 寒～ *cold pathogen* ㊀迷信的人指鬼神给予的灾祸 misfortune (caused by evil spirit)：驱～ *drive out evil spirits* | 避～ *counteract evil force*

⇨ see also yé on p.764

挟(挾) xié ㄒㄧㄝˊ ❶夹在胳膊底下 to hold under the arm：～山跨海逞英雄 *stride across the North Seas with Mount Tai under one's arm; (figurative) heroic posture* ❷倚仗势力或抓住人的弱点强迫使服从 to coerce：要（yāo）～ *to coerce* | ～制 *to dominate (by taking advantage of sb's weakness)* ❸心里怀着（怨恨等）to harbour (hatred, etc.)：～嫌 *bear a grudge* | ～恨 *harbour hatred*

偕 xié ㄒㄧㄝˊ (formerly pronounced jiē) 共同，在一块（㊥－同）together with; in the company of：～老 *(of a couple) grow old together* | ～行 *travel together*

谐(諧) xié ㄒㄧㄝˊ ❶协调，配合得适当（㊥和－）in harmony; in accord：～音 *homophonic; harmonic tone* | ～调（tiáo）*harmonious* ❷诙谐，滑稽 humorous：～趣 *humour; funniness* | ～谈 *humorous talk* | 亦庄亦～ *serious and facetious at the same time*

斜 xié ㄒㄧㄝˊ 不正，跟平面或直线既不平行也不垂直的 inclined; slanting：歪～ *askew* | ～坡 *slope* | 纸裁～了。*The paper is cut askew.* | ～对过 *diagonally across*

斜 xié ㄒㄧㄝˊ 用于地名 used in place names：麦～（在江西省新干）*Maixie (in Xingan, Jiangxi Province)*

絜 xié ㄒㄧㄝˊ 量度物体周围的长度，泛指量度 to measure the circumference; (generally) to measure：度（duó）长～大 *measure and compare*

⇨ see also jié on p.317

颉(頡) xié ㄒㄧㄝˊ ❶鸟往上飞 (of birds) to fly upwards; to soar [颉颃] (-háng) 1 鸟向上向下飞 fly up and down 2 不相上下 equally matched: 他的书法与名家相~。*His calligraphy matches that of famous calligraphers.* ㊕对抗 to rival: ~作用 *antagonistic action* ❷姓 (surname) Xie

⇨ see also jié on p.317

撷(擷) xié ㄒㄧㄝˊ ❶摘下, 取下(㊀采一) to pick; to pluck ❷用衣襟兜东西 to wrap in the front of a garment

缬(纈) xié ㄒㄧㄝˊ 有花纹的丝织品 patterned silk fabric

携(*攜、*擕、*攜、*擕) xié ㄒㄧㄝˊ ❶带(㊀一带) to carry; to take along: ~眷 *take along one's family* | ~款潜逃 *run off with money* ❷拉着手 to hold sb by the hand: 扶老~幼 *bring along the old and the young* [携手] 手拉着手 hand in hand ㊖合作 to cooperate; to make a concerted effort

鞋(*鞵) xié ㄒㄧㄝˊ 穿在脚上走路时着地的东西 shoe: 皮~ *leather shoes* | 拖~ *slippers* | 旅游~ *trainers*

勰 xié ㄒㄧㄝˊ 和谐, 协调。多用于人名。刘勰, 南朝人 harmonious (often used in given names, e.g., Liu Xie, of the Southern Dynasties)

写(寫) xiě ㄒㄧㄝˇ ❶用笔在纸或其他东西上做字 to write: ~字 *write (characters)* | ~对联 *write couplets* ❷写作 to compose (literary work, etc.): ~诗 *write poetry* | ~文章 *write an article* ❸描写 to describe: ~景 *describe scenery* | ~情 *write about emotions* ❹绘画 to paint: ~生 *paint from life or nature*

血 xiě ㄒㄧㄝˇ 义同"血"(xuè), 用于口语。多单用, 如"流了点儿血", 也用于口语常用词, 如"鸡血""血块子" in oral speech, same in meaning as 血 (xuè), often used alone such as in 流了点儿血, also in familiar oral words such as 鸡血 and 血块子

⇨ see also xuè on p.741

灺(**炧) xiè ㄒㄧㄝˋ 蜡烛烧剩下的部分 candle-end

泄(*洩) xiè ㄒㄧㄝˋ ❶液体、气体排出 to let out; to leak: ~洪道 *spillway* | 水~不通 *tightly packed* [泄劲] [泄气] 丧失干劲、勇气 to be disheartened; to slacken one's efforts ❷透露 to divulge; to leak: ~漏秘密 *divulge a secret* | ~底 (泄露内幕) *reveal what is at the bottom* ❸发泄 to vent: ~恨 *vent one's anger* | ~私愤 *give vent to personal resentment*

绁(紲、*絏) xiè ㄒㄧㄝˋ ❶绳索 rope; rein ❷系, 拴 to tie; to fasten

渫 xiè ㄒㄧㄝˋ ❶除去 to remove ❷泄, 疏通 to dredge

泻(瀉) xiè ㄒㄧㄝˋ ❶液体很快地流下 to flow

swiftly：一～千里 *(of rivers) rushing along* ❷ 拉稀屎 to have diarrhoea：～肚 *have diarrhoea*

契（△** 偰） xiè ㄒㄧㄝ 商朝的祖先，传说是舜的臣 Xie (ancestor of the Shang Dynasty, said to be an official under the legendary emperor Shun)

⇨ see also qì on p.523

偰 xiè ㄒㄧㄝ ❶ see 契 on page 722 ❷姓 (surname) Xie

禼（卨、** 离） xiè ㄒㄧㄝ 用于人名。万俟禼（mòqí－），宋代人 used in given names, e.g., Moqi Xie, of Song Dynasty

卸 xiè ㄒㄧㄝ ❶把东西去掉或拿下来 to unload; to remove：～货 *unload cargo* | ～车 *unload a vehicle* | 大拆大～ *dismantle everything* ❷解除 to get rid of; to be relieved of：～责 *shirk responsibility* | ～任 *leave office* | 推～ *to shirk*

屑 xiè ㄒㄧㄝ 碎末 bits; scraps; crumbs：煤～ *cinder* | 木～ *sawdust* ［琐屑］细小的事情 trifles ［不屑］由于轻视而不肯做或不接受 to disdain; to reject as unworthy：他～于做这件事。*He is above doing it.*

榍 xiè ㄒㄧㄝ ［榍石］矿物名，晶体，多呈褐色或绿色，有光泽，是提炼钛的原料 titanite

械 xiè ㄒㄧㄝ ❶器物，家伙 tool; instrument：机～ *machinery* | 器～ *apparatus* ❷武器 weapon：缴～ *to disarm* | ～斗 *(of two groups) fight with weapon* ❸刑具 fetters; shackles

齘（齘） xiè ㄒㄧㄝ ❶上下牙齿相磨 (of teeth) to grind ❷物体相接处参差不密合 (of joints) irregular

亵（褻） xiè ㄒㄧㄝ ❶轻慢，亲近而不庄重 to treat with irreverence：～渎 *blaspheme* ❷指贴身的衣服 underwear：～衣 *underwear* ❸淫秽 obscene; indecent：猥～ *obscene; act indecently*

谢（謝） xiè ㄒㄧㄝ ❶表示感激 ㊀to thank：～～你！ *Thank you!* ❷道歉或认错 to apologize; to excuse oneself：～罪 *apologize for an offence* ❸辞去，拒绝 to decline; to refuse：～客 *decline to receive guests* | ～绝参观。*Not open to visitors.* ❹凋落，衰退 to wither：花～了。*The flowers have withered away.* | 新陈代～ *metabolism; the new supersedes the old*

榭 xiè ㄒㄧㄝ 台上的屋子 house or pavilion built on a terrace：水～ *waterside pavilion*

解 xiè ㄒㄧㄝ ❶明白，懂得 to understand; to get the point：～不开这个理 *can not see the point* ❷姓 (surname) Xie ❸解县，旧县名，在山西省运城 Xiexian (old name for a county in Yuncheng, Shanxi Province)

⇨ see also jiě on p.318, jiè on p.320

薢 xiè ㄒㄧㄝ ［薢茩］（－hòu） 即菱 water chestnut (same as 菱)

獬 xiè ㄒㄧㄝ ［獬豸］（－zhì） 传说中的异兽名 a legendary creature in Chinese mythology

邂 xiè ㄒㄧㄝ ［邂逅］（—hòu）没有约定而遇到，偶然遇到 to encounter by chance

廨 xiè ㄒㄧㄝ 古代通称官署 (ancient) government office：官～ *government office* | 公～ *public functionary's office*

澥 xiè ㄒㄧㄝ ❶糊状物或胶状物由稠变稀 to thin down：糨糊～了。*The paste has lost its stickiness.* ❷加水使糊状物或胶状物变稀 to thin with water：粥太稠，加点儿水～一～。*The porridge is too thick, add some water to it.* ❸渤澥，古代海的别称，也指渤海 (another name for 海 in ancient times) sea; Bohai Sea

懈 xiè ㄒㄧㄝ 松懈，不紧张（㊀—怠）slack; lax：始终不～ *unremitting* ㊁漏洞 loophole：无～可击 *with no chink in one's armour*

蟹（*蠏）xiè ㄒㄧㄝ 螃蟹，节肢动物，水陆两栖，全身有甲壳。前面的一对脚呈钳状，叫螯。横着走。腹部分节，俗叫脐，雄的尖脐，雌的团脐。种类很多 crab：河～ *river crab* | 海～ *sea crab*

薤 xiè ㄒㄧㄝ 草本植物，又叫藠头（jiàotou），叶细长，花紫色。鳞茎和嫩叶可用作蔬菜 Chinese onion (also called 藠头 jiàotou)

瀣 xiè ㄒㄧㄝ see 沆瀣 (hàng—) at 沆 on page 243

燮（*爕）xiè ㄒㄧㄝ 谐和，调和 to mediate; to harmonize

瓕 xiè ㄒㄧㄝ 一种像玉的石头 a jade-like stone

躞 xiè ㄒㄧㄝ see 蹀躞 (dié—) at 蹀 on page 138

XIN ㄒㄧㄣ

心 xīn ㄒㄧㄣ ❶心脏，人和高等动物体内推动血液循环的器官 heart (see picture of 人体内脏 on page 819) ［心腹］㊂1 最要紧的部位 vital part：～之患 *serious hidden trouble (literally means 'disease in one's vitals')* 2 亲信的人 trusted subordinate; henchman ［心胸］指气量 magnanimity; breadth of mind：～宽阔 *broad-minded* ❷习惯上也指思想器官和思想感情等 mind; thought; feeling：～思 *thought; mind* | ～得 *knowledge gained; understanding* | 用～ *diligently* | ～情 *mood* | 开～（快乐）*happy* | 伤～ *sad* | 谈～ *have a heart-to-heart talk* | 全～全意 *whole heartedly* ❸中央，在中间的地位或部分 centre; core：掌～ *palm* | 江～ *middle of the river* | 圆～ *centre of a circle* ［中心］1 same as "心❸" 2 主要部分 central part：政治～ *political centre* | 文化～ *cultural centre* | ～任务 *central task* | ～环节 *key point; central link* ❹星宿名，又叫商，二十八宿之一 *xin* (also called 商, one of the twenty-eight constellations in ancient Chinese astronomy)

芯 xīn ㄒㄧㄣ 去皮的灯心草 rush pith：灯～ *wick* ㊃某些

物体的中心部分 core：机～ *core of a mechanical device* | 岩～ *rock core*

⇨ see also xìn on p.725

䜣(訢) xīn ㄒㄧㄣ 姓 (surname) Xin

忻 xīn ㄒㄧㄣ ❶same as "欣" ❷忻州，地名，在山西省 Xinzhou (a place in Shanxi Province)

昕 xīn ㄒㄧㄣ 太阳将要出来的时候 dawn; daybreak

欣 xīn ㄒㄧㄣ 快乐，喜欢 happy; joyful：欢～鼓舞 *elated and excited* | ～然前往 *go with pleasure* [欣赏] 用喜爱的心情来领会其中的意味，喜欢 to enjoy [欣欣] 1 高兴的样子 joyful：～然有喜色 *beam with delight* 2 草木生机旺盛的样子 (of plants) luxuriant：～向荣 *thriving; prosperous*

炘 xīn ㄒㄧㄣ 形容热气炽盛 blazing hot

焮 xīn ㄒㄧㄣ xìn ㄒㄧㄣˋ (又) 烧，灼 to burn; to scorch

辛 xīn ㄒㄧㄣ ❶辣 (in taste, flavour, etc.) hot; pungent ❷劳苦，艰难 hard; laborious：～勤 *industrious* ❸悲伤 sad; miserable：～酸 *miserable* ❹天干的第八位，用作顺序的第八 *xin* (the eighth of the ten Heavenly Stems, a system used in the Chinese calendar); eighth

莘 xīn ㄒㄧㄣ 古指细辛。草本植物，根细，有辣味，花暗紫色，可入药 (same as 细辛 in ancient times) *Asarum heterotropoides* [莘庄] 地名，在上海市 Xinzhuang (a place in Shanghai Municipality)

⇨ see also shēn on p.589

锌(鋅) xīn ㄒㄧㄣ 金属元素，符号 Zn，蓝白色，质脆。可用来制合金等 Zinc (Zn)

廞(廞) xīn ㄒㄧㄣ 陈设 decor; furnishing

歆 xīn ㄒㄧㄣ ❶鬼神享用祭品的香气 (of ghosts and gods) to enjoy the fragrance of offerings：～享 *to relish* ❷喜爱，羡慕 to like; to admire：～羡 *to adore*

新 xīn ㄒㄧㄣ ❶跟"旧"相对 new (opposite of 旧) ①刚有的或刚经验到的 fresh; recent：～办法 *new method* | 万象更～。*All things take on a new look.* | ～事物 *novelty* ②没有用过的 unused; new：～笔 *new pen* | ～房子 *new house* ③性质上改变得更好的，使变成新的 renewed; updated：～社会 *new society* | ～文艺 *new art and literature* | 粉刷一～ *painted anew* [自新] 改掉以往的过错，使思想行为向好的方面发展 turn over a new leaf ❷新近 recently; lately：这支钢笔是我～买的。*I have just bought this pen.* | 他是～来的。*He is a new arrival.* ❸结婚时的（人或物）relating to weddings：～郎 *bridegroom* | ～房 *bridal chamber*

薪 xīn ㄒㄧㄣ 柴火 firewood：杯水车～ *an utterly inadequate measure (literally means 'one cup of water for a cart of fire wood')* [薪水] [薪金] 工资 salary

馨 xīn ㄒㄧㄣ 散布很远的香气 pervasive fragrance：～香

fragrance; smell of burning incense | 芳～ *fragrance*

鑫 xīn ㄒㄧㄣ 财富兴盛。常用于商店字号、人名 prosperous; thriving (often used in names of shops or people)

镡（鐔） xín ㄒㄧㄣˊ ❶古代剑身与剑柄连接处突出的部分 (ancient) guard/pommel of a sword ❷古代兵器，似剑而小 an ancient weapon similar to sword but smaller

⇨ see also chán on p.66, tán on p.637

伈 xǐn ㄒㄧㄣˇ ［伈伈］形容恐惧 fearful

囟（顖）** xìn ㄒㄧㄣˋ 囟门，婴儿头顶骨未合缝（fèng）的地方 fontanel

芯 xìn ㄒㄧㄣˋ ❶（－子）装在器物中心的捻子之类的东西，如蜡烛的捻子、爆竹的引线等 fuse; wick ❷（－子）蛇的舌头 snake's tongue

⇨ see also xīn on p.723

信 xìn ㄒㄧㄣˋ ❶诚实，不欺骗 honest; true：～用 *credit; trustworthiness* | 失～ *break a promise* ❷信任，不怀疑，认为可靠 to believe; to trust：～赖 *to trust* | 这话我不～。*I don't believe this.* ㊀信仰，崇奉 to believe in：～徒 *believer; disciple* ❸（－儿）消息（㊥－息）message; information：报～ *to notify; deliver a message* | 喜～儿 *good news* ［信号］传达消息、命令、报告等的记号 signal：放～枪 *signal gun* ❹函件（㊥书－）letter; mail：给他写封～ *write him a letter* ❺随便 at will; without plan：～步 *to stroll* | ～口开河（随便乱说）*have a loose tongue* ❻信石，砒霜 arsenic ❼ same as "芯 (xìn)"

〈古 ancient〉 also same as 伸 (shēn)

衅（釁） xìn ㄒㄧㄣˋ ❶古代祭祀礼仪，用牲畜的血涂器物的缝隙 ancient sacrificial ritual of filling fissures of utensils with animal blood：～钟 *smear a bell with animal blood* | ～鼓 *spread animal blood onto a drum* ❷缝隙，争端 fissure; dispute：挑～ *to provoke* | 寻～ *pick a quarrel*

焮 xìn ㄒㄧㄣˋ（又）see xīn on page 724

XING ㄒㄧㄥ

兴（興） xīng ㄒㄧㄥ ❶举办，发动 to start; to launch：～工 *start construction* | ～利除弊 *promote the beneficial and abolish the harmful* | ～修水利 *build irrigation works* ❷起来 to get up; to rise：夙～夜寐（早起晚睡）*rise early and retire late* | 闻风～起 *rise up in action on hearing sth* ❸旺盛（㊥－盛、－旺）thriving：复～ *to revive* ［兴奋］精神振作或激动 to be excited ❹流行，盛行 to prevail; to become popular：时～ *be in vogue* ❺准许 to permit; to allow：不～胡闹。*Don't make mischief.* ❻〈方 dialect〉或许 maybe：他～来，～不来。*He may or may not come.* ❼姓 (surname) Xing

⇨ see also xìng on p.728

星 xīng ㄒㄧㄥ ❶天空中发光的或反射光的天体，如太阳、地球、北斗星等。通常指夜间天空中闪烁发光的天体 star：卫～ *satellite* | ～罗棋布 *scattered like stars* | 月明～稀。*The moon is bright and stars are few.* ⓔ称有名的演员、运动员等 celebrity; star: 明～ *star* | 球～ *star player (in ball games)* | 歌～ *star singer* ❷（－子、－儿）细碎或细小的东西 bit; particle：～火燎原。*A single spark can start a prairie fire.* | 火～儿 *(of fire) spark* | 唾沫～子 *spray of saliva* ❸星宿名，二十八宿之一 *xing* (one of the twenty-eight constellations in ancient Chinese astronomy)

猩 xīng ㄒㄧㄥ 猩猩，哺乳动物，略像人，毛赤褐色或黑色，前肢长，无尾。吃野果。产于苏门答腊等地 orang-utan

惺 xīng ㄒㄧㄥ 醒悟 to awake to; to realize［惺惺］1 清醒，聪明 clearheaded; awake 2 聪明的人 wise person：～惜～（指同类的人互相怜惜）*the clever appreciate each other*［假惺惺］虚情假意的样子 hypocritical

［惺忪］（*惺松）刚睡醒尚未清醒的样子 drowsy-eyed

瑆 xīng ㄒㄧㄥ 玉的光彩 lustre of jade

腥 xīng ㄒㄧㄥ ❶腥气，像鱼的气味 fishy smell：血～ *bloody* | ～膻（shān）*fishy smell* ❷鱼、肉一类的食品 raw meat or fish：荤～ *meat or fish*

煋 xīng ㄒㄧㄥ ❶火势猛烈 flaming ❷火光四射 glaring

骍（騂） xīng ㄒㄧㄥ 赤色的马或牛 bay horse; bay ox

刑 xíng ㄒㄧㄥˊ ❶刑罚，对犯人各种处罚的总称 punishment; penalty; sentence：判～ *to sentence* | 死～ *capital punishment; death penalty* | 徒～ *imprisonment* | 缓～ *probation* ❷特指对犯人的体罚，如拷打、折磨等 corporal punishment; torture：受～ *suffer corporal punishment* | 动～ *to torture* | 严～逼供 *extort confession by torturing*

邢 xíng ㄒㄧㄥˊ 姓 (surname) Xing

形 xíng ㄒㄧㄥˊ ❶样子 form; shape：三角～ *triangle* | 地～ *topography; terrain* | ～式 *form* | ～象 *image*［形成］逐渐发展成为（某种事物、状况或局面等）to form; to take shape：爱护公物已～一种风气。*It has become a common practice to care for public property.*［形势］1 地理上指地势的高低，山、水的样子 terrain 2 事物发展的状况 situation：国际～ *international situation* ❷体，实体 body; entity：～体 *shape; physique* | 无～ *shapeless* | ～影不离 *be inseparable (as form and shadow)* ❸表现 to show; to appear：喜怒不～于色 *not show one's emotions*［形容］1 面容 countenance：～枯槁 *appear thin and emaciated* 2 对事物的样子、性质加以描述 to describe［形容词］表示事物的特征、性质、状

态的词，如"大、小、好、坏、快、慢"等 adjective ❹对照，比较 to compare; to contrast：相～之下 *in comparison; by contrast* | 相～见绌（chù）*pale in comparison*

型 xíng ㄒㄧㄥˊ ❶铸造器物用的模子 mould; model：砂～ *sand mould* ❷样式 model; type; pattern：新～ *new model* | 小～汽车 *small car*

钘（鈃） xíng ㄒㄧㄥˊ 古代盛酒器。又用于人名 an ancient wine vessel; also used in given names

硎 xíng ㄒㄧㄥˊ ❶磨刀石 whetstone ❷磨制 to grind; to polish; to whet

铏（鉶） xíng ㄒㄧㄥˊ 古代盛羹的器具 ancient vessel for gruel

行 xíng ㄒㄧㄥˊ ❶走 to go; to walk：日～千里 *cover one thousand* li *a day* | 步～ *go on foot* ㊀出外时用的 relating to travel：～装 *outfit for a journey* | ～箧（qiè）*travelling suitcase*［行李］（-li）出外时所带的包裹、箱子等 luggage［一行］一组（指同行xíng的人）a group of people (travelling together)［行书］汉字的一种字体，形体和笔势介于草书和楷书之间 running script (in Chinese calligraphy) ❷流通，传递 to circulate：～销 *be on the market* | 通～全国 *go throughout the country* | 发～报刊、书籍 *publish and distribute newspapers, magazines and books* ❸流动性的，临时性的 mobile; temporary：～灶 *mobile cooking stove* | ～商 *travelling merchant* | ～营 *military camp; field headquarters* ❹进行 to carry out：另～通知 *will notify separately* | 即～查处 *investigate and treat forthwith* ❺实做，办 to perform; to implement：～礼 *to salute* | 举～ *to hold; to stage* | 实～ *carry out* ❻ (formerly pronounced xìng) 足以表明品质的举止行动 behaviour：言～ *words and deeds* | 品～ *conduct; behaviour* | 德～ *moral integrity* | 操～ *conduct; behaviour* | 罪～ *crime* ❼可以 to be all right; will do：不学习不～。*Not to study won't do.* ❽能干 capable; competent：你真～，这么快就解决了问题。*You are clever to have solved the problem so quickly.* ❾将要 soon：～将毕业 *soon to graduate* ❿乐府和古诗的一种体裁 a form in classical Chinese poetry and folk song ⓫姓 (surname) Xing

⇨ see also háng on p.242

饧（餳） xíng ㄒㄧㄥˊ ❶糖稀 treacle made from malt; molasses; syrup ❷糖块、面团等变软 to soften; to become sticky：刚和（huó）好的面～一会儿好擀（gǎn）。*The dough rolls well after resting for a while and becoming sticky.* ❸精神不振，眼睛半睁半闭 drowsy-eyed; sleepy：眼睛发～ *be drowsy-eyed*

陉（陘） xíng ㄒㄧㄥˊ 山脉中断的地方 defile; mountain pass

婞(婞) xíng ㄒㄧㄥˊ 女子身材高而美 (of a woman's figure) tall and pretty

荥(滎) xíng ㄒㄧㄥˊ [荥阳] 地名，在河南省 Xingyang (a place in Henan Province)

⇨ see also yíng on p.785

X

省 xǐng ㄒㄧㄥˇ ❶检查自己 to introspect：反～ *make a self-examination* ❷感觉 to feel; to be aware：不～人事 *lose consciousness* ❸省悟，觉悟 to become conscious; to realize：猛～前非 *suddenly wake up to one's former erroneous ways* ❹看望，问候（父母、尊长）to visit (parents or elders)：～亲 *pay a visit to one's parents*

⇨ see also shěng on p.593

醒 xǐng ㄒㄧㄥˇ ❶睡完或还没睡着（zháo）to be awake ❷头脑由迷糊而清楚（㊊一悟）to wake up：清～ *clear-headed; sober* | 惊～ *wake up with a start; be woken* [醒目] 鲜明，清楚，引人注意的 prominent; striking ❸酒醉之后恢复常态 to regain consciousness; to sober up：酒～了 *sobered up from drunkenness* 也指使醉酒的人恢复常态 to sober sb up：～酒 *sober sb up*

擤(揞)** xǐng ㄒㄧㄥˇ 捏住鼻子，用气排出鼻涕 to blow one's nose：～鼻涕 *blow one's nose*

兴(興) xìng ㄒㄧㄥˋ 兴趣，对事物喜爱的情绪 mood or desire for things; interest; excitement：游～ *mood for sight-seeing* | 助～ *enliven the mood* | ～高采烈 *be in good spirits* [高兴] 愉快，喜欢 happy; cheerful

⇨ see also xīng on p.725

杏 xìng ㄒㄧㄥˋ 杏树，落叶乔木，花白色或淡红色，果实叫杏ル或杏子，球形，味酸甜，可吃。核中的仁叫杏仁，甜的可吃，苦的供药用 apricot (its fruit is called 杏儿 or 杏子 and kernel called 杏仁)

幸(❶❺❻*倖) xìng ㄒㄧㄥˋ ❶意外地得到成功或免去灾害 fortunate; lucky：～存 *to survive* | ～免 *escape by luck* [幸亏] [幸而] 副词，多亏 (adverb) fortunately; luckily：～你来了。*Fortunately you came.* ❷幸福，幸运 happiness; good fortune：荣～ *honour* | 三生有～ *consider oneself most fortunate* ❸高兴 to rejoice：庆～ *congratulate oneself; rejoice* | 欣～ *be happy and thankful* ❹希望 hopefully：～勿推却。*I hope that you will not refuse.* ❺旧指宠爱 (old) to love; to dote on：宠～ *to favour;to love* | 得～ *win sb's favour* ❻旧指封建帝王到达某地 (old) (of an emperor) to arrive; to visit：巡～ *make imperial tour of inspection*

倖 xìng ㄒㄧㄥˋ ❶ see 幸 on page 728 ❷ see 傒倖 at 傒 on page 697

悻 xìng ㄒㄧㄥˋ [悻悻]怨恨，怒 resentful; angry：～而去 *walk off in a huff*

婞 xìng ㄒㄧㄥˋ 倔强，固执 stubborn; obstinate

性 xìng ㄒㄧㄥˋ ❶事物本身所具有的性质或性能 property; quality：碱～ *alkalinity* | 弹（tán）～ *elasticity* | 向日～ *heliotropism* | 药～ *property of a medicine* | 斗争～ *fighting spirit*［性命］生命 life ❷性格 nature; temperament：个～ *personality; individuality* | 天～ *nature (of a person)* | ～情 *disposition* | 本～难移。*One's nature can hardly be changed.* ❸男女或雌雄的特质 sex; gender：～别 *gender* | 男～ *male sex* | 女～ *female sex* | ～器官 *sexual organ; genital* | ～教育 *sexual education* ❹在思想、感情等方面的表现 spirit; sense：党～ *Party spirit* | 组织纪律～ *sense of organizational discipline*

姓 xìng ㄒㄧㄥˋ 表明家族系统的字 surname：～名 *surname and given name* | 复～"欧阳" *compound family name* 欧阳

荇（莕）** xìng ㄒㄧㄥˋ 荇菜，草本植物，叶浮在水面，花黄色。茎可以吃，全草可入药 yellow floating heart

XIONG ㄒㄩㄥ

凶（❸–❺*兇） xiōng ㄒㄩㄥ ❶不幸的，跟"吉"相对 ominous; unlucky (opposite of 吉)：～事（丧事）*funeral arrangement* | 吉～ *good or ill luck* ❷庄稼收成不好 crop failure：～年 *famine year* ❸恶，暴（㊀–恶、–暴）ferocious; fierce; brutal：～狠 *ferocious* | 穷～极恶 *utterly evil* ❹指杀伤人的行为，也指行凶作恶的人 act of violence; murder; ruffian; murderer：～器 *lethal/criminal weapon* | 行～ *commit physical assault or murder* | ～手 *assailant; murderer* | 帮～ *accomplice* ❺厉害，过甚 terrible：你闹得太～了。*You are making an unholy row.* | 雨来得很～。*The rain came down with a vengeance.*

匈 xiōng ㄒㄩㄥ (ancient) same as "胸"

［匈奴］我国古代北方的民族 Xiongnu (or Huns, an ancient ethnic group in northern China)

讻（訩、詾）** xiōng ㄒㄩㄥ 争辩 to dispute; to argue［讻讻］形容争论的声音或纷扰的样子 tumultuous; uproarious

汹（*洶） xiōng ㄒㄩㄥ 水向上翻腾（㊀–涌）(of waves) to surge［汹汹］1 形容水声或争吵声 (of waves or arguing) roaring 2 形容声势很大 violent; truculent：来势～ *with violent force*

胸（*胷） xiōng ㄒㄩㄥ 胸膛，躯干前部颈下腹上的部分 chest; breast (see picture of 人体 on page 647)［胸襟］指气量，抱负 breadth of mind

兄 xiōng ㄒㄩㄥ 哥哥 elder brother：～嫂 *elder brother and his wife* 敬辞 polite speech：老～ *my dear old friend* | 仁～ *my dear friend* | 某某～ *dear sb*［兄弟］1 兄和弟的统称 brothers (older and younger)：～三人 *three brothers* ㉄有亲密关系的 brotherly; fraternal：～单位 *brother unit* 2（—di）弟弟 younger brother

芎 xiōng ㄒㄩㄥ [芎䓖]（—qióng）草本植物，又叫川芎，叶像芹菜，秋天开花，花白色，全草有香味，地下茎可入药 *Ligusticum sinense* (also called 川芎)

雄 xióng ㄒㄩㄥˊ ❶公的，阳性的，跟"雌"相对 male (opposite of 雌)：～鸡 *cock* | ～蕊 *stamen* ❷强有力的 powerful; mighty：～师 *powerful army* | ～辩 *eloquence* ❸宏伟，有气魄的 grand; imposing：～心 *ambition* | ～伟 *magnificent* ❹强有力的人或国家 powerful person or state：英～ *hero* | 战国七～ *the seven powers of the Warring States Period*

熊 xióng ㄒㄩㄥˊ ❶兽名，身体大，尾短，能直立行走，也能爬树。种类很多 bear [大熊猫] 哺乳动物，又叫熊猫、猫熊，像熊而略小，尾短，眼周、耳、前后肢和肩部黑色，其余白色，耐寒。喜食竹叶、竹笋。生活在我国西南地区，是我国特有的珍贵动物 giant panda (also called 熊猫，猫熊）❷〈方 dialect〉斥责 to rebuke; to scold：～了他一顿 *gave him a scolding* ❸〈方 dialect〉怯懦，没有能力 cowardly; useless：这人真～，一上场就败了下来。*He is so useless, losing the match hardly after it started.*

[熊熊] 形容火势旺盛 flaming; ablaze：烈火～ *flames raging*

诇（詗）xiòng ㄒㄩㄥˋ 刺探 to spy on; to detect

敻 xiòng ㄒㄩㄥˋ 远，辽阔 remote; vast：～古 *remote antiquity*

XIU ㄒㄧㄡ

休 xiū ㄒㄧㄡ ❶歇息 to rest：～假 *take a vacation* | ～养 *to recuperate* ❷停止 to stop; to cease; to suspend：～业 *business closed* | ～学 *take time off school* | ～会 *recess* | 争论不～ *argue endlessly* ㉄完结（多指失败或死亡）to end; (usually) to die; to fail ❸旧社会丈夫把妻子赶回娘家，断绝夫妻关系 (old) to divorce (one's wife)：～书 *divorce letter (to wife)* | ～妻 *divorce one's wife* ❹副词，不要，别 (adverb) don't：～想 *don't even imagine* | ～要这样性急。*Don't be so impatient.* ❺吉庆，美善 good fortune; merit：～咎（吉凶）*good or bad luck* | ～戚（喜和忧）相关 *be linked together in common joys and sorrows*

咻 xiū ㄒㄧㄡ 吵，乱说话 to make a noise [咻咻] 1 形容喘气的声音 to pant noisily 2 形容某些动物的叫声 chirping; screeching：小鸭～地叫着。*The duckling is cheeping.*

庥 xiū ㄒㄧㄡ 庇荫，保护 to shelter; to protect

鸺（鵂）xiū ㄒㄧㄡ see 鸱鸺 (chī—) at 鸱 on page 79, and 鸺鹠 (—liú) at 鹠 on page

412
貅 xiū ㄒㄧㄡ see 貔貅 (pí—) at 貔 on page 501

髹(**髤) xiū ㄒㄧㄡ 把漆涂在器物上 to coat with lacquer

修(△*脩) xiū ㄒㄧㄡ ❶使完美或恢复完美 to repair; to mend; to overhaul: ～饰 *to embellish* | ～理 *to repair* | ～辞 *polish writing; rhetoric* | ～车 *repair a car* ❷建造 to build; to construct: ～铁道 *build a railway* | ～桥 *build a bridge* ❸写，编写 to write; to compile: ～书 *compile a book; write a letter* | ～史 *write history* ❹钻研学习，研究(㊊研—) to study: ～业 *pursue academic studies* | 自～ *study/review lessons on one's own* ❺长(cháng)(㊊—长) tall and slender: 茂林～竹 *thick forest and tall bamboos*

脩 xiū ㄒㄧㄡ ❶干肉 dried meat [束脩]一束干肉 a bundle of dried meat ㊟旧时指送给老师的薪金 (old) a private tutor's remuneration ❷ see 修 on page 731

蟰 xiū ㄒㄧㄡ 昆虫，即竹节虫，外形像竹节或树枝，头小，无翅。生活在树上，吃树叶 stick insect (same as 竹节虫)

羞 xiū ㄒㄧㄡ ❶耻辱，感到耻辱(㊊—耻) to feel ashamed: ～辱 *humiliation; to humiliate* | 遮～布 *fig leaf* | ～与为伍 *feel ashamed to associate with sb* ❷难为情，害臊 to feel shy; to be bashful: 害～ *feel bashful* | ～得脸通红 *blush with embarrassment* ㊀使难为情 to embarrass; to shame: 你别～我。*Don't embarrass me.* ❸ same as "馐"

馐(饈) xiū ㄒㄧㄡ 美味的食品 tasty food; delicacy: 珍～ *rare delicacy* (also written as 羞)

朽 xiǔ ㄒㄧㄡˇ ❶腐烂，多指木头(㊊腐—) to decay; to rot: ～木 *rotten wood or tree* [不朽](精神、功业等)不磨灭 (of spirit or exploits) to never die or decay: 永垂～ *go down forever* ❷衰老 senile: 老～ *old and useless*

宿(*宿) xiǔ ㄒㄧㄡˇ 夜 night: 住了一～ *stayed one night* | 谈了半～ *chatted till midnight*

⇨ see also sù on p.624, xiù on p.732

滫 xiǔ ㄒㄧㄡˇ 泔水 swill; hogwash

秀 xiù ㄒㄧㄡˋ ❶植物吐穗开花，多指庄稼 (of cereal plants) to put forth flowers or ears: 高粱～穗了。*The sorghum has put forth ears.* | 六月六看谷～。*The sixth day of the sixth month is when millets form ears.* ❷特别优异的(㊊优—) excellent: ～异 *outstanding* | ～挺 *outstanding* ㊀特别优异的人才 talented person: 新～ *new talent* | 后起之～ *up-and-coming star* [秀才](—cai)封建时代科举初考合格的人。泛指书生 one who passed the imperial examination at the county level in the Ming and Qing Dynasties; (generally) scholar ❸聪明，灵

巧 clever; nimble：聪～ *clever* | 内～ *intelligent but unassuming* | 心～ *implicitly intelligent* ❹美丽（㊉一丽）elegant; beautiful：眉清目～ *have delicate features* | 山明水～ *green hills and clear waters* | ～美 *graceful* [秀气]（一qi）1 清秀 delicate and pretty：小姑娘很～。*The little girl is delicately pretty.* 2（器物）灵巧轻便 exquisite：这个东西做得很～。*This thing is exquisite.* ❺（外 loanword）表演，展示 to show：作～ *put on a show* | 服装～ *fashion show*

绣（綉、*繡） xiù ㄒㄧㄡˋ ❶用丝线等在绸、布上缀成花纹或文字 to embroider：～花 *embroider* | ～字 *embroider words* ❷绣成的物品 embroidery：湘～ *Hunan embroidery* | 苏～ *Suzhou embroidery*

琇 xiù ㄒㄧㄡˋ 像玉的石头 jade-like stone

锈（銹、*鏽） xiù ㄒㄧㄡˋ ❶金属表面所生的氧化物 rust：铁～ *rust* | 铜～ *verdigris* | 这把刀子长（zhǎng）～了。*The knife is rusted.* ❷生锈 to rust：门上的锁～住了。*The lock on the door is rusted in.*

岫 xiù ㄒㄧㄡˋ ❶山洞 cave; cavern ❷山 mountain

袖 xiù ㄒㄧㄡˋ ❶（一子、一儿）衣服套在胳膊上的部分 sleeve (see picture of 上衣 on page 767) [袖珍] 小型的 miniature; pocket-size：～字典 *pocket dictionary* | ～收录机 *pocket radio cassette player* ❷藏在袖子里 to tuck inside the sleeve：～着手 *hands tucked in sleeves* | ～手旁观 *fold one's arms and look on*

琇 xiù ㄒㄧㄡˋ 一种有瑕疵的玉 a kind of blemished jade

臭 xiù ㄒㄧㄡˋ ❶气味 odour; smell：空气是无色无～的。*Air is colourless and odourless.* ❷ same as "嗅"

⇨ see also chòu on p.86

嗅 xiù ㄒㄧㄡˋ 闻，用鼻子辨别气味 to smell; to scent; to sniff：～觉 *sense of smell*

溴 xiù ㄒㄧㄡˋ 非金属元素，符号 Br，赤褐色液体，能侵蚀皮肤和黏膜。可用来制染料、镇静剂等 bromine (Br)

宿（*宿） xiù ㄒㄧㄡˋ 我国古代的天文学家把天上某些星的集合体叫作宿 (ancient) constellation：星～ *constellation* | 二十八～ *the twenty-eight constellations in ancient Chinese astronomy*

⇨ see also sù on p.624, xiǔ on p.731

XU ㄒㄩ

讦（訏） xū ㄒㄩ ❶夸口 to boast; to brag ❷大 big; broad：～谟（大计）*grand plan*

圩 xū ㄒㄩ 闽粤等地区称集市。古书里作"虚" (in regions including Fujian and Guangdong Provinces) country fair; market (written as 虚 in ancient texts)

⇨ see also wéi on p.679

吁 xū ㄒㄩ ❶叹息 to sigh：长～短叹 *to moan and groan* ❷文言叹词，表示惊疑 (exclamation in classical Chinese) oh; why：～，是何言欤！*Oh my, what kind of talk is this!*

⇨ see also yù on p.801

盱 xū ㄒㄩ ❶太阳刚出时的样子 rising sun ❷盱江，水名，又地名，都在江西省抚州 Xujiang (a river, also a place, both in Fuzhou, Jiangxi Province)

盱 xū ㄒㄩ 睁开眼向上看 to look up; to stare

［盱眙］(－yí) 地名，在江苏省 Xuyi (a place in Jiangsu Province)

戌 xū ㄒㄩ ❶地支的第十一位 *xu* (the eleventh of the twelve Earthly Branches, a system used in the Chinese calendar) ❷戌时，指晚上七点到九点 *xu* (the period from 7 p.m. to 9 p.m.)

砉 xū ㄒㄩ 形容皮骨相离声 sound of skin and flesh torn from the bone

⇨ see also huā on p.262

须(須、❸❹鬚) xū ㄒㄩ ❶必须，必得(děi)，应当 must; have to：这事～亲自动手。*This matter needs to be handled in person.* | 务～ *be sure to* ❷等待 to await：～晴日，看红装素裹，分外妖娆。*On a fine day, the land, clad in white and adorned in red, becomes exceedingly enchanting.* ❸胡子(㊀胡－) beard ❹像胡须的东西 palpus; feeler; tassel：触～ *feeler* | 花～ *stamen* | ～根 *fibrous root*

［须臾］(－yú) 片刻，一会儿 moment; instant

媭(嬃) xū ㄒㄩ 古代楚国人对姐姐的称呼 (in the ancient state of Chu) elder sister

胥 xū ㄒㄩ ❶古代的小官 petty official in ancient China：～吏 *petty official* ❷全，都 all; each and every：民～然矣。*All would follow the example.* | 万事～备。*Everything is ready.*

谞(諝) xū ㄒㄩ ❶才智 ability and wisdom ❷计谋 scheme; stratagem

顼(頊) xū ㄒㄩ see 颛顼 (zhuān－) at 颛 on page 872

虚 xū ㄒㄩ ❶空(㊀空－) void; empty：弹不～发。*Not a single shot missed its target.* | 座无～席。*No seat is left untaken.* ［虚心］不自满，不骄傲 modest：～使人进步，骄傲使人落后。*Modesty leads one forward and conceit drags one behind.* ❷不真实的，跟"实"相对 false; nominal (opposite of 实)：～名 *false reputation* | ～荣 *vanity* | ～张声势 *play a false show of strength* ［虚词］意义比较抽象，有帮助造句作用的词，如副词、介词、连词等 function word ❸心里怯懦 diffident; timid：心里发～ *feel unsure of oneself* | 做贼心～ *have a guilty conscience* ❹衰弱 weak; feeble：～弱 *physically weak* | 他身子太～了。*He is quite frail physically.* ❺徒

然，白白地 in vain：～度年华 *dawdle away one's time* | 不～此行 *have a rewarding trip* ❻指政治思想、方针、政策等方面的道理 guiding principles：务～ *discuss principles or general guidelines* | 以～带实 *practical work guided with principles* ❼星宿名，二十八宿之一 xu (one of the twenty-eight constellations in ancient Chinese astronomy)

墟 xū ㄒㄩ ❶有人住过而现在已经荒废的地方 ruins：废～ *ruins* | 殷～ *Yin Dynasty ruins* [墟里][墟落]村落 village; hamlet ❷〈方 dialect〉集市，同"圩"（xū）fair;market (same as 圩 xū)

嘘 xū ㄒㄩ ❶从嘴里慢慢地吐气，呵气 to exhale slowly ❷叹气 to sigh：仰天而～ *look up at the sky and sigh* ❸火或汽的热力熏炙 (of fire, steam, etc.) to scald; to burn：小心别～着手。*Careful you don't burn your hand.* | 把馒头放在锅里～一～ *heat the buns in the steamer*

[嘘唏] see 唏嘘 at 唏 on page 696

⇨ see also shī on p.596

歔 xū ㄒㄩ see 欷歔 (xī－) at 欷 on page 696

欻 xū ㄒㄩ 忽然 suddenly：风雨～至 *wind and rain come all of a sudden*

⇨ see also chuā on p.90

需 xū ㄒㄩ ❶需要，必得用 to need; to want; to require：必～ *essential* | 急～钱用 *be in urgent need of money* | 按～分配 *distribution to each according to his/her need* ❷必用的财物 necessaries; indispensables：军～ *military supplies*

繻(繻) xū ㄒㄩ ❶彩色的丝织品 coloured silk product ❷古代一种用帛制的通行证 (ancient) silk pass

魆 xū ㄒㄩ [黑魆魆]形容黑暗 in pitch dark：山洞里～的。*It is very dark inside the cave.*

徐 xú ㄒㄩˊ 缓，慢慢地 ㊀ slowly：～步 *walk slowly* | 清风～来。*A refreshing breeze comes gently.* | 火车～～开动了。*The train slowly started.*

许(許) xǔ ㄒㄩˇ ❶应允，认可（㊀允－、准－）to allow; to permit：特～ *special permission* | 不～ *to forbid* ㊁称赞，承认其优点 to praise：赞～ *to praise* | 推～ *to commend* | ～为佳作 *be praised as a fine piece of writing* ❷预先答应给予 to promise：～配 *to betroth* | 我～给他一份礼物。*I promised him a present.* | 以身～国 *dedicate oneself to one's country* ❸或者，可能 maybe; perhaps：也～ *perhaps* | 或～ *maybe* | 他下午～来。*He may come this afternoon.* ❹处，地方 place：先生不知何～人也。*The gentleman's place of birth is not known.* ❺表示约数 around; approximately：少～（少量）*a little* | 年三十～（三十岁左右）*some thirty years old* ❻这样 so; like this：如～ *so* [许多] 1 这样多，这么多 this much; this many; of such a quantity 2 很多 many;

much; a great deal [许久] 1 时间这么长 this much time 2 时间很长 a long time

浒(滸) xǔ ㄒㄩˇ [浒墅关] 地名，在江苏省苏州 Xushuguan (a place in Suzhou, Jiangsu Province) [浒浦] 地名，在江苏省常熟 Xupu (a place in Changshu, Jiangsu Province)

⇨ see also hǔ on p.260

诩(詡) xǔ ㄒㄩˇ 说大话，夸张 to boast; to exaggerate：自～ *to brag; self-styled*

珝 xǔ ㄒㄩˇ 一种玉 a kind of jade

栩 xǔ ㄒㄩˇ [栩栩] 形容生动的样子 vivid; lively：～如生 *vivid and lifelike*

姁 xǔ ㄒㄩˇ ㊫安乐，和悦 peaceful; amiable

冔 xǔ ㄒㄩˇ 商代的一种帽子 a cap worn during the Shang Dynasty

湑 xǔ ㄒㄩˇ ❶滤过的酒 filtered wine ㊀清澈 clear; pure ❷茂盛 luxuriant

⇨ see also xù on p.736

糈 xǔ ㄒㄩˇ ❶粮食 food; provision; grain ❷古代祭神用的精米 (ancient) sacrificial rice

醑 xǔ ㄒㄩˇ ❶美酒 fine wine ❷醑剂（挥发性药物的乙醇溶液）的简称 (of medicine) spirit：樟脑～ *camphor spirit* | 氯仿～ *spirit of chloroform*

旭 xù ㄒㄩˋ 光明，早晨太阳才出来的样子 brilliance of the rising sun [旭日] 才出来的太阳 rising sun

序 xù ㄒㄩˋ ❶次第（㊥次一）order; sequence：顺～ *order* | 工～ *procedure* | 前后有～ *in order of precedence* ❷排列次第 to arrange in order：～齿（按年龄排次序）*in order of age* ❸在正式内容之前的 preface; prelude; introduction：～文 *preface* | ～曲 *overture* | ～幕 *prologue* 特指序文 preface：写一篇～ *write a preface* ❹庠序，古代的学校 (ancient) school

垿 xù ㄒㄩˋ 古时放食物、酒器等东西的土台子，又叫坫（diàn）或反坫。多用于人名 earthen platform to hold wine vessels in ancient times; often used in given names (also called 坫 diàn or 反坫)

昫 xù ㄒㄩˋ ❶(old) same as "煦" ❷用于人名 used in given names

煦 xù ㄒㄩˋ 温暖 warm：春风和～ *a warm spring breeze*

叙(*敘、*敍) xù ㄒㄩˋ ❶述说（㊥一述）to talk; to chat：～旧 *chat about the old days* | ～家常 *chat about family trivia* ❷记述 to narrate; to recount：～事 *to narrate; to recount* | 记～ *to narrate* ❸same as "序❶❷❸"

溆 xù ㄒㄩˋ 水边 waterside [溆浦] 地名，在湖南省 Xupu (a place in Hunan Province)

洫 xù ㄒㄩˋ 水流动的样子 (of water) streaming

洫 xù ㄒㄩˋ 田间的水道、沟渠 water course in a field

恤(*卹、*賉、*邺) xù ㄒㄩˋ ❶对别人表同情，怜悯 to pity; to sympathize with：体～ *understand and sympathize with* | 怜～ *take pity on* ❷救济 to give relief; to compensate：～金 *pension; relief payment* | 抚～ *comfort and compensate* ❸忧虑 worry

畜 xù ㄒㄩˋ 饲养 to raise (domestic animals)：～产 *livestock product* | ～牧业 *animal husbandry*

⇨ see also chù on p.89

蓄 xù ㄒㄩˋ 积聚，储藏(㊟储－) to store up; to save up：～财 *save up money* ㊀①保存 to keep in reserve：～电池 *storage battery* | ～洪 *store flood water* | 养精～锐 *conserve strength and store up energy* ②心里存着 to harbour; to entertain (an idea)：～意 *deliberate; premeditated* | ～志 *have long held the ambition* | ～谋 *to premeditate*

滀 xù ㄒㄩˋ [滀仕](－shì) 越南地名 Xushi (a place in Vietnam)

⇨ see also chù on p.89

酗 xù ㄒㄩˋ 撒酒疯 to behave drunkenly：～酒(没有节制地喝酒) *to drink excessively*

勖(*勗) xù ㄒㄩˋ 勉励(㊟－勉) to encourage

绪(緒) xù ㄒㄩˋ ❶丝的头 ends of silk threads ㊟开端 beginning; commencement：千头万～ *have a multitude of things to cope with* [绪论] 著作开头叙述内容要点的部分 introduction (to a book) ❷前人留下的事业 unfinished task; unfinished cause：续未竟之～ *continue an unfinished task* ❸指心情、思想等 mentality; emotion：情～ *mood* | 思～ *train of thought* ❹残余 remnant：～余 *surplus*

续(續) xù ㄒㄩˋ ❶连接，接下去(㊟继－) to continue; to extend：～假(jià) *extend a leave of absence* | ～编 *sequel* | ～家谱 *add entries to the family tree* ❷在原有的上面再加 to add：把茶～上 *add tea* | 炉子该～煤了。*The stove fire needs more coal.*

[手续] 办事的程序 procedure

漵 xù ㄒㄩˋ 漵水河，水名，在陕西省汉中 Xushuihe River (in Hanzhong, Shaanxi Province)

⇨ see also xǔ on p.735

婿(*壻) xù ㄒㄩˋ ❶夫婿，丈夫 husband ❷女婿，女儿的丈夫 son-in-law, daughter's husband

絮 xù ㄒㄩˋ ❶棉絮，棉花的纤维 cotton fibre; cotton wadding：被～ *quilt wadding* | 吐～ *(of bolls) to open* ❷像棉絮的东西 some thing like cotton：柳～ *willow catkin* | 芦～ *reed catkin* ❸在衣物里铺棉花 to pad with cotton：～被子 *pad a quilt with cotton* | ～棉袄 *pad a jacket with cotton* ❹连续重复，惹人厌烦 long-winded; garrulous：～烦 *wordy* [絮叨](－dao) 说话啰唆 long-winded

蓿 xu ·ㄒㄩ see 苜蓿 (mù－) at 苜 on page 464

XUAN ㄒㄩㄢ

轩(軒) xuān ㄒㄩㄢ ❶古代的一种有围棚而前顶较高的车 a high-fronted, enclosed carriage in ancient times [轩昂] 1 高扬，高举 high; lofty 2 气度不凡 dignified; imposing: 气宇～ *have an imposing appearance* [轩轾](－zhì)车前高后低叫轩，前低后高叫轾。轩 is a carriage with a high front and a low back, in opposition to 轾. ⓗ高低优劣 high or low; good or bad: 不分～ *be equal* ❷有窗的长廊或小室 covered walkway with windows or small house

宣 xuān ㄒㄩㄢ ❶发表，公开说出 to declare; to proclaim; to announce: ～誓 *take an oath* | ～传 *to publicize* | 心照不～ *have a tacit understanding* ❷疏通 to drain off: ～泄 *drain off; unburden oneself* ❸指宣纸，安徽省宣城等地产的一种高级纸张，吸墨均匀，能长期存放 *xuan* paper (a high quality paper from Xuancheng, Anhui Province, among other places, for Chinese painting and calligraphy): 生～ *unprocessed* xuan *paper* | 虎皮～ *lightly-coloured and spotted* xuan *paper*

揎 xuān ㄒㄩㄢ 捋(luō)起袖子露出胳膊 to roll up sleeves: ～拳捋袖 *stretch out one's hand and roll up one's sleeves*

萱(*藼、*萲、*蕿、*蘐) xuān ㄒㄩㄢ ❶萱草，草本植物，叶细长，花红黄色。花蕾可以吃，根可入药 tawny daylily ❷萱堂，代指母亲 used to refer to one's mother: 椿～(父母) *used to refer to one's parents*

喧(*諠) xuān ㄒㄩㄢ 大声说话，声音大而杂乱(㊀－哗) (of many people) to speak loudly: noisy: ～闹 *noisy* | 锣鼓～天 *deafening sound of gongs and drums* | ～宾夺主。*A garrulous guest usurps the host's role; (figurative) The secondary supersedes the primary.*

愃 xuān ㄒㄩㄢ ❶心广体胖的样子 be carefree and well-nourished ❷忘记 to forget

瑄 xuān ㄒㄩㄢ 古代祭天用的璧 round flat piece of jade used in ancient times for worshipping Heaven

暄 xuān ㄒㄩㄢ ❶太阳的温暖 (of the sun) warmth [寒暄] ⓩ见面时谈天气冷暖之类的应酬话 exchange greetings: 彼此～了几句 *exchanged greetings* ❷〈方dialect〉松散，松软 fluffy; soft: ～土 *soft earth* | 馒头又大又～。*The steamed buns are big and fluffy.*

煊 xuān ㄒㄩㄢ same as "暄❶"

谖(諼) xuān ㄒㄩㄢ ❶欺诈，欺骗 to cheat ❷忘记 to forget

镟(鋗) xuān ㄒㄩㄢ 一种盆形有环耳的加热用的器具 a basin-like heating vessel with ring handles

儇 xuān ㄒㄩㄢ 轻薄而有点ㄦ小聪明 frivolous and clever

谖(諼) xuān ㄒㄩㄢ 聪慧 wisdom

翾 xuān ㄒㄩㄢ 飞翔 to fly

禤 xuān ㄒㄩㄢ 姓 (surname) Xuan

玄 xuán ㄒㄩㄢˊ ❶深奥不容易理解的 profound; abstruse: ～理 *profound doctrine* | ～妙 *profound and mysterious* ❷虚伪，不真实，不可靠 unreliable; incredible: 那话太～了，不能信。*That's too tall a story to be believed.* [玄虚] 1 虚幻，不真实 unreal; illusory 2 欺骗的手段 ruse; trick: 故弄～ *deliberately mystify things* ❸黑色 black; dark: ～狐 *black fox* | ～青(深黑色) *deep black*

伭 xuán ㄒㄩㄢˊ (又) see xián on page 706

骇(駭) xuán ㄒㄩㄢˊ 黑色的马 black horse

玹 xuán ㄒㄩㄢˊ ❶一种次于玉的美石 a kind of inferior jade ❷玉的颜色 colour of jade

⇨ see also xián on p.707, xuàn on p.739

痃 xuán ㄒㄩㄢˊ [横痃] 由下疳(gān，一种性病)引起的腹股沟淋巴结肿胀、发炎的症状 bubo

悬(懸) xuán ㄒㄩㄢˊ ❶挂，吊在空中 to hang; to suspend: ～灯结彩 *hang up lanterns and decorations* ㊃没有着落，没有结果 unsettled; unresolved: ～案 *unsettled legal case* | 那件事还～着呢。*That matter is still pending.* [悬念] 1 挂念 to be concerned about 2 欣赏戏剧、电影或小说等文艺作品时，观众或读者对故事发展和人物命运关切和期待的心情。也泛指人们对事物发展关注和期待的心情 suspense: 他毫无～地夺得了冠军。*He won the first prize without suspense.* ❷凭空设想 to imagine: ～拟 *to conjecture* | ～揣 *to suppose; to guess* ❸距离远 far apart: ～隔 *be separated by a great distance* | ～殊 *greatly disparate* ❹〈方 dialect〉危险 dangerous: 真～! 差点ㄦ掉下去。*It was a close call, almost falling off the edge.*

旋 xuán ㄒㄩㄢˊ ❶旋转，转动 to revolve; to circle; to spin: 螺～ *spiral* | 回～ *circle round* ㊀圈子 circle: 打～ㄦ *whirl around in a circle* ❷回，归 to return; to come back: ～里 *return home* | 凯～ *triumphant return* ❸不久 soon; immediately: ～即离去 *leave forthwith* ❹姓 (surname) Xuan

⇨ see also xuàn on p.739

漩 xuán ㄒㄩㄢˊ (～ㄦ) 水流旋转的圆窝 whirlpool; eddy: ～涡 *whirlpool*

璇(*璿) xuán ㄒㄩㄢˊ 美玉 fine jade [璇玑] (－jī) 古代天文仪器 ancient astronomical instrument

暶 xuán ㄒㄩㄢˊ ❶明亮 shiny; bright ❷容貌美丽 attractive in appearance

咺 xuǎn ㄒㄩㄢˇ ❶哭泣不止 to cry incessantly ❷姓 (surname) Xuan

晅 xuǎn ㄒㄩㄢˇ ❶日光 sunlight ❷光明 bright ❸晒干 to dry in the sun

烜 xuǎn ㄒㄩㄢˇ ❶火盛 ablaze ❷光明，盛大 bright; grand [烜赫] 声威昭著 of great renown and influence ❸晒干 to dry in the sun

选（選） xuǎn ㄒㄩㄢˇ ❶挑拣，择（㊀挑一、一择）to select; to choose: ～种（zhǒng）*select seeds* [选举] 多数人推举认为合适的人担任代表或负责人 to elect; election: ～代表 *elect representatives* ❷被选中了的人或物 the selected ones: 人～ *persons selected* ❸被选出来编在一起的作品 selected works; anthology: 文～ *selected works* | 诗～ *collection of poems*

癣（癬） xuǎn ㄒㄩㄢˇ 由真菌引起的皮肤病，有头癣、体癣、甲癣（灰指甲）等多种，患处常发痒 tinea; ringworm

券 xuàn ㄒㄩㄢˋ 拱券，门窗、桥梁等的弧形部分 (of window, door, bridge, etc.) arch

⇨ see also quàn on p.552

泫 xuàn ㄒㄩㄢˋ 水珠下滴 to drip; to trickle: ～然流涕 *tears rolling down*

玹 xuàn ㄒㄩㄢˋ 一种玉 a kind of jade

⇨ see also xián on p.707, xuán on p.738

昡 xuàn ㄒㄩㄢˋ 日光 sunshine

炫（❷△衒）** xuàn ㄒㄩㄢˋ ❶强光照耀 to dazzle: ～目 *blindingly bright* ❷夸耀 to show off; to flaunt [炫耀] 1 照耀 to dazzle 2 夸耀 to show off; to make a display of: ～武力 *make a show of force*

眩 xuàn ㄒㄩㄢˋ ❶眼睛昏花看不清楚 dizzy; giddy: 头晕目～ *feel dizzy* ❷迷惑，迷乱 dazzled; bewildered: ～于名利 *dazzled by the prospect of fame and wealth*

铉（鉉） xuàn ㄒㄩㄢˋ 横贯鼎耳以举鼎或抬鼎的器具 device that passes through the handles of a *ding* and is used for lifting or carrying it

衒 xuàn ㄒㄩㄢˋ ❶沿街叫卖 to peddle ❷ see 炫 on page 739

绚（絢） xuàn ㄒㄩㄢˋ 有文彩的，色彩华丽 brilliant; colourful: ～烂 *splendid* | ～丽 *gorgeous*

琄 xuàn ㄒㄩㄢˋ 佩玉 jade ornament

旋（❸❹鏇） xuàn ㄒㄩㄢˋ ❶旋（xuán）转的 spinning; rotating: ～风 *whirlwind* ❷临时（做）at the time: ～吃～做 *cook for immediate eating* ❸（一子）温酒的器具 vessel for warming wine ❹用车床或刀子转（zhuàn）着圈地削 to turn sth on a lathe: 用车床～零件 *make a part on a lathe* | ～皮 *peel (fruit)*

⇨ see also xuán on p.738

渲 xuàn ㄒㄩㄢˋ 中国画的一种画法，把水墨淋在纸上再擦

得浓淡适宜 (technique in Chinese painting) wash with ink [渲染] 用水墨或淡的色彩涂抹画面 to apply colours to a drawing ⑩夸大地形容 to play up; to exaggerate

楦 (*楥) xuàn ㄒㄩㄢˋ ❶(-子、-头) 做鞋用的模型 shoe last ❷拿东西把物体中空的部分填满使物体鼓起来 to shape with a last or block: 用鞋楦子～鞋 *last a shoe* | 把这个猫皮～起来 *shape this cat skin on a block*

碹 xuàn ㄒㄩㄢˋ ❶桥梁、涵洞等工程建筑的弧形部分 (of bridge, culvert, etc.) arch ❷用砖、石等筑成弧形 to build an arch (with bricks or stones)

XUE ㄒㄩㄝ

削 xuē ㄒㄩㄝ 义同"削"(xiāo), 用于一些复合词 same in meaning as 削 (xiāo), used in some compound words: ～除 *to eliminate* | ～减 *to reduce* | ～弱 *to weaken* | 剥～ *to exploit*

⇨ see also xiāo on p.715

靴 (*鞾) xuē ㄒㄩㄝ (-子) 有长筒的鞋 boots: 马～ *riding boots* | 皮～ *leather boots* | 雨～ *rubber boots*

薛 xuē ㄒㄩㄝ 周代诸侯国名, 在今山东省滕州、薛城一带 Xue (a state in Zhou Dynasty, located around Tengzhou and Xuecheng, Shandong Province)

穴 xué ㄒㄩㄝˊ ❶窟窿, 洞 cave; cavern; grotto: 不入虎～, 焉得虎子? *Nothing ventured, nothing gained.* | ～居野处 *live a primitive life* ❷墓穴 grave; vault; coffin pit: 坟地里有五个～。*There are five graves in the graveyard.* ❸穴位, 又叫穴道, 人体或某些动物体可以进行针灸的部位, 多为神经末梢密集或较粗的神经纤维经过的地方 acupoint (also called 穴道): 太阳～ *temple*

茓 xué ㄒㄩㄝˊ (-子) 做囤用的窄而长的席, 通常是用秫秸篾或芦苇篾编成的。也作"踅" coarse mat (also written as 踅)

峃 (嶨) xué ㄒㄩㄝˊ [峃口] 地名, 在浙江省文成 Xuekou (a place in Wencheng, Zhejiang Province)

学 (學、**斈) xué ㄒㄩㄝˊ ❶学习 to learn; to study: ～本领 *learn skills* | 活到老, ～到老 *live and learn* [学生] 1 在校学习的人 pupil; student 2 向前辈学习的人 disciple; follower 3 对前辈谦称自己 (humble speech) I; me [学徒] 在工厂或商店里学习技能的人 apprentice; trainee ❷模仿 to imitate; to mimic; to copy: 他～赵体字, ～得很像。*He copies the Zhao style of calligraphy very well.* ❸学问, 学到的知识 learning; knowledge: 饱～ *learned; erudite; widely-read* | 博～多能 *widely-read and multitalented* [学士] 1 学位名, 在硕士之下 bachelor (academic degree) 2 古代官名 an ancient official post [学术] 比较专门而有系统的学问

(academic) learning; science ❹ 分门别类的有系统的知识 sphere of learning：哲～ *philosophy* | 物理～ *physics* | 语言～ *linguistics* ❺ 学校 school; educational institution：中～ *middle school* | 大～ *university* | 上～ *go to school*

茓(鷽) xué ㄒㄩㄝˊ 鸟名，像雀而羽毛颜色不同，叫声很好听 bullfinch

踅 xué ㄒㄩㄝˊ ❶ 折回，旋（xuán）转 to turn back; to rotate：～来～去 *walk to and fro* | 这群鸟飞向东去又～回来落在树上了。*This flock of birds flew eastward and then returned to the tree.* ❷ same as "茓"

噱 xué ㄒㄩㄝˊ 〈方 dialect〉笑 to laugh：发～ *amusing; funny* [噱头] 逗笑的话或举动 words/acts meant to amuse; wisecrack

⇨ see also jué on p.344

雪 xuě ㄒㄩㄝˇ ❶寒冷天天空落下的白色晶体，多为六角形，是空气中的水蒸气降至0℃以下凝结而成的 snow：～花 *snow flake* | 冰天～地 *a world of ice and snow* ❷ 洗去，除去 to wipe out; to eliminate：～耻 *avenge an insult* | ～恨 *wreak vengeance*

鳕(鱈) xuě ㄒㄩㄝˇ 鱼名，又叫鳘，俗称大头鱼。头大，尾小，下颌有一条须，肝可制鱼肝油 cod (also called 鳘, informal 大头鱼)

血 xuè ㄒㄩㄝˋ ❶血液，人和高等动物体内的红色液体（由红细胞、白细胞、血小板和血浆组成），周身循环，输送养分给各组织，同时把废物带到排泄器官内 blood：～压 *blood pressure* | ～泊（pō）*pool of blood* ❷ 同一祖先的 related by blood：～统 *lineage* | ～族 *blood relations* ❸指刚强热烈 firm and high-spirited; vigorous：～性 *courage and uprightness* | ～气方刚 *full of vigour* (Pronounced xuè when used in disyllabic or polysyllabic words or in idioms, such as 贫血, 呕心沥血.)

⇨ see also xiě on p.721

谑(謔) xuè ㄒㄩㄝˋ 开玩笑 to crack a joke; to banter; to tease：戏～ *to tease* | 谐～ *banter; pleasantry*

XUN ㄒㄩㄣ

勋(勛、*勳) xūn ㄒㄩㄣ ❶特殊功劳（㊀功一）meritorious service; exploits：～章 *medal; decoration* | 屡建奇～ *win unusual merits repeatedly* ❷ 勋章 medal; decoration：授～ *confer a decoration*

埙(塤、*壎) xūn ㄒㄩㄣ 古代用陶土烧制的一种吹奏乐器 an ancient earthen musical instrument

熏(❶❷*燻) xūn ㄒㄩㄣ ❶ 气味或烟气接触物品 to cure with smoke; to smoke; to fumigate：～豆腐 *smoked* tofu | ～肉 *smoked meat* | 把墙～黑了。*The wall is blackened by smoke.* | 用茉莉花～茶叶 *scent tea with*

jasmine ❷气味刺激人 to stink：臭气～人。*It stinks badly.* ❸和暖 warm：～风 *warm wind*

⇨ see also xùn on p.744

薰 xūn ㄒㄩㄣ ❶薰草，古书上说的一种香草 a fragrant plant in ancient Chinese texts ㊀花草的香气 fragrance of plants ❷ same as "熏 (xūn) ❶"

獯 xūn ㄒㄩㄣ ［獯鬻］（－yù）我国古代北方民族，战国后称匈奴 Xunyu (an ancient ethnic group in northern China, called 匈奴 after the Warring States Period)

纁(纁) xūn ㄒㄩㄣ 浅红色 pale red

曛 xūn ㄒㄩㄣ 日没（mò）时的余光 twilight; dim glow of the setting sun：～黄（黄昏）*dusk*

醺 xūn ㄒㄩㄣ 醉 drunk［醺醺］醉的样子 drunk; tipsy：喝得醉～的 *get dead drunk*

窨 xūn ㄒㄩㄣ 同"熏"，用于窨茶叶。把茉莉花等放在茶叶中，使茶叶染上花的香味 to scent (tea) (same as 熏)

⇨ see also yìn on p.783

旬 xún ㄒㄩㄣˊ ❶十天叫一旬，一个月有三旬，分称上旬、中旬、下旬 a period of ten days (there are three 旬 in a month, namely 上旬，中旬 and 下旬) ❷指十岁 a ten-year period; a decade：三～上下年纪 *about 30 years of age* | 年过六～ *over 60 years old*

郇 xún ㄒㄩㄣˊ ❶周代诸侯国名，在今山西省临猗西南 Xun (a state in the Zhou Dynasty, in the southwest of today's Linyi, Shanxi Province) ❷ 姓 (surname) Xun

⇨ see also huán on p.266

询(詢) xún ㄒㄩㄣˊ 问，征求意见（㊥－问）to ask; to inquire：探～ *make inquiries about* | 查～ *make inquiries*

荀 xún ㄒㄩㄣˊ 姓 (surname) Xun

峋 xún ㄒㄩㄣˊ see 嶙峋 (lín－) at 嶙 on page 407

洵 xún ㄒㄩㄣˊ 诚然，实在 truly; indeed：～属可敬 *truly respectable*

恂 xún ㄒㄩㄣˊ ❶诚信，信实 honest ❷恐惧 fearful

珣 xún ㄒㄩㄣˊ 一种玉 a kind of jade

栒 xún ㄒㄩㄣˊ ［栒邑］地名，在陕西省。今作"旬邑" Xunyi (now written as 旬邑, a place in Shaanxi Province)

寻(尋、*尋) xún ㄒㄩㄣˊ ❶找，搜求（㊥－找、－觅）to look for; to search for：～人 *look for a person* | 自～烦恼 *bring vexation to oneself* | ～求 *to seek* | 搜～ *search for*［寻思］（－si）想，考虑 to think over sth; to consider ❷ 古代长度单位，八尺（一说七尺或六尺）为一寻 an ancient measurement of length, equals 8 (or 6 or 7) 尺［寻常］㊕平常，素常 ordinary; common; usual：这不是～的事情。*This is no ordinary matter.*

郇（**郇**）xún ㄒㄩㄣˊ 姓 (surname) Xun

荨（**蕁**）xún ㄒㄩㄣˊ ［荨麻疹］俗叫风疹疙瘩，一种过敏性皮疹，症状是局部皮肤突然红肿，成块状，发痒 urticaria; hives, wind patches (informal 风疹疙瘩)

⇨ see also qián on p.527

㖊（**噚**）xún ㄒㄩㄣˊ 又读 yīngxún，现写作"英寻"，英美制计量水深的单位，1 㖊是 6 英尺，合 1.828 米 fathom (also pronounced as yīngxún, now written as 英寻)

浔（**潯**）xún ㄒㄩㄣˊ ❶水边 waterside：江～ *riverside* ❷江西省九江市的别称 Xun (another name for Jiujiang, Jiangxi Province)

珣（**璕**）xún ㄒㄩㄣˊ 一种美石 a kind of fine stone

燖（**燂**）xún ㄒㄩㄣˊ ❶把肉放在沸水中使半熟。也泛指煮肉 to half boil (meat); to boil (meat) ❷把宰后的猪、鸡等用热水烫后去毛 to soak (pig or chicken) in hot water for easy removal of hair or feathers

鲟（**鱘**、**鱏）xún ㄒㄩㄣˊ 鱼名，身体纺锤形，背部和腹部有大片硬鳞，其余各部无鳞，生活在淡水中 sturgeon

纼（**紃**）xún ㄒㄩㄣˊ 圆绦子 silk braid

巡（*巡）xún ㄒㄩㄣˊ ❶往来查看 to patrol：～夜 *go on night patrol* | ～哨 *to scout* ［巡回］按一定路线到各处 to go the rounds; to tour：～医疗队 *mobile medical team* | ～演出 *(go on a) performing tour* ❷量词，遍（用于给所有在座的人斟酒）(measure word) round (of drinks)：酒过三～。*There have been three rounds of alcohol.*

循 xún ㄒㄩㄣˊ 遵守，依照 to abide by; to comply with; to follow：～规蹈矩 *stick to all rules and conventions* | ～序渐进 *proceed step by step* | 遵～ *abide by* ［循环］周而复始地运动 to circulate; move in cycles：血液～ *blood circulation* | ～演出 *perform (a repertoire) in rotation*

训（**訓**）xùn ㄒㄩㄣˋ ❶教导，教诲 to lecture; to teach; to train：～话 *to admonish* | 教～ *(teach a) lesson; moral* ❷训练 to train; to drill; to practice：集～ *assemble for training* | 冬～ *winter training* ❸可以作为法则的话 teachings; instructions; model：遗～ *teachings of the deceased* | 不足为～ *not to be taken as an example* ❹解释词的意义 to explain; to define：～诂 *critical interpretation of ancient texts*

驯（**馴**）xùn ㄒㄩㄣˋ 驯服，顺从，使驯服 tame; docile：～顺 *tame and docile* | ～良 *tractable* | ～马 *break in a horse* | ～养 *to domesticate*

讯（**訊**）xùn ㄒㄩㄣˋ ❶问。特指法庭中的审问 to question; to interrogate：审～ *to interrogate* ❷消息，音

信 message; dispatch; information: 通～ *communication* | 新华社～ *Xinhua News Agency report*

汛 xùn ㄒㄩㄣˋ 江河定期的涨水 seasonal flood; high water: 防～ *flood control* | 秋～ *autumn flood* | 桃花～ *spring flood (on the Yellow River, literally means 'peach blossom flood', so named since it occurs during the peach blossom season)*

迅 xùn ㄒㄩㄣˋ 快(㊀-速) fast; swift: ～跑 *run fast* | ～猛 *fast and violent* | ～雷不及掩耳 *as sudden as lightning (leaving no time to cover one's ears)*

徇(*狥) xùn ㄒㄩㄣˋ ❶依从，曲从 to give in to; to submit to; to comply with: ～私舞弊 *engage in favouritism and commit irregularities* ❷ same as "殉❶"

殉 xùn ㄒㄩㄣˋ ❶为达到某种目的而牺牲性命 to sacrifice one's life for: ～国(为国捐躯) *die for one's country* | ～难(nàn) *die for a just cause* ❷古代逼迫活人陪葬，也指用偶人或器物随葬 (of humans, figures or objects) to be buried along with the dead in ancient times: ～葬 *be buried with the dead*

逊(遜) xùn ㄒㄩㄣˋ ❶退避，退让 to abdicate: ～位(让出帝王的位子) *to abdicate* ❷谦让，恭顺 modest: 谦～ *modest* | 出言不～ *speak insolently* ❸不及，差 to be inferior: ～色 *pale in comparison* | 稍～一筹 *be slightly inferior*

浚(*濬) xùn ㄒㄩㄣˋ 浚县，在河南省 Xunxian (in Henan Province)

⇨ see also jùn on p.346

巽 xùn ㄒㄩㄣˋ 八卦之一，符号是☴。代表风 *xun* (one of the Eight Trigrams used in ancient divination, symbol ☴, representing wind)

噀(潠)** xùn ㄒㄩㄣˋ 把含在口中的液体喷出来 to spray/spout (liquid) from the mouth: ～水 *spurt water from the mouth* | ～酒 *spout liquor from the mouth*

熏 xùn ㄒㄩㄣˋ 〈方 dialect〉(煤气)使人窒息中毒 to be poisoned or suffocated (by coal gas): 炉子安上烟筒，就不至于～着了。*With a chimney installed on the stove, (we) won't suffocate from coal gas.*

⇨ see also xūn on p.741

蕈 xùn ㄒㄩㄣˋ 生长在树林里或草地上的某些菌类，形状略像伞，种类很多，无毒的可以吃 mushroom: 松～ *pine mushroom* | 香～ *shiitake*

Y 丨

YA 丨丫

丫(❶△*椏、❶*枒) yā 丨丫 ❶上端分杈的东西 fork：～杈 *fork of a tree* | 树～巴 *crotch* ❷〈方 dialect〉女孩子 girl：小～ *little girl* [丫头]（－tou）1 女孩子 girl 2 旧时称供人役使的女孩子 (old) maidservant

➪ 椏 see also 椏 on p.746

压(壓) yā 丨丫 ❶从上面加重力，也指压力 to press; pressure：～住 *press down* | ～碎 *to crush* | 减～ *reduce pressure* ㉃搁置不动 lay aside：积～ *to overstock; keep long in stock* ❷用威力制服，镇服 to suppress：镇～ *put down* | ～制 *to suppress* ㉃胜过，超过 prevail over：～倒一切 *overpower everything* | 技～群芳 *be the best in doing sth* ❸抑制，控制 to hold back; to control：～咳嗽 *ease the cough* | ～住气 *control one's anger* | ～不住火 *cannot control one's anger* ❹逼近 close in on：～境 *(of enemy troops) press on to the border* | 太阳～树梢。*The sun hovers over the treetops.* ❺赌博时在某一门上下注 to risk; to stake (in gambling)：～宝 *to stake*

➪ see also yà on p.748

呀 yā 丨丫 ❶叹词，表示惊疑 (exclamation, used to express surprise) oh：～，这怎么办！*Oh, what to do with it?* ❷拟声词 onomatopoeia：门～的一声开了。*The door creaked open.*

➪ see also ya on p.748

鸦(鴉、*鵶) yā 丨丫 乌鸦，鸟名，身体黑色，嘴大，翼长，种类很多 crow：～雀无声（形容寂静）*as quiet as a mouse*

押 yā 丨丫 ❶在文书契约上签字或画符号，也指签的字或画的符号 to sign (on a deed of agreement); signature：～尾 *to mark in place of a signature* | 画～ *make one's cross* | 签～ *to sign* ❷把财物交给有关的人做担保 to mortgage; to pledge：～金 *deposit; advance payment* | 抵～ *to mortgage* ❸拘留 to detain：看～ *to detain* | 关～ *lock up* | ～起来 *take into custody* ❹跟随看管 to escort：～车 *escort a vehicle* | ～运货物 *transport goods under escort*

鸭(鴨) yā 丨丫（－子）水鸟名。通常指家鸭，嘴扁腿短，趾间有蹼，善游泳，不能高飞 (usually) duck

垭(埡) yā 丨丫 yà 丨丫̀(又) 〈方 dialect〉两山之间的狭窄地方，多用于地名 (often used in place names) mountain pass：黄桷（jué）～（在重庆市）*Huangjueya (a place in Chongqing Municipality)*

哑(啞) yā ㄧㄚ same as "呀(yā)" [哑哑]形容乌鸦叫声或小儿学语声 (of crow) to caw; (of baby) to babble

⇨ see also yǎ on p.747

桠(椏) yā ㄧㄚ ❶用于科技术语 used in technical terms：五～果科 *dillenia family* ❷用于地名 used in place names：～溪镇（在江苏省高淳）*Yaxizhen (in Gaochun, Jiangsu Province)*

⇨ 桠 see also 丫 on p.745

牙 yá ㄧㄚˊ ❶牙齿，人和高等动物嘴里咀嚼食物的器官 tooth：门～*front tooth* ❷（一子）像牙齿形状的东西 something like tooth：抽屉～子 *elevated edge of a drawer* ❸旧社会介绍买卖从中取利的人 broker (in the past)：～侩（kuài）*broker*｜～行（háng）*brokerage*

伢 yá ㄧㄚˊ 〈方 dialect〉（一子、一儿）小孩子 small child; kid

芽 yá ㄧㄚˊ ❶（一儿）植物的幼体，可以发育成茎、叶或花的那一部分 bud：豆～儿 *bean sprouts*｜发～儿 *to sprout*｜～茶 *young tea leaves* [萌芽] ㊖事情的开端 beginning ❷像芽的东西 something like bud：肉～ *granulation*｜银～（银矿苗）*silver mine outcrop*

岈 yá ㄧㄚˊ see 嵖岈 (chá—) at 嵖 on page 63

琊 yá ㄧㄚˊ [琅琊]（láng—）1 山名，在安徽省滁州 Langya Mountain (in Chuzhou, Anhui Province) 2 山名，在山东省胶南 Langya Mountain (in Jiaonan, Shandong Province)

琊 yá ㄧㄚˊ ❶用于地名 used in place names：～川（在贵州

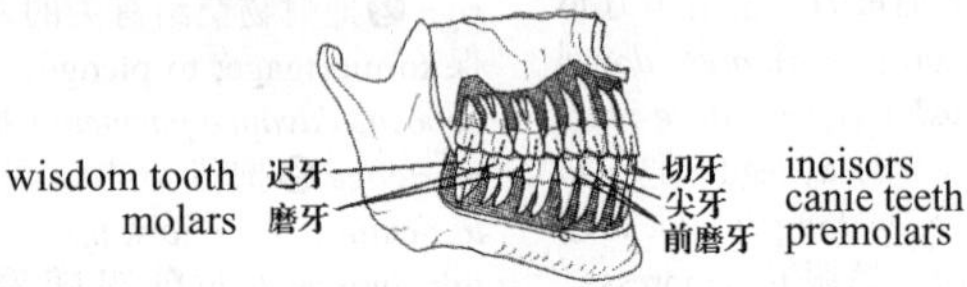

人的牙 human teeth

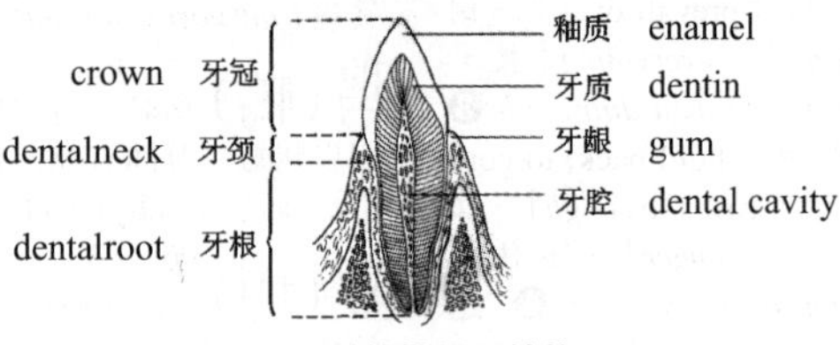

牙的纵切面结构

structure of the vertical section of the tooth

省凤冈）*Yachuan (in Fenggang, Guizhou Province)* ❷ same as "玡"

蚜 yá ㄧㄚˊ 蚜虫，昆虫，俗叫腻虫，身体小，绿色或棕色带紫红色，生活在植物嫩茎、叶片、花蕾上，吸食嫩芽的汁液，是害虫 aphid (informal 腻虫)

埡 yá ㄧㄚˊ 用于地名 used in place names：～东（在山东省利津）*Yadong (in Lijin, Shandong Province)* | ～西（在山东省利津）*Yaxi (in Lijin, Shandong Province)*

崖（**崕、**厓） yá ㄧㄚˊ (formerly pronounced ái) 高地或山石陡立的侧面 edge of a cliff：山～ *edge of a cliff* | 悬～勒马（喻到了危险的地步赶紧回头）*rein in at the brink of a precipice; wake up to and escape a disaster at the last moment*

涯 yá ㄧㄚˊ 水边 bank; waterside ㉄边际，极限 boundary; limit：天～海角 *end of the earth* | 一望无～ *stretch as far as the eye can see*

睚 yá ㄧㄚˊ 眼角 corner of the eye [睚眦]（-zì）发怒瞪眼 stare angrily ㉄小的怨恨 small grievance：～必报 *seek revenge for a petty grievance*

衙 yá ㄧㄚˊ 衙门，旧时指官署 (old) *yamen* (government office)：官～ *(old, generally) government office*

哑（**啞**） yǎ ㄧㄚˇ ❶由于生理缺陷或疾病而不能说话 mute：聋～ *deaf-mute* | ～口无言（喻无话可说）*be left speechless* ❷嗓子干涩发音困难或不清楚 hoarse：沙～ *hoarse* | 嗓子喊～了 *shout oneself hoarse* ❸无声的 mute; silent：～剧 *mime* | ～铃（一种运动器械）*dumb-bell* ❹ (formerly pronounced è) 笑声 laughter：～然失笑（不由自主地笑出声来）*cannot help laughing*

⇨ see also yā on p.746

雅 yǎ ㄧㄚˇ ❶正规的，标准的 standard：～声（指诗歌）*poetry* | ～言 *(old) standard language* ❷高尚不俗，美好大方 elegant：优～ *graceful and tasteful* | ～致 *tasteful* | ～观 *refined* ❸敬辞，用于称对方的情意、行动等 (polite speech) your (kindness, action, etc.)：～意 *your opinion; your kindness* | ～鉴 *for your inspection* | ～教（jiào）*give your esteemed opinion* ❹平素，素来 usually：～善鼓琴 *be good at playing the* qin *(a plucked musical instrument)* ❺极，甚 very; extremely：～以为美 *consider sth very beautiful* | ～不欲为 *be extremely unwilling to do sth* ❻交往 acquaintance：无一日之～ *not have the pleasure of knowing sb* ❼周代朝廷上的乐歌，《诗经》中诗篇的一类，分为大雅和小雅 *ya* (court songs in the Zhou Dynasty taken from the *Book of Songs*)

轧（**軋**） yà ㄧㄚˋ ❶圆轴或轮子等在东西上面滚压 to roll; to crush：把马路～平了 *rolled the road surface flat* | ～棉花 *to gin cotton* | ～花机 *cotton gin* ❷

排挤 squeeze out; push out：倾～ *engage in factional strife* ❸ 姓 (surname) Ya

⇨ see also gá on p.193, zhá on p.826

Y

亚(亞) yà ㄧㄚˋ ❶次，次一等的 inferior：～军 *runner-up (in sports)* | ～热带 *subtropical zone* ❷指亚洲，世界七大洲之一 Asia

垭(埡) yà ㄧㄚˋ（又） see yā on page 745

挜(掗) yà ㄧㄚˋ 〈方 dialect〉硬把东西送给或卖给别人 insist on giving or selling sth to sb

娅(婭) yà ㄧㄚˋ 连襟 brothers-in-law：姻～ *relatives by marriage*

氩(氬) yà ㄧㄚˋ 气体元素，符号 Ar，无色、无臭，不易跟其他元素化合。可用来充入电灯泡或真空管中 argon (Ar)

压(壓) yà ㄧㄚˋ ［压根儿］副词，根本，从来（多用于否定句）(adverb, often in negative sentences) in the first place; simply：我～没去过那个地方。*I have never been to that place before.*

⇨ see also yā on p.745

讶(訝) yà ㄧㄚˋ 惊奇，奇怪 to be surprised：惊～ *surprised*

迓 yà ㄧㄚˋ 迎接（㊀迎一）to welcome：～之于门 *meet one at the gate*

砑 yà ㄧㄚˋ 碾压 to press and smooth［砑光］用卵形或弧形的石块碾压或摩擦皮革、布帛等使紧密而光亮 press and smoothen (leather, cloth, etc.) with oval stones

揠 yà ㄧㄚˋ 拔 to pull up：～苗助长（zhǎng）（喻欲求速成反而做坏）*spoil things with excessive enthusiasm (literally means 'try to help the shoots grow by pulling them upward')*

猰(貏)** yà ㄧㄚˋ ［猰貐］（－yǔ）古代传说中的一种凶兽 a kind of ferocious beast in ancient Chinese legends

呀 ya ·ㄧㄚ 助词，"啊"受前一字韵母 a、e、i、o、ü 收音的影响而发生的变音 (auxiliary word) used instead of 啊 after a syllable ending in a vowel：大家快来～！ *Come quick, everybody!* | 你怎么不学一学～？ *Why don't you try to learn it?* | 这个瓜～，甜得很！ *This melon is really very sweet!*

⇨ see also yā on p.745

YAN ㄧㄢ

咽 yān ㄧㄢ 咽头，食物和气体的共同通道，位于鼻腔、口腔和喉腔的后方，通常混称咽喉 pharynx (usually interchangeably called 咽喉)

⇨ see also yàn on p.754, yè on p.766

胭(*臙) yān ㄧㄢ ［胭脂］（－zhi）一种红色颜料，多用作化妆品 rouge

烟(*煙、❺*菸) yān ㄧㄢ ❶（－儿）

物质燃烧时所产生的混有残余颗粒的气体 smoke：冒～ *belch smoke* | ～筒 *chimney* [烟火] 1 道教指熟食 cooked food (in Taoism)：不食人间～（现喻脱离现实）*live the life of an immortal; (figurative) be unrealistic* 2 在火药中掺上某些金属盐类制成的一种燃放物，燃烧时能发出灿烂的火花或呈现种种景物供人观赏，又叫烟花、焰火 (also called 烟花，焰火) firework [烟幕弹] 能放出大量烟雾的炸弹，供军事上做掩护用 smoke bomb ⑩用来掩盖真相或本意的言论或行为 smokescreen ❷（-子）烟气中间杂有碳素的微细颗粒，这些颗粒附着在其他物体上凝结成的黑灰 soot：松～ *pine soot* | 锅～子 *soot on the bottom of a pan* ❸像烟的东西 something like smoke：过眼云～ *as transient as fleeting clouds* | ～霞 *mist and clouds* ❹烟气刺激（眼睛）(of smoke) to irritate (eyes)：一屋子烟，～眼睛。*The room was full of smoke which irritated the eyes.* ❺烟草，草本植物，叶大有茸毛，可以制香烟和农业上的杀虫剂等 tobacco ❻烟草制成品 tobacco product：香～ *cigarette* | 旱～ *pipe tobacco* | 请勿吸～ *no smoking* ❼指鸦片 opium：～土 *crude opium*

恹（懨、懕）** yān ㄧㄢ [恹恹] 有病而衰弱无力、精神不振的样子 run-down：病～ *sickly*

殷 yān ㄧㄢ 黑红色 dark red：～红 *dark red* | 朱～ *dark red*

⇨ see also yīn on p.780

焉 yān ㄧㄢ 文言虚词 function word in classical Chinese ①跟介词"于"加代词"是"相当 (equivalent to 于是, where 于 is a preposition and 是 is a pronoun) here, this：心不在～ *absent-minded* | 罪莫大～。*There is no greater crime than this.* ②连词，乃，才 (conjunction) not until：必知疾之所自起，～能攻之。*You have to know the cause of the trouble before you can deal with it.* ③代词，表示疑问，怎么，哪儿 (pronoun, used to express doubt) how; why; where：～能如此？*How can (you) have done this?* | 其子～往？*Where could their children have gone?* ④助词，表示肯定语气 auxiliary word, used to express sth positive：因以为号～。*So I use this as my alias.* | 有厚望～。*I cherish high hopes.*

鄢 yān ㄧㄢ 用于地名 used in place names：～陵（在河南省）*Yanling (in Henan Province)*

嫣 yān ㄧㄢ 用于地名 used in place names：梁家～（在山西省灵石）*Liangjiayan (in Lingshi, Shanxi Province)*

⇨ see also yàn on p.755

漹 yān ㄧㄢ 用于地名 used in place names：～城（在四川省夹江县）*Yancheng (in Jiajiang County, Sichuan Province)*

嫣 yān ㄧㄢ 美好，鲜艳 beautiful; (of colours) brilliant：～然一笑 *give a sweet smile* | 姹紫～红 *a blaze of colours*

Y

崦 yān ㄧㄢ [崦嵫]（—zī）1山名，在甘肃省 Yanzi Mountain (in Gansu Province) 2古代指太阳落山的地方 (ancient) place where the sun sets：日薄～。*The sun is setting.*

阉(閹) yān ㄧㄢ ❶阉割，割去生殖腺 to castrate：～鸡 *capon*｜～猪 *castrated pig* ❷封建时代的宦官，太监 eunuch：～官 *eunuch*

淹(❶ 渰)** yān ㄧㄢ ❶浸没（mò）to flood：被水～了 *was flooded with water* ❷皮肤被汗液浸渍 (of skin) soaked by sweat ❸广 wide：～博 *knowledgeable*

腌(*醃) yān ㄧㄢ 用盐等浸渍食品 to pickle：～肉 *preserved meat*｜～咸菜 *pickled vegetables*

⇨ see also ā on p.1

阏(閼) yān ㄧㄢ [阏氏]（—zhī）汉代匈奴称君主的正妻 *yanzhi* (principal wife of a Hun monarch)

湮 yān ㄧㄢ 埋没（㊀—没）fall into oblivion：～灭 *bury in oblivion*

⇨ see also yīn on p.780

燕 yān ㄧㄢ ❶周代诸侯国名，在今河北省北部和辽宁省西南部 Yan (a state in the Zhou Dynasty, in the north of today's Hebei Province and southwest of today's Liaoning Province) ❷姓 (surname) Yan

⇨ see also yàn on p.755

延 yán ㄧㄢˊ ❶伸展变长 to prolong：～长 *to prolong*｜～年 *prolong life*｜蔓（màn）～ *to spread* ❷展缓，推迟 to postpone：～期 *to postpone; to extend*｜顺～ *to postpone*｜迟～ *to delay* ❸引进，请 to engage：～请 *to employ*｜～师 *engage a teacher*｜～医 *send for a doctor*

埏 yán ㄧㄢˊ ❶大地的边沿 edge of a land ❷墓道 path leading to a grave

⇨ see also shān on p.577

綖(綖) yán ㄧㄢˊ 古代指覆盖在冠冕上的装饰 (ancient) ornament covering an official hat

蜒 yán ㄧㄢˊ see 蚰蜒 (yóuyan) at 蚰 on page 793, and 蜿蜒 (wān—) at 蜿 on page 672

筵 yán ㄧㄢˊ ❶竹席 bamboo mat ❷酒席 banquet：喜～ *wedding banquet*｜～席 *banquet*

闫(閆) yán ㄧㄢˊ 姓 (surname) Yan

芫 yán ㄧㄢˊ [芫荽]（—sui）草本植物，俗叫香菜，又叫胡荽（—suī），花白色，果实球形，有香味，可以制药和香料，茎、叶可供调味用 (informal 香菜, also called 胡荽—suī) coriander

⇨ see also yuán on p.806

严(嚴) yán ㄧㄢˊ ❶紧密，没有空隙 tight：把罐子盖～了 *seal the jug*｜场地上的草都长（zhǎng）～了。*The ground was all covered with grass.*｜嘴～（不乱说话）*tight-lipped* ❷认真，不放松 strict：规矩～ *the rules are strict*｜～厉 *severe*｜～格

strict | ～办 punish with severity ⓩ指父亲 father：家～ my father [严肃]郑重，庄重 solemn：态度很～ be serious in attitude ❸程度深，厉害 intense：～冬 severe winter | ～寒 bitterly cold [严重]紧急，重大 serious：事态～ the situation is serious | ～的错误 serious mistake

言 yán ㄧㄢˊ ❶话（㊀语一）speech：发～ make a speech; speech | 格～ maxim | 名～ well-known saying | 谣～ rumour | 有～在先 to forewarn | 一～为定 it's a deal | 一～以蔽之 in a word ❷说（㊀一语）to say：知无不～ say all one knows ❸汉语的字 word; Chinese character：五～诗 poem with five characters to a line | 七～绝句 quatrain with seven characters to a line | 洋洋万～ a flood of words

蔷 yán ㄧㄢˊ ❶古书上说的一种草 a kind of grass in ancient Chinese texts ❷姓 (surname) Yan

阽 yán ㄧㄢˊ（又） see diàn on page 134

妍 yán ㄧㄢˊ 美丽 beautiful：百花争～。Countless flowers contend in beauty.

研 yán ㄧㄢˊ ❶细磨 to grind：～药 grind medicine | ～墨 rub an ink stick on an inkstone ❷研究，深入地探求 to research：钻～ study assiduously | ～求 study carefully

〈古 ancient〉 also same as 砚 (yàn)

岩(*巖、*巗、*嵒) yán ㄧㄢˊ ❶高峻的山崖 cliff ❷岩石，构成地壳的石头 rock：沉积～ sedimentary rock | 火成～ igneous rock

炎 yán ㄧㄢˊ ❶天气热（㊀一热）scorching：～夏 boiling hot summer | ～暑 hot summer; summer heat | ～凉 hot and cold; different attitudes towards people with different fortunes; snobbish ❷炎症，身体的某部位发生红、肿、热、痛、痒的现象 inflammation：发～ inflammation | 咽～ pharyngitis | 皮～ dermatitis ❸指炎帝，传说中的我国上古帝王 (in Chinese legend) Yandi, king of remote antiquity：～黄子孙 the Chinese people

沿 yán ㄧㄢˊ ❶顺着（道路、江河的边）along：～路 area along the road; on the way | ～江 area along the river | 铁路～线 area along the railway line ❷按照以往的规矩、式样等 to follow (a tradition, pattern, etc.)：～袭 to continue | 积习相～。Long-standing practice has been handed down. [沿革]事物发展和变化的历程 evolution ❸（一儿）边（㊀边一）edge：炕～儿 edge of a kang | 缸～儿 rim of a jar | 盆～儿 rim of a basin | 河～儿 river bank | 井～儿 rim of a well ❹在衣服等物的边上再加一条边 to trim (clothes, etc.)：～鞋口 trim the top of a shoe | ～个边 sew a hem

铅(鉛) yán ㄧㄢˊ [铅山]地名，在江西省 Yanshan (a place in Jiangxi Province)

⇨ see also qiān on p.526

Y

盐(**鹽**) yán ㄧㄢˊ ❶食盐，味咸，化学成分是氯化钠，有海盐、池盐、井盐、岩盐等 salt ❷盐类，化学上指酸类中的氢离子被金属离子（包括铵离子）置换而成的化合物 (in chemistry) salt

阎(**閻**) yán ㄧㄢˊ ❶里巷的门 gate of a lane ❷姓 (surname) Yan

颜(**顔**) yán ㄧㄢˊ ❶颜面，脸面 face：无～见人 *be too ashamed to face anyone* | 喜笑～开 *beam with joy* ❷颜色，色彩 colour：～料 *pigment* | 五～六色 *multicoloured*

虤 yán ㄧㄢˊ 老虎发怒的样子 (of tiger) angry

檐(****簷**) yán ㄧㄢˊ ❶（～儿）房顶伸出的边沿 eaves：房～儿 *eaves of a house* | 飞～走壁 *(in old swordman novels) leap onto roofs and vault over walls* ❷（～儿）覆盖物的边沿或伸出部分 edge：帽～儿 *visor of a cap*

沇 yǎn ㄧㄢˇ ❶沇水，古水名，即济水 Yanshui (an ancient river name, same as 济水) ❷用于地名 used in place names：～河村（在河南省孟州）*Yanhecun (in Mengzhou, Henan Province)*

兖 yǎn ㄧㄢˇ ［兖州］地名，在山东省 Yanzhou (a place in Shandong Province)

奄 yǎn ㄧㄢˇ ❶覆盖 to cover ❷忽然，突然 all of a sudden：～忽 *suddenly*

［奄奄］气息微弱 breathing feebly：～一息（生命垂危，快要断气）*be on the verge of death*

〈古 ancient〉also same as 阉 (yān)

掩(****揜**) yǎn ㄧㄢˇ ❶遮蔽，遮盖(㊀-盖、遮-) to cover：～鼻 *hold one's breath* | ～饰 *cover up* ［掩护］1 用炮火等压住敌方火力，或利用自然条件的掩蔽，以便进行军事上的活动 give cover 2 采取某种方式暗中保护 to shield ❷关，合 to close; to shut：把门～上 *shut the door* | ～卷 *close a book* ❸门窗箱柜等关闭时夹住东西 to get pinched：关门～住手了。*I got my fingers caught in the door when I closed it.* ❹乘其不备（进行袭击）to ambush and attack：～杀 *make a surprise attack* | ～取 *take by surprise*

罨 yǎn ㄧㄢˇ ❶覆盖，掩盖 to cover：冷～法（医疗的方法）*cold compress method* | 热～法（医疗的方法）*hot compress method* ❷捕鱼或捕鸟的网 net for catching fish or birds

龑(**龑**) yǎn ㄧㄢˇ 人名，五代时南汉刘龑为自己名字造的字 a given name coined for himself by Liu Yan in the Five Dynasties

俨(**儼**) yǎn ㄧㄢˇ 恭敬，庄严 solemn ㊕很像真的，活像 just like：～如白昼 *be as bright as day* ［俨然］1 庄严 solemn：望之～ *look dignified* 2 整齐 neatly arranged：屋舍～ *houses set out in neat order* 3 副词，表示很像 (adverb) just like：这孩子说起话来～是个大人。*The*

child spoke just like a grown-up.

衍 yǎn ㄧㄢˇ ❶延长，展开 to extend; to spread out：推～ *to deduce* ❷多余的（指文字）(of words) superfluous：～文（书籍中因缮写、刻版、排版错误而多出来的字句）*redundancy due to misprinting or miscopying*

弇 yǎn ㄧㄢˇ 覆盖，遮蔽 to cover

渰 yǎn ㄧㄢˇ 云兴起的样子 (of clouds) gathering

剡 yǎn ㄧㄢˇ 〈古 ancient〉❶尖，锐利 sharp ❷削，刮 to peel

⇨ see also shàn on p.578

琰 yǎn ㄧㄢˇ 美玉 a fine jade

棪 yǎn ㄧㄢˇ ❶古书上说的一种树，果实像柰 a kind of tree in ancient Chinese texts ❷用于地名 used in place names：～树村（在福建省云霄）*Yanshucun (in Yunxiao, Fujian Province)*

扊 yǎn ㄧㄢˇ ［扊扅］（－yí）门闩 latch; door bolt

厣(厴) yǎn ㄧㄢˇ 螺类介壳口圆片状的盖。蟹腹下面的薄壳有时也叫厣 operculum

魇(魘) yǎn ㄧㄢˇ 做可怕的梦，梦中觉得有什么东西压住不能动弹（tan）have a nightmare

黡(黶) yǎn ㄧㄢˇ 黑色的痣 black mole

郾 yǎn ㄧㄢˇ ［郾城］地名，在河南省 Yancheng (a place in Henan Province)

偃 yǎn ㄧㄢˇ ❶仰面倒下，放倒 fall on one's back; lay down：～卧 *lie on one's back*｜～旗息鼓 *(literally) lay down flags and stop beating war drums; (of troops) march stealthily; (now often) stop all activities* ❷停止 to cease：～武修文 *stop war preparations and promote culture and education*

鶠(鶠) yǎn ㄧㄢˇ 古书上说的凤的别名 another name for phoenix (in ancient Chinese texts)

蝘 yǎn ㄧㄢˇ 古书上指蝉一类的昆虫 cicada-like insect (in ancient Chinese texts)

［蝘蜓］（－tíng）古书上指壁虎 gecko (in ancient Chinese texts)

眼 yǎn ㄧㄢˇ ❶眼睛，人和动物的视觉器官 eye［眼光］见识，对事物的看法 insight：把～放远点ₙ *look at things with a broader perspective* ❷(－ₙ)孔洞，窟窿 small hole：炮～ *embrasure; blast hole*｜耳朵～ₙ *ear canal*｜针～ₙ *eye of a needle* ❸(－ₙ)指事物的关键处 salient point; crux：节骨～ₙ *critical juncture*｜字～ *wording* ❹戏曲中的节拍 unaccented beat：一板三～ *one accented and three unaccented beats in a bar* ❺量词，用于井、

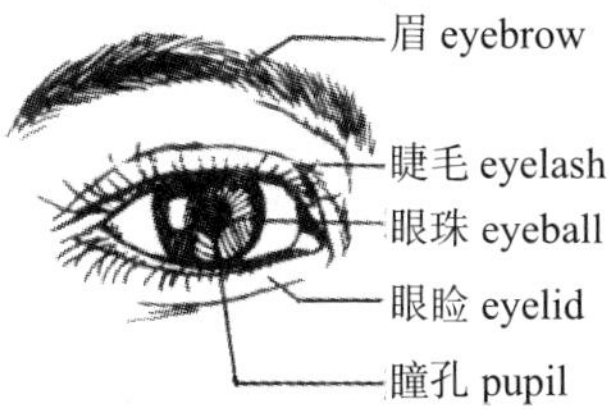

人的眼睛 human eye

Y

窑洞等 measure word for wells, cave dwellings, etc.: 一～井 *a well* | 两～窑洞 *two loess cave dwellings*

演 yǎn ㄧㄢˇ ❶把技艺当众表现出来 to perform: ～戏 *act in a play* | ～奏 *play a musical instrument* | ～唱 *perform a song/Chinese opera* ❷根据一件事理推广、发挥 to deduce: ～说 *make a speech; speech* | ～义 *extend the meaning on the basis of the text; historical novel* [演绎] 1 由普遍到特殊的推演过程 deduction 2 发挥 to elaborate ❸演习，依照一定程式练习 to practise (according to a set pattern): ～武 *practise traditional martial arts* | ～算习题 *do sums* ❹不断变化 to develop: ～变 *to develop* | ～进 *to develop and evolve* | ～化 *to evolve*

缜(縯) yǎn ㄧㄢˇ 延长 to extend

戭 yǎn ㄧㄢˇ 长枪，长戈 long spear

巘(巘) yǎn ㄧㄢˇ 〈古 ancient〉 ❶形状像甑（zèng，蒸锅）的山 pot-shaped mountain ❷山峰，山顶 peak: 绝～（极高的山顶）*high peak*

甗 yǎn ㄧㄢˇ 古代蒸煮用的炊具，陶制或青铜制 cooking utensil in ancient times

鼹(*鼴) yǎn ㄧㄢˇ 鼹鼠，哺乳动物，像老鼠，趾有钩爪，善掘土，生活在土中 mole

厌(厭) yàn ㄧㄢˋ ❶嫌恶，憎恶（㊀-恶）to detest: 讨～ *nasty; troublesome; to detest* | ～弃 *to reject* ❷满足 be satisfied: 贪得无～ *have an insatiable greed*

餍(饜) yàn ㄧㄢˋ 吃饱 eat one's fill ㊉ 满足 to satisfy: ～足（多指私欲）*to satisfy (often one's selfish desires)*

觃(覎) yàn ㄧㄢˋ [觃口] 地名，在浙江省富阳 Yankou (a place in Fuyang, Zhejiang Province)

砚(硯) yàn ㄧㄢˋ 砚台，写毛笔字研墨用的文具 inkstone

咽(*嚥) yàn ㄧㄢˋ 使嘴里的食物等通过咽喉到食道里去 to swallow: 细嚼慢～ *chew carefully and swallow slowly* | 狼吞虎～ *eat voraciously* [咽气] 人死时断气 breathe one's last breath

⇨ see also yān on p.748, yè on p.766

彦 yàn ㄧㄢˋ 古指有才学、德行的人 (ancient) man of ability and virtue: 俊～ *talent*

谚(諺) yàn ㄧㄢˋ 谚语，社会上流传的固定语句，用简单通俗的话反映出某种经验和道理 saying: 农～ *farmers' proverb* | 古～ *ancient proverb*

艳(艷、*豔、*艶、豓)** yàn ㄧㄢˋ ❶鲜艳，色彩鲜明 (of colours) brilliant: ～丽 *gorgeous* | ～阳天 *bright sunny spring* ❷旧时指关于爱情方面的 (old) romantic: ～情 *romance* | ～史 *love story*

[艳羡]非常羡慕 to envy

滟(灧、**灩) yàn ㄧㄢˋ [滟滪堆](-yùduī)长江瞿塘峡口的巨石，为便利长江航运，1958年将它炸除 Yanyudui (huge rocks in Qutang Gorge, in the Yangtze River, blasted away in 1958 for the convenience of navigation)

晏 yàn ㄧㄢˋ ❶晚，迟 late：～起 *get up late* ❷ same as "宴❹"

鴳(鷃、**鶠) yàn ㄧㄢˋ 鴳雀(què)，古书中说的小鸟 quail (in ancient Chinese texts)

唁 yàn ㄧㄢˋ 吊丧(sāng)，对遭遇丧事的人表示慰问(㊣吊－) extend one's condolences：～电(吊丧的电报) *telegram of condolence*

烻 yàn ㄧㄢˋ 光炽烈的样子 glowing

⇨ see also shān on p.577

宴(❶-❸*醼) yàn ㄧㄢˋ ❶用酒饭招待 entertain with food and drink：～客 *entertain guests with a feast* ❷聚会在一起吃酒饭 get together for food and drink：～会 *banquet* ❸酒席 feast：设～ *hold a banquet* ❹安乐 of ease and comfort：～安鸩(zhèn)毒(贪图享受等于喝毒酒自杀)。*Seeking a life of pleasure is like drinking poisoned wine.*

堰 yàn ㄧㄢˋ 挡水的低坝 dam：塘～ *pond* | 围～ *cofferdam*

验(驗、*騐) yàn ㄧㄢˋ ❶检查，察看 to examine：～血 *take a blood test* | ～收 *check and accept* | 考～ *to test* ❷有效果 produce the desired effect：屡试屡～ *prove successful in every test* | 应～ *be confirmed*

掞 yàn ㄧㄢˋ ❶光照 sunlit ❷美艳 gorgeous

⇨ see also shàn on p.579

焱 yàn ㄧㄢˋ 火焰 flame

雁(*鴈) yàn ㄧㄢˋ 大雁，鸟名，多指鸿雁。羽毛褐色，腿短，群居在水边，飞时排列成行。是候鸟 wild goose

赝(贋、*贗) yàn ㄧㄢˋ 假的，伪造的 fake：～品 *counterfeit*

焰(*燄) yàn ㄧㄢˋ 火苗 blaze：火～ *flame* [气焰]气势 arrogance：～万丈 *extremely arrogant*

墕 yàn ㄧㄢˋ ❶〈方 dialect〉两山之间的山地 area between two hills ❷ same as "堰"

⇨ see also yān on p.749

酽(釅) yàn ㄧㄢˋ 浓，味厚 (of taste) strong：这碗茶太～。*This cup of tea is too strong.*

谳(讞) yàn ㄧㄢˋ 审判定罪 to sentence：定～ *pronounce a sentence*

燕(❶*鷰) yàn ㄧㄢˋ ❶(－子)鸟名，背部黑色，翅膀长，尾巴像张开的剪刀，常在人家屋内或屋檐下用泥做巢，捕食昆虫。是候鸟 swallow ❷(ancient) same as "宴"：～居

stay at home idle | ～好 *(of a family) harmonious* | ～乐 *ease and comfort; banquet*

⇨ see also yān on p.750

谳(讌) yàn ㄧㄢˋ ❶相聚叙谈 gather and talk with each other ❷ same as "宴❶❷❸"

嬿 yàn ㄧㄢˋ 美好 fine; good

YANG ㄧㄤ

央 yāng ㄧㄤ ❶中心 centre: 大厅中～ *the centre of the hall* ❷恳求(㊀一求) to entreat; to beg: 只好～人去找 *have to beg sb to find* | ～告 *to beg* ❸尽，完了 end: 夜未～。*The night is not yet over.*

映 yāng ㄧㄤ 应答声 used in response to a call, etc.

⇨ see also yǎng on p.758

泱 yāng ㄧㄤ 深广，弘大㊀ vast; great: 河水～～ *mighty river* | ～～大国 *great and impressive country*

殃 yāng ㄧㄤ ❶祸害(㊀灾一) disaster: 遭～ *meet with disaster* | 城门失火，～及池鱼(喻牵连受害) *when the city gate catches fire, the fish in the moat are made victims; (figurative) embroil innocent bystanders in a disturbance* ❷使受祸害 bring disaster to: 祸国～民 *bring calamity to the country and the people*

鸯(鴦) yāng ㄧㄤ see 鸳鸯 (yuān—) at 鸳 on page 805

秧 yāng ㄧㄤ ❶(一儿)植物的幼苗 seedling: 树～儿 *sapling* | 茄子～ *aubergine seedling* 特指稻苗 (specifically) rice seedling: 插～ *transplant rice seedlings* [秧歌](—ge)我国民间歌舞的一种 *yangge* (a type of folk dance in China) ❷某些植物的茎 vine (of some plants): 瓜～ *melon vine* | 豆～ *bean stalks* ❸(一子)某些初生的饲养的动物 young (of some domesticated animals): 鱼～子 *young fish* | 猪～子 *piglet* ❹〈方 dialect〉栽植，畜养 to plant; to breed: ～几棵树 *plant several trees* | ～一池鱼 *keep a pond of fish*

鞅 yāng ㄧㄤ 古代用马拉车时套在马颈上的皮子 halter strap (in ancient times)

⇨ see also yàng on p.759

扬(揚、❷△*颺、*敭) yáng ㄧㄤˊ ❶高举，向上升 to raise: ～手 *wave one's hand* | ～帆 *set sail* | 趾高气～(骄傲的样子) *self-complacent and arrogant* [扬弃]事物在发展过程中，一面把积极因素提升到更高阶段，一面把消极因素抛弃 to sublate [扬扬]得意的样子 triumphant: ～自得 *triumphant* [扬汤止沸(fèi)]比喻办法不能根本解决问题 pour soup ladled out from the pot back, trying to stop the soup from boiling; (figurative) adopt half-measures ❷在空中飘动 to flutter: 飘～ *to flutter* | 飞～ *to float* ❸向上播撒 throw up and scatter: ～场(cháng) *to winnow* ㊁传布

（㊀宣一）to spread：～名 *make a name for oneself*｜赞～ *to praise*｜颂～ *sing praises*

［扬长而去］大模大样地离去 go off with a swagger

⇨ 颺 see also 飏 on p.757

玚(瑒) yáng ㄧㄤˊ 玉名 a kind of jade

杨(楊) yáng ㄧㄤˊ 杨树，落叶乔木，种类很多，有白杨、大叶杨、小叶杨等，有的木材可制器物 poplar

旸(暘) yáng ㄧㄤˊ ❶太阳出来 (of the sun) to rise ❷晴天 sunny day

飏(颺) yáng ㄧㄤˊ 用于人名 used in given names

⇨ 颺 see also 扬 on p.756

炀(煬) yáng ㄧㄤˊ ❶熔化金属 to smelt (metals) ❷火旺 big flame

钖(鍚) yáng ㄧㄤˊ 古代装饰在马额、盾牌上的金属饰物 a kind of metal ornaments on shields, foreheads of horses in ancient times

疡(瘍) yáng ㄧㄤˊ ❶疮 sore ❷溃烂 to ulcerate：溃～ *ulcer*

羊 yáng ㄧㄤˊ 家畜，反刍类，头上有角，常见的有山羊、绵羊等 sheep; goat

〈古 ancient〉also same as 祥 (xiáng)

佯 yáng ㄧㄤˊ 假装 to feign; to pretend：～攻 *feign an attack*｜～作不知 *feign ignorance*

垟 yáng ㄧㄤˊ 〈方 dialect〉田地。多用于地名 field (often used in place names)：翁～（在浙江省乐清）*Wengyang (a place in Yueqing, Zhejiang Province)*

徉 yáng ㄧㄤˊ see 徜徉 (cháng 一) at 徜 on page 70

洋 yáng ㄧㄤˊ ❶地球表面上比海更大的水域 ocean：海～ *sea*｜太平～ *Pacific Ocean* ❷广大，多 ㊀vast：～溢 *brim with*｜～～大观 *varied and spectacular* ❸外国，外国的 foreign country; foreign：留～ *(old, of Chinese) study abroad*｜～货 *imported goods*｜～为中用 *adapt foreign things for Chinese use* ❹现代化的 modern：土～结合 *combine the old-fashioned and the modern* ❺洋钱，银元 foreign coin; silver dollar

烊 yáng ㄧㄤˊ 熔化金属 to melt (metals) ㊀〈方 dialect〉溶化 to dissolve：糖～了。*The sweets have gone soft.*

⇨ see also yàng on p.759

蛘 yáng ㄧㄤˊ 〈方 dialect〉生在米里的一种小黑甲虫 rice weevil

阳(陽) yáng ㄧㄤˊ ❶明亮 bright ❷跟"阴"相对 opposite of 阴 ①阳性，男性的 masculine; male ②太阳 sun：～历 *solar calendar*｜～光 *sunshine* ③带正电的 positive：～电 *positive electricity*｜～极 *anode* ④山的南面，水的北面（多用于地名）south of a hill or north of a river (often used in place names)：衡～（地名，在湖南省衡山之南）*Hengyang (a place to the south of Hengshan Mountain,*

Hunan Province) | 洛～（地名，在河南省洛河之北）*Luoyang (a place to the north of Luohe River, Henan Province)* ⑤外露的，明显的 open：～沟 *open drain* | ～奉阴违 *comply in public but oppose in private* ⑥凸出的 convex：～文图章 *seal in relief* ⑦关于活人的（迷信）this world; concerned with living beings：～间 *this world* ❸指男性生殖器 male genitals ❹(ancient) same as "佯"

卬 yǎng ㄧㄤˇ same as "仰"

⇨ see also áng on p.7

仰 yǎng ㄧㄤˇ ❶脸向上，跟"俯"相对 face upward (opposite of 俯)：～起头来 *throw back one's head* | ～天大笑 *look up at the sky and laugh loudly* | 人～马翻 *suffer a crushing defeat; be in a bustle* ❷敬慕 to admire：久～ *(polite expression) have long admired sb* | 信～ *have belief in; faith* | 敬～ *to venerate* ❸依赖（㊀一赖）to rely on：～人鼻息（指依赖人，看人的脸色行事）*be at sb's beck and call* ❹旧时公文用语，对上行文用在"恳、祈、请"等之前，表示尊敬；对下行文表命令，如"仰即遵照"（指示下属机关遵照公文内容办事）(old, used before 恳, 祈 and 请 in an official letter to an office at a higher level to express respect or to an office at a lower level to express an order) respectfully; to be sure to

呹 yǎng ㄧㄤˇ [呹咽]（-yè）水流阻滞的样子 (of water flow) sluggish

⇨ see also yāng on p.756

养(養) yǎng ㄧㄤˇ ❶抚育，供给生活品（㊀一育）to support; to raise：～家 *keep a family* | 抚～ *to foster* | 赡～ *to support (one's elders)* ❷饲养（动物），培植（花草）to raise, to breed (animals); to grow (plants)：～鸡 *raise chickens* | ～鱼 *breed fish* | ～花 *grow flowers* ❸生育 give birth to：～了个儿子 *gave birth to a son* ❹（非血亲）抚养的 adoptive：～女 *foster daughter* | ～父 *foster father* ❺使身心得到滋补和休息 to convalesce; to recuperate：～神 *to repose* | ～精蓄锐 *conserve strength and build up one's energy* | ～病 *to convalesce* | 休～ *to convalesce* ㊀保护修补 to maintain：～路 *maintain a road/railway* ❻培养 to train：他～成了劳动习惯。*He has become used to physical labour.* ❼（品德学业等）良好的积累 (of character, education, etc.) cultivation：修～ *mastery; breeding* | 涵～ *breeding* | 教～ *bring up; upbringing* | 学～ *academic accomplishment and self-cultivation* ❽扶持，帮助 give aid to：以农～牧，以牧促农 *use agriculture to assist husbandry and use husbandry to boost agriculture*

氧 yǎng ㄧㄤˇ 气体元素，符号O，无色、无味、无臭，比空气重。能助燃，是动植物呼吸所必需的气体 oxygen (O)

痒(癢) yǎng ㄧㄤˇ 皮肤或黏膜受刺激想要抓

挠的感觉 ⓐ to itch：蚊子咬得身上直～～。*The mosquito bites itch terribly.* | 痛～相关 *share a common lot* ⓑ 想做某事的愿望强烈 itch to try：看见别人打球他心里发～。*He cannot resist the itch to play when he sees others playing ball game.* [技痒] 极想把自己的技能显出来 itch to exercise one's skill

漾 yǎng ㄧㄤˇ see 滉漾 (huàng —) at 滉 on page 271

怏 yàng ㄧㄤˋ 不服气，不满意 unhappy：～～不乐 *be in low spirits* | ～然不悦 *be unhappy about sth*

鞅 yàng ㄧㄤˋ 牛、马等拉东西时架在脖子上的器具 leather strap put around the neck of ox, horse, etc.

⇨ see also yāng on p.756

样(様) yàng ㄧㄤˋ ❶(一子、一儿) 形状 appearance：模～ *appearance* | 这～ *this way* | 不像～儿 *in poor shape* ❷(一儿) 量词，用于事物的种类 (measure word) kind：两～儿菜 *two dishes* | 四～儿果品 *four kinds of fruits* | ～～儿都行 *be good at everything* ❸(一子、一儿) 做标准的东西 sample：～品 *sample product* | 货～ *sample goods* | ～本 *sample*

恙 yàng ㄧㄤˋ 病 illness：偶染微～ *be unwell* | 安然无～(没受损伤或没发生意外) *safe and sound*

烊 yàng ㄧㄤˋ [打烊] 〈方 dialect〉 商店晚上关门停止营业 (of shops) to close for the night

⇨ see also yáng on p.757

羕 yàng ㄧㄤˋ 形容水流很长 (of water flow) long

漾 yàng ㄧㄤˋ ❶水面微微动荡 to ripple：荡～ *to ripple* ❷液体溢出来 (of liquids) to brim over：～奶 *(of babies) throw up milk* | ～酸水 *throw up gastric juice* | 汤太满，都～出来了。*The soup is brimming over.*

YAO ㄧㄠ

么 yāo ㄧㄠ same as "幺"

⇨ see also ma on p.433, me on p.441

幺 yāo ㄧㄠ ❶〈方 dialect〉小，排行最末的 youngest：～叔 *youngest uncle* | ～妹 *youngest sister* | ～儿 *youngest son* ❷在某些场合说数字时用来代替1。one (sometimes used instead of the numeral '1')

吆(吆)** yāo ㄧㄠ [吆喝] (一he) 喊叫，用于叫卖东西、赶牲口等 cry one's wares; loudly urge on (animals)

夭(❷*殀) yāo ㄧㄠ ❶茂盛 ⓐ luxuriant：桃之～～ *luxuriant peach blossoms; prosperous* ❷未成年的人死去 die young：～亡 *die young* | ～折 *die young*

妖 yāo ㄧㄠ ❶神话传说中称有妖术而害人的东西 demon (in Chinese mythology and legend)：～魔鬼怪 *all forces of evil* ⓑ 邪恶，荒诞，迷惑人的 evil and fraudulent: ～术 *witchcraft* | ～风 *evil wind* | ～言惑众 *deceive people with fallacies* ❷装束、神态不正派 (of dress, bearing, etc.) indecent: ～里～气 *seductive and bewitching* ❸媚，艳丽 gorgeous: ～娆 *bewitching*

约(約) yāo ㄧㄠ 用秤称 weigh with a steelyard: 你～～这条鱼有多重? *Will you please see how much the fish weighs?*

⇨ see also yuē on p.809

要 yāo ㄧㄠ ❶求 to ask; to demand; to request [要求] 提出具体事项，希望实现 to demand; to request: ～大家认真学习。*Everyone is asked to study earnestly.* | ～入党 *apply to join the Party* ❷强求，有所仗恃而强硬要求 to force; to coerce: ～挟(xié) *to blackmail; to threaten; to hold sth over sb* ❸ (ancient) same as "邀" "腰" ❹姓 (surname) Yao

⇨ see also yào on p.762

喓 yāo ㄧㄠ 用于地名 used in place names: 打石～(在山西省永和) *Dashiyao (in Yonghe, Shanxi Province)*

腰 yāo ㄧㄠ ❶胯上胁下的部分，在身体的中部 waist (see picture of 人体 on page 647) ❷裤、裙等围在腰上的部分 waist (of trousers, skirts, etc.): 裤～ *waist of trousers* ❸事物的中段，中间 middle: 山～ *halfway up a mountain* | 大树拦～折断。*The big tree broke in the middle.* ❹中间狭小像腰部的地势 waist-like terrain; narrow terrain: 土～ *isthmus* | 海～ *strait*

邀 yāo ㄧㄠ ❶约请 to invite: ～他来谈谈 *ask him to come and have a talk* | 特～代表 *specially invited representative* ❷求得 to solicit; to seek: ～赏 *seek rewards for one's achievements* | ～准 *get permission* | ～功 *seek rewards; take credit for someone else's achievements* ❸阻留 to intercept: ～截 *to intercept* | ～击 *to ambush*

爻 yáo ㄧㄠ (formerly pronounced xiáo) 组成八卦中每一个卦的长短横道，如"—"（阳爻）、"--"（阴爻）long and short linear symbols making up the Eight Trigrams in ancient divination

肴(*餚) yáo ㄧㄠ (formerly pronounced xiáo) 做熟的鱼肉等 cooked meat dish: 佳～ *delicious food; delicacy* | 酒～ *wine and dishes*

尧(堯) yáo ㄧㄠ 传说中上古帝王名 Yao, a legendary ruler in ancient China

侥(僥) yáo ㄧㄠ see 僬侥 (jiāo－) at 僬 on page 311

⇨ see also jiǎo on p.311

峣(嶢) yáo ㄧㄠ [岧峣] (tiáo－) 山高 (of mountain) high and steep

垚 yáo ㄧㄠ 高。多用于人名 (often used in given names) tall; high

轺(軺) yáo ㄧㄠ 轺车，古代一种轻便的小马车

a kind of small chariot in ancient times

姚 yáo ㄧㄠ 姓 (surname) Yao

珧 yáo ㄧㄠ 江珧，软体动物，又叫玉珧，壳三角形，生活在海里。肉柱叫江珧柱，干制后称干贝 pen shell (also called 玉珧)

铫(銚) yáo ㄧㄠ ❶古代一种大锄 a kind of big hoe in ancient times ❷ 姓 (surname) Yao

⇨ see also diào on p.137

陶 yáo ㄧㄠ ［皋陶］(gāo－) 传说中上古人名 Gaoyao (a legendary person in ancient times)

⇨ see also táo on p.642

窑(*窯、*窰) yáo ㄧㄠ ❶ 烧砖、瓦、陶瓷等的建筑物 kiln ❷为采煤而凿的洞 coal pit：煤～ *coal pit* ❸窑洞，在土坡上特为住人挖成的洞 cave dwelling ❹（－子）旧指妓院 (old) brothel

谣(謠) yáo ㄧㄠ ❶歌谣，随口唱出、没有伴奏的韵语 ballad：民～ *ballad* | 童～ *children's rhyme* ❷谣言，凭空捏造的话 rumour：造～ *start a rumour* | 辟～ *refute a rumour*

摇 yáo ㄧㄠ 摆动（㊀－摆、－晃）to rock; to shake：～头 *shake one's head* | ～船 *row a boat* ［摇曳］(－yè) 摇摆动荡 to flicker; to sway ［动摇］变动，不坚定 to waver：思想～ *waver in one's belief*

徭(傜)** yáo ㄧㄠ 徭役，古时统治者强制人民承担的无偿劳动 corvee; forced labour

遥 yáo ㄧㄠ 远㊂（㊀－远）far; distant; remote：～望 *look into the distance* | ～控 *control or instruct remotely* | 路～知马力。*Distance tests a horse's strength.* | ～～相对 *face each other at a distance* ［遥感］利用现代电子、光学仪器远距离探测、识别研究对象 to remotely sense

猺 yáo ㄧㄠ ［黄猺］哺乳动物，即青鼬，又叫黄喉貂，外形略像家猫，喉部及前胸部黄色。吃鼠类、蜜蜂等 (same as 青鼬，also called 黄喉貂) yellow-throated marten

媱 yáo ㄧㄠ ❶美好，美艳 beautiful ❷逍遥游乐 to have a good time

瑶 yáo ㄧㄠ 美玉 a fine jade ㊙ 美好，珍贵 fine; precious：～函 *precious ancient classics*

［瑶族］我国少数民族，参看附录四 the Yao people (one of the ethnic groups in China. See Appendix Ⅳ.)

飖(飆) yáo ㄧㄠ ［飘飖］(old) same as "飘摇" (see 飘 piāo on page 505 for reference)

繇 yáo ㄧㄠ same as "徭"

⇨ see also yóu on p.793, zhòu on p.865

鳐(鰩) yáo ㄧㄠ 鱼名，身体扁平，略呈圆形或菱形，有的种类有一对能发电的器官，生活在海里 skate

杳 yǎo ㄧㄠ 无影无声 distant and traceless：～无音信 *have*

lost contact | 音容已～ *(of a dead person) the voice and face are forgotten*

咬(*齩、**鱙) yǎo ㄧㄠˇ ❶上下牙对住，压碎或夹住东西 to bite: ～了一口馒头 *took a bite of the Chinese steamed bun* ❷钳子等夹住或螺丝齿轮等卡住 (of pincers or cogs) to grip; to fasten: 螺丝勚(yì)了，～不住扣。*The screw was worn and wouldn't fasten.* ❸受责问或审讯时拉扯上不相关的人 to implicate (innocent person when blamed or interrogated): 不许乱～好人。*Don't implicate innocent people indiscriminately.* ❹狗叫 to bark: 鸡叫狗～。*Cocks crow and dogs bark.* ❺读字音 to pronounce; to articulate: 这个字我～不准。*I cannot pronounce the character clearly.*

舀 yǎo ㄧㄠˇ 用瓢、勺等取东西(多指流质) to ladle; to scoop (often liquids): ～水 *scoop up water*| ～汤 *ladle out soup* [舀子](－zi)舀取液体的器具 ladle

窅 yǎo ㄧㄠˇ 眼睛眍(kōu)进去 (of eyes) sunken ㊖深远 deep and remote

窈 yǎo ㄧㄠˇ ❶深远 profound ❷昏暗 dim ❸美好 fine; beautiful [窈窕](－tiǎo) 1 形容女子文静而美好 (of woman) gentle and graceful 2(宫室、山水)幽深 (of palaces, mountains and rivers) secluded

疟(瘧) yào ㄧㄠˋ 疟子，即疟(nüè)疾 malaria (same as 疟 nüè 疾)

⇨ see also nüè on p.484

药(藥) yào ㄧㄠˋ ❶可以治病的东西 medicine; drug ❷有一定作用的化学物品 certain chemicals: 火～ *gunpowder* | 焊～ *weld flux* | 杀虫～ *insecticide* ❸用药物医治 to cure; to treat: 不可救～ *incurable; (figurative) hopeless* ❹毒死 to poison: ～老鼠 *kill rats with rat poison*

要 yào ㄧㄠˋ ❶索取，希望得到 to ask for; to want to get: ～账 *demand payment of a debt* | 我～这一本书。*I want this book.* ㊀希望保留 to like to keep: 这东西他还～呢。*He still needs this thing.* [要强]好胜心强，不愿落后 to be eager to excel ❷重大，值得重视的 essential; important: ～事 *important matter* | ～点 *main point* [要紧][紧要]急切重要 important and urgent ❸重大的值得重视的东西 essential: 纲～ *outline* | 提～ *summarise; summary* | 纪～ *summary* ❹应该，必须 must; should; have to: ～努力学习。*One must work hard.* ❺将要，将 to be about to: 我们～去学习了。*We are going to do our schoolwork.* ❻连词，要是，若，如果 (conjunction) if: 明天～下雨，我就不去了。*If it rains tomorrow, I will not go.* | 他～来了，你就交给他。*Give it to him if he comes.* ❼请求，叫 to request: 他～我给他买本书。*He asked me to buy him a book.*

⇨ see also yāo on p.760

崾 yào ㄧㄠ ［崾崄］(－xiǎn)〈方 dialect〉两山之间像马鞍子的地方，多用于地名 saddle-shaped place between two mountains (often used in place names)：～乡（在陕西省黄龙）*Yaoxiang (a place in Huanglong, Shaanxi Province)*｜白马～（在陕西省定边）*Baimayao (a place in Dingbian, Shaanxi Province)*

钥(鑰) yào ㄧㄠ ［钥匙］(－shi）开锁的用具 key

⇨ see also yuè on p.810

靿 yào ㄧㄠ 靴筒、袜筒 leg of a boot or stocking：高～靴子 *knee boot; high boot*

鹞(鷂) yào ㄧㄠ （－子）鹞鹰，鸟名，即雀鹰，像鹰而小，背部灰褐色，腹部白色，性凶猛，捕食鼠、兔和小鸟 sparrow hawk (same as 雀鹰)［纸鹞］风筝 kite

曜 yào ㄧㄠ ❶照耀 to shine; to illuminate ❷日、月、星都称"曜"，一个星期的七天用日、月、火、水、木、金、土七个星名排列，因此星期几也叫什么"曜日"，如星期日是"日曜日"，星期六是"土曜日"。Used to refer to the sun, the moon and stars. The seven days of the week are named for the seven heavenly bodies：Sun (日), Moon (月), Mars (火), Mercury (水), Jupiter (木),Venus (金) and Saturn (土). Thus Sunday is 日曜日 and Saturday is 土曜日 .

耀(*燿) yào ㄧㄠ ❶光线强烈地照射（㊀照－）to shine; to illuminate：～眼 *dazzling* ❷显扬，显示出来 to flaunt：～武扬威 *make a show of one's strength* ❸光荣 honourable：荣～ *honour*

YE ㄧㄝ

耶 yē ㄧㄝ 用于译音，如耶路撒冷 used in transliteration as in 耶路撒冷 (Jerusalem)

⇨ see also yé on p.764

倻 yē ㄧㄝ ［伽倻琴］(jiā－－）朝鲜族弦乐器，像筝 gayageum

椰 yē ㄧㄝ 椰子树，常绿乔木，树干很高，生长在热带。果实叫椰子，球形，里面有汁，可做饮料。果肉可吃，也可榨油。树干可做建筑材料 coconut tree; coconut palm

掖 yē ㄧㄝ 把东西塞在衣袋或夹缝里 to tuck in：把钱～在兜里 *tuck the money into the pocket*｜把书～在书包里 *tuck the books into the schoolbag*

⇨ see also yè on p.766

暍 yē ㄧㄝ 中暑，伤暑 to suffer sunstroke

噎 yē ㄧㄝ 食物堵住食道 to choke：吃得太快，～住了 *choked from eating too fast*｜因～废食（喻因为偶然出毛病而停止正常的活动）*stop doing anything to avoid making a mistake (literally means 'give up eating for fear of choking')* ㊀用话顶撞人，使对方说不出话来 to retort and render sb speechless：说话别～人。*Don't*

talk so aggressively that other people don't know how to reply.

邪 yé ㄧㄝ ❶ see 莫邪 at 莫 on page 461 ❷ (ancient) same as "耶 (yé) ❶"

⇨ see also xié on p.720

铘(鋣) yé ㄧㄝ see 镆铘 (mò—) at 镆 on page 461

爷(爺) yé ㄧㄝ ❶父亲 father: ～娘 *father and mother* ❷ 祖父 ㊂ grandfather; paternal grandfather: ～～奶奶 *(paternal) grandfather and grandmother* ❸对长辈或年长男子的敬称 polite speech, used to address one's male elders or an old man: 张大～(ye) *Uncle Zhang* | 李～ *Uncle Li* ❹旧时对官僚、财主等的称呼 (old) sir (used to address an official or a rich man): 老～ *lord* | 少～ *young master* | 县太～ *county magistrate* ❺迷信的人对神的称呼 god (used by superstitious people to address god): 土地～ *local village god* | 财神～ *God of Wealth*

耶 yé ㄧㄝ ❶文言助词，表示疑问 auxiliary word in classical Chinese, used to express doubt: 是～非～? *Yea or nay?* ❷ (ancient) same as "爷"

⇨ see also yē on p.763

揶 yé ㄧㄝ [揶揄](—yú) 耍笑，嘲弄 to deride; to ridicule: 被人～ *be in derision*

也 yě ㄧㄝ ❶副词 adverb ①表示同样、并行等意义 too; also; as well: 你去，我～去。*If you go, I will go there, too.* | ～好，～不好。*Not bad, but not perfect as well.* ②跟"再""一点儿""连"等连用表示语气的加强(多用在否定句里) often used in a negative sentence with 再，一点儿，连，etc. to express emphasis: 再～不敢闹了 *dare not make a scene again* | 这话一点儿～不错。*What was said was absolutely right.* | 连一个人影～没找到 *cannot find even one person* ③(跟前文的"虽然、即使"连用)表示转折或让步 used with 虽然 or 即使 in the above to express transition or concession: 我虽然没仔细读过这本书，～略知内容梗概。*I had a rough idea about the book even though I had not read it thoroughly.* | 即使天下雨，我～要出门。*Even if it rains, I will go out all the same.* ④表示委婉语气 used to soften the tone: 我看～只好如此了。*I suppose we'll have to leave it at that.* | 节目倒～不错。*The programme was not so bad.* ❷文言助词 auxiliary word in classical Chinese ①用在句末，表示判断语气 used at the end of a sentence to express judgement: 环滁皆山～。*Chuzhou is indeed surrounded by mountains.* ②表示疑问或感叹语气 used to express doubt or exclamation: 何～? *Why?* | 何为不去～? *Why don't you leave here?* | 是何言～? *What are you talking about?* ③用在句中，表示停顿 used in the middle of a sentence to express a pause: 向～不怒而今～怒，何也?

You were not angry then, but now you are angry. Why?

冶 yě ㄧㄝˇ ❶熔炼（金属）to smelt (metal)：～炼 *smelt*｜～金 *smelt* ❷装饰、打扮得过分艳丽（含贬义）(disapproving) seductively dressed or made up：～容 *seductively made up and dressed; flirtatious looks*｜妖～ *gorgeous and indecent*

野（*埜）yě ㄧㄝˇ ❶郊外，村外 open country：～营 *to camp; bivouac using a tent*｜～地 *wilderness*［野战军］适应广大区域机动作战的正规军 field army［分野］划分的范围，界限 demarcation; dividing line ❷指不当政的地位，跟"朝"相对 state of being out of office (opposite of 朝)：朝～ *the court and the common people; the government and the populace*｜下～ *(the President) be forced to step down*｜在～ *out of office* ❸不讲情理，没有礼貌，蛮横 rough; rude：撒～ *behave rudely*｜粗～ *rough* ❹不驯顺，狂妄非分 wild; untamed：狼子～心（狂妄狠毒的用心）*wild and evil ambitions* ❺不受约束或难于约束 unrestrained：～性 *wild nature*｜这孩子心都玩～了。*This kid has been having great fun and cannot concentrate on his study now.* ❻不是人所驯养或培植的（动物或植物）undomesticated (animals or plants)：～兽 *wild beast*｜～菜 *edible wild herbs*｜～草 *weeds*

业（業）yè ㄧㄝˋ ❶事业，事情，所从事的工作 line of business; cause; occupation ①国民经济中的部门 industry; line of business：农～ *agriculture*｜工～ *industry*｜渔～ *fishery*｜运输～ *transportation industry* ②职业，工作岗位 occupation：就～ *get a job* ③学业，学习的功课 course of study：毕～ *graduate* ❷从事某种工作 to engage in：～农 *engage in farming*｜～商 *engage in commerce* ❸产业，财产 estate; property：～主 *proprietor* ❹已经（㊣—已）already：～经公布 *have already been announced* ❺佛教称人的行为、言语、思想为业，分别叫作身业、口业、意业，合称三业，有善恶之分，一般指恶业 karma

邺（鄴）yè ㄧㄝˋ 古地名，在今河北省临漳西，河南省安阳北 Ye (an ancient place name, in the west of today's Linzhang, Hebei Province and the north of today's Anyang, Henan Province)

叶（葉）yè ㄧㄝˋ ❶（—子、—儿）植物的营养器官之一，多呈片状、绿色，长在茎上 leaf; foliage：树～ *tree leaf*｜菜～ *vegetable leaf* ❷像叶子的东西 leaf-shaped thing：铜～ *copper sheet*｜铁～ *iron sheet* ❸same as "页" ❹较长时期的分段 part of a historical period：明代末～ *closing period of the Ming Dynasty*｜20世纪中～ *in the middle of the 20th century* ❺姓 (surname) Ye

⇨ see also xié on p.719

Y

页(頁、**葉) yè ㄧㄝ ❶篇，张（指书、画、纸等）(of a book, picture or paper) leaf; sheet; page：活～ *loose-leaf* ❷指互联网网页 (of the internet) page：主～ *home page* | ～面 *page* ❸量词，旧指书本中的一张纸，现多指书本中一张纸的一面 (measure word) (old) a piece of paper in a book; (generally) page

曳(**抴) yè ㄧㄝ 拖，拉，牵引 to drag; to pull：～光弹 *tracer bullet* | 弃甲～兵 *flee helter-skelter (literally means 'cast off one's armour and drag one's weapon behind one')*

拽 yè ㄧㄝ same as "曳"

⇨ see also zhuāi on p.871, zhuài on p.871

夜(*亱) yè ㄧㄝ 从天黑到天亮的一段时间，跟"日""昼"相对 night (opposite of 日 or 昼)：日日～～ *day and night; day in, day out* | 白天黑～ *the day and the night* | 昼～不停 *round the clock*

掖 yè ㄧㄝ 用手扶着别人的胳膊 to support sb by the arm ⓘ扶助，提拔 to support; to promote：奖～ *reward and promote*

[掖县] 旧县名，今莱州，在山东省 Yexian (the old name of now Laizhou, Shandong Province)

⇨ see also yē on p.763

液 yè ㄧㄝ 液体，能流动、有一定体积而没有一定形状的物质 liquid：血～ *blood* | 溶～ *solution* [液晶] 一种同时具有液体的流动性和晶体的光学特性的有机化合物 liquid crystal

腋 yè ㄧㄝ ❶腋窝，上肢同肩膀相连处靠里凹入的部分 armpit ❷其他生物体上跟腋类似的部分 (of animal) armpit; (of plant) axil：～芽 *auxiliary bud*

咽 yè ㄧㄝ 呜咽，哽咽，悲哀得说不出话来 to choke with sobs

⇨ see also yān on p.748, yàn on p.754

晔(曄) yè ㄧㄝ ❶光明，多用于人名 (often used in given names) bright ❷ same as "烨"

烨(燁、*爗) yè ㄧㄝ 火光很盛的样子 (of firelight) flaming

谒(謁) yè ㄧㄝ 拜见 to visit; to pay respects：～见 *to visit (a superior)* | 拜～ *pay a formal visit*

馌(饁) yè ㄧㄝ 给在田里耕作的人送饭 to bring meal to people working in the fields

靥(靨) yè ㄧㄝ 酒窝儿，嘴两旁的小圆窝儿 dimple：脸上露出笑～。*There is a smile on her cheeks.*

YI ㄧ

一 yī ㄧ ❶数目字，最小的正整数 (number) one ❷纯，专 wholeheartedly：～心～意 *wholeheartedly* [一定] 1 特定 specific; certain：～的程序 *specified procedures* 2 相当的 considerable：

取得～的成绩 *make considerable achievements* 3 副词，必定 (adverb) certainly：～按期完成。*It will be done on schedule.* ❸满，全 all; whole：～屋子人 *a roomful of people* | ～冬 *throughout winter* | ～生 *all one's life* ❹相同 same：～样 *identical* | 大小不～ *different in size* ❺另外的 another：番茄～名西红柿。*'Fanqie' (tomato) is also known as 'xihongshi'(tomato).* ❻放在重叠的动词中间，表示稍微，轻微 used in the middle of a reduplicated verb to express the slightness of an action：看～看 *have a look* | 摸～摸 *have a feel* ❼与"就"呼应 used together with 就①表示两事时间紧接 as soon as; once：天～亮他就起来。*He gets up as soon as it is light.* ②表示每逢 whenever: ～想起大家的期望，就感到自己的责任重大。*Whenever one thinks of people's expectations, one feels a great responsibility.* ❽起加强语气的作用 used for emphasis：～至于此！ *How terrible it is!* | ～何怒！ *How angry they are!* | ～何悲！ *How sorrowful they are!*

弌 yī ㄧ same as "一"

伊 yī ㄧ ❶代词，彼，他，她 (pronoun) that; he; she ❷文言助词，用在某些词语前，加强语气 auxiliary word in classical Chinese, used before a word or an expression for emphasis：下车～始 *on getting off the car/bus*

[伊斯兰教] 宗教名。公元 7 世纪初阿拉伯人穆罕默德所创 Islam

咿 (*吚) yī ㄧ [咿呀]（—yā）小孩子学话的声音，摇桨的声音 babble;(of the oar) squeak [咿唔]（—wú）读书的声音 sound of reading aloud：～吟诵 *reading aloud*

洢 yī ㄧ ❶洢水，水名，在湖南省益阳，资水支流 Yishui River (a tributary of Zishui River, in Yiyang, Hunan Province) ❷古水名，即今伊河，在河南省洛阳 Yi River (same as today's 伊河, in Luoyang, Henan Province)

衣 yī ㄧ ❶衣服（fu），衣裳（shang）clothes ❷披在或包在物体外面的东西 coating：炮～ *gun cover* | 糖～炮弹 *sugar-coated bullet* ❸姓 (surname) Yi

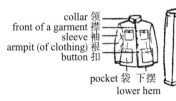

上衣 upper outer garment

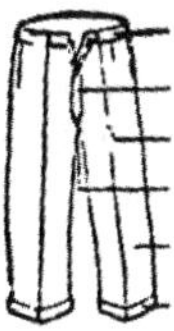

裤子 trousers

Y

⇨ see also yì on p.774

依 yī ㄧ ❶靠，仰赖（㊀－靠）to lean on; to depend on: 相～为命 *depend upon each other for survival* | 孤独无～ *be lonely without anyone or anything to rely on* ❷介词，按照（㊀－照）(preposition) according to: ～次前进 *move forward in turn* | ～我看，你最好不去。*In my opinion, you'd better not go.* ❸顺从，答应 to comply with: 不～不饶 *wouldn't let sb off*

[依依] 1 形容留恋，不忍分离 reluctant to part: ～不舍 *be reluctant to part* 2 柔软的东西摇动的样子 (of soft things) swaying gently: 杨柳～。*The willows are swaying in the breeze.*

铱（鉥） yī ㄧ 金属元素，符号 Ir，银白色，熔点高，质硬而脆。可用来制科学仪器等 iridium (Ir)

医（醫、毉）** yī ㄧ ❶医生，治病的人 doctor: 老中～ *veteran practitioner of traditional Chinese medicine* | 名～ *famous doctor* | 军～ *army surgeon* ❷医学，增进健康、预防和治疗疾病的科学 medical science: 中～ *traditional Chinese medicine* | 西～ *Western medicine* | 学～ *study medicine* ❸治病（㊀－疗、－治）to treat: ～术 *medical skill* | 有病早～ *get timely medical treatment*

鹥（鷖） yī ㄧ 古书上指鸥 gull (in ancient Chinese texts)

繄 yī ㄧ 文言助词，惟 (auxiliary word in classical Chinese) only: ～我独无。*Only I don't have that.*

祎（禕） yī ㄧ 美好。多用于人名 (often used in given names) glorious; fine

猗 yī ㄧ ❶文言助词，相当于"啊"(auxiliary word in classical Chinese, equivalent to 啊) ah: 河水清且涟～。*Ah, the clear river ripples on.* ❷文言叹词，表示赞美 exclamation in classical Chinese, used to express praise: ～欤休哉！*How wonderful!*

椅 yī ㄧ 落叶乔木，又叫山桐子，花黄色，果实球形，红色。木材可用来制器物 idesia (also called 山桐子)

⇨ see also yǐ on p.773

欹 yī ㄧ same as "猗❷"

⇨ see also qī on p.516

漪 yī ㄧ 水波纹 ripple: 清～ *clear ripples* | 涟～ *ripples* | ～澜 *ripples and waves*

揖 yī ㄧ 拱手礼 to bow with hands folded in front: 作～ *bow with hands folded*

壹 yī ㄧ "一"字的大写 (elaborate form of 一, used in commercial or financial context) one

噫 yī ㄧ 文言叹词 (exclamation in classical Chinese) alas

[噫嘻]（－xī）表示悲痛或叹息 (used to express sorrow or sigh) alas

黟 yī ㄧ 黟县，在安徽省 Yixian (a place in Anhui Province)

匜 yí ㄧˊ 〈古 ancient〉 ❶一种洗手用的器具 a container used to pour water when washing hands ❷一种盛酒的器具 a scoop for liquor

迤(迆)** yí ㄧˊ see 逶迤 (wēi—) at 逶 on page 677

⇨ see also yǐ on p.772

椸(箷)** yí ㄧˊ 衣架 hanger

仪(儀) yí ㄧˊ ❶人的容貌、举止 (of a person) appearance and behaviour: ～表 *appearance and behaviour* | ～容 *looks* | 威～ *dignified appearance and behaviour* ❷仪式，按程序进行的礼节 ceremony: 司～ *master of ceremonies* ❸礼物 present: 贺～ *congratulatory gift* | 谢～ *acknowledgement; honorarium* ❹仪器，供测量、绘图、实验等用的有一定准则的器具 apparatus: ～表 *instrument* | 光谱～ *spectrometer* | 地动～ *seismograph*

圯 yí ㄧˊ 桥 bridge

夷 yí ㄧˊ ❶我国古代称东方的民族 tribes in eastern China in ancient times ❷旧指外国或外国的 (old) foreign countries; foreign; barbaric ❸平坦，平安 flat; safe: 化险为～ *turn danger into safety (literally means 'make a dangerous and difficult road flat and safe')* ❹弄平 to raze: ～为平地 *raze to the ground* ㊀消灭 to exterminate: ～灭 *annihilate*

荑 yí ㄧˊ 割去田地里的野草 to weed

⇨ see also tí on p.646

咦 yí ㄧˊ 叹词，表示惊讶 (exclamation, used to express surprise) why: ～！这是怎么回事？ *Hey! What's all this about?*

姨 yí ㄧˊ ❶姨母，母亲的姊妹 aunt; one's mother's sister ❷（一子）妻的姊妹 one's wife's sister: 大～子 *one's wife's elder sister* | 小～子 *one's wife's younger sister* ❸称跟母亲年纪相近的无亲属关系的妇女 (used to address an unrelated woman of about the same age as one's mother) aunt: 阿～ *aunt* | 张～ *Aunt Zhang*

胰 yí ㄧˊ 胰腺，旧叫膵（cuì）脏，人和高等动物的腺体之一，能分泌胰液，帮助消化，还分泌一种激素（胰岛素），起调节糖类代谢作用 (formerly called 膵 cuì 脏) pancreas [胰子]〈方 dialect〉肥皂 soap: 香～ *perfumed soap* | 药～ *medicated soup*

痍 yí ㄧˊ 伤，创伤 wound; trauma: 疮～满目（喻到处是灾祸景象）。*Everywhere a scene of desolation meets the eye.*

沂 yí ㄧˊ 沂河，源出山东省，至江苏省入海 Yihe River (originating in Shandong Province and flowing into the sea from Jiangsu Province)

诒(詒) yí ㄧˊ 传给 to bequeath to; to pass on to: ～训 *teachings of the deceased*

饴(飴) yí ㄧˊ ❶糖浆，糖稀 syrup: 甘之如～ *enjoy*

sth bitter as if it were as sweet as sugar ❷饴糖，一种质软的糖 maltose：高粱～ *sorghum soft candy*

怡 yí ㄧˊ 和悦，愉快 joyful：心旷神～ *feel relaxed and happy* | ～然自得 *be happy and pleased with oneself*

贻(貽) yí ㄧˊ ❶赠给 to present (sb with a gift) ❷遗留 to bequeath：～害 *leave a legacy of trouble* | ～笑大方（让内行人笑话）*make a laughing stock of oneself before experts*

眙 yí ㄧˊ see 盱眙 (xū–) at 盱 on page 733

宜 yí ㄧˊ ❶适合，适当（㊀适–）suitable; appropriate：老少皆～ *good for both young and old* | 相～ *appropriate* ❷应该，应当（多用于否定式）should (often in the negative)：不～如此。*It is not appropriate to do so.* | 不～操之过急。*This should not be done in haste.* ❸当然，无怪 certainly; no wonder：～其无往而不利也！*Without any doubt they will meet success wherever they go.*

宧 yí ㄧˊ 古代称屋子里的东北角 (ancient) north-east corner of a room

颐(頤) yí ㄧˊ ❶面颊，腮 cheek：解～（开颜而笑）*smile* ❷休养，保养 to take care of oneself：～神 *rest one's mind* | ～养天年 *take good care of oneself so as to live out one's allotted life span*

扅 yí ㄧˊ see 扊扅 (yǎn–) at 扊 on page 753

移(*迻) yí ㄧˊ ❶挪动（㊀迁–）to move：～植 *transplant* | 愚公～山 *be resolute in one's endeavor, no matter what hardships one encounters (literally means 'an old man removes mountains')* | 转～ *shift* [移录] 抄录，过录 to make a copy of [移译] 翻译 to translate ❷改变，变动 to change：～风易俗 *change dated habits and customs* | 坚定不～ *firm and unshakable*

簃 yí ㄧˊ 楼阁旁边的小屋 small room next to a high building

蛇 yí ㄧˊ see 委蛇 (wēi–) at 委 on page 677

⇨ see also shé on p.585

遗(遺) yí ㄧˊ ❶丢失（㊀–失）to lose ❷漏掉（㊀–漏）to leave out：～忘 *forget* ❸丢失的东西，漏掉的部分 something lost; lost property; omission：路不拾～ *good social ethos (literally means 'no pocketing lost property on the road')* | 补～ *add missing information to a book* ❹余，留 to leave behind：不～余力 *spare no efforts* | ～憾 *regret; remorse* 特指死人留下的 (specifically) left to others at one's death：～嘱 *will* | ～产 *legacy* | ～像 *picture of the deceased* [遗传] 生物体的构造和生理机能由上一代传给下一代 to pass on to the next generation ❺不自觉地排泄大小便或精液 to emit (faeces, urine, or semen) involuntarily：～尿 *bedwetting* | ～精 *nocturnal* *emission*

⇨ see also wèi on p.684

疑 yí ㄧˊ ❶不信，因不信而猜度(duó)(㊃-惑) to doubt：可～ *suspicious* | 半信半～ *not quite convinced* | ～不能决 *cannot make up one's mind out of doubt* ❷不能解决的，不能断定的 doubtful：～问 *question; doubt* | ～案 *disputed case* | ～义 *doubt* | 存～(对怀疑的问题暂不做决定) *leave a question open*

嶷 yí ㄧˊ [九嶷]山名，在湖南省宁远 Mount Jiuyi (in Ningyuan, Hunan Province)

彝(彛)** yí ㄧˊ ❶古代盛酒的器具。也泛指古代宗庙的祭器 wine vessel in ancient times; (generally) sacrificial utensils：～器 *sacrificial vessel* | 鼎～ *bronze sacrificial utensils* ❷常规，法度 law; norms：～训 *regular exhortations* | ～宪 *law*

[彝族]我国少数民族，参看附录四 the Yi people (one of the ethnic groups in China. See Appendix Ⅳ.)

乙 yǐ ㄧˇ ❶天干的第二位，用作顺序的第二 *yi* (the second of the ten Heavenly Stems, a system used in the Chinese calendar); second：～等 *second grade* ❷画乙字形的符号，作用有二：1古时没有标点符号，遇有大的段落用墨笔勾一个∠符号，形似乙字。2遇有颠倒、遗漏的文字用∠符号改正过来或把遗漏的字勾进去。to draw a mark shaped like 乙 (used to indicate the end of a long paragraph stops in unpunctuated classical Chinese or to correct a transposition or an omission in writing)

钇(釔) yǐ ㄧˇ 金属元素，符号Y，暗灰色。可用来制特种玻璃和合金等 yttrium (Y)

已 yǐ ㄧˇ ❶止，罢了 to stop; to end：学不可以～。*Learning should be pursued without intermission.* | 如此而～。*That is all.* ❷副词，已经，已然，表过去 (adverb, used to express something in the past) already：时间～过。*It has expired.* ❸后来，过了一会儿，不多时 later on：～而 *soon after* | ～忽不见 *suddenly disappeared after a while* ❹太，过 too：其细～甚 *it is too trivial* ❺(ancient) same as "以❸"：～上 *the above* | ～下 *the following* | 自汉～后 *from the Han Dynasty on*

以(*㠯) yǐ ㄧˇ ❶介词 preposition ①用，拿，把，将 with; by; by means of：～少胜多 *use the few to defeat the many in a war* | 晓之～利害 *enable sb to see the advantages and disadvantages* | ～身作则 *set an example with one's own conduct* | ～理论为行动的指南 *use theory as a guide to action* | ～劳动为荣 *take labour as an honour* [以为]心里想，认为 think：意～未足 *not yet satiated* | 我～应该这样做。*I think we should do it like this.* ②依，顺，按照 according to：众人～次就座。*The people took their seats in due order.* | ～时启闭 *open and*

Y

close according to schedule ③因，由于 because of：不～失败自馁，不～成功自满 *not lose heart because of failure nor feel conceited because of success* ④在，于（指时日）at; on (of time and date)：中华人民共和国～1949年10月1日宣告成立。*The founding of the People's Republic of China was proclaimed on October 1, 1949.* ❷连词 conjunction ①表示目的关系 (used to express purpose) so that：大力发展生产，～提高人民生活水平。*Great efforts should be made to develop production to improve the living standards of the people.* ②表示并列关系，跟"而"用法相同 (used in the same way as 而, expressing coordinate relation) and：其责己也重～周，其待人也轻～约。*They were strict with themselves in all aspects but lenient to others without many requests.* ❸放在方位词前表明时间、地位、方向或数量的界限 used before words of locality to express the limits of time, place, direction or quantity：中等水平～上 *above intermediate level* | 五岭～南，古称百粤。*The area to the south of the Five Ridges was referred to as Baiyue in ancient times.* | 十天～后交货。*Delivery will be made in ten days' time.* | 三日～内完成 *accomplish the task within three days*

苡 yǐ ㄧˇ see 薏苡 (yì–) at 薏 on page 778

佁 yǐ ㄧˇ ❶痴呆的样子 silly ❷静止的样子 motionless

尾 yǐ ㄧˇ (–儿) ❶马尾 (wěi) 上的长毛 (of a horse) skirt; long tail hairs：马～罗 *sieve made of the long tail hair of horses* ❷蟋蟀等尾部的针状物 cercus：三～儿（雌蟋蟀）*female cricket (with three cerci on its tail)*

⇨ see also wěi on p.680

矣 yǐ ㄧˇ 文言助词 auxiliary word in classical Chinese ①直陈语气，与"了（le）❷"相当 equivalent to 了 (le) ❷, used to express an indicative mood：艰难险阻，备尝之～。*I have been through all kinds of hardships and hazards.* ②感叹语气 used in exclamation：大～哉！*How significant!* ③命令语气 used in imperatives：往～，毋多言！*Go and say no more about it.*

苢 yǐ ㄧˇ see 芣苢 (fú–) at 芣 on page 184

迤（迆）** yǐ ㄧˇ ❶地势斜着延长 (of terrain) to stretch in a curve ❷介词，表示延伸，向（专指方位）(preposition, used to express extension) towards：天安门～东（向东延伸）*to the east of Tian'anmen*

[迤逦]（–lǐ）曲折连绵 meandering：沿着蜿蜒的山势～而行 *go along the winding mountain*

⇨ see also yí on p.769

酏 yǐ ㄧˇ 酏剂，含有糖和挥发油或另含有主要药物的酒精溶液的制剂 elixir

蚁（蟻、螘）** yǐ ㄧˇ 蚂蚁 ant：雌～ *female ant; gyne* | 雄～ *male ant* |

工～ *worker ant; ergate* | 兵～ *soldier ant*

舣(艤、**檥) yǐ ǐ 停船靠岸 to pull a boat to shore

倚 yǐ ǐ ❶靠着 to lean on：～门 *lean against the door* ❷仗恃 to rely on：～势欺人 *rely on one's position to bully others* ❸偏，歪 partial：不偏不～ *impartial; even-handed*

椅 yǐ ǐ （－子）有靠背的坐具 chair

⇨ see also yī on p.768

旖 yǐ ǐ ［旖旎］（－nǐ）柔和美丽 charming and gentle：风光～。*The scene is enchanting.*

踦 yǐ ǐ 抵住 to prop up

齮(齮) yǐ ǐ 咬 to bite：～龁（hé）*bite*

扆 yǐ ǐ 古代一种屏风 a kind of screen in ancient times

顗(顗) yǐ ǐ 安静。古时多用于人名 (often used in given names in ancient times) quiet

乂 yì ì 治理，安定 to administer; to stabalize

刈 yì ì 割（草或谷类）to mow (grass or crops)：～麦 *mow wheat* | ～除杂草 *mow weeds*

艾 yì ì 治理 to administer［自怨自艾］本义是悔恨自己的错误，自己改正。现在只指悔恨 be full of remorse and self-reproach

⇨ see also ài on p.3

弋 yì ì 用带着绳子的箭来射鸟 shoot birds with retrievable arrows：～凫与雁 *shoot wild ducks and wild geese with retrievable arrows*

杙 yì ì 小木桩 small wooden post

钇(釴) yì ì ❶古代的一种方鼎 a kind of square *ding* in ancient times ❷姓 (surname) Yi

亿(億) yì ì 数目，一万万。旧时也指十万 (number) a hundred million; (old) a hundred thousand

忆(憶) yì ì ❶回想，想念 to recall; to remember：回～ *to recall* | ～苦思甜 *recall the past sorrows and savour the present joys* | ～故人 *remember one's old friends* ❷记得 to remember：记～力 *memory*

义(義) yì ì ❶公正合宜的道理或举动（㊥正一）justice; righteousness：见～勇为 *act bravely for a just cause* | ～不容辞 *be duty-bound* ㊊指合乎正义或公益的 righteous：～举 *righteous act*［义务］1 应尽的责任 duty 2 不受报酬的 voluntary：～劳动 *voluntary labour* ❷感情的联系 affection; relationship; friendly feeling：朋友的情～ *friendship* ❸意义，意思 meaning：定～ *definition* | 字～ *meaning of a character* | 歧～ *ambiguity* ❹指认作亲属的 adopted：～父 *adoptive father* | ～子 *adopted child* ㊊人工制造的（人体的某部分）artificial (parts of the body)：～齿（假牙）*false* *tooth* | ～肢（假肢）*artificial limb*

议（議）yì ㄧˋ ❶表明意见的言论（㊀–论）opinion：提～ *propose; proposal* | 建～ *suggest; suggestion* | 无异～ *have no objection* ❷商议，讨论 to discuss：会～ *meeting* | ～定 *agree on*

艺（藝）yì ㄧˋ ❶才能，技能（㊀技–）skill; talent：手～ *craftsmanship* | ～高人胆大 *boldness of execution stems from great skill* [艺术] 1 用形象来反映现实但比现实更有典型性的社会意识形态，包括音乐、舞蹈、美术、雕塑、文学、曲艺、戏剧、电影等 art 2 指富有创造性的方式、方法 skill：领导～ *the art of leadership* ❷限度 limit：贪贿无～ *be insatiably greedy for bribes*

呓（囈、**讛）yì ㄧˋ 梦话 somniloquy; sleep talking：梦～ *somniloquy; sleep talking* | ～语 *somniloquy*

仡 yì ㄧˋ [仡仡] 1 强壮勇敢 strong and brave 2 高大 tall and big

⇨ see also gē on p.203

屹 yì ㄧˋ 山势高耸 (of a mountain) towering ㊁坚定不可动摇 firm：～立 *stand erect and firm* | ～然不动 *stand erect and motionless*

亦 yì ㄧˋ 文言副词，也（表示同样），也是 (adverb in classical Chinese) also：人云～云 *parrot others' words* | 反之～然 *and vice versa* | ～步～趋（喻自己没有主张，跟着别人走）*follow slavishly*

㑊 yì ㄧˋ [解㑊]（xiè–）中医指困倦无力、懒得说话、抑郁不欢的症状 (in traditional Chinese medicine) symptoms of lethargy, weakness, unwillingness to speak, and depression

弈 yì ㄧˋ ❶古代称围棋 (ancient) *weiqi*; go ❷下棋 to play *weiqi*：对～ *play* weiqi *with sb*

奕 yì ㄧˋ ❶大 grand ❷美丽 beautiful [奕奕] 精神焕发的样子 radiating power and vitality：神采～ *glowing with health and vitality*

衣 yì ㄧˋ 穿（衣服），给人穿（衣服）to put on (clothes); to clothe (sb)：～布衣 *wear cotton clothes* | 解衣（yī）～我 *generous and considerate to others (literally means 'take off his own clothes and put it on me')*

⇨ see also yī on p.767

裔 yì ㄧˋ ❶后裔，后代子孙 descendant; posterity ❷边，边远的地方 border; remote area：四～ *borderlands; frontiers*

异（*異）yì ㄧˋ ❶不相同的 different：～议 *dissent; objection* | ～口同声 *speak in one voice* | 求同存～ *seek common ground on major issues while reserving differences on minor ones* ❷分开 to separate：离～ *divorce* | 分居～爨（cuàn）*(of brothers) live independently* ❸另外的，别的 other：～日 *some other day* | ～地 *foreign land* ❹特别的 strange：～味 *rare delicacy;*

strange odour | 奇才～能 *extraordinary talents and abilities* ❺奇怪 surprised：惊～ *astonished* | 深以为～ *strike one as very odd*

抑 yì ㄧˋ ❶压，压制 to curb：～制 *inhibit* | ～扬 *(of voice) rise and fall* | ～强扶弱 *curb the violent and help the weak* [抑郁] 忧闷 depressed ❷文言连词 conjunction in classical Chinese ① 表选择，还是 (used to indicate a choice) or：求之欤，～与之欤？*Is it that he asks for it or that he is asked for and told about it?* ② 表转折，只是 (used to express transition) but ③ 表递进，而且 (used to express progression) moreover：非惟天时，～亦人谋也。*It was not only because of a good opportunity but also because of skilful planning and preparation.*

邑 yì ㄧˋ ❶都城，城市 city：通都大～ *big city with convenient means of transportation* ❷县 county

挹 yì ㄧˋ ❶舀，把液体盛出来 to ladle out [挹注] ㊗从有余的地方取出来，以补不足 take from a surplus to supplement a deficiency ❷牵引，拉 to pull

浥 yì ㄧˋ 沾湿 to wet

悒 yì ㄧˋ 愁闷，不安 ㊟ sad; uneasy：忧～ *depressed* | ～～不乐 *feel depressed*

裛 yì ㄧˋ 〈古 ancient〉书套 slip case

佚 yì ㄧˋ same as "逸"

泆 yì ㄧˋ ❶放纵 wild; abandoned; unrestrained ❷ same as "溢❶"

轶(軼) yì ㄧˋ ❶超过 to excel：～群（比一般的强）*be head and shoulders above all others* | ～材（突出的才干）*outstanding talent* ❷散失 to be lost：～事（史书没有记载的事）*anecdote*

昳 yì ㄧˋ [昳丽] 美丽 beautiful：形貌～ *good-looking*

⇨ see also dié on p.137

役 yì ㄧˋ ❶战事 battle：战～ *campaign* ❷指需要出劳力的事 forced labour：劳～ *corvee* ❸兵役 military service：现～ *active service* | 预备～ *reserve duty* ❹使唤（㊟—使）to use as a servant：奴～ *enslave* ❺旧时称被役使的人 (old) servant：杂～ *odd-jobs man* | 差（chāi）～ *bailiff (in a yamen)*

疫 yì ㄧˋ 瘟疫，流行性急性传染病 epidemic; plague; pestilence：～情 *epidemic situation* | 防～ *prevent epidemics* | 鼠～ *bubonic plague*

毅 yì ㄧˋ 果决，志向坚定而不动摇 firm：刚～ *firm and resolute* | ～力 *willpower* | ～然决然 *resolutely and determinedly*

译(譯) yì ㄧˋ 把一种语言文字依照原义改变成另一种语言文字 to translate：翻～ *translate* | ～文 *translated text* 也指把代表语言文字的符号、数码转换成相应的语言文字 to decode：～电员 *decoder* | 破～

decipher

峄(嶧) yì ㄧˋ 峄山，山名，在山东省 Mount Yishan (in Shandong Province) 峄县，旧县名，在山东省枣庄 Yixian County (an old county in today's Zaozhuang, Shandong Province)

怿(懌) yì ㄧˋ 欢喜 pleased; happy

驿(驛) yì ㄧˋ 古代传递政府文书的人中途休息的地方 post station in ancient times：～站 *post house*

绎(繹) yì ㄧˋ 寻究，理出头绪 to unravel; to sort out：寻～ *explore repeatedly* | 演～ *deduct*

柃 yì ㄧˋ 古书上说的一种树 a kind of tree in ancient Chinese texts

易 yì ㄧˋ ❶容易，不费力 easy：通俗～懂 *easy to understand* | 轻而～举 *be easy to do* ❷平和 amiable：平～近人 *unassuming, amiable and approachable* ❸改变 to change：移风～俗 *change dated habits and customs* ❹交易，交换 to exchange：以物～物 *exchange one thing for another* ❺轻视 to despise ❻芟治草木 to get rid of weeds and trees：～其田畴 *rid the fields of weeds and trees*

埸 yì ㄧˋ ❶田界 field boundary ❷边境 border area：疆～ *border*

蜴 yì ㄧˋ see 蜥蜴 (xī—) at 蜥 on page 697

佾 yì ㄧˋ 古时乐舞的行列 a row of a certain number of dancers in ancient times

诣(詣) yì ㄧˋ 到。特指到尊长那里去 to visit (specifically one's superior)：～前请教 *call on sb for advice* [造诣] 学问或技术所达到的程度 attainments：他对于医学～很深。*He is well versed in medicine.*

狁 yì ㄧˋ [林狁]即猞猁(shēlì) lynx (same as 猞猁 shēlì)

羿 yì ㄧˋ 后羿，传说是夏代有穷国的君主，善于射箭 (in Chinese legend) Houyi (chief of a tribe named Youqiong during the Xia Dynasty, good at archery)

翊 yì ㄧˋ 辅佐，帮助 to assist：～戴（辅佐拥戴）*assist and support*

翌 yì ㄧˋ 次于今日、今年的 next (day, year)：～日 *next day* | ～年 *next year* | ～晨 *next morning*

翳(❷*瞖) yì ㄧˋ ❶遮盖 to cover：～蔽 *cover well; deep and vague* | 树林荫～ *shaded by dense forest* ❷（一子）眼角膜上所生障蔽视线的白斑 nebula

翼 yì ㄧˋ ❶翅膀或像翅膀的东西 wing; wing-like thing：鸟～ *wing of a bird* | 蝉～ *wing of a cicada* | 机～ *wing of an aeroplane* ❷左右两侧中的一侧 flank; wing：侧～ *flank* | 左～ *(of military) left flank; (of politics) left wing* | 右～ *(of military) right flank; (of politics) right wing* ❸帮助，辅佐 to assist ❹星宿名，二十八宿之一 *yi* (one of the twenty-eight constellations in ancient Chinese astronomy)

益 yì ì ❶增加 to increase：进～ *progress* | 延年～寿 *prolong life* ❷利，有好处的（㊟利一）beneficial：～处 *benefit* | ～虫 *beneficial insect* | 良师～友 *good teacher and worthy friend* ❸更（gèng）even more：日～壮大 *get stronger day by day* | 精～求精 *strive for perfection* | 多多～善 *the more the better*

嗌 yì ì 咽喉 throat
⇨ see also ài on p.4

溢 yì ì ❶充满而流出来 to overflow：河水四～。*The river overflowed in all directions.* | ～美（过分夸奖）*praise excessively* ㊕超出 to exceed：～出此数 *exceed the number* ❷ (ancient) same as "镒"

缢(縊) yì ì 用绳子勒死 to strangle; to hang：～杀 *strangle to death* | 自～ *hang oneself*

镒(鎰) yì ì 古代重量单位，一镒为二十两，一说是二十四两 an ancient Chinese unit for measuring weight, equal to 20 or 24 两

鹢(鷁) yì ì ❶古书上说的一种水鸟 a kind of aquatic bird in ancient Chinese texts ❷船头画有鹢的船，后泛指船 boat with a picture of such bird on the bow; (generally) boat

螠 yì ì 无脊椎动物，雌雄异体，身体呈圆筒状，不分节，生活在海底泥沙中 Echiura; spoon worm

谊(誼) yì ì 交情 friendship：友～ *friendship* | 深情厚～ *profound friendship*

勚(勩) yì ì ❶劳苦 toilsome ❷器物逐渐磨损，失去棱角、锋芒等 (of implement) gradually blunt：螺丝扣～了。*The thread of the screw was worn out.*

逸 yì ì ❶跑，逃跑 to escape：逃～ *escape* ❷散失（㊟亡一）to be lost：～书（已经散失的古书）*ancient works no longer extant* ❸安闲，安乐（㊟安一）leisurely：一劳永～ *manage to get sth done once and for all* | 劳～结合 *strike a proper balance between work and rest* ❹避世隐居 to be reclusive：～民 *recluse who refuses to take an official post* | 隐～ *lead the life of a hermit; hermit* ❺超过一般 to surpass：～群绝伦 *be head and shoulders above all others*

肄 yì ì 学习 to study：～业（指没能毕业或尚未毕业）*leave school before graduation or without qualification*

意 yì ì ❶意思，心思 meaning; purpose：来～ *purpose in coming* | 词不达～ *the words fail to convey the meaning* [意见] 见解，对事物的看法 idea; opinion ❷心愿，愿望 desire：中（zhòng）～ *be to one's liking* | 任～ *willfully* | 好～ *kindness* ❸料想 to expect：～外 *unexpected; accident* | 出其不～ *take sb by surprise*

薏 yì ㄧˋ ［薏苡］（-yǐ）草本植物，茎叶略像高粱，果实椭圆形，坚硬而光滑，种仁白色，叫薏仁米，可以吃，又可入药 Job's tears; *Coix lacryma-jobi*

繶（繶） yì ㄧˋ 古代鞋上装饰用的圆丝带 silk ribbon decorated on shoes in ancient times

臆（肊）** yì ㄧˋ ❶胸 chest：胸～（指心里的话或想法）*feelings or thoughts* ❷主观的，缺乏客观证据的 subjective：～见 *subjective view* | ～说 *assumption* | ～造 *fabricate* | ～测 *guess* | ～断 *assume*

镱（鐿） yì ㄧˋ 金属元素，符号 Yb，银白色，质软。可用来制特种合金，也用作激光材料等 ytterbium (Yb)

癔 yì ㄧˋ ［癔病］精神病的一种，又叫歇斯底里，发病时喜怒无常，感觉过敏，严重时手足或全身痉挛，说胡话，可出现类似昏迷的状态 hysteria (also called 歇斯底里)

埶 yì ㄧˋ 种植 to grow：树～五谷 *grow all food crops* | ～菊 *plant chrysanthemums*

廙 yì ㄧˋ ［廙廙］恭敬的样子 respectful

潩 yì ㄧˋ 清潩河，水名，在河南省中部，颍河支流 Qingyihe River (branch of Yinghe River, in the middle of Henan Province)

瘗（瘞） yì ㄧˋ 掩埋，埋葬 to bury

嫕 yì ㄧˋ 性情和善可亲 affable：婉～（和婉柔顺）*obedient and amiable*

鹝（鷊） yì ㄧˋ 古书中说的一种水鸟 a kind of water bird in ancient Chinese texts

虉（虉） yì ㄧˋ 虉草，草本植物，叶条形，嫩时可用作饲料，茎秆可用来编织器物 ribbon grass

熠 yì ㄧˋ 光耀，鲜明 ㊀ brilliant：光彩～～ *sparkling and shining*

殪 yì ㄧˋ ❶死 to die ❷杀死 to kill

懿 yì ㄧˋ 美，好（多指德、行）(often of morals and deeds) exemplary：～行 *exemplary conduct* | ～德 *moral excellence*

劓 yì ㄧˋ 古代割掉鼻子的酷刑 punishment by cutting off the nose in ancient times

燚 yì ㄧˋ 人名用字 used in given names

YIN ㄧㄣ

因（*囙） yīn ㄧㄣ ❶原因，缘故，事物发生前已具备的条件 cause; reason：事出有～。*There is good reason for it.* | 内～ *internal cause* | 外～ *external cause* ❷介词，因为，由于 (preposition) because of：会议～故改期。*The meeting was rescheduled for some reason.* | ～病缺席 *be absent because of illness* ❸连词，连接分句，表示因果关系 (conjunction, used to express cause and effect) because：～雾气太重，高速路暂时关闭。*The* *expressway was temporarily closed because of heavy fog.* [因为]连词，表示因果关系 (conjunction, used for cause and effect) because：～今天下雨，我没有出门。*I did not go out because it rained today.* ❹沿袭（㊀—袭）to follow：陈陈相～ *follow a dated set routine*[因循]1 沿袭，不改变 follow the old routine：～守旧 *stay in the same old rut* | ～成规 *follow the old routine* 2 拖沓（tà）to procrastinate：～误事 *procrastination causes trouble* ❺凭借，根据 on the basis of; due to：～势利导 *guide action according to the trend* | ～陋就简 *make do with whatever is available* | ～地制宜 *suit measures to local conditions*

茵 yīn ㄧㄣ 古代车子上的席、垫 mattress in ancient times ㊀铺（pū）的东西 bedding：～褥 *mattress* | 绿草如～。*The green grass looks like a carpet.*

洇 yīn ㄧㄣ 液体接触纸张等向周围渗透散开 to soak; to spread and sink in (paper, etc.)：这种纸写起来有些～。*This kind of paper is rather absorbent when written on.*

姻（*婣）yīn ㄧㄣ ❶婚姻 marriage：联～ *join by marriage* | ～缘 *happy fate which brings lovers together in marriage* ❷姻亲，由婚姻关系而结成的亲戚。古代专指婿家 relation by marriage; (ancient, specifically) son-in-law's family

骃（駰）yīn ㄧㄣ 浅黑带白色的杂毛马 greyish black horse with white spots

细（絪）yīn ㄧㄣ [细缊]（—yūn）same as "氤氲"

氤 yīn ㄧㄣ [氤氲]（—yūn）烟云弥漫的样子。也作"细缊"(of smoke, clouds) enshrouding (also written as 细缊)

铟（銦）yīn ㄧㄣ 金属元素，符号 In，银白色，质软。可用来制低熔点合金等 indium (In)

阴（陰、*隂）yīn ㄧㄣ ❶黑暗 dark ❷云彩遮住太阳或月、星，跟"晴"相对 cloudy (opposite of 晴)：天～了。*The sky is overcast.* ❸跟"阳"相对 opposite of 阳 ①阴性，女性的 female ②太阴，月亮 moon：～历 *lunar calendar* ③带负电的 negative：～电 *negative charge* | ～极 *negative electrode* ④水的南面，山的北面（多用于地名）(often used in place names) north of a hill or south of a river：江～（地名，在江苏省长江之南）*Jiangyin (a place to the south of the Yangtze River, in Jiangsu Province)* | 蒙～（地名，在山东省蒙山之北）*Mengyin (a place to the north of Mengshan Mountain in Shandong Province)* ⑤暗藏的，不露出来的 concealed：～沟 *sewer; drain* | ～私 *shameful secret* ⑥凹下的 in intaglio：～文 *characters or designs cut in intaglio* ⑦关于人死后的或鬼魂的（迷信）of the nether world：～宅 *grave* | ～间 *nether*

Y

world ❹（一儿）光线被东西遮住所成的影 shade：树～ *shade of a tree* | 背～ *shady* ❺背面 back：碑～ *back of a stone tablet* ❻诡诈，不光明 treacherous：～谋诡计 *schemes and intrigues* | 这家伙够～的。*The guy is indeed treacherous.* [阴险] 表面和善而内心险恶 treacherous ❼生殖器 genital organ

荫（蔭） yīn ㄧㄣ same as "阴❹"

⇨ see also yìn on p.783

音 yīn ㄧㄣ ❶声（㊥声一）sound; voice：口～ *accent* | 扩～器 *loudspeaker* ❷消息 news：佳～ *good news* | ～信 *news* ❸指音节 syllable：多～词 *polysyllabic word*

喑（*瘖） yīn ㄧㄣ ❶哑，不能说话 mute：～哑 *mute and dumb* ❷沉默不语，又指动物不鸣叫 to keep silent：～默 *keep silent* | 万马齐～ *an apathetic atmosphere (literally means 'ten thousand horses stand mute')*

愔 yīn ㄧㄣ [愔愔] 1 形容安静和悦 quiet and pleasant 2 形容沉默寡言 silent

殷（❷*慇） yīn ㄧㄣ ❶深厚，丰盛 ardent; abundant：情意甚～ *sincere hospitality* | ～切 *earnest* [殷实] 富足，富裕 abundant; rich：家道～。*The family is well off.* ❷[殷勤] 周到，尽心 keen to please：做事～ *do things wholeheartedly* | ～招待 *show solicitous hospitality* ❸殷代，商代的后期，由盘庚起称殷（公元前1300—公元前1046年）Yin Dynasty (the latter period of the Shang Dynasty, called Yin Dynasty from Pangeng onwards, 1300 BC—1046 BC) ❹姓 (surname) Yin

⇨ see also yān on p.749

溵 yīn ㄧㄣ [溵溜]（一liù）地名，在天津市蓟县 Yinliu (a place in Jixian, Tianjin Municipality)

禋（諲） yīn ㄧㄣ 恭敬 respectful

堙（*陻） yīn ㄧㄣ ❶堵塞 to block up; to stop up ❷土山 mound

闉（闉） yīn ㄧㄣ ❶瓮城，也指瓮城的门 enclosure for defence outside a city gate; gate of the enclosure ❷堵塞 to stop; to block

湮 yīn ㄧㄣ same as "洇"

⇨ see also yān on p.750

歅 yīn ㄧㄣ 用于人名。九方歅，春秋时人，善相马 used in given names, e.g. Jiufang Yin, a man in the Spring and Autunm Period

禋 yīn ㄧㄣ ❶古祭祀名，指祭天 a rite of offering a sacrifice to heaven in ancient times ❷泛指祭祀 (generally) to offer sacrifices

吟（*唫） yín ㄧㄣˊ ❶唱，声调抑扬地念 to chant：～诗 *recite poetry* ❷古代诗歌的一种 a type of poetry in ancient times：梁甫～ *Song of Liangfu* ❸呻吟，叹息 to groan; to sigh

垠 yín ㄧㄣˊ 边，岸，界限 bank; boundary：一望无～的麦田 *boundless wheat field*

琅 yín ㄧㄣˊ 像玉的石头 jade-like stone

硍 yín ㄧㄣˊ 用于地名 used in place names：六～（在广西壮族自治区浦北）*Liuyin (in Pubei, Guangxi Zhuang Autonomous Region)*

银（銀） yín ㄧㄣˊ ❶金属元素，符号 Ag，白色有光泽，质软，是热和电的良导体。可用来制货币、器皿、感光材料等 sliver (Ag) ❷（一子）旧时一种用银铸成块的货币 money (made of silver)：～两 *silver (as currency)* ❸像银子的颜色 silver-coloured：～发 *white hair* | ～燕（指银白色的飞机，也泛指飞机）*white aeroplane; (generally) aeroplane* | ～河（天河）*Milky Way*

龈（齦） yín ㄧㄣˊ 牙龈，牙床，牙根上的肉 gum

➪ see also kěn on p.358

狺 yín ㄧㄣˊ ［狺狺］狗叫的声音 yap; yelp

訚（誾） yín ㄧㄣˊ ㊀和颜悦色地进行辩论 to speak amiably in debate

崟（崯）** yín ㄧㄣˊ see 嵚崟 (qīn—) at 嵚 on page 537

淫（❷*婬、*滛） yín ㄧㄣˊ ❶过多，过甚 excessive：～威 *despotic power* | ～雨 *excessive rain* ❷在男女关系上不正当的 lascivious：～乱 *sexually promiscuous* | ～荡 *loose in morals* ❸放纵 unrestrained：骄奢～逸 *extravagant and dissipated* ❹迷惑，使昏乱 to puzzle; to bewilder：富贵不能～。*Neither riches nor honours can lead one astray.*

霪 yín ㄧㄣˊ ［霪雨］连绵不断下得过量的雨。现作“淫雨” excessive rain (now written as 淫雨)

寅 yín ㄧㄣˊ ❶地支的第三位 *yin* (the third of the twelve Earthly Branches, a system used in the Chinese calendar) ❷寅时，指夜里三点到五点 *yin* (the period from 3 a.m. to 5 a.m.)

夤 yín ㄧㄣˊ ❶深 deep：～夜 *the dead of night* ❷恭敬 respectful

［夤缘］攀缘上升 to climb up ㊥拉拢关系，向上巴结 attach oneself to sb powerful

龂（齗） yín ㄧㄣˊ ❶ same as “龈 (yín)” ❷㊀争辩的样子 to argue

鄞 yín ㄧㄣˊ 鄞州，地名，在浙江省宁波 Yinzhou (a place in Ningbo, Zhejiang Province)

蟫 yín ㄧㄣˊ 古书上指衣鱼，一种咬衣服、书籍的小虫。又叫蠹鱼 (in ancient Chinese texts) silverfish (also called 蠹鱼)

嚚 yín ㄧㄣˊ ❶愚蠢而顽固 stupid and stubborn ❷奸诈 sly and vicious

尹 yǐn ㄧㄣˇ 旧时官名 (old) official title：令～ *county magistrate* | 府～ *prefectural magistrate* | 道～ *prefect*

Y

引 yǐn ㄧㄣˇ ❶领，招来（㊥—导）to lead：～路 *to guide* | ～火 *ignite* | 抛砖～玉 *make some introductory remarks to set the ball rolling (literally means 'cast a brick to attract jade')* ㊥古时文体名，跟"序"差不多 a kind of literary style in ancient times, similar to preface or foreword [引子]（—zi）1 乐曲、戏剧开始的一段 first section or introductory part (in music or drama) 2 中医称主药以外的副药 (in traditional Chinese medicine) added ingredient enhancing the efficacy of medicine：这剂药用姜做～。*Ginger was added to this dose of medicine to enhance efficacy.* ❷拉，伸 to pull：～弓 *draw a bow* | ～颈（伸长脖子）*crane one's neck* [引申] 字、词由原义产生他义 extend the meaning of (words) ❸用来做证据、凭借或理由 to quote; to cite：～书 *quoted book* | ～证 *cite as evidence* | ～以为荣 *regard as a great honour* ❹诱发，惹 to induce：一句俏皮话，～得大家哄堂大笑。*One witty remark had everyone roaring with laughter.* ❺退却 to leave：～退 *to resign* | ～避 *make way (for sb)* ❻市制长度单位，1 引是 10 丈 a traditional Chinese unit for measuring length, with 10 丈 in 1 引 ❼古代柩车的绳索 rope for a hearse in ancient times：发～（出殡）*carry out the coffin for burial*

吲 yǐn ㄧㄣˇ [吲哚]（—duǒ）有机化合物，无色或淡黄色的片状晶体。可用来制香料和化学试剂等 indole

蚓 yǐn ㄧㄣˇ 指蚯（qiū）蚓 earthworm (see 蚯蚓 at 蚯 on page 543 for reference)

饮（飲、*歓） yǐn ㄧㄣˇ ❶喝，特指喝酒 to drink; (specifically) to drink wine：～水思源 *do not forget the source of one's happiness* | 畅～ *drink one's full* ❷可喝的东西 drink：冷～ *cold drink* ❸含忍 to nurse; to harbour：～恨 *nurse a grievance*

⇨ see also yìn on p.783

隐（隱） yǐn ㄧㄣˇ ❶藏匿，不显露（㊥—藏）to hide; to conceal：～蔽 *take cover* | ～痛 *secret anguish* | ～患 *hidden danger* ❷指隐秘的事 a secret：难言之～ *an unmentionable secret*

瘾（癮） yǐn ㄧㄣˇ 特别深的嗜好（shìhào）addiction; strong interest: 烟～ *addiction to smoking* | 看书看上～啦 *addicted to reading*

缫（繕） yǐn ㄧㄣˇ 〈方 dialect〉 绗（háng）to sew with long stitches：～棉袄 *sew long stitches on a padded jacket* | 在褥子中间～一行 *sew long stitches in the middle of a cotton-padded mattress*

印 yìn ㄧㄣˋ ❶图章，戳记 seal; stamp：盖～ *affix a seal* | 钢～ *embossing seal* | ～信 *official seal* | ～把（bà）子（也借指政权）*(seal of) authority* ❷（—子、—儿）痕迹 trace; mark：脚～儿 *footprint* |

烙～ *brand (burned on a farm animal)* ❸留下痕迹。特指把文字或图画等留在纸上或器物上 to leave a trace; (specifically) to print：～书 *print books* | 翻～ *to reprint* | 排～ *to typeset and print* [印刷]把文字图画等制成版，加油墨印在纸上，可以连续印出很多的复制品。印刷术是我国古代四大发明之一 to print; printing ❹合，符合 to tally; to conform：～证（互相证明）*to confirm* | 心心相～ *have mutual affinity*

茚 yìn 丨ㄣˋ 有机化合物，无色液体，容易产生聚合反应。是制造合成树脂的原料 indene

鲫(鮣) yìn 丨ㄣˋ 鱼名，身体细长，圆柱形，前半身扁平，背上有吸盘，可以吸在大鱼或船底上，生活在海洋里 remora

饮(飲、*歙) yìn 丨ㄣˋ 给牲畜水喝 to water (animals)：～马 *water a horse* | ～牛 *water a cow*

⇨ see also yǐn on p.782

荫(蔭、❷❸*廕) yìn 丨ㄣˋ ❶不见日光，又凉又潮 damp and shady：地下室很～。*The basement is very dank.* ❷封建时代帝王给功臣的子孙读书或做官的特权 (of emperors of the feudal times) to confer honours on one's descendants because of meritorious service：封妻～子 *confer titles of honour on an official's wife and hereditary ranks on his descendants* ❸保佑，庇护 to shield; to shelter：～庇 *to protect*

⇨ see also yīn on p.780

胤 yìn 丨ㄣˋ 后代 offspring

窨 yìn 丨ㄣˋ 地窨子，地下室 basement

⇨ see also xūn on p.742

憖(憗) yìn 丨ㄣˋ 〈古 ancient〉 ❶宁愿 would rather ❷损伤 to damage

[憖憖]谨慎的样子 cautious

YING 丨ㄥ

应(應) yīng 丨ㄥ ❶该，当（㊀一当、一该）should; ought to：～有尽有 *have all that one expects to find* ❷答应，应承（㊀一许、一允）to promise; to answer：我喊他喊不～。*I called out to him, but he didn't answer.* | ～他十天之内完工。*He was promised that the job would be completed within 10 days.* ❸姓 (surname) Ying

⇨ see also yìng on p.786

英 yīng 丨ㄥ ❶花 flower：落～ *fallen petals* ❷才能出众 outstanding：～俊 *outstanding; handsome* 又指才能出众的人 talented person：群～会 *gathering of talents* [英明]有远见卓识 wise [英雄]1 为人民利益英勇斗争而有功绩的人 hero 2 英武过人的人 very brave person

媖 yīng 丨ㄥ 妇女的美称 commendatory term for woman

瑛 yīng 丨ㄥ ❶似玉的美石 jade-like stone ❷玉的光彩

lustre of jade

锳(鍈) yīng ㄧㄥ 形容铃声 tinkle

莺(鶯、*鸎) yīng ㄧㄥ 鸟名，身体小，褐色，嘴短而尖，叫的声音清脆。吃昆虫，是益鸟 warbler［黄莺］鸟名，即黄鹂（lí）oriole (same as 黄鹂 lí)

罃(罃) yīng ㄧㄥ ❶古书上指一种长颈的瓶子 a kind of long-necked jar in ancient Chinese texts ❷ same as "罂"

罂(罌、*甖) yīng ㄧㄥ 大腹小口的瓶子 small-mouthed big-bellied jar［罂粟］草本植物，花有红、紫、白等颜色，果实球形，未成熟时有白浆，是制鸦片的原料，也可入药 opium poppy

婴(嬰) yīng ㄧㄥ ❶婴儿，才生下来的小孩儿 infant; baby：男～ *baby boy* | 女～ *baby girl* ❷触，缠绕 to touch; to harass：～疾（得病）*contract a disease*

撄(攖) yīng ㄧㄥ ❶接触，触犯 to contact; to offend：～其锋 *challenge the spearhead of an attack* | ～怒 *arouse one's anger* ❷扰乱，纠缠 to disturb; to harass

蘡(蘡) yīng ㄧㄥ ［蘡薁］（-yù）落叶藤本植物，枝条细长有棱角，叶子阔卵形，圆锥花序。茎、叶可入药 *Vitis bryoniifolia*

嘤(嚶) yīng ㄧㄥ 鸟叫的声音 ㊀ chirp; trill

缨(纓) yīng ㄧㄥ ❶（-子、-儿）用线、绳等做的穗状装饰品 tassel; ribbon (as an ornament)：帽～子 *hat tassel* | 红～枪 *red-tasselled spear* ❷（-子、-儿）像缨的东西 sth like a tassel：萝卜～子 *radish leaves* | 芥菜～儿 *mustard leaves* ❸带子，绳子 ribbon; rope：长～ *long rope*

璎(瓔) yīng ㄧㄥ 似玉的美石 jade-like stone［璎珞］（-luò）古代一种用珠玉穿成的戴在颈项上的装饰品 necklace of jade and pearls in ancient times

樱(櫻) yīng ㄧㄥ 樱花，落叶乔木，花淡红色或白色 flowering cherry［樱桃］樱桃树，落叶乔木，花淡红色或白色，果实也叫樱桃，成熟时为红色，可以吃 cherry tree

鹦(鸚) yīng ㄧㄥ ［鹦鹉］（-wǔ）鸟名，又叫鹦哥，羽毛美丽，嘴弯曲，能模仿人说话的声音。产于热带、亚热带 parrot (also called 鹦哥)

膺 yīng ㄧㄥ ❶胸 breast：义愤填～ *be filled with righteous indignation* ❷承受，当 to bear：～选 *be elected* | 荣～英雄称号 *receive a hero's title* ❸伐，打击 to strike：～惩 *to punish; send a punitive expedition against*

鹰(鷹) yīng ㄧㄥ 鸟名，嘴弯曲而锐利，四趾有钩爪，性凶猛，食肉。种类很多 hawk

迎 yíng ㄧㄥˊ ❶迎接，接 to welcome; to meet：欢～ *to*

welcome［迎合］为了讨好，使自己的言行符合别人的心意 to pander to ; to cater to ❷向着 to face：～面 *head-on*｜～头赶上 *try hard to catch up*

茔（塋）yíng ㄧㄥˊ 坟墓，坟地 grave：～地 *graveyard*

荥（滎）yíng ㄧㄥˊ ［荥经］地名，在四川省 Yingjing (a place in Sichuan Province)

⇨ see also xíng on p.728

荧（熒）yíng ㄧㄥˊ ❶微弱的光亮 glimmering［荧光］物理学上称某些物质受光或其他射线照射时所发出的可见光 fluorescence：～屏 *fluorescent screen; photoscope*｜～灯 *fluorescent lamp* ❷眼光迷乱 dazzled［荧惑］迷惑 to bewilder; to dazzle

莹（瑩）yíng ㄧㄥˊ ❶光洁像玉的石头 jade-like stone ❷光洁，透明 lustrous and transparent：晶～ *as clear as crystal*

萤（螢）yíng ㄧㄥˊ 萤火虫，昆虫，身体黄褐色，尾部有发光器，能发绿色的光 firefly

营（營）yíng ㄧㄥˊ ❶军队驻扎的地方 barracks：军～ *army barracks*｜安～扎寨 *pitch a camp*｜露（lù）～ *to camp (out)* ㉠为某种目的设置的集中居住的场所（多为临时性的）camp：夏令～ *summer camp*｜集中～ *concentration camp*｜难民～ *refugee camp* ❷军队的编制单位，是连的上一级 battalion ❸筹划管理（㊥经－）to manage：～业 *do business*｜～造防风林 *plant a windbreak forest* ❹谋求 to seek：～生 *earn a living*｜～救 *to rescue*

萦（縈）yíng ㄧㄥˊ 缠绕 to entangle: ～怀（挂心）*occupy one's mind*｜琐事～身 *get bogged down with trivial matters*

滢（瀅）yíng ㄧㄥˊ ［滢湾］地名，在湖南省长沙 Yingwan (a place in Changsha, Hunan Province)

蓥（鎣）yíng ㄧㄥˊ ［华蓥］山名，在四川省东南和重庆市交界处 Mount Huaying (at the junction of Southeast Sichuan and Chongqing Municipality)

滢（瀅）yíng ㄧㄥˊ 清澈 limpid

潆（瀠）yíng ㄧㄥˊ ［潆洄］水流回旋 (of water) to swirl

盈 yíng ㄧㄥˊ ❶充满 to be full of：恶贯满～ *be guilty of countless crimes and deserve damnation*｜热泪～眶 *one's eyes filled with tears* ❷多余（㊥－余）surplus：～利 *profit*

楹 yíng ㄧㄥˊ 堂屋前部的柱子 principal front columns of a hall：～联 *couplet on pillars*

蝇（蠅）yíng ㄧㄥˊ （－子）苍蝇，昆虫，种类很多，通常指家蝇，幼虫叫蛆。能传染痢疾等疾病 fly (its larva is called 蛆)：蚊～ *mosquitoes and flies*｜～头微利 *petty profits*

Y

嬴 yíng ㄧㄥˊ 姓 (surname) Ying

瀛 yíng ㄧㄥˊ 大海 ocean; sea: ～寰（五洲四海）*whole world* | 东～（指日本）*Japan*

籯 yíng ㄧㄥˊ ❶箱笼之类的器具 basket-shaped container ❷筷笼子 chopstick holder

赢（贏） yíng ㄧㄥˊ ❶获利，赚钱 to make a profit ❷胜，跟"输"相对 to win (opposite of 输): 那个篮球队～了。*That basketball team won.* | ～了三个球 *won by 3 goals* ㊀因成功而获得 to win: ～得全场欢呼喝（hè）彩 *win audience's applause*

郢 yǐng ㄧㄥˇ 郢都，楚国的都城，在今湖北省荆州 Yingdu (capital of the Chu state, in today's Jingzhou, Hubei Province)

颍（潁） yǐng ㄧㄥˇ 颍河，发源于河南省登封，东南流至安徽省注入淮河 Yinghe River (originating in Dengfeng, Henan Province, flowing southeast to Anhui Province and finally flowing into Huaihe River)

颖（穎、*頴） yǐng ㄧㄥˇ ❶禾的末端，指某些禾本科植物小穗基部的苞片 bract ❷东西末端的尖锐部分 tip; point: 短～羊毫笔 *goat hair brush with a short tip* | 脱～而出 *talent shows itself in a prominent way (literally means 'an awl-point sticks out through a bag')* ㊀才能出众 clever: 聪～ *clever* | ～悟 *clever* [新颖] 新奇，与一般的不同 new; original: 花样～ *new pattern*

影 yǐng ㄧㄥˇ ❶（－子、－儿）物体挡住光线时所形成的四周有光中间无光的形象 shadow ㊁不真切的形象或印象 vague sign or impression: 这件事在我脑子里没有一点～子了。*I have absolutely no memory of it.* [影响] 一件事物对其他事物发生作用，也指所发生的作用 to affect; effect ❷描摹 to photoprint: ～宋本 *copy of an edition printed in the Song Dynasty* ❸形象，图像 photograph; image: 摄～ *photograph* | 造～ *radiography* | 留～ *take a photo as a reminder of one's visit to a place* | 剪～ *(paper-cut) silhouette* [影印] 用照相方法制版印刷 photolithograph ❹指电影 film: ～视 *film and television* | ～评 *film review*

瘿（癭） yǐng ㄧㄥˇ ❶中医指生在脖子上的一种囊状的瘤子，多指甲状腺肿 (in traditional Chinese medicine, generally) goitre ❷虫瘿的简称，植物组织由于受害虫侵害发生变化而形成的瘤状物 (insect) gall; cecidium (short for 虫瘿)

应（應） yìng ㄧㄥˋ ❶回答或随声相和 to answer; to echo: ～声虫 *yesman* | 山鸣谷～ *echo on the mountains and in the valleys* | 呼～ *to echo* [反应] 1 又叫化学反应，指物质发生化学变化，产生性质和成分与原来不同的新物质 reaction (also called 化学反应) 2 人及动植物有机体受到刺激而发生的活动和变化 (of living things) reaction: 病人

对外界毫无～。*The patient did not respond to the outside world at all.* 3 回响，反响 reception; response：观众对影片～强烈。*The audience reacted strongly to the film.* ❷ 应付，对待 to deal with：～战 *meet an enemy attack*｜随机～变 *adjust according to changing circumstances*｜～接不暇 *be more than one's eyes can take in* [供应] 供给 to supply ❸ 适合，配合（㊟适一）to suit：～时 *follow the trend; in response to the call of the times*｜得心～手 *work with great skill* ❹ 接受，答应 to accept; to agree：～承 *to promise*｜～征 *be recruited*｜～邀 *accept an invitation*｜有求必～ *grant every request*

⇨ see also yīng on p.783

映（❶*暎）yìng ㄧㄥˋ ❶ 照射而显出 to reflect：影子倒～在水里。*The shadow was reflected in the water.*｜夕阳把湖水～得通红。*The setting sun turned the lake red.* [反映] 反照 to reflect ㊂ 1 把客观事物的实质表现出来 to reflect; to convey：文艺作品要～现实生活。*Literary and artistic works should reflect real life.* 2 向上级转达 to report; to make known (to one's superiors)：及时～群众的意见 *report the opinions of the masses in time* ❷放映电影或播放电视节目 to project a film or TV program：上～ *(of a film) to screen*｜播～ *to televise*｜首～式 *premiere*

硬 yìng ㄧㄥˋ ❶物体组织紧密，性质坚固，跟"软"相对 hard (opposite of 软)：～煤 *hard coal*｜～木 *hardwood* [硬件] 1 构成计算机的各个元件、部件和固定装置。是计算机系统的组成部分 computer hardware 2 借指生产、科研、经营等过程中的机器设备、物质材料等 material conditions ❷刚强有力，也指刚强不屈服的人或势力（㊟强一）tough; tough man：～汉子 *man of iron*｜态度很～。*(He) is very tough in his attitude.*｜欺软怕～ *bully the weak and fear the strong* ❸副词，强横地，固执地（多指不顾实际地）(adverb) forcibly; stubbornly (often impractically)：～抢 *snatch forcibly*｜～不承认 *shut one's eyes to*｜别干（gàn）不了～干（gàn）。*Don't insist if you cannot do it.* ❹ 能力强，质量好 good; competent：～手 *skilled hand*｜货色～ *quality product* ❺勉强 to manage to do sth with effort：这苦日子，他～熬过来了。*He managed to get through the hard times.*

媵 yìng ㄧㄥˋ 〈古 ancient〉 ❶ 陪送出嫁 to escort a bride to her new home ❷随嫁的人 maid accompanying a bride to her new home ❸妾 concubine

YO ㄧㄛ

哟（㗛）yō ㄧㄛ same as "唷"

⇨ see also yo on p.788

唷 yō ㄧㄛ 叹词，表示惊讶或疑问 exclamation, used to express surprise or doubt：～，这是怎么了？ *Why, what's wrong?*

Y

哟(喲) yo ·丨ㄛ ❶助词，用在句末或句中停顿处 auxiliary word used at the end of or pause in a sentence：大家齐用力～！ *All heave ho!* | 话剧～，京戏～，他都很喜欢。*Be it drama or Peking Opera, he likes them very much.* ❷歌词中做衬字 used as a syllable filler in a song：呼儿嗨～！ *Hu-er-hei-yo!*

⇨ see also yō on p.787

YONG ㄩㄥ

佣(傭) yōng ㄩㄥ ❶雇用，受雇用 to employ; to be employed：～工 *hired labour* ❷受雇用的人 servant：女～ *servant woman*

⇨ see also yòng on p.790

拥(擁) yōng ㄩㄥ ❶抱（㊥一抱）to embrace ❷围着 to gather round; to wrap around：～被而眠 *sleep in the quilt* | 前呼后～ *with large numbers of attendants crowding around* ❸拥护 to uphold; to support：～戴 *to support; uphold in esteem* | ～军优属 *support the army and give preferential treatment to the families of soldiers and martyrs* [拥护] 忠诚爱戴，竭力支持 to uphold; to support：～改革开放 *uphold reform and opening up* ❹聚到一块儿 to crowd：～挤 *crowded* | 一～而入 *come crowding in* ❺持有 to possess：～有 *to possess* | ～兵百万 *have an army of one million*

痈(癰) yōng ㄩㄥ 中医指一种毒疮，局部红肿，形成硬块并化脓 (in traditional Chinese medicine) carbuncle

邕 yōng ㄩㄥ ❶邕江，水名，在广西壮族自治区 Yongjiang River (in Guangxi Zhuang Autonomous Region) ❷广西壮族自治区南宁的别称 Yong (another name for Nanning, Guangxi Zhuang Autonomous Region)

滽 yōng ㄩㄥ 滽水，水名，在江西省 Yongshui River (in Jiangxi Province)

庸 yōng ㄩㄥ ❶平常，不高明的（㊥平一）commonplace; mediocre：～言 *trite remark* | ～俗 *vulgar* ❷用 to need：毋～讳言 *(there is) no need for reticence; to be frank* ❸岂，怎么 how：～可弃乎？ *How could this possibly be relinquished?*

鄘 yōng ㄩㄥ 周代诸侯国名，在今河南省卫辉一带 Yong (a state of the Zhou Dynasty, in today's Weihui, Henan Province)

墉(隦)** yōng ㄩㄥ ❶城墙 city wall ❷高墙 high wall

慵 yōng ㄩㄥ 困倦，懒 weary

镛(鏞) yōng ㄩㄥ 大钟，古代的一种乐器 large bell (musical instrument in ancient times)

鳙(鱅) yōng ㄩㄥ 鱼名，俗叫胖头鱼，头很大，生活在淡水中 variegated carp (informal 胖头鱼)

雍(*雝) yōng ㄩㄥ 和谐 harmonious

[雍容] 文雅大方、从容不迫的样子 elegant and posed: ～华贵 *be poised and stately*

壅 yōng ㄩㄥ ❶堵塞(sè)(㊥－塞)to block: 水道～塞。*The waterway is clogged.* ❷把土或肥料培在植物根上 to heap fertilizer around the roots

灉 yōng ㄩㄥ 古水名，一在今山东省菏泽东北，一在今河南省商丘一带 Yong River (ancient rivers, one in the northeast of today's Heze, Shandong Province, the other in today's Shangqiu, Henan Province)

臃 yōng ㄩㄥ [臃肿](－zhǒng)过于肥胖，动作不灵便 swollen; bloated ㊥ 1 衣服穿得太多 cumbersomely dressed 2 机构太庞大，妨碍工作 overstaffed

饔 yōng ㄩㄥ ❶熟食 cooked food ❷早饭 breakfast

喁 yóng ㄩㄥˊ 鱼口向上，露出水面 (of fish) to stick its mouth out of the water [喁喁] 众人景仰归向的样子 everyone looking up expectantly

⇨ see also yú on p.798

颙(顒) yóng ㄩㄥˊ ❶大头 big head ㊀大 big ❷仰慕 to admire: ～望 *look up respectfully*

永 yǒng ㄩㄥˇ ❶长 long: 江之～矣。*The river is so long.* ❷长久，久远(㊥－久、－远) eternal: ～不掉队 *never fall behind* | ～记历史的教训 *always remember the lessons of history*

咏(*詠) yǒng ㄩㄥˇ ❶声调抑扬地念，唱(㊥歌－、吟－) to chant ❷用诗词等来叙述 to express in poetic form: ～梅 *ode to plum blossom* | ～雪 *ode to snow*

泳 yǒng ㄩㄥˇ 在水里游动(㊥游－) to swim: 仰～ *backstroke* | 蛙～ *breaststroke*

栐 yǒng ㄩㄥˇ 古书上说的一种树，木材可以做笏板 a kind of tree in ancient Chinese texts

甬 yǒng ㄩㄥˇ 浙江省宁波的别称 Yong (another name for Ningbo, Zhejiang Province)

[甬道] 1 院落中用砖石砌成的路，又叫甬路 paved path in a courtyard (also called 甬路) 2 走廊，过道 corridor

俑 yǒng ㄩㄥˇ 古时殉葬用的木制或陶制的偶人 tomb figure

勇 yǒng ㄩㄥˇ ❶有胆量，敢干 brave: ～敢 *brave* | 英～ *heroic* | ～气 *courage* | 奋～ *summon up all one's courage* ㊀不畏避，不推诿 to brave; to face: ～于承认错误 *have the courage to admit one's mistakes* ❷清代称战争时期临时招募，不在平时编制之内的兵 temporary recruit in times of war in the Qing Dynasty: 散兵游～ *stragglers and disbanded soldiers*

埇 yǒng ㄩㄥˇ 用于地名 used in place names: ～桥(在安徽省宿州) *Yongqiao (in Suzhou, Anhui Province)*

涌(*湧) yǒng ㄩㄥˇ ❶水或云气冒出 (of water

or clouds) to gush; to pour：～泉 *fountain* | 泪如泉～ *tears streaming down one's face* | 风起云～ *erupt/spread like a storm* ❷像水涌般地出现 to surge：许多人从里面～出来。*Many people rushed out of it.* | 往事～上心头。*Memories of the past rushed through (my) mind.*

⇨ see also chōng on p.83

恿（*慂、*悀）yǒng ㄩㄥˇ see 怂恿 (sǒng—) at 怂 on page 620

蛹 yǒng ㄩㄥˇ 某些昆虫从幼虫过渡到成虫时的一种形态，在这个期间，不食不动，外皮变厚，身体缩短 pupa：蚕～ *silkworm chrysalis*

踊（踴）yǒng ㄩㄥˇ 跳，跳跃 to leap; to jump［踊跃］1 跳跃 to jump：～欢呼 *leap and cheer* 2 争先恐后 vie with each other：～发言 *eager to speak*

鲬（鯒）yǒng ㄩㄥˇ 鱼名，身体长，扁而平，黄褐色，有黑色斑点，无鳔，生活在海洋里 flathead

用 yòng ㄩㄥˋ ❶使用，使人、物发挥其功能 to use：～电 *consume electricity* | ～拖拉机耕田 *plough a field with a tractor* | 公～电话 *public telephone* | ～笔写字 *write with a pen* ❷进饭食 to eat; to drink：～茶 *drink some tea* | ～饭 *have a meal* ❸费用，花费的钱财 expenses：家～ *family expenses* | 零～ *pocket money* ❹物质使用的效果（㊀功－、效－）use; effect：有～之材 *useful materials* ❺需要（多用于否定或反问）to need (often used in the negative or rhetorical question)：不～说 *needless to say* | 还～你操心吗？*Is it really necessary for you to bother about it?* ❻因 hence：～此 *hence* | ～特函达。*Hence this letter.*

佣 yòng ㄩㄥˋ 佣金，佣钱，买卖东西时给介绍人的钱 commission

⇨ see also yōng on p.788

㶲 yòng ㄩㄥˋ 热力学上的一个参数，用来反映在实际状态变化过程中有用功的损失 exergy

YOU ｜ㄡ

优（優）yōu ｜ㄡ ❶美好的，跟"劣"相对 excellent (opposite of 劣)：～等 *first-rate* | ～良 *fine* | ～胜劣汰 *survival of the fittest* ❷充足，宽裕 abundant; ample：～裕 *affluent* | ～厚 *munificent* ❸优待 to give preferential treatment：拥军～属 *support the army and give preferential treatment to the families of soldiers and martyrs* ❹旧时指演戏的人（㊀－伶）(old) actor：名～ *famous actor*

［优柔］1 从容 leisurely 2 犹豫不决 hesitant：～寡断 *irresolute and hesitant*

忧（憂）yōu ｜ㄡ ❶发愁（㊀－愁）to worry：杞人～天（指过虑）*unnecessarily worried (literally means 'a man in Qi state worried that the sky might fall')* ❷使人忧愁的事 anxiety; nuisance：高枕无～ *sit back and relax*

攸 yōu ㄧㄡ 所 used like the particle 所 in certain phrases：责有～归。*The responsibility should lie where it belongs.* | 性命～关 *be a matter of life and death*

悠 yōu ㄧㄡ ❶长久（㊀一久）remote; long：～远 *long ago* | ～长 *long drawn-out* ❷闲适，闲散 leisurely：～闲 *leisurely and carefree* | ～然 *carefree and leisurely* ❸在空中摆动 to swing：站在秋千上来回～ *stand on the swing and swing back and forth* ❹稳住，控制 to take things easy：～着点儿劲儿。*Take things easy.*

[悠悠] 1 闲适，自由自在 leisurely：白云～。*White clouds drift quietly.* 2 忧郁 melancholy; gloomy：～我思。*Heavy is my heart.* 3 长久，遥远 long drawn-out：～岁月 *long years*

呦 yōu ㄧㄡ 叹词，表示惊异 exclamation, used to express surprise：～，你怎么也来了？*Oh, how come you are here too?* | ～，碗怎么破了！*Oh, how come the bowl was broken?*

[呦呦] 形容鹿叫声 (of deer) grunting; bleating：～鹿鸣。*Deer are grunting.*

幽 yōu ㄧㄡ ❶形容地方很僻静、光线暗 dim; secluded：～谷 *deep and secluded valley* | ～林 *secluded wood* | ～室 *quiet and tranquil room* ㊁隐藏，不公开的 hidden; secret：～居 *live as a hermit* | ～会 *tryst; assignation* ❷使人感觉沉静、安闲的 tranquil; serene：～香 *delicate/faint fragrance* | ～美 *serene and beautiful* | ～雅 *serene and elegant* ❸幽禁，把人关起来不让跟外人接触 to imprison ❹指阴间 nether world：～灵 *ghost; spirit* | ～明（阳间）永隔。*The dead and the living will be separated forever.* ❺幽州，古地名，大致在今河北省北部和辽宁省西南部 Youzhou (an ancient place, roughly in the north of today's Hebei Province and southwest of today's Liaoning Province)：～燕（yān）*Youyan (similar in meaning to 幽州)*

[幽默]（外 loanword）有趣或可笑而意味深长 humorous：～画 *humorous painting*

麀 yōu ㄧㄡ 古书上指母鹿 female deer (in ancient Chinese texts)

櫌 yōu ㄧㄡ ❶古代一种农具，用来弄碎土块，使田地平整 mallet-shaped farm implement in ancient times ❷播种后用櫌使土覆盖种子 to cover up the seeds with soil

尢 yóu ㄧㄡˊ ❶same as "尤" ❷姓 (surname) You

⇨ see also wāng on p.675

尤 yóu ㄧㄡˊ ❶特异的，突出的 exceptional：拔其～ *select and promote the excellent ones* ❷尤其，更，格外 particularly：～甚 *especially; more so* | ～妙 *even better* ❸过失 fault：勿效～（不要学着做坏事）。*Do not follow bad examples.* ❹怨恨，归咎 to blame：怨天～人 *blame everyone and everything but oneself*

犹(猶) yóu ㄧㄡˊ ❶如同（㊀一如）to be like：虽死～生 *still live in the hearts of the people though dead* | 过～不及。*Going too far is like falling short.* ❷还（hái），尚且 still：记忆～新 *remain fresh in one's memory* | 困兽～斗 *a cornered animal will turn and fight*

［犹豫］（－yù）迟疑不决 to hesitate; to vacillate

疣(肬)** yóu ㄧㄡˊ 皮肤病，俗叫瘊子，症状是皮肤上出现黄褐色的小疙瘩，不痛不痒 wart (informal 瘊子)

［赘疣］比喻多余而无用的东西 sth superfluous

莸(蕕) yóu ㄧㄡˊ ❶古书上说的一种有臭味的草 a kind of stinking grass in ancient Chinese texts：薰～不同器（喻好人和坏人搞不到一起）。*Good people cannot get along with bad.* ❷落叶小灌木，花蓝色，供观赏 bluebeard

鱿(魷) yóu ㄧㄡˊ 鱿鱼，软体动物，又叫枪乌贼，头像乌贼，尾端呈菱形，身体白色，有淡褐色斑点，生活在海洋里 squid (also called 枪乌贼)

由 yóu ㄧㄡˊ ❶经过 to pass through：必～之路 *path one must follow* | 观其所～ *observe one's deeds* ❷原因（㊀原－）reason; cause：情～ *hows and whys* | 理～ *reason* ❸顺随，听从 to follow; to be up to sb：～着性子 *do as one pleases* | ～不得自己 *be not up to one to decide* ❹介词 preposition ①自，从 from：～哪儿来？*Where do (you) come from?* | ～上到下 *from top to bottom* | ～浅入深 *proceed from the elementary to the profound* ②凭借 by means of：～此可知 *it can be concluded from this that...* ③归（某人去做）by (sb)：这事～你安排。*It is up to you to make the arrangements.* ［由于］1 介词，表示原因 (preposition) because of; due to：这项任务～大家的努力才圆满完成了。*Thanks to the efforts of everyone, the task was successfully completed.* 2 连词，跟"所以""因而"等呼应，表示因果关系 (conjunction, used together with 所以，因而，etc. to express cause and effect) since：～天气炎热，因而用电量猛增。*Because the weather is very hot, there has been a surge in electricity consumption.*

邮(郵) yóu ㄧㄡˊ ❶邮递，由国家专设的机构传递信件 to post; to mail：～信 *post a letter* ❷有关邮务的 postal：～票 *postage stamp* | ～费 *postage* | ～局 *post office*

油 yóu ㄧㄡˊ ❶动植物体内所含的脂肪物质 fat; oil; grease：猪～ *pork fat* | 花生～ *peanut oil* ❷各种碳氢化合物的混合物，一般不溶于水，容易燃烧 oil; petroleum：煤～ *kerosene* | 汽～ *petrol* ❸用油涂抹 to paint (with oil); to varnish：用桐油一～就好了。*Just paint it with tung*

oil and it will do. ❹被油弄脏 to be grease-stained：衣服～了一大片。*The dress has got a big oil stain on it.* ❺狡猾（㊀一滑）glib; oily：～腔滑调 *frivolous and insincere in speech* | 这个人太～。*This person is too slippery.*

[油然] 1 充盛地 densely; profusely：天～作云，沛然下雨。*If clouds are rising densely in the sky, then the rain will fall heavily.* 2（思想感情）自然而然地产生 (of emotions) welling up spontaneously：敬慕之情～而生。*Admiration wells up in one's heart.*

柚 yóu ㄧㄡˊ [柚木]落叶乔木，叶大，花白色。木质坚硬耐久，可用来造船、车等 teak

⇨ see also yòu on p.796

铀(鈾) yóu ㄧㄡˊ 放射性金属元素，符号U，银白色，质硬。可用作核燃料 uranium (U)

蚰 yóu ㄧㄡˊ [蚰蜒]（—yan）节肢动物，像蜈蚣而略小，足细长，触角长，多生活在阴湿的地方 house centipede

鲉(鮋) yóu ㄧㄡˊ 鱼名，身体侧扁，头部有许多棘状突起，生活在近海 scorpionfish

莜 yóu ㄧㄡˊ [莜麦]谷类作物，叶细长，花绿色。籽实可以吃，茎、叶可用作牧草。也作"油麦" naked oat (also written as 油麦)

滺 yóu ㄧㄡˊ ❶[滺滺]水流动的样子 (of water) flowing ❷姓 (surname) You

游(❷❹❺*遊) yóu ㄧㄡˊ ❶人或动物在水里行动（㊀一泳）to swim：～水 *to swim* | ～鱼可数（shǔ）。*The number of fish swimming can be counted.* ❷不固定 roving; unsettled：～资 *hot money* | ～牧 *live a nomadic life* | ～击战 *guerrilla warfare* [游移] 主意摇摆不定 to waver ❸河流的一段 part of river：上～ *upper reaches* | 下～ *lower reaches* ❹游逛，观赏 to travel：～玩 *to go sightseeing* | ～人 *tourist* | ～园 *visit a park* | 旅～ *to travel; tourism* | 春～ *go on a spring excursion* ❺交游，交往 to associate with ❻same as "圝(yóu)"

蝣 yóu ㄧㄡˊ see 蜉蝣 (fú—) at 蜉 on page 185

輶(輶) yóu ㄧㄡˊ ❶古代一种轻便的车 a kind of light cart in ancient times ❷轻 light

猷 yóu ㄧㄡˊ 计谋，打算 plan：鸿～（宏伟的计划）*great plan*

蝤 yóu ㄧㄡˊ [蝤蛑]（—móu）一种螃蟹，又叫梭子蟹，甲壳略呈梭形，生活在浅海里 swimming crab (also called 梭子蟹)

⇨ see also qiú on p.545

繇 yóu ㄧㄡˊ same as "由❹①②" in ancient Chinese texts

⇨ see also yáo on p.761, zhòu on p.865

圝 yóu ㄧㄡˊ （—子）捕鸟时用来引诱同类鸟的鸟 decoy

(also written as 游)：鸟～子 *decoy*

友 yǒu ㄧㄡˇ ❶朋友 friend：好～ *good friends* | 战～ *comrade-in-arms* | 网～ *online friend* ⓔ有友好关系的 friendly：～军 *friendly forces* | ～邦 *friendly nation* ❷相好，互相亲近 intimate：～爱 *affectionate* | ～好往来 *friendly exchanges*

有 yǒu ㄧㄡˇ ❶跟“无”“没”相对 opposite of 无 or 没 ①表所属 (used to express possession) to have：他～一本书。*He has a book.* | 现在～时间。*Now there is time.* ②表存在 to exist：那里～十来个人。*There are about 10 people there.* | ～困难 *have difficulties* | ～办法 *have a way* | ～意见 *be unhappy about sth or sb* ③表示发生或出现 used to express occurrence or appearance：～病了 *be sick* | 形势～了新的发展。*There have been new developments.* ④表示估量或比较 used to express estimation or comparison：水～一丈多深。*The water is more than one* zhang *in depth.* | 他～他哥哥那么高了。*He is as tall as his elder brother.* ⑤表示大，多 used to express great size or number：～学问 *be knowledgeable* | ～经验 *be experienced* [有的是] 有很多，多得很 have plenty of ❷用在某些动词前面表示客气 used before certain verbs in polite formulas：～劳 *please do me a favour of; thank you for having done me the favor of* | ～请 *polite formula used to express the host's desire to see the guest* ❸跟“某”相近 certain; some (similar in meaning to 某)：～一天晚上 *one evening* | ～人不赞成。*Some people disagree.* ❹用在“人、时候、地方”前面，表示一部分 used before 人，时候 or 地方 to express part of sth：～人性子急，～人性子慢。*Some are short-tempered while others have a sluggish disposition.* ❺古汉语词头 prefix in classical Chinese：～夏 *the Xia Dynasty* | ～周 *the Zhou Dynasty*

⇨ see also yòu on p.795

铕(銪) yǒu ㄧㄡˇ 金属元素，符号 Eu，铁灰色。用于核工业，也可制彩色显像管中的荧光粉 europium (Eu)

酉 yǒu ㄧㄡˇ ❶地支的第十位 *you* (the tenth of the twelve Earthly Branches, a system used in the Chinese calendar) ❷酉时，指下午五点到七点 *you* (the period from 5 p.m. to 7 p.m.)

槱 yǒu ㄧㄡˇ 聚积木柴以备燃烧 to gather wood

卣 yǒu ㄧㄡˇ 古代一种盛酒的器皿 a kind of wine vessel in ancient times

羑 yǒu ㄧㄡˇ [羑里] 古地名，在今河南省汤阴 Youli (an ancient place name, in today's Tangyin, Henan Province)

莠 yǒu ㄧㄡˇ （一子）狗尾草，草本植物，略像谷子，穗上有毛，像狗的尾巴 green bristlegrass ⓔ 品质坏的，不好的人 bad person：良～不齐。*The good is mixed up with the bad.*

牖 yǒu ㄧㄡˇ 窗户 window

黝 yǒu ㄧㄡˇ 黑色 dark：一张～黑的脸 *a swarthy face*

又 yòu ㄧㄡˋ 副词 adverb ①重复，连续，指相同的 again：他～立功了。*He did a good deed of merit again.* | 今天～下雨了。*Today it has rained again.* ②表示加重语气，更进一层 used for emphasis：他～不傻，怎么会不懂？ *He is not stupid, how can he not understand?* | 你～不是不会。*It isn't that you do not know how to do it.* ③表示并列关系 and; both：～高～大 *big and tall* | ～多～快 *numerous and fast* | ～好～省 *both good and economical* | 我～高兴，～着急。*I am both happy and worried.* ④再加上，还有 and：十～五年 *ten and five years* | 一～二分之一 *one and a half* ⑤表示某种范围之外另有补充 more; in addition：穿上了棉袄～加了一件皮背心 *put on a padded jacket and a leather vest as well* ⑥表示转折 but：刚还想说什么，可～把它忘了。*Just now I was thinking of saying something, but I've forgotten what to say.*

右 yòu ㄧㄡˋ ❶面向南时靠西的一边，跟"左"相对 right (opposite of 左)：～手 *right hand; to the right* | ～边 *right-hand side; on the right* ㊕西方（以面向南为准）west：江～ *west of the lower reaches of the Yangtze River* | 山～ *west side of a mountain; areas west of the Taihang Mountains* ❷政治思想上属于保守的或反动的 (of politics) right：～倾 *right deviation* ❸古以右为上，品质等级高的称右 superior (in quality or grade in ancient times)：无出其～ *second to none* ❹崇尚，重视 to value; to uphold：～文 *stress culture and learning* ❺ (ancient) same as "佑"

佑 yòu ㄧㄡˋ ❶辅助，保护 to assist; to protect：～助 *to assist* | ～护 *to protect* | 庇～ *to bless; to protect* ❷姓 (surname) You

祐 yòu ㄧㄡˋ ❶保佑，迷信的人指神帮助 to bless ❷用于地名 used in place names：吉～（在广东省顺德）*Jiyou (in Shunde, Guangdong Province)* ❸姓 (surname) You

幼 yòu ㄧㄡˋ ❶年纪小，初出生的，跟"老"相对（㊣－小）young (opposite of 老)：～儿 *infant; preschool child* | ～虫 *larva* | ～苗 *seedling* [幼稚] 年纪小的 young ㊗知识见解浅薄、缺乏经验的 childish; puerile：思想～ *naive* ❷小孩儿 child：扶老携～ *bring along the old and the young* | ～有所养。*The young will be provided for.*

蚴 yòu ㄧㄡˋ 绦虫、血吸虫等的幼体 larva (of a tapeworm, schistosome, etc.)：毛～ *miracidium* | 尾～ *cercaria*

有 yòu ㄧㄡˋ (ancient) same as "又④"

⇨ see also yǒu on p.794

侑 yòu ㄧㄡˋ 在筵席旁助兴，劝人吃喝 to urge sb to eat

or drink：～食 *urge sb to have food*

囿 yòu ㄧㄡˋ ❶养动物的园子 enclosure (for keeping animals)：鹿～ *deer park* ❷局限，被限制 to be fenced in：～于成见 *be blinded by prejudice* | 不为陈规所～ *not be constrained by outmoded conventions*

宥 yòu ㄧㄡˋ ❶宽容，饶恕，原谅（㊀原－、宽－）to pardon; to forgive：还请～我。*Please pardon me.* ❷帮助 to assist

狖 yòu ㄧㄡˋ 古书上说的一种猴子 a kind of monkey in ancient Chinese texts

柚 yòu ㄧㄡˋ 常绿乔木，种类很多。果实叫柚子，也叫文旦，比橘子大，多汁，味酸甜 pomelo; shaddock (its fruit is called 柚子 or 文旦)

⇨ see also yóu on p.793

釉 yòu ㄧㄡˋ （－子）以石英、长石、硼砂、黏土等为原料制成的物质，涂在瓷器、陶器外面，烧制后发出玻璃光泽，可增加陶瓷的机械强度和绝缘性能 glaze

鼬 yòu ㄧㄡˋ ［黄鼬］哺乳动物，俗叫黄鼠狼，身体细长，毛黄褐色，遇见敌人能由肛门附近分泌臭气自卫，常捕食田鼠 weasel (informal 黄鼠狼)

诱（誘） yòu ㄧㄡˋ (formerly pronounced yǒu) ❶劝导，教导 to induce; to guide：循循善～ *give guidance in a skilful and systematic fashion* ❷引诱，使用手段引人 to tempt; to lure：～敌 *entice the enemy* | 利～ *lure by promise of gain* ❸引发，导致 to lead to：～发 *bring out* | ～因 *incentive; inducement*

YU ㄩ

迂 yū ㄩ ❶曲折，绕远 circuitous：～回前进 *advance in a roundabout way* ❷言行、见解陈旧，不合时宜（㊀－腐）(of speech, act or opinion) impractical; doctrinaire：～论 *unrealistic argument* | ～见 *absurd view* | 思想太～ *be too impractical in thinking*

纡（紆） yū ㄩ ❶弯曲，绕弯 winding; circuitous ❷系，结 to tie：～金佩紫（指地位显贵）*be of high social rank (literally means 'wear gold ornaments and a purple gown')*

於 yū ㄩ 姓 (surname) Yu

⇨ see also wū on p.689, yú on p.798

淤 yū ㄩ ❶水里泥沙沉积 to silt up：～了好些泥。*There was a lot of silt.* ❷河沟中沉积的泥沙 silt：河～ *sludge from a riverbed* | 清～ *to dredge* ❸ same as "瘀"

瘀 yū ㄩ 血液凝滞 blood stasis extravasate：～血 *static blood*

于 yú ㄩˊ 介词 preposition ①在 at; in; on：写～北京 *written in Beijing* | 生～1949年 *born in 1949* ②对于，对 for; regarding：～人民有益 *beneficial for the people* | 忠～祖国 *be loyal to one's country* | 勇～负责 *be brave*

in shouldering responsibilities ③给 to：勿诿过～人。*Do not lay the blame on others.* | 光荣归～党。*The honour belongs to the Party.* | 取之于民，用之～民。*What is taken from the people is to be used for the good of the people.* ④自，由 from：出～自愿 *of one's own free will* | 取之～民，用之于民。*What is taken from the people is to be used for the good of the people.* ⑤向 to：问道～盲 *do sth in vain (literally means 'ask a blind person the way')* ⑥在形容词后，表示比较，跟"过"的意思相同 used after an adjective to express comparison, same in meaning as 过：霜叶红～二月花。*Frost-bitten leaves are more crimson than spring blooms.* | 人民的利益高～一切。*The interests of the people come before everything else.* ⑦在动词后，表示被动 used after a verb to express the passive voice：见笑～大方 *be exposed to ridicule* [于是] 连词，表示两件事前后紧接 (conjunction, used to show one thing happens right after another) so; then：他听完报告，～就回去了。*After listening to the lecture, he went straight back.*

邘 yú ㄩˊ ❶周代诸侯国名，在今河南省沁阳西北 Yu (a state in the Zhou Dynasty, in the north-west of today's Qinyang, Henan Province) ❷姓 (surname) Yu

盂 yú ㄩˊ 一种盛液体的器皿 broad-mouthed jar (for holding liquid)：痰～ *spittoon* | 漱口～ *mug for rinsing the mouth*

竽 yú ㄩˊ 古代的一种管乐器，像现在的笙 *yu* (ancient wind instrument, similar to *sheng*) [滥竽充数] 一个不会吹竽的人混在乐队里充数 pretend to play the *yu* in order to make up the numbers ㊘没有真本领，在行家里充数或以次充好 fill a post without real qualifications

与(與) yú ㄩˊ same as "欤" ⇨ see also yǔ on p.800, yù on p.801

玙(璵) yú ㄩˊ 玙璠 (fán)，美玉。也说璠玙 beautiful jade (also 璠玙)

欤(歟) yú ㄩˊ 文言助词 auxiliary in classical Chinese ①表示疑问语气 used in the interrogative：在齐～？在鲁～？*In Qi or in Lu state?* ②表示感叹语气 used in an exclamation：论者之言，一似管窥虎～！*Indeed, the speaker's argument was as one-sided as looking at a tiger through a bamboo tube!*

予 yú ㄩˊ 文言代词，我 (pronoun in classical Chinese) I; me ⇨ see also yǔ on p.800

妤 yú ㄩˊ see 婕妤 (jié－) at 婕 on page 318

余(❶－❸△餘) yú ㄩˊ ❶剩下，多出来 (㊖剩－) left-over; remaining：～粮 *surplus grain* | ～兴 (xìng) *lingering interest* | 业～ *spare time; amateur* | 不遗～力 *go all out* ❷十、百、千等整数或度量单位后面

的零头 over (a whole number)：十～人 *over ten people* | 三百～米 *over 300 metres* | 两吨～ *over two tons* ❸后 after：兴奋之～，高歌一曲 *sing a song loudly when excited* ❹文言代词，我 (pronoun in classical Chinese) I; me ❺姓 (surname) Yu

⇨ 餘 see also 馀 on p.798

馀(餘) yú ㄩˊ ❶ same as "余❶–❸" (餘 is simplified into 余, which is replaced by 馀 to avoid confusion, as in 馀年无多.) ❷姓 (surname) Yu

⇨ 餘 see also 余 on p.797

狳 yú ㄩˊ see 犰狳 (qiú–) at 犰 on page 544

畲 yú ㄩˊ 开垦过两年的地 land that has been cultivated for two years

⇨ see also shē on p.585

艅 yú ㄩˊ [艅艎] (–huáng) 古代一种大船 a kind of big ship in ancient times

臾 yú ㄩˊ [须臾] 片刻，一会儿 moment; instant

谀(諛) yú ㄩˊ 谄媚，奉承 to flatter; to toady to：～辞 *flattery* | 阿(ē)～ *to flatter*

萸 yú ㄩˊ see 茱萸 (zhū–) at 茱 on page 865

腴 yú ㄩˊ ❶肥，胖 fat：丰～ *plump* ❷肥沃 fertile：土地膏～ *fertile land*

鱼(魚) yú ㄩˊ 脊椎动物的一类，通常身体侧扁，大都有鳞和鳍，用鳃呼吸，体温随外界温度而变化，生活在水中。种类很多 fish

渔(漁、❶䰻)** yú ㄩˊ ❶捕鱼 to fish：～船 *fishing boat* | ～业 *fishery* ❷谋取（不应得的东西） to take (sth one is not entitled to)：～利 *profit at others' expense*

於 yú ㄩˊ same as "于"

⇨ see also wū on p.689, yū on p.796

禺 yú ㄩˊ ❶古书上说的一种猴子 a kind of monkey in ancient Chinese texts ❷ see 番禺 (pān–) at 番 on page 490

隅 yú ㄩˊ ❶角落 corner：城～ *corner of a city wall* [隅反] 由此知彼，能够类推，举一反三 draw inferences [向隅] 对着屋子的一个角落，比喻孤立或得不到机会而失望 to face a corner of the room; (figurative) feel left out or frustrated ❷靠边的地方 outlying place：海～ *seaboard*

喁 yú ㄩˊ [喁喁] 形容低声细语 in whisper：～私语 *to whisper*

⇨ see also yóng on p.789

嵎 yú ㄩˊ ❶山弯曲的地方 mountain recess ❷ same as "隅"

愚 yú ㄩˊ ❶傻，笨（连–蠢） foolish; stupid：～人 *fool* | ～昧 *ignorant* ❷谦辞 (humble speech) I; my：～见 *my humble opinion* ❸愚弄，欺骗 to make a fool of：为人所～ *be deceived* | ～民政策 *policy of keeping the people in ignorance*

髃 yú ㄩˊ 肩髃，针灸穴位名 *jianyu* (front of the shoulder, an acupuncture point)

舁 yú ㄩˊ 〈古 ancient〉共同抬东西 to raise/lift together

俞 yú ㄩˊ ❶文言叹词，表示允许 exclamation in classical Chinese, used for permission ❷姓 (surname) Yu

⇨ see also shù on p.611

揄 yú ㄩˊ 拉，引 to pull; to drag [揄扬] 称赞 to praise

嵛 yú ㄩˊ [昆嵛] 山名，在山东省东部 Mount Kunyu (in the east of Shandong Province)

逾 (❶* **踰**) yú ㄩˊ ❶越过，超过 (㊟一越) to exceed; to surpass: ～期 *exceed a time limit* ❷更，越发 even more: ～甚 *even more*

渝 yú ㄩˊ ❶变（多指感情或态度）(generally of feelings or attitudes) to change: 始终不～ *remain forever unchanged* ❷ 重庆市的别称 another name for Chongqing Municipality: 成～铁路 *Chengdu-Chongqing Railway*

愉 yú ㄩˊ 喜欢，快乐 (㊟一快) joyful; happy: ～快 *happy* | ～悦 *cheerful*

瑜 yú ㄩˊ ❶美玉 fine jade ❷玉石的光彩 lustre of jade ⓜ优点 virtue: 瑕（xiá）不掩～。*One flaw cannot obscure the splendour of the jade.*

榆 yú ㄩˊ 榆树，落叶乔木，果实外面有膜质的翅，叫榆荚或榆钱。木质坚硬，可供建筑或制器具用 elm (its fruit is called 榆荚 or 榆钱)

觎 (**覦**) yú ㄩˊ see 觊觎 (jì一) at 觊 on page 293

窬 (❷* **踰**) yú ㄩˊ ❶门边小洞 small hole beside a gate ❷从墙上爬过去 to climb over a wall: 穿～之盗（穿墙和爬墙的贼）*burglar*

褕 yú ㄩˊ ❶（衣服）华美 (of clothes) gorgeous ❷ see 襜褕 (chān一) at 襜 on page 65

蝓 yú ㄩˊ see 蛞蝓 (kuò一) at 蛞 on page 372

娱 yú ㄩˊ 快乐或使快乐（㊟一乐）amusing; to amuse: 文～活动 *cultural and recreational activities* | 自～ *amuse oneself* | ～亲（使父母快乐）*make one's parents happy*

虞 yú ㄩˊ ❶预料 to suppose; to expect: 以备不～ *in case of contingency* ❷忧虑 anxiety; worry: 无～ *have no worry* ❸欺骗 to deceive: 尔～我诈（互相欺骗）*each trying to cheat the other* ❹周代诸侯国名，在今山西省平陆东北 Yu (a state in the Zhou Dynasty, in the northeast of today's Pinglu, Shanxi Province)

雩 yú ㄩˊ 古代求雨的一种祭祀 a kind of sacrificial rite to pray for rain in ancient times

舆 (**輿**) yú ㄩˊ ❶车中载人载物的部分 part of the middle of a vehicle carrying people or goods ❷ 车 carriage: 舍～登舟 *change from carriage to boat* [肩舆] 轿子 sedan chair ❸众人 public: ～论 *public opinion* [舆情] 群众的意见和态度 public sentiment: 洞察～ *know public sentiment well* ❹ 地，疆域 land;

territory：～地 *land; earth* | 方～ *the earth* | ～图 *territory; map*

与(與) yǔ ㄩˇ ❶介词，跟 (preposition) with：～疾病做斗争 *combat a disease* | ～虎谋皮 *ask an enemy to act against his interests (literally means 'ask a tiger for its skin')* ❷连词，和 (conjunction) and：批评～自我批评 *criticism and self-criticism* | 父亲～母亲都来。*Father and mother are both coming.* ❸给 to give：赠～ *give a present* | 交～本人 *give to the person concerned* | ～人方便 *make things easy for others* ❹交往，交好 to get along with; to be on good terms with：此人易～。*This person is easy to get along with.* | 相～ *get along with* | ～国(相交好的国家) *friendly country* ❺赞助 to sponsor; to support：～人为善(原指赞助人学好，后多指善意助人) *(originally means supporting others to be good) aim at helping others out of good will*

[与其] 连词，常跟"宁""宁可""不如""不若"等连用，表示比较 (conjunction, often used together with 宁，宁可，不如，and 不若 to express comparison) rather than：～坐车，不如坐船。*Rather than go by train, it's better to go by ship.*

⇨ see also yú on p.797, yù on p.801

屿(嶼) yǔ ㄩˇ (formerly pronounced xù) 小岛(㊀岛—) islet

予 yǔ ㄩˇ 给予 to give：授～奖状 *award a certificate of merit* | ～以协助 *grant assistance* | ～以处分 *mete out punishment*

⇨ see also yú on p.797

伛(傴) yǔ ㄩˇ 驼背 hunched back：～人 *hunchback* | ～偻(lǚ) *hunched back*

宇 yǔ ㄩˇ ❶屋檐 eaves ㊀房屋 house：庙～ *temple* [眉宇] ㊁仪表，风度 bearing; manner ❷上下四方，所有的空间 space (between heaven and earth)：～内 *land under heaven* [宇宙] 1 same as "宇❷" 2 指所有的空间和时间 universe; cosmos ❸地层系统分类的最高一级，在"界"之上，是在地质年代"宙"的时期内形成的地层 eonothem (the highest division in stratigraphic classification)：显生～ *Phanerozoic* | 元古～ *Proterozoic* | 太古～ *Archean*

羽 yǔ ㄩˇ ❶羽毛，鸟的毛 feathers：～翼 *wing* ㊀翅膀 wing：振～高飞 *flutter and soar high* ❷量词，用于鸟类 measure word for birds：一～信鸽 *a carrier pigeon* ❸古代五音"宫、商、角(jué)、徵(zhǐ)、羽"之一 *yu* (one of the five notes in the ancient Chinese pentatonic scale)

雨 yǔ ㄩˇ 云层中的小水滴体积增大到不能悬浮在空气中时，就滴落下来成为雨 rain

⇨ see also yù on p.802

俣 yǔ ㄩˇ 大 large

禹 yǔ ㄩˇ 传说中的古代部落联盟首领，曾治服洪水 (in Chinese legend) Yu (the leader of an ancient tribal alliance who tamed floods)

郚 yǔ ㄩˇ 周代诸侯国名，在今山东省临沂 Yu (a state in the Zhou Dynasty, in today's Linyi, Shandong Province)

瑀 yǔ ㄩˇ 像玉的石头 jade-like stone

语(語) yǔ ㄩˇ ❶话(㊟—言) words：成～ *idiom*｜～文 *language and literature*｜外国～ *foreign language* ❷谚语或古语 proverb; saying：～云 *as the saying goes* ❸代替语言的动作或信号 sign; signal：手～ *sign language*｜旗～ *semaphore* ❹说 to say; to speak：不言不～ *keep silent*｜默默不～ *speak nothing*

⇨ see also yù on p.803

圄 yǔ ㄩˇ see 图圄 (líng—) at 图 on page 408

敔 yǔ ㄩˇ 古代的一种打击乐器，击敔使演奏停止 a kind of percussion musical instrument used to mark the end of a performance in ancient times

龉(齬) yǔ ㄩˇ see 龃龉(jǔ—) at 龃 on page 338

圉 yǔ ㄩˇ 养马的地方，也指养马的人 stable; sb who raises horses

庾 yǔ ㄩˇ 露天的谷仓 open-air granary

瘐 yǔ ㄩˇ 瘐死，旧时称囚犯在监狱里因受刑、冻饿、生病而死 (old, of a prisoner) to die of torture, cold, hunger or disease

貐(貐)** yǔ ㄩˇ see 猰貐 (yà—) at 猰 on page 748

窳 yǔ ㄩˇ 恶劣，坏 corrupt; bad：～劣 *inferior in quality*｜～败（败坏）*degenerate; ruined*

与(與) yù ㄩˋ 参与，参加 to take part in：～会 *participate in a conference*｜～闻此事（参与并且得知此事的内情）*have a participant's knowledge of a matter*

⇨ see also yú on p.797, yǔ on p.800

玉 yù ㄩˋ ❶矿物名，又叫玉石，质细而坚硬，有光泽，略透明，可制装饰品或做雕刻材料 jade (also called 玉石) ❷㊟洁白或美丽 pure; beautiful：～颜 *fair complexion*｜亭亭～立 *tall, slim and graceful* ❸敬辞，指对方的身体、言行等 (polite speech) your (health, language and behaviour, etc.)：～体 *your esteemed health*｜～言 *your valuable words*｜敬候～音 *look forward to your letter*

钰(鈺) yù ㄩˋ 宝物 treasure

驭(馭) yù ㄩˋ ❶驾驭（车马）to drive (a carriage)：～车 *drive a carriage*｜～马 *ride a horse*｜～手 *driver of a chariot* ❷统率，控制 to command; to control：～下无方 *not know how to keep one's subordinates under control*

芋 yù ㄩˋ 芋头，草本植物，叶略呈卵形，地下茎椭圆形，可以吃 taro

吁(籲) yù ㄩˋ 为某种要求而呼喊 to appeal; to plead：～求 *to implore*｜～请 *to*

plead | 呼～ *call on*

⇨ see also xū on p.733

聿 yù ㄩˋ 文言助词，用在一句话的开头，起顺承作用 (auxiliary word in classical Chinese, used at the beginning of a sentence to express transition) and then

谷 yù ㄩˋ ［吐谷浑］（tǔ—hún）我国古代西部民族名 the Tuyuhun people (one of the ethnic groups in the west of China in ancient times)

⇨ see also gǔ on p.219

峪 yù ㄩˋ 山谷，多用于地名 valley (often used in place names)：马兰～（在河北省）*Malanyu (a place in Hebei Province)*

浴 yù ㄩˋ 洗澡 to take a bath：～室 *bathroom* | 沐～ *take a bath*

欲(❶*慾) yù ㄩˋ ❶欲望，想得到某种东西或想达到某种目的的要求 desire：食～ *appetite* | 求知～ *thirst for knowledge* ❷想要，希望 to want; to wish：～盖弥彰（想要掩饰反而弄得更显明了）。*The harder one tries to conceal something, the more conspicuous it becomes.* ❸需要 to require; to need：胆～大而心～细 *be daring but also meticulous* ❹副词，将要，在动词前，表示动作就要开始 (adverb, used before a verb to indicate that an action begins soon) about to：摇摇～坠 *on the verge of collapse* | 山雨～来风满楼。*The rising wind foretells the coming storm.*

鹆(鵒) yù ㄩˋ see 鸲鹆 (qú—) at 鸲 on page 547

裕 yù ㄩˋ ❶丰富，宽绰（㊀富—、宽—）abundant; affluent：充～ *plentiful* ❷使富足 to enrich：富国～民 *enrich one's country and people*

［裕固族］我国少数民族，参看附录四 the Yugur people (one of the ethnic groups in China. See Appendix Ⅳ.)

饫(飫) yù ㄩˋ 饱 to have eaten one's fill

妪(嫗) yù ㄩˋ 年老的女人 old lady：老～ *old woman*

雨 yù ㄩˋ 下（雨、雪）to have a fall of (rain, snow)：～雪 *to snow*

⇨ see also yǔ on p.800

郁(❶❷鬱、❶❷*鬰、❶❷*欝) yù ㄩˋ ❶草木茂盛 ㊁ lush; luxuriant：～～葱葱 *lush and green* ❷忧愁，愁闷（㊀忧—）㊁ depressed; gloomy：～～不乐 *be depressed* ❸有文采 ㊁ refined; literarily elegant：文采～～ *displaying literacy elegance* ❹形容香气浓 intensely fragrant：馥（fù）～ *of rich fragrance*

育 yù ㄩˋ ❶生养（㊀生—）to breed; to give birth to：生儿～女 *bear children* | ～龄 *childbearing age* ❷养活（㊀养—）to rear; to raise：～婴 *raise babies* | ～蚕 *raise silkworms* | ～林 *to af-*

forest ❸教育 education: 德～ *moral education* | 智～ *intellectual education* | 体～ *physical education*

堉 yù ㄩˋ 〈古 ancient〉肥沃的土地 fertile soil

淯 yù ㄩˋ 淯河，水名，在河南省栾川 Yuhe River (in Luanchuan, Henan Province)

昱 yù ㄩˋ ❶日光 sunlight ❷光明 bright

煜 yù ㄩˋ 照耀 to illuminate; to shine

狱(獄) yù ㄩˋ ❶监禁罪犯的地方(㊀监－) prison; jail ❷官司，罪案 lawsuit: 冤～ *unjust verdict* | 断～ *hear and decide a case* | 文字～ *literary inquisition*

语(語) yù ㄩˋ 告诉 to tell; to inform: 不以～人 *not tell others about sth*

⇨ see also yǔ on p.801

彧 yù ㄩˋ 有文采 of literary elegance

域 yù ㄩˋ ❶在一定疆界内的地方 territory: 地～ *region* | 疆～ *territory* | ～外 *extraterritorial* ❷泛指某种范围 (generally) realm; domain: 音～ *compass; vocal range*

阈(閾) yù ㄩˋ ❶门槛 threshold ❷界限 limit: 视～ *visual threshold*

棫 yù ㄩˋ 古书上说的一种树 a kind of tree in ancient Chinese texts

蜮(魊)** yù ㄩˋ 传说中一种害人的动物 a kind of monster in Chinese legend: 鬼～(喻阴险的人) *evil spirit; (figurative) sinister person*

预(預) yù ㄩˋ ❶预先，事前 in advance; beforehand: ～备 *to prepare* | ～见 *to predict* | ～防 *guard against* | ～约 *make an appointment* ❷加入到里面去 to take part in: 干～ *to interfere*

蓣(蕷) yù ㄩˋ see 薯蓣 (shǔ－) at 薯 on page 609

滪(澦) yù ㄩˋ see 滟滪堆 (yàn－duī) at 滟 on page 755

豫 yù ㄩˋ ❶欢喜，快乐 happy; pleased: 面有不～之色 *look unhappy* ❷ same as "预❶" ❸安闲，舒适 ease; comfort: 忧劳兴国，逸～亡身。*Hard work leads to rejuvenation of the country while idleness leads to ruin.* ❹河南省的别称 another name for Henan Province

菀 yù ㄩˋ 茂盛的样子 (of plants) exuberant

⇨ see also wǎn on p.673

悆 yù ㄩˋ ❶喜悦 happy ❷舒适 comfortable

谕(諭) yù ㄩˋ ❶告诉，使人知道(旧指上级对下级或长辈对晚辈) (old, of superiors to inferiors) to instruct; to decree: 面～ *give orders personally* | 手～ *hand-written directive* | 上～(皇帝的命令) *imperial edict* ❷〈古 ancient〉same as "喻"

喻 yù ㄩˋ ❶比方(㊀比－) to draw an analogy: 用花朵～儿童 *compare children to flowers* ❷明

Y

白，了解 to understand; to know：不言而～ *it goes without saying* | 家～户晓 *known to everyone* ❸说明，使人了解 to explain：～之以理 *reason with sb*

愈(❸*瘉、❸*癒) yù ㄩˋ ❶更，越 even; more：～来～好 *become better and better* | 病情～甚。*(His) condition was getting even worse.* ❷贤，好 to surpass; be better：孰～（哪个好）？ *Which is better?* ❸病好了（㊥痊一）to recover; to be cured：病～ *to recover*

尉 yù ㄩˋ ［尉迟］复姓 (surname) Yuchi

［尉犁］地名，在新疆维吾尔自治区 Yuli (a place in Xinjiang Uygur Autonomous Region)

⇨ see also wèi on p.683

蔚 yù ㄩˋ ❶蔚县，在河北省 Yuxian (a place in Hebei Province) ❷姓 (surname) Yu

⇨ see also wèi on p.684

熨 yù ㄩˋ ［熨帖］（-tiē）1 妥帖舒服 fitting and comfortable 2〈方 dialect〉（事情）完全办妥 (of things) settled

⇨ see also yùn on p.814

遇 yù ㄩˋ ❶相逢，会面，碰到（㊥遭一）to meet：～雨 *be caught in the rain* | 百年不～ *not seen in a hundred years* | 不期而～ *bump into sb* ❷机会 opportunity：际～ *opportunity; favourable turn in life* | 佳～ *good opportunity* ❸对待，款待 to treat：可善～之。*(You) should treat (him) well.*

寓(*庽) yù ㄩˋ ❶居住 to reside; to inhabit：～所 *residence* | 暂～友人家 *stay in a friend's house for the time being* ❷住的地方 residence：张～ *Zhang's residence* | 公～ *flat; apartment* ❸寄托，隐含在内 to imply：～言 *fable* | ～意深刻 *have a deep message*［寓目］过目，看 look over

御(❹*禦) yù ㄩˋ ❶驾驶（车马）to drive; to ride：～车 *drive a carriage* | ～者（赶车的人）*carriage driver* ❷称与皇帝有关的 imperial：～用 *for imperial use* ❸封建社会指上级对下级的管理、使用 (in feudal society) to manage; to dominate：～下 *control one's subordinates* ❹抵挡 to resist; to defend：防～ *to defend* | ～敌 *resist the enemy* | ～寒 *keep out the cold*

矞 yù ㄩˋ 矞云，象征祥瑞的彩云 auspicious colourful clouds

潏 yù ㄩˋ 水涌出 (of water) to gush

遹 yù ㄩˋ 遵循。多用于人名 to follow; to obey (often used in given names)

燏 yù ㄩˋ 火光。多用于人名 flame (often used in given names)

鹬(鷸) yù ㄩˋ 鸟名，羽毛茶褐色，嘴、腿都很长，趾间无蹼，常在水边或田野中捕食小鱼、昆虫和贝类 sandpiper［鹬蚌相争，渔翁得利］比喻两败俱伤，便宜了第三者 two parties fight, and a third party reaps the advantage

誉(譽) yù ㄩˋ ❶名誉，名声 fame; reputation: 荣～ *glory* 特指好的名声 (specifically) good reputation: ～满中外 *be famed at home and abroad* ❷称赞(㊇称－、赞－) to praise: ～不绝口 *be full of praise*

毓 yù ㄩˋ 同"育"。多用于人名 same as 育 (often used in given names)

隩 yù ㄩˋ 河岸弯曲的地方 bend of a river

薁 yù ㄩˋ see 蘡薁 (yīng－) at 蘡 on page 784

⇨ see also ào on p.9

燠 yù ㄩˋ 暖，热 warm; hot: ～热（闷热）*muggy* | 寒～失时 *unseasonable weather*

鬻 yù ㄩˋ 卖 to sell: ～文为生 *make a living with one's pen* | 卖官～爵 *accept bribes in exchange for official ranks*

YUAN ㄩㄢ

鸢(鳶) yuān ㄩㄢ 鸟名，即老鹰 hawk (same as 老鹰) [纸鸢] 风筝 kite

眢 yuān ㄩㄢ 眼睛枯陷，失明 (of eyes) dry and sunken; blind ㊊干枯 dried up: ～井 *dry well*

鸳(鴛) yuān ㄩㄢ [鸳鸯] (－yang) 鸟名，像凫(fú)而小，雄的羽毛美丽，雌雄常在一起。文学上用来比喻夫妻 mandarin duck; (figurative) couple

涴 yuān ㄩㄢ 用于地名 used in place names: ～市（在湖北省松滋）*Yuanshi (in Songzi, Hubei Province)*

⇨ see also wò on p.689

鹓(鵷) yuān ㄩㄢ [鹓鶵] (－chú) 古代传说中的一种像凤凰的鸟 a kind of phoenix-like bird in Chinese legend

箢 yuān ㄩㄢ 箢箕，用竹篾等编成的盛东西的器具 bamboo basket

冤(*寃、*冤) yuān ㄩㄢ ❶冤枉，屈枉(㊇－屈) wrong; injustice; grievance: 鸣～ *voice grievance* | 伸～ *redress a grievance* | 不白之～ *unrighted wrong* ❷仇恨(㊇－仇) hatred; enmity: ～家 *enemy* | ～孽 *enmity and sin* ❸欺骗 to cheat; to kid: 不许～人。*Don't kid me.* ❹上当，不合算 not worth while: 白跑一趟，真～。*The trip came of nothing, what bad luck.* | 别花～钱。*Don't spend your money in vain.*

渊(淵) yuān ㄩㄢ 深水，潭 deep pool: 鱼跃于～ *fish springing up in a deep pool* ㊍深 deep; profound: ～博（学识深而广）*erudite*

蜎 yuān ㄩㄢ 古书上指孑孓 wiggler (in ancient Chinese texts)

元 yuán ㄩㄢˊ ❶开始，第一(㊇－始) first; initial: ～旦 *New Year's Day* | ～月 *the first month in a year* | ～年 *first year of*

an emperor's reign [元音] 发音的时候，从肺里出来的气使声带颤动，在口腔的通路上不受阻碍而发出的声音。汉语拼音字母 ɑ、o、u 等都是元音 vowel ❷为首的 leading; chief：～首 *monarch; head of state* | ～帅 *marshal* | ～勋 *founding father* ❸构成一个整体的 unit; component：单～ *unit* | ～件 *element* ❹朝代名（公元 1206—1368 年），公元 1206 年蒙古孛儿只斤·铁木真称成吉思汗，建蒙古汗国。1271 年忽必烈改国号为元，1279 年灭南宋 Yuan Dynasty (1206—1368) ❺ same as "圆❹"

芫 yuán ㄩㄢˊ 芫花，落叶灌木，花紫色，有毒，花蕾可入药 lilac daphne

⇨ see also yán on p.750

园（園） yuán ㄩㄢˊ ❶(一子、一儿) 种植菜蔬花果等的地方 garden [园地] 1 菜园、花园、果园等的统称 garden 2 借指开展某些活动的地方 place for certain activities：艺术～ *art garden* ❷供人游玩或娱乐的地方 park：公～ *park* | 动物～ *zoo*

沅 yuán ㄩㄢˊ 沅江，发源于贵州省，东北流至湖南省注入洞庭湖 Yuanjiang River (originating in Guizhou Province and flowing northeast into Dongting Lake in Hunan Province)

妧 yuán ㄩㄢˊ 人名用字 used in given names

⇨ see also wàn on p.675

鼋（黿） yuán ㄩㄢˊ 鼋鱼（也作"元鱼"），爬行动物，像龟而吻短，背甲暗绿色，上有许多小疙瘩。生活在水中 Asian giant soft-shelled turtle (also written as 元鱼)

员（員） yuán ㄩㄢˊ ❶指工作或学习的人 person engaged in a certain field of activity：演～ *actor* | 学～ *student* ❷指团体组织中的成员 member (of an organization)：党～ *Party member* | 团～ *member of the Communist Youth League of China* | 会～ *(of an organization) member* ❸量词，用于武将等 measure word, used to describe a brave soldier：一～大将 *a valiant general* ❹周围 surrounding; vicinity：幅～（指疆域）*area of a country's territory*

⇨ see also yún on p.812, yùn on p.813

圆（圓） yuán ㄩㄢˊ ❶圆形，从它的中心点到周边任何一点的距离都相等 circle ❷形状像球的 ball-shaped：滚～ *round as a ball* | 滴溜儿～ *perfectly round* ❸完备，周全 tactful; satisfactory：～满 *satisfactory* | 话说得不～。*What was said was not very tactful.* ㊂使之周全（多指掩饰矛盾）to justify; to make perfect：自～其说 *make one's statement consistent* | ～谎 *make a lie sound plausible* ❹我国的本位货币单位。也作"元" *yuan* (also written as 元, the standard monetary unit of China)

垣 yuán ㄩㄢˊ ❶墙，矮墙 wall; low wall：断瓦颓～ *debris* ❷城 city：省～（省城）*provincial capital*

爰 yuán ㄩㄢˊ ❶文言连词，于是 (conjunction in classical Chinese) thereupon; hence：～书其事以告。*Therefore I am writing to you about it.* ❷文言代词，何处，哪里 (pronoun in classical Chinese) where：～其适归？ *Where to?*

援 yuán ㄩㄢˊ ❶引，牵（㊥－引）to draw; to pull ❷帮助，救助（㊥－助）to help; to aid：支～ *to support* | 孤立无～ *isolated and cut off from outside help* ❸引用 to cite：～例 *cite an example*

湲 yuán ㄩㄢˊ see 潺湲 (chán－) at 潺 on page 66

媛 yuán ㄩㄢˊ ［婵媛］1（姿态）美好 (of posture) beautiful 2 牵连，相连 to be connected; to be related

⇨ see also yuàn on p.808

袁 yuán ㄩㄢˊ 姓 (surname) Yuan

猿（*猨、*蝯）yuán ㄩㄢˊ 哺乳动物，像猴而大，颊下没有囊，没有尾巴。如猩猩、大猩猩、长臂猿等 ape

辕（轅）yuán ㄩㄢˊ ❶车辕子，车前驾牲畜的部分 shafts (of a cart or carriage)：用牛驾～ *use an ox to pull a cart* ❷辕门，旧时称军营的门 (old) gate of barracks ㊀旧时军政大官的衙门 (old) *yamen*; an outer gate of the office for high-ranking government officials or military officers

原 yuán ㄩㄢˊ ❶最初的，开始的（㊥－始）original：～稿 *original copy; manuscript* | ～创 *to originate* ㊀没有经过加工的 raw; crude; unrefined：～油 *crude oil* | ～煤 *raw coal* ❷原来，本来 originally：这话～不错。*This remark was not wrong in the first place.* | ～打算去请他 *had thought of inviting him* | 放还～处 *put it back* ❸谅解，宽容（㊥－谅）to excuse; to pardon：情有可～ *excusable* ❹宽广平坦的地方 plain; flatland：～野 *open country* | 平～ *plain*| 高～ *plateau* | 大草～ *prairie* ❺ same as "塬"

塬 yuán ㄩㄢˊ 我国西北部黄土高原地区因流水冲刷而形成的高地，四边陡，顶上平 plateau in northwest China

源 yuán ㄩㄢˊ ❶水流所从出的地方 water source：泉～ *fountainhead* | 河～ *river source* ［源源］继续不断 continuously：～而来 *come in a steady stream* ❷事物的根由，来路 source; cause：来～ *source* | 货～ *source of supplies*

嫄 yuán ㄩㄢˊ 用于人名。姜嫄，传说是周代祖先后稷的母亲 used in given names, e.g. Jiangyuan, mother of Houji, the ancestor of Zhou Dynasty in Chinese legend

骦（騵）yuán ㄩㄢˊ 腹部白色，其他部位红色的马 red horse with a white abdomen

螈 yuán ㄩㄢˊ see 蝾螈 (róng－) at 蝾 on page 561

羱 yuán ㄩㄢˊ 羱羊，即北山羊，像山羊而大，生活在高山地

带 ibex (same as 北山羊)

缘(緣) yuán ㄩㄢˊ ❶因由，原因(㊀一故、一由) reason; cause：无～无故 *without rhyme or reason* ❷缘分，宿命论者指人与人命中注定的遇合机会，泛指人与人或人与事物之间结成关系的可能性 predestined relationship：姻～ *predestined marriage*｜有～相见 *have the chance to meet each other* ❸沿，顺着 along：～流而上 *go upstream*｜～木求鱼（喻必然得不到）*climb a tree to catch a fish; (figurative) to attempt the impossible* ❹边(㊀边一) edge; rim ❺因为 on account of：～何至此？ *Why so?*

橼(櫞) yuán ㄩㄢˊ see 枸橼 (jǔ一) at 枸 on page 338

圜 yuán ㄩㄢˊ same as "圆"
⇨ see also huán on p.266

远(遠) yuǎn ㄩㄢˇ ❶跟"近"相对 far; long (opposite of 近) ①距离长 (of distance) long: 路～ *a long way*｜住得～ *live far away* ②时间长(㊀永一、长一) (of time) long：做长～打算 *make a long-term plan* ❷不亲密，不接近 unfriendly; distant：～亲 *distant relative*｜敬而～之 *stay at a respectable distance from sb* ❸(差别)大 (of difference) big; great：差得～ *far from enough; distinctly inferior to* ❹深远 profound：言近旨～ *simple in language but deep in meaning*

苑 yuàn ㄩㄢˋ ❶养禽兽植林木的地方，旧时多指帝王的园林 enclosure (for animals or plants);(old) imperial garden：鹿～ *deer park* ❷(学术、文艺)荟萃之处 (of learning, art) centre：文～ *literary centre*｜艺～奇葩 *exquisite works of art*

怨 yuàn ㄩㄢˋ ❶仇恨(㊀一恨) hatred; resentment ❷不满意，责备 to complain; to blame：毫无～言 *without a word of complaint*｜任劳任～ *work hard and not be upset by criticisms*｜这事不能～他。*He is not to blame for this.*

院 yuàn ㄩㄢˋ ❶(一子、一儿)围墙里房屋四周的空地 courtyard ❷某些机关和公共场所的名称 used in names of certain government offices and public places：法～ *court of law*｜医～ *hospital*｜戏～ *theatre* ❸特指学院 (specifically) college：高等～校 *institutions of higher learning*

垸 yuàn ㄩㄢˋ 〈方 dialect〉(一子) 湖南省、湖北省在江湖地带挡水用的堤圩（wéi）protective embankments (in Hunan and Hubei provinces)

掾 yuàn ㄩㄢˋ 古代官署属员的通称 minor official; clerk (working in a government department in ancient times)

媛 yuàn ㄩㄢˋ 美女 beautiful woman
⇨ see also yuán on p.807

瑗 yuàn ㄩㄢˋ 大孔的璧 round flat piece of jade with a big hole in its centre

愿(❶-❸願) yuàn ㄩㄢˋ ❶乐意 to be willing：甘心情～ *be only too glad to do sth* | 自觉自～ *of one's own free will* ❷希望（㊣—望）hope：生平之～ *lifetime wish* | 如～以偿 *achieve one's heart's desire* [愿景]所向往的前景 vision; aspiration ❸迷信的人对神佛许下的酬谢 vow; pledge (to a deity)：许～ *make a vow to a deity* | 还～ *redeem a vow to a deity* ❹恭谨 respectful and cautious

YUE ㄩㄝ

曰 yuē ㄩㄝ ❶说 to say：子～：学而时习之。*The Master said, 'Learn and review it from time to time.'* | 其谁～不然？*Who can say it is not so?* ❷叫作 to be called：名之～文化室 *name it the cultural room*

约（約） yuē ㄩㄝ ❶拘束，限制（㊣—束）to restrict ❷共同议定的要遵守的条款 agreement：条～ *treaty* | 立～ *make a contract* | 公～ *pact* ❸预先说定 to make an appointment：预～ *make an appointment* | 和他～好了 *have made an appointment with him* ❹请 to invite：～他来 *ask him to come* | 特～记者 *special correspondent* ❺约分，用公约数去除分子和分母使分数简化 to reduce a fraction：5/10 可以～成 1/2。*5/10 can be reduced to 1/2.* ❻俭省 economical; frugal：节～ *to economize* ❼简单，简要 simple; brief：简～ *concise* | 由博返～ *from complexity to simplicity* ❽大约，大概，不十分确定的 about; around：～计 *come roughly to* | ～数 *approximate figure* | ～有五十人。*There are about 50 people.*

⇨ see also yāo on p.760

矱 yuē ㄩㄝ 尺度，标准 yardstick; measurement

彟（彠） yuē ㄩㄝ 尺度 yardstick; measurement

哕（噦） yuě ㄩㄝ 呕吐 to vomit：刚吃完药，都～出来了。*He had no sooner taken the medicine than he threw it all up.* [干哕]（gānyue）要吐（tù）而吐（tù）不出东西来 to retch

月 yuè ㄩㄝ ❶月亮，地球的卫星，本身不发光，它的光是反射太阳的光 moon [月食]（*月蚀）地球运行到太阳和月亮中间，遮住太阳照到月亮上的光，使得月亮看上去有亏缺或完全看不见的现象 lunar eclipse ❷计时单位，一年分十二个月 month ❸形状像月亮的，圆的 moon-shaped：～饼 *moon cake* | ～琴 *stringed instrument with a round sound box* ❹按月出现或完成的 every month; monthly：～经 *menstruation* | ～刊 *monthly (publication)* | ～票 *monthly ticket* | ～报表 *monthly report*

[月氏]（—zhī）我国古代西部民族名 *Yuezhi* (an ethnic group in the west of China in ancient times)

刖（ 跀）** yuè ㄩㄝ 古代把脚砍掉的酷刑 (ancient) to cut the feet as a punishment

Y

玥 yuè ㄩㄝ 古代传说中的一种神珠 a kind of magic pearl in Chinese legend

钥(鑰) yuè ㄩㄝ ❶锁 lock：门～ *door lock* ❷钥匙 key［锁钥］⑩1 做好事情的关键 key to sth：动员民众是革命的～。*The key to revolution is to mobilize the masses.* 2 边防要地 strategic place：北门～ *northern town of strategic importance*

⇨ see also yào on p.763

乐(樂) yuè ㄩㄝ ❶音乐 music：奏～ *play music*［乐清］地名，在浙江省 Yueqing (a place in Zhejiang Province) ❷ 姓 (surname) Yue

⇨ see also lè on p.383

栎(櫟) yuè ㄩㄝ ［栎阳］古地名，在今陕西省临潼 Yueyang (an ancient place, in today's Lintong, Shaanxi Province)

⇨ see also lì on p.394

轫(軏) yuè ㄩㄝ 古代车辕与车衡相连接的部件 part connecting a shaft and its horizontal bar in ancient times

岳(❶*嶽) yuè ㄩㄝ ❶高大的山 high mountain［五岳］我国五座名山，即东岳泰山，西岳华山，南岳衡山，北岳恒山，中岳嵩山 the Five Great Mountains (of China) ❷称妻的父母或妻的叔伯 wife's parents or paternal uncles：～父 *father-in-law*｜叔～ *wife's uncle*

娍 yuè ㄩㄝ 轻扬 to drift; to float lightly

钺(鉞、戉)** yuè ㄩㄝ 古代兵器名，像斧，比斧大些 large battle-axe in ancient times

越 yuè ㄩㄝ ❶度过，超出 to go beyond ①度过阻碍 to get over：爬山～岭 *trek over mountains* ②不按照一般的次序，超出范围 to overstep; to skip：～级 *skip a grade; to bypass ranks*｜～权 *overstep one's authority*｜～组(zǔ)代庖(páo)(喻越职做别人应做的事) *take sb else's business into one's own hands* ③经过 to go through：～冬作物 *over wintering crop* ❷扬起，昂扬 to be at high pitch：声音清～ *clear and melodious voice* ❸副词，越……越……，表示程度加深 (adverb) the more...the more...：～快～好 *the faster the better*｜～跑～有劲儿。*The more one runs, the more energetic one will become.*｜～战～强。*The more one fights, the stronger one grows.*｜天气～来～暖和。*The weather is getting warmer and warmer.*［越发］副词，更加 (adverb) more and more：由于水肥充足，今年的收成～好了。*Because of the abundance of water and fertilizer, the harvest is getting better this year.* ❹抢夺 to seize; to plunder：杀人～货 *rob and kill* ❺周代诸侯国名，在今浙江省东部，后扩展到浙江省北部、江苏全省、安徽省南部及山东省南部。后来用作浙江省东部的别称 Yue (a state in the Zhou Dynasty, originally located in the east of today's Zhejiang Province); eastern Zhejiang: ～剧 *Shaoxing opera*

樾 yuè ㄩㄝ 树阴凉儿 shade of a tree

说(說) yuè ㄩㄝ (ancient) same as "悦"

⇨ see also shuì on p.614, shuō on p.615

阅(閲) yuè ㄩㄝ ❶看，察看(㊥－览) to read; to inspect: ～报 *read newspapers* | 传～ *read and pass on* | 检～ *review troops* ❷经历，经过 to experience: ～历 *experience* | ～世 *see the world*

悦 yuè ㄩㄝ ❶高兴，愉快(㊥喜－) pleased: 和颜～色 *with a kind and pleasant countenance* | 心～诚服 *submit cheerfully; accept willingly* ❷使愉快 to please: ～耳 *sweet-sounding* | 赏心～目 *pleasing both the eye and the mind*

跃(躍) yuè ㄩㄝ 跳(㊥跳－) to leap: 飞～ *to leap* | 龙腾虎～(形容生气勃勃、威武雄壮的姿态) *vigorous and robust* | ～～欲试 *itch to have a go* [跃进] 1 跳着前进 to leap forward 2 极快地前进 to progress by leaps and bounds: 经济建设向前～。*The economy is developing by leaps and bounds.*

粤 yuè ㄩㄝ 广东省的别称 Yue (another name for Guangdong Province) [两粤] 指广东省和广西壮族自治区 Guangdong Province and Guangxi Zhuang Autonomous Region

鸑(鷟) yuè ㄩㄝ [鸑鷟] (－zhuó) 古书上指一种水鸟 a kind of water bird in ancient Chinese texts

龠 yuè ㄩㄝ ❶古代的一种管乐器 a kind of flute in ancient times ❷古代容量单位，两龠为一合(gě) an ancient Chinese unit for measuring capacity; there are two 龠 in one 合

瀹 yuè ㄩㄝ ❶煮 to boil: ～茗(烹茶) *make tea* ❷疏导(河道) to dredge (rivers): ～济(jǐ)漯(tà)(济、漯是古水名) *dredge Ji River and Ta River (both are ancient rivers)*

爚 yuè ㄩㄝ 火光 flame

籥 yuè ㄩㄝ same as "龠❶"

YUN ㄩㄣ

晕(暈) yūn ㄩㄣ 昏迷 to faint: ～厥(jué) *to faint* | ～倒 *fall down in a faint* | ～过去了 *went off in a faint* ㊀头脑不清 muddle-headed; dizzy: 头～ *feel dizzy* | ～头转向 *feel confused and disoriented*

⇨ see also yùn on p.814

缊(緼) yūn ㄩㄣ see 䌷缊 (yīn－) at 䌷 on page 779

⇨ see also yùn on p.814

氲 yūn ㄩㄣ see 氤氲 (yīn－) at 氤 on page 779

煴 yūn ㄩㄣ 微火，无焰的火 slow fire

Y

馧 yūn ㄩㄣ 香，香气 fragrance; aroma

頵(頵) yūn ㄩㄣ 头大的样子 big head

赟(贇) yūn ㄩㄣ 美好。多用于人名 fine; beautiful (often used in given names)

云(❸雲) yún ㄩㄣˊ ❶说 to say：诗～ *The Book of Songs says* | 人～亦～ *repeat what others say* ❷文言助词，句首、句中、句末都用 auxiliary word in classical Chinese：～谁之思？ *Whose idea is it?* | 岁～暮矣。*It is late in the year.* | 盖记时也～。*This is a description of the season.* ❸由微小的水滴或冰晶聚集形成的、在空中飘浮的成团的物体 cloud：～彩 *cloud* | ～消雾散 *the clouds vanish and the mists disperse; vanish into thin air* | ～集（形容许多人或事物聚集在一起）*to gather*

芸(❷蕓) yún ㄩㄣˊ ❶芸香，草本植物，花黄色，花、叶、茎有香味，可入药 rue ❷芸薹（tái），又叫油菜，草本植物，花黄色，种子可榨油 rape (also called 油菜)

[芸芸] 形容众多 innumerable：～众生 *all living things*

沄(❷澐) yún ㄩㄣˊ ❶[沄沄] 形容水流动 (of water) flowing ❷大波浪 billow; surging wave

妘 yún ㄩㄣˊ 姓 (surname) Yun

纭(紜) yún ㄩㄣˊ [纷纭] (fēn－)（言论、事情等）多而杂乱 (speeches, things, etc.) numerous and disorderly：众说～ *opinions vary*

耘 yún ㄩㄣˊ 除草 to weed：～田 *weed the fields* | 春耕夏～ *plough in spring and weed in summer*

匀 yún ㄩㄣˊ ❶平均，使平均（㊀均－）to even up：颜色涂得不～。*The colour is not evenly spread.* | 这两份儿多少不均，～一～吧。*The two shares are not equal, please even them up.* ❷从中抽出一部分给别人或做他用 to spare：把你买的纸～给我一些。*Spare me some of the paper you bought.* | 先～出两间房来给新来的同志。*Let's spare two rooms for our new comrades first.*

昀 yún ㄩㄣˊ 日光。多用于人名 sunlight (often used in given names)

畇 yún ㄩㄣˊ 田地平坦整齐的样子 ㊂ (of field) neatly arranged

筠 yún ㄩㄣˊ ❶竹皮 skin of a bamboo ❷竹子 bamboo

➪ see also jūn on p.345

鋆 yún ㄩㄣˊ （在人名中也读 jūn）金子 (also pronounced jūn in given names) gold

员(員) yún ㄩㄣˊ 用于人名。伍员（即伍子胥），春秋时人 used in given names, e.g. Wu Yun (same as Wu Zixu), who lived during the Spring and Autumn Period

➪ see also yuán on p.806, yùn on p.813

郧(鄖) yún ㄩㄣˊ 郧县，地名，在湖北省 Yunxian (a place in Hubei Province)

涢(溳) yún ㄩㄣˊ 涢水，水名，在湖北省北部 Yunshui River (in the north of Hubei Province)

筼(篔) yún ㄩㄣˊ [筼筜] (-dāng) 生长在水边的大竹子 tall bamboo growing by waterside

允 yǔn ㄩㄣˇ ❶答应，认可（㊟-许）to allow; to consent: ～诺 *to promise* | 应～ *to agree; to consent* | 不～ *not allow* ❷公平得当（dàng）fair; just: 公～ *fair and just*

狁 yǔn ㄩㄣˇ see 猃狁 (xiǎn-) at 猃 on page 709

陨(隕) yǔn ㄩㄣˇ 坠落 to fall down: ～石 *meteorite*

殒(殞) yǔn ㄩㄣˇ 死亡 to perish; to die: ～命 *to perish*

孕 yùn ㄩㄣˋ ❶怀胎 to be pregnant: ～妇 *pregnant woman* | ～期 *pregnancy* | ～育 *be pregnant with; to nurture* ❷胎，身孕 fetus; embryo: 有～ *be expecting a baby* | 怀～ *be pregnant*

运(運) yùn ㄩㄣˋ ❶旋转，循序移动 to move; to turn: 日月～行 *movement of the sun and the moon* [运动] 1 物体的位置不断变化的现象 (in physics) motion 2 哲学上指物质的存在形式和根本属性 (in philosophy) motion 3 体育活动，如体操、游泳等 sports; exercise 4 政治、文化、生产等方面开展的有组织的群众性活动 movement; campaign: 五四～ *the May 4th Movement* | 增产节约～ *campaign to increase production and to economize* 5 (-dong) 为求达到某种目的而钻营奔走 to manoeuvre; to arrange things through pull ❷搬送（㊟-输）to transport: ～货 *transport goods* | 客～ *passenger transport* | 陆～ *land transportation* ❸运用，灵活使用 to utilize: ～笔 *wield one's pen* | ～思 *conceive an idea* | ～筹 *to plan* ❹指人生死、福祸等一切的遭遇。特指迷信的人所说的命中注定的遭遇 fortune; fate: 幸～ *be lucky* | ～气 *luck* | 走好～ *be in luck*

酝(醖) yùn ㄩㄣˋ 酿酒，也指酒 to brew (wine); alcoholic drink: 佳～（好酒）*good wine* [酝酿] (-niàng) 造酒材料加工后的发酵过程 to brew ㊟事前考虑或磋商使条件成熟 to mull over (an issue); to hold exploratory discussion: 表决前要进行～。*Preliminary discussion is needed before the vote.*

员(員) yùn ㄩㄣˋ 姓 (surname) Yun

⇨ see also yuán on p.806, yún on p.812

郓(鄆) yùn ㄩㄣˋ [郓城] 地名，在山东省 Yuncheng (a place in Shandong Province)

恽(惲) yùn ㄩㄣˋ 姓 (surname) Yun

晕(暈) yùn ㄩㄣˋ ❶日光或月光通过云层时因折射作用而在太阳或月亮周围形成的光圈 halo：日～ *solar halo* | 月～而风。*A halo round the moon predicts the rising of wind.* ❷头发昏 to feel dizzy：一坐船就～ *feel dizzy whenever on ship*

⇨ see also yūn on p.811

愠 yùn ㄩㄣˋ 怒，怨恨 to be angry; to resent：面有～色 *wear an angry look*

缊(緼) yùn ㄩㄣˋ ❶新旧混合的丝绵 mixed silk wadding：～袍 *floss-padded robe* ❷碎麻 bits of hemp

⇨ see also yūn on p.811

韫(韞) yùn ㄩㄣˋ 藏，收藏 to hide sth away; to collect：～椟而藏诸（收在柜子里藏起来吗）？*Will it be hidden away in the cabinet?* | 石～玉而山辉。*Mountains are glorified for its rocks with hidden jade.*

蕴(藴) yùn ㄩㄣˋ ❶包含，储藏（㊥－藏）to accumulate; to contain：～含 *to contain* ❷事理的深奥之处 profundity：底～ *concrete details; erudition* | 精～ *profound meaning*

韵(*韻) yùn ㄩㄣˋ ❶语音名词 term of phonetics ①韵母，字音中声母、声调以外部分，包括介音在内，如"堂"（táng）的韵母是 ang，"皇"（huáng）的韵母是 uang。final (simple or compound vowel of a Chinese syllable) ②字音中声母、介音、声调以外的部分，如"堂皇"（tánghuáng）都是 ang 韵。又如 an、ian、uan、üan 是四个韵母，同是 an 韵。rhyme (the final sound of a Chinese syllable)：～文 *verse* | 押～ *to rhyme* | 叶（xié）～ *to rhyme* ❷有节奏的声音 rhythmic sound：琴～悠扬。*Sweet music was being played on the lute.* ❸风致，情趣 appeal; charm：风～ *charm* | ～味 *implicit richness* | 神～ *charm; grace; intrinsic interest*

熨 yùn ㄩㄣˋ 用烙铁、熨斗把衣布等烫平 to iron (clothes) [熨斗]（－dǒu）加热后用来烫平衣服的金属器具 an iron

⇨ see also yù on p.804

Z ㄗ

ZA ㄗㄚ

扎(*紮、*紥) zā ㄗㄚ ❶捆，缠束 to tie; to bind：～辫子 *braid one's hair* | ～裤腿 *fasten one's trousers legs* ❷把儿，捆儿 bundle：一～线 *a bundle of thread*

⇨ see also zhā on p.825, zhá on p.826

匝(*帀) zā ㄗㄚ ❶周 circle：绕树三～ *circle a tree three times* ❷满，环绕 to fill; to encircle：～地 *cover the ground* | ～月 *a full month*

咂 zā ㄗㄚ ❶舌尖与腭接触发声 click one's tongue：～嘴 *click one's tongue (to express awe or praise)* ❷吸，呷 to suck; to drink：～一口酒 *take a sip of wine* ❸仔细辨别 to discern：～滋味 *discern flavours*

拶 zā ㄗㄚ 逼迫 to force：债务～逼 *squeezed by debts*

⇨ see also zǎn on p.818

杂(雜、*襍) zá ㄗㄚˊ ❶多种多样的，不单纯的 mixed：～色 *mixed colours* | ～事 *miscellaneous matters* | ～技 *acrobatics* | 人多手～ *many people are working on sth; many stealing hands* [杂志] 把许多文章集在一起印行的期刊 magazine ❷掺杂，混合 to mix：夹～ *be mixed with* ❸正项或正式以外的 miscellaneous; unofficial：～费 *miscellaneous fees; incidental expenses* | ～牌儿军 *ragtag army*

砸 zá ㄗㄚˊ ❶打，捣 to hit：～钉子 *hammer a nail* | ～地基 *tamp a foundation* ❷打坏，打破 to smash：碗～了。*The bowl is smashed.* | ～碎铁锁链 *smash the chains* ㊕失败 to fail：这件事搞～了。*This matter has been messed up.*

咋(**㗅) zǎ ㄗㄚˇ 〈方 dialect〉代词，怎，怎么 (pronoun) what; how：不知～好 *don't know what to do* | 这可～办? *How do we get out of this?*

⇨ see also zé on p.823, zhā on p.825

臜(臢) za ·ㄗㄚ see 腌臜 (ā–) at 腌 on page 1

ZAI ㄗㄞ

灾(*災、*烖) zāi ㄗㄞ ❶水、火、荒旱等所造成的祸害 natural disaster：战胜～害 *overcome the effects of disaster* | 旱～ *drought* ❷个人的不幸遭遇 personal misfortune：飞～ *unexpected misfortune* | 招～惹祸 *be a magnet for disaster*

Z

甾 zāi ㄗㄞ 有机化合物的一类，又叫类固醇，广泛存在于动植物体内。胆固醇和许多种激素都属于甾类化合物 (also called 类固醇) steroid

哉 zāi ㄗㄞ 文言助词 auxiliary word in classical Chinese ①表疑问或反问语气 used in questions or rhetorical questions：有何难～？ *How difficult can it be?* | 岂有他～？ *What else is there?* ②表感叹语气 used in exclamations：呜呼哀～！ *Alas!* | 诚～斯言！ *Verily, these words are the truth!*

栽 zāi ㄗㄞ ❶种植 to plant：～菜 *plant vegetables* | ～树 *plant trees* ㊀安上，插上 to install; to insert：～绒 *tufting; knotting* | ～赃 *plant stolen goods on sb* ❷（－子）秧子，可以移植的植物幼苗 seedling：桃～ *peach seedling* | 树～子 *tree seedling* ❸跌倒 to fall：～跟头 *tumble and fall* | ～了一跤 *took a tumble*

仔 zǎi ㄗㄞˇ 〈方 dialect〉 same as "崽"

⇨ see also zī on p.879, zǐ on p.882

载(載) zǎi ㄗㄞˇ ❶年 year：一年半～ *six months to a year* ❷记在书报上（㊥记－）to print：登～ *to publish; be published (in a newspaper or magazine)* | 刊～ *to print; be printed (in a newspaper or magazine)* | 转～ *to reprint sth that has been published elsewhere* | ～入史册 *record in history*

⇨ see also zài on p.817

宰 zǎi ㄗㄞˇ ❶杀牲畜（㊥－杀、屠－）to slaughter (livestock)：～猪 *slaughter a pig* | ～鸡 *slaughter a chicken* ㊁向买东西或接受服务的人索取高价 rip off (a customer)：挨～ *get ripped off* | ～人 *rip people off* ❷主管，主持 to manage; preside over：主～ *to dominate; master* | ～制 *to rule* ❸古代官名 minister (in ancient times)：太～ *Great Steward* [宰相] 古代辅佐君王掌管国家大事的最高的官 (ancient) Prime Minister

崽 zǎi ㄗㄞˇ ❶〈方 dialect〉小孩子 child ❷（－子、－儿）幼小的动物 the young (of animals)：猪～儿 *piglet* | 虎～儿 *tiger cub*

再(*再、*再) zài ㄗㄞˋ ❶两次，第二次 twice; the second time：一而～，～而三 *again and again* ❷第二次出现，重复发生 to return; occur repeatedly：良辰难～。 *Once gone, a beautiful moment is lost forever.* | 青春不～。 *Youth doesn't return.* ❸副词 adverb ①表示又一次 again：～版 *publish a second edition; (sometimes) to reprint* | ～接～厉 *make persistent efforts* | 一错～错 *repeat a mistake* [再三] 副词，不止一次地，一次又一次地 (adverb) repeatedly：～考虑 *carefully reconsider* ②表示事情或行为重复、继续，多指未然（与"又"不同）again (different from 又)：明天～来。 *Come again tomorrow.* | 雨不会～下了。 *It will not rain again.* ③用在两个

动词之间，表示动作的先后关系 (used to indicate sequence of actions between two verbs) then：吃完饭～去学习 *finish one's meal and then go do one's homework* | 把材料整理好了～动笔写 *finish organizing one's materials before beginning to write* ④ 更，更加 more than：～好没有了 *nothing could be better* | 字～大一点儿就好了。*It would be better if the characters were a bit larger.* ⑤表示另外有所补充 and; as well as (used to indicate addition)：～则 *in addition* | 盘里放着葡萄、鸭梨，～就是苹果。*There are grapes and Chinese white pears on the tray, as well as apples.*

在 zài ㄗㄞˋ ❶存在 to exist：革命者青春常～。*Revolutionaries are forever youthful.* | 人～阵地～。*As long as soldiers remain, the position remains.* ❷存在于某地点 to be (somewhere)：书～桌子上呢。*The book is on the table.* | 我今天晚上～家。*I will be at home tonight.* ㉁留在，处在 to be：～职 *be employed* ❸在于，决定于 depend on：事～人为。*Success depends on effort.* | 学习进步，主要～自己努力。*Progress in one's studies depends on one's own efforts.* [在乎]（-hu）1 在于 depend on 2 在意，介意 be concerned：满不～ *totally unconcerned* | 不要～别人的看法。*Do not be concerned about what others think.* ❹副词，正在，表示动作的进行 adverb indicating ongoing action：会议～进行。*The meeting is in progress.* | 我～看报。*I am reading the newspaper.* ❺介词，表示事情的时间、地点、情形、范围等 preposition indicating time, place, situation, scope, etc.：～晚上读书 *study at night* | ～礼堂开会 *hold the meeting in the assembly hall* | ～这种条件之下工作 *work under such conditions* ❻"在"和"所"连用，表示强调 used with 所 to indicate emphasis：～所不辞 *will not refuse under any circumstances* | ～所不计 *irrespective of* | ～所难免 *cannot be avoided*

载（載） zài ㄗㄞˋ ❶用交通工具装 to carry using a means of transportation：装～ *to load* | ～货 *to freight* | ～重汽车 *lorry; truck* | 满～而归 *return with an abundance of things/results* ❷充满 to fill：怨声～道 *discontent fills the street* | 风雨～途 *arduous journey* ❸载……载……，用在动词前，表示两个动作同时进行 used before two verbs to indicate two simultaneous actions：～歌～舞 *singing while dancing* ❹姓 (surname) Zai

⇨ see also zǎi on p.816

ZAN ㄗㄢ

糌 zān ㄗㄢ [糌粑]（-ba）青稞麦炒熟后磨成的面，是藏族的主食 *zanba* (flour made with roasted highland barley, a Tibetan staple food)

Z

簪（*簮）zān ㄗㄢ ❶（一子、一儿）用来绾（wǎn）住头发的一种首饰，古时也用它把帽子别在头发上 hairpin; (ancient) hatpin ❷插，戴 to wear (in one's hair)：～花 *wear flowers in one's hair*

咱（*喒、*偺）zán ㄗㄢˊ 代词 pronoun ①我 I：～不懂他的话。*I don't understand what he's saying.* ②咱们 we; us; our：～村全都富起来了。*All of us in the village have become rich.*［咱们］"我"的多数，跟"我们"不同，包括听话的人在内 us (including those present, different from 我们)：同志，你别客气，～军民是一家嘛！*Don't mention it, comrade. We, the army and the people, are one family!*

拶 zǎn ㄗㄢˇ 压紧 to squeeze［拶指］旧时用拶子夹手指的酷刑 (old) to torture with thumbscrews［拶子］旧时夹手指的刑具 (old) thumbscrews

⇨ see also zā on p.815

昝 zǎn ㄗㄢˇ 姓 (surname) Zan

寁 zǎn ㄗㄢˇ jié ㄐㄧㄝˊ（又）迅速，快捷 quick

噆 zǎn ㄗㄢˇ ❶叼，衔 to hold in one's mouth ❷咬 to bite

攒（攢、**儹）zǎn ㄗㄢˇ 积聚，积蓄（㊟积一）to collect：～粪 *gather manure*｜～钱 *save money*

⇨ see also cuán on p.102

趱（趲）zǎn ㄗㄢˇ ❶赶，快走 to hurry：～路 *make haste on a journey*｜紧～了一程 *hurried on the journey* ❷催促，催逼 to hasten; to press：～马向前 *hasten the horse forward*

暂（暫、*蹔）zàn ㄗㄢˋ ❶时间短，跟"久"相对 short (in duration) (opposite of 久)：短～ *brief* ❷副词，暂时 (adverb) temporarily：～停 *to pause; call a timeout (in a sports game)*｜会议～不举行。*The meeting will not be held for the time being.*

錾（鏨）zàn ㄗㄢˋ ❶（一子）凿石头的小凿子 stone chisel ❷在金石上雕刻 to engrave (on metal or stone)：～花 *(metalwork) chasing*｜～字 *engrave words*

赞（贊、*賛、❷❸*讚）zàn ㄗㄢˋ ❶帮助 to help：～助 *to sponsor*［赞成］1 表示同意 to agree：大家都～他的意见。*Everyone agrees with his views.* 2 助人成功 help sb to succeed ❷夸奖，称扬（㊟一许、一扬、称一）to praise：～不绝口 *praise effusively* ❸旧时文体的一种，以颂扬人物为主旨 tribute; eulogy (old literary form)：像～ *eulogy (written in praise of sb's portrait or appearance)*｜小～ *short eulogy*

酂（酇）zàn ㄗㄢˋ 古地名，在今湖北省老河口一带 Zan (an ancient place name, in the area around today's Laohekou, Hubei Province)

⇨ see also cuán on p.102, cuó

on p.105

瓒(瓚) zàn ㄗㄢˋ 古代祭祀时用的一种像勺的玉器 (ancient) spoon-shaped jade item used in religious sacrifices

ZANG ㄗㄤ

赃(贜、**賍) zāng ㄗㄤ 赃物，贪污受贿或偷盗所得的财物 stolen property; ill-gotten gains：追～ *seek the return of stolen property* | 退～ *surrender stolen property* | 人～俱获 *seize both the criminal and stolen property*

脏(髒) zāng ㄗㄤ 不干净 dirty：衣服～了。*The clothes have got dirty.* | 把～东西清除出去 *clear out the dirty stuff*

⇨ see also zàng on p.819

牂 zāng ㄗㄤ 母羊 doe; nanny

臧 zāng ㄗㄤ 善，好 good [臧否]（－pǐ）褒贬，评论，说好说坏 to appraise：～人物 *appraise people*

驵(駔) zǎng ㄗㄤˇ 好马，壮马 fine steed [驵侩]（－kuài）马侩，进行牲畜交易的中间人，也泛指经纪人 livestock broker; (general) broker

脏(臟) zàng ㄗㄤˋ 身体内部器官的总称 internal organs：内～ (see picture of 人体内脏 on page 819) *internal organs* | 五～六腑（五脏：心、肝、脾、肺、肾）*the five* Zang *and six* Fu *viscera (five* Zang *viscera: heart, liver, spleen, lungs, and kidneys)*

⇨ see also zāng on p.819

奘 zàng ㄗㄤˋ ❶壮大，多用于人名。玄奘，唐代一位高

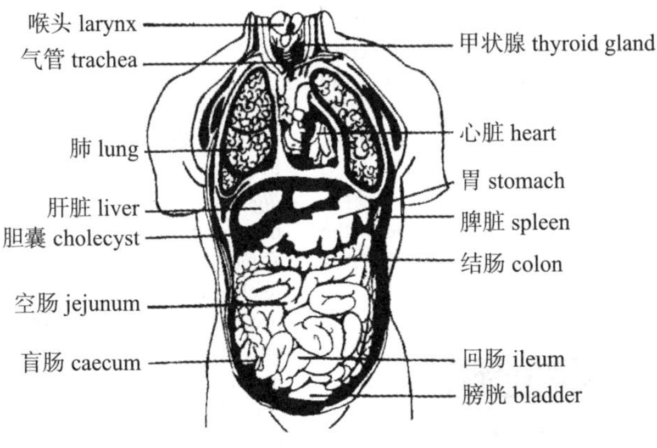

人体内脏 internal organs of human body

Z

僧的法名 big and powerful; often used in given names, e.g. Xuanzang, a revered Buddhist monk in the Tang Dynasty ❷〈方 dialect〉说话粗鲁，态度生硬 rough in speech and stiff in manner

⇨ see also zhuǎng on p.874

葬(*塟、*葬) zàng ㄗㄤˋ 掩埋死人，泛指处理死者遗体 to bury; (generally) dispose of a dead body：埋～ *to bury (the dead)* | 火～ *to cremate* [葬送] ⑩断送，毁灭 to ruin：～前程 *ruin one's future* | ～幸福 *ruin one's happiness*

藏 zàng ㄗㄤˋ ❶储放东西的地方 storage：宝～ *treasure* ❷佛教、道教经典的总称 collective term for Buddhist and Taoist scriptures：大～经 *Tripitaka (the Chinese Buddhist canon)* | 道～ *Taoist canon* [三藏] 佛教经典，包括"经""律""论"三部分，总称三藏 the Tripitaka (Buddhist canon that includes the three components of scriptures, laws, and discourse) ❸西藏自治区的简称 Zang (abbreviated term for the Tibet Autonomous Region)

[藏族] 我国少数民族，参看附录四 the Tibetan people (one of the ethnic groups in China. See Appendix Ⅳ.)

⇨ see also cáng on p.58

ZAO ㄗㄠ

遭 zāo ㄗㄠ ❶遇见，碰到(㊤—遇) to encounter：～灾 *suffer calamity* | ～难 *meet with misfortune* | ～殃 *meet with disaster* ❷(—儿)量词 measure word ①圈儿，周 circle：用绳子绕两～ *encircle twice with a rope* | 转了一～ *went round once* ②回，次 number of times：一～生，两～熟。*Strangers at the first meeting become familiar at the next.*

糟 zāo ㄗㄠ ❶做酒剩下的渣子 lees [糟粕] ⑩无价值的东西 dregs：取其精华，去其～ *take the essence and discard the dregs* ❷用酒或酒糟腌制食品 to pickle (in wine or with distiller's grains)：～鱼 *fish pickled with distiller's grains* | ～豆腐 *beancurd pickled with distiller's grains* ❸腐烂，朽烂 decayed：木头～了。*The wood has decayed.* | 布～了。*The fabric has decayed.* ❹坏 bad：事情～了。*The situation has turned bad.* [糟蹋] [糟踏] (—tɑ)作践，不爱惜 to waste：不许～粮食 *must not waste food*

凿(鑿) záo ㄗㄠˊ ❶(—子)挖槽或穿孔用的工具 chisel ❷穿孔，挖掘 to bore; to dig：～个眼儿 *bore a hole* | ～井 *dig a well* [穿凿] (formerly pronounced zuò)对于讲不通的道理，牵强附会，以求其通 give a far-fetched interpretation ❸ (formerly pronounced zuò)〈古 ancient〉器物上的孔，是容纳枘(ruì)的 mortise ❹ (formerly pronounced zuò) 明确，真实 ㊂(㊤确—) clear-cut; authentic：言之～～ *say sth with certainty*

早 zǎo ㄗㄠˇ ❶太阳出来的时候（㊖—晨）morning：一大～就开会去了 *went to a meeting early in the morning* | ～饭 *breakfast* | ～操 *morning exercises* ❷时间靠前，在一定时间以前 early：～起～睡 *go to bed early and wake up early* | 那是很～的事了。*This happened a long time ago.* | 我～就预备好了。*I was already prepared very early on.* | 开车还～着呢。*It is still early for the bus/train to depart.*

枣（棗） zǎo ㄗㄠˇ 枣树，落叶乔木，枝有刺，花黄色，果实叫枣子或枣儿，椭圆形，熟时红色，可以吃 Chinese date

蚤 zǎo ㄗㄠˇ ❶蛇蚤（gèzao），昆虫，即跳蚤，身体赤褐色，善跳跃，寄生在人畜的身体上，吸血液，能传染鼠疫等疾病 flea (same as 跳蚤) ❷ (ancient) same as "早"

澡 zǎo ㄗㄠˇ 洗澡，沐浴，洗全身 to bathe：～盆 *bathtub* | ～堂 *bathhouse*

璪 zǎo ㄗㄠˇ ❶古代刻有水藻花纹的玉制饰物 ancient jade decoration engraved with algae patterns ❷古代垂在冕上穿玉的五彩丝绦 (ancient) five-coloured ribbons threaded with jade and attached to an emperor's official hat

藻 zǎo ㄗㄠˇ ❶藻类植物，没有真正的根、茎、叶的分化，有叶绿素，可以自己制造养料。种类很多，大多生活在水里 algae ❷华丽的文辞 ornamented style of writing：～饰 *to embellish (one's writing)* | 辞～ *rhetoric language* [藻井] 我国传统建筑中的一种顶棚形式，一般呈方形、多边形或圆形的凹面，上有各种花纹、雕刻和彩画 (in traditional Chinese architecture) domed coffered ceiling

皂（*皁） zào ㄗㄠˋ ❶黑色 black：～鞋 *black cloth shoes* | 不分～白（喻不问是非）*do not differentiate between right and wrong* ❷差役 (old) bailiff in a magistrate's office：～隶 *runner in a magistrate's office* ❸皂角，落叶乔木，即皂荚。枝上有刺，结的长荚也叫皂角或皂荚，可供洗衣去污用 (same as 皂荚) Chinese honeylocust ❹有洗涤去污作用的日用化工制品 soap：肥～ *soap* | 香～ *scented soap* | 药～ *medicated soap*

唣（*唕） zào ㄗㄠˋ [啰唣] 吵闹 make a noise

灶（竈） zào ㄗㄠˋ 用土坯、砖或金属等制成的生火做饭的设备 kitchen stove：～台 *kitchen stove top* | 垒个～ *build a stove* | 煤气～ *gas stove*

造 zào ㄗㄠˋ ❶制作，做（㊖制—）to make：～船 *build a ship* | ～林 *plant a forest* | ～预算 *create a budget* ㊕ 瞎编 make sth up：～谣 *start a rumour* | 捏～ *to fabricate* ❷成就 achievement：～诣（yì）*attainment (in academic research, arts, etc.)* ❸培养 to train; to cultivate：深～ *pursue further study* | 可～之材 *promising talent* ❹到，去 to go：～访

pay a visit to | 登峰～极 reach the highest level ❺相对两方面的人，特指诉讼的两方 parties from the opposite sides; (specifically) plaintiff and defendant：两～ plaintiff and defendant | 甲～ Party A | 乙～ Party B ❻〈方 dialect〉稻子等作物从播种到收割一次叫一造 agricultural cycle：一年两～ two agricultural cycles a year

[造次] 仓卒，匆促 hurried：～之间 in a moment of haste ㊂鲁莽，草率 rash：不敢～ do not dare to be rash

慥 zào ㄗㄠˋ ㊎忠厚诚实的样子 sincere and honest in appearance

簉 zào ㄗㄠˋ 副，附属的 deputy; subordinate

噪(❷*譟) zào ㄗㄠˋ ❶许多鸟或虫子乱叫 (of many birds or insects) to call：鹊～ magpies' call (traditionally considered a good omen) | 蝉～ cicada's call ㊂声音杂乱 cacophony：～音 noise ❷许多人大声吵嚷 loud noises made by many people：聒～ noisy | 鼓～而进 to advance amidst a din ❸（名声）广为传扬 (of reputation) widely known：名～一时 become famous for a time

燥 zào ㄗㄠˋ 干（gān）(㊟干一) dry：～热 dry and hot | 口干舌～ parched with thirst

磲 zào ㄗㄠˋ 用于地名 used in place names：～都（在江西省靖安）Zaodu (in Jing'an, Jiangxi Province)

躁 zào ㄗㄠˋ 急躁，性急，不冷静 impetuous：暴～ short-tempered | 浮～ giddy and hot-tempered | 戒骄戒～ guard against conceit and rashness

ZE ㄗㄜ

则(則) zé ㄗㄜˊ ❶模范，规范 standard：准～ standard | 以身作～ set an example by one's own actions ❷规则，制度，规程 rules and regulations：细～ detailed rules and regulations | 原～ principle | 守～ rules; regulations [法则] 又叫规律，事物之间内在的必然的联系 (also called 规律) rule; law (of natural and social phenomena) [四则] 指加、减、乘、除四种运算方法 four basic arithmetic operations ❸效法 to imitate：～先烈之言行 follow the examples of our martyrs' speech and actions ❹连词 conjunction ①表示因果关系，就，便 then (used to indicate cause and effect)：兼听～明，偏信～暗。If one hears from multiple sides, then one will be enlightened; if one believes in a single opinion, then one remains in the dark. ②表示转折，却 but：今～不然 but it is not true in the present time ③表示两件事在时间上前后相承 then (used to indicate one action following the other)：预备铃一响，～学生陆续走进教室。When the school bell rings, the students files gradually into the classrooms. ❺副词，

表示肯定的判断，就是 (adverb) definitely：此～余之罪也。*This is definitely my fault.* ❻用在“一、二（再）、三”等后面，列举原因或理由 used after 一，二（再），三，etc. to list reasons：一～房子小，二～人太多，所以室内拥挤不堪。*It is very cramped indoors because firstly, the house is too small, and secondly, there are too many people.* ❼量词，用于成文的条数 measure word for texts：试题三～ *three test questions* | 新闻两～ *two pieces of news* | 随笔一～ *a short piece of writing*

责（責） zé ㄗㄜˊ ❶责任，分（fèn）内应做的事 responsibility; duty：负～ *be responsible* | 尽～ *be conscientious* | 爱护公物，人人有～。*It is everyone's responsibility to take good care of public property.* ❷要求 to demand：求全～备 *demand perfection* | ～己严于～人 *hold oneself to higher standards than others* [责成] 要求某人负责办好 to ask (sb to complete a task)：这个问题已～专人研究解决。*Someone has been asked to study and resolve this problem.* ❸指摘过失，责备 to reprimand：～罚 *to punish* | 斥～ *to rebuke* ❹责问，质问，诘（jié）问 to call to account ❺旧指为惩罚而打 (old) to administer corporal punishment：鞭～ *lashing* | 杖～ *flogging*

〈古 ancient〉also same as 债 (zhài)

啧（嘖） zé ㄗㄜˊ 争辩 to argue：～有烦言（很多人说不满意的话）*chorus of complaints* [啧啧] 1 形容咂嘴或说话声 used to indicate tutting, clicking, or the sound of voices：～称美 *to tut in admiration* | 人言～ *hubbub of voices* 2 形容鸟鸣声 tweet (sound of birdcall)

帻（幘） zé ㄗㄜˊ 古代的一种头巾 (ancient) a type of headscarf

箦（簀） zé ㄗㄜˊ 床席 bed mat

赜（賾） zé ㄗㄜˊ 深奥 profound：探～索隐 *investigate the mysterious and unknown*

咋 zé ㄗㄜˊ ❶大声呼叫 to shout ❷咬，啃 to bite [咋舌] 形容因惊讶、害怕而说不出话来 be speechless (out of surprise or fear)

⇨ see also zǎ on p.815, zhā on p.825

迮 zé ㄗㄜˊ ❶〈古 ancient〉狭窄 narrow：～狭 *narrow* ❷姓 (surname) Ze

笮 zé ㄗㄜˊ 姓 (surname) Ze

⇨ see also zuó on p.891

舴 zé ㄗㄜˊ [舴艋]（一měng）小船 small boat

择（擇） zé ㄗㄜˊ 挑拣，挑选（㊥选一）to choose：不～手段 *be unscrupulous* | ～善而从 *choose what is good and follow it* | ～友 *choose one's friends* | ～业 *choose one's job*

⇨ see also zhái on p.829

泽（澤） zé ㄗㄜˊ ❶水积聚的地方 pool; lake;

Z

march：大～ *big lake* | 水乡～国 *watery land* ❷光泽，金属或其他物体发出的光亮 lustre：色～ *colour and lustre* ❸湿 wet：润～ *moist; to moisten* ❹恩惠 favour：恩～ *favour bestowed from above*

仄 zè ㄗㄜˋ ❶倾斜 slanting［仄声］古汉语里上声、去声、入声的总称 oblique tones (collective term for rising, departing, and entering tones in ancient Chinese) ❷狭窄 narrow：逼～ *narrow* ❸心里不安 ashamed：歉～ *ashamed of oneself*

昃 zè ㄗㄜˋ 太阳偏西 (of the sun) to sink to the west

侧（側） zè ㄗㄜˋ same as "仄"［侧声］same as "仄声"

⇨ see also cè on p.60, zhāi on p.828

ZEI ㄗㄟ

贼（賊） zéi ㄗㄟˊ ❶偷东西的人，盗匪 thief㊀严重危害人民和国家的坏人 traitor：奸～ *wicked person* | 卖国～ *traitor to one's nation* ❷伤害 to hurt：戕（qiāng）～ *to ruin* ❸邪的，不正派的 bad：～眼 *furtive glance* | ～头～脑 *behave like a thief* ❹〈方 dialect〉狡猾 cunning：老鼠真～。*Rats are so cunning.* ❺〈方 dialect〉很，非常 very：～冷 *very cold* | ～亮 *very bright*

鲗（鰂） zéi ㄗㄟˊ 乌鲗，同"乌贼"，软体动物，又叫墨鱼、墨斗鱼，有墨囊，遇危险时能放出黑色液体逃走，生活在海里 cuttlefish (same as 乌贼, also called 墨鱼，墨斗鱼）

ZEN ㄗㄣ

怎 zěn ㄗㄣˇ 如何 how：～样？ *How?* | ～办？ *What does one do?*［怎么］（—me）代词，询问性质、状态、方式、原因等 (pronoun) what; how：你～也知道了？ *How on earth did you find out?* | 这是～回事？ *What is going on here?* | "难"字～写？ *How does one write the character 难？*

谮（譖） zèn ㄗㄣˋ 说坏话诬陷别人 to slander：～言 *slanderous words* | ～害 *to harm by slander* | ～毁 *to slander*

ZENG ㄗㄥ

曾 zēng ㄗㄥ ❶重（chóng），用来指与自己中间隔着两代的亲属 great- (relative two generations removed from oneself)：～祖 *great-grandfather* | ～孙 *great-grandson* ❷ (ancient) same as "增" ❸姓 (surname) Zeng

⇨ see also céng on p.61

鄫 zēng ㄗㄥ 周代诸侯国名，故城在今山东省苍山县 Zeng (a state in the Zhou Dynasty; in today's Cangshan County, Shandong Province)

增 zēng ㄗㄥ 加多，添（㊥—加）to increase：为国～光 *bring glory to the nation* | ～产节约 *increase production and practise*

Z

thrift [增殖] 繁殖 to breed：～耕牛 *breed draught cattle* ㊉ 大量地增添 to greatly increase：～财富 *grow wealth exponentially*

憎 zēng ㄗㄥ 厌恶（wù），嫌，跟"爱"相对（㊉一恶、一恨）to hate (opposite of 爱)：爱～分明 *have clear likes and dislikes* | 面目可～ *appearance is repugnant*

缯（繒） zēng ㄗㄥ 古代丝织品的总称 (ancient) collective term for silk products

⇨ see also zèng on p.825

罾 zēng ㄗㄥ 一种用竹竿或木棍做支架的方形渔网 square fishing net (with a bamboo or wood frame)

矰 zēng ㄗㄥ 古代射鸟用的一种拴着丝绳的箭 (ancient) an arrow with a string attached (for shooting birds)

翻 zēng ㄗㄥ 高飞 to soar

综（綜） zèng ㄗㄥˋ 织布机上使经线交错着上下分开以便梭子通过的装置 heddle

⇨ see also zōng on p.884

锃（鋥） zèng ㄗㄥˋ 器物等经过擦磨或整理后闪光耀眼 burnished：～亮 *burnished* | ～光 *gleaming*

缯（繒） zèng ㄗㄥˋ 〈方 dialect〉捆，扎 to bind：把那根裂了的棍子～起来 *tie up that split pole*

⇨ see also zēng on p.825

赠（贈） zèng ㄗㄥˋ 把东西无代价地送给别人 to give (a gift)：～品 *free gift* | ～阅 *(of editor or publishing house) to give complimentary copy*

甑 zèng ㄗㄥˋ (formerly pronounced jìng) ❶ 古代蒸饭的一种瓦器。现在称蒸饭用的木制桶状物 (ancient) clay pot for steaming rice; (now) wooden bucket for steaming rice) ❷ 蒸馏或使物体分解用的器皿 (apparatus) distiller：曲颈～ *retort*

ZHA ㄓㄚ

扎（❷*紮、❷*紥） zhā ㄓㄚ ❶刺 to poke：～针 *give acupuncture* | ～花（刺绣）*to embroider* ❷驻扎 be stationed：～营 *to encamp* ❸钻 to plunge/dive into：～猛子（游泳时头朝下钻入水中）*to dive (when one is swimming)*

[扎煞]（-sha）same as "挓挲"

⇨ see also zā on p.815, zhá on p.826

吒 zhā ㄓㄚ ❶用于神话中的人名，如金吒、木吒 Zha (used in given names in Chinese mythology, e.g. Jinzha, Muzha) ❷ 用于地名 Zha (used in place names)：～祖村（在广西壮族自治区东兴）*Zhazucun (in Dongxing, Guangxi Zhuang Autonomous Region)*

⇨ see also zhà 咤 on p.828

挓 zhā ㄓㄚ [挓挲]（-sha）〈方 dialect〉张开 to spread：～着手 *with one's arms spread out*

咋 zhā ㄓㄚ [咋呼]（-hu）〈方 dialect〉1 吆喝 to shout at 2 炫耀 to brag

⇨ see also zǎ on p.815, zé on p.823

吒 zhā ㄓㄚ see 啁吒 (zhāo—) at 啁 on page 836

查(*查) zhā ㄓㄚ ❶ same as "楂 (zhā)" ❷ 姓 (surname) Zha

⇨ see also chá on p.63

揸(摣、**叡)** zhā ㄓㄚ ❶用手指撮东西 pick up with one's fingers ❷把手指伸张开 spread one's fingers

喳 zhā ㄓㄚ 鸟叫声 bird call：唧唧～～ *chattering; warbling*｜喜鹊～～叫。*The magpie is singing.*

⇨ see also chā on p.62

渣 zhā ㄓㄚ （一子、一儿）提出精华或汁液后剩下的东西（㊀一滓）dregs：豆腐～ *beancurd dregs; soy pulp* ㊁碎屑 broken bits：点心～儿 *broken pieces of snacks*

楂(樝)** zhā ㄓㄚ ［山楂］（*山查）落叶乔木，花白色，果实也叫山楂，深红色有白点，味酸，可以吃，也可入药 hawthorn

⇨ see also chá on p.63

奓 zhā ㄓㄚ 奓山，地名，在湖北省武汉 Zhashan (a place in Wuhan, Hubei Province)

⇨ see also zhà on p.828

劄 zhā ㄓㄚ (old) same as "扎❶❷"

⇨ see also zhá on p.827, zhá 札 on p.826

齇(皻)** zhā ㄓㄚ 鼻子上长的红色小疮，就是酒糟鼻上的红斑 rhinophyma

扎 zhá ㄓㄚˊ ［扎挣］（—zheng）〈方 dialect〉勉强支持 to struggle; to move with difficulty (because of weakness)

⇨ see also zā on p.815, zhā on p.825

札(❸△*劄、❸*剳) zhá ㄓㄚˊ ❶古代写字用的木片 (ancient) wooden strip (used for writing on) ［札记］读书时记下的要点和心得 study notes ❷信件（㊀信一、书一）correspondence：手～ *handwritten letter*｜来～ *your letter* ❸（一子）旧时的一种公文 (old) a kind of official document

⇨ 劄 see also zhā on p.826, zhá on p.827

轧(軋) zhá ㄓㄚˊ 义同"轧"（yà），用于轧辊、轧钢、轧钢机等 same in meaning as 轧 (yà), used in 轧辊，轧钢，轧钢机，etc.

⇨ see also gá on p.193, yà on p.747

闸(閘、*牐) zhá ㄓㄚˊ ❶拦住水流的建筑物，可以随时开关 sluice：～口 *sluice gate*｜河里有一道～。*There is a sluice in the river.* ❷把水截住 to block water ❸使机械减速或停止运行的装置，也指较大型的电源开关 brake; (also) large power switch：刹～ *to brake*｜自行车～ *bicycle brake*｜拉～限电 *electricity rationing*

炸(煠)** zhá ㄓㄚˊ 把食物放在煮沸的油或

水里弄熟 to deep-fry; to scald: ～糕 *a famous deep-fried pastry from Tianjin Metropolis* | ～鱼 *deep-fried fish* | 把菠菜～一～ *wilt the spinach*

⇨ see also zhà on p.827

铡(鍘) zhá ㄓㄚˊ ❶铡刀，一种切草或切其他东西的器具 guillotine cutter (for grass, etc.) ❷用铡刀切 to cut with a guillotine cutter: ～草 *cut grass with a guillotine cutter*

喋 zhá ㄓㄚˊ see 唼喋 (shà–) at 唼 on page 575

⇨ see also dié on p.138

劄 zhá ㄓㄚˊ ❶[目劄]中医指不停地眨眼的病，多见于儿童 (in traditional Chinese medicine) frequent blinking ❷ see 札 on page 826

⇨ see also zhā on p.826

拃 zhǎ ㄓㄚˇ ❶张开大拇指和中指量长度 measure with one's thumb and middle finger outstretched ❷张开大拇指和中指两端的距离 *zha* (distance between outstretched thumb and middle finger): 两～宽 *two* zha *wide*

苲 zhǎ ㄓㄚˇ 苲草，指金鱼藻等水生植物 general term for aquatic plants such as hornwort

砟 zhǎ ㄓㄚˇ (–子)某些坚硬成块的东西 lump: 煤～子 *lump of coal* | 炉灰～子 *solidified lump of ashes*

鲊(鮓) zhǎ ㄓㄚˇ 一种用盐和红曲(调制食品的材料)腌(yān)的鱼 fish pickled in salt and *hongqu (fermentum rubrum)*

眨 zhǎ ㄓㄚˇ (–巴)眼睛很快地一闭一开 to blink: 一～眼(时间极短)就看不见了 *vanished in a blink of an eye* | 杀人不～眼(形容凶残) *kill a person without batting an eye*

鲝(鮺) zhǎ ㄓㄚˇ ❶ same as "鲊" ❷[鲝草滩]地名，在四川省乐山 Zhacaotan (a place in Leshan, Sichuan Province)

乍 zhà ㄓㄚˋ ❶忽然 suddenly: ～冷～热 *sudden changes in temperature* ❷刚刚 just now: 新来～到 *recently arrived* ❸张开 to spread: ～翅 *spread wings*

诈(詐) zhà ㄓㄚˋ ❶假装 to feign: ～死 *feign death* | ～降(xiáng) *feign surrender* ❷使手段诓(kuāng)骗(㊥欺–、–骗) to cheat: ～财 *swindle money* | 你不必拿话～我。*You don't have to deceive me with words.*

柞 zhà ㄓㄚˋ [柞水]地名，在陕西省 Zhashui (a place in Shaanxi Province)

⇨ see also zuò on p.892

炸 zhà ㄓㄚˋ ❶突然破裂(㊥爆–) to explode: ～弹 *bomb* | 玻璃杯～了。*The glass shattered.* ❷用炸药、炸弹爆破 to blast: ～碉堡 *blast the pillbox* ❸发怒 be angry: 他一听就～了。*He became furious as soon as he heard it.* ❹因受惊而四处逃散 to escape in fear; to scamper: ～市 *escape the market in fear* | ～窝 *to scatter and flee in fear*

Z

⇨ see also zhá on p.826

痄 zhà ㄓㄚˋ ［痄腮］（－sai）流行性腮腺炎的俗称 informal name for mumps

蚱 zhà ㄓㄚˋ ［蚱蜢］（－měng）昆虫，像蝗虫，身体绿色或褐色，触角短，不能远飞，吃稻叶等 grasshopper

榨（❶*搾）zhà ㄓㄚˋ ❶用力压出物体里的汁液 to press (to extract liquid)：～油 *press oil* | 压～ *to squeeze; to oppress and exploit* | ～汁机 *juicer* ❷压出物体里汁液的器具 press (machine)：油～ *oil press* | 酒～ *wine press*

栅（*柵）zhà ㄓㄚˋ 栅栏，用竹、木、铁条等做成的阻拦物 fence：篱笆～ *hedge* | 木～ *wooden fence* | 铁～ *iron fence*

⇨ see also shān on p.577

奓 zhà ㄓㄚˋ 张开 to spread：头发～着 *hair is spread out* | 这件衣服下摆太～了。*The hem of this piece of clothing is too wide.*

⇨ see also zhā on p.826

砟 zhà ㄓㄚˋ ［大水砟］地名，在甘肃省景泰 Dashuizha (a place in Jingtai, Gansu Province)

咤（△*吒）zhà ㄓㄚˋ 生气时对人大声嚷 shout angrily at sb

⇨ 吒 see also zhā on p.825

溠 zhà ㄓㄚˋ 溠水，水名，在湖北省随州 Zhashui River (in Suizhou, Hubei Province)

蜡（**䄍）zhà ㄓㄚˋ 古代年终的一种祭祀名 year-end religious sacrifice in ancient times

⇨ see also là on p.374

霅 zhà ㄓㄚˋ 霅溪，水名，在浙江省 Zhaxi River (in Zhejiang Province)

ZHAI ㄓㄞ

侧（側）zhāi ㄓㄞ 〈方 dialect〉倾斜 to incline［侧棱］（－leng）向一边倾斜 to lean sideways：～着身子睡觉 *sleep on one's side*［侧歪］（－wai）倾斜 inclined：车在山坡上～着走。*The vehicle is tipping sideways as it ascends the slope.*

⇨ see also cè on p.60, zè on p.824

斋（齋）zhāi ㄓㄞ ❶书房或校舍 study; school house：书～ *a study* | 第一～ *Number One Study* ❷祭祀前整洁身心，以示虔诚 purify oneself (before a religious sacrifice)：～戒 *(old) abstinence before a religious event* ㊀佛教、道教等教徒吃的素食 vegetarian diet (of Buddhists, Taoists, etc.)：吃～ *eat a vegetarian diet* ❸舍饭给僧人 give food (to monks)：～僧 *give food to monks*

摘 zhāi ㄓㄞ ❶采下，拿下 to pluck：～瓜 *pluck a gourd* | ～梨 *pluck a pear* | ～帽子 *remove one's hat* ❷选取 to select：～要 *to summarise; summary* | ～记 *to summarise; to quote*［指摘］指出缺点 to censure ❸临时借 borrow temporarily：东～西借 *borrow from multiple sources*

宅 zhái ㄓㄞˊ 住所 residence：住～ *residence* | 深～大院 *cavernous mansions and extensive gardens*

择(擇) zhái ㄓㄞˊ 义同"择"（zé），用于口语 (spoken) same in meaning as 择 (zé)：～菜 *discard unwanted parts of vegetables* | ～席（换个地方就睡不安稳）*sleep badly in an unfamiliar place*

⇨ see also zé on p.823

翟 zhái ㄓㄞˊ 姓 (surname) Zhai

⇨ see also dí on p.128

窄 zhǎi ㄓㄞˇ ❶狭，不宽，宽度小，跟"宽"相对（㊀—狭、狭—）narrow (opposite of 宽)：路太～。*The road is too narrow.* | 地方太～，放不下双人床。*The space is too confined to accommodate a double bed.* ㊁气量小，心胸不开阔 petty-minded：他的心眼儿太～。*He is too petty-minded.* ❷生活不宽裕 poor：以前的日子很～，现在可好了。*One was poor in the past, but all is well now.*

鉙 zhǎi ㄓㄞˇ（一儿）〈方 dialect〉器物残缺损坏的痕迹，水果伤损的痕迹 damage; bruise (on fruit)：碗上有块～儿。*There is a chip on the bowl.* | 苹果没～儿。*The apple is not bruised.*

豸 zhài ㄓㄞˋ ［冠豸山］（guàn — —）山名，在福建省连城 Guanzhaishan Mountain (in Liancheng, Fujian Province)

⇨ see also zhì on p.857

债(債) zhài ㄓㄞˋ 所欠下的钱财 debt：还～ *repay debt* | 公～ *government bond*

砦 zhài ㄓㄞˋ ❶ see 寨 on page 829 ❷姓 (surname) Zhai

寨(❶–❸△*砦) zhài ㄓㄞˋ ❶防守用的栅栏 stockade［鹿寨］军事上常用的一种障碍物，古代多用削尖的竹木，现多用铁蒺藜等做成 abattis ❷旧时军营 (old) military camp：安营扎～ *set up a military camp* ❸村子 village：山～ *fortified mountain village* | 村村～～ *every village* ❹姓 (surname) Zhai

摖 zhài ㄓㄞˋ 〈方 dialect〉缝纫方法，把衣服上附加的物件缝上 to sew onto clothing：～纽扣儿 *sew on a button* | ～花边 *sew a piece of lace on clothing*

瘵 zhài ㄓㄞˋ 病，多指痨病 illness (often phthisis)

ZHAN ㄓㄢ

占 zhān ㄓㄢ 古代用龟甲、蓍（shī）草等，后世用铜钱或牙牌等判断吉凶 to divine (using tortoise shells, yarrow, etc. in ancient times and coins, dominoes, etc. later)：～卦 *divine using the Eight Trigrams* | ～课 *to divine (by tossing coins, counting Heavenly Stems and Earthly Branches with one's fingers, etc.)*

⇨ see also zhàn on p.831

沾(❶❷*霑) zhān ㄓㄢ ❶浸湿 to wet; to soak：泪流～襟 *weep copious tears* | 汗出～背 *sweat soaks one's back* ❷因接触而附着（zhuó）

Z

上 to be stained/soiled with：～水 *wet with water*｜～了一身泥 *splattered one's whole body with mud* ㊀ ①染上 to acquire：～染了坏习气 *acquired bad habits* ②凭借某种关系而得到好处 to benefit from association：～光 *benefit from association* ❸稍微碰上或接触上 to touch slightly：～边儿 *to touch slightly*｜脚不～地 *to walk quickly*

［沾沾自喜］形容自己觉得很好而得意的样子 pleased with oneself

毡（氈、*氊）zhān ㄓㄢ （一子）用兽毛砑（yà）成的片状物，可做防寒用品和工业上的垫衬材料 felt：炕～ *felt lining for* kang｜～靴 *felt boots*｜油毛～ *linoleum*

粘 zhān ㄓㄢ ❶黏的东西互相连接或附着在别的东西上 to stick：几块糖都～在一起了。*A few pieces of candy are stuck together.*｜不～锅 *non-stick frying pan* ❷用胶水或糨糊等把一种东西胶合在另一种东西上 to glue：～贴 *to stick*｜～上信封 *seal the envelope*

⇨ see also nián on p.477

栴 zhān ㄓㄢ ［栴檀］古书上指檀香 sandalwood (in ancient Chinese texts)

旃 zhān ㄓㄢ ❶文言助词，等于"之焉"两字的合音 auxiliary word in classical Chinese, fusion of 之 and 焉：勉～！*Courage!* ❷ (ancient) same as "毡"

詹 zhān ㄓㄢ 姓 (surname) Zhan

谵（譫）zhān ㄓㄢ 多说话。特指病中说胡话 to rave; (specifically) to be delirious：～语 *to rave; raving*｜～妄 *delirium*

瞻 zhān ㄓㄢ 往上或往前看 look up; look forward：～仰 *look at with reverence*｜高～远瞩 *look far ahead and aim high*

饘（饘、**飦）zhān ㄓㄢ 稠粥 thick porridge

邅 zhān ㄓㄢ ❶难走 hard to walk ❷转，改变方向 to turn direction：～彼南道兮！*I make a turn and go on the road that leads to the south!*

鹯（鸇）zhān ㄓㄢ 古书中说的一种猛禽，似鹞（yào）鹰 a kind of bird of prey in ancient Chinese texts, similar to a hen harrier

鳣（鱣）zhān ㄓㄢ 古书上指鳇（huáng）鱼 kaluga (in ancient Chinese texts)

〈古 ancient〉also same as 鳝 (shàn)

斩（斬）zhǎn ㄓㄢˇ 砍断 to cut off：～首 *to decapitate*｜～草除根 *to root out thoroughly*｜～钉截铁 *resolute and decisive*

崭（嶄、*嶃）zhǎn ㄓㄢˇ ❶高峻，突出 high; prominent：～露头角 *(often of teenagers) to show one's talent prominently* ❷非常，极 very：～新 *brand new*

𫇭（𫇭）zhǎn ㄓㄢˇ 〈方 dialect〉眼皮开合，眨眼 to

blink

飐(颭) zhǎn ㄓㄢˇ 风吹物体使颤动 to quiver (because of the wind)：风～竹枝。*The wind causes the bamboo branches to quiver.*

盏(盞、❶*琖、*醆) zhǎn ㄓㄢˇ ❶小杯子 small cup：酒～ *wine cup*｜茶～ *tea cup* ❷量词，用于灯 measure word for lamps：一～灯 *a lamp*

展 zhǎn ㄓㄢˇ ❶张开，舒张开 to spread：～翅 *spread wings*｜～望 *look into the distance; look into the future*｜～开 *to unfold; to launch*｜舒～ *to stretch; comfortable* [展览] 把物品陈列起来让人参观 to exhibit ❷施展 give free play to：一筹莫～ *at the end of one's tether* ❸放宽 to ease：～缓 *to postpone; to extend (a deadline)*｜～期 *extend a time limit*｜～限 *extend a deadline*

搌 zhǎn ㄓㄢˇ 轻轻地擦抹或按压，以吸去液体 to dab：～布 *dishcloth*｜用药棉花～一～ *dab with absorbent cotton*

辗(輾) zhǎn ㄓㄢˇ [辗转] (*展转)(－zhuǎn) 1 身体翻来覆去地来回转动 to toss and turn：～反侧 *toss about (in bed)* 2 经过许多人或许多地方 pass through many people/places：～传说 *disseminate by word of mouth*｜～于大半个中国 *travel over most of China*

黵 zhǎn ㄓㄢˇ 弄脏，染上污点 to stain：墨水把纸～了。*The ink stained the paper.*｜这种布颜色暗，禁(jīn)～(脏了不容易看出来)。*Stains are not easily visible on such dark coloured fabrics.*

占(*佔) zhàn ㄓㄢˋ ❶据有，用强力取得(㊀－据) to occupy：～领 *to capture*｜强～ *to forcibly occupy*｜攻～ *to attack and occupy* ❷处于某种地位或情势 to occupy (a certain status or situation)：～上风 *have an advantage*｜～优势 *be at an advantage*｜～多数 *be in the majority*

⇨ see also zhān on p.829

战(戰) zhàn ㄓㄢˋ ❶战争，通常指打仗(㊀－斗) war; battle; to fight (a war or battle)：宣～ *declare war*｜～时 *wartime*｜～役 *military campaign*｜持久～ *protracted warfare*｜作～ *fight a war*｜百～百胜 *victorious in every battle* [战略] 1 指导战争全局的计划和策略 military strategy 2 比喻决定全局的策略 strategy [战术] 进行战斗的原则和方法 military tactic ㊉解决局部问题的方法 tactic [战国] 我国历史上的一个时代(公元前475—公元前221年) Warring States Period (475BCE—221 BCE) ❷发抖 to tremble：～栗(害怕发抖) *tremble with fear*｜打冷～ *to shiver*｜寒～ *shiver*

站 zhàn ㄓㄢˋ ❶直立 to stand：～岗 *be on sentry duty*｜中国人民～起来了。*The people of China have stood up.* ❷停 to stop：不怕慢，就怕～ *being slow is better than stopping* ❸为乘客

Z

上下或货物装卸而设的停车的地方 stop; station (for passengers or cargo)：车～ *bus/train stop* | 起点～ *starting station/stop* ❹ 分支办事处 branch office; station：工作～ *work station (for a specific purpose)* | 保健～ *health station*

栈(棧) zhàn ㄓㄢˋ ❶ 储存货物或供旅客住宿的房屋 warehouse; inn：货～ *warehouse* | 客～ *inn* ❷ 养牲畜的竹木棚或栅栏 pen (for animals)：马～ *horse pen*

[栈道] 在悬崖峭壁上凿孔架木桩，铺上木板而成的道路 trestle road along cliff

僝 zhàn ㄓㄢˋ 齐整 tidy

湛 zhàn ㄓㄢˋ ❶深 deep：精～的演技 *superb acting* ❷清澈 clear：清～ *clear*

绽(綻) zhàn ㄓㄢˋ 裂开 to split：破～ *burst seam; flaw* | 鞋开～了。*The shoe has burst at the seams.*

颤(顫) zhàn ㄓㄢˋ same as "战❷"

⇨ see also chàn on p.68

蘸 zhàn ㄓㄢˋ 在汁液、粉末或糊状物里沾一下就拿出来 to dip (in liquid, powder, or paste)：～墨水 *dip in ink* | ～酱 *dip in sauce*

ZHANG ㄓㄤ

张(張) zhāng ㄓㄤ ❶ 展开，打开 to open：～嘴 *open one's mouth* | ～弓搭箭 *nock an arrow and draw one's bow* | 纲举目～ *once a net is lifted, all its meshes are open; (figurative) when the key issue is grasped, everything else falls into place; (of articles) well-organized* | ～牙舞爪 *to act aggressively* ㊀①扩大，夸大 to exaggerate：虚～声势 *make a false display of strength* | ～大其词 *to exaggerate* ②放纵，无拘束 undisciplined; unrestrained：乖～ *eccentric and unreasonable* | 嚣(xiāo)～ *rampant* [开张] 开始营业 (of businesses) to open ❷铺排陈设 to decorate：～灯结彩 *decorate with lanterns and coloured streamers; (figurative) festive and uproarious* ❸看，望(㊁一望) to look：东～西望 *look in all directions* ❹ 量词 measure word ①用于纸、皮子、床、桌子等 used for paper, leather, beds, tables, etc.：一～画 *a painting* | 两～纸 *two pieces of paper* | 一～桌子 *a table* ②用于嘴、脸 used for mouths, faces, etc.：一～嘴 *a mouth* ③用于弓 used for archery bows：一～弓 *a bow* ❺星宿名，二十八宿之一 *zhang* (one of the twenty-eight constellations in ancient Chinese astronomy)

章 zhāng ㄓㄤ ❶诗歌文辞的段落 chapter; stanza：乐(yuè)～ *(in music) movement* | 篇～ *sections and chapters; (generally) articles* | 第一～ *Chapter One* ❷奏章，臣子呈给皇帝的意见书 memorial (submitted to the throne) ❸ 章程，法规 regulation: 简～ *general regulations*| 党～ *party constitution* | 规～制度 *rules and regulations* ㊀ ① 条理 order; orderliness: 杂乱无～ *messy* ②条目 clause; sub-clause: 约法三～ *make a compact of three legal provisions; (generally) draw up a simple agreement* ❹ 戳记 stamp; mark: 图～ *seal; stamp* | 盖～ *put one's seal on sth* ❺佩带在身上的标志 badge: 徽～ *badge; insignia* | 袖～ *arm badge*

鄣 zhāng ㄓㄤ 周代诸侯国名，在今山东省东平东 Zhang (a state in the Zhou Dynasty, in the east of today's Dongping, Shandong Province)

獐(*麞) zhāng ㄓㄤ 哺乳动物，又叫牙獐，像鹿而小，头上无角。雄的犬齿发达，露出嘴外 Chinese water deer (also called 牙獐)

彰 zhāng ㄓㄤ ❶明显，显著 obvious: 欲盖弥～ *the more one tries to hide sth, the more it is revealed* | 相得益～ *complement each other; bringing out each other's talents* ❷表彰 to commend: ～善瘅(dàn)恶 *commend the good and abhor the evil*

漳 zhāng ㄓㄤ 漳河，发源于山西省，流至河北省入卫河 Zhanghe River (originates in Shanxi Province and flows into the Weihe River in Hebei Province)

嫜 zhāng ㄓㄤ 丈夫的父亲 father-in-law (one's husband's father) [姑嫜] 古时女子称丈夫的母亲和父亲 (old) parents-in-law (one's husband's parents)

璋 zhāng ㄓㄤ 一种玉器，形状像半个圭 a trapezoid-shaped jade object

樟 zhāng ㄓㄤ 樟树，常绿乔木，树干高大，木质坚硬细致，有香味，做成箱柜，可以防蠹虫 camphor tree

暲 zhāng ㄓㄤ 明亮 bright

蟑 zhāng ㄓㄤ [蟑螂](－láng) 昆虫，又叫蜚蠊(fěilián)，黑褐色，有光泽，常咬坏衣物、污染食物，能发臭气 cockroach (also called 蜚蠊 fěilián)

长(長) zhǎng ㄓㄤˇ ❶生，发育 to grow: ～疮 *develop a sore* | 庄稼～得很旺。*The crops are growing very well.* ❷增加 to increase: ～见识 *increase one's knowledge and experience*| 增～ *to increase* ❸排行中第一的 eldest: ～兄 *eldest brother* | ～孙 *eldest grandson* [长子] 1 排行第一的儿子 eldest son 2 地名，在山西省 Zhangzi (a place in Shanxi Province) ❹辈分高或年纪大的 senior; elderly: ～者 *elderly person; venerable old person* | ～辈 *elder member of a family* 也指辈分高或年纪大的人 (also) senior/elderly person: 师～ *teachers* 敬辞 polite speech: 学～ *fellow student (often a senior schoolmate)* ❺主持人，机关、团体等单位的负责人 head (of an organization): 部～ *minister* | 校～ *school principal*

⇨ see also cháng on p.69

Z

涨(漲) zhǎng ㄓㄤˇ ❶水量增加，水面高起来 (of water level) to rise：水～船高。*A rising tide lifts all boats.* | 河里～水了。*The river has risen.* ❷价格提高 (of prices) to rise：～钱 *to rise in price; to rise in pay* | ～价 *rise in price*

⇨ see also zhàng on p.835

仉 zhǎng ㄓㄤˇ 姓 (surname) Zhang

掌 zhǎng ㄓㄤˇ ❶巴掌，手心，握拳时指尖触着的一面 palm (of one's hand)：鼓～ *clap one's hands* ㉚脚的底面 sole (of one's foot)：脚～ *sole of one's foot* | 熊～ *bear's paw* ❷用巴掌打 slap with one's hand：～嘴 *slap sb's face* ❸把握，主持，主管 to hold; to manage：～印 *be in power* | ～舵 *take the helm* | ～权 *wield power* | ～管 *be in charge of* [掌故] 关于古代人物、典章、制度等的故事 anecdote (relating to ancient figures, institutions, systems, etc.) [掌握] 把握，拿稳 to possess; to grasp：～政策 *have a good grasp on policy* | ～原则 *adhere to principles* ❹(－儿) 鞋底前后钉或缀上的皮子等 half sole (of a shoe)：钉两块～儿 *nail in two half soles* ❺马蹄铁，钉在马、驴、骡子等蹄子底下的铁 horseshoe：马～ *horseshoe* ❻ same as "礃"

礃 zhǎng ㄓㄤˇ [礃子] 煤矿里采煤或隧道工程中掘进的工作面。也作"掌子" (in mining or tunnelling) face (also written as 掌子)

丈 zhàng ㄓㄤˋ ❶市制长度单位，1丈是10尺，约合3.33米 a traditional Chinese unit for measuring length, equal to 3.33 metres. There are 10 尺 in 1 丈. ❷测量长度、面积 to measure length and area：～量 *measure land area* | ～地 *measure the land* ❸对成年或老年男子的尊称 Sir (honorific speech)：老～ *Old Sir* [丈夫] 1 成年男子的通称 man 2 (－fu) 妇女的配偶，跟"妻子"相对 husband (opposite of 妻子) [丈人] 1 旧称老年男子 (old) elderly man 2 (－ren) 称妻子的父亲 father-in-law (one's wife's father)

仗 zhàng ㄓㄤˋ ❶古代兵器的总称 (ancient) weapon：兵～ *weapon* | 仪～ *ceremonial weapon* | 明火执～ *blatant robbery* ㉝战争 war：打～ *fight a war* | 胜～ *victory in battle* | 败～ *defeat in battle* ❷凭借，依靠 (㉛倚－、－恃) to rely on：～着大家的力量 *with everybody's efforts* | ～势欺人 *use one's or sb else's power to bully others* ❸拿着 (兵器) to carry (weapons)：～剑 *carry a sword*

杖 zhàng ㄓㄤˋ ❶拐杖，扶着走路的棍子 walking stick：手～ *walking stick* | 扶～而行 *walk with a stick* ❷泛指棍棒 (generally) stick：擀面～ *rolling pin*

帐(帳) zhàng ㄓㄤˋ ❶(－子) 用布或其他材料做成的帷幕 curtain：蚊～ *mosquito net* | 圆顶～子 *round-top bed canopy* | 营～ *tent* | ～篷 *tent* ❷ same as "账"

账(賬) zhàng ㄓㄤˋ ❶关于银钱财物出入的记载 accounts：记～ *keep accounts; charge sth to sb's account* | 流水～ *single-entry bookkeeping account* ❷指记载银钱财物出入的本子或单子 accounts journal：一本～ *a book of accounts* | 一篇～ *a page of accounts* ❸债务 debt：欠～ *be in debt* | 不认～（喻不承认自己做的事）*refuse to admit what one has done*

胀(脹) zhàng ㄓㄤˋ ❶膨胀，体积变大 to expand：热～冷缩 *expand when hot and contract when cold* ❷身体内壁受到压迫而产生不舒服的感觉 bloating：肚子～ *bloated stomach* | 肿～ *swelling*

涨(漲) zhàng ㄓㄤˋ ❶体积增大 to expand：豆子泡～了。*The beans have expanded after being soaked.* ❷弥漫 to cover：烟尘～天 *smoke and dust cover the sky* ❸多出来 additional：～出十块钱 *an extra ten* yuan ❹头部充血 (of one's head) to fill with blood：头昏脑～ *one's head swims* | 他气得～红了脸。*He was so angry that his face turned red.*

⇨ see also zhǎng on p.834

障 zhàng ㄓㄤˋ ❶阻隔 to obstruct［障碍］阻挡进行的事物 obstacle：扫除～ *remove an obstacle* ❷用作遮蔽、防卫的东西 barrier：风～ *wind barrier* | 屏～ *barrier*

嶂 zhàng ㄓㄤˋ 形势高险像屏障的山峰 barrier-like mountain：层峦叠～ *extensive range of tall mountains*

幛 zhàng ㄓㄤˋ （－子）上面题有词句的整幅绸布，用作庆贺或吊唁的礼物 silk banner (with writing on it, given as a gift of congratulation or condolence)

瘴 zhàng ㄓㄤˋ 瘴气，热带山林中的湿热空气 hot and humid air (in tropical mountains and forests)

ZHAO ㄓㄠ

钊(釗) zhāo ㄓㄠ 勉励。多用于人名 to encourage (often used in given names)

招 zhāo ㄓㄠ ❶打手势叫人来或致意 to beckon：用手一～他就来了。*He came as soon as one beckoned him over.* | ～之即来 *come as soon as one is beckoned* | ～手示意 *wave one's hand in acknowledgment*［招待］应接宾客 to greet (guests)［招呼］(－hu) 1 召唤 to summon：有人～你。*Someone is calling for you.* 2 照料，扶助 to take care of：～老人 *take care of the elderly* ❷用公开的方式使人来 to attract (to sth)：～集 *assemble* | ～生 *enroll new students* | ～兵买马 *recruit troops* | ～商引资 *attract business and investment* 引①惹起 to provoke：～事 *bring trouble on oneself* | ～笑 *provoke laughter* | 别～他。*Don't provoke him.* ②引来 to attract：～蚂蚁 *attract ants* ❸承认自己的罪状 to confess：不打自～ *confess voluntarily; inadvertently reveal one's*

Z

wrongdoing ❹武术上的动作 move (in *wushu*) ⑩计策，办法 plan; method：花～儿 *flourish; trick*｜绝～儿 *unique skill; surprise move*

昭 zhāo ㄓㄠ ❶明显，显著 obvious：罪恶～彰 *evil is manifestly obvious*｜～然若揭 *abundantly clear* ❷表明，显示 to indicate：以～信守 *in witness whereof*［昭昭］1 光明，明亮 bright：日月～ *sun and moon are bright* 2 明白 to understand：使人～ *make others understand*

铝（鉊） zhāo ㄓㄠ 镰刀 sickle

啁 zhāo ㄓㄠ ［啁哳］［嘲哳］（-zhā）形容声音杂乱细碎 a discordant and disjointed sound

⇨ see also zhōu on p.863

着 zhāo ㄓㄠ ❶（-儿）下棋时下一子或走一步叫一着 move (in chess) ⑩计策，办法 plan：你出个高～儿。*Could you give me a brilliant plan?*｜我没～儿了。*I'm at my wit's end.* ❷〈方 dialect〉放，搁进去 to put in：～点儿盐 *add a little salt* ❸〈方 dialect〉用于应答，表示同意 yes (when indicating agreement)：～，你说得真对。*Yes, what you said is so right.*

⇨ see also zháo on p.836, zhe on p.841, zhuó on p.878

朝 zhāo ㄓㄠ 早晨 morning：只争～夕 *seize what little time one has*｜～思暮想 *think about sb/sth day and night* ⑪日，天 day：今～ *today*［朝气］精神振作、努力进取的气概 full of vigour：～蓬勃 *vigorous*

⇨ see also cháo on p.71

嘲 zhāo ㄓㄠ ［嘲哳］（-zhā）same as "啁哳"

⇨ see also cháo on p.72

着 zháo ㄓㄠ ❶接触，挨上 to touch：上不～天，下不～地 *touch neither the sky nor the earth; (figurative) be in a dilemma* ❷感受，受到 to feel：～慌 *be alarmed*｜～凉 *catch a cold*｜～急 *be anxious* ❸燃烧，也指灯发光 to ignite; (of a light) to turn on：～火 *catch fire*｜柴火～了。*The firewood has started burning.*｜天黑了，路灯都～了。*It is dark and all the street lights are on.* ❹入睡，睡着 to fall asleep：躺下就～了 *fall asleep as soon as one lies down* ❺用在动词后表示达到目的或有结果 used after a verb to indicate achievement of a goal or result：猜～了 *guessed correctly*｜打～了 *hit the target*

⇨ see also zhāo on p.836, zhe on p.841, zhuó on p.878

爪 zhǎo ㄓㄠ ❶指甲或趾甲 fingernail; toenail：手～ *fingernail* ❷鸟兽的脚趾 claw; paw：鹰～ *eagle's talons*［爪牙］⑩党羽，狗腿子 lackey

⇨ see also zhuǎ on p.871

找 zhǎo ㄓㄠ ❶寻求，想要得到或见到 to look for; to try to find：～东西 *look for sth*｜～事做 *seek job*｜丢了不好～ *hard to find if lost*｜～麻烦 *look for trouble*｜～人 *look for sb*｜～经理 *ask to see the manager* ❷把超出的部分

退回或把不足的部分补足 to give change：～钱 *give change* | ～零 *give small change* | ～齐 *make up a shortfall*

沼 zhǎo ㄓㄠˇ 水池子（㊀池一）pond［沼气］有机物在地下隔绝空气的条件下分解而产生的气体，可以燃烧。多产生于池沼，也产生于煤矿井、石油井中。主要成分是甲烷 marsh gas (mainly methane)［沼泽］水草茂密的泥泞地带 swamp

召 zhào ㄓㄠˋ ❶呼唤，招呼 to call：号～ *call on* | ～见 *summon (a subordinate)* | ～唤 *summon* | ～集 *call together* | ～开会议 *call a meeting* ❷姓 (surname) Zhao

⇨ see also shào on p.584

诏（詔） zhào ㄓㄠˋ ❶告诉 to tell：～示 *instruct* ❷皇帝所发的命令 order issued by an emperor：～书 *imperial decree* | ～令 *imperial order*

照（❶*炤） zhào ㄓㄠˋ ❶光线射在物体上 (of light) to shine on：拿灯～一～。*Shine on it with a lamp.* | 阳光普～。*The sun shines everywhere.* ❷对着镜子或其他反光的东西看自己或其他人物的影像 to look (in mirrors or reflective surfaces)：～镜子 *look in a mirror* ❸照相，摄影 to take (a photograph)：天安门前～张相 *take a photograph in front of Tian'anmen* | 拍～ *take a photograph* ❹画像或相片 portrait (painting or photograph)：小～ *small portrait* ❺照管，看顾 to take care of：～应 *look after*［照料］关心，料理 take care of：病人需要～。*Patients need taking care of.* ❻查对，对比 to verify：比～ *compare* | 对～ *contrast* | 参～ *refer to as a modal* ❼凭证 certificate：护～ *passport* | 牌～ *licence* ❽知晓 to know：心～不宣 *have a tacit understanding* ❾通告，通知 to notify：知～ *to inform*［关照］1 关心照顾 look after 2 口头通知 to tell：请～他一声，我明天来。*Please tell him I'll come tomorrow.*［照会］外交上用以表明立场、达成协议或通知事项的公文 diplomatic note ❿介词 preposition ①对着，向着 at; in; towards：～敌人开枪 *shoot at the enemy* | ～着这个方向走 *walk in this direction* ②按照，依照 according to：～计划执行 *execute according to plan* | ～他的意思办。*Do it according to his wishes.* ⓫副词，表示按原样或某种标准做 (adverb) used to indicate doing sth according to an original model or a certain standard：～抄 *copy word for word; imitate wholesale* | ～办 *act accordingly*

兆 zhào ㄓㄠˋ ❶古代占验吉凶时灼龟甲所成的裂纹（迷信）(ancient superstition) cracks on heated tortoise shells used in divination ❷预兆 augury：征～ *omen* | 佳～ *good omen* ❸预示 to forecast：瑞雪～丰年。*Auspicious snow forecasts a year of abundance.* ❹数目名 number ①百万 one million ②古代指万亿 (ancient) trillion ❺法定计量单位

Z

中十进倍数单位词头之一，表示10^6，符号M。(unit of measurement) mega (M)

旐 zhào ㄓㄠˋ 古代的一种旗子 (ancient) a type of flag

鮡(鮡) zhào ㄓㄠˋ 鱼名，无鳞，头部扁平，种类很多，有的种类胸部前方有吸盘，生活在溪水中 sisorid catfish

赵(趙) zhào ㄓㄠˋ 战国国名，在今河北省南部和山西省中部、北部一带 Zhao (a state in the Warring States Period, in the south of today's Hebei Province and the centre and north of today's Shanxi Province)

笊 zhào ㄓㄠˋ ［笊篱］(—li) 用竹篾、柳条、金属丝等编成的一种用具，可以在汤水里捞东西 strainer (made of bamboo, wicker or wire)

棹(*櫂) zhào ㄓㄠˋ 划船的一种工具，形状和桨差不多 oar 引①船 boat ②〈方 dialect〉划(船) to row (a boat)

罩 zhào ㄓㄠˋ ❶(—子、—儿)覆盖物体的东西 cover：口～ *face mask* | 灯～子 *lampshade* ❷扣盖，覆盖，套上 to cover：把菜～起来 *cover the vegetables* | 外面～了件白大褂儿 *wear a lab coat over one's other clothing* ❸穿在其他衣服外面的单衣 unlined garment worn over clothing：外～ *outer garment* | ～衣 *dust coat* | 袍～儿 *robe* ❹养鸡用的竹笼子 bamboo chicken basket ❺捕鱼用的竹器，圆筒形，无顶无底，下略大，上略小 bamboo fish trap

肇(肈)** zhào ㄓㄠˋ ❶开始 to start：～端 *beginning* ❷发生 to cause sth to happen：～祸(闯祸) *cause trouble* | ～事 *create a disturbance*

曌 zhào ㄓㄠˋ 同"照"。唐代女皇帝武则天为自己名字选用的新造字 (same as 照) a character coined by Empress Regnant Wu Zetian of the Tang Dynasty as her personal name

ZHE ㄓㄜ

折 zhē ㄓㄜ 翻转，倒腾 to roll; to turn upside down：～跟头 *do cartwheels* | 用两个碗把开水～一～就凉了。*Pour boiling water from one bowl to the other several times and it will cool down.*

⇨ see also shé on p.585, zhé on p.838

蜇 zhē ㄓㄜ ❶有毒腺的虫子刺人或牲畜 to sting：被蝎子～了 *stung by a scorpion* ❷某些东西刺激皮肤或器官使感觉不适 to irritate (the skin or organs)：切洋葱～眼睛 *cutting onions irritates the eyes*

⇨ see also zhé on p.839

遮 zhē ㄓㄜ 掩盖，掩蔽，挡 to cover; to shield：～丑 *hide one's shame; cover up one's defects* | ～人耳目 *hide the truth from others* | 乌云～不住太阳的光辉。*Dark clouds cannot block the radiance of the sun.*

折(❹❺△摺) zhé ㄓㄜˊ ❶断，弄断 to

break：骨～ *bone fracture* | 禁止攀～花木。*Climbing trees and plucking flowers are prohibited.* ㊥幼年死亡 to die in infancy：夭～ *die young; (figurative) come to a premature end* [折磨]（－mó）使在肉体或精神上受痛苦 to torment：受尽～ *suffer a great deal of torment* ❷损失 to lose：损兵～将 *suffer heavy casualties in battle* ❸弯转，屈曲 to bend：～腰 *to bow; debase oneself* | 转～ *turn in the course of events; transition* ㊀返转，回转 to turn back：走到半路又～回来了 *turned back after going halfway* [折中]（*折衷）对不同意见采取调和态度 to compromise ❹叠，折叠 to fold：～衣服 *fold clothes* | ～尺 *folding ruler* ❺（－子、－儿）用纸折叠起来的本子 book made of folded paper：存～ *passbook; deposit book* ❻杂剧一本分四折，一折相当于现代戏曲的一场 act (a section of a *zaju* play, which contains four acts) ❼心服 to be convinced：～服 *convince; be convinced* | 心～ *be convinced; admire* ❽折扣，按成数减少 discount：打～ *offer a discount* | 九～ *10% discount* ❾抵作，对换，以此代彼 to exchange：～账 *pay a debt in kind* | ～变（变卖）*sell off* ❿汉字的一种笔形（㇕）(in a Chinese character) turning stroke："买"字的第一笔是～。*The first stroke of the character 买 is a turning stroke.*

⇨ see also shé on p.585, zhē on p.838

哲（△*喆）zhé ㄓㄜˊ ❶有智慧 wise：～人 *sage* [哲学]社会意识形态之一，它研究自然界、社会和思维的普遍规律，是关于自然知识和社会知识的概括和总结，是关于世界观的理论 philosophy ❷聪明有智慧的人 wise person：先～ *great thinker of the past*

晢（**晣）zhé ㄓㄜˊ 明亮 bright

蜇 zhé ㄓㄜˊ 海蜇，腔肠动物，外形像张开的伞，生活在海里 flame jellyfish

⇨ see also zhē on p.838

篎 zhé ㄓㄜˊ 〈方 dialect〉（－子）一种粗的竹席 a type of coarse bamboo mat

辄（輒、*輙）zhé ㄓㄜˊ 总是，就 always; then：每至此，～觉心旷神怡。*I always feel relaxed and happy whenever I come here.* | 所言～听 *always heed sb's advice* | 动～得咎 *be blamed for every action*

喆 zhé ㄓㄜˊ ❶ see 哲 on page 839 ❷用于人名 used in given names

蛰（蟄）zhé ㄓㄜˊ 动物冬眠，藏起来不食不动 to hibernate：～伏 *hibernate; (figurative) hide from view* | 入～ *hibernate* | ～虫 *hibernating insect*

詟（讋）zhé ㄓㄜˊ 〈古 ancient〉恐惧 fear

谪（謫、*讁）zhé ㄓㄜˊ ❶谴责，责罚 to reprimand ❷封建时代特指贬

Z

官 (old) to demote (a government official)

摺 zhé ㄓㄜˊ see 折 (zhé) on page 838 (摺 has been simplified to 折, though 摺 is still used when there is a possibility of confusion.)

磔 zhé ㄓㄜˊ ❶古代分裂肢体的酷刑 quartering (ancient punishment) ❷汉字的一种笔形，即捺(nà) (in a Chinese character) right falling stroke (same as 捺 nà)

辙(轍) zhé ㄓㄜˊ 车辙，车轮轧的痕迹 rut 引 ①(一儿)车辆行走的一定路线 route：戗(qiāng)～儿(逆着规定的路向) *go against a prescribed direction* | 顺～儿 *follow a prescribed direction* ②歌词、戏曲、杂曲所押的韵 rhyme (in song lyrics, Chinese opera and *zaqu*)：合～ *to rhyme* | 十三～ *the Thirteen Rhymes (rhyming patterns in traditional storytelling and singing in northern China)* ③〈方 dialect〉办法 way; means：没～了 *can't find any way out*

者 zhě ㄓㄜˇ ❶助词，用在形容词、动词或词组后，指人或事物 (auxiliary word) used after adjectives, verbs, or phrases to indicate a person or thing：学～ *scholar* | 读～ *reader* | 作～ *author* | 强～ *the strong* | 符合标准～ *those who meet standards* ❷助词，表示语气停顿 (auxiliary word) used to indicate a pause：陈胜～，阳城人也。*Chen Sheng was a native of Yangcheng.* | 云～，水汽蒸腾而成。*Clouds are formed by evaporation of water.* ❸代词，这，此(多用在古诗词中) (pronoun) this (often used in ancient poems)：～回 *this time* | ～番 *this time* | ～边走 *walk this way* ❹用在"二、三、数"等数词后，指上文所说的几件事 used after numbers to indicate things mentioned previously：二～必居其一 *either one or the other* | 三～缺一不可。*None of these three things can be done without.*

啫 zhě ㄓㄜˇ [啫喱](一lí)(外 loanword) 从天然海藻或某些动物皮、骨中提取制作的胶性物质，可以作为某些食品和某些化妆品的原料 jelly

锗(鍺) zhě ㄓㄜˇ 金属元素，符号 Ge，银灰色，质脆。是重要的半导体材料 germanium (Ge)

赭 zhě ㄓㄜˇ 红褐色 (colour) maroon：～石(矿物名，可用作颜料) *(mineral) ochre*

褶(襵)** zhě ㄓㄜˇ (一子、一儿) ❶衣服经折叠而缝制成的印痕 pleat：百～裙 *pleated skirt* ❷泛指折皱的部分 fold; wrinkle：衣服上净是～子。*The clothes are full of wrinkles.* | 这张纸有好多～子。*There are so many fold lines on this piece of paper.* | 满脸的～子 *face covered in wrinkles*

这(這) zhè ㄓㄜˋ ❶代词，此，指较近的时间、地方或事物，跟"那"相对 (pronoun) this (opposite of 那)：

Z

～里 *here* | ～些 *these* | ～个 *this* | ～是英汉词典。*This is an English-Chinese dictionary.*[这么](－me)代词，如此 (pronoun) like this：～办就好了。*Just do it this way.* ❷这时候，指说话的同时 now：我～就走。*I'm going now.*

⇨ see also zhèi on p.841

柘 zhè ㄓㄜˋ 柘树，落叶灌木或小乔木，叶卵形或椭圆形，可以喂蚕，根、皮可入药，柘木可制黄色染料，叫柘黄 mandarin melon berry

浙(*淛) zhè ㄓㄜˋ ❶浙江，古水名，又叫浙江、之江或曲江，即今钱塘江，是浙江省第一大河流 Zhejiang River (ancient name for Qiantangjiang River, also called 浙江，之江 or 曲江) ❷浙江省的简称 Zhe (abbreviated form of Zhejiang Province)

蔗 zhè ㄓㄜˋ 甘蔗，草本植物，茎圆柱形，有节，含甜汁很多，可以吃，也用来制糖 sugarcane

嗻 zhè ㄓㄜˋ 叹词，旧时表示答应，"是"的意思 (old exclamation) used to indicate response

鹧(鷓) zhè ㄓㄜˋ [鹧鸪](－gū)鸟名，背部和腹部黑白两色相杂，头顶棕色，脚黄色。吃谷粒、昆虫、蚯蚓等 Chinese francolin

䗪 zhè ㄓㄜˋ 䗪虫，昆虫，即土鳖，身体扁，棕黑色，雄的有翅，雌的无翅。可入药 *Eupolyphaga sinensis* (a type of cockroach used as an ingredient for Chinese medicine, same as 土鳖)

着 zhe ·ㄓㄜ 助词 auxiliary ①用在动词后 used after a verb 1 表示动作正进行 indicates an action in progress：走～ *walking* | 等～ *waiting* | 开～会呢。*The meeting is in progress.* 2 表示状态的持续 indicates a continuous condition：桌上放～一本书。*A book has been placed on the table.* | 墙上挂～一幅画。*A painting is hanging on the wall.* ②用在形容词后，表示程度深，常跟"呢"(ne)连用 placed after an adjective to indicate intensity, often used with 呢 (ne)：好～呢 *very good* | 这小孩儿精～呢！*This child is so clever!* ③用在动词或表示程度的形容词后，表示祈使 placed after a verb or adjective indicating degree to make imperative statements：你听～。*Listen up.* | 步子大～点儿！*Take bigger strides!* ④加在某些动词后，使变成介词 placed after certain verbs to form prepositions：顺～ *along with* | 照～ *according to* | 沿～ *along* | 朝～ *towards*

⇨ see also zhāo on p.836, zháo on p.836, zhuó on p.878

ZHEI ㄓㄟ

这(這) zhèi ㄓㄟˋ "这(zhè)一"的合音，但指数量时不限于 combination of 这 (zhè) and 一, but not limited to

Z

one when denoting quantity: ～个 *this one* | ～些 *these* | ～年 *this year* | ～三年 *these three years*
⇨ see also zhè on p.840

ZHEN ㄓㄣ

贞(貞) zhēn ㄓㄣ (formerly pronounced zhēng) ❶ 坚定，有节操 firm; moral: 忠～ *loyal and staunch* | 坚～不屈 *resolute in not surrendering* ❷ 旧礼教中指女子不改嫁或不失身 (old) chastity; virginity (of a woman): ～女 *chaste woman* | ～节 *female chastity* ❸ 占，卜，问卦 to divine: ～卜 *divination*

侦(偵、*遉) zhēn ㄓㄣ (formerly pronounced zhēng) 探听，暗中察看 to investigate (secretly): ～探 *detective* | ～查案件 *investigate a case* | ～察机 *reconnaissance aircraft*

帧(幀) zhēn ㄓㄣ (formerly pronounced zhèng) 量词，幅（用于字画、照片等） measure word for calligraphy, paintings, photographs, etc.: 一～彩画 *a coloured drawing* [装帧] 书画等物的装潢设计 binding and layout (of books, paintings, etc.)

浈(湞) zhēn ㄓㄣ (formerly pronounced zhēng) 浈江，水名，在广东省北部 Zhenjiang River (in northern Guangdong Province)

桢(楨) zhēn ㄓㄣ (formerly pronounced zhēng) 古代打土墙时所立的木柱 (ancient) wooden posts erected for the construction of rammed earth walls [桢干]（－gàn）㊗能担重任的人才 pillar (of society, organisations, etc.)

祯(禎) zhēn ㄓㄣ (formerly pronounced zhēng) 吉祥 auspicious

针(針、*鍼) zhēn ㄓㄣ ❶缝织衣物引线用的一种细长的工具 needle [针对] 对准 to target: ～着工作中的缺点，提出改进的办法。*Suggest improvements that target flaws in one's work.* ❷细长像针形的东西 sth like a needle: 大头～ *drawing pin* | 松～ *pine needle* | 钟表上有时～、分～和秒～。*Clocks and watches have an hour hand, a minute hand, and a second hand.* [指南针] 我国古代发明的一种利用磁石制成的指示方向的仪器 compass ❸用针刺的方法治病 to treat with acupuncture: ～灸 *acupuncture* ❹西医注射用的器具 hypodermic needle: ～头 *needle* ❺针剂 injection: 打～ *have an injection* | 防疫～ *vaccine injection*

珍(*珎) zhēn ㄓㄣ ❶宝贝，宝贵的东西 valuable thing: 奇～异宝 *rare treasure* ❷贵重的，宝贵的 valuable: ～禽异兽 *rare and precious animals* ❸重视，看重 to value: 世人～之 *the world values it* | ～惜 *to treasure* | ～视 *to cherish*

胗 zhēn ㄓㄣ 鸟类的胃 gizzard: 鸭～ *duck gizzard* | 鸡～

Z

肝儿 *chicken gizzard*

真 zhēn ㄓㄣ ❶真实，跟客观事物相符合，跟“假”相对 real; true (opposite of 假)：～相大白 *the whole truth has emerged* | 千～万确 *absolutely true* [真理] 正确反映客观世界发展规律的思想 truth [天真] 1 心地单纯，性格很直率 innocent; artless 2 头脑简单，容易被假象迷惑 naive：这种想法太～。*This way of thinking is too naive.* ❷人和物的本样 original image of person or thing：写～ *portray a person; portrait* | 传～ *facsimile (fax)* ❸副词，确实，的确 (adverb) truly; indeed：～好 *so good* | ～高兴 *so happy* ❹清楚，显明 clear; obvious：字太小，看不～。*The characters are too small to read properly.* | 听得很～ *hear sth clearly* ❺真书（楷书）regular script (a style of Chinese calligraphy)：～草隶篆 *regular, cursive, clerical, and seal scripts* ❻本性，本原 natural character：返璞归～ *return to simplicity and one's nature*

禛 zhēn ㄓㄣ 吉祥。多用于人名 (often used in given names) auspicious

砧(*碪) zhēn ㄓㄣ 捶、砸或切东西的时候，垫在底下的器具 board/sheet used as a base for hammering/cutting：铁～ *anvil* | ～板 *chopping board* [砧木] 嫁接植物时把接穗接在另一个植物体上，这个植物体叫砧木 stock (in grafting)

葴 zhēn ㄓㄣ 古代指马蓝 (ancient) Chinese rain bell

箴 zhēn ㄓㄣ ❶same as “针❶” ❷劝告，劝诫 to admonish：～言 *admonition* ❸一种文体，以告诫规劝为主 literary form containing admonitions and warnings

蓁 zhēn ㄓㄣ ❶㊂草木茂盛(of plants) luxuriant：其叶～～ *its leaves are luxuriant* ❷ same as “榛❷”：深～（荆棘丛）*thorny thicket*

溱 zhēn ㄓㄣ 溱头河，水名，在河南省驻马店。今作“臻头河” Zhentouhe River (in Zhumadian, Henan Province)(now written as 臻头河)

⇨ see also qín on p.538

瑧 zhēn ㄓㄣ 一种玉 a type of jade

榛 zhēn ㄓㄣ ❶落叶灌木或小乔木，叶椭圆形，花黄褐色。果实叫榛子，果皮坚硬，果仁可以吃 Asian hazel ❷泛指丛生的荆棘 (generally) thorny bush：～莽 *luxuriant vegetation* ❸草木丛杂㊂ (of vegetation) dense and varied：草木～～ *a profusion of plants*

臻 zhēn ㄓㄣ 到，达到 to reach：日～完善 *gradually approach perfection*

斟 zhēn ㄓㄣ 往杯子里倒（酒或茶）to pour (wine or tea)：～酒 *pour wine* | ～茶 *pour tea* | 给我～上碗水。*Pour me a bowl of water.* [斟酌]（-zhuó）㊕度(duó)量，考虑 to consider. 请～办理。*Please act as you see fit.*

椹 zhēn ㄓㄣ same as “砧”

⇨ see also shèn on p.591

Z

甄 zhēn ㄓㄣ 审查 to examine: ～别 *to discern; to screen* | ～拔人才 *screen and select talent*

诊(診) zhěn ㄓㄣˇ 医生为断定病症而察看病人身体的情况 to examine (a patient): ～断 *diagnose* | ～脉 *take one's pulse* | 门～ *outpatient service* | 出～ *(of a doctor) make a house call*

轸(軫) zhěn ㄓㄣˇ ❶古代车后的横木 (ancient) horizontal wooden beam at the back of a carriage ❷悲痛 sorrowful: ～悼 *grieve sorrowfully* | ～怀（悲痛地怀念）*miss sb or sth with great sadness* | ～恤（怜悯）*take pity on* ❸星宿名，二十八宿之一 *zhen* (one of the twenty-eight constellations in ancient Chinese astronomy)

昣 zhěn ㄓㄣˇ 明亮 bright

畛 zhěn ㄓㄣˇ 田地间的小路 path in-between fields ㉡ 界限 border: 不分～域 *make no distinctions between self and others; set no boundaries*

疹 zhěn ㄓㄣˇ 皮肤上起的小疙瘩，多为红色，小的像针尖，大的像豆粒 rash: 湿～ *eczema*

袗 zhěn ㄓㄣˇ ❶单衣 unlined clothing ❷（衣服）华美 (of clothing) gorgeous

枕 zhěn ㄓㄣˇ ❶枕头，躺着时垫在头下的东西 pillow [枕木] 铁路路基上承受铁轨的横木 railway sleeper ❷躺着的时候把头放在枕头或器物上 to lay one's head on sth: ～着枕头 *with one's head on a pillow* | ～戈待旦（形容时刻准备投入战斗）*ready for battle at any time*

缜(縝) zhěn ㄓㄣˇ 周密，细致（㉤－密）detailed: ～密的思考 *careful deliberation*

稹 zhěn ㄓㄣˇ same as "缜"

鬒(黰)** zhěn ㄓㄣˇ 头发浓密而黑 (of hair) thick and black: ～发 *thick and black hair*

圳(甽)** zhèn ㄓㄣˋ 〈方 dialect〉田边水沟。多用于地名 ditch by the side of a field (often used in place names): 深～（在广东省）*Shenzhen (in Guangdong Province)*

阵(陣) zhèn ㄓㄣˋ ❶军队作战时布置的局势 military formation: ～线 *battlefront; alliance* | 布～ *array troops for battle* | 严～以待 *be ready in full battle array* | 一字长蛇～ *Single Long Snake Battle Formation; (figurative) a long line of people/things* ㉡战场 battleground: ～亡 *die in battle* [阵营] 两军交战对立的阵势 camp (in battles) ㊗利益和斗争目标相同的集团 camp (of people sharing the same interests and goals): 革命～ *revolutionary camp* ❷量词，表示事情或动作经过的段落 measure word for time taken for an event or action: 刮了一～风 *a moment of gusty winds* ㉣（－子）一段时间 period of time: 这一～子工作正忙。*I've been* *busy with work recently.*

纼(紖) zhèn ㄓㄣˋ 〈方 dialect〉 拴牛、马等的绳索 tether

鸩(鴆、❷❸△*酖) zhèn ㄓㄣˋ ❶传说中的一种毒鸟，相传把它的羽毛泡在酒里，喝了可以毒死人 a legendary bird whose poisonous feathers are lethal ❷用鸩的羽毛泡成的毒酒 poisoned wine：饮～止渴（喻满足一时需要，不顾严重后果）*seek immediate gratification without thinking about future consequences (literally means 'drinking poison to quench one's thirst')* ❸用毒酒害人 to poison sb with wine

⇨ 酖 see also dān on p.115

振 zhèn ㄓㄣˋ ❶摇动，挥动 to wave; to brandish：～笔直书 *pick up a pen/brush and write with furious speed* | ～铃 *ringing* | ～臂高呼 *raise one's arms and cry out* ❷奋起，兴起 to raise：～兴 *invigorate* | ～作 *buck up* | 精神一～ *invigorate one's spirits* ❸救 to rescue：～乏绝 *help the poor and destitute* ❹振动 to vibrate：共～ *resonance* | 谐～ *resonance*

赈(賑) zhèn ㄓㄣˋ 赈济，救济 to provide relief：～灾 *provide relief to people in disaster-stricken areas* | 以工代～ *provide relief through employment instead of direct handouts*

震 zhèn ㄓㄣˋ ❶迅速或剧烈地颤动 to shake violently：～耳 *earsplitting* | ～天动地 *momentous (literally means 'shaking heaven and earth')* 特指地震 (specifically) earthquake：～中 *epicentre* | 防～ *earthquake-proof* ❷惊恐或情绪过分激动 alarm; overexcited：～惊 *be shocked* | ～怒 *be enraged* ❸八卦之一，符号是☳，代表雷 *zhen* (one of the Eight Trigrams used in ancient divination, symbol ☳, representing thunder)

朕 zhèn ㄓㄣˋ ❶我，我的，由秦始皇时起专用作皇帝自称 I; my (pronoun used by Chinese sovereigns to refer to themselves since the Qin Dynasty) ❷预兆 omen

揕 zhèn ㄓㄣˋ 用刀剑等刺 to stab with a sword, sabre, etc.

瑱 zhèn ㄓㄣˋ [瑱圭] 古代帝王朝会时所拿的一种圭 a jade tablet held by the Emperor at court

⇨ see also tiàn on p.650

镇(鎮) zhèn ㄓㄣˋ ❶压 to press down：～尺 *paperweight* ⊜ 压制，抑制 to suppress：～痛 *relieve pain* | 警察一到，闹事的人就被～住了。*The troublemakers were subdued immediately after the police arrived.* [镇压] 用强力压制 to suppress by force：～叛乱 *suppress a revolt* ❷用武力维持安定 to maintain stability with military force：～守 *guard (a strategically important location)* | 坐～ *assume personal command* 也指镇守的地方 (also) guarded location：军事重～ *key military stronghold* ❸安定 calm; stable：～静 *composed* |

Z

～定 *calm* ❹把饮料等放在冰箱里或同冰、冷水放在一起使凉 to chill (a drink)：冰～汽水 *chilled soft drink* ❺行政区划单位，一般由县一级领导 town：城～居民 *residents of cities and towns* | 乡～企业 *enterprises in villages and towns* ❻较大的集市 large market place ❼时常 often：十年～相随 *always together for ten years*

ZHENG ㄓㄥ

丁 zhēng ㄓㄥ ［丁丁］形容伐木、弹琴等的声音 used to describe the sound of cutting trees, playing stringed instruments, etc.

⇨ see also dīng on p.138

正 zhēng ㄓㄥ 正月，农历一年的第一个月 the first month of the traditional Chinese calendar：新～ *the first month of the traditional Chinese calendar*

⇨ see also zhèng on p.847

征（❸–❻△徵）zhēng ㄓㄥ ❶远行 to go on a long journey：～帆（远行的船）*ship on a long voyage* | ～途 *long journey* ❷用武力制裁 to go on a military campaign：出～ *go on an expedition* | ～讨 *go on a punitive military campaign*［征服］用力制服 to conquer：～病魔 *conquer illness* ❸由国家召集或收用 to conscript (troops); to levy (taxes)：应（yìng）～入伍 *be drafted into the military* | ～税 *levy taxes* ❹寻求，希望得到（㊀—求）to seek：～稿 *call for papers* | ～求群众意见 *seek the public's opinion* ❺证明，证验 to prove：有实物可～ *have concrete evidence to prove it* ❻现象，迹象 sign：特～ *distinguishing feature* | ～兆 *omen*

⇨ 徵 see also zhǐ on p.855

怔 zhēng ㄓㄥ ［怔忡］（—chōng）中医指心悸，患者感到心脏跳动得很厉害 (in traditional Chinese medicine) palpitations［怔忪］（—zhōng）惊惧 panic; fear

⇨ see also zhèng on p.848

钲（鉦）zhēng ㄓㄥ 古代一种打击乐器，多用铜做成，在行军时敲打 ancient percussion instrument used by troops on the march, usually made of bronze

⇨ see also zhèng on p.848

症（癥）zhēng ㄓㄥ ［症结］中医指腹内结块的病 (in traditional Chinese medicine) lump in the abdomen ⑩事情难解决的关键所在 crux：制度不健全是问题的～。*The crux of the problem is the inadequate system.*

⇨ see also zhèng on p.849

争 zhēng ㄓㄥ ❶力求获得，互不相让 to vie：～夺 *to contend* | ～先恐后 *rush to the front for fear of lagging behind* ❷争执 to dispute：意气之～ *dispute caused by personal feelings* | ～论 *argument* ❸〈方 dialect〉差，欠 short of ❹怎么，如何（多用在古诗词曲中）(often used in ancient poems) how; why: ～不 *why not*| ～知 *how does one know* | ～奈 *however; but*

挣 zhēng ㄓㄥ [挣扎](—zhá) 尽力支撑或摆脱 to struggle: 垂死～ *be in one's death throes*

⇨ see also zhèng on p.849

峥 zhēng ㄓㄥ [峥嵘](—róng) 1 高峻，突出 towering: 山势～ *mountains towering high* 2 不平常 extraordinary: ～岁月 *extraordinary times*

狰 zhēng ㄓㄥ [狰狞](—níng) 样子凶恶 ferocious: 面目～ *ferocious appearance*

睁 zhēng ㄓㄥ 张开眼睛 to open (one's eyes)

铮(錚) zhēng ㄓㄥ 形容金属相击的声音 ⓐ clang (the sound of metal objects hitting each other): 刀剑相击，～～作响。*The sabre and sword struck each other with a clang.*

筝 zhēng ㄓㄥ 古代的一种弦乐器 an ancient stringed instrument [风筝](—zheng) 玩具的一种，用竹篾做架，糊上纸，牵线放在空中，可以飞得很高。装上弓弦或哨子，迎着风能发声 kite

烝 zhēng ㄓㄥ ❶众多 many: ～民 *the masses* ❷古代冬祭名 winter sacrifice offering ceremony in ancient times ❸ (ancient) same as "蒸"

蒸 zhēng ㄓㄥ ❶热气上升 (of hot air, etc.) to rise: ～发 *evaporate* | ～气 *steam* [蒸蒸] 像气一样向上升 to rise like gas: ～日上 *(the business) become more prosperous every day* ❷利用水蒸气的热力使食物变熟或变热 to steam: ～馒头 *steam* mantou; *steamed bun*

拯 zhěng ㄓㄥˇ 援救，救助(㊀—救) to rescue; to save: ～民于水火之中 *save the people from deep distress*

整 zhěng ㄓㄥˇ ❶整齐，有秩序，不乱 orderly: ～洁 *neat and clean* | 仪容不～ *dishevelled appearance* ❷不残缺，完全的，跟"零"相对 (㊀完—) intact; whole (opposite of 零): ～套的书 *full set of books* | 忙了一～天 *was busy all day* [整数] 算术上指不带分数、小数的数或不是分数、小数的数。一般指没有零头的数目 whole number; integer ❸整理，整顿 to tidy; to rectify: 休～ *rest and reorganize* | ～装待发 *have already packed the clothes and bedclothes for travelling and is ready to set off* | ～风 *rectify wrong practices, ideologies, etc.* [整合] 调整，重组，使和谐一致 to integrate ⓑ修理，搞，弄 to repair: 桌子坏了～一～。*The table is broken, please repair it.* | ～旧如新 *repair sth old or broken to make it look new* ❹使吃苦头 to torment: 挨～ *be tormented* | 不要～人。*Do not give other people a hard time.*

正 zhèng ㄓㄥˋ ❶不偏，不斜，使不歪斜 middle; straight; to straighten: ～午 *high noon* | ～中

Z

dead centre | ～一～帽子 *straighten one's hat* ㊂ ①合于法则、规矩的 proper; regular: ～派 *decent*| ～当 *honest; reasonable* | ～楷 *regular script (a style of Chinese calligraphy)* ②图形的各个边和各个角都相等的 (of a polygon) regular: ～方形 *square* ❷副词，表示恰好 (adverb) just; exactly: ～合我意 *exactly what I want* ❸副词，表示动作在进行中 (adverb) used to indicate an action in progress: 现在～开着会。*There is a meeting going on now.* | 我～吃饭，他来了。*I was eating when he came.* ❹改去偏差或错误 (㊀改一) to correct: ～误 *correct errors* | 给他～音 *correct his pronunciation* ❺纯，不杂（指色、味）(of colour, taste) pure: ～黄 *pure yellow* | 味道不～ *the taste is not right* ❻大于零的，跟"负"相对 positive (opposite of 负): ～数 *positive number* ❼指相对的两方面中积极的一面 positive of two sides ①跟"反"相对 opposite of 反: ～面 *front; positive side* | ～比 *direct proportion* ②跟"负"相对 opposite of 负: ～电 *positive electricity* | ～极 *positive pole* ③跟"副"相对 opposite of 副: ～本 *(of documents) original copy* | ～册 *(old) the regular register of law-abiding residence* ❽姓 (surname) Zheng

⇨ see also zhēng on p.846

证（證） zhèng ㄓㄥˋ ❶用人、物、事实来表明或断定 to prove: ～明 *prove* | 查～ *investigate and verify* | ～几何题 *prove a geometry question* [公证] 被授以权力的机关根据当事人的申请，证明法律行为或有法律意义的文书和事实的合法性、真实性 to notarize [认证] 证明产品达到某种质量标准的合格评定 to authenticate: 国际～ *international authentication*| ～书 *certificate* ❷凭据，帮助断定事理或情况的东西 proof: ～据 *evidence* | 工作～ *employee identification card* | 毕业～ *diploma* | 结婚～ *marriage certificate*

⇨ 證 see also 症 on p.849

怔 zhèng ㄓㄥˋ 〈方 dialect〉发愣，发呆 to be in a daze: 发～ *to be in a daze*

⇨ see also zhēng on p.846

政 zhèng ㄓㄥˋ ❶政治 politics: ～策 *policy* | ～权 *regime*| ～府 *government* | ～党 *political party* | ～纲 *political programme* | 参～ *participate in government and political affairs* [政治] 阶级、政党、社会集团、个人在国家生活和国际关系方面的活动，是经济的集中表现 politics ❷国家某一部门主管的业务 (of a state body) business: 财～ *finance* | 民～ *civil administration* | 邮～ *postal service* ❸指家庭或集体的事务 (of a family or collective) business: 家～ *household duties* | 校～ *school administration*

钲（鉦） zhèng ㄓㄥˋ 金属元素，镄（fèi）的旧称 (old) fermium (Fm)

⇨ see also zhēng on p.846

症(**證) zhèng ㄓㄥˋ 病 disease: ～候 *disease; symptom* | 霍乱～ *cholera* | 急～ *acute disease; medical emergency* | 不治之～ *incurable disease* | 对～下药 *apply the right solution for the problem (literally means 'prescribe the right medicine for the disease')*

⇨ see also zhēng on p.846

⇨ 證 see also 证 on p.848

郑(鄭) zhèng ㄓㄥˋ 周代诸侯国名，在今河南省新郑一带 Zheng (a state in the Zhou Dynasty, around today's Xinzheng, Henan Province)

[郑重] (－zhòng) 审慎，严肃 serious; solemn: ～其事 *deal with the matter seriously* | ～声明 *solemnly declare*

诤(諍) zhèng ㄓㄥˋ 谏，照直说出别人的过错，叫人改正 to point out sb's fault directly and urge him to correct it: 谏～ *criticise sb's faults frankly* | ～言 *forthright advice* [诤友] 能直言规劝的朋友 friend who gives forthright advice

挣 zhèng ㄓㄥˋ ❶用力支撑或摆脱 to struggle (to support sth or let go): ～脱 *break free from* | ～开 *wriggle oneself free* [挣揣] (－chuài) 挣扎 to struggle [挣命] 为保全性命而挣扎 to struggle for one's life ❷出力量而取得报酬 to earn: ～钱 *earn money*

⇨ see also zhēng on p.847

阐(闓) zhèng ㄓㄥˋ [阐阓] (－chuài) 同"挣揣" (多见于元曲) (usually in Yuan Drama) same as 挣揣

ZHI ㄓ

之 zhī ㄓ ❶助词 auxiliary word ①表示修饰关系，在形容词、名词或数量词后 indicates modification when used after an adjective, noun, or number: 光荣～家 *family of honour* | 淮河～南 *south of Huaihe River* | 三分～一 *one-third* | 三天～后 ("之"也可省略) *three days later (之 is optional)* ②表示领属关系，在名词或代词后 used after a noun or pronoun to indicate possession: 人民～子 *son of the people* | 余～身体大不如前。*My health is not good as before.* ③置于主谓结构之间，使其变成偏正结构 used between subject and predicate structures to transform it into an attributive structure: 大道～行也，天下为公。*When the Great Way (the ultimate political ideal) is implemented, the whole world belongs to everyone.* ❷代词，代替人或事物，限于做宾语 (pronoun) used to replace person or matter, only as an object: 爱～重～ *love and cherish (a person/thing)* | 取～不尽 *(of resources) inexhaustible* | 偶一为～ *do sth once by chance* ❸代词，虚指 (pronoun) used to indicate an unspecified reference: 总～ *in short* | 久而久～ *over a long period of time* ❹文言代词，这，这个 (pronoun in classical Chinese)

Z

this：～二虫又何知！ *What do these two little creatures know!* ❺往，到 to go：尔将何～？ *Where will you go?*

芝 zhī ㄓ ❶灵芝，长在枯树上的一种蕈，菌盖赤褐色，有光泽，可入药。古代以为瑞草 *lingzhi* mushroom (considered an auspicious plant in ancient times); *Ganoderma Lucidum* ❷古书上指白芷 (in ancient Chinese texts) *Angelica dahurica*：～兰 *noble character; true friendship; good environment (literally means 'two kinds of fragrant herb')*

支 zhī ㄓ ❶撑，支持 to support; to prop up：把帐篷～起来 *prop up the tent* ㊀受得住 to be able to endure：乐不可～ *overwhelmed with joy* [支援] 支持，援助 to support; to aid：～灾区 *provide relief to a disaster area* | 互相～ *support one another* ❷领款或付款 to draw money; to pay money：～走了工资 *drew one's salary* | 把工资～给他。*Pay him his wages.* ❸用话敷衍，使人离开 to use an excuse to get sb to leave：把来人都～出去 *use an excuse and get all the attendants out* [支配] 指挥，调度 to control; to allocate：人员由你～。*The staff is at your disposal.* ❹分支的，附属于总体的 branch：～流 *tributary* | ～行（háng）*sub-branch of a bank* [支离破碎] 形容事物零散破碎，不成整体 in broken pieces ❺量词 measure word ①用于队伍、歌曲或杆形的东西等 used for teams, songs, rod-shaped objects, etc.：一～军队 *an army* | 一～曲子 *a tune* | 一～笔 *a pen* ②各种纤维纺成的纱（如棉纱）粗细程度的计量单位，纱越细，支数越多，质量越好 (unit of measurement for fineness of yarn; the finer the yarn, the higher the measurement) S number ❻地支，历法中用的"子、丑、寅、卯、辰、巳、午、未、申、酉、戌、亥"十二个字，也用于编排次序 the Twelve Earthly Branches (a system used in the Chinese calendar); also used to indicate sequence

[支吾] 用话搪塞、应付，说话含混躲闪 to prevaricate：～其词 *speak evasively* | 一味～ *keep speaking evasively*

吱 zhī ㄓ 形容某些尖细的声音 ㊟ (used to describe high-pitched sounds) creak; screech; squeak：门～的一声开了。*The door opened with a creak.* | 车轮～～地响。*The wheels of the vehicle make a screeching sound.*

⇨ see also zī on p.879

枝 zhī ㄓ ❶（～子、～儿）由植物的主干上分出来的茎条 (of plants) branch：树～ *tree branch* | 柳～ *willow branch* | 节外生～（喻多生事端）*new problems crop up unexpectedly (literally means 'new branches grow out from a branch')* [枝节] ㊜1 由一事件引起的其他问题 side issues：这事又有了～了。*Another complication has cropped up in this matter.* 2 细碎的，不重要的 trivial：～问

题 *minor problem* ❷量词 measure word ①用于带枝子的花朵 used for flowers attached to stalks：一～杏花 *a sprig of apricot flowers* ②用于杆状物 used for nod-shaped objects：一～铅笔 *a pencil*

肢 zhī ㄓ 人的胳膊、腿，也指某些动物的腿 limb：～体 *limbs (and trunk)* | 四～ *four limbs* | 后～ *hindlimb* | 断～再植 *limb replantation*

氏 zhī ㄓ see 阏氏 (yān—) at 阏 on page 750, and 月氏 (yuè—) at 月 on page 809

⇨ see also shì on p.599

泜 zhī ㄓ 泜河，水名，在河北省邢台 Zhihe River (in Xingtai, Hebei Province)

胝 zhī ㄓ see 胼胝 (pián—) at 胼 on page 504

祗 zhī ㄓ 恭敬 to respect：～仰 *revere* | ～候光临 *wait respectfully for sb's arrival*

只(隻) zhī ㄓ ❶量词 measure word ①用于某些成对的东西中的一个 one of a pair of certain objects：两～手 *two hands* ②用于动物 used for animals：一～鸡 *a chicken* ③用于船只和某些器具 used for boats and certain implements：一～小船 *a small boat* | 两～箱子 *two boxes* ❷单独的，极少的 alone; very few：～身（一个人）*alone* | 片纸～字 *fragments of writing* [只眼] ㊕特别的见解 unique perspective：独具～ *have a unique perspective*

⇨ see also zhǐ on p.854

芨 zhī ㄓ 用于地名 used in place names：～芨(jī)梁(在内蒙古自治区土默特左旗) *Zhijiliang (in Tumed Left Banner, Inner Mongolia Autonomous Region)*

织(織) zhī ㄓ 用丝、麻、棉纱、毛线等编成布或衣物等 to weave：～布 *weave cloth* | ～毛衣 *knit a sweater* | ～席 *weave a mat*

卮(*巵) zhī ㄓ 古代盛酒的器皿 ancient wine vessel

栀(*梔) zhī ㄓ 栀子树，常绿灌木，花白色，香味浓，果实叫栀子。叶、花、果、根都可入药 Cape jasmine

汁 zhī ㄓ 含有某种物质的液体 juice：墨～ *liquid ink* | 橘～ *tangerine juice*

知 zhī ㄓ ❶知道，明了 to know; to understand：～无不言 *say everything that one knows* | 自～之明 *self-knowledge (especially about one's own weakness)* [知觉] 随着感觉而产生的反映客观物体或现象的心理过程 consciousness ❷使知道 to make known：通～ *notify* | ～照 *inform* ❸知识，学识，学问 knowledge：求～ *seek knowledge* | 无～ *ignorant* ❹主管 governor; director：～县（主管县里的事务，旧时指县长）*(old) governor of a county* | ～府 *(old) mayor of a prefecture-level city* ❺彼此相互了解而情谊深厚的人 close friend：新～ *newly made friend*

〈古 ancient〉also same as 智 (zhì)

Z

椥 zhī ㄓ [槟椥](bīn–)越南地名。今作"槟知" Ben Tre (a place in Vietnam)(now written as 槟知)

蜘 zhī ㄓ [蜘蛛](–zhū) see 蛛 on page 866

脂 zhī ㄓ ❶动物体内或油料植物种子内的油质(㊀–肪、–膏) fat; oil [脂肪]油质有机化合物，存在于人体和动物的皮下组织以及植物体中，是生物体内储存能量的物质 fats; oils ❷胭脂 rouge (used for colouring the cheeks and lips); a dark red colour in traditional Chinese painting：～粉 *rouge*

稙 zhī ㄓ 〈方 dialect〉❶庄稼种得较早 (of crops) early planted：～谷子 *early planted millet* ❷庄稼熟得较早 (of crops) early maturing：白玉米～ *early maturing white maize*

禔 zhī ㄓ ❶安宁 peace ❷福 happiness

榰 zhī ㄓ ❶柱下的木础或石础 (wood or stone) pillar base ❷支撑 to prop up

执(執) zhí ㄓˊ ❶拿着，掌握 to hold：～笔 *write* | ～政 *wield state power* ㊂固执，坚持(意见) to stubbornly insist on：～意要去 *stubbornly insist on going* | ～迷不悟 *stubbornly adhere to one's mistakes* [争执]争论中各执己见，不肯相让 dispute ❷行，施行 to implement：～法 *enforce the law* | ～礼甚恭 *act politely and respectfully* [执行]依据规定的原则、办法办事 execute; implement ❸凭单 proof：回～ *receipt* | 收～ *receipt* [执照]由机关发给的正式凭证 licence ❹捕捉，逮捕 to catch; to arrest

絷(縶) zhí ㄓˊ ❶拴，捆 to tie up ❷拘捕，拘禁 to arrest; to incarcerate ❸马缰绳 rein

直 zhí ㄓˊ ❶像拉紧的线那样不弯曲，跟"曲"相对 straight (opposite of 曲)：～线 *straight line* | ～立 *stand up straight* ㊃公正合理 just：正～ *upright* | 是非曲～ *right and wrong* | 理～气壮 *righteously confident* [直接]不经过第三者而发生关系的，跟"间接"相对 direct (opposite of 间接) ❷使直，把弯曲的伸开 to straighten：～起腰来 *straighten one's back* ❸爽快，坦率(㊀–爽) forthright：～言 *speak bluntly* | 心～口快 *straightforward and outspoken* ❹副词 adverb ①径直，一直 directly：～通北京 *directly to Beijing* | ～达客车 *through train/bus* ②一个劲儿地，连续不断 continuously：～哭 *keep crying* | 逗得大家～笑 *keep everyone in constant laughter* ❺竖，跟"横"相对 vertical (opposite of 横) ❻汉字自上往下写的一种笔形(丨) vertical stroke (in a Chinese character)(丨) ❼ (ancient) same as "值"

值 zhí ㄓˊ ❶价格，价钱 price：两物之～相等。*The prices of both things are equal.* ❷物和价相当 to be worth：～一百元 *worth 100* yuan ㊂值得，有意义或有价值 to be worthwhile：不～一提 *not worth a mention* ❸用数字

表示的量，数学演算所得的结果 (in mathematics) value ❹ 遇到 to meet：相～ *meet* | 正～新春佳节 *on the occasion of the Spring Festival* ㊂ 当，轮到 to be one's turn：～日 *be on duty for the day* | ～班 *be on duty*

埴 zhí ㄓ 黏土 clay

植 zhí ㄓ ❶栽种（㊀种一）to plant：～树 *plant trees* | 种～五谷 *plant the Five Grains* ㊂培养 to cultivate：培～ *foster; train* | 扶～ *foster and support* ❷指植物 plants：～被 *vegetation* | ～保 *plant protection* ❸戳（chuō）住，立住 to stand (sth); to erect：～其杖于门侧 *stand the pole at the side of the door*

殖 zhí ㄓ 生育，滋生（㊀生一）to breed：繁～ *reproduce; propagate* [殖民地] 被帝国主义国家剥夺了政治、经济的独立权力，并受它控制和掠夺的国家或地区 colony

⇨ see also shi on p.604

侄（*姪） zhí ㄓ （一子、一儿）弟兄的儿子，同辈男性亲属的儿子。也称朋友的儿子 nephew (son of one's brother); son of the male relatives of the same generation as oneself; (also) son of one's friend

职（職） zhí ㄓ ❶职务，分（fèn）内应做的事 duty：尽～ *fulfil one's duty* ❷职位，执行事务所处的一定的地位 position; post：调（diào）～ *be transferred to another post* | 兼～ *hold two or more jobs; part-time job* [职员] 机关、企业、学校、团体里担任行政或业务工作的人员 staff member ❸旧时公文用语，下属对上司的自称 (in old official documents) I; me (when addressing one's superior)：～奉命前往。*I will go as ordered.* ❹由于 because of：～是之故 *because of this* | ～此 *because of this* ❺掌管 to be in charge of：～掌 *be in charge of*

跖（*蹠） zhí ㄓ ❶脚面上接近脚趾的部分 midfoot：～骨 *metatarsal bone* ❷脚掌 (of a foot) sole

摭 zhí ㄓ 摘取，拾取 to pick up：～拾 *pick; collect*

踯（躑） zhí ㄓ [踯躅]（一zhú）徘徊不进 pace up and down; hesitate：～街头 *loiter in the streets*

蹢 zhí ㄓ [蹢躅]（一zhú）same as "踯躅"

⇨ see also dí on p.128

止 zhǐ ㄓˇ ❶停住不动（㊀停一）to stop：～步 *halt; stop* | 血流不～ *bleed non-stop* | 学无～境。*There's no limits to acquiring knowledge.* ❷拦阻，使停住 to block; to stop：制～ *prevent; stop* | ～血 *stop one's bleeding* | ～痛 *relieve pain* ❸截止 to end：报名日期自6月20日起至7月1日～。*Registration begins on 20 June and ends on 1 July.* ❹仅，只 only; just：不～一回 *not just once*

址（*阯） zhǐ ㄓˇ 地址，地基，地点 address;

Z

foundation; location：旧～ *site (of a former edifice)* | 住～ *residential address*

芷 zhǐ ㄓˇ 白芷，草本植物，花白色，根圆锥形，有香味，可入药 *Angelica dahurica*

沚 zhǐ ㄓˇ 水中的小块陆地 islet; small sandbank; small sandbar

祉 zhǐ ㄓˇ 福 happiness：福～ *happiness*

趾 zhǐ ㄓˇ ❶脚 foot：～高气扬（得意忘形的样子）*too proud and confident to control oneself (literally means 'swaggering with one's feet lifted high')* ❷脚指头 toe：～骨 *phalanx* | 鸭子脚～中间有蹼。*Ducks have webbing between their toes.*

只（衹、△*祇、*秖） zhǐ ㄓˇ 副词 adverb ①表示限于某个范围 used to indicate a limited scope：～知其一，不知其二 *only know one aspect of an issue but not the other* | 万事俱备，～欠东风。*Everything is ready except for the final key factor.* ②唯一，仅有 only：家里～我一个人。*There's only me at home.*［只是］1 连词，但是 (conjunction) but：我很想看戏，～没时间。*I really want to go to the theatre but I don't have the time.* 2 副词，就是 (adverb) simply; just：人家问他，他～不开口。*He simply kept quiet when others asked him.* 3 仅仅是 only：对抗～矛盾斗争的一种形式。*Resistance is only one form of contradiction and struggle.*

➪ see also zhī on p.851

➪ 祇 see also qí on p.518

枳 zhǐ ㄓˇ 落叶灌木或小乔木，通称枸橘，小枝多硬刺，叶为三小叶的复叶，果实球形，味酸苦。果实和叶可入药 trifoliate orange (usually known as 枸橘)

轵（軹） zhǐ ㄓˇ 古代指车轴的末端 (ancient) end of an axle

咫 zhǐ ㄓˇ 古代指八寸 an ancient Chinese unit for measuring length, equal to 8 寸［咫尺］形容距离很近 very near：远在天边，近在～。*What one is looking for is right under one's nose.*

疻 zhǐ ㄓˇ 殴伤 bruise (from a beating)

旨（❶指）** zhǐ ㄓˇ ❶意义，目的（㊀意一）meaning; aim：要～ *gist* | ～趣（目的和意义）*objective and meaning* | 主～ *gist; main point* ❷封建时代称帝王的命令 rulers' orders in feudal times：圣～ *imperial edict* ❸美味 delicious：～酒 *fine wine*

指 zhǐ ㄓˇ ❶手指头 finger：食～ *forefinger; index finger* | 首屈一～ *the best (literally means 'the thumb is the first finger to bend when counting with fingers')* | 屈～可数 *can be counted on one's fingers* ❷一个手指头的宽度叫一指 finger breadth：下了四～雨。*Four fingerbreadth deep rain has fallen.* ❸用手指或物体的尖端对着 to point：用手一～ *point with* *one's finger* | 时针～着十二点。*The hour hand is pointing to twelve o'clock.* ❹ 点明，告知 to point out; to inform：～导 *guide* | ～出他的错误 *point out his mistakes* [指示] 上级对下级做有关原则和方法的说明，也指所做的说明 to instruct; instructions ❺ 仰仗，倚靠 to depend on：不应～着别人生活 *should not depend on others for one's living* | 单～着一个人是不行的。*Depending on just one person doesn't work.* ❻ 直立起来 stand up：令人发（fà）～ *make sb bristle with anger* ❼向，意思上针对 to refer to; to：直～峰顶 *right to the peak* | 他是～你说的。*When he said that, he was referring to you.*

酯 zhǐ ㄓ 有机化合物的一类，是酸中的氢原子被烃基取代而成的。脂肪的主要成分就是几种不同的酯 ester

扺 zhǐ ㄓ 侧手击 to strike with the side of one's hand [扺掌] 击掌（表示高兴）to clap one's hands (in happiness)：～而谈 *chat cordially* (扺 and 抵 are different in their written forms, pronunciations, and meanings.)

纸(紙、*帋) zhǐ ㄓ ❶ 纸张，多用植物纤维制成。造纸是我国四大发明之一，起源很早，东汉时蔡伦曾加以改进 paper ❷量词，用于书信、文件等 measure word for letters, documents, etc.：一～公文 *an official document*

茋 zhǐ ㄓ 古书上指嫩的蒲草 young cattail (in ancient Chinese texts)

➪ see also dǐ on p.129

黹 zhǐ ㄓ 缝纫、刺绣等针线活 needlework：针～ *needlework*

徵 zhǐ ㄓ 古代五音"宫、商、角（jué）、徵、羽"之一 *zhi* (one of the five notes in the ancient Chinese pentatonic scale)

➪ see also zhēng 征 on p.855

至 zhì ㄓ ❶ 到 to; till：由南～北 *from south to north* | ～今未忘 *still have not forgotten* [至于] 1 指可能达到某种程度 go so far as to：他还不～不知道。*It goes too far to say he doesn't know.* | 我～这么小气吗？ *Would I really be so petty?* 2 介词，表示另提一事 (preposition) as for：～个人得失，他根本不考虑。*As for personal gains or losses, he doesn't even think about them.* [以至] 连词，一直到 (conjunction) up to：看一遍不懂，就看两遍、三遍，～更多遍。*If you don't understand it the first time, read it a second, a third, or even more times.* ❷ 最好的 the best：～宝 *most precious treasure* | ～理名言 *wisest saying* ❸ 极，最 the most; extremely：～尊 *the most exalted* | ～少 *at least* | ～高无上 *supreme*

厔 zhì ㄓ see 盩厔 (zhōu－) at 盩 on page 864

郅 zhì ㄓ 最，极 the most; extremely

桎 zhì ㄓ 古代拘束犯人两脚的刑具 (ancient) ankle shackles [桎梏]（－gù）脚镣和手铐，比喻束缚人或事物的东西 fetters

Z

and handcuffs; ankle and wrist shackles; (figurative) restriction

轾(輊) zhì ㄓˋ see 轩轾 (xuān–) at 轩 on page 737

致(❹緻) zhì ㄓˋ ❶给予，送给 to give; to extend: ～函 *write a letter to* | ～敬 *salute; pay one's respects to* 引(力量、意志等)集中于某个方面 to focus (one's strength, willpower, etc.): ～力于学业 *concentrate on studies* | 专心～志 *concentrate on sth wholeheartedly* [致命] 可使丧失生命 fatal: ～伤 *fatal injury* [致意] 向人表示问候的心意 to extend one's greetings to: 点头～ *greet sb with a nod* ❷招引，使达到 to cause; to achieve: ～病 *cause illness* | ～富 *become rich* | 学以～用 *study sth in order to apply it* [以致] 连词，因而 (conjunction) therefore: 由于没注意克服小缺点，～犯了严重错误。*The negligence to overcome minor faults resulted in major errors.* ❸样子，情趣 appeal; interest: 景～ *scenery* | 别～ *original; novel* | 风～ *demeanour and bearing; special flavour* | 兴～ *mood* | 雅～ *refined; elegant* | 错落有～ *irregularly arranged but charming* | 毫无二～ *identical* [大致] 大概，大体情形 roughly: ～已结束 *more or less ended* | ～不差。*It's about right.* [一致] 一样，没有分歧 same; consistent: 行动～ *uniformed action* ❹细密，精细(㊂细－) intricate; delicate: 他做事很细～。*He pays much attention to details at work.* | 这东西做得真精～。*This object is so intricately made.*

晊 zhì ㄓˋ 大。多用于人名。汉代有岑晊 great (often used in given names, e.g. Cen Zhi in the Han Dynasty)

铚(銍) zhì ㄓˋ ❶古代一种短的镰刀 (ancient) short sickle ❷割禾穗 to harvest grain ❸古地名，在今安徽省宿州西南 Zhi (ancient place name, southwest of today's Suzhou, Anhui Province)

窒 zhì ㄓˋ 阻塞不通 to obstruct: ～息(呼吸被阻停止) *suffocate*

蛭 zhì ㄓˋ ❶环节动物，俗叫蚂蟥，大都吸其他动物的血或体液，生活在水里或潮湿的陆地上，有的在医学上用来吸血治病 leech (informal 蚂蟥) ❷肝蛭，肝脏里的一种寄生虫，通常由螺蛳和鱼等传到人体内 liver fluke

膣 zhì ㄓˋ 阴道的旧称，女性生殖器的一部分 (old) vagina

志(❷–❹*誌) zhì ㄓˋ ❶意向，要有所作为的决心 aspiration: 立～ *determine to do sth* | ～同道合 *have common interest and goals* | 有～者事竟成。*Where there's a will there's a way.* [意志] 为了达到既定目的而自觉地努力的心理状态 will ❷记在心里 to keep in one's heart: ～喜 *(congratulatory greeting) remember the happiness* | ～哀 *express one's mourning for the deceased* | 永～不忘 *will* *always remember* ❸记载的文字 written records：杂～ *magazine* | 地理～ *geographical almanac* ❹记号 mark; sign：标～ *mark; sign* ❺〈方 dialect〉称轻重，量长短多少 to weigh; to measure：用秤～～ *weigh with a scale* | 拿碗～～ *measure with a bowl*

栺 zhì ㄓ ［栺木山］地名，在湖南省邵阳 Zhimushan (a place in Shaoyang, Hunan Province)

痣 zhì ㄓ 皮肤上生的斑痕，有青、红、褐等色，也有突起的 mole (on skin)

豸 zhì ㄓ 古书上指没有脚的虫子 legless worms in ancient Chinese texts ［虫豸］旧时对虫子的通称 (old) generic word for insects and worms

⇨ see also zhài on p.829

忮 zhì ㄓ 嫉妒 to be jealous

识(識) zhì ㄓ ❶记住 to remember：博闻强～ *erudite with a good memory* ❷标志，记号 mark; sign：款～ *words carved on ancient bronzeware; inscriptions on calligraphy works and paintings*

⇨ see also shí on p.597

帜(幟) zhì ㄓ 旗子（㊀旗－）flag：独树一～ *fly one's own flag; be unique*

帙(*袠、*袟) zhì ㄓ ❶包书的布套子 cloth book cover ❷量词，用于装套的线装书 measure word for sets of thread-bound books

秩 zhì ㄓ ❶有条理、不混乱的情况 order：～序良好 *orderly* ❷十年 ten years：七～寿辰 *seventieth birthday* ❸旧时指俸禄，也指官的品级 (old) official salary; (also) official rank：厚～ *high salary*

制(❹製) zhì ㄓ ❶规定，订立 to stipulate; to set：～定计划 *draw up a plan* ❷限定，约束，管束 to limit; to restrict：～止 *prevent; stop* | ～裁 *punish; sanction* | 限～ *limit* ❸制度，法度，法则 system; regulation：民主集中～ *democratic centralism* | 全日～学校 *full-time school* ❹造，作（㊀－造）to make：猪皮～革 *leather made from pig skin* | ～版 *make a printing plate* | ～图表 *make graphs and charts*

质(質) zhì ㄓ ❶本体，本性 nature; character：物～ *matter; material* | 流～ *liquid* | 铁～ *iron* | 实～ *essence* ［质量］1 产品或工作的优劣程度 quality：提高～ *improve quality* 2 物理学上指物体所含物质的量。过去习惯上称为重量 (in physics) mass (used to be called 重量) ［质子］原子核内带有正电的粒子，如氢原子核 proton ［本质］跟"现象"相对，指事物的内在联系，是这一事物和其他事物相区别的根本属性。它是由事物内部矛盾所规定的 nature; essence (opposite of 现象) ❷朴实（㊀－朴）down-to-earth; simple ❸依据事实来问明或辨别是非 to question：～询 *to question* | ～问 *to question* | ～疑

to doubt | ～之高明 *enquire from a more informed source* ❹抵押，抵押品 to pledge; collateral：～押 *to pledge* | 人～ *hostage* | 以房子为～ *use a house as collateral*

榰(櫍) zhì ㄓ ❶钟鼓架子的足，也泛指器物的足 leg (of a bell or drum frame); (generally) leg (of an object) ❷砧板 chopping board

锧(鑕) zhì ㄓ ❶〈古 ancient〉砧板 chopping board ❷铡刀座 base of a cutter [斧锧] 斩人的刑具 axe and seat (used to cut a criminal in half at the waist in ancient times)

踬(躓) zhì ㄓ 被东西绊倒 to trip on sth：颠～ *to trip; (figurative) be impoverished* ㊀事情不顺利，受挫折 be frustrated：屡试屡～ *fail at every try*

炙 zhì ㄓ ❶烤 to roast; to grill [亲炙] 直接得到某人的教诲或传授 to learn directly from sb ❷烤熟的肉 grilled/roasted meat：脍（kuài）～人口（喻诗文等受人欢迎）*(of literary works, etc.) universally appreciated (literally means 'everyone loves to eat grilled meat')*

治 zhì ㄓ ❶管理，处理（㊎－理）to manage：～国 *govern a state* | ～丧（sāng）*make funeral arrangements* | 自～ *autonomy; self-government* [统治] 1 凭借政权来控制、管理国家或地区 to rule 2 占绝对优势，支配别的事物 to dominate ❷整理，治理 to administer; to put in order：～山 *manage mountainous areas* | ～水 *dredge rivers to prevent flooding* | ～淮工程 *engineering works to regulate the Huaihe River* ❸惩办（㊎惩－）to punish：～罪 *punish for crime* | 处（chǔ）～ *punish; penalise* ❹医治 to cure; to treat (a disease)：～病 *treat an illness* | 不～之症 *incurable disease* ㊀消灭农作物的病虫害 to eliminate (agricultural pests)：～蝗 *eliminate locusts* | ～蚜虫 *eliminate aphids* ❺从事研究 to do research：～学 *do academic research* ❻社会治理有序，跟"乱"相对 stable and peaceful (opposite of 乱)：～世 *times of peace and prosperity* | 天下大～ *whole country is politically stable* [治安] 社会的秩序 public security ❼旧称地方政府所在地 (old) location of local government：省～ *provincial capital* | 县～ *seat of county government*

栉(櫛) zhì ㄓ ❶梳子和篦子的总称 comb：～比（像梳子齿那样挨着）*arranged like the teeth of comb* ❷梳头 to comb hair：～风沐雨（形容辛苦勤劳）*be on the run and undergo all kinds of hardships (literally means 'be combed by the wind and washed by the rain')*

峙 zhì ㄓ 直立，耸立 to stand up straight; to tower：～立 *tower* | 两峰相～ *two towering mountains next to each other*

⇨ see also shì on p.602

庤 zhì ㄓ 储备 to stock up

Z

畤 zhì ㄓ 古时祭天、地、五帝的固定处所 (ancient) fixed location to offer sacrifices to the Heaven, Earth and Five Emperors

痔 zhì ㄓ 痔疮，一种肛管疾病。因肛管或直肠末端静脉曲张、瘀血而形成 haemorrhoids

跱 zhì ㄓ 〈古 ancient〉站立，伫立 to stand

陟 zhì ㄓ 登高，上升 to climb：～山 *climb a mountain*

骘（騭） zhì ㄓ 排定 to place in position：评～高低 *to rank*

贽（贄） zhì ㄓ 古时初次拜见人时所送的礼物 (ancient) gift (given the first time one meets sb)：～见 *visit sb bearing presents*｜～敬（旧时拜师送的礼）*(old) gift (given when one formally acknowledged sb as one's teacher)*

挚（摯） zhì ㄓ 亲密，诚恳（㊀真～）sincere; earnest：～友 *bosom friend*

鸷（鷙） zhì ㄓ 鸷鸟，凶猛的鸟，如鹰、雕等 raptor ㊕凶猛 fierce：勇～ *brave and fierce*

掷（擲） zhì ㄓ 扔，投，抛（㊀投～）to throw：～铁饼 *throw a discus*｜～手榴弹 *throw a grenade*

智 zhì ㄓ 聪明，智慧，见识 intelligence; wisdom; knowledge：～勇双全 *both intelligent and courageous*｜不经一事，不长（zhǎng）一～ *one cannot gain wisdom without experience*［智慧］迅速、灵活、正确地理解事物和解决问题的能力 wisdom

滞（滯） zhì ㄓ 凝积，积留，不流通 to stagnate：～留 *be detained*｜停～ *to stagnate*｜～销（销路不畅）*sell poorly*

彘 zhì ㄓ 〈古 ancient〉猪 pig

置（❶*寘） zhì ㄓ ❶放，搁，摆 to place; to put：～于桌上 *place on the table*｜～之不理 *ignore*｜～若罔闻 *deliberately ignore what one has heard* ❷设立，装设 to install：装～电话 *install a telephone* ❸购买 to buy：～地 *buy land*｜新～了一些家具 *bought new pieces of furniture*｜～了一身衣裳 *bought an outfit*

雉 zhì ㄓ ❶鸟名，即野鸡。雄的羽毛很美，尾长。雌的淡黄褐色，尾较短。善走，不能久飞。种类很多 pheasant (same as 野鸡) ❷古代城墙长三丈高一丈叫一雉 (ancient) a measurement unit of city wall (a 雉 equal to three 丈 long and one 丈 high)

稚（*穉、*稺） zhì ㄓ 幼小 immature; young：～子 *child*｜～气 *childishness*｜幼～ *childish; naive*

滍 zhì ㄓ 滍水，古水名，在河南省平顶山市。现称沙河 Zhishui River (ancient river in Pingdingshan City, Henan Province, now called 沙河)［滍阳］地名，在河南省平顶山市 Zhiyang (in Pingdingshan City, Henan Province)

疐(**疐) zhì ㄓˋ ❶遇到障碍 to be hindered ❷跌倒 to fall：跋前～后（形容进退两难）*be in a dilemma*

瘈 zhì ㄓˋ 疯狂（特指狗）(specifically of dogs) mad

⇨ see also chì on p.82

觯(觶) zhì ㄓˋ 古时饮酒用的器皿 ancient wine vessel

擿 zhì ㄓˋ ❶搔，抓 to scratch ❷ same as "掷"

⇨ see also tī on p.646

ZHONG ㄓㄨㄥ

中 zhōng ㄓㄨㄥ ❶和四周、上下或两端距离同等的位置 centre：～心 *centre* | ～途 *midway* | 路～ *middle of the road* [中央] 1 中心的地方 centre 2 政党、国家等的最高领导机构 (of party, state, etc.) highest leadership：党～ *Central Committee of the Communist Party of China* ❷在一定的范围内，里面 in; within：空～ *in the air* | 房～ *in the house* | 水～ *in the water* ❸性质、等级在两端之间的 middle：～等 *medium* | ～学 *middle school* ㊀不偏不倚 right in the middle; impartial：～庸 *(of Confucianism) the golden mean; mediocre* | 适～ *moderate; well-situated* [中子] 构成原子核的一种不带电荷的微粒 neutron ❹用在动词后，表示动作正在进行 placed after a verb to indicate continuous action：在研究～ *being studied* | 在印刷～ *being printed* | 前进～ *advancing* | 发展～ *developing* ❺指中国 China：～文 *Chinese language and literature* | 古今～外 *all times and all places* ❻适于，合于 pleasing to：～看 *pleasing to the eye* | ～听 *pleasing to the ear* [中用] 有用，有能力 useful ❼〈方 dialect〉成，行，好 all right：～不～？～。*Is it all right? It's all right.*

⇨ see also zhòng on p.862

忠 zhōng ㄓㄨㄥ 赤诚无私，诚心尽力 loyal; faithful：～诚 *loyal; devoted* | ～言 *earnest advice* | ～告 *sincerely advise; sincere advice* | ～于人民，～于祖国 *loyal to the people and the Motherland*

盅 zhōng ㄓㄨㄥ 没有把儿的小杯子 small handless cup：酒～ *small wine cup* | 茶～ *small tea cup*

钟(❶-❸鐘、❹❺△鍾) zhōng ㄓㄨㄥ ❶金属制成的响器，中空，敲时发声 bell：警～ *alarm bell* ❷计时的器具 clock：座～ *desk clock* | 闹～ *alarm clock* ❸指钟点，时间 time (in hours, minutes or seconds)：两点～ *two o'clock* | 三个～头 *three hours* ❹杯子 cup ❺集中，专一 focused：～情 *be deeply in love with*

⇨ 鍾 see also 锺 on p.861

舯 zhōng ㄓㄨㄥ 船体的中部 midship

衷 zhōng ㄓㄨㄥ 内心 heart; inner feelings：由～之言 *heartfelt words* | 苦～ *private suf-*

fering/difficulty (that one is reluctant to discuss with others or that is not easy for others to understand) | ～心拥护 *wholeheartedly support*

忪 zhōng ㄓㄨㄥ [怔忪](zhēng－)惊惧 fear

⇨ see also sōng on p.619

终(終) zhōng ㄓㄨㄥ ❶末了(liǎo),完了,跟"始"相对 end (opposite of 始): ～点 *end; destination* | 年～ *end of the year* ⓘ人死 (of humans) to die: 临～ *on one's deathbed* ❷到底,总归 in the end: ～将成功 *will succeed in the end* | ～必奏效 *will work in the end* ❸从开始到末了的(整段时间)(of time) entire; all: ～日 *the whole day* | ～年 *the whole year* | ～生 *all one's life* | ～身 *all one's life*

柊 zhōng ㄓㄨㄥ [柊叶]草本植物,根状茎块状,叶长圆形,可用来包粽子,根和叶可入药 *Phrynium capitatum* (the leaves can be used to wrap sticky rice dumplings; the root and leaves can be used as medicine)

螽 zhōng ㄓㄨㄥ 螽斯,昆虫,身体绿色或褐色,善跳跃,雄的前翅有发声器,振翅能发声 long-horned grasshopper; katydid

锺(鍾) zhōng ㄓㄨㄥ 姓 (surname) Zhong

⇨ 鍾 see also 钟 on p.860

肿(腫) zhǒng ㄓㄨㄥˇ 皮肉浮胀 (of skin) swollen: 手冻～了 *hands are swollen because of low temperature*

种(種) zhǒng ㄓㄨㄥˇ ❶(－子、－儿)植物果实中能长(zhǎng)成新植物的部分,泛指生物传代的东西 (of plants) seed; (generally) gamete: 选～ *select seed; select breed* | 撒～ *scatter seeds* | 配～ *breeding* | 优良品～ *fine variety* [有种]有胆量或有骨气 have balls ❷人种,具有共同起源和共同遗传特征的人群 race: 黄～ *mongoloid* | 白～ *Caucasian* | ～族 *race* ❸事物的类别 category: ～类 *type* | 工～ *type of work (in industry and mining)* | 军～ *services (namely the army, navy and air force)* | 剧～ *genre of drama* | 语～ *language* ❹生物的分类单位之一,在"属"之下,其下还可分出"亚种""变种" species (a category in taxonomic classification) ❺量词,表示种类,用于人和任何事物 (measure word) kind; type: 两～面料 *two types of clothing materials* | 各～东西 *all kinds of things*

⇨ see also chóng on p.83, zhòng on p.862

冢(*塚) zhǒng ㄓㄨㄥˇ 坟墓 tomb: 衣冠～ *tomb containing the personal effects, for example the clothes, etc., but not the body of the deceased*

踵 zhǒng ㄓㄨㄥˇ ❶脚后跟 heel: 继～而至 *arrive in a constant stream (literally means 'people follow each other so close that one's toe touches someone's heel')* | 摩肩接～ *packed with a moving crowd* ❷走到 to walk to:

Z

～门相告 *visit one's home to inform one* | ～谢 *thank in person* ❸跟随，追随 to follow：～至 *arrive one after another*

中 zhòng ㄓㄨㄥˋ ❶正对上，恰好合上 hit (a target); fit exactly：～的（dì，箭中靶心，比喻切中要害）*(of an arrow) hit the bullseye; (figurative) hit the nail on the head* | ～肯 *to the point; hitting home* | 正～下怀 *accord exactly with one's wishes* ❷感受，受到 to feel; to suffer from：～毒 *be poisoned* | ～暑 *suffer from heatstroke* | ～弹（dàn）*be hit with a bullet*

⇨ see also zhōng on p.860

仲 zhòng ㄓㄨㄥˋ ❶兄弟排行常用伯、仲、叔、季做次序，仲是老二 second eldest among brothers (伯，仲，叔，季 are often used to indicate the birth order of brothers)：～兄 *second eldest brother* ❷在当中的 in the middle of：～冬（冬季第二月）*midwinter (second month of the winter)* | ～裁（居间调停，裁判）*arbitrate*

茽 zhòng ㄓㄨㄥˋ 〈古 ancient〉草丛生 grass growing thickly

种（種） zhòng ㄓㄨㄥˋ 种植，把种子或幼苗等埋在泥土里使生长 to plant (seeds or seedlings)：～庄稼 *plant crops* | ～瓜得瓜，～豆得豆 *one reaps what one sows*

⇨ see also chóng on p.83, zhǒng on p.861

众（衆、*眾） zhòng ㄓㄨㄥˋ ❶许多 many：～人 *multitude; everybody* | ～志成城（喻团结力量大）*in unity lies strength (literally means 'with a strong common will, people can build a strong fortress')* | 寡不敌～ *be outnumbered* ❷许多人 many people：群～ *the masses* | 大～ *the public* | 观～ *audience*

重 zhòng ㄓㄨㄥˋ ❶分量大，跟"轻"相对 heavy (opposite of 轻)：铁很～ *iron is heavy* | ～于泰山 *of great importance (literally means 'heavier than Mount Taishan')* [重力] 又叫地心引力，地球对物体的吸引力。力的方向指向地心 gravity (also called 地心引力) [重心] 1 物体各部分受到的重力作用集中于一点，这一点叫作这个物体的重心 centre of gravity 2 事物的主要部分 core ❷重量，分量 weight：体～ *body weight* | 箱子～二十斤。*The chest weighs twenty* jin. ❸程度深 deep; serious：色～ *the colour is deep* | ～病 *serious illness* | ～伤 *seriously injured* ❹价格高 expensive：～金收买 *bribe with a huge sum of money* ❺数量多 many; thick; heavy：眉毛～ *eyebrows are thick* | 工作很～ *workload is heavy* ❻主要，要紧 main; important：～镇 *place of importance* | 军事～地 *place of military importance* | ～任 *important task* ❼认为重要 to value：～视 *to value* | ～男轻女是错误的。*It is wrong to value males more than females.* ㊀敬重，尊重，尊敬 to respect：人皆～之 *be respected by all* ❽言行不轻率 grave; serious：慎～ *prudent*

⇨ see also chóng on p.84

ZHOU ㄓㄡ

舟 zhōu ㄓㄡ 船 boat：轻～ *canoe* | 龙～ *dragon boat* | 一叶扁（piān）～ *a light small boat*

侜 zhōu ㄓㄡ 欺骗 to deceive [侜张] 作伪，欺骗 to deceive：～为幻 *confuse by deceptive means*

辀(輈) zhōu ㄓㄡ 车辕 shaft (of a carriage)

鸼(鵃) zhōu ㄓㄡ see 鹘鸼（gǔ－）at 鹘 on page 220

州 zhōu ㄓㄡ ❶旧时的一种行政区划。多用于地名，如杭州、柳州 (old) an administrative division; often used in place names, e.g. Hangzhou, Liuzhou ❷一种民族自治行政区划单位 autonomous prefecture

洲 zhōu ㄓㄡ ❶水中的陆地 island; islet: 沙～ *sandbank* ❷大陆 continent：亚～ *Asia* | 地球上有七大～。*There are seven continents on Earth.*

诌(謅) zhōu ㄓㄡ 随口编 to cook up stories：胡～ *cook up stories* | 瞎～ *talk nonsense*

周(❶-❻*週) zhōu ㄓㄡ ❶量词，用于圈数 (measure word) round; circle; circuit：绕场一～ *go once round the location* | 环绕地球一～ *encircle the Earth once* ❷周围 around：圆～ *circumference* | 学校四～都种着树。*Trees have been planted all around the school.* ❸环绕，绕一圈 to encircle：～而复始 *move in circles* [周旋] 1 打交道 to deal with：四处～ *deal with people all over* 2 交际，应酬 to socialise：与客人～ *mingle with the guests* ❹指一个星期 a week：～末 *weekend* | ～刊 *weekly (publication)* ❺普遍，全面 widespread; general：众所～知 *everyone knows* | ～身 *all over the body* ❻完备 complete; perfect：～到 *attentive and thorough* | 计划不～。*The plan is not well-thought-out.* ❼给，接济 to give; to help：～济 *give money, food, clothes, etc. to the needy* | ～急 *give money, food, clothes, etc. to those who are desperately needy* ❽朝代名 name of dynasty ①周武王姬发所建立（公元前 1046—公元前 256 年）Zhou Dynasty (1046 BCD—256 BCD, founded by Ji Fa, King Wu) ②北朝之一，宇文觉取代西魏称帝，国号周（公元 557—581 年），史称北周 Northern Zhou Dynasty (557—581, one of the Northern Dynasties, founded by Yuwen Jue) ③五代之一，郭威所建立（公元 951—960 年），史称后周 Later Zhou Dynasty (951—960, one of the Five Dynasties, founded by Guo Wei)

啁 zhōu ㄓㄡ [啁啾]（－jiū）形容鸟叫的声音 chirp; tweet

⇨ see also zhāo on p.836

婤 zhōu ㄓㄡ 用于人名。婤姶（－è），东周时卫襄公的宠妾 used in given names, e.g.

Z

Zhou'e, a concubine favoured by Duke Xiang of Wei during the Eastern Zhou Dynasty

赒(賙) zhōu ㄓㄡ 接济 to help (financially): ～恤 *give help to others*

诪(譸) zhōu ㄓㄡ ❶诅咒 to curse ❷［诪张］same as "侜张"

粥 zhōu ㄓㄡ 用米、面等煮成的半流质食品 porridge; congee

〈古 ancient〉 also same as 鬻 (yù)

盩 zhōu ㄓㄡ ［盩厔］(－zhì)地名，在陕西省。今作"周至" (now written as 周至) Zhouzhi (a place in Shaanxi Province)

妯 zhóu ㄓㄡˊ ［妯娌］(－li) 兄和弟的妻子的合称 sisters-in-law (wives of brothers): 她们俩 (liǎ) 是～。*They are sisters-in-law (their husbands are brothers).*

轴(軸) zhóu ㄓㄡˊ ❶穿在轮子中间的圆柱形物件 axle (see picture of 旧式车轮 on page 426) ❷ (－儿) 用来缠绕东西的像车轴的器物 spindle: 线～儿 *spool* | 画～ *scroll painting* 引 量词，用于缠在轴上的线及带轴子的字画 measure word for spools of thread or scroll paintings: 一～儿线 *a spool of thread* ❸把平面或立体分成对称部分的直线 axis: 天安门在北京城的中～线上。*Tian'anmen is located along the central axis of the city of Beijing.*

⇨ see also zhòu on p.865

肘 zhǒu ㄓㄡˇ 上臂与前臂相接处向外凸起的部分 elbow (see picture of 人体 on page 647) ［肘子］指用作食品的猪腿上半部 pork shoulder

帚(*箒) zhǒu ㄓㄡˇ 扫除尘土、垃圾的用具 broom

纣(紂) zhòu ㄓㄡˋ ❶牲口的后鞧 (qiū) crupper: ～棍 (系在驴、马等尾下的横木) *crupper bar* ❷古人名，殷朝末代君主 Zhou (last ruler of the Yin Dynasty)

酎 zhòu ㄓㄡˋ 多次酿成的醇酒 multiple-fermented wine

㑇(㑳) zhòu ㄓㄡˋ 乖巧，伶俐，漂亮 (元曲中常用) (usually used in Yuan drama) clever; pretty

㤘(㥮) zhòu ㄓㄡˋ 〈方 dialect〉性情固执，不听劝说 stubborn: ～脾气 *pig-headed*

绉(縐) zhòu ㄓㄡˋ 一种有皱纹的丝织品 crepe silk

皱(皺) zhòu ㄓㄡˋ ❶脸上起的褶 (zhě) 纹 wrinkle 引 物体上的褶纹 crease: 褶～ *fold; wrinkle* ❷生褶纹 to wrinkle: ～眉头 *furrow one's eyebrows* | 衬衫～了。*The shirt is wrinkled.*

咒(*呪) zhòu ㄓㄡˋ ❶某些宗教或巫术中的密语 incantation: ～语 *incantation* ❷说希望人不顺利或遭厄运的话 to curse: ～骂 *to curse* | ～人倒霉 *curse sb with bad luck*

宙 zhòu ㄓㄡˋ ❶古往今来，指所有的时间 all time ❷地质

年代分期的最高一级，在“代”之上 eon (the highest division in geological time scale, divided into 代, i.e. eras)：显生～ *Phanerozoic Eon* | 元古～ *Proterozoic Eon* | 太古～ *Archean Eon*

轴(軸) zhòu ㄓㄡˋ [（大）轴子] 一次戏曲演出的节目中排在最末的一出戏 final act (of a *xiqu* performance)：压～（倒数第二出戏）*penultimate act*

⇨ see also zhóu on p.864

胄 zhòu ㄓㄡˋ ❶盔，古代作战时戴的帽子 (ancient) war helmet ❷古代指帝王或贵族的后代 (ancient) descendants of royalty or nobility

咮 zhòu ㄓㄡˋ 鸟嘴 beak

昼(晝) zhòu ㄓㄡˋ 白天，跟“夜”相对 daytime (opposite of 夜)：～夜不停 *not to stop day or night*

甃 zhòu ㄓㄡˋ ❶井壁 well wall ❷用砖砌 to build (by laying bricks)

繇 zhòu ㄓㄡˋ 古时占卜的文辞 (ancient) divination text

⇨ see also yáo on p.761, yóu on p.793

骤(驟) zhòu ㄓㄡˋ ❶快跑(④驰一) to run fast ❷急，疾速，突然 quick; sudden：暴风～雨 *violent storm* | 天气～冷 *temperature suddenly drops* | 狂风～起 *violent gusts suddenly blow up*

籀 zhòu ㄓㄡˋ ❶籀文，古代的一种字体，即大篆，相传是周宣王时太史籀所造 seal script of calligraphy (a type of written script in ancient times, same as 大篆) ❷阅读 to read：～绎 *to deduce* | ～读 *to read aloud*

碡 zhou ・ㄓㄡ see 碌碡 (liù—) at 碌 on page 414

ZHU ㄓㄨ

朱(❷硃) zhū ㄓㄨ ❶大红色 bright red ❷朱砂，即辰砂，矿物名。化学成分是硫化汞，颜色鲜红，是提炼汞的重要原料，又可用作颜料或药材 cinnabar (same as 辰砂)

邾 zhū ㄓㄨ 周代诸侯国名，后改称“邹” Zhu (a state in the Zhou Dynasty, later renamed 邹)

侏 zhū ㄓㄨ [侏儒] 身材特别矮小的人 dwarf

诛(誅) zhū ㄓㄨ ❶把罪人杀死 to execute (a criminal)：～戮 *put to death* | 伏～ *(of criminal) be executed* | 罪不容～ *even death cannot atone for the crime* ❷责罚 to punish; to condemn：口～笔伐 *condemn verbally and in writing*

茱 zhū ㄓㄨ [茱萸] (—yú) 植物名 plant name 1 山茱萸，落叶小乔木，花黄色。果实红色，味酸，可入药 asiatic cornelian cherry fruit 2 吴茱萸，落叶乔木，花白色。果实红色，可入药 medicinal evodia fruit 3 食茱萸，落叶乔木，花淡绿色。果实红色，味苦，可入药 ailan-

Z

thus-like prickly ash

洙 zhū ㄓㄨ 洙水河，在山东省西南部 Zhushuihe River (in southwest Shandong Province)

珠 zhū ㄓㄨ ❶(一子)珍珠(也作"真珠")，淡水里的三角帆蚌和海水里的某些贝类因沙粒进入壳内，受到刺激而分泌珍珠质，逐层包起来形成的圆粒，有光泽，可入药，又可做装饰品 pearl (also written as 真珠)：～宝 *jewellery* | 夜明～ *fluorescent pearl (in ancient Chinese legend)* | 鱼目混～ *pass off fish eyes as pearls; (figurative) pass a fake off as genuine* ❷(一儿)像珠子的东西 sth like pearl：眼～儿 *eyeball* | 水～儿 *water drop* [珠算]用算盘计算的方法 calculation with abacus

株 zhū ㄓㄨ ❶露出地面的树根 exposed root：守～待兔(比喻妄想不劳而得，也指拘泥不知变通) *wait for a windfall; (also) rigid and unable to adapt to circumstances* [株连]指一人犯罪牵连到许多人 to incriminate ❷棵儿，植物体 a plant：～距 *plant spacing* | 植～ *a plant* | 病～ *diseased plant* ❸量词，用于植物 measure word for plants：一～桃树 *a peach tree*

铢(銖) zhū ㄓㄨ 古代重量单位，二十四铢等于一两 an ancient Chinese unit for measuring weight (There are 24 铢 in 1 两.)：锱～ *a very small quantity* | ～积寸累(lěi)(喻一点一滴地积累) *build up little by little*

蛛 zhū ㄓㄨ 蜘蛛，节肢动物，俗叫蛛蛛。有足四对，腹部下方有丝腺开口，能分泌黏液，织网粘捕昆虫作为食物，种类很多 spider：～网 *spider web* | ～丝马迹(喻不明显的线索) *faint traces*

诸(諸) zhū ㄓㄨ ❶众，许多 multiple; many：～位 *everybody* | ～子百家 *various schools of thought from the Pre-Qin Period to the early Han Dynasty; all trades and professions* ❷"之于"或"之乎"二字的合音 fusion of 之于 or 之乎：付～实施 *put into operation* | 藏～名山 *(of written work) of much value to future generations* | 公～社会 *make public* | 有～？ *Is that so?*

猪(*豬) zhū ㄓㄨ 家畜，鼻子长，耳朵大，体肥多肉。肉可吃，皮和鬃是工业原料 pig

槠(櫧) zhū ㄓㄨ 常绿乔木，花黄绿色。木质坚硬，可制器具 evergreen chinkapin

潴(瀦)** zhū ㄓㄨ ❶(水)积聚 (of water) to accumulate ❷水停聚的地方 pool

橥(櫫)** zhū ㄓㄨ 用作标志的小木桩 wooden peg used as a sign

术 zhú ㄓㄨˊ 植物名 plant name ①白术，草本植物，秋天开紫色花。根状茎可入药 *Atractylodes macrocephala* (a plant used in traditional Chinese medicine) ②苍术，草本植物，秋

天开白色花，根状茎可入药 *Atractylodes lancea* (a plant used in traditional Chinese medicine) ③ 莪术 see 莪术 (é—) at 莪 on page 157

⇨ see also shù on p.610

竹 zhú ㄓㄨˊ （—子）常绿植物，茎节明显，中空，质地坚硬，可做器物，又可做建筑材料 bamboo：茂林修～ *thick forest of tall bamboo* | ～苞松茂 *solid foundation and spreading branches; congratulatory greeting for the completion of one's new house or for one's birthday* | 势如破～ *overcome the enemy with ease*

竺 zhú ㄓㄨˊ 姓 (surname) Zhu [天竺] 我国古代称印度 Tianzhu (ancient Chinese name for India)

逐 zhú ㄓㄨˊ ❶追赶（㊥追—）to chase：～鹿 *contend for power; to compete* | ～臭之夫 *eccentric person who runs after stinkiness* ❷赶走，强迫离开（㊥驱—）to drive out：～客令 *order for guests to leave* | 追亡～北（追击败逃的敌人）*pursue fleeing enemies* ❸依照先后次序，一一挨着 one by one：～日 *day by day* | ～步 *step by step* | ～字～句 *word by word, line by line* | ～渐 *gradually*

瘃 zhú ㄓㄨˊ 古书上指冻疮 chilblain (in ancient Chinese texts)

烛(燭) zhú ㄓㄨˊ ❶蜡烛，用线绳或苇子做中心，周围包上蜡油，点着取亮的东西 candle ❷照亮，照见 to illuminate：火光～天 *flames light up the sky* ㊀明察 to scrutinise：洞～其奸 *see through the deception*

蠋 zhú ㄓㄨˊ 蝴蝶、蛾子等的幼虫 caterpillar

躅 zhú ㄓㄨˊ see 踯躅 (zhí—) at 踯 on page 853

舳 zhú ㄓㄨˊ 船尾 stern (of a boat) [舳舻]（—lú）船尾和船头，也指首尾相接的船只 stern and prow; (also) boats arranged end to end：～千里 *a large number of ships*

主 zhǔ ㄓㄨˇ ❶主人 master ①权力或财物的所有者 owner：人民是国家的～人。*The people are the masters of the country.* | 物～ *owner of sth* ②接待客人的人，跟"宾、客"相对 host (opposite of 宾，客)：宾～ *guest and host* | 东道～ *host* ③事件中的当事人 person concerned：事～ *victim of crime* | 失～ *owner of lost property* ④旧社会占有奴隶或雇用仆役的人 (old) master (of slaves or servants)：奴隶～ *slave owner* | ～仆 *master and servant* [主观] 1 属于自我意识方面的，跟"客观"相对 subjective (opposite of 客观)：人类意识属于～，物质世界属于客观。*Human consciousness is subjective; the material world is objective.* 2 不依据客观事物，单凭自己的偏见的 biased：他的意见太～了。*His views are too biased.* 3 属于自身方面的 relating to oneself：～努力 *one's own efforts* [主权] 一个国家的独立自主的权力 sover-

Z

eignty ❷主张，决定 standpoint; decision：～见 *one's own definite opinion* | ～和 *advocate peaceful resolution* | 婚姻自～ *decide independently on one's own marriage* [主义] 1 人们对于自然界、社会以及学术、文艺等问题所持的有系统的理论与主张 -ism; doctrine：马克思～ *Marxism* | 达尔文～ *Darwinism* | 现实～ *realism* 2 思想作风 ideology and behaviour：革命乐观～ *revolutionary optimism* ❸最重要的，最基本的 most important; fundamental：～力 *main force* | 以预防为～，治疗为辅 *prevention is better than cure* ❹主持，负主要责任 in charge of: ～办 *to organise* | ～讲 *give a lecture* ❺预示 to portend：早霞～雨，晚霞～晴。*Red sky at night, shepherd's delight; red sky at morning, shepherd's warning.* ❻对事情的定见 definite view：六神无～ *in a state of utter confusion* | 心里没～ *have no idea what to do*

拄 zhǔ ㄓㄨˇ 用手扶着杖或棍支持身体 to support oneself (with a stick)：～拐棍 *use a walking stick*

让(詝) zhǔ ㄓㄨˇ 智慧 wisdom

渚 zhǔ ㄓㄨˇ 水中间的小块陆地 islet; small sandbank

煮(*煑) zhǔ ㄓㄨˇ 把东西放在水里，用火把水烧开 to boil：～面 *cook noodles* | ～饭 *cook rice* | 病人的碗筷餐后要～一下。*Patients' bowls and chopsticks must be put in boiling water after meals.*

褚 zhǔ ㄓㄨˇ ❶在衣服里铺丝绵 stuff clothing (with padding) ❷囊，口袋 bag; pocket

⇨ see also chǔ on p.88

属(屬) zhǔ ㄓㄨˇ ❶连缀 to join：～文 *to write* | 前后相～ *start and finish are connected* ❷(意念)集中在一点 to focus (thoughts)：～意 *fix one's mind on* | ～望 *to hope; to expect* ❸ (ancient) same as "嘱"

⇨ see also shǔ on p.609

嘱(囑) zhǔ ㄓㄨˇ 托付，告诫 to entrust; to admonish：以事相～ *entrust sb with sth* | ～托 *to entrust* | ～咐 *to enjoin* | 叮～ *to urge repeatedly* | 遗～ *will; testament*

瞩(矚) zhǔ ㄓㄨˇ 注视 to gaze：～目 *focus one's attention on* | ～望 *to expect; to gaze* | 高瞻远～ *far-sighted*

麈 zhǔ ㄓㄨˇ 古书上指鹿一类的动物，尾巴可以当作拂尘 deer-like animal in ancient Chinese texts, whose tail could be used as a duster

伫(*佇、*竚) zhù ㄓㄨˋ 长时间站着 stand for a long time：～立 *stand for a long time* | ～候 *stand waiting*

苎(△苧) zhù ㄓㄨˋ 苎麻，草本植物，茎皮纤维可以制绳索，又是纺织工业的重要原料 ramie

⇨ 苧 see also níng on p.480

纻(紵) zhù ㄓㄨˋ ❶ same as "苎" ❷苎麻织成的

布 ramie fabric

贮(貯) zhù ㄓㄨˋ 储存(㊊—存、—藏) to store

助 zhù ㄓㄨˋ 帮(㊊帮—), 协助 to help: 互～ *help each other* | ～理 *assistant* | ～我一臂之力 *lend me a helping hand* [助词] 不能独立使用，只能依附在别的词、词组或句子后面表示一定语法意义的词，如"的""了""吗"等 auxiliary word

住 zhù ㄓㄨˋ ❶长期居留或暂时留宿 to live; or stay: ～了一夜 *stayed for a night* | 他家在这里～了好几代。*His family has been living here for generations.* | 我家～在城外。*I live outside the city.* ❷停，止 to stop: ～手 *to stop (doing sth)* | 雨～了。*The rain has stopped.* ❸用作动词的补语 used as a complement after a verb ①表示稳当或牢固 used to indicate stability: 站～ *stand still* | 把～方向盘 *hold the steering wheel firmly* ②表示停顿或静止 used to indicate a pause or lack of motion: 把他问～了 *the question left him dumbstruck* ③表示力量够得上(跟"得"或"不"连用) used to indicate ability to withstand sth (used with 得 or 不): 禁(jīn)得～ *able to bear* | 支持不～ *unable to hold up*

注(❸–❺*註) zhù ㄓㄨˋ ❶灌进去 to pour: ～入 *pump into; feed into* | ～射 *to inject* | 大雨如～ *be raining cats and dogs* ❷集中在一点 to focus: ～视 *gaze at* | ～意 *pay attention to* | 引人～目 *conspicuous* | 全神贯～ *totally absorbed* ❸用文字来解释词句 to annotate: 下边～了两行小注。*There are two lines of annotations below.* | ～解 *to annotate; annotation* | 校(jiào)～ *to check and annotate* ❹解释词、句所用的文字 annotation: 加～ *to annotate* | 附～ *annotation* ❺记载，登记 to record; to register: ～册 *to register* | ～销 *to cancel* ❻赌博时所押的财物 stake (in gambling): 下～ *place bets* | 孤～一掷(喻拿出所有的力量希望最后侥幸成功) *risk everything on a single venture*

驻(駐) zhù ㄓㄨˋ ❶(车马等)停止，泛指停止或停留 (of carriages, horses, etc.) to stop; (generally) to stop/stay: ～马 *bring one's horse to a stop* | ～足 *stop in one's tracks* | 青春永～ *be forever youthful* ❷停留在一个地方 to station: ～军 *to station troops; troops (stationed at a place)* | ～外使节 *overseas envoy*

柱 zhù ㄓㄨˋ ❶(—子)建筑物中直立的起支撑作用的构件，多用木、石等制成 pillar; column ❷像柱子的东西 sth like pillar: 水～ *water column* | 花～ *style (of flowers)* | 水银～ *column of mercury*

炷 zhù ㄓㄨˋ ❶灯心 wick ❷烧 to burn ❸量词，用于线香 measure word for incense sticks: 一～香 *a stick of incense*

砫 zhù ㄓㄨˋ [石砫] 地名，在重庆市。今作"石柱"(now

Z

written as 石柱) Shizhu (a place in Chongqing Municipality)

疰 zhù ㄓㄨˋ [疰夏] 1 中医指夏季长期发热的病，多由排汗功能发生障碍引起，患者多为小儿 (in traditional Chinese medicine) summer non-acclimatization 2〈方 dialect〉苦夏 tiredness and appetite loss during summer

蛀 zhù ㄓㄨˋ ❶蛀虫，咬木器、谷物或衣物的小虫 borer ❷虫子咬坏 (of boring insects) to damage：木头被虫～了。*The wood was damaged by insects.*

杼 zhù ㄓㄨˋ 织布机上的筘(kòu)。古代也指梭 reed (of a loom); (ancient) shuttle

柷 zhù ㄓㄨˋ 古代乐器，木制，形状像方形的斗 ancient percussion instrument made of wood

⇨ see also chù on p.89

祝 zhù ㄓㄨˋ ❶削，断绝 to cut：～发为僧 *take the tonsure and become a Buddhist monk* ❷表示对人对事的美好愿望 give one's good wishes：～愿 *to wish*｜～福 *to bless*｜～身体健康 *wish one good health*

著 zhù ㄓㄨˋ ❶显明，显出(㊀显一、昭一) outstanding：卓～ *outstanding*｜～名 *famous*｜颇～成效 *prove rather effective* ❷写文章，写书 to write (an essay or a book)：～书立说 *write books to establish one's own theory; (generally) produce academic works* ❸著作，写出来的文章或书 written work：名～ *famous book*｜译～ *translated book*

[土著] 1 世代居住在一定的地方 indigenous; aboriginal 2 世代居住在本地的人 aborigine; native

⇨ see also zhuó on p.878

翥 zhù ㄓㄨˋ 鸟向上飞 (of birds) fly upwards：龙翔凤～ *dragons and phoenixes flying high; (figurative) be in high spirits*

箸(*筯) zhù ㄓㄨˋ 筷子 chopsticks

铸(鑄) zhù ㄓㄨˋ 把金属熔化后倒在模子里制成器物 casting (in metallurgy)：～一口铁锅 *cast an iron pot*｜～成大错(造成大错误) *commit a grave error* [铸铁] 由铁矿砂最初炼出来的铁。含碳量在 2.0% 以上，质脆，易熔化，多用来铸造器物。旧时又叫铣(xiǎn)铁 (formerly also called 铣 xiǎn 铁) cast iron

筑(❶築) zhù ㄓㄨˋ ❶建造，修盖(㊀建一) to construct; to build：～路 *build a road*｜～堤 *build a dyke*｜建～ *to build; building* ❷古代的一种弦乐器，像琴，有十三根弦 ancient stringed instrument with thirteen strings ❸ (formerly pronounced zhú) 贵州省贵阳的别称 Zhu (another name for Guiyang, Guizhou Province)

ZHUA ㄓㄨㄚ

抓 zhuā ㄓㄨㄚ ❶用指或爪挠(náo) to scratch：～耳挠腮 *scratch one's ears and cheeks (because of anxiety, helplessness, or joy)* ❷用手或爪拿取 to grab：老鹰～小鸡 *eagle catching chicks (a*

Z

children's game) | ～一把米 *grab a handful of rice* 引①捕捉（连一捕）to capture：～贼 *catch a thief* | ～逃犯 *catch an escaped criminal* ②把握住，不放过 to seize：～工夫 *find time (to do sth)* | ～紧时间 *make the best use of one's time* ❸着力办理 put all one's effort into：～农业 *focus on agriculture* | ～工作 *go all out in one's work* | ～重点 *focus on key points* ❹引人注意 attract attention：这个演员一出场就～住了观众。*This actor captivated the audience as soon as he/she came on the stage.*

挝（撾）zhuā ㄓㄨㄚ 打，敲打 to hit

⇨ see also wō on p.687

髽 zhuā ㄓㄨㄚ ［髽髻］（一ji）［髽鬏］（一jiu）女孩子梳在头两旁的发结。也作"抓髻""抓鬏"(also written as 抓髻，抓鬏) double bun (girl's hairstyle with one bun on each side of the head)

爪 zhuǎ ㄓㄨㄚˇ ❶（一子、一儿）禽兽的脚（多指有尖甲的）animal foot (often with claws)：鸡～子 *chicken foot* | 狗～儿 *dog's paw* ❷（一儿）某些器物上像爪的东西 sth like claw：这个锅有三个～儿。*This pot has three feet.*

⇨ see also zhǎo on p.836

ZHUAI ㄓㄨㄞ

拽 zhuāi ㄓㄨㄞ 〈方 dialect〉❶用力扔 to throw (with some force)：～了吧，没用了。*Throw it away; it's useless.* | 把球～过来 *throw the ball over here* ❷胳膊有毛病，动转不灵 (of one's arm) stiff

⇨ see also yè on p.766, zhuài on p.871

跩 zhuǎi ㄓㄨㄞˇ 走路像鸭子似的摇摆 to waddle：走路一～一～的 *walk with a waddling gait*

拽（**攠）zhuài ㄓㄨㄞˋ 拉，拖，牵引 to pull：～不动 *cannot be moved by pulling* | 把门～上 *pull the door shut* | 生拉硬～ *drag sb kicking and screaming; draw a forced analogy*

⇨ see also yè on p.766, zhuāi on p.871

ZHUAN ㄓㄨㄢ

专（專、❶❷△*耑）zhuān ㄓㄨㄢ ❶单纯，独一，集中在一件事上 specialized; focused：～心 *concentrated* | ～卖 *monopolise the sale of; specialize in the sale of a particular (brand-name) commodity* | ～修科 *special training course* ［专家］学术技能有专长的人 expert ❷独自掌握或享有 to monopolise：～权 *monopolise power* | ～政 *dictatorship* ❸姓 (surname) Zhuan

⇨ 耑 see also duān on p.149

肫（膞）zhuān ㄓㄨㄢ 〈方 dialect〉鸟类的胃 gizzard：鸡～ *chicken gizzard*

砖（磚、*甎、*塼）zhuān ㄓㄨㄢ ❶用土坯烧成的建筑材料 brick

Z

❷像砖的东西 sth like brick：茶～ *brick tea* | 冰～ *ice cream block* | 金～ *gold bullion; a square paving brick used for traditional Chinese buildings* | 煤～ *briquette*

颛(顓) zhuān ㄓㄨㄢ ❶愚昧 foolish ❷ same as "专❶❷"

［颛顼］（—xū）传说中上古帝王名 Zhuanxu (a legendary emperor in ancient times)

转(轉) zhuǎn ㄓㄨㄢˇ ❶旋动，改换方向或情势 to turn：～身 *turn round* | 运～ *to revolve; to operate* | 向左～ *turn to the left* | ～眼之间 *in a blink of an eye* | ～危为安 *turn a critical situation around* ❷不直接地，中间再经过别人或别的地方 to pass on indirectly：～送 *pass sth on; to regift* | ～达 *to convey*

⇨ see also zhuàn on p.872

传(傳) zhuàn ㄓㄨㄢˋ ❶旧时一般指解说儒家经书的文字 (old) commentary (on Confucian classics) ❷记载。特指记载某人一生事迹的文字 record (specifically biography)：小～ *brief biography* | 别～ *anecdotal biography* | 外～ *unofficial biography* ❸叙述历史故事的作品 historical fiction (used in titles)：《儿女英雄～》The Tale of Heroic Sons and Daughters | 《水浒～》Outlaws of the Marsh

⇨ see also chuán on p.91

转(轉) zhuàn ㄓㄨㄢˋ ❶旋转，绕着圈儿动，围绕着中心运动 to rotate; to turn：轮子～得很快。*The wheel is turning very fast.* ❷绕着某物移动，打转 to revolve around sth：～圈子 *turn in circles* | ～来～去 *walk back and forth* ❸量词，绕几圈儿叫绕几转 (measure word) circuit

⇨ see also zhuǎn on p.872

啭(囀) zhuàn ㄓㄨㄢˋ 鸟婉转地叫 (of a bird) to tweet：莺啼鸟～ *birds twitter*

沌 zhuàn ㄓㄨㄢˋ 用于地名 used in place names：～口（在湖北省武汉）*Zhuankou (in Wuhan, Hubei Province)* | ～阳（在湖北省武汉）*Zhuanyang (in Wuhan, Hubei Province)*

⇨ see also dùn on p.153

瑑 zhuàn ㄓㄨㄢˋ 玉器上隆起的雕刻花纹 relief carving (on jade objects)

篆 zhuàn ㄓㄨㄢˋ ❶篆字，古代的一种字体，有大篆、小篆 seal script (ancient style of Chinese calligraphy, divided into 大篆 and 小篆) ❷书写篆字 to write in seal script：～额（用篆字写碑额）*write the inscription on the top part of a tablet in seal script* ❸指印章 stamp; seal

赚(賺) zhuàn ㄓㄨㄢˋ ❶做买卖得利，跟"赔"相对 to profit (opposite of 赔)：～钱 *make money* ❷做买卖得的利 profit：有～儿 *with profit* | ～头 *profit* ❸占便宜 gain advantage：这回出差真～，顺便游了庐山。*One got something extra out of this business trip: one visited Lushan*

Mountain on the way.

⇨ see also zuàn on p.889

僎 zhuàn ㄓㄨㄢˋ 具备 have everything ready

撰(*譔) zhuàn ㄓㄨㄢˋ 写文章，著书 to write (an essay or a book)：～文 *write an essay* | ～稿 *write an article*

馔(饌、*篹) zhuàn ㄓㄨㄢˋ 饮食，吃喝 food and drink：盛～ *lavish feast* | 设～招待 *food will be served (for the guest)*

ZHUANG ㄓㄨㄤ

妆(妝、*粧) zhuāng ㄓㄨㄤ ❶修饰，打扮 to dress up：梳～ *dress and put on make-up* | 化～ *put on make-up* ❷妇女脸上、身上的装饰 jewellery and make-up：卸～ *remove make-up; (old) remove adornments* | 素～ *simple, discreet outfit and make-up; put on simple make-up* | 红～ *elaborate, fancy outfit* ❸出嫁女子的陪送衣物 dowry：送～ *send the dowry from the bride's family to the groom's family* | 嫁～ *dowry*

庄(莊) zhuāng ㄓㄨㄤ ❶村落，田舍(㊀村一) village ❷商店的一种名称 shop：布～ *fabric shop* | 饭～ *restaurant* | 茶～ *tea shop* ❸封建社会君主、贵族等所占有的成片土地 (old) land owned by rulers, the nobility, etc.：皇～ *crown lands* | ～园 *demesne* ❹庄家，打牌时每一局的主持人 banker (in gambling)：轮流坐～ *take turns to be banker* ❺严肃，庄重(㊀一严、端一) solemn

桩(樁) zhuāng ㄓㄨㄤ ❶(一子)一头插入地里的木棍或石柱 wood or stone pile (in construction)：打～ *drive a pile into the ground* | 牲口～子 *hitching post for farm animals* | 桥～ *bridge pillar* ❷量词，用于事件 measure word for events or incidents：一～事 *an incident* | 两～买卖 *two transactions*

装(裝) zhuāng ㄓㄨㄤ ❶穿着的衣物(㊀服一) clothing：军～ *military uniform* | 春～ *spring clothing* | 泳～ *swimming costume* 特指演员演出时的打扮 (specifically) stage makeup and costume：上～ *put on makeup and costume* | 卸～ *remove makeup and costume* [行装] 出行时带的衣物 luggage ❷打扮，用服饰使人改变原来的外貌(㊀一扮) to dress up; to disguise oneself [装饰] 1 加上一些附属的东西使美观 to decorate：～房间 *decorate a room* 2 修饰用的物品 decoration [化装] 改变装束 to disguise oneself ❸故意做作，假作 to pretend：～听不见 *pretend not to hear* | ～模作样 *put on an act* ❹安置，安放，通常指放到器物里面去 to install (often by inserting)：～电灯 *fit a light bulb* | ～车 *load cargo onto a vehicle* | ～箱 *load cargo into a box or container* ㊁把零部件安在一起构成整体 to assemble：～配 *as-*

Z

semble | ～了一台电脑 *assembled a computer* [装备] 1 生产上或军事上必需的东西 equipment：工业～ *industrial equipment* | 军事～ *military equipment* 2 配备 to equip：学校正在～多媒体教室。*The school is fitting out a multi-media classroom.* ❺对书籍、字画加以修整或修整成的式样 to bind a book; to mount a calligraphic work or painting; binding; mounting: ～订 *to bind; binding* | 精～ *(of book) hardback* | 线～书 *thread-bound book*

奘 zhuǎng ㄓㄨㄤˇ 粗大 stout：这棵树很～。*This tree is big.* | 这人真～。*This person is very stout.*

⇨ see also zàng on p.819

壮(壯) zhuàng ㄓㄨㄤˋ ❶健壮，有力（㊥强－）strong; forceful：～士 *heroic man; warrior* | 年轻力～ *young and strong* | 庄稼长得很～。*The crops are very sturdy.* [壮年] 习惯指人三四十岁的时期 prime of one's life (usually refers to a person in their thirties and forties) ❷雄伟，有气魄 magnificent: ～观 *magnificent sight* | ～志凌云 *soaring aspiration* ❸增加勇气或力量 to boost one's courage or strength：～一～胆子 *boost one's courage*

[壮族] 我国少数民族，参看附录四 the Zhuang people (one of the ethnic groups in China. See Appendix Ⅳ.)

状(狀) zhuàng ㄓㄨㄤˋ ❶形态（㊥形－、－态）condition; state：奇形怪～ *strange in shape and appearance* ❷事情表现出来的情形（㊥－况）condition：病～ *symptom* | ～况 *condition* ❸陈述或描摹 to describe; to depict：写情～物 *write about emotions and things* | 风景奇丽，殆不可～。*The scenery is so fantastically beautiful that it almost defies description.* ❹叙述事件的文字 written account：行～（指死者传略）*brief biography of a deceased person* | 诉～ *plaint* ❺褒奖、委任等的凭证 certificate (of commendation, appointment, etc.)：奖～ *certificate of award* | 委任～ *certificate of appointment*

僮 zhuàng ㄓㄨㄤˋ 我国少数民族壮族的"壮"字旧作"僮" the Zhuang people (now written as 壮)

⇨ see also tóng on p.658

撞 zhuàng ㄓㄨㄤˋ ❶击打 to strike：～钟 *strike a bell* ❷碰 to collide：别让汽车～了。*Be careful not to be hit by the car.* ㊀无意中遇到 to bump into (sb)：让我～见了 *I bumped into* ❸莽撞地行动，闯 to act rashly; to rush：横冲直～ *dash around madly*

幢 zhuàng ㄓㄨㄤˋ 〈方 dialect〉量词，用于房子 measure word for buildings：一～楼 *one building*

⇨ see also chuáng on p.92

戇(戆) zhuàng ㄓㄨㄤˋ 刚直 upright and outspoken：性情～直 *upright and outspoken personality*

⇨ see also gàng on p.201

ZHUI ㄓㄨㄟ

隹 zhuī ㄓㄨㄟ 短尾巴的鸟 birds with short tails

骓(騅) zhuī ㄓㄨㄟ 毛色青白相杂的马 piebald horse

椎 zhuī ㄓㄨㄟ 椎骨，构成人和高等动物脊柱的短骨 vertebra：颈～ *cervical vertebrae*｜胸～ *thoracic vertebrae*｜腰～ *lumbar vertebrae*｜尾～ *caudal vertebrae; coccyx*

⇨ see also chuí on p.94

锥(錐) zhuī ㄓㄨㄟ ❶（一子）一头尖锐，可以扎窟窿的工具 awl：针～ *awl*｜无立～之地（形容赤贫）*extremely poor* ❷像锥子的东西 sth like an awl：改～ *screwdriver*｜冰～ *icicle* ❸用锥子形的工具钻 to bore with an awl or similar tool：用锥子～个眼儿 *bore a hole with an awl*

追 zhuī ㄓㄨㄟ ❶赶，紧跟着（㊥一逐）to chase：～随 *follow*｜～击敌人 *pursue and attack the enemy*｜急起直～ *start quickly and surge forward*｜他走得太快，我～不上他。*I cannot catch up with him because he walks too fast.* ❷追溯过去，事后补做 to look back at the past; to add on afterwards：～念 *to recollect*｜～悼 *mourn*｜～认 *subsequently confirm; posthumously confer*｜～加预算 *add to the original budget*｜～肥 *top application of fertiliser* ❸竭力探求，寻求 to seek with great effort：～问 *ask closely*｜～根 *get to the bottom of sth*｜这件事不必再～了。*It is no longer necessary to get to the bottom of this matter.*｜～求真理 *seek the truth*

坠(墜) zhuì ㄓㄨㄟˋ ❶落，掉下 to fall：～马 *fall from a horse*｜摇摇欲～ *tottering* ❷往下沉 to sink：船锚往下～。*The ship's anchor is sinking.* ❸（一儿）系在器物上垂着的东西 sth that is tied to and hangs off an object：扇～ *fan pendant*｜表～ *watch pendant* [坠子] 1 耳朵上的一种装饰品。又叫耳坠子、耳坠儿 ear pendent; earring (also called 耳坠子，耳坠儿) 2 流行于河南、山东的一种曲艺形式 a musical art form popular in Henan and Shandong provinces

缀(綴) zhuì ㄓㄨㄟˋ ❶缝（féng）to sew：～扣子 *sew a button*｜补～ *mend (by sewing)* ❷连接 to connect; to link：～字成文 *link words together to create a piece of writing* [词缀] 加在词根上的构词成分。常见的有前缀（也叫词头）和后缀（也叫词尾）两种 affix (usually including prefix [前缀，also 词头] and suffix [后缀，also 词尾]) ❸装饰 to decorate：点～ *embellish*

醊 zhuì ㄓㄨㄟˋ 祭奠 memorial ceremony for the dead

惴 zhuì ㄓㄨㄟˋ 又忧愁，又恐惧 ㊖ worried and fearful：～～不安 *nervous and worried*

缒(縋) zhuì ㄓㄨㄟˋ 用绳子拴住人、物从上往下

Z

送 to lower sb or sth on a rope：工人们从楼顶上把空桶～下来。*The workers lowered the empty barrel down with a rope from the top of the building.*

膇 zhuì ㄓㄨㄟˋ 脚肿 swelling of the feet

赘(贅) zhuì ㄓㄨㄟˋ ❶多余的，多而无用的 superfluous：～述 *give unnecessary details; say more than is needed* | ～言 *unnecessary talk* | ～疣 *wart; (figurative) superfluous thing* ❷男子到女家结婚并成为女家的家庭成员叫入赘，女家招女婿叫招赘 a man marrying into and living with his wife's family is called 入赘; a woman's family receiving a groom who lives with the family is called 招赘：～婿 *a man who lives with his wife's family*

ZHUN ㄓㄨㄣ

屯 zhūn ㄓㄨㄣ 困难 trouble [屯邅](－zhān) same as "迍邅"

⇨ see also tún on p.666

迍 zhūn ㄓㄨㄣ [迍邅](－zhān) 1 迟迟不前 at a standstill; not moving forward 2 处在困难中，十分不得志 in deep trouble

肫 zhūn ㄓㄨㄣ ❶〈方 dialect〉鸟类的胃 gizzard：鸡～ *chicken gizzard* | 鸭～ *duck gizzard* ❷恳切，真挚㊀ earnest; sincere：～～ *sincerely* | ～笃 *sincere and faithful*

窀 zhūn ㄓㄨㄣ [窀穸](－xī) 墓穴 grave (for the dead)

谆(諄) zhūn ㄓㄨㄣ 恳切 earnest [谆谆] 恳切，不厌倦地 earnestly; tirelessly：～告诫 *caution sb tirelessly* | ～教导 *instruct sb tirelessly* | 言之～ *speak earnestly*

衠 zhūn ㄓㄨㄣ 〈方 dialect〉纯粹，纯 pure

准(❷-❿準) zhǔn ㄓㄨㄣˇ ❶允许，许可 to permit：批～ *approve* | 不～他来。*He is not allowed to come.* ❷依照，依据 to follow; in accordance with：～此办理 *handle it this way* ❸定平直的东西 level; yardstick：水～ *level* | ～绳 *yardstick; criterion* ❹标准，法则，可以作为依据的 standard：～则 *norm; standard* | 以此为～。*Use this as the standard.* ❺ same as "埻" ❻正确(㊥－确) correct：瞄～ *take aim at* | 他枪打得很～。*He is a sharp shooter.* ❼副词，一定，确实 (adverb) definitely：我～来。*I shall definitely come.* | ～能完成任务。*The mission can certainly be accomplished.* ❽鼻子 nose：隆～(高鼻子) *high-bridged nose* ❾(－儿) 把握 confidence：心里没～儿 *not feel confident* ❿可作为某类事物看待的 quasi-; para-：～将 *brigadier general* | ～平原 *peneplain*

埻 zhǔn ㄓㄨㄣˇ 箭靶上的中心 bull's eye (in archery)

綧(綧) zhǔn ㄓㄨㄣˇ 〈古 ancient〉标准，准则 standard; norm

ZHUO ㄓㄨㄛ

拙 zhuō ㄓㄨㄛ ❶笨，不灵巧（㊀—笨）clumsy：～嘴笨舌 *awkward in speech* | 手～ *clumsy with one's hands* | 弄巧成～ *try to be clever and mess things up* | 勤能补～ *hard work makes up for lack of skill* ❷ 谦辞 (humble speech) my：～作 *my (poor) work* | ～见 *my (humble) opinion*

捉 zhuō ㄓㄨㄛ ❶抓，逮 to capture：～老鼠 *catch a mouse/ rat* | 捕风～影 *speak/act on shaky grounds* [捉弄] 玩弄，戏弄 to tease ❷ 握 to hold：～刀 *ghostwrite; be a proxy* | ～笔 *write*

桌（*槕） zhuō ㄓㄨㄛ ❶（—子、—儿）一种日用家具，上面可以放东西 table：书～ *desk* | 饭～ *dining table* | 八仙～ *square table that seats eight people* ❷量词，用于成桌的饭菜或围着桌子坐的客人 (measure word) table：一～酒席 *a table of victuals* | 来客可坐三～。*The guests could fill three tables.*

倬 zhuō ㄓㄨㄛ ❶显著 noticeable ❷大 big

焯 zhuō ㄓㄨㄛ 显明，明白 clear; obvious

⇨ see also chāo on p.71

棁 zhuō ㄓㄨㄛ 梁上的短柱 short support on a rafter or beam

涿 zhuō ㄓㄨㄛ 涿州，地名，在河北省 Zhuozhou (a place in Hebei Province)

镯（鐲） zhuō ㄓㄨㄛ〈方 dialect〉❶镯钩，刨地的镐（gǎo）hoe ❷用小镐刨 to dig with a small pickaxe：～高粱 *dig out sorghum* | ～玉米 *dig out maize*

汋 zhuó ㄓㄨㄛˊ 形容水激荡的声音 gurgle (used to describe the sound of rushing water)

灼 zhuó ㄓㄨㄛˊ ❶烧，炙 to burn：～伤 *be burned; burn* | 心如火～ *feel very anxious* ❷明亮，透彻 clear and bright：目光～～ *clear and bright eyes* | 真知～见 *correct and insightful opinions*

酌 zhuó ㄓㄨㄛˊ ❶斟酒 to pour wine：自～自饮 *drink by oneself* ㊁酒饭 meal with wine：便～ *casual meal* ❷度量，考虑(㊀—量) to consider：～办 *do as one thinks fit* | ～情 *take into consideration the circumstances* | ～加修改 *make changes as one thinks fit*

茁 zhuó ㄓㄨㄛˊ 植物才生长出来的样子 (of a plant) thriving [茁壮] 1 强壮茂盛 strong and vigorous：庄稼长得～。*The crops are growing healthily.* 2 健壮 healthy and strong：牛羊～。*The cows and goats are healthy and strong.* | 青少年～成长 *the strong and healthy development of youths*

卓 zhuó ㄓㄨㄛˊ ❶高而直 tall and straight：～立 *stand tall* ❷高明，高超，杰出，不平凡 outstanding; extraordinary：～见 *brilliant opinion* | ～越 *outstanding* [卓绝] 超过寻常，没有能比的

Z

incomparable：坚苦～ *incomparable tenacity in hardship*

䓬 zhuó ㄓㄨㄛˊ 化学上指环庚三烯（一种环烃）的正离子 tropylium ion

晫 zhuó ㄓㄨㄛˊ 明亮，昌盛 bright; flourishing

叕 zhuó ㄓㄨㄛˊ ❶连缀 to connect ❷短 short

斫（*斲、*斵、*斮） zhuó ㄓㄨㄛˊ 砍削 to chop; to cut：～伐树木 *fell trees*｜～轮老手（指经验多的人）*person with vast experience*

浊（濁） zhuó ㄓㄨㄛˊ ❶水、空气等含杂质，不清洁，不干净，跟"清"相对（㊟浑～）(of water, air, etc.) impure; unclean (opposite of 清) ❷混乱 chaos：～世（形容混乱的时代）*chaotic times* ❸（声音）低沉粗重 (of one's voice) deep and rough-sounding：～声～气 *deep, gravelly voice* ❹浊音，发音时声带颤动的音 voiced sound

镯（鐲、**鋜） zhuó ㄓㄨㄛˊ（～子）套在腕子上的环形装饰品 bangle：手～ *bangle*｜玉～ *jade bangle*

浞 zhuó ㄓㄨㄛˊ 〈方 dialect〉淋，使湿 to wet：让雨～了 *got wet in the rain*

诼（諑） zhuó ㄓㄨㄛˊ 造谣毁谤 to slander

啄 zhuó ㄓㄨㄛˊ 鸟类用嘴叩击或吃食 (of birds) to peck：鸡～米 *chickens peck rice*｜～木鸟 *woodpecker*

琢 zhuó ㄓㄨㄛˊ 雕刻玉石，使成器物 to carve (jade or stone)：精雕细～ *be meticulous in doing sth*［琢磨］1 雕刻和打磨（玉石）carve and polish (jade or stone) 2 加工使精美（指文章等）to embellish (writing, etc.)

⇨ see also zuó on p.891

椓 zhuó ㄓㄨㄛˊ ❶击 to strike ❷古代宫刑，割去男性的生殖器 (ancient) castration as punishment

著 zhuó ㄓㄨㄛˊ 附着，穿着。后作"着"（zhuó）(later written as 着 zhuó) to adhere to; one's outfit

⇨ see also zhù on p.870

着 zhuó ㄓㄨㄛˊ ❶穿（衣）to wear (clothes)：～衣 *wear clothes*｜～装 *one's outfit* ❷接触，挨上 to touch; to contact：附～ *adhere to*｜～陆 *to land*｜不～边际 *not to the point; irrelevant* ❸使接触别的事物，使附着在别的物体上 to apply; to attach sth：～眼 *fix attention on; have sth in mind*｜～手 *put one's hands to; set about*｜～色 *to colour*｜不～痕迹 *leave no trace* ❹着落 whereabouts：寻找无～ *cannot find*［着落］（-luò）下落，来源 whereabouts; source：遗失的东西有了～了。*The whereabouts of the lost objects are known.*｜这笔费用还没有～。*The money for this expense has yet to be sourced.* ❺派遣 to send：～人前来办理 *send someone here to deal with it* ❻公文用语，表示命令的语气 used in official documents to indicate an order: ～即施行 *for immediate implementation*

⇨ see also zhāo on p.836, zháo on p.836, zhe on p.841

禚 zhuó ㄓㄨㄛˊ 姓 (surname) Zhuo

鷟(鷟) zhuó ㄓㄨㄛˊ see 鸑鷟 (yuè—) at 鸑 on page 811

缴(繳) zhuó ㄓㄨㄛˊ 系在箭上的丝绳 silk thread tied to an arrow

⇨ see also jiǎo on p.312

擢 zhuó ㄓㄨㄛˊ ❶ 拔 to pull out: ～发(fà)难数(shǔ)(形容罪恶多得像头发那样数不清) *innumerable evil deeds* ❷ 提拔 to promote: ～用 *promote* | ～升 *promote*

濯 zhuó ㄓㄨㄛˊ 洗 to wash: ～足 *wash one's feet*

ZI ㄗ

仔 zī ㄗ [仔肩] 所担负的职务，责任 duties and responsibilities

⇨ see also zǎi on p.816, zǐ on p.882

孖 zī ㄗ 双生子 twins

⇨ see also mā on p.431

孜 zī ㄗ [孜孜] 勤勉，不懈怠 diligent: ～不倦 *diligently; industriously*

吱 zī ㄗ same as "嗞"

⇨ see also zhī on p.850

呲 zī ㄗ same as "龇"

⇨ see also cī on p.96

赀(貲) zī ㄗ 计量(多用于否定) to count (often used in negative phrases): 所费不～ *spend an incalculable amount of money* | 不可～计 *uncountable*

⇨ 貲 see also 资 on p.879

觜 zī ㄗ 星宿名，二十八宿之一 *zi* (one of the twenty-eight constellations in ancient Chinese astronomy)

⇨ see also zuǐ on p.889

訾 zī ㄗ 姓 (surname) Zi

⇨ see also zǐ on p.882

龇(齜) zī ㄗ 张开嘴露出牙 to bare one's teeth: ～牙咧嘴 *show teeth; look fierce; grimace with pain*

髭 zī ㄗ 嘴上边的胡子 moustache: ～须皆白 *both moustache and beard are white*

咨 zī ㄗ 跟别人商议，询问(㊀—询) to discuss; to enquire: ～商 *consult* | ～议 *(old) advisor*

[咨文] 旧时用于同级机关的一种公文 (old) official document used between organisations of the same rank

姿 zī ㄗ ❶容貌 looks: ～容 *appearance* | 丰～ *charm; good looks* ❷形态，样子(㊀—态、—势) state; appearance: 雄～ *heroic appearance* | ～势 *posture*

资(資、❶△*貲) zī ㄗ ❶财物，钱财 material wealth; money: ～源 *resource* | 投～ *invest; investment* | 工～ *salary* ㊀费用 expense: 车～ *bus/train fare* | 邮～ *postage*

[资金] 1 国民经济中物资的货

Z

币表现 funds 2 经营工商业的本钱 capital [资料] 1 生产、生活中必需的东西 means; resources 2 用作依据的材料 data：统计～ *statistical data* | 研究～ *research data* ❷ 供给 to provide：～助 *aid financially* | 以～参考 *provided for reference* ❸ 智力 intelligence：天～聪明 *naturally intelligent* ❹资历，指出身、经历 qualifications; background; experience：年～ *seniority* | ～格 *qualification* | 论～排辈 *place in a hierarchy according to seniority* [资质] 人的素质，智力 natural endowments ⓘ泛指从事某种工作或活动所应具备的条件、资格、能力等 qualification：管理～ *management qualification* | 设计～ *design qualification* | ～等级 *qualification level*

⇨ 貲 see also 赀 on p.879

谘(諮) zī ㄗ same as "咨"

粢 zī ㄗ 古代供祭祀用的谷类 (ancient) grain for religious sacrifices

趑 zī ㄗ [趑趄] (－jū) 1 行走困难 walking with difficulty 2 犹豫不前 hesitant：～不前 *hesitant about moving forward*

兹(玆)** zī ㄗ ❶文言代词，这，这个 (pronoun in classical Chinese) this：～日 *on this day* | ～理易明 *the argument is easy to grasp* ❷现在 now：～不赘述 *will not be elaborated on now* | ～订于明日召开全体职工大会。*It is decided that the general staff meeting will be held tomorrow.* ❸年 year：今～ *this year* | 来～ *next year*

⇨ see also cí on p.97

嗞 zī ㄗ (－儿) 拟声词 ㊟ (onomatopoeia) squeak：老鼠～的一声跑了。*The mouse ran off with a squeak.* | 小鸟～～地叫。*The little bird keeps squeaking.*

嵫 zī ㄗ see 崦嵫 (yān－) at 崦 on page 750

孳 zī ㄗ 滋生，繁殖 to breed; to propagate：～生得很快 *breed very quickly*

滋 zī ㄗ ❶生出，长(zhǎng) to grow：～芽 *germinate* | ～事 *make trouble* | ～蔓 *grow and spread* ❷益，增益，加多 to gain; to increase：～益 *increase* | ～补 *nourish* [滋润] 1 润泽，湿润，使不干枯 to moisturise 2〈方 dialect〉舒服 comfortable：日子过得挺～ *life is quite comfortable* [滋味] 味道 taste [滋养] 补益身体 nourish ❸〈方 dialect〉喷射 to spurt：水管往外～水。*Water is gushing out of the pipe.*

镃(鎡) zī ㄗ [镃錤] (－jī) 古代的锄头 (ancient) hoe

菑 zī ㄗ ❶已经开垦了一年的田地 farmland that has been cultivated for a year ❷ 除草 to weed ❸茂盛的草 exuberant grass：～榛秽聚 *thick lush vegetation*

〈古 ancient〉 also same as 灾 (zāi)

淄 zī ㄗ 淄河，水名，在山东省中部 Zihe River (in central

Shandong Province)

缁(緇) zī ㄗ 黑色 black: ～衣 *black clothes*

辎(輜) zī ㄗ 辎车，有帷子的车 covered carriage

[辎重] (－zhòng) 行军时携带的器械、粮草、被服等 supplies and gear carried by troops on the march

锱(錙) zī ㄗ 古代重量单位，六铢等于一锱，四锱等于一两 an ancient Chinese unit for measuring weight, equal to 6 铢 (There are 4 锱 in 1 两.)

[锱铢] (－zhū) ㊞琐碎的事或极少的钱 trivial matter; tiny amount of money: ～必较 *very petty-minded*

鲻(鯔) zī ㄗ 鱼名，背部青灰色，腹部白色，嘴宽而短，生活在海水和河水交界处 flathead grey mullet

鄑 zī ㄗ 用于地名 used in place names: 夏家～水（在山东省昌邑）*Xiajiazishui (in Changyi, Shandong Province)*

鼒 zī ㄗ 上端收敛而口小的鼎 ancient cooking utensil, the top of which narrows into a small mouth

子 zǐ ㄗˇ ❶古代指儿女，现在专指儿子 (ancient) son or daughter; (today) son [子弟] 后辈人，年轻人 young people; younger generation ❷对人的称呼 form of address ①一般的人 for an ordinary person: 男～ *man* | 女～ *woman* ②旧称某种行（háng）业的人 (old) for a person of a certain occupation: 士～ *official; scholar* | 舟～ *boatman* ③古代指著书立说，代表一个流派的人 (ancient) founder or representative of a school of thought: 孔～ *Confucius* | 诸～百家 *various schools of thought during the Spring and Autumn Period and the Warring States Period* ④古代图书四部（经、史、子、集）分类法中的第三类 philosophical works (the third category in the ancient Chinese book classification system of 经, 史, 子 and 集): ～部 *philosophical works category* | ～书 *book on philosophy* ⑤古代对对方的敬称，相当于"您" (ancient polite speech equivalent to 您) you: ～试为之。*You may try doing it.* | 以～之矛，攻～之盾 *use your ideas to rebut your argument* ⑥古代称老师 (ancient) teacher: ～墨子 *Master Mozi* [子虚] ㊕虚无的，不实在的 unreal: 事属～ *the matter is fictitious* ❸（－儿）植物的种子 seed (of a plant): 莲～ *lotus seed* | 瓜～儿 *melon seed* | 结～ *bear seed* ❹（－儿）动物的卵 animal egg: 鱼～ *fish roe* | 鸡～儿 *chicken egg* | 蚕～ *silkworm egg* | 下～儿 *lay eggs* ❺幼小的 young: ～鸡 *chick* | ～姜 *young ginger* ❻派生的，附属的 derivative; subsidiary: ～金 *interest (on a sum of money)* | ～公司 *subsidiary company* ❼地支的第一位 zi (the first of the twelve Earthly Branches, a system used in the Chinese calendar) ❽子时，指夜里十一点到一点 zi (the period

Z

from 11 p.m. to 1 a.m.) [子夜] 深夜 midnight ❾古代五等爵位（公、侯、伯、子、男）的第四等 viscount (the fourth rank in the ancient Chinese nobility ranks of 公，侯，伯，子 and 男) ❿ (zi) 名词词尾 noun suffix ①加在名词性语素后 added after nominal morphemes: 孩～*child*| 珠～*bead; pearl* | 桌～ *table* | 椅 ～ *chair* ②加在形容词或动词性语素后 added after adjectival or verbal morphemes: 胖 ～ *fat person* | 拐 ～ *cripple* | 瞎 ～ *blind person*| 乱 ～ *trouble* | 垫 ～ *cushion; mat* ⓫ (zi) 某些量词词尾 suffix for certain measure words: 一档～事 *a matter* | 敲了两下～门 *knocked on the door twice*

仔 zǐ ㄗˇ 幼小的（多指家畜、家禽）young (often of livestock, poultry): ～鸡 *chick* | ～猪 *piglet* [仔密] 衣物等质地紧密 (of clothing, etc.) closely woven/knitted: 袜子织得十分～。*The sock is knitted very densely.* [仔细] 1 周密，细致 detailed; meticulous: ～研究 *detailed research* | ～考虑 *careful consideration* 2 俭省 thrifty: 日子过得～ *live a frugal life* 3 当心，注意 to be careful: 路很滑，～点ル。*Be careful. The road is slippery.*

⇨ see also zǎi on p.816, zī on p.879

耔 zǐ ㄗˇ 培土 to hill up; to earth up

虸 zǐ ㄗˇ [虸蚄]（ －fāng ）黏虫 armyworm

籽 zǐ ㄗˇ same as “子❸”

姊（*姉）zǐ ㄗˇ 姐姐 elder sister [姊妹] 1 姐姐和妹妹 sisters: ～三个 *three sisters* ㊂有密切关系的 intimately related: ～篇 *companion volume* | ～ 城 *sister city* 2 同辈女朋友间亲热的称呼 sister (term of endearment between female friends of the same generation)

秭 zǐ ㄗˇ 古代数目，指一万亿，也指十亿或千亿等 (ancient) one trillion; (also) one billion, 100 billion, etc.

[秭归] 地名，在湖北省 Zigui (a place in Hubei Province)

笫 zǐ ㄗˇ 竹子编的床席 woven bamboo bed mat: 床～ *woven bamboo bed mat; bed*

茈 zǐ ㄗˇ 茈草，草本植物，即紫草，叶椭圆形，花白色，根皮紫色。根可入药，又可用作紫色染料 purple gromwell (same as 紫草)

⇨ see also cí on p.96

紫 zǐ ㄗˇ 蓝和红合成的颜色 purple

訾 zǐ ㄗˇ 说别人的坏话，诋毁 (㊀—毁)to slander: 不苟～议 *not rashly criticise others' faults*

⇨ see also zī on p.879

梓 zǐ ㄗˇ ❶梓树，落叶乔木，花黄色，木材可供建筑或制器物用 yellow catalpa [梓里] [桑梓] 故乡 hometown ❷印书用的木版 wooden block used for book-printing ㊕雕版，把木头刻成印书的版，泛指制版印刷 to carve wooden blocks for printing; (generally) to make plates for printing: 付～ *send to the press* | ～行 *publish*

滓 zǐ ㄗˇ 渣子，沉淀物 sediment: 渣～ *sediment*

自 zì ㄗˋ ❶自己，己身，本人 oneself: ～给～足 *self-sufficiency* | 独立～主 *independence and self-determination* | ～力更生 *self-reliance* | ～动 *automatic* [自个儿] (*自各儿) (-gěr) 〈方 dialect〉代词，自己 (pronoun) myself [自然] 1 一切天然存在的东西 nature: 大～ *nature; Mother Nature* | ～景物 *natural scenery* 2 不勉强 natural; not contrived: ～而然 *naturally* | 功到～成 *an endeavour will naturally succeed with effort* | 他笑得很～。*His smile is very natural.* 3 当然，没有疑问 of course; naturally: 学习不认真，～就要落后。*If one is not serious in one's studies, one naturally falls behind.* [自由] 1 人们在法律规定的范围内，随意安排自己活动的权利 liberty 2 哲学上指人们在实践中认识了客观规律，并能有意识地运用到实践中去 (in philosophy) freedom 3 不受拘束和限制 free: ～活动 *move freely* | ～发言 *speak freely* ❷介词，从，由 (㊥一从) (preposition) from: ～古到今 *from ancient times to the present* | ～天津到北京 *from Tianjin to Beijing* ❸副词，自然，当然 (adverb) naturally: 借债还钱，～不待言。*When one borrows money, one pays it back: that goes without saying.* | 公道～在人心 *justice and fairness is imbued in everyone's heart* | 久别重逢，～有许多话要讲。*Meeting again after such a long absence, there is naturally a lot to talk about.*

字 zì ㄗˋ ❶文字，用来记录语言的符号 written language: 汉～ *Chinese characters* | ～眼儿 *word; expression* | ～体 *style of writing; typeface* | 常用～ *common words* [字典] 注明文字的音义，列举词语说明用法的工具书 dictionary [字符] 表示数据和信息的字母、数字及各种符号 character [字母] 表语音的符号 letter; alphabet: 拼音～ *Pinyin* | 拉丁～ *Latin (or Roman) alphabet* ❷字音 pronunciation: 咬～清楚 *clear enunciation* | ～正腔圆 *speak clearly with a rich tone* ❸字体 style of calligraphy: 篆～ *seal script* | 柳～ *the calligraphy of Liu Gongquan (778—865)* ❹书法作品 calligraphic work: ～画 *calligraphic works and paintings* ❺根据人名中的字义另取的别名叫"字"，又叫"表字" courtesy name (also called 表字): 李白～太白 *Li Bai, courtesy name Taibai* | 岳飞～鹏举 *Yue Fei, courtesy name Pengju* ❻字据，合同，契约 written pledge; contract: 立～为凭 *write a note as pledge* ❼旧时称女子许嫁 (old) a woman's acceptance of a marriage proposal: 待～闺中 *unmarried*

牸 zì ㄗˋ 雌性的牲畜 female livestock: ～牛 *cow*

Z

恣 zì ㄗˋ ❶放纵，无拘束 indulge oneself; unrestrained：～意 *wilfully; unbridled* | ～情 *do as one pleases* ❷〈方 dialect〉舒服 comfortable：你看，他睡得多～。*Look, he is sleeping so comfortably.*

眦（*眥） zì ㄗˋ 眼角，上下眼睑的接合处，靠近鼻子的叫内眦，靠近两鬓的叫外眦 corners of the eye (inner corners are 内眦; outer corners are 外眦)

胔 zì ㄗˋ ❶带腐肉的尸骨 skeletal remains with decomposed flesh ❷腐烂的肉 decomposed flesh

渍（漬） zì ㄗˋ ❶浸，沤 to soak：～麻 *ret flax* ❷地面的积水 ponding：～水 *waterlogging* | 防洪排～ *flood prevention and drainage* ❸油、泥等积在上面难以除去 (of oil, mud, etc.) to build up：烟袋里～了很多油子。*The inside of the Chinese smoking pipe is full of tar.* | 手表的轮子～住了。*The wheels of the watch are clogged up.* ㊀浸积在物体上的污垢 stain：血～ *blood stain* | 污～ *stain* | 油～ *oil stain*

胾 zì ㄗˋ 切成的大块肉 large piece of cut meat

ZONG ㄗㄨㄥ

枞（樅） zōng ㄗㄨㄥ ［枞阳］地名，在安徽省 Zongyang (a place in Anhui Province)

⇨ see also cōng on p.99

宗 zōng ㄗㄨㄥ ❶旧指宗庙，祖庙 (old) ancestral temple ［祖宗］先人 ancestor ❷家族，同一家族的 clan; of the same clan：同～ *of the same clan* | ～兄 *elder male relative of one's generation* ［宗法］封建社会以家族为中心，按血统远近区别亲疏的制度 (old) Chinese patriarchal system：破除～观念 *break with old patriarchal views* ❸宗派，派别 school; sect：禅(chán)～ *Chan school of Buddhism* | 北～山水画 *Northern School of Chinese landscape painting* ❹宗旨，主要的目的和意图 object; aim：开～明义 *state the purpose at the very beginning* | 万变不离其～ *essence remains the same despite myriad changes* ❺尊奉，向往，也指尊奉的人 to venerate; (also) object of veneration：～仰 *to respect* | ～师 *great master* ❻量词，件，批 (measure word) piece; case：一～事 *a matter* | 大～货物 *a large load of goods* | 三～传染病例 *three cases of infectious disease*

倧 zōng ㄗㄨㄥ 传说中的上古神人 Zong (ancient divine being in legends)

综（綜） zōng ㄗㄨㄥ 总合 to put together; to sum up：～述 *to summarize* | ～观全局 *take a comprehensive look over the whole situation* | 错～(纵横交错) *intricate; complex* ［综合］1 把各个独立而互相关联的事物或现象进行分析、归纳、整理 to synthesize 2 不同种类、不同性质的事

物组合在一起 to integrate：～利用 *integrated use* | ～大学 *comprehensive university*

⇨ see also zèng on p.825

棕（*椶）zōng ㄗㄨㄥ 指棕榈（lú）树或棕毛 palm tree; palm fibre［棕榈］常绿乔木，树干高而直，不分枝，叶大，叶鞘上的毛叫棕毛，可以制绳索和刷子等 palm tree［棕色］像棕毛的颜色 brown

腙 zōng ㄗㄨㄥ 有机化合物的一类，由羰（tāng）基与肼（jǐng）缩合而成 hydrazone

踪（*蹤）zōng ㄗㄨㄥ 人或动物走过留下的脚印（㊟－迹）footprint; paw print：～影 *trace* | 追～ *to trace* | 失～ *be missing*

鬃（*騌、*騣、*鬉）zōng ㄗㄨㄥ 马、猪等兽类颈上的长毛，可制刷、帚等 mane

鬷 zōng ㄗㄨㄥ ❶古代的一种锅 (ancient) a type of cooking pot ❷姓 (surname) Zong

总（總、**縂）zǒng ㄗㄨㄥˇ ❶聚合，聚集在一起 to gather together：～在一起算 *calculate everything together* | ～共三万 *thirty thousand in total* | ～起来说 *sum it up*［总结］把一段工作过程中的经验教训分析、研究，归纳出结论 to summarize：要认真～经验 *sum up one's experience properly* ❷概括全部的，主要的，为首的 general; main：～纲 *general principles* | ～司令 *commander-in-chief* ❸副词，经常，一直 (adverb) always：为什么～来晚？*Why do you always arrive late?* | ～不肯听 *always refuse to listen* ❹副词，一定，无论如何 (adverb) must; no matter what：这件事～是要办的。*This matter must be dealt with no matter what.* | 明天他～该回来了。*Surely he must return tomorrow.*

偬（*傯）zǒng ㄗㄨㄥˇ see 倥偬 (kǒng－) at 倥 on page 360

纵（縱）zòng ㄗㄨㄥˋ ❶ (formerly pronounced zōng) 竖，直，南北方向，跟"横"相对 vertical; north-south direction (opposite of 横)：～线 *longitudinal line* | 排成～队 *form up in columns* | ～横各十里 *10 li in both length and breadth* | ～剖面 *longitudinal profile/section* ❷放 to release：～虎归山 *release the tiger back to the mountain; (figurative) store up trouble for the future* ❸放任，不加拘束 to indulge; to let loose：～目 *look as far as one's eyes can see* | ～情 *to one's heart's content* | ～欲 *over-indulge in sensual pleasure* ❹身体猛然向前或向上 to lunge; to jump：～身一跳 *make a sudden leap* ❺连词，即使 (conjunction) even if; despite：～有千山万水，也拦不住勘探队员。*Even the long journey and challenging terrain could not stop the prospecting team.* ❻〈方 dialect〉起皱纹 to get wrinkled：这张纸都～了。*This piece of paper* *is crumpled.* | 衣服压～了。*The clothes are creased from pressure.*

疭(瘲) zòng ㄗㄨㄥˋ see 瘛疭(chì–) at 瘛 on page 82

粽(*糉) zòng ㄗㄨㄥˋ 粽子，用箬叶或苇叶裹糯米做成的多角形的食品。民俗端午节吃粽子 *zongzi* (a leaf-wrapped glutinous rice dumpling traditionally eaten during the Dragon Boat Festival)

ZOU ㄗㄡ

邹(鄒) zōu ㄗㄡ 周代诸侯国名，在今山东省邹城东南 Zou (a state in the Zhou Dynasty, in today's southeastern Zoucheng, Shandong Province)

驺(騶) zōu ㄗㄡ 驺从，封建时代贵族官僚出门时所带的骑马的侍从 (old) attendants on horseback (accompanying travelling aristocrats and officials)

诹(諏) zōu ㄗㄡ 在一起商量事情 to discuss; to consult：～吉（商订好日子）*discuss and agree on an auspicious date* | 咨～（询问政事）*seek advice on political matters*

陬 zōu ㄗㄡ 角落，山脚 corner; foot of a mountain

缬(緅) zōu ㄗㄡ 黑里带红的颜色 reddish black

鲰(鯫) zōu ㄗㄡ 小鱼 fry; fingerling (fish) [鲰生] 古代对人的蔑称，义为小子、小人。也用作谦辞 (ancient) derogatory form of address, also used in humble speech

鄹(❶**聊) zōu ㄗㄡ ❶古地名，在今山东省曲阜东南 Zou (an ancient place in today's southeastern Qufu, Shandong Province) ❷周代诸侯国名，即邹 Zou (a state in the Zhou Dynasty; same as 邹)

走 zǒu ㄗㄡˇ ❶走路，步行 to walk：～得快 *walk quickly* | 小孩子会～了。*The child can walk now.* ⑬ ①往来 to socialize with：～亲戚 *call on relatives* ②移动，挪动 to move：～棋 *move a chess piece* | 钟不～了。*The clock has stopped.* ③往来运送 to transport; to deliver：～信 *deliver the mail* | ～货 *to smuggle* | ～私 *to smuggle* ❷离去 to leave：他刚～。*He has just left.* | 我明天要～了。*I am leaving tomorrow.* ❸通过，由 through; via：咱们～这个门出去吧。*Let's leave through this door.* ❹经过 go through：这笔钱不～账了。*Leave this amount of money off the account books.* ❺透漏出，越过范围 to reveal; to exceed：～漏消息 *leak information* | ～气 *leak gas; to deflate* | 说话～了嘴 *make a slip of the tongue* ❻失去原样 to lose original state：衣服～样子了。*The piece of clothing has lost its shape.* | 茶叶～味了。*The tea leaves have lost their flavour.* ❼古代指跑（⑬奔—）(ancient) to run：～马看花 *give a passing glance; have a superficial understanding of sth* [走狗] 善跑的猎狗 fast hunting hound ⑭受

人豢养而帮助作恶的人 lackey; running dog

奏 zòu ㄗㄡˋ ❶演奏，依照曲调吹弹乐器 to play (a musical instrument); to perform：～乐 *play music* | 提琴独～ *violin solo* | 伴～ *(in music) accompany; accompaniment* ❷封建时代臣子对皇帝进言或上书 (old) to submit a memorial to the emperor in feudal times：上～ *submit a memorial* ❸呈现，做出 to show; to achieve：～效 *prove effective* | ～功 *achieve success; yield result*

揍 zòu ㄗㄡˋ ❶打人 to beat (sb); to hit (sb) ❷〈方 dialect〉打碎 to smash; to break：小心别把玻璃～了。*Take care not to smash the glass.*

ZU ㄗㄨ

租 zū ㄗㄨ ❶出代价暂用别人的东西 to rent：～房 *rent a house* | ～家具 *rent furniture* [租界] 帝国主义者强迫被侵略国家在通商都市以"租借"名义划给他们直接统治的地区 foreign concession ❷出租 to lease：～给人 *lease sth to sb* | ～出去 *to lease* [出租] 收取一定的代价，让别人暂时使用房地器物等 to lease ❸出租所收取的钱或实物 rent; rental：房～ *rent (for house, apartment, etc.)* | 收～ *collect rent* ❹田赋 land tax：～税 *land tax and other levies*

菹 (**葅) zū ㄗㄨ ❶酸菜 pickled vegetables ❷切碎的肉、菜 minced meat; diced vegetables

足 zú ㄗㄨˊ ❶脚 foot：～迹 *footmark; footprint* | 画蛇添～ *ruin sth by adding sth that is unnecessary (literally means 'paint a snake and add legs')* | ～不出户 *not take a step out of one's home* ㊀器物下部的支撑部分 foot (of a utensil)：鼎～ *feet of the* ding ❷满，充分，够量 (㊥充一) full; sufficient：～数 *full amount* | 心满意～ *be thoroughly satisfied* | 丰衣～食 *have ample food and clothing* | 分量不～ *insufficient amount* ㊀副词 adverb ①尽情地，尽量地 to the maximum：～玩了一天 *enjoyed oneself for the whole day* ②完全 totally：他～可以担任翻译工作。*He can absolutely do the translation work.* | 两天～能完成任务。*Two days is definitely enough to complete the mission.* ❸值得 worthwhile：不～为凭 *cannot be taken as proof* | 微不～道 *insignificant*

卒 (*卆) zú ㄗㄨˊ ❶古时指兵 (ancient) soldier：小～ *low-ranking soldier* | 士～ *soldiers* ❷旧称差役 (old) bailiff in a *yamen*：走～ *servant; lackey* | 狱～ *jailer; prison guard* ❸死亡 death：生～年月 *dates of sb's birth and death* ❹完毕，终了 to complete; to end：～业 *to graduate* ㊀究竟，终于 at last; finally：相持半月，～胜敌军。*After half a month's impasse, (we) finally prevailed over the enemy in battle.*

⇨ see also cù on p.101

Z

崒(崪)** zú ㄗㄨˊ 险峻 precipitous

族 zú ㄗㄨˊ ❶民族 nationality; ethnic group: 汉～ *the Han people* | 回～ *the Hui people* | 各～人民 *people of all ethnic groups* ❷聚居而有血统关系的人群的统称 family; clan: 宗～ *patriarchal clan* | 家～ *family* ❸事物有共同属性的一大类 a group of things with common features: 水～ *aquatic animals* | 芳香～ *(in chemistry) aromatic* ⑩有共同特点的某类人 a group of people with common features: 上班～ *office workers* | 追星～ *celebrity fans* ❹灭族，古代的一种残酷刑法，一人有罪把全家或包括母家、妻家的人都杀死 (ancient punishment) clan extermination (by killing the criminal's entire family)

镞(鏃) zú ㄗㄨˊ 箭镞，箭头 arrowhead

诅(詛) zǔ ㄗㄨˇ ❶迷信的人求神加祸于别人 to curse; to swear [诅咒] 咒骂，说希望人不顺利的话 to curse ❷盟誓 oath of alliance

阻 zǔ ㄗㄨˇ 拦挡(㊥－挡) to block; to impede: ～止 *to prevent; to stop* | 通行无～ *pass without any obstruction* | 山川险～ *dangerous and difficult mountains and rivers*

组(組) zǔ ㄗㄨˇ ❶结合，构成 to combine; to form: ～成 *to form; to constitute* | ～建 *to organize; to set up* | 改～ *to reorganize; to reshuffle (post,etc.)* [组织] 1 有目的、有系统、有秩序地结合起来 to organise: ～群众 *organise the people* 2 按照一定的政治目的、任务和系统建立起来的集体 organisation: 党团～ *party and group organisation* 3 有机体中由形状、性质和作用相同的若干细胞结合而成的单位 (in biology) tissue: 神经～ *nerve/nervous tissue* | ～疗法 *histotherapy* ❷由若干人员结合成的单位 group: 小～ *small group* | 教研～ *teaching and research group* ❸合成一组的（文学艺术作品）series; set (of literary or artistic works): ～诗 *poem series* | ～画 *set of paintings* ❹量词，用于成组的事物 (measure word) set; series: 一～照片 *a set of photographs*

珇 zǔ ㄗㄨˇ ❶珪玉、琮玉上的浮雕花纹 relief patterns on ceremonial jadeite tablets ❷美好 fine

俎 zǔ ㄗㄨˇ ❶古代祭祀时放祭品的器物 (ancient) vessels for holding offerings during religious sacrifices ❷切肉或菜时垫在下面的砧（zhēn）板 cutting board: 刀～ *knife and cutting board; (figurative) person who controls and persecutes sb*

祖 zǔ ㄗㄨˇ ❶称父母亲的上一辈 the generation above one's parents: ～父 *paternal grandfather* | 外～母 *maternal grandmother* | ～孙三代 *three generations including grandparents and grandchildren* ㉂先代 ancestor: ～宗 *ancestor* | 始～ *progenitor; forefather* [祖国] 对自己国家的亲切称呼 motherland;

fatherland ❷某种事业或流派的开创者 progenitor; founding father: 鼻～ *originator* | ～师 *founder (of a school of learning or religious sect)*

ZUAN ㄗㄨㄢ

钻(鑽、*鑚) zuān ㄗㄨㄢ ❶用锥状的物体在另一物体上转动穿孔 to drill; to bore: ～个眼儿 *bore a hole* | ～探 *drilling* ㊀穿过，进入 go through; to enter: ～山洞 *enter a cave* | ～到水里 *dive into water* | ～空（kòng）子 *exploit a loophole* [钻营] 指攀附权势取得个人好处 to curry favour with sb in authority for personal gain ❷钻研，仔细深入研究 study intensively: ～书本 *delve deep into books* | 他肯～，学得快。*He learns very quickly because he is willing to study intensively.*

⇨ see also zuàn on p.889

躜(躦) zuān ㄗㄨㄢ 向上或向前冲 to jump up; to lunge forward

缵(纘) zuǎn ㄗㄨㄢˇ 继承 to inherit

纂(❶*篹) zuǎn ㄗㄨㄢˇ ❶编纂，搜集材料编书 (of books) to compile: ～修 *edit and revise* ❷（一儿）梳在头后边的发髻 chignon ; bun

钻(鑽、*鑚) zuàn ㄗㄨㄢˋ ❶穿孔洞的工具 drill: ～床 *drilling machine* | 电～ *electric drill* | 风～ *pneumatic drill* | 手摇～ *hand drill* ❷钻石，经过琢磨的金刚石，又指硬度高的人造宝石 diamond; (also) man-made jewel: ～戒 *diamond ring* | 十七～的手表 *seventeen-jewel watch*

⇨ see also zuān on p.889

赚(賺) zuàn ㄗㄨㄢˋ 骗 to deceive; to hoax: ～人 *deceive sb*

⇨ see also zhuàn on p.872

攥 zuàn ㄗㄨㄢˋ 用手握住 to hold ; to grip: 手里～着一把斧子 *hold an axe in one's hand*

ZUI ㄗㄨㄟ

咀 zuǐ ㄗㄨㄟˇ informal written form for 嘴

⇨ see also jǔ on p.337

觜 zuǐ ㄗㄨㄟˇ same as "嘴"

⇨ see also zī on p.879

嘴 zuǐ ㄗㄨㄟˇ ❶same as "口": 张～ *open one's mouth* ❷（一子、一儿）形状或作用像嘴的东西 sth like a mouth: 山～ *mountain spur* | 壶～儿 *spout of a pot* ❸指说的话 spoken words: 别多～。*Don't speak out of turn.* | ～甜 *honey-tongued*

最(*冣) zuì ㄗㄨㄟˋ ❶副词，极，无比的 (adverb) most: ～大 *biggest* | ～好 *best* | ～要紧 *most important* ❷指居首位的、没有比得上的人或事物 top; the acme of sth: 中华之～ *top in China; best of China* | 世界之～ *top in the world; best of the world* | 以此为～ *take sth as the best*

蕞 zuì ㄗㄨㄟˋ 小的样子 small: ～尔小国 *small country*

晬 zuì ㄗㄨㄟˋ 婴儿周岁 baby's first birthday

醉 zuì ㄗㄨㄟˋ ❶喝酒过多，神志不清 drunk：他喝～了。*He is drunk.* ❷沉迷，过分地爱好 to indulge in：陶～ *be infatuated* | 沉～ *be intoxicated* | ～心文学 *revel in literature* ❸用酒泡制（食品）preserve with wine：家家忙着～鱼。*Every household is busy preserving fish in wine.* 也指用酒泡制的（食品）food that has been preserved with wine：～蟹 *wine-preserved crab* | ～虾 *wine-preserved shrimp* | ～枣 *wine-preserved dates*

罪（*辠）zuì ㄗㄨㄟˋ ❶犯法的行为 crime; guilt：犯～ *commit a crime* ㊀过失 wrongdoing：不应该归～于人 *should not put the blame on others* ❷刑罚 penalty; punishment：判～ *to convict* | 死～ *capital offense* ❸苦难，痛苦 suffering; pain：受～ *endure hardship* ❹把罪过归到某人身上 to blame ; to put the blame on：～己 *blame oneself*

槜（**檇）zuì ㄗㄨㄟˋ ［槜李］1 一种李子，果皮鲜红，浆多味甜 a kind of plum 2 古地名，在今浙江省嘉兴一带 Zuili (an ancient place, near today's Jiaxing, Zhejiang Province)

ZUN ㄗㄨㄣ

尊 zūn ㄗㄨㄣ ❶地位或辈分高 senior; high (in status)：～卑 *seniors and juniors; superiors and inferiors* | ～亲 *one's senior relative* | ～长（zhǎng）*elders and seniors* 敬辞 (polite speech) your：～姓 *your family name* | ～著 *your (written) work* | ～府 *your residence* ［令尊］对对方父亲的尊称 (polite speech) your father ❷敬重（㊀－敬）to respect：～师爱徒 *respect the teacher and love the student* ❸量词，用于神佛塑像或炮等 measure word for statues of deities, cannons, etc.：一～佛像 *a statue of the Buddha* | 一～大炮 *a cannon* ❹ same as "樽"

嶟 zūn ㄗㄨㄣ 山石高峻陡峭 (of a mountain) precipitous

遵 zūn ㄗㄨㄣ 依照，按照 to abide by; to obey; to follow：～纪守法 *observe laws and regulations* | ～医嘱 *follow medical advice* | ～从 *to obey* | ～循 *comply with*

樽（*罇）zūn ㄗㄨㄣ 古代的盛酒器具 an ancient wine vessel

镈（鐏）zūn ㄗㄨㄣ ❶戈柄下端圆锥形的金属套 pointed metal guard attached to the lower end of the staff of a dagger-axe ❷盛酒的器皿 wine vessel ❸姓 (surname) Zun

鳟（鱒）zūn ㄗㄨㄣ 鱼名，身体银白色，背略带黑色 trout

僔 zǔn ㄗㄨㄣˇ ❶聚集 to gather ❷谦恭 humble and courteous

撙 zǔn ㄗㄨㄣˇ 撙节，从全部财物里节省下一部分 to make

savings

噂 zǔn ㄗㄨㄣˇ 聚在一起议论 to gather and discuss

ZUO ㄗㄨㄛ

作 zuō ㄗㄨㄛ 作坊（fang），手工业制造或加工的地方 workshop：油漆～ *lacquer workshop* | 洗衣～ *laundry*

⇨ see also zuò on p.892

嘬 zuō ㄗㄨㄛ 聚缩嘴唇吸取 to suck：小孩～奶。*The infant is suckling.*

⇨ see also chuài on p.90

昨 zuó ㄗㄨㄛˊ ❶昨天，今天的前一天 yesterday：～夜 *last night* ❷泛指过去 (generally) the past：觉今是而～非 *realise that one is correct now and was mistaken in the past*

笮（**筰）zuó ㄗㄨㄛˊ 用竹子做成的绳索 rope made with bamboo［笮桥］用竹索编成的桥 bridge made with bamboo rope

⇨ see also zé on p.823

捽 zuó ㄗㄨㄛˊ 〈方 dialect〉揪，抓 to grab：～他的头发 *grab his hair*

琢 zuó ㄗㄨㄛˊ ［琢磨］（－mo）反复思索、考虑 to think over; to turn sth over in one's mind：这个问题我～了很久。*I have turned this issue over in my mind for a long time.* | 你～一下，是不是这个理儿？*Think about it. Is this reasonable?*

⇨ see also zhuó on p.878

左 zuǒ ㄗㄨㄛˇ ❶面向南时靠东的一边，跟"右"相对 left (opposite of 右)：～手 *left hand* ㊕东方（以面向南为准）east (left side when one is facing south)：山～ *east of the mountain; east of Taihang Mountains* | 江～ *east of the river; east of the lower reaches of Yangtze River*［左右］1 上下，表示约数 approximately：三十岁～ *around thirty years old* 2 横竖，反正 anyhow：～是要去的，你还是早点去吧。*You have to go anyhow, so it's better if you go early.* 3 身边跟从的人 attendant 4 支配，操纵 to control; to manipulate：～局势 *manipulate the situation* ❷政治思想上属于较激进的或进步的 (of political ideology) the left：～派 *leftist* | ～翼 *left-wing* ❸斜，偏，错 slanting; wrong：～脾气 *obstinate and eccentric temperament* | 越说越～ *wander further away from the point the longer one speaks* | 你想～了。*You are mistaken.* | ～道旁门 *heretical sect; improper channels* ❹相反 opposite; contrary：彼此意见相～ *hold distinctly different views*

佐 zuǒ ㄗㄨㄛˇ (formerly pronounced zuò) ❶辅佐，帮助 to assist; to help：～理 *help to rule* | ～助 *to help; to support* ❷辅助别人的人 assistant：僚～ *aide*［佐证］（*左证）证据 evidence

撮 zuǒ ㄗㄨㄛˇ （－子、－儿）量词，用于成丛的毛发 (measure word for hair) tuft：剪下一～子头发 *cut off a tuft of hair*

Z

⇨ see also cuō on p.104

作 zuò ㄗㄨㄛˋ ❶起，兴起 to rise：振～ *be invigorated; cheer up*｜锣鼓大～ *drums and gongs strike up loudly*｜日出而～ *rise at dawn*｜一鼓～气 *press on to the end without pause* [作用] 功能，使事物发生变化的力量 function; effect：起～ *have an effect*｜带头～ *leading role* ❷劳作，制造 to work; to make：深耕细～ *deep ploughing and intensive cultivation*｜操～ *to operate* ❸写作 to write; to compose：～文 *write a composition; composition*｜～画 *paint a painting*｜～曲 *compose music*｜吟诗～赋 *recite and compose poetry* ❹作品，指文学、艺术方面的创作 (of literature or art) work：佳～ *excellent work (of art or literature)*｜杰～ *masterpiece* ❺进行某种活动 to engage in (certain activities)：～乱 *stage an armed revolt* [作风] 人们在工作或行动中表现出来的态度和风格 style; way of thing/doing

⇨ see also zuō on p.891

阼 zuò ㄗㄨㄛˋ 古代指大堂前东面的台阶 (ancient) eastern flight of steps in front of the main hall

岞 zuò ㄗㄨㄛˋ [岞山] 地名，在山东省潍坊 Zuoshan (a place in Weifang, Shandong Province)

怍 zuò ㄗㄨㄛˋ 惭愧（㊀愧－）ashamed

柞 zuò ㄗㄨㄛˋ 柞树，即栎树 lea oak (same as 栎树)：～蚕 *Chinese tussah moth*｜～丝（柞蚕吐的丝）*tussah silk* (see 栎 lì on page 394 for reference)

⇨ see also zhà on p.827

胙 zuò ㄗㄨㄛˋ 古代祭祀时用过的酒肉等祭品 (ancient) used sacrificial offerings (of wine, meat, etc.)

祚 zuò ㄗㄨㄛˋ ❶福 blessing; happiness：门衰～薄 *family in straitened circumstances* ❷皇帝的地位 throne：卒践帝～（终于登上帝位）*finally ascend to the imperial throne*

酢 zuò ㄗㄨㄛˋ 客人用酒回敬主人 (of a guest) to return the host's toast：酬(chóu)～ *exchange of toasts*

⇨ see also cù on p.101

坐 zuò ㄗㄨㄛˋ ❶臀部放在椅子等物体上以支持身体 to sit：席地而～ *sit on the floor/ground*｜～在凳子上 *sit on the bench* ㊀①乘，搭 to take; to travel by：～车 *take a bus/train*｜～船 *take a boat* ②坐落 to be located; to be situated：房屋～北朝南。*The house faces south.* ❷物体向后施压力 to lean back; to push back：房子往后～了。*The house is leaning back.*｜这枪～力很小。*This gun has low recoil.* ❸把锅、壶等放在炉火上 to place (pots, etc., on the stove)：～锅 *place a pot on the stove*｜～水 *boil water on the stove* ❹因 because of：～此解职 *relieved of one's position because of this*｜停车～爱枫林晚。*I stop the carriage because I love the maple forest at night.* ❺旧指定罪 (old) to convict：连～*implicate others related to the one found guilty* | 反～*sentence the accuser to the punishment for the crime he/she had falsely accused sb else of committing* ❻植物结实（jiēshí）to bear (fruit)：～果 *bear fruit* | ～瓜 *bear gourds/melons* ㉖形成（疾病）to develop (an illness)：打那以后就～下了病。*(He) has been sick since that time.* ❼自然而然 naturally：孤蓬自振，惊沙～飞。*The lone fleabane soars by itself; the agitated sand flies of its own accord.* ❽ same as "座❶"

唑 zuò ㄗㄨㄛˋ see 噻唑 (sāi—) at 噻 on page 570

座 zuò ㄗㄨㄛˋ ❶（一儿）座位 seat：入～*take one's seat* | ～无虚席 *not a seat left empty* 敬辞，旧时称高级长官 (old) polite form of address for senior officials：军～*sir (addressing a superior military officer)* | 处～*sir (addressing the head of one's department)* [座右铭] 写出来放在座位旁边的格言。泛指警戒、激励自己的话 motto; maxim ❷（一子、一儿）托着器物的东西 stand; pedestal：钟～儿 *clock stand* ❸星座 constellation：天琴～*Lyra* ❹量词，用于较大或固定的物体 measure word for large or fixed objects：一～山 *a mountain* | 三～楼 *three buildings*

做 zuò ㄗㄨㄛˋ ❶干（gàn），进行工作或活动 to do; to conduct：～活 *do physical labour* | ～工 *do physical labour* | ～买卖 *do business* | ～报告 *give a lecture* | ～斗争 *engage in struggle* ❷写作 to write：～诗 *write poetry* | ～文章 *write an essay* ❸制造 to make; to produce：～制服 *make a uniform* | 甘蔗能～糖。*Sugar can be made from sugar cane.* ❹当，为（wéi）to be; to become：～父母的 *as parents* | ～革命事业接班人 *be a successor to the revolutionary cause* ❺装，扮 to pretend; to play a part：～样子 *put on an act* | ～好～歹 *persuade by kindness and threats* [做作] 故意装出某种表情或神态 affected; contrived; unnatural ❻举行 to hold; to organise：～生日 *organise a birthday celebration* | ～寿 *organise a birthday celebration (for an elderly person)* ❼用为 to be used as：芦苇可以～造纸原料。*Reeds can be used as the raw material for making paper.*

附　　录
Appendices

附录一 汉语拼音方案
Appendix I Chinese Phonetic Alphabet

（1957 年 11 月 1 日国务院全体会议第 60 次会议通过）
（1958 年 2 月 11 日第一届全国人民代表大会第五次会议批准）
(Passed by the 60th meeting of the State Council of the People's Republic of China on November 1st, 1957; Approved by the 5th meeting of the First National People's Congress of China on February 11th, 1958.)

一 字母表
I The Alphabet

字母 Letter	Aa	Bb	Cc	Dd	Ee	Ff	Gg
名称 Name	ㄚ	ㄅㄝ	ㄘㄝ	ㄉㄝ	ㄜ	ㄝㄈ	ㄍㄝ
	Hh	Ii	Jj	Kk	Ll	Mm	Nn
	ㄏㄚ	ㄧ	ㄐㄧㄝ	ㄎㄝ	ㄝㄌ	ㄝㄇ	ㄋㄝ
	Oo	Pp	Qq	Rr	Ss	Tt	
	ㄛ	ㄆㄝ	ㄑㄧㄡ	ㄚㄦ	ㄝㄙ	ㄊㄝ	
	Uu	Vv	Ww	Xx	Yy	Zz	
	ㄨ	ㄪㄝ	ㄨㄚ	ㄒㄧ	ㄧㄚ	ㄗㄝ	

v 只用来拼写外来语、少数民族语言和方言。
字母的手写体依照拉丁字母的一般书写习惯。
The letter v is only used in loanwords, ethnic group languages and dialects. The letters are written in the same way as the Latin alphabet.

二 声母表
II The Consonants

b	p	m	f	d	t	n	l
ㄅ玻	ㄆ坡	ㄇ摸	ㄈ佛	ㄉ得	ㄊ特	ㄋ讷	ㄌ勒
g	k	h		j	q	x	
ㄍ哥	ㄎ科	ㄏ喝		ㄐ基	ㄑ欺	ㄒ希	
zh	ch	sh	r	z	c	s	
ㄓ知	ㄔ蚩	ㄕ诗	ㄖ日	ㄗ资	ㄘ雌	ㄙ思	

在给汉字注音的时候，为了使拼式简短，zh ch sh可以省作 ẑ ĉ ŝ。

When phonetic notations are given to Chinese characters, zh, ch and sh can be abbreviated to ẑ, ĉ and ŝ to simplify the spelling.

三　韵母表
III　The Vowels

	i ㄧ　衣	u ㄨ　乌	ü ㄩ　迂
a ㄚ　啊	ia ㄧㄚ　呀	ua ㄨㄚ　蛙	
o ㄛ　喔		uo ㄨㄛ　窝	
e ㄜ　鹅	ie ㄧㄝ　耶		üe ㄩㄝ　约
ai ㄞ　哀		uai ㄨㄞ　歪	
ei ㄟ　欸		uei ㄨㄟ　威	
ao ㄠ　熬	iao ㄧㄠ　腰		
ou ㄡ　欧	iou ㄧㄡ　忧		
an ㄢ　安	ian ㄧㄢ　烟	uan ㄨㄢ　弯	üan ㄩㄢ　冤
en ㄣ　恩	in ㄧㄣ　因	uen ㄨㄣ　温	ün ㄩㄣ　晕
ang ㄤ　昂	iang ㄧㄤ　央	uang ㄨㄤ　汪	
eng ㄥ　亨的韵母 vowel of 亨	ing ㄧㄥ　英	ueng ㄨㄥ　翁	
ong （ㄨㄥ）轰的韵母 vowel of 轰	iong ㄩㄥ　雍		

(1) “知、蚩、诗、日、资、雌、思”等七个音节的韵母用 i，即：知、蚩、诗、日、资、雌、思等字拼作 zhi，chi，shi，ri，zi，ci，si。
The vowel i is used in the syllables of 知，蚩，诗，日，资，雌，思，etc. to form their pronunciation as zhi，chi，shi，ri，zi，ci，si，etc.

(2) 韵母儿写成 er，用作韵尾的时候写成 r。例如：“儿童”拼作 ertong，“花儿”拼作 huar。
The vowel 儿 is written as er，but as r when used as a tail vowel. For example，儿童 is noted as ertong，花儿 is noted as huar.

(3) 韵母ㄝ单用的时候写成 ê。
The vowel ㄝ is written as ê when used independently.

(4) i 行的韵母，前面没有声母的时候，写成 yi(衣)，ya(呀)，ye(耶)，yao(腰)，you(忧)，yan(烟)，yin(因)，yang(央)，ying(英)，yong(雍)。
The vowels in the i row are written as yi(衣)，ya(呀)，ye(耶)，yao(腰)，you(忧)，yan(烟)，yin(因)，yang(央)，ying(英)，yong(雍) if no consonants precede them.
u 行的韵母，前面没有声母的时候，写成 wu(乌)，wa(蛙)，wo(窝)，wai(歪)，wei(威)，wan(弯)，wen(温)，wang(汪)，weng(翁)。
The vowels in the u row are written as wu(乌)，wa(蛙)，wo(窝)，wai(歪)，wei(威)，wan(弯)，wen(温)，wang(汪)，weng(翁) if no consonants precede them.
ü 行的韵母，前面没有声母的时候，写成 yu(迂)，yue(约)，yuan(冤)，yun(晕)；ü 上两点省略。
The vowels in the ü row are written as yu(迂)，yue(约)，yuan(冤)，yun(晕) if no consonants precede them，and the two dots of ü are omitted.
ü 行的韵母跟声母 j，q，x 拼的时候，写成 ju(居)，qu(区)，xu(虚)，ü 上两点也省略；但是跟声母 l，n 拼的时候，仍然写成 lü(吕)，nü(女)。
When the vowels in the ü row are used together with the consonants of j，q and x，they are written as ju(居)，qu(区)，xu(虚)，with the two dots of ü being omitted. When they are used together with the consonants of l and n，the two dots of ü are retained as in lü

(吕) and nü(女).

(5) iou, uei, uen 前面加声母的时候,写成 iu, ui, un。例如 niu(牛), gui(归), lun(论)。
When iou, uei and uen are preceded by consonants, they are written as iu, ui and un, such as in niu(牛), gui(归) and lun(论).

(6) 在给汉字注音的时候,为了使拼式简短,ng 可以省作 ŋ。
When phonetic notations are added to Chinese characters, ng may be abbreviated to ŋ to simplify the spelling.

四 声调符号
IV The Symbols of Tones

阴平 high and level tone ˉ	阳平 rising tone ˊ
上声 falling-rising tone ˇ	去声 falling tone ˋ

声调符号标在音节的主要母音上。轻声不标。例如:

The symbol of each tone is marked on the main vowel of a syllable, but it is omitted when the pronunciation is light. For example:

妈 mā (阴平) (high and level tone)	麻 má (阳平) (rising tone)	
马 mǎ (上声) (falling-rising tone)	骂 mà (去声) (falling tone)	吗 ma (轻声) (light)

五 隔音符号
V The Syllable-Dividing Mark

a, o, e 开头的音节连接在其他音节后面的时候,如果音节的界限发生混淆,用隔音符号(')隔开,例如:pi'ao(皮袄)。

When a syllable beginning with a, o, e follows another syllable, and the boundary of the two syllables are confusing, the syllable-dividing mark (') is used to separate then, i.e. pi'ao (皮袄).

附录二　常用标点符号用法简表*

Appendix II Table for the Use of Punctuation Marks

一　基本定义 Basic Definitions

句子:前后都有停顿,并带有一定的句调,表示相对完整意义的语言单位。

Sentence: a tonal linguistic unit, with a pause before and after it, which conveys a relatively complete meaning.

陈述句:用来说明事实的句子。

Declarative sentence: a sentence that is used to state a fact.

祈使句:用来要求听话人做某件事情的句子。

Imperative sentence: a sentence that is used to request the hearer to do something.

疑问句:用来提出问题的句子。

Interrogative sentence: a sentence that is used to raise a question.

感叹句:用来抒发某种强烈感情的句子。

Exclamatory sentence: a sentence that is used to express some strong emotion.

复句、分句:意思上有密切联系的小句子组织在一起构成一个大句子。这样的大句子叫复句,复句中的每个小句子叫分句。

Composite sentence and clause: a composite sentence is a big sentence formed from small sentences that are closely related in meaning. Each of those small sentences is called a clause.

词语:词和短语(词组)。词,即最小的能独立运用的语言单位。短语,即由两个或两个以上的词按一定的语法规则组成的表达一定意义的语言单位,也叫词组。

Word and phrase (word group): A word is a minimum linguistic unit that can be used independently. A phrase (word group) is a linguistic unit that is formed from two or more

---

* 本表参考了中华人民共和国国家标准《标点符号用法》。

This table refers to the *National Standard Use of Punctuation Marks of the People's Republic of China*.

words and conveys certain meaning.

二 用法简表 Table of Uses

名称 Name	符号 Mark	用法说明 Use	举例 Example
句号① Period	。	1.用于陈述句的末尾。 Used at the end of a declarative sentence.	北京是中华人民共和国的首都。 Beijing is the capital of the People's Republic of China.
		2.用于语气舒缓的祈使句末尾。 Used at the end of a mildly imperative sentence.	请您稍等一下。 Wait a moment, please.
问号 Question mark	?	1.用于疑问句的末尾。 Used at the end of an interrogative sentence.	他叫什么名字? What's his name?
		2.用于反问句的末尾。 Used at the end of a rhetorical sentence.	难道你还不了解我吗? Don't you understand me?
叹号 Exclamation mark	!	1.用于感叹句的末尾。 Used at the end of an exclamatory sentence.	为祖国的繁荣昌盛而奋斗! Struggle for the thriving and prosperity of our motherland!
		2.用于语气强烈的祈使句末尾。 Used at the end of a strong imperative sentence.	停止射击! Stop shooting!
		3.用于语气强烈的反问句末尾。 Used at the end of a strong rhetorical sentence.	我哪里比得上他呀! How could I match him!

名称 Name	符号 Mark	用法说明 Use	举例 Example
逗号 Comma	，	1.句子内部主语与谓语之间如需停顿，用逗号。 Used when a pause is needed between the subject and its predicate in a sentence.	我们看得见的星星，绝大多数是恒星。 Most of the stars we see are fixed stars.
		2.句子内部动词与宾语之间如需停顿，用逗号。 Used when a pause is needed between the verb and its object in a sentence.	应该看到，科学需要一个人贡献出毕生的精力。 We should know that scientific research needs a person's lifelong devotion.
		3.句子内部状语后边如需停顿，用逗号。 Used when a pause is needed after an adverbial in a sentence.	对于这个城市，他并不陌生。 He is not unfamiliar with this city.
		4.复句内各分句之间的停顿，除了有时要用分号外，都要用逗号。 Used for pauses between the clauses in a composite sentence except where the semicolon is required occasionally.	据说苏州园林有一百多处，我到过的不过十多处。 It is said that there are more than 100 gardens in Suzhou, but I have only visited over a dozen.
顿号 Slight-pause mark	、	用于句子内部并列词语之间的停顿。 Used for pauses between parallel words or phrases.	正方形是四边相等、四角均为直角的四边形。 A square is a quadrilateral with equal side lines and four right angles.

名称 Name	符号 Mark	用法说明 Use	举例 Example
分号② Semi-colon	；	1.用于复句内部并列分句之间的停顿。 Used for pauses between parallel clauses in a composite sentence.	语言，人们用来抒情达意；文字，人们用来记言记事。 Speech is used to express emotions and ideas while writing is used to record words and events.
		2.用于分行列举的各项之间。 Used for items listed in separate lines.	下列情形，应当以国家通用语言文字为基本的用语用字： (一)广播、电影、电视用语用字； (二)公共场所的设施用字； (三)招牌、广告用字； (四)企业事业组织名称； (五)在境内销售的商品的包装、说明。 In following cases, the national standard Chinese language and characters should be used: 1. In broadcasts, TV programs and movies; 2. On public facilities; 3. On public signs and advertisement; 4. In names of organizations and enterprises; 5. On the package and in specifications of goods sold in China.

名称 Name	符号 Mark	用法说明 Use	举例 Example
冒号 Colon	：	1.用于称呼语后边，表示提起下文。 Used for a term of address to introduce what follows.	同志们，朋友们：现在开会了…… Comrades and friends, now the meeting begins ...
		2.用于“说、想、是、证明、宣布、指出、透露、例如、如下”等词语后边，表示提起下文。 Used after such words or phrases as “说，想，是，证明，宣布，指出，透露，例如，如下，” etc. to introduce what follows.	他十分惊讶地说：“啊，原来是你！” He says in great surprise：“Oh，it's you!”
		3.用于总说性话语的后边，表示引起下文的分说。 Used after a summary expression to introduce a list of items.	北京紫禁城有四座城门：午门、神武门、东华门和西华门。 There are four gates in the Forbidden City of Beijing：*Wumen* Gate，*Shenwu* Gate，*Donghua* Gate and *Xihua* Gate.
		4.用于需要解释的词语后边，表示引出解释或说明。 Used after a word or phrase that needs explanation or illustration.	外文图书展销会 日期：10 月 20 日至 11 月 10 日 时间：上午 8 时至下午 4 时 地点：北京朝阳区工体东路 16 号 主办单位：中国图书进出口总公司

名称 Name	符号 Mark	用法说明 Use	举例 Example
冒号 Colon	：		Foreign Language Book Fair Dates：Oct. 20—Nov. 10 Time：8:00 a.m.—4:00 p.m. Location：16 East Gongti Road，Chaoyang District，Beijing Sponsor：China National Publications Import & Export (Group) Corporation
		5.用于总括性话语的前边，以总结上文。 Used for a summarizing expression to sum up what has been discussed in the proceeding text.	张华考上了北京大学；李萍进了中等技术学校；我在百货公司当售货员：我们都有光明的前途。 Zhang Hua has been admitted into Beijing University，Li Ping is now attending a secondary technical school，and I have become a salesman in a department store. All of us have a bright future.
引号③ Quotation marks	“ ” ‘ ’	1.用于行文中直接引用的部分。 Used for quotations in a text.	“满招损，谦受益”这句格言，流传到今天至少有两千年了。 The dictum “complacency spells loss，while modesty brings benefits” has been circulating for at least 2 000 years.

名称 Name	符号 Mark	用法说明 Use	举例 Example
引号③ Quotation marks	“ ” ‘ ’	2.用于需要着重论述的对象。 Used for what needs to be emphasized in a discussion.	古人对于写文章有个基本要求，叫作“有物有序”。“有物”就是要有内容，“有序”就是要有条理。 There has been a basic requirement from the ancient times on how to write an article — “to have substance and be arranged in good order.” The former means that the article should have content while the latter means that the article should be well-organized.
		3.用于具有特殊含义的词语。 Used for words or phrases with implied meaning.	这样的“聪明人”还是少一点好。 It is better to have fewer “wise persons” like these.
		4.引号里面还要用引号时，外面一层用双引号，里面一层用单引号。 When quotation marks are embedded in quotation marks, single quotation marks are used for the embedded ones and double quotation marks for the embedding ones.	他站起来问：“老师，‘有条不紊’的‘紊’是什么意思？” He stands up and asks, “Professor, what does ‘紊’ in the idiom ‘有条不紊’ mean?”

名称 Name	符号 Mark	用法说明 Use	举例 Example
括号④ Parentheses	( )	用于行文中注释性的部分。注释句子中某些词语的,括注紧贴在被注释词语之后;注释整个句子的,括注放在句末标点之后。 Used for an annotation in a text. If the annotation in parentheses is applied to words or phrases, it is placed immediately after them; but if it is applied to a whole sentence, it is placed after the final punctuation mark of the sentence.	(1)中国猿人(全名为"中国猿人北京种",或简称"北京人")在我国的发现,是对古人类学的一个重大贡献。 The discovery of Chinese ape-men ("Beijing species of Chinese ape-men" for the full name or "Beijing men" for short) in our country is a great contribution to palaeoanthropology. (2)写研究性文章跟文学创作不同,不能摊开稿纸搞"即兴"。(其实文学创作也要有素养才能有"即兴"。) The research article writing, different from literary creation, is not to be done in an improvisational way. (In fact literary creation also depends on cultural attainment for "improvisation".)
破折号 Dash	——	1.用于行文中解释说明的部分。 Used to introduce an explanation in a text.	迈进金黄色的大门,穿过宽阔的风门厅和衣帽厅,就到了大会堂建筑的枢纽部分——中央大厅。 Stepping into the great golden gate and passing through the lobby and the cloakroom, we came to the main quarters of the Great Hall of the People — the central hall.

名称 Name	符号 Mark	用法说明 Use	举例 Example
破折号 Dash	——	2.用于话题突然转变。Used for a sudden turn of topic.	"今天好热啊！——你什么时候去上海？"张强对刚刚进门的小王说。"How hot it is today! — When are you going to Shanghai?" Zhang Qiang said to Xiao Wang who had just entered the room.
		3.用于声音延长的拟声词后面。Used after a prolonged onomatopoeic word.	"呜——"火车开动了。The train sets off with a "hoot—".
		4.用于事项列举分承的各项之前。Used before each of a list of items.	根据研究对象的不同，环境物理学分为以下五个分支学科： ——环境声学； ——环境光学； ——环境热学； ——环境电磁学； ——环境空气动力学。 According to the differences of its study objects, environmental physics is classified into five branches: —environmental acoustics; —environmental optics; —environmental thermodynamics; —environmental electromagnetics; —environmental aerodynamics.

名称 **Name**	符号 **Mark**	用法说明 **Use**	举例 **Example**
省略号⑤ Ellipsis	……	1.用于引文的省略。 Used for omissions in a quotation.	她轻轻地哼起了《摇篮曲》:“月儿明,风儿静,树叶儿遮窗棂啊……” “Bright is the moonlight, gentle is the wind, and shelter are the tree leaves ...” she hummed *The Cradle Song*.
		2.用于列举的省略。 Used for omissions in listed items.	在广州的花市上,牡丹、吊钟、水仙、梅花、菊花、山茶、墨兰……春秋冬三季的鲜花都挤在一起啦! In the Guangzhou Flower Fair, there are peonies, bellflowers, narcissi, Chinese plum flowers, chrysanthemums, camellias, dark orchids ... All the fresh flowers in spring, autumn and winter are displayed there.
		3.用于话语中间,表示说话断断续续。 Used in a speech to indicate intermittence.	“我……对不起……大家,我……没有……完成……任务。” “I am sorry ... to all of you ... I have failed to ... fulfill ... my task.”
着重号 Emphasis mark	·	用于要求读者特别注意的字、词、句的下面。 Used under the Chinese characters, phrases or sentences to which special attention is required of the readers.	事业是干出来的,不是吹出来的。 Your achievement in the cause lies in working hard, not in bragging.

名称 Name	符号 Mark	用法说明 Use	举例 Example
连接号⑥ Hyphen	—	1.两个相关的名词构成一个意义单位,中间用连接号。 Used between two related nouns to constitute a semantic unit.	我国秦岭—淮河以北地区属于温带季风气候区,夏季高温多雨,冬季寒冷干燥。 The North of Mount Qinling-Huaihe River is an area of temperate monsoon. It is hot and rainy in summer, and cold and dry in winter.
		2.相关的时间、地点或数目之间用连接号,表示起止。 Used between related times, places, or numbers to indicate the beginning and the ending.	鲁迅(1881—1936)原名周树人,字豫才,浙江绍兴人。 Lu Xun (1881-1936), with the original name of Zhou Shuren and the style name of Yucai, was from Shaoxing County, Zhejiang Province.
		3.相关的字母、阿拉伯数字等之间,用连接号,表示产品型号。 Used between related letters, Arabic numerals, etc. to indicate product model.	在太平洋地区,除了已建成投入使用的 HAW—4 和 TPC—3 海底光缆之外,又有 TPC—4 海底光缆投入运营。 In the Pacific Region, the optical cable TPC-4 has become operational in addition to HAW-4 and TPC-3.

名称 Name	符号 Mark	用法说明 Use	举例 Example
连接号⑥ Hyphen	—	4.几个相关的项目表示递进式发展，中间用连接号。 Used between related items to indicate progressive development.	人类的发展可以分为古猿—猿人—古人—新人这四个阶段。 The evolution of mankind can be divided into four stages: Aegyptopithecus, Pithecanthropus, Palaeoanthropus and Neoanthropus.
间隔号 Separation dot	·	1.用于外国人和某些少数民族人名内各部分的分界。 Used to separate the different parts of the name of a foreigner or a person from certain minority ethnic group.	列奥纳多·达·芬奇 Leonardo da Vinci 爱新觉罗·努尔哈赤 Aisin Gioro Nurhachi
		2.用于书名与篇(章、卷)名之间的分界。 Used to separate the title of a book and its chapter or volume.	《中国大百科全书·物理学》 *Encyclopedia of China, Vol. Physics* 《三国志·蜀书·诸葛亮传》 *History of Three Kingdoms, History of Shuhan, A Biography of Zhuge Liang*

名称 Name	符号 Mark	用法说明 Use	举例 Example
书名号 Double angle brackets	《 》 〈 〉	用于书名、篇名、报纸名、刊物名等。 Used to enclose the title of a book, an article, a newspaper, a journal, etc.	(1)《红楼梦》的作者是曹雪芹。 The author of *A Dream of Red Mansions* is Cao Xueqin. (2)课文里有一篇鲁迅的《从百草园到三味书屋》。 In the textbook, there is an article entitled *From the Garden of a Hundred Kinds of Grasses to Sanwei Study* by Lu Xun. (3)他的文章在《人民日报》上发表了。 His article has been published in the *People's Daily*. (4)桌上放着一本《中国语文》。 There is a copy of *Chinese Language and Writing* on the desk. (5)《〈中国工人〉发刊词》发表于1940年2月7日。 Opening Remarks to *Chinese Workers* was published on Feb. 7th, 1940.
专名号⑦ Proper noun mark	——	用于人名、地名、朝代名等专名下面。 Used to underline the names of a person, place, dynasty, etc.	司马相如者，汉蜀郡成都人也，字长卿。 Sima Xiangru, with the style name of Changqing, was from Chengdu, Shu Prefecture, in the Han Dynasty.

附注 Notes:① 句号还有一种形式,即一个小圆点“.”,一般在科技文献中使用。
Another form of full stop is a small dot “.”, which is usually used in scientific and technological writings.

② 非并列关系(如转折关系、因果关系等)的多重复句,第一层的前后两部分之间,也用分号。
The semicolon is also used between the two first-level clauses of a complex sentence (to express transition, cause-and-effect, etc.).

③ 直行文稿引号改用双引号“﹃﹄”和单引号“﹁﹂”。
The double quotation marks “﹃﹄” and single quotation marks “﹁﹂” are used in vertically written or printed text.

④ 此外还有方括号“[ ]”、六角括号“〔 〕”和方头括号“【 】”。
In addition, there are square brackets “[ ]”, hexagon brackets “〔 〕”, and square-head brackets “【 】”.

⑤ 如果是整段文章或诗行的省略,可以使用十二个小圆点来表示。
Twelve small dots (............) can be used to indicate omission of whole paragraphs of a text or omission of whole lines of a poem.

⑥ 连接号另外还有三种形式,即长横“——”(占两个字的位置)、半字线“-”(占半个字的位置)和浪纹“~”(占一个字的位置)。
The hyphen has three more variants, i.e. a long horizontal line “——” (occupying a two-character space), a half-character line “-” (occupying a half-character space), a wavy line “~”(occupying a one-character space).

⑦ 专名号只用在古籍或某些文史著作里面。为了跟专名号配合,这类著作里的书名号可以用浪线“﹏﹏”。
The proper noun mark is only used in ancient books and certain literary and historical books. To go with the proper noun marks the wavy line “﹏﹏”can be used for double angle brackets in such books.

附录三 中国历代纪元简表

Appendix III Dynastic Chronology of Chinese History

夏 Xia Dynasty		约前 2070—前 1600 Around 2070 BC—1600 BC
商 Shang Dynasty		前 1600—前 1046 1600 BC—1046 BC
周 Zhou Dynasty	西周 Western Zhou Dynasty	前 1046—前 771 1046 BC—771 BC
	东周 Eastern Zhou Dynasty	前 770—前 256 770 BC—256 BC
	春秋时代 Spring and Autumn Period	前 770—前 476 770 BC—476 BC
	战国时代 Warring States Period①	前 475—前 221 475 BC—221 BC
秦 Qin Dynasty		前 221—前 206 221 BC—206 BC
汉 Han Dynasty	西汉 Western Han Dynasty②	前 206—公元 25 206 BC—25 AD
	东汉 Eastern Han Dynasty	25—220
三国 Three Kingdoms	魏 Kingdom of Wei	220—265
	蜀 Kingdom of Shu	221—263
	吴 Kingdom of Wu	222—280
西晋 Western Jin Dynasty		265—317
东晋 Eastern Jin 十六国 Sixteen States	东晋 Eastern Jin Dynasty	317—420
	十六国 Sixteen States Periods③	304—439

南北朝 Southern and Northern Dynasties	南朝 Southern Dynasties	宋 Song Dynasty	420—479
		齐 Qi Dynasty	479—502
		梁 Liang Dynasty	502—557
		陈 Chen Dynasty	557—589
	北朝 Northern Dynasties	北魏 Northern Wei Dynasty	386—534
		东魏 Eastern Wei Dynasty	534—550
		北齐 Northern Qi Dynasty	550—577
		西魏 Western Wei Dynasty	535—556
		北周 Northern Zhou Dynasty	557—581
隋 Sui Dynasty			581—618
唐 Tang Dynasty			618—907
五代十国 Five Dynasties Ten States Periods	后梁 Later Liang Dynasty		907—923
	后唐 Later Tang Dynasty		923—936
	后晋 Later Jin Dynasty		936—947
	后汉 Later Han Dynasty		947—950
	后周 Later Zhou Dynasty		951—960
	十国 Ten States Periods[4]		902—979
宋 Song Dynasty	北宋 Northern Song Dynasty		960—1127
	南宋 Southern Song Dynasty		1127—1279
辽 Liao Dynasty[5]			907—1125
西夏 Western Xia Dynasty[6]			1038—1227
金 Jin Dynasty			1115—1234
元 Yuan Dynasty[7]			1206—1368
明 Ming Dynasty			1368—1644
清 Qing Dynasty[8]			1616—1911
中华民国 Republic of China			1912—1949

中华人民共和国 1949 年 10 月 1 日成立

Founding of the People's Republic of China on October 1, 1949

附注 Notes：① 这时期，主要有秦、魏、韩、赵、楚、燕、齐等国。
In this period, the main states are Qin, Wei, Han, Zhao, Chu, Yan, Qi, etc.

② 包括王莽建立的“新”王朝(公元9年—23年)和更始帝(公元23年—25年)。王莽时期，爆发大规模的农民起义，建立了农民政权。公元23年，新莽王朝灭亡。公元25年，东汉王朝建立。
This period includes the “New” Dynasty (9—23) established by Wang Mang and the period of Gengshi Emperor (23—25). Under Wang Mang's reign, a large-scale peasant uprising broke up and a peasant regime was established. In 23 AD, the new Dynasty of Wang Mang was overthrown. In 25 AD, Eastern Han Dynasty was established.

③ 这时期，在中国北方和巴蜀，先后存在过一些封建割据政权，其中有：汉(前赵)、成(成汉)、前凉、后赵(魏)、前燕、前秦、后燕、后秦、西秦、后凉、南凉、南燕、西凉、北凉、北燕、夏等国，历史上叫作“十六国”。
In this period, some feudal separatist regimes existed consecutively in the north and Bashu regions of China. Among them are Han (Former Zhao), Cheng (Cheng Han), Former Liang, Later Zhao (Wei), Former Yan, Former Qin, Later Yan, Later Qin, Western Qin, Later Liang, Southern Liang, Southern Yan, Western Liang, Northern Liang, Northern Yan, Xia, etc. In history, these states are called “the Sixteen States”.

④ 这时期，除后梁、后唐、后晋、后汉、后周外，还先后存在过一些封建割据政权，其中有：吴、前蜀、吴越、楚、闽、南汉、荆南(南平)、后蜀、南唐、北汉等国，历史上叫作“十国”。
In this period, besides Later Liang, Later Tang, Later Jin, Later Han and Later Zhou, there were other feudal separatist regimes. They were Wu, Former Shu, Wu Yue, Chu, Min, South-

ern Han, Jing Nan (Nan Ping), Later Shu, Southern Tang, Northern Han, etc. In history, they are called "the Ten States".

⑤ 辽建国于公元 907 年,国号契丹,916 年始建年号,938 年(一说 947 年)改国号为辽,983 年复称契丹,1066 年仍称辽。
The Liao Dynasty was known as the Qidan Kingdom when it was first established in 907. The dynasty began to use a reign title in 916 and renamed itself Liao in 938 (or 947 according to another source), but it resumed the name of Qidan in 983, before changing back to Liao in 1066.

⑥ 1032 年(北宋明道元年)元昊嗣夏王位,1034 年始建年号,1038 年称帝,国名大夏。在汉籍中习称西夏。1227 年为蒙古所灭。
Yuanhao succeeded the throne of King of Xia in 1032 (the first year of Mingdao, Northern Song dynasty) , started the title of his reign in 1034 and proclaimed himself emperor with Daxia as his kingdom name in 1038, which is traditionally called Western Xia in historical documents of Han Dynasty. This kingdom was ended by Mongolian army in 1227.

⑦ 铁木真于公元 1206 年建国;公元 1271 年忽必烈定国号为元,1279 年灭南宋。
Temuzin, a Mongol general, founded a kingdom in 1206. Kublai Khan renamed the kingdom Yuan in 1271, and overthrew the Southern Song Dynasty in 1279.

⑧ 清建国于 1616 年,初称后金,1636 年始改国号为清,1644 年入关。
Qing was founded in 1616 and called Later Jin originally and changed the title to Qing in 1636. They entered China proper through Shanhaiguan pass from the Northeast in 1644.

附录四 中国少数民族简表

Appendix IV Table of Ethnic Groups in China

中国是统一的多民族的社会主义国家，由 56 个民族组成。除汉族外，有 55 个少数民族，约占全国总人口的 8%。

China is a unified, multi-ethnic, socialist country, which is made up of 56 ethnic groups. Other than Hans, there are 55 ethnic Groups, accounting for about 8% of the entire population in China.

民族名称 **Names of Ethnic Groups**	主要分布地区 **Main Distribution Areas**
蒙古族 Mongol	内蒙古、辽宁、新疆、黑龙江、吉林、青海、甘肃、河北、河南等地 Inner Mongolia, Liaoning, Xinjiang, Heilongjiang, Jilin, Qinghai, Gansu, Hebei, Henan, etc.
回族 Hui	宁夏、甘肃、河南、新疆、青海、云南、河北、山东、安徽、辽宁、北京、内蒙古、天津、黑龙江、陕西、吉林、江苏、贵州等地 Ningxia, Gansu, Henan, Xinjiang, Qinghai, Yunnan, Hebei, Shandong, Anhui, Liaoning, Beijing, Inner Mongolia, Tianjin, Heilongjiang, Shaanxi, Jilin, Jiangsu, Guizhou, etc.
藏族 Tibetan	西藏及四川、青海、甘肃、云南等地 Tibet, Sichuan, Qinghai, Gansu, Yunnan, etc.
维吾尔族 Uygur	新疆 Xinjiang
苗族 Miao	贵州、云南、湖南、重庆、广西、四川、海南、湖北等地 Guizhou, Yunnan, Hunan, Chongqing, Guangxi, Sichuan, Hainan, Hubei, etc.

民族名称 **Names of Ethnic Groups**	主要分布地区 **Main Distribution Areas**
彝族 Yi	云南、四川、贵州、广西等地 Yunnan, Sichuan, Guizhou, Guangxi, etc.
壮族 Zhuang	广西及云南、广东、贵州、湖南等地 Guangxi, Yunnan, Guangdong, Guizhou, Hunan, etc.
布依族 Bouyei	贵州 Guizhou
朝鲜族 Korean	吉林、黑龙江、辽宁等地 Jilin, Heilongjiang, Liaoning, etc.
满族 Manchu	辽宁及黑龙江、吉林、河北、内蒙古、北京等地 Liaoning, Heilongjiang, Jilin, Hebei, Inner Mongolia, Beijing, etc.
侗族 Dong	贵州、湖南、广西等地 Guizhou, Hunan, Guangxi, etc.
瑶族 Yao	广西、湖南、云南、广东、贵州等地 Guangxi, Hunan, Yunnan, Guangdong, Guizhou, etc.
白族 Bai	云南、贵州、湖南等地 Yunnan, Guizhou, Hunan, etc.
土家族 Tujia	湖北、湖南、重庆等地 Hubei, Hunan, Chongqing, etc.
哈尼族 Hani	云南 Yunnan
哈萨克族 Kazak	新疆、甘肃、青海等地 Xinjiang, Gansu, Qinghai, etc.
傣族 Dai	云南 Yunnan
黎族 Li	海南 Hainan
傈僳族 Lisu	云南、四川等地 Yunnan, Sichuan, etc.
佤族 Va	云南 Yunnan
畲族 She	福建、浙江、江西、广东等地 Fujian, Zhejiang, Jiangxi, Guangdong, etc.
高山族 Gaoshan	台湾及福建 Taiwan, Fujian

民族名称 **Names of Ethnic Groups**	主要分布地区 **Main Distribution Areas**
拉祜族 Lahu	云南 Yunnan
水族 Sui	贵州、广西 Guizhou, Guangxi
东乡族 Dongxiang	甘肃、新疆 Gansu, Xinjiang
纳西族 Naxi	云南、四川 Yunnan, Sichuan
景颇族 Jingpo	云南 Yunnan
柯尔克孜族 Kirgiz	新疆、黑龙江 Xinjiang, Heilongjiang
土族 Tu	青海、甘肃 Qinghai, Gansu
达斡尔族 Daur	内蒙古、黑龙江、新疆等地 Inner Mongolia, Heilongjiang, Xinjiang, etc.
仫佬族 Mulam	广西 Guangxi
羌族 Qiang	四川 Sichuan
布朗族 Blang	云南 Yunnan
撒拉族 Salar	青海、甘肃等地 Qinghai, Gansu, etc.
毛南族 Maonan	广西 Guangxi
仡佬族 Gelao	贵州、广西 Guizhou, Guangxi
锡伯族 Xibe	辽宁、新疆、吉林、黑龙江等地 Liaoning, Xinjiang, Jilin, Heilongjiang, etc.
阿昌族 Achang	云南 Yunnan
塔吉克族 Tajik	新疆 Xinjiang
普米族 Pumi	云南 Yunnan
怒族 Nu	云南 Yunnan
乌孜别克族 Uzbek	新疆 Xinjiang
俄罗斯族 Russian	新疆、黑龙江 Xinjiang, Heilongjiang
鄂温克族 Ewenki	内蒙古、黑龙江 Inner Mongolia, Heilongjiang
德昂族 De'ang	云南 Yunnan
保安族 Bonan	甘肃 Gansu
裕固族 Yugur	甘肃 Gansu
京族 Gin	广西 Guangxi
塔塔尔族 Tatar	新疆 Xinjiang

民族名称 **Names of Ethnic Groups**	主要分布地区 **Main Distribution Areas**
独龙族 Derung	云南 Yunnan
鄂伦春族 Oroqen	内蒙古、黑龙江 Inner Mongolia, Heilongjiang
赫哲族 Hezhen	黑龙江 Heilongjiang
门巴族 Monba	西藏 Tibet
珞巴族 Lhoba	西藏 Tibet
基诺族 Jino	云南 Yunnan

附录五 中国各省、直辖市、自治区及省会(或首府)名称表

Appendix V Table of Provinces, Municipalities, Autonomous Regions and Provincial Capitals in China

(按汉语拼音字母顺序排列)

(Arranged in Chinese phonetic alphabetical order)

省、市、自治区名 Province, Municipality, Autonomous Region	简称(或别称) Alternative Name	省会(或首府)名 Provincial Capital
安徽 Anhui	(皖)Wan	合肥 Hefei
北京 Beijing	京 Jing	
重庆 Chongqing	(渝)Yu	
福建 Fujian	(闽)Min	福州 Fuzhou
甘肃 Gansu	甘(陇)Gan (Long)	兰州 Lanzhou
广东 Guangdong	(粤)Yue	广州 Guangzhou
广西 Guangxi	(桂)Gui	南宁 Nanning
贵州 Guizhou	贵(黔)Gui (Qian)	贵阳 Guiyang
海南 Hainan	(琼)Qiong	海口 Haikou
河北 Hebei	(冀)Ji	石家庄 Shijiazhuang
河南 Henan	(豫)Yu	郑州 Zhengzhou
黑龙江 Heilongjiang	黑 Hei	哈尔滨 Harbin
湖北 Hubei	(鄂)E	武汉 Wuhan
湖南 Hunan	(湘)Xiang	长沙 Changsha
吉林 Jilin	吉 Ji	长春 Changchun

省、市、自治区名 Province, Municipality, Autonomous Region	简称(或别称) Alternative Name	省会(或首府)名 Provincial Capital
江苏 Jiangsu	苏 Su	南京 Nanjing
江西 Jiangxi	(赣)Gan	南昌 Nanchang
辽宁 Liaoning	辽 Liao	沈阳 Shenyang
内蒙古 Inner Mongolia	蒙 Meng	呼和浩特 Huhehaote
宁夏 Ningxia	宁 Ning	银川 Yinchuan
青海 Qinghai	青 Qing	西宁 Xining
山东 Shandong	(鲁)Lu	济南 Jinan
山西 Shanxi	(晋)Jin	太原 Taiyuan
陕西 Shaanxi	陕(秦)Shaan (Qin)	西安 Xi'an
上海 Shanghai	(沪)(申)Hu (Shen)	
四川 Sichuan	川(蜀)Chuan (Shu)	成都 Chengdu
台湾 Taiwan	台 Tai	台北 Taibei
天津 Tianjin	津 Jin	
西藏 Tibet	藏 Zang	拉萨 Lasa
新疆 Xinjiang	新 Xin	乌鲁木齐 Urumqi
云南 Yunnan	云(滇)Yun (Dian)	昆明 Kunming
浙江 Zhejiang	浙 Zhe	杭州 Hangzhou
香港 Hongkong (特别行政区 Special Administrative Region)	港 Gang	
澳门 Macao (特别行政区 Special Administrative Region)	澳 Ao	

附录六 世界各国和地区及首都(或首府)一览表*

Appendix VI Table of Capitals for Countries and Regions Worldwide

国家或地区 **Country / Region**	首都(或首府) **Capital**
亚洲 **Asia**	
中国 China (the People's Republic of China)	北京 Beijing
蒙古 Mongolia (the State of Mongolia)	乌兰巴托 Ulan Bator
朝鲜 North Korea (the Democratic People's Republic of Korea)	平壤 Pyongyang
韩国 South Korea (the Republic of Korea)	首尔 Seoul
日本 Japan	东京 Tokyo
老挝 Lao (the Lao People's Democratic Republic)	万象 Vientiane
越南 Vietnam (the Socialist Republic of Vietnam)	河内 Hanoi

* 本资料主要依据 2009/2010《世界知识年鉴》(世界知识出版社,2010)整理。

This is mainly based on *The World Factbook* 2009/2010 by World Affairs Press, 2010.

柬埔寨 Cambodia (the Kingdom of Cambodia)	金边 Phnom Penh
缅甸 Myanmar (the Union of Myanmar)	内比都 Naypyitaw
泰国 Thailand (the Kingdom of Thailand)	曼谷 Bangkok
马来西亚 Malaysia	吉隆坡 Kuala Lumpur
新加坡 Singapore (the Republic of Singapore)	新加坡 Singapore City
文莱 Brunei (Negara Brunei Darussalam)	斯里巴加湾市 Bandar Seri Begawan
菲律宾 Philippines (the Republic of the Philippines)	大马尼拉市 Manila
印度尼西亚 Indonesia (the Republic of Indonesia)	雅加达 Jakarta
东帝汶 East Timor (the Democratic Republic of East Timor)	帝力 Dili
尼泊尔 Nepal (the Kingdom of Nepal)	加德满都 Kathmandu
不丹 Bhutan (the Kingdom of Bhutan)	廷布 Thimphu
孟加拉国 Bangladesh (the People's Republic of Bangladesh)	达卡 Dhaka
印度 India (the Republic of India)	新德里 New Delhi
斯里兰卡 Sri Lanka (the Democratic Socialist Republic of Sri Lanka)	科伦坡 Colombo
马尔代夫 Maldives (the Republic of Maldives)	马累 Male
巴基斯坦 Pakistan (the Islamic Republic of Pakistan)	伊斯兰堡 Islamabad

阿富汗 Afghanistan (the Islamic State of Afghanistan)	喀布尔 Kabul
伊朗 Iran (the Islamic Republic of Iran)	德黑兰 Tehran
科威特 Kuwait (the State of Kuwait)	科威特城 Kuwait City
沙特阿拉伯 Saudi Arabia (the Kingdom of Saudi Arabia)	利雅得 Riyadh
巴林 Bahrain (the State of Bahrain)	麦纳麦 Manama
卡塔尔 Qatar (the State of Qatar)	多哈 Doha
阿拉伯联合酋长国 United Arab Emirates (the United Arab Emirates)	阿布扎比 Abu Dhabi
阿曼 Oman (the Sultanate of Oman)	马斯喀特 Muscat
也门 Yemen (the Republic of Yemen)	萨那 Sana'a
伊拉克 Iraq (the Republic of Iraq)	巴格达 Baghdad
叙利亚 Syrian (the Syrian Arab Republic)	大马士革 Damascus
黎巴嫩 Lebanon (the Republic of Lebanon)	贝鲁特 Beirut
约旦 Jordan (the Hashemite Kingdom of Jordan)	安曼 Amman
巴勒斯坦 Palestine (the State of Palestine)	耶路撒冷① Jerusalem
以色列 Israel (the State of Israel)	特拉维夫② Tel Aviv
土耳其 Turkey (the Republic of Turkey)	安卡拉 Ankara
乌兹别克斯坦 Uzbekistan (the Republic of Uzbekistan)	塔什干 Tashkent

哈萨克斯坦 Kazakhstan (the Republic of Kazakhstan)	阿斯塔纳 Astana
吉尔吉斯斯坦 Kyrgyzstan (the Kyrghyz Republic)	比什凯克 Bishkek
塔吉克斯坦 Tadzhikistan (the Republic of Tadzhikistan)	杜尚别 Dushanbe
亚美尼亚 Armenia (the Republic of Armenia)	埃里温 Yerevan
土库曼斯坦 Turkmenistan (the Republic of Turkmenistan)	阿什哈巴德 Ashkhabad
阿塞拜疆 Azerbaijan (the Republic of Azerbaijan)	巴库 Baku
格鲁吉亚 Georgia (the Republic of Georgia)	第比利斯 Tbilisi

欧　洲
Europe

冰岛 Iceland (the Republic of Iceland)	雷克雅未克 Reykjavik
法罗群岛(丹) Faroe Islands (Danish Faroe Islands)	托尔斯港 Torshavn
丹麦 Denmark (the Kingdom of Denmark)	哥本哈根 Copenhagen
挪威③ Norway (the Kingdom of Norway)	奥斯陆 Oslo
瑞典 Sweden (the Kingdom of Sweden)	斯德哥尔摩 Stockholm
芬兰 Finland (the Republic of Finland)	赫尔辛基 Helsinki
俄罗斯联邦 Russia (the Russian Federation)	莫斯科 Moscow
乌克兰 Ukraine	基辅 Kiev
白俄罗斯 Belarus (the Republic of Belarus)	明斯克 Minsk

摩尔多瓦 Moldova (the Republic of Moldova)	基希讷乌 Kishinev
立陶宛 Lithuania (the Republic of Lithuania)	维尔纽斯 Vilnius
爱沙尼亚 Estonia (the Republic of Estonia)	塔林 Tallinn
拉脱维亚 Latvia (the Republic of Latvia)	里加 Riga
波兰 Poland (the Republic of Poland)	华沙 Warsaw
捷克 Czech (the Czech Republic)	布拉格 Prague
匈牙利 Hungary (the Republic of Hungary)	布达佩斯 Budapest
德国 Germany (the Federal Republic of Germany)	柏林 Berlin
奥地利 Austria (the Republic of Austria)	维也纳 Vienna
列支敦士登 Liechtenstein (the Principality of Liechtenstein)	瓦杜兹 Vaduz
瑞士 Switzerland (the Confederation of Switzerland)	伯尔尼 Berne
荷兰 the Netherlands (the Kingdom of the Netherlands)	阿姆斯特丹 Amsterdam
比利时 Belgium (the Kingdom of Belgium)	布鲁塞尔 Brussels
卢森堡 Luxembourg (the Grand Duchy of Luxembourg)	卢森堡 Luxembourg
英国 Britain (the United Kingdom of Great Britain and Northern Ireland)	伦敦 London
直布罗陀(英) Gibraltar (UK)	

爱尔兰 Ireland (the Republic of Ireland)	都柏林 Dublin
法国 France (the Republic of France)	巴黎 Paris
摩纳哥 Monaco (the Principality of Monaco)	摩纳哥 Monaco-Ville
安道尔 Andorra (the Principality of Andorra)	安道尔城 Andorra la Vella
西班牙 Spain (the Kingdom of Spain)	马德里 Madrid
葡萄牙 Portugal (the Portuguese Republic)	里斯本 Lisbon
意大利 Italy (the Italian Republic)	罗马 Rome
梵蒂冈 Vatican (the Vatican City State)	梵蒂冈城 the Vatican City
圣马力诺 San Marino (the Republic of San Marino)	圣马力诺 San Marino
马耳他 Malta (the Republic of Malta)	瓦莱塔 Valletta
克罗地亚 Croatia (the Republic of Croatia)	萨格勒布 Zagreb
斯洛伐克 Slovak (the Slovak Republic)	布拉迪斯拉发 Bratislava
斯洛文尼亚 Slovenia (the Republic of Slovenia)	卢布尔雅那 Ljubljana
波斯尼亚和黑塞哥维那,简称波黑 Bosnia and Herzegovina (the Republic of Bosnia and Herzegovina)	萨拉热窝 Sarajevo
马其顿 Macedonia (the Republic of Macedonia)	斯科普里 Skopje
塞尔维亚 Serbia (the Republic of Serbia)	贝尔格莱德 Belgrade
黑山 Montenegro (the Republic of Montenegro)	波德戈里察 Podgorica
罗马尼亚 Romania	布加勒斯特 Bucharest

保加利亚 Bulgaria (the Republic of Bulgaria)	索非亚 Sofia
阿尔巴尼亚 Albania (the Republic of Albania)	地拉那 Tirana
希腊 Greece (the Republic of Greece)	雅典 Athens
塞浦路斯 Cyprus (the Republic of Cyprus)	尼科西亚 Nicosia

非 洲
Africa

埃及 Egypt (the Arab Republic of Egypt)	开罗 Cairo
利比亚 Libya (the Great Socialist People's Libyan Arab Jamahiriya)	的黎波里 Tripoli
突尼斯 Tunisia (the Republic of Tunisia)	突尼斯 Tunis
阿尔及利亚 Algeria (the Democratic People's Republic of Algeria)	阿尔及尔 Algiers
摩洛哥 Morocco (the Kingdom of Morocco)	拉巴特 Rabat
西撒哈拉 West Sahara	阿尤恩 Lá Youne
毛里塔尼亚 Mauritania (the Islamic Republic of Mauritania)	努瓦克肖特 Nouakchott
塞内加尔 Senegal (the Republic of Senegal)	达喀尔 Dakar
冈比亚 Gambia (the Republic of Gambia)	班珠尔 Banjul
马里 Mali (the Republic of Mali)	巴马科 Bamako
布基纳法索 Burkina Faso	瓦加杜古 Quagadougou

佛得角	普拉亚
Cape Verde (the Republic of Cape Verde)	Praia
几内亚比绍	比绍
Guinea-Bissau (the Republic of Guinea-Bissau)	Bissau
几内亚	科纳克里
Guinea (the Republic of Guinea)	Conakry
塞拉利昂	弗里敦
Sierra Leone (the Republic of Sierra Leone)	Freetown
利比里亚	蒙罗维亚
Liberia (the Republic of Liberia)	Monrovia
科特迪瓦	亚穆苏克罗[4]
Cote d'Ivoire (the Republic of Cote d'Ivoire)	Yamoussoukro
加纳	阿克拉
Ghana (the Republic of Ghana)	Accra
多哥	洛美
Togo (the Republic of Togo)	Lomé
贝宁	波多诺伏
Benin (the Republic of Benin)	Porto-Novo
尼日尔	尼亚美
Niger (the Republic of Niger)	Niamey
尼日利亚	阿布贾
Nigeria (the Federal Republic of Nigeria)	Abuja
喀麦隆	雅温得
Cameroon (the Republic of Cameroon)	Yaoundé
赤道几内亚	马拉博
Equatorial Guinea (the Republic of Equatorial Guinea)	Malabo
乍得	恩贾梅纳
Chad (the Republic of Chad)	N'Djamena
中非	班吉
Central Africa (the Central African Republic)	Bangui
苏丹	喀土穆
Sudan (the Republic of Sudan)	Khartoum
南苏丹	朱巴
(the Republic of South Sudan)	Juba

埃塞俄比亚 Ethiopia (the Federal Democratic Republic of Ethiopia)	亚的斯亚贝巴 Addis Ababa
吉布提 Djibouti (the Republic of Djibouti)	吉布提市 Djibouti
索马里 Somali (the Somali Republic)	摩加迪沙 Mogadishu
肯尼亚 Kenya (the Republic of Kenya)	内罗毕 Nairobi
乌干达 Uganda (the Republic of Uganda)	坎帕拉 Kampala
坦桑尼亚 Tanzania (the United Republic of Tanzania)	达累斯萨拉姆 Dar es Salaam
卢旺达 Rwanda (the Republic of Rwanda)	基加利 Kigali
布隆迪 Burundi (the Republic of Burundi)	布琼布拉 Bujumbura
刚果(金) Congo (K) (the Democratic Republic of Congo)	金沙萨 Kinshasa
刚果(布) Congo (B) (the Republic of the Congo)	布拉柴维尔 Brazzaville
加蓬 Gabon (the Republic of Gabon)	利伯维尔 Libreville
圣多美和普林西比 Sao Tome and Principe (the Democratic Republic of Sao Tome and Principe)	圣多美 Sao Tome
安哥拉 Angola (the Republic of Angola)	罗安达 Luanda
赞比亚 Zambia (the Republic of Zambia)	卢萨卡 Lusaka
马拉维 Malawi (the Republic of Malawi)	利隆圭 Lilongwe
莫桑比克 Mozambique (the Republic of Mozambique)	马普托 Maputo

科摩罗 Comoros (the Federal Islamic Republic of the Comoros)	莫罗尼 Moroni
马达加斯加 Madagascar (the Republic of Madagascar)	塔那那利佛 Antananarivo
塞舌尔 Seychelles (the Republic of Seychelles)	维多利亚 Victoria
毛里求斯 Mauritius (the Republic of Mauritius)	路易港 Port Louis
留尼汪(法) Reunion (Overseas Department and Region of France)	圣但尼 Saint-Denis
津巴布韦 Zimbabwe (the Republic of Zimbabwe)	哈拉雷 Harare
博茨瓦纳 Botswana (the Republic of Botswana)	哈博罗内 Gaborone
纳米比亚 Namibia (the Republic of Namibia)	温得和克 Windhoek
南非 South Africa (the Republic of South Africa)	比勒陀利亚⑤ Pretoria
斯威士兰 Swaziland (the Kingdom of Swaziland)	姆巴巴内 Mbabane
莱索托 Lesotho (the Kingdom of Lesotho)	马塞卢 Maseru
圣赫勒拿(英)⑥ Saint Helena (UK)	詹姆斯敦 Jamestown
厄立特里亚 Eritrea (the State of Eritrea)	阿斯马拉 Asmara
法属南部领地 French Southern Territories	
英属印度洋领地 British Indian Ocean Territory	

大 洋 洲
Oceania

澳大利亚 Australia (the Commonwealth of Australia)	堪培拉 Canberra

新西兰 New Zealand	惠灵顿 Wellington
巴布亚新几内亚 Papua New Guinea (the Independent State of Papua New Guinea)	莫尔斯比港 Port Moresby
所罗门群岛 Solomon Islands	霍尼亚拉 Honiara
瓦努阿图 Vanuatu (the Republic of Vanuatu)	维拉港 Port Vila
新喀里多尼亚(法) New Caledonia (France)	努美阿 Noumea
斐济 Fiji (the Republic of the Fiji Islands)	苏瓦 Suva
基里巴斯 Kiribati (the Republic of Kiribati)	塔拉瓦 Tarawa
瑙鲁 Nauru (the Republic of Nauru)	亚伦区⑦ Yaren District
密克罗尼西亚 Micronesia (the Federated States of Micronesia)	帕利基尔 Palikir
马绍尔群岛 Marshall Islands (the Republic of the Marshall Islands)	马朱罗 Majuro
北马里亚纳群岛⑧ the Northern Mariana Islands (the Commonwealth of the Northern Mariana Islands)	塞班岛 Saipan Island
关岛(美) Guam (US)	阿加尼亚 Agana
图瓦卢 Tuvalu	富纳富提 Funafuti
瓦利斯和富图纳(法) Wallis and Futuna Islands (France)	马塔乌图 Mata-Utu
萨摩亚 Samoa (the Independent State of Samoa)	阿皮亚 Apia
美属萨摩亚⑨ American Samoa (Territory of American Samoa)	帕果帕果 Pago-Pago

纽埃(新) Niue (NZ)	阿洛菲 Alofi
诺福克岛 Norfolk Island	金斯敦 Kingstown
帕劳 Palau (the Republic of Palau)	梅莱凯奥克 Melekeok
托克劳(新) Tokelau (NZ)	⑩
库克群岛(新) the Cook Islands (NZ)	阿瓦鲁阿 Avarua
汤加 Tonga (the Kingdom of Tonga)	努库阿洛法 Nukualofa
法属波利尼西亚 French Polynesia	帕皮提 Papeete
皮特凯恩群岛(英) Pitcairn Islands Groups (UK)	亚当斯敦 Adamston
赫德岛和麦克唐纳群岛[11] Heard Island and McDonald Islands (the Territory of Heard Island and McDonald Islands)	
科科斯(基林)群岛(澳) Cocos (Keeling) Islands (Australia)	西岛 West Island
美国本土外小岛屿[12] United States Minor Outlying Islands	
圣诞岛(澳) Christmas Island (Australia)	

北 美 洲
North America

格陵兰(丹) Greenland (Denmark)	努克,前称戈特霍布 Nuuk (formerly called Godthaab)
加拿大 Canada	渥太华 Ottawa
圣皮埃尔和密克隆(法) The Islands of St. Pierre and Miquelon (France)	圣皮埃尔市 St. Pierre

美国 United States (the United States of America)	华盛顿哥伦比亚特区 Washington D.C.
百慕大(英) the Bermuda Islands (UK)	汉密尔顿 Hamilton
墨西哥 Mexico (the United States of Mexico)	墨西哥城 Mexico City
危地马拉 Guatemala (the Republic Guatemala)	危地马拉城 Guatemala City
伯利兹 Belize	贝尔莫潘 Belmopan
萨尔瓦多 El Salvador (the Republic of El Salvador)	圣萨尔瓦多市 San Salvador
洪都拉斯 Honduras (the Republic of Honduras)	特古西加尔巴 Tegucigalpa
尼加拉瓜 Nicaragua (the Republic of Nicaragua)	马那瓜 Managua
哥斯达黎加 Costa Rica (the Republic of Costa Rica)	圣何塞 San Jose
巴拿马 Panama (the Republic of Panama)	巴拿马城 Panama City
巴哈马 Bahamas (the Commonwealth of the Bahamas)	拿骚 Nassau
特克斯和凯科斯群岛(英) Turks and Caicos Islands (UK)	科伯恩城 Cockburn Town
古巴 Cuba (the Republic of Cuba)	哈瓦那 La Havana
开曼群岛(英) the Cayman Islands (UK)	乔治敦 Georgetown
牙买加 Jamaica	金斯敦 Kingstown
海地 Haiti (the Republic of Haiti)	太子港 Port-au-Prince
多米尼加 the Dominican Republic	圣多明各 Santo Domingo

波多黎各(美) Puerto Rico (US) (the Commonwealth of Puerto Rico)	圣胡安 San Juan
美属维尔京群岛 the Virgin Islands of the United States	夏洛特·阿马里 Charlotte Amalie
英属维尔京群岛 the British Virgin Islands	罗德城 Road Town
圣基茨和尼维斯 Saint Kitts and Nevis (the Federation of Saint Kitts and Nevis)	巴斯特尔 Basseterre
安圭拉(英) Anguilla (UK)	瓦利 Valley
圣巴泰勒米(法) Saint Barthelemy (Fr.)	古斯塔维亚 Gustavia
圣马丁(法) St. Martin (Fr.)	马里戈特 Marigot
安提瓜和巴布达 Antigua and Barbuda	圣约翰 St. John's
蒙特塞拉特(英) Montserrat (UK)	普利茅斯[13] Plymouth
瓜德罗普(法) Guadeloupe (France)	巴斯特尔 Basse-Terre
多米尼克 Dominica (the Commonwealth of Dominica)	罗索 Roseau
马提尼克(法) Martinique (France)	法兰西堡 Fort-de-France
圣卢西亚 Saint Lucia	卡斯特里 Castries
圣文森特和格林纳丁斯 Saint Vincent and Grenadines	金斯敦 Kingstown
巴巴多斯 Barbados	布里奇顿 Bridgetown
格林纳达 Grenada	圣乔治 St. George's

特立尼达和多巴哥 Trinidad and Tobago (the Republic of Trinidad and Tobago)	西班牙港 Port of Spain
荷属安的列斯 the Netherlands Antilles	威廉斯塔德 Willemstad
阿鲁巴(荷) Aruba (Dutch)	奥拉涅斯塔德 Oranjestad

南美洲
South America

哥伦比亚 Columbia (the Republic of Columbia)	波哥大 Santa Fe Bogota
委内瑞拉 Venezuela (the Republic of Venezuela)	加拉加斯 Caracas
圭亚那 Guyana (the Cooperative Republic of Guyana)	乔治敦 Georgetown
苏里南 Suriname (the Republic of Suriname)	帕拉马里博 Paramaribo
法属圭亚那 French Guyana	卡宴 Cayenne
厄瓜多尔 Ecuador (the Republic of Ecuador)	基多 Quito
秘鲁 Peru (the Republic of Peru)	利马 Lima
巴西 Brazil (the Federative Republic of Brazil)	巴西利亚 Brasilia
玻利维亚 Bolivia (the Republic of Bolivia)	苏克雷[14] Sucre
智利 Chile (the Republic of Chile)	圣地亚哥 Santiago
阿根廷 Argentina (the Republic of Argentina)	布宜诺斯艾利斯 Buenos Aires
巴拉圭 Paraguay (the Republic of Paraguay)	亚松森 Asuncion

乌拉圭 Uruguay (the Oriental Republic of Uruguay)	蒙得维的亚 Montevideo
马尔维纳斯群岛⑮ Malvinas Islands	阿根廷港⑯ Port Argentina
南乔治亚和南桑德韦奇群岛(英) South Georgia and South Sandwich Islands (UK)	

附注 Notes：① 1988年11月，巴勒斯坦全国委员会第19次特别会议通过《独立宣言》，宣布耶路撒冷为新成立的巴勒斯坦国首都。目前，巴勒斯坦国政府机构设在拉马拉。
In November 1988, the 19th session of the Palestine National Council meeting approved the Declaration of Independence of the State of Palestine, claiming Jerusalem as its capital. At present, Palestinian government headquarters are mainly located in Ramallah.

② 1948年建国时在特拉维夫，1950年迁往耶路撒冷。1980年7月30日，以色列议会通过法案，宣布耶路撒冷是以色列"永恒的与不可分割的首都"。对此，阿拉伯国家同以色列一直有争议。目前，绝大多数同以色列有外交关系的国家仍把使馆设在特拉维夫。
Tel Aviv was the capital of the State of Israel when the state was founded in 1948. Then in 1950, Israel designated Jerusalem as its capital. On 30 July, 1980, Israel passed a law proclaiming Jerusalem "the eternal and undivided capital of Israel", but there has long been a dispute between many Arab countries and Israel about the status of Jerusalem. At present, most countries that have established diplomatic relations with Israel locate their embassies in Tel Aviv.

③ 包括斯瓦尔巴群岛、扬马延岛等属地。
This includes Svalbard, Jan Mayen, and other dependencies.

④ 政治首都亚穆苏克罗，经济首都阿比让。

Yamoussoukro is the political capital and Abidjan the economic capital.

⑤ 行政首都比勒陀利亚,立法首都开普敦,司法首都布隆方丹。

Pretoria is the administrative capital, Cape Town the legislative capital, and Bloemfontein the judicial capital.

⑥ 阿森松岛、特里斯坦—达库尼亚群岛为属岛。

Ascension and Tristan da Cunha are its dependencies.

⑦ 不设首都,行政管理中心在亚伦区。

There is no official capital. The government offices are located in the Yaren District.

⑧ 拥有美国联邦领土地位。

It has the status as a United State commonwealth territory.

⑨ 又称东萨摩亚。

It is also called Eastern Samoa.

⑩ 行政中心随首席部长办公室轮流设于三个环礁岛。

Its administrative center is located in turn at one of the three atolls.

⑪ 无常住人口,为澳大利亚海外领地。

These islands are overseas territories of Australia and there are no permanent residents.

⑫ 包括太平洋上的贝克岛、豪兰岛、贾维斯岛、约翰斯顿岛、金曼礁、中途岛、巴尔米拉环礁、威克岛及加勒比海上的纳瓦萨岛。

These islands include Baker Island, Howland Island, Jarvis Island, Johnston Atoll, Kingman Reef, Midway Island, Palmyra Atoll, and Wake Atoll in the Pacific Ocean, and Navassa Island in the Caribbean.

⑬ 首府普利茅斯毁于 1997 年火山爆发。政府临时所在地为该岛北部的布莱兹。

Its previous capital Plymouth was destroyed in a volcanic eruption in 1997. The temporary government headquarters are now situated at

Brades in the north of the island.

⑭ 苏克雷为法定首都(最高法院所在地),政府、议会所在地在拉巴斯。

Sucre is the statutory capital (where the Supreme Court is located). The government and Parliament are situated in La Paz.

⑮ 英国称福克兰群岛。

This is referred to as Falkland Islands by UK.

⑯ 英国称斯坦利。

This is referred to as Stanley by UK.

附录七　计量单位简表
Appendix VII
Tables of Weights and Measures

一　法定计量单位表
I　Tables of Legal Units of Weights and Measures

长度 Length

名称 Name	纳米 nano- metre	微米 micron	毫米 milli- metre	厘米 centi- metre	分米 deci- metre	米 metre	千米(公里) kilometre
符号 Symbol	nm	μm	mm	cm	dm	m	km
等数 Equi- valent		1 000 纳米 nm	1 000 微米 μm	10 毫米 mm	10 厘米 cm	10 分米 dm	1 000 米 m

面积 Area

名称 Name	平方毫米 square millimetre	平方厘米 square centimetre	平方分米 square decimetre	平方米 square metre	平方千米 (平方公里) square kilometre
符号 Symbol	mm^2	cm^2	dm^2	m^2	km^2
等数 Equi- valent		100 平方毫米 mm^2	100 平方厘米 cm^2	100 平方分米 dm^2	1 000 000 平方米 m^2

体积 Cubic Measure

名称 Name	立方毫米 cubic millimetre	立方厘米 cubic centimetre	立方分米 cubic decimetre	立方米 cubic metre
符号 Symbol	mm^3	cm^3	dm^3	m^3
等数 Equivalent		1 000 立方毫米 mm^3	1 000 立方厘米 cm^3	1 000 立方分米 dm^3

容积(容量) Capacity (Volume)

名称 Name	毫升 millilitre	厘升 centiliter	分升 decilitre	升 litre
符号 Symbol	mL, ml	cL, cl	dL, dl	L, l
等数 Equivalent		10 毫升 ml	10 厘升 cl	10 分升 dl

质量(重量) Mass (Weight)

名称 Name	纳克 nano-gramme	微克 micro-gramme	毫克 milli-gramme	厘克 centi-gramme	分克 deci-gramme	克 gramme	千克(公斤) kilo-gramme	吨 ton
符号 Symbol	ng	μg	mg	cg	dg	g	kg	t
等数 Equivalent		1 000 纳克 ng	1 000 微克 μg	10 毫克 mg	10 厘克 cg	10 分克 dg	1 000 克 g	1 000 千克(公斤) kg

二 市制计量单位表
II Tables of Traditional Chinese Units of Weights and Measures

长度 Length

名称 Name	毫 *hao*	厘 *li*	分 *fen*	寸 *cun*	尺(市尺) *chi*	丈 *zhang*	里(市里) *li*
等数 Equi-valent		10 毫 *hao*	10 厘 *li*	10 分 *fen*	10 寸 *cun*	10 尺 *chi*	150 丈 *zhang*

面积 Area

名称 Name	平方毫 square *hao*	平方厘 square *li*	平方分 square *fen*	平方寸 square *cun*	平方尺 square *chi*	平方丈 square *zhang*	平方里 square *li*
等数 Equi-valent		100 平方毫 square *hao*	100 平方厘 square *li*	100 平方分 square *fen*	100 平方寸 square *cun*	100 平方尺 square *chi*	22 500 平方丈 square *zhang*

地积 Acreage

名称 Name	毫 *hao*	厘 *li*	分 *fen*	亩 *mu*	顷 *qing*
等数 Equi-valent		10 毫 *hao*	10 厘 *li*	10 分 *fen*	100 亩 *mu*

质量(重量) Mass (Weight)

名称 Name	丝 *si*	毫 *hao*	厘 *li*	分 *fen*	钱 *qian*	两 *liang*	斤 *jin*	担 *dan*
等数 Equi-valent		10 丝 *si*	10 毫 *hao*	10 厘 *li*	10 分 *fen*	10 钱 *qian*	10 两 *liang*	100 斤 *jin*

容积(容量) Capacity (Volume)

名称 Name	撮 *cuo*	勺 *shao*	合 *he*	升 *sheng*	斗 *dou*	石 *dan*
等数 Equivalent		10 撮 *cuo*	10 勺 *shao*	10 合 *he*	10 升 *sheng*	10 斗 *dou*

三 计量单位比较表
III Conversion Tables of Legal Units of Weights and Measures

长度比较表
Conversion Table of Length

1 千米(公里)km=2 市里 *li*=0.621 英里 mi=0.540 海里 nautical mi 1 米(公尺)m=3 市尺 *chi*=3.281 英尺 ft 1 海里 nautical mi=1.852 千米(公里) km=3.704 市里 *li*=1.150 英里 mi
1 市里 *li*=150 丈 *zhang*=0.5 千米(公里) km=0.311 英里 mi=0.270海里 nautical mi 1 市尺 *chi*=10 市寸 *cun*=0.333 米 m=1.094 英尺 ft
1 英里 mi=1.609 千米(公里)km=3.219 市里 *li*=0.869 海里 nautical mi 1 英尺 ft=12 英寸 in=0.305 米 m=0.914 市尺 *chi*

面积比较表
Conversion Table of Area

1 平方千米(平方公里)km^2=100 公顷 ha=4 平方市里 square *li*=0.386 平方英里 mi^2 1 平方米 m^2=1 平米 m^2=9 平方市尺 square *chi*=10.764 平方英尺 ft^2
1 市顷 *qing*=100 市亩 *mu*=6.666 7 公顷 ha 1 市亩 *mu*=10 市分 *fen*=60 平方市丈 square *zhang*=6.666 7 公亩 a=666.67 平方米 m^2
1 公顷 ha=10 000 平方米 m^2=100 公亩 a=15 市亩 *mu* 1 公亩 a=100 平方米 m^2=0.15 市亩 *mu*

质量(重量)比较表
Conversion Table of Mass (Weight)

1 千克(公斤)kg=2 市斤 *jin*=2.205 磅 lb
1 市斤 *jin*=10 市两 *liang*=0.5 千克(公斤)kg=1.102 磅 lb
1 磅 lb=16 盎司 oz=0.454 千克(公斤) kg=0.907 市斤 *jin*

容积(容量)比较表
Conversion Table of Capacity (Volume)

1 升(公制)l=1 公升 l=1 立升 litre=1 市升 *sheng*=0.220 加仑(英制)UK gal 1 毫升 ml=1 西西 cc=0.001 升(公制)l
1 加仑(英制)Uk gal=4.546 升 l=4.546 市升 *sheng*

附录八　地质年代简表

Appendix VIII
Table of the Geological Time Scale

宙 Eon	代 Era	纪 Period	符号 Sym-bol	同位素年龄 Isotopic age (单位:百万年) (million years) 开始时间 Start (距今 up to now)	持续时间 Duration	生物发展的阶段 Development of organism
显生宙 (PH) Phane-rozoic	新生代 (Kz) Ceno-zoic	第四纪 Quater-nary	Q	1.6	1.6	人类出现 appearance of man
		新近纪 Neogene	N	23	21.4	动植物都接近现代 fauna and flora approaching mod-ern forms
		古近纪 Paleogen	E	65	42	哺乳动物迅速繁衍，被子植物繁盛 rapid mammal pro-creation; flourish-ing angiosperms

显生宙 (PH) Phanerozoic	中生代 (Mz) Mesozoic	白垩纪 Cretaceous	K	135	70	被子植物大量出现，爬行类后期急剧减少 appearance of abundant angiosperms; rapid decrease of reptiles in the Late Mesozoic
		侏罗纪 Jurassic	J	205	70	裸子植物繁盛，鸟类出现 flourishing gymnosperms; appearance of birds
		三叠纪 Triassic	T	250	45	哺乳动物出现，恐龙大量繁衍 appearance of mammals; abundant dinosaur procreation
	古生代 (Pz) Palaeozoic	二叠纪 Permian	P	290	40	松柏类开始发展 rise of pines and cypresses
		石炭纪 Carboniferous	C	355	65	爬行动物出现 appearance of reptiles
		泥盆纪 Devonian	D	410	55	裸子植物出现，昆虫和两栖动物出现 appearance of gymnosperms, insects and amphibians
		志留纪 Silurian	S	438	28	蕨类植物出现，鱼类出现 appearance of pteridophytes and fish

显生宙 (PH) Phane-rozoic	古生代 (Pz) Palaeo-zoic	奥陶纪 Ordo-vician	O	510	72	藻类广泛发育,海生无脊椎动物繁盛 extensive development of algae; abundance of marine invertebrates
		寒武纪 Cam-brian	€	570	60	海生无脊椎动物门类大量增加 great increase of marine inverte-brates
元古宙 (PT) Prote-rozoic				2 500	1 930	蓝藻和细菌开始繁盛,无脊椎动物出现 prosperity of blue green algae and bacteria; appear-ance of inverte-brates
太古宙 (AR) Archeo-zoic				4 000	1 500	细菌和藻类出现 appearance of bac-teria and algae

附录九　节气表

Appendix IX　Table of Solar Terms

（按公元月日计算）

(Calculated according to the months and dates of the Christian Era)

春季 spring	立春 Beginning of Spring 2月3—5日交节 Reaching on 3－5 February	雨水 Rain Water 2月18—20日交节 Reaching on 18－20 February	惊蛰 Waking of Insects 3月5—7日交节 Reaching on 5－7 March
	春分 Spring Equinox 3月20—22日交节 Reaching on 20－22 March	清明 Pure Brightness 4月4—6日交节 Reaching on 4－6 April	谷雨 Grain Rain 4月19—21日交节 Reaching on 19－21 April
夏季 summer	立夏 Beginning of Summer 5月5—7日交节 Reaching on 5－7 May	小满 Grain Full 5月20—22日交节 Reaching on 20－22 May	芒种 Grain in Ear 6月5—7日交节 Reaching on 5－7 June
	夏至 Summer Solstice 6月21—22日交节 Reaching on 21－22 June	小暑 Slight Heat 7月6—8日交节 Reaching on 6－8 July	大暑 Great Heat 7月22—24日交节 Reaching on 22－24 July

秋季 autumn	立秋 Beginning of Autumn 8 月 7—9 日交节 Reaching on 7—9 August	处暑 Limit of Heat 8 月 22—24 日交节 Reaching on 22—24 August	白露 White Dew 9 月 7—9 日交节 Reaching on 7—9 September
	秋分 Autumn Equinox 9 月 22—24 日交节 Reaching on 22—24 September	寒露 Cold Dew 10 月 8—9 日交节 Reaching on 8—9 October	霜降 Frost's Descent 10 月 23—24 日交节 Reaching on 23—24 October
冬季 winter	立冬 Beginning of Winter 11 月 7—8 日交节 Reaching on 7—8 November	小雪 Slight Snow 11 月 22—23 日交节 Reaching on 22—23 November	大雪 Great Snow 12 月 6—8 日交节 Reaching on 6—8 December
	冬至 Winter Solstice 12 月 21—23 日交节 Reaching on 21—23 December	小寒 Slight Cold 1 月 5—7 日交节 Reaching on 5—7 January	大寒 Great Cold 1 月 20—21 日交节 Reaching on 20—21 January

二十四节气歌

Song of the Twenty-four Solar Terms

春雨惊春清谷天，夏满芒夏暑相连，
秋处露秋寒霜降，冬雪雪冬小大寒。
每月两节不变更，最多相差一两天，
上半年来六、廿一，下半年是八、廿三。
Beginning of Spring, Rain Water, and Waking of Insects,
Spring Equinox, Pure Brightness, and Grain Rain following,
Beginning of Summer, Grain Full, and Grain in Ear,
Summer Solstice, Slight Heat and Great Heat connecting,
Beginning of Autumn, Limit of Heat, and White Dew,
Autumn Equinox, Cold Dew, and Frost's Descent following,
Beginning of Winter, Slight Snow, and Great Snow,
Winter Solstice, Slight Cold, and Great Cold following.
Two solar terms always begin
On every 6th and 21st days
In the first half of the year,
And on every 8th and 23rd days
In the second half of the year,
With difference of only one or two days.

附录十 元

Appendix X The Periodic

原子序数 atomic number ← 19 K → 元素符号 symbol of eleme

钾 potassium → 元素名称 name of elemen

原子量 atomic weight ← 39.0983 (1)

注*的是人造元

Those marked w

族 Group / 周期 Period	IA	IIA	IIIB	IVB	VB	VIB	VIIB	VIIIB	
1	1 H 氢 hydrogen 1.00794(7)								
2	3 Li 锂 lithium 6.941(2)	4 Be 铍 beryllium 9.012182(3)							
3	11 Na 钠 sodium 22.989770(2)	12 Mg 镁 magnesium 24.3050(6)							
4	19 K 钾 potassium 39.0983(1)	20 Ca 钙 calcium 40.078(4)	21 Sc 钪 scandium 44.955910(8)	22 Ti 钛 titanium 47.867(1)	23 V 钒 vanadium 50.9415	24 Cr 铬 chromium 51.9961(6)	25 Mn 锰 manganese 54.938049(9)	26 Fe 铁 iron 55.845(2)	27 Co 钴 cobalt 58.933200(9)
5	37 Rb 铷 rubidium 85.4678(3)	38 Sr 锶 strontium 87.62(1)	39 Y 钇 yttrium 88.90585(2)	40 Zr 锆 zirconium 91.224(2)	41 Nb 铌 niobium 92.90638(2)	42 Mo 钼 molybdenum 95.94(2)	43 Tc 锝 * technetium 97.907	44 Ru 钌 ruthenium 101.07(2)	45 Rh 铑 rhodium 102.90550(2)
6	55 Cs 铯 cesium 132.90545(2)	56 Ba 钡 barium 137.327(7)	57—71 La-Lu 镧系 lanthanides	72 Hf 铪 hafnium 178.49(2)	73 Ta 钽 tantalum 180.9479(1)	74 W 钨 tungsten 183.84(1)	75 Re 铼 rhenium 186.207(1)	76 Os 锇 osmium 190.23(3)	77 Ir 铱 iridium 192.217(3)
7	87 Fr 钫 * francium 223.02	88 Ra 镭 radium 226.03	89—103 Ac-Lr 锕系 actinides	104 Rf 𬬻 * rutherfordium 261.11	105 Db 𬭊 * dubnium 262.11	106 Sg 𬭳 * seaborgium 263.12	107 Bh 𬭛 * Bohrium 264.12	108 Hs 𬭶 * hassium 265.13	109 Mt 鿏 * meitnerium 266.13

镧系 lanthanides	57 La 镧 lanthanum 138.9055(2)	58 Ce 铈 cerium 140.116(1)	59 Pr 镨 praseodymium 140.90765(2)	60 Nd 钕 neodymium 144.24(3)	61 Pm 钷 * promethium 144.91	62 Sm 钐 samarium 150.36(3)	63 Eu 铕 europium 151.964(1)
锕系 actinides	89 Ac 锕 actinium 227.03	90 Th 钍 thorium 232.0381(1)	91 Pa 镤 protactinium 231.03588(2)	92 U 铀 uranium 238.02891(3)	93 Np 镎 neptunium 237.05	94 Pu 钚 plutonium 244.06	95 Am 镅 * americium 243.06